Maeve Binchy was born in Co Dublin and was educated at the Holy Child convent in Killiney and at UCD. After a spell as a teacher in various girls' schools, she joined the *Irish Times*, for whom she still writes occasional columns. Her first novel, *Light a Penny Candle*, was published in 1982, and since then she has written more than a dozen novels and short story collections, each one of them bestsellers. Several have been adapted for cinema and television, most notably *Circle of Friends* in 1995. She was awarded the Lifetime Achievement award at the British Book Awards in 1999. She is married to the writer and broadcaster Gordon Snell.

Also by Maeve Binchy

Light a Penny Candle
Echoes
London Transports
Dublin 4
The Lilac Bus
Firefly Summer
Silver Wedding
Circle of Friends
The Copper Beech
The Glass Lake
Tara Road
Scarlet Feather

Aches & Pains (non-fiction)
Cross Lines (short stories)

Maeve Binchy
Three Great Novels
Evening Class
The Copper Beech
Tara Road

ORION

First published in Great Britain in 2002 by
Orion
An imprint of Orion Books Ltd
Orion House, 5 Upper St Martin's Lane, London WC2H 9EA

ISBN 0 75285 284 1

A CIP catalogue record for this book is available
from the British Library

Printed and bound in Great Britain by
Clays Ltd, St Ives plc

Contents

Evening Class

To dear, generous Gordon,
grazie per tutto
and with all my love

Aidan

There was a time back in 1970 when they would love filling in a questionnaire.

Aidan might find one in a newspaper at a weekend. Are You A Thoughtful Husband? or possibly What Do You Know About Show Biz? They scored high on the answers to Are You Well Suited? and How Well Do You Treat Your Friends?

But that was long ago.

Nowadays if Nell or Aidan Dunne saw a list of questions they didn't rush eagerly to fill them in and see how they scored. It would be too painful to answer How Often Do You Make Love? a) More than four times a week? b) Twice a week on average? c) Every Saturday night? d) Less than this? Who would want to acknowledge how very much less than this, and look up what kind of interpretation the questionnaire sages had applied to this admission?

The page would be turned nowadays if either of them saw a survey asking Are You Compatible? And there had been no row, no falling out. Aidan had not been unfaithful to Nell, and he assumed that she had not strayed either. Was it arrogant to assume this? She was an attractive looking woman; other men would definitely find her worth a second glance, as they always had.

Aidan knew that a great many men who were genuinely astounded when it was proved that their wives had been having affairs, were just smug and unobservant. But not him. He knew Nell wouldn't meet anyone else, make love to another man. He knew her so well he would know if this was the case. Anyway, where would she have met anyone? And if she had met someone she fancied where would they have gone? No, it was a ludicrous idea.

Possibly everyone else felt like this. It could well be one of the things they didn't tell you about getting older. Like having aches and pains in the backs of your legs after a long walk, like not being able to hear or understand the lyrics of pop songs any more. Maybe you just drifted apart from the person that you had thought was the centre of the world.

It was quite likely that every other man of forty-eight going on forty-nine felt the same. All over the world there could be men who wanted their wives to be eager and excited about everything. It wasn't only about lovemaking, it was about enthusiasm for other things as well.

It had been so long now since Nell had asked about his job, and his hopes and dreams in the school. There was a time when she had known the name of every teacher and many of the pupils, when she would talk about the large classes, and the posts of responsibility and the school excursions and plays, about Aidan's projects for the Third World.

But now she hardly knew what was happening. When the new Minister for Education was appointed Nell just shrugged. 'I suppose she can't be worse than the last one,' was her only comment. Nell knew nothing of the Transition Year except to call it a bloody luxury. Imagine giving children all that time to think and discuss and . . . find themselves . . . instead of getting down to their exams.

And Aidan didn't blame her.

He had become very dull explaining things. He could hear his own voice echoing in his ears; there was a kind of drone to it, and his daughters would raise their eyes to heaven wondering why at the ages of twenty-one and nineteen they should have to listen to any of this.

He tried not to bore them. Aidan knew it was a characteristic of teachers; they were so used to the captive audience in the classroom they could go on for far too long, approaching every subject from several sides until they were sure that the listener had grasped the drift.

He made huge efforts to key into their lives.

But Nell never had any stories or any issues to discuss about the restaurant where she worked as a cashier. 'Ah, for heaven's sake, Aidan, it's a job. I sit there and I take their credit cards, or their cheque cards or their cash, and I give them change and a receipt. And then at the end of the day I come home and at the end of the week I get my wages. And that's the way it is for ninety per cent of the world. We don't have issues and dramas and power struggles; we're normal, that's all.'

It was not intended to wound him or put him down, but still it was a slap in the face. It was obvious that he himself must have been going on and on about confrontations and conflicts in the staffroom. And the days were gone – obviously long gone – when Nell was waiting eagerly to know what had happened, always rooting for him, championing his cause and declaring that his enemies were her enemies. Aidan ached for the companionship, the solidarity and the teamwork of other times.

Perhaps when he became Principal it would return.

Or was this fooling himself? Possibly the headship would still hold little interest for his wife and two daughters. His home just ticked along easily. Recently he had felt this odd feeling that he had died some time ago, and they were all managing perfectly well. Nell went to and from the restaurant. She went to see her mother once a week; no, Aidan needn't come, she had said, it was just a nice family chat. Her mother liked to see them all regularly to know were they all right.

'And *are* you all right?' Aidan had asked anxiously.

'You're not with the Fifth Years now doing amateur philosophy,' Nell had said. 'I'm as all right as anyone, I suppose. Can't you leave it at that?'

But of course Aidan couldn't leave it. He told her it wasn't amateur philosophy it was Introduction to Philosophy, and it wasn't Fifth Years, it was Transition Years. He would never forget the look Nell had given him. She had begun to say something but then changed her mind. Her face was full of distant pity. She looked at him as she might have looked at a poor tramp sitting on the street, his coat tied with a rope and drinking the dregs of a ginger wine bottle.

He fared no better with his daughters.

Grania worked in the bank but had little to report from it, to her father at any rate. Sometimes he came across her talking to her friends, and she seemed much more animated. And it was the same with Brigid. The travel agency is fine, Dad, stop going on about it. Of course it's fine, and the free holiday twice a year, and the long lunch hours because they worked a rota.

Grania didn't want to talk about the whole system of banking and whether it was unfair to encourage people to take loans that they would find it difficult to repay. She didn't invent the rule, she told him, she had an In basket on her desk and she dealt with what was in it each day. That was it. Dead simple. Brigid didn't have any views on whether the travel trade was selling tourists some kind of dream it could never deliver. 'Dad, if they don't want a holiday nobody's twisting their arms, they don't have to come in and buy one.'

Aidan wished he were more observant. When had all this happened . . . this growing apart? There was a time when the girls had sat all clean and shiny after their bath time in pink dressing gowns while he told them stories and Nell would look on pleased from across the room. But that was years back. There had been good times since then. When they were doing their exams, for example, Aidan remembered doing out revision sheets for them, planning how they should study to the best advantage. They had been grateful then. He remembered the celebrations when Grania got her Leaving Certificate and later when she was accepted in the bank. There had been a lunch on each occasion in a big hotel, the waiter had taken photographs of them all. And it had been the same with Brigid, a lunch and a picture session. They looked a perfectly happy family in those pictures. Was it all a façade?

In a way it must have been, because here he was now only a few short years later, and he could not sit down with his wife and two daughters, the people he loved most in the world, and tell them his fears that he might not be made Principal.

He had put in so much time in that school, worked so many extra hours, involved himself in every aspect of it, and somewhere in his bones he felt that he would be passed over.

Another man, a man almost precisely his own age, might well get the post. This was Tony O'Brien, a man who had never stayed on after hours to support a school team playing a home match, a man who had not involved himself in the restructuring of the curriculum, in the fundraising for the new building project. Tony O'Brien who smoked quite openly in the corridors of a school which was meant to be a smoke-free zone, who had his lunch in a pub, letting everyone know it was a pint and a half and a cheese sandwich. A bachelor, in no sense a family man, often seen with a girl half his age on his arm, and yet he was being suggested as a very possible candidate for head of the school.

Many things had confused Aidan in the last few years, but nothing as

5

much as this. By any standards Tony O'Brien should not be in the running at all. Aidan ran his hands through his hair, which was thinning. Tony O'Brien of course had a huge shock of thick brown hair falling into his eyes and resting on his collar. Surely the world hadn't gone so mad that they would take this into consideration when choosing a Principal?

Lots of hair good, thinning hair bad ... Aidan grinned to himself. If he could laugh to himself at some of the worst bits of the paranoia maybe he could keep self-pity at bay. And he would have to laugh to himself. Somehow, there was no one else to laugh with these days.

There was a questionnaire in one of the Sunday papers, Are You Tense? Aidan filled in the answers truthfully. He scored over 75 on the scale, which he knew was high. He wasn't however quite prepared for the terse and dismissive verdict. If you scored over 70 you are in fact a clenched fist. Lighten up, friend, before you explode.

They had always said that these tests were just jokes really, space fillers. That's what Aidan and Nell used to say when they emerged less well than they had hoped from a questionnaire. But this time, of course, he was on his own. He told himself that newspapers had to think of something to take up half a page, otherwise the edition would appear with great white blanks.

But still it upset him. Aidan knew that he was jumpy, that was one thing. But a clenched fist? No wonder they might think twice about him as headmaster material.

He had written his answers on a separate sheet of paper lest anyone in the family should find and read his confessional of worries and anxieties and sleeplessness.

Sundays were the days that Aidan now found hardest to bear. In the past when they were a real family, a happy family, they had gone on picnics in the summer and taken healthy, bracing walks when the weather was cold. Aidan boasted that his family would never be like those Dublin families who didn't know anywhere except the area they lived themselves.

One Sunday he would take them on a train south and they would climb Bray Head, and look into the neighbouring county of Wicklow, another Sunday they would go north to the seaside villages of Rush and Lusk and Skerries, small places each with their own character, all on the road that would eventually take them up to the Border. He had arranged day excursions to Belfast for them too, so that they would not grow up in ignorance of the other part of Ireland.

Those had been some of his happiest times, the combination of schoolteacher and father, explainer and entertainer. Daddy knew the answer to everything: where to get the bus out to Carrickfergus Castle, or the Ulster Folk Museum, and a grand place for chips before getting on the train back home.

Aidan remembered a woman on the train telling Grania and Brigid that they were lucky little girls to have a daddy who taught them so much. They had nodded solemnly to agree with her and Nell had whispered to him that the woman obviously fancied Aidan but she wasn't going to get her hands on him. And Aidan had felt twelve feet tall and the most important man on earth.

Now on a Sunday he felt increasingly that he was hardly noticed in his home.

They had never been people for the traditional Sunday lunch, roast beef or lamb or chicken and great dishes of potatoes and vegetables, like so many other families were. Because of their outings and adventures, Sunday had been a casual day in their home. Aidan wished that there were some fixed point in it. He went to Mass. Nell sometimes came with him, but usually she was going on somewhere afterwards to meet one of her sisters or a friend from work. And of course nowadays the shops were open on Sundays, so there were plenty of places to go.

The girls never went to Mass. It was useless to talk to them. He had given up when they were seventeen. They didn't get up until lunchtime and then they made sandwiches, looked at whatever they had videoed during the week, lounged around in dressing gowns, washed their hair, their clothes, spoke on the phone to friends, asked other friends in for coffee.

They behaved as if they lived in a flat together with their mother as a pleasant, eccentric landlady who had to be humoured. Grania and Brigid contributed a very small amount of money each for bed and board, and handed it over with a bad grace as if they were being bled dry. To his knowledge they contributed nothing else to the household budget. Not a tin of biscuits, a tub of ice cream nor a carton of fabric softener ever came from their purses, but they were quick to grizzle if these things weren't readily available.

Aidan wondered how Tony O'Brien spent his Sundays.

He knew that Tony certainly didn't go to Mass, he had made that clear to the pupils when they questioned him: 'Sir, sir, do you go to Mass on Sundays?'

'Sometimes I do, when I feel in the mood for talking to God,' Tony O'Brien had said.

Aidan knew this. It had been reported gleefully by the boys and girls, who used it as ammunition against those who said they had to go every Sunday under pain of Mortal Sin.

He had been very clever; too clever, Aidan thought. He didn't deny the existence of God, instead he had made out that he was a friend of God's and friends only drop in to have a chat when they are in good form. It made Tony O'Brien have the inside track somehow while Aidan Dunne was left on the outside, no friend of the Almighty, just a time server. It was one of the many annoying and unfair things about it all.

On a Sunday Tony O'Brien probably got up late ... he lived in what they called a 'townhouse' nowadays, which was the equivalent of a flat. Just one big room and kitchen downstairs, and one big bedroom and bathroom upstairs. The door opened straight onto the street. He had been observed leaving in the morning accompanied by young women.

There was a time when that would have ended his career, let alone his chances of promotion – back in the 1960s teachers had been sacked for having relationships outside marriage. Not, of course, that this was right. In fact, they had all protested very strongly at the time. But still, for a man who had never committed to any woman, to parade a succession of them through his townhouse, and still be considered headmaster material, a role model for the students ... that wasn't right either.

What would Tony O'Brien be doing now, at two thirty on a wet Sunday? Maybe round to lunch at one of the other teachers' houses. Aidan had never been able to ask him since they literally didn't *have* lunch, and Nell would reasonably have enquired why he should impose on them a man he had been denouncing for five years. He might still be entertaining a lady from last night. Tony O'Brien said he owed a great debt of gratitude to the people of China since there was an excellent takeaway only three doors away – lemon chicken, sesame toast and chilli prawns were always great with a bottle of Australian Chardonnay and the Sunday papers. Imagine, at his age, a man who could be a grandfather, entertaining girls and buying Chinese food on a Sunday.

But then again, why not?

Aidan Dunne was a fair man. He had to admit that people had a choice in such matters. Tony O'Brien didn't drag these women back to his townhouse by their hair. There was no law that said he should be married and bring up two distant daughters as Aidan had done. And in a way it was to the man's credit that he wasn't a hypocrite, he didn't try to disguise his lifestyle.

It was just that things had changed so very much. Someone had moved the goalposts about what was acceptable and what was not, and they hadn't consulted Aidan first.

And how would Tony spend the rest of the day?

Surely they wouldn't go back to bed again for the afternoon? Maybe he would go for a walk or the girl would go home and Tony would play music, he often spoke of his CDs. When he had won £350 on the Match Four of the Lotto he had hired a carpenter who was working on the school extension, and paid him the money straight out to make a rack that would hold 500 CDs. Everyone had been impressed. Aidan had been jealous. Where would you get the money to buy that number of CDs? He knew for a fact that Tony O'Brien bought about three a week. When would you get the time to listen to them? And then Tony would stroll down to the pub and meet a few friends, or go to a foreign language movie with subtitles, or to a jazz club.

Maybe it was all this moving around that made him more interesting and gave him the edge on everyone else. Certainly on Aidan. Aidan's Sundays were nothing that would interest anyone.

When he came back from late Mass around one o'clock and asked would anyone like bacon and egg, there was a chorus of disgust from his daughters: 'God no, Daddy!' or 'Daddy, please don't even mention something like that, and could you keep the kitchen door closed if you're going to have it?' If Nell were at home she might raise her eyes from a novel and ask 'Why?' Her tone was never hostile, only bewildered, as if it were the most unlikely suggestion that had ever been made. Left to herself Nell might make a salad sandwich at three.

Aidan thought back wistfully to his mother's table, where the chat of the week took place and no one was excused without a very good reason. Of course, dismantling this had all been his own doing. Making them into free spirits who would discover the length and breadth of County Dublin and even the neighbouring counties on their one full day off. How could he have known it would lead to his being displaced and restless, wandering from the kitchen where everyone heated up their own food in a microwave, to the sitting room where there was some programme that he didn't want to see on television, to the bedroom where it was so long since he had made love with his wife he could barely endure looking at it until it was time to go to sleep.

There was of course the dining room. The room with the heavy dark furniture that they had hardly used since they bought the house. Even if they had been people who entertained, it was too small and poky. Once or twice recently Nell had suggested casually that Aidan should make it into a study for himself. But he had resisted. He felt that if he turned it into a copy of his room at the school he might somehow lose his identity as head of this house, as father, provider and man who once believed that this was the centre of the world.

He also feared that if he made himself too much at home there then the next step would be that he should sleep there too. After all, there was a downstairs cloakroom. It would be perfectly feasible to leave the three women to roam the upstairs area.

He must never do that, he must fight to keep his place in the family as he was fighting to keep his presence in the minds of the Board of Management, the men and women who would choose the next Principal of Mountainview College.

His mother had never understood why the school wasn't called Saint something college. That's what all schools were called. It was hard to explain to her that things were different now, a changed set-up, but he kept reassuring her that there were both a priest and a nun on the Board of Management. They didn't make all the decisions but they were there to give a voice to the role the religious had played in Irish education over the years.

Aidan's mother had sniffed. Things had come to a strange state when priests and nuns were meant to be pleased that they had a place on the Board instead of running it like God intended. In vain Aidan had tried to explain about the fall in vocations. Even secondary schools ostensibly run by religious orders had in the nineties only a very few religious in teaching positions. The numbers just weren't there.

Nell had heard him arguing the situation with his mother once and had suggested that he save his breath. 'Tell her they still run it, Aidan. It makes for an easier life. And of course in a way they do. People are afraid of them.' It irritated him greatly when Nell spoke like this. Nell had no reason to fear the power of the Catholic Church. She had attended its services for as long as it had suited her, had abandoned confession and any of the Pope's teachings on contraception at an early stage. Why should she pretend that it had been a burden that lay heavily on her? But he didn't fight her on this. He was calm and accepting as in so many things. She had no time for his mother; no hostility, but no interest in her at all.

Sometimes his mother wondered when she would get invited for dinner and Aidan had to say that the way things were they were in a state of flux, but once they got organised . . .

He had been saying this for over two decades and as an excuse it had worn thin. And it wasn't fair to fault Nell over this. It wasn't as if she was constantly inviting her own mother around or anything. His mother had been asked to any family celebration in hotels, of course. But it wasn't the same. And it had been so long since there was anything to celebrate. Except, of course, the hope that he would be made Principal.

'Did you have a good weekend?' Tony O'Brien asked him in the staffroom.

Aidan looked at him, surprised. It was so long since anyone had enquired. 'Quiet, you know,' Aidan said.

'Oh well, lucky you. I was at a party last night and I'm suffering after it. Still, only three and a half hours till the good old rehydrating lunchtime pint,' Tony groaned.

'Aren't you marvellous, the stamina I mean.' Aidan hoped the bitterness and criticism were not too obvious in his voice.

'Not at all, I'm far too long in the tooth for this, but I don't have the consolations of wife and family like all the rest of you do.' Tony's smile was warm. If you didn't know him and his lifestyle you'd have believed that he was genuinely wistful, Aidan thought to himself.

They walked together along the corridors of Mountainview College, the place his mother would like to have been called Saint Kevin's or even more particularly Saint Anthony's. Anthony was the saint who found lost things, and his mother had increasing calls on him as she got older. He found her glasses a dozen times a day. The least that people could do was thank him by naming the local school after him. Still, when her son was Principal . . . she lived in hope.

The children ran past them, some of them chorusing 'good morning', others looking sullenly away. Aidan Dunne knew them all, and their parents. And remembered many of their elder brothers and sisters. Tony O'Brien knew hardly any of them. It was so unfair.

'I met someone who knew you last night,' Tony O'Brien said suddenly.

'At a party? I doubt that,' Aidan smiled.

'No, definitely she did. When I told her I taught here she asked did I know you.'

'And who was she?' Aidan was interested in spite of himself.

'I never got her name. Nice girl.'

'An ex-pupil possibly?'

'No, then she'd have known me.'

'A mystery indeed,' Aidan said, and watched as Tony O'Brien went into Fifth Year.

The silence that fell immediately was beyond explanation. Why did they respect him so much, fear to be caught talking, behaving badly? Tony

O'Brien didn't remember their names, for heaven's sake. He barely marked their work, he lost not an hour's sleep over their examination results. Basically he didn't care about them very much. And yet they sought his approval. Aidan couldn't understand it. In sixteen-year-old boys and girls.

You always heard that women were meant to like men who treated them hard. He felt a flicker of relief that Nell had never crossed Tony O'Brien's path. Then it was followed by another flicker, a sense of recognition that somehow Nell had left him long ago.

Aidan Dunne went into the Fourth Years and stood at the door for three minutes until they gradually came to a sort of silence for him.

He thought that Mr Walsh, the old Principal, may have passed by behind him in the corridor. But he may have imagined it. You always imagined that the Principal was passing by when your class was in disorder. It was something every single teacher he ever met admitted to. Aidan knew that it was a trivial worry. The Principal admired him far too much to care if the Fourth Years were a bit noisier than usual. Aidan was the most responsible teacher in Mountainview. Everyone knew that.

That was the afternoon that Mr Walsh called him into the Principal's office. He was a man whose retirement could not come quickly enough. Today for the first time there was no small talk.

'You and I feel the same about a lot of things, Aidan.'

'I hope so, Mr Walsh.'

'Yes, we look at the world from the same viewpoint. But it's not enough.'

'I don't know exactly what you mean?' And Aidan spoke only the truth. Was this a philosophical discussion? Was it a warning? A reprimand?

'It's the system, you see. The way they run things. The Principal doesn't have a vote. Sits there like a bloody eunuch, that's what it amounts to.'

'A vote?' Aidan thought he knew where this was going, but decided to pretend not to.

It had been a wrong calculation. It only annoyed the Principal. 'Come on, man, you know what I'm talking about. The job, the job, man.'

'Well, yes.' Aidan now felt foolish.

'I'm a non-voting member of the Board of Management. I don't have a say. If I did you'd be in this job in September. I'd give you a few bits of advice about taking no nonsense from those louts in Fourth Year. But I still think you're the man with the values, and the sense of what's right for a school.'

'Thank you, Mr Walsh, that's very good to know.'

'Man, will you listen to me before you mouth these things ... there's nothing to thank me for. I can't *do* anything for you, that's what I'm trying to tell you, Aidan.' The elder man looked at him despairingly as if Aidan were some very slow-learning child in First Year.

The look was not unlike the way Nell looked at him sometimes, Aidan realised with a great feeling of sadness. He had been teaching other people's children since he was twenty-two years of age, over twenty-six years now, yet he did not know how to respond to a man who was trying hard to help him; he had only managed to annoy him.

The Principal was looking at him intently. For all that Aidan knew Mr Walsh might be able to read his thoughts, recognise the realisation that had just sunk into Aidan's brain. 'Come on now, pull yourself together. Don't look so stricken. I might be wrong, I could have it all wrong. I'm an old horse going out to grass, and I suppose I just wanted to cover myself in case it didn't go in your favour.'

Aidan could see that the Principal deeply regretted having spoken at all. 'No, no. I greatly appreciate it, I mean you are very good to tell me where you stand in all this . . . I mean . . .' Aidan's voice trickled away.

'It wouldn't be the end of the world you know . . . suppose you didn't get it.'

'No no, absolutely not.'

'I mean, you're a family man, many compensations. Lots of life going on at home, not wedded to this place like I was for so long.' Mr Walsh had been a widower for many years, his only son visited him but rarely.

'Utterly right, just as you say,' Aidan said.

'But?' the older man looked kind, approachable.

Aidan spoke slowly. 'You're right, it's not the end of the world, but I suppose I thought . . . I hoped that it might be a new beginning, liven everything up in my own life. I wouldn't mind the extra hours, I never did. I spend a lot of hours here already. In a way I am a bit like you, you know, wedded to Mountainview.'

'I know you are.' Mr Walsh was gentle.

'I never found any of it a chore. I like my classes and particularly the Transition Year when you can bring them out of themselves a bit, get to know them, let them think. And I even like the parent teacher evenings which everyone else hates, because I can remember all the kids and . . . I suppose I like it all except for the politics of it, the sort of jostling for position bit.' Aidan stopped suddenly. He was afraid there would be a break in his voice, and also he realised that *his* jostling hadn't worked.

Mr Walsh was silent.

Outside the room were the noises of a school at four thirty in the afternoon. In the distance the sounds of bicycle bells shrilling, doors banging, voices shouting as they ran for the buses in each direction. Soon the sound of the cleaners with their buckets and mops, and the hum of the electric polisher, would be heard. It was so familiar, so safe. And until this moment Aidan had thought that there was a very sporting chance that this would be his.

'I suppose it's Tony O'Brien,' he said in a defeated tone.

'He seems to be the one they want. Nothing definite yet, not till next week, but that's where their thinking lies.'

'I wonder why?' Aidan felt almost dizzy with jealousy and confusion.

'Oh search me, Aidan. The man's not even a practising Catholic. He has the morals of a tom cat. He doesn't love the place, care about it like we do, but they think he's the man for the times that are in it. Tough ways of dealing with tough problems.'

'Like beating an eighteen-year-old boy nearly senseless,' Aidan said.

'Well, they all think that the boy was a drug dealer, and he certainly didn't come anywhere near the school again.'

'You can't run a place like that,' Aidan said.

'You wouldn't and I wouldn't, but our day is over.'

'You're sixty-five, with respect, Mr Walsh. I am only forty-eight, I didn't think my day was over.'

'And it needn't be, Aidan. That's what I'm telling you. You've got a lovely wife and daughters, a life out there. You should build on all that. Don't let Mountainview become like a mistress to you.'

'You're very kind and I appreciate what you say. No, I'm not just mouthing words. Truly I do appreciate being warned in advance, makes me look less foolish.' And he left the room with a very straight back.

At home he found Nell in her black dress and yellow scarf, the uniform she wore for work in the restaurant.

'But you don't work Monday night,' he cried in dismay.

'They were short-handed, and I thought why not, there's nothing on television,' she said. Then possibly she saw his face. 'There's a nice bit of steak in the fridge,' she said. 'And some of Saturday's potatoes ... they'd be grand fried up with an onion. Right?'

'Right,' he said. He wouldn't have told her anyway. Maybe it was better that Nell was going out. 'Are the girls home?' he asked.

'Grania's taken possession of the bathroom. Heavy date tonight, apparently.'

'Anyone we know?' He didn't know why he said it. He could see her irritation.

'How would it be anyone we know?'

'Remember when they were toddlers and we knew all their friends?' Aidan said.

'Yes, and remember too when they kept us awake all night roaring and bawling. I'll be off now.'

'Fine, take care.' His voice was flat.

'Are you all right, Aidan?'

'Would it matter all that much if I were or I weren't?'

'What kind of an answer is that? There's very little point in asking you a civil question if this is all the response I get.'

'I mean it. Does it matter?'

'Not if you're going to put on this self-pitying thing. We're all tired, Aidan, life's hard for everyone. Why do you think you're the only one with problems?'

'What problems do you have? You never tell me.'

'And as sure as hell I'm not going to tell you now with three minutes before the bus.'

She was gone.

He made a cup of instant coffee and sat down at the kitchen table. Brigid came in. She was dark-haired, freckled like he was but fortunately less square. Her elder sister had Nell's blonde good looks.

'Daddy, it's not fair, she's been in the bathroom for nearly an hour. She was home at five thirty and she went in at six and now it's nearly seven. Daddy, tell her to get out and let me in.'

'No,' he said quietly.

'What do you mean, no?' Brigid was startled.

What would he usually have said? Something bland, trying to keep the peace, reminding her there was a shower in the downstairs cloakroom. But tonight he hadn't the energy to placate them. Let them fight, he would make no effort to stop them.

'You're grown-up women, sort out the bathroom between you,' he said, and walked out with his coffee into the dining room, closing the door behind him.

He sat still for a while and looked around him. It seemed to signify all that was wrong with the life they lived. There were no happy family meals around this big bleak table. Friends and extended family never drew up those dark chairs to talk animatedly.

When Grania and Brigid brought friends home they took them up to their bedrooms or giggled with Nell in the kitchen. Aidan was left in the sitting room looking at television programmes that he didn't want to see. Wouldn't it be better if he had his own little place, somewhere he could feel at peace?

He had seen a desk that he would love in a second-hand shop, one of those marvellous desks with a flap that came down and you sat and wrote on it like people were meant to do. And he would have fresh flowers in the room because he liked their beauty and he didn't mind changing the water every day which Nell said was a bore.

And there was a nice light that came in the window here during the daytime, a soft light which they never saw. Maybe he could get a windowseat or sofa and put it there, and get big drapey curtains. And he could sit and read, and invite friends in, well, whoever there was, because he knew now there would be no life for him from the family any more. He would have to realise this and stop hoping that things would change.

He could have a wall with books on it, and maybe tapes until he got a CD player. Or maybe he would never get a CD player, he didn't have to try to compete with Tony O'Brien any more. He could put up pictures on the wall, frescoes from Florence, or those heads, those graceful necks and heads of Leonardo da Vinci. And he could play arias to himself, and read articles in magazines about the great operas. Mr Walsh thought he had a life. It was time for him to get this life. His other life was over. He would not be married to Mountainview from now on. He sat warming his hands on the coffee cup. This room would need more heating, but that could be seen to. And it would need some lamps, the harsh centre light gave it no shadows, no mystery.

There was a knock on the door. His blonde daughter Grania stood there, dressed for her date. 'Are you all right, Daddy?' she asked. 'Brigid said you were a bit odd, I was wondering if you were sick.'

'No, I'm fine,' he said. But his voice seemed to come from far away. If it seemed far to him it must be very far to Grania; he forced a smile. 'Are you going somewhere nice?' he asked.

She was relieved to see him more himself. 'I don't know, I met a gorgeous fellow, but listen, I'll tell you about it sometime.' Her face was soft, kinder than it had been for a long while.

'Tell me now,' he said.

She shuffled. 'No, I can't yet, I have to see how we get on. If there's anything to tell, you'll be the first to know.'

He felt unbearably sad. This girl whose hand he had held for so long, who used to laugh at his jokes and think he knew everything, and she could hardly wait to get away. 'That's fine,' he said.

'Don't sit in here, Daddy. It's cold and lonely.'

He wanted to say it was cold and lonely everywhere, but he didn't. 'Enjoy your night,' he said.

He came back and sat by the television.

'What are you watching tonight?' he asked Brigid.

'What would you like, Daddy?' she countered.

He must have taken this blow much worse than he believed, his naked disappointment and sense of in-justice had to be showing in his face if both his daughters . . .

He looked at his younger child, her freckled face and big brown eyes so dear and loved and familiar since she was a baby in the pram. Normally so impatient with him, tonight she looked at him as if he were someone on a stretcher in a hospital corridor, with that wave of sympathy that washes over you for a complete stranger going through a very bad time.

They sat beside each other until 11.30 pm, looking at television programmes that neither of them liked, but both with an air of pleasure that they were pleasing the other.

Aidan was in bed when Nell came home at one o'clock. The light was out but he was not asleep. He heard the taxi pulling up outside the door; they paid for a cab home when she was on the late shift.

She came into the room quietly. He could smell toothpaste and talcum powder, so she had washed in the bathroom rather than disturb him by using the hand basin in their bedroom. She had a bedside light which pointed downwards at whatever book she was reading and didn't shine in his eyes, so often he had lain there listening as she turned the pages. No words between them would ever be as interesting as the paperbacks she and her friends and sisters read, so nowadays he didn't offer them.

Even tonight when his heart was like lead and he wanted to hold her in his arms and cry into her soft clean skin and tell her about Tony O'Brien who should not be allowed do dinner duty but who was going to get the headship because he was more upfront, whatever that might mean. He would have liked to tell her that he was sorry that she had to go in and sit in a cash desk watching rich people eat and get drunk and pay their bills because it was better than anything else a Monday night might offer a married couple with two grown daughters. But he lay there and heard the faraway town hall clock strike the hours.

At two o'clock Nell put down her book with a little sigh and went to sleep,

15

as far from him on her side of the bed as if she were sleeping in the next room. When the town hall said it was four o'clock Aidan realised that Grania would only have three hours' sleep before she went to work.

But there was nothing he could do or say. It was clearly understood that the girls lived their own lives without interrogation. He had not liked to think about it but had accepted that they had been to the Family Planning Association. They came home at the times that suited them and if they did *not* come home then they called at eight o'clock during breakfast to say they were all right, that they had stayed over with a girlfriend. This was the polite fiction that covered the Lord knew what. But as Nell said, it was often the actual truth, and she much preferred Grania and Brigid staying in some other girl's flat rather than risking being driven home by a drunk, or not getting a taxi in the small hours of the morning.

Still, Aidan was relieved when he heard the hall door click and the light footsteps running up the stairs. At her age she could survive on three hours' sleep. And it would be three hours more than he would have.

His mind was racing with foolish plans. He could resign from the school as a protest. Surely he could get work in a private college, Sixth Year Colleges, for example, where they did intensive work. Aidan as a Latin teacher would be useful there, there were so many careers where students still needed Latin. He could appeal to the Board of Management, list the ways in which he had helped the school, the hours he had put in to see that it got its rightful place in the community, his liaising with Third Level education so that they would come and give the children talks and pointers about the future, his environmental studies backed up by the wildlife garden.

Without appearing to do so, he could let it be known that Tony O'Brien was a destructive element, that the very fact of using violence against an ex-pupil on the school premises sent the worst possible signal to those who were meant to follow his leadership. Or could he write an anonymous letter to the religious members of the Board, to the pleasant open-faced priest and the rather serious nun, who might have no idea of Tony O'Brien's loose moral code? Or could he get some of the parents to set up an action group? There were many, many things he could do.

Or else he would accept Mr Walsh's view of him and become a man with a life outside the school, do up the dining room, make it his last-ditch stand against all the disappointments that life had thrown at him. His head felt as if someone had attached a lead weight to it during the night, but since he hadn't closed his eyes he knew that this could not have happened.

He shaved very carefully; he would not appear at school with little bits of Elastoplast on his face. He looked around his bathroom as if he had never seen it before. On every inch of available wall were prints of Venice, big shiny reproductions of Turners that he had bought when he went to the Tate Gallery. When the children were young they used to talk of going to the Venice Room not the bathroom; now they probably didn't see them at all, they were literally the wallpaper that they almost obscured.

He touched them and wondered would he ever go there again. He had been there twice as a young man, and then they had spent their honeymoon in Italy, where he had shown Nell his Venice, his Rome, his Florence, his Siena. It had been a wonderful time, but they had never gone back. When the children were young there hadn't been the money or the time, and then lately . . . well . . . who would have come with him? And it would have been a statement to have gone alone. Still, in the future there might have to be statements, and surely his soul was not so dead that it would not respond to the beauty of Italy?

Somewhere along the line they had all agreed not to talk at breakfast. And as a ceremony somehow it worked well for them. The coffee percolator was ready at eight, and the radio news switched on. A brightly coloured Italian dish of grapefruit was on the table. Everyone helped themselves and prepared their own. A basket of bread was there and an electric toaster sat on a tray with a picture of the Trevi Fountain on it. It had been a gift from Nell on his fortieth birthday. By twenty past eight Aidan and the girls had gone, each of them leaving their mug and plates in the dishwasher to minimise the clearing up.

He didn't give his wife a bad life, Aidan thought to himself. He had lived up to the promises he had made. It wasn't an elegant house but it had radiators and appliances and he paid for the windows to be cleaned three times a year, the carpet to be steamed every two years, and the house painted on the outside every three years.

Stop thinking in this ridiculous petty-clerk way, Aidan warned himself, and forcing a smile on his face began his exit.

'Nice evening last night, Grania?' he asked.

'Yeah, okay.' There was no sign of the hesitant confidences of last night. No wondering about whether people were sincere or not.

'Good, good,' he nodded. 'Was it busy in the restaurant?' he asked Nell.

'Fair for a Monday night, you know, nothing spectacular,' she said. She spoke perfectly pleasantly but as if to a stranger she had met on a bus.

Aidan took up his briefcase and left for school. His mistress, Mountain-view College. What a fanciful idea. She certainly didn't have the allures of a lover to him this morning.

He stood for a moment at the gates of the school yard, scene of the disgraceful and brutal fight between Tony O'Brien and that boy whose ribs were broken and who needed stitches over his eye and in his lower lip. The yard was untidy, with litter blowing in the early morning breezes. The bicycle shed needed to be painted, the bikes were not properly stacked. Outside the gates the bus stop was open and exposed to the winds. If Bus Eireann would not provide a proper bus shelter for the children who waited there after school, then the Vocational Education Committee should do so, and if they refused a parents' committee would raise the funds. These were the kind of things Aidan Dunne had intended to do when he was Principal. Things that would never be done now.

He nodded gruffly to the children who saluted him, instead of addressing them all by name which was his usual way, and he walked into the staffroom to find no one there except Tony O'Brien mixing a headache seltzer in a glass.

'I'm getting too old for these nights,' he confided to Aidan.

Aidan longed to ask him why he didn't just cut them out, but that would be counterproductive. He must make no false stupid moves, in fact no moves at all until he had worked out what his plan was to be. He must continue in his bland, good-natured way.

'I suppose all work and no play . . .' he began.

But Tony O'Brien was in no mood to hear platitudes. 'I think forty-five is a sort of watershed. It's half of ninety after all, it's telling you something. Not that some of us listen.' He drained the glass and smacked his lips.

'Was it worth it, I mean the late night?'

'Who knows if it's ever worth it, Aidan. I met a nice little girl, but what's the good of that when you have to face the Fourth Years.' He shook his head like a dog coming out of the sea trying to get rid of the water. And this man was going to run Mountainview College for the next twenty years while poor old Mr Dunne was expected to sit by and let it happen. Tony O'Brien gave him a heavy clap on the shoulder. 'Still, *ave atque vale* as you Latinists say. I have to be getting on, only four hours and three minutes before I stand with that healing pint in my hand.'

Aidan would not have thought that Tony O'Brien would have known the Latin words for hallo and goodbye. He himself had never used any Latin phrases in the staffroom, aware that many of his colleagues might not have studied it and fearing to show off in front of them. It just showed you must never underestimate the enemy.

The day passed as days always pass, whether you have a hangover like Tony O'Brien, or a heavy heart like Aidan Dunne, and the next passed, and the next. Aidan had still settled on no definite plan of action. He could never find the right moment to tell them at home that his hopes of being Principal had been misplaced. In fact, he thought it would be easier to say nothing until the decision was announced, let it appear a surprise to everyone.

And he had not forgotten his plans to make himself a room. He sold the dining table and chairs and bought the little desk. When his wife worked in Quentin's restaurant and his daughters went out on their dates, he sat and planned it for himself. Gradually he assembled little bits of his dream: second-hand picture frames, a low table for near the window, a big cheap sofa that fitted the space exactly. And one day he would get loose covers, something in gold or yellow, a sunny colour, and he would get a square of carpet that would be a splash of some other colour, orange, purple, something with life and vigour.

They weren't very interested at home so he didn't tell them his plans. In a way he felt that his wife and daughters thought it was yet another harmless little interest for him, like the projects in Transition Year and his long struggle to get a few metres of wildlife garden up and running in Mountainview.

'Any word of the big job above in the school?' Nell asked unexpectedly one evening when the four of them were seated around the kitchen table.

He felt his heart lurch at the lie. 'Not a whisper. But they'll be voting next week, that's for sure.' He seemed calm and unruffled.

'You're bound to get it. Old Walsh loves the ground you walk on,' Nell said.

'He doesn't have a vote, as it happens, so that's no use to me.' Aidan gave a nervous little laugh.

'Surely you'll get it, Daddy?' Brigid said.

'You never know, people want different things in Principals. I'm sort of slow and steady, but that mightn't be what's needed these days.' He spread out his hands in a gesture to show that it was all beyond him but wouldn't matter very much either way.

'But who would they have if they didn't have you?' Grania wanted to know.

'Wouldn't I be doing the horoscope column if I knew that? An outsider maybe, someone inside that we hadn't reckoned on . . .' He sounded good-natured and full of fair play. The job would go to the best man or woman. It was as simple as that.

'But you don't think they'll pass you over?' Nell said.

There was something that he hated in her tone. It was a kind of disbelief that he could possibly let this one slip. It was the phrase 'passed over', so dismissive, so hurtful. But she didn't know, she couldn't guess, that it had already happened.

Aidan willed his smile to look confident. 'Passed over? Me? Never!' he cried.

'That's more like it, Daddy,' said Grania, before going upstairs to spend further time in the bathroom where she possibly never saw any more the beautiful images of Venice on the wall, only her face in the mirror and her anxieties that it should look well for whatever outing was planned tonight.

It was their sixth date. Grania knew now that he definitely wasn't married. She had asked him enough questions to have tripped him up. Every night so far he had wanted her to come back to his place for coffee. Every night so far she had said no. But tonight could be different. She really liked him. He knew so much about things, and he was far more interesting than people of her own age. He wasn't one of those middle-aged ravers who pretended they were twenty years younger.

There was only one problem. Tony worked at Dad's school. She had asked him the very first time she met him whether he knew an Aidan Dunne, but hadn't said he was her father. It seemed an ageist sort of thing to say, putting herself in a different generation. And there were loads of Dunnes around the place, it wasn't as if Tony would make the connection. There wasn't any point in mentioning it to Dad, not yet anyway, not until it developed into anything if it did. And if it were the real thing then everything else like him working in the same place as Dad would fall into place, and Grania made a silly face at herself in the mirror and thought that maybe Tony would have to be even nicer than ever to her if she was going to be the Principal's daughter.

Tony sat in the bar and dragged deep on his cigarette. This was one thing he was going to have to cut down on when he was Principal. There really couldn't be any more smoking on the premises. And probably fewer pints at lunchtime. It hadn't been actually spelled out but it had been hinted at. Heavily. But that was it. Not a huge price to pay for a good job. And they weren't going to ask about his social life. It might still be Holy Catholic Ireland, but it was the 1990s after all.

And by extraordinary timing he had just met a girl who really did hold his attention, and might well be around for more than a few weeks' duration. A bright lively girl called Grania, worked in the bank. Sharp as anything, but not at all hard or tough. She was warm and generous in her outlook. They didn't come in that kind of a package often. She was twenty-one, which was of course a problem. Less than half his age, but she wouldn't always be that. When he was sixty she'd be thirty-five, which was half of seventy when you came to think of it. She'd be catching up all the time.

She hadn't come back to the townhouse with him, but she had been very frank. It wasn't because she was afraid of sex, it was just that she wasn't ready for it with him yet, that was all, and if they were to get along together then they must respect each other and not one of them force the other. He had agreed with her, that seemed perfectly fair. And for once it did. Normally he would have regarded such a response as a challenge, but not with Grania. He was quite ready to wait. And she had assured him that she wasn't going to play games.

He saw her come into the bar and he felt lighter and happier than he had for a long time. He wasn't going to play games either. 'You look lovely,' he said. 'Thank you for dressing up for me, I appreciate it.'

'You're worth it,' she said simply.

They drank together, like people who had always known each other, interrupting, laughing, eager to hear what the other would say.

'There are lots of things we could do this evening,' Tony O'Brien said. 'There's a New Orleans evening, you know, Creole food and jazz in one of the hotels, or there was this movie we were talking about last night . . . or I could cook for you at home. Show you what a great chef I am.'

Grania laughed. 'Am I to believe that you'll be making me Won Tons and Peking Duck? You see, I remember that you said you had a neighbouring Chinese restaurant.'

'No, if you come home with me I'll cook for you myself. To show you how much it means to me. I won't just get menu A or menu B, good and all as they may be.' Tony O'Brien had not spoken so directly for a long time.

'I'd love to come home with you, Tony,' Grania said very simply, without a hint of playing games.

Aidan slept in fits and starts. And then near dawn he felt wide awake and clear headed. All he had was the doddering word of a retiring Principal, a man fussed and confused by the way the world was going. The vote had not been taken, there was nothing to be depressed about, no excuses to make, action to take, career to abandon. Today would be a much, much better day now that he was clear about all this.

He would speak to Mr Walsh, the present Principal, and ask him briefly and directly if his remarks of some days ago had any substance and intent, or if they were mere speculation. After all, as a non-voting member he might also have been a non-listening member to their deliberations. He would be brief, Aidan told himself. That was his weakness, a tendency to go on at too great a length. But he would be crystal clear. What was it that the poet Horace said? Horace had a word for every occasion. *Brevis esse laboro/ obscurus fio.* Yes, that was it, the more I struggle to be brief, the more unintelligible I become. In the kitchen Brigid and Nell exchanged glances and shrugs when they heard him whistling. He wasn't a very good whistler, but nobody could remember when he had last even attempted it.

Just after eight o'clock the phone rang.

'Three guesses,' Brigid said, reaching for more toast.

'She's very reliable, you both are,' Nell said, and went to answer it.

Aidan wondered was it very reliable for one of his daughters to spend the night with a man who had been described by the other as a heavy date. About whom only a week ago she had raised tentative worries, whether he was reliable ... sincere. Aidan didn't voice these wonderings. He watched Nell at the phone.

'Sure, fine, good. Do you have proper clothes to go into the bank in or will you come back here? Oh, you brought a sweater, how lucky. Righto, love, see you this evening.'

'And how did she seem?' Aidan asked.

'Now, Aidan, don't start taking attitudes. We've always agreed that it's much wiser that Grania should stay with Fiona in town instead of getting a dodgy lift home.'

He nodded. None of them thought for a moment that Grania was staying with Fiona.

'No problems, then?' Tony asked.

'No, I told you ... they treat me as a grown up.'

'And so do I in a different way.' He reached out for her as she sat on the edge of the bed.

'No, Tony, I can't possibly. We have to go to work. I have to get to the bank, you have to go to Mountainview.'

He was pleased that she remembered the name of the place he worked. 'No, they won't mind, they're very lax there, let the teachers do what they like most of the time.'

She laughed at him. 'No that's not true, not even a little bit true. Get up and have a shower, I'll put on some coffee. Where's the machine?'

'It's only instant, I'm afraid.'

'Oh, that's not classy enough for me at all, I'm afraid, Mr O'Brien,' she said, shaking her head at him in mock disapproval. 'Things will have to improve round here if I am to visit again.'

'I was hoping you'd pay a visit this evening,' he said.

Their eyes met. There was no guile.

'Yes, if you have real coffee,' she said.

'Consider it done,' he said.

Grania had toast, Tony had two cigarettes.

'You really should cut down on those,' she said. 'I could hear your wheeze all night.'

'That was passion,' he said.

'No, it was cigarettes.' She was firm.

Perhaps, perhaps for this lively bright young woman he might, he just might, be able to cut them out. It was bad enough to be so much older than her, he didn't want to be so much wheezier as well. 'I might change, you know,' he said seriously. 'There are going to be a lot of changes in my life at work for one thing, but more important, now that I've met you I think I might have the strength to cut out a lot of the rubbishy bits.'

'Believe me, I'll help you,' Grania said, reaching for his hand across the table. 'And you must help me too. Help me to keep my mind alert and busy. I've stopped reading since I left school. I want to read again.'

'I think we should both take the day off to cement this promise,' he said, only half joking.

'Hey, you won't even be thinking about suggesting that next term,' she laughed.

'Why next term?' How could she have known of his promotion? Nobody knew except the Board who had offered him the job. It was to be kept totally secret until it was announced.

She had not meant to tell him yet about her father being on the staff, but somehow with all they had shared it seemed pointless to keep it secret any longer. It would have to come out some time, and anyway she was so proud of Dad's new post. 'Well, you'll want to keep well in with my father, he's going to be the Principal of Mountainview.'

'Your father's going to be *what*?'

'Principal. It's a secret until next week but I think everyone expected it.'

'What's your father's name?'

'Dunne, like mine. He's the Latin teacher, Aidan Dunne. Remember, I asked you did you know him the first time we met?'

'You didn't say he was your father.'

'No, well it was a crowded place and I didn't want to be making myself sound too babyish. And later it didn't matter.'

'Oh my God,' said Tony O'Brien. He didn't look at all pleased.

Grania bit her lip and regretted that she had ever mentioned it. 'Please don't say to him that you know, please.'

'He told you this? That he was going to be Principal?' Tony O'Brien's face was hardly able to register the shock. 'When? When did he tell you this? Was it a long time ago?'

'He's been talking about it for ages, but he told us last night.'

'Last night? No, you must be mistaken, you must have misunderstood.'

'Of course I didn't misunderstand, we were just talking about it before I came out to meet you.'

'And did you tell him that you were meeting me?' He looked almost wild.

'No. Tony, what is it?'

He held both her hands in his and spoke very slowly and carefully. 'This is the most important thing I have ever said in my whole life. In my whole long life, Grania. You must never, never tell your father what you told me now. Never.'

She laughed nervously and tried to draw her hands away. 'Oh come on, you're behaving like someone in a melodrama.'

'It's a bit like that, honestly.'

'I'm never to tell my father I met you, know you, like you . . . What kind of relationship is that?' Her eyes blazed at him across the breakfast table.

'No, of course we'll tell him. But later, not a lot later, but there's something else I have to tell him first.'

'Tell me,' she asked.

'I can't. If there's any dignity to be left anywhere in this whole world it depends on your trusting me this minute and believing I want the best, the very, very best for you.'

'How can I believe anything if you won't tell me what all the mystery is about?'

'It's about faith and trust.'

'It's about keeping me in the dark, that's what it is, and I hate it.'

'What have you to lose by trusting me, Grania? Listen, two weeks ago we hadn't even met, now we think we love each other. Can't you give it just a day or two till I sort something out?' He was standing up and putting on his jacket. For a man who had said Mountainview College was a lax place where it didn't matter what time you rolled in, Tony O'Brien seemed in a very great hurry.

Aidan Dunne was in the staffroom. He looked slightly excited, feverish even. His eyes were unnaturally bright. Was it possible that he could be suffering from some kind of delusions? Or did he suspect that his beloved daughter had been seduced by a man as old as himself but ten times as unreliable?

'Aidan, I want to talk to you very very urgently,' Tony O'Brien hissed in an undertone.

'After school hours possibly, Tony . . .'

'This very minute. Come on, we'll go to the library.'

'Tony, the bell will go in five minutes.'

'To hell with the bell.' Tony half pulled, half dragged him out of the staffroom.

In the library two studious girls from Sixth Year looked up, startled.

'Out,' Tony O'Brien said in a voice that wasn't going to be argued with.

One of them tried to argue. 'But we're *studying* here, we were looking up . . .'

'Did you hear me?'

This time she got the message and they were gone.

'That's no way to treat children, we're meant to encourage them, lead them *into* the library, for heaven's sake, not throw them out of it like some bouncer in these night clubs you go to. What example is that for them to follow?'

'We're not here to be some example to them, we're here to teach them. To put some information into their heads. It's as simple as that.'

Aidan looked at him aghast, and then he spoke. 'I'll thank you not to give me the benefit of your half-baked hungover philosophies at this time in the morning, or any time. Let me back to my classes this minute.'

'Aidan.' Tony O'Brien's voice had changed. 'Aidan, listen to me. I'm going to be the Principal. They were going to announce it next week, but I think it's better if I make them do it today.'

'What, what . . . Why do you want to do that?' Aidan felt he had a blow in the stomach. This was too soon, he wasn't ready for it. There was no proof. Nothing was fixed yet.

'So that all this nonsense in your head can be knocked out if it, so that you don't go round believing that it's you who's getting the job . . . upsetting yourself, upsetting other people . . . that's why.'

Aidan looked at Tony O'Brien. 'Why are you doing this to me, Tony, why? Suppose they do give you the job, is your first response to drag me in here and start rubbing my nose in it, the fact that you . . . you who don't give a tuppenny damn about Mountainview are going to get the job? Have you no dignity at all? Can't you even wait until the Board offer you the job before you start gloating? Are you so bloody confident, so eager . . . ?'

'Aidan, you can't have gone on believing that it was going to be you. Did that old blatherer Walsh not tell you? They all thought he would mark your card about it, he actually said that he *had* told you.'

'He said it was likely that you might get it, and I might add that he said he would be very sorry indeed if you did.'

A child put his head around the library door and stared with amazement at the two red-faced teachers facing each other across a table.

Tony O'Brien let out a roar that nearly lifted the child up in the air. 'Get the hell out of here, you interfering young pup, and back to your classroom.'

White-faced, the boy looked at Aidan Dunne for confirmation.

'That's the boy, Declan. Tell the class to open their Virgil, I'll be along shortly.' The door closed.

'You know all their names,' Tony O'Brien said wonderingly.

'You hardly know *any* of them,' Aidan Dunne said flatly.

'Being Principal doesn't have anything to do with being a Dale Carnegie figure, a Mister Nice Guy, you know.'

'Evidently not,' Aidan agreed. They were much calmer now, the heat and fury had gone from both of them.

'I'm going to need you, Aidan, to help me, if we're going to keep this place afloat at all.'

But Aidan was stiff, rigid with his disappointment and humiliation. 'No, it's too much to ask. I may be easy-going but I can't do this. I couldn't stay on here. Not now.'

'But what will you do, in the name of God?'

'I'm not completely washed up you know, there *are* places who would be glad of me, even though this one doesn't seem to be.'

'They rely on you here, you great fool. You're the cornerstone of Mountainview, you know that.'

'Not cornerstone enough to want me as Principal.'

'Do I have to spell it out for you? The job of Principal is changing. They don't want a wise preacher up in that office ... they need someone with a loud voice, who's not afraid to argue with the VEC, with the Department of Education, to get the guards in here if there's vandalism or drugs, to deal with the parents if they start bleating...'

'I couldn't work under you, Tony, I don't respect you as a teacher.'

'You don't have to respect me as a teacher.'

'Yes I would. You see, I couldn't go along with the things that you would want or the things you'd ignore.'

'Give me one example, one, now this minute. What did you think of as you were coming in the school gate ... what one thing would *you* do as Principal?'

'I'd get the place painted, it's dirty, shabby...'

'Okay, snap. That's what I'd do too.'

'Oh you just say that.'

'No, Aidan, I don't bloody say that, but even better I know how I'm going to do it. You wouldn't know where to start. I'm going to get a young fellow I know on the evening paper to come up here with a photographer and do an article called Magnificent Mountainview, showing the peeling paint, the rusty railings, the sign with the letters missing.'

'You'd never humiliate the place like that?'

'It wouldn't be humiliation. The day after the article appears I'll have the Board agree to a huge refurbishing job. We can announce details of it, say it was all on line and that local sponsors are going to take part ... list who is going to do what ... you know, garden centres, paint shops, that wrought-iron place for the school sign ... I've a list as long as my arm.'

Aidan looked down at his hands. He knew that he himself could not have set up something like this, a plan that was sure to work. This time next year Mountainview would have a facelift, one that he would never have been able to organise. It left him more bereft than ever. 'I couldn't stay, Tony. I'd feel so humbled, passed over.'

'But no one here thought you were going to get it.'

'I thought it.' He said it simply.

'Well then, the humiliation that you speak of is only in your mind.'

'And my family, of course ... they think it is in the bag for me ... they're waiting to celebrate.'

There was a lump in Tony O'Brien's throat. He knew this was true. This man's glowing daughter was so proud of her father's new post. But there was no time for sentiment, only action.

'Then give them something to celebrate.'

'Like what, for example?'

'Suppose there was no race to be Principal. Suppose you could have some

position in the school, bring in something new ... set up something ...
What would you like to do?'

'Look, I know you mean well, Tony, and I'm grateful to you for it, but I'm
not into let's pretend at the moment.'

'I'm the Principal, can't you get that into your head. I can do what I like,
there's no let's pretend about it. I want you on my side. I want you to be
enthusiastic, not a Moaning Minnie. Tell me what you'd do for God's sake,
man – if you were given the go-ahead.'

'Well, you wouldn't wear it because it's not got much to do with the
school, but I think we should have evening classes.'

'What?'

'There, I knew you wouldn't want it.'

'I didn't say I didn't want it. What kind of evening classes?'

The two men talked on in the library, and oddly, their classrooms were
curiously quiet. Normally the noise of any room left without a teacher could
reach a very high decibel level indeed. But the two studious girls who had
been thrown out of the library by Mr O'Brien had scuttled to their classroom
with news of their eviction and of Mr O'Brien's face. It was agreed that the
Geography teacher was on the warpath and it was probably better to keep
things fairly low until he arrived. They had all seen him in a temper at some
stage, and it wasn't something you'd want to bring on yourselves.

Declan, who had been instructed to tell his class to get out their Virgil,
spoke in low tones. 'I think they were arm wrestling,' he said. 'They were
purple in the face, both of them, and Mr Dunne spoke as if there was a knife
held in his back.'

They looked at him, round-eyed. Declan was not a boy with much
imagination, it must be true. They got out their Virgils obediently. They
didn't study them or translate them or anything, that had not been part of
the instructions, but every child in the class had an open copy of *The Aeneid
Book IV* ready, and they looked at the door fearfully in case Mr Dunne
should come staggering in with blood coming down his shoulder blades.

The announcement was made that afternoon. It was in two parts.

A pilot scheme for Adult Education Classes would begin in September
under the supervision of Mr Aidan Dunne. The present Principal Mr John
Walsh having reached retirement age would now stand down, and his post
would be filled by Mr Anthony O'Brien.

In the staffroom there seemed to be as many congratulations for Aidan as for
Tony. Two bottles of sparkling wine were opened, and people's health was
drunk from mugs.

Imagine evening classes. The subject had been brought up before but
always to be knocked down. It was the wrong area, too much competition
from other Adult Education Centres, trouble heating the school, the business
of keeping on the caretaker after hours, the whole notion of classes being
self-funding. How had it happened now?

'Apparently Aidan persuaded them,' Tony O'Brien said, pouring more
fizzy drink into the school mugs.

It was time to go home.

'I don't know what to say,' Aidan said to his new Principal.

'We made a deal. You got what you wanted, you are to go straight home to your wife and family and present it as that. Because this *is* what you want. You don't want all the shit of fighting with people morning, noon and night, which is what being the Principal is about. Just remember that, present it to them as it is.'

'Can I ask you something, Tony? Why does it matter to you one way or the other how I present things to my family?'

'Simple. I need you, I told you that. But I need you as a happy, successful man. If you present yourself in this old self-pitying I-was-passed-over role, then you'll begin to believe it all over again.'

'That makes sense.'

'And they'll be pleased for you that you have got what you really wanted all along.'

As Aidan walked out the school gate he paused for a moment and felt its peeling paint and looked at the rusting locks. Tony was right, he wouldn't have known where to begin on a project like this. Then he looked at the annexe where he and Tony had decided the evening classes should be held. It had its own entrance, they wouldn't have to trek through the whole school. It had cloakrooms and two big classrooms. It would be ideal.

Tony was an odd guy, there were no two ways about it. He had even suggested to him that he come home and meet the family but Tony had said not yet. Wait until September when the new term began, he had insisted.

'Who knows what will have happened by September?'

Those were his words. As odd as two left shoes, but quite possibly the best thing that could happen to Mountainview.

Inside the building Tony O'Brien inhaled deeply. He would smoke in his own office from now on, but never outside it.

He watched Aidan Dunne hold the gate and even stroke it lovingly. He was a good teacher and a good man. He was worth the sacrifice about the evening classes. All the bloody work that lay ahead, the fights with this committee and that Board, and the lying promises that the classes would be self-financing when everyone knew there wasn't a chance that they would be.

He sighed deeply and hoped that Aidan would handle it right at home. Otherwise, his own future with Grania Dunne, the first girl to whom he could even consider a real commitment, would be a very rocky future indeed.

'I have very good news,' Aidan said at supper.

He told them about the evening classes, the pilot scheme, the annexe, the funds at his disposal and how he would have Italian Language and Culture.

His enthusiasm was catching. They asked him questions. Would he have walls to put up pictures, posters, maps? Would these things remain up all week? What kind of experts should he invite to lecture? Would there be Italian cookery? And arias from operas as well?

'Won't you find this a lot of extra work as well as being Principal?' Nell asked.

'Oh no, I'm doing it instead of being Principal,' he explained eagerly and he looked at their faces. Nobody missed a beat, it seemed to them a perfectly reasonable alternative. And oddly it began more and more to seem that way to him too. Maybe that crazy Tony O'Brien was more intelligent than people gave him credit for. They talked on like a real family. What numbers would they need? Should it be more conversational Italian suitable for holidays? Or something more ambitious? The dishes were pushed aside on the table as Aidan made notes.

Later, much later it seemed, Brigid asked: 'Who will become Principal now if you're not going to do it?'

'Oh a man called Tony O'Brien, the Geography teacher, a good fellow. He'll do all right for Mountainview.'

'I knew it wouldn't be a woman,' Nell said, sniffing.

'Now there *were* two women, I believe, in the running, but they gave it to the right person,' Aidan said. He poured them another glass of wine from the bottle he had bought to celebrate his good news. Soon he would move into his room; he was going to measure it tonight for the shelves. One of the teachers at school did carpentry in his spare time, he would build the bookshelves and little racks for Italian plates.

They didn't notice Grania getting up quietly and leaving the room.

He sat in the sitting room and waited. She would have to come, just to tell him how much she hated him. That if nothing else. The doorbell rang and she stood there, eyes red from weeping.

'I bought a coffee machine,' he said. 'And some fine ground Colombian blend. Was that right?'

She walked into the room. Young but not confident, not any more. 'You are such a bastard, such a terrible deceitful bastard.'

'No, I'm not.' His voice was very quiet. 'I am an honourable man. You must believe me.'

'Why should I believe the daylight from you? You were laughing all the time at me, laughing at my father, even at the notion of a coffee percolator. Well, laugh as much as you like. I came to tell you that you are the lowest of the low, and I hope you are the worst I meet. I hope I have a very long life and that I meet hundreds and hundreds of people and that this is the very worst that will ever happen to me, to trust someone who doesn't give a damn about people's feelings. If there *is* a God then please, please God let this be the very lowest I ever meet.' Her hurt was so great he didn't even dare to stretch out a hand to her.

'This morning I didn't know you were Aidan Dunne's daughter. This morning I didn't know that Aidan thought he was getting the headship,' he began.

'You *could* have told me, you *could* have told me,' she cried.

Suddenly he was very tired. It had been a long day. He spoke quietly. 'No, I could not have told you. I could not have said: "Your father's got it wrong, actually it's yours truly who is getting the job." If there was loyalty involved, mine was to him, my duty was to make sure he didn't make a fool of himself, didn't set himself up for disappointment, and that he got what was rightfully his – a new position of power and authority.'

'Oh I see.' Her voice was scornful. 'Give him the evening classes, a little pat on the head.'

Tony O'Brien's voice was cold. 'Well, of course, if that's the way you see it I can't hope to change your mind. If you don't see it for what it is, a breakthrough, a challenge, possibly the beginning of something that will change people's lives, most of all your father's life, then I'm sorry. Sorry and surprised. I thought you would have been more understanding.'

'I'm not in your classroom, Mr O'Brien, sir. I'm not fooled by this shaking your head more in sorrow than in anger bit. You made a fool of my father and of me.'

'How did I do that?'

'He doesn't know that you slept with his daughter, heard of his hopes and ran in and took his job. That's how.'

'And have you told him all these things to make him feel better?'

'You know I haven't. But the sleeping with his daughter bit isn't important. If ever there was a one-night stand, that was it.'

'I hope you'll change your mind, Grania. I am very, *very* fond of you, and attracted to you.'

'Yeah.'

'No, not "Yeah". It's true what I say. Odd as it may seem to you, it's not your age and your looks that appeal to me. I have had many young attractive girlfriends and should I want company I feel sure I could find more. But you are different. If you walk out on me I'll have lost something very important. You can believe it or not as you will, but very truthfully that's what I feel.'

This time she was silent. They looked at each other for a while. Then he spoke. 'Your father asked me to come and meet the family but I said we should wait until September. I said to him that September was a long way away and who knows what could have happened by then.' She shrugged. 'I wasn't thinking of myself, actually, I was thinking of you. Either you'll still be full of scorn and anger about me, and you can be out the day I call. Or maybe we will love each other fully and truly and know that all that happened here today was just some spectacularly bad timing.'

She said nothing.

'So September it is,' he said.

'Right.' She turned to go.

'I'll leave it to you to contact me, Grania. I'll be here, I'd love to see you again. We don't have to be lovers if you don't want to be. If you were a one-night stand I'd be happy to see you go. If I didn't feel the way I do I'd think that maybe it was all too complicated and it would be for the best that we end it now. But I'll be here, hoping you come back.'

Her face was still hard and upset. 'Ringing first, of course, to make sure you haven't company, as you put it,' she said.

'I won't have company until you come back,' he said.

She held out her hand. 'I don't think I'll be back,' she said.

'No, well, let's agree never say never.' His grin was good-natured. He stood at the doorway as she walked down the road, her hands in the pockets of her jacket, her head down. She was lonely and lost. He wanted to run and swoop her back to him, but it was too soon.

And yet he had done what he had to do. There could have been no future for them at all if he had sat down behind Aidan's back and told the man's daughter what he didn't know himself. He wondered what a betting man would give as odds on her ever coming back to him. Fifty-fifty he decided.

Which were much more hopeful odds than anyone would get on whether the evening classes would succeed. That was a bet that no sane person would take. They were doomed before they even began.

Signora

For years, yes years, when Nora O'Donoghue had lived in Sicily, she had received no letter at all from home.

She used to look hopefully at *il postino* as he came up the little street under the hot blue sky. But there was never a letter from Ireland, even though she wrote regularly on the first of every month to tell them how she was getting on. She had bought carbon paper; it was another thing hard to describe and translate in the shop where they sold writing paper and pencils and envelopes. But Nora needed to know what she had told them already, so that she would not contradict herself when she wrote. Since the whole life she described was a lie, she might as well make it the same lie. They would never reply but they would read the letters. They would pass them from one to the other with heavy sighs, raised eyebrows and deep shakes of the head. Poor stupid headstrong Nora who couldn't see what a fool she had made of herself, wouldn't cut her losses and come back home.

'There was no reasoning with her,' her mother would say.

'The girl was beyond help and showed no remorse,' would be her father's view. He was a very religious man, and in his eyes the sin of having loved Mario outside marriage was greater far than having followed him out to the remote village of Annunziata even when he had said he wouldn't marry her.

If she had known that they wouldn't get in touch at all she would have pretended that she and Mario *were* married. At least her old father would have slept easier in his bed and not feared so much the thought of meeting God and explaining the Mortal Sin of his daughter's adultery.

But then she would not have been able to do that, because Mario had insisted on being upfront with them.

'I would love to marry your daughter,' he had said, with his big dark eyes looking from her father to her mother, backwards and forwards. 'But sadly, sadly it is not possible. My family want me very much to marry Gabriella and her family also want the marriage. We are Sicilians; we can't disobey what our families want. I'm sure it is very much the same in Ireland.' He had pleaded for an understanding, a tolerance and almost a pat on the head.

He had lived with their daughter for two years in London. They had come over to confront him. He had been in his own mind admirably truthful and fair. What more could they want of him?

Well, they wanted him gone from her life for one thing.

They wanted Nora to come back to Ireland and hope and pray that no one would ever know of this unfortunate episode in her life, or her marriage chances which were already slim would be further lessened.

She tried to make allowances for them. It was 1969, but then they did live in a one-horse town; they even thought coming up to Dublin was an ordeal. What had they made of their visit to London to see their daughter living in sin, and then accept the news that she would follow this man to Sicily?

The answer was they had gone into complete shock and did not reply to her letters.

She could forgive them. Yes, part of her really did forgive them, but she could never forgive her two sisters and two brothers. They were young; they must have understood love, though to look at the people they had married you might wonder. But they had all grown up together, struggled to get out of the lonely remote little town where they lived. They had shared the anxiety of their mother's hysterectomy, their father's fall on the ice which had left him frail. They had always consulted each other about the future, about what would happen if either Mam or Dad were left alone. Neither could manage. They had always agreed that the little farm would be sold and the money used to keep whoever it was that was left alive in a flat in Dublin somewhere adjacent to them all.

Nora realised that her having decamped to Sicily didn't suit that long-term plan at all. It reduced the helpforce by more than twenty per cent. Since Nora wasn't married the others would have assumed that she might take sole charge of a parent. She had reduced the helpforce by one hundred per cent. Possibly that was why she never heard from them. She assumed that they would write and tell her if either Mam or Dad was very ill, or even had died.

But then sometimes she didn't know if they would do that. She seemed so remote from them, as if she herself had died already. So she relied on a friend, a good kind friend called Brenda, who had worked with her in the hotel business. Brenda called from time to time to visit the O'Donoghues. It was not difficult for Brenda to shake her head with them over the foolishness of their daughter Nora. Brenda had spent days and nights trying to persuade, cajole, warn and threaten Nora about how unwise was her plan to follow Mario to his village of Annunziata and face the collective rage of two families.

Brenda would be welcome in that house because nobody knew she kept in touch and told the emigrant what was happening back home. So it was through Brenda that Nora learned of new nieces and nephews, of the outbuilding on the farm house, of the sale of three acres, and the small trailer that was now attached to the back of the family car. Brenda wrote and told her how they watched television a lot, and had been given a microwave oven for Christmas by their children. Well, by the children they acknowledged.

Brenda did try to make them write. She had said she was sure Nora would love to hear from them; it must be lonely for her out there. But they had laughed and said: 'Oh no, it wasn't at all lonely for Lady Nora who was having a fine time in Annunziata, living the life of Reilly with the whole place probably gossiping about her and ruining the reputation of all Irishwomen in front of these people.'

Brenda was married to a man whom they had both laughed at years back, a man called Pillow Case, for some reason they had all forgotten. They had no children and they both worked in a restaurant now. Patrick, as she now called Pillow Case, was the chef and Brenda was the manageress. The owner lived mainly abroad and was content to leave it to them. She wrote that it was as good as having your own place without the financial worries. She seemed content, but then perhaps she wasn't telling the truth either.

Nora certainly never told Brenda about how it had turned out; the years of living in a place smaller than the village she had come from in Ireland and loving the man who lived across the little *piazza*, a man who could come to visit her only with huge subterfuge, and as the years went on made less and less effort to try and find the opportunities.

Nora wrote about the beautiful village of Annunziata and its white buildings where everyone had little black wrought-iron balconies and filled them with pots of geraniums or Busy Lizzies, but not just one or two pots like at home, whole clusters of them. And how there was a gate outside the village where you could stand and look down on the valley. And the church had some lovely ceramics which visitors were coming to see more and more.

Mario and Gabriella ran the local hotel and they did lunches now for visitors and it was very successful. Everyone in Annunziata was pleased because it meant that other people, like wonderful Signora Leone who sold postcards and little pictures of the church and Nora's great friends Paolo and Gianna who made little pottery dishes and jugs with Annunziata written on them, made some money. And people sold oranges and flowers from baskets. And even she, Nora, benefited from the tourists since, as well as making her lace-trimmed handkerchiefs and table runners for sale, she also gave little guided tours for English-speaking visitors. She took them round the church and told of its history, and pointed out the places in the valley where there had been battles and possibly Roman settlements and certainly centuries of adventure.

She never found it necessary to tell Brenda about Mario and Gabriella's children, five of them in all, with big dark eyes looking at her suspiciously with sullen downcast glances from across the *piazza*. Too young to know who she was and why she was hated and feared, too knowing to think she was just another neighbour and friend.

Brenda and Pillow Case didn't have any children of their own, they wouldn't be interested in these handsome, unsmiling Sicilian children who looked across from the steps of their family hotel at the little room where Signora sat sewing and surveying all that passed by.

That's what they called her in Annunziata, just Signora. She had said she was a widow when she arrived. It was so like her own name Nora anyway, she felt she had been meant to be called that always.

And even had there been anyone who truly loved her and cared about her life, how hard it would have been to try and explain what her life was like in this village. A place she would have scorned if it were back in Ireland, no cinema, no dance hall, no supermarket, the local bus irregular and the journeys when it did arrive positively endless.

But here she loved every stone of the place because it was where Mario lived and worked and sang in his hotel, and eventually raised his sons and daughters, and smiled up at her as she sat sewing in her window. And she would nod at him graciously, not noticing as the years went by. And the passionate years in London that ended in 1969 were long forgotten by everyone except Mario and Signora.

Of course, Mario must have remembered them with love and longing and regret as she did, otherwise why would he have stolen into her bed some nights using the key that she had made for him? Creeping across the dark square when his wife was asleep. She knew never to expect him on a night there was a moon. Too many other eyes might have seen a figure crossing the *piazza* and known that Mario was wandering from the wife to the foreign woman, the strange foreign woman with the big wild eyes and long red hair.

Occasionally Signora asked herself was there any possibility that she *could* be mad, which was what her family at home thought and was almost certainly the view of the citizens of Annunziata.

Other women would surely have let him go, cried over the loss of his love and got on with their lives. She had only been twenty-four back in 1969, and she lived through her thirties, sewing and smiling and speaking Italian, but never in public to the man she loved. All that time in London when he had begged her to learn his language, telling her how beautiful it was, she had learned hardly a word, telling him that he was the one who must learn English so that they could open a twelve-bedroom hotel in Ireland and make their fortune. And all the time Mario had laughed and told her that she was his redheaded *principessa*, the loveliest girl in the world.

Signora had some memories that she did not run past herself in the little picture-show of memories which she played in her mind.

She didn't think of the white-hot anger of Mario when she followed him to Annunziata and got off the bus that day, recognising his father's little hotel immediately from the description. His face had hardened in a way that frightened her to think about. He had pointed to a van that was parked outside and motioned her to get in. He had driven very fast, taking corners at a terrible speed, and then turned suddenly off that road into a secluded olive grove where no one could see them. She reached for him, yearning as she had been yearning since she had set out on her journey.

But he pushed her away from him and pointed to the valley down below.

'See those vines, those belong to Gabriella's father, see the ones there, they belong to my father. It has always been known that we will marry. You have no right to come here like this and make things bad for me.'

'I have every right. I love you, you love me.' It had been so simple.

His face was working with the emotion of bewilderment. 'You cannot say that I have not been honest, I *told* you this, I *told* your parents. I never pretended that I was not involved with and promised to Gabriella.'

'Not in bed you didn't, you spoke of no Gabriella then,' she had pleaded.

'Nobody speaks of another woman in bed, Nora. Be reasonable, go away, go home, go back to Ireland.'

'I can't go home,' Nora had said simply. 'I have to be where you are. It's just the way things are. I will stay here forever.'

And that was the way it was.

The years passed and by sheer grit Signora became a part of the life of Annunziata. Not really accepted, because nobody knew exactly why she was there and her explanation that she loved Italy was not considered enough. She lived in two rooms in a house on the square. Her rent was low because she kept an eye on the elderly couple who owned the house, brought them steaming cups of *caffè latte* in the morning and she did their shopping for them.

But she was no trouble. She didn't sleep with the menfolk or drink in the bars. She taught English in the little school every Friday morning. She sewed little fancies and took them every few months to a big town to sell them.

She learned Italian from a little book and it became tattered as she went over and over the phrases, asking herself questions and answering them, her soft Irish voice eventually mastering the Italian sounds.

She sat in her room and watched the wedding of Mario and Gabriella, sewing all the time and letting no tear fall on the linen that she was embroidering. The fact that he looked up at her as the bells rang from the little campanile of the church in the square was enough. He was walking with his brothers and Gabriella's brothers to be married because it was their way. A tradition that involved families marrying each other to keep the land. It had nothing to do with his love for her or hers for him. That couldn't be affected by something like this.

And she watched from this window as his children were carried to the church to be christened. Families needed sons in this part of the world. It didn't hurt her. She knew that if he could have it another way then she would have been his *principessa irlandese* for all to see.

Signora realised that many of the men in Annunziata knew that there was something between Mario and herself. But it didn't worry them, it made Mario more of a man than ever in their eyes. She always believed that the women knew nothing of their love. She never thought it odd that they didn't invite her to join them when they went to market together, or to gather the grapes that were not used for wine, or to pick the wild flowers for the festival. They were happy when she made beautiful clothes to deck the statue of Our Lady.

They smiled at her over the years as she stumbled through and then mastered their language. They had stopped asking her when she was going home, back to her island. It was as if they had been watching her and she had passed some test. She wasn't upsetting anyone, she could stay.

And after twelve years she started hearing from her sisters. Inconsequential letters from Rita and Helen. Nothing that referred to anything that *she* had written herself. No mention that they had heard from her on birthdays and at Christmas and read all the letters she had written to their parents. Instead they wrote about their marriages and their children and how times were hard and everything was expensive and time was short, and everything was pressure these days.

At first Signora was delighted to hear from them. She had long wanted something that brought her two worlds together. The letters from Brenda went a little way along the road but didn't connect with her past, with her family life. She replied eagerly, asking questions about the family and how her parents were, and had they become at all reconciled to the Situation. Since this drew no response, Signora wrote different kinds of questions, seeking their views on subjects from the IRA hunger strikers, to Ronald Reagan being elected President of America, and the engagement of Prince Charles and Lady Di. None of these were ever answered, and no matter how much she told them about Annunziata, they never commented on it at all.

Brenda's note said she wasn't at all surprised by the arrival of letters from Rita and Helen.

'Any day now you'll be hearing from the brothers as well,' she wrote. 'The hard truth is that your father is very frail. He may have to go into hospital on a permanent basis, and then what will become of your mother? Nora, I tell you this harshly, because it is harsh and sad news. And you know well that I think you were foolish to go to that godforsaken spot on a mountain and watch the man who said he loved you flaunt his family in front of you . . . but still by God I don't think you should come home to be a minder to your mother who wouldn't give you the time of day or even reply to your letters.'

Signora read this letter sadly. Surely Brenda must be mistaken. And surely she had read the situation all wrong. Rita and Helen were writing because they wanted to keep in touch. Then came the letter saying that Dad was going to hospital and wondering when Nora would come home and take things over.

It was springtime and Annunziata had never looked more beautiful. But Signora looked pale and sad. Even the people who did not trust her were concerned. The Leone family who sold the postcards and little drawings called to see her. Would she like a little soup, *stracciatella*, it was a broth with beaten egg and lemon juice? She thanked them but her face was wan and her tone was flat. They worried about her.

Across the *piazza* in the hotel, the word reached dark handsome Mario and Gabriella his solid dutiful wife that Signora was not well. Perhaps someone should send for the *dottore*.

Gabriella's brothers frowned. When a woman had a mystery frailty in Annunziata it often meant one thing. Like that she was pregnant.

The same thought had crossed Mario's mind. But he met their glances levelly. 'Can't be that, she's nearly forty,' he said.

Still they waited for the doctor, hoping he would let fall some information over a glass of sambucca, which was his little weakness.

'It's all in the head,' the doctor said confidentially. 'Strange woman, nothing physical wrong with her, just a great sadness.'

'Why does she not go home to where she comes from then?' asked the eldest brother of Gabriella. He was the head of the family since his father had died. He had heard the odd troublesome rumour about his brother-in-law and Signora. But he knew it couldn't possibly be true. The man could not be so stupid as to do something like that right on his doorstep.

The people of the village watched as Signora's shoulders drooped and not even the Leone family were able to throw any light on it. Poor Signora. She just sat there, her eyes far away.

One night when his family slept Mario crept in and up the stairs to her bed.

'What has happened? Everyone says that you have an illness and that you are losing your mind,' he said, as he put his arms around her and pulled up the quilt that she had embroidered with the names of Italian cities, Firenze, Napoli, Milano, Venezia, Genova. All in different colours and with little flowers around them. It was a labour of love, she told Mario. When she did the stitching she thought how lucky she was to have come to this land and to live near the man she loved; not everyone was as lucky as she was.

That night she didn't sound like one of the luckiest women in the world. She sighed heavily and lay like lead on the bed instead of turning to welcome Mario joyfully. She said nothing at all.

'Signora.' He called her that too, like everyone else. It would have marked him out if he had used her real name. 'Dear, dear Signora, many many times I have told you to go away from here, that there is no life for you in Annunziata. But you insist that you stay and it is your decision. People here have begun to know and like you. They tell me you had the doctor. I don't want you to be sad, tell me what has happened.'

'You know what has happened.' Her voice was very dead.

'No, what is it?'

'You asked the doctor. I saw him go into the hotel after he left me. He told you I am sick in the mind, that's all.'

'But why? Why now? You have been here so long when you couldn't speak Italian, when you knew nobody. That was the time to be sick in the mind, not now when you have been ten years as a part of this town.'

'Over eleven years, Mario. Nearly twelve.'

'Yes, well whatever.'

'I am sad because I thought my family missed me and loved me, and now I realise that they just want me to be a nursemaid to my old mother.' She never turned to look at him. She lay cold and dead without response to his touches.

'You don't want to be with me, happy like it always is and so good?' He was very surprised.

'No, Mario, not now. Thank you very very much but not tonight.'

He got out of bed and came around to look at her. He lit the candle in the pottery holder; her room did not run to a bedside light. She lay there white-faced, her long red hair on the pillow under the absurd coverlet with all the cities' names on it. He was at a loss for words. 'Soon you must do the places of Sicily,' he said. 'Catania, Palermo, Cefalù, Agrigento . . .'

She sighed again.

He left troubled. But the hills around Annunziata, with their daily carpet of new flowers, had healing powers. Signora walked among them until the colour came back to her face.

The Leone family sometimes packed her a little basket with bread and cheese and olives, and Gabriella the stony-faced wife of Mario gave her a bottle of Marsala, saying that some people drank it as a tonic. The Leone family invited her to lunch on a Sunday and cooked pasta Norma, with aubergines and tomatoes.

'Do you know why it's called pasta Norma, Signora?'

'No, Signora Leone. I'm afraid I don't.'

'Because it's so good it is reaching the same height of perfection as the opera *Norma* by Bellini.'

'Who was, of course, Sicilian,' Signora finished proudly.

They patted her hand. She knew so much about their country, their village. Who could fail to be delighted with her?

Paolo and Gianna, who had the little pottery shop, made her a special jug. They had written *Signora d'Irlanda* on it. And they put a little piece of gauze over it with beads at the edge. It was to keep her water fresh at night. No flies could get in, or dust in the hot summers. People came in and did little jobs for the old couple whose house she lived in, so that Signora would not have to worry about earning her rent. And, bathed in all this friendship and indeed love, she became well and strong again. And she knew she was loved here even if she wasn't loved back home in Dublin, where the letters were written with greater frequency, wanting to know her plans.

She wrote back almost dreamily of life in Annunziata, and how she was so needed here, by the old people upstairs who relied on her. By the Leone family who fought so often and so volubly, she had to go to lunch there every Sunday to make sure they didn't kill each other. She wrote about Mario's hotel and how much it depended on tourism so everyone in the village had to pull together to get the visitors to come. Her own job was to guide tourists around and she had found a lovely place to take them on a little escorted walk, to a kind of ledge that looked down over the valleys and up at the mountain.

She had suggested that Mario's younger brother open a little café there. It was called Vista del Monte, mountain view – but didn't it sound so much more wonderful in Italian?

She expressed sympathy for her father, who now spent much of his time in hospital. How right it had been for them to sell the farm and move to Dublin. And for mother now struggling, they told her, to manage in a flat in Dublin. So often they had explained that the flat had an extra bedroom, and so often she ignored the information, only enquiring after her parents' health and wondering vaguely about the postal services, saying that she had written so regularly since 1969 and now here they were in the eighties and yet her parents had never been able to reply to a letter. Surely the only explanation was that all the letters must have gone astray.

Brenda wrote a letter of high approval.

'Good girl yourself. You have them totally confused. I'd say you'll have a letter from your mother within the month. But stick to your guns. Don't come home for her. She wouldn't write unless she had to.'

The letter came, and Signora's heart turned over at her mother's familiar writing. Yes, familiar even after all these years. She knew every word had been dictated by Helen and Rita.

It skated over twelve years of silence, of obstinate refusal to reply to the beseechings of her lonely daughter overseas. It blamed most of it on 'your father's very doctrinaire attitudes to morality'. Signora smiled wanly to herself at the phrase. If she were to look at a writing pad for a hundred years, her mother could not have come up with such an expression.

In the last paragraph the letter said: 'Please come home, Nora. Come home and live with us. We will not interfere with your life but we need you, otherwise we would not ask.'

And otherwise they would not have written, Signora thought to herself. She was surprised that she did not feel more bitter, but that had all passed now. She had been through it when Brenda had written saying how they didn't care about her as a person, only as someone who would look after elderly and unbending parents.

Here in her peaceful life she could afford to feel sorry for them. Compared to what she had in life, her own family had nothing at all. She wrote gently and explained that she could not come. If they had read her letters they would realise how much she was needed here now. And that of course if they had let her know in the past that they wanted her as part of their life then she would have made plans not to get so involved in the life of this beautiful peaceful place. But of course how could she have known that they would call on her? They had never been in touch, and she was sure they would understand.

And the years went on.

Signora's hair got streaks of grey in the red. But unlike the dark women who surrounded her it didn't seem to age her. Her hair just looked bleached by the sun. Gabriella looked matronly now. She sat at the desk of the hotel, her face heavier and rounder, her eyes much more beady than when they had flashed with jealousy across the *piazza*. Her sons were tall and difficult, no longer the little dark-eyed angels who did whatever they were asked to do.

Probably Mario had got older too, but Signora didn't see it. He came to her room – less frequently, and often just to lie there with his arm around her.

The quilt had hardly any space on it now for more cities. Signora had put in smaller places that appealed to her.

'You should not put Giardini-Naxos there among the big places, it's only a tiny place,' Mario complained.

'No, I don't agree. When I went to Taormina I went out there on the bus, it was a lovely place ... its own atmosphere, its own character, a lot of tourism. No, no, it deserves a place.' And sometimes Mario would sigh heavily as if he had too many problems. He told her his worries. His second boy was wild. He was going to New York, aged only twenty. He was too young, he would get in with all the wrong people. No good would come of it.

'He's in with all the wrong people here,' Signora said soothingly. 'Possibly in New York he will be more timid, less assured. Let him go with your blessing because he'll go anyway.'

'You are very, very wise, Signora,' he said, and lay with his head tucked companionably on her shoulder.

She didn't close her eyes, she looked at the dark ceiling and thought of the times in this room when he had told her she was foolish, the most foolish stupid woman in the world, to have followed him here. Here where there was no future for her. And the years had turned it all into wisdom. How strange the world was.

And then the daughter of Mario and Gabriella became pregnant. The boy was not at all the kind of husband they would have wanted for her, a boy from the countryside who washed pots in the kitchen of the hotel in the *piazza*. Mario came and cried in her room about this, his daughter, a child, a little child herself. The disgrace, the shame.

It was 1994, she told him. Even in Ireland it was no longer a disgrace and a shame. It was the way life went on. You coped with it. Perhaps the boy could come and work in Vista del Monte, expand it a little, then he would be seen to have his own place.

That was her fiftieth birthday, but Signora didn't tell Mario, she didn't tell anyone. She had embroidered herself a little cushion cover with *BUON COMPLEANNO*, Happy Birthday, on it. She fingered it when Mario had gone, his tears for his defiled daughter dried. 'I wonder am I really mad as I feared all those years ago?'

She watched from her window as the young Maria was married to the boy who worked in the kitchen, just as she had watched Mario and Gabriella go to the church. The bells of the campanile were still the same, ringing over the mountain like bells should ring.

Imagine being in her fifties. She didn't feel a day older than she had when she came here. She didn't have a single regret. Were there many people in this or any other place who could say the same?

And of course she had been right in her predictions. Maria was married to the man who was not worthy of her and her family, but the loss was made up by the boy having to work night and day in Vista del Monte. And if people gossiped about it, it was only for a few days.

And their second son, the boy who was wild, went to New York and the news was that he was as good as gold. He was working in his cousin's trattoria and saving money every week for the day when he would buy his own place back home on the island of Sicily.

Signora always slept with her window on the square slightly open, so she was one of the first to hear the news when the brothers of Gabriella, thickset men, middle-aged now, came running from their cars. First she heard them wake the *dottore* in his house. Signora stood in the shadows of her shutter and watched. There had been an accident, that much was obvious.

She peered to see what had happened. Please God may it not be one of their children. They had already had too many problems with that family.

And then she saw the solid figure of Gabriella on the doorstep, in her nightdress, with a shawl around her shoulders. Her hands were to her face and the sky was rent apart by her cries.

'MARIO, MARIO . . .'

The sound went up into the mountains around Annunziata and down into the valleys.

And the sound went into Signora's bedroom, and chilled her heart as she watched them lift the body out of the car.

She didn't know how long she stood there, like stone. But soon, as the square filled up in the moonlight with his family and neighbours and friends, she found herself amongst them, the tears flowing unchecked. She saw his face with the bloodstains and the bruising. He had been driving home from a village not far away. He had missed a corner. The car had turned over many times.

She knew she must touch his face. Nothing would ever settle down in the world unless she touched him, kissed him even as his sisters and children and wife were doing. She moved towards him unaware of anyone looking at her, forgetful entirely of the years of secrecy and covering up.

When she was quite near him she felt hands reaching out to her, and keen bodies in the crowd pulled her back. Signora Leone, her friends the pottery makers, Paolo and Gianna, and, strange as it seemed ever afterwards, two of the brothers of Gabriella. They just moved her away, back from where the eyes of Annunziata would see her naked grief and the memories of the village would store yet one more amazing happening, the night when the *Signora irlandese* broke down and admitted in public her love for the man who ran the hotel.

She was in houses that night where she had never been before, and people gave her strong brandy to drink and someone stroked her hand. Outside the walls of these houses she could hear the wailing and the prayers, and sometimes she stood to go and stand at her rightful place by his body but always gentle hands held her back.

On the day of his funeral, she sat pale and calm at her window, her head bowed as they carried his coffin out from the hotel and across the square to the church with the frescoes and ceramics. The bell was one lonely mournful sound. Nobody looked up at her window. Nobody saw the tears fall down her face and splash on to the embroidery that lay in her lap.

And after that they all assumed that she should now be leaving, that it was time for her to go home.

Little by little she realised it. Signora Leone would say: 'Before you go back you must come once with me to the great passion procession in my home town Trapani . . . you will be able to tell the people back in Ireland about it all.'

And Paolo and Gianna gave her a big plate they had made specially for her return. 'You can put on it all the fruits that are grown in Ireland and the plate will remind you of your time in Annunziata.' They seemed to think that this is what she would do.

But Signora had no home to go to, she didn't want to move. She was in her fifties, she had lived here since before she was thirty. This was where she would die. One day the church bell here would ring for her funeral too, she had money to pay for it all ready in a little carved wooden box.

So she took no notice of the hints that were getting heavier, and the advice that was trembling on lips waiting to be given.

Not until Gabriella came to see her.

Gabriella crossed the square in her dark mourning clothes. Her face looked old, as if it were set in lines of grief and sorrow. She had never come to

Signora's rooms before. She knocked on the door as if she had been expected. Signora fussed to make her guest welcome, offering her a little fruit juice and water, a biscuit from the tin. Then she sat and waited.

Gabriella walked around the two small rooms. She fingered the coverlet on the bed with all its intricately woven place names.

'It's exquisite, Signora,' she said.

'You are too kind, Signora Gabriella.'

Then there was a long silence.

'Will you go back soon to your country?' Gabriella asked eventually.

'There is nobody for me to go back to,' Signora said simply.

'But there is nobody here, nobody that you should want to stay for. Not now.' Gabriella was equally direct.

Signora nodded as if to agree. 'But in Ireland, Signora Gabriella, there is nobody at all. I came here when I was a young girl, now I am a woman, middle-aged, about to approach the beginning of old age. I thought I would stay here.' Their eyes met.

'You do not have friends here, not a real life, Signora.'

'I have more than I have in Ireland.'

'You could pick up a life again in Ireland. Your friends there, your family, would be happy to see you return.'

'Do you want me to go away from here, Signora Gabriella?' The question was very straight. She just wanted to know.

'He always said you would go if he were to die. He said you would go back to your people and leave me here with my people to mourn my husband.'

Signora looked at her in amazement. Mario had made this promise on her behalf, without any guarantee. 'Did he say that I had agreed to do this?'

'He said it was what would happen. And that if I, Gabriella, were to die, he told me that he would not marry you, because it would cause a scandal, and my name would be lessened. They would think that always he had wanted to marry you.'

'And did this please you?'

'No, these things didn't please me, Signora. I didn't want to think of Mario dead, or of my being dead. But I suppose it gave me the dignity that I need. I didn't need to fear you. You would not stay on here against the tradition of the place and share in the mourning for the man who was gone.'

The sounds of the square went on outside, meat deliveries to the hotel, a van of clay supplies being carried into the pottery shop, children coming home from school laughing and calling to each other. Dogs barking, and somewhere birds singing too. Mario had told her about dignity and tradition and how important they were to him and his family.

It was as if he were speaking to her now from the grave. He was sending her a message, asking her to go home.

She spoke very slowly. 'I think at the end of the month, Signora Gabriella. That is when I will go back to Ireland.'

The other woman's eyes were full with gratitude and relief. She reached out both her hands and took Signora's. 'I am sure you will be much happier, much more at peace,' she said.

'Yes, yes,' Signora said slowly, letting the words hang there in the warm afternoon air.

'*Sì sì . . . veramente.*'

She only barely had the money for the fare. Somehow her friends knew this.

Signora Leone came and pressed the bundles of lire into her hand. 'Please, Signora. Please. It's thanks to you I have such a good living, please take it.'

It was the same with Paolo and Gianna. Their pottery business would not have got started if it had not been for Signora. 'Regard it as a tiny commission.'

And the old couple who owned the room where she had lived most of her adult life. They said she had improved the property so well she deserved some compensation.

On the day that the bus came to take her with her belongings to the town with the airport, Gabriella came out on her steps. She didn't speak and nor did Signora, but they bowed to each other. Their faces were grave and respectful. Some of those who watched the little scene knew what was being said. They knew that one woman was thanking the other with all her heart in a way that could never be put into words, and wishing her good fortune in whatever lay ahead.

It was loud and crowded in the city, and the airport was full of noise and bustle, not the happy, easy bustle of Annunziata but people rushing without meeting each other's gaze. It would be like this in Dublin too, when she got back there, but Signora decided not to think about it.

She had made no plans, she would just do what seemed the right thing to do when she got there. No point in wasting her journey planning what could not be planned. She had told no one that she was coming. Not her family, not even Brenda. She would find a room and look after herself as she had always done, and then she would work out what to do next.

On the plane she began talking to a boy. He was about ten, the age of Mario and Gabriella's youngest son, Enrico. Automatically she spoke to him in Italian, but he looked away confused.

Signora looked out the window. She would never know what would happen to Enrico, or his brother in New York, or his sister married to the kitchen help and up in Vista del Monte. She would not know who came to live in her room. And whoever it was would never know of her long years there, and why she had spent them.

It was like swimming out to sea and not knowing what would happen where you had left and what was going to happen where you would arrive.

She changed planes in London. She had no wish to spend any time there. Not to visit the old haunts where she had lived with Mario in a different life. Not to look up people long forgotten, and places only barely remembered. No, she would go on to Dublin. To whatever lay ahead.

It had all changed so much. The place was much, much bigger than she remembered. There were flights arriving from all over the world. When she had left, most of the big international flights had gone in and out of Shannon

Airport. She hadn't known that things would be so different. Like the road in from the airport. When she had left the bus had wound its way out through housing estates; now it came in on a motorway with flowers planted on each side. Heavens, how Ireland was keeping up with the times!

An American woman on the bus asked her where she was staying.

'I'm not absolutely sure,' Signora explained. 'I'll find somewhere.'

'Are you a native or a visitor?'

'I came from here a long time ago,' Signora said.

'Same as me . . . looking for ancestors.' The American woman was pleased. She was giving a week to finding her roots, she thought that should be long enough.

'Oh definitely,' Signora said, realising how hard it was to find instantly the right response in English. She had been about to say *certo*. How affected it would sound breaking into Italian, they would think she was showing off. She must watch for it.

Signora got out of her bus and walked up the quays beside the Liffey to O'Connell Bridge. All around her there were young people, tall, confident, laughing, in groups. She remembered reading somewhere about this youthful population, half the country under the age of twenty-four was it?

She hadn't expected to see such proof of it. And they were dressed brightly too. Before she had gone to England to work, Dublin had been a grey and drab place. A lot of the buildings had been cleaned, there were smart cars, expensive cars in the busy traffic lanes. She remembered more bicycles and second-hand cars. The shops were bright and opened up. Her eye caught the magazines, girls with big bosoms, surely these had been banned when she was last here or was she living in some kind of cloud cuckoo land?

For some reason she kept walking down the Liffey after O'Connell Bridge. It was almost as if she were following the crowd, and there she found Temple Bar. It was like the Left Bank in Paris when once she had gone there so many years ago with Mario for a long weekend. Cobbled streets, outdoor cafés, each place full of young people calling to each other and waving at those they knew.

Nobody had told her Dublin was like this. But then would Brenda, married to Pillow Case and working in a much more settled kind of place, have even visited these streets?

Her sisters and their hard-up husbands, her two brothers and their inert wives . . . they were not people who'd have discovered Temple Bar. If they knew of it, then it would be surely only to shake their heads.

Signora thought it was wonderful. It was a whole new world, she couldn't get enough of it. Eventually she sat down to have a coffee.

A girl of about eighteen with long red hair, like her own many years ago, served her coffee. She thought Signora was a foreigner.

'What country are you from?' she asked in slow English, mouthing the words.

'Sicilia, in Italia,' Signora said.

'Beautiful country, but I tell you I'm not going there until I can speak the language though.'

'And why is that?'

'Well, I'd want to know what the fellows are saying, I mean you wouldn't know what you were letting yourself in for if you didn't know what they were saying.'

'I didn't speak any Italian when I went there, and I sure didn't know what I was letting myself in for,' Signora said. 'But you know it worked out all right . . . no, more than all right. It was wonderful.'

'How long did you stay for?'

'A long time. Twenty-six years.' Her voice sounded wondering.

The girl who wasn't born when she had set out on this adventure looked at her in amazement. 'You stayed all that time, you must have loved it.'

'Oh I did, I did.'

'And when did you come back?'

'Today,' Signora said.

She sighed heavily and wondered had she imagined that the girl looked at her slightly differently, as if she had somehow revealed herself to be a little strange. Signora knew she must watch that she didn't let people think that. No letting Italian phrases fall, no sighing, no saying strange, disconnected things.

The girl was about to move away.

'Excuse me, this seems a very nice part of Dublin. Is this the kind of place I could rent a room, do you think?' Now the girl knew she was odd. Perhaps people didn't call them rooms any more. Should she have said apartment? Flat? Place to stay? 'Just somewhere simple,' Signora said.

She listened glumly as she learned that this was one of the most fashionable parts of town; everyone wanted to live here. There were penthouse apartments, pop stars had bought hotels, business people had invested in townhouses. The place was coming down with restaurants. It was the last word now.

'I see.' Signora did see something, she saw she had a lot to learn about the city she had returned to. 'And please could you tell me where *would* be a place that would be good value to stay, somewhere that hasn't become the last word?'

The girl shook her head of long, dark red hair. It was hard to know. She seemed to be trying to work out whether Signora had any money at all, whether she would have to work for her keep, how long she would perch in wherever she landed.

Signora decided to help her. 'I have enough money for bed and breakfast for a week, but then I'll have to find a cheap place and maybe somewhere I could do some jobs . . . maybe mind children.'

The girl was doubtful. 'They usually want young ones to mind kids,' she said.

'Or maybe over a restaurant and work in it?'

'No, I wouldn't get your hopes up over that, honestly . . . we all want those kind of places. They're very hard to get.'

She was nice, the girl. Her face was pitying, of course, but Signora would have to get used to a lot of that in what lay ahead. She decided to be brisk to hide her messiness, anything to make her acceptable and not to appear like a doddery old bag lady.

'Is that your name there on your apron? Suzi?'

'Yes. I'm afraid my mother was a Suzi Quatro fan.' She saw the blank look. 'The singer, you know? She was big years ago, maybe not in Italy.'

'I'm sure she was, it's just that I wasn't listening then. Now, Suzi, I can't take up your day with all my problems, but if you could give me just half a minute I'd love you to tell me what area would be a nice cheap one where I should start looking.'

Suzi listed off the names of places that used to be small areas, suburbs if not exactly villages, well outside the city when Signora was young, but now apparently they were big sprawling working-class estates. Half the people there would take someone in to rent a room if their kids had left home maybe. As long as it was cash. It wouldn't be wise to mention that she herself was badly off. Be fairly secretive about things, they liked that.

'You're very good to me, Suzi. How do you know all about things like this at your age?'

'Well, that's where I grew up, I know the scene.'

Signora knew she must not tire the patience of this nice child. She reached for her purse to get out the money for the coffee.

'Thank you very much for your help – I do appreciate it. And if I do get settled I'll come in and give you a little gift.'

She saw Suzi pause and bite her lip as if to decide something.

'What's your name?' Suzi asked.

'Now I know this sounds funny, but my name is Signora. It's not that I'm trying to be formal, but that's what they called me and what I like to be called.'

'Are you serious about not minding what kind of a place it is?'

'Absolutely serious.' Her face was honest. It was quite clear that Signora couldn't understand people who cared about their surroundings.

'Listen. I don't get on with my family myself, so I don't live at home any more. And only a couple of weeks ago they were talking about trying to get someone to take my room. It's empty, and they could well do with a few pounds a week – it would have to be cash, you know, and you'd have to say you were a friend in case anyone asked . . . because of income tax.'

'Do you think I could?' Signora's eyes were shining.

'Listen, now.' Suzi was anxious there should be no misunderstandings. 'We're talking about a very ordinary house in an estate of houses that look the same, some a bit better, some a bit worse . . . it wouldn't be gracious or anything. They have the telly on all the time, they shout to each other over it and of course my brother's there, Jerry. He's fourteen and awful.'

'I just need a place to stay. I'm sure it would be lovely.'

Suzi wrote down the address and told her which bus to take. 'Why don't you go down their road and ask a few people who I know definitely won't be able to have you and then go by chance as it were to my house and ask. Mention the money first and say it won't be for long. They'll like you because you're a bit older like, respectable is what they'll say. They'll take you, but don't say you came from me.'

Signora gave her a long look. 'Did they not like your boyfriend?'

'Boyfriends.' Suzi corrected her. 'My father says I'm a slut, but please don't try to deny it when he tells you because it will show you've met me.' Suzi's face looked hard.

Signora wondered had her own face been hard like that when she set out for Sicily all those years ago.

She took the bus and wondered at how the city she had once lived in had grown and spread so wide. In the evening light children played in the streets amongst the traffic, and then they went further afield, in where there were small gardens and children cycled round in circles leaning on gates and running in and out of each other's gardens.

Signora called at the houses that Suzi had suggested. Dublin men and women told her that their houses were full and they needed all the space they had.

'Can you suggest anyone?' she asked.

'Try the Sullivans,' someone suggested.

Now she had her reason. She knocked on the door. Would this be her new home? Was this the roof she would lie under and hope to ease the pain of losing her life in Annunziata? Not only the man she loved but her whole life, her future, her burial with the bells ringing for her. Everything. She must not try to like it in case they said no.

Jerry opened the door, his mouth full. He had red hair and freckles and he had a sandwich in his hand.

'Yeah?' he said.

'Could I speak to your mother or your father please?'

'What about?' Jerry asked.

This was a household where he had obviously welcomed in people who should not have been welcomed in the past.

'I was wondering if I could rent a room?' Signora began. She knew that inside they had turned down the television to hear what was happening on the doorstep.

'A room *here*?' Jerry was so utterly disbelieving that Signora thought maybe he was right, it did seem a foolish notion. But then her life had been based on a series of foolish notions. Why stop now?

'So perhaps I could talk to them?'

The boy's father came to the door. A big man with tufts of hair on each side of his head, looking like handles that he could be lifted by. He was about Signora's age, she supposed, but red-faced and looked as if the years had taken their toll. He was wiping his hands down the sides of his trousers, as if about to shake hands.

'Can I help you?' he said suspiciously.

Signora explained that she had been looking for a place in the area, and that the Quinns in number 22 had sent her over here in case they might have a spare room. She sort of implied that she had known the Quinns; it gave her an introduction.

'Peggy, will you come out here?' he called. And a woman with tired, dark shadows under her eyes and straight hair pushed behind her ears came out smoking and coughing at the same time.

'What is it?' she asked unwelcomingly.

It was not very promising, but Signora told her tale again.

'And what has you looking for a room up in this area?'

'I have been away from Ireland for a long time, I don't know many places now but I do need somewhere to live. I had no idea that things had become so expensive and ... well ... I came out this way because you can see the mountains from here,' she said.

For some reason this seemed to please them. Maybe it was because it was so without guile.

'We never had boarders,' the woman said.

'I would be no trouble, I would sit in my room.'

'You wouldn't want to eat with us?' The man indicated a table with a plate of very thick unappetising sandwiches, butter still in its foil paper and the milk still in the bottle.

'No, no thank you so much. Suppose I were to buy an electric kettle, I eat mainly salads, and I suppose I could have an electric ring thing. You know, to heat up soups?'

'You haven't even seen the room,' the woman said.

'Can you show it to me?' Her voice was gentle but authoritative.

Together they all walked up the stairs, watched by Jerry from below.

It was a small room with a wash hand basin. An empty wardrobe and an empty book case, no pictures on the walls. Not much memory of the years that the beautiful vibrant Suzi with her long dark red hair and her flashing eyes had spent in this room.

Outside the window it was getting dark. The room was on the back of the house. It looked out over wasteland which would soon be more houses, but at the moment there was nothing between her and the mountains.

'It's good to have a beautiful view like this,' Signora said. 'I have been living in Italy, they would call this Vista del Monte, mountain view.'

'That's the name of the school the young lad goes to, Mountainview,' said the big man.

Signora smiled at him. 'If you'll have me, Mrs Sullivan, Mr Sullivan ... I think I've come to a lovely place,' she said.

She saw them exchange glances, wondering was she cracked in the head, were they wise to let her into the house.

They showed her the bathroom. They would tidy it up a bit, they said, and give her a rack for her towel.

They sat downstairs and talked, and it was as if her very gentleness seemed to impose more manners on them. The man cleared the food away from the table, the woman put out her cigarette, and turned off the television. The boy sat in the far corner watching with interest.

They explained that there was a couple across the road who made a living out of informing the tax offices on other people's business, so if she did come she would have to be a relation, so that the busybodies couldn't report there was a paying guest contributing to the household expenses.

'A cousin maybe.' Signora seemed excited at the thought of the subterfuge.

She told them she had lived long years in Italy, and having seen several pictures of the Pope and the Sacred Heart on the walls she added that her Italian husband had died there recently and she had come home to Ireland to make her life here.

'And have you no family here?'

'I do have some relations. I will look them up in time,' said Signora, who had a mother, a father, two sisters and two brothers living in this city.

They told her that times were hard and that Jimmy worked as a driver, freelance sort of, hackney cabs, vans, whatever was going, and that Peggy worked in the supermarket at the checkout.

And then the conversation came back to the room upstairs.

'The room belonged to someone else in the family?' Signora enquired politely.

They told her of a daughter who preferred to live nearer the city. Then they talked of money, and she showed them her wallet. She had five weeks' rent. Would they like a month in advance? she wondered.

They looked at each other, the Sullivans, faces anxious. They were suspicious of unworldly people like this who showed you their entire wallet.

'Is that all you have in the world?'

'It's all I have now but I will have more when I get some work.' Signora seemed unruffled by the thought of it. They were still uneasy. 'Perhaps I could step outside while you talk it over,' she said, and went out to the back garden where she looked at the distant, faraway mountains that some people called hills. They weren't rugged and sharp and blue like her mountains were back in Sicily.

People would be going about their business there in Annunziata. Would any of them wonder about Signora and where she was going to lay her head tonight?

The Sullivans came to the door, their decision made.

'I suppose, being a bit short and everything, you'll want to stay immediately, if you are going to be here, that is?' said Jimmy Sullivan.

'Oh, tonight would be great,' Signora said.

'Well, you can come for a week and if you like us and we like you we can talk about it being for a bit longer,' Peggy said.

Signora's eyes lit up. '*Grazie, grazie*,' she said before she could help herself. 'I lived there so long, you see,' she said apologetically.

They didn't mind, she was obviously a harmless eccentric.

'Come on up and help me make the bed,' Peggy said.

Young Jerry's eyes followed them wordlessly.

'I'll be no trouble, Jerry,' Signora said.

'How did you know I was called Jerry?' he asked.

Surely his parents must have spoken to him. This was a slip-up, but

Signora was used to covering her tracks. 'Because it's your name,' she said simply.

And it seemed to satisfy him.

Peggy got out sheets and blankets. 'Suzi had one of those candlewick bedspreads but she took it with her when she went,' Peggy said.

'Do you miss her?'

'She comes round once a week, but usually when her father's out. They never saw eye to eye, not since she was about ten years of age. It's a pity but that's the way it is. Better for her to live on her own rather than all the barneys they had here.'

Signora unpacked the coverlet with all the Italian place names embroidered on it. She had wrapped it in tissue paper and had used it to keep her jug safe. She had brought few possessions with her; she was happy to unpack them so that Peggy Sullivan could see how blameless and innocent was her lifestyle.

Peggy's eyes were round with amazement.

'Where on earth did you get that? It's beautiful.' She gaped.

'I made it myself over the years, adding names here and there. Look there's Rome, and that's Annunziata, the place I lived.'

Peggy's eyes had tears in them. 'And you and he lay under this . . . how sad that he died.'

'Yes, yes it was.'

'Was he sick for a long time?'

'No, killed in an accident.'

'Do you have a picture of him, to put up here maybe?' Peggy patted the top of the chest of drawers.

'No, I have no pictures of Mario, only in my heart and mind.'

The words hung there between them.

Peggy Sullivan decided to talk of something else. 'I tell you if you can do sewing like that it won't be long till you get a job. Anyone would take you on.'

'I never thought of earning my living by sewing.' Signora's face was far away.

'Well what were you going to take up?'

'Teaching maybe, being a guide. I used to sell little embroidered things, fine detailed work for tourists in Sicily. But I didn't think they'd want them here.'

'You could do shamrocks and harps, I suppose,' Peggy said. But neither of them liked the thought of it very much. They finished the room. Signora hung up her few garments and seemed well pleased with it all.

'Thank you for giving me a new home so quickly. I was just saying to your son I'll be no trouble.'

'Don't mind him, he's trouble enough for us all, bone idle lazy. He has our hearts broken. At least Suzi's bright, that fellow will end in the gutter.'

'I'm sure it's just a phase.' Signora had talked like this to Mario about his sons, soothing, optimistic. It was what parents wanted to hear.

'It's a long phase if that's what it is. Listen, will you come down and have a drink with us before you go to bed?'

'No, thank you. I'll start as I mean to go on. I'm tired now. I'll sleep.'

'But you don't even have a kettle to make yourself a cup of tea.'

'Thank you, truly I am fine.'

Peggy left her and went downstairs. Jimmy had a sports programme on television. 'Turn it down a bit, Jimmy. The woman's tired, she's been travelling all day.'

'God almighty, is it going to be like when those two were babies, shush this and shush that?'

'No it's not, and you're as anxious for her money as I am.'

'She's as odd as two left shoes. Did you get anything out of her at all?'

'She says she was married and her husband was killed in an accident. That's what she says.'

'And you don't believe her obviously?'

'Well, she has no picture of him. She doesn't *look* married. And she's got this thing on the bed. It's like a priest's vestment, a quilt. You'd never have time to do that if you were married.'

'You read too many books and see too many films, that's your trouble.'

'She is a bit mad though, Jimmy, not the full shilling.'

'She's hardly an axe murderer, is she?'

'No, but she might have been a nun, she has that sort of still way about her. I'd say that's what she was. Is, even. You never know these days.'

'It could be.' Jimmy was thoughtful. 'Well in case she *is* a nun, don't be too free with telling her all that Suzi gets up to. She'd be out of here in a flash if she knew how that young rossie that we reared carries on.'

Signora stood at her window and looked across the wasteground at the mountains.

Could this place ever be her home?

Would she give in when she saw a mother and father more frail and dependent than when she had left? Would she forgive their slights and their coldness, the lack of response once they knew she was not going to run home obediently and do the single daughter's duty for them?

Or would she stay in this small shabby house with noisy people banging around downstairs, a sullen boy, a disaffected daughter? Signora knew she *would* be kind to this family, the Sullivans whom she had never met before this day.

She would try to bring about a reconciliation between Suzi and her father. She would find some way to interest the sullen child in his work. In time she would hem the curtains, she would mend the frayed cushions in the sitting room, and put ribbon on the edges of the towels in the bathroom. But she would do it slowly. Her years in Annunziata had taught her patience.

She would not go tomorrow and look at her mother's house or visit the home where her father lived.

She would however go to see Brenda and Pillow Case, and she would remember to refer to him as Patrick. They would be even more pleased to see her once they realised she had found herself accommodation and was about to look for work. Maybe they might even have something in their restaurant.

She could wash up and prepare vegetables in the kitchen like the boy who had married Mario's daughter.

Signora washed and undressed. She put on the white nightdress with the little rosebuds she had embroidered around the neckline. Mario had said he loved it; she remembered his hands stroking the rosebuds before he would stroke her.

Mario, asleep now in a graveyard that looked out over the valleys and mountains. He had known her well in the end, known she would follow his advice after his death even though she had not done so in his lifetime. Still, all in all he was probably glad she had stayed, glad she had come and lived in his village for twenty-six years, and he would be glad to know that she had left as he wanted her to do, to give his widow dignity and respect.

She had made him happy so often under this very quilt and wearing this very nightdress. She had made him happy by listening to his worries, stroking his head and giving him gentle thoughts and suggestions. She listened to the strange unfamiliar dogs barking and the children shouting to each other.

Soon she would sleep and tomorrow her new life would start.

Brenda always walked through the dining room of Quentin's at midday. It was a routine. In a nearby church the Angelus rang over a Dublin that rarely paused to acknowledge it by saying prayers these days, as people had done when Brenda was a young girl. She wore a plain coloured dress always, with a crisp clean white collar. Her make-up was freshly applied and she checked each table carefully. The waiters knew they might as well get it right in the beginning because Brenda had such high standards. Mr Quentin who lived abroad always said that his name was good in Dublin entirely due to Brenda and Patrick, and Brenda wanted to keep it that way.

Most of the staff had been there for a while; they knew each other's ways and worked well as a team. There were regular customers, who all liked to be addressed by name, and Brenda had stressed how important it was to remember small details about the customers. Had they enjoyed their holiday? Were they writing a new book? Glad to see their photograph in the *Irish Times*, nice to hear their horse won at the Curragh.

Although her husband Patrick thought that they came for the food Brenda knew that their clientele came to be welcomed, and to be made much of as well. She had spent too many years being nice to people who were nobodies, watching them turn into somebodies and always remembering the flattering reception they got in Quentin's. This was the basis of the regular lunch trade, even when economic times were meant to be hard and belts were reported to be in need of tightening.

Brenda adjusted the flowers on a table by the window and heard the door opening. Nobody came to lunch at this time. Dubliners were late lunch eaters anyway, and Quentin's never saw anyone until well after twelve thirty.

The woman came in hesitantly. She was about fifty or maybe more, long hair streaked in grey but with the remains of red in it, and it was tied back loosely with a coloured scarf. She wore a long brown skirt almost to her ankles and an old-fashioned jacket, like people wore way back in the seventies. She was neither shabby nor smart, she was just totally different. She was about to approach Nell Dunne, already seated in her place at the cash desk, when Brenda realised who she was.

'Nora O'Donoghue!' she called out excitedly. It had been a lifetime since she had seen her friend. The young waiters and Mrs Dunne at the desk looked surprised to see Brenda, the impeccable Brenda Brennan, running across to embrace this unlikely looking woman. 'My God, you actually left that place, you actually got on a plane and came home.'

'I came back, yes,' Signora said.

Suddenly Brenda looked worried. 'It's not . . . I mean your father didn't die or anything?'

'No, not that I know of.'

'So you haven't gone back to them?'

'Oh no. No, not at all.'

'Great, I knew you wouldn't give in. And tell me, how's the love of your life?'

And then Signora's face changed. All the colour and life seemed to go out of it. 'He's dead, Brenda. Mario died. He was killed on the road, on a corner. He's in a churchyard in Annunziata now.'

Even saying it had drained her; she looked as if she were about to faint. In forty minutes the place would fill up. Brenda Brennan had to be out there, the face of Quentin's, not crying with a friend over a lost love. She thought quickly. There was one booth that she usually reserved for lovers, or people having discreet lunches. She would take it for Nora. She led her friend to the table, and called for a large brandy and a glass of iced water. One of them would surely help.

With a practised eye and hand she changed the reservation list, and asked Nell Dunne to photocopy the new version.

Nell was almost too interested in events. 'Is there anything at all we can do to help . . . the situation, Ms Brennan?'

'Yes, thank you, Nell. Photocopy the new seating plan, make sure the waiters have it and that there's a copy in the kitchen. Thank you.' She was brisk and barely courteous. Sometimes Nell Dunne annoyed her, although she never knew quite why.

And then Brenda Brennan, who was known as the Ice Maiden by staff and customers alike, went into the booth and cried tears with her friend over the death of this man Mario whose wife had crossed the square to tell Nora to go home to where she belonged.

It was a nightmare and yet it was a love story. Brenda wondered wistfully for a while what it must have been like to have loved like this, so wildly and without care for the consequences, without planning for the future.

The guests wouldn't see Signora in her booth any more than they ever saw the Government Minister and his lady friend who often dined there, or the head-hunters lunching a likely candidate from another company. It was safe to leave her there alone.

Brenda dried her eyes, touched up her make-up, straightened her collar and went to work. Signora, peering around from time to time, saw with amazement her friend Brenda escorting wealthy confident people to tables, asking them about their families, their business deals . . . And the prices on the menu! It would have kept a family for a whole week in Annunziata. *Where* did these people get the money?

'Chef has some very fresh brill today which he recommends highly, and there's a medley of wild mushrooms . . . but I'll leave it with you, and Charles will come and take your order when you're ready.'

How had Brenda learned to talk like this, to refer to Pillow Case as Chef in some kind of awe, to hold herself so straight? To be *so* confident? While Signora had lived striving to be deferential, to find a background to live in, other people had been putting themselves forward. This is what she would have to learn in her new life. If she were to survive.

Signora blew her nose and straightened herself up. She didn't hunch over the table any more, looking at the menu with frightened eyes. Instead she ordered a tomato salad followed by beef. It had been *so* long since she had eaten meat. Her budget hadn't run to it, and probably would not ever run to it again. She closed her eyes, feeling almost faint at the prices on the menu, but Brenda had insisted. Have what she liked, this was her welcome home lunch. Without her asking for it, a bottle of Chianti appeared. Signora steeled herself not to look it up on the price list. It was a gift and she would accept it as such.

Once she began to eat she realised just how hungry she was. She had hardly had anything to eat on the plane, she was too excited, nervous rather. And then last night in the Sullivans' she had not eaten. The tomato salad was delicious. Fresh basil sprinkled over the plate. When had they heard about things like this in Ireland? The beef was served rare, the vegetables crisp and firm, not soft and swimming in water like she had thought all vegetables used to be before she learned how to cook them properly.

When she had finished she felt much stronger.

'It's all right, I won't cry again,' she said, when the lunchtime crowd had left and Brenda slid in opposite her.

'You're not to go back to your mother, Nora. I don't want to come between families, but really and truly she was never a mother to you when you needed it, why should you be a daughter to her now when she needs it?'

'No, no I don't feel any sense of duty about it at all.'

'Thank God for that,' Brenda said, relieved.

'But I will need to work, to earn a living, to pay my way. Do you need anyone here to peel potatoes, clean up or anything?'

Gently Brenda told her friend that it wouldn't work out, and they had youngsters, trainees. They had been themselves trainees all those years ago. Before . . . well, before everything changed.

'Anyway, Nora, you're too old to do that, you're too well trained. You can do all kinds of things, work in an office, teach Italian maybe.'

'No, I'm too old, that's the problem. I never used a typewriter, let alone a computer. I don't have any qualifications to teach.'

'You'd better sign on to get some money, anyway.' Brenda was always practical.

'Sign on?'

'For the dole, for unemployment benefit.'

'I can't do that, I'm not entitled.'

'Yes, you are. You're Irish, aren't you?'

'But I lived away for so long, I contributed nothing to the country.' She was adamant.

Brenda looked worried. 'You can't start being like Mother Teresa here, you know. This is the real world, you have to look to yourself and take what's being offered.'

'Brenda, don't worry about me, I'm a survivor. Look what I survived for nearly a quarter of a century. Most people would not have done that. I found a place to live within hours of coming back to Dublin. I'll find a job too.'

Signora was brought into the kitchen to meet Pillow Case, whom she managed to call Patrick with difficulty. He was courteous and grave as he welcomed her back and sympathised formally on the death of her husband. Did he think Mario really had been her husband or was it just for appearances in front of these young people who watched him with reverence?

Signora thanked them for the delicious meal and said she would return to eat there again under her own steam.

'We are going to have an Italian season of cooking soon. Perhaps you would translate the menus for us?' Patrick suggested.

'Oh I'd be delighted.' Signora's face lit up. This would go some way towards paying for a meal that would have cost more than she could hope to earn in two weeks.

'It would be all done officially, for a fee and everything,' Patrick insisted. How had the Brennans become so smooth and sophisticated? Offering her money without being seen to give her a handout.

Signora's will strengthened even further. 'Well, we'll discuss that when the time comes. I won't delay you, and I'll be in touch next week to tell you my progress.' She left swiftly without protracted goodbyes. That was something she had learned over the years in her village. People liked you more if you didn't stay on interminably, if they realised that a conversation was going to have an end.

She bought teabags and biscuits, and as a luxury a cake of nice soap.

She asked several restaurants for kitchen work and was politely refused everywhere. She tried a supermarket for shelf stacking and newsagents for a job as an assistant or someone to open the piles of papers and magazines for them. She felt that they looked at her puzzled. Sometimes they asked her why she wasn't going through the Job Centre and she looked at them with vague eyes which confirmed their view that she might be a bit simple.

But she did not give in. Until five o'clock she sought work. Then she took a bus to where her mother lived. The flats were in their own grounds, raised flower beds with little bushes and ground cover provided the landscaping, as it was called. A lot of the doors had ramps as well as steps. This was a development, purpose built for the needs of the elderly. With mature trees and bushes around it and built in red brick it looked solid and safe, something that would appeal to those who had sold their family homes to end their days here.

Signora sat quietly hidden by a large tree. She held her paper bag of possessions on her lap and watched the doorway of number 23 for what must have been a long time. She was so used to being still she never noticed time pass. She never wore a watch so time and its passing were not important to her. She would watch until she saw her mother, if not today then another day, and once she saw her then she would know what to do. She could make no decision until she had seen her mother's face. Perhaps pity would be uppermost in her heart, or love from the old days, or forgiveness. Perhaps she might see her mother only as another stranger and one who had spurned love and friendship in the past.

Signora trusted feelings. She knew she would know.

Nobody went in or out of number 23 that evening. At ten o'clock Signora gave up her post and took a bus back to the Sullivans'. She let herself in quietly and went upstairs, calling goodnight into the room where the television blared. The boy Jerry sat with them watching. No wonder the child didn't pay much attention at school if he was up till all hours watching Westerns.

They had found her an electric ring and an old kettle. She made herself tea and looked out at the mountains.

Already in thirty-six hours there was a little veil in her mind over the memory of Annunziata and the walk out to Vista del Monte. She wondered would Gabriella ever be sorry that she had sent Signora away. Would Paolo and Gianna miss her? Would Signora Leone wonder how her friend the Irishwoman was faring far across the sea? Then she washed with the nice soap that smelled of sandalwood, and slept. She didn't hear the sound of the gunfights in the saloons or the flight of the covered wagons. She slept long and deeply.

When she got up the house was empty. Peggy gone to her supermarket, Jimmy out on a driving job and Jerry putting in the day at his school. She set out on her journey. This time she would target her mother's home for a morning stake-out. She would look for jobs later on. Again she sat behind her familiar tree, and this time she didn't have long to wait. A small car drew up outside number 23 and a matronly woman, thickset, with very tightly permed red hair, got out. With a gasp she realised this was her younger sister Rita. She looked so settled in her ways, so middle-aged even though she must only be forty-six. She had been a girl when Signora left, and of course there had been no photograph, any more than there had been warm family letters in the meantime. She must remember that. They only wrote when they needed her, when the comfort of their own lives seemed bigger than the effort of getting in touch with the madwoman who had disgraced herself by fleeing to Sicily to follow a married man.

Rita looked stiff and tense.

She reminded Signora of Gabriella's mother, a small angry woman whose eyes darted around her seeing faults everywhere but not being able to define them. She was meant to suffer with her nerves, they said. Could this really be

Rita, her little sister, this woman with shoulders hunched, with feet squashed into shoes that were too tight, taking a dozen short fussy steps when four would have done? Signora watched aghast from behind her tree. The door of the car was open, she must be going in to collect Mother. She braced herself for the shock. If Rita looked old, what must mother be like now?

She thought of the old people in Annunziata. Small, bent often over sticks, sitting out in the square watching people go by, always smiling, often touching her skirt and looking at the embroidery . . . 'Bella bellissima', they would say.

Her mother would not be like that. Her mother was a well preserved seventy-seven. She wore a brown dress and brown cardigan over it. Her hair was pulled back as it had always been into that unfashionable bun Mario had commented on all those years ago. 'Your mother would be handsome if she let her hair be more free.'

Imagine, her mother then must have only been a little older than she was now. So hard, so set in her ways, so willing to go along with the religious line although she did not feel it in her heart. If her mother had just stood up for her things would have been different. For years Signora could have had a lifeline to home, and she might well have come back and looked after them even in the country, the small farm that they hated leaving.

But now? They were only yards away from her . . . she could have called out and they would have heard.

She saw Rita's body stiffen still further in irritation and resentment as their mother scolded. 'All right, all *right*. I'm getting in, no need to rush me. You'll be old one day yourself, you know.' There was no pleasure at seeing each other, no gratitude for the lift to the hospital, no shared solidarity or sympathy about going to see an old man who could no longer live at home.

This must be Rita's day, the next one would be Helen's, and the sisters-in-law did a small amount of the joyless transporting and minding. No wonder they wanted the madwoman back from Italy. The car drove off with the two stern figures upright in it, not talking to each other, animatedly or at all. How had she learned to love so much, Signora wondered, coming as she did from such a loveless family? It had indeed made up her mind for her. Signora walked out of the neatly landscaped gardens, her head held high. It was clear to her now. She would have no regret, no residual guilt.

The afternoon was as dispiriting as the previous one in terms of job hunting, but she refused to let it get her down. When her journeying brought her towards the River Liffey again she sought out the coffee shop where Suzi worked. The girl looked up, pleased.

'You actually went there! My Mam told me they had got a lodger out of a clear blue sky.'

'It's very nice, I wanted to thank you.'

'No, it's not very nice, but it'll tide you over.'

'I can see the mountains from your bedroom.'

'Yeah, and about twenty tons of waste earth waiting for more little boxes to be built on it.'

'It's just what I need, thank you again.'

'They think you might be a nun, are you?'

'No, no. Far from a nun, I'm afraid.'

'Mam says you say your husband died.'

'In a sort of a way that's true.'

'He sort of died . . . is that what you mean?'

Signora looked very calm; it was easy to see why people might mistake her for a nun. 'No, I meant that in a sort of a way he was my husband, but I didn't see any need to explain all that to your mother and father.'

'No need at all, much wiser not to,' Suzi said, and poured her a cup of coffee. 'On the house,' she whispered.

Signora smiled to herself, thinking that if she played her cards right she might be able to eat for nothing all around Dublin. 'I had a free lunch in Quentin's; I am doing well,' she confided to Suzi.

'That's where I'd love to work,' Suzi said. 'I'd dress up in black trousers just like the waiters. I'd be the only woman apart from Ms Brennan.'

'You know of Ms Brennan?'

'She's a legend,' said Suzi. 'I want to work with her for about three years, learn everything there is to know, then open my own place.'

Signora gave a sigh of envy. How great to think this was possible, rather than a further series of refusals as a washer-up. 'Tell me why can't I get a job, just an ordinary job cleaning, tidying up, anything. What's wrong with me? Is it just that I'm too old?'

Suzi bit her lip. 'I think it's that you look a bit too good for the jobs you're looking for. Like, you look a bit too smart for staying in my parents' house, it makes people uneasy. They might think that it's a bit odd. And they're afraid of odd people.'

'So what should I do, do you think?'

'Maybe you should aim for something a bit higher up, like a receptionist or maybe . . . My Mam says you've an embroidered bedspread that would take the sight out of your eyes. Maybe you could take that to a shop and show them. You know, the right kind of shop.'

'I wouldn't have the confidence.'

'If you lived with a fellow out in Italy at your age, a fellow that wasn't your husband, you've all the confidence that it needs,' said Suzi.

And they made a list of the designers and fashion shops where really top market embroidery might find a home. As she watched Suzi sucking the pencil to think of more places to write down, Signora felt a huge fantasy flood over her. Maybe some day she might bring this lovely girl back with her to Annunziata, say that she was her niece, they had the same red hair. She could show the people there she had a life in Ireland and let the Irish know she was a person of importance in Italy. But it was only a dream, and there was Suzi talking about her hair.

'I have this friend who works in a real posh place cutting hair and they need guinea pigs on training nights. Why don't you go down there? You'll get a great styling for only two pounds. It costs you twenty – thirty times that if you go for real.'

Could people really pay £60 to have their hair cut? The world had gone mad. Mario had always loved her long hair. Mario was dead. He had sent her a message telling her go back to Ireland, he would expect her to cut her hair if it was necessary to do so. 'Where is this place?' Signora asked, and took down the address.

'Jimmy, she's cut her hair,' whispered Peggy Sullivan.

Jimmy was listening to an in-depth interview with a soccer manager. 'Yeah, great,' he said.

'No honestly, she's not what she pretends, I saw her coming in. You wouldn't know her, she looks twenty years younger.'

'Good, good.' Jimmy raised the volume a bit, but Peggy took the control and turned it down.

'Have some respect. We're taking the woman's money, we don't have to deafen her as well.'

'All right, but hush talking.'

Peggy sat brooding. This Signora as she called herself was very odd altogether. No one could be as simple as she was and survive. No one with that little money could get a haircut that must have cost a fortune. Peggy hated mysteries and this was a very deep mystery indeed.

'You'll have to forgive me if I take my bedspread with me today. I didn't want you to think I was taking away all the furnishings or anything,' Signora explained to them at their breakfast next morning. 'You see, I think people are a bit confused by me. I have to show them that I can do *some* kind of work. I got my hair cut in a place that needed people to experiment on. Do you think it makes me look more ordinary?'

'It's very nice indeed, Signora,' said Jimmy Sullivan.

'It looks most expensive, certainly.' Peggy approved.

'Is it dyed?' asked Jerry with interest.

'No, it's got henna in it, but they said it was an unusual colour already, like a wild animal,' Signora said, not at all offended by Jerry's question or the verdict of the young hairdressers.

It was pleasing that everyone liked her work so much and admired the intricate stitching and the imaginative mingling of place names with flowers. But there were no jobs. They said they would keep her name on file and were surprised by the address, as if they thought she would live somewhere more elegant. It was a day of refusals like other days but somehow they seemed to be given with more respect and less bewilderment. Dress designers, boutiques and two theatre companies looked at her handiwork with genuine interest. Suzi had been right that she should aim high.

Could she dare try to be a guide or a teacher as she had been so confidently for half her adult life in a Sicilian village?

She got into the habit of talking to Jerry in the evenings.

He would come and knock on her door. 'Are you busy, Mrs Signora?'

'No, come in, Jerry. It's nice to have company.'

'You could always come downstairs, you know. They wouldn't mind.'

'No, no. I rented a room from your parents, I want them to like having me here in the house not living on top of them.'

'What are you doing, Mrs Signora?'

'I'm making little baby dresses for a boutique. They told me they would take four. They have to be good because I spent some of my savings on the material so I can't afford for them not to take them.'

'Are you poor, Mrs Signora?'

'Not really, but I don't have much money.' It seemed quite a natural, reasonable answer. It satisfied Jerry totally. 'Why don't you bring your homework up here, Jerry?' she suggested. 'Then you could be company for me and I could give you a hand if you needed it.'

They sat together all through the month of May, chatting easily. Jerry advised her to make five baby dresses and pretend she thought they ordered five. It had been great advice, they took all five and wanted more.

Signora showed huge interest in Jerry's homework. 'Read me that poem again, let's see what does it mean?'

'It's only an old poem, Mrs Signora.'

'I know but it must mean *something*. Let's think.' Together they would recite: 'Nine bean rows will I have there'. 'I wonder why he wanted nine?'

'He was only an old poet, Mrs Signora. I don't suppose he knew what he wanted.'

'"And live alone in the bee loud glade." Imagine that, Jerry. He only wanted to hear the sound of the bees around him, he didn't want the noise of the city.'

'He was old, of course,' Jerry explained.

'Who was?'

'Yeats, you know, who wrote the poem.'

Little by little she made him interested in everything.

She pretended her own memory was bad. As she sewed she asked him to say it to her over and over. So Jerry Sullivan learned his poetry, wrote his essays, attempted his maths. The only thing he was remotely interested in was Geography. It had to do with a teacher, Mr O'Brien. He was a great fellow apparently. Mr O'Brien used to teach about river beds and soil strata and erosion and a rake of things, but he always expected you to know it. The other teachers didn't expect you to, that was the difference.

'He's going to be the Head, you know, next year,' Jerry explained.

'Oh. And are people in Mountainview school pleased about that?'

'Yeah, I think so. Old Walsh was a terrible bollocks.'

She looked at him vaguely, as if she didn't understand the word. It worked every time.

'Mr Walsh, the old fellow who's Head at the moment, he's not good at all.'

'Ah, I see.'

Jerry's language had improved beyond all recognition, Suzi reported to

Signora. And what was more some teacher at school had said that his work had taken a turn for the better as well. 'It's they should be paying you,' Suzi said. 'You're like a private governess. Isn't it a pity you couldn't get a job teaching.'

'Your mother's asking me to tea on Thursday so that I can meet you,' Signora said. 'I think Jerry's teacher is calling then too. She probably wanted a bit of support.'

'He's a real ladies' man, Tony O'Brien is. I've heard a tale or two about him, you'd want to watch yourself there, Signora. With your smart new hairdo and all, he could have his way with you.'

'I'm not ever going to be interested in a man again.' She spoke simply.

'Oh, I said that after the second-last fellow, but suddenly the interest came back.'

The tea party began awkwardly.

Peggy Sullivan was not a natural hostess, so Signora took over the conversation, gently, almost dreamily talking about all the changes in Ireland she noticed and most of them were for the better. 'The schools are all so bright and cheerful nowadays, and Jerry tells me of the great projects you do in Geography class. We had nothing like that when I was at school.'

And after that everything thawed. Peggy Sullivan had seen the visit of the schoolteacher as a possible list of complaints against her son. She hadn't hoped that her daughter and Signora would get on so well. Or that Jerry would actually tell Mr O'Brien that he was doing a project on place names, trying to find out why all the streets around here were called what they were. Jimmy came home in the middle of it all, and Signora explained that Jerry was lucky to have a father who knew the city so well, he was better than any map.

They talked like a normal family. More polite than many Tony O'Brien had visited. He had always thought young Jerry Sullivan was part of the group for whom there was no hope. But this odd, unsettling woman who seemed to have taken over the household obviously had a good effect on the kid too.

'You must have loved Italy to stay there so long.'

'I did, very, very much.'

'I've never been there myself, but a colleague of mine above in the school, Aidan Dunne, now he'd live, sleep and breathe Italy to you if you let him.'

'Mr Dunne, he teaches Latin,' Jerry said in a glum voice.

'Latin? You could learn Latin, Jerry.' Signora's eyes lit up.

'Oh it's only for brainy people, ones going on to University to be lawyers and doctors and things.'

'No, it's not.' Signora and Tony O'Brien spoke at the same time.

'Please . . .' he motioned her to speak.

'Well, I wish I had learned Latin because it's sort of the root of all other languages, like French and Italian and Spanish. If you know the Latin word you know where everything comes from.' She spoke enthusiastically.

Tony O'Brien said: 'God, you really should meet Aidan Dunne, that's what he's been saying for years. I like kids to learn it because it's logical. Like doing a crossword, trains them to think, and there's no problem with an accent.'

When the teacher had gone they all talked together eagerly. Signora knew that Suzi would come home a little more regularly now, and wouldn't have to avoid her father. Somehow fences had been mended.

Signora met Brenda for a walk in St Stephen's Green. Brenda brought stale bread for the ducks and they fed them together, peaceable in the sunshine.

'I go to see your mother every month, will I tell her you're home?' Brenda asked.

'What do you think?'

'I think no, but then that's just because I'm still afraid you'll go and live with her.'

'You don't know me at all. I am as hard as hell. Do you like her as a person? Truthfully now?'

'No, not very much. I went to please you in the beginning and then I got sucked into it because she seems so miserable, complaining about Rita and Helen and the awful daughters-in-law, as she calls them.'

'I'll go and see her. I won't have you trying to cover over for me.'

'Don't go, you'll give in.'

'Believe me, that will not happen.'

She called on her mother that afternoon. Just went and rang on the bell of number 23.

Her mother looked at her, confused. 'Yes?' she said.

'I'm Nora, Mother. I've come to visit you.'

No smile, no arms outstretched, no welcome. Just hostility in the small brown eyes that looked back at her. They stood almost frozen in the doorway. Her mother had not moved back to let her enter, and Nora would not ask could she come in.

But she did speak again. 'I came to see how you are and to ask whether Daddy would like me to go and see him in the home or not. I want to do what's best for everyone.'

Her mother's lip curled. 'When did you ever want to do what was best for anyone except yourself?' she said. Signora stood calm in the doorway. It was at times like this that her habit of stillness came into its own. Eventually her mother moved back into the apartment. 'Come in as you're here,' she said ungraciously.

Signora recognised a few, but not many, pieces from her home. There was a cabinet, where the good china and the few small bits of silver were kept. You could hardly see into it years ago, any more than you could see now. There were no pictures on the wall, or books on the bookshelf. A big television set dominated the room, a bottle with orange squash stood on a tin tray on the dining table. There were no flowers, no sign at all of any enjoyment of life. Her mother did not offer her a seat so Signora sat at the dining table. She wondered had it known many meals served on it, but then she was not in a position to criticise. For twenty-six years she had lived in rooms where nobody was entertained to a dinner. Maybe it ran in the family.

'I suppose you'll want to smoke all over the place.'

'No, Mother. I never smoked.'

'How would I know what you do or don't do?'

'Indeed, Mother, how would you?' Her voice was calm, not challenging.

'And are you home on a holiday or what?'

In the level voice which was driving her mother mad, Signora explained that she had come home to live, that she had found a room and some small sewing jobs. She hoped to get further work to keep herself. She ignored her mother's scornful sniff at the area she was living. She paused then and waited politely for some reaction.

'And did he throw you out in the end, Mario or whatever his name is?'

'You know his name was Mario, Mother. You met him. And no, he didn't throw me out. If he were alive I would still be there. He was killed very tragically, Mother, I know you'll be sorry to hear, in an accident on a mountain road. So then I decided to come home and live in Ireland.' Again she waited.

'I suppose they didn't want you there in that place once he wasn't there to protect you, is that what happened?'

'No, you're wrong. They wanted what was best for me, all of them.'

Her mother snorted again. The silence hung between them.

Her mother couldn't take it. 'So you're going to live with these people up in that tough estate, full of the unemployed and criminals rather than with your own flesh and blood. Is this what we are to expect?'

'It's very kind of you to offer me a home, Mother, but we have been strangers for too long. I have developed my little ways and I am sure you have yours. You didn't want to know about my life so I would only bore you talking about it, you made that clear. But perhaps I can come and see you every now and then, and tell me if Father would like me to visit or not?'

'Oh, you can take your talk of visits with you when you go. None of us want you and that is a fact.'

'I would hate to think that. I tried to keep in touch with everyone. I wrote letter after letter. I know nothing about my six nieces and five nephews. I would love to get to know them now that I am home.'

'Well, none of them want anything to do with you, I can tell you that, half cracked as you were thinking you can come back here and take up as if nothing has happened. You could have turned out a somebody. Look at that friend of yours, Brenda, a nice groomed person, married and a good job and all. *She's* the kind of girl any woman would like as a daughter.'

'And of course you have Helen and Rita,' Signora added. There was a half snort this time, showing that they had been less than totally satisfactory. 'Anyway, Mother, now that I'm back perhaps I could take you out somewhere for a meal sometimes, or we could go into town for afternoon tea. And I'll enquire at the home whether Father would like a visit or not.'

There was a silence. It was all too much for her mother to take in. Signora had not given her address, just the area. Her sisters could not come and track her down. She felt no qualms. This was not a woman who had loved her or thought of her welfare, not at any time during the long years she had pleaded for friendship and contact.

She stood up to leave.

'Oh, you're very high and mighty. But you're a middle-aged woman, don't think any man in Dublin will have you after all you've been through. I know there's divorce and all now for all it broke your father's heart, but still you wouldn't find many men in Ireland willing to take on a fifty-year-old woman like yourself, another man's leavings.'

'No indeed, Mother, so it's just as well I don't have any plans in that direction. I'll write you a little note and come and see you in a few weeks' time.'

'Weeks?' her mother said.

'Yes indeed, and maybe I'll bring along a cake or a cherry log from Bewleys with me and we could have tea. But we'll see. And give my warmest wishes to Helen and Rita, and tell them I'll write to them too.'

She was gone before her mother could realise it. She knew she would be on the phone to one of her daughters within minutes. Nothing as dramatic as this had happened in years.

She felt no sadness. That was all over long ago. She felt no guilt. Her only responsibility now was to keep herself sane and strong and self-employed. She must not learn to be dependent on the Sullivan family, no matter how attracted she felt to their handsome daughter and protective to their surly son. She must not be a burden to Brenda and Patrick who were obviously the success story of their generation in Dublin, and she could not rely on the boutiques who would give her no guarantees that they could sell her intricate embroidery.

She must get a teaching job of some sort. It didn't matter that she had no real qualifications, at least she knew how to teach Italian to beginners. Had she not taught herself? Perhaps this man up in Jerry's school, the one that Tony O'Brien said was a lover of Italy . . . He might know some group, some little organisation that could do with Italian lessons. It didn't matter if it wasn't well paid, she would love to be speaking that beautiful language again, letting it roll around her tongue.

What was his name? Mr Dunne? That was it. Mr Aidan Dunne. Nothing could be lost by asking, and if he loved Italian he would be on her side already.

She took the bus to the school. What a different place from her own Vista del Monte, where the summer flowers would all be cascading down the hills already. This was a concrete yard, a shambles of a bicycle shed, litter everywhere, and the whole building needed badly to be painted. Why couldn't they have had some greenery growing over the walls?

Signora knew that a community school or college or whatever it was did not have any funds or legacies or donations to make the place more stylish. But really, was it any wonder that children like Jerry Sullivan didn't feel any great sense of pride in their school?

'He'd be in the staffroom,' a group said when she asked for Mr Dunne the Latin teacher.

She knocked on the door and a man came to answer it. He had thinning brown hair and anxious eyes. He was in his shirt sleeves but she could see his jacket hanging on a chair behind him. It was lunch hour and all the other teachers were obviously out, but Mr Dunne seemed to be guarding the fort. Somehow she had thought he would be an old man. Something to do with teaching Latin possibly. But he only looked around her own age or younger. Still, by today's standards that *was* old, much nearer to retirement than starting out.

'I've come to talk to you about Italian, Mr Dunne,' she said.

'Do you know, I *knew* some day someone would knock at the door and say that to me,' Aidan Dunne said.

They smiled at each other and it was quite clear that they were going to be friends. They sat in the big untidy staffroom that looked out on the mountains and they talked as if they had known each other always. Aidan Dunne explained about the evening class which was his heart's desire, but that he had got terrible news that very morning. The funding had not been passed by the authorities. They would never now be able to afford a qualified teacher. The new Principal-Elect had promised a small sum from his own funds, but that would go to do up the classrooms and get the place ready. Aidan Dunne said that his heart had been low in case the whole project might have to be scrapped but now he felt a glimmer of hope again.

Signora told how she had lived so long in the Sicilian hills and that she could teach not just the language but perhaps something of the culture as well. Could there be a class on Italian artists and sculptors and frescoes for example, that would be three topics and then there could be Italian music, and opera and religious music. And then there could be wines and food, you know the fruits and vegetables and the *frutti di mare* and really there was so much as well as the conversation and the holiday phrases, so much to add to the grammar and the learning of the language itself.

Her eyes were bright, she looked a younger woman than the tall person with anxious eyes who had stood at the door. Aidan heard the swelling sounds of children's voices in the corridor. It meant that the lunch hour was nearly over. The other teachers would be in soon, the magic would end.

She seemed to understand this without his saying it. 'I'm staying too long, you have work to do. But do you think we might talk of it again?'

'We get out at four o'clock. Now I sound like the children,' Aidan said.

She smiled at him. 'That's what must be wonderful about working in a school, you are always young and think like the children.'

'I wish it were always like that,' Aidan said.

'When I taught English in Annunziata I used to look at their faces and I might think, they don't know something but when I have finished they will know it. It was a good feeling.'

He was admiring her openly now, this man struggling into his jacket to go back to the classroom. It had been a long time since Signora had felt herself admired. In Annunziata they respected her in some strange way. And of course Mario had loved her, there was no question of that. He had loved her with all his heart. But he had never admired her. He had come to her in the dark. He had held her body to him and he had told her his worries but there had never been a look of admiration in his eyes.

Signora liked it, as she liked this good man struggling to share his own love of another land with the people hereabouts. His fear was that they didn't have enough money for leisure time education themselves to make such a study worthwhile.

'Will I wait outside the school for you?' she asked. 'We could talk more then after four o'clock.'

'I wouldn't want to keep you,' he began.

'I have nothing else to do.' She had no disguises.

'Would you care to sit in our library?' he asked.

'Very much.'

He walked her along the corridor as crowds of children shoved past them. There were always strangers in a big school like this, a new face wasn't interesting enough to make them look twice. Except of course for young Jerry Sullivan, who did a double take.

'Jesus, Signora . . .' he said in amazement.

'Hallo, Jerry,' she said pleasantly, as if she were here in this school the whole time.

She sat in the library reading through what they had in their Italian section, mainly second-hand books obviously bought with his own money by Aidan Dunne. He was such a kind man, an enthusiast, perhaps he could help her. And she could help him. For the first time since she had come back to Ireland Signora felt relaxed, not just holding on by her fingernails. She stretched and yawned in the summer sunshine.

Even though she was going to teach Italian, she felt sure of it, she didn't think of Italy. She thought of Dublin, she wondered where they would find the people to attend the class. She and Mr Dunne. She and Aidan. She pulled herself together a little. She must not be fanciful. That had been her undoing, people said. She was full of mad notions and didn't see reality.

Two hours had passed and Aidan Dunne stood at the door of the big room. He was smiling all over his face. 'I don't have a car,' he said. 'I don't suppose you do?'

'I've barely my bus fare,' Signora said.

Bill

Life would have been much easier, Bill Burke thought, if only he could have been in love with Grania Dunne.

She was about twenty-three, his own age. She came from a normal kind of home, her father was a teacher up in Mountainview school, her mother worked in the cash desk of Quentin's restaurant. She was good looking and easy to talk to.

They used to grumble together about the bank sometimes, and wonder how it was that greedy selfish people always got on well. Grania used to ask about his sister, and give him books for her. And perhaps Grania might have loved him too if things had only been different.

It was easy to talk about love to a good friend who understood. Bill understood when Grania told him about this very old man she just couldn't get out of her mind even though she had tried and tried. He was as old as her own father, and smoked and wheezed and would probably be dead in a couple of years the way he went on, but she had never met anyone who attracted her so much.

She couldn't possibly get together with him because he had lied to her and not told her that he was going to be Principal of the school when he knew all along. And Grania's father would have a stroke and drop dead if he knew that she had been seeing this Tony O'Brien and even slept with him. Once.

She had tried going out with other people but it just hadn't worked. She kept thinking about him and the way the lines came out from the side of his eyes when he smiled. It was so unfair. What part of the human mind or body was so inefficient that it could make you think you loved someone so wildly unsuitable?

Bill agreed in the most heartfelt way possible. He too was a victim of this unsuitable streak. He loved Lizzie Duffy, the most improbable person in the world. Lizzie was a beautiful, troublesome bad debt, who had broken every rule and was still somehow allowed more credit than any customer in this or any branch.

Lizzie loved Bill too. Or *said* she did, or *thought* she did. She said she had never met anyone so serious and owlish and honourable and silly in her whole life. And indeed, compared to Lizzie's other friends, he was all of these things. Most of them just laughed at nothing, and had very little interest in getting or keeping jobs but huge interest in travel and having fun. It was idiotic loving Lizzie.

But Bill and Grania told each other seriously over coffee that if life was all about loving suitable people then it would be both very easy and very dull.

Lizzie never asked about Bill's big sister, Olive. She had met her of course, once when she came to visit. Olive was slow, that was all, just slow. She didn't have any disease or illness that had a name. She was twenty-five and she behaved as if she were eight. A very nice eager eight.

Once you knew this there was no problem with Olive. She would tell you stories from books like any eight-year-old, she would be enthusiastic about things she had seen on television. Sometimes she was loud and awkward, and because Olive was big she knocked things over. But there were never any scenes or moods with Olive, she was interested in everything and everyone and thought that there was nobody on earth like her family. 'My mother makes the best cakes in the world,' she would tell people and Bill's mother who had never done more than decorate a bought sponge cake would smile proudly. 'My father runs the big supermarket,' Olive said, and her father who worked at the bacon counter there smiled indulgently.

'My brother Bill's a bank manager,' was the one that got a wry smile from Bill, and indeed Grania, when he told her. 'That'll be the day,' he said.

'You don't want it, it will only show you've given in, compromised,' Grania said encouragingly.

Lizzie shared Olive's view. 'You must rise high in banking,' she said to Bill often. 'I can only marry a successful man, and when we are twenty-five and get married you'll have to be well on your way to the top.'

Even though it was said with Lizzie's wonderful sparkling laugh showing all her tiny white teeth, and a toss of the legendary blonde curls, Bill knew that Lizzie meant it. She said she could never marry a failure; it would be so cruel, because she would just drag them both down. But she would seriously consider marrying Bill in two years' time when they were both a quarter of a century old, because she would be getting past her sell-by date then and it would be time to settle down.

Lizzie had been refused a loan because she had not repaid the first one, her Visa card had been withdrawn and Bill had seen letters go out to her saying: 'Unless you lodge by five o'clock tomorrow the bank will have no option . . .' But somehow the bank always found an option. Lizzie would arrive tearful on some occasions, brimming with confidence and a new job on others. She never went under. And always she was entirely unrepentant.

'Oh for heaven's sake, Bill, banks don't have a heart or a soul. They only want to make money and not to risk losing money. They are the enemy.'

'They're not my enemy,' Bill said. 'They're my employers.'

'Lizzie, don't,' he would say despairingly as she ordered another bottle of wine. Because he knew that she didn't have the money to pay for it he would have to, and it was becoming increasingly difficult. He wanted to contribute at home, his salary was so much better than his father's wages and they had sacrificed a lot to give him the kind of start he had got. But with Lizzie it was impossible to save. Bill had wanted to buy a new jacket but it was out of the question. He wished Lizzie would stop talking about a holiday, there literally wasn't the money for one. And how was he meant to put aside the money to be wealthy at the age of twenty-five so that he and Lizzie could get married?

Bill was hoping it would be a warm summer. Lizzie might just about tolerate staying in Ireland if the sun shone. But if it were overcast and all her friends were talking about this Greek island, that Greek island and how cheap it was to live in Turkey for a month, then she would become very restless indeed. Bill could not get a loan from the bank he worked in. It was a diamond hard rule. But of course it was always possible elsewhere. Possible and highly undesirable. He wondered if he were a mean man. He thought not, but then who really knew what they were like themselves?

'I suppose we are only what other people think we are,' he said to Grania at coffee.

'I don't think so, that would mean we might be acting the whole time,' she said.

'Do I look like an owl?' he asked.

'Of course not,' Grania sighed. She had been through this before.

'It's not even as if I wore glasses,' Bill complained. 'I suppose I have a round face and sort of straight hair.'

'Owls don't have hair at all, they have feathers,' Grania said.

This only served to confuse Bill further. 'Then what makes them think I'm like one?' he said.

There was a lecture that evening at the bank on opportunities. Grania and Bill sat together. They heard of courses and schemes, and how the bank wanted the staff to specialise in different areas, and how the world was open to bright young men and women with a command of languages and different skills and training. The salary working abroad would of course be greater since it would include an overseas allowance. The opportunities would present themselves in a year and interested staff were advised to prepare themselves well in advance since the competition would be keen.

'Are you going to apply for any course?' Bill asked.

Grania looked troubled. 'There are ways I want to, because it might get me out of here, get me away from chances of seeing Tony O'Brien. But then I don't want to be thinking about him in some other part of the world. What's the point of that? I might as well be miserable here where I know what he's up to than in some far off place where I don't.'

'And he wants you back?' Bill had heard the story many times.

'Yes, he sends me a postcard every week to the bank. Look, here's this week's one.' Grania took out a picture of a coffee plantation. On the back were three words: 'Still waiting, Tony.'

'He doesn't *say* very much,' Bill complained.

'No, but it's a kind of series,' Grania explained. 'There was one that said: "Still brewing", and another that said: "Still hoping". It's a message that he's leaving it all up to me.'

'Is it a code?' Bill was bewildered.

'It's a reference to the fact that I said I wouldn't go back to him unless he bought a proper coffee percolator.'

'And he did?'

'Yes, of course he did, Bill. But that wasn't the point.'

'Women are very complicated,' Bill sighed.

'No they're not. They're perfectly ordinary and straightforward. Not necessarily little Miss Retail Therapy that you've got yourself involved with, but most of us are.'

Grania thought that Lizzie was hopeless. Bill thought that Grania should go back to this old man and have coffee and bed and whatever else he was sending messages about, because she sure as hell wasn't enjoying life without him.

The lecture had started Bill thinking. Suppose he were to get a posting abroad. Suppose he actually *did* succeed in being chosen as one of the experimental task force going to a European capital as part of the expansion process. Imagine the difference it would make. He would be earning real money for the first time in his life. He would have freedom. He need not spend the evenings at home playing with Olive and telling his parents choice bits of the day which would show him in a successful light.

Lizzie might come and live with him in Paris or Rome or Madrid, they could have a little flat, and sleep together every night rather than his just going to her place and then coming home again afterwards . . . a habit that Lizzie found screamingly funny and quite suitable since she didn't get up until just before noon and it was nice not to be wakened by someone leaving to go to something as extraordinary as the bank.

He began to look at brochures about intensive language courses. They were very expensive. The language laboratory ones were out of the question. He didn't have time or energy for them either. A day in the bank took it out of him, he felt tired in the evening and not able to concentrate. And since the whole point was to make enough money to build a life for Lizzie, he must not risk losing her by absenting himself from her and her crowd of friends.

Not for the first time he wished that he loved a different kind of person. But it was like measles, wasn't it. Once you got love it was there. You had to wait to get cured of it or it worked itself out someday. As usual he consulted his friend Grania and for once she had something specific to offer, rather than what he felt was a vague threat that he was on a helter-skelter to hell through loving Lizzie.

'My father is starting an evening class in Italian up in his school,' she said. 'It begins in September and they're looking far and wide for pupils.'

'Would it be any good?'

'I don't know. I'm meant to be drumming up a bit of business for it.' Grania was always so honest. It was one of the many things he liked about her. She wouldn't pretend. 'At least it's cheap,' she said. 'They've put as much money as they can into it and unless he gets thirty pupils the class will fall on its face. I couldn't bear that for my father.'

'Are you signing up then?'

'No, he said that would be humiliating for him. If his whole family had to join it would look pathetic.'

'I suppose it would. But would it be any help at all in banking? Do you think it would have the terms and the technical kind of phrases?'

'I doubt that, but they'd have hallo and goodbye and how's your father. And I suppose if you were out in Italy you'd have to be able to say all that to people like we do here.'

'Yes.' Bill was doubtful.

'Jesus, Bill, what technical phrases do you and I use here every day, except debit and credit? I bet she'd teach you those.'

'Who?'

'The one he's hired. A real Italian, he calls her Signora. He says she's great altogether.'

'And when does the class start?'

'September fifth, if they have the numbers.'

'And do you have to pay the whole year in advance?'

'Only the term. I'll get you a leaflet. If you were going to do it then you might as well do it there, Bill. You'd be keeping my poor old father sane.'

'And will I see Tony, the one who writes all these long passionate letters?' Bill asked.

'God, don't mention Tony, you're only told this in great secrecy.' Grania sounded worried.

He patted her hand. 'I'm only having a bit of fun with you, of course I know it's a secret. But I'll have a look at him if I see him, and tell you what I think.'

'I hope you'll like him.' Grania looked suddenly very young and vulnerable.

'I'm sure he's so fabulous that I'll be sending you postcards about him myself,' said Bill with his smile of encouragement that Grania was relying on so much in a world that knew nothing of Tony O'Brien.

Bill told his parents that night that he was going to learn Italian.

Olive was very excited. 'Bill's going to Italy. Bill's going to Italy to run a bank,' she told the next-door neighbours.

They were used to Olive. 'That's great,' they said indulgently. 'Will you miss him?'

'When he goes there he'll bring us all over to Italy to stay with him,' Olive said confidently.

From his bedroom Bill heard and his heart felt heavy. His mother had thought learning Italian was a great idea. It was a beautiful language. She loved to hear the Pope speak it, and she loved the song O Sole Mio. His father had said that it was great to see a boy bettering himself all the time, and he had always known that those extra grinds for the Leaving Certificate had been an investment. His mother asked casually whether Lizzie would go to the Italian classes.

Bill had never thought of Lizzie as being disciplined or organised enough to spend two sessions of two hours each learning something. Surely she would prefer to be out with her friends laughing and drinking very expensive multi-coloured cocktails. 'She hasn't decided yet,' he said firmly. He knew how much they disapproved of Lizzie. Her one visit had not been a success.

Her skirt too short, her neckline too low, her laughter too wide and non-specific and her grasp of their life so minimal.

But he had been resolute. Lizzie was the girl he loved. She was the woman he would marry in two years' time when he was twenty-five. He would hear no disparaging word about Lizzie in his home and they respected him for this. Sometimes Bill wondered about his wedding day. His parents would be so excited. His mother would talk for ages about the hat she was going to buy and perhaps buy several before settling on the right one. There would be a lot of discussion too about an outfit for Olive, something which would be discreet and yet smart. His father would discuss the timing of the wedding, hoping that it was convenient for the supermarket. He had worked in this store since he was a boy, watching it change character all the time, never realising his own worth and always fearing that change of manager might mean his walking papers. Sometimes Bill wanted to shake him and tell him that he was worth more than the rest of the employees combined, and that everyone would realise this. But his father, in his fifties without any of the qualifications and skills of young men, would never have believed him. He would remain fearful of the supermarket and grateful to it for the rest of his days.

Lizzie's family on her side of the church was always fairly vague in Bill's dream of a wedding day. She talked of her mother who lived in West Cork because she preferred it there, and her father who lived in Galway because that's where his pals were. She had a sister in the States and a brother who was working in a ski resort and hadn't come home for ages. Bill couldn't quite imagine them all gathering together.

He told Lizzie about the class. 'Would you like to learn too?' he asked hopefully.

'Whatever for?' Lizzie's infectious laughter had him laughing too although he didn't know why.

'Well, so that you could speak a bit of it if we went there, you know.'

'But don't they speak English?'

'Some of them, but wouldn't it be great to speak to them in their own language?'

'And we'd learn to do that up in a ropey old school like Mountainview?'

'It's meant to be quite a good school, they say.' He felt stung with loyalty for Grania and her father.

'It may be, but look at the place it's in. You'd need a flak jacket to get through those housing estates.'

'It's a deprived area certainly,' Bill said. 'But they're just poor, that's all.'

'Poor,' cried Lizzie. 'We're all poor, for heaven's sake, but we don't go on like they do up there.'

Bill wondered, as he so often did, about Lizzie's values. How could she compare herself with the families who lived on welfare and social security? The many households where there had never been a job? Still, it was part of her innocence. You didn't love people to change them. He had known that for a long time.

'Well, I'm going to do it anyway,' he said. 'There's a bus stop right outside the school and the lessons are on Tuesdays and Thursdays.'

Lizzie turned over the little leaflet. 'I would do it to support you Bill, but honestly I just don't have the money.' Her eyes were enormous. It would be wonderful to have her sitting beside him mouthing the words, learning the language.

'I'll pay for your course,' Bill Burke said. Now he would definitely have to go to another bank and get a loan.

They were nice in the other bank and sympathetic. They had to do the same themselves, they all had to borrow elsewhere. There was no problem about setting it up.

'You can get more than that,' the helpful young bank official said, just as Bill would have said himself.

'I know, but the bit about paying it back ... I seem to have so many calls each month.'

'Tell me about it,' said the boy. 'And the price of clothes is disgraceful. Anything you'd want to be seen in costs an arm and a leg.'

Bill thought of the jacket, and he thought of his parents and Olive. He'd love to give them some little end of summer treat. He got a loan exactly twice what he had gone into the bank intending to borrow.

Grania told Bill that her father was absolutely delighted about her recruiting two new members for the class. There were twenty-two already. Things were looking good and still a week to go. They had decided that even if they didn't make the full thirty they would have the first term's lessons anyway so as not to disappoint those who had enrolled, and to avoid embarrassing themselves at the very outset.

'Once it gets going there might be word of mouth,' Bill said.

'They say there's usually a great fall-off after lesson three,' Grania said. 'But let's not be downhearted. I'm going to work on my friend Fiona tonight.'

'Fiona who works in the hospital?' Bill had a feeling that Grania was match-making for him here. She always mentioned Fiona in approving terms, just after something Lizzie had done turned out to have been particularly silly or difficult.

'Yeah, you know about Fiona, I'm always talking about her. Great friend of mine and Brigid's. We can always say we're staying with her when we're not, if you know what I mean.'

'I know what you mean, but do your parents?' Bill asked.

'They don't think about it, that's what parents do. They put these things to the back of their minds.'

'Is Fiona asked to cover for you often?'

'Not for me since ... well since that night with Tony ages ago. You see, it was the very next day I discovered about him being such a rat and taking my father's job. Did I tell you?'

She had, many times, but Bill was very kind. 'I think you said that the timing was bad.'

'It couldn't have been worse,' Grania fumed. 'If I had known earlier I wouldn't have given him the time of day, and if it were later then I might have been so committed to him that there was no turning back.' She fumed at the unfairness of it all.

'Suppose you did decide to go back to him, would that finish your father off entirely?'

Grania looked at him sharply. Bill must be psychic to know that she had tossed and turned all last night thinking that she might approach Tony O'Brien again. He had left the ball so firmly in her court and he had sent encouraging messages in the form of postcards. In a way it was discourteous not to respond to him in some manner. But she had thought of the damage it would do to her father. He had been so sure that the post of Principal was his; he *must* have felt it more keenly than he had shown. 'You know I *was* thinking about that,' Grania said slowly. 'And I worked out that I might wait a bit, you know, until things are better in my dad's life. Then he might be able to face up to something like that.'

'Does he talk about things with your mother, do you think?'

Grania shook her head. 'They hardly talk at all. My mother's only interested in the restaurant and going to see her sisters. Dad spends most of his time doing up a sort of study for himself. He's very lonely these days, I couldn't bear to bring anything else on him. But maybe if these evening classes are a huge success and he gets a lot of praise for that . . . then I could face him with the other thing. Were I to go ahead with it, of course.'

Bill looked admiringly at Grania. Like himself she was more confident than her parents, and also like him she didn't want to upset them. 'We have so much in common,' he said suddenly. 'Isn't it a pity that we don't fancy each other.'

'I *know*, Bill.' Grania's sigh was heartfelt. 'And you're a very good looking guy, specially in that new jacket. And you've got lovely shiny brown hair and you're young, you won't be dead when I'm forty. Isn't it awful that we couldn't fancy each other but I don't, not even a bit.'

'I know,' Bill said. 'Neither do I, isn't it a crying shame?'

As a treat he decided to take the family to lunch, out to the seaside. They took the train called the DART.

'We're darting out to the seaside,' Olive told several people on the train and they smiled at her. Everyone smiled at Olive, she was so eager. They explained to her that DART meant Dublin Area Rapid Transit but she didn't take it in.

They walked down to look at the harbour and the fishing boasts. There were still summer visitors around and tourists snapping the scene. They walked through the windy main street of the little town and looked at the shops. Bill's mother said it must be wonderful to live in a place like this.

'When we were young anyone could have afforded a place out here,' Bill's father said. 'But it seemed very far away in those days and the better jobs were nearer the city so we didn't come.'

'Maybe Bill would live somewhere like this one day when he got promotion,' his mother suggested, almost afraid to hope.

Bill tried to see himself living in one of the new flats or the old houses here with Lizzie. What would she do all day as he commuted into Dublin City on the DART? Would she have friends out here as she had everywhere? Would they have children? She had said one boy and one girl, and then curtains. But that was a long time ago. Whenever he brought the subject up nowadays she was much more vague. 'Suppose you got pregnant now,' Bill had suggested one night. 'Then we'd have to advance our plans a bit.'

'Absolutely wrong, Bill sweetheart,' she had said. 'We would have to cancel all our plans.'

And he saw for the first time the hint of hardness behind her smile. But of course he dismissed this notion. Bill knew that Lizzie wasn't hard. Like any woman she feared the dangers and accidents of her own body. It wasn't fair really the way it was organised. Women could never be as relaxed about love-making, knowing it might result in something unexpected like pregnancy.

Olive was not a good walker and his mother wanted to visit the church anyway so Bill and his father walked up to the Vico Road, an elegant curved road that swept the bay which had often been compared to the Bay of Naples. A lot of the roads here had Italian names like Vico and Sorrento, and there were houses called La Scala, Milano, Ancona. People who had travelled had brought back memories of similar seaside views. Also it was full of hills like they said the Italian coastline was.

Bill and his father looked at the gardens and homes and admired them without envy. If Lizzie had been here she would have said it was unfair for some people to have houses like that, with two big cars parked outside. But Bill who worked as a bank clerk, and his father who sliced bacon and wearing plastic gloves inserted it into little transparent bags and weighed them out at so many grams each, were able to see these properties without wanting them for themselves.

The sun shone and they looked far down. The sea was shimmering. A few yachts were out. They sat on the wall and Bill's father puffed a pipe.

'Did it all turn out as you wanted when you were young?' Bill said.

'Not *all* of course, but most of it.' His father puffed away.

'Like what bits?'

'Well, having such a good job and keeping it in spite of everything. That was something I'd never have bet money on if I was a gambling man. And then there was your mother accepting me, and being such a marvellous wife, and making us such a great home. And then there was Olive and you, and that was a great reward to us.'

Bill felt a strange choking sensation. His father lived in an unreal world. All these things were blessings? Things to be delighted with? An educationally sub-normal daughter. A wife who could barely fry an egg and this was called making a great home? A job that they would never get anyone of his competence to do, and to do so well . . .

'Dad, why am I part of the good bits?' Bill asked.

'Come on now, you're just asking for praise.' His father smiled at him as if the lad had been teasing him.

'No, I mean it, why are you pleased with me?'

'Who could ask for a better son? Look at the way you take us all out for a day's trip today with your hard earned money, and you contribute to the house plenty, and you're so good to your sister.'

'Everyone loves Olive.'

'Yes they do, but you are specially good to her. Your mother and I have no fears and worries. We know that in the fullness of time when we've gone to Glasnevin cemetery, you'll look after Olive.'

Bill heard himself speak in a tone he didn't recognise as his own. 'Ah, don't you know Olive will always be looked after. You would never worry about a thing like that, would you?'

'I know there are plenty of homes and institutions, but we know that you'd never send Olive off to a place like that.'

And as they sat in the sun with the sea shimmering below a little breeze came up and blew around them and it went straight into Bill Burke's heart. He realised what he had never faced in his twenty-three years of living. He knew now that Olive was his problem, not just theirs. That his big simple sister was his for life. When he and Lizzie married in two years' time, when he went abroad with Lizzie to live, when their two children were born, Olive would be part of their family.

His father and mother might live for another twenty years. Olive would only be forty-five then, with the mind of a child. He felt very cold indeed.

'Come on, Dad, Mam will have said three rosaries in the church and they'll be in the pub waiting for us.'

And indeed there they were, Olive's big face shining to see her brother come in.

'That's Bill, the bank manager,' she said.

And everyone in the pub smiled. As they would always smile at Olive when they didn't have to take her on for life.

Bill went up to Mountainview to register for the Italian lesson. He realised with a heavy heart how lucky he had been that his father had saved money to send him to a smaller and better school. In Bill's school there were proper games pitches and the parents had paid a so-called Voluntary Subscription to maintain some of the frills and extras that would never be known in Mountainview.

He looked at the shabby paint and the ugly bicycle shed. Few boys who went to school here would find it easy to get into the bank as he had done. Or was he just being snobbish? Perhaps things had changed. Perhaps he was guiltier than others because he was trying to keep a system going in his mind. It was something he could talk to Grania about. Her father taught here after all.

It was not something he could talk to Lizzie about.

Lizzie had become excited about the lessons. 'I'm telling everyone that we'll be speaking Italian shortly,' she laughed happily. For an instant she reminded him of Olive. The same innocent belief that once you mentioned something that was it, it had happened, and you were somehow in command. But who could compare the beautiful feckless wild-eyed Lizzie to poor Olive, the lumpen slow smiling sister who would be his for evermore?

Part of Bill hoped that Lizzie would change her mind about the lessons. That would be a few pounds saved anyway. He was beginning to feel panicky about the amount of his salary that was promised in debts before he took home anything at all at the end of the month. His new jacket gave him pleasure, but not *that* much pleasure. Possibly it had been a foolish extravagance that he would live to regret.

'What a beautiful jacket, is it pure wool?' asked the woman at the desk. She was old of course, over fifty. But she had a nice smile and she felt the sleeve just above his wrist.

'Yes it is,' Bill said. 'Light wool, but apparently you pay for the cut. That's what I was told.'

'Of course you do. It's Italian isn't it?' Her voice was Irish but slightly accented, as if she had lived abroad. She seemed genuinely interested. Was she the teacher? Bill had been told that they were going to have a real Italian. Was this the first cut-back?

'Are you the teacher?' he asked. He hadn't parted with his money yet. Possibly this was not the week to hand over fees from Lizzie and himself. Suppose it was a cheapskate kind of thing. Wouldn't that have been typical? Just to throw his money away foolishly without checking.

'Yes indeed. I am Signora. I lived twenty-six years in Italy, in Sicilia. I still think in Italian and dream in it. I hope that I will be able to share all this with you and the others who come to the class.'

Now it was going to be harder still to back out. Bill wished he wasn't such a Mister Nice Guy. There were people in the bank who would know exactly how to get out of this situation. The sharks, he and Grania called them.

Thinking of Grania reminded him of her father. 'Do you have enough numbers to make the class workable?' he asked. Perhaps this could be his out. Maybe the class would never take place.

But Signora's face was alive with enthusiasm. '*Si si*, we have been so fortunate. People from far and near have heard about it. How did you hear, Signor Burke?'

'In the bank,' he said.

'The bank.' Signora's pleasure was so great he didn't want to puncture it. 'Imagine, they know of us in the bank.'

'Will I be able to learn bank terms, do you think?' He leaned across the table his eyes seeking reassurance in her face.

'What kind exactly?'

'You know, the words we use in banking . . .' But Bill was vague, he didn't know the terms he might use in banking in Italy one day.

'You can write them down for me and I could look them up for you,' Signora explained. 'But to be very truthful the course will not concentrate on banking terms. It will be more about the language and the feel of Italy. I want to make you love it and know it a little so that when you go there it will be like going home to a friend.'

'That will be great,' Bill said, and handed over the money for Lizzie and himself.

'*Martedì*,' Signora said.

'I beg your pardon?'

'*Martedì*, Tuesday. Now you know one word already.'

'*Martedì*,' Bill said and walked to the bus stop. He felt that even more than his fine wool, well cut jacket, this was good money being thrown away.

'What will I wear for the evening class?' Lizzie asked him on Monday night. Only Lizzie would want to know that. Other people might want to know whether to bring notebooks or dictionaries or name badges.

'Something that won't distract everyone from their studies,' Bill suggested.

It was a pretty vain hope and a foolish suggestion. Lizzie's wardrobe did not include clothes that would not distract. Even now at the end of summer she would have a short skirt that would show her long tanned legs, she would have a tight top and a jacket loosely around her shoulders.

'But what exactly?'

He knew it wasn't a question of style. It was a matter of choosing a colour. 'I love the red,' he said.

Her eyes lit up. It was very easy to please Lizzie. 'I'll try it on now,' she said, and got her red skirt and red and white shirt. She looked marvellous, fresh and young, like an advertisement for shampoo with her golden hair.

'I could wear a red ribbon in my hair?' She seemed doubtful.

Bill felt a huge protective surge well up in him. Lizzie really did need him. Owlish and obsessed with paying debts as he was, she would be lost without him.

'Tonight's the night,' he told Grania at work next day.

'You'll tell me honestly, won't you? You'll tell me what it's like.' Grania seemed very serious. She was wondering how it would go for her father, whether he might look good or just foolish.

Bill assured her he would tell the truth, but somehow he knew it was unlikely. Even if it was a disaster Bill would not feel able to blow the whistle. He would probably say that it was fine.

Bill did not recognise the dusty school annexe when they arrived. The place had been transformed. Huge posters festooned the walls, pictures of the Trevi Fountain and the Colosseum, images of the *Mona Lisa* and of Michelangelo's *David*, and mixed amongst them mighty vineyards and plates of Italian food. There was a table covered in red, white and green crepe paper which held paper plates covered with cling film.

They seemed to have real food in them, little pieces of salami and cheese. There were paper flowers too, each one with a big label giving its name. Carnations were *garofani* . . . Somebody had taken immense pains.

Bill hoped that it would all work out well. For the strange woman with the odd-coloured red and grey hair called simply Signora, for the kind, hovering man in the background who must be Grania's father, for all the people who sat awkwardly and nervously around waiting for it to start. All of them with some hope or dream like his own. None of them, by the look of it, wanting to make a career in international banking.

Signora clapped her hands and introduced herself. '*Mi chiamo Signora. Come si chiama?*' she asked the man who must be Grania's father.

'*Mi chiamo Aidan,*' he said. And so on around the classroom.

Lizzie loved it. '*Mi chiamo Lizzie,*' she cried and everyone smiled admiringly as if she had achieved a great feat.

'Let's try to make our names more Italian. You could say: '*Mi chiamo Elizabetta.*'

Lizzie loved that even more and could hardly be stopped from repeating it.

Then they all wrote *Mi chiamo* and their names on huge pieces of paper and pinned them on. And they learned how to ask each other how they were, what time it was, what day it was, what date, where they lived.

'*Chi è?*' pointing at Bill.

'*Guglielmo,*' the class all shouted back.

Soon they knew everyone's names in Italian and the class had visibly relaxed. Signora handed out pieces of paper. There were all the phrases they had been using, familiar to the sound, but they would never have been able to pronounce them had they seen them written first.

They went through them over and over, what day, what time, what is your name, and they answered them. People's faces were taking on a look of near smugness.

'*Bene,*' said Signora. 'Now we have ten minutes more.' There was a gasp. The two hours could not truly be over. 'You have all worked so hard there is a little treat, but we have to pronounce the salami before we eat it, and the *formaggio.*'

Like children, the thirty adults fell on the sausage and cheese and pronounced the words.

'*Giovedì,*' Signora was saying.

'*Giovedì,*' they were all chorusing. Bill began to put the chairs away neatly by the wall in a stack. Signora seemed to look at Grania's father as if to know whether this was what was needed. He nodded quietly. Then the others helped. In minutes the classroom was tidy. The porter would have little to do in terms of clearing up.

Bill and Lizzie went out to the bus stop.

'*Ti amo,*' she said to him suddenly.

'What's that?' he asked.

'Oh go on, you're the one with the brains,' Lizzie said. She was smiling fit to break his heart. 'Go on guess. *Ti* . . . what's that?'

'It's "you", I think,' said Bill.

'And what's "*amo*"?'

'Is it love?'

'It means *I love you!*'

'How do you know?' He was amazed.

'I asked her just before we left. She said they were the most beautiful two words in the world.'

'They are, they are,' said Bill.

Perhaps the Italian classes might work after all.

'It was really and truly great,' Bill told Grania next day.

'My father came home high as a kite, thank God,' Grania said.

'And she's really good, you know, she makes you think you can speak the language in five minutes.'

'So you're off to run the Italian section then,' Grania teased.

'Even Lizzie liked it, she was really interested. She kept saying the sentences over and over on the bus, everyone was joining in.'

'I'm sure they were.' Grania was clipped.

'No, stop being like that. She took much more notice of it than I thought she would. She calls herself Elizabetta now.' Bill was proud.

'I bet she does,' Grania said grimly. 'I'd also like to bet she'll have dropped out by lesson three.'

As it happened Grania was right, but not because Lizzie wasn't interested. It was because her mother came to Dublin.

'She hasn't been for ages and I have to meet her off the train,' she said to Bill apologetically.

'But can't you tell her you'll be back at half past nine?' Bill begged. He felt sure that if Signorina Elizabetta were to miss out on one lesson that would be it. She would claim that she was far too far behind to catch up.

'No honestly, Bill, she doesn't come to Dublin very often. I have to be there.' He was silent. 'You care about your mother enough to *live* with her for heaven's sake, why shouldn't I meet mine at Heuston Station? It's not much to ask.'

Bill was very reasonable. 'No,' he agreed. 'It's not.'

'And Bill, could you lend me the money for a taxi? My mother hates travelling on a bus.'

'Won't she pay for the taxi?'

'Oh don't be so mean, you're mean and tight-fisted and penny-pinching.'

'That's not fair, Lizzie. It's not true and it's not fair.'

'Okay,' she shrugged.

'What do you mean, "Okay"?'

'Just that. Enjoy the lesson, give my love to Signora.'

'Have the money for the taxi.'

'No, not like that, not with a bad grace.'

'I'd love you and your mother to travel by taxi, I'd love it. It would make you feel happy and generous and welcoming. Please take it, Lizzie, please.'

'Well, if you're sure.'

He kissed her on the forehead. 'Will I meet your mother this time?'

'I hope so, Bill, you know we wanted you to last time but she had so many friends around. They took all her time. She knows so many people, you see.'

Bill thought to himself that Lizzie's mother might know a lot of people but none of them well enough to meet her at the railway station with a car or taxi. But he didn't say it.

'*Dov'è la bella Elizabetta?*' Signora asked.

'*La bella Elizabetta è andata alla stazione,*' Bill heard himself say. '*La madre di Elizabetta arriva stasera.*'

Signora was overwhelmed. '*Benissimo, Guglielmo. Bravo, bravo.*'

'You've been cramming, you little sneak,' said an angry-faced thickset fellow with Luigi on his blue name tag. His real name was Lou.

'We did *andato* last week, it was on the list, and we did *stasera* the first day. They're all words we know. I *didn't* cram.'

'Oh Jesus, keep your shirt on,' said Lou, who frowned more than ever and joined with the class shouting that in this *piazza* there were many beautiful buildings. 'There's a lie for a start,' he muttered, looking out the window at the barrack-like school yard.

'It's getting better, they are painting it up,' Bill said.

'You're a real cheerful Charlie, aren't you?' Lou said. 'Everything's always bloody marvellous as far as you're concerned.'

Bill longed to tell him that everything was far from cheerful, he was trapped in a house where everyone depended on him, he had a girlfriend who didn't love him enough to introduce him to her mother, he had no idea how he was going to pay his term loan next month.

But of course he said none of these things. Instead he joined in the chorus chanting that *in questa piazza ci sono molti belli edifici.* He wondered where Lizzie and her mother had gone. He hoped beyond reason that she hadn't taken her mother to a restaurant and cashed a cheque. This time there would be real trouble in the bank.

They had little bits of bread with topping of some sort on them. Signora said they were *crostini.* 'What about the *vino?*' someone asked.

'I wanted to have *vino, vino rosso, vino bianco.* But it's a school you see, they don't want any alcohol on the premises. Not to give a bad example to the children.'

'A bit late for that round here,' Lou said.

Bill looked at him with interest. It was impossible to know why a man like that was learning Italian. Although it was difficult to see why any of them were there, and he felt sure that a lot of them must puzzle about Lizzie, there seemed to be no reason that anyone could fathom why Lou, now transformed to Luigi, should come to something that he obviously despised, two nights a week, and glower at everyone from beginning to end. Bill decided he would have to regard it as part of the rich tapestry of life.

One of the paper flowers was broken and on the floor.

'Can I have this, Signora?' Bill asked.

'*Certo, Guglielmo,* is it for *la bellissima Elizabetta?*'

'No, it's for my sister.'

'*Mia sorella, mia sorella,* my sister,' Signora said. 'You are a kind, good man, Guglielmo.'

'Yeah, but where does that get you these days?' Bill asked as he went out to the bus stop.

Olive was waiting for him at the door. 'Speak in Italian,' she cried.

'*Ciao, sorella*,' he said. 'Have a *garofano*. I brought it for you.'

The look of pleasure on her face made him feel worse than he had been feeling already, which had been pretty bad.

Bill was taking sandwiches to work this week. There was no way he could afford even the canteen.

'Are you okay?' Grania asked him concerned. 'You look tired.'

'Oh, we international linguists have to learn to take the strain,' he said with a weak smile.

Grania looked as if she were about to ask him about Lizzie but changed her mind. Lizzie? Where was she today? With her mother's friends maybe, having cocktails in one of the big hotels. Or somewhere down in Temple Bar discovering some new place that she would tell him about, eyes shining. He wished she would ring and speak to him, ask about last night at the class. He would tell her how she had been missed and called beautiful. He would tell her about the sentence he had made up, saying she had gone to the station to meet her mother. She would tell him what she did. Why this silence?

The afternoon seemed long and tedious. After work he began to worry. A whole day never passed like this without any contact. Should he go round to her flat? But then if she were entertaining her mother, might she not regard this as intrusive? She had said she hoped they would meet. He mustn't force it.

Grania was working late too. 'Waiting for Lizzie?' she asked.

'No, her mother's in town, she's probably tied up. Just wondering what to do.'

'I was wondering what to do too. Great fun being in the bank, isn't it? When the day ends you're such a zombie you can't think what to do next.' Grania laughed at the whole notion of it.

'You're always rushing here and there, Grania.' He sounded envious.

'Well, not tonight. I haven't a notion of going home. My mother will be on her way out to the restaurant, my father disappeared into his study and Brigid like some kind of wild animal because she's put on weight again. She's kicking the scales and saying that the house is full of the smell of frying, and she talks about food for about five hours each evening. She'd make your hair go white overnight listening to her.'

'Is she really worried about it?' Bill was always so kind and interested in people's problems.

'I don't know whether she is or not. She's always looked the same to me, a bit squarish but fine. When she has her hair done and she's smiling she's as good as anyone, but there's this dreary litany of a pound here or a kilo there or a zip that broke or tights that split. Jesus, she'd drive you insane. I'm not going home to listen to that, I tell you.'

There was a pause. Bill was on the point of asking her to have a drink when he remembered his finances. This would be a good excuse to go home on his season ticket and spend not a single penny.

At that moment Grania said: 'Why don't I take you to the pictures and chips, my treat?'

'I can't do that, Grania.'

'Yes you can. I owe you for signing up for those classes, it was a great favour.' She made it sound reasonable.

They went through the film listings in the evening paper and argued good naturedly about what might be good and what might be rubbish. It would have been so easy to be with someone like this all the time, Bill thought yet again. And he felt sure that Grania was thinking the same thing. But when it wasn't there it wasn't there. She would remain loving this awkward older man and endure the problems that lay ahead when her father found out. He would stay with Lizzie who had his heart broken morning, noon and night. That's what happened to people.

When he got back home his mother had an anxious face. 'That Lizzie's been here,' she said. 'Whatever time you came in you were to go to her flat.'

'Is anything wrong?' He was alarmed. It wasn't like Lizzie to come to the house, not after her uncertain welcome on her one official visit.

'Oh, I'd say there's plenty wrong, she's a troubled girl,' his mother said.

'But was she sick, had anything happened?'

'Troubled in herself, I mean,' his mother repeated.

He knew he would get nothing but a general mood of disapproval, so he went down the road and caught a bus in the other direction.

She was sitting there in the warm September night outside the house where she had her bedsitter. There were big stone steps leading up to the door, and Lizzie sat hugging her knees swaying backwards and forwards. To his relief she wasn't crying and didn't seem upset or in a state.

'Where were you?' she asked accusingly.

'Where were *you*?' Bill said. '*You* are the one who says I'm not to call you, not to turn up.'

'I was here.'

'Yes, well I was out.'

'Where did you go?'

'To the pictures,' he said.

'I thought we had no money, we weren't meant to be doing anything normal like going to the pictures.'

'I didn't pay. Grania Dunne took me as a treat.'

'Oh yes?'

'Yes. What's wrong, Lizzie?'

'Everything,' she said.

'Why did you come to my house?'

'I wanted to see you, to make things right.'

'Well, you succeeded in frightening the life out of my mother and out of me. Why didn't you ring me at work?'

'I was confused.'

'Did your mother arrive?'

'Yes, she did.'

'And did you meet her?'

'Yes.' Her voice was very flat.

'And take the taxi?'

'Yes.'

'So, what's wrong?'

'She laughed at my flat.'

'Oh Lizzie. Come *on*. You didn't drag me all the way here, twenty-four hours later, to tell me that, did you?'

'Of course,' she laughed.

'It's her way, it's your way . . . people like you and your mother laugh all the time, it's what you do.'

'No, not that kind of laughing.'

'Well, what kind?'

'She just said it was too funny and asked could she go now that she'd seen it. She said I'd never let the taxi go and marooned her in this neck of the woods, had I?'

Bill was sad. Lizzie had obviously been very upset. What a thoughtless bloody woman. She hardly ever saw her daughter, couldn't she have been nice for the few hours she *was* in Dublin?

'I know, I know,' he said soothingly. 'But people always say the wrong thing, they're known for it. Come on, let's not worry about it, let's go upstairs. Hey, come on.'

'No, we can't.'

She was going to need a bit of persuading.

'Lizzie, I have people in the bank all day from nine o'clock in the morning saying the wrong thing, they're not evil people, they just upset others. The trick is not to let them. And then when I go home my mother tells me she's worn out pouring tinned sauce over the frozen chicken, and my father tells me of all the chances he never had as a boy and Olive tells anyone who will listen that I am the head of the bank. And sometimes it's a bit hard to take, but you just put up with it, that's what it's all about.'

'For you yes, but not for me.' Again her voice was very dead.

'So did you have a row? Is that it? It'll pass, family rows always do. Honestly Lizzie.'

'No, we didn't exactly have a row.'

'Well?'

'I had her supper ready. It was chicken livers and a miniature of sherry, and I had the rice all ready too. I showed it to her and she laughed again.'

'Yes well, as I said . . .'

'She wasn't going to stay, Bill, not for supper. She said she had only called in to keep me quiet. She was going to some art gallery, some opening, some exhibition. She'd be late. She tried to push past me.'

'Um . . . yes . . . ?' Bill didn't like this at all.

'So, I couldn't take it any more.'

'What did you do, Lizzie?' He was amazed that he could keep so calm.

'I locked the door and threw the key out the window.'

'You *what*?'

'I said, now you *have* to stay and sit and talk to your daughter. I said, now you can't get out and run away as you've run away from us all, all your life, from Daddy and from the rest of us.'

'And what did she do?'

'Oh, she got into a terrible temper and kept screaming and beating the door and saying I was cracked and like my father and you know, the usual.'

'No I don't know. What else?'

'Oh, what you'd expect.'

'And what happened then?'

'Well she wore herself out, and eventually she did have supper.'

'And was she still shouting then?'

'No, she was just worried in case the house went on fire and we'd be burned to a crisp. That's what she kept saying, burned to a crisp.'

Bill's mind was working slowly but surely. 'You *did* let her out eventually.'

'No, I didn't. Not at all.'

'But she's not still there?'

'Yes she is.'

'You can't be serious, Lizzie.'

She nodded several times. 'I'm afraid I am.'

'How did you get out?'

'The window. When she was in the bathroom.'

'She slept there?'

'She had to. I slept in the chair. She had the whole bed.' Lizzie sounded defensive.

'Let me get this straight. She came here yesterday, Tuesday, at seven o'clock and it's now eleven o'clock at night on Wednesday and she's *still* here, locked in against her will?'

'Yes.'

'But God almighty, why?'

'So that I could talk to her. She never makes time to talk to me. Never, not once.'

'And *has* she talked to you? I mean now that she's locked in?'

'Not really, not in a satisfactory way, she just keeps giving out and saying I'm unreasonable, unstable, whatever.'

'I don't believe this, Lizzie, I don't. She's been there not only all night but all day and all tonight?' His head was reeling.

'What else could I do? She never has a moment, always in a rush . . . to go somewhere else, to meet other people.'

'But you can't do this. You can't lock people in and expect them to talk.'

'I know it mightn't have been the right thing to do. Listen, I was wondering could you come and talk to her . . . She doesn't seem very reasonable.'

'Me, talk to her? *Me?*'

'Well, you did say you wanted to meet her, Bill. You asked several times.'

He looked into the beautiful troubled face of the woman he loved. Of course he had wanted to meet his future mother-in-law. But not when she was locked into a bedsitter. Not when she had been kidnapped for over thirty hours and was about to call the Guards. This was going to be a meeting which called for diplomacy like Bill Burke had never known to exist.

He wondered how his heroes in fiction would have handled it and knew with a great certainty that nobody would ever have put them in a position where they might have to.

They walked up the stairs to Lizzie's flat. No noise came from inside.

'Could she have got out?' Bill whispered.

'No. There's a sort of bar under the window. She couldn't have opened it.'

'Would she have broken the glass?'

'No, you don't know my mother.'

True, Bill thought, but he was about to get to know her under very strange circumstances indeed. 'Will she be violent, rush at me or anything?'

'No, of course not.' Lizzie was scornful of his fears.

'Well, speak to her or something, tell her who it is.'

'No, she's cross with me, she'd be better with someone new.' Lizzie's eyes were huge with fear.

Bill squared his shoulders. 'Um, Mrs Duffy, my name is Bill Burke, I work in the bank,' he said. It produced no response. 'Mrs Duffy, are you all right? Can I have your assurance that you are calm and in good health?'

'Why should I be either calm or in good health? My certifiably insane daughter has imprisoned me in here and this is something she will regret every day, every hour, from now until the end of her life.' The voice sounded very angry, but strong.

'Well, Mrs Duffy, if you just stand back from the door I will come in and explain this to you.'

'Are you a friend of Elizabeth's?'

'Yes, a very good friend. In fact I am very fond of her.'

'Then you must be insane too,' said the voice.

Lizzie raised her eyes. 'See what I mean,' she whispered.

'Mrs Duffy, I think we can discuss this much better face to face. I am coming in now, so please stand well away.'

'You are not coming in. I have put a chair under the door handle in case she was going to bring back some other drug addicts or criminals like you. I am staying here until somebody comes to rescue me.'

'I have come to rescue you,' Bill said desperately.

'You can turn the key all you like, you won't get in.'

It was true, Bill found. She had indeed barricaded herself in.

'The window?' he asked Lizzie.

'It's a bit of a climb but I'll show you.'

Bill looked alarmed. 'I meant *you* to go in the window.'

'I can't, Bill, you've heard her. She's like a raging bull. She'd kill me.'

'Well, what will she do to me, suppose I did get in? She thinks I'm a drug addict.'

Lizzie's lip trembled. 'You said you'd help me,' she said in a small voice.

'Show me the window,' said Bill. It was a bit of a climb and when he got there he saw the pole that Lizzie had wedged under the top part of the window. He eased it out, opened the window, and pulled the curtain back. A blonde woman in her forties, with a mascara-stained face, saw him just as he got in and ran at him with a chair.

'Stay away from me, get off, you useless little thug,' she cried.

'Mummy, Mummy,' Lizzie shouted from outside the door.

'Mrs Duffy, please, please.' Bill took up the lid of the bread bin to defend himself. 'Mrs Duffy, I've come to let you out. Look here's the key. Please, please put the chair down.'

He did indeed seem to be offering her a key; her eyes appeared to relax slightly. She put down the chair, and watched him warily.

'Just let me open the door, and Lizzie can come in and we can all discuss this calmly,' he said, moving towards the door.

But Lizzie's mother had picked up the kitchen chair again. 'Get away from that door. Who knows what kind of a gang there is? I've told Lizzie I have no money, I have no credit cards . . . it's useless kidnapping *me*. No one will pay a ransom. You've really picked the wrong woman.' Her lip was trembling; she looked so like her daughter that Bill felt the familiar protective attitude sweeping over him.

'It's only Lizzie outside, there's no gang. It's all a misunderstanding.' His voice was calming.

'You can say that again. Locked in here with that lunatic girl since last night and then she goes off and leaves me here, all on my own, wondering what's next in the door, and you come in the window with a bread bin coming at me.'

'No, no, I just picked that up when you picked up the chair. Look, I'll put it down now.' His voice was having a great effect. She seemed ready to talk reason. She put the red kitchen chair down and sat on it, exhausted, frightened and unsure what to do next.

Bill began to breathe normally. He decided to let the moment last rather than introducing any new elements into it like opening the door. They looked at each other warily.

Then there was a cry from outside. 'Mummy? Bill? What's happening? Why aren't you talking, shouting?'

'We're resting,' Bill called. As an explanation he wondered was it adequate. But Lizzie seemed to think so. 'Okay,' she said from outside.

'Is she on some kind of drugs?' her mother asked.

'No. Heavens no, not at all.'

'Well, what was it all about? All this locking me in, saying she wanted to talk and then not talking any sense.'

'I think she misses you,' Bill said slowly.

'She'll be missing me a lot more from now on in,' said Mrs Duffy.

Bill looked at her, trying to take her in. She was young and slim, she looked a different generation to his own mother. She wore a floaty kind of caftan dress, with some glass beads around the neckline. It was the kind of thing you saw in pictures of New Age people, but she didn't have open sandals or long flowing hair. Her curls were like Lizzie's, but with little streaks of grey. Apart from her tearstained face she could have been going to a party. Which was of course what she *had* been doing when she was waylaid.

'I think she was sorry that you had grown a bit apart,' Bill said. There was a snort from the figure in the caftan. 'Well, you know, you live so far away and everything.'

'Not far enough, I tell you. All I did was ask the girl to come out and meet me for a quick drink and she insists on coming to the station in a taxi, and bringing me here. I said, well only for a little while because we had to go to Chester's opening . . . Where Chester thinks I am now is beyond worrying about.'

'Who is Chester?'

'He's a friend, for God's sake, a friend, one of the people who lives near where I live, he's an artist. We all came up, no one will know what happened to me.'

'Won't they think of looking for you here – in your daughter's house?'

'No, of course not, why would they?'

'They know you have a daughter in Dublin?'

'Yes, well maybe. They know I have three children but I don't bleat on and on about them, they wouldn't know where Elizabeth *lived* or anything.'

'But your other friends, your real friends?'

'These are my real friends,' she snapped.

'Are you all right in there?' Lizzie called.

'Leave it for a bit, Lizzie,' Bill said.

'By God, you're going to pay for this, Elizabeth,' her mother called.

'Where are they staying – your friends?'

'I don't know, that's the whole bloody problem, we said we'd see how it went at the opening and maybe if Harry was there we might all go to Harry's. He lives in a big barn, we once stayed there before. Or if all else failed Chester would know some marvellous little B & Bs for half nothing.'

'And will Chester have called the Guards, do you think?'

'Why on earth should he have done that?'

'To see what had happened to you.'

'The Guards?'

'Well, if he was expecting you and you had disappeared.'

'He'll think I just drifted off with someone at the exhibition. He might even think I hadn't bothered to come up at all. That's what's so bloody maddening about it all.'

Bill let out a sigh of relief. Lizzie's mother was a floater and a drifter. There would not be a full-scale alert looking for her. No Garda cars would cruise by, eyes out for a blonde in a caftan. Lizzie would not spend the rest of the night in a cell in a Garda station.

'Will we let her in, do you think?' He managed to make it appear that they were together in this.

'Will she go on with all that stuff about never talking and never relating and running away?'

'No, I'll see to it that she doesn't, believe me.'

'Very well. But don't expect me to be all sunshine and light after this trick she's pulled.'

'No, you have every right to be upset.' He moved past her to the door.

And there was Lizzie cowering outside in the dark corridor. 'Ah, Lizzie,' Bill said in the voice you would use if you found an unexpected but delightful guest on your doorstep. 'Come in, won't you. And perhaps you could make us all a cup of tea.'

Lizzie scuttled by him into the kitchen, avoiding the eye of her mother. 'Wait until your father hears about this carry-on,' her mother said.

'Mrs Duffy, do you take your tea with milk and sugar?' Bill interrupted. 'Neither, thank you.'

'Just black for Mrs Duffy,' Bill called as if he were giving a command to the staff. He moved around the tiny flat tidying things up, straightening the counterpane on the bed, picking up objects from the floor, as if establishing normality in a place which had temporarily abandoned it. Soon they were sitting, an unlikely threesome, drinking mugs of tea.

'I bought a tin of shortbread,' Lizzie said proudly, taking out a tartan-patterned box.

'They cost a fortune,' Bill said aghast.

'I wanted to have something for my mother's visit.'

'I *never* said I was coming to visit, that was all your idea. Some idea it was, too.'

'Still, they're in a tin,' Bill said. 'They could last for a long time.'

'Are you soft in the head?' Lizzie's mother suddenly asked Bill.

'I don't think so. Why do you ask?'

'Talking about biscuits at a time like this. I thought you were meant to be the one in charge.'

'Well, isn't it better than screaming and talking about needing and relating and all the things you said you didn't want talked about?' Bill was stung with the unfairness of it.

'No it's not, it's insane if you ask me. You're just as mad as she is. I've got myself into a lunatic asylum.'

Her eyes darted to the door, and he saw her grip bag beside it. Would she make a run for it? Would that perhaps be for the best? Or had they gone so far into this that they had better see it through to the end. Let Lizzie tell her mother what was wrong, let her mother accept or deny all this. His father had always said that they should wait and see. It seemed a poor philosophy to Bill. What were you waiting for? What would you see? But his father seemed pleased with the end product, so perhaps it had its merits.

Lizzie munched the biscuit. 'These are beautiful,' she said. 'Full of butter, you can tell.' She was so endearing, like a small child. Could her mother not see that in her too?

Bill looked from one to the other. He hoped he wasn't imagining that the mother's face seemed to be softening a little.

'It's quite hard, Lizzie, in ways, a woman alone,' she began.

'But you didn't have to be alone, Mummy, you could have had us all with you, Daddy and me and John and Kate.'

'I couldn't live in a house like that, trapped all day waiting for a man to come home with the wages. And then your father often *didn't* come home with the wages, he went to the betting shop with them. Like he does still over in Galway.'

'You didn't have to go.'

'I had to go because otherwise I would have killed somebody, him, you, myself. Sometimes it's safer to go and get a bit of air to breathe.'

'When *did* you go?' Bill asked conversationally, as if he were enquiring about the times of trains.

'Don't you know, don't you know every detail of the wicked witch who ran away abandoning everyone?'

'No I don't, actually. I didn't even know you *had* ever gone until this moment. I thought you and Mr Duffy had separated amicably and that all your children had scattered. It seemed very grown up and what families should do.'

'What do you mean, what families should do?' Lizzie's mother looked at him suspiciously.

'Well, you see, I live at home with my mother and father and I have a handicapped sister, and honestly I can't ever see any way of *not* being there, or nearby anyway, so I thought what Lizzie's family had was very free . . . and I kind of envied it.' He was so transparently honest. Nobody could put on an act like that.

'You could just get up and go,' Lizzie's mother suggested.

'I suppose so, but I wouldn't feel easy about it.'

'You've only one life.' They were both ignoring Lizzie now.

'Yes, that's it. I suppose, if we had more than one then I wouldn't feel so guilty.'

Lizzie tried to get back into the conversation. 'You never write, you never stay in touch.'

'What's there to write *about*, Lizzie? You don't know my friends. I don't know yours, I don't know John's or Kate's. I still love you and want the best for you even though we don't see each other all the time.' She stopped, almost surprised at herself that she had said this much.

Lizzie was not convinced. 'You couldn't love us otherwise you'd come to see us. You wouldn't laugh at me and this place I live in, and laugh at the idea of staying with me, not if you loved us.'

'I think what Mrs Duffy means . . .' Bill began.

'Oh, for Jesus' sake call me Bernie.' Bill was so taken aback he forgot his sentence. 'Go on, you were saying what I meant was . . . What *do* I mean?'

'I think you mean that Lizzie *is* very important to you, but you have sort of drifted away a bit, what with West Cork being so far from here . . . and that last night was a bad time to stay because your friend Chester was having an art exhibition, and you wanted to be there in time to give him moral support. Was it something like that?' He looked from one to the other with his round face creased in anxiety. Please may she have meant something like this, and not have meant that she was going for the Guards or that she was never going to see Lizzie as long as she lived.

'It was a *bit* like that,' Bernie agreed. 'But only a bit.'

Still, it was something, Bill thought to himself. 'And what Lizzie meant when she threw away the key was that she was afraid life was passing too quickly and she wanted a chance to get to know you and talk properly, make up for all the lost time, wasn't that it?'

'That was it,' Lizzie nodded vigorously.

'But God almighty, whatever your name is . . .'

'Bill,' he said helpfully.

'Yes, well, Bill, it's not the act of a sane person to lure me here and lock me in.'

'I didn't lure you here, I borrowed the money from Bill to get a taxi for you. I invited you here, I bought shortbread and bacon and chicken livers and sherry. I made my bed for you to sleep in. I wanted you to stay. That wasn't all that much, was it?'

'But I couldn't.' Bernie Duffy's voice was gentler now.

'You could have said you'd come back the next day. You just laughed. I couldn't bear that, and then you got crosser and crosser and said awful things.'

'I wasn't talking normally because I wasn't talking to a normal person. I was really shaken by you, Lizzie. You seemed to be losing your mind. Truly. You weren't making any sense. You kept saying that the last six years you had been like a lost soul . . .'

'That's just the way it was.'

'You were seventeen when I left. Your father wanted you to go to Galway with him, you wouldn't . . . You insisted you were old enough to live in Dublin, you got a job in a dry cleaner's, I remember. You had your own money. It was what you wanted. That was what you said.'

'I stayed because I thought you'd come back.'

'Back to where? Here?'

'No, back to the house. Daddy didn't sell it for a year, remember?'

'I remember, and then he put every penny he got for it on horses that are still running backwards somewhere on English racetracks.'

'Why didn't you come back, Mummy?'

'What was there to come back *to*? Your father was only interested in a form book, John had gone to Switzerland, Kate had gone to New York, you were running with your crowd.'

'I was waiting for you, Mummy.'

'No, that's not true, Lizzie. You can't rewrite the whole thing. Why didn't you write and tell me if that was the way it was?'

There was a silence.

'You only liked hearing from me if I was having a good time, so I told you about the good times. On postcards and letters. I told you when I went to Greece, and to Achill Island. I didn't tell you about wanting you to come back in case you got annoyed with me.'

'I would have liked it a hell of a lot more than being hijacked, imprisoned . . .'

'And is it nice where you are in West Cork?' Again Bill was being conversational and interested. 'It always sounds a lovely place to me, the pictures you see of the coastline.'

'It's very special. There are a lot of free spirits there, people who have gone back to the land, people who paint, express themselves, make pottery.'

'And do you specialise in any of the arts . . . er . . . Bernie?' He was owlish and interested, she couldn't take offence.

'No, not myself personally, but I have always been interested in artistic people, and places. I find myself stifled if I'm cooped up anywhere. That's why this whole business . . .'

Bill was anxious to head her off the subject. 'And do you have a house of your own or do you live with Chester?'

'No, heavens no,' she laughed just like her daughter laughed, a happy peal of mirth. 'No, Chester is gay, he lives with Vinnie. No, no. They're my dearest friends. They live about four miles away. No, I have a room, a sort of studio I suppose, outhouse it once was, off a bigger property.'

'That sounds nice, is it near the sea?'

'Yes, of course. Everywhere's near the sea. It's very charming. I love it. I've been there for six years now, made a real little home of it.'

'And how do you get money to live, Bernie? Do you have a job?'

Lizzie's mother looked at him as if he had made a very vulgar noise. 'I beg your pardon?'

'I mean, if Lizzie's father didn't give you any money you have to earn a living. That's all.' He was unrepentant.

'It's because he works in a bank, Mummy.' Lizzie apologised. 'He's obsessed with earning a living.'

Suddenly it became too much for Bill. He was sitting in this house in the middle of the night trying to keep the peace between two madwomen and they thought that *he* was the odd one because he actually had a job and paid his bills and lived according to the rules. Well, he had had just about enough. Let them sort it out. He would go home, back to his dull house, with his sad family.

He would never be transferred into international banking no matter how much he learned about 'How are you' and 'beautiful buildings' and 'red carnations'. He would not try any more to make selfish people see some good in each other. He felt an entirely unfamiliar twitching in his nose and eyes, as if he were about to cry.

There was something about his face that both women noticed at the same time. It was as if he had opted out, left them.

'I didn't mean to laugh at your question,' Lizzie's mother said. 'Of course I have to earn money. I do some help in the home where I have my studio, you know, cleaning, light housework, and when they have parties I help with the . . . well, with the clearing up. I love ironing, I always have, so I do all their ironing too, and for this I don't have to pay any rent. And of course they give me a little spending money too.'

Lizzie looked at her mother in disbelief. This was the arty lifestyle, mixing with the great and the rich, the playboys and the glittery set who had second homes in the south-west of Ireland. Her mother was a maid.

Bill was in control of himself again. 'It must be very satisfying,' he said.

'Means you can have the best of both worlds, a nice place to live, independence, and no real worries about how to put food on the table.'

She searched his face for sarcasm, but did not find any. 'That's right,' Bernie Duffy said eventually. 'That's the way it is.'

Bill thought he must speak before Lizzie blurted out something that would start them off again. 'Perhaps some time when the weather gets finer Lizzie and I could come down and see you there. It would be a real treat for me. We could come on the bus, and change at Cork city.' Eager, boyish and planning it as if this were a social call long overdue.

'And, are you two . . . I mean, are you Lizzie's boyfriend?'

'Yes, we are going to get married when we are twenty-five, two years' time. We hope to get a job in Italy so we are both learning Italian at night.'

'Yes, she told me that amongst all the other ramblings,' Bernie said.

'That we were getting married?' Bill was pleased.

'No, that she was learning Italian. I thought it was more madness.'

There seemed little more to be said. Bill stood up as if he were a normal guest taking his leave of a normal evening. 'Bernie, as you may have noticed it's very late now. There won't be more buses running, and it might be difficult to find your friends even if there were buses. So I suggest that you stay here tonight, at your own wish of course, with the key in the door. And then tomorrow when you've both had a good rest, you and Lizzie, say goodbye to each other nice and peaceably and I probably won't see you until next summer when it would be lovely if we could come and see you in West Cork.'

'Don't go,' Bernie begged. 'Don't go. She's nice and quiet while you're here but the moment you are out the door she'll be ranting and raving and saying she was abandoned.'

'No, no. It won't be a bit like that now.' He spoke with conviction. 'Lizzie, could you give your mother the key? Now Bernie, you keep that and then you know you can come and go as you please.'

'How will *you* get home, Bill?' Lizzie asked.

He looked at her in surprise. She never usually asked or seemed to care that he had to walk three miles when he left her at night.

'I'll walk, it's a fine starry night,' he said. They were both looking at him. He felt an urge to say something more, to make the peaceful moment last. 'At Italian class last night Signora taught us a bit about the weather, how to say it's been a great summer. *E stata una magnifica estate.*'

'That's nice,' Lizzie said. '*E stata una magnifica estate.*' She repeated it perfectly.

'Hey, you got it in one, the rest of us had to keep saying it over.' Bill was impressed.

'She always had a great memory, even as a little girl. You said a thing once and Elizabeth would remember it always.' Bernie looked at her daughter with something like pride.

On the way home Bill felt quite light-hearted. A lot of the obstacles that had seemed huge were less enormous now. He didn't need to fear some classy mother in West Cork who would regard a lowly bank clerk as too humble for her daughter. He didn't have to worry any more that he might be too dull for Lizzie. She wanted safety and love and a base and he could give her all of those things. There would of course be problems ahead. Lizzie would not find it easy to live on a budget. She would never change in her attitude to spending and wanting things now. All he had to do was to try and make it happen somehow within reason. And to head her towards work. If her dizzy mother actually earned a living doing other people's ironing and cleaning, then perhaps Lizzie's own goalposts might move.

Attitudes might change.

They might even go to Galway and visit her father some time. Let her know that she was already part of a family, she didn't have to pretend and wish. And that soon she would be part of his family.

Bill Burke walked on through the night as other people drove by in cars or hailed taxis. He had no envy for any of them. He was a lucky man. So all right, he had people who needed him. And people who relied on him. But that was fine. That meant he was just that sort of person, and maybe in the years to come his son would be sorry for him and pity him as Bill pitied his own father. But it wouldn't matter. It would only mean that the boy wouldn't understand. That was all.

Kathy

Kathy Clarke was one of the hardest working girls in Mountainview. She frowned with concentration in class, she puzzled things out, she hung back and asked questions. In the staffroom they often made good-natured fun of her. 'Doing a Kathy Clarke' meant screwing up your eyes at a notice on the bulletin board trying to understand it.

She was a tall awkward girl, her navy school skirt a bit too long, none of the pierced ears and cheap jewellery of her classmates. Not really bright but determined to do well. Almost too determined. Every year they had parent–teacher meetings. Nobody could really remember who came to ask about Kathy.

'Her father's a plumber,' Aidan Dunne said once. 'He came and put in the cloakroom for us, great job he made of it too, but of course it had to be paid for in cash. Didn't tell me till the end . . . nearly passed out when he saw the cheque book.' 'I remember her mother never took the cigarette out of her mouth during the whole chat,' said Helen the Irish teacher. 'She kept saying what *good* will all this do her, will it earn her a living.'

'That's what they all say.' Tony O'Brien the Principal-Elect was resigned. 'You're surely not expecting them to talk about the sheer intellectual stimulation of studying for its own sake.'

'She has a big sister who comes too,' someone else remembered. 'She's the manageress in the supermarket, I think she's the only one who understands about poor Kathy.'

'God, wouldn't it be a great life if the only worries we had were about them working too hard and frowning too much with concentration,' said Tony O'Brien, who as Principal-Elect had many more trying problems on his desk every day. And not only on his desk.

In his life of moving on from one woman to another there had been very few women he had wanted to stay with, and now that it had finally happened and he had met one, there was this goddamned complication. She was the daughter of poor Aidan Dunne who had thought that he was going to be Principal. The misunderstanding and the confusions would have done credit to a Victorian melodrama.

Now young Grania Dunne wouldn't see him because she accused him of having humiliated her father. It was farfetched and wrong, but the girl believed it. He had left the decision to her, saying for the first time in his life that he would remain unattached waiting until she came back to him. He

95

sent her joky postcards to let her know that he was still there, but there was no response. Perhaps he was stupid to go on hoping. He knew how many other fish there were in the sea, and he had never been short of female fishes in his life.

But somehow none of them had the appeal of this bright eager girl with the dancing eyes and the energy and quick response that made him feel genuinely young again. She hadn't thought he was too old for her, not that night she had stayed. The night before he knew who she was and that her father had expected the job that could never be his.

The last thing Tony O'Brien had expected as Principal of Mountainview was that he would live a near-monastic life at home. It was doing him no harm, early nights, less clubbing, less drinking. In fact he was even trying to cut down on his smoking in case she came back. At least he didn't smoke in the mornings now. He didn't reach out of the bed, eyes closed, hands searching for the packet, he managed to wait till break and have his first drag of the day in the privacy of his own office with a coffee. That was an advance. He wondered should he send her a card with a picture of a cigarette on it saying 'Not still smoking', but then she might think he was totally cured which he was far from being. It was absurd how much of his thoughts she took up.

And he had never realised what an exhausting job it was running a school like Mountainview, the parent–teacher meetings and Open Nights were only two of the many things that cried out for his being there.

He had little time left to worry about the Kathy Clarkes of this world. She would leave school, get some kind of a job; maybe her sister might get her into the supermarket. She would never get third-level education. There wasn't the background, there wasn't the brains. She would survive.

None of them knew what Kathy Clarke's home life was like. If they thought at all, they might have assumed that it was one of the houses on the big sprawling estate with too much television and fast food and too little peace and quiet, too many children and not enough money coming in. That would be the normal picture. They could not know that Kathy's bedroom had a built-in desk and a little library of books. Her elder sister Fran sat there every evening until homework was finished. In winter there was a gas heater with portable cylinders of bottled gas which Fran bought at a discount in the supermarket.

Kathy's parents laughed at the extravagance, all the other children had done their homework at the kitchen table and hadn't it been fine? But Fran said it had not been fine. She had left school at fifteen with no qualifications, it had taken her years to build her way up to a position of seniority and there were still huge gaps in her education. The boys had barely scraped by, two working in England and one a roadie with a pop group. It was as if Fran had a mission to get Kathy to make more of herself than the rest of the family.

Sometimes Kathy felt she was letting Fran down. 'You see, I'm not really very bright, Fran. Things don't come to me like they do to some of them in the class. You wouldn't believe how quick Harriet is.'

'Well, her father's a teacher, why wouldn't she be bright?' Fran sniffed.

'Yes, this is what I mean, Fran. You're so good to me. When you should be dancing you give time to hearing my homework, and I'm so afraid I'll fail all my exams and be a disgrace to you after all your work.'

'I don't want to go dancing,' Fran would sigh.

'But you're still young enough surely to go to discos?' Kathy was sixteen, the baby of the family, Fran was thirty-two, the eldest. She really should be married now with a home of her own like all her friends were, and yet Kathy never wanted Fran to leave. The house would be unthinkable without her. Their mam was out a lot in town, getting things done was what it was called. In fact it was playing slot machines.

There would have been very few comforts in this house if Fran were not there to provide them. Orange juice for breakfast, and a hot meal in the evening. It was Fran who bought Kathy's school uniform and who taught the girl to polish her shoes and to wash her blouses and underwear every night. She would have learned nothing like this from her mother.

Fran explained the facts of life to her and bought her the first packet of Tampax. Fran said that it was better to wait until you found someone you liked a lot to have sex with rather than having it with anyone just because it was expected.

'Did you find someone you liked a lot to have it with?' the fourteen-year-old Kathy had asked with interest.

But Fran had an answer for that one too. 'I've always thought it best not to talk about it, you know the magic sort of goes out of it once you start speaking about it,' she said, and that was that.

Fran took her to the theatre, to plays in the Abbey, the Gate and the Project. She brought her up and down Grafton Street and through the smart shops as well. 'We must learn to do everything with an air of confidence,' Fran said. 'That's the whole trick, we mustn't look humble and apologetic as if we hadn't a right to be here.'

There was never a word of criticism from Fran about their parents. Sometimes Kathy complained: 'Mam takes you for granted, Fran, you bought her a lovely new cooker and she still never makes anything in it.'

'Ah, she's all right,' Fran would say.

'Dad never says thank you when you bring him home beer from the supermarket. He never brings you home a present.'

'He's not the worst,' Fran said. 'It's not a great life with your head stuck down pipes and round S bends all the time.'

'Will you get married, do you think?' Kathy asked her once, anxiously.

'I'll wait until you're a grown up then I'll put my mind to it.' Fran laughed when she said it.

'But won't you be too old?'

'Not at all. By the time you're twenty I'll only be thirty-six, in my prime,' she assured her sister.

'I thought you were going to marry Ken,' Kathy had said.

'Yes, well I didn't. And he went to America, so he's out of the picture.' Fran was brisk.

Ken had worked in the supermarket too and was very go-ahead. Mam and Dad said that he and Fran were sure to make a go of it. Kathy had been very relieved when Ken had left the picture.

At the summer parent–teacher meeting Kathy's father wasn't able to go. He said he had to work late that night.

'Please, Dad, please. The teachers want a parent there. Mam won't come, she never does, and you wouldn't have to do anything, only listen and tell them it's all fine.'

'God, Kathy, I hate going into a school, I feel out of place.'

'But Dad, it's not as if I had done anything bad and they were giving out about me, I just want them to think you're all interested.'

'And we are, we are, child . . . but your mother's not herself these days and she'd be worse than useless and you know the way they go on about smoking up there, it sets her back . . . maybe Fran will go again. She'd know more than we would anyway.'

So Fran went and spoke about her little sister to the tired teachers who had to see legions of parents in a confessional situation and give a message of encouragement laced with caution to all of them.

'She's too serious,' they told Fran. 'She tries too hard, she might take more in if she were to relax more.'

'She's very interested, really she is,' Fran protested. 'I sit with her when she does her homework, she never neglects any of it.'

'She doesn't play any games, does she?' The man who was going to be the new headmaster was nice. He seemed to have the vaguest knowledge of the children and spoke in generalities. Fran wondered if he really remembered them all or was making wild guesses.

'No, she doesn't want to take the time from her studying, you see.'

'Maybe she should.' He was brusque and good-natured about it.

'I don't think she should continue with Latin,' the pleasant Mr Dunne said.

Fran's heart fell. 'But Mr Dunne, she tries so hard. I never studied it myself and I'm trying to follow it in the book with her and she really does put in hours on it.'

'But you see, she doesn't understand what it's about.' Poor Mr Dunne was trying hard not to offend her.

'Could I get her a couple of private lessons? It would be great for her to have Latin in her Leaving. Look at all the places she could go with a subject like that.'

'She may not get the points for University.' It was if he was letting her down lightly.

'But she *has* to. None of us have got anywhere, she must get a start in life.'

'You have a very good job yourself, Miss Clarke. I see you when I go to the supermarket, couldn't you get Kathy a job there?'

'Kathy will *never* work in the supermarket.' Fran's eyes were blazing.

'I'm sorry,' he said quietly.

'No, I'm sorry, it is very kind of you to take such an interest. Please forgive me for shouting like this. Just advise me what would be best for her.'

'She should do something that she would enjoy, something she wouldn't have to strain at,' Mr Dunne said. 'A musical instrument, has she shown any interest?'

'No.' Fran shook her head. 'Nothing like that. We're all tone deaf, even the brother who's working for a pop group.'

'Or painting?'

'I can't see it myself, she'd only fret over that too, to know was she getting it right.' It was easy to talk to this kind man, Mr Dunne. It was probably hard for him to tell parents and family that a child wasn't bright enough to get third-level education. Maybe his own children were at university and he wished that others would also get the chance. And it was good of him to care that poor Kathy should be happy and relaxed. She hated being so negative to all his suggestions. The man meant so well. He must have great patience too, being a teacher.

Aidan looked back at the thin handsome face of this girl who showed much more interest in her sister than either of the parents could summon up. He hated having to say that a child was slow, because truthfully he felt guilty about it. He always thought that if the school were smaller, or there were better facilities, if there were bigger libraries, extra tuition when called for, maybe then there would be far fewer slow pupils. He had discussed this with Signora when they planned the Italian classes. She said it had a lot to do with people's expectations. It took more than a generation of free education to stop people believing there were barriers and obstacles in the way.

It had been the same in Italy, she said. She had seen the children of a local hotelier and his wife grow up. The village had been small and poor, nobody ever thought that the children from the little school there should do more than their fathers or mothers had. She had taught them English only so that they could greet tourists and be chambermaids or waiters. She had wanted so much more for them. Signora understood what Aidan wanted for the people around Mountainview school.

She was such an easy person to talk to. They had many a coffee as they planned the evening classes. She was undemanding company, asking no questions about his home and family, telling little of her own life in that Jerry Sullivan household. He had even told her about the study he was making for himself.

'I'm not very interested in possessions,' Signora said. 'But a lovely quiet room with light coming in a window and a desk in good wood, and all your memories, and books and pictures on a wall . . . that would be very satisfying indeed.' She spoke as if she were a gypsy or a bag lady who might never aspire to something so wonderful, but would appreciate it as a reward for others.

He would tell her about this Kathy Clarke, the girl with the anxious face trying hard because her sister expected so much and thought she was clever. Maybe Signora would come up with an idea, she often did.

But he took his mind away from the pleasant chats he had with her and so enjoyed and back to the present. There was a long night ahead of him. 'I'm sure you'll think of something, Miss Clarke.' Mr Dunne looked beyond her to the line of parents still to be seen.

'I'm very grateful to you all here.' Fran sounded as if she meant it. 'You really do give your time, and care about the children. Years ago when I was at school it wasn't like that, or maybe I'm only making excuses.' She was serious and pale-faced. Young Kathy Clarke was lucky to have such a concerned sister.

Fran went to the bus stop hands in pockets and head down. She had to pass an annexe on the way out and saw a notice up advertising Italian lessons next September. A course to introduce you to the colours and paintings and music and language of Italy. It promised to be fun as well as educational. Fran wondered whether something like that might be a good idea. But it was too dear. She had so many outgoings. It would be very hard to pay a whole term in advance. And suppose Kathy decided to take the whole thing too seriously like she had taken everything else. Then it might be a case of the cure being worse than the disease. No, she would have to think of something else. Fran sighed and walked to the bus stop.

There she met Peggy Sullivan, one of the women who worked at the checkout. 'They'd put years on you, these meetings, wouldn't they?' said Mrs Sullivan.

'There's a lot of hanging about certainly, but it's better than when we were young and no one knew where we were half the time. How's your own little fellow getting on?' As manageress Fran had made it her business to know personally as many of the staff as possible. She knew that Peggy had two children, both of them severe trials. A grown-up daughter who didn't get on with the father and a youngster who wouldn't open a book.

'Well, Jerry's not going to believe this but apparently he's much improved. They all said it. He's started to join the human race again, as one of them put it.'

'That's a bit of good news.'

'Well, it's all down to this cracked one we have living with us. Not a word to anyone, Miss Clarke, but we have a lodger, half Italian half Irish. Says she was married to an Italian and he died but that's not true at all. I think she's a nun in disguise. But anyway, didn't she take an interest in Jerry and she has him a changed man, it would appear.' Peggy Sullivan explained that Jerry hadn't understood that poetry was meant to *mean* something until Signora came to the house, and this had made all the difference. His English teacher was delighted with him. And he hadn't understood that History really happened and now he did, and *that* had made all the difference.

Fran thought sadly that her own sister on whom she had lavished such attention had not realised that Latin was a language people spoke. Perhaps this Signora might open doors for her, too. 'What does she do for a living, your lodger?' she asked.

'Oh, you'd need a fleet of detectives to find out. A bit of sewing here and a bit of work up in a hospital I believe, but she's going to be teaching an Italian class here in the school next term and she's high as a kite over it. You'd think it was the World Cup she'd won all by herself, singing little Italian songs. She's spending the whole summer getting ready for it. Nicest woman that ever wore shoe leather, but off the wall I tell you, off the wall.'

Fran decided there and then. She would sign up for the course. She and Kathy would go there every Tuesday and Thursday, they'd bloody learn Italian that's what they'd do, and they'd enjoy doing it, with this madwoman who was singing songs and getting ready for it so excitedly. It might make the poor, nervous, tense Kathy relax a bit, and it might help Fran to forget Ken who had gone to America without her.

'They said Kathy was a great girl,' Fran said proudly at the kitchen table.

Her mother, despondent over some heavy losses at the machines, tried to show enthusiasm. 'Well, why wouldn't they? She *is* a great girl.'

'They didn't say anything bad about me?' Kathy asked.

'No, they didn't. They said you were great at your homework and that it was a pleasure to teach you. So now!'

'I'd like to have been there, child, it's just that I didn't think I'd get off in time.' Kathy and Fran forgave their Dad. It didn't matter now.

'I have a great treat for you, Kathy, we're going to learn Italian. Yourself and myself.'

If she had suggested they fly to the moon nothing could have surprised the Clarke family more.

Kathy flushed with pleasure. 'The two of us?'

'Why not? I always fancied going to Italy, and wouldn't my chances of picking up an Italian fellow be much better if I could speak the language!'

'Would I be able for it?'

'Of course you would, it's for eejits like myself who haven't learned anything, you'd probably be top of the class, but it's meant to be fun. There's this woman and she's going to play us operas and show us pictures and give us Italian food. It'll be terrific.'

'It's not very dear, is it, Fran?'

'No, it's not, and look at the value we'll get from it,' said Fran, who was already wondering was she verging on madness to have made such an announcement.

During the summer Ken settled himself in the small town in New York State. He wrote again to Fran. 'I love you, I will always love you. I do understand about Kathy but couldn't you come out here? We could have her out for holidays, you could teach her then. Please say yes before I get a little service flat for myself. Say yes and we'll get a little house. She's sixteen, Fran, I can't wait another four years for you.'

She wept over the letter but she couldn't leave Kathy now. This had been her dream, to see one of the Clarkes get to University. True, Ken had said wait until their children were born then they could plan it from the word go, to give them all the chances in the world, but Ken didn't understand. She had invested too much in Kathy. The girl was not an intellectual, but she was not stupid. If she had been born to wealthy parents she would have had all the advantages that would cushion her. She would get her place in University merely because there would be enough time, there would be books in the house, people would have expectations. Fran had raised Kathy's hopes. She couldn't go now, and leave her to her mother who would look up vaguely from the gambling machines and her father who would mean well but see no further than the next cash-in-hand job for the few simple comforts he wanted from life.

Kathy would drown without her.

It was a warm summer, visitors came to Ireland in greater numbers than before. The supermarket arranged special picnic lunches that people could take out to the park. It had been Fran's idea, and it was a great success.

Mr Burke at the bacon counter had been doubtful. 'I don't want to go on about being in this business man and boy, Miss Clarke, but really I can't think it's a good idea to slice bacon and fry it and serve it cold in a sandwich. Why wouldn't they make do with nice lean ham like they always did?'

'There's a taste now, Mr Burke, that people like their bacon crispy and you see if we keep the pieces nice and warm and fill the sandwiches as they come in, I can tell you they'll want more and more.'

'But suppose I cut it and it's fried and nobody buys it, what then, Miss Clarke?' He was such a nice man, anxious and very willing to please but fearful of change.

'Let's give it a three-week trial, Mr Burke, and see,' she said.

She had been totally correct. People flocked for the great sandwiches. They lost money on them, of course, but that didn't matter; once you got people into the supermarket they bought other things on the way to the checkout.

She took Kathy to the Museum of Modern Art and on her day off they went on a three-hour bus tour of Dublin. Just so that we know about where we live, Fran had said. They loved it, the two Protestant cathedrals that they had never been inside, and they drove around the Phoenix Park and they looked on proudly as the Georgian doors and fanlight windows were pointed out.

'Imagine, we're the only Irish people on the bus,' Kathy whispered. 'This is all ours, the others are visitors.'

And without being too bossy Fran organised the sixteen-year-old to get a smart yellow cotton dress, and to get her hair cut. At the end of the summer she was tanned and attractive looking, her eyes had lost the haunted look.

Kathy did have friends, Fran noticed, but not close, giggly friends as she had known when she was young, what seemed like a whole generation ago. Some of these friends went to a noisy disco on a Saturday, a place that Fran knew about from the youngsters at work.

She knew enough to know it was not at all well run and that drugs circulated freely. She always happened to be passing by at one o'clock in the morning to collect her sister. She asked Barry, one of the young van drivers in the supermarket, to pick her up on several of these Saturdays and to drive past the disco. He had said it wasn't a place for a youngster.

'What can I do?' Fran shrugged at him. 'Tell her not to go and she feels a victim. I think I'm lucky that I can have you to act as an excuse to get her home.' Barry was a great kid, mad for overtime since he wanted to buy a motorbike. He said he had saved enough for one third of it, as soon as he had half the price he'd go and choose it, and then when he had two-thirds he would buy it and pay the rest later.

'And what do you want it for, Barry?' Fran asked.

'For freedom, Miss Clarke,' he said. 'You know, freedom, all that air rushing past and everything.'

Fran felt very old. 'My sister and I are going to learn Italian,' she told him one night as they waited outside the disco, edging the advent of his motorbike nearer.

'Oh that's great, Miss Clarke. I'd like to do that myself. I went to the World Cup, I made the greatest of friends, the nicest people you'd meet in a day's walk, Miss Clarke, much the way we'd be, I often think, if we had the weather.'

'Maybe you'll learn Italian too.' She spoke absently. She was watching tough-looking people come out of the disco. Why did Kathy and her friends want to go there? Imagine the freedom they had at sixteen, to go to such places, compared to her day.

'I might if I have the bike paid for, because one of the first places I'm going to take it is Italy,' Barry said.

'Well, it's up in Mountainview School and it begins in September.' She spoke in a slightly distracted tone because she had just seen Kathy, Harriet and their friends come out. She leaned over and hooted the horn. Immediately they looked over. The regular Saturday lift home was becoming part of the scene. What about the parents of all these girls, she thought? Did any of them care? Was she just a fusspot herself? Lord, but it would be such a relief when the term started again and all these outings were over.

The Italian classes began on a Tuesday at seven o'clock. There had been a letter from Ken that morning. He was settled in his little apartment; a flat didn't mean a flat, it meant a flat tyre over there. The stock control was totally different. There were no deals with suppliers; you paid what was asked. People were very friendly, they invited him around to their homes. Soon it would be Labor Day and they would have a picnic to define that the summer was over. He missed her. Did she miss him?

There were thirty people in the class. Everyone got a huge piece of cardboard to put their names on but this marvellous woman said they should be called by the Italian version. So Fran became *Francesca*, and Kathy *Caterina*. They had great games of shaking hands and asking people what their names were. Kathy seemed to be enjoying it hugely. It would be worth it in the end, Fran said, putting the memory of Ken going to Labor Day picnics out of her mind.

'Hey, Fran, do you see that guy who says *Mi chiamo Bartolomeo*? Isn't that Barry from your supermarket?' It was indeed. Fran was pleased, the overtime must have been good enough to sort out the bike. They waved at each other across the room.

What an extraordinary assortment of people. There was that elegant woman, surely she was the one who gave those huge lunches at her house. What on earth could she be doing at a place like this? And the beautiful girl with the golden curls *Mi chiamo Elizabetta* and her nice staid boyfriend in his good suit. And the dark, violent-looking *Luigi* and the older man called *Lorenzo*. What an amazing mixture.

Signora was delightful. 'I know your landlady,' Fran said to her when they were having little snacks of salami and cheese.

'Yes, well Mrs Sullivan is a relation, I am a relation,' Signora said nervously.

'Of course. How stupid, yes, I know she is.' Fran was reassuring. It was her own father's lifestyle, she knew it well. 'She said you were very helpful to her son.'

Signora's face broke into a wide smile. She was very beautiful when she smiled. Fran didn't think she could be a nun. She was sure Peggy Sullivan had got it wrong.

They loved the lessons, Fran and Kathy. They went together on the bus laughing like children at their mispronunciations and at the stories Signora told them. Kathy told the girls at school and they could hardly believe it.

There was an extraordinary bond amongst the people in the class. It was as if they were on a desert island and their only hope of rescue was to learn the language, and remember everything they were taught. Possibly because Signora believed that they were all capable of great feats they began to believe it too. She begged them to use the Italian words for everything, even if they couldn't form the whole sentence. They found themselves saying that they had to get back to the *casa* or that the *camera* was very warm or that they were *stanca* instead of tired.

And all the time Signora watched and listened, pleased but not surprised. She had never thought that anyone faced with the Italian language would feel anything but delight and enthusiasm for it. With her was Mr Dunne, whose special project all this was. They seemed to get on together very well.

'Maybe they were friends from way back,' Fran wondered.

'No, he's got a wife and grown-up children,' Kathy explained.

'He could still have a wife and be her friend,' Fran said.

'Yes, but I think he could be having it off with her, they're always giving special little smiles. Harriet says that's a dead giveaway.' Harriet was Kathy's friend at school who was very interested in sex.

Aidan Dunne watched the flowering of the Italian class with a pleasure that he had not known possible. Week after week they came to the school, bicycles, motorbikes, vans and bus, even the amazing woman in the BMW. And he loved planning the various surprises for them too. The paper flags they made, she would give everyone a blank flag then call out colours that they were to fill in. Each person would hold up a flag and the rest of the class had to call out the colours. They were like children, eager enthusiastic pupils. And when the class was over that tough-looking fellow, called Lou or Luigi or whatever, used to help tidy up, tough type, the last one you'd ever think would be hanging around to tidy up, put away boxes and stack chairs.

But that was Signora for you. She had this simple way of expecting the best and getting it. She had asked him if she could make cushion covers for him.

'Come and see the room,' Aidan suggested suddenly.

'That's a good idea. When will I come?'

'Saturday morning. I've no school, would you be free?'

'I can be free any time,' she said.

He spent all Friday evening cleaning and polishing his room. He took out the tray with the two little red glasses that came from Murano, beside Venice. He had bought a bottle of Marsala. They would toast the success of the room and the classes.

She came at midday and brought some sample fabrics. 'I thought that yellow would be right from what you told me,' she said, holding up a glowing rich colour. 'It costs a little more a metre than the others, but then it's a room for life, isn't it?'

'A room for life,' Aidan repeated.

'Do you want to show it to your wife before I begin?' she asked.

'No, no. Nell will be pleased. I mean, this is *my* room really.'

'Yes, of course.' She never asked questions.

Nell was not at home that morning, nor were either of his daughters. Aidan hadn't told them of the visit, and he was glad they weren't there. Together he and Signora toasted the success of the Italian class and the Room for Life.

'I wish you could teach in the school itself, you can create such enthusiasm,' he said admiringly.

'Ah, that's only because they want to learn.'

'But that girl Kathy Clarke, they say she's as bright as a button these days, all due to the Italian classes.'

'*Caterina* . . . a nice girl.'

'Well, I hear that she has them all entertained in the classroom with stories of your class, they all want to join.'

'Isn't that wonderful?' said Signora.

What Aidan did not report, because he didn't know it, was that Kathy Clarke's description of the Italian class included an account of his playing footsie with the ancient Italian teacher, and that he looked at her with the adoring eyes of a puppy. Kathy's friend Harriet said she had always suspected it. It was the quiet ones that you had to watch. That's where real passion and lust were lurking.

Miss Hayes was taking a history class and was anxious to relate things to the modern day. Something the children might recognise. Telling them the Medicis were patrons of the arts was no use, she called them sponsors. That would mean something.

'Can anyone think of the people that they sponsored?' she asked.

They looked at each other blankly.

'Sponsor?' Harriet asked. 'Like a drinks company or an insurance company?'

'Yes. You must know the names of some of the famous artists of Italy, don't you?' The history teacher was young, she was not yet hardened to how much children had forgotten or what they had never known.

Quietly Kathy Clarke stood up. 'One of the most important was Michelangelo. When one of the Medicis was Pope Sixtus V he asked Michelangelo to do the ceiling of the Sistine Chapel, and he wanted all the different scenes.' In a calm confident voice she told the class about the scaffolding that was built, the rows and the fallings-out. The problems that there still were keeping the colours alive.

There was no frown, there was just enthusiasm. Since she had obviously gone further than Miss Hayes the young history teacher could have attempted, it was soon time to bring it to an end.

'Thank you for that, Katherine Clarke, now can anyone else name any other artist of the period?'

Kathy's hand went up again. The teacher looked around to see if there was any other taker but there was no one. The boys and girls looked on amazed as Kathy Clarke explained about Leonardo da Vinci's notebooks, five thousand pages of them, all in mirror writing maybe because he was left-handed or maybe because he wanted them kept secret. And how he applied to the Duke of Milan for a job saying he could design cannon-proof ships in wartime and statues in peace time.

Kathy knew all this and was telling it as if it was a story.

'Jesus Mary and Joseph, those Italian culture classes must be something else,' said Josie Hayes in the staffroom.

'What do you mean?' they asked.

'I've had Kathy Clark standing up giving me a run-down of the Renaissance like nobody's ever heard.'

Across the room Aidan Dunne who had dreamed up the classes stirred his coffee and smiled to himself. A big happy smile.

It brought them even closer together, Kathy and Fran, the hours spent at the Italian class. Matt Clarke came home from England in the autumn to tell them that he was getting married to Tracey from Liverpool but that they weren't having much of a do, they were going to go to the Canaries instead. Everyone was relieved that it didn't mean a trek to England for the wedding. They giggled a bit when they heard that the honeymoon was going to be before, not after, the marriage.

Matt thought it was sensible. 'She wants a suntan for the wedding snaps, and of course if we hate each other out there then we can call it off,' he said cheerfully.

Matt gave his mother money for the slot machines and took his father for a few pints. 'What's all this business about learning Italian?' he asked.

'Search me,' said his father. 'I can't make head nor tail of it. Fran is worn out above in the supermarket early mornings, late nights. The fellow she was going with has gone off to the States. I haven't a notion why she wants to bring all this on herself, specially since they say over in the school that young Kathy works too hard already. But they're mad about it. Planning to go there next year and all. So let them at it.'

'Kathy's turning into a grand little looker, isn't she?' Matt said.

'I suppose she is. Do you know, seeing her every day I never noticed,' his father said with an air of surprise.

Kathy was indeed becoming more attractive. At school her friend Harriet commented on it. 'Do you have a fellow or something at this Italian class? You seem different somehow.'

'No, but there are lots of older men there all right,' Kathy laughed. 'Very old, some of them. We have to pair into couples to do the asking for a date bit. It's a scream. I had this man, he must be about a hundred, called Lorenzo. Well, I think it's Laddy in real life. Anyway Lorenzo says to me "*E libera questa sera?*" and he rolls his eyes and twirls an imaginary moustache and everyone was sick with laughter.'

'Go on. And does she teach you anything really useful like How's about it and what you'd say?'

'Sort of.' Kathy searched her memory for the phrase. 'There's things like *Vive solo* or *sola*, that's do you live alone. And there's one I can't quite remember . . . *Deve rincasare questa notte*? Do you have to go home tonight.'

'And she's the old one we see in the library sometimes, with the funny coloured hair?'

'Yes, Signora.'

'Imagine,' said Harriet. Things were getting stranger all the time.

'Do you still go to those classes in Mountainview, Miss Clarke?' Peggy Sullivan was handing in her till's takings.

'They're really terrific, Mrs Sullivan. Do pass that on to Signora, won't you? Everyone just loves them. Do you know that nobody at all has fallen out of the class. That must be unheard of.'

'Well, she sounds very cheerful about them, I must say. An extraordinarily secretive person, of course, Miss Clarke. Claims she was married to some Italian for twenty-six years in a village out there . . . never a letter from Italy . . . not a picture of him in sight. *And* it turns out she has a whole family living in Dublin, a mother in those expensive flats down by the sea, a father in a home and brothers and sisters all over the place.'

'Yes, well . . .' Fran didn't want to hear anything even mildly critical or questioning about Signora.

'It just seems odd, doesn't it. What's she living in one room in our estate for if she has all this family dotted all over the place?'

'Maybe she doesn't get on with them. It could be as simple as that.'

'She goes to see her mother every Monday and her father twice a week up in the home. She wheels him out in his chair, one of the nurses told Suzi. She sits and reads to him under a tree and he just sits and stares ahead, even though he makes an effort to talk to the others who only come once in a blue moon.'

'Poor Signora,' said Fran suddenly. 'She deserves better than that.'

'Well she does, now that you say it, Miss Clarke,' said Peggy Sullivan.

She had good reason to be grateful to this strange visitor, nun or not a nun. She had been a great influence on their lives. Suzi got on great with her and came home much more regularly, Jerry regarded her as his own private tutor. She had made net curtains for them and matching cushion covers. She had painted the dresser in the kitchen and planted window boxes. Her room was immaculate and neat as a new pin. Sometimes Peggy Sullivan had gone in to investigate. As one would. But Signora seemed to have acquired no more possessions than those she had when she arrived. She was an extraordinary person. It was good that they all liked her in the class.

Kathy Clarke was the youngest of her students by far. The girl was eager to learn and asked about the grammar which the others didn't know or didn't bother about. She was attractive, too, in that blue-eyed, dark-haired way that she had never seen in Italy. There the dark beauties all had huge brown eyes.

She wondered what Kathy would do when she left school. Sometimes she saw the girl studying in the library. She must have hopes of getting a third-level education.

'What does your mother think you might do when you leave school?' she asked Kathy one evening when they were all tidying up the chairs after the lesson. People stayed and chatted, no one was anxious to run away, which was good. She knew for a fact that some of them went for a drink in a pub up the hill and others for coffee. It was all as she had hoped.

'My mother?' Kathy seemed surprised.

'Yes, she seems so eager and enthusiastic about everything,' Signora said.

'No, she doesn't really know much about the school or what I'm doing. She doesn't go out much, she'd have no idea what there was to do or study or anything.'

'But she comes here to the class with you, doesn't she, and she goes out to work in the supermarket? Mrs Sullivan where I stay says she's the boss.'

'Oh, that's Fran. That's my *sister*,' Kathy said. 'Don't let her hear you said that, she'd go mad.'

Signora looked puzzled. 'I'm so sorry, I get everything wrong.'

'No, it's an easy mistake.' Kathy was anxious for the older woman not to be embarrassed. 'Fran's the oldest of the family, I'm the youngest. Of course you thought that.'

She didn't say anything to Fran about it. No point in making Fran go to the mirror to look for lines. Poor Signora was a bit absent-minded, and she did get a lot of things wrong. But she was so marvellous as a teacher. Everyone in the class including Bartolomeo, the one of the motorbike, loved her.

Kathy liked Bartolomeo, he had a lovely smile and he told her all about football. He asked where she went dancing and when she told him about the disco in the summer he said it was a date when it came to half term and they could go out dancing again, he'd tell her a good place.

She reported this to Harriet. 'I knew you joined that class just for sex,'

Harriet said. And they laughed and laughed over it long after anyone else would have thought it remotely funny.

There was a bad rainstorm in October, and a leak came in the roof of the annexe where the evening class was held. With huge solidarity they all managed to cope with it by getting newspapers, and moving tables out of the way and finding a bucket in one of the cloakrooms. All the time they shouted *Che tempaccio* at each other and *Che brutto tempo*. Barry said he would wait outside in his rain gear at the bus stop and flash his lights when the bus arrived so that everyone would not get soaked to the skin.

Connie, the woman with the jewellery that Luigi said would buy a block of flats, said she could give four people a lift. They scrambled into her beautiful BMW – Guglielmo, the nice young man from the bank, his dizzy girlfriend Elizabetta, Francesca and young Caterina. They went first to Elizabetta's flat and there was a lot of chorusing of *ciao* and *arrivederci* as the two young lovers scampered up the steps in the rain.

And then it was on to the Clarkes' house. Fran in front gave directions. This was not the kind of territory that would be familiar to Connie. When they got there Fran saw her mother putting out the dustbin, a cigarette still in her mouth despite the rain that would fall on it and make it soggy, the same scuffed slippers and sloppy housecoat that she wore all the time. She then felt ashamed of herself for feeling ashamed of her mother. Just because she was getting a lift in a smart car didn't mean that she should change all her values. Her mother had had a hard life and had been generous and understanding when it was needed.

'There's Mam getting drenched. Wouldn't the bins have done in the morning?' Fran said.

'*Che tempaccio, che tempaccio,*' Kathy said dramatically.

'Go on, Caterina. Your Granny's holding the door open for you,' Connie said.

'That's my mother,' Kathy said.

There was so much rain, so much confusion of banging doors and clattering dustbins nobody seemed to take much notice.

Inside the house Mrs Clarke was looking with surprise and disgust at her wet cigarette. 'I got drowned waiting for you to come in from that limousine.'

'God, let's have a cup of tea,' said Fran, running to the kettle.

Kathy sat down suddenly at the kitchen table.

'*Due tazze di te,*' Fran said in her best Italian. 'Come on, Kathy. *Con latte? Con zucchero?*'

'You know I don't take milk and sugar.' Kathy's voice was remote. She looked very pale. Mrs Clarke said there was no point in a person staying up if this is all you were to hear, she was going off to her bed and to tell that husband of hers when and if he ever came in from the pub not to be leaving any frying pan to clean up in the morning.

She was gone, complaining, coughing and creaking up the stairs.

'What is it, Kathy?'

Kathy looked at her. 'Are you my mother, Fran?' she asked.

There was a silence in the kitchen. They could hear the flushing of the lavatory upstairs and the rain falling on the concrete outside.

'Why do you ask this now?'

'I want to know. Are you or aren't you?'

'You know I am, Kathy.' A long silence.

'No, I didn't know. Not until now.' Fran came towards her, reaching out. 'No, go away from me. I don't want you to touch me.'

'Kathy you knew, you felt it, it didn't need to be said, I thought you knew.'

'Does everyone else know?'

'What do you mean everyone else? The people who need to, know. *You* know how much I love you, how I'd do everything on earth for you and get you the best that I could get.'

'Except a father and a home and a name.'

'You have a name, you have a home, you have another father and mother in Mam and Dad.'

'No I haven't. I'm a bastard that you had and never told me about.'

'There's no such word as bastard, as you well know. There's no such thing any more as an illegitimate child. And you were legally part of this household since the day you were born. This is your home.'

'How could you . . .' Kathy began.

'Kathy, what are you saying – that I should have given you away to strangers for adoption, that I should have waited until you were eighteen before I got to know you and only then if you sought me out?'

'And all of these years letting me think that Mam was my mother. I can't believe it.' Kathy shook her head as if to clear it, to take this new and frightening idea out of her mind.

'Mam was a mother to you and to me. She welcomed you from the day she knew about you. She said won't it be grand to have another baby round here. That's what she said and it was. And, Kathy, I thought you knew.'

'How would I have known? We both called Mam and Dad Mam and Dad. People said you were my sister and that Matt and Joe and Sean were my brothers. How was I to know?'

'Well, it wasn't a big thing. We were all together in the house, you were only seven years younger than Joe, it was the natural way to do things.'

'Do all the neighbours know?'

'Some of them maybe, they've forgotten I imagine.'

'And who was my father? Who was my real father?'

'Dad is your real father in that he brought you up and looked after both of us.'

'You know what I mean.'

'He was a boy who was at a posh school and his parents didn't want him to marry me.'

'Why do you say was? Is he dead?'

'No he's not dead, but he's not part of our lives.'

'He's not part of your life, he might be part of mine.'

'I don't think that's a good idea.'

'It doesn't matter what you think. Wherever he is, he's still my father. I have a right to know him, to meet him, to tell him I'm Kathy and that I exist because of him.'

'Please have some tea. Or let me have some anyway.'

'I'm not stopping you.' Her eyes were cold.

Fran knew she needed more tact and diplomacy than had ever been called on in work. Even the time when one of the director's children, there on a holiday job, was found pilfering. This was vastly more important.

'I'll tell you every single thing you want to know. Everything,' she said, in as calm a voice as she could manage. 'And if Dad comes in in the middle of it I suggest we move up to your room.'

Kathy's room was much bigger than Fran's. It had the desk, the bookshelf, the hand basin that had been put in lovingly by the plumber in the house years ago.

'You did it all from guilt, didn't you, the nice room, the buying my uniform and the extra pocket money and even the Italian classes. You paid for it all because you were so guilty about me.'

'I have never had a day's guilt about you in my life,' Fran said calmly. She sounded so sure that she stopped Kathy in the slightly hysterical tone she was taking. 'No, I have felt sad for you sometimes, because you work so hard and I hoped I would be able to give you everything to start you off well. I worked hard so that I could always provide a good living for you. I've saved a little every single week in a building society, not much but enough to give you independence. I have loved you every day of my life, and honestly it got kind of blurred whether you were my sister or my daughter. You're just Kathy to me and I want the very, very best for you. I work long and hard to get it and I think about it all the time. So I assure you whatever I feel I don't feel guilty.'

Tears came into Kathy's eyes. Fran reached her hand over tentatively and patted the hand that clutched the mug of tea.

Kathy said, 'I know, I shouldn't have said that. I got a shock, you see.'

'No, no it's all right. Ask me anything.'

'What's his name?'

'Paul. Paul Malone.'

'Kathy Malone?' she said wonderingly.

'No, Kathy Clarke.'

'And how old was he then?'

'Sixteen. I was fifteen and a half.'

'When I think of all the bossy advice you gave me about sex and how I listened.'

'Look back on what I said, you'll find that I didn't preach what I didn't practise.'

'So you loved him, this Paul Malone?' Kathy's voice was very scornful.

'Yes, very much. Very much indeed. I was young but I thought I knew what love was and so did he, so I won't dismiss it and say it was nonsense. It wasn't.'

'And where did you meet him?'

'At a pop concert. We got on so well then I used to sneak out to meet him from school sometimes and we'd go to the pictures, and he was meant to be having extra lessons so he could skip that. And it was a wonderful happy time.'

'And then?'

'And then I realised I was pregnant, and Paul told his mother and father and I told Mam and Dad and all hell broke out everywhere.'

'Did anyone talk about getting married?'

'No, nobody talked about it. I thought about it a lot up in the room that's your room now. I used to dream that one day Paul would come to the door with a bunch of flowers and say that as soon as I was sixteen we would marry.'

'But it didn't happen, obviously?'

'No, it didn't.'

'And why did he not want to stay around and support you even if you didn't marry?'

'That was part of the deal.'

'Deal?'

'Yes. His parents said that since this was an unlikely partnership and that there was no future in it, it might be kindest for everyone to cut all ties. That's what they said. Cut all ties or maybe sever all ties.'

'Were they awful?'

'I don't know, I'd never met them until then, any more than Paul had met Mam and Dad'

'So the deal was that he was to get away with it, father a child and never see her again.'

'They gave four thousand pounds, Kathy, it was a lot of money then.'

'They bought you off!'

'No, we didn't think it was like that. I put two thousand in a building society for you. It's grown a lot as well as what I added myself, and we gave the other two thousand pounds to Mam and Dad because they would be bringing you up.'

'And did Paul Malone think that was fair? To give four thousand pounds to get rid of me?'

'He didn't know you. He listened to his parents, they told him sixteen was too young to be a father, he had a career ahead of him, it was a mistake, he must honour his commitment to me. That's the way they saw it.'

'And did he have a career?'

'Yes, he's an accountant.'

'My father the accountant,' Kathy said.

'He married and he has children now, his own family.'

'You mean he has other children?' Kathy's chin was in the air.

'Yes, that's right. Two, I believe.'

'How do you know?'

'There was an article about him in a magazine not long ago, you know, lifestyles of the rich and famous, that is.'

'But he's not famous.'

'His wife is, he married Marianne Hayes.' Fran waited to see the effect this would have.

'My father is married to one of the richest women in Ireland?'

'Yes.'

'And he gave a measly four thousand pounds to get rid of me.'

'That's not the point. He wasn't married to her then.'

'It is the point. He's rich now, he should give something.'

'You have enough, Kathy, we have everything we want.'

'No, of course I haven't everything I want, and neither do you,' Kathy said, and suddenly the tears that were waiting came and she cried and cried, while Fran, whom she had thought for sixteen years was her sister, stroked her head and her wet cheeks and her neck with all the love a mother could give.

The next morning at breakfast Joe Clarke had a hangover.

'Will you give me a can of cold Coca Cola from the fridge, Kathy, like a good girl? I've a bugger of a job to do today out in Killiney, and the van will be here for me any minute.'

'You're nearer to the fridge than I am,' Kathy said.

'Are you giving me cheek?' he asked.

'No, I'm just stating a fact.'

'Well, no child of mine is going to be stating facts in that tone of voice, let me tell you,' he said, face flushed with anger.

'I'm not a child of yours,' Kathy said coldly.

They didn't even look up startled, her grandparents. These old people she had thought of as her mother and father. The woman went on reading the magazine and smoking, the man grumbled. 'I'm as good as any other goddamn father you ever had or will have. Go on, child, give me the Coke now to save me getting up, will you.'

And Kathy realised that they weren't in the business of secrecy or pretending. Like Fran, they had assumed she knew the state of affairs. She looked across at Fran standing with a rigid back looking out the window.

'All right, Dad,' she said, and got him the can and a glass to pour it into,

'There's a good girl,' he said, smiling at her as he always did. For him nothing had changed.

'What would you do if you discovered you weren't your parents' child?' Kathy asked Harriet at school.

'I'd be delighted, I tell you that.'

'Why?'

'Because then I won't grow up to have an awful chin like my mother and my grandmother, and I wouldn't have to listen to Daddy droning on and on about getting enough points in the Leaving.' Harriet's father, a teacher, had great hopes that she would be a doctor. Harriet wanted to own a night club.

They let the matter drop.

'What do you know about Marianne Hayes?' Kathy asked later.

'She's like the richest woman in Europe, or is it only Dublin? And she's good looking too. I suppose she bought all those things like good teeth and a suntan and all that shiny hair.'

'Yeah, I'm sure she did.'

'Why are you interested in her?'

'I dreamed about her last night,' Kathy said truthfully.

'I dreamed that I had sex with a gorgeous fellow. I think we should get started on it, you know we are sixteen.'

'You're the one who said we should concentrate on our studies,' Kathy complained.

'Yeah, that was before this dream. You look awful pale and tired and old, don't dream about Marianne Hayes again, it's not doing you any good.'

'No, it's not,' Kathy agreed, thinking suddenly of Fran with her white face and the lines under her eyes, and no suntan and no holidays abroad. She thought of Fran saving money every week for her for sixteen years. She remembered Fran's boyfriend Ken going off to America, had he too found some rich woman? Someone who wasn't a plumber's daughter who had dragged herself up to the top in a supermarket, someone who wasn't struggling to support an illegitimate child. Ken had known about her. It didn't appear that Fran had gone to any trouble to keep it all a secret.

As she had said last night there were many, many households all over Dublin where the youngest child was really a grandchild. And Fran had said that in many cases the mother had not stayed at home, the eldest sister had left to start a new life. It wasn't fair.

It just wasn't fair that Paul Malone should have his pleasure and no responsibility. Three times that day in class she was reprimanded for not paying attention. But Kathy Clarke had no interest in her studies. She was planning how she should best visit Paul Malone.

'Talk to me,' Fran said that evening.

'What about? You said there was nothing more to say.'

'So nothing's changed?' Fran asked. Her eyes were anxious. She didn't have expensive creams to take away the lines on her face. She never had anyone to help her bring up a child. Marianne Hayes, now Marianne Malone, must have had help everywhere. Nurses, nannies, au pairs, chauffeurs, tennis coaches. Kathy looked at her mother with a level glance. Even though her world had turned upside down she wouldn't add this to Fran's trouble.

'No, Fran,' she lied. 'Nothing's changed.'

It wasn't hard to find out where Paul and Marianne lived.

There was something about them in a paper almost every week. Everyone knew of their house. But she didn't want to go and see him at home. She must go to his office. Talk to him in a businesslike way. There was no need to involve his wife in what she wanted to say.

Armed with a phonecard she began to telephone large accountancy firms. On the second call she got the name of where he worked. She had heard of the company, they were accountants to all the film stars and theatre people. This was a show business kind of place. Not only did he have all the money, he had all the fun too.

Twice she went to the offices and twice her courage failed. The building was so enormous. She knew they only occupied floors five and six, but somehow she didn't have the confidence. Once in she could talk to him, tell him who she was, how her mother had worked and saved. She would beg for nothing. She would point out the injustice, that was all. But the place was too impressive. It overawed her. The commissionaire in the foyer, the girls at the information desk downstairs who called up to see if you were allowed access to the prestige offices above.

She would need to look different to get past these groomed dragons at the desk if she were to meet Paul Malone. They wouldn't let a schoolgirl in a navy skirt up to see a senior accountant, particularly one married to a millionaire.

She telephoned Harriet.

'Can't you bring in some posh clothes of your mother's tomorrow to school?'

'Only if you tell me why.'

'I'm going to have an adventure.'

'A sexual adventure?'

'Possibly.'

'Do you want nighties and knickers then?' Harriet was very practical.

'No, a jacket. And gloves even.'

'God almighty,' said Harriet. 'This must be something very kinky altogether.'

Next day the clothes arrived slightly crushed in a games bag. Kathy tried them on in the girls' cloakroom. The jacket was fine but the skirt seemed wrong.

'Where's the adventure?' Harriet was breathless with excitement.

'In an office, a smart office.'

'You could sort of hitch your skirt up, you know the school one. It would look okay if it was meant to be short. Will he be undressing you or will you be doing it yourself?'

'What? Oh, yes, I'll be doing it myself.'

'That's all right then.' Together they made Kathy look like someone who might gain access anywhere. She had already taken Fran's lipstick and eyeshadow.

'Don't put it all on now,' Harriet hissed.

'Why not?'

'I mean you've got to go to class, they'll know something's up if you go in like that.'

'I'm not going to class. You're to say you got a message that I had the flu.'

'No. I don't believe it.'

'Go on, Harriet. I did it for you when you wanted to go down and see the pop stars.'

'But where are you going at nine o'clock in the morning?'

'To the office to have the adventure,' Kathy said.

'You are something else,' said Harriet, whose mouth was round in admiration.

This time she didn't falter.

'Good morning. Mr Paul Malone, please.'

'And the name?'

'The name will mean nothing to him but if you could say it is Katherine Clarke, come here about the matter of Frances Clarke, a client from a long time ago.' Kathy felt that this was an office where people had full names not Kathys and Frans.

'I'll speak to his secretary. Mr Malone doesn't see anyone without an appointment.'

'You may tell her that I will wait until he's free.' Kathy spoke with a quiet intensity that was far more effective than her attempts to dress for the part.

One of the gorgeous receptionists seemed to shrug slightly at the other and make the call in a low voice.

'Miss Clarke, would you care to speak to Mr Malone's secretary?' she said eventually.

'Certainly.'

Kathy walked forward, hoping that her school skirt would not fall suddenly below Harriet's mother's jacket.

'It's Penny here. Can I help you?'

'Have you been given the relevant names?' Kathy said. How wonderful that she remembered that word relevant. It was a great word, it covered everything.

'Well, yes . . . but this is not actually the point.'

'Ah, but I think it is. Please mention these names to Mr Malone and please tell him that it will not take very long. Only ten minutes at the very most of his time, but I will wait here until he can see me.'

'We don't make appointments like this.'

'Please give him the names.' Kathy felt almost dizzy with excitement.

She waited politely for three more minutes then there was a buzz.

'Mr Malone's secretary will meet you on the sixth floor,' said one of the goddesses at the desk.

'Thank you so much for your help,' said Kathy Clarke, hitching up her school skirt and going into the lift that would take her to meet her father.

'Miss Clarke?' Penny said. Penny was like someone from a beauty contest. She wore a cream-coloured suit and had very high-heeled black shoes. Around her neck she wore a thick black necklace.

'That's right.' Kathy wished she were better looking and older and well dressed.

'Come this way, please. Mr Malone will see you in the conference room. Coffee?'

'That would be very nice, thank you.'

She was shown into a room with a pale wood table, and eight chairs around it. There were paintings on the wall, not just pictures behind glass like they had in school but real paintings. There were flowers on the windowsill, fresh flowers, arranged that morning. She sat and waited.

In he came, young, handsome, younger looking than Fran although he had been a year older.

'Hallo,' he said, with a big smile from ear to ear.

'Hallo,' she said. There was a silence.

At that moment Penny arrived with the coffee. 'Shall I leave it?' she asked, dying to stay.

'Thanks, Pen,' he said.

'Do you know who I am?' she asked when Penny had left.

'Yes,' he said.

'Were you expecting me?'

'Not for about two or three more years to be honest.' His grin was attractive.

'And what would you have done then?'

'What I'll do now – listen.'

It was a clever thing to say, he was leaving it all to her.

'Well, I just wanted to come and see you,' she said a little uncertainly.

'Absolutely,' he said.

'To know what you looked like.'

'And now you do.' He was warm as he said it, he was warm and welcoming. 'What do you think?' he asked.

'You look fine,' she said reluctantly.

'And so do you, very fine,' he said.

'I only just found out, you see,' she explained.

'I see.'

'So, that's why I had to come and talk to you.'

'Sure, sure.' He had poured them coffee and left her to add milk and sugar if she wished.

'You see, until this week I honestly thought I was Mam and Dad's daughter. It's been a bit of a shock.'

'Fran didn't tell you that she was your mother?'

'No, she didn't.'

'Well, when you were younger I can understand, but when you were older, surely . . . ?'

'No, she thought I sort of understood, but I didn't. I thought she was just a marvellous elder sister. I wasn't too bright, you see.'

'You look fine and bright to me.' He seemed genuinely to admire her.

'I'm not, as it happens. I'm a hard worker and I'll get there in the end, but I don't have quick leaps of understanding, not like my friend Harriet. I'm a bit of a plodder.'

'So am I, as it happens. You take after your father then.'

It was such an extraordinary moment there in this office. He was admitting he was her father. She felt almost light-headed. But she had no idea where to go now. He had taken away all her arguments. She thought he would have blustered, and denied things and excused himself. But he had done nothing like this.

'You wouldn't have got a job like this if you were just a plodder.'

'My wife is very wealthy, I am a charming plodder, I don't upset people. In a way that's why I am here.'

'But you got to be an accountant all by yourself before you met her, didn't you?'

'Yes, I got to be an accountant, not here exactly. And I hope you'll meet my wife one day, Katherine. You'll like her, she's a very, very nice woman.'

'It's Kathy, and I couldn't like her. I am sure she is very nice, but she wouldn't want to meet me.'

'Yes, if I tell her I would like it. We do things to please each other, I would meet someone to please her.'

'But she doesn't know I exist.'

'Yes, she does. I told her, a long time ago. I didn't know your name but I told her that I had a daughter, a daughter I didn't see, but would probably meet when she was grown up.'

'You didn't know my name?'

'No. When all the business happened Fran said she would just tell me if it was a girl or a boy, that was all.'

'That was the deal?' Kathy said.

'You put it very well. That was the deal.'

'She's very kind about you, she thinks you were great in all this.'

'And what message does she send me?' He was very relaxed, gentle, not watchful or anything.

'She has no idea I'm here.'

'Where does she think you are?'

'At school up in Mountainview.'

'Mountainview? Is that where you are?'

'There isn't much money out of four thousand pounds sixteen years ago to send me to a posh place,' Kathy said with spirit.

'So you know about the deal?'

'I heard it all at the same time, in one night. I realised she was not my sister and that you had sold me.'

'Is that how she put it?'

'No. It's how it is, she puts it differently.'

'I'm very sorry. It must have been a bad, bleak kind of thing to hear.'

Kathy looked at him. That's exactly what it had been. Bleak. She had thought about the unfairness of the deal. Her mother was poor, and could be paid off. Her father was the son of privileged people and didn't have to pay for his fun. It had made her think the system was always loaded against people like her, and always would be. Odd that he understood exactly the feeling.

'Yes, it was. It is.'

'Well, tell me what you want from me. Tell me and we can talk about it.'

She had been going to demand everything under the sun for Fran and for herself. She had been going to make him realise that it was too late in the twentieth century for the rich to get away with everything. But somehow it wasn't easy to say all this to the man who sat easily and warmly giving every impression of being pleased to see her rather than horrified.

'I'm not sure yet what I want. It's all a bit soon.'

'I know. You haven't had time to work out how you feel yet.' He didn't look relieved or off the hook, he sounded sympathetic.

'It's still hard for me to take in, you see.'

'And for me, meeting you too. That's hard to take in.' He was putting himself in the same boat.

'Aren't you annoyed I came?'

'No, you couldn't be more wrong. I'm delighted you came to see me. I'm only sorry that life was hard up to now and then it got worse with this shock. That's what I feel.'

She felt a lump in her throat. He couldn't have been more different than she had thought. Was it possible that this man was her father? That if things had been different he and Fran would have been married and she would be their eldest girl?

He took out a business card and wrote a number on it. 'This is my direct line. Ring this and you won't have to go through the whole system,' he said. It seemed almost too slick, as if he were arranging not to have explanations. Avoiding the people at work knowing about his nasty little secret.

'Aren't you afraid I might ring you at home?' she asked, sorry to break the mood of his niceness but determined that she would not allow herself to be conned by him.

He still had his pen in his hand. 'I was about to write down my home number as well. You can call me any time.'

'And what about your wife?'

'Marianne will be happy to speak to you too, of course. I shall tell her tonight that you came to see me.'

'You're very cool, aren't you?' Kathy said with a mixture of admiration and resentment.

'I'm calm, I suppose, on the exterior, but inside I'm very excited. Who wouldn't be? To meet a handsome grown-up daughter for the first time and to realise that it was because of me you came into the world.'

'And do you ever think of my mother?'

'I thought of her for a while, as we all think of our first love, and more than that because of what happened and because you had been born. But then since it wasn't going to happen, I went on and thought of other things and other people.'

It was the truth, Kathy couldn't deny that.

'What will I call you?' she asked suddenly.

'You call Fran, Fran, can't you call me Paul?'

'I'll come and see you again, Paul,' she said, standing up to leave.

'Any time you want me I'll be here, Kathy,' said her father.

They put out a hand each but when they touched he drew her to him and hugged her. 'It will be different from now on, Kathy,' he said, 'Different and better.'

As she went back to school in the bus Kathy scraped off her lipstick and eyeshadow. She rolled up Harriet's mother's jacket in to the canvas bag and went along to rejoin the classes.

'Well?' hissed Harriet.

'Nothing.'

'What do you mean nothing?'

'Nothing happened.'

'You mean you took all that gear and went to his office and he didn't touch you?'

'He sort of hugged me,' Kathy said.

'I expect he's impotent,' Harriet said wisely. 'In the magazines you always hear of women writing in about that sort of thing, there seems to be a lot of it about.'

'It could be, I suppose,' said Kathy, and took out her geography textbook.

Mr O'Brien, who still took senior geography even though he was Principal, looked at her over his half glasses. 'Your flu better all of a sudden, Kathy?' he said suspiciously.

'Yes, thank God, Mr O'Brien,' Kathy said. It wasn't actually rude or defiant, but she spoke to him as an equal not a pupil.

That child had come on a lot since the beginning of term, he said to himself. He wondered had it anything to do with the Italian classes, which by some miracle had proved not to be the total disaster he had predicted but a huge success.

Mam had gone to Bingo, Dad was at the pub. Fran was at home in the kitchen.

'You're a bit late, Kathy. Everything all right?'

'Sure, I took a bit of a walk. I learned all the parts of the body for class tonight. You know, she's going to put us into pairs and ask *Dov'è il gomito* and you have to touch your partner's elbow.'

Fran was pleased to see her happy. 'Will I make us a toasted sandwich to give us energy for all this?'

'Great. Do you know the feet?'

'*I piedi*. I learned them at lunchtime,' Fran grinned. 'We're going to be teacher's pets, you and I.'

'I went to see him today,' Kathy said.

'Who?'

'Paul Malone.'

Fran sat down. 'You're not serious.'

'He was very nice, very nice indeed. He gave me his card. Look, he gave me his direct line and his home number.'

'I don't think it was a wise thing to do,' Fran said eventually.

'Well, he seemed quite pleased. In fact he said he was glad I did.'

'He did?'

'Yes. And he said I could come any time and go to his house and meet his wife if I wanted to.' Fran's face seemed empty suddenly. As if all the life had gone out of it. It was as if someone had put a hand into her head and switched something off. Kathy was puzzled. 'Well, aren't you pleased? There was no row, no scene, just normal and natural as you said it was. He understood that it had all been a bit of a shock, and he said from now on it would be different. Different and better, those were his words.'

Fran nodded, it was as if she wasn't able to speak. She nodded again and got out the words. 'Yes, that's good. Good.'

'Why aren't you glad? I thought this is what you'd like.'

'You have every right to get in touch with him and to be part of all he has. I never meant to deny you that.'

'It isn't a question of that.'

'It is a question of that. You're right to feel short-changed when you see a man like that who has everything, tennis courts, swimming pools, chauffeurs probably.'

'That's not what I was looking for,' Kathy began.

'And then you come back to a house like this, and go to a school like Mountainview and you're meant to think that going to some bloody evening class that I scrimp and save for is a treat. No wonder you hope things are going to be ... what is it, different and better?'

Kathy looked at her in horror. Fran thought she wanted Paul Malone instead of her. That she had been swayed and dazzled by a momentary meeting with a man she had not heard of until a few days ago.

'It's only better because now I know everything. Nothing else will change,' she tried to explain.

'Of course.' Fran was clipped and tight now. She was spreading the cheese on bread, with two slices of tomato each and putting it under the grill as if she were a robot.

'Fran, stop. I don't want any of that. Listen, don't you understand? I had to see him. You were right, he's not a monster, he's nice.'

'I'm glad I told you.'

'But you've got it wrong. Look, ring him yourself, ask him. It's not that I want to be with him rather than you. It's only just to see him the odd time. That's all. Talk to him on the phone then you'll understand.'

'No.'

'Why? Why not? Now that I've sort of paved the way.'

'Sixteen years ago I made a bargain. There was a deal I would not contact them again, and I never did.'

'But I didn't make that deal.'

'No, and am I criticising you? I said you had every right. Isn't that what I said?' Fran served them the cheese on toast and poured a glass of milk each.

Kathy felt inexpressibly sad. This kind woman had slaved for her, making sure that there was everything she needed. There would have been no pints of nice cold milk at the ready, no hot suppers cooked, if it were not for Fran. Now she had even let slip that she had scrimped and saved for the Italian classes. No wonder she was hurt and upset at the thought that Kathy might, after all this sacrifice, be prepared to forget the years of love and commitment. That she might be blinded by the unaccustomed thought of access to real wealth and comfort.

'We should go now for the bus,' Kathy said.

'Sure, if you want to.'

'Of course I want to.'

'Right then.' Fran put on a coat which had seen better days. She changed into her good shoes, which weren't all that good. Kathy remembered the soft Italian leather shoes that her father wore. She knew that they were very, very expensive.

'*Avanti*,' she said. And they ran for the bus.

At the lesson Fran was paired with Luigi. His dark menacing frown seemed somehow more sinister than ever tonight.

'*Dov'è il cuore?*' Luigi asked. His Dublin accent made it hard to know which part of the body he was talking about. '*Il cuore*,' said Luigi again, annoyed. '*Il cuore*, the most important part of the body, for God's sake.'

Fran looked at him vaguely. '*Non so*,' she said.

'Of course you know where your bloody cuore is.' Luigi was getting more unpleasant by the moment.

Signora helped her out. '*Con calma per favore*,' Signora came in to make the peace. She lifted Fran's hand and put it on her heart. '*Ecco il cuore.*'

'It took you long enough to find it,' Luigi grumbled.

Signora looked at Fran. She was quite different tonight. Normally she was part of everything and encouraging the child to participate as well.

Signora had checked with Peggy Sullivan. 'Did you tell me that Miss Clarke was the mother of the sixteen-year-old girl?' she asked.

'Yes, she had her when she was only that age herself. Her mam brought the girl up, but she's Miss Clarke's child, it's well known.'

Signora realised that it had not been known to Kathy. But they were both different this week. Perhaps it was known now. Guiltily she hoped she had played no part in it.

Kathy waited a week before she called Paul Malone on his private line.

'Is this a good time to talk?' she asked.

'I have someone with me at the moment but I do want to speak, so please can you hold on a moment?' She heard him getting rid of someone else. An important person maybe. A well-known personality, for all she knew.

'Kathy?' His voice was warm and welcoming.

'Did you mean it that we could meet somewhere sometime, not rushed like in an office?'

'Of course I meant it. Will you have lunch with me?'

'Thank you, when?'

'Tomorrow. Do you know Quentin's?'

'I know where it *is*.'

'Great. Will we say one o'clock? Does that fit in with school?'

'I'll make it fit in with school.' She was grinning and she felt him smile too.

'Sure, but I don't want you getting into trouble.'

'No, I'll be fine.'

'I'm glad you rang,' he said.

She washed her hair that night and dressed with care, her best school blouse and she had taken the stain remover to her blazer.

'You're meeting him today,' Fran said as she watched Kathy polish her shoes.

'I've always said you should have been in Interpol,' Kathy said.

'No, you've never said that.'

'It's just for lunch.'

'I told you, it's your right if you want to. Where are you going?'

'Quentin's.' She had to tell the truth. Fran would have to know sooner or later. She wished he hadn't picked somewhere quite as posh, somewhere so far from their ordinary world.

Fran managed to find the words of encouragement. 'Well, that will be nice, enjoy it. All of it.'

Kathy realised how little part in their lives Mam and Dad seemed to play these days, they were just there in the background. Had it always been like that and she just hadn't noticed? She told the duty teacher that she had a dentist's appointment.

'You have to show these in writing,' the teacher said.

'I know, but I was so frightened thinking about it I forgot to take the card. Can I bring it to you tomorrow?'

'All right, all right.'

Kathy realised that it had paid off to have been a good hard-working pupil all those years. She was not one of the school troublemakers. She could get away with anything now.

Naturally she told Harriet that she was skipping classes.

'Where are you going this time? To dress up as a nurse for him?' Harriet wanted to know.

'No, just to lunch in Quentin's,' she said proudly.

Harriet's jaw fell open. 'Now you *are* joking.'

'Not a bit of it, I'll bring you back the menu this afternoon.'

'You have the most exciting sex life of anyone I ever met,' Harriet said in envy.

It was dark and cool and very elegant.

A good looking woman in a dark suit came forward to meet her.

'Good afternoon, I'm Brenda Brennan and you're most welcome. Are you meeting somebody?'

Kathy wished she could be like this, she wished that Fran could. Confident and assured. Maybe her father's wife was like this. Something you had to be born to, not something that could be learned. Still, you could learn to pretend to be confident.

'I am meeting a Mr Paul Malone. He said he'd book a table for one o'clock, I'm a little early.'

'Let me show you to Mr Malone's table. A drink while you're waiting?'

Kathy ordered a Diet Coke. It came in a Waterford Crystal glass with ice and slices of lemon. She must remember every moment of it for Harriet.

He came in nodding to this table and smiling at that one. A man stood up to shake his hand. By the time he got to her he had greeted half the place.

'You look different, lovely,' he said.

'Well, at least I'm not wearing my friend's mother's jacket and a ton of make-up to get past reception,' she laughed.

'Should we order quickly? Do you have to rush back?'

'No, I'm at the dentist, it can take ages. Do you have to rush back?'

'No, not at all.'

They got the menus and Ms Brennan came to explain the dishes of the day. 'We have a nice *insalata di mare*,' she began.

'*Gamberi, calamari?*' Kathy asked before she could stop herself. Only last night they had been doing all the sea food ... '*Gamberi*, prawns, *calamari*, squid ...'

Both Paul and Brenda Brennan looked at her in surprise.

'I'm showing off. I go to Italian evening classes.'

'I'd show off if I knew all that off the top of my head,' Ms Brennan said. 'I had to learn them from my friend Nora who helps us write the menus when we have Italian dishes.' They seemed to look at her admiringly, or maybe she was just getting big-headed.

Paul had his usual, which was a glass of wine mixed with mineral water.

'You didn't have to bring me to somewhere as smart as this,' she said.

'I'm proud of you, I wanted to show you off.'

'Well, it's just Fran thinks ... I suppose she's jealous that I can go to somewhere like this with you. I'd never go anywhere except Colonel Sanders or McDonald's with her.'

'She'd understand. I just wanted to bring you somewhere nice to celebrate.'

'She says it's my right and she said I was to enjoy it all. That's what she said this morning, but I think in her heart she's a bit upset.'

'Does she have anyone else, any boyfriend or anything?' he asked. Kathy looked up surprised. 'What I'm trying to say ... it's none of my business but I hope she has. I'd hoped she would have married and given you sisters and brothers. But if you don't want to tell me then don't, because as I say I don't have any right to ask.'

'There was Ken.'

'And was it serious?'

'You'd never know. Or at least I'd never know, because I see nothing, understand nothing. But they went out a lot, and she used to laugh when he came to the house in the car to collect her.'

'And where is he now?'

'He went to America,' Kathy said.

'Was she sorry, do you think?'

'Again I don't know. He writes from time to time. Not so much lately but he did a lot in the summer.'

'Could she have gone?'

'It's funny you should say that ... she asked me once if I'd like to go and live in some small town in the backwoods of America. It's not New York City or anywhere. And I said Lord no, give me Dublin any day, at least it's a capital city.'

'Do you think she didn't go with Ken because of you?'

'I never thought of that. But then all that time I thought she was my sister. Perhaps that could have had something to do with it.' She looked troubled now and guilty.

'Stop worrying about it, if it's anyone's fault it's mine.' He had read her thoughts.

'I asked her to ring you but she won't.'

'Why not? Did she give a reason?'

'She said because of the deal ... she was going to keep her part of the bargain, you kept yours.'

'She was always straight as a die,' he said.

'So it looks as if you two will never talk.'

'We'll never get together and walk into the sunset, that's for sure, because we're both different people now. I love Marianne and she may or may not love Ken, or she'll love someone else. But we will talk, I'll see to that. Now you and I are going to have a real lunch as well as solving the problems of the world.'

He was right, there wasn't much more to be said. They talked of school and show business, and the marvellous Italian classes, and his two children who were seven and six.

As they paid the bill the woman at the cash desk looked at her with interest. 'Excuse me, but is that a Mountainview blazer you're wearing?' Kathy looked guilty. 'It's just that my husband teaches there, that's how I recognise it,' she continued.

'Oh really, what's his name?'

'Aidan Dunne.'

'Oh, Mr Dunne's very nice, he teaches Latin and he set up the Italian classes,' she told Paul.

'And your name ... ?' the woman behind the desk asked.

'Will be for ever a mystery. Girls who take time off for lunch don't want tales brought back to their teachers.' Paul Malone's smile was charming but his voice was steely. Nell Dunne at the cash desk knew she was being criticised for taking too much interest. She just hoped that Ms Brennan hadn't overheard.

'Don't tell me about it,' Harriet yawned. 'You had oysters and caviar.'

'No. I had *carciofi* and lamb. Mr Dunne's wife was on the cash desk, she recognised the blazer.'

'Now you're done for,' said Harriet with a smirk.

'Not a bit of it, I didn't tell her who I was.'

'She'll know. You'll be caught.'

'Stop saying that, you don't want me to be caught, you want me to go on having these adventures.'

'Kathy Clarke, I tell you if I had been burned at the stake I'd have said you were the last person on earth to have adventures.'

'That's the way it goes,' said Kathy cheerfully.

'Personal call for Miss Clarke on line three,' went the tannoy. Fran looked up in surprise. She moved into the surveillance room, a place where they could see shoppers without being seen themselves.

She pressed the button and got line three. 'Miss Clarke, Supervisor,' she said.

'Paul Malone,' said the voice.

'Yes?'

'I'd love to talk. I don't suppose you'd like to meet?'

'You're right, Paul. No bitterness, just no point.'

'Fran, can I talk to you a little on the phone?'

'It's a busy time.'

'It's always a busy time for busy people.'

'Well, you've said it.'

'But what's more important than Kathy?'

'To me, nothing.'

'And she is hugely important to me too, but . . .'

'But you don't want to get too involved.'

'Absolutely wrong. I would love to get as involved as I can, but you brought her up, you made her what she is, you are the person who cares for her most in the world. I don't want to muscle in suddenly. I want you to tell me what would be best for her.'

'Do you think I know? How could I know? I want everything in the world for her, but I can't get it. If you can get more, then do it, get it, give it to her.'

'She thinks the world of you, Fran.'

'She's pretty taken with you too.'

'She's only known about me a week or two, she's known you all her life.'

'Don't break her heart, Paul. She's a great girl, she's had such a shock. I thought she sort of knew, guessed, absorbed it or something. It's not such an unusual situation around here. But apparently not.'

'No, but she's coped with it. She's got your genes. She can cope with things, fair or unfair.'

'And yours too, lots of courage.'

'So what will we do, Fran?'

'We have to leave it to her.'

'She can have as much of me as she wants, but I promise you I won't try to take her away from you.'

'I know.' There was a silence.

'And are things . . . well, all right?'

'Yeah, they're, well, all right.'

'She tells me you're both learning Italian, she spoke Italian in the restaurant today.'

'Good for her,' Fran sounded pleased.

'Didn't we do well in a way, Fran?'

'We sure did,' she said, and hung up before she burst into tears.

'What are *carciofi*, Signora?' Kathy asked at Italian class.

'Artichokes, Caterina. Why do you ask?'

'I went to a restaurant and they had them on the menu.'

'I wrote that menu for my friend Brenda Brennan,' Signora said proudly. 'Was it Quentin's?'

'That's right, but don't tell Mr Dunne. His wife works there, a bit of a prune, I think.'

'I believe so,' said Signora.

'Oh, by the way, Signora, you know the way you said you thought Fran was my mother and I said she was my sister?'

'Yes, yes . . .' Signora was ready to apologise.

'You were quite right, I hadn't understood,' Kathy said, as if it were the most natural mistake in the world anyone could have made, mistaking a mother for a sister.

'Well, it's good to have it all sorted out.'

'I think it *is* good,' Kathy said.

'It must be.' Signora was serious. 'She's so young, and so nice and you'll have her around for years and years, much longer than if she were an older mother.'

'Yes. I wish she'd get married, then I wouldn't feel so responsible for her.'

'She may in time.'

'But I think she missed her chance. He went to America. I think she stayed because of me.'

'You could write to him,' said Signora.

Signora's friend Brenda Brennan was thrilled to hear how well the classes were going. 'I had one of your little pupils in the other day, well, she was wearing a Mountainview blazer and said that she was learning Italian.'

'Did she have artichokes?'

'How do you know these things, you must be psychic!'

'That's Kathy Clarke . . . She's the only child, the rest of them are grown ups. She said that Aidan Dunne's wife works there. Is that right?'

'Oh, this is the Aidan you talk about so much. Yes, Nell is the cashier. Odd sort of woman, I don't know what she's at, to be honest.'

'What do you mean?'

'Well, highly efficient, honest, quick. Nice mechanical smile at the customers, remembers their names. But she's miles away.'

'Miles away where?'

'I think she's having an affair,' Brenda said eventually.

'Never. Who with?'

'I don't know, she's so secretive and she meets someone after work often.'

'Well, well.'

Brenda shrugged it off. 'So if you're thinking of making a play for her husband, go ahead, the wife isn't going to be able to cast any stones at you.'

'Heavens, Brenda, what an idea. At my age. But tell me, who was Kathy Clarke having lunch with in your elegant restaurant?'

'It's funny . . . she was with Paul Malone, you know, or maybe you wouldn't, very trendy accountant married to all that Hayes money. Buckets of charm.'

'And Kathy was with him?'

'I know. She could have been his daughter,' Brenda said. 'But honestly, the longer I work in this business the less surprised I am about anything.'

'Paul?'

'Kathy, it's been ages.'

'Will you come to have lunch with me, my treat? Not Quentin's.'

'Sure, where do you suggest?'

'I won a voucher at Italian class to this place, lunch for two including wine.'

'I can't have you missing school like this.'

'Well, I was going to suggest a Saturday, unless that's a problem.'

'It's never a problem, I told you that.'

She showed him the prize she had won at the Italian class. Paul Malone said he was very pleased to have been chosen as her guest.

'I want to put something to you. It's got a bit to do with money but it's not begging.'

'You put it to me,' he said.

She told him about this flight to New York for Christmas. Ken would pay most of it but he literally didn't have all of it and he couldn't borrow out there; it wasn't like here where people sort of lived on credit.

'Tell me about it,' said Paul Malone the accountant.

'He was so pleased when I wrote and told him that I knew about everything now, and I was so sorry if I had stood in their way. He wrote back and said that he loved Fran to bits and that he had been thinking of coming back to Ireland for her but he felt he would have messed it up all ways if he did that. Honestly, Paul, I couldn't let you see the letter because it's private but you'd love it, you really would, you'd be pleased for her.'

'I know I would.'

'So I'll tell you exactly how much it is. It's about three hundred pounds. I know it's enormous. And I know all that's in this building society account Fran has for me, so you see it's only a loan. When we get them together I can give it straight back to you.'

'How will we give it so that it doesn't look the way it is?'

'You'll do it.'

'I'd give you anything, Kathy, and your mother too. But you can't take away people's pride.'

'Could we send it to Ken?'

'That might be taking away his pride.'

There was a silence. The waiter came to ask were they enjoying the meal.

'*Benissimo*,' Kathy said.

'My ... my young friend has taken me here on a voucher she won at Italian class,' Paul Malone said.

'You must be clever,' said the waiter.

'No, I'm just good at winning things,' Kathy said.

Paul looked as if an idea had just struck him. 'That's it, you could win a couple of air tickets,' he suggested.

'How could I do that?'

'Well, you won us two lunches here.'

'That's because Signora organised it that someone in the class should get a prize.'

'Well, maybe I could organise it that someone could win two air tickets.'

'It would be cheating.'

'It would be better than being patronising.'

'Can I think about it?'

'Don't think too long, we have to set up this imaginary competition.'

'And should we tell Ken?'

'I don't think so,' said Paul. 'What do you think?'

'I don't think he has any need to know the whole scenario,' Kathy said. It was a phrase Harriet used a lot.

Lou

When Lou was fifteen, three men with sticks had come into his parents' shop, taken all the cigarettes, the contents of the till and, as the family cowered behind the counter, there came the noise of a Garda car.

Quick as a flash Lou said to the biggest of the men, 'Out the back, over the wall.'

'What's in it for you?' the fellow hissed.

'Take the fags, leave the money. Go.'

And that's exactly what they did.

The Guards were furious. 'How did they know there was a back way?'

'They must have known the area,' Louis shrugged.

His father was very angry indeed. 'You let them away with it, you bloody let them away, the Guards could have had them in gaol if it hadn't been for you.'

'Get real, Da.' Lou always spoke like a gangster anyway. 'What's the point? The prisons are full, they'd get the Probation Act, and they'd come back and smash the place up. This way they owe us. It's like paying protection money.'

'Living in a bloody jungle,' his father said. But Lou was certain he had done the right thing, and secretly his mother agreed with him.

'No point in attracting trouble,' was her motto. Delivering aggressive thieves with sticks to the Guards would have been attracting trouble as far as she was concerned.

Six weeks later a man came in to buy cigarettes. About thirty, burly with a nearly shaved head. It was after school and Lou was serving.

'What's your name?' the man asked.

Lou recognised the voice as the one that had asked him what was in it for him. 'Lou,' he said.

'Do you know me, Lou?'

Lou looked him straight in the eye. 'Not from a bar of soap,' he said.

'Good lad, Lou, you'll be hearing from us.' And the man who had taken over fifty packets of cigarettes six weeks ago while waving a stick paid nice and politely for his packet. Not long after, the big man came in with a plastic bag. 'Leg of lamb for your mother, Lou,' he said and left.

'We won't say a thing to your father,' she said, and cooked it for their Sunday lunch.

Lou's father would have said that they would not appreciate someone distributing the contents of *their* shop around the neighbourhood like some modern day Robin Hood, and presumably the butcher's shop that had been done over felt the same.

Lou and his mother thought it easier not to go too far down that road. Lou thought of the big man as Robin Hood and when he saw him around the place he would just nod at him. 'Howaya.'

And the big man would laugh back at him and say, 'How's it going, Lou?'

In a way Lou hoped that Robin would get in touch again. He knew that the debt had been paid by the gift of the lamb. But he felt excited at the thought of being so close to the underworld. He wished Robin would give him some kind of task. He didn't want to do a smash and grab himself. And he couldn't drive a getaway car. But he did want to be involved in something exciting.

The call didn't come while he was at school. Lou was not a natural student, at sixteen he was out of the classroom and into the Job Centre without very much hope there either. One of the first people he saw was Robin studying the notices on the board.

'Howaya, Robin,' Lou said, forgetting that was only a made up name.

'What do you mean, Robin?' the man asked.

'I have to call you something. I don't know your name so that's what I call you.'

'Is it some kind of a poor joke?' The man looked very bad-tempered indeed.

'No, it's like Robin Hood, you know the fellow . . .' his voice trailed away. Lou didn't want to talk about Merry Men in case Robin thought he might be saying he was gay, he didn't want to say a band or a gang. Why had he ever said the name at all?

'As long as it's not a reference to people robbing things . . .'

'Oh God no, NO,' Lou said, as if such an idea was utterly repulsive.

'Well then,' Robin seemed mollified.

'What is your real name?'

'Robin will do fine, now that we know there's no misunderstanding.'

'None, none.'

'Good, well how are things, Lou?'

'Not great, I had a job in a warehouse but they had stupid rules about smoking.'

'I know, they're all the same.' Robin was sympathetic. He could read the story of a boy's first job ending after a week. It was probably his own.

'I'll tell you, there's a job here.' He pointed at an advertisement offering a cleaning job in a cinema.

'It's for girls, isn't it?'

'It doesn't say, you can't say nowadays.'

'But it would be a desperate job.' Lou was disappointed that Robin thought so little of him as to point him in such a lowly direction.

'It could have its compensations,' Robin said, looking vaguely into the distance.

'What would they be?'

'It could mean leaving doors open.'

'Every night? Wouldn't they cop on?'

'Not if the bolt was just pulled slightly back.'

'And then?'

'And then if other people, say, wanted to go in and out, they would have a week to do so.'

'And after that?'

'Well, whoever had that cleaning job could move on in a bit, not too quickly, but in a bit. And would find that people were very grateful to him.'

Lou was so excited he could hardly breathe. It was happening. Robin was including him in his gang. Without another word he went up to the counter and filled in the forms for the post as cleaner.

'Whatever made you take a job like that?' his father said.

'Someone's got to do it,' Lou shrugged.

He cleaned the seats and picked up the litter. He cleaned the lavatories and used scouring powder to get rid of the graffiti. Each evening he loosened the bolt on the big back door. Robin didn't even have to tell him which, it was quite obvious that this was the only way that people could get in.

The manager was a nervous, fussy little man. He told Lou that the world was a wicked place now, totally different from when he was growing up.

'True enough,' Lou said. He didn't engage in much conversation. He didn't want to be remembered one way or another after the event.

The event happened four days later. Thieves had got in, broken into the little covered-in cash desk and got away with the night's takings. They had sawn through a bolt, apparently. They must have been able to reach through a crack in the door. The Guards asked was there any way that the door could have been left unlocked but the nervous fussy manager, who was by this stage nearly hysterical and confirmed in his belief of the wickedness of the world, said that was ridiculous. He always checked at night and why would they have had all the sawing if they had got in an open door. Lou realised they organised that to protect him. Nobody could finger the new cleaner as being the inside contact.

He stayed on at the cinema, carefully locking the newly fitted bolt for two weeks to prove that he was in no way connected. Then he told the manager he had got a better position.

'You weren't the worst of them,' the manager said, and Lou felt slightly ashamed because he knew that in a way he was the worst of them. His predecessors hadn't opened the doors to admit the burglars. But there was no point whatsoever in feeling guilty about that now. What was done was done. It was a matter of waiting to see what happened next.

What happened next was that Robin came in to buy a pack of cigarettes and handed him an envelope. His father was in the shop so Lou took it quietly without comment. Only when he was alone did he open it. There were ten ten-pound notes. A hundred pounds for loosening a bolt four nights in succession. As Robin had promised, people were being grateful to him.

*

Lou never asked Robin for a job. He went about his own work, taking bits here and there. He felt sure that if he were needed he would be called on. But he longed to run into the big man again. He never saw Robin any more at the Job Centre.

He felt sure that Robin was involved in the job at the supermarket where they had got almost the entire contents of the off licence into a van and away within an hour of late closing. The security firm just couldn't believe it. There was no evidence of an inside job.

Lou wondered how Robin had managed it, and where he stashed what he stole. He must have premises somewhere. He had gone up in the world since the time years ago when he had come into their shop. Lou had only been fifteen. Now he was nearly nineteen. And in all that time he had only done one job for big Robin.

He met him again unexpectedly at a disco. It was a noisy place and Lou hadn't met any girls he fancied. More truthfully he hadn't met any girls who fancied him. He couldn't understand it, he was being as nice as anything, smiling, buying them drinks, but they went for mean-looking fellows, people who scowled and frowned. It was then he saw Robin dancing with a most attractive girl. The more she smiled and shimmered at him the deeper and darker and more menacing Robin appeared to be. Maybe this was the secret. Lou practised his frown as he stood at the bar, frowning at himself in the mirror, and Robin came up behind him.

'Looking well, Lou?'

'Good to see you again, Robin.'

'I like you, Lou, you're not a pushy person.'

'Not much point. Take it easy, I always say.'

'I hear there was a bit of trouble in your parents' shop the other day.'

How had Robin heard that? 'There was, kids, brats.'

'Well they've been dealt with, the hide has been beaten off them, they won't touch the place again. Small call to our friends the Gardai telling them where the stuff can be found, should be sorted out tomorrow.'

'That's very good of you, Robin, I appreciate it.'

'Not at all, it's a pleasure.' he said. Lou waited. 'Working at the moment?'

'Nothing that can't be altered if needs be,' Lou said.

'Busy place here, isn't it?' Robin nodded at the bar where they stood. Ten-pound notes and twenty-pound notes were flashing back and forward. The night's takings would be substantial.

'Yeah, I'd say they have two guys and an Alsatian to take all that to a night safe.'

'As it happens they don't,' said Robin. Lou waited again. 'They have this van that drives the staff home, about three in the morning, and the last to be left off is the manager, who looks as if he's carrying a duffel bag with his gear in it but that's the takings.'

'And does he put it in a safe?'

'No, he takes it home and someone comes to his house to pick it up a bit later and they put it in a safe.'

'Bit complicated, isn't it?'

'Yeah, but this is a tough kind of an area.' Robin shook his head disapprovingly. 'No one would want to be driving a security van round here, too dangerous.' Robin frowned darkly, as if this were a monstrous shadow over their lives.

'And most people don't know this set-up, about the manager with the sports bag?'

'I don't believe it's generally known at all.'

'Not even to the driver of the van?'

'No, not at all.'

'And what would people need, do you think?'

'Someone to reverse in front of the van accidentally, and prevent the van leaving the lane for about five minutes.' Lou nodded. 'Someone who has a car and a clean driving licence and a record of coming here regularly.'

'That would be a good idea.'

'You have a car?'

'Sadly no, Robin, a licence yes, a record of coming here but not a car.'

'Were you thinking of buying one?'

'I was indeed, a second-hand car ... thinking a lot, but it hasn't been possible.'

'Until now.' Robin raised a glass to him.

'Until now,' Lou said. He knew he must do nothing until he heard from Robin. He felt very pleased that Robin had said he liked him. He frowned vaguely at a girl nearby and she asked him to dance. Lou hadn't felt so good for a long time

Next day his father said that you wouldn't believe it but the Guards had found every single thing that had been taken by those young pups. Wasn't it a miracle? Three days later a letter and hire purchase agreement form came from a garage. Mr Lou Lynch had paid a deposit of two thousand pounds and agreed to pay a monthly sum. The car could be picked up and the agreement signed within the next three days.

'I'm thinking of getting a car,' Lou told his parents.

'That's great,' said his mother.

'Bloody marvellous what people can do on the dole,' his father said.

'I'm not on the dole as it happens,' Lou said, stung.

He was working in a big electrical appliances store, carrying fridges and microwaves out to the back of people's cars. He had always hoped it might be the kind of place where Robin would come and find him. How could he have guessed it would be in a discotheque?

He drove his car around proudly. He took his mother out to Glendalough one Sunday morning, and she told him that when she was a young girl she always dreamed that she might meet a fellow with a car but it never happened.

'Well, it's happened now, Mam,' he said soothingly.

'Your Da thinks you're on the take, Lou, he says there's no way you could have a car like this on what you earn.'

'And what do you think Ma?'

'I don't think at all, son,' she said.

'And neither do I, Ma,' he said.

It was six weeks before he ran into Robin again. He called to the big store and bought a television. Lou carried it to his car for him.

'Been going to that disco regularly?'

'Twice, three times a week. They know me by name now.'

'Bit of a dump though.'

'Still. You've got to dance somewhere, drink somewhere.' Lou knew that Robin liked people to be relaxed.

'Very fair point. I was wondering if you'd be there tonight?'

'Certainly I will.'

'And maybe not drink anything because of breathalysers.'

'I think a night on the mineral water's very good for everyone from time to time.'

'Maybe I'd show you a good place to park the car there tonight.'

'That would be great.' He asked no other details, that was his strength. Robin seemed to like him wanting as little information as possible.

About ten o'clock that night he parked the car where Robin indicated. He could see how it would obstruct the exit from the alley into the main road if he pulled out. He realised he would be in full view of everyone in the staff van. The car would have to stall. And refuse to start despite his apparent best efforts. But there were about five hours before that happened.

So he went into the disco, and within fifteen minutes he met the first girl that he ever thought he could love and live with for the rest of his life. Her name was Suzi and she was a tall, stunning redhead. It was her first time at the disco, she told him. But she was beginning to vegetate at home in her flat, and she decided she would go out and see what the night brought.

And the night had brought Lou. They danced and they talked, and she said she loved that he drank mineral water, so many fellows just stank of beer. And he said he did drink beer sometimes but not in great quantities.

She worked in a café in Temple Bar, she told him. They liked the same kind of films and they liked the same music and they loved curries and they didn't mind swimming in the cold sea in the summer and they each hoped to go to America one day. You can learn a lot about other people in four and a half hours if you are sober. And everything that Lou learned about Suzi he liked. Under normal circumstances he would have driven her home.

But these were not normal circumstances. And the only reason that he had a car at all was that the circumstances were so very far from normal.

'I'd offer you a lift home but I have to meet this guy here a bit later.' Could he say that, or would it be suspicious later when he was questioned? Because questioned he would be. Could he walk her home and then come back? That might have been possible, but Robin wanted him to establish his presence as being on the scene all night.

'I'd really like to see you again, Suzi,' he said.

'Well, I'd like that, too.'

'So will we say tomorrow night? Here, or somewhere quieter?'

'So is tonight over now?' Suzi asked.

'For me it is, but listen, tomorrow night can go on as long as we like it to.'

'Are you married?' Suzi asked.

'No, of course I'm not. Hey, I'm only twenty. Why would I be married?'

'Some people are.'

'I'm not. Will I see you tomorrow?'

'Where are you going now?'

'To the men's room.'

'Do you do drugs, Lou?'

'Jesus, I don't. What is this, an interrogation?'

'It's just that you've been going to the loo all night.' It was true he had, just to get himself noticed, seen, remembered.

'No, I don't. Listen, sweetheart, you and I'll have a great night out tomorrow, go wherever you want, I mean it.'

'Yeah,' she said.

'No, not Yeah ... Yes. I mean it.'

'Goodnight, Lou,' she said, hurt and annoyed. And picked up her jacket and walked out into the night.

He longed to run after her. Was there ever such bad timing? How miserably unfair it all was.

The minutes crept by until it was time for action, then he went to his car, the last to leave the club. He waited until the minivan filled and the lights went on. At that very moment he shot backwards in its path. Then he revved the engine over and over, flooding it, ensuring that it wouldn't start.

The operation worked like clockwork. Lou looked at none of it, all the time he played the part of a man desperate to start his car, and when he realised that dark figures had climbed a wall and got away he watched astounded as the scarlet-faced manager came running out crying help and wanting the Guards and panicking utterly.

Lou sat helpless in the car. 'I can't get it out of here, I'm trying.'

'He's one of them' shouted somebody, and strong hands held him, bouncers, barmen, until they realised who it was.

'Hey, that's Lou Lynch,' they said releasing him.

'What *is* all this, first my car won't start and then you all jump on me. What's happening?'

'The takings have been snatched, that's what's happened.' The manager knew his career was over. He knew there would be hours ahead with the Guards. And there were, for everybody.

One of the Guards recognised Lou's address. 'I was up there not long back, a crowd of kids broke in and stole all before them.'

'I know, Guard, and my parents were very grateful you retrieved it all.'

The Guard was pleased to be so publicly praised for what had been, after all, a tip-off out of the blue. Lou was regarded as the most unlucky accident to have happened for a long time. The staff told detectives that he was a very nice fellow, couldn't be involved in anything like that. He got a good report from the big electrical store, his car payments were up to date, he hadn't an ounce of alcohol in his body. Lou Lynch was in the clear.

But he didn't spend all the next day thinking about Robin and wondering when the next envelope would come and how much it would contain. He thought instead about the beautiful Suzi Sullivan. He would have to lie to her and tell her the official account of what had happened. He hoped she wasn't too annoyed with him.

He went to her restaurant in his lunch break with a red rose. 'Thank you for last night.'

'There wasn't much *of* last night,' Suzi complained. 'You were such a little Cinderella we all had to come home early.'

'It won't happen tonight,' he said. 'Unless you want to, of course.'

'We'll see,' said Suzi darkly.

They met almost every night after that.

Lou wanted them to go back to the disco where they had met. He said that it was out of sentimental reasons. In reality it was because he didn't want the staff to think that he never came back again after the Incident.

He heard all about the Incident. Apparently four men with guns had got into the van and told them to lie down. They had taken everyone's carrier bag and left in minutes. Guns. Lou felt a bit sick in his stomach when he heard that. He had thought that Robin and his friends were still in sticks. But of course that was all five years ago, and the world had moved on. The manager lost his job, the system of banking the takings was changed, a huge van with barking dogs picked them up each night. You'd need an army to take that on.

It was three weeks later when he was leaving work that he saw Robin in the car park. There was again an envelope. Again Lou pocketed it without looking.

'Thank you very much,' he said.

'Aren't you going to see what's in it?' Robin seemed disappointed.

'No need to. You've treated me well in the past.'

'There's a thousand quid,' Robin said proudly.

That was something to get excited about. Lou opened the envelope and saw the notes. 'That's absolutely terrific,' he said.

'You're a good man, Lou, I like you,' said Robin, and drove away.

A thousand pounds in his pocket and the most beautiful redhead in the world waiting for him. Lou Lynch knew he was the luckiest man in the world.

His romance with Suzi developed nicely. He was able to buy her nice things and take her to good places with his stash of money. But it seemed to alarm her when he pulled out twenty-pound notes.

'Hey, Lou, where do you get money like that to throw around?'

'I work, don't I?'

'Yeah, and I know what they pay you in that place. That's the third twenty you've split this week.'

'Are you watching me?'

'I like you, of course I watch you,' she said.

'What are you looking for?'

'I'm hoping not to find that you're some sort of a criminal,' she said quite directly.

'Do I look the type?'

'That's not a yes or a no.'

'And there are some questions to which there are no yes-and-no answers,' Lou said.

'Okay, let me ask you this, are you involved in anything at the moment?'

'No.' He spoke from the heart.

'And do you plan to be?' There was a pause. 'We don't need it, Lou, you've got a job, I've got a job. Let's not get caught up in something messy.' She had beautiful creamy skin and huge dark green eyes.

'All right, I won't get involved in anything again,' he said.

And Suzi had the sense to let it rest there. She asked no questions about the past. The weeks went on and they saw more and more of each other, Suzi and Lou. She brought him to meet her parents one Sunday lunchtime.

He was surprised by where they lived.

'I thought you were posher than this place,' he said as they got off the bus.

'I made myself seem posher to get the job in the restaurant.'

Her father was not nearly as bad as she had said he was, he supported the right football team and he had cans of beer in the fridge.

Her mother worked in that supermarket that Robin and his friends had done over a while back. She told them the story, and how Miss Clarke the supervisor had always thought there must be someone in the shop who had left the door open for them but nobody knew who it was.

Lou listened, shaking his head at it all. Robin must have people all over the city loosening bolts, parking cars in strategic places. He looked at Suzi, smiling and eager. For the first time he hoped that Robin wouldn't contact him again.

'They liked you,' Suzi said, surprised, afterwards.

'Well, why not? I'm a nice fellow,' Lou said.

'My brother said you had a terrible frown but I told him it was a nervous tic and he was to shut up about it.'

'It's *not* a nervous tic, it's a deliberate attempt to look important,' Lou said crossly.

'Well, whatever it is, it was all they could find fault with so that's something. When am I going to meet yours?'

'Next week,' he said.

His mother and father were alarmed that he was bringing a girl to lunch. 'I suppose she's pregnant,' his father said.

'She most certainly is not, and there'll be none of that talk when she comes to the house.'

'What kind of things would she eat?' His mother was doubtful.

He tried to remember what he had to eat at the Sullivans' house.

'Chicken,' he said. 'She just loves a bit of chicken.' Even his mother could hardly destroy a chicken.

'They liked you,' he said to her afterwards, putting on exactly the same note of surprise as she had.

'That's good.' She pretended indifference but he knew she was pleased.

'You're the first, you see,' he explained.

'Oh, yeah?'

'No, I mean the first I brought home.'

She patted him on the hand. He had been very, very lucky to have met a girl like Suzi Sullivan.

At the beginning of September he met Robin by accident. But of course it wasn't by accident. Robin was parked near his parents' shop and just got out of the car.

'A half pint to end the day?' Robin said, jerking his head towards the nearby pub.

'Great,' Lou said with fake enthusiasm. He sometimes feared Robin could read minds, he hoped he couldn't see the insincerity in Lou's tone.

'How are things?'

'Great, I've got a smashing girl.'

'So I see, she's a real looker, isn't she?'

'Absolutely. We're quite serious about it all.'

Robin punched him on the arm. It was meant to be a punch of solidarity but somehow it hurt. Lou managed not to rub where it felt bruised. 'So you'll be needing a deposit on a house soon?' Robin asked casually.

'We're not in any hurry with that, she's got a grand bedsit.'

'But *eventually*, of course?' Robin wasn't taking any argument.

'Oh yes, way down the line.' There was a silence. Did Robin know that Lou was trying to get off the hook?

Robin spoke. 'Lou, you know I always said I liked you.'

'Yes, and I always liked you too. It was mutual. And is mutual,' Lou added hastily.

'Considering how we met, as it were.'

'You know the way it is, you forget how you met people.'

'Good, good.' Robin nodded. 'What I'm looking for, Lou, is a place.'

'A place. To live in?'

'No, no. I've got a place to live in, a place that our friends the Guards turn over with great regularity. They sort of regard it as part of their weekly routine, go in and search my place.'

'It's harassment.'

'I know it is, they know it is. They never find anything, so they know well it's harassment.'

'So if they don't find anything . . . ?' Lou had no idea where all this was going.

'It means that things have to be somewhere else and that's getting increasingly difficult,' Robin said. In the past Lou had always waited. Robin would say what he wanted in time. 'The kind of place I want is somewhere that there's a lot of activity two or three times a week, a place where people wouldn't be noticed going in and out.'

'Like the warehouse where I work?' Lou asked nervously.

'No, there's proper security there.'

'What would this place have to have, in terms of facilities?'

'Not very much space at all, like enough for . . . Imagine five or six cases of wine – packages about that size, in all.'

'That shouldn't be hard, Robin.'

'I'm watched like a hawk. I'm spending weeks going round talking to everyone I know that they don't have a file on, just to confuse them. But there's something coming in soon, and I really do need a place.'

Lou looked anxiously out the door of the pub in the direction of his parents' shop.

'I don't think it would be possible in my Ma and Da's place.'

'No, no that's not what I want at all, it's a place with bustle, doors in and out, lots of people moving through.'

'I'll think,' Lou said.

'Good, Lou. Think this week will you, and then I'll give you the instructions. It's very easy, no driving cars or anything.'

'Well actually, Robin, this is something I meant to bring up, but I'm thinking of . . . um . . . well not being involved any more.'

Robin's frown was terrible to see. 'Once you're involved you're *always* involved,' he said. Lou said nothing. 'That's the way it is,' Robin added.

'I see,' said Lou, and he frowned hard in response to show how seriously he took it.

That night Suzi said she wasn't free, she had promised to help the mad old Italian woman who lived as a lodger in their house to do up an annexe up in Mountainview school for some evening class.

'*Why* do you have to do that?' Lou grumbled. He had wanted to go to the pictures and then for some chips and then back to bed with Suzi in her little bedsitter. He did not want to be on his own thinking about the fact that once you were involved you could never get uninvolved again.

'Come with me,' Suzi suggested, 'that'll make it quicker.'

Lou said he would, and they went to this annexe attached to the school but slightly separate from it. It had an entrance hall, a big classroom, two lavatories and a small kitchen space. In the hall there was a store room with a few boxes in it. Empty boxes.

'What are all these?' he asked.

'We're trying to tidy up the place so it looks more festive and not so much like a rubbish dump for when the classes start,' said the deranged woman they called Signora. Harmless but very odd, and some most peculiar coloured hair, like a piebald mare.

'Should we throw out the boxes?' Suzi suggested.

Slowly Lou spoke. 'Why don't I just tidy them up and leave them in a neat stack in there? You never know when you might need a few boxes.'

'For Italian classes?' Suzi said in disbelief.

But at this moment Signora interrupted. 'No, he's right. We could use them to be tables when we are learning the section on what to order in an Italian restaurant, they could be counters in the shops, or a car at the garage.' Her face seemed radiant at all the uses there would be for boxes.

Lou looked at her with amazement. She was obviously missing her marbles but at this moment he loved her. 'Good woman, Signora,' he said, and tidied the boxes into neat piles.

He couldn't contact Robin but he wasn't surprised to get a phone call at work.

'Don't want to come and see you, the toy soldiers are going mad with excitement these days. I can't move without five of them padding after me.'

'I found somewhere,' said Lou.

'I knew you would, Lou.'

Lou told him where it was, and about the activity every Tuesday and Thursday, thirty people.

'Fantastic,' Robin said. 'Have you enrolled?'

'For what?'

'For the class, of course.'

'Oh Jesus, Robin, I scarcely speak English, what would I be doing learning Italian?'

'I'm relying on you,' said Robin, and hung up.

There was an envelope waiting for him at home that night. It contained five hundred pounds and a note. 'Incidental expenses for language learning.' He had been serious.

'You're going to do *what*?'

'Well you're the one who said I should better myself, Suzi. Why not?'

'When I said better yourself, I meant smarten yourself up, get a better paid job. I didn't mean go mad and learn a foreign language.' Suzi was astounded. 'Lou, you have to be off your head. It costs a fair amount. Poor Signora is afraid that it will be too dear for people and suddenly out of the blue, you decide to take it up. I can't take it in.'

Lou frowned a mighty frown. 'Life would be very dull if we all understood everyone,' he said.

And Suzi said that it would be a lot easier to get on with.

Lou went to the first Italian lesson as a condemned man walks to Death Row. His years in the classroom had not been glorious. Now he would face further humiliation. But it had been surprisingly enjoyable. First the mad Signora asked them all their names and gave them ridiculous pieces of coloured cardboard to write them on, but they had to write Italianised versions.

Lou became Luigi. In a way he liked it. It was important.

'*Mi chiamo Luigi*,' he would say, and frown at people, and they seemed impressed.

They were an odd bunch, a woman dripping in jewellery that no one in their sane senses would have worn to Mountainview school, and driving a

BMW. Lou hoped that Robin's friends wouldn't steal the BMW. The woman who drove it was nice as it happened, and she had sad eyes.

There was a very nice old fellow, a hotel porter called Laddy though he had Lorenzo written on his badge, a mother and daughter, a real dizzy blonde called Elizabetta who had a serious boyfriend with a collar and tie, and dozens of others that you'd never expect to find at a class like this. Perhaps they wouldn't think it odd that he was there. They might not even question it for a moment why he was there.

For two weeks he questioned it himself, then he heard from Robin. Some boxes would be coming in on Tuesday, just around seven thirty when the classroom was filling up. Maybe he could see to it that they got into the store cupboard in the hall.

He didn't know the man in the anorak. He just looked out for the van. There were so many people arriving, parking bikes, motorbikes, the dame with the BMW, two women with a Toyota Starlet . . . the van didn't cause any stir.

There were four boxes, they were in in a flash, the van and the man in the anorak were gone.

On Thursday he had the four boxes ready to be pulled out quickly. The whole thing was done in seconds. Lou had made himself teacher's pet by helping with the boxes. Sometimes they covered them with red crepe paper and put cutlery on them.

'*Quanto costa il piatto del giorno?*' Signora would ask and they would all repeat it over and over until they could ask for any damn thing and lift knives and say '*Ecco il coltello!*'

Babyish it might have been but Lou liked it, he even saw himself and Suzi going to Italy one day and he would order her a *bicchiere di vino rosso* as quick as look at her.

Once Signora lifted a heavy box, one of the consignment.

Lou felt his heart turn over but he spoke quickly. 'Listen, Signora, will you let *me* lift those for you, it's the empty ones we want.'

'But what's in it, this is so heavy?'

'Could you be up to them in a school? Come on, here we are. What are they going to be today?'

'They are doing hotels, *alberghi. Albergo di prima categoria, di seconda categoria.*'

Lou was pleased that he understood these things. 'Maybe I wasn't just thick at school,' he told Suzi. 'Maybe I was just badly taught.'

'Could be,' Suzi said. She was preoccupied. There had been some trouble with Jerry; her mam and dad had been called to see the headmaster. They said it sounded serious. And just after he had been getting on so well and doing so well since Signora had come to the house, and actually doing his homework and everything. It couldn't have been stealing, or anything. They had been very mysterious up at the school.

One of the nice things about working in a café was listening to people's conversations. Suzi said that she could write a book about Dublin just from the bits of overheard conversation.

People were talking about secret weekends, and plans for further dalliances, and cheating their income tax. And incredible scandal about politicians and journalists and television personalities ... maybe none of it true, but all of it hair-raising. But it was often the most ordinary conversations that were the most fascinating. A girl of sixteen determined to get pregnant so that she could leave home and get a council flat, a couple who made fake ID cards explaining the economics of buying a good laminator. Lou hoped that Robin and his friends would never use this café to discuss their plans. But then it was a bit up market for them, he was probably in the clear as regards this.

Suzi would spend a lot of time clearing a nearby table when people were saying interesting things. A middle-aged man and his daughter came in, good looking blonde girl with a bank uniform. The man was craggy and had longish hair, hard to know what he did, maybe a journalist or a poet. They seemed to have had a row. Suzi hovered nearby.

'I'm only agreeing to meet you because it's a half hour off work and I'd love a cup of good coffee compared to that dishwater we get in the canteen,' the girl said.

'There's a new and beautiful percolator with four different kinds of coffee waiting for you any time you would like to call,' he said. He didn't sound like a father, he sounded more like a lover. But he was so old. Suzi kept shining up the table so that she could hear more.

'You mean you've used it?'

'I keep practising, waiting for the day you'll come back and I can make you Blue Mountain or Costa Rica.'

'You'll have a long wait,' said the girl.

'Please, can't we talk?' he was begging. He was quite a handsome old man, Suzi admitted.

'We are talking, Tony.'

'I think I love you,' he said.

'No, you don't, you just love the memory of me and you can't bear that I don't just troop back there like all the others.'

'There are no others now.' There was a silence. 'I never said I loved anyone before.'

'You didn't say you loved me, you only said you *thought* you loved me. It's different.'

'Let me find out. I'm almost certain,' he smiled at the girl.

'You mean let's get back into bed together until you test it?' she sounded very bitter.

'No, I don't, as it happens. Let's go out for dinner somewhere and talk like we used to talk.'

'Until bedtime, and then it's let's get back into bed like we used to do that.'

'We only did that once, Grania. It's not just about that.' Suzi was hooked now. He was a nice old guy, the girl Grania should give him a chance, just for dinner. She was dying to suggest it but knew she had to say nothing.

'Just dinner then,' Grania said, and they smiled at each other and held hands.

It was not always the same man, the same van or the same anorak. But the contact was always minimal and the speed great.

The weather became dark and wet and Lou provided a big hanging rail for the wet coats and jackets that might otherwise have been stacked in the hall cupboard. 'I don't want to drip all over Signora's boxes,' he would say.

Weeks of boxes in on Tuesday and out on Thursday. Lou didn't want to think about what was in them. It wasn't bottles, that was for sure. If Robin were involved in bottles it would be a whole off licence full of them like the time in the supermarket. Lou couldn't deny it any more. He knew it must be drugs. Why else was Robin so worried? What other kind of business involved one person delivering and another collecting? But God almighty, drugs in a school. Robin must be mad.

And then by chance there was this matter of Suzi's young brother, a young red head with an impudent face. He had been found with a crowd of the older boys in the bicycle shed. Jerry had sworn that he was only being their delivery boy, they had asked him to pick up something at the school gates because they were being watched by the headmaster. But the Mr O'Brien who terrorised them all nearly lifted the head off Suzi's entire family about the whole thing.

Only the pleas of Signora had succeeded in keeping Jerry from being expelled. He was so very young, the whole family would ensure that he didn't hang around after school but came straight home to do his lessons. And in fact, because he had shown such improvement and because Signora gave her personal guarantee, Jerry had been spared.

The older boys were out, expelled that day. Apparently Tony O'Brien said that he didn't give one damn about what happened to their futures. They didn't have much of a future, but what they had of it would not be spent in his school.

Lou wondered what hell would break loose if it were ever discovered that the school annexe was acting as a receiving depot for drugs every Tuesday and was passing them on the next stage of their journey on a Thursday. Perhaps some of these very consignments were the ones that had been handled by young Jerry Sullivan, his future brother-in-law.

Suzi and he decided that they would marry next year.

'I'll never like anyone more,' Suzi said.

'You sound fed up, as if I'm only the best of a bad bunch,' Lou said.

'No, that's not true.' She had become even fonder of him since he had taken up Italian. Signora always spoke of how helpful he was at the class. 'He's full of surprises certainly,' Suzi had said. And indeed he was. She used to hear him recite his Italian homework, the parts of the body, the days of the week. He was so earnest about it, he looked like a little boy. A good little boy.

It was just when he was thinking of getting a ring that he heard from Robin.

'Maybe a nice jewel for your red-haired girlfriend, Lou,' he said.

'Yes, well, Robin, I was thinking of buying it myself, you know, wanting to take her to the shop so that we could discuss . . .' Lou didn't know if there were to be further payment for his work up in the school. In one way it was so simple that he didn't really *need* any more. In another he was doing something so *dangerous* that he really should be paid very well for it. To make it worth the risk.

'I was going to say that if you went into that big place near Grafton Street and chose her a ring, you'd only have to leave a deposit on it, the rest would be paid.'

'She'd know, Robin. I don't tell her anything.'

Robin smiled at him. 'I know you don't, Lou, and she wouldn't know. There's this guy who'd show you a tray of really good stuff, no prices mentioned, and then she'd always have something really nice on her finger. And paid for absolutely legitimately because the balance would be sorted out.'

'I don't think so, listen, I know how good this is, but I think . . .'

'Think when you have a couple of kids and things are hard how glad you'll be that you once met a fellow called Robin and got a deposit for a house and your wife is wearing a rock that cost ten big ones on her finger.'

Did Robin really mean ten thousand pounds? Lou felt dizzy. And there was the mention of a deposit for a house as well. You'd have to be stark staring mad to fly in the face of this.

They went into the jeweller's. He asked for George.

George brought a tray. 'These are all in your price range,' he said to Lou.

'But they're enormous,' hissed Suzi. 'Lou, *you* can't afford these.'

'Please don't take away the pleasure of giving you a nice ring,' he said, his eyes big and sad.

'No but, Lou, listen to me. We save twenty-five a week between us and we find it hard going. These must be two hundred and fifty pounds at least, that's ten weeks' saving. Let's get something cheaper, really.' She was so nice he didn't deserve her. And she didn't have an idea she was looking at serious jewellery.

'Which one do you like best?'

'This isn't a real emerald is it, Lou?'

'It's an emerald-*type* stone,' he said solemnly.

Suzi waved her hand backwards and forwards, it caught the light and it flashed. She laughed with pleasure. 'God, you'd swear it was the real thing,' she said to George.

Lou went into a corner with George where he paid over £250 in notes and saw that an extra £9,500 had already been paid towards a ring to be bought by a Mr Lou Lynch on that day.

'I wish you every happiness, sir,' said George without changing a line of the expression on his face.

What did George know or not know? Was George someone who once got involved and now couldn't get uninvolved? Had Robin really been in to a respectable place like this and paid all that money in cash? Lou felt faint and dizzy.

Signora admired Suzi's ring. 'It's very, very beautiful' she said.

'It's only glass, Signora, but wouldn't you think it was an emerald?'

Signora, who had always loved jewellery but never owned any, knew it was an emerald. In a very good setting. She began to worry about Luigi.

Suzi saw the good looking blonde girl called Grania come in. She wondered how the dinner with the older man had gone. As usual she longed to ask but couldn't.

'Table for two?' she enquired politely.

'Yes, I'm meeting a friend.'

Suzi was disappointed that it wasn't the old man. It was a girl, a small girl with enormous glasses. They were obviously old friends.

'I must explain, Fiona, that nothing is settled, nothing at all. But I might be calling on you in the weeks ahead to say that I am staying with you, if you know what I mean.'

'I know only too well what you mean. It's been ages since either of you called on me to be the alibi,' Fiona said.

'Well, it's just that this fellow . . . well, it's a very long story. I really do fancy him a lot but there are problems.'

'Like he's nearly a hundred, is that it?' Fiona asked helpfully.

'Oh, Fiona, if only you knew . . . that's the least of the problems. His being nearly a hundred isn't a problem at all.'

'You live very mysterious lives, you Dunnes,' Fiona said in wonder. 'You're going out with a pensioner and you don't notice what age he is. Brigid is obsessed with the size of her thighs which seem perfectly ordinary to me.'

'It's all because of that holiday she went on where they had a nudist beach,' Grania explained. 'Some eejit said that if you could hold a pencil under your boobs and it didn't fall down then you were too floppy and you shouldn't go topless.'

'And . . . ?'

'Brigid said that she could hold a telephone directory under hers and it wouldn't fall.'

They giggled at the thought.

'Well, if she said it herself,' said the girl in the enormous spectacles.

'Yeah, but the awful point was that nobody denied it, and now she's got a complex the size of a house.' Suzi tried not to laugh aloud. She offered them more coffee. 'Hey, that's a beautiful ring,' Grania said.

'I just got engaged.' Suzi was proud.

They congratulated her and tried it on.

'Is it a real emerald?' Fiona asked.

'Hardly. Poor Lou works as a packer up in the big electrical place. No, but it's terrific glass, isn't it?'

'It's gorgeous, where did you get it?'

Suzi told her the name of the shop.

When she was out of hearing Grania said in a whisper to Fiona, 'That's funny, they only sell precious stones in that shop. I know because they have an account with us. I bet that's not glass, I bet it's the real thing.'

It was coming up to the Christmas party in the Italian class. They wouldn't be seeing each other for two weeks. Signora asked them all to bring something to the last lesson and they would make it into a party. Huge banners with *Buon Natale* hung all over the room, and banners for the New Year too. They had all dressed up. Even Bill, the serious fellow from the bank, Guglielmo as they all called him, had entered into the spirit of it all and had brought paper hats.

Connie, the woman with the car and the jewellery, brought six bottles of Frascati which she said she found in the back of her husband's car and she felt that he might have been taking them off somewhere for his secretary so they had better be drunk. No one quite knew whether or not to take her seriously and there had been this restriction about drink earlier. But Signora said it had all been cleared with Mr O'Brien the Principal so they needn't worry about that aspect of things.

Signora didn't feel it necessary to add that Tony O'Brien had said that since the school seemed to be crawling with hard drugs and kids laying their hands on crack with ease, it seemed fairly minor if some adults had a few glasses of wine as a Christmas treat.

'What did you do last Christmas?' Luigi asked Signora, for no reason except that he was sitting near her when all the *salute* and *molto grazie* and *va bene* were going on around them.

'Last year I went to midnight mass at Christmas and watched my husband Mario and his children from the back of the church,' Signora said.

'And why weren't you sitting with them?' he asked.

She smiled at him. 'It wouldn't have been proper,' she said.

'And then he went and died,' Lou said. Suzi had filled him in on Signora, a widow, apparently, even though Suzi's mother thought she was a plain-clothes nun.

'That's right, Lou, he went and died,' she said gently.

'*Mi dispiace*,' Lou said. '*Troppo triste*, Signora.'

'You're right, Lou, but then life was never going to be easy for anyone.'

He was about to agree with her when a horrifying thought struck him. It was a Thursday and there had been no man with an anorak. No van. The school would be locked up for two weeks with all of whatever it was in the store cupboard in the hall. What in the name of God was he to do now?

Signora had brought them the words of Silent Night in Italian and the evening was coming to a close. Lou was frantic. He had no car with him, even if he could get a taxi at this late stage what on earth would he do to explain why he was carrying four heavy boxes from the store cupboard. There was no way that he could come in here again until the first week of January. Robin would kill him.

But then it was Robin's fault. He had given no contact number, no fall-back position. Something must have happened to whoever was due to pick up. That was where the weak link was. It wasn't Lou's fault. No one could blame him. But he was paid, very well paid, to think quickly and stay cool. What would he do?

The clear-up was beginning. Everyone was shouting their goodbyes.

Lou offered to get rid of the rubbish. 'I can't have you do all that, Luigi, you're far too good already,' said Signora.

Guglielmo and Bartolomeo helped him. In no other place would he have been friendly with two fellows like this, a serious bank clerk and a van driver. Together they carried black sacks of rubbish out into the night and found the big school bins.

'She's terribly nice, your one, Signora, isn't she?' said Bartolomeo.

'Lizzie thinks she's having a thing with Mr Dunne, you know, the man in charge of the whole thing,' Guglielmo whispered.

'Get away.' Lou was amazed. The lads speculated about it.

'Well, wouldn't it be great if it were true.'

'But at their age . . .' Guglielmo shook his head.

'Maybe when we get to their age we'll think it the most natural thing in the world.' Lou somehow wanted to stand up for Signora. He didn't know whether he should deny this ridiculous suggestion or confirm it as the most normal thing in the world.

His heart was still racing about the boxes. He knew he had to do something he hated; he had to deceive this nice kind woman with the amazing hair. 'How are you getting home, will Mr Dunne be picking you up?' he asked casually.

'Yes, he did say he might drop by.' She looked a little pink and flustered. The wine, the success of the evening, and the directness of his question.

Signora thought that if Luigi, not the brightest of pupils, had seen something in the way she related to Aidan Dunne then it must be very well known in the class. She would hate it to be thought that she was his lady friend. After all, it wasn't as if words or anything else except companionship had been exchanged between them. But if his wife were to find out, or his two daughters. If they were to be a subject of gossip that Mrs Sullivan would hear about, as she well might considering how her daughter was engaged to Luigi.

Having lived so discreetly for years, Signora was nervous of stepping out of her role. And also, it was so unnecessary. Aidan Dunne didn't think of her as anything except a good friend. That was all. But it might not look that way to people who were, how would she put it, more basic, people like Luigi.

He was looking at her quizzically. 'Right, will I lock up for you? You go ahead and I'll catch you up, we're all a bit late tonight.'

'*Grazie, Luigi. Troppo gentile.* But be sure you *do* lock it. You know there's a watchman comes round an hour after we've all gone. Mr O'Brien is a stickler for this. So far we've never been caught leaving it unlocked. I don't want to fall at the last fence.'

So he couldn't leave it open and come back when he thought up a plan. He *had* to lock the bloody thing. He took the key. It was on a big heavy ring shaped like an owl. It was a silly childish thing but at least it was big, no one would be able to forget it, or think they had it in a handbag if it weren't there.

Like lightning he put his own key on to the silly owl ring and took off Signora's. Then he locked the school, ran after her and dropped the key into her handbag. She wouldn't need it until next term, and even if before, he could always manage to substitute something, get the real key back into her handbag somehow. The main thing was to get her home thinking she had the key.

He did not see Mr Dunne step out of the shadows and take her arm tonight, but wouldn't it be amazing if it were true. He must tell Suzi. Which reminded him, he had better stay with Suzi tonight. He had just given away his mother and father's key.

'I'll be staying with Fiona tonight,' Grania said.

Brigid looked up from her plate of tomatoes.

Nell Dunne didn't look up from the book she was reading. 'That's nice,' she said.

'So, I'll see you tomorrow evening then,' Grania said.

'Great.' Her mother still didn't look up.

'Great altogether,' Brigid said sourly.

'You could go out too if you wanted to, Brigid. You don't have to sit sighing over tomatoes, there are plenty of places to go and you could stay in Fiona's too.'

'Yes, she has a mansion that will fit us all,' Brigid said.

'Come on, Brigid, it's Christmas Eve tomorrow. Cheer up.'

'I can cheer up without getting laid,' Brigid hissed.

Grania looked across anxiously, but her mother hadn't registered it. 'Yes, so can we all,' Grania said in a low voice. 'But we don't go round attacking everyone over the size of our thighs which, it may be said in all cases, are quite normal.'

'Who mentioned my thighs to you?' Brigid was suspicious.

'A crowd of people came by the bank today to protest about them. Oh, Brigid, do shut up, you're gorgeous, stop all this anorexic business.'

'Anorexic?' Brigid gave a snort of laugher. 'Suddenly you're all sweetness and light because lover boy has materialised again.'

'Who is lover boy? Come on, who? You know nothing.' Grania was furious with her younger sister.

'I know you've been moping and moaning. And you talk of *me* sighing over tomatoes, you sigh like the wind over everyone and you leap ten feet in the air when the phone rings. Whoever it is he's married. You're as guilty as hell.'

'You have been wrong about everything since you were born,' Grania told her. 'But you were never more wrong in your life about this. He is not married, and I would lay you a very good bet that he never will be.'

'That's the kind of crap people talk when they're dying for an engagement ring,' said Brigid, turning the tomatoes over with no enthusiasm.

'I'm off now,' Grania said. 'Tell Dad I'll not be coming in so that he can lock the door.'

Their father was hardly ever at the kitchen supper any more. He was either away in his room planning colours and pictures for the wall, or up in the school talking about the evening class.

Aidan Dunne had gone to the school in case Signora might be there but the place was all locked up. She never went to the pub on her own. The coffee shop would be too crowded with last-minute shoppers. He had never telephoned her at the Sullivans' house, he couldn't start now.

But he really wanted to see her before Christmas to give her a little gift. He had found a locket with a little Leonardo da Vinci face inside. It wasn't expensive but it seemed entirely suitable. He hoped she would have it for Christmas Day. It was wrapped up with *Buon Natale* printed on the gold paper. It wouldn't be the same afterwards.

Or perhaps it would, but he felt like talking to her for a while. She had once said to him that at the end of the road where she lived there was a wall where she sat sometimes and looked across at the mountains, and thought how different her life had become, and how *vista del monte* meant the school to her now. Perhaps she might be there tonight.

Aidan Dunne walked up through the busy estate. There were Christmas lights in the windows, cartons of beer being delivered at houses. It must be so different to Signora from last year, when she had spent Christmas with all those Italians in the village in Sicily.

She was sitting there, very still. She didn't seem a bit surprised. He sat down beside her.

'I brought your Christmas present,' he said.

'And I brought yours,' she said, holding a big parcel.

'Will we open them now?' He was eager.

'Why not?'

They unwrapped the locket and the big coloured Italian plate with yellow and gold and a dash of purple, perfect for his room. They thanked each other and praised the gifts. They sat like teenagers with nowhere to go.

It got cold and somehow they both stood up at the same time.

'*Buon natale*, Signora.' He kissed her on the cheek.

'*Buon natale*, Aidan, *caro mio*,' she said.

Christmas Eve they worked long hard hours in the electrical store. Why did people wait until then to decide on the electric carving knife, the video, the electric kettle? Lou toiled all day and it was at closing time that Robin came in to the warehouse with a docket. Lou had somehow expected him.

'Happy Christmas, Lou.'

'*Buon natale*, Robin.'

'What do you mean?'

'It's the Italian you made me learn, I can hardly think in English any more.'

'Well I came to tell you that you can give it up any time you like,' Robin said.

'*What?*'

'Sure. Another premises has been located, but the people have been very grateful indeed for the smooth way your premises were organised.'

'But the last one?' Lou's face was white.

'What about the last one?'

'It's still in there,' Lou said.

'You are joking me in this matter.'

'Would I joke about a thing like this? Nobody ever came on the Thursday. Nothing was picked up.'

'Hurry along there, get the man his appliance.' The foreman wanted to close up.

'Give me your docket,' hissed Lou.

'It's a television for you and Suzi.'

'I can't take it,' Lou said. 'She'd know it was nicked.'

'It's not nicked, haven't I just paid for it?' Robin was hurt.

'No, but you know what I mean. I'll go and put it into your car.'

'I was going to drive you back to her flat with the surprise Christmas present.'

It *was*, as Lou would have guessed, the most expensive in the whole store. The top of the range. Suzi Sullivan would never have accepted any explanation for something like that being carried up the stairs into her bedsitter.

'Listen, we've much bigger problems than the telly, wait till I get my wages and then we'll see what were going to do about the school.'

'I presume you have taken some steps.'

'Some, but they mightn't be the right ones.'

Lou went in and stood with the lads. They got their money, a drink and a bonus; after what seemed for ever he came to where the big man sat in his station wagon, the huge television set in the back.

'I have the key to the school, but God knows what kind of lunatics they employ to walk round and test doors at odd times. The Principal there is some kind of maniac apparently.'

He produced the key which he carried with him at all times since the day he took it from Signora's key ring.

'You're a bright boy, Lou.'

'Brighter than those who didn't tell me what to do if a bloody man in an anorak doesn't turn up.' He was angry and aggrieved and frightened now. He was sitting with a criminal in the car park of his workplace with a giant television set that he could not accept. He had stolen a key, left a shipment of drugs in a school. He didn't feel like a bright man, he felt like a fool.

'Well, of course there are always problems with people,' Robin said. 'People let you down. Somebody has let us down. He will not work again.'

'What will happen to him?' Lou asked fearfully. He had visions of the offending anorak who hadn't turned up ending up dead, weighed down with cement blocks in the River Liffey.

'As I said, he will never work again for people.'

'Maybe he had a car crash, or maybe his child went to hospital.' Why was Lou defending him? This was the man who had broken all their hearts.

He could have been off the hook if it hadn't been for this. Robin's people had found new premises. Oddly, he thought he might have continued with the lessons. He enjoyed them anyway. He might even have gone on the trip that Signora was planning to Italy next summer. There would have been no need to have stayed on as a cover. Nothing had been proved. It had been a successful resting place. No accusation of an inside job would have been made because nothing had been discovered, apart from this fool who had not turned up on the last Thursday.

'His punishment will be that he never works again,' Robin shook his head in sorrow.

Lou saw a chink of light at the end of the tunnel. That was what you had to do to get uninvolved. Just screw up on a deal. Just do one job badly and you were never called again. If only he had known it would be so simple. But this job wasn't his to falter on. The anorak man was already suffering for this, and Lou had got the key and probably saved the day. It would have to be the next one.

'Robin, is this your car?'

'No, of course it isn't. You know that. I got it off a friend just so that I could transport the television to you and Suzi. But there you are.' He looked sulky, like a child.

'The Guards won't be watching for you in this car,' Lou said. 'I have an idea. It might not work but it's all I can think of.'

'Tell it to me.'

And Lou told him.

It was almost midnight when Lou drove up to the school. He reversed the station wagon up to the door of the annexe, and looking left and right to see was he being watched he let himself into the school annexe.

Almost afraid to breathe, he went to the store cupboard and there they were, four boxes. Just like they always were, looking indeed as if they held a dozen bottles of wine each but there was no sign saying this way up. Nothing saying handle with care. Tenderly he lifted them one by one outside the door. Then, straining and panting he carried the huge television in to the classroom. It had a built in video, it was state of the art. He had written the note already in coloured pencils which he had bought in a late night shop.

'*Buon natale a Lei, Signora, e a tutti,*' it said.

The school would have a television. The boxes had been rescued. He would drive them in Robin's car to a place where a different man in a different van would meet him and take them silently.

Lou wondered about the lifestyle of people who were suddenly available on Christmas Eve. He hoped he would never be one of them.

He wondered what Signora would say when she saw it. Would she be the first in? Perhaps that madman Tony O'Brien, who seemed to prowl the place night and day, would find it first. They would wonder about it for ever. The number had been filed off it. It could have been bought in any of two dozen stores.

The box revealed nothing of its origin. They would realise it had not been stolen when they began to enquire. They would guess for ever and not be able to come up with a solution. The mystery of how the place had been entered would fade in time. After all, nothing had been stolen. There had been no vandalism.

Even tetchy Mr O'Brien would have to give up eventually.

Meanwhile there would be a great television and video for the use of the school and presumably the evening class where it had appeared.

And the next job that Robin asked Lou to do would be botched. And then sadly Lou would be told that he could never work again, and he could get on with his life.

It was Christmas morning and he was exhausted. He went around to Suzi's parents' house for tea and Christmas cake. Signora was there quietly in the background playing chess with Jerry.

'Chess!' whispered Suzi in amazement. 'That fellow can understand the pieces and the moves of chess. Wonders will never cease.'

'Signora!' he said.

'Luigi.' She seemed delighted to see him.

'You know, I got a present of a key ring just like yours,' he said. They weren't all that uncommon, it was hardly something to be marvelled at.

'My owl key ring.' Signora was always pleasant and responded to any conversation that was presented to her.

'Yeah, let me see, are they the same?' he said.

She took it from her bag and he pretended to make a comparison as he made the switch. He was safe now, and so was she. No one would ever remember this harmless little conversation. He must talk about other gifts and confuse them.

'God, I thought that Lou would never stop talking tonight,' Peggy Sullivan said as she and Signora washed up. 'Do you remember when they used to say people were vaccinated with a gramophone needle, they can't say that today I suppose, what with CDs and tapes.'

'I remember that phrase. I once tried to explain it to Mario, but like so many things it got lost in the translation and he never knew what I meant.'

It was a moment for confidences. Peggy never dared to ask this odd woman a personal question but she had sort of lowered the guard here. 'And did you not think of being with your own people at all, Signora, on Christmas Day?' she asked.

Signora did not look at all put out. She answered the question thoughtfully, with deliberation, as she answered Jerry's questions. 'No, you know, it wasn't something I would have liked. It would have been artificial. And I have seen my mother and sisters many times and none of them suggested it. They have their own ways and customs now. It would be hard to try and add me to them. It would have been very false. None of us would have enjoyed it. But I did enjoy myself here today with your family.' She stood there calm and untroubled. She wore a new locket around her neck. She had not said where she got it and nobody had liked to ask. She was much too private a person.

'And we liked having you very, very much, Signora,' said Peggy Sullivan, who wondered nowadays what she had ever done before this odd woman had come to live there.

The class began again on the first Tuesday of January. A cold evening, but they were all there. Nobody was missing from the thirty who had signed on in September. It must be a record in any evening class.

And all the top brass were there, the Principal, Tony O'Brien, and Mr Dunne, and they were beaming all over their faces. The most extraordinary thing had happened. The class had been given a gift. Signora was like a child, almost clapping her hands with pleasure.

Who could have done it? Was it anyone here? Was it one of the class? Would they say so that they could thank him or her? Everyone was mystified, but of course they all thought it was Connie.

'No, I wish it had been. I really do wish I had been nice enough to think of it.' Connie seemed almost embarrassed now that she hadn't been responsible.

The Principal said he was delighted but he was anxious in terms of security. If nobody owned up to having given this generous present then they would have to have the locks changed because somebody somewhere must have a key to the place. There had been no sign of a break-in.

'That's not the way the bank would look at it,' Guglielmo said. 'They'd say leave things as they are, whoever it is might give us a hi-fi next week.'

Lorenzo, who was actually Laddy the hotel porter, said that you'd be surprised how many keys there were walking round the city of Dublin that would open the same doors.

And suddenly Signora looked up and looked at Luigi and Luigi looked away.

Please may she say nothing, he said. Please may she know it will do no good, only harm. He didn't know if he were praying to God or just muttering to himself, but he meant it. He really meant it.

And it seemed to have worked. She looked away too.

The class began. They were revising. What a lot they had forgotten, Signora said, how much work there was to be done if they were all going to make the promised trip to Italy. Shamed, they struggled again with the phrases that had come so easily before the two-week break.

Lou tried to slip out when the class was over.

'Not helping me with the boxes tonight, Luigi?' Her look was unfaltering.

'Scusi, Signora, where are they? I forgot.'

They lifted them into the now blameless store cupboard, an area that would never again house anything dangerous.

'Is um ... Mr Dunne coming to walk you home, Signora?'

'No, Luigi, but you on the other hand are walking out with Suzi who is the daughter of the house where I stay.' Her face looked cross.

'But you know that, Signora. We're engaged.'

'Yes, that's what I wanted to discuss with you, the engagement, and the ring. *Un anello di fidanzamento*, that's what we call it in Italian.'

'Yes, yes, a ring for the fiancée,' Lou was eager.

'But not usually emeralds, Luigi. Not a real emerald. That is what is so strange.'

'Aw, go on out of that, Signora, real emerald? You have to be joking. It's glass.'

'It's an emerald, *uno smeraldo*. I know them. I love to touch them.'

'They're making them better and better, Signora, no one can tell the real thing from the fakes now.'

'It cost thousands, Luigi.'

'Signora, listen to me . . .'

'As that television set cost hundreds and hundreds . . . maybe over a thousand.'

'What are you saying?'

'I don't know. What are *you* saying to me?'

No schoolteacher in the past had ever made Lou Lynch feel like this, humbled and ashamed. His mother and father had never been able to get him to conform, no priest or Christian Brother, and suddenly he was terrified of losing the respect and the silence of this strange woman.

'I'm saying . . .' he began. She waited with that curious stillness. 'I suppose I'm saying it's over, whatever it was. There won't be any more of it.'

'And are these things stolen, the beautiful emerald and the magnificent television set?'

'No, no they're not, as it happens,' he said. 'They were paid for, not exactly by me but by other people that I worked for.'

'But that you don't work for any more?'

'No, I don't, I swear it.' He desperately wanted her to believe him. His soul was all in his face as he spoke.

'So, no more pornography.'

'No more *what*, Signora?'

'Well, of course I opened those boxes, Luigi. I was so worried with the drugs in the school, and young Jerry, Suzi's little brother . . . I was afraid that's what you had in the store cupboard.'

'And it wasn't?' He tried to take the question out of his voice.

'You know it wasn't. It was ridiculous filthy stuff, judging by the pictures on the covers. Such a fuss getting them in and out, so silly, and for young impressionable people probably very harmful.'

'You looked at them, Signora?'

'I told you I didn't play them, I don't have a video, and even if I did . . .'

'And you said nothing?'

'For years I have lived silently saying nothing. It becomes a habit.'

'And did you know about the key?'

'Not until tonight, then I remembered the nonsense about a key ring. Why did you need it?'

'There were some boxes accidentally left over Christmas,' he said.

'Couldn't you have left them there, Luigi, rather than steal keys and get them back?'

'It was always a bit complicated,' he said repentantly.

'And the television?'

'It's a long story.'

'Tell me some of it.'

'Well, it was given to me as a present for ... er, storing the ... er, boxes of tapes. And I didn't want to give it to Suzi because ... well, you know I couldn't have. She'd know, or guess or something.'

'But there's nothing for her to find out now.'

'No, Signora.' He felt as if he were four years old with his head hanging down.

'*In bocca al lupo*, Luigi,' said Signora, and locked the door behind them firmly, leaning against it and testing to make quite sure it was closed.

Connie

When Constance O'Connor was fifteen her mother stopped serving desserts at home. There were no cakes at tea, a low fat spread was on the table instead of butter, and sweets and chocolate forbidden from the house.

'You're getting a bit hippy, darling,' her mother said when Constance protested.

'All the tennis lessons, all the smart places we go, will be no use at all if you have a big bum.'

'No use for what?'

'To attract the right kind of husband,' her mother had laughed. And then, before Connie could persist, she said: 'Believe me, I know what I'm saying. I'm not saying it's fair, but it's the way things are, so if we know the rules why not play by them?'

'They might have been the rules in your day, Mother, back in the forties, but everything's changed since then.'

'Believe me,' her mother said. It was a great phrase of hers, she ordered people to believe her on this and on that. 'Nothing has changed, 1940s, 1960s, they still want a slim, trim wife. It looks classy. The kind of men *we* want, want women who look the part. Just be glad you know that and lots of your friends at school don't.'

Connie had asked her father. 'Did you marry Mother because she was slim?'

'No, I married her because she was lovely and delightful and warm and because she looked after herself. I knew someone who looked after herself would look after me, and you when you came along, and the home. It's as simple as that.'

Connie was at an expensive girls' school.

Her mother always insisted she invite her friends around to supper or for the weekend. 'That way they'll invite you and you can meet their brothers and their friends,' Mother said.

'Oh, Mother, it's idiotic. It's not like some kind of Society where we are all presented at court. I'll meet whoever I meet, that's the way it is.'

'That's not the way it is,' her mother said.

And when Connie was seventeen or eighteen she found herself going out with exactly the people her mother would have chosen for her; doctors' sons, lawyers' sons, young people whose fathers were very successful in business. Some of them were great fun, some of them were very stupid, but Connie knew it would all be all right when she went to university. Then she could really meet the kind of people she knew were out there. She could make her own friends, not just pick from the tiny circle that her mother had thought suitable.

She had registered to go to University College Dublin just before her nineteenth birthday. She had gone in and walked around the campus several times and attended a few public lectures there so that she wouldn't feel nervous when it all started in October.

But in September the unbelievable happened. Her father died. A dentist who spent a great deal of his time on the golf course, and whose successful practice had a lot to do with being a partner in his uncle's firm, should have lived for ever. That's what everyone said. Didn't smoke, only the odd drink to be sociable, took plenty of exercise. No stress in his life.

But of course they hadn't known about the gambling. Nobody had known until later the debts that existed. That the house would have to be sold. That there would be no money for Connie or any of them to go to university.

Connie's mother had been ice cold about it all. She behaved perfectly at the funeral, invited everyone around to the house for salads and wine. 'Richard would have wanted it this way,' she said.

Already the rumours were beginning to spread, but she kept her head up high. When she was alone with Connie, and only then, she let her public face fall. 'If he weren't dead I would kill him,' she said over and over. 'With my own bare hands I would choke the life out of him for doing this to us.'

'Poor Daddy.' Connie had a softer heart. 'He must have been very upset in his mind to throw money away on dogs and horses. He must have been looking for something.'

'If he were still here to face me, he would have known what he was looking for,' her mother said.

'But if he had lived, he would have explained, won it back maybe, told us.' Connie wanted a good memory of her father who had been kind and good-tempered. He hadn't fussed as much as Mother, and made so many rules and laid down so many laws.

'Don't be a fool, Connie. There's no time for that now. Our only hope is that you will marry well.'

'Mother! Don't be *idiotic*, Mother. I'm not going to get married for years. I have all my college years to get through, then I want to travel. I'm going to wait until I'm nearly thirty before I settle down.'

Her mother looked at her with a very hard face. 'Let's get this understood here and now, there will be no university. Who will pay the fees, who will pay your upkeep?'

'What do you want me to do instead?'

'You'll do what you have to do. You'll live with your father's family, his uncles and brothers are very ashamed about this weakness of his. Some of them knew, some didn't. But they're going to keep you in Dublin for a year while you do a secretarial course, and possibly a couple of other things as well, then you'll get a job and marry somebody suitable as soon as possible.'

'But Mother ... I'm going to do a degree, it's all arranged, I've been accepted.'

'It's all unarranged now.'

'That's not fair, it can't be.'

'Talk to your late father about it, it's his doing, not mine.'

'But couldn't I get a job and go to college at the same time?'

'It doesn't happen. And that crowd of his relatives aren't going to put you up in their house if you're working as a cleaner or a shopgirl, which is all you can hope to get.'

Maybe she should have fought harder, Connie told herself. But it was hard to remember how times were then. And how shocked and upset they all were.

And how frightened she was going to live with her cousins whom she didn't know, while Mother and the twins went back to the country to live with Mother's family. Mother said that going back to the small town she had left in triumph long ago was the hardest thing a human should be asked to do.

'But they'll be sorry for you so they'll be nice to you,' Connie had said.

'I don't want their pity, their niceness. I wanted my pride. He took that away. That's what I will never forgive him for, not until the day I die.'

At her secretarial course Connie met Vera, who had been at school with her.

'I'm desperately sorry about your father losing all his money,' Vera said immediately, and Connie's eyes filled with tears.

'It was terrible,' she said. 'Because it's not like the awfulness of your father dying anyway, it's as if he were a different person all the time and none of us ever knew him.'

'Oh, you *did* know him, it's just you didn't know him liking a flutter, and he'd never have done it if he thought you were all going to be upset,' said Vera.

Connie was delighted to meet someone so kind and understanding. And even though she and Vera had never been close at school they became very firm friends at that moment.

'I think you don't know how nice it is having someone being sympathetic,' she wrote to her mother. 'It's like a warm bath. I bet people would be like that to you around Grannie's home if you let them and told them how awful you felt.'

The letter back from her mother was sharp and to the point. 'Kindly don't go weeping for sympathy on all and sundry. Pity is no comfort to you, nor are fine soft words. Your dignity and your pride are the only things you need to see you into your middle age. I pray that you will not be deprived of them as I was.'

Never a word about missing Father. About the kind husband he was, the good father. The photographs were taken out of the frames. The frames were sold in the auction. Connie didn't dare to ask whether the pictures of her childhood had been saved.

Connie and Vera got on very well at their secretarial college. They did the

159

shorthand and typing classes, together with the book-keeping and office routine that were all part of such a comprehensive type of training. The family of cousins that she stayed with were embarrassed by her plight and gave her more freedom than her mother would have done.

Connie enjoyed being young and in Dublin. She and Vera went to dances where they met great people. A boy called Jacko fancied Connie and his friend Kevin fancied Vera, so they often went out together as a four. But neither she nor Vera were serious while both the boys were. There was a lot of pressure on both of them to have sex. Connie refused but Vera agreed.

'Why do you do it if you don't enjoy it, if you're afraid of getting pregnant?' Connie asked, bewildered.

'I didn't say I didn't enjoy it,' Vera protested. 'I said it's not as great as it's made out to be and I can't see what all the puffing and panting is about. And I'm not afraid of getting pregnant, I'm going to go on the Pill.'

Even though birth control was still officially banned in Ireland in the early 1970s, the contraceptive pill could be prescribed for menstrual irregularity. Not surprisingly a large number of the female population were found to suffer from this. Connie thought it might be a good idea to go the same route. You never knew the day or the hour you might need to sleep with someone, and it would be a pity to have to hang around and wait until the Pill started to work.

Jacko had not been told that Connie was taking the contraceptive pill. He remained hopeful that she would eventually realise that they were meant for each other just like Kevin and Vera. He dreamed up more and more ideas that he thought would please her. They would travel to Italy together – they would learn Italian before they left at some night school or from records. When they got there they would Scusi and Grazie with the best of them. He was good looking, eager and besotted with her. But Connie was firm. There would be no affair, no real involvement. Taking the Pill was just part of her own practicality.

Whatever version of the Pill Vera was taking did not agree with her, and in the time when she was changing over to another brand she became pregnant.

Kevin was delighted. 'We always meant to get married anyway,' he kept saying.

'I wanted to have a bit of a life first,' Vera wept.

'You've *had* a bit of a life, now we'll have a real life, you and the baby and me.' Kevin was overjoyed that they didn't need to live at home any more. They could have their own place.

It didn't turn out to be a very comfortable place. Vera's family were not wealthy and were very annoyed indeed with their daughter having, as they considered it, thrown away her expensive education and costly commercial course before she ever worked for a day in her life.

They were also less than pleased with the family that Vera was about to marry into. While they considered Kevin's people extremely worthy, they were definitely not what they had hoped for their daughter.

Vera didn't need to explain this tension to Connie, Connie's own mother would have been fit to be tied. She could imagine her screaming: 'His father a house painter. And he's going into the business! They call *that* a business to be going into.' It was useless for Vera to point out that Kevin's father owned a small builder's provider and decorator that in time might well become fairly important.

Kevin had earned a living every week of his life since he had been seventeen. He was twenty-one now and extremely proud of being a father. He had painted the nursery of the two-up two-down house with three coats. He wanted it to be perfect when the baby arrived.

At Vera's wedding, where Jacko was best man and Connie was the bridesmaid, Connie made a decision. 'We can never go out with each other ever again after today,' she said.

'You're not serious, what did I do?'

'You did nothing, Jacko, except be nice and terrific, but I don't want to get married, I want to work and go abroad.'

His open, honest face was mystified. 'I'd let you work, I'd take you away every year to Italy on a holiday.'

'No, Jacko. Dear Jacko, no.'

'And I thought we might even make an announcement tonight,' he said, his face drawn in lines of disappointment.

'We hardly know each other, you and I.'

'We know each other just as much as the bride and groom here, and look how far down the road they are.' Jacko spoke enviously.

Connie didn't say that she thought her friend Vera was very unwise to have signed on for life with Kevin. She felt Vera would tire of this life soon. Vera, with the laughing dark eyes and the dark fringe still in her eyes, as it had been at school, would soon be a mother. She was able to face down her stiff-faced mother and father, and force everyone to have a good time at her wedding party. Look at her now, with the small bump in her stomach obvious to all, leading the singing of 'Hey Jude' at the piano. Soon the whole room was singing 'la la la la la la, Hey Jude'.

She swore to Connie that it was what she wanted.

And amazingly it turned out to be what she *did* want. She finished the rest of her course and went to work in Kevin's father's office. In no time she had organised their rather rudimentary system of accounts. There was a proper filing cabinet, not a series of spikes, there was an appointment book which everyone had to fill in. The arrival of the tax man was no longer a source of such dread. Slowly Vera moved them into a different league.

The baby was an angel, small and dark-eyed with loads of black hair like Vera and Kevin. At the christening Connie felt her first small twinge of envy. She and Jacko were the godparents. Jacko had another girl now, a pert little thing. Her skirt was too short, her outfit not right for a christening.

'I hope you're happy,' Connie whispered to him at the font.

'I'd come back to you tomorrow. Tonight, Connie,' he said to her.

'That's not only not on, it's not fair to think like that,' she said.

'She's only to get me over you,' he pleaded.

'Maybe she will.'

'Or the next twenty-seven, but I doubt it.'

The hostility that Vera's family had been showing to Kevin's had disappeared. As so often happened, a tiny innocent baby in a robe being handed from one to the other made all the difference ... the looking for family noses and ears and eyes in the little bundle. There was no need for Vera to sing 'Hey Jude' to cheer them up, they were happy already.

The girls had not lost touch. Vera had asked: 'Do you want to know how much Jacko yearns over you or not?'

'Not, please. Not a word.'

'And what should I say when he asks are you seeing anyone?'

'Tell him the truth, that I do from time to time but you think I'm not all that interested in fellows, and certainly not in settling down.'

'All right,' Vera promised. 'But for me, tell me have you met anyone you fancied since him?'

'Ones I half fancy, yes.'

'And have you gone all the way with them?'

'I can't talk to a respectable married woman and mother about such things.'

'That means no,' Vera said, and they giggled as they had when they learned typing.

Connie's good looks and cool manner were an asset at interviews. She never allowed herself to look too eager, and yet there was nothing supercilious about her either. She refused quite an attractive job in the bank since it was only a temporary one.

The man who interviewed her had been surprised and rather impressed. 'But why did you apply if you didn't intend to take it?' he asked.

'If you see the wording of your advertisement, there was nothing to suggest that my job would be in the nature of temporary relief,' she said.

'But once with a foot in the bank, Miss O'Connor, surely that would be to your advantage.'

Connie was unflustered. 'If I were to go in for banking I would prefer to be part of the natural intake and be part of a system,' she said.

He remembered her and spoke of her that night to two friends in the golf club. 'Remember Richard O'Connor, the dentist who lost his shirt? His daughter came in to see me, real little Grace Kelly, cool as anything. I wanted to give her a job, out of decency for poor old Richard, but she wouldn't take it. Bright as a button though.'

One of the men owned a hotel. 'Would she be good at a front desk?'

'Exactly what you're looking for, maybe even too classy for you.'

So next day Connie was called for another interview.

'It's very simple work, Miss O'Connor,' the man explained.

'Yes, but what could I learn then? I wouldn't like to do something that didn't stretch me, require me to grow with it.'

'This job is in a new top-grade hotel, it can be what you make of it.'

'Why do you think I would be suitable for it?'

'Three reasons: you look nice, you talk well, and I knew your dad.'

'I didn't mention anything about my late father in this interview.'

'No, but I know who he was. Don't be foolish, girl, take the job. Your father would like you to be looked after.'

'Well, if he would have, he certainly didn't do much during his lifetime to see that this would be the case.'

'Don't talk like that, he loved you all very much.'

'How do you know?'

'He was for ever showing us pictures on the golf course of the three of you. Brightest children in the world, we were told.'

She felt a stinging behind her eyes. 'I don't want a job from pity, Mr Hayes,' she said.

'I would want my daughter to feel the same way, but also I wouldn't want her to make a big thing about pride. You know it's a deadly sin, but that's not as important as knowing it's a very poor companion on a winter's evening.'

This was one of the wealthiest men in Dublin sharing his views with her. 'Thank you, Mr Hayes, and I do appreciate it. Should I think about it?'

'I'd love you to take it now. There are a dozen other young women waiting for it. Take it and make it into a great job.'

Connie rang her mother that night.

'I'm going to work for the Hayes Hotel starting on Monday. When the hotel opens I'll be introduced as their first hotel receptionist, chosen from hundreds of applicants. That's what the public relations people say. Imagine, I'm going to have my picture in the evening papers.' Connie was very excited.

Her mother was not impressed. 'They just want to make you into some kind of little dumb blonde, you know, simpering for the photographers.'

Connie felt her heart harden. She'd followed her mother's instructions to the letter, done her secretarial course, stayed with her cousins, got herself a job. She was not going to be insulted and patronised in this way. 'If you remember, Mother, what *I* wanted was to go to university and be a lawyer. That didn't happen so I'm doing the best I can. I am sorry you think so poorly of it, I thought you'd be pleased.'

Her mother was immediately contrite. 'I'm sorry, I really am. If you knew how sharp tongued I'm getting ... They say here I'm like our great Aunt Katie, and you remember what a legend she was in the family.'

'It's all right, Mother.'

'No, it's not, I'm ashamed. I'm very proud of you. I just say these hard things because I can't bear to have to be grateful to people like that Hayes man your father played golf with. He probably knows you're poor Richard's daughter and gave you the job out of charity.'

'No, I don't think he would know that at all, Mother,' Connie lied in a cool tone.

'You're right, why would he? It's nearly two years ago.' Her mother sounded sad.

'I'll ring and tell you about it, Mother.'

'Do that, Connie dear, and don't mind me. It's all I have left, you know, my pride. I won't apologise to any of them round here, my head is as high as ever.'

'I'm glad you're pleased for me, give my love to the twins.' Connie knew she would grow up a stranger now from the two fourteen-year-old boys who went to a Brothers school in a small town and not the private Jesuit college which had been planned.

Her father was gone, her mother was going to be no help. She was on her own. She would do what Mr Hayes said. She would make a great job of this, her first serious position. She would be remembered in the Hayes Hotel as the first and best receptionist they ever had.

She was an excellent appointment. Mr Hayes congratulated himself over and over. And so like Grace Kelly. He wondered how long it would take before she met her Prince.

In fact it took two years. There were of course endless offers of all kinds of things. Businessmen staying regularly in the hotel longed to escort the elegant Miss O'Connor at the front desk to some of the smarter restaurants and indeed night clubs that were starting up around the city. But she was very detached. She smiled and talked to them warmly and said she didn't mix business with pleasure.

'It doesn't have to be business,' Teddy O'Hara cried in desperation. 'Look, I'll stay in some other hotel if you just come out with me.'

'That would hardly be a good way to repay Hayes Hotel for my good job here.' Connie would smile at him. 'Sending all the clients off to rival establishments.'

She would tell Vera all about them. She called every week to see Vera, Kevin and Deirdre, who was shortly to be joined by another baby.

'Teddy O'Hara asked you out?' Vera's eyes were round. 'Oh please marry him, Connie, then we can get the contract for all the decorating on his shops. We'd be made for life. Go on, marry him for our sake.'

Connie laughed, but she realised she had not been putting any business in her friends' way which she could have been doing. Next day she said to Mr Hayes that she knew a very good small firm of painters and decorators if they wanted to add them to their list of service suppliers. Mr Hayes said that he left all that to the relevant manager but he did need someone to do a job for him in his own house out in Foxrock.

Kevin and Vera never stopped talking about the size and splendour of the house, and the niceness of the Hayes family, who had a little girl themselves called Marianne, Kevin and his father had done up the girl's bedroom for her with every luxury you could think of. Her own little pink bathroom off it, for a child!

Vera and Kevin never sounded jealous, and always grateful for the introduction. Mr Hayes had been pleased with the work done and because of that recommended the small firm to others. Soon Kevin drove a smarter van. There was even talk of a bigger house when the new baby arrived.

They were still friendly with Jacko, who was in the electrical business. Could I put a bit of work *his* way? Connie had wondered. Vera said she'd test the water. What Jacko actually said was: 'You can tell that stuck-up bitch to take her favours and stuff them.' 'He didn't seem keen' was the way Vera reported it, being someone who liked to keep the peace.

And just when Vera and Kevin's new baby, Charlie, was born Connie met Harry Kane. He was the most handsome man she had ever seen, tall with thick brown hair which curled on his shoulders, very unlike the business people she mixed with. He had an easy smile for everyone and a manner that seemed to expect that he would get good attention everywhere. Doormen rushed to open doors for him, the girl in the boutique left other customers to get him his copy of the newspaper and even Connie, who knew she was regarded as an ice maiden, looked up and smiled at him welcomingly.

She was particularly pleased that he saw her dealing with some difficult business travellers very efficiently. 'Quite the diplomat, Miss O'Connor,' he said admiringly.

'Always good to see you here, Mr Kane. Everything's arranged in your meeting room.'

Harry Kane with two older partners ran a new and very successful insurance business. It was taking a lot of business from the more established companies. Some people looked on it with suspicion. Growing too big too fast, they said, bound to be in trouble. But it showed no signs of it. The partners worked in Galway and Cork, they met every Wednesday in Hayes Hotel. They worked from nine until twelve thirty with a secretary in their conference room, then they entertained people to lunch.

Sometimes it was government ministers, or heads of industry or of big trade unions. Connie wondered why they didn't have their meeting in the Dublin office. Harry Kane had a big prestige office in one of the Georgian squares, with almost a dozen people working there. It must be for privacy, she decided, that and lack of disturbance. The hotel had strict instructions that no calls whatsoever be put through to the conference room on a Wednesday. Obviously this secretary must know all their secrets and where the bodies were buried. Connie looked at her with interest as she went in and out with them each week. She would carry a briefcase of documents away with her and never joined the partners at lunch. Yet she must be a highly trusted confidante.

Connie would like to work like that for someone. Someone very like Harry Kane. She began to talk to the woman, using all her charm and every skill she could rustle up.

'Everything in the room to your satisfaction, Miss Casey?'

'Certainly, Miss O'Connor, otherwise Mr Kane would have mentioned it to you.'

'We have just stocked quite a new range of audio-visual equipment, in case any of it would be of use for your meetings.'

'Thank you, but no.'

Miss Casey always seemed anxious to leave, as if her briefcase contained hot money. Maybe it did. Connie and Vera talked it over for hours.

'She's obviously a fetishist, I'd say,' Vera suggested, as they bounced baby Charlie on their knees and assured Deirdre that she was much more beautiful and much more loved than Charlie would ever be.

'*What?*' Connie had no idea what Vera was suggesting.

'Sado-masochism, whips them within an inch of their life every Wednesday. That's the only way they can function. That's what's in the case. Whips!'

'Oh, Vera, I wish you could see her.'

Connie laughed till the tears came down her face at the thought of Miss Casey in that role. And, oddly, at the same time she felt a wave of jealousy in case the quiet, elegant Miss Casey did have an intimate relationship with Harry Kane. She had not felt that way about anyone before.

'You fancy him,' Vera said sagely.

'Only because he doesn't look at me. You know that's the way of it.'

'Why do you like him, do you think?'

'He reminds me a bit of my father,' Connie said suddenly, before she realised that this was what she had felt.

'All the more reason to keep a sharp eye on him then,' said Vera, who was the only person allowed to mention the late Richard O'Connor's little gambling habit without getting a withering look from his daughter.

Without appearing to ask, Connie found out more and more about Harry Kane. He was almost thirty, single, his parents were from the country, small farmers. He was the first of his family to get into business in a big way. He lived in a bachelor apartment overlooking the sea, he went to first nights and to gallery openings, but always in a group.

His name had been mentioned in newspaper columns and always as part of a group, or sharing a box at the races with the highest of the land. When he married it would be into a family like that of Mr Hayes. Thank God that *his* daughter was only a young schoolgirl, otherwise she would have been ideal for him.

'Mother, why don't you come up to Dublin some Wednesday on the train and take a few of your friends for lunch in Hayes Hotel? I'll see they make the most enormous fuss of you.'

'I don't have any friends left in Dublin.'

'Yes, you do.' She listed a few.

'I don't want their pity.'

'What pity would there be if you invited them to a nice lunch? Come on, try it. Maybe *they'll* suggest it another time. You can take the day excursion ticket.'

Grudgingly her mother agreed.

They were placed near Mr Kane's party, which included a newspaper owner and two cabinet ministers. The ladies thoroughly enjoyed their lunch, and the fact that they seemed to be even more fêted than the amazingly important people nearby.

As Connie had hoped it would be, the lunch was pronounced a huge success and one of the others said that next time it must be her treat. It would also be a Wednesday, in a month's time. And so it went on, her mother becoming more confident and cheerful since nobody mentioned her late husband apart from saying 'Poor Richard', as they would to any widow about the deceased.

Connie always arranged to pass their table and offer them a glass of port with her compliments. Very publicly she would sign the docket for it so that everyone knew it was accountable for. She would flash a smile at the Kane table too.

After the fourth time she realised that he really *did* notice her. 'You're very kind to those older women, Miss O'Connor,' he said.

'That's my mother and some of her friends. They do enjoy their lunch here, and it's a pleasure to see her, she lives in the country, you see.'

'Ah, and where do *you* live?' he asked, his eyes alert waiting for her reply.

It was her cue to say: 'I have my own flat,' or 'by myself'. But Connie was prepared. 'Well, I live in Dublin of course, Mr Kane, but I do hope to travel sometime, I would love to see other cities.' She was giving nothing away. She saw further interest in his face.

'And so you should, Miss O'Connor. Have you been to Paris?'

'Sadly not yet.'

'I'm going next weekend, would you like to come with me?'

She laughed pleasantly, as if she were laughing with him not at him. 'Wouldn't that be nice! But out of the question, I'm afraid. I hope you have a good time.'

'Perhaps I could take you to dinner when I come back and tell you about it?'

'I'd like that very much indeed.'

And so it began, the courtship of Connie O'Connor and Harry Kane. And throughout it all she knew that Siobhan Casey, his faithful secretary, hated her. They kept the relationship as private as they could, but it wasn't easy. If he were invited to the opera he wanted to take her, he didn't want to go with a crowd of singles hand-picked for him. It wasn't long before their names were linked. She was described by one columnist as his blonde companion.

'I don't like this,' she said when she saw it in a Sunday paper. 'It makes me look flashy, trash almost.'

'To be my companion?' He raised his eyebrows.

'You know what I mean, the word companion and all it suggests.'

'Well, it's not my fault that they're not right about that.' He had been urging her to bed and she had been refusing for some time now.

'I think we should stop seeing each other, Harry.'

'You can't mean it.'

'I don't want it but I think it's best. Look, I'm not just going to have a fling with you, and then be thrown aside. Seriously, Harry, I like you too much. I more than like you, I think of you all the time.'

'And I of you.' He sounded as if he meant it.

'So isn't it better if we stop now?'

'I don't know what the phrase is . . . ?'

'Get out in time,' she smiled at him.

'I don't want to get out,' he said.

'Neither do I, but it will be harder later.'

'Will you marry me?' he asked.

'No, it's not that, I'm not putting a gun to your head. This isn't an ultimatum or anything, it's for our own good.'

'I am putting a gun to *yours*. Marry me.'

'Why?'

'I love you,' he said.

The wedding was to be in Hayes Hotel. Everyone insisted, Mr Kane was like part of the family there, and Miss O'Connor was the heartbeat of the place since it had opened.

Connie's mother had nothing to pay for except her outfit. She was able to invite her friends, the ladies with whom she had regained contact. She even invited some of her old enemies. Her twin sons were ushers at the smartest wedding Dublin had seen in years, her daughter was a beauty, the groom was the most eligible man in Ireland. On that day Connie's mother almost forgave the late Richard. If he turned up alive now she might not choke him to death after all. She had become reconciled to the hand that fate had dealt.

She and Connie slept in the same hotel room the night before the wedding. 'I can't tell you how happy I am to see you so happy,' she said to her daughter.

'Thank you, Mother, I know you've always wanted the best for me.' Connie was very calm. She was having a hairdresser and beautician come to the room in the morning to look after her mother and Vera and herself. Vera was the matron of honour, and utterly overawed by the splendour of it all.

'You *are* happy?' her mother said suddenly.

'Oh, Mother, for goodness' sake.' Connie tried to control her anger. Was there no occasion, no timing, no ceremony, that her mother could not try to spoil? Yet she looked into the kind, concerned face. 'I'm very, very happy. But just afraid I might not be enough for him, you know. He's a very successful man, I might not be able to keep up with him.'

'You've kept up with him so far,' her mother said shrewdly.

'But that's a matter of tactics, I didn't sleep with him like everyone else did from what I hear. I didn't give in easily, it might not be the same when I'm married.'

Her mother lit another cigarette. 'Just remember this one thing I said to you tonight and don't ever talk about it again, but remember it. Make sure he gives you money for yourself. Invest it, have it. Then in the end whatever happens won't be too bad.'

'Oh, Mother.' Her eyes were soft and filled with pity for a mother who had been betrayed. A mother whose whole life had to be rewritten in the light of the fact that her husband had frittered away the future.

'Would money have made that much difference?'

'You'll never know how much, and my prayer for you tonight is that you will never have to know.'

'I'll think about what you say,' Connie said. It was a very useful phrase, she used it a lot at work when she had no intention whatsoever of thinking about what anyone said.

*

The wedding was a triumph. Harry's two partners and their wives said it was the best wedding they had ever been at, and this was like a seal of approval. Mr Hayes from the hotel said that since the bride's father was sadly no longer with us, could he say that Richard would be so happy and proud to be here today and see his beautiful daughter so happy and radiant. It was the good fortune of the Hayes Hotel Group that Connie Kane, as she would now be known, had agreed to continue working until something might stop her doing so.

There was a titter of excitement at the thought of such a rich man's wife working as a hotel receptionist until she got pregnant. Which would be in the minimum time it took.

They had a honeymoon in the Bahamas, two weeks that Connie had thought would be the best in her life. She liked talking to Harry and laughing with him. She liked walking along the beach with him, making sandcastles in the morning sunshine just by the water edge, hand in hand at sunset before they went to dinner and dance.

She did not enjoy being in bed with him, not even a little bit. It was the last thing she would have expected. He was rough and impatient. He was terribly annoyed with her failure to respond. Even when she realised what he would like and tried to pretend an excitement she did not feel, he saw through it.

'Oh, come off it, Connie, stop all that ludicrous panting and groaning, you'd embarrass a cat.'

She had never felt more hurt or more alone. To give him his due he tried everything. He was gentle and wooing and flattering. He tried just holding her and stroking her. But as soon as penetration seemed likely she tensed up and seemed to resist it, no matter how much she told herself it was what they both wanted.

Sometimes she lay awake in the dark warm night listening to the unfamiliar cicadas and the Caribbean sounds in the distance. She wondered did all women feel like this. Was it perhaps just a giant conspiracy for centuries, women pretending they enjoyed it when all they wanted was children and security? Was this what her mother had meant by telling her to demand that security? In today's world in the 1970s, it didn't automatically exist for women. Men could leave home now without being considered villains, men could lose all their savings in gambling like her father and still be remembered as a good fellow.

In those long, warm, sleepless nights when she dared not stir for fear of wakening him and starting it all over again, Connie wondered too about the words of her friend Vera. 'Go on, Connie, sleep with him now for God's sake. See if you like it. Suppose you don't – imagine a lifetime of it.'

She had said no, it seemed cheating to hold back sex as if it was a prize, and then deliver it in consideration of an engagement ring. He had respected her wish to be a virgin when she married. There had been times in the last few months when she had felt aroused by him. Why had she not gone ahead then instead of waiting for this? A disaster. A disappointment that was going to scar both of them for life.

After eight days and nights of what should have been the best time for two young healthy people but which was actually becoming a nightmare of frustration and misunderstanding, Connie decided to become her old cool self, the woman who had attracted him so much. Wearing her best lemon and white dress, and sitting with the fruit basket and the china coffee pot on their balcony, she called to him: 'Harry, get up and shower will you, you and I need to have a talk.'

'That's all you ever want to do,' he muttered into his pillow.

'Soon, Harry, the coffee won't stay hot for ever.'

To her surprise he obeyed her and came tousled and handsome in his white towelling robe to breakfast. It was a sin, she thought, that she could not please this man and make him please her. But more than that, it was something that had to be dealt with.

After the second cup of coffee she said: 'At home in your work and indeed in my work, if a problem arose we would have a meeting and a discussion, do you agree?'

'What's this?' He didn't sound as if he were going to play along.

'You told me about your partner's wife who drank too much and would talk about your business. How you had to make sure she knew nothing important. It was a strategy . . . you all told her in deepest secrecy things that never mattered at all. And she was perfectly happy and is perfectly happy to this day. You worked that out by a strategy, all three of you. You sat down and said we don't want to hurt her, we can't talk to her, what do we do? And you solved it.'

'Yes?' He didn't know where this was leading.

'And in my job, we had this problem with Mr Hayes' nephew. Thick as two short planks . . . he was there, being groomed for a position of power. A vet with a curry comb couldn't groom him. How do we tell Mr Hayes? We talked about it; three of us who cared sat down and had a meeting and said what do we do? We found out that the kid wanted to be a musician not a hotel manager. We employed him to play the piano in one of the lounges, he brought in all his rich friends, it worked like a dream.'

'So what's all this about, Connie?'

'You and I have a problem. I can't understand it. You're gorgeous, you're an experienced lover, I love you. It must be my fault, I may need to see a doctor or a shrink or something. But I want to sort it out. Can we talk about it without fighting or sulking or getting upset?' She looked so lovely there, so eager, explaining things that were hard and distasteful to articulate, he struggled to reply.

'Say *something*, Harry, say that after eight days and eight nights we will not give up. It's a happiness that's there waiting to happen for me, tell me that you know it will be all right.' Still the silence. Not accusing, just bewildered. 'Say anything,' she begged. 'Just tell me what you want.'

'I want a honeymoon baby, Connie. I am thirty years of age, I want a son who can take over my business by the time I'm fifty-five. I want a family there over the next years; when I need them I come home to them. But you *know* all this. You and I have talked of aims and dreams for so long, night after night before I knew . . .' he stopped.

'No, go on,' she said, her voice quiet.

'Well then, before I knew you were frigid,' he said. There was a silence. 'Now, you *made* me say it. I don't see the point of talking about these things.' He looked upset.

She was still calm. 'You're right, I did make you say it. And is that what I am, do you think?'

'Well, you said yourself you might need a shrink, a doctor, something. Maybe it's in your past. Jesus, I don't know. And I'm as sorry as hell because you're absolutely beautiful and I couldn't be more upset that it's no good for you.'

She was determined not to cry, scream, run away, all the things she wanted to do. She had got by by being calm, she must continue like this.

'So in many ways we want the same thing. I too want a honeymoon baby,' she said. 'Come on, it's not that difficult. Lots of people do it, let's keep trying.' And she gave him the most insincere smile she had ever given anyone and led him back to the bedroom.

When they got back to Dublin she assured him she would get it sorted out. Still smiling bravely she said it made sense, she would consult the experts. First she made an appointment with a leading gynaecologist. He was a very courteous and charming man, he showed her a diagram of the female reproductive area pointing out where there might be blockages or obstructions. Connie studied the drawings with interest. They might have been plans for a new air-conditioning system in the hotel, for all the relevance they had to what she felt in her own body. She nodded at his explanations, reassured by his easy manner and discreet way of implying that almost everyone in the world had similar problems.

But at the physical examination the problems began. She tensed so much that he could not examine her at all. He stood there despairing, his hand in its plastic glove, his face kind and impersonal at the same time. She did not feel that he was a threat to her, it would be such a relief to discover some membrane that could be easily removed, but every muscle in her body had seized up.

'I think we should do an examination under anaesthetic,' he said. 'Much easier for everyone, and very probably a D and C, then you'll be as right as rain.'

She made the appointment for the next week. Harry was loving and supportive. He came to the nursing home to settle her in. 'You're all that matters to me, I never met anyone like you.'

'I bet you didn't,' she tried to joke about it. 'Beating them off was your trouble, not like you have with me.'

'Connie, it will be fine.' He was so gentle and handsome and concerned. If she couldn't be loving to a man like this there was no hope for her. Suppose she had given in to the persuasion of people like Jacko in the past, would it have been better or worse? She would never know now.

The examination showed that there was nothing physically wrong with Mrs Constance Kane. At work Connie knew if you went down one avenue and came to a dead end you had to go back to where you started from and go down another. She made an appointment with a psychiatrist. A very pleasant woman with a genuine smile and a matter-of-fact approach. She was easy to talk to, she seemed to ask shortish questions and expected longer answers. At work Connie was more accustomed to be in a listening mode, but gradually she responded to the interested questions of the psychiatrist, which never seemed intrusive.

She assured the older woman that there had not been any unpleasant sexual experiences in her past because there hadn't been any. No, she hadn't felt deprived, or curious or frustrated by not having had sex. No she had never felt drawn to anyone of her own sex, nor had an emotional relationship that was so strong it overshadowed anything heterosexual. She told the woman about her great friendship with Vera, but said that in all honesty there wasn't a hint of sexuality or emotional dependency in it, it was all laughter and confiding. And how it began because Vera was the only person to treat the whole business of her father as if it were a normal kind of thing that could happen to anyone.

The psychiatrist was very understanding and sympathetic and asked more and more about Connie's father, and her sense of disappointment after his death. 'I think you're making too much of this whole business about my Dad,' Connie said at one point.

'It's quite possible. Tell me about when you came home from school each day. Did he get involved in your homework, for example?'

'I know what you're trying to say, that maybe he interfered with me or something, but it was not remotely like that.'

'No, I'm not saying that at all. Why do you think I'm saying that?'

They went around in circles. At times Connie cried. 'I feel so disloyal talking about my father like this.'

'But you haven't said anything against him, just how kind and good and loving he was, and how he showed your picture to people at the golf course.'

'But I feel he's accused of something else, like my not being able to be good in bed.'

'You haven't accused him of that.'

'I know, but I feel it's hanging there over me.'

'And why is that, do you think?'

'I don't know. I suppose it's because I felt so let down, I had to write my whole life story all over again. He didn't love us at all. How could he have, if he was more interested in some horse or dog?'

'Is that the way it looks now?'

'He never laid a hand on me, I can't tell you that enough. It's not that I've suppressed it or anything.'

'But he let you down, disappointed you.'

'It couldn't be just that, could it? Because one man let us down as a family I'm afraid of all men?' Connie laughed at the notion.

'Is that so unlikely?'

'I deal with men all day, I work with men. I've never been afraid of them.'

'But then you've never let any of them come close to you.'

'I'll think about what you say,' Connie said.

'Think about what *you* say,' said the psychiatrist.

'Did she find anything?' His face was hopeful.

'A load of nonsense. Because my father was unreliable I think all men are unreliable.' Connie laughed in scorn.

'It might be true,' he said to her surprise.

'But Harry, how could it be? We are so open with each other, you would never let me down.'

'I hope I wouldn't,' he said, so seriously that she felt a shiver go the whole way up and down her spine.

And the week went on. Nothing got any better, but Connie clung to him and begged, 'Please don't give up on me, please Harry. I love you, I want our child so much. Maybe when we have our child I'll relax and love it all like I should.'

'Shush, shush,' he would say, stroking the anxious lines away from her face, and it wasn't all repulsive or painful, it was just so very difficult. And they had surely had sex often enough now for her to have become pregnant. Look at all the people who got pregnant who were doing everything on earth to avoid it. In the wakeful night Connie wondered could fate have also decided that she be infertile on top of everything else. But no. She missed her period, and hardly daring to hope she waited until she was sure. Then she told him the news.

His face lit up. 'You couldn't have made me a happier man,' he said. 'I'll never let you down.'

'I know,' she said. But she didn't know, because she felt sure that there was a whole part of his life that she could never share and that sooner or later he would share that side at least with someone else. But in the meantime she must do all she could to shore up the parts of his life she *could* share.

Together they attended many public functions, and Connie insisted that she be described as Mrs Constance Kane of Hayes Hotel as well as just Harry's wife. She raised money for two charities with the wives of other successful men. She entertained in her own new and splendid home, where all the decorating had been done by Kevin's family.

She told her mother nothing about the situation between them. She told Vera everything. 'When the baby's born,' Vera advised, 'go off and have a fling with someone else. You might get to like it and then come back and do it properly with Harry.'

'I'll think about it,' said Connie.

The baby's nursery was ready. Connie had given up her job. 'No hope we could tempt you back, even part time, when the baby is old enough to leave with a nurse?' Mr Hayes pleaded.

'We'll see.' She was more calm and controlled than ever, Mr Hayes thought. Marriage to a tough man like Harry Kane hadn't taken away any of her spirit.

Connie had made a point of keeping well in touch with Harry's family. She had driven to see them more often in one year than they had been visited by their son in the previous ten. She kept them informed about all the details of her pregnancy, their first grandchild, a very important milestone, she told them. They were quiet people, in awe of the hugely successful Harry. They were delighted and almost embarrassed to be so well included and to have their opinions sought about names.

Connie also made sure that she had the partners and their wives well within her own area. She took to giving light suppers in their house on a Wednesday night. The partners would all have wined and dined well at lunchtime after their weekly meeting, they would not want a huge meal. But each week there was something delicious for them to eat. Not too fattening because one of them was always on a diet, and not too much alcohol served since the other was inclined to hit the bottle.

Connie asked questions and listened to the answers. She assured these women that Harry thought so highly of their husbands that she was almost jealous of all his praise. She remembered every tiresome detail of their children's examinations and their home improvements and their holidays, the clothes they had bought. They were almost twenty years older than her. They had been resentful and suspicious at the outset. Six months after her marriage, they were her devoted slaves. They told their husbands that Harry Kane could not have found a more suitable wife, and wasn't it great that he hadn't married that hard-faced Siobhan Casey who had such high hopes of him.

The partners were unwilling to have a word said against the entirely admirable Siobhan. Because of discretion and male bonding they didn't see any need to explain that Miss Casey's high hopes might not have resulted in marriage but there was distinct evidence that a romantic dalliance that had once existed between them had begun again. Neither of the partners could understand it. If you had a beautiful wife like Connie at home, why go out for it?

When Connie realised that her husband was sleeping with Siobhan Casey she got a great shock. She hadn't expected anything like this so soon. It hadn't taken long before he had let her down. He hadn't given the life they had together much of a chance. She was seven months married, three months pregnant, and she had kept her part of the bargain perfectly. No man ever had a better companion and a more comfortable lifestyle. Connie had brought all her considerable knowledge of the hotel industry to bear on their house. It was elegant and comfortable. It was filled with people and flowers and festivity when he wanted. It was quiet and restful when he wanted that. But he wanted more.

She could possibly have put up with it if it had been a one-night stand, at a conference or visit abroad. But this woman who had obviously always wanted him! How humiliating that she should get him back. And so quickly.

His excuses were not even devious. 'I'll be in Cork on Monday, think I'll stay,' he had said, only the Cork partner had rung looking for him. So he wasn't in Cork after all.

Connie had played it down, and appeared to accept Harry's casual explanation. 'That fellow couldn't remember his own name if it wasn't written on his briefcase. I must have told him three times I was overnighting in the hotel. That's age for you.'

And then shortly afterwards when he was going to Cheltenham the travel agency sent the ticket around to the house, and she saw there was a ticket for Siobhan Casey as well.

'I didn't realise she was going.' Her voice was light.

Harry shrugged. 'We go to make contacts, to see the races, to meet people. Someone has to stay sober and write it all down.'

And after that he was away from home at least one night a week. And perhaps two nights a week so late that it was obvious he had been with somebody else. He suggested separate bedrooms so as not to disturb her, let her have all the sleep she needed in her condition. It was, Connie realised, as lonely as hell.

The weeks went on and their communication grew less. He was always courteous and praising. Particularly of her Wednesday suppers. That had really helped to cement the partnership, he told her. It also meant that he spent Wednesday night at home, but she didn't tell him that was her aim. She arranged taxis to take the partners and their wives to Hayes Hotel, where they had suites at a special discount.

She would sit with Harry when they left and talk about his business, but often with only part of her mind. She wondered did he sit in Siobhan Casey's flat and talk about his successes and failures like this. Or did he and Siobhan feel such a swelling of lust that they took the clothes off each other as soon as they got in the door and were at it on the hearthrug because they couldn't wait until they got to the bedroom?

One Wednesday evening he stroked the large bump of her stomach and there were tears in his eyes. 'I'm so sorry,' he said.

'What for?' Her face was blank. He paused as if considering whether to tell her something or not, so she spoke quickly. She wanted nothing admitted, acknowledged or accepted. 'What are you sorry about? We have everything, almost everything, and what we don't have, we may have in time.'

'Yes, yes of course,' he said pulling himself together.

'And soon our baby will be born,' she said soothingly.

'And we'll be fine,' he said, unconvinced.

Their son was born after eighteen hours of labour. A perfect healthy child. He was baptised Richard. Connie explained that by chance this was Harry's father's name and her father's name too, so it was the obvious choice. The fact that Mr Kane senior had been called Sonny Kane all his life was never mentioned.

The christening party in their home was elegant and simple at the same time. Connie stood welcoming people, her figure apparently slim again a week after the birth, her mother overdressed and happy, her friend Vera's children Deirdre and Charlie honoured guests.

The parish priest was a great friend of Connie's. He stood there proudly. Would that all his parishioners were as generous and charming as this young woman. A middle-aged lawyer friend of Connie's father was there too, a distinguished member of the Bar, with a very high reputation. He wasn't known for losing cases.

As Connie stood there in her elegant navy silk dress with its smart white trimmings, flanked by the priest and the lawyer and holding his baby son, Harry felt a frisson of alarm. He didn't know what it was and dismissed it. It might be the beginnings of flu. He hoped not, he had a lot of work in the weeks ahead. But he couldn't take his eyes off the tableau. It was as if they represented something. Something that threatened him.

Almost against his will he approached them. 'This looks very nice,' he said in his usual easy manner. 'My son surrounded by the clergy and the law on his christening day, what more does he need as a start in life in Holy Ireland?'

They smiled and Connie spoke. 'I was just telling Father O'Hara and Mr Murphy here that you should be a happy man today. I was telling them what you said eight days after we were married.'

'Oh yes, what was that?'

'You said you wanted a honeymoon baby that would be able to take over your business when you were fifty-five, and a family that would be there for you when you needed it.' Her voice seemed pleasant and admiring enough to the others. He could hear the hardness of steel in it. They had never discussed that conversation again. He had not known she would recall the words which, he remembered thinking at the time, were untempered. He had never believed it possible that she would repeat them to him in public. Was it a threat?

'I'm sure I said it more lovingly than that, Connie,' he smiled. 'It was the Bahamas, we were newly-weds.'

'That's what you said, and I was just pointing out to Father O'Hara and Mr Murphy that I hope it doesn't seem like tempting fate, but it does seem to be more or less on course so far.'

'Let's just hope that Richard likes the insurance business.'

It was some sort of threat; he knew it but didn't realise where it was coming from.

It was months later that a solicitor asked him to come to a consultation in his office. 'Are you arranging a corporate insurance plan?' Harry asked.

'No, it's entirely personal, it's a personal matter, and I will have a Senior Counsel there,' the solicitor said.

In the office was T. P. Murphy, the friend of Connie's father. Smiling and charming, he sat silently as the solicitor explained that he had been retained by Mrs Kane to arrange a division of the joint property, under the Married Women's Property Act.

'But she knows that half of mine is hers.' Harry was more shocked than he had ever been in his life. He had been in business deals where people had surprised him, but never to this extent.

'Yes, but there are certain other factors to be taken into consideration,' the solicitor said. The distinguished barrister said nothing, just looked from one face to the other.

'Like what?'

'Like the element of risk in your business, Mr Kane.'

'There's an element of risk in every bloody business, including your own,' he snapped.

'You will have to admit that your company started very quickly, grew very quickly, some of the assets might not be as sound as they appear on paper.'

God damn her, she had told these lawyers about the group that was dodgy, the one area that he and the partners worried about. They couldn't have known otherwise.

'If she has been saying anything against our company in order to get her hands on something for herself she'll answer for it,' he said, letting his guard drop completely.

It was at this point that the barrister leaned forward and spoke in his silky voice. 'My dear Mr Kane, you shock us with such a misunderstanding of your wife's concern for you. You may know a little of her own background. Her father's own investments proved insufficient to look after his family when . . .'

'That was totally different. He was a cracked old dentist who put everything he got from filling teeth onto a horse or a dog.' There was a silence in the law office. Harry Kane realised he was doing himself no good. The two lawyers looked at each other. 'Decent man by all accounts, all the same,' he said grudgingly.

'Yes, a very decent man as you say. One of my closest friends for many years,' said T. P. Murphy.

'Yes. Yes, of course.'

'And we understand from Mrs Kane that you and she are expecting a second child in a few months' time?' the solicitor spoke without looking up from his papers.

'That's true, yes. We're both very pleased.'

'And Mrs Kane of course has given up her successful career in Hayes Hotel to look after these children, and any more you and she may have.'

'Listen, it's a goddamn receptionist job, handing people their keys, saying have a nice stay with us. It's not a career. She's married to *me*, she can have anything she wants. Do I deny her anything? Does she say that in her list of complaints?'

'I'm really very glad that Mrs Kane isn't here to listen to your words,' said T. P. Murphy. 'If you knew how much you have misrepresented the situation. There is no list of complaints, there is a huge concern on her part for you, your company and the family you wanted so much to create. Her anxiety is all on your behalf. She fears that if anything were to happen to the company you would be left without the things you have worked so hard for, and continue to work so hard for, involving a lot of travel and being away from the family home so much.'

'And what does she suggest?'

They were down to it now. Connie's lawyers wanted almost everything put in her name, the house and a certain high percentage of the annual pre-tax profit. She would form a company with its own directors. Papers were shuffled, obviously names were already in place.

'I can't do that.' Harry Kane had got where he was by coming straight to the point.

'Why not, Mr Kane?'

'What would it mean to my own two partners, the men who set this thing up with me? I have to tell them "Listen lads, I'm a bit worried about the whole caboodle so I'm putting my share in the wife's name so that you won't be able to touch me if the shit hits the fan"? How would that look to them? Like a vote of confidence in what we do?'

Harry had never known a voice as soft and yet effective as T. P. Murphy's. He spoke at a barely audible level and yet every word was crystal clear. 'I am sure you are perfectly happy for both of your partners to spend their profits as they wish, Mr Kane. One might want to put all his into a stud farm in the West, one might want to buy works of art and entertain a lot of film and media people, for example. You don't question that. Why should they question that you invest in your wife's company?'

She had told them all that. How had she known anyway? The wives at the Wednesday evenings . . . Well, by God, he'd put an end to this.

'And if I refuse?'

'I'm sure you won't do that. We may not have divorce on the statute book but we do have Family Law Courts, and I can assure you that anyone who would represent Mrs Kane would get a huge settlement. The trouble, of course, would be that there would be all that bad publicity, and the insurance business is so dependent on the good faith and trust of the public in general . . .' His voice trailed away.

Harry Kane signed the papers.

He drove straight back to his large comfortable home. A gardener came every day, he was wheeling plants across towards a south-facing wall. He let himself in the front door and looked at the fresh flowers in the hall, the bright clean look of the paintwork, the pictures they had chosen together on the walls. He glanced into the large sitting room which would host forty easily for drinks without opening the double doors into the dining room. There were cabinets of Waterford glass. Only dried flowers in the dining room, they didn't eat there unless it was a dinner party. Out to the sunny kitchen where Connie sat feeding baby Richard little spoonfuls of strained apple and laughing at him, delighted. She wore a pretty flowered maternity dress with a white collar. Upstairs there was the sound of the vacuum cleaner. Soon the delivery van from the supermarket would arrive.

It was by any standards a superbly run home. Domestic arrangements never bothered him nor intruded on his life. His clothes were taken and returned to his wardrobe and drawers. He never needed to buy new socks or underpants, but he chose his own suits and shirts and ties.

He stood and looked at his beautiful wife and handsome little son. Soon they would have another child. She had kept every part of her bargain. In a way she was right to protect her investment. She didn't see him standing there and when he moved she gave a little jump.

But he noticed that her first reaction was one of pleasure. 'Oh good, you were able to get home for a bit, will I put on some coffee?'

'I saw them,' he said.

'Saw who?'

'Your legal team.' He was crisp.

She was unmoved. 'Much easier to let them do all the paperwork. You've always said that yourself, don't waste time, pay the experts.'

'I'd say we'll be paying T. P. Murphy well to be an expert, judging by the cut of his suits and the watch he was wearing.'

'I've known him a long time.'

'Yes, so he said.'

She tickled Richard under his chin. 'Say hallo to your Daddy, Richard. He doesn't often get home to see you in the daytime.'

'Is it going to be like this all the time, barbed remarks, snide little references to the fact that I'm not home? Will he grow up like this and the next one, bad daddy, neglectful daddy . . . is that the way it's going to be?'

Her face was contrite. And in as much as he understood her at all, he thought she was sincere.

'Harry, I can't tell you how much I didn't mean that to be a barbed remark. I swear I didn't. I was pleased to see you, I was speaking stupid baby talk telling *him* to be pleased too. Believe me it's not going to be full of barbed remarks, I hate it in other people, we won't have it.'

For months she hadn't approached him, made a gesture of affection to him. But she saw him standing there desolate and her heart went out to him. She crossed to where he was standing. 'Harry, please don't be like this, please. You are so good to me, we have such a nice life. Can't we get the best from it, get joy from it, instead of acting watchful and guarded the way we do?'

He didn't raise his hands to her even though her arms were around his neck. 'You didn't ask me did I sign,' he said.

She pulled away. 'I know you did.'

'Why do you know that? Did they call the moment I left the office?'

'No, of course they wouldn't.' She looked scornful of such a thought.

'Why not, a job well done?'

'You signed because it was fair, and because you realise it was for your own good in the end,' she said.

Then he pulled her towards him and felt the bump in her stomach resting against him. Another child, another Kane for the dynasty he wanted in this fine house. 'I wish you loved me,' he said.

'I do.'

'Not in the way that matters,' he said. And his voice was so sad.

'I try. I try, you know I'm there every night if you want me. I'd like you to sleep in the same bed in the same room, it's you who wants to be separate.'

'I came home very, very angry, Connie. I wanted to tell you that you were a bitch going behind my back like that, taking me for every penny I have. I kept thinking you were well named Connie, a real con woman all right . . . I wanted to tell you a lot of things.' She stood there waiting. 'But honestly I think you made just as big a mistake as I did. You are just as unhappy.'

'I'm more lonely than unhappy,' she said.

'Call it whatever you like,' he shrugged. 'Will you be less lonely now that you've got your money?'

'I imagine I'll be less frightened,' she said.

'What were you frightened of? That I'd lose it all like your old man did, that you'd have to be poor again?'

'No, that's totally wrong.' She spoke with great clearness. He knew she was telling the truth. 'No, I never minded being poor. I could earn a living, something my mother couldn't do. But I was afraid of being bitter like she became, I was afraid that I would hate you if I had to go back to a job that you made me leave, and go in at the bottom rung again. I couldn't bear the children to have grown up in expectation of one kind of life and end up in another. I know that from experience, so those were things I was frightened of. We had so much going for us, we were always so well suited, everywhere except in bed. I wanted that to go on until we died.'

'I see.'

'Can't you be my friend, Harry? I love you and want the best for you, even if I don't seem to be able to show it.'

'I don't know,' he said, picking up his car keys to leave again. 'I don't know. I'd like to be your friend, but I don't think I can trust you and you have to trust friends.' He spoke to the gurgling Richard in his high chair. 'Be good to your mummy, kid, she may look as if she has it nice and easy, but it's not all that great for her either.' And when he had gone Connie cried until she thought her heart would break.

The new baby was a girl. She was called Veronica, and then a year later there were the twins. When the scan showed two embryos Connie was overjoyed. Twins had run in her family, how marvellous. She thought Harry too would be delighted. 'I can see you're pleased,' he said very coldly. 'That makes four. Bargain completed. Curtains drawn on all that nasty, messy business. What a relief.'

'You can be very, very cruel,' she said.

To the outside world they were of course the perfect couple. Mr Hayes, whose own daughter Marianne was growing up as a young beauty much sought after by the fortune-hunting young men of Dublin, was still a good friend of Connie's and often consulted her about the hotel business. If he suspected that her eyes were sometimes sad he said nothing.

He heard rumours that Harry Kane was not an entirely faithful man. He had been spotted here and there with other women. He still had the pathetic devoted secretary in tow. But as the years went on the watchful Mr Hayes decided the couple must have come to some accommodation.

The eldest boy, Richard, was doing well at school and even playing on the first fifteen in the schools rugby cup, the girl Veronica was determined to do medicine and had no other aim since she was twelve, and the twins were fine boisterous boys.

The Kanes still hosted marvellous parties and were seen together in public a lot. Connie went through her thirties more elegantly than any other well-dressed woman of her generation. She never seemed to spend much time studying fashion, nor did she specialise in buying the designer outfits she could well afford, but she always looked perfectly groomed.

She wasn't happy. Of course she wasn't happy. But then Connie thought that a lot of people lived life hoping that things would get better, and that lights would turn on, or the film turn into Technicolor.

Maybe that's the way most people lived, and all this talk about happiness was for the birds. Having worked in a hotel for so long she knew how many people were lonely and inadequate. You saw that side of life amongst the guests. Then on the various charity committees she saw many members who were there only to banish the hours of emptiness, people who suggested more and more coffee-morning meetings because there was nothing else to fill their lives.

She read a lot of books, saw every play that she wanted to, and made little trips to London or down to Kerry.

Harry never had time for a family holiday, he said. She often wondered whether the children realised that his partners went on family holidays with their wives and children. But children could be very unobservant. Other women went abroad with their husbands, but Connie never did. Harry went abroad a lot. It was connected with work, he said. She wondered wryly what work there could be for his investment company in the south of Spain or on a newly developed resort in the Greek Islands. But she said nothing.

Harry only went out for sex. He loved it. She had not been able to give it to him, it was unfair of her to deny it to him elsewhere. And she was not at all jealous of his sexual intimacy with Siobhan Casey and whoever else there might be. One of Connie's friends had once cried and cried over a husband's infidelity. She said that the very thought of him doing with another woman what he did with her made her sick to the point of madness. It didn't bother Connie at all.

What she would have liked was for him to get that side of things over with outside the home and be a loving friend within it. She would have been happy to share his bedroom and his plans and hopes and dreams. Was this utterly unreasonable? It seemed a hard punishment to be cut off from everything because she wasn't able to mate with him in a way that gave him pleasure. She had after all produced four fine children for him, and surely he could see that this rated some way in his evaluation of things.

Connie knew that some people thought she should leave Harry. Vera, for example. She didn't say it straight out, but she hinted at it. And so had Mr Hayes in the hotel. They both assumed she stayed with him only for security.

They didn't know how well her finances were organised and that she could have left that house a woman of independent means.

So why did she stay?

Because it was better for the family. Because the children needed both parents there. Because it required so much bloody effort to change everything and there was no guarantee that she would be any happier elsewhere. And it wasn't as if this was a *bad* life. Harry was courteous and pleasant when he was there. There was plenty to do, she had no trouble filling the hours that turned into weeks, months and years.

She visited her own mother and Harry's parents. She still entertained the partners and their wives. She provided a home for her children's friends. The sound of tennis balls on the court, or music from their rooms, was always in the background. The Kane household was highly regarded by the next generation because Mrs Kane didn't fuss and Mr Kane was hardly ever there, two things people liked in their friends' parents.

And then when Richard Kane was nineteen, the same age that Connie had been when her father died and left them bankrupt, Harry Kane came home and told them the dream was over. The company was closing the very next day with the maximum of scandal, and the minimum of resources. They would leave bad debts all over the country, people whose investments and life savings were lost. One of his partners had to be restrained from committing suicide, the other from fleeing the country.

They sat in the dining room, Connie, Richard and Veronica. The twins were away on a school trip. They sat in silence while Harry Kane laid out how bad it would be. Across seven or eight columns in the newspapers. Reporters at the door, photographers struggling to capture images of the tennis court, the luxurious lifestyle of the man who had swindled the country. There would be names of politicians who had favoured them, details of trips abroad. Big names associated once now denying any real relationship.

What had caused it? Cutting corners, taking risks, accepting people whom others had thought unreliable. Not asking questions where they should have been asked. Not noticing things that should have been noticed by more established companies.

'Will we have to sell the house?' Richard asked. There was a silence.

'Will there be any money for university?' Veronica wanted to know. Another silence.

Then Harry spoke. 'I should say to you both now at this point that your mother always warned me that this could happen. She warned me and I didn't listen. So when you look back on this day, remember that.'

'Oh Dad, it doesn't matter,' Veronica said in exactly the same tone that Connie would have used had her own father been alive when his financial disasters emerged. She saw Harry's eyes fill with tears.

'It could happen to anyone,' Richard said bravely. 'That's business for you.'

Connie's heart felt glad. They had brought up generous children, not little pups expecting the world as a right. Connie realised it was time to speak. 'As soon as your father began to tell me this bad news I asked him to wait until you could be there, I wanted us all to hear it together and react to it as a family. In a way it's a blessing the twins aren't here, I'll sort them out later. What we are going to do now is leave this house, this evening. We are going to pack small suitcases, enough to do us for a week. I'll ask Vera and Kevin to send round vans to pick us up so that any journalists already outside won't see us leaving in our cars. We'll put a message on the machine saying that all telephone queries are to be addressed to Siobhan Casey. I presume that's right, Harry?'

He nodded, astounded. 'Right.'

'You will go to stay with my mother in the country. Nobody will know where she is or bother her. Use her phone to call your friends and tell them that it's all going to be fine in the end, but until it dies down you're going to be out of sight for a bit. Say you'll be back in ten days. No story lasts that long.' They looked at her, open-mouthed.

'And yes of course you'll both go to university, and the twins. And we will probably sell this house but not immediately, not at the whim of any bank.'

'But won't we have to pay what's owing?' Richard asked.

'This house doesn't belong to your father,' Connie said simply.

'But even if it's yours, wouldn't you have to . . . ?'

'No, it's not mine. It was long ago bought by another company of which I am a director.'

'Oh Dad, aren't you clever!' Richard said.

There was a moment. 'Yes, your father is an extremely clever businessman, and when he makes a bargain he keeps it. He won't want people to be out of pocket, so I feel sure that we won't end up as villains out of all this. But for the moment it's going to be quite hard, so we're going to need all the courage and faith we can gather.'

And then the evening became a blur of gathering things and making phone calls. They moved out of the house unseen in the back of decorators' vans.

A white-faced Vera and Kevin welcomed them both into their home. There was no small chat to be made, no sympathy to be offered or received, so they went straight to the room that had been prepared for them, the best guest room with its large double bed. A plate of cold supper and a flask of hot soup had been left out for them.

'See you tomorrow,' Vera said.

'How do people know exactly what to say?' Harry asked.

'I suppose they wonder what they'd like themselves.' Connie poured him a small mug of soup. He shook his head. 'Take it, Harry. You may need it tomorrow.'

'Does Kevin have all his insurance tied up with us?'

'No, none of it,' Connie spoke calmly.

'How's that?'

'I asked them not to, just in case.'

'What am I going to do, Connie?'

'You're going to face it. Say it failed, you didn't want it to happen, you're going to stay in the country and work at whatever you can.'

'They'll tear me to pieces.'

'Only for a while. Then it will be the next story.'

'And you?'

'I'll go back to work.'

'But what about the money all those lawyers salted away for you?'

'I'll keep as much as I need to get the children sorted, then I'll put the rest back in to pay the people who lost their savings.'

'God, you're not doing the Christian martyr bit on top of everything else?'

'What would you suggest I do with what is after all my money, Harry?' Her eyes were hard.

'Keep it. Thank your lucky stars that you saved it, don't plough it back in.'

'You don't mean that. We'll talk about it tomorrow.'

'I mean it. This is business, it's not a gentleman's cricket match. That's the whole point of having a limited company, they can only get what's in it. You took your bit out, what in God's name was the point if you're going to throw it back in again?'

'Tomorrow,' she said.

'Take that prissy po-faced look off you, Connie, and be normal for once in your whole goddamned life. Stop acting for five minutes and let's have less of the pious crap about giving the poor investors back their money. They knew what they were doing like anyone knows. Like your father knew what he was doing when he put your university fees on some horse that's still running.'

Her face was white. She stood up and walked to the door. 'Very high and mighty. Go on, leave rather than talk it out. Go down to your friend Vera and talk about the pure badness of men. Maybe it was Vera you should have moved in with in the first place. Could be that it was a woman you needed to get you going?'

She hadn't intended to do it, but she hit him right across the face. It was because he was shouting about Vera in her own house, when Vera and Kevin had rescued them, asked no questions. Harry didn't seem like a person any more, he was like an animal that had turned wild.

Her rings drew blood from his cheek, a long smear of red. And to her surprise she felt no shock at the blood, no shame at what she had done.

She closed the door and went downstairs. At the kitchen table they had obviously heard the shouting from above, possibly even the words he had been saying. Connie, who had been so calm and in control during the previous hours, looked around the little group. There was Deirdre, Vera's handsome dark-eyed daughter, who worked in a fashion boutique, and Charlie, who had joined the family business of painting and decorating.

And between Kevin and Vera in front of a bottle of whiskey was Jacko. Jacko with a collar wide open and red wild eyes. Jacko who had been crying and drinking and hadn't finished doing either. She realised in seconds that he had lost every penny in her husband's investment company. Her first boyfriend, who had loved her simply and without complication, who had stood outside the church the day she was marrying Harry in the hope that she wouldn't go through with it, he sat now at his friends' kitchen table, bankrupt. How had all this happened, Connie wondered, as she stood there with her hand at her throat for what seemed an age?

She couldn't stay in this room. She couldn't go back upstairs to where Harry waited like a raging lion with further abuse and self-disgust. She couldn't go outside into the real world, she would never be able to do that again and look people in the eye. Did people attract bad luck and encourage others to behave badly? She thought that the statistics against someone having both a father and a husband who lost everything must be enormous unless you decided that it was something in your own personality that drew you to exactly the same kind of weakness in the second as you had known in the first.

She remembered suddenly the open-faced friendly psychiatrist asking all those questions about her father. Could there have been anything in it? She thought she had been there a long time but they didn't seem to have moved, so perhaps it had only been a couple of seconds.

Then Jacko spoke. His voice was slurred. 'I hope you're satisfied now,' he said.

The others were silent.

In a voice that was clear and steady as always, Connie spoke. 'No, Jacko, this is an odd thing to say, but I have never been satisfied, not in my whole life.' Her eyes seemed far away. 'I may have had twenty years of money, which should have made me happy. Truthfully, it didn't. I've been lonely and acting a part for most of my adult life. Anyway, that's no help to you now.'

'No, it's not.' His face was mutinous. He was still handsome and eager. His marriage had failed, she knew from Vera, and his wife had taken the boy he cared about.

His business had been everything to him. And now that was gone. 'You'll get it all back,' she said.

'Oh yes?' His laugh sounded more like a bark.

'Yes, there *is* money there.'

'I bet there is, in Jersey or the Cayman Islands or maybe in the wife's name,' Jacko sneered.

'Quite a lot of it *is* in the wife's name, as it happens,' she said.

Vera and Kevin looked at her open-mouthed. Jacko couldn't take it in.

'So I got lucky by being an old boyfriend of the wife, is that what you're telling me?' He didn't know whether to believe it was a lifeline or throw it back in her face.

'I suppose I'm telling you that a lot of people got lucky because of the wife. If he's sane enough in the morning, I'll get him to the bank before his press conference.'

'If it's yours why don't you keep it?' Jacko asked.

'Because I'm not, despite what you might think, a total shit. Vera, can I sleep somewhere else, like on the couch in the television room?'

Vera came in with her and handed her a rug. 'You're the strongest woman I ever met,' Vera said.

'You're the best friend anyone ever had,' said Connie.

Would it have been good to have loved Vera? To have lived together for years with flower gardens, and maybe a small crafts business to show for their commitment. She smiled wanly at the thought.

'What has you laughing in the middle of all this?' Vera asked.

'Remind me to tell you one day, you'll never believe it,' said Connie as she kicked off her shoes and lay down on the couch.

Amazingly she slept, and only woke to the sound of a cup and saucer rattling. It was Harry, pale-faced with a long dark red scar standing out from his cheek. She had forgotten that particular part of last night.

'I brought you coffee,' he said.

'Thank you.' She made no move to take it.

'I'm so desperately sorry.'

'Yes.'

'I am so sorry. Jesus, Connie, I just went mad last night. All I ever wanted was to be somebody and I nearly was and then I blew it.' He had dressed carefully and shaved around the wound on his face. He was up and ready for the longest day he would ever have to live through. She looked at him as if she had never seen him before, as the people who saw him on television would see him, all the strangers who had lost their savings, and the people who had come across him in business deals or at social gatherings. A handsome hungry man, all he wanted was to be somebody and he didn't care how he got there.

Then she saw he was crying.

'I need you desperately, Connie. You've been acting all your life with me, could you just act for a little bit longer and pretend you have forgiven me? Please, Connie, I need you. You're the only one who can help me.' He laid his face with the livid scar on her knees, and he sobbed like a child.

She couldn't really remember the day. It was like trying to put together the pieces of a horror movie that you have covered your eyes for, or a nightmare that won't go away. There was some of it set in the lawyer's office, where the terms of the trust she had set up for her children's education were explained to him. The money had been well invested. There was plenty. The rest had been equally well placed for her. Constance Kane was a very wealthy woman. She could see the scorn that the solicitor had for her husband. He hardly bothered to disguise it. Her father's old friend T. P. Murphy was there, silent and more silver-haired than ever. His face was set in a grim line. There was an accountant and an investment manager. They spoke in front of the great Harry Kane as they would before a common swindler. In their eyes this is what he was. This time yesterday morning, Connie reflected, those people would have treated her husband with respect. How quickly things changed in business.

Then they went to the bank. Never were bankers more surprised to see funds appear from nowhere. Connie and Harry sat silently while their advisers told the bank that not one penny of this *need* be recovered, and that it was being given only if the bank promised a package to rescue the investors.

By midday they had a deal. Harry's partners were summoned and ordered to remain silent during the press conference at Hayes Hotel. It was agreed that neither of the partners' wives would attend. They watched it together on a television set in one of the hotel bedrooms. Connie's name was not mentioned. It was just stated that emergency funds had been put aside against just such a contingency.

By the one o'clock news the morning papers' headlines were obsolete. One of the journalists asked Harry Kane about the wound on his face. Was it a creditor?

'It was someone who didn't understand what was happening, who didn't realise we would do everything under the sun to safeguard the people who had trust in us,' Harry said, straight to camera.

And Connie felt a little sick, a wave of nausea sweeping over her. If he could lie like that, what else could he not do? As part of the audience Connie saw Siobhan Casey at the back of the big hotel room where the press conference was being held. She wondered how much Siobhan had known, and whether money would be taken from Connie's fund to provide for her. But she would never find out. She had assured the bank that since the whole thing would be administered by them, there would be no need for a policing operation from her side. She knew the money would be fairly and wisely distributed. It wasn't up to her to say that Siobhan Casey's shares should not be honoured because she was sleeping with the boss.

They were able to go back to their house. In a week they were all beginning to breathe again. In three months things were almost back to normal.

Veronica asked him from time to time about his poor face. 'Oh that will always be there to remind your father what a foolish man he was,' he would say, and Connie saw the look of affection pass between them.

Richard seemed to have nothing but admiration for his father as well. Both children thought he had grown from the whole experience.

'He spends much more time at home now, doesn't he, Mum?' Veronica said, as if asking for Connie's approval and blessing on something.

'Indeed he does,' Connie said. Harry spent one night away each week and came home late to his bedroom two or three nights. This was going to be the pattern of their future.

Something in Connie wanted to change it but she was tired. She was weary from the years of pretence, she knew no other life.

She telephoned Jacko one day at work.

'I suppose I'm meant to go down on my knees to thank her ladyship for the fact that I got my own money back.'

'No, Jacko, I just thought you might want to meet or something.'

'For what?' he asked.

'I don't know, to talk, go to the pictures. Did you ever learn Italian?'

'No, I was too busy earning a living.' She was silent. She must have made him feel guilty. 'Did you?' he asked.

'No, I was too busy not earning a living.'

He laughed. 'Jesus, Connie, there'd be no point in our meeting. I'd only fall for you all over again, and start pestering you to come to bed with me as I was doing all those years back.'

'Not *still*, Jacko, are you still into all that sort of thing?'

'By God I am, and why not? Aren't I only in my prime?'

'True, true.'

'Connie?'

'Yes?'

'Just, you know. Thank you. You know.'

'I know, Jacko.'

The months went by. Nothing had changed very much but if you looked closely you would know that a lot of the life had gone out of Connie Kane.

Kevin and Vera talked about it. They were among the few who knew how she had rescued her husband. They felt strongly that he was not showing any serious gratitude. Everyone knew that he was seen publicly with his one-time personal assistant, the enigmatic Siobhan Casey, who was now a director of the company.

Connie's mother knew that her daughter had lost a lot of her spirit. She tried to cheer her up. 'It wasn't permanent, the damage he did to you, not like in my case, and he did have that emergency fund ready. Your father never had that.' Connie never told her. A sort of loyalty to Harry was one reason, but mainly she didn't want to admit that her mother had been right all those years ago about demanding her own money and getting independence from it.

Her children didn't notice. Mother was just Mother, marvellous and always here when you wanted her. She seemed happy in herself and meeting her friends.

Richard qualified as an accountant and Mr Hayes got him a splendid position with his son-in-law's firm. The beloved only daughter Marianne had married a handsome and very charming man called Paul Malone. The Hayes money and his own personality had helped him high up a ladder. Richard was happy there.

Veronica was racing through her medical studies. She was thinking of specialising in psychiatry, she said, most of people's troubles were in the heads and in their past.

The twins had finally separated in identity, one to go to Art College, one to join the Civil Service. Their big house was still in Connie's name. It had not been necessary to sell it when the money was being raised for the rescue package. Connie's solicitors kept pressurising her to draw up another formal document with similar provisions to the original arrangement, guaranteeing her part of the profits, but she was loath to do it.

'That was all years ago when I needed to assure the children's future,' she said.

'Strictly speaking it should be done again. If there was a problem a court would almost certainly decide for you within the spirit of the law, but ...'

'What sort of problem could there be now?' Connie had asked.

The solicitor, who had often seen Mr Kane dining in Quentin's with a woman who was not Mrs Kane, was tight-lipped. 'I would much prefer it done,' he said.

'All right, but not with big dramas and humiliating him. The past is the past.'

'It will be done with the minimum of drama, Mrs Kane,' the solicitor said.

And it was. Papers were sent to Harry's office to be signed. There were no confrontations. His face was hard the day he signed them. She knew him so well and could read his moods. He wouldn't tell her straight out, he would somehow try to punish her for it.

'I'll be away for a few days,' he said that evening. No explanation, no pretence. She was preparing their supper but she knew he wasn't going to stay and share it. Still, old habits die hard. Connie was used to pretending everything was fine even when it was not. She went on tossing the tomato and fennel salad carefully, as if it were something that required a huge amount of care and concentration.

'Will that be tiring?' she asked, careful not to ask where and why and with whom.

'Not really,' his voice was brittle. 'I decided to combine it with a few days' rest as well.'

'That will be good,' she said.

'It's in the Bahamas,' he said. The silence hung between them.

'Oh,' she said.

'No objection? I mean you don't consider it our special place or anything?' She didn't answer but went to take the warm bacon flan from the oven. 'Still, of course you'll have all your investments, your handcuffs, your share of everything, your rights, to console you when I'm away.' He was so angry he could hardly speak.

Only a few short years ago he had cried to her on his knees with gratitude, said that he didn't deserve her, sworn that she would never know another lonely hour. Now he was white-lipped with rage that she continued to protect her investment after it had been shown to be only too necessary.

'You know that's only a formality,' she said.

His face had turned to a sneer. 'As this business trip I'm going on is a formality,' he said. He went upstairs to pack.

She realised he was going to Siobhan's flat tonight, they would leave tomorrow. She sat down and ate her supper. She was used to eating supper alone. It was a late summer evening, she could hear the birds in the garden, the muffled sound of cars out on the road beyond their high garden walls. There were a dozen places she could go this evening if she wanted to.

What she would like to do was meet Jacko and go to the pictures. Just stand in O'Connell Street looking at what was on and arguing with him over which film they would choose. But it was such a ludicrous notion. He had been right, there was nothing left to say now. It would be playing games, going up to the working-class estate where he lived and hooting the horn of the BMW outside his house. Only fools thought they might have been happier if they had taken a different turning and wasted a lifetime regretting it. She might not have been at all happier if she had married Jacko, she would possibly have hated being in bed with him too. But somehow it might have been less lonely.

She was reading the evening paper when Harry came back downstairs with two suitcases. It was going to be a serious holiday in the Bahamas. He seemed to be both relieved and piqued at the same time that there was going to be no scene about his leaving.

She looked up and smiled at him over her glasses. 'When will I say you'll be back?' she asked.

'Say? Who do you need to say it to?'

'Well, your children for one thing, but I'm sure you'll tell them you're going, and friends or anyone from the office or the bank.'

'The office will know,' he said.

'That's fine, then I can refer them to Siobhan?' Her face was innocent.

'Siobhan's going to the Bahamas too, as you very well know.'

'So, to someone else then?'

'I wouldn't have gone at all, Connie, if you'd behaved reasonably, not like some kind of tax inspector, hedging me here and confining me there.'

'But if it's a business trip you have to go, don't you?' she said, and he went out, slamming the door. She tried to go on reading the paper. There had been too many scenes like this, where he left and she cried. It was no way to live a life.

She read an interview with a schoolmaster who was setting up an evening class in Italian up in Mountainview school, a big community school or college in a tough area. It was Jacko's area. Mr Aidan Dunne said he thought people from the neighbourhood would be interested in learning about the life and culture of Italy as well as the language. Since the World Cup there had been a huge interest in Italy among ordinary Dubliners. They would offer a very varied programme. Connie read the piece again. It was quite possible that Jacko might enrol. And if not, she would be in his part of the forest two nights a week. There was a telephone number, she would book now before she changed her mind.

Of course Jacko hadn't signed on for the class. That kind of thing only happened in fantasy. But Connie enjoyed it. This wonderful woman, Signora, not much older than she was, had all the gifts of a born teacher. She never raised her voice, yet she had everyone's attention. She never criticised but she expected people to learn what she marked out for them.

'*Constanza* ... I'm afraid you don't know the clock properly, you only know *sono le due, sono le tre* ... that would be fine if it was always something o'clock but you have to learn half past and a quarter to.'

'I'm sorry, Signora,' Mrs Constance Kane would say, abashed. 'I was a bit busy, I didn't get it learned.'

'Next week you will know it perfectly,' Signora would cry and Connie found herself with her fingers in her ears saying *sono le sei e venti*. How had it come about that she was going up to this barracks of a school miles away and sitting in a classroom with thirty strangers chanting and singing and identifying great paintings and statues and buildings, tasting Italian food and listening to Italian operas? And what's more, loving it.

She tried to tell Harry about it when he returned tanned and less acerbic from the West Indies. But he didn't show much interest.

'What's taking you up to that bloody place, you want to watch your hubcaps up there,' he said. His only comment on the whole undertaking.

Vera didn't like it either. 'It's a tough place, you're tempting fate bringing your good car up there, and God, Connie, take off that gold watch.'

'I'm not going to regard it as a ghetto, that would be patronising.'

'I don't know what has you there at all, aren't there plenty of places nearer to you where you could learn Italian if you want to?'

'I like this one, I'm always half hoping I'll meet Jacko at one of the classes,' Connie smiled mischievously.

'God Almighty, haven't you had enough trouble in one lifetime without inviting more in?' Vera said, raising her eyes to heaven. Vera had her hands full, she was still running the office for Kevin and minding her grandson as well. Deirdre had produced an enormous and gorgeous baby but had said that she didn't want to be shackled by outdated concepts of marriage and slavery.

Connie liked the other people in the class, the serious Bill Burke, Guglielmo, and his dramatic girl friend Elizabetta. He worked in the bank which had put together the rescue package for Harry and his partners, but he was too young to have known about it. And even if he had, how would he have recognised her as Constanza? The gutsy young couple of women Caterina and Francesca, hard to know if they were sisters or mother and daughter, they were good company.

There was the big, decent Lorenzo with hands the size of shovels playing the part of a guest in a restaurant, with Connie as the waitress.

Una tavola vicina alla finestra, Lorenzo would say, and Connie would move a cardboard box to where there was a drawing of a window and seat him there, waiting while Lorenzo thought up dishes he would like to order. Lorenzo learned all kinds of new dishes, like eels, goose liver and sea urchins. Signora would remonstrate and tell him to learn only the list she had provided.

'You don't understand, Signora, these people I'll be meeting in Italy, they'll be classy eaters, they wouldn't be your pizza merchants.'

Then there was the terrifying Luigi with the dark scowl and particular way of murdering the Italian language. He was someone she would never have met in the ordinary run of things, yet sometimes he was her partner, like the time they were playing doctors and nurses with pretend stethoscopes, telling each other to breathe deeply. *Respiri profondamente per favore*, *Signora* Luigi would shout, listening to one end of a rubber hose. *Non mi sento bene*, Connie would reply.

And gradually they were all getting less self-conscious and more united in this far-fetched dream of a holiday in Italy next summer. Connie, who could have paid for everyone in the class to take a scheduled flight, joined in the discussions of sponsorship and cost-cutting and putting down early deposits for a group charter. If they got the trip together she would certainly go.

Connie noticed that the school was improving week by week. It was getting a definite face-lift, a new coat of paint, trees planted, the school yard smartened up. The broken bicycle sheds were replaced.

'You're doing a real make-over here,' she said approvingly to the shaggy, attractive looking Principal Mr O'Brien, who came in from time to time to give his general praise to the Italian class.

'Uphill work, Mrs Kane, if you could put a word in for us to those financiers you and your husband meet we'd be grateful.' He knew who she was all right, there was no calling her Constanza like all the others. But he was pleasantly incurious about what she was doing there.

'They are people without hearts, Mr O'Brien. They don't understand about schools being a country's future.'

'Tell me about it,' he sighed. 'Don't I spend half my life in bloody banks and filling in forms. I've forgotten how to teach.'

'And do you have a wife and family, Mr O'Brien?' Connie didn't know why she had asked him such a personal question. It was out of character for her to be intrusive. In the hotel business she had learned the wisdom of listening rather than enquiring.

'No, I don't as it happens,' he said.

'Better, I suppose, if you're kind of wedded to a school. I think a lot of people should never marry. My own husband is a case in point,' she said.

He raised an eyebrow. Connie realised she had gone too far for pleasant casual conversation. 'Sorry,' she laughed. 'I'm not doing the lonely wife bit, I was just stating a fact.'

'I would love to be married, that's a fact too,' he said. It was polite of him to exchange a confidence. One had been given, it was courtesy to return one. 'Problem was, I never met anyone that I wanted to marry until I was too old.'

'You're not too old now, surely?'

'I am, because it's the wrong person, like she's a child. She's Mr Dunne's child actually,' he said, nodding his head back at the school where Aidan Dunne and Signora were saying goodnight to the members of the class.

'And does she love you?'

'I hope so, I think so, but I'm wrong for her, far too old. I'm *so* wrong for her. And there are other problems.'

'What does Mr Dunne think?'

'He doesn't know, Mrs Kane.'

She let out a deep breath. 'I see what you mean about there being problems,' she said. 'I'll leave you to try and sort them out.'

He grinned at her, grateful that she asked no more. 'Your husband is a madman to be married to his business,' he said.

'Thank you, Mr O'Brien.' She got into her car and drove home. Since joining this class she was learning the most extraordinary things about people.

That amazing girl with the curls, Elizabetta, had told her that Guglielmo was going to manage a bank in Italy next year when he had a command of the language; the glowering Luigi had asked her would an ordinary person know if someone was wearing a ring worth twelve grand. Aidan Dunne had asked her did she know where you could buy brightly coloured second-hand carpets. Bartolomeo wanted to know if she had ever come across people who committed suicide and did they always try it again. It was just for a friend, he had said several times. Caterina, who was either the sister or the daughter of Francesca, impossible to know, had said that she had lunch in Quentin's one day and the artichokes were terrific. Lorenzo kept telling her that the family he was going to stay with in Italy were so rich that he hoped he wouldn't disgrace himself. And now Mr O'Brien said that he was having an affair with Mr Dunne's daughter.

A couple of months back she had known none of these people or their lives.

When it rained she would give people a lift home, but she didn't do it regularly in case she became an unofficial taxi service. But she had a soft spot for Lorenzo, who had to take two buses to get back to his nephew's hotel. This was where he lived and worked as an odd-job man and night porter. Everyone else went home to bed or television or to the pub or a café after class. But Lorenzo went back to work. He had said that the lift had made all the difference in the world, so Connie made sure she drove him.

His real name was Laddy, she learned. But they all called each other their Italian names, it made it easier in class. Laddy had been invited by some Italians to come and visit them in Rome. He was a big, simple, cheerful man of around sixty who found nothing odd about being driven back to his hotel porter's job by a woman in a top-of-the-range car.

Sometimes he talked of his nephew Gus, his sister's boy, a lad who had worked every hour God sent, and now there was every possibility he would lose his hotel.

There had been a scare a while back, an insurance and investment company that had failed. But at the last moment hadn't it all come right and they were all to get their money after all. Lorenzo's sister was in the Hospice at the time, and it nearly broke her heart. But God had been good, she lived long enough to know that her only son Gus would not be bankrupt. She died happy after that. Connie bit her lip as the story was being told. These were the people that Harry would have walked out on.

So what was the new problem, she wondered? Well, it was all part of the old problem. The company that had been in trouble and that had honoured its debts in the end had made them all re-invest, a very large sum. It was as if to thank the company for having stood by them when it hadn't needed to. Lorenzo's understanding of it was vague, but his concern was enormous. Gus was at the end of his tether, he had been down every avenue. The hotel needed improvement, the Health Authorities had said that it could well be a fire hazard, there were no resources left. Everything that he could have called on was gone in this new investment, and there was no way he could cash it in. Apparently there was some law in the Bahamas that you needed an unholy amount of advance notice before you could get at it.

Connie pulled the car into the side of the road when she heard this.

'Could you tell me about it again, please, Lorenzo.' Her face was white.
'I'm no financial expert myself, Constanza.'
'Can I talk to your nephew? Please.'
'He mightn't like my telling his business . . .' Lorenzo was almost sorry he had confided in this kind woman.
'Please, Lorenzo.'
During the conversation with the worried Gus Connie had to ask for a brandy. The story was so squalid, so shabby. For the last five years since their investment had been saved Gus, and presumably many, many others like him, had been persuaded to invest in two entirely separate companies based in Freeport and Nassau.
With tears in her eyes Connie read that the directors were Harold Kane and Siobhan Casey. Gus and Lorenzo looked at her uncomprehending. First she took out her chequebook and wrote Gus a very substantial cheque, then she gave them the address of builders and decorators who were good friends of hers and would do an expert job. She wrote the name of an electrical firm as well, but suggested that they should not use her name in this context.
'But why are you doing all this, Constanza?' Gus was totally bewildered.
Connie pointed at the names on the stationery. 'That man is my husband, that woman is his mistress. I have turned a blind eye to their affair for years. I don't *care* that he sleeps with her, but by God I do care that he has used my money to defraud decent people.' She knew she must look mad and wild eyed to them.
Gus spoke gently. 'I can't take this money, Mrs Kane, I can't. It's far too much.'
'See you Tuesday, Lorenzo,' she said, and she was gone.

So many Thursday nights when she had let herself into the house she had hoped he would be at home and he so rarely was. Tonight was no exception. It was late, but she telephoned her father's old friend the barrister T. P. Murphy. Then the solicitor. She fixed a meeting for the following morning. There were no apologies or recriminations. It was eleven o'clock at night when they had finished talking to her.
'What will you do now?' she asked the solicitor.
'Phone Harcourt Square,' he said succinctly. That was where the Garda Fraud Investigation Unit was based.
He had not come home that night. She had not slept.

She realised that it had been a ridiculous house to have kept for so long. The children all lived in their own apartments. Pale-faced, she drove herself into the city and parked her car. Taking a deep breath she walked up the steps of her husband's office to a meeting that would end his life as he knew it.
They had told her that there would be a lot of publicity, most of it unfavourable, the mud would stick to her too. They suggested she find somewhere else to stay. Years ago she had bought a small apartment in case her mother had ever wanted to come and live in Dublin. It was on the ground floor and near the sea. It would be ideal. She could move her things in there in a matter of hours.

'Hours is what it will be,' they told her.

She saw him on his own at her request.

He sat in his office watching as files and software were taken away. 'All I wanted was to be somebody,' he said.

'You told me that before.'

'Well, I'm telling you again. Just because you say something twice doesn't mean it's not true.'

'You were somebody, you were always somebody. That's not what you wanted, you wanted to have everything.'

'You didn't have to do it, you know, you were all right.'

'I was always all right,' she said.

'No, you weren't, you were a tense frigid jealous bitch and still are.'

'I was never jealous of what Siobhan Casey could give you, never,' she spoke simply.

'So why did you do it?'

'Because it wasn't fair. You had your warning, you were rescued, wasn't that enough?'

'You know nothing of men. Nothing.' He almost spat the words. 'Not only do you not know how to please them, you actually think that a man could be a real man and accept your money and pats on the head.'

'It would be a help if you were strong for the children's sake,' she said.

'Get out of here, Connie.'

'They loved you all through the last time, they really did. They have lives of their own but you are their father. You didn't care much about your father, but most people do.'

'You really hate me, don't you, you'll rejoice that I'm in gaol.'

'No, and you probably won't serve much time, if any. You'll get away with things, you always do.' She left the office.

She saw Siobhan Casey's name on a brass plate on her door. Inside that office files and software were also being removed. Siobhan apparently had no family or friends to give her support. She was sitting with bankers, inspectors in the Fraud Squad and lawyers.

Connie's steps never faltered as she walked out the door and pressed the remote switch that opened her car. Then she got in and drove to her new apartment by the sea.

Laddy

When Signora was choosing Italian names for people she tried to make sure that they had the same initial rather than being too purist about the translation. There was a woman there called Gertie. Strictly speaking that should have been Margaret, then Margaretta. But Gertie would never have recognised her own name in that form so she was called Gloria. In fact, she decided that she liked the name Gloria so much that she might keep it ever after.

The big man with the eager face said he was called Laddy. Signora paused. No future in trying to work out the origins. Give him something that he might like to roll around. 'Lorenzo,' she cried.

Laddy liked it. 'Is that what all the people called Laddy in Italy call themselves?' he asked.

'That's it, Lorenzo,' Signora rolled out the name again for him.

'Lorenzo, would you credit it?' Laddy was delighted with the name. He said it over and over. '*Mi chiamo Lorenzo.*'

When Laddy was christened in the 1930s the name they gave him at the font was John Matthew Joseph Byrne, but he was never called anything except Laddy. The only boy after five girls, his arrival meant that the small farm would be safe. There would be a man to run it.

But things don't always turn out the way people think.

Laddy was coming home from school, the mile and a half through puddles and under dripping trees, when he saw his sisters coming out to meet him and he knew that something terrible had happened. He thought first that something had happened to Tripper, the collie dog he loved so much. Maybe it had hurt its paw or been bitten by a rat.

He tried to run past them, the crying girls, but they held him back and told him that Mam and Dad had gone to heaven, and that from now on they would look after him.

'They can't have both gone at the same time.'

Laddy was eight, he knew things. People went to heaven one by one and everyone wore black and cried.

But it had happened. They had been killed at a level crossing, pulling a cart that had got stuck in the rails, and the train was on top of them before they realised it. Laddy knew that God had wanted them, that it was their time, but all through the years he wondered why God had chosen that way.

It had caused such upset and hurt for everyone. The poor man who had been driving the train was never the same again and went to a mental home. The people who had found Mam and Dad never spoke of it to anyone. Laddy once asked a priest why God couldn't have given his Mam and Dad heavy winter colds if He had wanted them to die. And the priest had scratched his head and said that it was a mystery, and that if we understood all the things that happened on earth we would be as wise as God Himself, which of course couldn't happen.

Laddy's eldest sister Rose was a nurse in the local hospital. She gave up her job and came back to look after the family. It was lonely for her, and the boy who was courting her didn't continue the romance when it meant a mile and a half walk to see her and a family of children in the house dependent on her.

But Rose made a good home for them. She supervised the homework every night in the kitchen, she washed and mended their clothes, she cooked and cleaned the house, she grew vegetables, kept hens, and she employed Shay Neil as the farm man.

Shay worked with the small herd of cattle, and kept the place ticking over. He went to fairs and markets, he did deals. He lived silently in a converted outhouse separate from the farmhouse. It had to look right when people called. No one would like to think of a man, a working farm-hand, living in the same house as all those girls and a child.

But the Byrne girls did not stay on the little farm. Rose made sure they got their exams and with her encouragement one by one they left. One for nursing, another to be trained as a teacher, one to a job in a shop in Dublin and one to a post in the Civil Service.

They had done well for the Byrne girls, the nuns and Rose. Everyone said that. And she was making a great fist of bringing up young Laddy. A big boy now, sixteen years of age, Laddy had almost forgotten his parents. He could only remember life with Rose, patient and funny and never thinking he was thick.

She would sit for ages with him at his books going over and over a thing until he could remember it, and she was never cross if he sometimes forgot it the next morning. From what he heard from other fellows at school, Rose was better than any mother.

There were two weddings the year that Laddy was sixteen, and Rose did all the cooking and entertaining for her younger sisters. They were great occasions and the photographs hung on the wall, pictures taken outside the house which had been newly painted by Shay for the festivities. Shay was there of course, but in the background. He didn't really mix, he was the hired man.

And then Laddy's sister who was working in England said she was having a very quiet wedding, which meant that she was pregnant and it would be in a Register office. Rose wrote and said that she and Laddy would be happy to come over if it would help. But the letter back was full of gratitude and underlined words saying that it wouldn't be at all helpful.

And the sister who was nursing went out to Africa. So that was the Byrne family settled, people said, Rose running the farm until poor Laddy grew up and was able to take over, God bless him if that were ever to happen.

Everyone assumed that Laddy was slow. That was, everyone except Rose and Laddy himself.

Now that he was sixteen Laddy should have been right in the middle of all the fuss getting ready for his Intermediate Certificate, but there seemed to be no mention of it at all.

'Lord, but they take things very easily above in the Brothers,' Rose said to him one day. 'You'd think there'd be all sorts of revision and plans and studying going on, but not a squeak out of them.'

'I don't think I'm doing it this year,' Laddy said.

'Well, of course you are, fourth year. When else would you do it?'

'Brother Gerald didn't say a word about it.' He looked worried now.

'I'll sort it out, Laddy.' Rose had always sorted everything out.

She was nearly thirty now, a handsome dark-haired woman, cheerful and good-natured. Over the years there had been a fair share of interest in her. But she never responded. She had to look after the family. When that was all sorted out she would think of romance ... she would say this with a happy laugh, never offending anyone because overtures were turned down at an early stage before they had become serious and before anyone could be offended.

Rose went to see Brother Gerald, a small, kind man who had always been spoken well of by Laddy.

'Ah Rose, would you not open your eyes, girl,' he said. 'Laddy's the most decent boy that ever wore shoe leather into this school, but the poor divil hasn't two brains to rattle together.'

Rose felt a flush of annoyance come to her face. 'I don't think you understand, Brother,' she began. 'He's so eager and he wants to learn, maybe the class is too big for him.'

'He can't read without putting his finger under the words, and only with difficulty then.'

'That's a habit, we can get him out of it.'

'I've been trying to get him out of it for ten years and I haven't got anywhere.'

'Well, that's not the end of the world. He hasn't failed any exams. He hasn't had any tests that he did very badly in, he'll get the Inter, won't he?' Brother Gerald began to speak and then paused as if changing his mind. 'No, go on, Brother please, we're not fighting over Laddy. We both want the best for him. Tell me what I should know.'

'He's never failed a test, Rose, because he's never done a test. I wouldn't put a humiliation like that on Laddy. Why let the boy be last all the time?'

'And what do you do with Laddy when the others are doing a test?'

'I ask him to do messages for me, he's a good-natured reliable lad.'

'What kind of messages, Brother?'

'Ah, you know, carrying boxes of books and stoking up the fire in the teachers' room, and bringing something down to the post office.'

'So I'm paying fees in this school for my brother to be a skivvy to the Brothers, is this what you're telling me?'

'Rose Byrne,' the man's eyes were full of tears. 'Will you stop getting the wrong end of things. And what fees are you talking about? A few pounds a year. Laddy's happy with us, you know that. Isn't that the best we can do for him? There isn't a notion of putting him in for the Inter or any exam, you must know that. The boy is slow, that's all I'm saying. I wish that was all I had to say about many a boy that went through the school.'

'What will I do with him, Brother? I thought he might go to an agricultural college, you know, to learn about farming.'

'It would be over his head, Rose, even if he were to get in which he wouldn't.'

'But how will he run the farm?'

'He won't run the farm. You'll run the farm. You've always known that.'

She hadn't known. Not until that minute.

She came home with a heavy heart.

Shay Neil was forking manure into a heap. He nodded his usual dour jerk of the head. Laddy's old dog Tripper barked a welcome home. Laddy himself came to the door.

'Did Brother Gerald say anything against me?' he asked fearfully.

'He said you were the most helpful lad that ever came into the school.' Without realising it she had almost started to talk to him as if he were a toddler, speaking down to him in soothing baby talk. She fought to check it.

But Laddy hadn't noticed. His big face was one huge smile. 'He did?'

'Yes, he said you were great to make up a fire and carry the books and do the messages.' She tried to keep the bitterness out of her tone.

'Well, he doesn't trust a lot of them, but he does trust me.' Laddy was proud.

'I've a bit of a headache, Laddy. Do you know what would be great, could you make me a cup of tea and bring it up to me with a slice of soda bread, and then maybe make Shay's tea for him?'

'Will I cut him two bits of ham and a tomato?'

'That's right, Laddy, that would be great.'

She went upstairs and lay on her bed. How had she not seen how backward he was? Did parents feel this about children, fiercely overprotective?

Well she'd never know now. She wasn't going to marry anyone, was she? She was going to live here with her slow brother and the dour hired man. There was no future to look forward to. It would always be just more of the same. The light had gone out of a lot of what she did now.

Every week she wrote a letter to one of her sisters, so they all heard from her once a month. She had been telling the little titbits about the farm and about Laddy. She found the letters hard to write now. Did they realise that their brother was slow? Was all their praise and gratitude because she had given up her life to look after him?

She hadn't *known* this was what she was doing; she had thought she had taken time out of her youth, cut short her nursing career because of the accident. She felt bitter about her parents. Why were they pulling a bloody cart across, and why didn't they leave it and run to save themselves?

She had a birthday card for a niece with a ten-shilling note to send, and as she put it in the envelope she realised that the others must think she was well paid for her trouble. She had a farm of land. If they only knew how much she didn't want it, that she would have handed it to the first person who passed by if she thought they would give Laddy a happy home for the rest of his life.

The carnival came to town every summer. Rose took Laddy and they went on the bumpers and the chair-o-planes. They went in the ghost train and he clung onto her with cries of terror, but then wanted another shilling so that they could do it again. She saw various people from the town, all of them saluting her warmly. Rose Byrne was someone who was admired. Now she saw why. They were praising her for having signed on for life.

Her brother was having a great day

'Can we spend the egg money?' he asked.

'Some of it, not all of it.'

'But what would be better to spend it on than a carnival?' he asked, and she watched him go to the Three Ring stall and win her a statue of the Sacred Heart. He carried it back to her bursting with pride.

A voice beside her said, 'I'll take that back to the farm, you won't want to be carrying it round all day,' and there was Shay Neil. 'I can put it in the bicycle bag,' he said.

It was kind of him, because the big statue, hopelessly wrapped in newspaper, would have been a cumbersome weight to carry.

Rose smiled at him gratefully. 'Well, Shay, aren't you the great fellow, always there when you're wanted?'

'Thank you, Rose,' he said.

There was something about his voice, as if he had been drinking. She looked at him sharply. Well, why not? It was his day off, he was allowed to drink if he wanted to. It couldn't have been a great life for him either, living in that outhouse, forking dung, milking cows. He didn't have any friends, any family that she knew of. Wasn't a few whiskeys on a day out only a bit of comfort to him?

She moved away and directed Laddy towards the fortune teller. 'Will we give it a try?' she asked.

He was so pleased that she was staying at the carnival. He had feared she might want to go home. 'I'd love my fortune told,' he said. Gypsy Ella looked for a long time at his hand. She saw great successes at games and sport ahead for him, a long life, a job working with people. And travel. There would be travel over the water. Rose sighed. It had been fine so far, why had she mentioned travel? Laddy would never go abroad unless she were to take him. It didn't look like anything that would happen.

'Now you, Rose,' he said.

Gypsy Ella looked up, pleased.

'Ah, but we know my future, Laddy.'

'Do we?'

'My future is running the farm with you.'

'But I'll be meeting people and going over the water travelling,' he said.

'True, true,' Rose agreed.

'So have your hand read, go on, Rose.' He waited eagerly.

Gypsy Ella saw that Rose would marry within a year, that she would have one child and that this would bring her great happiness.

'And will I be going over the water?' she asked, more from politeness than anything else.

No, Gypsy Ella saw no travel for Rose. She saw some poor health, but not for a long time. The two half crowns were paid and they got another ice cream before going home. The walk seemed long tonight, she was glad she didn't have to carry the statue.

Laddy talked on about the great day and how he wasn't really frightened by the ghost train. Rose looked into the fire and thought about Gypsy Ella, what a strange way to make a living moving on from town to town with the same set of people. Maybe she was married to the man in the bumpers.

Laddy went to bed with the comics she had bought him and Rose wondered what they were all doing in the carnival now. It would be closing soon. The coloured lights would be switched off, the people would go to their caravans. Tripper lay beside the fire snoring gently, upstairs Laddy would have fallen asleep. Outside it was dark. Rose thought of the marriage and the one child and the ill health late in life. They should really put a stop to these kind of sideshows. Some people were foolish enough to believe them.

She woke in the dark thinking she was being suffocated. A great weight lay on top of her, she began to struggle and panic. Had the wardrobe fallen over? Had some of the roof fallen down? As she started to move and cry out a hand went across her mouth. She smelled alcohol. She realised in a moment of sick recognition that Shay Neil was in her bed, lying on top of her.

She struggled to free her head from his hand. 'Please Shay,' she whispered. 'Please, Shay, don't do this.'

'You've been begging for it,' he said, still pushing at her, trying to get her legs apart.

'Shay, I haven't. I don't want you to do this. Shay, leave now we'll say no more about it.'

'Why are you whispering then?' He spoke in a whisper too.

'So as not to wake Laddy, frighten him.'

'No, so that we can do it, that's why, that's why you don't want him to wake.'

'I'll give you anything.'

'No, it's what I'm going to give you that we're talking about now.' He was rough, he was heavy, he was too strong for her. She had two choices. One was to shout for Laddy to come and hit him. But did she want Laddy to see her like this, her nightdress torn, her body pinned down? The other choice was to let him get it over with. Rose made the second choice.

Next morning she washed every item of bedclothes, burned her nightdress and opened the windows of her room.

'Shay must have come upstairs in the night,' Laddy said at breakfast.

'Why do you say that?'

'The statue I won for you is on the landing. He must have brought it up,' Laddy said pleased.

'That's right, he must have,' Rose agreed.

She felt bruised and sore. She would ask Shay to leave. Laddy would ask endless questions, she must get a story together that would cover it, and cover it for the neighbours too. Then a wave of anger came over her. Why should *she*, Rose, who was blameless in all this, have to invent excuses, explanations, cover stories? It was the most unjust thing she had ever heard in her life.

The morning passed as so many mornings had passed for Rose. She made Laddy's sandwiches and he went to school, to do errands for the teachers, as she now realised. She collected the eggs, fed the hens. All the time the sheets and pillowcases flapped on the line, the blanket lay spread on a hedge.

The custom had been that Shay ate bread and butter and boiled tea in his own quarters at breakfast time. After he heard the Angelus ring from the town he washed his hands and face at the pump in the yard and came in for a meal. It wasn't meat every day, sometimes it was soup. But there was always a bowl of big floury potatoes, a jug of water on the table and a pot of tea afterwards. Shay would take his plate and cutlery to the sink and wash it.

It had been a fairly joyless business. Sometimes Rose had read through it, Shay had never been one for conversation. Today she prepared no lunch. When he came in she would tell him that he must leave. But the bells of the Angelus rang and Shay did not come in. She knew he was working. She had heard the cows come in to be milked, she had seen the churns left out for the creamery to collect.

Now she began to get frightened. Maybe he was going to attack her again. Perhaps he took the fact that she had not ordered him out this morning as encouragement. Perhaps he took the whole of last night's passivity as encouragement, when all she was doing was trying to save Laddy from something he would not understand. That no normal sixteen-year-old would understand in relation to his own sister, but especially not Laddy of all people.

By two o'clock she was very uneasy. There had never been a day when Shay had not come in for his midday meal. Was he waiting for her somewhere, would he grab her and hurt her again? Well if he did, by God this time she would defend herself. Outside the kitchen door was a pole with some curved nails in it. They used it to rake twigs and branches off the thatched roof. It was the perfect thing to have to hand. She brought it inside and sat at the kitchen table trying to plan her next move.

He had opened the door and was in the kitchen before she realised it. She moved for the stick but he kicked it out of her way. His face was pale and she could see his Adam's apple moving up and down in his throat. 'What I did last night should not have been done,' he said. She sat trembling. 'I was very drunk. I'm not used to strong drink. It was the drink that made me do it.'

She searched for the words that would make him leave their lives, the actual phrase of dismissal that would not goad him into attacking her again. But she found she still couldn't speak. They were used to silences. Hours, days, weeks, of her life had been spent in this kitchen with Shay Neil and no words being said, but today was different. The fear and the memory of the grunts and obscenities of last night hung between them. 'I would like if last night had not happened,' he said eventually.

'And so would I, by God so would I,' she said. 'But since it did . . .' Now she could say it, get him out from their place.

'But since it did,' he said, 'I don't think I should come in and eat dinner with you any more in your house. I'll make my own food over beyond. That would be best from now on.'

He seriously intended to stay on after what had happened between them. After the most intimate and frightening abuse of another human being, he thought that it could be put aside with just a minor readjustment of the meal schedule. The man must be truly mad.

She spoke gently and very deliberately. She must not allow the fear to be heard in her voice. 'No, Shay, I don't think that would be enough, I really think you had better leave. It would not be easy for us to forget what happened. You should start somewhere else.'

He looked at her in disbelief. 'I can't go,' he said.

'You'll find another place.'

'I can't go, I love you,' he said.

'Don't talk nonsense.' She was angry and even more frightened now. 'You don't love me or anyone. What you did had nothing to do with love.'

'I've told you that was the drink, but I do love you.'

'You'll have to go, Shay.'

'I can't leave you. What is to happen to you and Laddy if I go?'

He turned and left the kitchen.

'Why didn't Shay come in for his dinner?' Laddy asked on Saturday.

'He says he prefers to have it on his own, he's a very quiet sort of person,' Rose said.

She had not spoken to Shay since. The work went on as it always did. A fence around the orchard had been mended. He had put a new bolt on the kitchen door, for her to fasten at night from the inside.

Tripper, the old collie dog, took to die.

Laddy was very upset. He sat stroking the dog's head and trying to administer him little sips of water on a spoon. Sometimes he would cry with his arms around the dog's neck. 'Get better, Tripper. I can't bear to hear you breathing like this.'

'Rose?' It was the first time that Shay had spoken to her in weeks.

She jumped. 'What?'

'I think I should take Tripper out to the field and shoot him through the head. What do you think?' Together they looked at the wheezing dog.

'We can't do it without telling Laddy.' Laddy had gone to school that day with the promise that he was going to buy a small piece of steak for Tripper, it might build him up. He would call at the butcher's on his way home. The dog would never be able to eat steak or anything, but Laddy didn't want to believe this.

'So will I ask him then?'

'Do.'

He turned away. That evening Laddy dug a grave for Tripper and they carried him out to the back field. Shay put the gun to the dog's head. It was over in a second. Laddy made a small wooden cross, and the three of them stood in silence around the little mound. Shay went back to his quarters.

'You're very quiet, Rose,' Laddy said. 'I think you loved Tripper as much as I did.'

'Oh I did, definitely,' she said.

But Rose was quiet because she had missed her period. Something that had never happened to her before.

In the week that followed Laddy was anxious. There was something very wrong with Rose. It had to be more than just missing Tripper.

There were three routes open to her in Ireland of the fifties. She could have the child and live on in the farm, a disgraced woman, with the gossip of the parish ringing in her years. She could sell the farm and move with Laddy to somewhere else, start a new life where nobody knew them. She could bring Shay Neil to the priest, and marry him.

There was something wrong with all these options. She could not bear to think of her changed status after all these years, if she were to be known as the unwed mother of a child for whom no father had ever been acknowledged. Her few pleasures like a visit to the town, a coffee in the hotel, a chat after Mass, would end. She would be a matter of speculation and someone to be pitied. Heads would shake. Laddy would be confused. But could she sell the farm and leave under such circumstances? In a way the farm belonged to all of them, her four sisters as well. Suppose they were to hear that she had taken all the proceeds and gone to live with Laddy and an illegitimate child in some rooms in Dublin? What would they feel about it?

She married Shay Neil.

Laddy was delighted about it all. And overjoyed to think he would be an uncle. 'Will the baby call me Uncle Laddy?' he wanted to know.

'Whatever you like,' Rose said.

Nothing had changed much at home except that Shay slept up in Rose's bedroom now. Rose went less often to town than she used to. Perhaps it was because she felt tired now that she was expecting the baby, or maybe she had lost interest in seeing people there. Laddy wasn't sure. And she wrote less to her sisters even though they wrote more to her. They had been very startled by the marriage. And the fact that there had been no big wedding breakfast as Rose had organised for them. They had come to visit and shaken Shay's hand awkwardly. They had found no satisfactory explanations in the conversation of their normally outgoing eldest sister.

And then the baby was born, a healthy child. Laddy was his godfather and Mrs Nolan from the hotel his godmother. The child was baptised Augustus. They called him Gus. The smile came back to Rose's face again as she held her son. Laddy loved the little boy and never tired of trying to entertain him. Shay was silent and uncommunicative about the baby as well as everything else. The strange household got on with their lives. Laddy went to work for Mrs Nolan in the hotel. The grandest help she ever had, Mrs Nolan said. Nothing was too much trouble for him, they would be lost without Laddy.

And young Gus learned to walk and staggered around the farmyard after the chickens, and Rose stood at the door admiring him. Shay Neil was morose as ever. Sometimes at night Rose would look at him while pretending not to. He lay for long times with his eyes open. What was he thinking about? Was he happy in this marriage?

There had been very little sexual activity involved. Firstly she had been unwilling because of her pregnancy. But after the birth of Gus she had said to him very directly: 'We are man and wife and putting the past behind us, we should have a normal married life.'

'That's right,' he had said, with no great enthusiasm at all.

Rose had found to her surprise that he did not revolt or frighten her. It did not bring up memories of that night of violence. In fact it was the only time they seemed to be in any way close. He was a complicated, withdrawn man. Conversation would never be easy with him, on any subject.

They never had alcohol at home, apart from the half bottle of whiskey on the top shelf in the kitchen to be used in an emergency or for soaking cotton wool if someone had a toothache. The drunkenness of that one night was never mentioned between them. The events had such a strange nightmarish quality that Rose had put them as far from her mind as possible. She didn't even pause to rationalise that they had resulted in the birth of her beloved Gus, the child that had brought her more happiness than she would ever have believed possible.

So she was entirely unprepared to face a drunken, violent Shay when he came home from a Fair almost incapable of speech. Slurred and maddened by her criticism of him he took his belt from his trousers and beat her. The beating seemed to excite him and he forced himself on her in exactly the same way as the night she had managed to put out of her mind. Every memory came rushing back, the disgust and the terror. And even though she was familiar with his body now and had welcomed it to her own this was something horrifying. She lay there bruised and with a cut lip.

'And you can't come the high and mighty lady tomorrow telling me to pack my bags and go. Not this time. Not now that I'm married in,' he said. And turned over to fall asleep.

'Whatever happened to you, Rose?' Laddy was concerned.

'I fell out of bed, half asleep and I hit my head against the bedside table,' she said.

'Will I ask the doctor to come out to you when I'm in town?' Laddy had never seen a bruise like it.

'No, Laddy, it's fine,' she said, and joined the ranks of women who accept violence because it's easier than standing up to it.

Rose had hoped for another child, a sister for little Gus, but it didn't happen. How strange that a pregnancy could result from one night of rape and not from months of what was called normal married life.

Mrs Nolan of the hotel said to Dr Kenny that it was strange how often Rose seemed to fall and hurt herself.

'I know, I've seen her.'

'She says she's got clumsy, but I don't know.'

'I don't know either, Mrs Nolan, but what can I do?' He had lived long enough to notice that a lot of women claimed they had got clumsy and had fallen over.

And the strange coincidence was that it often happened after the Fair Day or the market had been in town. If Dr Kenny had his way alcohol would be barred from fairs. But then, who listened to an old country doctor who picked up the pieces and was rarely if ever told the truth about what happened?

Laddy fancied girls but he was no good with them. He told Rose that he'd love to have slicked-down hair and wear pointed shoes, then the girls would love him. She bought him pointed shoes and tried to grease his hair. But it didn't work.

'Do you think I'll ever get married, Rose?' he asked her one evening. Shay was in another town buying stock. Gus was asleep, excited because tomorrow he would start school. It was just Rose and Laddy by the fire, as so often in the past.

'I don't know, Laddy, I really never expected to, but you remember that fortune teller we went to years ago, she said I'd be married within the year and I was. I certainly didn't expect that, and that I'd have a child and love him, and I didn't think that would happen. She said to you that you'd be in a job meeting people and you are in the hotel. And that you'd travel across the water and be good at sport, so all that is ahead of you.' She smiled at him brightly reminding him of all the good things, glossing over what was left out, deliberately not mentioning that Gypsy Ella had forecast ill health for Rose, but not yet.

When it happened, it happened very unexpectedly. There was no Fair, there would be no drinking, none of those large whiskeys thrown back in the company of men who were more jovial and who were made merry by drink. She didn't fear his return that night which was why it was such a shock to see him drunk, his eyes blurring, not focusing, his mouth drooping at one side.

'Don't look at me like that,' he began.

'I'm not looking at you at all,' she said.

'Yes, you are, yes you bloody are.'

'Did you get any heifers?'

'I'll give you heifers,' he said taking off his belt.

'No, Shay, no. I'm having a conversation with you, I'm not saying a word against you. NO!' Tonight she screamed rather than speaking in the demented pleading whisper to prevent her brother and her son knowing what was happening.

The scream seemed to excite him more. 'You are a slut,' he said. 'A coarse slut. You can't get enough of it, that's always been your problem even before you were a married woman. You are disgusting.' He raised the belt and brought it down first on her shoulders, then on her head.

At the same time his trousers fell to the floor and he ripped at her nightdress. She moved to get the bedroom chair to protect herself but he got there first and, raising the chair, he broke it on the edge of the bed and came at her with it raised aloft.

'Don't, Shay, in the name of God don't do this.' She didn't care who heard. Behind him at the door she saw the small frightened figure of Gus, his hand in his mouth with terror, and behind that was Laddy. Wakened by the screams, both of them transfixed by the scene in front of them. Before she could stop herself Rose cried, 'Help, Laddy, help me!' And then she saw Shay being pulled back, Laddy's huge arm around his neck restraining him.

Gus was screaming in terror. Rose gathered her torn nightdress and, uncaring about the blood flowing down her forehead, ran to pick her son up in her arms.

'He's not himself,' she said to Laddy. 'He doesn't know what he's doing, we'll have to lock him in somewhere.'

'Daddy,' screamed Gus.

Shay broke free and came at the mother and child. He still had the leg of the chair in his hand.

'Laddy, for God's sake,' she implored.

Shay stopped to look at Laddy, the big boy with his face red and sweating, standing in his pyjamas, uncertain, frightened.

'Well, Lady Rose, don't you have a fine protector here. The town simpleton in his pyjamas, that's great to see, isn't it. The village idiot going to look after his big sister.' He looked from one to the other, taunting Laddy. 'Come on then, big boy, hit me now. Hit me, Laddy, you big fat queer. Come on.' He had the chair leg with the spiky pointy bit where it had snapped making it a dangerous weapon.

'Hit him, Laddy,' Rose cried, and Laddy's big fist came out and hit Shay hard across the jaw. As Shay fell his head hit the marble washstand. There was a crunching sound and his eyes were open as he lay on the floor. Rose put Gus down on the floor gently, the child had stopped crying now. The silence lasted for ever.

'I think he's dead,' Laddy said.

'You did what you had to do, Laddy.' Laddy looked at her in disbelief. He thought that he had done something terrible. He had hit Shay too hard, he had knocked the life out of him. Often Rose had said to him: 'You don't know your own strength, Laddy, go easy with this or that.' But this time there wasn't a word said against him. He could hardly believe what had happened. He turned his face away from the staring eyes on the floor.

Rose spoke slowly. 'Now, Laddy, I want you to get dressed and cycle into town and tell Dr Kenny that poor Shay had a fall and hit his head and he'll tell Father Maher and then they'll drive you back here.'

'And will I say . . . ?'

'You'll say that you heard a lot of shouting and that Shay fell and that I asked you to go for the doctor.'

'But isn't he . . . I mean, will Dr Kenny be able to . . . ?'

'Dr Kenny will do what he can and then he'll close poor Shay's eyes for him. Will you get dressed and go now, Laddy, there's a good fellow?'

'Will you be all right, Rose?'

'I'll be fine, and Gus is fine.'

'I'm fine,' Gus said, his finger still in his mouth and holding on to Rose's hand.

Laddy cycled furiously through the dark, the light on his bicycle bobbing up and down through the frightening shadows and shapes of the night.

Dr Kenny and Father Maher put his bicycle on the roof of the doctor's car. When they got home Rose was very calm. She had dressed in a neat dark cardigan and skirt with a white blouse, she had combed her hair slightly over her forehead to hide the cut. The fire was burning brightly, she had built it up and burned the broken bedroom chair. It was in ashes now. No one would ever see that it had been used as a weapon.

Her face was pale. She had a kettle ready for tea, and candles for the Last Sacraments. The prayers were said, Laddy and Gus joining Rose in the responses. The death certificate was written, and it was obviously by misadventure and due to intoxication.

The women who would lay him out would be there in the morning. The sympathies that were offered and accepted were formal and perfunctory. Both the doctor and the priest knew that this was a loveless marriage of convenience, where the hired hand had made the woman of the house pregnant. Shay Neil couldn't hold his drink, that was known.

Dr Kenny was not going to speculate about how Shay had fallen, nor was he going to discuss the fresh blood on her face. When the priest was busy elsewhere the doctor took out his black bag and without waiting to be asked to do so, gave the wound a quick examination and dabbed antiseptic on it. 'You'll be fine, Rose,' he said. And she knew he wasn't just talking about the cut on her forehead. He meant about everything.

After the funeral Rose asked all her family back to the farm, and they sat around the table in the kitchen to a meal that she had prepared carefully. There had been only a few of Shay's relations at the funeral and they had not been invited back to the farm.

Rose had a proposition to make. The place had no happy associations for her now, she and Gus and Laddy would like to sell it and live in Dublin. She had discussed it with an estate agent and had been given a realistic idea of what it would sell for. Did any of them have any objection to the place being sold? Would any of them like to live in it? No, none of them wanted to live there, and yes they were all enthusiastic and happy for Rose to sell the farm.

'Good.' She was brisk.

Were there any keepsakes or mementoes they might like to take?

'Now?' They were surprised at the speed.

'Yes, today.'

She was going to put the house on the market next day.

Gus settled in a Dublin school, and Laddy, armed with a glowing reference from Mrs Nolan, got a job as a porter in a small hotel. He was soon regarded as part of the family and invited to live in. This suited everyone. And the years passed peacefully enough.

Rose took up nursing again. Gus did well at school and went into a Hotel Management course. Rose was still a presentable woman in her forties, she could have her chances of marrying again in Dublin. The widower of a woman she had nursed seemed very interested in her, but Rose was firm. One loveless marriage behind her was enough. She wouldn't join again unless it was someone she really loved. She didn't mind missing out on love, because she didn't really think she had. Most people didn't have anything nearly as good as Gus and Laddy in their lives.

Gus loved his work, he was prepared to do the longest hours and the hardest jobs to learn the hotel business. Laddy had always taken the boy to football matches and boxing matches. He remembered the fortune teller. 'Maybe she meant I was going to be interested in sports,' he told Gus. 'Maybe she didn't mean good at it, more involved in it.'

'Could be.' Gus was very fond of the big kind man who looked after him so well.

None of them ever talked about the night of the accident. Sometimes Rose wondered how much Gus remembered. He had been six, old enough to have taken it all in. But he didn't appear to have nightmares as a child and later on he could listen to talk about his father without looking awkward. He did not, however, ask many questions about what his father had been like, which was significant. Most boys would surely have wanted to know. Possibly Gus knew enough.

The hotel where Laddy worked was owned by an elderly couple. They told Laddy that they would soon retire, and he became very agitated. This had been his home now for years. It coincided with Gus meeting the girl of his dreams, a bright sparky girl called Maggie, a trained chef with Northern Ireland wit and confidence. She was ideal for him in Rose's mind; she would give him all the support he needed.

'I always thought I'd be jealous when Gus found himself a proper girl but it's not so, I'm delighted for him.'

'And I always thought I'd have some wee bat out of hell as a mother-in-law and I got you,' Maggie said.

All they needed now was a hotel job together. Even to buy a small run-down place and build it up.

'Couldn't you buy my hotel?' Laddy suggested. It would be exactly what they wanted, but of course they couldn't afford it.

'If you give me a room in it to live in, I'll give you the money,' Rose said.

What better could she do with what she had saved and the proceeds of her Dublin flat when she sold it? It would be a home for Laddy and Gus, a start in business for the young couple. A place to rest her limbs when this ill health that had been foretold finally came. She knew it was sinful and even stupid to believe in fortune tellers, but that whole day, the day of Gypsy Ella, was still very clear in her mind.

It had been, after all, the day that Shay had raped her.

It was not easy to get business at the start. They spent a lot of time studying the accounts. They were paying out more than was coming in.

Laddy understood that business was not good. 'I can carry more coal upstairs,' he said, anxious to help.

'Not much use, Laddy, when we've no one to light fires for.' Maggie was very kind to her husband's Uncle Laddy. She always made him feel important.

'Could we go out in the street, Rose, and I would wear a sandwich board with the name of the hotel and you could give people leaflets?' He was so eager to help.

'No, Laddy. This is Gus and Maggie's hotel. They'll come up with ideas, they'll get it going. Soon it will be very busy, as many guests as they can handle.'

And eventually it was.

The young couple worked at it night and day. They built up a clientele of faithful visitors. They attracted people from the North, the word of mouth spread. And whenever they had a foreign visitor from the continent Maggie would give them a card saying: 'We have friends who speak French, German, Italian.'

It was true. They knew a German bookbinder, a French teacher in a boys' school and an Italian who ran a chip shop. When they needed translation these people were immediately found on the telephone to interpret for them.

Gus and Maggie had two children, angelic little girls, and Rose thought herself one of the happiest women in Ireland. She would take her little granddaughters to feed the ducks in St Stephen's Green on a sunny morning.

One of the hotel guests asked Laddy was there a snooker hall nearby, and Laddy, eager to please, found one.

'Have a game with me,' said the man, a lonely businessman from Birmingham.

'I'm afraid I don't play, sir.' Laddy was apologetic.

'I'll show you,' the man said.

And then it happened. The fortune teller's forecast came true. Laddy had a natural eye for the game. The man from Birmingham didn't believe he had never played before. He learned the order, yellow, green, brown, blue, pink, black. He potted them all easily and stylishly. People gathered to watch.

Laddy was the sportsman that had been foretold for him.

He never wagered money on a game. Other people bet on him, but he worked too hard for his wages and they all needed them, Rose, Gus, Maggie and the little girls. But he won competitions and he had his picture in the paper. And he was invited to join a club. He was a minor snooker celebrity.

Rose watched all this with delight. Her brother a person of importance at last. She didn't even need to ask her son to look after Laddy when she was gone. She knew it wasn't necessary. Laddy would live with Gus and Maggie until the end. She made a scrapbook of his snooker triumphs, and together they would read it.

'Would Shay have been proud of all this, do you think?' Laddy asked one evening. He was a middle-aged man now and he had hardly ever spoken of the dead Shay Neil. The man he had killed that night with a violent blow.

Rose was startled. She spoke slowly. 'I think he might have been pleased. But you know, with him it was very hard to know what he thought. He said very little, who knows what he was thinking in his head.'

'Why did you marry him, Rose?'

'To make a home for us all,' she said simply.

As an explanation it seemed to satisfy Laddy. He had never given any more thought to marriage himself, or women, as far as Rose knew. He must have had sexual desires and needs like any man but they were never acknowledged in any way. And nowadays the snooker seemed a perfectly adequate substitute. So by the time Rose realised that the women's trouble she complained of meant hysterectomy and then that hysterectomy hadn't solved the problem, she was a woman with no worries about the future.

The doctor was not accustomed to people taking a diagnosis and sentence like this so calmly.

'We'll make sure that there's as little pain as possible,' he said.

'Oh, I know you will. Now, what I'd really like is to go to a hospice, if that's possible.'

'You have a very loving family who would want to nurse you,' the doctor said.

'True, but they have a hotel to run. I'd much prefer not to be there, just because they would give me too much time. Please, Doctor, I'll be no trouble up in the hospice, I'll help all I can.'

'I don't doubt that,' he said blowing his nose hard.

Rose had her moments of rage and anger like anyone else. But they were not shared with her family or her fellow patients in the hospice. The hours that she spent brooding on the unfair hand that had been dealt to her were short compared to the time spent planning for the months that were left.

When the family came to visit they got hardly any information about pain and nausea, but a lot of detail about the place she was in and the work it was doing. The hospice was a happy place, open to ideas and receptive to anything new. This is what she wanted them to channel their energy into, not to bringing her sweets or bed jackets. Something practical, something that would help. That's what Rose wanted from her family.

So they set about organising it.

Laddy got them a second-hand snooker table and gave lessons, and Gus came with Maggie to do cookery demonstrations. And the months passed easily and happily. Even though Rose was very thin now and her step was slower she said she was in no pain, and she wanted no sympathy, only company and enthusiasm. At least her mind was fine, she said.

It was too fine for Gus and Maggie, they couldn't hide from her the catastrophe that happened to them. They had insured and invested with a company that had gone bankrupt. They would lose the hotel, their hopes and dreams and future. Perhaps there was a hope that they could keep it from Rose. Maybe she could die without knowing what had happened to them. After all, she was so frail now that they could not take her back home to the hotel, as they had been able to do in the early months, for a Sunday lunch with her grandchildren. The only thing they could save from the disaster was the fact that Rose might not know how her investment in them had been lost.

But they could not hide it.

'You *have* to tell me what it is,' she said to Gus and Maggie. 'You cannot leave this room without telling me what's happening. I only have weeks left of my life, you won't let me spend them in torment, trying to work out what is. Letting me imagine it even worse than it is.'

'What would be the worst thing that you might think it is?' Maggie asked.

'That there's something wrong with one of the children?' They shook their heads 'Or with either of you? Or Laddy? Some illness?' Again they said no. 'Well, we can face anything else,' she said, her thin face smiling and her eyes burning brightly out at them.

They told her the story. How it was in the papers that the assets were gone. There was nothing left in the funds to meet the calls that were being made. Then the plausible man Harry Kane had said on television that nobody would lose their investment, the banks would rescue them, but people still feared they would. Nothing was clear.

Tears poured down Rose's face. Gypsy Ella had never told her this. She cursed herself for believing the fortune teller in the beginning. She cursed Harry Kane and all belonging to him for his greed and theft. They had never seen her so angry.

'I knew we shouldn't have told you,' Gus said dismally.

'No, of course you had to tell me. And swear you'll tell me every single thing that happens from now on. If you tell me that it's fine and it isn't, I'll know, and I'll never forgive you.'

'I'll show you every page of the paperwork, Mam,' he said.

'And if he doesn't, I will,' Maggie promised.

'And Mam, suppose it *does* go down you know, and we have to get another job, you know we'll take Laddy with us.'

'Of course she knows that,' said Maggie scornfully.

And as the days passed they brought her letters from the bank. And there did seem to be a rescue package. Their investment had been shaken but not lost. She read the small print carefully to make sure there was nothing she had missed.

'Does Laddy understand how near we came to losing everything?' she asked.

'He understands at a level of his own,' said Maggie, and with a great rush of relief Rose realised that whatever happened when she was gone, Laddy would be in safe, understanding hands.

She died peacefully.

She never knew that a woman called Siobhan Casey would call to the hotel and explain that a substantial reinvestment would now be called for, to make up for the hotel having been rescued. Miss Casey pointed out that in similar circumstances when a limited company had failed investors had not been recompensed, and that the money payable to the Neils for their hotel had come from the personal finances of Mr Kane, who was now being supported in his new venture by all those whose businesses he had saved.

There was an element of secrecy about it which was called confidentiality. The paperwork looked impressive but it was requested that it should not be put through the books in the normal way. It was a gentleman's agreement, nothing for the accountants to be involved in.

At first the amount suggested was not large, but then it increased. Gus and Maggie worried about it. But they *had* been pulled out of the fire when they assumed everything was gone. Perhaps in the swings and roundabouts of business this was accepted practice. Miss Casey spoke of her associates in a slightly respectful tone as if these were people of immense power, people it might be foolish to cross.

Gus knew that if his mother were alive she would be against it. This made him worry about why he was being so naive as to go ahead with it. They told Laddy nothing. They just made economies. They couldn't get a new boiler when they needed one, and they didn't replace the hall carpet, they bought a cheap rug instead to cover the worn bit. But Laddy realised that something was wrong and it worried him. It couldn't be that they didn't have enough business, the customers were coming in thick and fast. But the Hearty Irish Breakfasts weren't as hearty as they used to be, and Maggie said there was no need for Laddy to go to the market for fresh flowers any more, they were too dear. And when one of the waitresses left she wasn't replaced.

They were getting a fair few Italians now, and Paolo who worked in the chip shop was worn out coming to translate. 'One of you should learn to speak the language,' he said to Gus. 'I mean, we're all Europeans, but none of you are even trying.'

'I had hoped the girls might be interested in languages,' Gus had apologised. But it hadn't happened.

An Italian businessman, his wife and two sons came to stay in the hotel. The man was holed up in offices with the Irish Trade Board all day, his wife was in the shops fingering soft Irish tweed and examining jewellery. Their two teenage sons were bored and discontented. Laddy offered to take them to play snooker. Not in a hall where there would be smoking and drinking and gambling but in a Catholic Boys' Club where they would come to no harm. And he completely transformed their holiday.

From Paolo he got a written list ... *tavola da biliardo, sala da biliardo, stecca da biliardo*. The boys responded by learning the words in English: billiard table, cue.

They were a wealthy family. They lived in Roma, that was all Laddy could get from them. When they were leaving they had their photograph taken with him outside the hotel. Then they got into their taxi and went to the airport. On the footpath when the taxi pulled away Laddy saw the roll of notes. Irish banknotes tightly wrapped together with a rubber band. He looked up to see the taxi disappearing. They would never know where they had dropped it. They might not notice it until they got home. They were wealthy people, they wouldn't miss it. The woman had spent a fortune in Grafton Street every time she had got near the place.

They wouldn't need this money.

Not like Maggie and Gus, who badly needed some things. Nice new menu holders, for example. Theirs had become very stained and tattered. They needed a new sign over the door. He thought along these lines for about four minutes, then he sighed, and got the bus out to the airport to give them back the money they had lost.

He found them checking in all their lovely expensive soft leather luggage. For a moment he wavered again but then he thrust out his big hand before he could change his mind.

The Italian family all hugged him. They shouted out to everyone around about the generosity and the marvellousness of the Irish. Never had they met such good people in their lives. Some notes were peeled off and put into Laddy's pocket. That wasn't important.

'*Può venire alla casa. La casa a Roma,*' they begged him.

'They're asking you to go to Rome to stay with them,' translated people in the queue, pleased to hear such enthusiasm for one of their own.

'I know,' said Laddy, his eyes shining. 'And what's more I'll go. I had my fortune told years ago, and she said I'd go abroad across the water.' He beamed at everyone. The Italians all kissed him again and he went back on the bus. He could hardly wait to tell them his good news.

Gus and Maggie talked about it that night.

'Maybe he'll forget it in a few days,' Gus said.

'Why couldn't they just have given him the tip and left it?' Maggie wondered. Because they knew in their hearts that Laddy would think he was invited to stay with these people in Rome and that he would prepare for it and then his heart would break.

'I'll need to get a passport, you know,' Laddy said next day.

'Won't you need to learn to speak Italian first?' Maggie said with a stroke of genius.

If they could delay the whole expedition for some time, Laddy might be persuaded that the trip to Rome was only a dream.

In his snooker club Laddy asked around about Italian lessons.

A van driver he knew called Jimmy Sullivan said there was a great woman altogether called Signora who had come to live with them, and she was starting Italian lessons up in Mountainview school.

Laddy went up to the school one evening and booked. 'I'm not very well educated, do you think I'd be able to keep up with the lessons?' he asked the woman called Signora when he was paying his money.

'Oh, there'll be no problem about that. If you love the whole idea of it we'll have you speaking it in no time,' she said.

'It'll only be two hours off on Tuesday and Thursday evening,' Laddy said in a pleading tone to Gus and Maggie.

'Take all the time you like, for God's sake, Laddy. Don't you work a hundred hours a week as it is?'

'You were quite right that I shouldn't go out there like a fool. Signora says she'll have me speaking it in no time.'

Maggie closed her eyes. *What* had made her open her mouth and get him to go to Italian lessons? The notion of poor Laddy keeping up with an evening class was ludicrous.

He was very nervous on the first evening so Maggie went with him.

They looked a decent crowd going into the rather bleak-looking school yard. The classroom was all decorated with pictures and posters and there even seemed to be plates of cheese and meat that they would eat later. The woman in charge was giving them big cardboard labels with their names on, translating them into an Italian form as she went along.

'Laddy,' she said. 'Now that's a hard one. Do you have any other name?'

'I don't think so.' Laddy sounded fearful and apologetic.

'No, that's fine. Let's think of a nice Italian name that sounds a bit like it. Lorenzo! How about that?' Laddy looked doubtful, but Signora liked it. 'Lorenzo,' she said again and again, rolling the word. 'I think that's the right name. We don't have any other Lorenzos in the class.'

'Is that what all the people called Laddy in Italy call themselves?' he asked eagerly.

Maggie waited, biting her lip.

'That's it, Lorenzo,' said the woman with the strange hair and the huge smile.

Maggie went back to the hotel. 'She was a nice person,' she told Gus. 'There'd be no way she'd make poor Laddy feel a fool or anything. But I'd give it three lessons before he has to give it up.'

Gus sighed. It was just one more thing to sigh about these days.

They couldn't have been more wrong about the class. Laddy loved it. He learned the phrases that they got as homework each week as if his very life depended on it. When any Italians came to the hotel he greeted them warmly in Italian, adding *mi chiamo Lorenzo* with a sense of pride, as if they should have expected the porter at a small Irish hotel to be called something like that. The weeks went on and often on nights when it rained they saw Laddy being driven home to the door in a sleek BMW.

'You should ask your lady friend in, Laddy.' Maggie had peered out a few times and just seen the profile of a handsome woman driving the car.

'Ah no, Constanza has to get back. She has a long drive home,' he said.

Constanza! How had this ridiculous teacher hypnotised the whole class into her game-playing. She was like some pied piper. Laddy missed a snooker competition which he would definitely have won because he couldn't let down the Italian class. It was parts of the body that week and he and Francesca would have to point out to the class things like their throats and elbows and ankles. He had them all learned: *la gola* he had his hand on his neck, *i gomiti* one hand on each elbow and he bent down to touch *la caviglia* on each foot. Francesca would never forgive him if he didn't turn up. He'd miss the snooker competition, there'd be another. There wouldn't be another day with parts of the body. *He* would be furious if Francesca didn't turn up because she was in some sort of competition or other.

Gus and Maggie looked at each other, amazed. They decided that it was good for him. They had to believe that, other things were so grim at the moment. There were improvements that were now pressing and they just couldn't afford to make them. They had told Laddy that things were difficult but he didn't appear to have taken it on board. They were trying to live one day at a time. At least Laddy was happy for the moment. At least Rose had died thinking all was well.

Sometimes Laddy found it hard to remember all the vocabulary. He hadn't been used to it at school where the Brothers hadn't seemed to need too much studying from him. But in this class he was expected to keep up.

Sometimes he sat, fingers in ears on the wall of the school yard, learning the words. Trying to remember the emphasis. *Dov'è il dolore*, you must say that in a questioning way. It was the thing the doctor would say to you when you ended up in hospital. You wouldn't want to be an eejit and not know where you were hurting, so remember what he would ask. *Dov'è il dolore*, he said over and over.

Mr O'Brien who was the Principal of the whole school came and sat beside him. 'How are you?' he asked.

'*Bene, benissimo.*' Signora had told them to answer every question in Italian.

'Great stuff ... And do you like the classes? What's your name again?'

'*Mi chiamo Lorenzo.*'

'Of course you do. Well, Lorenzo, is it worth the money?'

'I'm not sure how much it costs, Signor. My nephew's wife pays it for me.'

Tony O'Brien looked at the big simple man with the beginnings of a lump in his throat. Aidan Dunne had been right to fight for these classes. And they seemed to be going like a dream. All kinds of people coming there. Harry Kane's wife of all people, and gangsters like the fellow with the low brow.

He had said as much to Grania but she still thought that he was patronising her, patting her father on the head for his efforts. Maybe he should learn something specific so that he could prove to Grania that he was interested.

'What are you doing today, Lorenzo?'

'Well, all this week it's parts of the body for when we get heart attacks or have accidents in Italy. The first thing the doctor will say when you're wheeled in is *Dov'è il dolore*? Do you know what that means?'

'No, I don't. I'm not in the class. The doctor would say to you *Dov'è il dolore*?'

'Yes, it means: where is the pain? And you tell him.'

'*Dov'è* is where, is that it?'

'Yes, it must be, because you have *Dov'è il banco; Dov'è l'albergo*. So you're right, *Dov'è* must be where is?' Laddy seemed pleased, as if he hadn't made the connection before.

'Are you married, Lorenzo?'

'No, Signor, I wouldn't be much good at it. My sister said I should concentrate on snooker.'

'Well, it doesn't have to be one or the other, man. You could have had both.'

'That's all right if you're very clever, and run a school like you do. But I wouldn't be able to do too many things at the one time.'

'I'm not either, Lorenzo.' Mr O'Brien looked sad.

'And are you not married, then? I'd have thought you'd have big grown-up children by now,' Laddy said.

'No, I'm not married.'

'Maybe teaching's a job where people don't get married,' Laddy speculated. 'Mr Dunne in the class, he's not married either.'

'Oh, is that so?' Tony O'Brien was alert to this piece of news.

'No, but I think he's having a romance with Signora!' Laddy looked around him as he spoke in case he was overheard. It was so daring to say such a thing aloud.

'I'm not sure that's the situation.' Tony O'Brien was astounded.

'*We* all think it is. Francesca and Guglielmo and Bartolomeo and I were talking about it. They laugh a lot together and go home along the road after class.'

'Well, now,' said Tony O'Brien.

'It would be nice for them, wouldn't it?' Laddy liked everyone pleased about things.

'It would be very interesting, yes,' Tony O'Brien agreed. Whatever he had wanted to find out to tell Grania, he had never expected this. He wondered about the piece of information. It might be this poor fellow's over-simple interpretation, or it might in fact be true. If it were true then things were looking up. Aidan Dunne could not be too critical if he himself were involved in something a little unusual to put it mildly. There was no high moral ground he could claim and preach from. After all, Tony O'Brien was a straightforward single man wooing a single woman. Compared to the Aidan–Signora relationship, this was totally straight and uncomplicated.

But it wasn't something he would mention to Grania yet. They had met and the conversation had been stilted, both of them trying to be polite and forget the cruel timing that had upset them before.

'Are you going to stay the night?' he had asked.

'Yes, but I don't want to make love.' She spoke without coyness or any element of game-playing.

'And shall we sleep in the same bed or will I sleep on the sofa?'

She had looked very young and confused. He had wanted to take her in his arms, stroke her and tell her that it would all work out in the end, it would be all right eventually. But he didn't dare.

'I should sleep on the sofa, it's your house.'

'I don't know what to say to you, Grania. If I beg you to sleep in my bed with me it looks as if I am just being a beast and after your body. If I don't it looks as if I don't care. Do you see what a problem it is for me?'

'Please let me sleep on the sofa this time?' she had asked.

And he tucked her in and kissed her on the forehead. In the morning he had made her Costa Rican coffee and she looked tired with dark circles under her eyes.

'I couldn't sleep,' she said. 'I read some of your books. You have amazing things I've never heard of.'

He saw *Catch*-22 and *On The Road* beside her bed. Grania would not have read Heller or Kerouac. Possibly the gulf between them *was* too great. She had looked mystified at his collection of traditional jazz. She was a child.

'I would love to come back for supper again,' she had said as she left.

'You tell me when and I'll cook it for you,' he had said.

'Tonight? Would that be too soon?'

'No, tonight would be great,' he had said. 'But a little later because I like to look in on the Italian class. And before we fight again I go because I want to, nothing to do with you or your father.'

'Peace,' she said. But her eyes had been troubled.

Now Tony O'Brien had gone home and got everything ready. The chicken breasts were marinating in ginger and honey, the table was set. There were clean sheets on the bed and a rug left on the sofa to cover every eventuality.

Tony had hoped to have something more appropriate to report from his visit to the class than the news that Grania's father was rumoured to be having an affair with the very strange-looking Italian teacher. He had better go into the bloody classroom quick and find some damn thing to tell her about.

'*Dov'è il dolore?*' he said as a farewell to Lorenzo.

'*Il gomito*,' shouted Laddy, clutching his elbow.

'Right on,' said Tony O'Brien.

The whole thing was getting madder by the minute.

The parts of the body class was great fun. Tony O'Brien had to keep his hand over his face to stop laughing as they poked at each other and shouted *eccola*. But to his surprise they seemed to have learned a hell of a lot of vocabulary and to be quite unselfconscious about using it.

The woman was a good teacher; she would suddenly hark back to the days of the week or the ordering of a drink in the bar. 'We won't spend all our time in hospital when we go on the *viaggio* to Roma.'

These people really thought they were going on an excursion to Rome.

Tony O'Brien, who could cope with the Department of Education, the various teachers' unions, the wrath of priests and nuns, the demands of parents, the drug dealers and the vandals, and the most difficult and deprived of schoolchildren, was speechless. He felt slightly dizzy at the thought of the excursion.

He was about to tell Aidan Dunne that he was leaving when he saw Aidan and Signora laughing over some boxes that were changing from being hospital beds into seats in a train. The way they stood was the way people who cared about each other might stand. Intimate without touching each other. Jesus God, suppose it was true!

He grabbed his coat and continued with his plans to wine, dine and hopefully bed Aidan Dunne's daughter.

Things were so bad in the hotel that Gus and Maggie found it very hard to cope with Laddy's learning problems. His mind was full of words, he told them, and some of them were getting jumbled.

'Never mind, Laddy. Learn what you can,' Gus was soothing. Just like the Brothers years ago were soothing to Laddy, telling him not to push himself.

But Laddy would have none of it. 'You don't understand. Signora says this is the stage we must be confident and no humming and hahing. We're having another lesson on parts of the body and I keep forgetting them. Please hear me, *please.*'

Two guests had left today because they said that the rooms were not up to standard, one said she would write to the Tourist Board. They had barely enough to pay the wages this week and there was Laddy, his big face working with anxiety, wanting to be heard his Italian homework.

'I'd be all right if I knew I were going to be with Constanza. She sort of helps me along, but we can't have the same partners. I could be with Francesca or Gloria. But very probably with Elizabetta, so can we go over them, please?'

Maggie picked up the piece of paper. 'Where do we begin?' she asked. There was an interruption. The butcher wanted to discuss when if ever his bill was going to be paid. 'Let me deal with it, Gus,' Maggie said.

Gus took the paper. 'Right, Laddy. Will I be the doctor or the patient?'

'Could you be both, Gus, until I get the sound of it back. Could you say the words to me like you used to?'

'Sure. Now I have come in to the surgery and there's something wrong with me and you're the doctor, so what do you say?'

'I have to say: "Where is the pain?" Elizabetta will be the patient, I'll be the doctor.'

Gus never knew how he kept his patience. *Dov'è il dolore*, he said through clenched teeth. *Dove le fa male?* And Laddy repeated it all desperately over and over. 'You see Elizabetta used to be a bit silly when she came first and not learning properly but Guglielmo has forced her to take it seriously and now she does all her homework too.' These people sounded like the cast of a pantomime to Gus and Maggie. Grown people calling each other ridiculous names and pointing to their elbows and having pretend stethoscopes.

And that, of all nights, was the night he invited Constanza in. The most elegant woman that they had ever seen, with a troubled face. Of all the bloody nights of the year, Laddy would have to choose this one. When they had spent three hours in the back room going over and over the columns of figures trying not to face what was obvious, which was that they must sell the hotel. Now they would have to make small talk to some half cracked woman.

But there was no small talk. This was the angriest person they had ever met. She told them that she was married to Harry Kane, the name on the papers, the contracts, the documents. She told them that Siobhan Casey was his mistress.

'I don't see how that could be, you're much better looking,' Maggie said suddenly.

Constanza thanked her briefly, and took out her chequebook. She gave them the name of friends whom she would like them to use in doing the work. Never for a moment did they doubt that she was sincere. She said without them she might never have had the information and courage to do what she was about to do. Lives would change and they must believe that the money was theirs by right and would be recovered by her when the wheels started to turn.

'Did I do right telling Constanza?' Laddy looked around fearfully at the three of them. He had never spoken of their business outside before. He had been afraid that they did not look welcoming when he had arrived in with her beside him. But now, in as much as he could follow it all, everything seemed to have sorted itself out marvellously. Far better than he could have hoped.

'Yes, Laddy, you did right,' Gus said. It was very quiet but Laddy knew that there was high praise hidden in there somehow.

Everyone seemed to be breathing more easily. Gus and Maggie had been so tense when they were helping him with his Italian words a few hours ago. Now it seemed to have gone away, whatever the problem was.

He must tell them how well he had done in class. 'It all went great tonight. You know I was afraid I wouldn't remember the words but I did, all of them,' he beamed around.

Maggie nodded, not trusting herself to speak. Her eyes were very bright.

Constanza decided to rescue the conversation. 'Did you know Laddy and I were partners tonight? We were very good,' she said.

'The elbow and the ankle and the throat?' Gus said.

'Oh, and much more, the knee and the beard,' said Constanza.

'*Il ginocchio e la barba*,' Laddy cried.

'Did *you* know Laddy has hopes of seeing this family in Rome?' Maggie began.

'Oh, we all know about it, yes. And next summer when we all go to Rome we'll certainly see them. Signora has it all under control.'

Constanza left.

They sat together, the three of them who would always live together, as Rose had known they would.

Fiona

Fiona worked in the coffee shop of a big city hospital.

She often said it was as bad as being a nurse without any of the good bits, like making people better. She saw the pale, anxious faces of people waiting for their appointment, the visitors who had come to see someone who was not getting better, the children troublesome and noisy, knowing that something was wrong but not sure what it was.

From time to time nice things happened, like the man who came out crying: 'I don't have cancer, I don't have cancer.' And he kissed Fiona and went round the room shaking people's hands. Which was of course fine for him and everyone smiled for him. But some of those who smiled *did* have cancer, and that was something he hadn't thought of. And some of those who did have cancer would get better, but when they saw him rejoicing over his sentence being lifted they forgot that they could get better and envied his reprieve.

You had to pay for tea, coffee and biscuits but Fiona knew that you never pressed for payment if someone was upset. In fact you pressed hot sweet tea into the hands of anyone suffering from shock. She wished they didn't have paper cups, but it would have been impossible to have washed cups and saucers for the numbers that passed through every day. A lot of them knew her by name and made conversation just to take their minds off whatever else they were thinking.

Fiona was always bright and cheerful, it was what they needed. She was a small pixie-like girl with enormous glasses that made her eyes look even bigger than ever, and she wore her hair tied back with a big bow. It was warm in the big waiting room so Fiona wore T-shirts and a short black skirt. She had bought shirts which had the day of the week on them and she found people liked that. 'I don't know what day it is unless I look at Fiona's chest,' they would say. 'Lucky you don't just have January, February, March on them,' others would say. It was always a talking point, Fiona and her days of the week.

Sometimes Fiona had happy fantasies that one of the handsome doctors would stop and look into her huge eyes and say that she was the girl he had been looking for all his life.

But this didn't happen. And Fiona realised that it was never likely to happen. These doctors had friends of their own, other doctors, doctors' daughters, smart people. They wouldn't look into the eyes of a girl wearing a

T-shirt and handing out paper cups of coffee. Stop dreaming, she told herself.

Fiona was twenty and rather disillusioned about the whole business of meeting men. She just wasn't good at it. Look at her friends Grania and Brigid Dunne now. They only had to go out the door and they met fellows, fellows they sometimes stayed the night with. Fiona knew this because she was often asked to be the alibi. 'I'm staying with Fiona,' was the great excuse.

Fiona's mother knew nothing of this. She would not have approved. Fiona's mother was very firmly in the Nice Girls Wait Until They Are Married school of thought. Fiona realised that she herself had no very firm views on the matter at all. In theory she felt that if you loved a fellow and he loved you then you should have a proper relationship with him. But since the matter had never come up she had never been able to put the theory to the test.

Sometimes she looked at herself in the mirror. She wasn't *bad* looking. She was possibly a little too small, and maybe it didn't help to have to wear glasses, but people said they *liked* her glasses, they said she looked sweet in them. Were they patting her on the head? Did she look idiotic? It was so hard to know.

Grania Dunne told her not to be such a fool, she looked fine. But then Grania only had half a mind on anything these days. She was so infatuated with this man who was as old as her father! Fiona couldn't understand it. Grania had her pick of fellows, why did she go for this old, old man?

And Brigid said that Fiona looked terrific and she had a gorgeous figure, unlike Brigid who put on weight as soon as she ate a sandwich. Why was it, then, that Brigid with the chubby hips was never without a date or a partner at everything? And it wasn't just people she met in the travel agency. Brigid said she never met a chap that you'd fancy in the line of work. There were just crowds of girls coming in booking sunshine holidays, and old women booking pilgrimages, and honeymoon couples that would make you throw up talking about somewhere Very Private. And it wasn't a question of Grania and Brigid sleeping with *everyone* they met. That wasn't the explanation of their popularity with men. It was a great puzzle to Fiona.

The morning was very busy and she was rushed off her feet. There were so many teabags and biscuit-wrapping papers in her litter bin she needed to move it. She struggled with the large plastic bag to the door. Once she got it out to the bin area she would be fine. A young man stood up and took it from her.

'Let me carry that,' he said. He was dark and quite handsome apart from rather spiky hair. He had a motorcycle helmet under one arm, almost as if afraid to leave it out of his sight.

She held the door open to where the bins were lined up. 'Any of those would be great,' she said, and waited courteously for him to return.

'That was very nice of you,' she said.

'It keeps my mind off other things,' he said.

She hoped there wasn't something bad wrong with him, he looked so fit and young. But then Fiona had seen the fit and the well go through her waiting room to be told bad news.

'Well, it's a great hospital,' she said. She didn't even know if it was. She supposed it was all right as hospitals go, but she always said that to people to cheer them and give them hope.

'Is it?' he sounded eager. 'I just brought her here because it was nearest.'

'Oh, it's got a great reputation.' Fiona didn't want to end the conversation. He was pointing to her chest. '*Giovedi*,' he said eventually.

'I beg your pardon?'

'It's the Italian for Thursday,' he explained.

'Oh, is it? Do you speak Italian?'

'No, but I go to an evening class in Italian twice a week.' He seemed very proud of this and eager and enthusiastic. She liked him and wanted to go on talking.

'Who did you say you brought in here?' she asked. Better clear the whole thing up at the start. If it were a wife or a girlfriend, no point in getting interested.

'My mother,' he said, his face clouding. 'She's in Emergency. I'm to wait here.'

'Did she have an accident?'

'Sort of.' He didn't want to talk about it.

Fiona went back to Italian classes. Was it hard work? Where were they held?

'In Mountainview, the big school there.'

Fiona was amazed. 'Isn't that a coincidence! My best friend's father is a teacher there.' It seemed like a bond.

'It's a small world all right,' the boy said.

She felt she was boring him, and there were people waiting at the counter for tea and coffee. 'Thanks for helping me with the rubbish, that was very nice of you,' she said.

'You're very welcome.'

'I'm sure your mother will be fine, they're just terrific in Emergency.'

'I'm sure she will,' he said.

Fiona served the people and smiled at them all. Was she perhaps a very boring person? It wasn't something you would automatically know about yourself.

'Am I boring?' she asked Brigid that night.

'No, you're a scream. You should have your own television show.' Brigid was looking with no pleasure at a zip that had parted company with the skirt. 'They just don't make them properly, you know, I couldn't be so fat that this actually burst. That's impossible.'

'Of course it's impossible,' Fiona lied. Then she realised that Brigid was probably lying to her too. 'I *am* boring,' poor Fiona said, in a sudden moment of self-realisation.

'Fiona, you're thin, isn't that all anybody in the whole bloody world wants to be? Will you shut up about being boring, you were never boring until you started yammering on that you were.' Brigid had little patience with this complaint when faced with the incontrovertible evidence that she'd put on more weight.

'I met this fellow, and he started to yawn and go away from me two minutes after he met me.' Fiona looked very upset.

Brigid relented. 'Where did you meet him?'

'At work, his mother was in Emergency.'

'Well, for God's sake, his mother had been knocked down or whatever. What did you expect him to do, make party conversation with you? Cop yourself on, Fiona, really and truly.'

Fiona was only partly convinced. 'He's learning Italian up in your father's school.'

'Good. Thank God someone is, they were afraid they wouldn't get enough pupils for the class; he was like a weasel all the summer,' Brigid said.

'I blame my parents, of course. I couldn't be anything else but boring, they don't talk about anything. There are no subjects of discussion at home. What would I have to say after years of that?'

'Oh, will you shut up, Fiona, you're *not* boring, and nobody's parents have anything to say. Mine haven't had a conversation for years. Dad goes into his room after supper and stays there all night. I'm surprised he doesn't sleep there. Sits at his little desk, touches the books and the Italian plates and the pictures on the wall. In the sunny evenings he sits on the sofa in the window just looking ahead of him. How's that for dull?'

'What would I say if I ever saw him again?' Fiona asked.

'My father?'

'No, the fellow with the spiky hair.'

'God, I suppose you could ask him how his mother was. Do I have to go in and sit beside you as if you were a puppet saying speak now, nod now?'

'It mightn't be a bad idea . . . Does your father have an Italian dictionary?'

'He must have about twenty, why?'

'I want to look up the days of the week,' Fiona explained, as if it should have been obvious.

'I was up seeing the Dunne family tonight,' Fiona said at home.

'That's nice,' her mother said.

'Wouldn't want to see too much of them, not to appear to live in the house,' her father warned.

Fiona wondered what he could mean. She hadn't been there in weeks. If only her parents knew how often the Dunne girls claimed to be staying overnight in *this* house! Now that would really cause them problems.

'Would you say Brigid Dunne is pretty?' she asked.

'I don't know, it's hard to say,' her mother said.

Her father was reading his paper.

'But *is* it hard to say, suppose you saw her would you say that's a good looking girl?'

'I'd have to think about it,' said Fiona's mother.

That night in bed Fiona thought about it over and over.

How did Grania and Brigid Dunne get to be so confident and sure of things? They had the same kind of home, they went to the same school. Yet Grania was as brave as a lion. She had been having an affair with a man, an old, old man, for ages now. On off, on off, but it was the real thing. She was going to tell her father and mother about it, say that she was going to move in with him and even get married.

The really terrible thing was that he was Mr Dunne's boss. And Mr Dunne didn't like him. Grania didn't know whether she should pretend to begin the affair now so as to give her father time to get accustomed to it, or tell him the truth. The old man said people should be told the truth straight out, that they were often more courageous than you thought.

But Grania and Brigid had their doubts.

Brigid had her doubts, anyway. He was so terribly old. 'You'll be a widow in no time,' she had said.

'I'll be a rich widow, that's why we're getting married. I'll have his pension,' Grania had laughed.

'You'll want other fellows, you'll go off and be unfaithful to him and he'll come after you and find you in someone's bed and do a double slaying.' Brigid looked almost enthusiastic at the prospect.

'No, I never really wanted anyone before. When it happens you'll all know.' Grania looked unbearably smug about it.

Fiona and Brigid raised their eyes to heaven over it all. True love was a very exhausting and excluding thing to have to watch from the sideline. But Brigid wasn't always on the sidelines. She had plenty of offers.

Fiona lay in the dark and thought of the nice boy with the spiky hair who had smiled so warmly at her. Wouldn't it be wonderful to be the kind of girl who could get a boy like that to fancy her.

It was over a week before she saw him again.

'How's your mother? Fiona asked him.

'How did you know about her?' He seemed annoyed, and worried that she had made the enquiry. So much for Brigid's great suggestion.

'When you were here last week you helped me carry out the rubbish bag and you told me your mother was in Emergency.'

His face cleared. 'Yes, of course, I'm sorry. Well she's not great actually, she did it again.'

'Got knocked down?'

'No, took an overdose.'

'Oh, I'm very, very sorry.' She sounded very sincere.

'I know you are.'

There was a silence. Then she pointed to her tee shirt. '*Venerdi*,' she said proudly. 'Is that how you pronounce it?'

'Yes, it is.' He said it in a more Italian way and she repeated it.

'Are you learning Italian too then?' he asked with interest.

Fiona spoke without thinking, 'No, I just learned the days of the week in case I met you again,' she said. Her face got red and she wanted to die that moment, beside the coffee and tea machines.

'My name's Barry,' he said. 'Would you like to come to the pictures tonight?'

Barry and Fiona met in O'Connell Street and looked at the cinema queues.

'What would you like?' he asked.

'No, what would *you* like?'

'I don't mind, honestly.'

'Neither do I.' Did Fiona see a look of impatience crossing his face? 'Perhaps the one with the shortest queue,' she suggested.

'But that's Martial Arts,' he protested.

'That's fine,' she said foolishly.

'You *like* Martial Arts?' He was unbelieving.

'Do you like them?' she countered.

As a date it wasn't a great success so far. They went to a film which neither of them enjoyed. Then came the problem of what to do next.

'Would you like pizza?' he offered.

Fiona nodded eagerly. 'That would be great.'

'Or would you prefer to go to a pub?'

'Well, I'd like that, too.'

'Let's have a pizza,' he said, in the tone of a man who knew that if any decision was ever going to be made it would have to be made by him.

They sat and looked at each other. The choosing of the pizza had been a nightmare. Fiona had said yes to both the *pizza margherita* and the *pizza napoletana*, so Barry had eventually ordered them a *quattro stagioni* each. This one had four different fillings he said, one in each corner. You could eat them all, no further decisions would be called for.

He told her that at the Italian class Signora the teacher had brought in pizzas one evening. He said that she must spend all the money she earned on bringing them gifts. They all sat there eating and chanting the names of the various pizzas aloud, it had been wonderful. He looked boyish and so enthusiastic about it all. Fiona wished she could have that kind of life in her face and her heart. About anything.

It was of course all her mother and father's fault. They were nice kind people but they had nothing to say to anyone. Her father said that 'Least said soonest mended' should be tattooed on to everyone's arm at birth and then people wouldn't go round saying the wrong thing. It did mean that her father hardly said anything at all. Her mother had a different rule to live by. It had to do with not getting carried away over things. She had always told Fiona not to get carried away by the Irish dancing class, or the holiday in Spain, or anything at all that she got enthusiastic about. That's why she had no opinions, no views.

She had ended up as the kind of person who couldn't decide what film to see, what pizza to eat, and what to say next. Should she talk to him about his mother's suicide attempts, or was he just trying to have some time off to forget about it? Fiona frowned with the concentration of it all.

'I'm sorry, I suppose I'm a bit boring about the Italian classes.'

'Oh no, heavens no you're not,' she cried. 'I just love hearing you talk about them. You see, I wish I cared about things like you do. I was envying you and all the people who bothered to go to that class, I feel a bit dull.' Very often, when she least expected it, she appeared to have said something that pleased people.

Barry smiled from ear to ear and patted her hand. 'No, you're not a bit dull, you're very nice and there's nothing to stop you going to any evening class yourself, is there?'

'No, I suppose not. Is your one full?' Again she wished she had not spoken. It looked too eager, chasing him, not being able to find an evening class of her own. She bit her lip as he shook his head.

'It wouldn't be any good joining ours now. It's too late, we're all too far ahead,' he said proudly. 'And anyway, everyone joined for some kind of reason, you know. They all had a *need* to learn Italian. Or that's the way it looks.'

'What was your need to learn it?' she asked.

Barry looked a bit awkward. 'Oh well, it has to do with being there for the World Cup,' he said. 'I went with a crowd but I met a lot of nice Italian people and I felt as thick as a plank not being able to speak their language.'

'But the World Cup won't be there again, will it?'

'No, but the Italians will still be there. I'd like to go back to the place I was in and talk to them,' he said. There was a faraway look on his face.

Fiona wondered whether to ask him about his mother but she decided against it. If he had wanted to tell her he would have. It could be too personal and private. She thought he was very, very nice and would love to see him again. How did these girls who were great with fellows manage it? Was it by saying something witty? Or by not saying anything at all? She wished she knew. Fiona would love to have said something that would make this nice kind boy realise that she liked him and would love to be his friend. And even more in time. Why was there no way of sending out a signal?

'I suppose we should be thinking of going home,' Barry said.

'Oh yes. Of course.' He was tired of her, she could see.

'Will I walk you to the bus?'

'That would be nice, thank you.'

'Or would you rather a lift home on my motorbike?'

'Oh, that would be terrific.' She realised she had agreed to both things. What a fool he would think she was. Fiona decided to explain. 'I mean when you offered to walk me to the bus I didn't know that there was a chance of a lift on the bike. But I would prefer the bike actually.' She was shocked at her own courage.

He seemed to be pleased. 'Great,' he said 'You'll hang on to me tight then. Is that a promise?'

'It's a promise,' said Fiona, and smiled at him from behind her big glasses. She asked him to leave her at the end of the road, because it was a quiet place where motorbikes didn't often travel. She wondered would he ask to see her again.

'I'll see you,' Barry said.

'Yes, that would be nice.' She prayed that her face didn't look too hopeful, too beseeching.

'Well, you might run across me in the supermarket,' he said.

'What? Oh sure. Yes. Easily.'

'Or I might see you in the hospital?' he added as another possibility.

'Well, yes. Yes, of course, if you were passing by,' she said sadly.

'I'll be passing by every day,' Barry said. 'They've kept my mother in. Thank you for not asking about her . . . I didn't want to talk about it.'

'No, no of course not.' Fiona held her breath with relief. She had been within a whisper of leaning on the table in the pizza place and asking him every detail.

'Goodnight, Fiona.'

'Goodnight, Barry, and thank you,' she said.

She lay awake in her bed for a long time. He did like her. And he admired her for not prying into his life. All right, she had made a few silly mistakes, but he *had* said he would see her again.

Brigid called by the hospital to see Fiona. 'Could you do us a favour, come up to the house tonight?'

'Sure, why?'

'Tonight's the night. Grania's going to tell them about the Old Age Pensioner. There should be fur and feathers flying.'

'What good will I be?' Fiona asked anxiously.

'They might tone it down a bit if there's an outsider in the house. *Might.*' Brigid seemed doubtful.

'And will he be there, the old man?'

'He'll be parked in a car outside in case he's needed.'

'Needed?' Fiona sounded fearful.

'Well, you know, needed to be welcomed in as a son-in-law, or to come in and rescue Grania if Dad beats her senseless.'

'He wouldn't do that?' Fiona's mouth was an O of horror.

'No, Fiona, he wouldn't. You take everything so literally. Have you no imagination?'

'No, I don't think I have,' Fiona said sadly.

During the day Fiona made enquiries about Mrs Healy, Barry's mother. She knew Kitty, one of the nurses on the ward, who told her. Heavy stomach-pumping job, second time. She seemed determined to do it. Kitty had no time for her, let them finish themselves off if they were intent on it. Why spend all that time and money telling them they were loved and needed? They probably weren't. If they only knew all the really sick people, decent people who didn't *bring* it on themselves, then they'd think again.

Kitty had no sympathy for would-be suicides. But she said Fiona wasn't to tell anyone that. She didn't want to get the reputation for being as hard as nails. And she did give this bloody woman her medication and was as nice to her as she was to all the patients.

'What's her first name?'

'Nessa, I think.'

'What's she like?' Fiona asked.

'Oh, I don't know. Weak mainly, in shock a bit. Watches the door of the ward all the time waiting for the husband to come in.'

'And does he?'

'Not so far, her son does but that's not what she's looking for, she wants to see the husband's face. That's why she did it.'

'How do you know?'

'That's why they all do it,' Kitty said sagely.

In the Dunnes' kitchen they sat around the kitchen table. There was a macaroni cheese on it but hardly anyone was eating. Mrs Dunne had her paperback folded back on itself as she so often had. She gave the impression of someone waiting in an airport rather than being in the centre of her own home.

Brigid as usual was eating nothing officially but pulling little bits off the edge of the dish and taking bread and butter to mop up a bit of juice that spilled, and in the end eating more than if she had been able to take a sensible portion. Grania looked pale, and Mr Dunne was about to head off to his room that he loved so much.

'Dad, wait a minute,' Grania said. Her voice sounded strangulated. 'I want to tell you something, all of you in fact.'

Grania's mother looked up from her book. Brigid looked down at the table. Fiona felt herself go red and look guilty. Only Grania's father seemed unaware that anything of moment was to be said.

'Yes, of course.' He sat down, almost pleased that there was to be general conversation.

'You'll all find this very hard to take, I know, so I'll try to explain it as simply as I can. I love somebody and I want to get married.'

'Well, isn't that great,' her father said.

'Married?' her mother said, as if it was the most unexpected thing that anyone who loved anyone might consider.

Brigid and Fiona said nothing, but gave little grunts and sounds of surprise and pleasure that anyone would have known were not a serious reaction to the news.

Before her father could ask who she loved Grania told him. 'Now, you're not going to like this in the beginning, you're going to say he's too old for me, and a lot of other things, but it's Tony O'Brien.'

The silence was worse than even Grania could have believed.

'Is this a joke?' her father said eventually.

'No, Dad.'

'Tony O'Brien! The wife of the Principal, no less.' Her mother gave a snort of laughter.

Fiona couldn't bear the tension. 'I hear he's very nice,' she said pleadingly.

'And who do you hear that from, Fiona?' Mr Dunne spoke like a typical schoolteacher.

'Well, just around,' Fiona said feebly.

'He's not that bad, Dad. And she's got to marry someone,' Brigid said, thinking this was helping somehow.

'Well, if you think Tony O'Brien will marry you, you have another think coming.' Aidan Dunne's face was in a hard, bitter line.

'We wanted you to know about it first, and then we thought we might get married next month.' Grania tried to keep the shake out of her voice.

'Grania, that man tells at least three girls a year that he's going to marry them. Then he takes them back to his bordello and he does what he likes with them. Well, you probably know that, you've been there often enough when you're telling us that you stay with Fiona.'

Fiona cowered at the lie being unmasked.

'It's not like that. It's been going on for ages, well, it's been in the air for ages. I didn't see him any more after he became Principal because I thought he had sort of cheated us both, you and me, but he says he didn't and that things are fine now.'

'Does he, by God?'

'Yes, he does. He cares about you and he has great admiration for you and the way the evening class is going.'

'I know a boy who goes to it, he says it's just great,' squeaked Fiona. She gathered from the looks she got that the interruption had not been hugely helpful.

'It took him a long time to persuade me, Dad. I was on your side and I didn't want to have anything to do with him. And he explained that there *were* no sides ... you were all in it for the same reason ...'

'I'm sure it took him a long time to persuade you. Usually about three days, he boasts. He boasts, you know, about how he gets young girls to bed with him. That's the kind of man we have running Mountainview.'

'Not nowadays, Dad. Not now. I bet he hasn't. Think about it.'

'Only because he's not in the staffroom, because he's in his little God Almighty tinpot throne room, the Principal's Office as he calls it.'

'But Dad, wasn't it always the Principal's Office, even when Mr Walsh was there?'

'That was different. He was a man worthy of the post.'

'And hasn't Tony been worthy of it? Hasn't he painted the school, got it all smartened up? Started new things everywhere, given you money for your wild garden, set up the Italian class, got the parents to campaign for a better bus service ...?'

'Oh, he has you well indoctrinated.'

'What do you think, Mam?' Grania turned to her mother.

'What do I think? What does it matter what I think? You're going to do whatever you want to anyway.'

'I wish you would understand it's not easy for him either. He wanted to tell you a long time ago, he didn't like it being all secret, but I wasn't ready.'

'Oh, yes.' Her father was very scornful.

'Truly, Dad. He said he didn't feel good seeing you and knowing that sooner or later he would have to face you, knowing he had been keeping something from you.'

'Oh dear me, the poor man, the poor worried soul.' They had never seen their father as sarcastic and bitter as this. His face was literally twisted in a sneer.

Grania straightened her shoulders. 'As Mam said, I am of course over twenty-one and I can and will do what I like, but I had hoped to do it with your ... well, your encouragement.'

'And where is he, the great Sir Galahad, who didn't dare to come and tell us himself?'

'He's outside, Dad, in his car. I told him that I'd ask him to come in if it were appropriate.' Grania was biting her lip. She knew he would not be asked in.

'It's *not* appropriate. And no, Grania, I will *not* give you the blessing or encouragement you ask for. As your mother says, you'll go your own way and what can we do about it?' Angry and upset, he got up and left the table. They heard the door of his room bang behind him.

Grania looked at her mother. Nell Dunne shrugged. 'What did you expect?' she said.

'Tony *does* love me,' Grania protested.

'Oh, he may or he may not. But do you think that matters to your father? It's just that you picked on the one person out of all the billions in the world that he will never get reconciled to. Never.'

'But you, you understand?' Grania was dying for someone to support her.

'I understand that he's what you want at the moment. Sure. What else is there to understand?'

Grania's face was stony. 'Thanks, that's a lot of help,' she said. Then she looked at her sister and her friend. 'And thank you too, what a great support you were.'

'God, what could we do, go down on our knees and say we always knew you were made for him?' Brigid was stung with the unfairness of the accusation.

'I did try to say he was well thought of,' poor Fiona bleated.

'You did.' Grania was grim. She stood up from the table with her face still hard.

'Where are you going? Don't go after Dad, he won't change,' Brigid said.

'No, I'm going to pack some things and go to Tony's house.'

'If he's so mad for you he'll still be there tomorrow,' her mother said.

'I don't want to stay here any more,' Grania said. 'I didn't realise it until five minutes ago, but I haven't ever been really happy here.'

'What's happy?' Nell Dunne said.

And they were silent as they heard Grania's footsteps going upstairs and into her room to pack a case.

Outside in a car a man strained to see if he could get any indication of what was going on in the house, and wondered whether movement back and forth in the side bedroom was a good sign or a bad sign.

Then he saw Grania leaving the house with a case.

'I'll take you home, sweetheart,' he said to her. And she cried on his shoulder and into his jacket as she had cried on her father not very long ago when she was a child.

Fiona thought about it all for hours afterwards. Grania was only a year older than her. How had she been able to face up to her parents like that? Compared to the dramas in Grania's life, Fiona's were very small. What she must do now was something to get her locked into Barry and his life again.

She would think when she got into work next morning.

If you worked in the hospital you could often get flowers cheap at the end of the day from the florist, blooms that had passed their best. She got a small bunch of freesias and wrote 'Get well soon, Nessa Healy' on it. When nobody was looking she left them at the Nurses' Station in the ward. Then she hurried back to her coffee shop.

She didn't see Barry for two days, but he looked cheerful when he came in. 'She's much better, she'll be coming home at the end of the week,' he said.

'Oh, I am glad . . . has she got over it, whatever it was?'

'Well, it's my father, you see. She thinks . . . well, she thought . . . anyway, he wouldn't come and see her. He said he wasn't going to be blackmailed by these suicide attempts. And she was very depressed at first.'

'But now?'

'Now it seems that he gave in. He sent her flowers. A bunch of freesias. So she knows he cares and she's going home.'

Fiona felt herself go cold. 'And he didn't come in himself . . . with the flowers?'

'No just left them in the ward and went away. Still, it did the trick.'

'And what does he say about it all, your Dad?' Fiona's voice was faint.

'Oh, he keeps saying he never sent her flowers, but that's part of the way they go on.' He looked a bit worried about it.

'Everyone's parents are very odd, my friend was just saying that to me the other day. You couldn't understand what goes on in their minds at all.' She looked eager and concerned.

'When she's settled in back at home will we go out again?' he asked.

'I'd love that,' said Fiona. Please, please God, may no one ever find out about the flowers, may they decide to take the easy way out and go along with the notion that he had sent them.

Barry took her to a football match. Before they went he told her which was the good team and which was the bad one. He explained the offside rule and said that the referee had been blind on some previous matches and it was hoped that his sight might have returned to him by now.

At the match Barry met a dark, thickset man. 'Howaya, Luigi, I didn't know you followed this team.'

Luigi couldn't have been more pleased to meet him. 'Bartolomeo, me old skin, I've been with these lads since time began.'

Then they both broke into Italian, *mi piace giocare a calcio*. They laughed immoderately at this, and Fiona laughed too.

'That means I like to play football,' Luigi explained.

Fiona thought it must, but she sounded as if it was news to her. 'You're all getting on great at the Italian, then?'

'Oh sorry, Luigi, this is my friend Fiona,' Barry said.

'Aren't you lucky your girlfriend will go to a match. Suzi says she'd prefer to stand and watch paint dry.'

Fiona wondered should she explain to this odd man with the Dublin accent and the Italian name that she wasn't *really* Barry's girlfriend. But she decided to let it pass. And why was he calling Barry this strange name?

'If you're meeting Suzi later, maybe we'd all have a drink?' Barry suggested, and Luigi thought that was the greatest idea he'd ever heard and they named a pub.

All through the match Fiona struggled hard to understand it, and to cheer and be excited at the right time. In her heart she thought that this was great, it was what other girls did, went to matches with fellows and met other fellows and joined up with them and their girlfriends later.

She felt terrific.

She must just remember now the different circumstances which led to a goal kick or a corner, and which to a throw-in. And even more important she must remember not to ask Barry about his mother and his father and the mysterious bunch of freesias.

Suzi was gorgeous, she had red hair and she was a waitress in one of those posh places in Temple Bar.

Fiona told her about serving coffee in the hospital. 'It's not in the same league,' she said apologetically.

'It's more important,' said Suzi firmly. 'You're serving people who need it, I'm just putting it in front of people who are there to be seen.'

The men were happy to see the girls talking so they left them to it and analysed the match down to the bone. Then they started talking about the great trip to Italy.

'Does Bartolomeo talk night and day about this *viaggio*?' Suzi wanted to know.

'Why do you call him that?' Fiona whispered.

'It's his name, isn't it?' Suzi seemed genuinely surprised.

'Well, it's Barry actually.'

'Oh. Well, it's this Signora, she's marvellous altogether. She lives as a lodger in my mother's house. She runs it all and she calls Lou Luigi. It's an improvement as it happens, I sometimes call him that myself. But are you going?'

'Going where?'

'To Roma?' Suzi said, rolling her eyes and the letter R.

'I'm not sure. I don't really know Barry all that well yet. But if things go on well between us, I might be able to go. You never know.'

'Start saving, it'll be great fun. Lou wants us to get married out there or at least have it as a honeymoon.' Suzi waved her finger with a beautiful engagement ring on it.

'That's gorgeous,' Fiona said.

'Yeah, it's not real but a friend of Lou's got some great deal on it.'

'Imagine a honeymoon in Rome.' Fiona was wistful.

'The only snag is that I'll be sharing a honeymoon with fifty or sixty people,' said Suzi.

'Then you'll only have to entertain him at night, not in the day as well,' said Fiona.

'Entertain *him*? What about *me*? I was expecting him to entertain me.'

Fiona wished she hadn't spoken, as she so often wished. Of course someone like Suzi would think that way. She'd expect this Luigi to dance attendance on her. She wouldn't try to please him and fear she was annoying him all the time like Fiona would. Wouldn't it be wonderful to be as confident as that. But then, if you looked like Suzi with all that gorgeous red hair, and if you worked in such a smart place, and probably had a history of fellows like Luigi giving you great rocks of rings ... Fiona sighed deeply.

Suzi looked at her sympathetically. 'Was the match very boring?' she enquired.

'No, it wasn't bad. I'd never been to one before. I'm not sure if I understand offside though, do you?'

'Jesus no. And I haven't a notion of understanding it. You'd find yourself stuck out in the freezing cold with people bursting your eardrums if you could understand that. Meet them afterwards, that's my motto.' Suzi knew everything.

Fiona looked at her with undisguised admiration and envy. 'How did you get to be ... you know, the way you are, sure of things? Was it just because you were good looking?'

Suzi looked at her. This girl with the eager face and the huge glasses wasn't having her on. She was quite sincere. 'I have no idea what I look like,' Suzi said truthfully. 'My father told me I looked like a slut and a whore, my mother said I looked a bit fast, places I tried to get jobs in said I wore too much make-up, fellows who wanted to go to bed with me said I looked great. How would you know what you looked like?'

'Oh I know, I know,' Fiona agreed. Her mother said she looked silly in the T-shirts, people in the hospital loved them. Some people said her glasses were an asset – they magnified her eyes; other people asked could she not afford contact lenses. And sometimes she thought her long hair was nice and sometimes she thought it was like an overgrown schoolgirl.

'So I suppose in the end I realised that I was a grown up and that I was never going to please everyone,' Suzi explained. 'And I decided to please myself, and I have good legs so I wear short skirts, but not stupid ones, and I did tone down the make-up a bit. And now that I've stopped worrying about it nobody seems to be giving out to me at all.'

'Do you think I should get my hair cut?' Fiona whispered to her trustingly.

'No I don't, and I don't think you should leave it long. It's your hair and your face and you should do what *you* think about it, don't take my advice or Bartolomeo's advice or your mother's advice, otherwise you'll always be a child. That's my view anyway.'

Oh it was so easy for the beautiful Suzi to talk like that. Fiona felt like a mouse in spectacles. A long-haired mouse. But if she got rid of the glasses and the long hair, she would just be a blinking short-haired mouse. What would make her grown up, and able to make decisions like ordinary people? Maybe something would happen, something that would make her strong.

Barry had enjoyed the evening. He drove Fiona home on his motorbike and as she clung to his jacket she wondered what she would say if he asked her to another match. Should she be courageous and, like Suzi, say she'd prefer to meet him afterwards? Or should she work out the offside rule with someone at work and go with him? Which was the better thing to do? If only she could choose which she wanted to do herself. But she hadn't grown up yet like Suzi, she was someone who had no opinions.

'It was nice to meet your friends,' she said, when she got off the bike at the end of her street.

'Next time we'll do something that you choose,' he said. 'I'll drop in and see you tomorrow. That's the day I'm taking my mother home.'

'Oh, I thought she'd be home by now.' Barry had said he would ask her out when his mother had settled in at home, obviously she had thought Mrs Healy had been discharged. Fiona had not dared to go near the ward in case of being identified as the woman who had left the freesias.

'No. We thought she'd be well enough but she had a set-back.'

'Oh I'm sorry to hear that,' Fiona said.

'She got it into her head that my dad had sent her flowers. And of course he hadn't, and when she realised that she had a relapse.'

Fiona felt hot and cold at the same time. 'How awful,' she said. And then in a small voice: 'Why did she think he had?'

Barry's face was sad. He shrugged his shoulders. 'Who knows. There *was* a bunch of flowers with her name printed on it. But the doctors think she got them for herself.'

'Why do they think that?'

'Because nobody else knew she was in there,' Barry said simply.

Another night without sleeping for Fiona. Too much had happened. The match, the rules, the meeting with Luigi and Suzi, the possibility of a trip to Italy, people thinking she was Barry's girlfriend. The whole idea that once you grow up you know what to do and think and decide for yourself. And then the horrible, awful realisation that she had set Barry's mother back by her gift of the flowers. She had thought it would be something nice for the woman to wake up to. Instead it had made everything a thousand times worse.

Fiona was very pale and tired-looking when she went into work. She had taken the wrong day from her pile of tee-shirts. She created great confusion. People kept saying that they thought it was Friday and other people told her that she must have got dressed in the dark. One woman who saw Monday on Fiona's chest left before her appointment because she thought she had got the wrong day. Fiona went to the cloakroom and turned her shirt back to front. She just made sure that nobody saw her from the back.

Barry came in around lunchtime. 'Miss Clarke the supervisor let me have a couple of hours off, she's really nice. She's in the Italian class too, I call her Francesca there and Miss Clarke at work, it's a scream,' he said.

Fiona was beginning to think that half of Dublin was in this class masquerading under false names. But she had more on her mind than to feel envious of all these people who were playing childish games up in that tough school in Mountainview. She must find out about his mother without appearing to ask.

'Everything all right?'

'No, it's not, as it happens. My mother doesn't want to come home and she's not bad enough for them to keep here, so they'll have to get her referred to a mental home.' He looked very bleak and sad.

'That's bad, Barry,' she said, her face tired with lack of sleep and anxiety.

'Yes well, I'll have to cope somehow. I just wanted to say, that you know I said we'd have another outing and you could choose what we did . . . ?'

Fiona began to panic, she hadn't dared to choose yet. God, he wasn't going to ask her now on top of everything else.

'I haven't exactly made up my mind what . . .'

'No I mean, we may have to put it off a bit, but it's not that I'm going out with anyone else, or don't want to or anything . . .' he was stammering his eagerness.

Fiona realised that he *did* like her. About three-quarters of the weight on her heart lifted. 'Oh *no*, for heaven's sake, I understand, whenever things have sorted themselves out, well I'll hear from you then.' Her smile was enormous, the people waiting for their tea and coffee were ignored.

Barry smiled just as broadly and left.

Fiona learned the rules for offside in soccer but she couldn't understand how you could make sure there were always two people between you and the goal. No one gave her a satisfactory answer.

She rang her friend Brigid Dunne.

Brigid's father answered the phone. 'Oh yes. I'm glad to have an opportunity of talking to you, Fiona. I'm afraid I was rather discourteous to you when you were in our house last. Please forgive me.'

'That's fine, Mr Dunne. You were upset.'

'Yes, I was very upset and still am. But it's no excuse for behaving badly to a guest. Please accept my apologies.'

'No, maybe I shouldn't have been there.'

'I'll get Brigid for you,' he said.

Brigid was in great form. She had lost a kilo in weight, she had found a fantastic jacket that made you look positively angular, and she was going on a free trip to Prague. No awful nude beaches there showing people up for what they were.

'And how's Grania getting on?'

'I haven't an idea.'

'You mean you haven't been to see her?' Fiona was shocked.

'Hey, that's a good idea. Let's go up to Adultery Mews and see her tonight. We might meet the geriatric as well.'

'Shush, don't call it that. Your father might hear.'

'That's what *he* calls it, it's his expression.' Brigid was unrepentant.

They fixed a place to meet. It would be a laugh anyway, Brigid thought. Fiona wanted to know if Grania had survived.

Grania opened the door. She wore jeans and a long black sweater. She looked amazed to see them. 'I don't believe it,' she said, delighted. 'Come in. Tony, the first sign of an olive branch has come to the door.'

He came out smiling, good looking, but very old. Fiona wondered how could Grania see her future with this man.

'My sister Brigid, and our friend Fiona.'

'Come in, you couldn't have come at a better time. I wanted to open a bottle of wine. Grania said we were drinking too much, which meant that I was drinking too much ... so now we have to.' He led them into a room filled with books, tapes and CDs. There was some Greek music on the player.

'Is that the Zorba dance?' Fiona asked.

'No, but it's the same composer. Do you like Theodorakis?' His eyes lit up at the thought that he might have found someone who liked his era of music.

'Who?' said Fiona, and the smile fell sadly.

'It's very plush.' Brigid looked around in grudging admiration.

'Isn't it? Tony got all these shelves made, same man who did the shelves for Dad. How is he?' Grania really wanted to know.

'Oh, you know, the same.' Brigid was no help.

'Is he still ranting and raving?'

'No, more sighing and groaning.'

'And Mam?'

'You know Mam, hardly notices you're gone.'

'Thanks, you know how to make someone feel wanted.'

'I'm only telling you the truth.'

Fiona was trying to talk to the old man so that he wouldn't hear all this intimate detail about the Dunne family. But he probably knew it all already.

Tony poured them a glass of wine each. 'I'm delighted to see you girls, but I have a bit of business up in the school to attend to, and you'll want a chat, so I'll leave you at it.'

'You don't have to go, love.' Grania called him love quite unselfconsciously.

'I know I don't have to, but I will.' He turned to Brigid. 'And if you're talking to your father, tell him ... well ... tell him ...' Brigid looked at him expectantly. But the words didn't come easily to Tony O'Brien. 'Tell him ... she's fine,' he said gruffly, and left.

'Well,' said Brigid. 'What do you make of that?'

'He's desperately upset,' said Grania. 'You see, Dad doesn't speak to him at school, just walks out if he comes in, and it's hard for him there. And it's hard for me here not being able to go home.'

'Can you not go home?' Fiona asked.

'Not really, there'd be a scene, and the no daughter of mine speech all over again.'

'I don't know, he's quietened down a bit,' Brigid said. 'Maybe he'd only moan and groan for the first few visits, after that he might be normal again.'

'I hate him saying things about Tony.' Grania looked doubtful.

'Bringing up his lurid past, do you mean?' Brigid asked.

'Yeah, but then I had a bit of a past too. If I was as old as he is I'd hope to have a very substantial past. It's just that I haven't been around long enough.'

'Aren't you lucky to have a past?' Fiona was wistful.

'Oh shut up, Fiona. You're as thin as a rake, you must have a past to beat the band,' said Brigid.

'I've never slept with anyone, made love, done it,' Fiona blurted out.

The Dunne sisters looked at her with interest.

'You must have,' Brigid said.

'Why must I have? I'd have remembered it if I did. I didn't, that's it.'

'Why not?' Grania asked.

'I don't know. Either people were drunk or awful or it was the wrong place, or by the time I had decided I would it was too late. You know me.' She sounded full of self-pity and regret. Grania and Brigid seemed at a loss for words. 'But I'd like to now,' Fiona said eagerly.

'Pity we let the stud of all time out, he could have obliged,' Brigid said, jerking her head towards the door that Tony O'Brien had closed behind him.

'I want you to know that I don't find that even remotely funny,' Grania said.

'Nor do I,' said Fiona disapprovingly. 'I wasn't thinking of doing it with just anybody, it's someone I'm in love with.'

'Oh well, excuse *me*,' Brigid said huffily.

Grania poured another glass of wine for them. 'Let's not fight,' she said.

'Who's fighting?' Brigid asked, stretching out her glass.

'Remember when we were at school we used to have truth or dare?'

'You always took dare,' Fiona remembered.

'But tonight let's do truth.'

'What should I do, the two of you tell me.'

'You should go home and see Dad. He does miss you,' Brigid said.

'You should talk about other things like the bank and politics and the evening class he runs, not things that would remind him of . . . er . . . Tony, until he gets more used to it,' Fiona said.

'And Mam? Does she really not care?'

'No, I only said that to annoy you. But you know she's got something on her mind, maybe it's work or the menopause, you're not the Big Issue there like you are for Dad.'

'That's fair enough,' Grania said. 'Now, let's do Brigid.'

'I think Brigid should zip up her mouth about being fat,' Fiona said.

'Because she's not fat, she's sexy. A huge bum and big boobs, isn't that what men just love?' said Grania.

'And a very small waist in between,' Fiona added.

'But very, very boring about bloody calories and zip fasteners,' Grania said with a laugh.

'Easy to say when you're like a brush handle.'

'Boring and sexy, an unexpected combination,' Grania said.

And Brigid was smiling a bit, she could see they meant it. 'Right. Now Fiona,' Brigid said, visibly cheered.

The sisters paused. It was easier to attack a member of your own family.

'Let me have another drink to prepare for it,' Fiona said unexpectedly.

'Too humble.'

'Too apologetic.'

'No views on things.'

'Not able to make up her mind on anything.'

'Never really grew up and realised we all have to make up our own minds.'

'Probably going to remain a child all her life.'

'Say that again,' Fiona interrupted.

Grania and Brigid wondered had they got too carried away.

'It's just that you're too nice to people and nobody really knows what *you* think,' Grania said.

'Or *if* you think,' Brigid added darkly.

'About being a child?' Fiona begged.

'Well, I suppose I meant that we have to make decisions, don't we. Otherwise other people make them for us and it's like being a child. That's all I meant,' Grania said, afraid that she had offended funny little Fiona.

'That's extraordinary. You're the second person who's said that to me. This girl, Suzi, she said it too when I asked her should I cut my hair. How amazing.'

'So do you think you'll do it?' Brigid asked.

'Do what?'

'Make up your own mind in time about things, sleep with your man, get your hair cut, have views?'

'Will *you* stop bellyaching about calories?' Fiona said with spirit.

'Yeah, I will if it's that boring.'

'Okay then,' said Fiona.

Grania said she'd go out for a Chinese takeaway if Fiona promised she wouldn't dither about what she wanted and if Brigid didn't say one word about things being deep fried. They said that if Grania agreed to go and see her father next day they would obey her rules.

They opened another bottle of wine and laughed until the old man came home and said that at his age he had to have regular sleep so he would chase them away.

But they knew by the way he was looking at Grania that he wasn't thinking about regular sleep.

'Well, that was a great idea to go and see them.' Brigid thought it was her idea by the time they were on the bus home.

'She seems very happy,' Fiona said.

'He's so old though, isn't he?'

'Well, he's what she wants,' Fiona said firmly.

To her surprise Brigid agreed with her vehemently. 'That's the point. It doesn't matter if he's from Mars with pointed ears if it's what she wants. If more people had the guts to go after what they want the world would be a better place.' She spoke very loudly, due perhaps to the wine.

A lot of people on the bus heard her and laughed, some of them even clapped. Brigid glared at them ferociously.

'Aw come on, sexy. Give us a smile,' one of the fellows shouted.

'They called me sexy,' Brigid whispered, delighted, to Fiona.

'What did we tell you?' Fiona said.

She resolved that she would be a different person when Barry Healy asked her out again. As he undoubtedly would.

The time seemed very long, even though it was only a week. Then Barry turned up again.

'Are things all right at home?' she asked.

'No, not really. My mother has no interest in anything, she won't even cook. And in the old days she'd have you demented baking this and that and wanting to force-feed you. Now I have to buy her instant meals in the supermarket or she'd eat nothing.'

Fiona was sympathetic. 'What do you think you'll do?' she asked.

'I've no idea, honestly I'm getting madder than she is herself. Listen, have you decided what you'd like to do when we go out?'

And suddenly there and then Fiona decided. 'I'd like to come and have tea in your house.'

'No, that wouldn't be a good idea,' he said startled.

'You did ask me what I'd like, that's what it is. Your mother would have to stir herself to get something for me if you said you were bringing a girl to supper, and I could be nice and cheerful and talk about things normally.'

'No, Fiona, not yet.'

'But isn't this the very time it would be a help? How's she going to think that things will ever be normal if you don't make it look as if they are?'

'Well, I suppose you have a point,' he began doubtfully.

'So what evening then?' With grave misgivings Barry fixed the date.

Then he expected Fiona to dither and say that she'd like anything at all, and really it didn't matter. But to his surprise she said that she'd be tired after a long day at work and she'd love something substantial like say spaghetti or maybe shepherd's pie, something nice and comforting. Barry was amazed. But he delivered the message.

'I wouldn't be able to do anything like that,' Barry's mother said.

'Of course you would, Mam, aren't you a great cook?'

'Your father doesn't think so,' she said. And Barry's heart turned to lead again. It was going to take much more than Fiona coming to supper to make his mother turn the corner. He wished that he weren't an only child, that he had six brothers and sisters to share this with. He wished that his father would just say the bloody things that his mother wanted to hear, that he loved her and that his heart was broken when she tried to take her own life. And that he would swear never to leave her for anyone else. After all his father was terribly old, nearly fifty for heaven's sake, of course he wasn't going to leave Mam for anyone else. Who would have him for a start? And why did he have to take this attitude that suicide attempts were blackmail and he wouldn't give in to blackmail. His father had no firm opinions on anything else. When there was an election or a referendum his father would sigh and go back to his evening paper rather than express a view. Why did he have to feel so strongly about this of all things? Couldn't he say the words that would please her?

This bright idea of Fiona's wasn't going to work. He could see that.

'Well, all right, Mam, I suppose I could try to cook something myself. I'm not much good, but I'll try. And I'll pretend you made it. After all, I wouldn't want her to think you weren't welcoming her.'

'I'll cook it,' said his mother. 'You couldn't make a meal for Cascarino.' Cascarino was their big cat with only one eye. He had been called after Tony Cascarino who played football for the Republic of Ireland, but the cat was not as fleet of foot.

Fiona brought a small box of chocolates for Barry's mother.

'Oh, you shouldn't have, they'll only make me put on weight,' the woman said to her. She was pale-looking and had tired eyes. She wore a dull brown dress and her hair was flat and listless.

But Fiona looked at her with admiration. 'Oh Mrs Healy, you're not fat. You've got lovely cheekbones, that's how you know if a person's going to put on weight or not, the cheekbones,' she said.

Barry saw his mother touch her face with some disbelief. 'Is that right?' she said.

'Oh, it's a fact, look at all the film stars who had good cheekbones ...' Together they listed them happily. The Audrey Hepburns who never put on a pound, the Ava Gardners, the Meryl Streeps, then they examined the so-called pretty women whose cheekbones were not apparent.

Barry hadn't seen his mother so animated in weeks. Then he heard Fiona talk about Marilyn Monroe, who might not have stood the test of time if she had allowed herself to grow older. He wished she hadn't let the conversation get round to people who had committed suicide.

His mother naturally took up the theme. 'But that's not why she killed herself of course, not over her cheekbones.'

Barry could see the colour rising on Fiona's face but she fought back. 'No, I suppose she did it because she thought she wasn't loved enough. Lord, it's just as well the rest of us don't do that, the world would be empty in no time.' She spoke so casually and lightly about it that Barry held his breath.

But unexpectedly his mother answered in quite a normal voice. 'Maybe she hoped she'd be found and whoever it was she loved would be sorry.'

'I'd say he'd have been more pissed off with her than ever,' Fiona said cheerfully.

Barry looked at Fiona with admiration. She had more spark about her today. It was hard to say what it was, but she didn't seem to be waiting to take her cue from him all the time. It had been a very good idea to insist on coming to supper. And imagine Fiona of all people telling his mother she had good cheekbones.

He felt it was a lot less disastrous than it might have been. He let himself relax a little and wondered what they would talk about next, now that they had been through the minefield of Marilyn Monroe's suicide.

Barry ran a list of conversational topics past himself without success. He couldn't say Fiona worked in the hospital, that would remind everyone of the stomach pumping and the stay there, he couldn't suddenly start talking about the Italian Class, the supermarket, or his motorbike because they would know he was trying to get on to other less controversial subjects. He was going to tell his mother about Fiona's tee-shirts but he didn't think she'd like that, and Fiona had dressed up in her good jacket and nice pink blouse for the meeting so perhaps it would be letting her down.

At that moment the cat came in and fixed his one good eye on Fiona.

'I'd like to introduce you to Cascarino,' Barry said, never having loved the big angry cat so much in his life. Please may Cascarino not claw at Fiona's new skirt, or pause to lick his nether regions in full view of everyone. But the cat laid his head on Fiona's lap and began a purr that sounded like a light aircraft revving up.

'Do you have a cat at home yourselves?' Barry's mother asked.

'No, I'd love one but my father says you never know what trouble they lead to.'

'That's a pity, I find them a great consolation. Cascarino may not look much but for a male he's very understanding.'

'I know,' Fiona agreed with her. 'Isn't it funny the way men are so difficult. I honestly don't think they mean to be, it's just the way they're made.'

'They're made without heart,' Mrs Healy said, her eyes dangerously bright. 'Oh, they have something in there all right beating away and sending the blood out, but it's not a heart. Look at Barry's father, he's not even here this evening even though he knew Barry was having a friend to supper. He *knew* and he's still not here.'

This was worse than Barry could have believed possible. He had no idea that his mother would go in at the deep end in the first half an hour.

But to his amazement Fiona seemed to be able to cope with it quite easily.

'That's men for you. When I bring Barry home to my house to meet my family, my father will let me down too. Oh, he'll be there all right, he's always there. But I bet you within five minutes he'll tell Barry it's dangerous to ride a motorbike, it's dangerous to drive a supermarket van, it's stupid to follow football. If he can think of anything wrong with learning Italian he'll say that. He only sees all the things that are wrong with everything, not the things that are right. It's very depressing.'

'And what does your mother say to all this?' Barry's mother was interested in the situation, her own attack on her husband seemed to be put aside for the moment.

'Well, I think over the years she started to agree with him. They're old you see, Mrs Healy, much older than you and Barry's father. I'm the youngest of a big family. They're set in their ways, you won't change them now.' She looked so eager with her glasses glinting and a big pink bow tying back her nice shiny hair. Any mother would be glad to have a warm girl like this for her son.

Barry saw his mother beginning to relax.

'Barry, like a good lad will you go into the kitchen and put the pie into the oven, and do what has to be done out there.'

He left them and clattered around, then he crept back to the door to hear what was going on in the sitting room. They were speaking in low voices and he couldn't make it out. Please God may Fiona not be saying anything stupid. And may his mother not be telling all the fantasies about Dad having another woman. He sighed and went back to the kitchen to set the table for the three of them. He felt annoyed with his father for not being there. It was after all an attempt at restoring the situation to normal. He *could* have made an effort. Did Dad not see he was only giving fuel to Mam's suspicions by all this?

Why couldn't he just come in and act the part for an evening? But still, his mother had made a chicken pie and an apple tart for afterwards. This was an advance.

The supper went better than he dared hope. Fiona ate everything that was put in front of her and almost licked the plate. She said she'd love to know how to make pastry. She was no good at cooking, and then suddenly a thought struck her. '*That's* what I could do, go to a cookery class,' she cried. 'Barry was asking what I'd really like to learn, and now that I see this spread I know what I'd enjoy.'

'That's a good idea,' Barry said, delighted at the praise for his mother's cooking.

'You'd want to make sure that you got someone with a light hand to teach you pastry,' his mother said.

Finding fault with the idea, of course. Barry fumed inside.

But Fiona didn't seem to mind. 'Yes, I know, and of course it would be the middle of the term and all. Listen ... no, I couldn't ask ... but maybe ...' She looked at Barry's mother eagerly.

'Go on, what is it?'

'I don't suppose on Tuesday or Thursday when Barry's at his evening class, that *you* would show me, you know give me a few hints?' The older woman was silent for a moment. Fiona rushed in. 'I'm sorry, that's typical of me, open my big mouth before I think what I'm going to say.'

'I'd be delighted to teach you to cook, Fiona,' said Barry's mother 'We'll start next Tuesday, with bread and scones.'

Brigid Dunne was very impressed. 'Getting his mother to teach you cooking, now that's a clever move,' she said admiringly.

'Well, it sort of came out naturally, I just said it.' Fiona was amazed at her own daring.

'And you're the one who says she's no good with men. When are we going to meet this Barry?'

'Soon, I don't want to overpower him with all my friends, particularly sexy, over-confident ones like you.'

'You have changed, Fiona,' Brigid said.

*

'Grania? It's Fiona.'

'Oh great, I thought it was Head Office. How are you? Have you done it yet?'

'Done what?'

'You know,' Grania said.

'No, not yet, but soon. It's all on course, I just rang to thank you.'

'Whatever for?'

'For saying I was a bit dopey.'

'I never said that, Fiona.' Grania was stung.

'No, but you told me to get my act together and it worked a dream. He's mad about me, and his mother is. And it couldn't be better.'

'Well, I'm glad.' Grania sounded pleased.

'I just rang to ask did you do your bit, go back to see your father?'

'No. I tried, but I lost my nerve at the last moment.'

'Grania!' Fiona sounded stern.

'Hey, you of all people lecturing me.'

'I know, but we did promise to keep each other up to all the things we said that evening.'

'I know.'

'And Brigid hasn't talked about low cal sweetener since then, and I've been as brave as a tiger about things. You wouldn't believe it.'

'Oh bloody hell, Fiona. I'll go tonight,' said Grania.

Grania took a deep breath and knocked on the door. Her father answered. She couldn't read his face.

'You still have your key, you don't have to have the door answered for you,' he said.

'I didn't like to waltz in as if I still lived here,' she said.

'Nobody said you couldn't live here.'

'I know, Dad.' They still stood in the hall. An awkward silence all around them. 'And where's everyone else? Are they all at home?'

'I don't know,' her father said.

'Come on, Dad. You must know.'

'I don't. Your mother may be in the kitchen reading, and Brigid may be upstairs. I was in my room.'

'How's it getting along?' she asked, to try and cover the loneliness. This wasn't a big house, not big enough for the man not to know whether his wife and daughter were at home or not. And not to care.

'It's fine,' he said.

'Will you show it to me?' Grania wondered was it going to be like this for ever, making conversation with her father like drawing teeth.

'Certainly.'

He led her into the room and she literally gasped in surprise. The evening sun came through the window, the yellow and gold colours all around the windowseat picked up the light, and the curtains in purple and gold looked as if they were for a stage in a theatre. His shelves were full of books and ornaments, and the little desk shone and glowed in the evening light.

'Dad, it's beautiful. I never knew you could make anything like this,' Grania said.

'There's a lot we never knew about each other,' he said.

'Please, Dad, let me admire your lovely, lovely room, and look at those frescoes, they're marvellous.'

'Yes.'

'And all those colours, Dad. It's like a dream.'

Her enthusiasm was so genuine he couldn't keep cold and stiff. 'It is a bit of a dream, but then I've always been a stupid sort of dreamer, Grania.'

'I inherited it from you then.'

'No, I don't think you did.'

'Not in this artistic way, I couldn't make a room like this in a million years. But I do have my dreams, yes.'

'They're not proper dreams, Grania. Truly they're not.'

'I tell you this, Dad, I never loved anyone before, apart from you and Mam, and to be honest, you more. No, I want to say this because you might not let me talk again. Now I know what love is about. It's wanting the best for someone else, it's wanting them to be happier than you are, isn't that it?'

'Yes.' He spoke in a very dead voice.

'You felt that for Mam once, didn't you? I mean, you probably still do.'

'I think it changes as you get older.'

'But I won't have much time for it to get older. You and Mam have had nearly twenty-five years, Tony'll be dead and buried in twenty-five years' time. He smokes and drinks and is hopeless. You know that. If I get a good ten years I'll be lucky.'

'Grania, you could do so much better.'

'You couldn't do better than to be loved by the person you love, Dad. I know that, you know that.'

'He's not reliable.'

'I rely on him absolutely, Dad. I would trust him with my life.'

'Wait until he leaves you with a fatherless child. You'll remember these words then.'

'More than anything else on earth I would love to have his child.'

'Well, go ahead. Nothing's going to stop you.'

Grania bent and examined the flowers on the little table. 'You buy these for yourself, Dad?'

'Who else do you think would buy them for me?'

There were tears in her eyes. 'I'd buy them for you if you'd let me, I'd come here and sit with you, and if I had your grandchild I would bring him or her here.'

'You're telling me you're pregnant, is that it?'

'No, that's not it. I'm in control of whether I will be or not, and I won't until I know the child would be welcomed by everyone.'

'That could be a long wait,' he said. But she noticed that this time there were tears in his eyes too.

'Dad,' she said, and it was hard to say which of them moved first towards the other until their arms were around each other and their tears were lost in each other's shoulders.

Brigid and Fiona went to the pictures.

'Have you been to bed with him yet?'

'No, but there's no rush, it's all going according to plan,' Fiona said.

'Longest plan since time began,' Brigid grumbled.

'No, believe me, I know what I'm doing.'

'I'm glad someone does,' Brigid said. 'Dad and Grania have gone all emotional on us. Grania's sitting in Dad's room talking to him as if a cross word had never been said between them.'

'Isn't that good?'

'Yes, it's good, of course it's good, but it's a mystery,' Brigid complained.

'And what does your mother say about it?'

'Nothing. That's another mystery. I used to think that we were the dullest, most ordinary family in the western world. Now I think I live in a madhouse. I used to think that you were the odd one, Fiona. But there you are, the little pet of the house, learning to be a gourmet chef from the mother and planning to bed the son. How did it all happen?'

Brigid hated mysteries and being confused by things. She sounded very disgruntled indeed.

The cookery classes were a great success. Sometimes Barry's father was there. Tall and dark and watchful, he looked a lot younger than his wife, but then his mind was not so troubled. He worked in a big nurseries and vegetable farm, delivering produce and flowers to restaurants and hotels around the city. He was perfectly pleasant to Fiona but not enthusiastic. He was not curious about her and he gave the impression of someone passing through rather than someone who lived there.

Sometimes Barry came back from his own Italian class and ate the results of their cooking, but Fiona said he shouldn't hurry back specially. It was too late for eating anyway, and he liked talking to the people afterwards. She would take the bus home herself. After all, they would meet on other nights.

Bit by bit she began to hear the story of the Great Infidelity. She tried not to listen at first. 'Don't tell me all this, Mrs Healy please, you'll wish you hadn't when you're all nice and friendly with Mr Healy again and then you'll be sorry.'

'No, I won't, you're my friend. Chop those a lot finer, Fiona. You don't want great lumps in it. You have to hear. You have to know what Barry's father is like.'

Everything had been fine until two years ago. Well, you know, fine in a manner of speaking. His hours had always been difficult, she had lived with that. Sometimes up for the four-thirty run in the morning, sometimes working late at night. But there had been time off. Grand time in the middle of the day sometimes. She could remember when they had gone to the cinema for the two o'clock show, and then had tea and buns afterwards and she was the envy of every other woman around. None of them ever went to the pictures in the daylight with their husbands. And he had never wanted her to work in the old days. He had said that he brought in plenty for the two of them and the child. She should keep the home nice and cook for them and be there when he got time off. That way they could have a good life.

But two years ago it had all changed. He had met someone and started having an affair.

'You can't be sure, Mrs Healy,' Fiona said as she weighed out the raisins and sultanas for the fruit cake. 'It could be anything, you know, like pressure at work, or the traffic getting worse, you know the way everyone's giving out about rush hour.'

'There's no rush hour at four a.m. when he comes home.' Her face was grim.

'But isn't it these awful hours?'

'I checked with the company, he works twenty-eight hours a week. He's out of here nearly twice that much.'

'The travelling to and fro?' Fiona said desperately

'He's about ten minutes from work,' Barry's mother said.

'He might just want a bit of space.'

'He has that all right, he sleeps in the spare room.'

'Maybe not to wake you?'

'Maybe not to be near me.'

'And if she exists who do you think she is?' Fiona spoke in a whisper.

'I don't know but I'll find out.'

'Would it be someone at work, do you think?'

'No, I know all of them. There's no one likely there. But it's someone he met *through* work though, and that could be half of Dublin.'

It was very distressing to listen to her. All that unhappiness, and according to Barry it was all in her mind.

'Does she talk to you at all about it?' Barry asked Fiona.

Fiona thought there as a sort of sacredness about the conversations over the floured boards and the bubbling casseroles, over cups of coffee after the cooking when Fiona would sit on the sofa and the huge half-blind Cascarino would lie purring on her lap.

'A bit here and there, not much,' she lied.

Nessa Healy thought that Fiona was her friend, it wasn't the action of a friend to repeat conversations back.

Barry and Fiona saw a lot of each other. They went to football matches and to the cinema and as the weather got nicer they went on the motorbike out to Wicklow or Kildare and saw places that Fiona had never been.

He had not asked her to come on the trip to Rome, the *viaggio* as they kept calling it. Fiona hoped that at some stage soon he would, and so she had applied for a passport just in case.

Sometimes they went out in a foursome with Suzi and Luigi, who had invited them to their wedding in Dublin the middle of June. Suzi said that mercifully the idea of a Roman wedding had been abandoned. Her parents said no, Luigi's parents said no, and all their friends who weren't in the

Italian class said they were off their skulls. So it would be a Roman honeymoon instead.

'Are you learning any Italian yourself?' Fiona enquired.

'No. If they want to talk to me they have to speak my language,' said Suzi, the confident handsome girl who would have expected Eskimos to learn her language if she were passing the North Pole.

Then there was the big fund-raising party. The Italian class, all thirty of them, were to provide the food. Drink was being sponsored by various off licences and the supermarket. Somebody knew a group which would play free in return for their picture in the local paper. Each pupil was expected to invite at least five people who would pay £5 a head for the party. That would raise £750 for the *viaggio* and then there would be a huge raffle. The prizes were enormous, and that might raise another £150 or even more. The travel agency was bringing the price down all the time. The accommodation had been booked in a *pensione* in Rome. There would be the trip to Florence staying overnight at a hostel, and on to Siena before they went back to Rome.

Barry was drumming up his five for the party.

'I'd like you to come, Dad,' he said. 'It means a lot to me, and remember Mam and I always went to your works outings.'

'I'm not sure I'll be free, son. But if I am I'll be there, I can't say fairer than that.'

And Barry would have Fiona, his mother, a fellow from work and a next-door neighbour. Fiona was going to ask her friends Grania and Brigid but they were going already because of their father. And Suzi was going with Luigi. It would be a great night.

The cookery lessons continued. Fiona and Barry's mother were going to make a very exotic dessert for the party; it was called *cannoli*. Full of fruit and nuts and ricotta cheese in pastry and deep fried.

'Are you sure that's not one of the pastas?' Barry asked anxiously.

No, the women assured him, that was *cannelloni*. He knew nothing. They asked him to check with Signora. Signora said that *cannoli alla siciliana* was one of the most mouth-watering dishes in the world, she couldn't wait to taste it.

The confidences continued to be exchanged between Fiona and Nessa Healy as they cooked. Fiona said that she really did like Barry a lot, he was a generous kind person, but she didn't want to rush him because she didn't think he was ready to settle down.

And Barry's mother told Fiona that she couldn't give up on her husband. There was a time she might have been able to say he didn't love her, and let him go to whoever it was that he did love. But not now.

'And why is that?' Fiona wanted to know.

'When I was in hospital that time, when I was a bit foolish you know, he brought me flowers. A man doesn't do that unless he cares. He brought a bunch of freesias in and left them for me. He says he didn't, but I know he did. For all his blustering and all his saying that he's not going to be railroaded into things, he *does* care, Fiona. That's what I'm holding on to.'

And Fiona sat, her eyes enormous behind her glasses and her hands floury.

And cursed herself to the pit of hell and back for having been so stupid. She knew that if she spoke it would have to be at that very minute, and she did consider it.

But when she looked at Nessa Healy's face and saw all the life and hope in it she realised what a problem she had. How could she tell this woman that she, the girl who worked selling coffee in the hospital waiting room, had delivered the bloody freesias? She, Fiona, who wasn't even meant to know about the suicide attempt. It had never been discussed. Whatever Fiona was going to attempt in order to try and undo the harm she had managed to create, it could not involve taking all this hope and life away. She would find some other way.

Some other way, Fiona said to herself desperately, as the days went by and the woman who might one day be her mother-in-law told how love could never be dead if someone sent a bunch of flowers.

Suzi would know what to do, but Fiona would not ask her, not in a million years. Suzi might well tell Luigi, and Luigi would tell his old pal Bartolomeo, as he insisted on calling Barry. And anyway, Suzi would despise her, and Fiona didn't want that.

Brigid and Grania Dunne would be no use in a situation like this. They'd just say that Fiona was reverting to her old ways and getting into a tizz about nothing. There was an old teacher at school who used that word. Don't get in a tizz, girls, she would cry, and they would have to stuff their fists down their throats to stop laughing. But later on Brigid and Grania said that tizz was a good word for Fiona's temperament, sort of fussy and dizzy and troubled. She couldn't let them know how frightening and upsetting the tizz was this time because they would say it was all her own fault. And of course it undoubtedly was.

'You are fond of me, Fiona?' Mrs Healy asked after they had made a lemon meringue pie.

'Very fond,' Fiona said eagerly.

'And you'd tell me the truth?'

'Oh, yes.' Fiona's voice was a squeak at this stage. She waited for the blow to fall. Somehow the flowers had been traced back to her. Maybe it was all for the best.

'Do you think I should get my colours done?' Mrs Healy asked.

'Your colours?'

'Yes. You go to a consultant and they tell you what shades suit you and what drain the colour from your face. It's quite scientific, apparently.'

Fiona struggled for speech. 'And how much does it cost?' she asked eventually.

'Oh, I have the money,' Mrs Healy said.

'Well, I'm not much good at these things but I have a very smart friend, I'll ask her. She'll know if it's a good idea or not.'

'Thanks, Fiona,' said Mrs Healy, who must be about forty-five and who looked seventy-five and still thought her husband loved her because of Fiona.

*

Suzi said that it was a brilliant idea. 'When are you going?' she asked.

Fiona didn't have the courage to admit that she hadn't been talking about herself. She was also a little upset that Suzi felt she needed advice. But she was trying so hard to be grown up these days and not to dither that she said firmly yes, it had been something she was thinking of.

Nessa Healy was pleased with this news. 'Do you know another thing I think we should do?' Mrs Healy said confidingly. 'I think we should go to an expensive hair stylist's and have a whole new look.'

Fiona felt faint. All the money she had been saving so painstakingly for the *viaggio*, if she ever went on it, would trickle away on these huge improvements that she and Barry's mother were about to embark on.

Fortunately Suzi saved the day here by knowing a hairdressing school.

And as the weeks went on Mrs Healy stopped wearing brown but dug out all her pale-coloured clothes and wore nice dark-coloured scarves with them. Her hair was coloured and cut short, and she looked fifty instead of seventy-five.

Fiona had her dark, shiny hair cut very short and thick, dead straight with a fringe, and everyone said she looked terrific. She wore bright reds and yellows, and one or two of the house surgeons said flirtatious things to her, which she just laughed at good-naturedly instead of thinking that they might be going to marry her as she might have done in the old days.

And Barry's father stayed at home a little more, but not a lot more, and seemed perfectly pleasant any time Fiona was in the house.

But it didn't look as if the colours or the new hairstyle were going to win him back to the way things had been before the Affair began two years ago.

'You're very good to my mother, she looks terrific,' Barry said.

'And what about me, don't I look terrific too?'

'You always looked terrific. But listen, never let her know that I told you about the suicide. She often asks me to swear that I never told you. She'd hate to lose your respect, that's what it is.'

Fiona swallowed when he said this. She could never tell Barry either. There must be people who lived with a lie for ever. It was quite possible. It wasn't even that important a lie, it was just that it had led to such false hopes.

Nothing prepared Fiona for the revelation that came as they were separating eggs and beating the whites for a meringue topping.

'I've discovered where she works.'

'Who?'

'The woman. Dan's woman, the mistress.' Mrs Healy spoke with satisfaction, as if of a detection job well done.

'And where is it?' Did this all mean that Barry's poor mother would get another attack of nerves and try to kill herself again? Fiona's face was anxious.

'In one of the smartest restaurants in Dublin, it would seem. Quentin's no less. Have you heard of it?'

'Yes, you often see it in the papers,' poor Fiona said.

'And you might see it in the papers again,' said the older woman darkly.

She couldn't mean she was going to go there to Quentin's Restaurant and make a scene. Could she?

'And are you sure that's where she is? I mean, how do you know exactly, Mrs Healy?'

'I followed him,' she said triumphantly.

'You followed him?'

'He went out in his van last night. He often does on a Wednesday. Stays in and watches television and then after twelve he says he has to go and do late night work. I know it's a lie, I've always known that about Wednesday – there's no night work, and anyway he's all dressed up, brushing his teeth, clean shirt. The lot.'

'But how did you follow him, Mrs Healy? Didn't he go out in his van?'

'Indeed he did. But I had a taxi waiting, with its lights off, and away we went.'

'A taxi waiting all that time? Until he was ready to go out?' The sheer, mad extravagance of it stunned Fiona more than the act itself.

'No, I knew it would be about midnight so I booked it for fifteen minutes earlier just in case. Then I got in and followed him.'

'And merciful Lord, Mrs Healy, what did the taxi-driver think?'

'He thought about the nice sum clicking up on his meter, that's what he thought.'

'And what happened?'

'Well, the van went off and turned into the lane behind Quentin's.' She paused. She didn't *look* very upset. Fiona had often seen Mrs Healy more strained, more stressed than this. What could she have seen on this extraordinary mission?

'And then?'

'Well, then we waited. I mean he waited, and the taxi driver and I waited. And a woman came out. I couldn't see her, it was so dark. And she got straight into the van as if she knew it was going to be there, and they took off so quickly that we lost them.'

Fiona felt vastly relieved. But Mrs Healy was practical. 'We won't lose them next Wednesday,' she said determinedly.

Fiona had been very unsuccessful in trying to head off this second excursion. 'Would you look at the cost of it? You could get a lovely new check skirt for what you pay the taxi-driver.'

'It's my housekeeping money, Fiona. I'll spend what I save on what gives me pleasure.'

'But suppose he sees you, suppose you're discovered.'

'I'm not the one that's doing anything wrong, I'm just going out for a drive in a taxi.'

'But what if you do see her? What difference will it make?'

'I'll know what she's like, the woman he *thinks* he loves.' And her voice sounded so sure that Dan Healy only thought he loved another that Fiona's blood ran chill.

'Doesn't your mother work in Quentin's?' Fiona asked Brigid.

'Yeah, she does. Why?'

'Would she know people who work there at night, like waitresses, young ones?'

'I suppose she would, she's been there long enough. Why?'

'If I were to give you a name would you be able to ask her about them, like without saying why you were asking?'

'I might, why?'

'You never stop asking why.'

'I don't do anything without asking why,' Brigid said.

'Okay, forget it then,' said Fiona with spirit.

'No, I didn't say I wouldn't.'

'Forget it. Forget it.'

'All right, I'll check it out with her. Is it your Barry? Is that what it is? Do you think he has someone else who works in Quentin's?' Brigid was all interest now.

'Not exactly.'

'Well, I could ask her of course.'

'No, you ask too many questions. Let's leave it, you'd give everything away.'

'Oh, come on Fiona, we've all been friends for ever. You cover for us, we cover for you. I'll find out, just give me the name and I'll ask dead casual like to my mum.'

'Maybe.'

'What is her name anyway?' Brigid asked.

'I don't know yet, but I will soon,' said Fiona, and it was obvious to Brigid and anyone else who might have been listening that she was telling the truth.

'How could we find out her name?' Fiona asked Mrs Healy.

'I don't know. I think we just have to confront them.'

'No, I mean knowing her name would give us an advantage. There might be no need to confront her.'

'I don't see how that could be.' Nessa Healy was confused. They sat in silence thinking about it.

'Suppose,' said Fiona. 'Suppose you were to say that someone from Quentin's rang and asked him to ring back, but whoever it was, she didn't leave a name, said he'd know who it was. Then we could listen who he asks for.'

'Fiona, you're wasted in that hospital,' Barry's mother said. 'You should have been a private eye.'

They did it that very evening, when Dan had been welcomed and given a little bit of peanut brittle to taste. Then, as if she had just remembered it, his wife told him about the message from Quentin's.

He went to the hall to phone and Fiona kept the sounds of the electric mixer at high blast, while Barry's mother crept to listen at the door.

They were both amongst the ingredients when Dan Healy came back into the kitchen. 'Are you sure she said Quentin's?'

'That's what she said.'

'It's just that I rang them now and they say that no one there was looking for me.'

His wife shrugged. It implied that this was business for you. He seemed troubled and he left soon to go upstairs.

'Did you hear him ask for anyone?' said Fiona.

Mrs Healy nodded, her eyes bright and feverish. 'Yes, we have the name. He spoke to her.'

'And who was it? What was her name?' Fiona could hardly breathe with the excitement and the danger of it all.

'Well, whoever it was answered the phone and he said, "Jesus, Nell, why did you ring me at home?" That's what he said. Her name is Nell.'

'WHAT?'

'Nell. Little bitch, selfish, thoughtless little cow. Well, she needn't think he loves her, he sounded furious with her.'

'Yes,' said Fiona.

'So now we know her name, that gives us power,' said Nessa Healy.

Fiona said nothing.

Nell was the name of Brigid and Grania's mother. It was Nell Dunne who worked at the reception desk in Quentin's and answered the phone when it rang.

Barry's father was involved with her friends' mother. Not a silly little good-time girl as they had thought, a woman as old as Nessa Healy. A woman with a husband and grown-up daughters of her own. Fiona wondered were the complications of this ever going to end.

'Fiona? It's Brigid.'

'Oh yes, listen, I'm not meant to get phone calls at work.'

'If you'd done your Leaving Cert and got a proper job you'd have been able to have people phone you,' Brigid complained.

'Yeah, well, I didn't. What is it, Brigid? There's a crowd of people here waiting to be served.' There was nobody as it happened, but she felt ill at ease talking to her friend now that she knew such a terrible secret about their family.

'This bird, the one that you think Barry fancies, the one working in Quentin's . . . you were going to tell me her name and I was going to get the low-down on her from my mam.'

'No!' Fiona's voice was almost a screech.

'Hey, you were the one who asked me.'

'I've changed my mind.'

'Well, if he is having a bit on the side you should know. People should know, it's their right.'

'Is it, Brigid? Is it?' Fiona knew she sounded very intense.

'Of course it is. If he says he loves you and if he tells her he loves her, then for God's sake . . .'

'But it's not exactly like that, you see.'

'He doesn't say he loves you?'

'Yes he does. But well, what the hell!'

'Fiona?'

'Yes?'

'You are becoming quite seriously mad. I think you should know this.'

'Sure, Brigid,' said Fiona, grateful for once that she had always been considered a person in a permanent tizz.

'Would you mind more if she were young or old?' Fiona asked Barry's mother.

'Nell? She has to be young, why else would he have strayed?'

'There's no understanding men, everyone says that. She could be as old as a tree, you know.'

Nessa Healy was very serene. 'If he had a dalliance it was because some young one threw herself at him. Men go for flattery. But he loves me. That was always clear. When I was unavoidably in hospital that time I told you about, he came in when I was asleep and left me flowers. Whatever else there is to hold on to, there's that.'

Barry came in full of excitement. The party on Thursday had been so well subscribed, you would never believe it. It was going to be fantastic. *Magnifico*. Mr Dunne had said that he would be able to announce that with a success like this on their hands a whole new programme in adult education might start next year.

'Mr Dunne?' Fiona said in a hollow voice.

'He was the one who set it up, he's a great pal of Signora's. You told me you knew his daughters.'

'Yes, I do.' Fiona spoke in a hollow voice.

'So he's delighted about the whole thing. It makes him look good too.'

'And he'll be there?'

'Hey, Fiona are you asleep or something? Didn't you tell me we couldn't sell tickets to his daughters because they're going with him?'

'Did I say that?' She must have, but it was long ago, before she knew all that she knew now.

'And do you *think* his wife is coming?' she asked.

'Oh, I'd say so. Any of us who have a wife or a husband, a mother or a father, not to mention a loving girlfriend . . . well, we're making sure they're coming.'

'And your father is coming?' Fiona said.

'As of today he says he is,' said Bartolomeo, Italian speaker, pleased and happy that he was able to field a good team.

The night of the *festa* in Mountainview school was eagerly awaited.

Signora had been going to buy a new dress but she decided at the last moment to spend the money on coloured lights for the school hall.

'Aw, come on Signora,' said Suzi Sullivan. 'I have a great dress picked out for you in the Good as New shop. Let them have whatever old lights are there, up in the school.'

'I want them to remember this evening always. If there are nice coloured lights it will add to the romance of it . . . What will anyone care if I spend forty pounds on a dress? Nobody will notice.'

'If I can get you the lights will you get the dress?' Suzi asked.

'You're not going to suggest that Luigi . . .' Signora looked very doubtful about it indeed.

'No, I swear I won't let him get in touch with the underworld again. It took me long enough to get him out of it. No, I really do know someone in the electrical business, a fellow called Jacko. I needed someone to rewire the flat and Lou asked in the Italian class and Laddy knew this guy who did up the hotel where he works. He'd know what you want, will I send him up to you?'

'Well, Suzi . . .'

'And if he's cheap, as he will be, then you'll buy the dress?' She looked so eager.

'Of course, Suzi,' Signora said, wondering why people set such a store by clothes.

Jacko came up to look at the school hall. 'Built like a bloody barn, of course,' he said.

'I know, but I thought if we had three or four rows of coloured lights, you know, a bit like Christmas lights . . .'

'It would look pathetic,' Jacko said.

'Well, we don't have enough money to buy anything else.' Signora looked distressed now.

'Who said anything about buying? I'll light the place properly for you. Bring proper gear up, do it like a disco. Install it for the night, take it away after.'

'But you can't do that. It would cost a fortune. There'd have to be someone to operate it.'

'I'll come and see it doesn't blow up. And it's only for a night, I won't charge you.'

'But we couldn't expect you to do all that.'

'Just a nice big board advertising my electrical business,' Jacko said, grinning from ear to ear.

'Could I give you a couple of tickets, in case you would like to bring a partner or anything?' Signora was desperate to return his kindness.

'No, I travel alone these days, Signora,' he said with his crooked smile. 'But you never know what I might pick up at the party. Minding the lights won't take up all my time.'

Bill Burke and Lizzie Duffy had to get ten people between them and Bill found it hard to sell tickets at the bank because Grania Dunne had got in first. As it happened, Lizzie's mother was going to be in Dublin for the night.

'Do you think we dare?' Bill said. Mrs Duffy was very much a loose cannon, the dangers might be greater than the rewards.

Lizzie thought about it seriously. 'What's the very worst she could do?' she wondered.

Bill gave it serious thought. 'She could get drunk and sing with the band?' he suggested.

'No, when she gets drunk she tells everyone what a bastard my father is.'

'The music will be very loud, no one will hear her. Let's ask her,' said Bill.

Constanza could have bought every ticket and not noticed the dip in her bank balance, but that wasn't the point. She had to invite people, that's what it was about.

Veronica would come, of course, and bring a friend from work. Daughters were marvellous. More diffidently she asked her son, Richard, would he like to take his girlfriend, and to her surprise he sounded eager. The children had been a huge support to her after the trial and sentence. Harry was serving a minimum prison sentence, as she had foretold. Every week in her small seaside apartment she got phone calls and visits from her four children. She must have done something right.

'You won't believe this.' Richard rang her a couple of days later. 'But you know your Italian *festa* thing up in Mountainview school? Mr Malone, my boss, is going. He was just talking to me about it today.'

'What a small world,' said Connie. 'Maybe I'll ask his father-in-law, then. Is Paul bringing his wife?'

'I imagine so,' said Richard. 'Older people always do.' Connie wondered who on earth at their Italian class could have invited Paul Malone.

Gus and Maggie told Laddy that *of course* they would come to the *festa*. Nothing would keep them away. They would ask their friend who ran the chip shop to come too, to thank him for all his interpreting, and they would give prizes of free dinners in the hotel with wine for the raffle.

Jerry Sullivan in the house where Signora stayed wanted to know what was the lower age limit.

'Sixteen, Jerry. I keep telling you that,' Signora said. She knew there was an inordinate interest in the school in a dance in their school hall which would have disco lights and real liquor.

Mr O'Brien, the Principal, had discouraged even the older children from attending. 'Don't you all spend enough time on these premises?' he had said. 'Why don't you go to your horrible smoke-filled basements listening to ear-injuring music as usual?'

Tony O'Brien was like a devil these days. In order to please Grania Dunne, the love of his life, he had given up smoking and it didn't suit him. But Grania had worked a miracle for him so in fairness he had to trade the smoking business. She had gone to visit her father and got him on their side.

He never knew how she had managed it, but the following day Aidan Dunne had strode into his office and offered his hand.

'I've been behaving like a father in a Victorian melodrama,' he had said. 'My daughter is old enough to know her own mind and if you make her happy then that's a good thing.'

Tony had nearly fallen out of his chair with the shock. 'I've lived a rackety old life, Aidan, and you know this. But honestly, Grania is the turning point for me. Your daughter makes me feel good and young and full of hope and happiness. I'll never let her down. If you believe anything you must believe that.'

And they had shaken hands with such vigour that both of their arms were sore for days.

It made everything much simpler both at school and at home. She had stopped taking her contraceptive pill. He knew it had taken a lot for Aidan to make that gesture. He was an odd man ... If he hadn't known him better Tony O'Brien would have believed that the Latin master really did have a thing going with Signora.

But there wasn't a chance of that.

Signora's friends Brenda and Patrick Brennan were both coming to the party. What was the point of being successful, they said, if they could not delegate? There was an under chef, there was another greeter, the place could survive one evening without them or it wasn't run properly in the first place. And of course Nell Dunne from the cash desk would be there too, so Quentin's would be really running on the B team, they laughed to each other.

'I don't know why we're all going at all, we must be touched in the head,' Nell Dunne said.

'For solidarity and support of course, what else?' Ms Brennan said, looking at Nell oddly.

Nell felt, as she so often felt, that Ms Brennan didn't really like her. It was after all a reasonable question. Smart people like the Brennans and yes, even herself, Nell Dunne, a person who mattered in Dublin in her black dress and yellow scarf sitting like a queen in Quentin's, and all of them traipsing up to that barracks of a school Mountainview, where Aidan had soldiered on so long and for nothing.

But she wished she hadn't spoken. The Brennans thought less of her for it somehow.

Still, she might well go. Dan wasn't free that night, he had to go to something with his son he said, and her own children would be annoyed with her if she didn't make the effort.

It would be dreary, like everything always had been in that school. But at least it wasn't the kind of outing that you'd bother dressing up for. Five pounds for a bit of pizza and a band that would deafen you belting out Italian songs. God almighty, what she did for her family!

Grania and Brigid were getting dressed for the *festa*.

'I hope it goes well, for Dad's sake,' Grania said.

'Dad can take anything if he accepts that you go to bed with his boss. Nothing's going to knock him off his perch now.' Brigid was back combing her hair in front of the sitting-room mirror.

Grania was annoyed. 'I wish you'd stop dwelling on the going to bed bit. There's a lot more to it than that.'

'At his age would he not get exhausted?' Brigid giggled.

'If I were into talking about it I'd have you green with jealousy,' Grania said, putting on her eyeshadow. Their mother came in. 'Hey, Mam, get a move on, we're going in a few minutes,' Grania said.

'I'm ready.'

They looked at their mother, hair barely combed, no make-up, an ordinary dress with a loose cardigan over her shoulders. There was no point in saying anything. The sisters exchanged a glance and made no comment.

'Right then,' said Grania. 'Off we go.'

This was Nessa Healy's first outing since she had been in hospital. The woman who had done her colours had given her very good advice.

Barry thought he hadn't seen his mother looking so well in years. There was no doubt but that Fiona had been a wonderful influence on her. He wondered should he ask Fiona to go on the *viaggio* with him. It was implying a lot, like they would share a room, and that side of things had not progressed very far in the weeks they had been together. He wanted to, but there was never the opportunity or the place or the right occasion.

His father looked uneasy. 'What kind of people will be there, son?'

'All the people who go to the class, Dad, and whoever they could drag like I'm dragging you. It'll be great, honestly.'

'Yes, I'm sure.'

'And, Dad, Miss Clarke says I can drive the supermarket van even though it's a social outing. So I can take you home or Mam home if you get bored or tired or anything.'

He looked so eager and grateful that his father felt ashamed. 'When did Dan Healy ever leave a party while there was still drink on the table?' he asked.

'And Fiona's meeting us there?' Mrs Healy would have liked the moral support of this lively young girl she had grown so fond of. Fiona had made her promise to hold off about confronting everyone with Nell. Just for a week. One week. And reluctantly Nessa Healy had agreed.

'Yes, she was very insistent. She wanted to go on her own,' said Barry. 'Right, are we off?'

They were off.

Signora was there in the hall.

She had looked at herself in the long mirror before she left the Sullivans' house. Truly she hardly recognised herself as the woman who had come to Ireland a year ago. The widow, as she saw herself, weeping for her dead Mario, her long hair trailing behind her, her long skirt hanging unevenly. Timid, unable to ask for work or a place to live, frightened of her family.

Today she stood tall and elegant, her coffee and lilac dress somehow perfect with her odd-coloured hair. Suzi had said that this dress might have cost £300. Imagine. She had let Suzi make up her face.

'Nobody will see me,' she had protested.

'It's your night, Signora,' Peggy Sullivan had insisted.

And it was. She stood there in a hall with flashing coloured lights, with pictures and posters all over it, with the sound system playing a loop tape of Italian songs and music until the live band would arrive with a flourish. They had decided that *Nessun Dorma, Volare* and *Arrivederci Roma* should be played often on the tape. Nothing too unfamiliar.

Aidan Dunne came in. 'I'll never be able to thank you,' he said.

'It's I who have to thank you, Aidan,' He was the only person around them who had not been given an Italianised form of his name. It made him more special.

'Are you nervous?' he asked.

'A little. But then, we are surrounded by friends, why should I be nervous? Everyone is for us, there's nobody against us.' She smiled. She was putting out of her mind the fact that not one of her family, her own family, would come to support her tonight. She had asked them gently but had not begged. It would have been so nice, just once, to have said to people, this is my sister, this is my mother. But no.

'You look really terrific, Nora. Yourself, I mean, not just the whole place.'

He had never called her Nora before. She hadn't time to take it in because people were arriving. At the door a friend of Constanza, an extremely efficient woman called Vera, was taking the tickets.

In the cloakrooms, young Caterina from the Italian class and her friend, a bright girl called Harriet, were busy giving people cloakroom tickets and telling them not to lose them. Strangers were coming in and marvelling over the place.

The Principal, Tony O'Brien, was busy passing all compliments their way. 'Nothing to do with me, I'm afraid, all down to Mr Dunne whose project this is, and to Signora.'

They stood there like a bride and groom accepting compliments.

Fiona saw Grania and Brigid come in with their mother. She gasped. She had met Mrs Dunne many times before, but tonight she hardly recognised her. The woman looked a complete wreck. She had barely bothered to wash her face.

Good, thought Fiona grimly. She felt a horrible sensation in her chest, as if she'd swallowed a lump of something that would not go up or down, like a piece of very hard potato or a piece of raw celery. She knew it was fear. Fiona, the mouse in spectacles, was going to interfere in everyone else's life. She was going to tell a whole lot of people a pack of lies and frighten them to death. Would she be able for it, or would she fall on the floor in a swoon and make everything worse?

Of course she would be able for it. Remember that night around in the townhouse when the old man had gone out and Grania had bought the Chinese takeaway. Fiona had changed her whole style then, and look how much good had come out of it. She had single-handedly persuaded Nessa Healy to dress up and come to this party. That wasn't the action of a mouse in spectacles. She had gone so far she must get over this last fence. She must end the affair that was breaking everyone's heart. As soon as she had done this then she could get on with her own life and begin her own affair properly.

Fiona looked around her, trying to fasten a confident smile on her face. She would just wait until it began to warm up a bit.

It took no time at all for it all to warm up. There was the roar of conversation, the clink of glasses and then the band arrived. The dancing started to serious sixties music which suited every age group.

Fiona went up to Nell Dunne, who was standing on her own looking very scornful. 'Do you remember me, Mrs Dunne?'

'Oh, Fiona?' she seemed to drag up the name with difficulty and not great interest.

'Yes, you were always nice to me when I was young, Mrs Dunne, I remember that.'

'Was I?'

'Yes, when I'd come to tea. I wouldn't want you to be made a fool of.'

'Why would I be made a fool of?'

'Dan, the man over there.'

'WHAT?' Nell looked to where Fiona was pointing.

'You know he goes round telling everyone he has this frump of a wife, and that she's always committing suicide and he can't wait to leave her. But he has a string of women, and he tells them all the same story.'

'I don't know what you're talking about.'

'And you're probably, let me see, Wednesday's woman and one other day. That's the way he works it.'

Nell Dunne looked at the smart woman with Dan Healy, laughing easily. This couldn't be the wife he had spoken of. 'And what makes *you* think you know anything about him?' she asked Fiona.

'Simple,' Fiona said. 'He had my mother too. Used to come up in the van and collect her outside work and take her off. She was besotted over him. It was awful.'

'Why are you telling me this?' Her eyes were wild, her voice was hushed. She was looking to the right and left of her.

Fiona realised that Mrs Dunne was greatly rattled. 'Well, he delivers vegetables and flowers to where I work you see, and he's always talking about his women, even you, and how you're just mad for it. "Posh lady from Quentin's", he calls you. And then I realised it was Brigid and Grania's mum he was talking about, just like it was once my mum ... and I felt sick.'

'I don't believe a word of this. You're a very dangerous and mad girl,' Mrs Dunne said, her eyes narrow as slits.

Luigi was dancing up a storm with Caterina from the class. Caterina and her friend Harriet had been released from cloakroom duty now and were making up for lost time.

'Excuse me.' Fiona dragged Luigi off the dance floor.

'What is it? Suzi doesn't mind, she *likes* me to dance.' He looked indignant.

'Do me one big favour,' Fiona begged. 'One thing without asking any questions at all.'

'That's me,' Luigi said.

'Could you go over to that dark man over there near the door, and tell him that if he knows what's good for him, he'll leave his Wednesday night lady alone.'

'But . . . ?'

'You said you wouldn't ask why!'

'I'm not asking why, I'm only asking would he hit me?'

'No, he won't. And Luigi?'

'Yeah?'

'Two things. Could you not say anything at all about this to Suzi or Bartolomeo?'

'That's done.'

'And could you try and look a bit ferocious when you're talking to him?'

'I'll try,' said Luigi, who thought it was something he might have to work at.

Nell Dunne was about to approach Dan. He was talking to a thickset, jowlish man with a very angry expression. She thought she would walk by and speak to him out of the corner of her mouth. Say she needed a word. Jerk her head to the corridor outside.

Why hadn't he told her he was coming to this anyway? So secretive. So hidden. There could be a lot more she didn't know. But just before she approached him he looked up and saw her, and a look of fear came into his eyes. He started to move away from her. She saw him grab his wife's arm and ask her to dance.

The band was playing *Ciao Ciao Bambino*. They hated it but a job was a job. They were going to appear in tomorrow's evening paper.

And Fiona stood on a chair so that she could observe it all. And remember it for ever. Barry had just asked her if she would come on the *viaggio* with him and she had said yes. Her future mother- and father-in-law were dancing with each other.

Grania and Brigid's mother was struggling to get out and look for her coat. She was demanding that Caterina and her friend Harriet open up the cloakroom for her. Only Fiona saw her go. Barry certainly didn't notice her. Maybe he might never have to know about her any more than anyone ever had to know about the freesias.

'Will you dance with me?' he said. It was *Three Coins in the Fountain*. Sugary and sentimental.

Barry held her very tight. '*Ti amo, Fiona, carissima Fiona.*'

'*Anch'io,*' she said.

'WHAT?' He could hardly believe it.

'*Anch'io.* It means me too. I love you too. *Ti amo da morire.*'

'God, how did you learn that?' he asked, impressed as he never had been.

'I asked Signora. I practised it. Just in case.'

'In case?'

'In case you said it, so that I'd know what to say.'

Around them people danced and sang the silly words of the song. Grania and Brigid's father hadn't gone hunting for his wife, he was talking to Signora. They looked like people who might dance at any moment if it occurred to one of them. Barry's father wasn't looking around anxiously, he was talking to his wife as if she were a real person again. Brigid wasn't laced into some tight skirt tugging at it, she wore a scarlet, loose dress and had her arms around the neck of a man who would not escape. Grania was leaning on the arm of Tony, the old man. They didn't dance but they were getting married. Fiona had been invited to the wedding.

Fiona thought it was wonderful to be grown up at last. She hadn't made *all* this happen, but she had made a very important part of it happen.

Viaggio

'Why are we asking Mr Dunne to our wedding?' Lou wanted to know.

'Because it would be nice for Signora, she won't have anyone.'

'Won't she have everyone else? Doesn't she live with your family, for God's sake?'

'You know what I mean.' Suzi was adamant.

'Do we have to have his wife as well? The list is getting longer every minute. You *do* know it's seventeen pounds a head and that's before a drink passes their lips?'

'Of course we're not asking his wife. Are you soft in the head?' Suzi said, and the look came over her face that Lou didn't like, the look that said she wondered was she marrying someone as thick as the wall.

'Certainly not his wife,' Lou said hastily. 'I must have been dreaming, that's all.'

'Is there anyone else from your side that you'd like?' Suzi asked.

'No, no. In a way they're my side as well, and aren't they coming on the honeymoon with us?' Lou said brightening up.

'Together with half of Dublin,' said Suzi, rolling her eyes.

'A Register office, I see' said Nell Dunne when Grania told her the date.

'Well, it would be hypocritical to get the job done in a church, neither of us ever going into one.' Nell shrugged. 'You will be there, Mam, won't you?' Grania sounded concerned.

'Of course I will, why do you ask?'

'It's just ... it's just ...'

'What is it, Grania? I've said I'll be there.'

'Well, you left that party up in the school before it even got going, and it was Dad's big night. And you're not going on his trip to Italy or anything.'

'I wasn't asked on his trip to Italy,' Nell Dunne said in a tight hard voice.

'Can everyone come on this holiday to Rome and Florence?' Bernie Duffy asked her daughter Lizzie.

'No, Mother. I'm sorry, but it's restricted to the people in the class,' Lizzie apologised.

'Wouldn't they want more people to swell the numbers?' Bernie had enjoyed herself boisterously at the *festa*. She thought the *viaggio* might be more of the same.

263

'What will we do, she's at me all the time?' Lizzie asked Bill later.

'We'll take her to Galway to see your father instead,' Bill said suddenly.

'We can't do that, can we?'

'Wouldn't it sort a lot of things out? It would distract her, and one way or the other it would take up her time and she wouldn't feel she was being left out of any fun if she was in the thick of all that drama.'

'That's a great idea.' Lizzie was full of admiration.

'And anyway, I should meet him, shouldn't I?'

'Why? We're not getting married till we're twenty-five.'

'I don't know. Luigi's getting married and Mr Dunne's daughter is getting married . . . I think we should get married sooner, don't you?'

'*Perché non?*' said Lizzie with a huge smile all over her face.

'I've asked Signora to write the letter to the Garaldis for me,' Laddy said. 'She said she'd explain everything.'

Maggie and Gus exchanged glances. Surely Signora would realise how casual the invitation had been to Laddy, the exuberance and gratitude of a warm-hearted family touched at the honesty of an Irish porter. They'd never expect him to take it so seriously, to go to Italian classes and to expect a huge welcome.

Signora was a mature woman who would understand the situation, wasn't she? Yet there was something childlike about the woman in the coffee and lilac dress, the woman at the *festa* that night who was so innocently thrilled with the success of the lessons and the support that had been given to her evening class. She was an unworldly sort of person, perhaps she would be like Laddy and think that these Garaldis were waiting with open arms for someone they must have well forgotten by now.

But nothing would let Gus and Maggie take from Laddy's excitement. He had his passport in the hotel safe and he had changed money into *lire* already. This trip meant everything to him, not a shadow must be allowed to fall on it. It will all be fine, Gus and Maggie told each other, willing it to be so.

'I've never been abroad in my life and imagine, I'm going twice this summer,' Fran told Connie.

'Twice?'

'Yes, as well as the *viaggio* Kathy won two tickets to America. You wouldn't believe it, she entered a competition in some business magazine that her friend Harriet brought into the school, and she won two tickets to New York, so we're both going.'

'Isn't that great. And have you anywhere to stay when you get there?'

'Yes. I have a friend, a fellow I used to go out with, he's going to drive to meet us. It's over four hundred miles, but they think nothing of that over there.'

'He must like you still if he's going to drive that distance.'

Fran smiled. 'I hope so, I still like him,' she said. 'Wasn't it a miracle that Kathy won the tickets?'

'Yes.'

'Do you know, when she told me I thought her father had given them to her. But no, when they came they were paid for by this magazine and all, so it's all above board.'

'Why would her father have given them and not told you?'

'Well, I don't see him now, and he's married to one of the richest women in Ireland, but I wouldn't take them from him as a pat on the head.'

'No, of course not. And do you still have feelings for Kathy's father?'

'Not at all, it was all years and years ago. No, I wish him well, for all that he's married to Marianne Hayes and owns a quarter of Dublin.'

'Bartolomeo, will you and Fiona be able to share a room, do you think?' Signora asked.

'*Si, grazie*, Signora, that's all sorted out.' Barry blushed a bit at the memory of how very pleasurably it had been sorted out.

'Good, that makes it all easier, single rooms are a big problem.'

Signora was going to share with Constanza and Aidan Dunne with Lorenzo. Everyone else had partners of some sort.

The travel agency had been marvellous, it was the place where Brigid Dunne worked. They had given the best price when it had all been analysed down to the bone. Brigid Dunne said she almost wished she was going herself.

'Why don't you and the Old Man of the Sea go?' she asked Grania.

Grania just laughed at her now when she made these remarks. 'Tony and I don't want to crowd Dad out on this, and anyway we're getting ready for the geriatric wedding of the century.'

Brigid giggled. Grania was so happy that you couldn't offend her.

They were both thinking how odd it was that no mention at all of their mother had been made in the planning of this famous *viaggio*. But it was something they didn't speak of. It was somehow too trivial and too serious at the same time. Did it mean that Mam and Dad were over? Things like that didn't happen to families like theirs.

Fiona brought Barry home to supper in her house shortly before the *viaggio*.

'You practically live in my house,' he complained, 'and I'm never allowed into yours.'

'I didn't want you to meet my parents until it was too late.'

'What do you mean too late?'

'Too late for you to abandon me. I wanted you to be consumed with physical lust for me, as well as liking me and admiring me as a person.'

She spoke so seriously and earnestly Barry found it hard to keep a straight face. 'It's just as well then that the physical lust bit has taken over so strongly,' he said. 'I'll be able to put up with them however awful they are.'

And they were fairly awful. Fiona's mother said that Ireland was very nice for a holiday because you wouldn't get yourself sunburned or people wouldn't snatch your handbag.

'They do here just as much as anywhere else.'

'But at least they speak English here,' her father said.

Barry said he had been learning Italian in readiness, he would be able to order food and deal with police stations, hospitals and breakdowns of the bus.

'See what I mean?' Fiona's father was triumphant. 'Must be a very dangerous place if that is what they taught you.'

'How much is the supplement for a single room?' her mother asked.

'Five pounds a night,' Fiona said.

'Nine pounds a night,' Barry said at exactly the same time. They looked at each other wildly. 'It's . . . um . . . more for the men you see,' poor Barry said in desperation.

'Why is that?' Fiona's father was suspicious.

'Something to do with the Italian character, really. They insist men have bigger rooms for all their clothes and things.'

'Wouldn't you think women would have more clothes?' Fiona's mother was now suspicious. What kind of a peacock was her daughter involved with, needing a huge room for all his wardrobe?

'I know, that's what my mother was saying . . . By the way, she's very much looking forward to meeting you, getting to know you.'

'Why?' asked Fiona's mother.

Barry couldn't think why so he said: 'She's like that, she just loves people.'

'Lucky for her,' said Fiona father.

'What's the Italian for "Good luck, Dad"?' Grania asked her father the night before the *viaggio*.

'*In bocca al lupo, Papà.*' She repeated it. They sat in his study. He had all his maps and guidebooks out. He would bring a small suitcase which he would carry with him containing all this. It didn't really matter, he said, if his clothes got lost, but this was what counted.

'Mam working tonight?' Grania said casually.

'I suppose so, love.'

'And you'll have a suntan for the wedding?' She was determined to keep the mood cheerful.

'Yes, and you know we'd have it here for you, you know that.'

'We'd prefer it in a pub, really, Dad.'

'I always thought you'd marry from here and I'd pay for it all.'

'You're paying for a big cake and champagne, isn't that enough?'

'I hope so.'

'It's plenty. And listen, are you nervous about this trip?'

'A little, in case it's not as good as we all promised, hoped, and remembered even. The class went so well, I'd hate this to be an anticlimax.'

'It can't be, Dad, it will be great. I wish I were going in many ways.'

'In many ways I wish you were too.' And neither of them said a word about the fact that Aidan's wife of twenty-five years was not going, and according to herself had not been invited to go.

Jimmy Sullivan had a driving job on the Northside, so he drove Signora to the airport.

'You're miles too early,' he said.

'I'm too excited. I couldn't stay at home, I want to be on my way.'

'Will you go at all to see your husband's people in that village you lived in?'

'No, no, Jimmy, there won't be time.'

'It's a pity to go all the way to Italy and not visit them though. The class would let you off for a day or two.'

'No, it's too far away, right at the far end of Italy on the island of Sicily.'

'So they won't hear you're there and take a poor view?'

'No, no they won't hear I'm there.'

'Well, that's all right then, so long as there's no offence.'

'No, nothing like that. And Suzi and I will tell you every detail when we get back.'

'God, the wedding was something else, wasn't it Signora?'

'I did enjoy it, and I know everyone else did too.'

'I'll be paying for it for the rest of my life.'

'Nonsense, Jimmy, you loved it. You've only one daughter and it was a real feast. People will talk about it for years.'

'Well, they were days getting over their hangovers all right,' he said, brightening at the thought of his legendary hospitality. 'I hope that Suzi and Lou will get themselves out of that bed and make it to the airport.'

'Oh, you know newly-weds,' Signora said diplomatically.

'They were in that bed for many a month before they were newly-weds,' Jimmy Sullivan said, brow darkening with disapproval. It always annoyed him that Suzi was so utterly uncontrite about her bad behaviour.

When she was alone at the airport Signora found a seat and took out the badges she had made. Each one had Vista del Monte – the Italian for Mountainview – on it, and the person's name. Surely nobody could get lost. Surely if there was a God he would be delighted that all these people were visiting the Holy City and he wouldn't let them get lost or killed or into fights. Forty-two people including herself and Aidan Dunne, just enough to fill the coach they had arranged to meet them. She wondered who would be the first to arrive. Maybe Lorenzo? Could be Aidan. He said he would help her distribute the badges.

But it was Constanza. 'My room mate,' Constanza said eagerly and pinned on her badge.

'You could easily have afforded the single room, Constanza,' Signora said, something that had not been mentioned before.

'Yes, but who would I have talked to . . . isn't that half the fun of a holiday?'

Before she could answer Signora saw the others arriving. A lot of them had come on the airport bus. They came to collect their badges and seemed pleased to see that they were from such an elegant-sounding place.

'No one will know in Italy what kind of a dump Mountainview really is,' Lou said.

'Hey, Luigi be fair, it's improved in leaps and bounds this year.' Aidan was referring to the rebuilding, the paint job, the new bicycle sheds. Tony O'Brien had delivered all he had promised.

'Sorry, Aidan, I didn't realise you were in earshot,' Lou grinned. Aidan had been good company at the wedding. He had sung *La donna è mobile* and knew all the words.

Brenda Brennan had come to the airport to wave them off. Signora was very touched. 'You're so good, everyone else has a normal family.'

'No, they don't.' Brenda Brennan jerked her head towards where Aidan was talking to Luigi. 'He doesn't for one thing. I asked his pill of a wife why she wasn't going to Rome with the rest of you, and she shrugged and said that she hadn't been asked, wouldn't push herself where she wasn't wanted and wouldn't have enjoyed it anyway. So how's that for normal?'

'Poor Aidan.' Signora was sympathetic.

Then the flight was called.

The sister of Guglielmo was waving like mad to everyone. For Olive just going to the airport was a treat. 'My brother is a bank manager, he's going to see the Pope,' she said to strangers.

'Well, if he lays his hands on some of that money they'll be pleased with him,' said a passer-by. Bill just smiled, and he and Lizzie waved to Olive while they could still see her.

'Forty-two people, we'll have to lose one of them,' Aidan said as they counted the flock into the departure lounge.

'Aren't you optimistic! I keep thinking we'll lose all of them,' Signora smiled.

'Still, the counting system should work.' Aidan tried to sound more convinced than he felt. He had divided them into four groups of ten and appointed a leader of each. When they arrived anywhere or left anywhere the leader had to report that all were present. It worked for children, but adults might resent it.

They didn't seem at all put out by it, in fact some of them positively welcomed it.

'Imagine, Lou is a leader,' Suzi said in admiration to Signora.

'Well, a responsible married man like Luigi, who better?' Signora asked. The truth was of course that she and Aidan had chosen him because of his fierce scowl. Nobody in his team would be late if they were reporting to Luigi.

He marched them on to the plane as if he were taking them into war. 'Can you raise your passports?' he asked them. Obediently they did 'Now, put them away very carefully. Zip them away, I won't want to see them unzipped until we get to Roma.'

The announcements were made in Italian on the plane as well as in English. Signora had prepared all this with them so it was familiar. When the air stewardess began to speak the evening class all nodded at each other, pleased to hear familiar words and phrases. The girl pointed out the emergency doors on the right and the left, the class repeated them all happily, *destra, sinistra*. Even though they had heard it all in English already.

When it was over and she said *grazie* all the evening class shouted *prego* and Aidan's eyes met Signora's. It was really happening. They were going to Rome.

Signora was seated beside Laddy. Everything was new and exciting to him, from the safety belt to the meal with its little portions of food.

'Will the Garaldis be at the airport?' he asked eagerly.

'No, Lorenzo. The first few days we get to know Roma . . . we do all the tours we talked about, remember?'

'Yes, but suppose they want me straight away?' His big face was worried.

'They know you're coming. I've written to them, they know we'll be in touch on Thursday.'

'*Giovedi,*' he said.

'*Bene, Lorenzo, giovedi.*'

'Aren't you going to eat your dessert, Signora?'

'No, Lorenzo. Please have it.'

'It's just that I'd hate to waste it.'

Signora said she would have a little sleep now. She closed her eyes. Please may it go well. May they all find magic there. May the Garaldis remember Lorenzo and be nice to him. She had put her heart into the letter and was distressed that there had been no reply.

The bus was there. '*Dov'è l'autobus?*' Bill asked to show he remembered the phrase.

'It's here in front of us,' Lizzie said.

'I know, but I wanted to talk about it,' Bill explained.

'Don't the girls all have enormous bosoms and bums,' Fiona whispered admiringly to Barry as she looked around her.

'I think it's rather nice actually,' Barry said defensively. This was his Italy, he was the expert on the place since his visit for the World Cup, he didn't want any aspersions cast.

'No, I think it's great,' Fiona explained. 'It's just that I'd love Brigid Dunne to see them . . . the way she's always bellyaching about herself.'

'You could tell her father to tell her, I suppose.' Barry was doubtful of the suitability of this.

'Of course I couldn't, she'd know I was talking about her. She says the hotel isn't going to be any great shakes. She says we're not to be disappointed.'

'I won't be disappointed,' Barry said, putting his arm around Fiona.

'Neither will I. I was only in a hotel once before, in Majorca. And it was so noisy that none of us could sleep at all, so we all got up and went back to the beach.'

'I suppose they had to keep the prices down.' Barry was terrified that there would be any criticism.

'I know it's dead cheap, and Brigid was telling me that some half cracked one came in wanting to know where we were all staying, so the word must be out that we got good value.'

'Did she want to join the group?'

'Brigid said she couldn't join, that we had been booked at this rate for ages. But she just insisted on knowing the name of the hotel.'

'Well, now.' Barry was pleased as they stepped out into the sunshine and the head counting began. *Uno, due, tre*. The team leaders were very serious about their roles for Signora.

'Did you ever stay in a hotel, Fran?' Kathy asked as the bus sped through the traffic, which seemed to be full of very impatient drivers.

'Twice, ages ago.' Fran was vague.

But Kathy probed. 'You never told me.'

'It was in Cork, with Ken if you must know.'

'Oho, when you said you were staying with a schoolfriend?'

'Yes, I didn't want them thinking I was going to produce yet another child for them to look after.' Fran nudged her good-naturedly.

'You'd be far too old for that sort of thing surely?'

'Listen here to me, if I get together with Ken again for a bit in America, now that you've won me a ticket there . . . I may well produce a little sister or brother for you to take home with us.'

'Or maybe even stay there with?' Kathy said.

'It's a return ticket, remember.'

'They're not born overnight, remember,' Kathy said.

The two laughed and pointed out sights to each other as the bus pulled up at a building in the Via Giolitti.

Signora was on her feet and an excited conversation took place.

'She's telling him that we must be left at the hotel itself, not here at the terminus,' Suzi explained.

'How do you know, you're not even in the evening class?' Lou was outraged.

'Oh, if you work as a waitress you get to understand everything sooner or later.' Suzi dismissed her skill. Then, looking at Lou's face she added, 'Anyway, you're always speaking bits of it at home so I pick up words here and there.' That seemed entirely more suitable.

And Suzi was indeed right. The bus lurched off again and dropped them at the *Albergo Francobollo*.

'The Stamp Hotel,' Bill translated for them. 'Should be easy to remember. '*Vorrei un francobollo per l'Irlanda*,' they all chorused aloud and Signora gave them a broad smile.

She had got them to Rome without any disaster, the hotel had their booking and the class were all in high good spirits. Her anxiety was not necessary. Soon she would relax and enjoy being back in Italy again, its colours and sounds and excitement. She began to breathe more easily.

The *Albergo Francobollo* was not one of the smarter hotels in Rome but its welcome was gigantic. Signor and Signora Buona Sera were full of admiration and praise over how well they all spoke Italian.

'*Bene, bene benissimo*,' they cried as they ran up and down the stairs to the rooms.

'Are we really saying "Good evening Mr Good Evening"?' Fiona asked Barry.

'Yes, but look at the names at home like Ramsbottom, and we've even a customer in the supermarket called O'Looney.'

'But we don't have people called Miss Goodmorning and Mr Goodnight,' Fiona insisted.

'We do have a place in Ireland called Effin, and they talk about the Effin football team and the Effin choir will sing at eleven o'clock Mass ... what would outsiders make of that?' Barry asked.

'I love you, Barry,' Fiona said suddenly. They had just arrived at their bedroom and Mrs Good Evening heard the remark.

'Love. Very, very good,' she said, and ran down the stairs to settle more people in their rooms.

Connie hung her clothes up carefully on her side of the small cupboard. Out the window she could see the roofs and windows of tall houses in the little streets that led off the Piazza del Cinquecento. Connie washed at the small hand basin in the room. It had been years since she had stayed in a hotel without its own bathroom. But it had also been years since she had gone on a trip with such an easy heart. She did not feel superior to these people because she had more money. She wasn't even remotely tempted to hire a car which she could have done easily, or to treat them to a meal in a five star restaurant. She was eager to join in the plans that had been made in such detail by Signora and Aidan Dunne. Like every other member of the evening class Connie sensed that their friendship was deeper than a merely professional one. Nobody had been surprised when Aidan's wife had not joined the group.

'*Signor Dunne, telefono*,' Signora Buona Sera called up the stairs.

Aidan had been advising Laddy not to suggest *immediately* that he should clean the brasses on the door, maybe they should wait until had been there for a few days.

'Would that be your Italian friends?' Laddy asked eagerly.

'No, Lorenzo, I have no Italian friends.'

'But you were here before.'

'A quarter of a century ago, no one who would remember me.'

'I have friends here,' Laddy said proudly. 'And Bartolomeo has people he met during the World Cup.'

'That's great,' Aidan said. 'I'd better go and see who it is that *does* want me.'

'Dad?'

'Brigid? Is everything all right?'

'Sure. You all got there then?'

'Absolutely, all in one piece. It's a gorgeous evening, we're going to walk down to the Piazza Navona and have a drink.'

'Great, I'm sure it'll be terrific.'

'Yes. Brigid, is anything . . . you know . . . ?'

'It's probably stupid, Dad, but a kind of loopy woman came in twice wanting to know what hotel you're all staying at. It might be nothing but I didn't like the feel of her, I thought she was off her rocker.'

'Did she say why?'

'She said that it was a simple question and could I answer her and give her the name of the hotel or would she have to speak to my boss.'

'And what did you do?'

'Well, Dad, I did think she was out of a funny farm so I said No. I said my father was out there and if she wanted a message passed to anyone I'd get in touch.'

'Well, that's it then.'

'No, it's not. She went to the boss and said it was very urgent she contact a Mr Dunne with the Mountainview party, and he gave the hotel name to her and gave me a ticking off.'

'She must know me if she knew my name.'

'No, I saw her reading my name Brigid Dunne from my badge. Look, I suppose I just wanted to say . . .'

'Say what, Brigid?'

'That she's sort of crazy and you should look out.'

'Thank you very much, my dear, dear Brigid,' he said, and realised that it had been a long time since he had called her that.

It was a warm evening as they set out to walk through Rome.

They passed near Santa Maria Maggiore, but not near enough to stop and go in.

'Tonight is just a social night . . . we all have a drink in the beautiful square. Tomorrow we look at culture and religion for those who want to, and for those who want to sit and sip coffee they can do that too.' Signora was anxious to remind them that they were not going to be herded, but she saw in their eyes that they wanted a little looking after still. 'What do you think we might say when we see the wonderful square with all the fountains and statues in the Piazza Navona?' she asked, looking around.

And there on the side of the street they all shouted out, '*In questa piazza ci sono molti belli edifici!*'

'*Benissimo,*' said Signora. '*Avanti,* let's go and find them.'

They sat at peace, forty-two of them, and watched the night fall on Rome. Signora was beside Aidan. 'No problems with the phone call?' she asked.

'No, no, just Brigid ringing to know if the hotel was all right for us. I told her it was wonderful.'

'She was very helpful over it all, she really wanted it to be a success for you, for all of us.'

'And it will.' They sipped their coffees. Some of the group had a beer, others a *grappa*. Signora had said there were tourist prices here and she advised only one drink for the atmosphere. They had to keep *something* to spend when they got to Firenze and Siena. They smiled almost unbelievingly when she mentioned the names. They were here in Italy to begin the *viaggio*. It wasn't just talk any more in a classroom on a wet Tuesday and Thursday.

'Yes, it will be a success, Aidan,' Signora said.

'Brigid said something else too. I didn't want to bother you with it, but some kind of madwoman came into the agency and wanted to know where we were all staying. Brigid thought she was someone who might cause trouble.'

Signora shrugged. 'We've got this lot here, we'll cope with whatever else turns up, don't you think?'

In small groups, the evening class were posing with each other by the Fountain of the Four Rivers.

He reached out his hand and took hers. 'We can cope with anything,' he said.

'Your friend arrived, Signor Dunne,' said Signora Buona Sera.

'Friend?'

'The lady from Irlanda. She just wanted to check the hotel and that all of you were staying here.'

'Did she leave her name?' Aidan asked.

'No name, just interested to know if everyone was staying here. I said you were going on a tour tomorrow morning in the bus. That's right, yes?'

'That's right,' Aidan said.

'Did she look like a madwoman?' he asked casually.

'Mad, Signor Dunne?'

'*Pazza?*' Signora explained.

'No, no, not at all *pazza*.' Signora Buona Sera seemed offended that a madwoman might be assumed to have called at the Hotel Francobollo.

'Well then,' Aidan said.

'Well then,' Signora smiled back at him.

The younger people would have smiled if they had known how much it had meant to them to sit there with their hands in each other's as the stars came out over the Piazza Navona.

The bus tour was to give them the feel of Rome, Signora said, then they could all go back at their leisure to see particular places. Not everyone wanted to spend hours in the Vatican museum.

Signora said that since they served cheese at breakfast people often made themselves a little sandwich to eat later on in the day. And then there would be a big dinner tonight in the restaurant not far from the hotel. Somewhere they could all walk home from. Again, nobody *had* to come she said. But she knew that everyone would.

There was no mention of the woman who had called to look for them. Signora and Aidan Dunne were too busy discussing the bus route with the driver to give it any thought.

Would there be time to get out and throw a coin into the famous Trevi fountain? Was there room for the bus to park near the Bocca della Verità? The party would enjoy putting their hands into the mouth of the great weatherbeaten face of stone which was meant to bite the fingers off liars. Would he leave them at the top of the Spanish Steps to walk down or at the bottom to walk up? They hadn't time to think of the woman who was looking for them. Whoever she might be.

And when they came back exhausted from the tour everyone had two hours' rest before they assembled for dinner. Signora walked around to the restaurant, leaving Connie asleep in their bedroom. She wanted to check about the menu and to arrange that there would be no grey areas. Only a fixed menu was to be offered.

On the door she saw a notice draped in black crepe *CHIUSO: morte in famiglia*. Signora fumed with rage. Why couldn't the family member have died at some other time? Why did he or she have to die just as forty-two Irish people were coming to have supper? Now she had less than an hour to find somewhere else. Signora could feel no sympathy for the family tragedy, only fury. And why had they not telephoned the hotel as she had asked them to do if there was any hitch in arrangements?

She walked up and down the streets around Termini. Small hotels, cheap accommodation suitable for the people who got off trains at the huge station. But no jolly restaurant like the one she had planned. Biting her lip she went towards a place with the name Catania. It must be Sicilian. Was this a good omen? Could she throw herself on their mercy and explain that in an hour and a half, forty-two Irish people were expecting a huge inexpensive meal? She could but try.

'*Buona sera,*' she said.

The square young man with dark hair looked up. '*Signora?*' he said. Then he looked at her again in disbelief. '*Signora?*' he said again, his face working. '*Non è possibile, Signora,*' he said coming towards her with hands stretched out. It was Alfredo, the eldest son of Mario and Gabriella. She had walked into his restaurant by accident. He kissed her on both cheeks. '*È un miracolo,*' he said, and pulled out a chair.

Signora sat down. She felt a great dizziness come over her, and she gripped the table in case she fell.

'*Stock Ottanta Quattro,*' he said and poured her a great glass of the strong sweet Italian brandy.

'*Non grazie . . .*' she held it to her mouth, and she sipped. 'Is this your restaurant, Alfredo?' she asked.

'No, no, Signora, I work here, I work here to make money . . .'

'But your own hotel. Your mother's hotel. Why do you not work there?'

'My mother is dead, Signora. She died six months ago. Her brothers, my uncles, they try to interfere, to make decisions . . . they know nothing. There is nothing for us to do. Enrico is there, but he is still a child, my brother in America will not come home. I came here to Rome to learn more.'

'Your mother dead? Poor Gabriella. What happened to her?'

'It was cancer, very, very quick. She went to the doctor only a month after my father was killed.'

'I am so sorry,' Signora said. 'I can't tell you how sorry I am.' And suddenly it was all too much for her. Gabriella to die now instead of years ago, the hot brandy in her throat, no place for dinner tonight, Mario in his grave near Annunziata. She cried and cried while Mario's son stroked her head.

In her bedroom Connie lay on her bed, each foot wrapped in a face cloth wrung through in cold water. Why had she not brought some foot balm with her, or those soft leather walking shoes that were like gloves? She had not wanted to unpack a spongebag full of luxury cosmetics in front of the unworldly Signora, that was probably it. But who would have known that her soft shoes had cost what none of her companions would have been able to earn in three weeks? She should have taken them, she was paying the penalty now. Tomorrow she might slip away to the Via Veneto and buy herself some beautiful Italian shoes as a treat. Nobody would notice, and if they did what the hell? These weren't people obsessed by wealth and differences in standards of living. Not everyone thought about the whole business of wealth. They weren't all like Harry Kane.

How strange to be able to think about him without emotion. He would be out of gaol by the end of the year. She had heard from old Mr Murphy that he intended to go to England. Some friends would look after him. Would Siobhan Casey go with him? she had enquired, almost as you ask after strangers who have no meaning to you, or characters in a television series. Oh no, hadn't she heard, there had been a definite cooling of relationships there. He had refused to see Miss Casey when she went to visit him in prison. He blamed her for everything that had happened, apparently.

It had given Connie Kane no huge pleasure to hear this. In a way it might have been easier to think of him in a new life with a woman he had been involved with for ever. She wondered had they ever come here together, the two of them, Siobhan and Harry. And had they felt touched by this beautiful city, the way everyone did whether or not they were in love? It was something she would never know now, and it was of no importance really.

She heard a gentle knock at the door. Signora must be back already. But no, it was the small bustling Signora Buona Sera. 'A letter for you,' she said. And she handed her an envelope.

It was written on a plain postcard. It said: 'You could easily die in the Roman traffic and you would not be missed.'

The leaders were counting heads to go to dinner. Everyone was present and correct except for three, Connie and Laddy and Signora. They assumed Connie and Signora were together and they would be there any moment.

But where was Laddy? Aidan had not been in the room they shared, he had been busy getting his notes together for the tour the next day to the Forum and the Colosseum. Perhaps Laddy had fallen asleep. Aidan ran lightly up the stairs but he was not to be found.

At that moment Signora arrived, pale-faced and with the news that the venue had been changed but the price was the same. She had managed to secure a booking at the Catania. She looked stressed and worried. Aidan didn't want to tell her about the disappearances. At that moment Connie arrived down the stairs, full of apologies. She too looked pale and worried. Aidan wondered was it all too much for these women, the heat, the noise, the excitement. But then he realised he was being fanciful. It was his job to find Laddy. He would take the address of the restaurant and join them later. Signora gave him a card; her hand was shaking.

'All right, Nora?'

'Fine, Aidan,' she lied to him.

They were gone chattering down the street, and Aidan began the hunt for Laddy. Signor Buona Sera knew Signor Lorenzo, he had offered to clean windows with him. A very nice gentleman, he worked in a hotel in Irlanda too. He had been pleased to hear that there was a visitor for him.

'A visitor?'

'Well, somebody had come and left a letter for one of the Irish party. His wife had mentioned it. Signor Lorenzo had said this must be the message he was waiting for and he was very happy.'

'But was it for him? *Did* he get a message?'

'No, Signor Dunne, my wife she told him she had given the letter to one of the ladies but Signor Laddy said it was a mistake, it was for him. There was no problem, he said, he knew the address, he would go there.'

'God Almighty,' Aidan Dunne said. 'I left him for twenty bloody minutes to do my notes and he thinks that bloody family have sent for him. Oh Laddy, I'll swing for you yet, I really will.'

First he had to go to the restaurant where they were all sitting down and then standing up again to take pictures of the banner saying *Benvenuto agli Irlandesi*.

'I need the Garaldis' address,' he hissed to Signora.

'No. He's never gone there?'

'So it would appear.'

Signora looked up at him anxiously. 'I'd better go.'

'No, let me. You stay here and look after the dinner.'

'I'll go, Aidan. I can speak the language, I've written to them.'

'Let's both go,' he suggested.

'Who will we put in charge? Constanza?'

'No, there's something upsetting her. Let's see. Francesca and Luigi between them.'

The word was out. Signora and Mr Dunne had gone to hunt for Lorenzo and two new people were in command, Francesca and Luigi.

'Why those?' someone muttered.

'Because we were the nearest,' Fran said, a peacemaker.

'And the best,' said Luigi, a man who liked to win.

They got a taxi and they arrived at the house. 'It's even smarter than I thought,' Signora whispered.

'He never got into a place like this.' Aidan looked amazed at the big marble entrance hall and the courtyard beyond.

'*Vorrei parlare con la famiglia Garaldi.*' Signora spoke with a confidence she didn't feel to the splendid-looking uniformed commissionaire. He asked her name and business and Aidan marvelled as she told him and stressed the importance of it. The man in the grey and scarlet went to a phone and spoke into it urgently. It seemed to take for ever.

'I hope they're managing back in the restaurant,' Signora said.

'Of course they are. Weren't you great to find a place so quickly? They seem very welcoming.'

'Yes, it was extraordinary.' She seemed miles away.

'But everyone's been so nice everywhere, it's not really extraordinary,' Aidan said.

'No. The waiter, I knew his father. Can you believe that?'

'Was that in Sicily?'

'Yes.'

'And did you know him?'

'From the day he was born ... I saw him going to the church to be baptised.'

The commissionaire returned. 'Signor Garaldi says he is very confused, he wants to speak to you personally.'

'We must go in, I can't explain things on the telephone,' Signora said. Aidan understood and marvelled at her courage. He felt a little confused by this rediscovering of a Sicilian past.

Soon they were walking through a courtyard and up another wide staircase to a fountain and some large doors. These were seriously wealthy people. Had Laddy really penetrated in here?

They were shown into an entrance hall where a small angry man in a brocade jacket seemed to hurtle out of a room and demand an explanation. Behind him came his wife trying to placate him and inside, wretched and totally at a loss, was poor Laddy sitting on a piano stool.

His face lit up when he saw them. 'Signora,' he called. 'Mr Dunne. Now you can tell them everything. You'll never believe it but I lost all my Italian. I could only tell them the days and the seasons and order the dish of the day. It's been terrible.'

'*Sta calmo, Lorenzo,*' Signora said.

'They want to know am I O'Donoghue, they keep writing it down for me.' He had never looked so anxious and disturbed.

'Please Laddy, I am O'Donoghue, that's my name, that's why they thought it was you. That was what I put on my letter.'

'You're not O'Donoghue,' Laddy cried. 'You're Signora.'

Aidan put his arm around Laddy's shaking shoulders and let Signora begin. The explanation, and he could understand most of it, was clear and unflustered. She told of the man who had found their money in Ireland a year ago, a man who had worked hard as a hotel porter and had believed their kind words of gratitude to be an invitation to come to Italy. She described the efforts he had made to learn Italian. She introduced herself and Aidan as people who ran an evening class and how worried they had been that due to some misunderstanding their friend Lorenzo had believed there was a message for him to call. They would all go now, but perhaps out of the kindness of his heart Signor Garaldi and his family might make some affectionate gesture to show they remembered his kindness, and indeed spectacular honesty, in returning a wad of notes to them, money that many a man in many a city including Dublin might not have felt obliged to return.

Aidan stood there, feeling Laddy's shaking shoulder and wondering about the strange turnings life took. Suppose he had become Principal of Mountainview? That's what he had wanted so much, not long ago. Now he realised how much he would have hated it, how far better a choice was Tony O'Brien, a man, not evil incarnate as he had once believed, but a genuine achiever, heartbroken in his battle against nicotine and shortly to become Aidan's son-in-law. Aidan would never have notes for a lecture in the Forum stuck in his pocket, he would never be standing here in this sumptuous Roman townhouse reassuring a nervous hotel porter and looking with pride and admiration at this strange woman who had taken up so much of his life. She had brought clarity and understanding to the face that had so recently been creased with anger and confusion.

'Lorenzo,' Signor Garaldi said, and approached Laddy who sat terrified at his approach. '*Lorenzo, mio amico.*' He kissed him on both cheeks.

Laddy didn't harbour a grudge long. 'Signor Garaldi,' he said and grabbed him by the shoulders. '*Mio amico.*'

There were quickfire explanations and the rest of the family realised what had happened. Wine was brought, and little Italian biscuits.

Laddy was beaming from ear to ear now. '*Giovedì,*' he kept saying happily.

'Why does he say that?' Signor Garaldi was raising his glass and toasting next Thursday as well, but he wanted to know why.

'I told him that we would be in touch with you then, I wanted to prevent him from coming here on his own. I put that in my letter, that we might call by the house for ten minutes on Thursday. Did you not get it?'

The little man looked ashamed. 'I have to tell you I get so many begging letters I thought it was something like that, if he came some money would have been given. You have to forgive me but I didn't read it properly. Now I am so ashamed.'

'No please, but do you think he could come on Thursday? He is so eager, and maybe I could take his photograph with you and he could show it to people afterwards.'

Signor Garaldi and his wife exchanged glances. 'Why don't you all come here on Thursday, for a drink and a celebration?'

'There are forty-two of us,' Signora said.

'These houses were built for gatherings like that,' he said with a little bow.

A car was called and they were soon crossing Rome to the Catania, in a street where a car like the Garaldis' had hardly ever driven before. Signora and Aidan looked at each other, as proud as parents who had rescued a child from an awkward situation.

'I wish my sister could see me now,' Laddy said suddenly.

'Would she have been pleased?' Signora was gentle.

'Well, she knew it would happen. We went to a fortune teller, you see, and she said she would be married and have a child, and die young, and that I would be great at sport and I would travel across the sea. So it wouldn't have been a surprise or anything, but it's a pity she didn't live to see it.'

'It is indeed, but maybe she sees now.' Aidan wanted to be reassuring.

'I'm not at all sure that there are people in heaven, you know, Mr Dunne,' said Laddy as they purred through Rome in the chauffeur-driven car.

'Aren't you, Laddy? I'm getting more sure of it every day,' said Aidan.

At the Catania everyone was singing 'Low Lie the Fields of Athenry'. The waiters stood in an admiring group and clapped mightily when it was over. Any other guests brave enough to dine in the Catania that night had been absorbed into the group, and as the threesome came in there was a huge shout of welcome.

Alfredo ran to get the soup.

'*Brodo*,' Laddy said.

'We'll go straight to the main course if you like,' Aidan said.

'Excuse me, Mr Dunne. I'm in charge until relieved of it, and I say that Lorenzo is to have his *brodo*.' Luigi looked fiercer than he had ever looked. Aidan quailed and said of course it had been a mistake. 'That's all right, then,' Luigi said generously.

Fran explained to Signora that one of the younger waiters kept asking young Kathy to go out with him later and Fran was worried. Could Signora say that they all had to return together when the night was over.

'Certainly, Francesca,' Signora said. Wasn't it amazing, none of them asked what had happened to Laddy, they had just assumed that she and Aidan would rescue him in Rome.

'Lorenzo has had us all invited to a party on Thursday,' she said. 'In a magnificent house.'

'*Giovedì*,' Laddy said, in case anyone should mistake the day. They seemed to take that for granted too. Signora finished her soup quickly. She looked around for Constanza and saw her, not animated like she normally was but looking absently into the distance. Something had happened, but she was such a private person and would not say what it was. Signora was that kind of person herself, she would not make any enquiries.

Alfredo said that there was going to be a surprise for the Irlandesi. There was going to be a cake in the Irish colours, they had arranged it because all the people had been so happy and they wanted to make it a memory for them. They knew the Irish colours since the World Cup.

'I can't thank you enough, Alfredo, for making the evening so special for us.'

'You can, Signora, can you come and talk with me tomorrow? Please?'

'Not tomorrow, Alfredo, Signor Dunne is giving his talk about the Forum.'

'You can hear Signor Dunne any time. I have only a few days to talk to you. Please, Signora, I am begging.'

'Perhaps he'll understand.' Signora looked over at Aidan. She hated letting him down, she knew how much he had put into this lecture. He was determined that everyone would see Rome as it was when chariots raced through it. But the boy did look very anxious, as if he had something to tell her. For the sake of the past and of everyone, she must listen.

Signora managed to get Caterina back to the hotel and out of the clutches of the waiter very easily; she just told Alfredo that the boy was to be called off immediately. So the soulful Roman eyes had beseeched Caterina for another evening and he had given her a red rose and a kiss on the hand.

The mystery of the message had not been sorted out by Connie. Signora Buona Sera said she had delivered to Signora Kane. Neither she nor her husband knew whether it was a man or a woman who had left it. It would always be a mystery, Signora Buona Sera said. But during the night Connie Kane lay awake and worried. She wondered why some things should always be mysterious. She longed to tell Signora, but didn't want to intrude on the quiet woman who lived such a private life.

'No, of course, if you have business of your own. Business to do with Sicily,' Aidan said next day.

'I am so sorry, Aidan, I was looking forward to it.'

'Yes.' He turned away shortly so she wouldn't see the naked hurt and disappointment in his face, but it was too late. Signora had seen it.

'We don't have to go to this lecture,' Lou said, pulling Suzi back to bed.

'I want to go.' She struggled to get up.

'Latin, Roman gods and old temples . . . of course you don't.'

'Mr Dunne's been getting it ready for weeks, and anyway Signora'd like us to be there.'

'She's not going to be there herself.' Lou spoke knowledgeably.

'How on earth do you know that?'

'I heard her telling him last night,' Lou said. 'He was sour as a lemon.'

'That's not like her.'

'Well, now we don't have to go,' Lou said, snuggling back into the bed.

'No, now it's more important that we go to support him.' Suzi was out of bed and into her dressing gown before he could protest. She was halfway down the corridor to the bathroom before he could reach out and catch her.

Lizzie and Bill were making their sandwiches carefully. 'Isn't it a great idea?' Bill said eagerly, hoping that it was something that might be extended to their own life at home. The idea of saving money by any means at all was something that he prayed would catch on in Lizzie's mind. She had been very good on this visit and not even looked at a shoeshop. She had noted the cost of Italian ice cream in lire, translated it and said it wasn't a good idea.

'Oh, Bill, don't be an idiot. If we were to buy ham and eggs and great chunks of bread like this to make sandwiches it would be dearer than having a bowl of soup in a pub like we do already.'

'Maybe.'

'But when you're an international banker out here, then we might consider it. Will we be living in a hotel do you think, or having our own villa?'

'A villa, I imagine,' Bill said glumly. It all seemed so unlikely and far from reality.

'Have you made any enquiries yet?'

'About villas?' Bill looked at her wildly.

'No, about opportunities in banking, remember that's why we are learning Italian.' Lizzie was prim.

'It *was*, in the first place,' Bill admitted, 'but now I'm only learning it because I enjoy it.'

'Are you trying to tell me we'll never be rich?' Lizzie's huge beautiful eyes were troubled.

'No, no, I'm not trying to tell you that. We *will* be rich. This very day I'll go into banks and ask relevant words. Believe me, I will.'

'I believe you. Now I have all these done and wrapped, we can eat them in the Forum after the lecture, and we might send our postcards too.'

'This time you'll be able to send one to your Dad,' Bill Burke said, always seeing the silver lining.

'You got on well with him, didn't you?'

They had had a brief visit to Galway and a reasonably successful attempt to reunite Lizzie's parents. At least they were speaking to each other and on visiting terms now.

'Yes, I liked him, he was very comical.' Bill thought this was a masterly way to describe a man who had almost crushed Bill's whole hand in his, and who had borrowed a ten-pound note from him within minutes of their meeting.

'It's *such* a relief that you like my family,' Lizzie said.

'And you mine,' Bill agreed.

His own parents were warming more to Lizzie's ways. She wore longer skirts and higher necklines. She asked questions of his father about cutting bacon, and the difference between smoked and green bacon. She played noughts and crosses endlessly with Olive, letting her win about half the time, which gave the games an air of frenzied excitement. The wedding wouldn't be nearly as fraught as Bill had once thought it would be.

'Let's go hear about Vestal Virgins,' he said, smiling from ear to ear.

'What?'

'Lizzie! Didn't you read your notes? Mr Dunne gave us one page, he said we'd all be able to remember that much.'

'Give it to me quick,' said Lizzie.

Aidan Dunne had drawn a little map highlighting the places they would visit and which he would describe. She read it speedily and returned it.

'Do you think he's in bed with Signora?' she asked, eyes shining.

'If so, Lorenzo and Constanza will be feeling a bit in the way,' said Bill.

Constanza and Signora had dressed and were about to come down to breakfast. There was an air that something was about to be said.

'Constanza?'

'*Sì, Signora?*'

'Could I ask you to take notes when Aidan is speaking today? I can't go, and I'm upset and, well, I think he's upset. He went to such trouble, such great trouble.' Signora's face looked very sad.

'And you have to miss it?'

'Yes, I do.'

'I'm sure he'll understand but I will pay great attention, and yes, of course I'll tell you everything.' There was a pause, then Connie spoke again. 'Oh, and Signora?'

'*Sì, Constanza?*'

'It's just that ... Well, did you ever hear anyone in our group saying anything bad about me, resentful, or possibly caught up in losing money to my husband or anything?'

'No, never. I never heard anyone saying anything about you. Why do you ask?'

'Someone left me a rather horrible note. It's probably a joke, but it upset me.'

'What did it say? Please tell me.'

Connie unfolded it and showed it to the other woman. Signora's eyes filled with tears. 'When did this happen?'

'It was left at the desk yesterday evening before we went out. Nobody knows who left it. I have asked but the Buona Seras don't know.'

'It can't be anyone in this group, Constanza, I tell you that.'

'But who else knows we are in Rome?'

Signora remembered something. 'Aidan said there was a madwoman back in Dublin enquiring what hotel we were all staying in. Could that be it? Someone who followed us here?'

'That's hard to believe, it's very far-fetched.'

'But it's even harder to believe that it's any member of our group,' Signora said.

'Why me? Now? And in Rome?'

'Is there anyone with a grievance, do you think?'

'Hundreds because of what Harry did, but he's locked up in gaol.'

'Not someone mad, disturbed possibly?'

'Not that I know.' Connie shook herself deliberately. She must spend no time speculating and worrying Signora as well. 'I'll just walk well away from the traffic side of things and be watchful. And Signora, I'll take notes. I promise you, it will be just as good as being there.'

'Alfredo, this had better be important. You have no idea how much I have upset somebody by missing a lecture.'

'There are many lectures, Signora.'

'This one was special. A great deal of trouble had been taken. Anyway?'

He made them coffee and sat down beside her. 'Signora, I have a very big favour to ask of you.'

She looked at him, anguished. He was going to ask her for money. He could not know that she had nothing. Literally nothing. When she got back to Dublin she would be penniless. She would have to ask the Sullivans to let her live free in their house until September when payment would start again in the school. Every last coin she had, had been changed into lire so that she could pay her way on this *viaggio*. How could this boy from his simple village and working as a waiter in a shabby restaurant in Rome know this? He must see her as responsible for forty people, a person of importance. Power even.

'It may not be easy. There's a lot you do not know,' she began.

'I know everything, Signora. I know my father loved you, and that you loved him. That you sat in that window sewing while we all grew up. I know that you behaved so well to my mother and that even though you didn't want to go, when she and my uncles said it was time to leave, you left.'

'You know all this?' Her voice was a whisper.

'Yes, we all knew.'

'For how long?'

'As long as I remember.'

'It's so hard to believe. I thought ... well, it doesn't matter what I thought ...'

'And we were all so sad when you went away.'

She lifted her face and smiled at him. 'You were? Truly?'

'Yes, all of us. You helped us all. We know.'

'How do you know?'

'Because my father did things he would not have done otherwise, Maria's wedding, the shop in Annunziata, my brother going to America ... everything. It was all you.'

'No, not all. He loved you, he wanted the best. Sometimes we talked. That was all.'

'We wanted to find you when Mama died. We wanted to write and tell you. But we didn't even know your name.'

'That was good of you.'

'And now, now God sends you into this restaurant. It was God who sent you, I really believe that.' She was silent. 'And now I can ask you the great, great favour.' She held tightly onto the table. *Why* had she no money? Most women of her age had some money, even a little. She had been so uncaring about possessions. If there was anything she could sell for this boy, who must be very desperate to ask her ...

'The favour, Signora ...'

'Yes, Alfredo.'

'You know what it is?'

'Ask me, Alfredo, and if I can I will.'

'We want you to come back. We want you to come home, Signora. Home where you belong.'

Constanza didn't eat breakfast, she went off to the shops. She bought the soft shoes she yearned for, she got a long silk scarf for Signora, and cut off the designer label in case Elizabetta would recognise the name and exclaim at how much it must have cost. And then she bought what she had set out to buy and went back to join the trip to the Forum.

They all loved the lecture. Luigi said you could nearly see the poor Christians being led into the Colosseum. Mr Dunne said that he was only a crusty old Latin teacher and he promised he wouldn't keep them long, but when it was over they clapped and wanted more. His smile was surprised. He answered all their questions, and occasionally looked at Constanza, who seemed to be waving a camera near him all the time but never took a picture.

They separated for lunch to eat their sandwiches in little groups. Connie Kane watched Aidan Dunne. He had no sandwiches with him, he just walked to a wall and sat there looking absently out into the distance before him. He had told everyone the route back to the hotel. He made sure that Laddy was in the hands of Bartolomeo and his funny little girlfriend Fiona. Then he just sat there, sad that the person he had prepared the lecture for had not turned up.

Connie wondered whether to join him or not. But she didn't think that there was anything she could say that might help. So she walked to a restaurant and ordered herself grilled fish and wine. It was good to be able to do so easily. But she barely tasted the food as she wondered who could have come from Dublin to frighten her. Could Harry have sent someone? It was too alarming to think about. It would be preposterous to try and explain it to the Italian police, and difficult to get any detectives in Ireland to take her seriously either. An anonymous letter in a hotel in Rome? It was impossible to take seriously. But she walked very close to the walls and shops as she returned to the hotel.

And she enquired nervously at the desk had there been any more messages.

'No, Signora Kane, nothing at all.'

Barry and Fiona were going to the bar where Barry had met all the wonderful Italians during the World Cup. He had pictures taken that summer, flags and bunting and Jack Charlton hats.

'Have you written and told them we're coming?' Fiona asked.

'No, it's not that kind of scene, you just turn up and they're all there.'

'Every night?'

'No, but you know . . . most nights.'

'But suppose they came looking for you in Dublin, you mightn't be in the pub the night they came. Don't you have any names and addresses?'

'Names and addresses aren't important in something like this,' Barry said.

Fiona hoped he was right. He had set so much store by meeting them all and living through those glory days again. He would be very disappointed if it turned out that nobody ever gathered there any more. Or worse if they had forgotten him.

That was the evening that everyone was at leisure. If things had been different Connie might have gone window-shopping with Fran and Kathy and had coffee at a pavement café. But Connie was afraid to go out at night in case somebody really was waiting to push her in front of the cars that sped up and down the Roman streets.

If things had been different Signora and Aidan would have had supper together and planned the visit to the Vatican next day. But he was hurt and lonely and she had to be somewhere quiet until she could think over the turbulent proposal that had been made to her.

They wanted her to go back and help in the hotel, bring them English-speaking visitors, be part of the life she had looked on for so long as an outsider. It would have made sense of all those years she had watched and waited. It would be a future for her now as well as a past. Alfredo had begged her to come back. Even for a visit first, so that she could see how things were. She would realise all that she could contribute and know how much people had admired her. So Signora sat alone in a café thinking about what it would be like.

And a few streets away Aidan Dunne sat and tried to think about all the good things that had come out of this trip. He had managed to create a class that had not only stayed together for the year but had travelled in a block to Rome at the end of it. These people would never have done that without him. He had shared his love of Italy with them, nobody had been bored at his lecture today. He had done all he had set out to do. It had in fact been a year of triumph. But of course he had to listen to the other voice, the voice that said it was all Nora's doing. It was she who had created the real enthusiasm, with her silly games and her boxes pretending to be hospitals and railway stations and restaurants. It was Nora who had called them these fancy names and believed that one day they would go on a *viaggio*. And now that she was back here in Italy its magic had worked too strongly for her.

She had to talk business, she told him. What business could she have with a waiter from Sicily, even if she *had* known him as a child? He ordered a third beer without even noticing. He looked out at the crowds walking around on the hot Roman night. He had never felt so lonely in his life.

Kathy and Fran said they were going for a walk, they had planned a route and it would end up in the Piazza Navona where they went the first night. Would Laddy like to come?

Laddy looked at the route. It would pass the street where his friends the Garaldis lived. 'We won't go in,' Laddy said. 'But I can point out the house to you.'

When they saw the house Fran and Kathy were dumbfounded.

'We can't possibly be going to a party in a place like that,' Kathy said.

'*Giovedì*,' Laddy said proudly. 'Thursday, you'll see. He wants all of us, the whole forty-two. I said to him *quarantadue* but he said *sì, sì, benissimo*.'

It was only one more extraordinary thing about this holiday.

Connie waited for a while in her room for Signora to return; she wanted to give her the information and the surprise. But it got dark and she never came back. From outside the window came the sounds of chatter and people calling to each other as they went along the street, the distant sound of traffic and of cutlery clinking in a nearby restaurant. Connie decided that she would not allow herself to feel imprisoned by this mean, cowardly letter-writer.

Whoever it was would not kill her in a public place even if it was someone sent by Harry.

'To hell with him, if I stay in tonight he's won,' she said aloud. She walked around the corner to a pizza parlour and sat down. She didn't notice someone following her from outside the door of the Hotel Francobollo.

Lou and Suzi were across the river in Trastevere. They had walked with Bill and Lizzie around the little Piazza but, as Signora had warned, the restaurants were a bit too pricey for them. Wasn't it wonderful that they had learned all that about the *piatto del giorno*, and how to think in lire rather than translating it back into Irish money all the time.

'Maybe we should have kept our sandwiches from lunchtime,' Lizzie said sadly.

'We can't go in the door of these places,' Suzi said philosophically.

'It's not fair as a system, you know,' Lou said. 'Most of those people are on the take somehow, they all have an angle, a scene for themselves. Believe me, I know ...'

'Sure, Lou, but it doesn't matter.' Suzi didn't want the murky past brought up. It was never discussed but it was hinted at wistfully when Lou might sometimes tell her how the living could have been very easy had she not been so righteous.

'Do you mean like stolen credit cards?' Bill asked, interested.

'No, nothing like that, just doing favours, someone does a favour and they get a dinner, or a big favour and they get many dinners or a car. It's as simple as that.'

'You'd have to do a lot of favours to get a car,' Lizzie said.

'Yes and no. It's not doing a lot, it's just being reliable. I think that's what people want when favours are being exchanged.'

They all nodded, mystified. Sometimes Suzi looked at her huge emerald engagement ring. So many people had claimed it was the real thing that she had begun to believe that it might have been the result of a huge favour Lou had done for somebody. There was a way of finding out, like having it valued. But then she would know one way or the other. Far better to leave it as part of the unknown.

'I wish someone would ask us to do them a favour,' Lizzie said, looking at the restaurant with the musicians going from table to table, and the flower sellers passing amongst the diners selling long-stemmed roses.

'You keep your eyes peeled, Elizabetta,' said Lou with a laugh.

And at that moment a man and woman rose to their feet at a table near the road, the woman slapped the man across the face, the man snatched her handbag and leaped over the little hedge that formed the restaurant wall.

In two seconds Lou had caught him. He held one of the man's arms behind his back in a lock that was obviously extremely painful, he raised the other hand, the one holding the stolen handbag, high for all to see. Then he marched him through all the guests right up to the proprietor.

Huge explanations in Italian were exchanged, leading to the arrival of the *carabinieri* in a van and enormous excitement all around. They never got to know what had happened. Some Americans nearby said they thought the woman had picked up a gigolo. Some English people said that he was the woman's boyfriend who had been taking a cure for drug addiction. A French couple said that it was just a lovers' tiff but it was good that the man should be taken to a police station.

Lou and his friends were the heroes of the hour. The woman was offering him a reward. Lou was quick to translate it into a meal for four. This seemed entirely suitable to all parties.

'*Con vino, se è possibile?*' Lou added. They drank themselves into a stupor and had to take a taxi home.

'It wash the besht time I ever had,' Lizzie said as she fell twice before getting into the taxi.

'It's all a matter of looking for opportunities,' said Lou.

Connie looked around the pizza place. They were mainly young people, her children's age. They were animated and lively, interrupting each other laughing. Very alive and aware. Suppose this were to be the last place she was to see. Suppose it were really true and someone stalked after her leaving frightening messages at the hotel. But she couldn't be killed in front of everyone here? It wasn't possible. And yet how else to explain the letter? It was still in her handbag. Maybe if she were to write a note to leave with it just in case, a note explaining how she feared it might be from Harry, or one of his associates, as he always called them. But was this madness? Or was he just trying to make her go mad? Connie had seen films where this happened. She must not let it happen to her.

A shadow fell over the table and she looked up, expecting the waiter or someone to ask for one of the spare chairs. But her eyes met those of Siobhan Casey, her husband's mistress of many years. The woman who had helped Harry salt away money not once but twice.

Her face was different now, older and much more tired. There were lines where they had never been before. Her eyes were bright and wild. Connie suddenly felt very afraid indeed. Her voice dried in her throat. No words would come out.

'You're still alone,' Siobhan said, her face scornful. Connie still couldn't speak. 'It doesn't matter what city or how many deadbeats you travel with, you still end up having to go out by yourself.' She gave a little bark of a laugh with no humour in it.

Connie struggled to remain calm, she must not let the fear show in her face. Years of pretending that everything was normal stood to her now. 'I'm not by myself any more,' she said, pushing a chair towards Siobhan.

Siobhan's brow darkened further. 'Always the grand lady with nothing to back it up. Nothing.' Siobhan spoke loudly and angrily. People began to look at them, sensing a scene about to begin.

Connie spoke in a low voice. 'This is hardly the setting for a grand lady,' she said. She hoped her voice wasn't shaking.

'No, it's part of the slumming duchess routine. You have no real friends so you go and patronise a crowd of no-hopers, and you come on their cheapo trip with them and even then they don't want you. You'll always be alone, you should prepare for it.'

Connie breathed a little more easily. Perhaps Siobhan Casey did not intend to launch a murderous attack on her after all. She wouldn't speak about an empty, lonely future if she were about to kill her. It gave Connie a little courage. 'I am prepared for it. Haven't I been alone for years?' she said simply.

Siobhan looked at her, surprised. 'You're very cool, aren't you?'

'No, not really.'

'You knew the letter was from me?' Siobhan asked. Did she seem disappointed, or was she pleased she had instilled such fear? Her eyes still glinted madly. Connie was unsure which way to react. Would it be better to admit that she had no idea, or was it more clever to say that she had rumbled Siobhan from the start? It was a nightmare trying to guess which way would be the right one.

'I thought it must be, I wasn't sure.' She marvelled at how steady her own voice was.

'Why me?'

'You're the only one who really cared enough about Harry to write it.'

There was a silence. Siobhan stood leaning on the back of the chair. Around them the babble and laughter of the restaurant went on as before. The two foreign woman did *not* appear to be about to have a fight, as had looked possible. There was nothing of interest there any more. Connie would not ask her to sit down. She would not pretend that matters were so normal between them that they could sit together as ordinary people. Siobhan Casey had threatened to kill her, she was literally mad.

'You know he never loved you at all, you do know that?' Siobhan said.

'In truth possibly he did, the very beginning, before he knew I didn't enjoy sex.'

'Enjoy it!' Siobhan snorted at the word. 'He said you were pathetic, lying there whimpering, tight and terrified. That was the word he used about you. Pathetic.'

Connie's eyes narrowed. This was disloyalty of a spectacular sort. Harry knew how she had tried, how she had yearned for him. It was very cruel to tell Siobhan all the details. 'I did try, you know, to get something done about it.'

'Oh yes?'

'Yes. It was upsetting and distressing and painful, and in the end did no good at all.'

'They told you that you were a dyke, was that it?' Siobhan stood swaying, mocking, her lank hair falling over her face. She was hardly recognisable as the efficient Miss Casey of former times.

'No, and I don't think that *was* it.'

'So what *did* they say?' Siobhan seemed interested in spite of herself.

'They said that I couldn't trust men because my father had gambled away all our money.'

'That is pure bullshit,' Siobhan said.

'That's what I said too. A little more politely, but it's what I meant,' Connie said, with weak attempt at a smile.

Unexpectedly, Siobhan pulled out the chair and sat down. Now that Connie didn't have to look up at her any more she saw close up the ravages that the past months had worked on Siobhan Casey. Her blouse was stained, her skirt ill-fitting, her fingernails bitten and dirty. She wore no make-up and her face was working and moving all the time. She must be two or three years younger than I am, Connie thought; she looks years older.

Was it true that Harry had told her that he was finished with her? This was what must have unhinged her. Connie noticed the way she picked up the knife and fork and fingered them, moving them from hand to hand. She was very disturbed. They were not out of the wood yet.

'It was all such a waste when you look back on it. He should have married you,' Connie said.

'I don't have the style, I couldn't have been the kind of hostess he wanted.'

'That was only a small and very superficial part of his life. He practically lived with you.' Connie was hoping that these tactics would work. Flatter her, tell Siobhan that she was central to Harry's life. Don't let her brood and realise it was all over now.

'He had no love at home, of course, he had to go somewhere,' Siobhan said. She was drinking now, the Chianti from Connie's glass.

Connie with a glance and an indication of her finger managed to let the waiter know they needed more wine and a further glass. Something about her also communicated itself, so that instead of the usual friendly greetings and banter of a place like this he just left the bottle and glass on the table and went away.

'I did love him for long time.'

'Fine way you showed it, shopping him and sending him to gaol.'

'I had stopped loving him by then.'

'I never did.'

'I know. And for all you may hate me, I didn't hate you.'

'Oh yeah?'

'No, I knew he needed you, and still does, I imagine.'

'Not any more, you put paid to that too. When he gets out he'll go to England. That's all your fault. You made it impossible for him to live in his own land.' Siobhan's face was blotched and unhappy.

'I presume you'll go with him.'

'You presume wrong.' Again the sneer and the very, very mad look.

Connie had to get it right now. It was desperately important. 'I was jealous of you but I didn't hate you. You gave him everything, a proper love life, loyalty, total understanding about work. He spent most of his time with you, for God's sake, why wouldn't I have been jealous?' She had Siobhan's interest now. So she continued. 'But I didn't *hate* you, believe me.'

Siobhan looked at her with interest. 'I suppose you felt it was better that he should have just been with me than having lots of women, is that it?'

Connie knew she must be very careful here. Everything could depend on it. She looked at the ruined face of Siobhan Casey, who had loved Harry Kane for ever and still loved him. Was it possible that Siobhan, who was so close to him, didn't know about the girl from the airline, the woman who owned the small hotel in Galway, the wife of one of the investors? She searched the other woman's face. In as much as she could see, Siobhan Casey believed herself to have been the only woman in Harry Kane's life.

Connie spoke thoughtfully. 'I suppose that's true, it would have been humiliating to think he was running around with everyone . . . but even though I didn't like it . . . I knew that what you and he had was something special. As I said, he should have been married to you from the start.'

Siobhan listened to this. And thought it over. Her eyes were narrow and very mad when she finally spoke. 'And when you realised that I had followed you here and written that note, why were you not afraid?'

Connie was very afraid still. 'I suppose I thought you realised that whatever the difficulties were or maybe are, you were the only one who ever counted in Harry's life.' Siobhan listened. Connie continued. 'And of course I left a sort of insurance policy, so that you'd be punished if you did do me any harm.'

'You what?'

'I wrote a letter to my solicitor to be opened in case I died suddenly in Rome, or indeed anywhere, enclosing a copy of your note, and I said I had reason to suspect that it might have come from you.'

Siobhan nodded almost in admiration. It would have been marvellous to think that she saw reason. But the woman was still too distraught for that. It was not the time to give her a woman to woman talk about smartening herself, setting her appearance to rights, and providing a home for him in England to await his release. Connie was very sure that there was still money that had escaped any detection. But she wasn't going to run Siobhan's life for her. In fact her legs were still weak. She had managed to remain so normal and calm when faced with someone dangerous enough to follow her and make death threats, but Connie didn't know how much more she could take. She longed for the safety of the Hotel Francobollo.

'I won't do anything to you,' Siobhan said in a small voice.

'Well, it would sure be a pity for you to have to go in one door of the gaol as Harry is coming out another,' Connie said, as casually as if they were talking about shopping for souvenirs.

'How did you get to be so cool?' Siobhan asked.

'Years and bloody years of loneliness,' Connie said. She wiped an unexpected tear of self-pity from her eye and walked purposefully towards the waiter. She gave him lire that would cover the bill.

'Grazie, tante grazie, Signora,' he said.

Signora! She would be back now surely, and Connie wanted to give her the surprise. It all seemed much more real to her than the sad woman sitting in this pizza house, the woman who had been her husband's mistress for most of her life, who had come to Rome to kill Connie. She glanced at Siobhan Casey briefly, but she didn't say goodbye. There was nothing more to say.

*

It was very noisy in the bar where Barry and Fiona were looking for the friends from the World Cup.

'This is the corner we sat in,' Barry said.

Great crowds of young people were gathered and the giant television set was being moved into a position of even greater prominence. There was a match, and everyone was against Juventus. It didn't matter who they were for, Juventus was the enemy. The game began and Barry got drawn into it in spite of his quest. Fiona too was interested, and howled with rage at a decision that went against everyone's wishes.

'You like the football?' a man said to her.

Barry immediately put his arm around her shoulder. 'She understands a little, but I was here, here in this very bar for the World Cup. Irlanda.'

'Irlanda!' the man cried with delight. Barry produced the pictures, great happy shouting throngs then as now, but more bedecked. The man said his name was Gino, and he showed the pictures to other people and they came and clapped Barry on the back. Names were exchanged. Paul McGrath, Cascarino, Houghton, Charlton. A.C. Milan was mentioned tentatively and proved to have been a good way to go. These were good guys. More and more beer kept flowing.

Fiona lost all track of the conversation. And she was getting a headache. 'If you love me, Barry, let me go back to the hotel. It's only a straight line along the Via Giovanni and I know where to turn left.'

'I don't know.'

'Please, Barry. I don't ask much.'

'Barry, Barry,' his friends were calling.

'Take great care,' he said.

'I'll leave the key in the door,' she said, and blew him a kiss.

It was as safe as the streets in her own part of Dublin. Fiona walked happily back to the hotel, rejoicing that Barry had found his friends. They seemed to be fairly casual in their great reunion, none of them remembering anyone's names at first. But still, maybe that's the way men were. Fiona looked at the window boxes with the geraniums and busy lizzies in them, clustered in little pots. They looked so much more colourful than at home. Of course it was the weather. You could do anything if you had all this sunshine.

Then passing a bar she saw Mr Dunne sitting on his own, a glass of beer in front of him, his face sad and a million miles away. On an impulse Fiona suddenly turned in the door to join him. 'Well, Mr Dunne . . . the two of us on our own.'

'Fiona!' he seemed to drag himself back. 'And where's Bartolomeo?'

'With his football friends. I got a headache so he let me go home.'

'Oh, he found them. Isn't that marvellous!' Mr Dunne had a kind, tired smile.

'Yes, and he's delighted with himself. Are you enjoying it all, Mr Dunne?'

'Yes, very much.' But his voice sounded a bit hollow.

'You shouldn't be out here on your own, you organised it with Signora. Where is she, by the way?'

'She met some friends from Sicily, that's where she used to live, you see.' His voice sounded bitter and sad.

'Oh, that's nice.'

'Nice for her, she's spending the evening with them.'

'It's only one evening, Mr Dunne.'

'As far as we know.' He was mutinous, like a twelve-year-old.

Fiona looked at him, wondering. She knew so much. She knew for example all about Mr Dunne's wife Nell, who had been having an affair with Barry's father. It was over now, but apparently there were still bewildered letters and phone calls from Mrs Dunne, who had no idea that Fiona had been responsible for breaking everything up. Fiona knew from Grania and Brigid Dunne that their father was not happy, that he withdrew into his own little Italian sitting room all the time and hardly ever came out. She knew like everyone on the *viaggio* knew that he was in love with Signora. Fiona remembered that divorce was now possible in Ireland.

She recalled that the old Fiona, the timid Fiona, would have left things as they were, would not interfere. But the new Fiona, the happy version, went in there fighting. She took a deep breath. 'Signora was telling me the other day that you had made the dream of her life come true. She said she never felt of any importance until you gave her this job.'

Mr Dunne didn't respond, not as she would have liked. 'That was before she met all these Sicilians.'

'She said it again today at lunchtime,' Fiona lied.

'She did?' He was like a child.

'Mr Dunne, could I speak to you frankly and in total secrecy?'

'Of course you can, Fiona.'

'And will you never tell anyone what I said, particularly not Grania or Brigid?'

'Sure.'

Fiona felt weak. 'Maybe I need a drink,' she said.

'A coffee, a glass of water?'

'A brandy, I think.'

'If it's as bad as that I'll have a brandy myself,' Aidan Dunne said, and they ordered it flawlessly from the waiter.

'Mr Dunne, you know that Mrs Dunne isn't here with you.'

'I had noticed,' Aidan said.

'Well, there's been a bit of unfortunate behaviour. You see, she's friendly, rather over-friendly actually, with Barry's father. And Barry's mother, she took it badly. Well, very badly. She tried to kill herself over it all.'

'*What?*' Aidan Dunne looked utterly shocked.

'Anyway, it's all over now, it was over on the night of the *festa* up in Mountainview. If you remember, Mrs Dunne went home in a bit of a hurry, and now Barry's mother is all cheered up and his father isn't, well, unsuitably friendly, with Mrs Dunne any more.'

'Fiona, none of this is true.'

'It is actually, Mr Dunne, but you swore and promised you'd tell nobody.'

'This is nonsense, Fiona.'

'No it's not, it's utterly true. You can ask your wife when you get home. She's the only person you can tell about it. But maybe better not bring it up at all. Barry doesn't know, and Grania or Brigid don't, no point in getting everyone upset about it.' She looked so straightforward with her huge glasses reflecting all the lights in the bar that Aidan believed her utterly.

'So why are you telling me if no one is to know and no one is to get upset about it?'

'Because . . . because I want you and Signora to be happy, I suppose. Mr Dunne, I don't want you to think that you were the one to make the first move cheating on your wife. I suppose I wanted to say that the cheating had started and it was open season.' Fiona stopped abruptly.

'You're an amazing child,' he said. He paid the bill and they walked back to the Hotel Francobollo in total silence. In the hall he shook her hand formally. 'Amazing,' he said again.

And he went upstairs to the bedroom where Laddy had arranged all the items that would be blessed by the Pope tomorrow. The Papal audience in St Peter's. Aidan put his head in his hands. He had forgotten all about it. Laddy had six sets of Rosary Beads to be blessed by the Pope. He was sitting in the little anteroom sorting them out. He had already polished the shoes for the Buona Seras, who didn't know what to make of him. *'Domani mercoledi noi vedremo Il Papa,'* he said happily.

Upstairs Lou had to admit to Suzi that he was full of desire for her but didn't think that the performance would live up to it. 'A bit too much drink,' he explained, as if this were an insight.

'Never mind, we need our energy to see the Pope tomorrow,' Suzi said.

'Oh God, I'd forgotten the damn Pope,' said Lou, and fell asleep suddenly.

Bill Burke and Lizzie had fallen asleep with their clothes on, lying on the bed. They woke frozen at five o'clock in the morning.

'Is today a quiet day, by any chance?' Bill asked.

'After the Papal Audience I think it is.' Lizzie had an inexplicable headache.

Barry fell over the chair and Fiona woke in alarm. 'I forgot where we were living,' he said.

'Oh Barry, it was a straight line from the pub and then you turn left.'

'No, I meant in the hotel. I kept opening the wrong people's doors.'

'You're so drunk,' Fiona said sympathetically. 'Was it a nice night?'

'Yesh, but there's a myshtery,' Barry said.

'I'm sure there is. Drink some water.'

'I'll be going to the loo all night.'

'Well go, you will anyway after all the beer.'

'How did *you* get home?' he asked suddenly.

'As I told you, it was only a straight line. Drink up.'

'Did you have a convershashun with anyone?'

'Only Mr Dunne, I met him along the way.'

'He's in bed with Signora,' Barry reported proudly.

'He never is? How do you know?'

'I could hear them talking when I passed the door,' Barry explained.

'What was he saying?'

'It was about the temple of Mars the Avenger?'

'Like the lecture?'

'Just like that. I think he was giving her the lecture again.'

'God,' said Fiona. 'Isn't that weird?'

'I'll tell you something even more weird,' Barry said. 'All those fellows in the bar, they're not from here at all, they're from somewhere else . . .'

'What do you mean?'

'They're from a place called Messagne, way down at the bottom of Italy, near Brindisi where you get the boat from. Full of figs and olives, they say.' He sounded very troubled.

'What's wrong with that? We all have to be from somewhere.' Fiona gave him more water.

'This is their first time in Rome, they say, I couldn't have met them when I was here before.'

'But you were such friends.' Fiona was sad.

'I *know*.'

'Could it have been a different bar, honestly?'

'I don't know.' He was very glum.

'Maybe they forgot they'd been to Rome,' she said brightly.

'Yes, it's not the kind of thing you'd forget though, is it?'

'But they remembered you.'

'And *I* thought I remembered them.'

'Come on, go to bed. We have to be bright-eyed for the Pope,' Fiona said.

'Oh God, the Pope,' said Barry.

In their bedroom Connie had given her surprise to Signora. It was a full tape-recording of Aidan's speech. She had bought the tape recorder and got every word of it for her.

Signora was touched to the heart. 'I'll listen to it under my pillow here so that it won't disturb you,' she said, after they had tried some of it out.

'No, I'm happy to hear it again,' Connie said.

Signora looked at the other woman. Her eyes were bright and she seemed flushed. 'Is everything all right, Constanza?'

'What? Oh yes, absolutely, Signora.'

And they sat there, each of them having had an evening that might change their lives. Was Connie Kane in any real danger from the mentally disturbed Siobhan? And would Nora O'Donoghue go back to the small town in Sicily which had been the centre of her life for twenty-three years? Even though they had confided in each other a little, they both had a strong tradition of keeping troubles to themselves. Connie wondered what had kept Signora from Aidan's lecture, and indeed out so late on her own tonight. Signora longed to ask if Constanza had heard anything more from the person who had written the unpleasant letter.

They got into bed and discussed the time for the alarm.

'Tomorrow is the Papal Audience,' Signora said suddenly.

'Oh God, I'd forgotten,' Connie admitted.

'So had I, aren't we a disgrace?' said Signora with a giggle.

They loved seeing the Pope. He looked a little frail but in good spirits. They all thought he was looking directly at them. There were hundreds and hundreds of people in St Peter's Square, and yet it seemed very personal.

'I'm glad it wasn't a Private Audience,' Laddy said, as if such a thing could ever have been possible. 'This big one is better somehow. It shows you religion isn't dead, and what's more you wouldn't have to think of anything to say to him, yourself like.'

Lou and Bill Burke had three cold beers each before they went and when Barry saw them he joined in quickly. Suzi and Lizzie had two very cold ice creams each. They all took photographs. There was an optional lunch which everyone took. Most of them had been too hungover or upset to have thought of making sandwiches at breakfast time.

'I hope they'll all be in better shape for the party at Signor Garaldi's tomorrow,' Laddy said disapprovingly to Kathy and Fran.

Lou was passing by when he said it. 'God Almighty, the party,' he said holding his head.

'Signora?' Aidan spoke to her after lunch.

'That's a bit formal, Aidan, you used to call me Nora,' she said.

'Ah well.'

'Ah well what?'

'How was your meeting yesterday, Nora?'

She paused for moment. 'It was interesting, and despite the fact that it was in a restaurant, I managed to stay sober, unlike almost everyone else in the group. I'm surprised the Holy Father wasn't lifted out of his chair with the fumes of alcohol from our group.'

He smiled. 'I went to a bar and drowned my sorrows.'

'What are these sorrows, now?'

He tried to keep it light. 'Well, the main one was that you weren't there for my talk.'

Her face lit up and she reached into her big handbag. 'But I *was*. Look what Constanza did for me. I've heard the whole thing. It was wonderful, Aidan, and they clapped so much at the end and they loved it. It was so clear, I could see it all. In fact, when we have a little free time I'm going back there and I'll play the tape just for myself. It will be as if I got a special tour all for myself.'

'I'd give you a repeat, you know that.' His eyes were full of warmth, he was reaching out for her hand, but she pulled away.

'No, Aidan don't, please don't, it's not fair. To make me think things I shouldn't think, like that you ... well, like that you care about me and my future.'

'But God, Nora, you know I do.'

'Yes, but we've been over a year fond of each other in this way, and it's impossible. You live with your wife and family.'

'Not for much longer,' he said.

'Ah well, Grania's getting married, but nothing else has changed.'

'Yes it has. A lot has changed.'

'I can't listen to you, Aidan. I have to make up my mind about something huge.'

'They want you to go back to Sicily, don't they?' he said, his heart heavy and his face rigid.

'Yes, they do.'

'I never asked you why you left.'

'No.'

'Nor why you stayed so long there either.'

'So doesn't that show something? I don't ask about you either. I don't ask questions I might like to know the answers to.'

'I'd answer them, I promise you, and I'd hold nothing back.'

'Let's wait. It's too hothouse to ask each other questions and answer them here in Rome.'

'But if we don't, then you may go away and live in Sicily, and then . . .'

'And then what?' her voice was gentle.

'And then the whole point of my life will have gone away,' he said, and his eyes filled with tears.

The forty-two guests arrived at the Garaldi residence at five o'clock on Thursday. They had dressed in their best finery, and they all carried cameras. Word had got around that this was the kind of house that you might see in *Hello!* magazine. They wanted it recorded.

'Will we be able to take photos do you think, Lorenzo?' Kathy Clarke asked.

Laddy was the authority on all aspects of the visit. He thought about it for a while. 'There should be an official group photograph certainly, to record the occasion, and as many shots of the outside as we like. But I somehow feel that we shouldn't take pictures of their possessions, you know, in case they were to be seen and stolen later.'

They nodded their agreement. Laddy had certainly worked it all out. When they saw the building they all stopped, amazed. Even Connie Kane, who was used to visiting splendid places, was knocked backwards.

'We can't be allowed in here,' Lou whispered to Suzi, loosening his tie which had begun to choke him.

'Shut up, Lou, how are we going to go up in the world if you panic in front of a bit of money and class,' Suzi hissed back at him.

'This is the kind of life I was born to,' Lizzie Duffy said, bowing graciously at the staff who conducted them in, and up the steps.

'Don't be ridiculous, Lizzie.' Bill Burke was anxious. He hadn't learned any really good phrases about international banking that would advance his career. He knew she would be disappointed in him.

*

The Garaldi family were there and they had invited a photographer of their own. Would anyone mind if they took pictures, then these could be developed and given to the guests as they departed? Mind? They were thrilled. First there was Lorenzo and Signor Garaldi. Then one of Lorenzo and the whole Garaldi family. Then that group plus Signora and Aidan and after that, everyone ranked on the stairs. This was a house that had seen the need for group photography before.

The two sullen sons of the family whom Laddy had entertained in the snooker halls of Dublin had cheered up mightily, and they bore him away to show him their own games room. There were trays of wine and soft drinks. There was beer in tall elegant glasses, plates of crostini and little cakes and tartlets.

'May I take a picture of the food?' Fiona asked.

'Please, please.' Signor Garaldi's wife seemed touched.

'It's my future mother-in-law, she's teaching me to cook, I'd like her to see something elegant like this.'

'Is she a kind person, *la suocera* . . . the mother-in-law?' Signora Garaldi was interested.

'Yes, very kind. She was a bit unstable, she tried to commit suicide you see, because her husband was having an affair with that man's wife. But it's all over now. Actually, I ended it. Myself personally!' Fiona's eyes were bright with excitement and marsala wine.

'*Dio mio.*' Signora Garaldi had her hand to her throat. All this in Holy Catholic Ireland!

'I met her through the suicide,' Fiona continued. 'She was brought to my hospital. In many ways I pulled her around, and she's very grateful to me, so she's teaching me high-class cooking.'

'High class,' Signora Garaldi murmured.

Lizzie passed by her eyes wide with admiration. '*Che bella casa,*' she said.

'*Parla bene Italiano,*' Signora Garaldi said warmly.

'Yes, well I'll need it when Guglielmo is appointed to an international banking post, quite possibly in Rome.'

'Really he might be sent to Rome?'

'We *could* choose Rome, or anywhere he wants really, but this is such a beautiful city,' Lizzie was gracious in her praise.

There was going to be a speech, people were gathered together, Laddy from the games room, Connie from the picture gallery, Barry from the car and motorbikes down in the underground garage.

While they assembled Signora took Aidan's arm. 'You won't believe what the Garaldis have made of this, I heard the wife explaining that someone in the group is an international surgeon who saves lives, and Elizabetta has said that Guglielmo is a famous banker contemplating settling in Rome.'

Aidan smiled. 'And do they believe any of it?' he asked.

'I doubt it. For one thing, Guglielmo has asked three times can he cash a cheque and what is today's rate of exchange. It wouldn't inspire huge confidence.' She smiled back at him too. Anything either of them said seemed warm or funny or full of insights.

'Nora?' he said.

'Not yet ... Let's try and get the show on the road.'

The speech was warm in the extreme. Never had the Garaldis been made so welcome as in Ireland, never had they met such honesty and friendship. Today was just one more example of it. People had come to their house as strangers and would leave as friends. '*Amici*,' a lot of them said when he said friends.

'*Amici sempre*,' said Signor Garaldi.

Laddy's hand was raised high in the air. He would come to this house for ever. They would visit his nephew's hotel again.

'We could have a party for *you* when you come to Dublin,' Connie Kane said, and at this they all nodded eagerly, promising to take part. The pictures arrived. Marvellous big pictures on elegant steps in the courtyard. Amongst the thousands of shots taken on this *viaggio*, snaps of people squinting into the sun, these would have pride of place in all the different homes over Dublin.

There were a lot of *ciaos* and *arrivedercis* and *grazies*, and the evening class from Mountainview were out again on the streets of Rome. It was after eleven o'clock, the crowds were beginning to have their little *passeggiata*, the evening stroll. Nobody felt like going home; they had been having too exciting a time.

'I'm going back to the hotel. Will I take everyone's pictures?' Aidan said suddenly. He looked across the group, waiting for her to speak.

Signora spoke slowly. 'So am I, we can carry them back for you and so if you all get drunk again you won't lose them.'

They smiled at each other knowingly. What they had all suspected over the past year was about to happen.

They walked hand in hand until they found an open-air restaurant with strolling players. 'You warned us against these,' Aidan said.

'I only said they were expensive, I didn't say they weren't wonderful,' said Nora O'Donoghue.

They sat and talked. She told him about Mario and Gabriella, and how she had lived happily in their shadow for so long.

He told her about Nell, and how he could never see when and why the good times had gone from their marriage. But gone they had. They lived now like strangers under the same roof.

She told him how Mario had died first and Gabriella then, how their children wanted her to go back and help with the hotel. Alfredo had said the words she had ached to hear, that they had always thought of her as a kind of mother anyway.

He told her that he knew now Nell had been having an affair. That he had neither been shocked or hurt by this, but just surprised. It did seem a very male response, he thought, a little arrogant and very insensitive, but that's the way it was.

She said that she would have to meet Alfredo again and talk to him. She didn't know yet what she was going to say.

He told her that when they got home he would tell Nell that they would sell their house and give her half the proceeds. He didn't know yet where he was going to live.

They went slowly back to the Hotel Francobollo. They were too old to have the where-do-we-go problem of youngsters. Yet that was exactly what they had. They couldn't lock Laddy out of his room for the night. Nor Constanza. They looked at each other.

'*Buona sera*, Signor Buona Sera,' began Nora O'Donoghue. '*C'è un piccolo problema . . .*'

It wasn't a problem for long. Signor Buona Sera was a man of the world. He found them a room with no delays and no questions asked.

The days flew by in Rome, and then it was just a short walk across to Termini and the train to Florence.

'*Firenze*,' they all chorused when they saw the name come up on the noticeboard at the station. They didn't mind leaving because they knew they were coming back. Hadn't they all put their coins in the Trevi Fountain? And there would be so much more to see and do once they had mastered Intermediate or Improvers' Italian. They hadn't decided what to call it, but everyone was signing on.

They settled in the train, their picnics packed. The Buona Seras had left out plenty of supplies. This group had been no trouble. And imagine the unexpected romance between the two leaders! Far too old for it, of course, and it would never last when they went back to their own spouses, but still, part of the madness of a holiday.

Next year's *viaggio* they would go south from Rome, not north. Signora said they must see Naples, and then they would go to Sicily to a hotel she had known when she lived there. She and Aidan Dunne had promised Alfredo. They had also agreed to tell him that Aidan's daughter Brigid or one of her colleagues would come out and see if they could set up package holidays to his hotel.

At Signora's insistence Aidan had telephoned his home. The conversation with Nell had been easier and shorter than he could ever have believed.

'You had to know sometime,' Nell said curtly.

'So we'll put the house on the market when I get home and split it down the middle.'

'Right,' she said.

'Don't you care, Nell? Doesn't it mean anything to you, all these years?'

'They're over, isn't this what you're saying?'

'I was saying we should discuss the fact that they will be over.'

'What's there to discuss, Aidan?'

'It's just that I didn't want you to be getting ready for my coming home and preparing for it . . . and then this being a bombshell.' He was always too courteous, and possibly too self-centred, he realised.

'I don't want to upset you, but truly I don't even know what day you *are* coming back,' Nell said.

They sat apart from the others on the train, Aidan Dunne and Signora, in a world of their own with a future to plan.

'We won't have much money,' he said.

'I never had any money at all to speak of, it won't bother me.' Signora spoke from the heart.

'I'll take all the things from the Italian room. You know, the desk, the books, and the curtains and sofa.'

'Yes, better to put back a dining-room table in there, for the sale, even just borrow one.' Signora was practical.

'We could get a small flat, I'm sure, as soon as we get back.' He was anxious to show her that she wasn't going to lose out by refusing to go back to Sicily, her only real home.

'A room would do,' Signora said.

'No, no, we must have more than a room,' he protested.

'I love you, Aidan,' she said.

And for some reason, the others were all quiet and the train wasn't making any of its noises so everyone heard. For a second they exchanged glances. But the decision was made. To hell with discretion. Celebration was more important. And the other passengers on the train would never know why forty people wearing badges saying Vista del Monte cheered and cheered and sang a variety of songs in English including 'This Is Our Lovely Day', and eventually ended up in a tuneless version of 'Arrivederci Roma'.

And they would never understand why so many of them were wiping tears quickly away from their eyes.

The Copper Beech

For Gordon, who has made my life so good and happy,
with all my gratitude and love.

Shancarrig School

Father Gunn knew that their housekeeper Mrs Kennedy could have done it all much better than he would do it. Mrs Kennedy would have done *everything* better in fact, heard Confessions, forgiven sins, sung the *Tantum Ergo* at Benediction, buried the dead. Mrs Kennedy would have looked the part too, tall and angular like the Bishop, not round and small like Father Gunn. Mrs Kennedy's eyes were soulful and looked as if they understood the sadness of the world.

Most of the time he was very happy in Shancarrig, a peaceful place in the midlands. Most people only knew it because of the huge rock that stood high on a hill over Barna Woods. There had once been great speculation about this rock. Had it been part of something greater? Was it of great geological interest? But experts had come and decided while there may well have been a house built around it once all traces must have been washed away with the rains and storms of centuries. It had never been mentioned in any history book. All that was there was one great rock. And since Carrig was the Irish word for rock that was how the place was named – Shancarrig, the Old Rock.

Life was good at the Church of the Holy Redeemer in Shancarrig. The parish priest, Monsignor O'Toole, was a courteous, frail man who let the curate run things his own way. Father Gunn wished that more could be done for the people of the parish so that they didn't have to stand at the railway station waving goodbye to sons and daughters emigrating to England and America. He wished that there were fewer damp cottages where tuberculosis could flourish, filling the graveyard with people too young to die. He wished that tired women did not have to bear so many children, children for whom there was often scant living. But he knew that all the young men who had been in the seminary with him were in similar parishes wishing the same thing. He didn't think he was a man who could change the world. For one thing he didn't *look* like a man who could change the world. Father Gunn's eyes were like two currants in a bun.

There had been a Mr Kennedy long ago, long before Father Gunn's time, but he had died of pneumonia. Every year he was prayed for at mass on the anniversary of his death, and every year Mrs Kennedy's sad face achieved what seemed to be an impossible feat, which was a still more sorrowful appearance. But even though it was nowhere near her late husband's anniversary now she was pretty gloomy, and it was all to do with Shancarrig school.

Mrs Kennedy would have thought since it was a question of a visit from the Bishop that *she*, as the priests' housekeeper, should have been in charge of everything. She didn't want to impose, she said many a time, but really had Father Gunn got it quite clear? Was it really expected that those teachers, those lay teachers above at the schoolhouse and the children that were taught in it, were really in charge of the ceremony?

'They're not used to bishops,' said Mrs Kennedy, implying that she had her breakfast, dinner and tea with the higher orders.

But Father Gunn had been adamant. The occasion was the dedication of the school, a bishop's blessing, a ceremony to add to the legion of ceremonies for Holy Year, but it was to involve the children, the teachers. It wasn't something run by the presbytery.

'But Monsignor O'Toole is the manager,' Mrs Kennedy protested. The elderly frail parish priest played little part in the events of the parish, it was all done by his bustling energetic curate, Father Gunn.

In many ways, of course, it would have been much easier to let Mrs Kennedy take charge, to have allowed her to get her machine into motion and organise the tired sponge cases, the heavy pastries, the big pots of tea that characterised so many church functions. But Father Gunn had stood firm. This event was for the school and the school would run it.

Thinking of Mrs Kennedy standing there hatted and gloved and sorrowfully disapproving, he asked God to let the thing be done right, to inspire young Jim and Nora Kelly, the teachers, to set it up properly. And to keep that mob of young savages that they taught in some kind of control.

After all, God had an interest in the whole thing too, and making the Holy Year meaningful in the parish was important. God must want it to be a success, not just to impress the Bishop but so that the children would remember their school and all the values they learned there. He was very fond of the school, the little stone building under the huge copper beech. He loved going up there on visits and watching the little heads bent over their copy books.

'Procrastination is the thief of time' they copied diligently.

'What does that mean, do you think?' he had asked once.

'We don't know what it means, Father. We only have to copy it out,' explained one of the children helpfully.

They weren't too bad really, the children of Shancarrig – he heard their Confessions regularly. The most terrible sin, and the one for which he had to remember to apportion a heavy penance, was scutting on the back of a lorry. As far as Father Gunn could work out this was holding on to the back of a moving vehicle and being borne along without the driver's knowledge. It not unnaturally drew huge rage and disapproval from parents and passers-by, so he had to reflect the evilness of it by a decade of the Rosary, which was almost unheard of in the canon of children's penances. But scutting apart they were good children, weren't they? They'd do the school and Shancarrig credit when the Bishop came, wouldn't they?

The children talked of little else all term. The teachers told them over and over what an honour it was. The Bishop didn't normally go to small schools like this. They would have the chance to see him on their own ground, unlike so many children in the country who had never seen him until they were confirmed in the big town.

They had spent days cleaning the place up. The windows had been painted, and the door. The bicycle shed had been tidied so that you wouldn't recognise it. The classrooms had been polished till they gleamed. Perhaps His Grace would tour the school. It wasn't certain, but every eventuality had to be allowed for.

Long trestle tables would be arranged under the copper beech tree which dominated the school yard. Clean white sheets would cover them and Mrs Barton, the local dressmaker, had embroidered some lovely edging so that they wouldn't look like sheets. There would be jars of flowers, bunches of lilac and the wonderful purple orchids that grow wild in Barna Woods in the month of June.

A special table with Holy Water and a really good white cloth would be there so that His Grace could take the silver spoon and sprinkle the Water, dedicating the school again to God. The children would sing 'Faith of Our Fathers', and because it was near to the Feast of Corpus Christi they would also sing 'Sweet Sacrament Divine'. They rehearsed it every single day, they were word perfect now.

Whether or not the children were going to be allowed to partake of the feast itself was a somewhat grey area. Some of the braver ones had enquired but the answers were always unsatisfactory.

'We'll see,' Mrs Kelly had said.

'Don't always think of your bellies,' Mr Kelly had said.

It didn't look terribly hopeful.

Even though it was all going to take place at the school they knew that it wasn't really centred around the children. It was for the parish.

There would be something, of course, they knew that. But only when the grown-ups were properly served. There might be just plain bits of bread and butter with a little scraping of sandwich paste on them, or the duller biscuits when all the iced and chocolate-sided ones had gone.

The feast was going to be a communal effort from Shancarrig and so they each knew some aspect of it. There was hardly a household that wouldn't be contributing.

'There are going to be bowls of jelly and cream with strawberries on top,' Nessa Ryan was able to tell.

'That's for grown-ups!' Eddie Barton felt this was unfair.

'Well, my mother is making the jellies and giving the cream. Mrs Kelly said it would be whipped in the school and the decorations put on at the last moment in case they ran.'

'And chocolate cake. Two whole ones,' Leo Murphy said.

It seemed very unfair that this should all be for the Bishop and priests and great crowds of multifarious adults in front of whom they had all been instructed, or ordered, to behave well.

Sergeant Keane would be there, they had been told, as if he was about to take them all personally to the gaol in the big town if there was a word astray.

'They'll have to give some to us,' Maura Brennan said. 'It wouldn't be fair otherwise.'

Father Gunn heard her say this and marvelled at the innocence of children. For a child like young Maura, daughter of Paudie who drank every penny that came his way, to believe still in fairness was touching.

'There'll be bound to be *something* left over for you and your friends, Maura,' he said to her, hoping to spread comfort, but Maura's face reddened. It was bad to be overheard by the priest wanting food on a holy occasion. She hung back and let her hair fall over her face.

But Father Gunn had other worries.

The Bishop was a thin silent man. He didn't walk to places but was more inclined to glide. Under his long soutane or his regal-style vestments he might well have had wheels rather than feet. He had already said he would like to process rather than drive from the railway station to the school. Very nice if you were a gliding person and it was a cool day. Not so good however if it was a hot day, and the Bishop would notice the unattractive features of Shancarrig.

Like Johnny Finn's pub where Johnny had said that out of deference to the occasion he would close his doors but he was not going to dislodge the sitters.

'They'll sing. They'll be disrespectful,' Father Gunn had pleaded.

'Think what they'd be like if they were out on the streets, Father.' The publican had been firm.

So much was spoken about the day and so much was made of the numbers that would attend that the children grew increasingly nervous.

'There's no proof at all that we'll get *any* jelly and cream,' Niall Hayes said. 'I heard no talk of special bowls or plates or forks.'

'And if they let people like Nellie Dunne loose they'll eat all before them.' Nessa Ryan bit her lip with anxiety.

'We'll help ourselves,' said Foxy Dunne.

They looked at him round-eyed. Everything would be counted, they'd be murdered, he must be mad.

'I'll sort it out on the day,' he said.

Father Gunn was not sleeping well for the days preceding the ceremony. It was a great kindness that he hadn't heard Foxy's plans.

Mrs Kennedy said that she would have some basic emergency supplies ready in the kitchen of the presbytery, just in case. Just in case. She said it several times.

Father Gunn would not give her the satisfaction of asking just in case *what*. He knew only too well. She meant in case his foolish confidence in allowing lay people up at a small schoolhouse to run a huge public religious ceremony was misplaced. She shook her head and dressed in black from head to foot, in honour of the occasion.

There had been three days of volunteer work trying to beautify the station.

No money had been allotted by CIE, the railways company, for repainting. The stationmaster, Jack Kerr, had been most unwilling to allow a party of amateur painters loose on it. His instructions did not include playing fast and loose with company property, painting it all the colours of the rainbow.

'We'll paint it grey,' Father Gunn had begged.

But no. Jack Kerr wouldn't hear of it, and he was greatly insulted at the weeding and slashing down of dandelions that took place.

'The Bishop likes flowers,' Father Gunn said sadly.

'Let him bring his own bunch of them to wear with his frock then,' said Mattie the postman, the one man in Shancarrig foolhardy enough to say publicly that he did not believe in God and wouldn't therefore be hypocritical enough to attend mass, or the sacraments.

'Mattie, this is not the time to get me into a theological discussion,' implored Father Gunn.

'We'll have it whenever you're feeling yourself again, Father.' Mattie was unfailingly courteous and rather too patronising for Father Gunn's liking.

But he had a good heart. He transported clumps of flowers from Barna Woods and planted them in the station beds. 'Tell Jack they grew when the earth was disturbed,' he advised. He had correctly judged the stationmaster to be unsound about nature and uninterested in gardening.

'I think the place is perfectly all right,' Jack Kerr was heard to grumble as they all stood waiting for the Bishop's train. He looked around his transformed railway station and saw nothing different.

The Bishop emerged from the train gracefully. He was shaped like an S hook, Father Gunn thought sadly. He was graceful, straightening or bending as he talked to each person. He was extraordinarily gracious, he didn't fuss or fumble, he remembered everyone's name, unlike Father Gunn who had immediately forgotten the names of the two self-important clerics who accompanied the Bishop.

Some of the younger children, dressed in the little white surplices of altar boys, stood ready to lead the procession up the town.

The sun shone mercilessly. Father Gunn had prayed unsuccessfully for one of the wet summer days they had been having recently. Even that would be better than this oppressive heat.

The Bishop seemed interested in everything he saw. They left the station and walked the narrow road to what might be called the centre of town had Shancarrig been a larger place. They paused at the Church of the Holy Redeemer for His Grace to say a silent prayer at the foot of the altar. Then they walked past the bus stop, the little line of shops, Ryan's Commercial Hotel and The Terrace where the doctor, the solicitor and other people of importance lived.

The Bishop seemed to nod approvingly when places looked well, and to frown slightly as he passed the poorer cottages. But perhaps that was all in Father Gunn's mind. Maybe His Grace was unaware of his surroundings and was merely saying his prayers. As they walked along Father Gunn was only too conscious of the smell from the River Grane, low and muddy. As they crossed the bridge he saw out of the corner of his eye a few faces at the window of Johnny Finn Noted for Best Drinks. He prayed they wouldn't find it necessary to open the window.

Mattie the postman sat laconically on an upturned barrel. He was one of the only spectators since almost every other citizen of Shancarrig was waiting at the school.

The Bishop stretched out his hand very slightly as if offering his ring to be kissed.

Mattie inclined his head very slightly and touched his cap. The gesture was not offensive, but neither was it exactly respectful. If the Bishop understood it he said nothing. He smiled to the right and the left, his thin aristocratic face impervious to the heat. Father Gunn's face was a red round puddle of sweat.

The first sign of the schoolhouse was the huge ancient beech tree, a copper beech that shaded the playground. Then you saw the little stone schoolhouse that had been built at the turn of the century. The dedication ceremony had been carefully written out in advance and scrutinised by these bureaucratic clerics who seemed to swarm around the Bishop. They had checked every word in case Father Gunn might have included a major heresy or sacrilege. The purpose of it all was to consecrate the school, and the future of all the young people it would educate, to God in this Holy Year. Father Gunn failed to understand why this should be considered some kind of doctrinal minefield. All he was trying to do was to involve the community at the right level, to make them see that their children were their hope and their future.

For almost three months the event had been heralded from the altar at mass. And the pious hope expressed that the whole village would be present for the prayers and the dedication. The prayers, hymns and short discourse should take forty-five minutes, and then there would be an hour for tea.

As they plodded up the hill Father Gunn saw that everything was in place.

A crowd of almost two hundred people stood around the school yard. Some of the men leaned against the school walls but the women stood chatting to each other. They were dressed in their Sunday best. The group would part to let the little procession through and then the Bishop would see the children of Shancarrig.

All neat and shining – he had been on a tour of inspection already this morning. There wasn't a hair out of place, a dirty nose or a bare foot to be seen. Even the Brennans and the Dunnes had been made respectable. They stood, all forty-eight of them, outside the school. They were in six rows of eight; those at the back were on benches so that they could be seen. They looked like little angels, Father Gunn thought. It was always a great surprise the difference a little cleaning and polishing could make.

Father Gunn relaxed, they were nearly there. Only a few more moments then the ceremony would begin. It would be all right after all.

The school looked magnificent. Not even Mrs Kennedy could have complained about its appearance, Father Gunn thought. And the tables were arranged under the spreading shade of the copper beech.

The master and the mistress had the children beautifully arranged, great emphasis having been laid on looking neat and tidy. Father Gunn began to relax a little. This was as fine a gathering as the Bishop would find anywhere in the diocese.

The ceremony went like clockwork. The chair for Monsignor O'Toole, the elderly parish priest, was discreetly placed. The singing, if not strictly tuneful, was at least in the right area. No huge discordancies were evident.

It was almost time for tea – the most splendid tea that had ever been served in Shancarrig. All the eatables were kept inside the school building, out of the heat and away from the flies. When the last notes of the last hymn died away Mr and Mrs Kelly withdrew indoors.

There was something about the set line of Mrs Kennedy's face that made Father Gunn decide to go and help them. He couldn't bear it if a tray of sandwiches fell to the ground or the cream slid from the top of a trifle. Quietly he moved in, to find a scene of total confusion. Mr and Mrs Kelly and Mrs Barton, who had offered to help with carrying plates to tables, stood frozen in a tableau, their faces expressing different degrees of horror.

'What is it?' he asked, barely able to speak.

'Every single queen cake!' Mrs Kelly held up what looked from the top a perfectly acceptable tea cake with white icing on it, but underneath the sign of tooth marks showed that the innards had been eaten away.

'And the chocolate cake!' gasped Una Barton, who was white as a sheet. The front of the big cake as you saw it looked delectable, but the back had been propped up with a piece of bark, a good third of the cake having been eaten away.

'It's the same with the apple tarts!' Mrs Kelly's tears were now openly flowing down her cheeks. 'Some of the children, I suppose.'

'That Foxy Dunne and his gang! I should have known. I should have bloody known.' Jim Kelly's face was working itself into a terrible anger.

'How did he get in?'

'The little bastard said he'd help with the chairs, brought a whole gang in with him. I said to him, "All those cakes are counted very carefully." And I did bloody count them when they went out.'

'Stop saying bloody and bastard to Father Gunn,' said Nora Kelly.

'I think it's called for.' Father Gunn was grim.

'If only they could have just eaten half a dozen. They've wrecked the whole thing.'

'Maybe I shouldn't have gone on about counting them.' Jim Kelly's big face was full of regret.

'It's all ruined,' Mrs Barton said. 'It's ruined.' Her voice held the high tinge of hysteria that Father Gunn needed to bring him to his senses.

'Of course it's not ruined. Mrs Barton, get the teapots out, call Mrs Kennedy to help you. She's wonderful at pouring tea and she'd like to be invited. Get Conor Ryan from the hotel to start pouring the lemonade and send Dr Jims in here to me quick as lightning.'

His words were so firm that Mrs Barton was out the door in a flash.

Through the small window he saw the tea pouring begin and Conor Ryan happy to be doing something he was familiar with, pouring the lemonade.

The doctor arrived, worried in case someone had been taken ill.

'It's your surgical skills we need, Doctor. You take one knife, I'll take another and we'll cut up all these cakes and put out a small selection.'

'In the name of God, Father Gunn, what do you want to do that for?' asked the doctor.

'Because these lighting devils that go by the wrong name of innocent children have torn most of the cakes apart with their teeth,' said Father Gunn.

Triumphantly they arrived out with the plates full of cake selections.

'Plenty more where that came from!' Father Gunn beamed as he pressed the assortments into their hands. Since most people might not have felt bold enough to choose such a wide selection they were pleased rather than distressed to see so much coming their way.

Out of the corner of his mouth Father Gunn kept asking Mr Kelly, the master, for the names of those likely to have been involved. He kept repeating them to himself, as someone might repeat the names of tribal leaders who had brought havoc and destruction on his ancestors. Smiling as he served people and bustled to and fro, he repeated as an incantation – 'Leo Murphy, Eddie Barton, Niall Hayes, Maura Brennan, Nessa Ryan, and Foxy Bloody Dunne.'

He saw that Mattie the postman had consented to join the gathering, and was dangerously near the Bishop.

'Willing to eat the food of the Opium of the People, I see,' he hissed out of the corner of his mouth.

'That's a bit harsh from you, Father,' Mattie said, halfway through a plate of cake.

'Speak to the Bishop on any subject whatsoever and you'll never deliver a letter in this parish again,' Father Gunn warned.

The gathering was nearing its end. Soon it would be time to return to the station.

This time the journey would be made by car. Dr Jims and Mr Hayes, the solicitor, would drive the Bishop and the two clerics, whose names had never been ascertained.

Father Gunn assembled the criminals together in the school. 'Correct me if I have made an error in identifying any of the most evil people it has ever been my misfortune to meet,' he said in a terrible tone.

Their faces told him that his information had been mainly correct.

'Well?' he thundered.

'Niall wasn't in on it,' Leo Murphy said. She was a small wiry ten-year-old with red hair. She came from The Glen, the big house on the hill. She could have had cake for tea seven days a week.

'I did have a bit, though,' Niall Hayes said.

'Mr Kelly is a man with large hands. He has declared his intention of using them to break your necks, one after the other. I told him that I would check with the Vatican, but I was sure he would get absolution. Maybe even a *medal.*' Father Gunn roared the last word. They all jumped back in fright. 'However, I told Mr Kelly not to waste the Holy Father's time with all these dispensations and pardons, instead I would handle it. I told him that you had all volunteered to wash every dish and plate and cup and glass. That it was your contribution. That you would pick up every single piece of litter that has fallen around the school. That you would come to report to Mr and Mrs Kelly when it is all completed.'

They looked at each other in dismay. This was a long job. This was something that the ladies of the parish might have been expected to do.

'What about people like Mrs Kennedy? Wouldn't they want to . . . ?' Foxy began.

'No, they wouldn't want to, and people like Mrs Kennedy are *delighted* to know that you volunteered to do this. Because those kinds of people haven't seen into your black souls.'

There was silence.

'This day will never be forgotten. I want you to know that. When other bad deeds are hard to remember this one will always be to the forefront of the mind. This June day in 1950 will be etched there for ever.' He could see that Eddie Barton's and Maura Brennan's faces were beginning to pucker; he mustn't frighten them to death. 'So now. You will join the guard of honour to say farewell to the Bishop, to wave goodbye with your hypocritical hearts to His Grace whose visit you did your best to undermine and destroy. *Out.*' He glared at them. '*Out* this minute.'

Outside, the Bishop's party was about to depart. Gracefully he was moving from person to person, thanking them, praising them, admiring the lovely rural part of Ireland they lived in, saying that it did the heart good to get out to see God's beautiful nature from time to time rather than being always in a bishop's palace in a city.

'What a wonderful tree this is, and what great shade it gave us today.' He looked up at the copper beech as if to thank it, although it was obvious that he was the kind of man who could stand for hours in the Sahara Desert without noticing anything amiss in the climate. It was the boiling Father Gunn who owed thanks to the leafy shade.

'And what's all this writing on the trunk?' He peered at it, his face alive with its well-bred interest and curiosity. Father Gunn heard the Kellys' intake of breath. This was the tree where the children always inscribed their initials, complete with hearts and messages saying who was loved by whom. Too secular, too racy, too sexual to be admired by a bishop. Possibly even a hint of vandalism about it.

But no.

The Bishop seemed by some miracle to be admiring it.

'It's good to see the children mark their being here and leaving here,' he said to the group who stood around straining for his last words. 'Like this tree has been here for decades, maybe even centuries back, so will there always be a school in Shancarrig to open the minds of its children and to send them out into the world.'

He looked back lingeringly at the little stone schoolhouse and the huge tree as the car swept him down the hill and towards the station.

As Father Gunn got into the second car to follow him and make the final farewells at the station he turned to look once more at the criminals. Because his heart was big and the day hadn't been ruined he gave them half a smile. They didn't dare to believe it.

Maddy

When Madeleine Ross was brought to the church in Shancarrig to be baptised she wore an old christening robe that had belonged to her grandmother. Such lace was rarely seen in the Church of the Holy Redeemer – it would have been more at home in St Matthew's parish church, the ivy-covered Protestant church eleven miles away. But this was 1932, the year of the Eucharistic Congress in Ireland. Catholic fervour was at its highest and everyone would expect fine lace on a baby who was being christened.

The old priest did say to someone that this was a baby girl not likely to be lacking in anything, considering the life she was born into.

But parish priests don't know everything.

Madeleine's father died when she was eight. He was killed in the War. Her only brother went out to Rhodesia to live with an uncle who had a farm the size of Munster.

When Maddy Ross was eighteen years old in 1950 there were a great many things lacking in her life: like any plan of what she was going to do – like any freedom to go away and do it.

Her mother needed somebody at home and her brother had gone, so Maddy would be the one to stay.

Maddy also thought she needed a man friend, but Shancarrig was not the place to find one.

It wasn't even a question of being a big fish in a small pond. The Ross family were not rich landowners – people of class and distinction. If they had been then there might have been some society that Maddy could have moved in and hunted for a husband.

It was a matter of such fine degree.

Maddy and her mother were both too well off and not well enough off to fit into the pattern of small-town life. It was fortunate for Maddy that she was a girl who liked her own company, since so little of anyone else's company was offered to her.

Or perhaps she became this way because of circumstances.

But ever since she was a child people remembered her gathering armfuls of bluebells all on her own in the Barna Woods, or bringing home funny-shaped stones from around the big rock of Shancarrig.

The Rosses had a small house on the bank of the River Grane, not near the rundown cottages, but further on towards Barna Woods which led up to the

Old Rock. Almost anywhere you walked from Maddy Ross's house was full of interest, whether it was up a side road to the school, or past the cottages to the bridge and into the heart of town, where The Terrace, Ryan's Commercial Hotel and the row of shops all stood. But her favourite walk was to head out through the woods, which changed so much in each season they were like different woods altogether. She loved them most in autumn when everything was golden, when the ground was a carpet of leaves.

You could imagine the trees were people, kind big people about to embrace you with their branches, or that there was a world of tiny people living in the roots, people who couldn't really be seen by humans.

She would tell stories, half wanting to be listened to and half to herself – stories about where she found golden and scarlet branches in autumn and the eyes of an old woman watching her through the trees, or of how children in bare feet played by the big rock that overlooked the town and ran away when anyone approached.

They were harmless stories, the Imaginary Friend stories of all children. Nobody took any notice, especially since it all died down when she went off to boarding school at the age of eleven. Shancarrig school was much too rough a place for little Madeleine Ross. She was sent to a convent two counties away.

Then they saw her growing up, her long pale hair in plaits hanging down her back and when she got to seventeen the plaits were wound around her head.

She was slim and willowy like her mother but she had these curious pale eyes. Had Maddy had good strong eyes of any colour she would have been beautiful. The lightness somehow gave her a colourless quality, a wispy appearance, as if she wasn't a proper person.

And if anyone in Shancarrig had thought much about her they might have come to the conclusion that she was a weak girl who had few views of her own.

A more determined young woman might have made a decision about finding work for herself, or friends. No matter how complex the social structure of Shancarrig you'd have thought that young Maddy Ross would have had some friends.

There were cousins of course, aunts and uncles to visit. Maddy and her mother went to see families in four counties, always her mother's relations. Her father's people lived in England.

But at home she was really only on the fringe of things. Like the day they had the dedication of the school, the day the Bishop came.

Maddy Ross stood on the edge with her straw sunhat to keep the rays of the sun from her fair skin. She watched Father Gunn bowing his way up the hill towards the school. She watched the elderly Monsignor O'Toole in his wheelchair. But she stood slightly apart from the rest of Shancarrig as they waited for the procession to arrive.

The Kellys with their little niece Maria, all of them dressed to kill. Nora Kelly should have worn a hat like Maddy had, not a hopeless lank mantilla that made her look out of place in the Irish countryside.

Still it would be nice to belong somewhere, like the Kellys did. They had come to that school and made it their own. They were the centre of the community now while Maddy, who had lived here all her life, was still on the outside.

She accepted her plate of cakes, all served for some reason sliced and on a plate, rather than letting people choose what they wished.

Mrs Kelly looked at her speculatively.

'I think the time has come to get a JAM,' she said.

Maddy was mystified. 'I hardly think you need any more,' she said, looking at her plate.

'A Junior Assistant Mistress,' Mrs Kelly explained, as if to a five-year-old.

'Oh, sorry.'

'Well, do you think we should talk to your mother about it?'

Maddy began to wonder was the heat affecting all of them.

'I . . . think she's a bit set in her ways now . . . she mightn't be able to teach,' she explained kindly.

'I meant you, Miss Ross.'

'Oh. Of course. Yes, well . . .' Maddy said.

It proved how little she must have been planning her life. She had *no* immediate plans.

There had been much talk that year of visiting Rome. It was the Holy Year. It would be a special time. Aunty Peggy had been, the pictures were endless, the stories often repeated, the lack of good strong tea regretted over and over.

But Mother could never make up her mind about little things like whether to have strawberry jam or gooseberry jam for tea, so how could she make up her mind about something huge like a visit to Rome? The autumn came, the evenings started to get cooler, and everyone agreed that there would be grave danger of catching a chill.

It was just as well they hadn't gone to all the trouble of getting passports and booking tickets. And as Mother often said, you could love God just as well from Shancarrig as you could from a city in Italy.

Maddy Ross had been disappointed at first when the often discussed plans looked as if they were coming to nothing. But then she didn't think about it any more. She was good at putting disappointments behind her, there had been many of them even by the time she was eighteen.

Her best friend at school, Kathleen White, hadn't even told Maddy when she decided to enter the convent and become a nun. Everyone else in the school knew first. Maddy had been shaking with emotion when she challenged Kathleen with the news.

Kathleen had become unhealthily calm, too serene for her own good.

'I didn't tell you because you're so intense about everything,' Kathleen said simply. 'You'd either have wanted to join with me or you'd have been too dramatic about it. It's just what I want to do. That's all.'

Maddy decided to forgive Kathleen after a while. After all, a Vocation was a huge step. Obviously Kathleen had too much on her mind to care about the sensibilities of her friend. Maddy wrote her long letters forgiving her and talking about the commitment to religious life. Kathleen had written one short note. In two months' time she would be a postulant at the convent. She could neither write nor receive letters then. Perhaps it would be better to get ready for that by not beginning a very emotional correspondence now.

And there had been other disappointments that summer. At the tennis club dance Maddy had thought she looked well and that a young man had admired her. He had danced with her for longer than anyone else. He had been particularly attentive about glasses of fruit punch. They had sat in the swinging seat and talked easily about every subject. But nothing had come of it. She had gone to great trouble to let him know where she lived and even found two occasions to call at his house. But it was as if she had never existed.

Sometimes when Maddy Ross went for her long lonely walks up the tree-covered hill to the Old Rock that stood guarding the town she felt that she handled everything wrong. It was all so different to things that happened to girls in the pictures.

Maddy had always known that there wouldn't be the money to send her to university, so she had thought it just as well that she didn't have any burning desire to be a professor, or a doctor or lawyer. But there was nothing else that fired her either. Other girls had gone to train as nurses, some of them had done secretarial courses and gone into the bank or big insurance offices. There were others who went to be radiographers, or physiotherapists.

Maddy, the girl with the long pale hair and the slow smile that went all over her face once it began, thought that sooner or later something would turn up.

Probably at the end of the holidays.

Mrs Kelly had been serious on that hot day, and in the very first week of September Mr and Mrs Kelly from the school came to see Mother.

Shancarrig's small stone schoolhouse was a little way out of the town. That was to make it easier for the children of the farmers, it had been said. Mr and Mrs Kelly had come as newly marrieds to the school in answer to Father Gunn's appeal. The last teachers had left in some disarray. Maddy had heard stories about drinking and dismissals, but as usual, only a very edited version of events, filtered through her mother. Mother never seemed to grasp the full end of any stick.

Mr and Mrs Kelly were a strange couple. He was big and innocent-looking, like a farmer's boy. She was small and taut-looking, her mouth often in a narrow line of disapproval.

Maddy Ross had looked at her more than once, wondering what it was about Mrs Kelly that had attracted the big, simple, good-natured man by her side. They were only about ten years older than she was.

She wondered if Mrs Kelly had looked about her and then, finding nobody more suitable, settled for the teacher. She certainly looked as if something had displeased her. Even when they came uninvited to see Mother they both looked as if they were going to issue some complaint.

Maddy found nothing odd about their asking Mother rather than asking her. After all, it was the kind of thing Mrs Ross would have a view on.

Perhaps she thought her daughter Madeleine was intended for something more elevated than working in Shancarrig school. It was better to sound out the opinions before making a direct approach.

But Mother thought it would be an excellent idea. 'Fallen straight into their laps' was the way she described it when the cousins came to supper the following day.

'And won't Madeleine need to be trained to teach?' the cousins asked.

'Nonsense,' said Mother. 'What training would anyone need to put manners on unfortunates like the young Brennans or the young Dunnes?'

They agreed. It wasn't a real career like the cousins' children were embarking on: one in a bank, one doing a very advanced secretarial course, with Commercial French thrown in, which could lead to any kind of a position almost anywhere in the world.

To her surprise Maddy loved it.

She had neither the roar of Mr Kelly nor the confident firm voice of his wife. She spoke gently and almost hesitantly but the children responded to her. Even the bold Brennan children, whose father was Paudie Brennan, drunk and layabout, seemed easy to handle. And the Dunnes, whose faces were smeared with jam, agreed quite meekly to having their mouths wiped before class began.

There were three classsrooms in the little schoolhouse, one for Mrs Kelly's class, one for Mr Kelly's, and the biggest one for Maddy Ross. It was called Mixed Infants and it was here that she started the young minds of Shancarrig off on what might be a limited kind of educational journey. There would be some, of course, who would advance to a far greater education than she had herself. The young Hayes girls, whose father was a solicitor, might well get professions, as might little Nuala Ryan from the hotel. But it was only too obvious that the Dunnes and Brennans would say goodbye to any hopes of education once they left this school. They would be on the boat abroad or into the town to get whatever was on offer for children of fourteen years of age.

They all looked the same at five, however. There was nothing except the difference of clothing to mark out those who would have the money to go further and those who would not.

Before she had gone into the school Maddy Ross barely noticed the children of her own place. Now she knew everything about them, the ones that sniffled and seemed upset, the ones who thought they could run the place, those that had the doorsteps of sandwiches for their lunch, those who had nothing at all. There were children who clung to her and told her everything about themselves and their families, and there were those who hung back.

She had never known that there would be a great joy in seeing a child work out for himself the letters of a simple sentence and read it aloud, or in watching a girl who had bitten her pencil to a stub suddenly realise how you did the great long tots or the subtraction sums. Each day it was a pleasure to point to the map of Ireland with a long stick and hear them chant the places out.

'What are the main towns of County Cavan? All right. All together now. Cavan, Cootehill, Virginia . . .' all in a sing-song voice.

There were two cloakrooms, one for the girls and one for the boys. They smelled of Jeyes Fluid, as the master obviously poured it liberally in the evenings when the children had left.

It would have been a bleak little place had it not been for the huge copper beech which dwarfed it and looked as if it was holding the school under its protective arm. Like she felt safe in Barna Woods as a child, Maddy felt safe with this tree. It marked the seasons with its colouring and its leaves.

The days passed easily, each one very much like that which had gone before. Madeleine Ross made big cardboard charts to entertain the children. She had pictures of the flowers she collected in Barna Woods, and she sometimes pressed the flowers as well and wrote their names underneath. Every day the children in Shancarrig school sat in their little wooden desks and repeated the names of the ferns, and foxgloves, cowslips and primroses and ivies. Then they would look at the pictures of St Patrick and St Brigid and St Colmcille and chant their names too.

Maddy made sure that they remembered the saints as well as the flowers.

The saints were higher on Father Gunn's list of priorities. Father Gunn was a very nice curate. He had little whirly glasses, like looking through the bottom of a lemonade bottle. Now the school manager he was a frequent visitor – he had to guard the faith and morals of the future parishioners of Shancarrig. But Father Gunn liked flowers and trees too, and he was always kind and supportive to the Junior Assistant Mistress.

Maddy wondered how old he was. With priests, as with nuns, it was always so hard to know. One day he unexpectedly told her how old he was. He said he was born on the day the Treaty was signed in 1921.

'I'm as old as the State,' he said proudly. 'I hope we'll both live for ever.'

'It's good to hear you saying that, Father.' Maddy was arranging a nature display in the window. 'It shows you enjoy life. Mother is always saying that she can't get her wings soon enough.'

'Wings!' The priest was puzzled.

'It's her way of saying she'd like to be in heaven with God. She talks about it quite a lot.'

Father Gunn seemed at a loss for words. 'It's wholly admirable, of course, to see this world only as a shadow of the heavenly bliss Our Father has prepared for us but . . .'

'But Mother's only just gone fifty. It's a bit soon to be thinking about it already, isn't it?' Maddy helped him out.

He nodded gratefully, 'Of course, I'm getting on myself. Maybe I'll start thinking the same way.' His voice was jokey. 'But I have so much to do I don't feel old.'

'You should have someone to help you.' Maddy said only what everyone else in Shancarrig said. The old priest was doddery now. Father Gunn did everything. They definitely needed a new curate.

And it wasn't as if the priests' housekeeper was any help. Mrs Kennedy had a face like a long drink of water. She was dressed in black most of the time, mourning for a husband who had died so long ago hardly anyone in Shancarrig could remember him. A good priests' housekeeper should surely be kind and supportive, fill the role of mother, old family retainer and friend.

It had to be said that Mrs Kennedy played none of these roles. She seemed to smoulder in resentment that she herself had not been given charge of the parish. She snorted derisively when anyone offered to help out in the parish work. It was a tribute to Father Gunn's own niceness that so many people stepped in to help with the problems caused by Monsignor O'Toole being almost out of the picture, and Mrs Kennedy being almost too much in it.

Then the news came that there was indeed a new priest on the way to Shancarrig. Someone knew someone in Dublin who had been told definitely. He was meant to be a very nice man altogether.

About six months later, in the spring of 1952, the new curate arrived. He was a pale young man called Father Barry. He had long delicate white hands, light fair hair and dark, startling blue eyes. He moved gracefully around Shancarrig, his soutane swishing gently from side to side. He had none of the bustle of Father Gunn, who always seemed uneasily belted into his priestly garb and distinctly ill at ease in the vestments.

When Father Barry said mass a shaft of sunlight seemed to come in and touch his pale face, making him look more saintly than ever. The people of Shancarrig loved Father Barry and in her heart Maddy Ross often felt a little sorry for Father Gunn, who had somehow been overshadowed.

It wasn't *his* fault that he looked burly and solid. He was just as good and attentive to the old and the feeble, just as understanding in Confession, just as involved in the school. And yet she had to admit that Father Barry brought with him some new sense of exhilaration that the first priest didn't have.

When Father Barry came to her classroom and spoke he didn't talk vaguely about the missions and the need to save stamps and silver paper for mission stations, he talked of hill villages in Peru where the people ached to hear of Our Lord, where there was only one small river and that dried up during the dry seasons, leaving the villagers to walk for miles over the hot dry land to get water for the old and for their babies.

As they sat in the damp little schoolhouse in Shancarrig, Maddy and Mixed Infants were transported miles away to another continent. The Brennans had broken shoes and torn clothes, they even bore the marks of a drunken father's fist, but they felt rich beyond the dreams of kings compared to the people in Vieja Piedra, thousands of miles away.

The very name of this village was the same as their own. It meant Old Rock. The people in this village were crying out to them across the world for help.

Father Barry fired the children with an enthusiasm never before known in that school. And it wasn't only in Maddy Ross's class. Even under the sterner eye of Mrs Kelly, who might have been expected to say that we should look after our own first before going abroad to give help, the collections increased.

And in Mr Kelly's class the fierce master echoed the words of the young priest, but in his own way.

'Come out of that, Jeremiah O'Connor. You'll want your arse kicked from here to Barna and back if you can't go out and raise a shilling for the poor people of Vieja Piedra.'

When he gave the Sunday sermon Father Barry often closed his disturbing blue eyes and spoke of how fortunate his congregation were to live in the green fertile lands around Shancarrig. The church might be full of people sneezing and coughing, wearing coats wet from the trek across three miles of road and field to get there, but Father Barry made their place sound like a paradise compared to its namesake in Peru.

Some of them began to wonder why a loving God had been so unjust to the good Spanish-speaking people in that part of the world, who would have done anything to have a church and priests in their midst.

Father Barry had an answer for that whenever the matter was raised. He said it was God's plan to test men's love and goodness for each other. It was easy to love God, Father Barry assured everyone. Nobody had any problem in loving Our Heavenly Father. The problem was to love people in a small lonely village miles away and treat them as brothers and sisters.

Maddy and her mother often talked about Father Barry and his saintliness. It was something they both agreed on, which meant they talked about him more than ever. There were so many subjects which divided them.

Maddy wondered would there be the chance for them to go out to Rhodesia to Joseph's wedding. Her brother was marrying a girl from a Scottish family in Bulawayo. There would be nobody from the Ross side of the family. He had sent the money, and the wedding was during the school holidays, but Mrs Ross said she wasn't up to the journey. Dr Jims had said that Maddy's mother was fit as a fiddle and well able to make the trip. In fact, the sea journey would do nothing except improve her health.

Father Gunn had said that family solidarity would be a great thing at a time like this and that truly she should make the effort. Major and Mrs Murphy who lived in The Glen, the big house with the iron railings and the wonderful glasshouses, said that it was a chance of a lifetime. Mr Hayes the solicitor said that if it was his choice he'd go.

But Mother remained adamant. It was a waste, she said, to spend the money on a trip for such an old person as she was. She would soon be getting her wings. She would see enough and know enough then.

Maddy was becoming increasingly impatient with this attitude of her mother's. The wings theory seemed to apply to everything. If Maddy wanted a new coat, or a trip to Dublin, or a perm for her light straight hair, her mother would sigh and say there would be plenty of time for that and money to spend on it after Mother had gone.

Mother was in her fifties and as strong as anyone in Shancarrig, but giving the aura of frailty. Maddy did the housework, because until Mother had got her wings there would be no money to spend on luxuries like having a maid.

Maddy's own wages as a Junior Assistant Mistress were so small as to be insignificant.

She was twenty-three and very restless.

The only person in the whole of Shancarrig who understood was Father Barry. He was thirty-three and equally restless. He had been called to order for preaching too much about Vieja Piedra, by no less an authority than the Bishop. He burned with the injustice of it. Monsignor O'Toole was doting, and knew nothing of what was being preached or what was not. Father Gunn must have gone behind his back and complained about him. Father Gunn was only a fellow curate, he had no authority over him.

Father Brian Barry roamed the woods of Barna, swishing angrily against the bushes that got in his way. What right had men, the pettiest and most jealous of men, to try to halt God's work for dying people, for brothers and sisters who were calling out to them?

If Brian Barry's own health had been better he would have been a missionary priest. He would have been amongst the people of Vieja Piedra, like his friend from the seminary, Cormac Flynn, was. Cormac it was who wrote and told him at first hand of the work that had to be done.

In the Church of the Holy Redeemer there was a window dedicated to the memory of the Hayes family relations who had gone to their eternal reward. There had been many priests in that family. On the window the words were written *The Harvest is Great but the Labourers are Few.* There it was, written in stained glass, in their own church, and the mad parish priest and the selfish complacent Father Gunn were so blind they couldn't see it.

In one of these angry walks Father Barry came across Miss Ross from the school, sitting on a tree trunk and puzzling over a letter. He calmed himself for a minute before he spoke. She was a gentle girl and he didn't want to let her know the depth of his rage and resentment in the battle for people's souls, and all the obstacles that were being put in his way.

She looked up startled when she saw him, but made room on the log for him to sit down.

'Isn't it beautiful here? You can often find a solution in this place, I think.'

He reached through the slit in his cassock to take cigarettes out of his pocket and sat beside her without speaking.

Somehow, she seemed to understand the need for silence. She sat, hugging her knees and looking out ahead of her, as the summer afternoon light came in patches between the rowan trees and beeches that made up Barna Woods. A squirrel came and gazed at them, inquisitively looking from one to the other before he hopped away.

They laughed. The tension and the silence broken, they could talk to each other easily.

'When I was young I'd never seen a squirrel,' Father Barry said. 'Only in picture books, and there was a giraffe on the same page so I always thought they were the same size. I was terrified of meeting one.'

'When did you?'

'Not until I was in the seminary . . . someone said there was a squirrel over there and I urged everyone to take cover . . . they thought I was mad.'

'Well, that's nothing,' she encouraged him. 'I thought guerrilla warfare was sending gorillas out to fight each other instead of people.'

'You're saying that to make me feel good,' he teased her.

'Not a bit of it. Did they all laugh or didn't any of them understand?'

'I had a friend, Cormac. He understood. He understood everything.'

'That's Father Cormac out in Peru?'

'Yes. He understood everything. But how can I tell him what's happening now?'

As the shadows got longer they sat in Barna Woods and talked. Brian Barry told of his anguish over the work that had to be done and the burden of guilt he felt about the people of this place that seemed to call to him, but what did he do about Obedience to superiors? Maddy Ross told of her brother Joseph who had sent money and expected his mother and sister to come and be there for the happiest day of his life.

'How can I find the words to tell him?' Maddy asked.

'How can I find the words to tell Cormac there'll be no more support from Shancarrig?' asked Father Barry.

That was the day that began their dependence on each other – the knowledge that only the other understood the pressures, the pain and the indecision. The very thought that somebody else understood gave each of them courage.

Maddy Ross found herself able to write to her brother Joseph and say that she would love to come to his wedding, but that Mother did not consider herself strong enough to travel. It meant a lot of silences and sulks at home, but Maddy weathered it. She assembled a simple wardrobe and made her bookings.

Eventually her mother relented and began to show some enthusiasm for the trip. She didn't take this enthusiasm to the point of going with her daughter, but at least the stony silences ended and the atmosphere had cleared.

Father Barry too showed courage. He spoke directly to Father Gunn, and said that he accepted the ruling of the diocese that there was not to be exceptional emphasis on the missions in general or on one mission field in particular. He agreed that other themes such as tolerance and charity on the home front and devotion to Our Blessed Lady, Queen of Ireland, be brought to the forefront.

He also said that in his spare time, if he could run sales of work, he could set up charitable projects in aid of Vieja Piedra. He felt sure that there could be no objection. To this Father Gunn, with a sigh of pure relief, said that there would no objection.

In the summer of 1955 Maddy Ross and Brian Barry wished each other well, she on her journey to Africa, he on his fund-raising efforts so that Cormac Flynn would not be let down. When they met again in the autumn they would tell each other everything.

'We'll meet in the woods with the giant squirrels,' said Father Barry.

'Watching out for the military gorillas,' laughed Maddy Ross.

They were both looking forward to the meeting even as they were saying goodbye.

They were very much changed when they met again. They knew this just from the briefest meeting in the church porch after ten o'clock mass. Father Barry was rearranging the pamphlets that the Catholic Truth Society published, which were in racks for sale, but were always mixed up whenever he passed them by. The problem was that everyone wanted to read 'The Devil at Dances' and 'Keeping Company', but nobody wanted to buy them. Copies of these booklets were always well thumbed and returned to some position or other.

He saw Madeleine come out with her mother. Mrs Ross spent a lengthy time at the holy water font, blessing herself as if she were giving the *Urbi et Orbi* blessing from the papal balcony in Rome.

'Welcome back, stranger. Was it wonderful?' He smiled at her.

'No. It couldn't have gone more differently than was planned.'

They looked at each other, both surprised by the intense way the other had spoken. Father Barry looked over at Mrs Ross, still far enough away not to hear.

'Barna Woods,' he said, his eyes dark and huge.

'At four o'clock,' Maddy said.

She hadn't felt like this since gym class back at school, where they did the wall bars and all the blood ran to her head, making her feel dizzy and faint.

When she found herself deliberating over which blouse to wear she pulled herself up sharply. He's a priest, she said. But she still wore the striped one which gave her more colour and didn't make her look wishy-washy.

When her mother asked her where she was going, she said she wanted to pick the great fronds of beech leaves in Barna Woods. They could put them in glycerine later and preserve them to decorate the house for the winter.

'I'll look for some really good ones that have turned,' she explained. 'I might be some time.'

She found him sitting on their log with his head in his hands. He told of a summer where everything he had done for Vieja Piedra had been thwarted, not just by Father Gunn, who had turned up dutifully at the bring and buy sale, at the whist drive and the general knowledge quiz, but because the interest simply wasn't there. And since he could no longer use the parish pulpit to preach of the plight of these poor people he didn't have the ear and the heart of the congregation any more. His face was troubled. Maddy felt there was more he wasn't telling. She didn't push him. He would tell what he wanted to tell. Now he asked about her: had her brother Joseph been delighted to see her?

'Yes, and no.' Her brother's fiancée was of the Presbyterian faith and had only agreed to be married in a Catholic Church to please Joseph. Now that his mother wasn't coming to the wedding Joseph had decided that he shouldn't put Caitriona through all this since, really and truly as long as it was Christian, one service was the same as another in the eyes of God.

So Maddy had gone the whole way to Africa to see her brother commit a mortal sin. There had been endless arguments, discussions and tears on both their parts. Joseph said that since they hardly knew each other their tie as brother and sister was not like a real family. Maddy had asked why then had he paid for her to come out to see him.

'To show people that I am not alone in the world,' he had said.

Oh yes, she had attended the ceremony, and smiled, and been pleasant to all the guests. She had told her mother nothing of this. In fact, she was worn out remembering to call the priest Father McPherson rather than Mr McPherson, which was the name of the Presbyterian minister who had married the young couple, in a stiflingly hot church under a cloudless sky – a church with no tabernacle, and no proper God in it at all.

They walked together to find the kind of sprays she wanted. She explained that she had made a sort of excuse to her mother for going to the woods. Then she wished she hadn't said that – it might appear to him as if she needed an excuse for something so perfectly innocent as a meeting with a friend.

But, oddly, it struck a chord with him.

'I made an excuse too, to Father Gunn and Mrs Kennedy, of course. I told him that I wanted to make a couple of parish calls, the Dunnes and the Brennans. Both of them are sure to be out, or at any rate unlikely to invite me in.'

They looked at each other and looked away. A lot had been admitted.

Speaking too quickly she told him about how you preserved flowers and leaves, and how the trick was to put very few in a vase with a narrow opening.

Speaking equally quickly he nodded agreement and perfect understanding of the process, and said that parish calls were an imposition on the priest and the people, everyone dreaded them, and how much better it would be to spend our life in a place where people really needed you rather than worrying had they a clean tablecloth and a slice of cake to give you. His face looked very bitter and sad as he spoke and she felt such huge sympathy for him that she touched him lightly on the arm.

'You *do* a great deal of good here. If you knew how much you touch all our lives.'

To her shock his eyes filled with tears.

'Oh, Madeleine,' he cried. 'Oh God, I'm so lonely. I've no one to talk to, I've no friends. No one will listen.'

'Shush, shush.' She spoke as to a child. 'I'm your friend. I'll listen.'

He put his arms around her and laid his head on her shoulder. She felt arms around her waist and his body close to hers as he shook with sobs.

'I'm so sorry. I'm so foolish,' he wept.

'No. No, you're not. You're good. You care. You wouldn't be you unless you were so caring,' she soothed him. She stroked his head and the back of his neck. She could feel his tears wet against her face as he raised his head to try to apologise.

'Shush, shush,' she said again. She held him until the sobs died down.

Then she took out her handkerchief, a small white one with a blue flower in the corner, and handed it to him.

They walked wordlessly to their tree trunk. He blew his nose very hard.

'I feel such a fool. I should be strong and courageous for you, Madeleine, tell you things that will console you about your brother's situation, not cry like a baby.'

'No, you *do* make me feel courageous and strong, really, Father Barry...'

He interrupted her sharply. 'Now, listen here. If I'm going to cry in your arms, the least you can do is call me Brian.'

She accepted it immediately. 'Yes, but Brian, you must believe that you have helped me. I didn't think I was any use to anyone, a disappointment to my mother, no support to my brother...'

'You must have friends. You of all people, so generous and giving. You're not locked up in rigid rules and practices like I am.'

'I have no friends,' Madeleine Ross said simply.

That afternoon there wasn't time to tell each other all the millions of things there were still to tell – like how Brian had a letter from his great friend Cormac Flynn in Peru saying for heaven's sake not to be so intense about Vieja Piedra, it was just one place on the globe – Father Brian Barry hadn't been born into the world thousands of miles away with a direct instruction to save the place single-handed.

Father Brian Barry had been more hurt than he could ever express by that letter. But when he told Maddy and she tumbled out her own information about Kathleen White and how she had begged Maddy, her friend, not to write to her so intensely, they saw it as one further common bond between them.

She learned about his childhood – his mother who had always wanted a son as a priest, but who had died a month before his ordination and never received his blessing.

He heard of life with a mother who was becoming increasingly irrational – of a life lived more and more in fantasy – in a world where her cousins were people of great wealth and high breeding – where all kinds of niceties were important, the wearing of gloves, the owning of a coach and horses in the old days, the calling with visiting cards. None of it had any basis in reality, Maddy said, but Dr Jims said it was harmless. Lots of middle-aged women had notions and delusions of grandeur, and those harboured by Mrs Ross were no worse than a lot of people's, and better than most.

Their meetings had to be more and more conspiratorial. Maddy would stay late in the school, decorating her window displays. Father Barry would call with some information for the Kellys and happen to see her in the classroom. The door would be left open. He would sit on the teacher's desk, swinging his legs. If Mrs Kelly were to look in, and her anxious face seemed to look everywhere, then she would see nothing untoward.

But when they walked together in Barna Woods away from the eyes of the town they walked close together. Sometimes they would stop by chance at exactly the same time and she would lay her head companionably on his shoulder, and lean against him as they peeled the bark from a tree or looked at a bird's nest hidden in the branches.

Night after night Maddy lay alone in her narrow bed remembering that day he had cried and she had held him in the woods. She could remember the way his body shook and how she could feel his heart beat against her. She could bring back the smell of him, the smell of winegums and Gold Flake tobacco, of Knight's Castile soap. She could remember the way his hair had tickled her neck and how his tears had wet her cheeks. It was like seeing the same scene of a film over and over.

She wondered did he ever think of it, but supposed that would be foolishly romantic. And for Father Barry . . . for Brian . . . it might even be a sin.

Because of this new centre to her life Maddy Ross was able to do more than ever before. She could scarcely remember the days when the time had seemed long and hung heavily around her. Now there weren't enough hours in the week for all that had to be done. She had long back hired young Maura Brennan from the cottages, a solemn poor child who loved stroking the furniture, to do her ironing and that worked out very well. Now on a different day she got young Eddie Barton to come and do her garden for her.

Eddie was a funny little fellow of about fourteen, interested in plants and nature. He would often want to talk to her about the various things that grew in her garden.

'What do you spend the money on?' she asked him one day. He reddened. 'It doesn't matter. It's yours to spend any way you like.'

'Stamps,' he said eventually.

'That's nice. Have you a big collection?'

'No. To put on letters. Father Barry said we should have a pen-friend overseas,' he said.

It was wonderful to think how much good Father Barry was doing. Imagine a boy with wiry sticky-up hair like Eddie, a boy who would normally be kicking a ball up against a house wall, or writing messages on it, now had a Catholic pen-friend overseas. She gave him extra money that day.

'Tell him about Shancarrig, what a great place it is.'

'I do,' Eddie said simply. 'I write all about it.'

When Eddie got flu and his mother wouldn't let him out, Foxy Dunne offered to do the chore.

'I believe you're a great payer, Miss Ross,' he said cheerfully.

'You won't get as much as Eddie – you don't know which are flowers and which are weeds.' She was spirited and cheerful herself.

'Ah but you're a teacher, Miss Ross. It'd only take you a minute to show me.'

'Only till Eddie comes back,' she agreed.

By the time Eddie was better and came back to fume over the desecration he claimed Foxy had done in the garden, Foxy had got himself several odd jobs, mending doors, fixing locks on an outhouse. Her mother didn't like having one of the Dunnes around the place in case he was sizing it up for a job for himself or one of his brothers.

'Oh Mother! They shouldn't all be tarred with the same brush,' Maddy cried.

'You're nearly as unworldly as Father Barry himself,' said her mother.

There had once been a Dramatic Society in Shancarrig but it had fallen into inactivity. There was some vague story behind this, as there was behind everything. It had to do with the previous teacher having become very inebriated at a performance and some kind of unpleasantness was meant to have taken place. Nellie Dunne always said she could tell you a thing or two about the play-acting that went on in this town. It was play-acting in every sense of the word, she might say. But though she threatened she never in fact did tell anybody a thing or two about what had gone on; and whatever it was had gone on long before Father Gunn had come to Shancarrig. And Monsignor O'Toole wasn't likely to remember it.

Maddy thought that very possibly the members of whatever it had been were sufficiently cooled to start again. She was surprised and pleased at the enthusiasm – Eddie Barton's mother said she'd help with the wardrobe; you always needed a professional to stop the thing looking like children playing charades. Biddy, the maid up at The Glen, said that if there was any call for a step dance she would be glad to oblige. It was a skill which her position didn't give her much chance to use, and she didn't want to get too rusty. Both Brian and Liam Dunne from the hardware store said they would join, and Carrie who looked after Dr Jims' little boy said she'd love to try out for a small part, but nothing with too many lines. Sergeant Keane and his wife both said it was the one thing they had been waiting for and the Sergeant pumped Maddy's hand up and down in gratitude.

So Maddy started the Shancarrig Dramatic Society and they were always very grateful for the kind interest that Father Barry took in their productions. Nobody thought it a bit odd that the saintly young priest with the sad face should throw himself whole-heartedly into anything that was for the parish good. And of course the proceeds went to the charity of the missions in South America. And it was just as well to have Father Barry, everyone agreed, laughing a little behind Father Gunn's back, because poor Father Gunn, in spite of his many other great qualities, didn't know one side of the stage from the other, while Father Barry could turn his hand to anything. He could design a set, arrange the lighting, and best of all, direct performances. He coaxed the townspeople of Shancarrig to play everything from *Pygmalion* to *Drama at Inish*, and the Christmas concerts were a legend.

Only Maddy knew how his heart wasn't in any of it.

Only she knew the real man, who hid his unhappiness. Soon she found she was thinking of him all the time, and imagining his reaction to the smallest and most inconsequential things she did. If she was telling the story of the Flight into Egypt to the Mixed Infants at school she imagined him leaning against the door smiling at her approvingly. Sometimes she smiled back as if he were really there. The children would look around to see if someone had come in.

Then at home, when she was preparing her mother's supper, she would decorate the plate with a garnish of finely sliced tomato, or chopped hard-boiled egg and fresh parsley. Her mother barely noticed, but she could see how Brian Barry would respond. She would put words of praise in his mouth and say them to herself.

She spent her time in what she considered was a much more satisfactory relationship than anyone else around her. Mr and Mrs Kelly were locked in a routine marriage if ever she saw one. Poor Maura Brennan of the cottages, who married a flash harry of a barman, was left alone with her Down's syndrome child to rear. Major Murphy in The Glen had a marriage that defied description. They never went anywhere outside their four walls. In any other land they would have been called recluses, but here, because The Glen was the big house, they were admired for their sense of isolation.

There was nobody that Madeleine Ross envied. Nobody she knew had as dear and pure a love as she had known, a man who depended on her utterly and who would have been lost to his vocation if it had not been for her.

And then one night all of a sudden, when she least expected it, came a strange thought. It was one of those sleepless nights when the moon seemed unnaturally bright and visible even through the curtains, so it was easier to leave them open.

Maddy saw a figure walking past going to the woods. She thought first that it was Brian, and she was about to slip into some clothes and follow him. But then she saw at the last moment that it was Major Murphy, on goodness knew what kind of outing. It was easy to mistake them, tall men in dark clothes. But Brian was asleep in the presbytery, or possibly not asleep, maybe looking at the same moon and feeling the same restlessness.

That was when it came to Maddy Ross that Father Barry should leave Shancarrig.

He could no longer be wasted passing plates of sandwiches, rigging up old curtains, praising a tuneless choir, welcoming yet another bishop or visiting churchmen. There was only one life to be lived. He must go on and live it as best he could, serving the people of Vieja Piedra. The whole notion of there being only one life to live buzzed around in her head all night. There was no more sleep now. She sat hugging a mug of tea, remembering how her brother Joseph had said those very words to her, all that while ago when she had gone to Rhodesia for his wedding, about there being only one chance to live your life.

And Joseph, who had been given the same kind of education as she had had, and who came from the same parents, had been able to seize at the life he wanted. Joseph and Caitriona Ross had children out in Africa. Sometimes they sent pictures of them outside their big white house with the pillars at the front door. Maddy had never told her mother that these little children weren't Catholics and might not even have been properly baptised. She and Brian had agreed that it was better not to trouble an already troubled mind with such information.

If Joseph Ross had only one life so had Maddy Ross and so had Brian

Barry. Why couldn't Father Brian leave and go to South America? After a decent interval Maddy could leave too and be with him.

For part of the night as she paced the house she told herself that things need not change between them. They would be as they were here, true friends doing the work they felt was calling across the land and sea to them. And Brian could remain a priest. Once a priest always a priest. He wouldn't have to leave, just change the nature and scope of his vocation.

And then as dawn came up over Barna Woods Maddy Ross admitted to herself what she had been hiding. She acknowledged that she wanted Brian Barry to be her love, her husband. She wanted him to leave the priesthood. If he could get released from his vows by Rome so much the better. But even if he could not Maddy wanted him anyway. She would take him on any terms.

It was a curious freedom realising this.

She felt almost light-headed and at the same time she stopped playing games. She took her mother breakfast on a tray without fantasising what Brian would say if he had been standing beside them looking on. It was as if she had come out of the shadows, she thought, and into the real world.

She could barely wait to meet Brian. No day had ever seemed longer. Mrs Kelly had never been sharper or more inquisitive about everything Maddy was doing.

Why was she putting greetings on the blackboard in different languages? Spanish. And French, no less. Wasn't it enough for these boneheaded children to try and learn Irish and English like the Department laid down without filling their heads with how to say good day and goodbye in tongues they'd never need to use?

Maddy looked at her levelly. Normally, she would have seen Brian in her mind's eye standing by the blackboard, congratulating her on her patience and forbearance, and then the two of them wandering together in Barna Woods crying 'Buenos dias Vieja Piedra, we are coming to help you.'

But today she saw no shadowy figure. She saw only the small quivering Mrs Kelly, who was wearing a brown and yellow striped dress and looked for all the world like a wasp.

Maddy Ross was a different person today.

'I'm putting some phrases in foreign languages on the blackboard, Mrs Kelly, because, despite what you and the Department of Education think, these children may well go to lands where they use them. And I shall put them on the blackboard every day until they feel a little bit of confidence about themselves instead of being humble and content to remain in Shancarrig pulling their caps and saying *good morning* in Irish and English until they are old men and women.'

Mrs Kelly went red and white in rapid succession.

'You'll do nothing of the sort, Miss Ross. Not in the timetable that is laid down for you.'

'I had no intention of doing it in school time, Mrs Kelly.' Maddy smiled a falsely sweet smile. 'I am in the fortunate position of being able to hold the children's interest *outside* school hours as well as when the bell rings. They will learn it before or after school. That will be clearly understood.'

She felt twenty feet tall. She felt as if she were elevated above the small stone schoolhouse and the town. She could hardly bear the slow noise of the clock ticking until she could go to Brian and tell him of her new courage, her hope and her belief that they had only one chance at life.

She met him at rehearsal under the eyes of the nosey people in town.

'How is your mother these days, Miss Ross?' he asked. It was part of their code. They had never practised it; it just came naturally to them, as so much else would now.

'She's fine, Father, always asking for you, of course.'

'I might drop in and see her later tonight, if you think she'd like that.'

'She'd love it, Father. I'll just let her know. I'm going out myself, but she'd be delighted to see you, like everyone.'

Her eyes danced with mischief as she said the words. She thought she saw the hint of a frown on Brian Barry's face, but it passed.

Miss Ross left the rehearsal and she imagined people thinking that she was a dutiful daughter, and very good also to the priest, to go home and prepare a little tray for her mother to offer him. As Maddy walked home, her cheeks burning, she thought that she had been a bloody good daughter for all her life, nearly thirty years of life in this small place. And come to think of it she had been good to the priest too. Good for him and a good friend.

Nobody could blame her for wanting her chance at life.

She sat in the wood and waited on their log. He came gently through the leafy paths. His smile was tired. Something had crossed him during the day; she knew him so very well, every little change, every flicker in his face.

'I'm late. I had to go into your mother's,' he said.

'What on earth for? You know I didn't mean ...'

'I know, but Father Gunn said to me, this very morning, that he thought I should see less of you.'

'What!'

Brian Barry was nervous and edgy. 'Oh, he said it very nicely of course, not an accusation, nothing you could take offence at ...'

'I most certainly do take offence at it,' Maddy blazed. 'How dare he insinuate that there has been anything improper between us. How *dare* he!'

'No, he didn't. He was very anxious that I should know he wasn't suggesting that.' He walked up and down as he talked, agitated, and anxious to get over the mildness of the message, the lack of blame and the motive behind it. It was just that Father Gunn wanted to protect them both from evil minds and idle wagging tongues. In a place this size when people had little real news to speculate about they made up their own. It would be better for Father Barry not to be seen so obviously sharing the same interests as Miss Ross, for both of them to make other friends.

'And what did you say, Brian?' Her pale eyes had flecks of light in them tonight.

'I said that he had a very poor opinion of people if he thought they would give such low motives to what was an obvious and proper friendship.'

But it was clear that Brian Barry had not found his own answer satisfactory. He looked confused and bewildered. She had never loved him more. 'I am sorry, Maddy, I couldn't think of what else to say.' He had never called her Maddy before, always Madeleine like her mother did.

She moved over to him and closed her arms around his neck. He smelled still of cigarette smoke, but his soap was Imperial Leather now, and he hadn't been eating the winegums. It was the chocolate cake given to him, Maddy realised, by her mother.

'It was perfect,' she whispered.

He looked very startled and moved as if to get away.

'What was perfect?' he asked, his eyes large and alarmed.

'What you said. It is a proper friendship and a proper love...'

'Yes... well...' He hadn't raised his arms to hold her.

She moved nearer to him and pressed herself towards him. 'Brian, hold me. Please hold me.'

'I can't, Maddy. I can't. I'm a priest.'

'I held you years ago when you had no friend. Hold me now; now that I have no friend and they are trying to take you away.' Her eyes filled with tears.

'No, no, no.' He soothed her as she had stroked him all that time ago. He held her head to his shoulder and comforted her. 'No, it's not a question of being taken away ... it's just ... well, you know what it is.'

She snuggled closer to him. Again she could hear his heart beat in the way she had remembered so often from that first time. He was about to release her so she allowed sobs to shake her body again. He was so clumsy, and tender at the same time. Maddy knew that this was her man, and her one chance to take what life was presenting.

'I love you so much, Brian,' she whispered.

The answering words were not there. She changed direction slightly.

'You are the only person who understands me, who knows what I want to do in the world, and I think I'm the only person who knows what is best for you.' She gulped as she spoke so that he wouldn't think the storm was over, the need for consolation at an end. In the seven years since they had first held each other in these woods times had changed; when he offered her a handkerchief now it was a paper tissue, when he sat down beside her on their log to smoke it wasn't the flaky old Gold Flake, it was a tipped cigarette.

'You've been better to me than anyone in the world. I mean that.' His voice was sincere. He *did* mean it. She could see his brain clicking through all the people who had been good to him, his mother, some kind superior in the seminary possibly. She was the best of this pathetic little list. That was all. Why was she not his great love? She would have to walk very warily.

'I have wanted the best for you since the day I met you,' she said simply.

'And I for you. Truly.'

This was probably true, Maddy thought. Like he wanted the best for the people of Vieja Piedra, wanted it in his heart but wasn't able to do anything real and lasting about it.

'You must go there,' she said.

'Go where?'

'To Peru. To Father Cormac.'

He looked at her as if she was suggesting he fly to the moon. 'How can I go, Maddy? They'll never let me.'

'Don't ask them. Just go. You've often said that God isn't worried about some pecking order and lines of obedience. Our Lord didn't ask permission when he wanted to heal people.'

He still looked doubtful. Maddy got up and paced up and down beside him. With all the powers of persuasion she could gather she told him why he must go. She played back to him all his own thoughts and phrases about the small village where people had died waiting for someone to come and help them, where they looked up to the mountain pass each day hoping that a man of God would come, not just to visit but to stay amongst them and give them the sacraments. She could see the light coming to his eye: the magic was working.

'How would I get the fare to go there?' he asked.

'You can take it from the collection.' To her it was simple.

'I couldn't do that. It's for Vieja Piedra.'

'But isn't that exactly where you would be going? Isn't that why we're raising this money, so that they'd have someone to help them?'

'No, I don't believe that would be right. I've never been sure about the end justifying the means . . . remember we often discussed that.' They had, here in this wood, sitting in her classroom, having coffee after the rehearsals for the plays.

She looked at him, flushed and eager in the middle of yet another moral dilemma, but not moved by the fact that he had held her close to him and felt her heart beat, her hair against his face, her eyelashes on his cheek. Was he an ordinary man or had he managed to quell that side of himself so satisfactorily that it didn't respond any more? She had to know.

'And when you go you can write and tell me about it . . . until I come there too.'

His eyes were dark circles of amazement now. 'You come out there, Maddy? You couldn't. You couldn't come all that far and you can't be with me. I'm a priest.'

'We have only one life.' She spoke calmly.

'And I chose mine as a priest. You know I can't change that. Nothing will change that.'

'You can change it if you want to. Just like you can change the place you live.' There was something in the direct simple way she spoke that seemed to alarm him. This was not the over-excitable intense Maddy Ross he had known, it was a serious young woman going after what she wanted.

'Sit down, Maddy.' He too was calm. He squatted in front of her, holding both her hands in his. 'If I ever gave you the impression that I might leave the priesthood then I must spend the rest of my days making up for such a terrible misunderstanding . . .' His face was troubled as he sought some response in hers. 'Maddy, I am a priest for ever. It's the one thing that means anything to me. I've been selfish and impatient and critical of those around me, I don't have the understanding and generosity of a Father Gunn, but I do have this belief that God chose me and called me.'

'You also have the belief that the people of Vieja Piedra are calling you.'

'Yes, I do. If there was a way to go there I *would* go. You have given me that courage. I won't take the money that the people of Shancarrig raised. They didn't raise it for their priest to run away with.'

The moon came up as they talked. They saw a badger quite nearby, but it wasn't important enough for either of them to comment on. Brian Barry told Madeleine Ross that he would never leave his ministry. He had a few certainties in life. This was one of them. In vain did Maddy tell him that clerical celibacy was only something introduced long after Our Lord's time, it was more or less a Civil Service ruling, not part of the Constitution. The first apostles had wives and children.

'Children.' She stroked his hand as she said the word.

He pulled both hands away from her and stood up. This was something he was never going to think about. It was the sacrifice he had made for God, the one thing God wanted from his priests: to give up the happiness and love of a wife and family. Not that it had been hard to give up because he had never known it, and now he was heading for forty years of age so it wasn't something he would be thinking of, even if he weren't a priest.

'A lot of men marry around forty,' Maddy said.

'Not priests.'

'You can do anything. Anything.'

'I won't do this.'

'But you love me, Brian. You're not going to be frightened into some kind of cringing life for the rest of your days by a silly warning from Father Gunn, by Mrs Kennedy spying, by a promise made when you were a child . . . when you didn't know what love was . . . or anything about it.'

'I still don't really know.'

'You know.'

He shook his head and Maddy could bear it no more. She reached out for him and kissed him directly on the lips. She moved herself into his arms and opened her mouth to his. She felt his arms tighten around her . . . He stroked her back and then because she pulled away from his clasp a little he stroked the outline of her breasts. She peeped through her closed eyes and saw that his eyes were closed too.

They stood locked like this for a time. Eventually he pulled away.

They looked at each other for moments before he spoke. 'You've given me everything, Maddy Ross,' he said.

'I haven't begun to give you anything,' she said.

'No but you have, believe me. You've given me such bravery, such faith. Without you I'd be nothing. You've given me the courage to go. Now you must give me one more thing . . . the freedom.'

She looked at him with disbelief. 'You could hold me like that and ask me never to be in your arms again?'

'That is what I'm begging you. *Begging* you, Maddy. It was my only sure centre. The only thing I knew . . . that I was to be a priest of God. Don't take that away from me or all the other things you have given will totter like a house of cards.'

This man had been her best friend, her soul mate. Now he was asking her permission and her encouragement to leave her life entirely, to step out of it and away from Shancarrig to the village that they had both dreamed about and prayed for and saved for all these years.

Such monstrous selfishness couldn't be part of God's plan. It couldn't be part of any dream of taking your chance in life. Maddy looked at him, confused. It was all going wrong, very very wrong.

He saw her shock, he didn't run away from it. He spoke very gently.

'Since I came to Shancarrig and even before it I've known that women are stronger than men. We could list them in this town. And I know more than you because I hear them in the Confessional. I'm there at their deathbeds when they worry not about their own pain but about how a husband will manage or whether a son will go to the bad. I've been there when their babies have died at birth, when they bury a man who was not only a husband but their means of living. Women are very strong. Can you be strong and let me go with your blessing?'

She looked at him dumbly. The words would not come, the torrent of words welling up inside her. She must be able to explain that he could not be bound by these tired old rules, these empty vows made at another time by another person. Brian Barry was different now, he had come into his kingdom, he was a man who could love and give. But she said none of these things. Which was just as well because he looked at her and the dark blue of his eyes was hard.

'You see, I want to go with your blessing, because I'm *going* to go anyway.'

They didn't meet again in Shancarrig without other people being present.

There were no more walks in the woods, no visits to the classroom. The rehearsals had to do without the kind help of Father Barry, Shancarrig Dramatic Society was told. He had been advised to take it easy. Somehow that was the hardest place, the place she missed him most. They had started these plays together; she didn't know how she would have the heart to continue. In fact, she feared the whole organisation would fall apart without him.

The Shancarrig Dramatic Society continued to thrive without Father Barry. In many ways his leaving gave them greater scope. They were able to do more comedies. They had never liked to suggest anything too light-hearted when Father Barry was there, he was so soulful and good it seemed like being too flippant in his presence.

In the weeks that seemed endless to Maddy the society decided to enter the All Ireland contest for the humorous one-act play.

'Poor Father Barry. He'd have loved this,' said Biddy from The Glen, who was going to play a dancing washroom woman in the piece.

'Go on out of that,' said Sergeant Keane's wife, 'we'd be doing a tragedy if poor Father Barry was here. Not that I wish the man any harm, and I hope whatever's bothering him gets better.'

The rumour was that he had a spot on his lung. Heads nodded. Yes, it was true he did have that colour, the very pale complexion with occasional spots of high colour that could spell out TB. Still, the sanatorium was wonderful and anyway it hadn't been confirmed yet.

He didn't avoid her eye, Maddy realised. He was totally at peace with himself, and grateful to her that she had nodded her head that night in Barna Woods and left without trusting herself to speak a word.

He thought she had seen his way was the only way.

The days were endless as she waited to hear that he had gone. It was three whole months before she heard what she had been waiting for. Father Gunn, visiting the school in his usual way, had asked her pleasantly if she could drop in at the presbytery that evening. Nothing in his face had given a hint of what was to be said.

When she arrived she was startled to see Brian sitting in one of the chairs. Father Gunn motioned her to the other.

'Maddy, you know that Father Barry is going to Peru?'

'I knew he wanted to.' She spoke carefully, but smiled at Brian. His face was alive and happy. 'You mean, it's settled? You're going to be able to go, officially?'

'I'm going with everyone's blessing,' Brian said. His face was full of love, love and gratitude.

'The Bishop is very understanding and when he saw such missionary zeal he said it would be hard not to encourage it,' said Father Gunn.

It had always been impossible to see Father Gunn's eyes through those glasses, but they seemed more opaque than ever. Maddy wondered had Father Gunn told the Bishop that Vieja Piedra alone and on Church business was infinitely preferable to another alternative.

'I hope it's every bit as rewarding for you as you and I have always believed it would be.' Her voice choked slightly.

'I wanted to thank you, Maddy, for all your help and encouragement. Father Gunn has been so wise and understanding about everything. When I told him that I wanted you to be the first to know he insisted that we invite you here, to tell you that it has all finally gone through.'

Maddy looked at Father Gunn. She knew exactly why she had been invited to the presbytery, so that there could be no tearful farewells, implorings and highly charged emotion in Barna Woods, or anywhere on their own.

'That's very kind of you, Father,' she said to the small square priest, in a very cold tone.

'No, no, and I must just get some papers. I'll leave the two of you for a few minutes.' He fussed out of the room.

Brian didn't move from his chair. 'I owe it all to you, Maddy,' he said.

'Will you write?' she asked, her voice dull.

'To everyone, a general letter in response to whatever marvellous fund-raising you do for me . . .' He smiled at her winningly as he had smiled at so many people. As he would smile at the poor Peruvians in the dry valley, who had been calling out for him. She said nothing.

And for the first time in seven years they sat in silence. They willed the time to pass when Father Gunn would have found his letters and returned to the sitting room of the presbytery. The sitting-room door had been left open.

The farewells were endless. Father Barry wanted no present, he insisted. He didn't need any goodbye gift to remind him of Shancarrig, its great people and the wonderful years he had spent here. He said he would try to describe what the place was like, their namesake on the other side of the world.

He cried when they came to see him off at the station. Maddy was in the back of the crowd. She wanted to be sure he was actually going. She wanted to see it with her own eyes. He waved with one hand and dabbed his eyes with the other. Maddy heard Dr Jims saying to Mr Hayes that he was always a very emotional and intense young man. He hoped he would fare all right in that hot climate over there.

And the time went by, but it was like a summer garden when the sun has gone, and although there's daylight there's no point in sitting out in it. More children came and went in Mixed Infants. They left Miss Ross and went up to Mrs Kelly. They still learned how to say *bonjour* and *buenos dias* in their own time. Maddy Ross had won that victory hard from Mrs Kelly – she was not going to give it up.

The fund-raising continued, but Ireland was changing in the sixties. There was television for one thing . . . people heard about other parts of the world where there was famine and disaster. Suddenly Vieja Piedra was not the only place that called to them. Sometimes the collections were small that went in the money order to the Reverend Brian Barry at his post office in a hill town some sixty-seven miles from Vieja Piedra.

Yet his letters were always grateful and warm, and there were stories of the church being built, a small building. It looked like a shed with a cross on top, but Father Barry was desperately proud of it. Pictures were sent of it, badly focused snapshots taken from different angles.

And then there was the wonderful help of Viatores Christi, some lay Christians who were coming out to help. They were invaluable, as committed in every way as were the clergy.

Maddy heard the letters read aloud, and wondered why could Brian Barry not have become a lay missionary. Then there would have been the same dream and the same hope but no terrible promise about celibacy.

But she cheered herself up. If he had not been ordained as a priest he would never have come to Shancarrig, she would never have known him, never had her chance in life.

There had been five years of walking alone in Barna Woods, five plays in Shancarrig Dramatic Society, five Christmas concerts, there had been five sales of work, whist drives, beetle drives, treasure hunts. There had been five years of raffles, bingo, house to house collections. And then, one day, Brian Barry telephoned Maddy Ross.

'I thought you'd be home from school by now.' He sounded as if he were down the road. He couldn't be telephoning her from Peru!

'I'm in Dublin,' he said.

Her heart gave an uncomfortable lurch. Something was happening. Why had the communication not been through Father Gunn?

'I want to see you. Nobody knows I'm home.'

'Brian.' Her voice was only a whisper.

'Don't tell anyone at all. Just come tomorrow.'

'But why? What's happened?'

'I'll tell you tomorrow.'

'Tomorrow? All the way to Dublin, just like that?'

'I've come all the way from Peru.'

'Is anything wrong? Is there any trouble?'

'No no. Oh Maddy, it's good to talk to you.'

'I haven't talked to you for five years, Brian. You have to tell me why are you home? Are you going to leave the priesthood?'

'Please, Maddy. Trust me. I want to tell you personally. That's why I came the whole way back. Just get the early train, will you? I'll meet you.'

'Brian?'

'I'll be on the platform.' He hung up.

She had to cash a cheque at the hotel. Mrs Ryan was interested as usual in everything. Maddy gave her no information. Her mind was too confused. She knew there would be no sleep tonight.

For five years she had slept seven hours a night.

But tonight she would not close her eyes. No matter how tired and old she might look next morning Maddy knew that there was no point in lying in that same bed where she had lain for years, seeking sleep.

Instead she examined everything in her wardrobe.

She chose a cream blouse and a blue skirt. She wore a soft blue woollen scarf around her neck. It wasn't girlish but it was youthful. It didn't look like the ageing schoolteacher grown old in her love for the faraway priest.

Maddy smiled. At least she had kept her sense of humour. Whatever he was going to tell her he would like that.

He didn't seem to have got a day older. He was boyish, even at forty-five. His coat collar was up so she couldn't see whether he still wore his roman collar, but she had told herself not to read anything into that. Out in the missions priests wore no clerical garb and yet they were as firmly priests as ever they had been.

He saw her and ran to her. They hugged like a long-separated brother and sister, like old friends parted unwillingly, which is probably what they were. She pulled away from him to see his face, but still he hugged her. You can't kiss someone who is hugging the life out of you.

The crowd had thinned on the platform. Some caution seemed to seep back into him.

'There was no one from home on the train, was there?'

'Where's home?' She laughed at him. 'In all your letters you say Vieja Piedra is home.'

'And so it is.' He seemed satisfied that they weren't under surveillance. He tucked her arm into his and they walked to a nearby hotel. The lounge was small and dark, the coffee strong and scalding. Maddy Ross would remember for ever the way it stuck to the roof of her mouth when Brian Barry told her that he was going to leave the priesthood and marry Deirdre, one of the

337

volunteers. It was like a patch of red-hot tar in her mouth. It wouldn't go away as she nodded and listened and forced her face to smile through tales of growth, and understanding and love and the emptiness of vows taken at an early age before a boy was a man, and about a loving God not holding people to meaningless promises.

And she heard how there was still a lot to be decided. Deirdre and he had realised that laicisation took such a long time, and brought so much grief, destroying the relationships of those who waited.

But in South America the clergy had understood the core values. They had gone straight to the heart of things. They knew that a blessing could be given to a union of which God would patently approve. What was the expression that Maddy herself had used so many years ago? Something about thinking in terms of the Constitution rather than in petty Civil Service bye-laws.

And he owed it all to Maddy. So often he had told that to Deirdre, who wanted to send her gratitude. If Maddy hadn't proven to him that he could be courageous and open up his heart to the world and to love, this might never have happened.

'Did you ever love me?' Maddy asked him.

'Of course I love you. I love you with all my heart. Nothing will destroy our love, not my marrying Deirdre or you marrying whoever you will. Maybe you have someone in mind?' He was roguish now, playful even. She wanted to knock him down.

'No. No plans as yet.'

'Well you should, Maddy.' Gone was the light-hearted banter, now he was being serious and caring. 'A woman should get married, and have children. That's what a woman should do.'

'And have you and Deirdre decided to have children?' She tried to put the smile back in her voice. It was so easy to let a sneer creep in instead, to let him know how she could sense that Deirdre was already pregnant.

'Eventually,' he told her, which meant imminently.

He was going to leave Vieja Piedra, and they were going to a place further down the coast of Peru. He would teach in a town, there was just as much work needed there, but they had found a native born priest, a real Peruvian, to look after the valley of Vieja Piedra. He talked on. Nothing would be said to Father Gunn. The fund-raising would take a different style. Nothing would be said to anyone really. In today's world you didn't need to explain or to be intense. It was a matter of seizing what good there was and creating more good. It was taking your chance when it was offered.

The only person who *had* to be told face to face was Maddy. That's why he had taken Deirdre's savings to come back and tell her, to thank her in the way that a letter could never do for having put him on this road to happiness.

'And did Deirdre not feel afraid that once you saw your old love you might never return to her?' Maddy's tone was light, her question deadly serious.

But Brian hastened to put her anxieties at rest. 'Lord no. Deirdre knew that what *we* had wasn't love. It was childlike fumblings, it was heavy meaning-of-life conversation, it was part of growth, and for me a very important part.' He wanted to reassure her about that.

The train back to Shancarrig left in fifteen minutes. Maddy said she thought she should take it.

'But you can't go *now*. You've only been here an hour.' His dismay was enormous.

'But you've told me everything.'

'No, I haven't told you anything really. I have only skimmed the surface.'

'I have to go back, Brian. I would have, anyway, no matter what you told me. My mother hasn't been well.'

'I didn't know that.'

'Of course you didn't. You didn't know a great many things, like Mrs Murphy in The Glen died, and that Maura Brennan brings her poor son around with her and he sits in every house in Shancarrig while she cleans floors and does washing. There are many things you don't know.'

'Well, they don't tell me. *You* don't tell me. You don't write at all.'

'I was ordered not to. Don't you remember?'

'Not ordered, just advised.'

'To you it was the same once.'

'If you'd wanted to write to me enough you would have,' he said, head on one side, roguish again.

She closed her mind to his disbelief that she would return on the next train. He had thought she would spend the whole day, if not the weekend, in Dublin with him. What was he to do now? No relations were meant to know he was back.

'Did I do the wrong thing coming back to tell you?' He was a child again, confused, uncertain.

She was gentle. She could afford to be. She had a lifetime ahead of her with little to contemplate except why her one stab at living life had failed. She reached out and held his hand.

'No, you did the right thing,' she lied straight into his face. 'Tell Deirdre that I wish you well, all of you. Tell her I went back to Shancarrig on the train with my heart brimming over.'

It was the only wedding present she could give him.

And she held the tears until the train had turned the bend and until she could no longer see his eager hand waving her goodbye.

Maura

When the time came for Maura to go to school any small enthusiasm that there had ever been in the Brennan family for education had died down. Maura's mother was worn out with all the demands that were made on her to dress them up for this May Procession and that visit from the Bishop. Not to mention communion and confirmations. Mrs Brennan had been heard to say that the Shancarrig school had notions about itself being some kind of private college for the sons and daughters of the land-owning gentry rather than the National School it was, and that nature had always intended it to be.

And the young Maura didn't get much encouragement from her father either. Paudie Brennan believed that schools and all that were women's work and not things a man got involved with. And since Paudie Brennan was not a man ever continuously in work he couldn't be expected to take an interest financially and every other way in each and every one of his nine living children, and Maura came near the end of the trail. Paudie Brennan had too much on his mind what with a leaking roof missing a dozen slates, and a very different and worrying kind of slate altogether above in Johnny Finn Noted for Best Drinks, so what time was there to be wondering about young Maura and her book learning?

Maura had never expected there to be an interest. School was for books, home was for fights. The older brothers and sisters had gone to England – the really grown-up ones. They went as soon as they were seventeen or eighteen. They came home for holidays and it was great at first, but after a day it would wear off, the niceness, and there would be shouting again as if the returned sister or brother was an ordinary part of the family, not a visitor.

One day, Maura knew, she would be the eldest one at home – just herself and Geraldine left. But Maura wasn't going to England to work in a shoe factory like Margaret, or a fish shop like Deirdre. No, she was going to stay here in Shancarrig. She wouldn't get married but she would live like Miss Ross, who was very old and could do what she liked and stay up all night without anyone giving out or groaning at her. Of course, Miss Ross was a schoolteacher and must earn pots of money, but Maura would save whenever she started to work, and keep the money in the post office until she could have a house and freedom to go to bed at two in the morning if the notion took her.

Maura Brennan often stayed on late at school to talk to Miss Ross, to try to find out more about this magnificent lifestyle in the small house with the lilac bushes and the tall hollyhocks, where Miss Ross lived. She would ask endless questions about the dog or the cat. She knew their names and ages, which nobody else at school did. She would hope that one day Miss Ross might drop another hint or two about her life. Miss Ross seemed puzzled by her interest. The child was in no way bright. Even taking into account her loutish father and timid uneducated mother, young Maura must still be called one of the slower learners in the school. Even the youngest of that Brennan string of children, Geraldine, with the permanent cold and her hair in her eyes, was quicker. But Maura was the one who hung about, who found excuses to have meaningless little conversations.

One day Miss Ross let slip that she hated ironing.

'I love ironing,' Maura said. 'I love it, I'd do it all day but the one we have is broke, and my da won't pay to have it mended.'

'What do you like about it?' Miss Ross seemed genuinely interested.

'The way your hand goes on and on . . . it's like music almost . . . and the clothes get lovely and smooth, and it all smells nice and clean,' Maura said.

'You make it sound great. I wish you'd come and do mine.'

'Of course I will,' said Maura.

She was eleven then, a square girl with her hair clipped back by a brown slide, a high forehead and clear eyes. In a different family in another place she might have had a better chance, a start that would have brought her further along some kind of road.

'No, Maura, you can't, child. I don't want the other children to see you rating yourself as only fit to do my ironing. I don't want you making little of yourself before you have to.'

'How could that be making little of myself?' The question was without guile. Maura Brennan saw no lack of dignity in coming to the teacher's house to do household chores.

'The others . . . they don't have to know, Miss Ross.'

'But they do, they will. You know this place.'

'They don't know lots of things, like that my sister Margaret had a baby in Northampton. Geraldine and I are aunts, Miss Ross. Imagine!' Maura had told the family secret easily, as if she knew that there was no danger that Miss Ross would pass on this titbit. There was the same simplicity as when she had spoken of ironing.

'Once a week, and I'll pay you properly,' Miss Ross had said.

'Thank you, Miss Ross, I'll put it in the post office.' It was the beginning for Maura Brennan. She warned young Geraldine not to tell anyone. It would be their secret.

'Why has it to be a secret?' Geraldine wanted to know.

'I don't know.' Maura was truthful. 'But it has.'

So if ever Mrs Brennan asked what was keeping Maura above at the school, Geraldine said she didn't know. It seemed daft to her, all this sucking up to Miss Ross. It wasn't as if Maura ever got anywhere at her books. She was slow and was always asking people to help her, Leo Murphy or Nessa

Ryan, girls from important families, big houses. Geraldine would know better than to talk to them or their like. Maura was half daft a lot of the time.

When Maura started doing the ironing Miss Ross gave her a doll as well as the money. She said she had seen Maura admiring it and even taking off its crushed pink dress and giving it a good press. Anyone who thought that much of a doll should have it. Maura always told Geraldine that it was on loan. Miss Ross had lent it to her until the time Miss Ross married someone and had children of her own.

'Sure Miss Ross is a hundred. She'll never marry and have children,' Geraldine cried.

'People have them at all ages. Look at Mammy, look at St Elizabeth.'

Geraldine wasn't so sure about her ground on St Elizabeth, but she knew all about their mother. 'Mammy started having them and she couldn't stop. I heard her telling Mrs Barton. But after me she stopped all of a sudden.' Geraldine was nine and she knew everything.

Maura wished she had those kind of certainties.

The doll sat on a shelf in their bedroom. It had a china face and little china hands. When Geraldine wasn't there to laugh at her Maura would hug it and speak reassuring words, saying the doll was very much loved. Sometimes Miss Ross gave Maura things to wear, a nice coloured belt once, a scarf with a tassel.

'I never wore them in the school, Maura, no one will know they're mine.'

'But what would I mind if they knew?' Again the question was so honest and without guile that Miss Ross seemed taken aback.

'I wish I could help you with your lessons, Maura. I wish I could, but you don't really have the will to concentrate.'

Maura was eager to reassure her. 'I'll be fine, Miss Ross. There's no point in trying to put things into my head that won't go in, and what would I need with all those sums and knowing poems off by heart? It wouldn't be any use to me at all.'

'What's to become of you, though ... off to England like Deirdre and Margaret with no qualifications ... ?'

'No, I'm staying here. I'm going to get a house like this one, and have it the way you do, lovely and shiny and clean, and coloured china on a dresser and a smell of lavender polish everywhere.'

'It'll be some lucky man if you are going to do all that for him.'

'I won't be getting married, Miss Ross.' It was one of the few things she had ever said with conviction.

Her sister Geraldine believed her too, over this.

'Why don't you go the whole hog and be a nun?' Geraldine wanted to know. 'If you're so sure you're not going to get a fellow, hadn't you better be in a convent, singing hymns and getting three meals a day?'

'I can still pray in a house of my own. I'll have a Sacred Heart lamp on a small wooden shelf, and I'll have a picture of Our Lady, Queen of May on a small round table with a blue tablecloth and a vase of flowers in front of it.'

She didn't say that she was going to buy a chair for the doll too.

Geraldine shrugged. She was twelve now, and much more grown up than her sister of fourteen, who would be leaving school this year. Geraldine's confirmation was coming up and between wheedling and complaining she and her mother had managed to get Paudie Brennan to put up money for a lovely confirmation dress. This was the first item of clothing that had ever been bought new to celebrate the confirmation of any of his nine children. The dress hung on the back of the bedroom door and had been tried on a dozen times. Maura had managed to persuade Geraldine to keep the hair from hanging over her eyes.

Geraldine was going to look gorgeous on her confirmation day. She had written to her sisters and brothers in England telling them of this event and, getting the hint, they had sent a pound note or a ten-shilling note in an envelope with a couple of lines scrawled to wish her well. Maura hadn't done that and she looked with envy at the riches coming in. It took a lot of ironing in Miss Ross's house to make anything like that amount of money.

Three days before confirmation Paudie Brennan, on a serious drinking bout, found himself short of ready cash and, deciding that the Lord couldn't possibly be concerned what clothes young Christians decked themselves in for confirmation ceremonies, managed to take the new dress to a pawnbroker in the big town and raise the sum of two pounds on it.

The consternation was terrible. In the middle of the shouting, tears and accusations being hurled backwards and forwards, Maura realised that this was all that would happen. Bluster and hurt, disappointment and recriminations. There was no question of anyone getting the dress back for Geraldine. That kind of money could not appear by magic. Credit had been arranged in the first place to buy it. There was no possibility of more funds being made available.

'I'll get it for you,' Maura said simply to a red-eyed, near hysterical Geraldine who lay on her bed railing at the unfairness of life and the meanness of her father.

'How can you get it? Don't be stupid.'

'I have that saved. Just get the ticket from him. We'll go on the bus, but you must never tell them, never never.'

'Where will they think we got the money? They might say we stole it.' Geraldine didn't care to believe that there was a way out.

'Da's not going to be able to say much one way or the other after what he did,' said Maura.

On the day, Paudie Brennan was dressed and shaved and his neck squeezed into a proper shirt and collar for the visit of the Bishop. It was a sunlit day, and the children from Shancarrig looked a credit to their school, people said, as they gathered for the group photograph outside the cathedral in the big town. Geraldine Brennan, resplendent with her shiny blonde hair and her frilly white dress, caught the eye of a lot of people.

'You have dressed her up like a picture. She's a credit to you,' said Mrs Ryan, of Ryan's Hotel. Her own daughter Catherine looked far less resplendent. It was easy to see that she was mystified and even put out that the young Brennan girl, daughter of a known layabout and drunk, should look so well.

'Ah, sure, you have to do your best, Mrs Ryan, Ma'am,' Maura's mother said. Maura felt her heart harden. If her mam had been the one in charge Geraldine would have stood there in some limp handout dress that had been begged from a family who might not have used all its castoffs. There had been no word of apology from her father, no question of any promised repayment from Geraldine. No questions, no interest.

Any more than anyone had asked what Maura would do when she left school in a few short weeks' time. She wouldn't be going to the convent in the town like Leo Murphy and Nessa Ryan. There were no plans for her to go into the technical school. She wasn't smart enough to be taken on as a trainee in one of the shops, or the hairdressing salon.

Maura was going to work as a maid, the only question was where – and this, she realised, was something she would have to work out for herself as well as everything else. Maura would really have liked a job where she could live in. In a lovely big house, with beautiful furniture in it. Somewhere like The Glen, where Leo Murphy lived.

She would call and ask them had they a place. It wasn't fair to ask Leo at school and embarrass her in case the answer was no. Or she could possibly get a place in the kitchens of Ryan's Commercial Hotel, or as a chambermaid. She wouldn't like that as much. There was nothing beautiful to touch and polish.

'Are you thinking about your own confirmation, Maura?' Father Gunn from Shancarrig was standing beside her.

'Not really, I'm afraid, Father. I was thinking about where I'd go to work.'

'Is it time for you to leave school already?' He was a kindly man with very thick glasses that made him look vaguer and more confused than he was. It seemed impossible for him to believe that another of Paudie Brennan's brood was ready for the emigrant ship.

'It is. I'll be fifteen soon,' Maura said proudly. Father Gunn looked at her. She was a pleasant open-faced child. Not a pretty face like the one being confirmed today, but still easy enough on the eye. He hoped she wouldn't fall for a child the way the elder sister had in Northampton. There were few secrets kept from a priest in a small community.

'You'll be needing a reference I suppose,' he sighed, thinking of the numbers of young people that he had written about, praising their honesty and integrity to anonymous English employers.

'I suppose they'll all know me in Shancarrig,' she said. 'I'll be looking for a job as a maid, Father. If you hear of anyone, I'm great at cleaning altogether.'

'I will, Maura, I'll keep my eyes open for you.' He turned away, feeling unexpectedly sad.

Maura went first to the back door of The Glen and waited patiently as the dogs raced around her, barking the news of her arrival, but nobody came to see what was her business. She had seen two figures sitting in the front room.

Surely they must have heard. After a lot of thought she went around to the front and Leo, tall and confident, came running down the stairs.

'Maura, what on earth are you doing?' she asked.

'I came wondering do your parents want anyone to work for them in the house, Leo,' she said to the girl who had been sitting beside her in school for eight years.

'Work?' Leo seemed startled.

'Yes, like I have to have a job working somewhere, and this is a big house. I wondered . . . ?'

'No, Maura.'

'But, I know how to turn out a room . . .'

'There's Biddy here already.'

'I meant as well as Biddy, under her of course.'

Leo had always been nice at school. Maura couldn't understand why she spoke so brusquely. 'It wouldn't work. You couldn't come here and clear up after me.'

'I have to clear up after someone. Wouldn't your family be as nice as anyone else's? Let me ask them, Leo.' She didn't say the place could do with a clean. She didn't plead. She had always been quick to recognise when something was impossible. And a look at Leo Murphy's face told her that this was now the case.

'Right then,' she said cheerfully. 'I had to ask.'

She knew Leo was standing at the door with the dogs as she walked down the avenue. Maura thought that she should have been allowed to talk to the people of the house, rather than being sent off by her own schoolfriend. Still, Leo had the air of being the one who made the decisions in that house. They mightn't have hired her if they knew Leo disapproved.

Imagine being able to make the decisions at nearly fifteen. But then Maura told herself that that's what she was doing herself. There were very few decisions made in Brennans' by anyone except herself.

Maura went then to Mrs Hayes. Mr Hayes was a solicitor so the Hayes family were very wealthy. They had a big house covered with virginia creeper, and a lovely piano in the drawing room. Maura knew this because Niall Hayes went to the same school. He was very nice. He told her one day how much he hated the piano lessons that his mother arranged for him twice a week, and Maura told him how much she hated going to the pub to tell her father his dinner was ready on Saturday and Sunday lunchtimes. It was a kind of bond between them.

But Mrs Hayes didn't want a young girl, she told Maura. She'd need someone older, someone trained.

She went to Mrs Barton, Eddie Barton's mother, who ran a dressmaking business, but Mrs Barton said it was hard enough to put food on the table for herself and Eddie, without trying to find another few shillings for a child to be playing at pushing a brush around the floor. She had said it kindly, but the facts were the facts.

And Dr Jims said that he had not only Carrie to look after his son but there were many good years left in Maisie as well. So, everything now depended on going to the Ryans in the hotel. Maura had left that till last because she thought Mrs Ryan was very strong willed. She was a woman whom it might be easy to annoy.

She got the job, chambermaid. Mrs Ryan said she hoped Maura would be happy but there were three things they should get straight from the start – Maura was not to speak to Nessa just because they knew each other at school – Maura was to live on the premises, they didn't really want her going back to the cottages every night – and lastly, if there was a question of flirting or making free with any of the customers there would be words with Father Gunn about it and Maura would leave Shancarrig without a backward glance.

It suited Maura not to live at home. Her father was increasingly difficult these days. Geraldine had her friends in and out of the place, giggling in the bedroom. It would be nice to have a place of her own, a small room certainly, like a nun's cell, but all to herself.

Maura began work at once, and in her time off she did the ironing still for Miss Ross and she polished silver for Mrs Hayes, sitting quietly in the kitchen on her afternoon off from the hotel. She never spoke to Niall when he came home on holidays from his boarding school. Nobody would ever have known they had been schoolfriends and even companions in a kind of way too. If Niall ever saw her there he didn't seem to take any notice.

Not even as the years passed and Maura Brennan developed a small waist and began to look altogether more attractive. If you were born square and dull-looking in appearance you didn't ever think that things would change. Maura knew that her sister Geraldine was pretty but she didn't feel jealous. It was good that Geraldine had got a job up in the sawmills; they liked someone nice with a bright smile around the office. Maura never thought that it was bad luck to be square and making beds behind the scenes in a hotel.

In fact, she was so used to being square and dull-looking she was quite unaware that she had changed and had begun to look very attractive indeed.

The men who came to stay in Ryan's Commercial Hotel noticed, though. Maura had many an occasion to raise her voice sharply and speak in clear firm tones when men asked for an extra blanket, or complained of some imaginary fault in their rooms, just in order to give her a squeeze.

By the time she was eighteen years old, Mrs Ryan suggested to her husband that they put her behind the bar. She'd be able to attract custom. To their surprise, Maura refused. She'd prefer to continue the work she was doing, she had no head for figures. She would need a lot of smart clothes if she was to be in the public eye. She would be happier making beds and helping in the kitchen.

'At least, wait on the tables,' Mrs Ryan asked. But no, if her work was satisfactory she would prefer to keep in the background.

Breda Ryan shrugged. They had tried to better her, a girl from the cottages, poor Paudie Brennan's child, and yet she wouldn't seize the opportunity. Mrs Ryan had always thought that if the whole wealth of the world was taken back and divided out equally, giving the same amount to each person, you'd find in five years that the same people would end up having money and power and the same people would end up shiftless and hopeless. In a changing world, she found this view very comforting.

Maura didn't want to change because her life suited her just the way it was. She had three square meals a day. She could even choose what she wanted to eat in a hotel, which she mightn't have been able to do in a private house. She had the excuse which she could give her mother and father that the hotel needed her night and day. As a barmaid or waitress she might be expected to live out. And she wanted nothing to interfere with her savings and her plans.

Whenever she took the children she minded for walks she would always go the same way, past the places that she would buy when she had the money. There was the little gate lodge to The Glen. It was totally disused. People had lived there once, but now the ivy grew in the windows. That would be her first choice. Then there was the little house near where Miss Ross lived. It was painted a wishy-washy grey, but if Maura had it she would paint it pink and have window boxes full of red geraniums on each side of the hall door.

There wasn't much time for talking to friends these days. Not if you had to save as hard as Maura did. And she didn't go dancing – dances cost money, lots of money. First you had to buy something to wear, then the price of the bus fare to the town, and the admission to the dance hall, and the minerals. It would run away with your savings.

Maura had never been to a dance by the time her young sister Geraldine was ready to leave Shancarrig and join their sisters in England.

'Come on, just as my goodbye,' Geraldine had urged.

'I've nothing to wear.'

The sisters had remained friendly over the years as Maura had worked on in the hotel and Geraldine had worked in the office in the sawmills.

'I've plenty,' Geraldine said.

And indeed she had, Maura discovered. The bedroom they had once shared would never have held a second bed these days, with all the clothes strewn around it. Maura looked in wonder. 'You must have spent everything you earned on these,' she said.

'Don't be mean, Maura. There's nothing worse than a mean woman,' Geraldine said.

Was she mean? Maura wondered. It would indeed be terrible to be a mean woman. Yet, she didn't think she was mean. She gave a pound a week out of her wages to her mother and she always brought a cake or a half pound of ham when she came home to tea. She seemed to be giving Geraldine the price of the cinema for as long as she remembered. All she had been careful about was not spending on herself.

But perhaps that too was mean.

She fingered the dresses. A taffeta dress with shot silk in green and yellow colours, a red corduroy skirt, a black satin with little bits of diamanté at the shoulders. It was like Aladdin's cave.

'Do all your friends have clothes like this?' she asked.

'Well, Catherine Ryan from the place you work, she'd have different things. You know, well-cut, awful-looking garments you wouldn't be seen dead in. Some people have a ton of stuff. We swap a bit. What'll you wear?'

Maura Brennan wore the black satin with the diamanté decorations and set out for the dance in the big town. She looked at herself in the mirror of the ladies' cloakroom. She thought she looked all right. It was hard to tell what fellows would like, but she thought she'd get asked up to dance and not be left a fool by the side of the wall.

The first man who came over was Gerry O'Sullivan, the new barman in Ryan's Hotel.

'Well, don't tell me you're the same girl that I see in the kitchen in the back of beyond where we work,' he said, stretching out his arms to her.

And then the night flew by. They danced everything, sambas and tangos, and rock and roll, and old-time waltzes. She couldn't believe that it was time for the National Anthem.

'I have to find my sister and her friends,' she said.

'Aw, don't give me that. I've the loan of a car,' he said.

He was very handsome, Gerry O'Sullivan, small and dark with black hair and an easy laugh. But there was no question of it. They had all given five shillings to get their lift there and back in a big van.

'I'll see you tomorrow in the hotel,' she said, thinking that might cheer him up. She was wrong.

'Tomorrow you won't be looking like this, you'll be dressed like a streel and emptying chamber pots,' he grumbled, and went off.

Maura said very little on the way home. Geraldine's friends passed around a bottle of cider, but she shook her head. She supposed he was right: that was the way she dressed and that was what she did for a living.

'I'll write from England,' Geraldine said. Maura knew she wouldn't, any more than the others had.

A few days later Gerry O'Sullivan found her alone.

'I only said that because I was so mad wanting to be with you. I had a very bad mouth and I'm sorry.' He was so handsome and so upset. Maura's face lit up.

'I didn't mind a bit,' she said.

'You should have minded. Listen, will you come to the dance again, on Friday? I'll bring you there and back. Please?' She looked doubtful, because this time she literally didn't have anything to wear. Geraldine had taken her wardrobe across the sea to England. 'I'll be very nicely mannered all night long,' he said with a grin. 'And it's Mick Delahunty's Show Band and he won't be back this way for a good bit.'

She decided she could take the cost of one party dress from her savings. And the following week she took another, and the price of shoes and a nice bag. She'd never have her house at this rate, Maura told herself. But she found herself saying that you only live once. Gerry O'Sullivan told her that she was the loveliest girl in the dance hall.

'Don't be making a jeer of me,' she said.

'I'll show you I'm not making a jeer of you.' Gerry was indignant. 'I'll not dance with you and see how you'll be swept away . . .' Before she could say anything he picked a girl from the waiting line and began to dance.

Red-cheeked and unsure Maura was about to step aside but from three directions arms were stretched out and faces offered a dance. She laughed, confused, and picked the nearest one. He had been right. She *was* the kind of girl men danced with.

'What did I tell you,' he murmured in the back of the car that night. He seemed excited by the thought of other men wanting Maura and not being able to have her. His own intention of having her had now become a near reality. No protestations were going to be any use, and in honesty Maura didn't want to protest any further.

'Not in the car, please,' she whispered.

'You're right.' He seemed cheerful. Too cheerful, in fact. From his pocket he took out one of the hotel keys.

'Room Eleven,' he said triumphantly. 'There'll be no one there. We'll be fine as long as we keep the light off.' Maura looked at him trustingly.

'Will it be all right?' she asked in a whisper.

'I'll not let you down,' Gerry O'Sullivan said.

She knew he spoke the truth. She knew it again five months later, after many happy visits to Room Eleven and even Room Two, when she told him she was pregnant.

'We'll get married,' he said.

Father Gunn agreed that it should be as speedily as possible. His face seemed to say that it would be no better or worse than a lot of marriages he was asked to officiate at with speed. And at least in this case they seemed to have a deposit for a house, which was more than you might have hoped for in some cases. Father Gunn talked about it to Miss Ross.

'It could be a lot worse, I suppose,' he said.

'She'll never settle in a poor house. She wanted to be well away from those cottages. She had her eyes on great things,' the teacher said.

'Well, faith and she should have her eyes on being grateful the fellow married her and putting her mind to raising the child and being glad they have a roof over their heads.' Father Gunn knew he sounded like a stern old parish priest from thirty years ago, but somehow the whole thing had him annoyed and he didn't want to hear any fairy stories about people having their eyes set on great things.

Maura decided to work until the day before the wedding. She looked Mrs Ryan straight in the eye and refused to accept any hints about the work being tiring in her condition. She said she needed every penny she could earn.

Mrs Ryan was cross to be losing a hard-working maid, and at the same time having an attractive barman marry beneath him because of activities obviously carried out under her own roof. She began to look more sternly at her own daughters, Nessa and Catherine, lest anything untoward should happen in their lives.

Nessa, the same age as Maura, had been all through Shancarrig school with her. 'What should I give her as a present?' she said to her mother.

'Best present is to ignore it and the reason for it,' Mrs Ryan snapped.

This reaction ensured, of course, that Nessa would go to great trouble to find a nice present. She rang Leo Murphy up in The Glen. Maura, putting away mops and buckets in the room at the end of the corridor, heard Nessa on the phone.

'Leo, she *was* in our class. We have to do something. Of course it's shotgun. What else could it be? You choose something, anything at all. Poor Maura, she expects so little.'

That's not true, Maura thought as she put away the cleaning equipment. She didn't expect so little, she expected a lot and mainly she got it. She had wanted to stay in Shancarrig rather than emigrating like the rest of her brothers and sisters, and here she had stayed. She had wanted the one handsome man that she ever fancied in her life, and he had wanted her. He was standing by her now and marrying her.

She had got more than she expected. She certainly hadn't thought that she would be having a baby and yet there was one on the way. The very thought of it made her pleased and excited. It took away the ache of sorrow about the place they would be living in.

With Gerry and a baby it wouldn't matter anyway.

Leo Murphy and Nessa Ryan gave her a little glass-fronted cabinet.

She couldn't have liked it more. She stroked it over and over and said how lovely it would look on a wall when she got her own treasures to put in it.

'Have you any treasures yet?' Nessa asked.

'Only a doll. A doll with a china face and china hands,' Maura said.

'That'll be nice for the baby . . .' Leo gulped. 'If you ever have one, I mean,' she said hastily.

'Oh, I'm sure I will,' Maura said. 'But the baby won't be let play with this doll. It's a treasure, for the lovely cabinet.'

She could see that the girls thought their money had been well spent, and she was touched by how much they must have given for it. As part of her continuing fantasy about a house, Maura used to look at furniture and price it. She knew well that this cabinet was not inexpensive.

Maura hoped that Geraldine would come home from England. She even offered her the fare, but there was no reply. It would have been nice to have had her standing as a bridesmaid, but instead she had Eileen Dunne, who said she loved weddings and she'd be anyone's bridesmaid for them. And with a great nudge that nearly knocked Maura over she said she'd do godmother as well, and laughed a lot.

Gerry's brother came to do the best man bit. His parents were old and didn't travel, he said.

Maura saw nothing sad or shabby about her wedding day.

When she turned around in the church she saw Nessa Ryan, Leo Murphy, Niall Hayes and Eddie Barton sitting smiling at her. She was the first of their class to get married. They seemed to think this was like winning some kind of race rather than having been caught in a teenage pregnancy. When they went to Johnny Finn's for drinks Mr Ryan from the hotel came running in with a fistful of money to buy them all a drink. He said he came to wish them well from everyone in Ryan's Commercial Hotel.

There was no word of the haste or the disgrace or anything. Maura's father behaved in a way that, for Paudie Brennan, could be called respectable. This week he happened to be friendly with Foxy Dunne's father, so the two of them had their arms around each other as they sang tunelessly together in a corner. If it had been one of the weeks when they were fighting, things would have been terrible – insults hurling across Johnny Finn's all afternoon.

And Father Gunn and Father Barry were there smiling and talking to people as if it were a real wedding.

Maura didn't see anything less than the kind of wedding day she had dreamed about when she was at school, or when reading the women's magazines. All she saw was Gerry O'Sullivan beside her, smiling and saying everything would be grand.

And everything *was* grand for a while.

Maura left her job in the hotel. Mrs Ryan seemed to want it that way. Possibly there would be social differences now that Maura was the wife of the popular barman, instead of just the girl from the cottages cleaning the floors and washing potatoes. But Maura found plenty of work, hours here and hours there. When it was obvious that she was expecting a child many of her employers said they would be lost without her. Mrs Hayes, who hadn't wanted her in the start, was particularly keen to keep her.

'Maybe your mother could look after the child, and you'd still want to go out and work?' she said hopefully.

Maura had no intention of letting any child grow up in the same house as she had herself, with the lack of interest and love. But she had learned to be very circumspect in her life. 'Maybe indeed,' she said to Mrs Hayes and the others. 'We'll have to wait and see.'

It seemed a long time to wait for the baby, all those evenings on her own in the little cottage, sometimes hearing her father going home drunk, as she had when she was a child. She polished the little cabinet, took out the doll and patted the bump of her stomach.

'Soon you'll be admiring this,' she said to the unborn baby.

It was Dr Jims Blake who told her about the baby boy. The child had Down's syndrome. The boy, who was what was called a mongol, would still be healthy and loving and live a full and happy life.

It was Father Gunn who told her about Gerry, and how he had come from the cottage to the church and told the priest he was going. He took the wages owing to him from the hotel, saying his father had died and he needed time off for the funeral. But he told Father Gunn that he was getting the boat to England.

No entreaties would make him stay.

Maura remembered always the way that Father Gunn's thick round glasses seemed to sparkle as he was telling her. She didn't know if there were tears behind them, or if it was only a trick of the light.

People were kind, very kind. Maura often told herself that she had been lucky to have stayed in Shancarrig. Suppose all this had happened to her in some big city in England where she had known nobody. Here she had a friendly face everywhere she turned.

And of course she had Michael.

Nobody had told her how much she would love him because nobody could have known. She had never known a child as loving. She watched him grow with a heart that nearly burst with pride. Everything he learned, every new skill – like being able to do up his buttons – was a huge hurdle for the child, and soon everyone in Shancarrig got used to seeing them hand in hand walking around.

'Who's this?' people would ask affectionately, even though they knew well.

'This is Michael O'Sullivan,' Maura would say proudly.

'I'm Michael O'Sullivan,' he would say and, as often as not, hug the person who had asked.

If you wanted Maura to come and clean your house you took Michael as well. And as they walked from job to job each day Maura used to point out the houses that she loved to her son – the little gate lodge, ever more covered with ivy and choked with nettles, that stood at the end of the long avenue up to The Glen, and there was the one near Miss Ross which she was going to paint pink if she ever bought it.

At night she would take the doll with the china hands and face out from its cabinet and the two cups and saucers she had been given by Mrs Ryan. There was a little silver plate, which had EPNS on the back, that Eileen Dunne had given when she stood as godmother to Michael. She said that this meant it wasn't real silver, but since the S stood for silver Maura thought it deserved a place in the cabinet. There was a watch too, one that belonged to Gerry. A watch that didn't go, but might go one day if it were seen to, and would hang on a chain. When Michael got to be a man he could call it his father's watch.

Most people forgot that Michael ever had a father; the memory of Gerry O'Sullivan faded. And for Maura the memory began to fade too. Days passed when she didn't think of the handsome fellow with the dark eyes who had cared enough to marry her, but hadn't got the strength to stay when he knew his child was handicapped. She had never hated him, sometimes she even pitied him that he didn't know the great hugs and devotion of Michael his son, who grew in size but not greatly in achievement.

Maura had got glances and serious invitations out from other men in the town, but she had always told them simply that she wasn't free to accept any invitation. She had a husband living in England and really there could be no question of anything else.

Her dream remained constant. A proper little home, not the broken-down cottage where only the hopeless and the helpless lived, where she had grown up and wanted to escape.

Then the Darcys came to Shancarrig. They bought a small grocery shop like the one Nellie Dunne ran, and they put in all kinds of newfangled things. The world was changing, even in places like Shancarrig. Mike and Gloria

Darcy were new people who livened the place up. No one had ever met anyone called Gloria before and she lived up to her name. Lots of black curly hair like a gypsy, and she must have known this because she often wore a red scarf knotted around her neck and a full coloured skirt, as if she was going to break into a gypsy dance any moment.

Mike Darcy was easygoing and got on with everyone. Even old Nellie Dunne who looked on them as rivals liked Mike Darcy. He had a laugh and a word for anyone he met on the road. Mrs Ryan in the Commercial Hotel felt they were a bit brash for the town, but when Mike said he'd buy for her at the market as well as for himself she began to change her tune.

It was good to see such energy about the place, she said, and it wasn't long before she had the front of the hotel painted to make it the equal of the new shopfront in Darcy's. Mike's brother, Jimmy Darcy, had come with them. He was a great house-painter and Mrs Ryan claimed that even the dozy fellows from down in the cottages, who used to paint a bit when the humour took them, seemed to think Jimmy did a good job. Mike and Gloria had children, two tough dark little boys who used to get up to all kinds of devilment in the school.

Maura didn't wait to see whether the town liked the Darcys or not; she presented herself on the doorstep the moment they arrived.

'You'll be needing someone to work for you,' she said to Gloria.

Gloria glanced at the round eager face of Michael, who stood holding his mother's hand. 'Will you be able to make yourself free?' she asked.

'Michael would come with me. He's the greatest help you could imagine,' she said, and Michael beamed at the praise.

'I'm not sure if we really *do* need anyone . . .' Gloria was polite but unsure.

'You do need someone, but take your time. Ask around a bit about me. Maura O'Sullivan is the name, Mrs Maura O'Sullivan.'

'Well, yes, Mrs O'Sullivan . . .'

'No, I just wanted you to know, because you're new. Michael's daddy had to go and live in England. You'd call me Maura if you had me in the house.'

'And you'd call me Michael,' the boy said, putting both his arms around Gloria's small waist.

'I don't need to ask around. When will you start?'

The Darcys were better payers than anyone else in the town. They seemed to have no end of money. The children's clothes were all good quality, their shoes were new, not mended. The furniture they had was expensive, not lovely old wood which Maura would have enjoyed polishing, but dear modern furniture. She knew the prices of all these things from her trips to the big town, and her dreams of furnishing the house that she'd buy.

Back in the cottage she had hardly anything worth speaking of. The small slow savings were being kept for the day she moved into the place she wanted. Only the glass-fronted cabinet with its small trove of treasures showed any sign of the gracious living that Maura yearned for. Otherwise it was converted boxes and broken second-hand furniture.

The Darcys had been in lots of places. Maura marvelled at how quickly the children could adapt.

They were warm-hearted too. They didn't like to come across Michael cleaning their shoes. 'He doesn't have to do that, Missus,' said Kevin Darcy, who was nine.

'I'm doing them great,' Michael protested.

'Don't worry, Kevin, that's Michael's and my job. All we ask you to do is not to leave everything on the floor of your bedroom so as we have to bend and pick it up.'

It worked. Gloria Darcy said that Maura and her son had managed to put manners on her children, something no one in any house had ever done before.

'Don't you find it hard, Mam, all the moving from place to place?'

Gloria looked at her. 'No, it's interesting. You meet new people, and in each place we better ourselves. We sell the place at a profit and then move on.'

'And will you be moving on from here too, do you think?' Maura was disappointed. She wouldn't ever get the kind of hours and payments that the Darcys gave her from anyone else. Gloria Darcy said not for a while. She thought they would stay in Shancarrig until the children got a bit of an education before uprooting them.

And their business prospered. They built on a whole new section to the original building they had bought and they expanded their range of goods. Soon people didn't need to go into the big town for their shopping trips. You could buy nearly everything you needed in Darcy's.

'I don't know where they get the money,' Mrs Hayes said one day to Maura. 'They can't be doing that much business, nothing that would warrant the kind of showing off they're doing.'

Maura said nothing. She thought that Mrs Hayes was the kind of wife who might well disapprove of Gloria's low-cut blouses and winning ways with the men of Shancarrig.

It was around this time that Maura became aware of financial problems in the Darcy household. There were bills that were being presented over and over to them. She could hear Mike Darcy's voice raised on the phone. But at the same time he had bought Gloria some marvellous jewellery that was the talk of Shancarrig.

'She has me broke,' he'd say to anyone who came into the shop. 'Go on Gloria, show them that emerald.'

And laughing, Gloria would wave the emerald on the chain. It had been bought in the big town in the jeweller's. She had always wanted one. And it was the same with the little diamond earrings. They were so small they were only specks really, but the thought that they were real diamonds made her shiver with excitement.

Shancarrig looked on with admiration. And the Darcys weren't blowing or boasting either. Nessa Ryan had been in the big town and checked. They were the real thing. The Darcys were new rich, courageous and not afraid to spend. With varying degrees of envy the people of Shancarrig wished them good luck.

The tinkers came every year on the way to the Galway races. They didn't stay in Shancarrig. They stayed nearby. Maura was struck with how Gloria looked like the Hollywood version of a gypsy, not the real thing. The real women of the travelling people looked tired and weather-beaten, not the flashing eyes and colourful garb of Gloria Darcy, and certainly not the real diamonds in the ears and the real emerald around her neck.

But this particular year people said some tinker woman must be wearing the jewels because, at the very time they were encamped outside Shancarrig, Gloria Darcy's jewellery case was stolen.

All hell broke loose. It could only be the tinkers.

Sergeant Keane was in charge of the search, and the ill will created was enormous. Nothing was found. No one was charged. Everyone was upset. Even Michael was interrogated and asked about what he had seen and what he had touched in his visits to the Darcy house. It was a frightening time in Shancarrig; there had never been a robbery like this before.

There had never been anything like this to steal before.

A lot of tut-tutting and head-shaking went on. It was vulgar of the Darcys to have displayed that jewellery; it made people envious. It put temptation in the way of others. But then, how had the gypsies known about it? They had only just come to camp. They hadn't been given dazzling displays of the glinting emerald on the chain around Gloria's throat.

'I'm sorry if the guards frightened Michael,' Gloria said to Maura.

'I don't mind about that. Sergeant Keane has known Michael since he was in a pram, he wouldn't frighten him,' Maura said. 'But I'm sorry for you, Mrs Darcy. You put a lot of store by those jewels. It won't be the same without them.'

'No, but there will be the insurance money . . . eventually,' Gloria said. She said they weren't going to buy emeralds and diamonds again. Maybe put the money into paying off the extension and getting the place rewired and better stocked.

Maura remembered some of the conversations she had heard about the need to pay builders' bills. She went back over those financial difficulties she thought she had been aware of. Possibly the insurance money was exactly what the Darcys needed at this stage.

Indeed, it could be said to come at exactly the right time.

Maura had been used to keeping her own counsel for as long as she could remember. She had seen what the wild indiscretions of her own family had brought on themselves and everyone else around – her father's blustering revelations of any bit of gossip he knew, her mother's trying to play one member of the family off against the other.

Maura said very little.

She had sometimes suspected over the years that the envelope Father Gunn gave her each Christmas, saying that it was from Gerry O'Sullivan from no fixed address in England, actually came from the priest himself. But she never let Father Gunn know of her suspicions. She thanked him for acting as postman.

She sometimes wondered why she had become so secretive and close. When she was a youngster she had been open and would talk to everyone.

Maybe it was just the whole business of Gerry and having to be protective of Michael. And because there had never been a real friend to talk to.

The robbery of the jewels had been a nine-day wonder. Soon people stopped talking about it. There were other things to occupy their minds.

There was always something happening in Shancarrig. Maura never knew why people called it sleepy or a backwater. Only people who didn't know the place would have used words like that. Maura and Michael helped at the Dramatic Society and there was a drama a week there from the time that Biddy who worked at The Glen started to dance and went on like something wound up until no one could drag her from the stage. And there was all the business about Father Barry not being well, and then going off to the missions.

There was Richard, that handsome cousin of Niall Hayes, who had come to The Terrace and broken a few hearts – Nessa's maybe – and Maura thought there might be a bit of electricity between him and Mrs Darcy, not that she would ever mention a word of it. Yet Nellie Dunne hinted of it too so that rumour might well be going around the place. Eddie Barton had opened all their eyes with his unexpected romance, and the news of Foxy Dunne from London was always worth people pausing to discuss.

There was plenty to distract the minds of Shancarrig from the missing emerald and diamonds.

Maura O'Sullivan and her son Michael went from house to house – the ironing for Miss Ross, who had lines set in her face now, and had begun to look like a waxwork image of her old mother – there was the silver polishing for Mrs Hayes – the two hours on a Saturday for Mrs Barton – but mainly, the Darcys.

There was a lot to be done in a house where there were two boys and where the parents were hardly ever out of the shop. Maura didn't wait to be asked to do things. She had her own routine.

She was doing the master bedroom, as Gloria called it, when she found the jewellery. It was on top of the wardrobe in a big round hat box. Maura had been dusting the top of the wardrobe with sheets of newspapers spread below to catch the falling dirt. She saw a neater way to stack the suitcases, but it involved lifting them down. Michael stood willingly to take them from her. And it was only because the hat box rattled that she opened it. It was as if there was a big stone in it. She didn't want whatever it was to fall out.

It was a red silk scarf with two small black velvet bags wrapped up in it.

Michael saw her stop and hold the wardrobe top for support.

'Are you going to fall down?' he asked anxiously.

'No, love.' Maura climbed down and sat on the bed. Her heart was racing dangerously.

There was no way that she could have accidentally discovered the lost and much-mourned jewellery. There would be no cries of delight if the gems were recovered and the insurance claim had to be cancelled.

She also knew that they had not got into the hat box by accident. The description had been given over and over. The emerald on its chain had been in a box on the desk downstairs, and the little earrings in their black velvet bag beside them. The room they were in, the sitting room, had a pair of glass doors opening on to the small back garden. A light-fingered, light-footed tinker boy could have been in and out without anyone noticing.

That was how the story went.

In all her time cleaning in this house Maura had never known the valuables kept in this hat box. It was not a place someone would have put them and forgotten about them.

'Why aren't you speaking?' Michael wanted to know.

'I'm trying to think about something,' she said. She put her arm around his shoulder and drew him close.

She seemed to sit there for a long time, yellow duster in hand, her feet squarely on the spread newspaper, her son enclosed in her arm.

That evening Maura put the two little black velvet bags in her cabinet of treasures. She had to think it out very cleverly. She mustn't do the wrong thing and end up the worse for this great discovery.

Weeks went by before she brought up the subject of the lost jewels. She waited until she had Gloria in the house on her own. She had left Michael playing with the chickens outside.

'I was thinking, Mam, Mrs Darcy . . . what would happen if someone found your emerald chain say . . . thrown in a hedge by the tinkers?'

'What do you mean?' Gloria's voice was sharp.

'Well, now that you've done all the renovations here . . . and got used to not having it and wearing it round your neck . . . wouldn't it be bad for you if it turned up?'

'It won't turn up. That lot have it well sold by now, you can be sure.'

'But where would they sell it? If they brought it into a jeweller's shop, Mrs Darcy, wouldn't people know it was the one that was stolen from you? They'd call the guards, not give them the money.'

'That crowd travel far and wide. They could take it to a shop miles from here.'

There was a silence.

Then Gloria said, 'Anyway, it hasn't been found.'

'My head is full of dreams, Mrs Darcy. I go walking by the hedges. I often find things . . . what would happen if I were to find it?'

'I don't know what you mean.'

'Well, suppose I did find it, would I take it to Sergeant Keane and say where I came across it, or would I give it to you . . . ?'

Gloria's eyes were very narrow.

Maura saw her glance towards the stairs as if she were about to run up and check the hat box.

'This is fancy talk,' she said eventually. 'But I suppose the best would be, if you *were* to find it, to give it to me quietly. As you say, the insurance money was really more use to us than the jewellery itself at this stage.'

'What about a reward?' Maura looked confused and eager.

'We'd have to see.'

Maura went out to the chickens to find Michael, but she paused before she closed the door behind her and heard the light sound of Gloria Darcy's feet running up the stairs, and the sound of the suitcases being thrown from the high wardrobe to the floor.

Nothing was said.

It wasn't as hard for Maura as it might have been for others, because after a life of keeping her thoughts and opinions to herself it was relatively easy to work on in the house where Gloria and Mike Darcy obviously walked on a knife edge of anxiety around her.

They offered her cups of tea in the middle of her cleaning. They found things for Michael in the shop as gifts, but Maura said he mustn't be allowed to think of the shop as a wonderland where he could stroll and take whatever bar of chocolate he wanted. It would be very bad for him, and she had spent so much time trying to make him see what was his and what wasn't.

When she said this Maura O'Sullivan looked Mike and Gloria straight in the eye. She could see that she had them totally perplexed.

It was Gloria who broke eventually.

'Remember you were saying that you were a great one for finding things, Maura?'

'Yes indeed. I prayed to St Anthony for that good Parker pen of Mr Darcy's to turn up and didn't it roll out from behind where we keep the trays stacked in the kitchen.' Maura was proud and pleased with the results of her prayers.

'I was thinking about what you said . . . and in our business, well . . . we get to know a lot of people. Now, suppose you were to find the stuff that the tinkers took somewhere . . . ?'

'Yes, Mrs Darcy?'

'Do you know what the very best thing to do with it would be . . . ?'

'I do not. And I've been wondering and wondering.'

'You see, the insurance money has been paid and spent improving the shop, providing work for people, even for you in the house.' Maura held her head on one side, waiting. 'So, if it did turn up and you were able to give it to me I could get it sold for you, and give you some of it . . .' Her voice trailed away.

'Ah, but if I knew the right place to sell it myself, then I could get plenty of money. Because, as you say yourself, you got the insurance money out of it already. You wouldn't want to be getting things twice over . . . it wouldn't be fair.'

'But why would it be fair for *you* to get it all?'

'If I found it in a hedge, or wherever I found it, it's finders keepers, isn't it?'

'But no use of course if you didn't know where to sell it.'

This was the deal. They both knew it.

'I'll be going to the big town next week, Mrs Darcy.'

'Yes, for your Christmas shopping. Of course.'

'I get this envelope from Michael's father, through Father Gunn. I'll be spending whatever there is . . .'

'I know.'

'And I was thinking, suppose I found the lost jewels by then, I'd be able to sell the emerald on the chain and I could give you back the diamonds, on account of you taking me straight to the right place, and that way . . .' She let the sentence hang there.

'That way would be better, I suppose, than any other way.' Gloria's face was grim.

Niall Hayes was surprised when he heard that a Mrs O'Sullivan wanted to see him particularly. People usually wanted to see his father, Mr Hayes Senior, the real solicitor as he had heard him described.

He was more surprised when he discovered that it was Maura Brennan from the cottages. He welcomed the two of them into his office – hardly anyone in Shancarrig had ever seen them apart.

'How have you been keeping, Maura?' he said, always a kind open fellow, despite his sharp snobby mother.

'I couldn't be better, Niall,' she said. 'We've had a bit of good luck. Michael's father always sends a bit to help out at Christmas time, and this year he was able to send a lot more.'

'Well, that's good, very good.' Niall couldn't see where the conversation was leading.

'And I'll tell you what we'd love, Niall . . . You know the cottage at the gate of The Glen?'

'I do, indeed. And they're putting it up for sale.'

'I'd like to buy it for Michael and myself. Would you act for us?'

Niall paused. How could Maura have enough to buy and renovate a place like that?

'I'll talk to Leo,' he said.

'No, talk to me. Tell me what's fair to offer her. Fair to her, fair to me.'

That was the way Niall Hayes liked to do business. There wasn't enough of it around. People were changing, attitudes were different. They wanted sharp dealings here and there.

He patted Maura's hand. It would be done.

Maura told Father Gunn that Michael's father had given them a great deal of money this year, much more than other times. If the priest was surprised he didn't show it.

'I think that's the last payment, Father.' She looked into the priest's eyes behind the thick round glasses. 'I don't think you'll be getting any more envelopes to give out at Christmas.'

He looked after them as they went down the road – Maura and Michael, soon to be householders, soon to go into a place of dreams, and paint it and tidy it and fill it with treasures.

He knew that the longer he lived in this parish the less he would understand.

Eddie

Eddie Barton only had a birthday once every four years, which was highly unusual. In fact, he thought he was the only person in the world in this situation. It came as a shock to him that other children had been born on this day. He was ten before he accepted it properly. Up to that he had thought he was unique.

Miss Ross, who was so nice at school, had told them all about Leap Year. Mr Kelly had frightened the wits out of him by saying that if a woman proposed to you on February twenty-ninth you had to say yes, even if she was the most terrifyingly awful person in the world. Mr Kelly had laughed as he said it but Eddie wasn't sure if it was a real laugh or not. Mr Kelly often looked sad.

'Did Mrs Kelly propose to you on my birthday?' Eddie asked fearfully. If the answer was yes then this indeed was another bad aspect of growing up.

But Mr Kelly had put his finger on his lips in a jokey sort of way and said, 'Nonsense and don't let Mrs Kelly hear a whisper of this or there'd be trouble.' It was to be a secret between them.

'I thought you said it was a well-known fact?' Eddie was confused.

'I did,' the teacher sighed. 'I did but I keep forgetting, even after all my years in a classroom, how dangerous it is to say anything, anything at all, to children.'

When Eddie's tenth birthday was coming up, his mother said he could be ten on the day before or the day after.

'I'd better wait until the day after,' he told Leo Murphy, who walked home after school with him because she lived in the big house, The Glen, up the hill, and Eddie lived in the small pink house halfway up the road. Leo had said that Eddie's house reminded her of a child's drawing of a house. It had windows that looked as if they were painted on. Eddie didn't know whether this was praise or not.

'What's wrong with that?' he had asked ferociously.

'Nothing. It's nice. It looks safe and normal, not like a jungle,' Leo had replied.

That meant she liked it. He was pleased.

Eddie liked Leo Murphy. If *she* were to ask him to marry her when he had a real birthday he wouldn't say no. The Glen would be a great place to live, orchards and an old tennis court. Fantastic.

Leo took things seriously.

'Why wait until March first?' she asked Eddie about his birthday. 'Suppose you died on the night of the twenty-eighth then you'd have missed your birthday altogether.'

It was unanswerable.

Eddie's mother said she didn't mind which day he had it just so long as he knew there'd be a cake and an apple tart and no more. He could have ten people or he could have two.

Eddie measured the cake plate carefully. He'd have three and himself. That way they'd have lots. He invited Leo Murphy and Nessa Ryan and Maura Brennan. They were the people he sat beside at class and liked.

'No boys at all?' Eddie's mother was a dressmaker. She was rarely seen without pins in her mouth or a frown of concentration on her face.

'I don't sit near any boys,' Eddie said.

His mother seemed to accept this. Una Barton was a small dark woman with worried eyes. She always walked very quickly, as if she feared people might stop her and detain her in conversation. She had a kind heart and a good eye for colour and dress fabrics in the clothes she made for the women of Shancarrig and the farmers' wives from out the country. They said that Una Barton lived for her son Eddie and for him alone.

Eddie had hair that grew upwards from his head. Foxy Dunne had said he looked like a lavatory brush. Eddie didn't know what a lavatory brush was. They didn't have one in their house, but when he saw one in Ryan's Hotel he was very annoyed. His hair wasn't as bad as that.

He liked doing things that the other boys didn't like doing at all. He liked going up to Barna Woods and collecting flowers. He sometimes pressed them and wrote their names underneath, and then stuck them on a card. His mother said that he was a real artist.

'Was my father artistic?' Eddie asked.

'The less said about your father's artistry the better.' His mother's face was in that sharp straight line again. There would be no more said.

He had to make a wish when he cut the cake. He closed his eyes and wished that his father would come back, like he had wished last year and the year before.

Maybe if you wished it three times it happened.

Ted Barton had left when his son was five. He had left in some spectacular manner, because Eddie had heard it mentioned several times when people didn't know he was listening. People would say about something, 'There was nearly as much noise as the night Ted Barton was thrown out.'

And once he heard the Dunnes in their shop say that if someone didn't mind himself it would be another case of Ted Barton, with the suitcase flung down the stairs after him. Eddie couldn't imagine his mother shouting or throwing a suitcase. But then again she must have.

She told him everything else he asked, but never told him about his father. 'Let's just agree that he didn't keep his part of the bargain. He didn't look after his wife and son. He doesn't deserve our interest.'

It was easy for her to say that but hard for Eddie to agree. Every boy wanted to know where his father was, even if it was a terrible father like the Brennans' or a fierce one like Leo Murphy's, with his moustache and being called a Major and everything.

Sometimes Eddie saw people getting off the bus and dreamed that maybe it was his father coming for him – coming to take him on a long holiday, just the two of them, walking all round Ireland, staying where they felt like. And then he'd imagine his father saying, with his head on one side, 'How about it, Eddie son, will I come home?' In the daydream Eddie's mother would always be smiling and welcoming and there would be less work to make her tired because his father would be looking after them now.

After tea they played games. They had to play on the floor of Eddie's bedroom, because Mrs Barton needed to bring her sewing machine back on to the table downstairs.

They said if only Eddie had a birthday in the summer they could all have gone up to Barna Woods. Eddie showed them some of the pressed flowers.

'They're beautiful,' Nessa Ryan said.

Nessa never said anything nice just to please you. If Nessa Ryan said they were good then they must be.

'You could even do that for a living,' she added.

At ten they usually didn't think as far ahead as that, but today there had been a talk on careers in school and an encouragement to think ahead and try to get trained for something rather than just gazing out the window and letting the time pass by.

'How could I get trained to press flowers?' Eddie was interested, but Nessa's momentary enthusiasm had passed.

'We'll have another go at blow football,' she said.

It had been Eddie's birthday present. His one gift. He hadn't really wanted it but his mother had heard from the Dunnes in the shop that it was what every child wanted this year and she had paid it off over five weeks. She was pleased the game was being used. Eddie secretly thought it was silly and tiring and that there was too much spit trying to blow a paper ball through paper tubes that got chewy and soggy.

When the party was over he stood at the door of the pink house in the moonlight and watched Leo skipping up the hill to her home. You could see the walls of The Glen from here. She waved when she reached the gate.

Nessa and Maura went downhill, Maura to the row of cottages where she lived. Eddie hoped that her father wouldn't be drunk tonight. Sometimes Paudie Brennan fell around the town shouting and insulting people.

Nessa Ryan had run on ahead. She lived in Ryan's Hotel. She could have anything she wanted to eat any time. She had told that to Eddie when he had explained about the cake and the apple tart. But there must have been something of an apology in his face because Nessa had said quickly that she didn't get as much *cake* as she liked. It was really only chips and sandwiches.

The moon was shining brightly, even though it was only seven o'clock. His mother's sewing machine was already whirring away. There she would sit surrounded by paper patterns and the big dummy which used to frighten him when he was a child, always draped with some nearly finished garment, as she listened to the radio. She would smile at him a lot, but when he came upon her alone he thought her face looked sad and tired. He wished she didn't have to work so hard. And it would keep whirring until he slept. It had been like that as long as he remembered. Eddie wondered was his father looking at the moon somewhere. Did he remember his son was ten-years-old today?

That night Eddie wrote a letter to his father.

He told him about the day and the pressed flowers that Nessa Ryan had admired so much. Then he wondered would his father think that bit was sissy so he crossed it out. He told his father that there was a big wedding in the next town and that his mother had been asked to do not only the bride's dress but the two bridesmaids and the mother and aunt of the bride as well. The whole church nearly would be dressed by Mrs Barton. And that his mother had said it came just in the nick of time because something needed to be done to the roof and there wasn't enough money to pay for it.

Then he read that last bit again and wondered would his father think it was a complaint. He didn't want to annoy him now that he had just found him.

With a jolt Eddie realised that he hadn't found his father, he was only making it up. Still, it was kind of comforting. He crossed out the bit about the roof costing money and left in the good news about the wedding dresses. He told his father about the careers lecture at school and about there being lots of jobs for hard-working young fellows over in England when he got old enough. He thought that maybe his father might be in England. Wouldn't it be marvellous if he met him by accident over there in a good job with prospects.

He wrote often that year. He told his father that Bernard Shaw had died, in case he might be somewhere where they didn't get that kind of news. Mr Kelly at school had said he was a great writer but he had been a bit against the church. Eddie asked his father why people would be against the church.

His father didn't answer, of course, because the letters were never sent. There was nowhere to send them to.

It wasn't that Eddie was all *that* lonely and friendless. He did have friends, of course he did. He often went up to The Glen to play with Leo Murphy. They used to hit the ball across the net to each other on the tennis court, and Leo had a great swing on a big oak tree. She hadn't known it was an oak tree until he told her and showed her the leaves and the acorns. It was extraordinary to have all those trees and still not know what they were.

Eddie often took oak leaves and traced around them. He loved the shape – there were so many more zig-zags than in the leaves of the plane trees, or the poplar. He liked the chestnut leaves too, and he never played the silly game that the others did at school – peeling away the green bits to see who could have the most perfect fillet, like a fish with no flesh, only bones. Eddie liked the texture of the leaves.

He didn't write any of this to his father, but he did tell him when de Valera got back again and Nessa Ryan had said there had been a terrible shouting match one night in the hotel and they had to send for the guards because some people didn't agree that it was great he was back. He went on writing and told a lot of fairly private things.

Still, he didn't mention that he was afraid of someone proposing to him on his birthday when he was twelve. It seemed such a stupid thing to be afraid of. But Eddie had great fears of Eileen Dunne at school, who had a terribly loud laugh and about five brothers who would deal with him if he refused her.

'You weren't thinking of asking me to marry you on Friday, were you?' he asked Leo hopefully. She had just raised her head from a book.

'No,' Leo said. 'I was thinking about the King of England being dead and my father being all upset about it.'

'Would you?' he asked.

'Would I what? Be all upset?'

'No. Ask me to marry you.'

'Why should I? You never asked *me* to marry you.'

'It's the day, you see. It's the day women can.'

'Men can every other day of the year.'

Eddie had worked that out. 'Suppose I asked you now, and we were engaged, then if anyone asked me on Friday I could say that I wasn't free.'

He looked very worried. Leo wasn't concentrating one bit. She was reading her book. She always had a book with her. This time it was *Good Wives*. It seemed a fine coincidence to Eddie.

'What *is* it, Eddie?'

'Just say yes. You don't have to.'

'Yes, then.'

Eddie was flooded with relief. He wasn't having a party for his twelfth birthday, he was too old. He was getting a bicycle, a second-hand bicycle. His mother had told him he could cycle to school on the day. He thought he'd keep it until next day, he said. His mother looked at him affectionately. He was such a funny little thing, quirky and complicated but never a moment's trouble to her, which was more than she could have hoped the day that bastard had left her doorstep.

People sometimes said it must be hard for her to bring a boy up all on her own. But Una Barton thought they had a reasonable life together. Her son told her long rambling tales, he was interested in helping her cook what they ate and would dry the dishes dutifully. She wished there was more money or time to take him to the seaside or to Dublin to the zoo. But that wasn't for their kind. That was for boys who had fathers that didn't run away.

Eddie didn't want to remind anyone it was his birthday, just in case Eileen Dunne might get it into her head, or Maura Brennan's young sister Geraldine. But nobody seemed to have realised the opportunity they had of proposing to Eddie, or to anyone. They were far more interested in Father Barry, who had come to give them a talk about the missions and to show them a Missionary magazine which had competitions in it and a Pen-Friends Corner. There were people in every part of the world who wanted to exchange ideas with young Irish people, he said. They could have a great time writing to youngsters in different lands.

Father Barry was very nice. He seemed kind of dreamy when he spoke and he sometimes closed his eyes as if the place he was talking about was somehow nearer than the place where he was. Eddie liked that. He often thought about being out with trees and flowers when he should have been thinking about the sums on the blackboard. Father Barry pinned up the page with names of the boys and girls who wanted pen-friends. They could all speak English. They lived in far lands. One of them said he liked botany, flowers and plants. His name was Chris and he lived in Glasgow, Scotland.

'That's not very far to be writing,' Niall Hayes said dismissively. He had picked a boy in Argentina.

'There's more chance he might write back if he's not too far away,' Eddie said.

'That's stupid,' said Niall.

In his heart Eddie agreed that it was. Maybe the boy in Scotland wanted someone more exotic, not from a small town in Ireland. But the real reason he had picked Chris Taylor was that Scotland wouldn't be too dear a stamp and because he had said he liked plant life. Eddie had always thought botany was a kind of wool. He checked with Miss Ross. He didn't want to get involved in writing about knitting or sheep or anything. Not that a boy would like knitting. Miss Ross said botany was plants and things that grew.

He wrote to Chris, a long letter. It was extraordinary to be writing one that would actually go into the post box. Other twelve-year-olds might have had to suck their pens and think of something more to say to use up another sheet of paper, but not Eddie Barton. He was well used to writing long letters about the state of the world in general and Shancarrig in particular.

The letter came back very quickly but it came addressed to Miss E. Barton. It had a Glasgow postmark on it. Eddie looked at it for a long time. It must be for him. His mother's name was Una. But why had Chris Taylor called him Miss? Burning with shame he opened the letter.

Dear Edith,
  I couldn't read your name properly and maybe yours is an Irish name, but I hope I'm right in guessing Edith.

The letter went on, a friendly interesting letter, lots about Scottish fir trees and pine cones, a request to send some pressed flowers, an enquiry about whether it might be good to learn the Latin names of things in case it was going to be easier to find them when you looked them up – Chris had gone to the library and spent two hours looking up a very ordinary maple and couldn't find it because he didn't know it was called *Acer*.

Eddie read on, delighted. It was nice of Chris to take so much trouble to write, especially since he obviously thought that Eddie was a girl, and a girl called Edith. Ugh. He even asked what kind of a convent was it if the teachers were called Miss Ross and Mrs Kelly and weren't nuns.

Then on the last page Eddie got an even worse shock. Chris was closing in hope that there would be a letter soon, and saying that he was delighted to find a kindred spirit on the other side of the sea, and then signed his name

Christine

Chris was a girl.

He went hot and cold thinking about the stupid mistake. She wouldn't write to him any more once she knew he didn't go to a convent school like she did, once she knew he was a twelve-year-old boy with baggy trousers and spiky hair. It was a great pity because that was just the sort of person he would have liked to write to. And it was her fault. Not his. She was the one who had the name that could have been anything. He had a perfectly normal male name, Eddie. He could imagine what they'd say at school if they knew he had got himself a *girl* in Scotland as a pen-friend when they were all finding fellows in India or South America.

Typical sissy Eddie Barton, they'd say.

He'd love to have sent Chris, whether it was a boy Chris or a girl Chris, some of the pressed flowers. All of a sudden Eddie realised that's what he'd do, he'd *pretend* to be a girl. Just get her not to put the Miss on the envelopes any more.

And for four years Eddie Barton and Christine Taylor wrote to each other, long long letters, pouring out their hearts in a way that neither of them could to anyone else.

Chris told how her mother had this dream of moving out of the city and into a house on an estate, a place with a garden and a garage, even though they didn't have a car. Chris hated the idea, she would be miles from the library and the art gallery and the places she went to when school was over. The girls at school didn't want to do anything except go to the sweet shop and talk about the fellows. Chris sent a picture of herself in school uniform and wanted Edith to send one too. In desperation Eddie sent one of Leo which he stole from The Glen when he was visiting there.

Chris wrote and said she hadn't thought of him as tall like that. She had a feeling from what he wrote that he was short and stocky and had hair that stood up. Eddie trembled when he read this as if she had found him out. He thanked the heavens that Scotland was so far away and that she would never visit. It would have been better still if she had been in Argentina, then the thought needn't have crossed his mind.

It was hard to keep up the fiction of school life when he had left Shancarrig school at the age of fourteen and now went to the Brothers in the big town every day on the bus. He told Chris that truly he wasn't happy at school and he preferred to talk about other things in his letters, like the rowan tree, like the fact that his mother was getting headaches from working too hard, like he wondered was there any way of finding out where his father was, so that he could just let him know what things were like.

He wrote about Father Barry and how he had been preaching about this village in Peru called Vieja Piedra and then had to stop, and people said the Bishop didn't like money going out of the diocese to foreign places instead of being spent at home. Chris seemed to understand. She asked him why didn't he help his mother with the sewing – it wasn't hard, they could share it.

Eddie burned with frustration over that. He realised he had made himself sound selfish and unhelpful while his only crime was that he was a boy. Everyone knew boys didn't do sewing.

He was getting on very badly at school, but he couldn't tell Chris. How could he tell of Brothers who were loud and rough with him, who often hit him with a belt when he least expected it, and one who even mocked his stutter?

Chris asked him for another picture when he was sixteen. He had none of Leo. He couldn't bear to ask her personally so he wrote her a note.

'For a long complicated reason which I'll explain to you some time, I need a photograph of you. I want you to know that it has nothing at all to do with that promise of marriage I once forced you to give. You are free from that vow, but could I have a picture next week?'

She didn't reply, but then just before his sixteenth birthday he met her unexpectedly in the middle of the town.

'Did you forget the picture?' he asked.

Leo looked distracted. She hadn't remembered.

'Please Leo, it is very important. You know I wouldn't ask you unless it were. Can I come to the house and see if you have one?'

It *was* important. Chris had sent him a picture of herself on *her* sixteenth birthday a month back. A dark girl with big eyes and a nice smile.

'*No.*' He had never known her so adamant.

'Well then, will you bring me one?'

She looked at him, as if deciding what would be the way that would cause less interference in her life.

'Oh God, I'll bring you one,' she said.

He looked hurt. 'I thought we were friends in a sort of a way,' he said.

'Yes, yes of course we are,' she relented.

'So, don't bite my head off. It's got nothing to do with being engaged.'

'What?'

Eddie decided that Leo Murphy never listened to anything anyone said. She wasn't like Chris Taylor who cared about everything.

Except of course that she thought Eddie was a girl, a fellow conspirator in life. Eddie had been forced to write and say that yes he had got his periods when he was eleven. He had managed to say that he fancied the film star Fernando Lamas and that he liked red tartan as a colour for a winter skirt.

But mainly Chris wrote about interesting things – she only descended into these female things every now and then. It always gave him a start.

He posted the photograph and waited.

He knew that she would write with a card for his birthday, usually flowers and bows and entirely unsuitable things he couldn't show to anyone. This year it was a small envelope.

'Do not open until Wednesday 29th,' it said.

Eddie took it away to read when he was on his own. He had explained to his mother that he had this pen-friend, a boy in Scotland.

'What does the Scots boy say?' his mother asked him from time to time.
'Not much. All about flowers and trees,' Eddie would say.
'Keeps you out of harm's way, I suppose,' Mrs Barton would say.
Eddie knew she sounded gruffer than she was.

In his bedroom he opened the letter from Chris and got such a shock that he had to sit down.

'I always told myself that when we were both sixteen I would tell you that I have known since the very beginning that you were a boy. I was afraid to tell you that I knew in case you'd stop writing. I *like* you being a boy. You're the nicest boy I ever met in my whole life. Happy birthday dear Eddie and thank you for your friendship.'

His first feeling was shame. How dare she have made a fool of him for four years? Then bewilderment. *How* did she know? He had agreed to having periods, being at a convent, wearing a red plaid skirt. Then came an entirely different feeling. A feeling of excitement. She knew he was a boy, and she liked him. She was afraid she'd lose him. He went to the drawer where her letters were. He read bits over and over.

'You are so easy to talk to. You really understand. You have a marvellous mind, people here are so ignorant.'

Eddie Barton was sixteen years old and in love. He went to Barna Woods. It was icy cold but he didn't care. He found an old log which he sat on, and thought about the new turn of events in his life. He must put a letter in the post to her before six o'clock. There was no question of going to school, there was far too much to think about.

Through the day he felt overwhelming regret about some of the things he had written, whole paragraphs that she must have known were lies. Then he was swept with an irritation. Why had she asked him to help his mother with the sewing when she knew he was a boy? But he mainly wanted his letter to her to be perfect and to say what he felt without frightening her off. He took the picture out again. Huge dark eyes, like an Italian. Then his heart lurched. She had no idea what he looked like. She thought he looked like Leo Murphy. Well, no she didn't, but she had no idea. Eddie wished he was tall and strong, that he looked like Niall Hayes' cousin, Richard, who had come to visit. Everyone said he was so handsome. Eddie wished more than ever that he could find his father and ask his advice.

But his father didn't turn up on Eddie's sixteenth birthday any more than he had on any other anniversary, so he knew he would have to write it alone.

He decided to go to Miss Ross and her mother and ask if he could write the letter there. It would be warm and dry. There would be no fear of his mother asking him what he was doing, saying something that was bound to irritate him. He often did some work on the garden for Miss Ross, who wouldn't mind him coming in on a wild cold day like this.

She was just coming back from the school for her lunch when he arrived. She wore a belted raincoat which swished as she walked along. Eddie wondered if Chris wore a raincoat like that. He might ask her but somehow it seemed a bit personal, that swishy sound. Something he didn't want her to know about, and the feeling it gave him.

Miss Ross looked tired and pale. She said he was an answer to prayer. If he would just chop a few logs for her not only could he sit by the fire and write for the afternoon, she would give him a big bowl of soup as well.

'It's my birthday, Miss Ross. That's why,' he said.

She seemed to find the explanation perfectly satisfactory, and asked nothing about why he had absented himself from the Brothers without any permission. She couldn't imagine Brother O'Brien saying to a lad of sixteen that he should celebrate the day.

'What kind of a letter? Is it an application for a job?' Miss Ross asked.

'No. It's more a letter to a friend.' He was scarlet as he spoke.

'Yes, well if the friend's in a convent boarding school don't forget the nuns might read it.' Miss Ross was full of wisdom.

'No, the friend's not in a boarding school.' Eddie knew he sounded stiff.

'Well, you're all right then.' Eddie thought Miss Ross sounded as if she was trying to be cheerful for his sake. And maybe a little envious.

Eddie looked around the room before he began his letter. He had never noticed the house very much before, thinking of it as a place to take off his shoes before he came in from the garden. He remembered that Maura Brennan, who had been his friend at Shancarrig school, had always said she loved this house and that when she got old she would have one just like it, with lovely pieces of furniture that she would polish until they shone and china ornaments on shelves and thick rich velvet curtains. Eddie admired the colours; everything seemed to match with everything else, not like in his own home where the carpet was brown and the curtains were yellow and the table cloth was green; it looked as if everything was chosen to clash with everything else. He knew this was not the case, it was because they didn't have enough money to get things that would look nice. His mother had great taste in the clothes she made. She was always advising her customers what went well with their eyes or their complexion.

But still, that didn't help him to write to Chris Taylor.

He sat for a long time, the old grandfather clock ticking. Miss Ross had gone back to Shancarrig school; her mother was having her afternoon rest upstairs.

'Dearest Chris,' Eddie wrote. 'I can't tell you how good it is to be able to write as myself. I wanted to so often but once I had begun with the silly lie I had to keep it going in case you stopped writing. Your letters are the most important thing in my life. I couldn't bear them to stop.'

And then it was easy. Page after page. He tried to imagine himself sitting in this small house in Glasgow. She called it a two up two down, meaning the number of rooms. Her mother had never realised the dream of moving to an estate. Her father kept pigeons and hadn't much interest in anything else. Her two brothers were at sea and only came home for a very short visit now and then. She wanted to go to a school of art but she wasn't good enough. Her mother said to get a job in the florists and be grateful for it; most people had to do work they hated. At least Chris liked flowers so she'd be ahead of the game.

What would this girl like to read from Eddie, now revealed as a man? He knew one thing. There must be no more pretence.

'I'm small and square and have hair that sticks up. I don't think I ever told you properly about school and how much I hate it, because when I was meant to be a girl I couldn't tell you how rough they are there and how they think I'm as thick as the wall. I don't think I am, and your letters make me think I have something.'

There was no trouble finding the words. When he read it over he thought she would think it was a fair explanation for his years of deceit. Not too much apology, more setting the record straight.

He was surprised when Miss Ross came back from school.

'That's a letter and a half, Eddie,' she said approvingly.

'Would you have said I was thick, Miss Ross?'

'No, I wouldn't, and you're not,' she said.

He grinned at her and ran off. She looked out the door and saw him heading for the post office, skipping and jumping over puddles.

The letters came fast and thick. They wrote to each other about hopes and fears, about books and paintings, about colours and designs. They kept nothing back.

'If we ever meet I must show you the ferns of Barna Woods,' he wrote once.

'What do you mean "if we ever meet"? It's "when we meet"!' she wrote back, and his heart felt leaden because he knew he had made Shancarrig sound too beautiful, too exciting, too romantic for Christine Taylor.

'That boy must have nothing to do but write letters,' his mother said one day when the usual fat envelope arrived from Scotland.

'It's not a boy, it's a girl.' Eddie knew he'd have to explain some time.

'What do you mean? Did he turn into a girl all of a sudden?' Mrs Barton didn't like the sound of it being a girl.

'No, it's a different one.' Eddie didn't feel that any further explanation would help.

'Why Scotland?' his mother said.

'It's nice and far away,' he grinned. 'If I have to be writing to a girl, Ma, isn't it better that I write to one in a far off country?'

'At your age you shouldn't be writing to a girl at all. There'll be plenty of time for that later. Too much time if you're your father's son.'

There had been much mention over the years of Ted Barton's interest in women, always vague and generalised, never specific and detailed. Eddie had long given up the hope of getting any more information than the sketchy amount he already had. His father had been thrown out because of a known association with another woman. When he had left Shancarrig that night the woman had not gone with him. She might even be someone he knew. Someone he had spoken to. If only it was someone nice like Miss Ross then maybe she could have told him more about the man who had left their lives.

'Did my father ever like Miss Ross?' he asked his mother suddenly.

'Maddy Ross?' His mother looked at him in surprise.

'Yes. Could she have been his love?'

'Well, given that she was about twelve or thirteen when he left town it isn't entirely likely, but that doesn't say it should be ruled out either.' His mother had even managed a wry smile as she said this.

Eddie thought she was less bitter. He must remember to tell this to Chris when he wrote; they had no secrets. She told him about her father being laid off in the shipyard and her mother getting an extra shift in the factory. Chris was doing Saturdays in the local flower shop. It wasn't like she thought it would be, working with flowers. It was very mechanical, stiff little arrangements and awful cheaty ways of making flowers look alive when they were almost dead.

They wrote to each other when they should have been trying a last desperate effort at their books. Christine said that they were snobby in her convent and didn't like the girls whose mothers worked in factories. Eddie wrote that the Brothers had a down on anyone with a bit of soul at all and that they had him written off as a no-hoper. The results of the exams were a foregone conclusion to them both.

In the summer of 1957 they wrote and told each other of poor results, bad marks and limited futures.

'I had a word with Brother O'Brien. He doesn't think it worth trying to repeat the year,' Eddie's mother said glumly. She had taken the bus into the big town to buy materials, threads, zip fasteners and spare pieces for the sewing machine. She had used the opportunity to visit the school.

It hadn't been a happy encounter.

'I told him that other boys had fathers who could pay for this kind of thing, but that we weren't in the lucky position to know where your father is or has been for the last dozen years.' Her face had that old bitter look which Eddie hated.

'Ma, you threw him out. You asked him to go. You can't keep blaming him for everything after he went, only for what he did before he went.'

'And that was plenty for one lifetime, let me assure you.'

'You always *assure* me these things but you never explain them.'

'Oh, you've words at will, just like him.'

'And was Brother O'Brien sympathetic? I bet he wasn't. He couldn't care about anyone's father, or mother, or anyone at all.'

His mother gave him an odd look.

'He wasn't sympathetic. Neither to you nor to me. But I think he does care about people. He said there was no point in my lamenting the absence of a husband, that it was mainly women who did all the consulting whether their husbands were alive or around or whatever.'

'And what else?'

'He said that you had got it into your head you were too good for the school, above them and their plain ways. And that would have been fine if you were a real artist burning to paint or to write, but the way things were he didn't know what would become of you. He sounded sorry.'

To Eddie it had the ring of truth. That was exactly the way Brother O'Brien would speak, and there was some truth in it. He could see the big man with his red face regretting that he couldn't find a place for the boy. Brother O'Brien loved his boys to get into banks and insurance offices, the Civil Service, and the very odd time even into a university.

There would be nowhere for Eddie Barton.

If he hadn't had his lifeline of letters to hold him together as support and strength Eddie would have been very depressed that summer. But Chris wrote every day. She said they must get themselves out of this situation. She would not work in a factory like her mother, nor would she train to be a florist.

They had begun to talk of love now, they ended each letter with more and more yearning and wishes that they could meet. Eddie said that perhaps he had made Shancarrig sound too attractive. Maybe they could meet in some foreign land where there would be warm winds and palm trees. Chris said that nobody could love anybody if they met in the grey streets around her home. She was all for somewhere exotic too.

The world of fantasy became an important part of their letter-writing. It almost took over from the practical side. Chris Taylor went to work in a department store in Glasgow. She hated it, she said. It was very tiring. Her legs ached more than usual. Eddie wrote and asked did her legs usually ache, she had never mentioned it before. But she didn't mention it again so he thought it must have been just a phrase.

Eddie Barton went to work in Dunne's Hardware. He hated it. He wrote to Chris about the days talking to farmers who came in to buy chicken wire and plough parts. He said he was sick of harrows and rakes and if he had to talk about linseed oil or red oxide for painting a barn again he thought he might actually lie down and die. He wrote about how ignorant the Dunnes were. Their aunt, Nellie Dunne, ran a small grocery shop and she gave people credit which was the only reason why anyone shopped there. Eddie worked for old Mr Dunne and his sons Brian and Liam. Eileen, who was his own age, worked in Ryan's Hotel, but was always giving him the eye when she came in.

'I tell you this . . .' he wrote to Chris, 'not to make myself sound great or to make you jealous, but to remind myself how lucky I am that stupid girls like Eileen with her forward pushy ways form no part of my life now that I know what love is. Now that I have you.'

Sometimes she wrote about going to a dance, but she said she sat in a seat on the balcony most of the time and thought about what he had said in his last letter.

Sometimes Nessa Ryan and Leo Murphy came into the shop to talk to him. The Dunnes never minded him talking to them because they were as near to the Quality as Shancarrig possessed. If Maura Brennan came in, or anyone else from the cottages, it would be different. But old Mr Dunne seemed to take positive pleasure out of a visit from young Miss Ryan of the hotel and young Miss Murphy from The Glen.

'And how goes the good Major?' he would ask Leo about her father.

'Talking to himself as usual,' Leo muttered once and they all giggled. Mr Dunne didn't like such disrespect.

'And how are they all in Ireland's leading hostelry?' he would ask Nessa Ryan about her family's hotel.

Nessa always said it was doing fine thank you.

Eddie wrote to Chris about how strained and worried Leo Murphy looked when she should have had no worries in the world. She had got six honours in her Leaving Certificate. She had all the money in the world; she could have gone to university in Cork or Galway or Dublin, yet she always seemed to be biting her lip.

Chris wrote back and said you never knew what worries people had. Perhaps Leo wasn't well, maybe it was her health. What did she look like? In shame Eddie wrote and said that Leo looked like him, or rather, the pictures he had sent of him when he was meant to be a girl were of Leo.

'She's very good-looking,' Chris wrote back anxiously.

'I never noticed it,' he wrote. 'Perhaps I should have stayed a girl.'

'No. You're lovely as you are,' she said in the next letter.

They knew that they must talk. Neither household had a phone but Chris could use the public phone and Eddie could be in Ryan's Hotel waiting for the call. They rehearsed it in letters for some weeks.

'We mightn't like each other's voices,' Chris wrote. 'But it's important to remember that we like each other so the voice doesn't matter.'

'What do you mean we *like* each other?' wrote Eddie. 'We love each other. That's what we must remember on Saturday night.'

They made it Saturday so that they could look forward to it all week.

He dressed himself up and put on a clean shirt.

'On the town again I suppose.' His mother hardly seemed to look up but she had taken in that he was smartly turned out.

'Aw, no, Mam. There's nowhere much to go on the town in Shancarrig.'

'Well, where are you going if I might ask?' Her tone wasn't as sharp as the words. She was aching to know.

'Just down to Ryan's Hotel, Mam, for a cup of coffee.'

'Eddie. . . ?'

'Yes, Mam.'

'Eddie, I know I'm nagging you but you won't . . .'

'Mam, I told you I don't drink. I didn't like the smell of it or the taste of it the once I tried.'

'I don't mean drink.' She looked him up and down, a boy setting out for a date, for romance.

'What do you mean?'

'You wouldn't get involved with that Eileen Dunne, now would you? They'd be bad people to get on the wrong side of . . .'

'Who are you telling! Don't I work for them?'

'But Eileen . . . ?'

He knelt beside his mother and looked up into her face.

'If she were the last woman in Ireland I wouldn't want her.'

Anyone would have known that he was speaking the truth. Eddie's mother waved him off with a lighter heart.

Chris was to ring at eight. Eddie positioned himself in the hall. The telephone would ring at the reception desk, then whoever was on duty would look around and say, 'Eddie Barton, I don't know . . . oh yes, *there* he is,' and she'd motion Eddie to go into the booth. Then he would speak to her. To the girl he loved.

Another good thing about it being a Saturday was that awful Eileen Dunne wouldn't be working at the desk. She was in the dining room on Saturdays, her dress tight across the bottom and the bosom, and a small white apron making no attempt to cover her at all.

Eddie's heart was beating so strongly it reminded him of the big clock in Shancarrig school and the thudding sounds it made as the seconds ticked on.

Soon, soon. Ten minutes. Nine.

He jumped a foot in the air when he heard the phone ring. He hadn't noticed that Eileen Dunne *was* working at Reception tonight. Please may she not make any remark, may she not say something stupid that Chris would hear all the way away in Scotland.

'Yes, he's here. Hold on. *Edd* . . . *ie?*'

He was at the desk.

'Yes?'

'There's someone on the phone for you. Will you take it here at the desk? God, you're looking like a dog's dinner tonight.'

'I'll go into the box,' he said, his face red with fury.

'Right. Hold on till I get this bloody thing through. There's more plugs and wires than a hedgehog's backside. Are you going in to town to the dance?'

He ran in to the dark phone booth, his hands trembling. Damn Eileen Dunne to hell. Please may Chris not have heard.

'Hello?' he said tentatively.

It must be the Scottish telephone operator on the line. He could hardly understand her. She was saying something about difficulty in getting through.

'Can you put me on to Chris, please?' He knew his voice was shaky but it had been a bit of luck that she hadn't come straight through. She wouldn't have heard that stupid stupid Eileen. Any moment she'd talk to him.

'This *is* Chris,' he managed to decipher from the strange speech. 'Do you mean you canna hear me?'

It wasn't Chris's voice. It was like someone imitating a Scottish comedian. Every word was canna and wouldna.

'That's never you, not you yourself, Chris?' he said. She must be playing a joke.

'Och, Eddie, stop putting on that Irish blarney bit. You're like the fellows they have at Christmas concerts in the church, with their afther doing this and afther doing that.'

There was silence. They realised that neither of them was putting on an act. This is the way they were. The silence was broken by their laughter.

'Oh God, Eddie . . . I forgot. I had you talking normally in my mind.'

His heart was full of love. This strange way she spoke didn't matter a bit. 'I thought you'd be like a real person too,' he said.

Then it was back to the way they were in letters. Until the three minutes ran out.

'I love you, Chris, more than ever.'

'And I love you too,' she said.

They lived for Saturdays, and yet as they wrote to each other the phone calls were never as good as they expected. Sometimes they literally didn't understand what the other was saying and they wasted precious time explaining.

They were desperate to meet. The time was very long.

'We'd better meet soon before we're too old to recognise each other,' she wrote.

'While we still remember what we wrote to each other.'

They each kept their letters in shoe boxes. It seemed a small thing but a bond . . . another bond. Yet they hesitated each to ask the other to their town. Eddie couldn't bear the explanations, the doing up of the spare room, the questioning from his mother, the eyes of Shancarrig.

Chris said that if he had found it hard to understand her voice then her family and her neighbours in Glasgow would be incomprehensible.

She obviously yearned for Barna Woods and the hill with the big rock on it, the rock that gave its name to the town. She wanted to see Eddie's pink house and meet his mother.

He wanted her here and he didn't want her. He wanted to leave Shancarrig for ever, and yet he couldn't. One man had left his mother already, Eddie couldn't go.

Then at last he heard himself inviting her. He didn't really intend to, it just came out.

It had been a long hard day in Dunne's when nothing had gone right. Old Mr Dunne was like a devil, Liam had been scornful, Brian had been giving him orders, and to make matters worse their cousin Foxy who had been in Eddie's class at school had come back for a visit.

Foxy worked on the buildings in England. He was doing well by all accounts. He had started by making billycans of tea for Irishmen working on the lump, building the big roads over in Britain. He came home every year, eyes bright and darting around him as usual.

Normally Eddie was pleased to see Foxy, he had a quick wit and was always ready with a joke.

Today it hadn't been like that. 'Don't let him speak to you like that,' Foxy said to Eddie when Mr Dunne had called him an ignorant bosthoon.

'Fine words, Foxy. He's only an uncle to you, but he pays my week's wages.'

'Still and all, you're letting him walk over you. You'll be here for the rest of your life with a shop coat on you stuck behind a counter.'

'And what are you going to be?' Eddie had flared back.

'I've got the hell out of here. I wouldn't sit here listening to my uncle mumbling and bumbling, and my Aunt Nellie letting people run up bad debts because they're Quality. I'm in England and I'll make a pile of money. And then I'll come back and marry Leo Murphy.'

It was the longest speech that Foxy had ever made. Eddie had been surprised.

'And will Leo marry *you*?'

'Not now, she won't. Not the way I am. No one would marry either of us, Eddie. We're eejits. We have only one good suit each with an arse in the trousers of it. We have to *do* something with our lives instead of standing round here like fools. What class of a woman would want the likes of us?'

'I don't know. We might have a charm of our own.' Eddie was being light-hearted but he felt that Foxy was right.

Foxy turned away impatiently. 'I can see you in twenty years still saying that, Eddie. This place makes us all slow and stupid. It's like a muddy river dragging us down.'

Eddie had been thinking about it all day. He didn't dress up for the phone call that night. It was his turn to call the Glasgow phone box.

'Come over to Ireland. Come to Shancarrig,' he said when Chris answered the phone.

'When? When will I come?'

'As soon as you can. I'm sick of being without you,' he said. 'There's nothing at all else in my life except you.'

Their letters changed tone. It was confident now. It was 'when' not 'if'. It was definite. The love was there, the need, the surprise that one other person could feel exactly the same about everything as another.

There were the details.

Chris would take her two weeks holidays from the flower shop. Eddie could take his two weeks off from Dunne's. She would get the boat from Stranraer to Larne, and the train to Belfast maybe?

'Will I come to meet you there? I've never been to the North of Ireland. It'll be familiar to you, red buses, red pillar boxes. Like England.'

'Like Scotland,' she corrected him. She had never been to England in her life.

Or would she take a train to Wales, and get the boat from Holyhead? Maybe that would be a nicer way to go. She could see Dun Laoghaire and a bit of Dublin before taking the train to Shancarrig.

'I don't want you wandering around on your own, meeting Dublin fellows. I'll come and meet you off the boat,' he suggested.

Chris said no, she wanted to arrive in Shancarrig on the train herself. She knew about the station, and the flowers that now spelt out the word Shancarrig. He had written that long ago to her.

Eddie could be on the platform.

He prayed that it would be a fine fortnight, that the sun would shine into Barna Woods between the branches, that there would be a sparkle on the River Grane. He knew you shouldn't pray for something bad to happen to another human but he hoped that somehow Eileen Dunne would be in hospital when Chris arrived, and that Nessa Ryan wouldn't be superior towards him, and that he'd be free of Brian and Liam Dunne and their bad-tempered father because he was on holidays.

He hoped most of all that his mother would be nice to Chris. They had never had anyone to stay, and Eddie had distempered the walls, and painted the woodwork in the small stuffy room they had called a boxroom up to now. His mother had been curiously quiet.

'What kind of a girl is she?' was all she had asked.

'A girl I write to, I write to her a lot. I like her through the post and on the telephone. I've asked her to come over here so that ... well, so that I wouldn't be the one going off on you.'

His mother looked away so that he wouldn't see the look of gratitude in her face. But he saw all the same.

'I'll make curtains for the room,' she said.

Please let them like each other.

They had got ham for tea, cooked ham and tomatoes, and a Fullers chocolate cake with four chocolate buttons on the top.

His mother had cleared the sewing away so that the place would look like a normal house. There were blue curtains on the window of the boxroom, and a matching bedspread. On the makeshift dressing table there was a little blue cloth and Eddie had gathered a bunch of flowers.

It was nearly time. The train would be in at three. Only four hours. Three. Two. It was time.

Liam Dunne was on the platform; there was a delivery coming down with the guard on the train.

'What are you doing?' Liam asked. 'Aren't you meant to be on your holidays? If you're doing nothing you could give me a hand ... ?'

'I most definitely *am* on my holidays and I'm meeting a friend,' Eddie said firmly.

The train whistled and came around the corner. She got off. She carried a big suitcase, square with little firm bits over the corners like leather triangles to preserve it.

She had a red jacket and a navy skirt, a navy shoulder bag and a huge bright smile.

He had been afraid for a moment that she might think Liam Dunne was him. Liam was taller and good-looking in a rangy sort of way. Eddie felt like a barrel. He wished his spine would shoot up and make him willowy.

He started to walk towards her and saw her foot. Chris Taylor had a big built-up shoe. He willed his eyes away from it, and on to her smiling eager face.

Liam was busy with the guard, hauling things from the luggage van, and nobody was watching them.

Eddie had never kissed anyone in his life apart from fumbles at dances. He put his arms around Chris.

'Welcome to Shancarrig,' he said first, then he kissed her very gently. She clung to him.

'I didn't tell you about my foot,' she said, her face working anxiously.

'What about your foot?' He forced himself not to look at it again to see how bad it was. Could she walk? Did it drag? His head was whirling.

'I didn't want you to pity me,' she said.

'Me? Pity *you*? You must be mad,' he said.

'I can walk and everything, and I can keep up. I'll be able to see every bit of Barna Woods with you after tea.'

She looked very young and frightened. She must have been worried about this for ages, like he worried about the place not being as nice as he described.

'I don't know what you're going on about,' he tried to reassure her, but he knew it wasn't working.

'My leg, Eddie. I've got one shorter than the other, you see. I wear a special shoe.'

He could read how hard it was for her to say this. How often she must have rehearsed it. He urged himself to find the right words.

He looked down at her foot in its black shoe with the big thick raised sole and heel.

'Does it hurt?' he asked.

'No, of course not, but it's the way it looks.'

He took both her hands in his. 'Chris, are you mad?' he asked her. 'Are you off your head? It's me. It's Eddie, your best friend. Your love. Do you think for a moment that it's part of the bargain that our legs had to be the same length?'

It was, as it happened, exactly the right thing to say. Chris Taylor burst into tears and hugged Eddie to her as if she was never going to leave him go. 'I love you, Eddie.'

'I love you too. Come on, let's go home.' He carried her case and they walked to the gate of the station.

Chris was still wiping her eyes. Liam Dunne stood watching them.

'Don't mind him.' He nodded in Eddie's direction. 'That fellow's as thick as the wall. He's always upsetting people and making them cry. There's plenty of real men in Shancarrig.'

She gave him a bright smile.

'I bet there are. I've come all the way from Scotland to investigate them.' She tucked her arm into Eddie's and they went out the gate.

Eddie felt ten feet tall.

'Who was that?' she whispered.

'Liam Dunne. Desperate . . .'

'Don't tell me. I know all about him. The younger son, the one that'll take over if Brian goes to England and the old man dies.'

'You know it all,' he said in wonder.

'I feel like I'm coming home.'

As they walked up the road and he pointed out Ryan's Hotel where he had sat waiting for the phone calls, and the church where Father Gunn waved to him cheerfully, the pubs and Nellie Dunne's grocery, he knew that in many ways she had come home. He knew that he had been right, she was the centre of his life. It would be fine when he brought her home to his mother.

Afterwards nobody could ever tell you exactly how and why Chris Taylor came to live in Shancarrig. One day she had never been heard of and then the next there she was, as if she had been part of the place all her life.

If people asked Mrs Barton about her they were told that she was a marvellous girl altogether and a dab hand at the sewing. There was nothing she couldn't turn her hand to. Look at the way she had made them go into furnishings, for example. Chris Taylor had loved the curtains and bedspread in her little room the day she arrived. Her praise was unstinting. Mrs Barton was a genius.

Eddie never thought of his mother's dressmaking as anything except a way to make a living; he knew she didn't particularly like some of the women whose dresses she made. He hadn't realised that the work was artistic in itself.

Chris opened his eyes for him. 'Look at the way the ribbon falls, look at the colours she's put together . . . Eddie, it's easy to see where you got your artistic sense from . . .'

His mother reddened with pleasure. There were no derisory remarks about his father. In fact, Chris was able to introduce the first reasonable conversation about the long-departed Ted Barton that had ever been held in this house.

'I suppose he was a restless kind of a man. Better for him to be gone in a lot of ways.'

And to his surprise Eddie heard his mother agreeing. Things had really begun to change around here.

Chris was part of Shancarrig.

They knew her coming in and out of Dunnes to see Eddie or to give him a message, they knew her in the hotel where she became friendly with Nessa Ryan. No one ever spoke dismissively to Chris Taylor as people had been known to do to Eddie Barton. She talked furnishings and fabrics to Nessa's mother. There was going to be a grant for the hotel to make it smarter, the kind of a place where tourist visitors might stay as well as commercial travellers.

They couldn't stay in Ryan's the way it was. Chris seemed to know the way it should be – pelmets, nice wooden pelmets covered in fabric, she had seen it all in an American magazine, you stuck the fabric to the plywood, and then the curtains draped properly down below. And, of course, bed covers to match.

Nessa Ryan and her mother were very excited.

'How would we get it started? Would we need to call someone in from Dublin? Who'd do it?'

'We would,' Chris said simply.

'We?'

'Mrs Barton and I. Let us do one room as a sample and see.'

'Wooden pelmets . . . ? You couldn't do that . . . ?'

'Eddie could, he could get the plywood. Liam Dunne could help him . . .'

The room was a huge success. The whole hotel would be done the same way. They had chosen a fabric which would tone in with Eddie's pressed flowers, with his large bold designs, flowers from Barna Woods, a place in the locality, especially commissioned from a local artist.

'You can't call me a local artist,' Eddie had protested.

'You are local. You live here, don't you?' she said simply.

The plans were afoot. Chris and Eddie's mother would be able to do it between them, but they needed someone to organise it, someone who would go and choose the right fabrics, someone with an eye for colour, someone whose pictures were already on the wall.

Flushed and happy Chris told Eddie the plan.

'You can leave Dunne's. We'll have a business, all of us . . .'

'I can't leave . . . if we get married I have to support you.'

'What's this if? Are you changing your mind? I've come over here and lived with you, set myself up shamelessly in your house and you say "if"?'

'I want to ask you something properly.'

'Not here, Eddie. Let's go up to the woods.'

Eddie's mother stood by the window and watched the two of them walk together, the limping figure of this strange strong Scottish girl, the stocky figure of her own son, who had grown taller since Chris had arrived.

She knew nothing about the kind of family over in Scotland who let their daughter wander away to another land without seeming to care.

She cared little now about the past. Once she had lived in it and felt burdened by it, now she thought only about the future, the proposal that was going to be made in Barna Woods and accepted, the new life that was ahead of all of them.

Dr Jims

In Shancarrig they only knew him as Dr Blake for about six weeks. Then they all started to call him Dr Jims. It had to do with Maisie, of course. Maisie who couldn't pronounce any name properly, not even one as ordinary as James. She had been asked to call Dr James to the telephone and in front of the whole waiting room she had said that Dr Jims was wanted. Somehow, the name had stuck. James Blake was too young a man to be given a full title, not while the great Dr Nolan held sway in Shancarrig.

Jims Blake got very accustomed to people asking for the real doctor when they came to The Terrace, and if a call came in the night which Dr Jims answered, the gravest doubts were expressed. He learned to say that he was only holding the fort for the real doctor, and Dr Nolan would be along at a more convenient hour to give his approval.

But it was a good partnership – the wise old man who knew all the secrets of Shancarrig and the thin eager young man, son of a small farmer out the country. The old man who drank more brandy at night than was good for him and the young man who stayed up late reading the journals and reports ... they lived together peaceably. They had Maisie doting on both of them and resenting the fact that people kept getting sick and needing to disturb the two men in her life, the great Dr Nolan and poor young Dr Jims.

Dr Nolan was always saying that Jims Blake should find a wife for himself and Maisie was always saying that there was plenty of time.

Matters came to a head in 1940 when Dr Nolan was seventy and Dr Jims was thirty. It had been a busy time. There was a baby to be delivered in almost every house around them. A little girl Leonora up at The Glen, a first daughter to the Ryans at the hotel, another Dunne to the cottages, a son for the wife of wild Ted Barton, another Brennan to add to Paudie's brood.

Dr Jims would come back tired to the big house in The Terrace – the tall house, one of a line facing the hotel. It formed the centre of the town in a triangle with the row of shops. The bus stopped nearby and the movement of Shancarrig could be charted from any of the windows. Dr Jims' work took him to the far outlying districts as well, but the centre of life remained this small area around the place where he lived.

Even though it was comfortable there were ways in which it was not a real life. Dr Nolan was able to put it into words. 'I'm not going to let you make the same mistake as I did,' the old man said. 'A doctor needs a wife, really

381

and truly. I had my chances and my choices in the old days, like you do now. But I was both too set and too easy in my ways. I didn't want to disrupt everything by bringing a woman in. I didn't really need a woman, I thought.'

'And you didn't either,' Dr Jims encouraged him. 'Didn't you have a full life ... where was there room for a wife? I've seen too many doctors' wives neglected, left out ... maybe the medical profession should take a vow of celibacy, like the clerics. It might be something we could bring up at the Irish Medical Association.'

'Don't make a jeer out of it, Jims. I'm serious.'

'So am I. How could I marry? Where would I get the stake for a house? I still send a bit home to the farm. You know that. I have to be averting my eyes for a bit, in case I think I might want a wife.'

'And who are you averting them from?' The old man drank his brandy, looking deep into the glass and not at his partner.

'Not anybody in particular.'

'But Frances Fitzgerald, maybe?'

'Ah, come on out of that. What could I offer Frances Fitzgerald?'

But Jims Blake knew that the old man had seen through him. He most desperately wanted to advance things with Frances, to go further than the games of tennis with other people present, the card evenings at The Glen or in Ryan's Hotel.

He'd hoped it hadn't been as transparent to other people.

Yet again Dr Nolan seemed to read his mind.

'Nobody would know but myself,' he said reassuringly. 'And you could offer her half a house here.'

'It's your house.'

'I won't be here for ever. It's taking more of this stuff to ease the pain in my gut.' He raised his brandy glass to show what he was referring to.

'The pain in your gut would be less if you had less of that stuff.'

'So you say, with the arrogance of youth ... We'll get the top two floors done up for you. The Dunnes can come in on Monday and lean on their picks and shovels and we'll see what they can do. Frances will want her own kitchen ... she won't want Maisie traipsing around after her.'

'Charles, I can't ... we don't even know if Frances is interested ...'

'We do,' said Dr Nolan.

Jims Blake didn't even wait to let that sink in.

'But I can't afford ...' he began.

Charles Nolan's face winced with pain and anger. 'Stop being such a defeatist, such a sniveller ... I can't this, I can't that ... Is that how you made yourself a doctor ...?'

His face was red now proving his point.

'Listen here to me, Jims Blake, why do you think I took you on here? Think about it. It wasn't for your great moneyed connections and class. No. I took you on because you were a fighter, and a dogged little fellow. I liked your thin white face and your determination. I liked the way you forced them to let you study, and took jobs to make up the extra money that they couldn't give you. That's what people need in a doctor – someone who won't quit.'

'I could pay you so much a month for it, I suppose. I could take on more of the work.'

'Boy, aren't you doing almost all the work already. I'm only giving you what's fair . . .'

And it was settled like that. Dr Jims was to have the upstairs part of the house. Everyone said it was very sensible. After all, Dr Nolan wasn't getting any younger. Wasn't it sensible that a bedroom be built for him on the ground floor?

Maisie sniffed a bit, especially since it became known that Dr Jims was now courting Miss Fitzgerald.

The Dunne brothers were in regularly, wondering should the kitchen be facing the front or the back of the house. It might be good to have it looking out on the town. There was a nice view of Shancarrig from upstairs in The Terrace. But then, traditionally a kitchen was at the back. They puzzled at it.

Before they came to any solution their work was rendered unnecessary. Dr Charles Nolan died of the liver complaint he had been ignoring for some years, and he willed his house to his partner Dr Blake.

Before he died he spoke of it to Jims. 'You're a good lad. You'll keep it all going fine here, if only you'd learn to . . .'

'You've got years yet. Stop making a farewell speech,' Jims Blake said to the dying man.

'What I was *going* to say, if only you'd learn that there are people, myself included, who are quite glad to be coming to the end of their lives, who don't *want* to be told that there are years of pain and confusion ahead of them . . .'

Jims held his partner's hand – it was a simple gesture of solidarity where no words would have worked.

'That's more like it,' said Dr Nolan. 'Now, will you promise me to have a family and a real life for yourself? Don't be forced to leave this place to some whippersnapper of a junior partner, like I am!'

'You can't leave it all to me . . .' He was aghast.

'I was hoping to leave it to Frances as well. Tell me you've made some move in that direction . . .'

'Yes. We were hoping to marry . . .' His voice choked, realising that his benefactor wouldn't now be at the wedding.

'That's good, very good. I'm tired now. Get me into hospital tomorrow, Jims. I don't want to die in the house where she's coming as a bride.'

'It's your house. Die wherever you want to,' Jims blazed at him.

The old man smiled. 'I like to hear you talk that way. And where I would like to die is the hospital. Tell that young Father Gunn to come up there to me, not to be upsetting Maisie by coming here. And move that brandy bottle back to my reach.'

It didn't take Shancarrig long to recognise Dr Jims as the real doctor. Everything had changed. There was no old Dr Nolan any more to know their secrets so they told them to Dr Jims instead. He was a married man now, of course, and his wife a very gentle person – one of the Fitzgeralds who owned a big milling business.

It had been a good match – that's what outsiders thought. But they only knew the surface. They didn't know about passion and love and understanding. Frances, with her gentle solemn face transformed so often with a quick smile that lit up her whole being, was a wife that he never dreamed possible.

She would creep up behind him and lock her arms around his neck. She would feed him pieces of food from her plate when Maisie wasn't looking. When he was called out at night Frances sometimes left a note on his pillow saying, 'Wake me up. I want to welcome you home properly.' In every way she made him grow in confidence. Jims Blake walked with a lighter step and a smile in his eyes.

The fact that Dr Nolan had left him the house made Dr Jims even more respected in the community. If the old doctor had thought so much of him then this must be a good man. Sometimes Jims Blake felt unworthy of all the respect he got in Shancarrig.

When he visited his dour family on their small bleak farm and saw the lifestyle that he would have been condemned to had he not fought so hard to study medicine, he felt guilty. He was saddened that they had so little, and even the money he gave them was stored under a mattress, not used to buy his mother and father a better standard of life.

He had tried to explain this guilt to Frances but she calmed him down. He had done everything he could for the family. Surely that was as much as anyone was expected to do – he couldn't do any more.

Frances said that *they* were a family now she and Jims and the baby they were expecting. There was no tie that bound them to the bleak family of Blakes in the small wet farm, or the distant, undemonstrative Fitzgeralds wrapped up in their business affairs. They were a little unit in themselves.

And so it was for a while.

Jims often thought that the spirit of old Dr Nolan would have been pleased to hear the way that Number Three The Terrace rang with laughter. First Eileen was born, then Sheila. No son and heir yet, but as people said, God would send the boy in his own good time.

There were many attempts for the boy – all ending in miscarriage.

Frances Blake was a frail woman – the efforts to hold a child to full term were taking a great toll on her health.

Several times Jims asked himself what would the old doctor have advised if he had been involved in a family where this had been the situation. He could almost hear Dr Nolan's voice.

'This is a thing you could work out between the pair of you . . . Now the good God up in heaven doesn't have a book of rules saying you must do this or that, and so many times . . . The good God expects us to use our intelligence . . .'

And he might go on to explain some of the most elemental details of times of high fertility and low fertility, suggesting the latter as the wiser time to indulge in what he called the business of marriage.

But always he would urge the couple to talk to each other.

Jims Blake somehow found it hard to talk to his own wife.

The problem was all the greater because he loved her so much. He desired her *and* he wanted to protect her. A combination of that was hard to rationalise. He had worked out her ovulation as carefully as he could, they had tried to make love at the times she was least likely to conceive. He had held her face in his hands and assured her that his two little girls were plenty, they didn't need to try for a son. Let them live their lives without putting her to any additional strain, without placing her health in danger.

Sometimes she looked sad, he didn't know if it was because she feared that he didn't desire her as much as he once had. Perhaps it was because she really did yearn to give him a son. He found it impossible to believe that two people who loved each other so much could still have areas of misunderstanding. And yet, whenever he approached her she seemed so receptive and willing that he had to believe this was what she wanted too.

When Frances became pregnant again in 1946 the girls Eileen and Sheila were five and four – two cherubs sitting in their Viyella nightdresses and red flannel dressing gowns while he read them stories. This time he hoped for a son to join them.

In the coldest winter that Ireland had ever known Frances Blake gave birth to her son. And in the house with log fires burning in every room, with a midwife from the hospital in the big town in attendance, as well as her husband who had, even at the age of thirty-seven, delivered thousands of children into the world . . . she died.

They had never even discussed what to call the baby. They hadn't dared to hope it would live, nor had they dared to hope it would be a boy.

Father Gunn, arriving at the house to the news of the birth and death, enquired if the child was sickly, and whether there should be an emergency baptism.

'I think the child is healthy enough.' Jims Blake's voice was empty.

'Well, we'll leave it for a while then. It'll bring some cheer to the household to have a baptism.' Father Gunn was optimistic. He tried to see some light at the end of the seemingly endless dark tunnels of this particular winter. He had been burying far more than he baptised.

'Maybe you could get it over with, Father.' The young doctor looked white and strained.

'Not now, Jims. Wait a bit. Give the lad a start, find godparents for him. Think of a name. He has a life to live, Frances would want that for him.'

'He mightn't live, let's do it now.'

Something about the face of Jims Blake made Father Gunn know that this was not so. But he couldn't close the doors of heaven to a little soul.

He still had his stole on.

'Bill Hayes is downstairs, he could be the godfather. What about a godmother?'

'Maisie will stand for him . . .'

'But later, the boy might like to . . .'

'It doesn't matter what the boy might like later on. Will we do it or will we not?'

Father Gunn said the words of baptism while pouring the holy water on the head of Declan Blake. He had asked was there to be any other name – people usually had two.

'Declan will do,' said Jims Blake.

Maisie, her face red from crying, her voice almost inaudible from a heavy chest cold, made the vows together with Bill Hayes, the local solicitor – they would look after the spiritual welfare of this child.

Bill Hayes, the local solicitor in Shancarrig, had children the same age as Jims Blake's, including a newly born baby girl, safely delivered from a living wife not four weeks previously.

Never short of the right word in terms of the law, Bill Hayes found himself totally unable to give any meaningful sympathy at a time like this.

'If you were a drinking man I'd get you drunk, Jims,' he said.

'But you're not a drinking man either, Bill.'

'Still, I could become one if it would help you.'

The doctor shook his head.

He had seen too many people opting for this solution.

'Would I sit with you downstairs by the fire?'

Poor Bill Hayes was truly at a loss for the comforting small talk that came to him so easily in his office when consoling those who had been cut out of wills or who had lost a court case. Nothing seemed appropriate to say.

'No. Go home, Bill. I beg you. I'll sit by myself. There's a doctor coming in from the town. He'll be staying in the spare room tonight . . . in case I get a call-out. He'll do it for me tonight. I wouldn't be much good to anyone.'

'Did Frances know she had a son?' Bill Hayes asked. He knew his wife would want to know – it wasn't the kind of question he would normally ask.

'No. She knew nothing at all.'

'Well, well. He'll grow up a credit to you both. I know that.'

Jims tried to remember that he had a son, a boy who would grow in this house, as the girls had grown. A baby who would be fed with a bottle, and who would cry in the night. A baby who would smile and flail with little fists. A baby boy who would sit in a dressing gown and want to hear stories read aloud to him.

Suddenly it was all too much for him. He could see other pictures crowding in. A little boy with a school satchel, struggling along the road to Shancarrig school. A boy with a hurley going to a match. He almost felt dizzy with the responsibility of it all.

A wave of loneliness swept over him. There would be no Frances ever again. No Frances so proud of the girls in their little powder-blue coats, going up the church with them at mass. No Frances to talk to in the evening. She was lying ice-cold already. Tomorrow she would be taken to the church and then the whole of Shancarrig would process to the churchyard.

His father and mother would come, his sisters and his brother, rosary beads dangling from their hands, nudging each other, whispering. No help or support to anyone.

The Fitzgeralds would come, the women in hats looking down at the Blake women in headscarves. There would be stiff and stilted conversation in the house.

Not one of them knew how terrible it was that his wife had died, and that he felt responsible. If it hadn't been for that time . . . the time they must have conceived the child . . . Frances would be alive and well tonight.

He said goodbye to Bill Hayes, who left with some relief. And then Jims Blake sat down at his fire and tried to count his blessings, like he always urged his patients to do.

He listed a good marriage with Frances as a blessing. Nearly seven years of it. Great passion, great friendship, a happy time full of hope.

He listed his little girls, he listed the big house in The Terrace, left to him by his good, kind partner. And a big steady doctor's practice. He counted in having escaped from his own family as a blessing, and he added his own good health. He did not include his son, the baby not yet one day old.

Everyone said that it was the worst funeral they were ever at – the rain lashing against the church, the traces of old snow slippery on the ground, a freezing east wind as they walked to the cemetery.

Jims Blake insisted that the girls be taken home after the mass. In fact, as he stood shaking hands with the congregation of sympathisers, many of them with heavy colds and flu, he begged them not to come to the grave.

'Things are bad enough already, don't get pneumonia,' he urged them.

But in Shancarrig people felt it was only right and respectful to accompany a funeral to the final resting place. They stood, a wretched group, as the wind caught the coats of the gravediggers and blew the few flowers away from the top of the coffin, hurtling them in a macabre sort of dance around the gravestones.

Back in The Terrace they asked in hushed tones how he would manage. What was he going to do? The loss of Frances wasn't just that of a wife, it was the loss of the person who managed the home. Three little children. Every time they said three he got a shock.

He thought of Eileen and Sheila with their little faces. He had forgotten about the baby.

This wasn't at all healthy, he told himself. And as his relations and friends drank sherry and ate plates of sandwiches in the rooms downstairs he went up wearily to look at his son.

The child was sleeping as he went into the room.

Tiny and red as all children, he seemed swamped and smothered by the bedding, his tiny perfect little fists with their minuscule nails on the pillow. Was it his imagination or did the baby look more helpless and alone than any other child? As if he knew he was motherless from the moment he had come on earth.

'I'll do my best for you, Declan,' he promised aloud. It was curiously formal and he felt himself remote as he said it. It was like a contract or a bargain between strangers, not a father to his infant son.

He hadn't heard anyone come into the room they called the nursery, but turned to find Nora Kelly, the young schoolmistress married to the master.

'Can I pick him up?' she whispered softly, as if she were in a sickroom.

'Of course, Nora.'

He saw the woman who had been aching to have her own child lift the tiny baby and hold him to her breast.

She said nothing, just walked around the room.

Her stance was that of a woman who had always nursed a child. Her hold on the baby was sure, her love obvious. No one except Jims Blake would know the amount of examination she had undergone to try and discover why she could not conceive.

He watched, almost mesmerised, as she walked to and fro crooning a very soft sound to the baby boy.

He didn't know how long they were there – the strange tableau of the doctor, the teacher and child. But he felt this slow urge coming over him to give away his baby son. He wanted more than anything in the world to say to Nora Kelly: 'Take him home, you have none, you never will have any. I don't want this child that killed Frances . . . Bring him back home and rear him as your own.'

In a more civilised society that's what people would have done. Why would it be the scandal of Shancarrig, the talk of the county and, moreover, a crime against the law of the land, for someone to walk out of this room with the child they so desperately wanted, taking him from a home where he wasn't needed?

Then he pulled himself together.

'I'll go on down, Nora. Stay here a bit if you want to.'

'No, I'd better come down too, Doctor,' she said.

He knew that the same solution had crossed her mind, and she was banishing it, as he had.

It was on occasions like this that Mrs Kennedy, the mournful bleak-looking housekeeper to Father Gunn, came into her own. She slid almost invisibly into the house of the bereaved, suggesting, helping and organising. She would arrive with a supply of gleaming white tablecloths to hand them, then in a trice sum up what the house would need in order to give hospitality to those who would come to sympathise. A quick word with the hotel across the road from The Terrace about extra cups, glasses and plates while Maisie listened to it all wringing her hands. Mrs Kennedy had the authority of the clergy because she had worked with them for so long.

She never interfered, she just guided.

Maisie wouldn't have known about the need for good hot soup to serve with the sandwiches, nor that a room should be cleared for people's coats and umbrellas. Mrs Kennedy managed to imply that she was the voice of order and sanity in sad circumstances like these. And in houses rich and poor all over Shancarrig people had gone along with her, feeling a sense of overpowering relief that someone was taking charge.

Jims Blake greeted people, accepted their condolences, poured them more drinks, enquired about their health, but he did so with only part of his brain. He was working out what arrangements he was going to make. He did so by elimination. He would not have either of his unmarried sisters to live in the house, and he must make that clear before any offer was made. He would not have anyone from the Fitzgerald side of the family either, though they were less likely to present themselves.

Maisie couldn't manage a baby. It would be too expensive to have a live-in nurse. What was he to do?

As he had done so often, he asked himself what old Charles Nolan would have done. Again the voice came to him, booming as it would have been. 'Isn't the countryside crawling with young girls dying to get out from under their parents? Any one of them will have brought up a rake of brothers and sisters. They'll be well able to look after one small baby.'

He felt better then, and was even able to smile at Foxy Dunne, one of the boldest of the entire Dunne clan from the cottages – a red-haired boy in raggy trousers who had come to the door to sympathise.

'I'm sorry for your trouble,' Foxy had said, standing confidently in the cold outside Number Three The Terrace.

'Thank you, Foxy. It was good of you to call.'

The boy was looking past him to the table where there was food and orange squash.

'Well then . . .' Foxy said.

'Would you like to come in and . . . sympathise inside?'

'That's very good of you, Sir,' said Foxy, and was past him and at the table in two seconds.

Maisie looked disapproving and was on the point of ejecting him. Mrs Kennedy frowned heavily.

Dr Jims shook his head.

'Mr Dunne has come to sympathise, Maisie. Mrs Kennedy, can you please give him a slice of cake?'

The nurse was booked to stay for a month and Jims Blake began his search for the girl who would bring up his son. It didn't take long.

He found Carrie, a big-boned, dark-haired girl of twenty-four, living on the side of a hill, deeply discontented with a life that involved cooking for six unappreciative brothers. He had been to the house on several occasions, usually to deal with injuries from threshing machines or otherwise around the farm. He had never treated the girl, but when he was called to their place to stitch the father's head after yet another violent altercation with some farm machinery, it occurred to Jims Blake that Carrie might be glad of the offer of a place, and a better situation.

They walked to the farmyard gate and he told her what he had in mind.

'Why me, Doctor? I'd be a bit ignorant for the kind of house you run.'

'You'd be kind. You could manage a child. You managed all this lot.' He jerked his head back at the house where she had looked after brothers, older and younger than herself, since her own mother died.

'I'm not very smart,' she said.

'You're fine. But here's a few pounds anyway, in case you want to buy yourself some clothes to travel in.'

It was a nice way to put it. He knew the travelling which meant taking a few belongings on the next lift she could get to the town wasn't important, but it covered the fact that she hadn't an outfit to wear.

Maisie sniffed a bit at the news of the new arrival, but not too much. After all, the poor young doctor was still in mourning, and mustn't be upset. And it had been very clear from the outset that Carrie would help Maisie in the house. There would be no question of meals on a tray for a fancy nurse.

Declan Blake was only ten days old when Carrie took him in her arms.

'He's a bit like my own,' she said quietly to Dr Blake.

'You had one of your own?' The world was full of surprises. She had never consulted him about the pregnancy.

'Up in Dublin. He's given away, it was for the best. He's three now, somewhere.'

'As you say, it would have been hard to have reared him.' His voice held its usual gentle sympathetic tone, but it came from the heart. This gawky girl wouldn't think it was at all for the best that her three-year-old had been given away.

'I'll do a good job minding this little fellow, Dr Jims,' she said.

It reminded him of his own vow to the child. Everyone was promising this tiny baby some kind of care, as if the baby feared he wouldn't get any.

The summer eventually came that year, and Dr Jims took his little daughters by the hand up to Shancarrig school.

He walked around the three classrooms with them, and showed them the globe and the map of the world. He pointed out the ink wells in the desks and told them that soon they'd be dipping their own pens in there and doing their exercises. Solemnly they all studied the charts showing the Irish lettering for the alphabet.

'You'll be able to speak Irish when you leave here,' he promised them.

'Who would we speak it to?' Eileen asked.

Mrs Kelly was standing at the door and gave one of her rare smiles.

'It's a good question,' she said ruefully.

Dr Jims had sent her to Dublin again for further tests, none of the results being remotely helpful. There was no reason that specialists could find why the Kellys were not conceiving a child. He remembered his strange urge to bundle the baby into her arms on that unreal day back at The Terrace. He knew how near he had been to saying something so unsettling that it could never have been unsaid.

Again, this time she seemed to be thinking along the same lines.

'How is Declan?' she asked the children. 'It won't be long now until you'll be bringing him along to school with you.'

'Oh, he'd be useless. He never says anything at all,' Eileen said.

'And he'd wet the floor,' Sheila added, in case there was any question of enrolling the baby.

'Not now. The child's only ten weeks old on Friday. You were the same at that age.' Mrs Kelly spoke in her stern teacher's voice. Eileen and Sheila drew back in awe.

Jims Blake noted that Nora Kelly remembered the exact age of the baby boy he had wanted to give her.

If he had been asked he couldn't have said without counting back to the April day when Frances had died.

'Come on now, girls. We mustn't delay Mrs Kelly.' He began to shepherd them home.

'I'm sure you're dying to be back to him,' she said.

'Yes. Yes, of course.' His voice sounded false and he knew it.

As they closed the school gate he wondered was he unnatural not to hurry home to see a sleeping infant? He didn't think so. When Eileen and Sheila were babies he didn't see them for hours on end, and then only when presented with them by Frances after bathtime. Surely that was the way most men felt?

He mustn't dwell on that one highly charged moment on the day of his wife's funeral. Rationally of course he had no intention of giving away the baby that she had died bringing into the world. It was foolish to keep harking back to it with guilt.

He had perfectly normal feelings towards this child, and the hiring of Carrie had been inspired. She had indeed a natural instinct of motherhood, and she seemed to know that they wanted as little sign of a baby about the house as possible.

The girls went to the nursery each evening to play with him and to hear stories of Carrie's wild brothers, and the desperate injuries they had endured. She told them nothing of the child born in Dublin and given away. She sat rocking the substitute baby Declan in her arms.

Jims Blake called in from time to time. Not every day.

He knew that Mrs Kelly at the school would find this unbelievable.

That evening he went into the nursery.

Carrie was sitting at a table with pen and ink and several sheets of screwed-up paper.

'I was never one for writing, Doctor,' she said.

'We're all good at different things. Aren't you marvellous with the child?'

'Anyone would love a baby.' She shrugged it off.

'Yes,' he said.

Something in his voice made her look up. 'Well, it's different in your case ... I mean, being a man and everything, and your poor wife dying giving birth to him.'

'I don't blame him for that.' It was true. Jims Blake blamed himself, not his son, for the death of Frances.

'You'll grow to love him. Wait till he starts to call you Daddy . . . and clings to your legs. They're lovely at that age.'

She must have been thinking about her brothers, he realised. She didn't see her own child grow.

He changed the subject. 'Could I help you at all with the writing . . . or is it private?' He saw Carrie look at him. In many ways he had the same status as Father Gunn, a man who knew secrets, a man who could be told things.

Carrie had a brother in gaol. None of the rest of the family wrote to him. She wanted him to feel that he wasn't forgotten, that there'd be a place for him when he got out. It was told trustingly and simply.

He sat down at the table and took out his pen.

He wrote a letter to the boy, whose head he had stitched some years back, as if the letter came from Carrie. He told of the changes in the farm, the new barn, the way they had let the lower field go to grass. He told how Jacky Noone had got a new truck, and how Cissy had married. He said that Shancarrig looked fine in the summer sunshine and would be waiting to greet him when he came home.

Haltingly Carrie read it aloud, and tears came to her eyes. 'You're such a good man, Doctor. You knew what I wanted to say, even though I didn't know myself.'

'Here. You can have my fountain pen as a present. You'll get into less of a mess with it than trying to dip that thing there.' The baby began to cry and the doctor stood up. He walked to the door without going to see the child. 'Copy that out, Carrie, yourself. It's no use sending the boy my letter. You copy it and next time I'll give you more ideas.'

She picked the child up and looked at him with a face confused. A man so kind as to spend time writing a letter to her gaol-bird brother, a man who would give her his own good pen, but wouldn't pick up his son who was ten weeks old.

When Declan Blake was three Carrie had a cake for him with three candles and there was a party in the nursery. Maisie made special drop scones for the occasion. The girls got him presents of sweets and they all sang 'Happy Birthday' before he blew the candles out.

Jims Blake looked at the small excited face of his son, the snub nose and the straight shiny hair washed especially for the day. He was wearing a new yellow jumper which Carrie must have bought in the town. He left money for the children's clothes with Carrie and for the food with Maisie. Together they ran his house very well for him.

He had a curious empty feeling when the birthday song was over, as if something were expected of him.

It was only ten years ago in this house that Charles Nolan had urged him to marry. Ten years of visiting people and hearing their troubles and learning their hopes, realistic or wildly beyond their reach. He didn't know what his own hopes were. He had never had time to work them out, he told himself.

The children were still looking at him.

In his mind he asked old Charles Nolan what to do and he heard himself saying . . .

'Why don't we sing "For He's a Jolly Good Fellow" . . . ?'

Their eyes lit up, Carrie's face softened, the girls shouted the chorus and Declan clapped his hands to be the centre of such attention. Jims Blake felt the moment frozen for a long time.

The day came sooner than he ever thought it would when Declan should be brought to school.

'A great day for you, Doctor, to see your son setting out with a satchel,' Carrie had said.

Jims Blake looked at the child. 'It's a great day all right. Isn't it, Declan?'

Declan looked up at him solemnly, as if he were a stranger. 'It is, yes.' He spoke shyly, and half hid himself behind Carrie, scuffing his new shoes a little on the ground, and seeming awkward.

Probably all children that age are awkward with their fathers, the doctor told himself. He watched from the window as his son went off to school on wobbly legs.

The doctor meant to ask how the day went, but he was out on calls when Declan came home, and the next morning there wasn't time to talk either. It was a week before he even knew that there was a problem about Carrie delivering Declan to the school.

'The other children call him a baby,' Carrie explained.

'He's too young at five to walk all that way by himself,' his father protested.

'Other children do. All the young Dunnes come up from the cottages on their own . . .'

'Those Dunnes aren't children at all, they're like monkeys. They were climbing trees barefoot when they were two years old.'

Jims Blake was indignant that there should be any comparison.

'But it's terrible to have him made a jeer of. Maybe he could go with the girls . . . ?'

'The girls say they don't want him traipsing after them. They have their own friends . . .'

Carrie looked at him as if he had let her down. Jims Blake felt a wave of self-pity sweep over him. Why was he always made out to be in the wrong? He thought he was doing his best for all of them, not loading Eileen and Sheila down with dragging their baby brother, and now he was the worst in the world as a result.

None of his patients challenged what he said. They took their tablets, drank their medicine bottles, changed poultices and dressings, made journeys into hospitals for tests, without ever doubting him.

Only at home did his every action seem suspect.

Later, when he was helping Carrie with her letters, as he did every week, underlining a spelling mistake lightly in pencil, she looked at him, troubled.

'You're a very good man, Doctor.'

'Why do you say that?'

'You correct me without insulting me. I write "yez" meaning "you all" and you just say, "Wouldn't it be better to put you all, it might be clearer" . . . You don't say I'm pig ignorant!'

'But you're *not* pig ignorant.'

'Maybe you shouldn't be teaching me all the time. Maybe you should be doing pot hooks with Declan.'

'Pot hooks?'

'It's how they teach them to write.'

'I don't want to be cutting across Mrs Kelly and her ways.'

He did look at Declan's copy book though, and asked him knowledgeably, 'Are these pot hooks, then?'

'Yes, Daddy.'

'Very good. Very good, keep at them,' he said. There was the familiar feeling that it hadn't been the right thing to say.

Since he had organised them all to sing 'For He's a Jolly Good Fellow' when Declan was three, there had hardly been a time when he was sure that the right thing had been said.

Eileen and Sheila always asked about his patients, ever since they had been very young.

'Is Mrs Barton going to die?' They liked the quiet dressmaker who lived with her only son in the pink house on the hill.

'No, of course not. She's only got the flu.'

'Is Miss Ross going to have a baby?' They had seen her knitting and thought the two went together.

'Was there much blood in the car crash?'

He parried their questions, kept the secrecy and diffused the sense of drama, and always he was aware that his son never asked him questions.

As the years went by he was even more aware of it. The girls left Shancarrig school and went to be boarders at a good convent school fifty miles away. There was now only the doctor and Maisie and Declan left in the house.

Carrie had given her own notice when Declan made his first communion.

'He's seven now, Doctor. He's a grown lad. He can dress himself, keep his room tidy, do his homework and all. You don't need me.'

'And maybe you're thinking of getting married?' There was nothing Dr Jims didn't see or know.

'I'm not going to say much about it.'

'And is it the father of the little lad?'

'Yes, it is. Thanks to you, Doctor, I was able to write to him a bit, tell him things, speak my mind. You're a great man for getting people to say things out. There's far too many round here who bottle it all up.'

He was pleased at her praise. 'You'll have another child. I know you'll never forget the first one, but you'll be a family now.' He was full of happiness for this dark-haired angular girl, who had such a poor start in life.

'And you'll have a chance to get to know your son more, maybe, when I'm gone.'

'Ah, that will come, that will come. I was thinking of getting a desk up here for him to do his homework.'

'The girls always did it downstairs, you know, more in the hub of things.'

'But he'd like it here. More independent. Wouldn't he?'

'He might feel a bit shut away.' Her eyes were troubled.

'Not a bit of it, it would let him concentrate. Anyway, enough of such things. You'll come back and see us?'

'Of course I will. It was the best seven years of my life. I grew up properly in this house. I was very privileged.' He tried to brush it away. 'I mean it, Doctor Jims. I wouldn't even have been able to use a word like privileged when I came here. Isn't that living proof?'

When she was gone he made deliberate efforts to get involved in his son's world.

Always he seemed choked off.

Declan did his homework silently up in the room that used to be called the nursery, then he would come down and sit with Maisie in the kitchen while she prepared the supper. Dr Jims was out so often it seemed only sensible for the boy to eat with Maisie, after all he had eaten his meals with Carrie when she was there to look after him.

He tried to think of things to interest Declan. 'Are you on to fractions yet, lad?'

'I don't know.'

'You must know. Either you are or you aren't.' His voice was suddenly impatient.

'We might be. Sometimes you call things one thing and they call it another at school.'

'And how's your friend, Dinnie?'

'Vinnie.'

'Yes, Vinnie. How is he?'

'He's all right, I think, Dad.'

'Well, surely you know whether he's all right or not?' Again the impatience arising without control, the tone of his voice changing.

'I mean, I haven't seen him for ages.'

'Aren't you friends any more?'

'I don't know. We might be. He's living in the town, I'm here.'

Guilt then. Had he not listened? Had he ever been told? Surely other parents had this confusion about their children's friends.

And of course, girls were easier too, anyone knew that. There had never been any trouble about Eileen and Sheila. He knew who their friends were. They talked about them, they brought them to The Terrace. When they came home from boarding school they always sought out Nessa Ryan from the hotel, and Leo Murphy, the daughter of Major Murphy up at The Glen.

Boys were hard to fathom. They lived in a secretive world of their own, it seemed. Jims Blake looked back on his own childhood, on the small bleak farm with the dour uncommunicative father who had hardly ever thrown him a word. He was behaving so differently from that silent man, and still meeting rebuff, it seemed.

The girls talked to him very easily. Eileen came and sat on a footstool in his study, hugging her knees. 'Leo Murphy's got all odd and snooty this year,' she complained.

'Is that a fact?' Jims Blake had his own worries about the mental health of Miriam Murphy, the girl's mother.

'Yes. She wouldn't let me in when I went up to The Glen, just said she couldn't play today. *Play*, as if I was a child or she was a child.'

'I know, I know.' He was soothing.

'And Nessa Ryan says the same thing about her, snooty as anything. She won't let you into her house, as if anyone wanted to go.'

'Maybe Maisie could make you a nice tea here . . .'

'She doesn't want to go to anyone else's house either, Nessa says.'

'At least you have Nessa,' he said consolingly.

Eileen flounced. 'Yes, and who needs Leo Murphy and her big house? Ours is much smarter than theirs anyway.'

'Don't be boasting about our good fortune in having a nice house,' he said.

He had tried to tell them all about the good fortune in being given a house of such quality by the late Dr Nolan, but his loyal daughters dismissed it. They thought their father was worth it and more, they said.

Eileen was going to go to university if she got a lot of honours in her Leaving Certificate. She would be an architect. She would love that. The nuns said she had all the brains in the world and by the time she was qualified the world, and indeed Ireland, would be moving to the point where women architects would be quite acceptable. It would be the 1960s after all. Imagine.

And Sheila wanted to do nursing, so he was already sending out feelers for her to the better training hospitals in Dublin.

Declan would do medicine, of course, so the main thing was to get him into a good boarding school. He had spoken to the Jesuits, the Benedictines, the Vincentians and the Holy Ghost Fathers. There were advantages and drawbacks in all of them. He checked the records, the achievements, the teaching records and he chose the one that came out best overall. The bad side was that it was further away than any other school.

'You won't be able to go and see him much there,' Eileen said.

'He'll come home in the holidays.' Dr Jims knew he was being defensive. Again.

'But it's lovely to have visitors at school. We loved you coming on Sundays.'

He used to go every second week, a long, wet drive in winter. He had never taken Declan. At first he would have been too young and restless for the drive, and the girls would have hated him to be troublesome when he arrived in the parlour. Then later, it didn't seem the right thing to suggest.

A ten-year-old boy wouldn't *want* to be dragged off to a girls' school of a Sunday even if he had been invited. It would be a sissy sort of thing for a boy.

He intended to spend more time with the boy during the summer before

Declan went to boarding school, but there was so much to do. There was the whole business of Maura Brennan's child for one thing.

He had always liked Maura, the only Brennan girl to stay in Shancarrig. The others had long gone to unsatisfactory posts in England. Maura had a dreamy quality about her, an acceptance of what life had to offer. He remembered the day he had confirmed her pregnancy.

'He'll never marry me, Dr Jims,' she had said, big tears waiting to fall from her eyes.

'I wouldn't be sure of that. Aren't you a great catch for any man?' He had said it but his heart wasn't in the words. He had thought Gerry O'Sullivan would disappear but he had been wrong, Gerry stayed. There had been a wedding, he had gone in to Johnny Finn's to drink their health.

And then when he had delivered her child it was he who saw the epicanthic folds around the eyes. It was he who had to tell Maura O'Sullivan, as she so proudly called herself, that her son was a child with Down's syndrome.

He remembered how he had held the girl in his arms and told her it would all be all right. Even when Father Gunn had told him that Gerry O'Sullivan, father of the boy, had taken the train from Shancarrig station and was gone before the baptism, he remembered the sense of hearing his own voice mouth the words of comfort, telling Maura that everything would be fine.

And he had been right to say that she would always love young Michael with an overpowering love. That much had been true even if Gerry O'Sullivan was never seen in the streets of Shancarrig again.

There was a human story everywhere he turned . . . in the small houses and in the big ones.

There was something seriously wrong up at The Glen and he didn't know how to cope with it. Frank Murphy, a quiet man who bore his war injuries bravely, had something much more serious on his mind than the bad leg he dragged after him so uncomplainingly.

Jims Blake thought it had to do with his wife. But Miriam Murphy was someone he had never examined. She assured him she was as strong as a horse. She was an attractive woman with a dismissive manner if crossed, and he had liked her red-gold hair and her effortless way of looking elegant while walking around the big gardens with a shallow basket, an old silk scarf draped over her shoulders.

People in Shancarrig had long grown accustomed to the fact that Mrs Murphy never came down to the shops. There were accounts in the shops and the delivery boys who called on bicycles always got a friendly wave from the mistress of The Glen. They would deal with Biddy the maid, or with the Major himself.

But this summer there was something different about Miriam. A vacancy in her eyes that was more than disturbing. And a cautious protective look in Frank's that hadn't been there before. Charles Nolan had told him often enough about families who guarded their secrets, who kept their unstable people hidden. Often it was better not to pry.

Jims Blake wondered what old Charles would have made of the situation in The Glen. Not only was the Major in a state of distress, but their daughter Leo, who had been such a close friend of his daughters, had also begun to show signs of strain. He met the girl when driving past Barna Woods.

'Do you want a lift back up to the house, Leo?'

'Are you going that way?'

'A car goes whatever way you point it.'

'Thanks, Doctor.'

'Have you lots of new friends for yourself this summer, Leo?'

She was surprised. No, it turned out she hadn't any. Why did he ask? Without putting his own children in the role of complainers he hinted that she hadn't been around.

'We went on a bit of a holiday, you see, to the seaside.'

That was true. He had heard Bill Hayes say that the Major had packed dogs and all into the car and driven off without warning.

'Ah, but you're back now, and still no one ever sees you. I thought you'd gone off with the gypsies.' They had just driven in the gate of The Glen as he said this. She looked at him, as white as a sheet. 'It's all right, Leo. I was only joking.'

'I hate jokes about the gypsies,' she said.

He wondered had they frightened her in the woods. Dark, suspicious and always on guard, they had given him a pheasant once, when he had delivered a child for them. Unsmiling and proud they had handed him the bird, wrapped in grass, to thank him for the skill they hadn't sought, but had used because he was passing near during a difficult birth.

The Major appeared at the door. 'I won't ask you in,' he said.

'No, no.' His reputation as a discreet man who could be told anything rested on ending conversations when others wanted to. He never probed a step further, but his face was always open and ready to hear when others wanted to tell.

His son Declan never wanted to tell anything.

'Will you like being at the school do you think, Declan?'

'I won't know, not really, until I get there.'

Had there ever been a boy so pedantic, so unwilling to talk?

Maisie wanted to know had he settled in? Was the bed aired? Were there any other boys from this part of the world there?

Dr Jims Blake could answer none of this. His only memory was his son's hand waving goodbye. He wasn't clinging, like one or two other lads were, loath to leave mothers go. Nor was he chatting and making friends as some of the more outgoing boys seemed to be doing.

They had to write letters home every Sunday. Declan wrote of saints' days, and walks, and doing a play, making a relief map. Jims Blake knew that these letters were supervised by the priests, that they were intended to give a good impression of the school and all its activities. Sometimes the letter lay unopened on the hall table along with the advertising literature from pharmaceutical companies that was sent to all doctors on a mailing list.

Declan didn't write to Eileen, now in a hostel in Dublin while she studied architecture in University College. He didn't write to Sheila, now nursing in one of Dublin's best hospitals. He sent a birthday card to Maisie, but they knew very little about his world at school.

The reports said that he was satisfactory, his marks were average, his place in the class was in the top end of the lower half.

His school holidays seemed long and formless. The doctor got the impression that he was dying to be back at school.

'Would you like to ask any of your friends to stay?'

'Here?' Declan had been surprised.

'Well, there's plenty of room. They might like it.'

'What would they do, Daddy?'

'I don't know. Whatever they do, whatever you do anywhere.' He was irritated now. It was this habit of answering one question with another that he found hard to take.

It never came to anything, that suggestion. Nor the invitation to go to Dublin.

'What would I do in Dublin for two days?'

'What does anyone do in Dublin? We could see your sisters, take them out to lunch. That would be nice, wouldn't it?' He realised he sounded as if he was talking to a five-year-old, not a boy of fifteen. A boy who had grown apart from Eileen, now nearly qualified as an architect, from Sheila, now almost a qualified nurse.

The visit never happened. Neither did the outing to the Galway races, which had been long spoken of as a reward when Declan's Leaving Certificate was over.

Jims Blake said he could put his hand on his heart and swear that he had made every move to try and get close to his son, and that at every turn he was repelled.

It wasn't a thing that he would normally talk to another man about, but he did mention it to Bill Hayes. 'Do you find it like ploughing a hard field trying to get a word out of your fellow, Niall, or does he talk to you?'

'Niall would talk to the birds in the trees if he thought they'd listen. He has a yarn for every moment of the day. Not much knack of dealing with clients, though.'

Bill Hayes shook his head gloomily. His son too seemed a slight disappointment to him. Although a qualified solicitor he showed no signs of being able to attract new business or, indeed, cope with the business that was already there.

'And does he talk to *you*?' Dr Jims persisted.

'When he can get me to listen, which isn't often. I don't want to hear rambling tales about the mountains and the lakes when he goes out to make some farmer's will for him. I want to hear that it's been done properly, the man's affairs are settled and everything's in order.'

Dr Jims sighed. 'With me it's just the opposite. I can't even get him to talk about enrolling up at the university. He keeps making excuses.'

'Talk to him at a meal. Don't serve him until he answers your question ... That'll get an answer out of him. Boys love their food.'

Jims Blake was ashamed to say why this wouldn't work, to admit that his son still ate meals in the kitchen with Maisie, out of habit, out of tradition. No point in laying up two places in the dining room. Who knew when the poor doctor would have to be called out?

But the summer of 1964 was moving on. Arrangements would have to be made, fees must be paid, places in the Medical School reserved, living quarters booked.

'Declan? No one would ever think we lived in the same house, lad . . .'

'I'm always here,' the boy said. It wasn't mutinous or defensive, it was said as a simple fact.

Jims Blake was annoyed by it.

'I'm always here too,' he said. 'Except when I'm out working, as you will be.'

'I'm not going to do medicine, Dad.'

Somehow, it came as no surprise. He must have been expecting it.

'When did you decide against it?' His voice was cold.

'I never decided *for* it, it was only in your mind. It wasn't in mine.'

They talked like strangers, polite but firm.

Declan would like to join an auctioneering firm. His friend Vinnie O'Neill's father would take him on. He'd like the life. It was the kind of thing that appealed to him, looking at places, showing them to customers. He was good at talking to people, telling them the good points of a place. There'd be a very good living in it for him. Vinnie was going off to be a priest. There was no other boy in the family, only girls. Mr O'Neill liked him, got on well with him.

Jims Blake listened bleakly to the story of a man he didn't know, a man called Gerry O'Neill, whose estate agent's signs he had seen around the place. A man who got on well with Declan Blake and regarded him as a kind of son now that his own was going to enter the priesthood. Silently he accepted the plans, plans that involved Declan going to live in the big town. He could have Vinnie's room, apparently. It would be easier to have him on the spot, and the sooner the better.

Vinnie was going to the seminary next week. Declan thought he'd move in at the weekend.

Jims Blake heard that Maisie wouldn't miss him because so much of her life was now centred around the church. And she had got used to him being away at school.

'And what about me?' Jims Blake said. 'What about my missing you?'

'Aw, Dad, you're your own person. You wouldn't miss me.'

It was said with total sincerity, and when the boy realised that there actually was loneliness in his father's face, he seemed distressed.

'But even if I were going to be doing medicine wouldn't I be away all the time?'

'You'd be coming back to help me in the practice, and take over. That's what I thought.'

There was a silence. A long silence.

'I'm sorry,' Declan said.

Later Jims wondered should he have put his arm around the boy's shoulder. Should he have made some gesture to apologise for the coldness and distance of eighteen years, to hope that the next years would be better. But he shrugged. 'You must do as you want to,' he said. And then he heard himself saying, 'It's what you've always done.'

He knew it was the most final goodbye he could ever have said.

Sometimes when he was in the town Jims Blake called in to O'Neill's. Like someone probing a sore tooth he was anxious to see the man and the home where Declan Blake felt he belonged. Gerry O'Neill, a florid man with a fund of anecdotes about people and places, regarded himself as a great raconteur. Jims Blake found him boring and opinionated. He sat and watched unbelievingly while the man's wife and daughters and Declan laughed and encouraged him in these tales.

The eldest girl was Ruth, a good-looking girl, her Daddy's pet. She was doing a commercial course in the local secretarial college so that she could help in the business. They talked of O'Neill's Auctioneers as if it was a long-established and widely respected family firm, instead of a Mickey Mouse operation set up by Gerry O'Neill himself on the basis of being a fast talker.

'Invite Ruth to The Terrace some time, won't you?' Jims asked his son.

He could see that Declan was very attracted to the dark-eyed girl in his new family.

'I don't think so . . .'

'I'm not asking you to live there, I'm just asking you to bring the girl to Sunday lunch, for God's sake.' Again, the harsh ungracious words that he didn't mean to speak. His son looked taken aback.

'Yes, well. Of course . . . some time.'

Jims Blake contemplated getting an assistant. He realised now how the lonely old Charles Nolan must have relished him coming to stay in that house all those years ago. How he had felt able to will him the place, as well as the practice. Jims had thought the same thing would have happened with Declan. He had foreseen evenings like he had had with Charles, discussing articles in the *Lancet* and the *Irish Medical Times*, wondering about a new cure-all cream with apparently magical qualities that had come from one of the drug firms.

There was a phone call every week from Sheila in her Dublin hospital, and a letter every week from Eileen, now working in an architect's practice in England.

He had almost forgotten what Frances had looked like, or felt like in his arms. He should not have felt like an old man, after all he was only in his late fifties, yet he had the distinct feeling that his life, such as it was, was over.

Declan did bring Ruth to lunch eventually. And the girl chattered easily and eagerly, as she did in her own home. She asked questions, seemed interested in the answers. She asked Maisie about doing the flowers for the altar. Maisie said she was a girl of great breeding, and that Declan was very lucky to have met her and not some foolish fast girl, like he might well have met in the town.

On her third visit she took the initiative and leaned over to kiss him goodbye.

'Thank you, Dr Jims,' she said. She smelled of Knight's Castile soap, fresh and lovely. He was not surprised his son was so taken by her.

He was horrified when he saw Declan some weeks later. The boy arrived on a Thursday afternoon, Maisie's half day. He was ashen white, but the circles under his eyes were deep purple shadows.

He paced the house until the last patient left. 'Will there be any more?'

'I have to go out the country. One of Carrie's brothers. Do you remember Carrie?'

'Of course I do. Can I come with you?'

Somehow Jims Blake found the right silences and didn't choose the wrong words. He didn't ask what had the boy out on a working day, and looking so terrible. Instead he smiled and opened the hall door for him. They walked together to the car, father and son, down the steps of Number Three The Terrace, as he had always wanted to walk with a son.

They talked of nothing during the drive out to the farm where one of Carrie's brothers had impaled himself on yet another piece of rusting machinery. Declan watched wordlessly as his father cleaned the wound and stitched it.

The talk came on the way back.

They stopped under the shadow of the Old Rock, the big craggy monument from which Shancarrig took its name. They walked a little in the crisp afternoon with the shadows of the trees lengthening.

Jims Blake heard the story. The terrible tale of a boy invited into a good man's house. How Gerry O'Neill would lie down dead when he knew Ruth was pregnant. How her brother Vinnie, studying to be a priest, would never forgive such a betrayal.

The boy had not slept or eaten for a week, and presumably neither had the girl. It was the end of the road. Declan wanted them to run away, but Ruth wouldn't go, and in his saner moments he realised that she was right.

'You realise how bad things are, if I had to tell you,' he said to his father.

Jims Blake bit back the retort. At another time he might have made the remark that would drive the boy back into the shell from which he had painfully dragged himself. He didn't ask what Declan wanted of him. He knew that Declan himself barely knew. So instead he did what he had been intending to do all his life, he put his arm around his son's shoulder.

He pretended not to notice the flinching in surprise. 'I'll tell you what I think,' he said. His voice was calm, almost cheerful. He could feel his son's shoulders relaxing under his arm. 'I have this friend up in Dublin, we did our training together. He's in gynaecology and obstetrics. A specialist now. Quite a well-known man . . . I'll recommend that young Ruth go to see him for a D and C . . . Oh, don't worry, these names are always very alarming. It's called a dilatation and curettage, just an examination under anaesthetic of the neck of the womb. Clears up any disorders. A lot of girls have them . . .'

Declan turned to look at him.

'Is that . . . ? I mean is that the same as . . . ?'

Jims Blake had decided how to play it. 'As I was saying to you, there's no knowing what names all these things go by, the main thing is that Ruth will go in there and be out in a day or two and it can all go through this house and this address without having to bother anyone else.'

They walked back to the car and drove to Shancarrig. The mood was not broken.

His son came in to Number Three The Terrace and sat with him as they lit a fire, because the evening was getting chilly. Declan had a small brandy and some of the colour had returned to his face.

Jims Blake remembered how old Dr Nolan had often said to him that the ways of the world were stranger than anyone would ever believe. Dr Jims Blake agreed with him as he sat there and realised that the only companionable evening he had ever had with his son was the evening he had arranged to abort his own grandchild.

Nora Kelly

Nora and Jim Kelly had no pictures of their wedding. The cousin with the camera had been unreliable. There was something wrong with the film, he told them afterwards.

It didn't matter, they told him.

But to Nora it did. There was nothing to mark the day their marriage began. It hadn't been a very fancy wedding. During the Emergency of course people didn't go in for big flashy do's, not even people with more class and style than Nora and Jim. But theirs had been particularly quiet.

It took place in Lent, because they wanted to have a honeymoon in the Easter Holidays, the two young teachers starting out life together. Nora's mother had been tight-lipped. A Lenten wedding often meant one thing and one thing only, that the privileges of matrimony had been anticipated and that an unexpected pregnancy had resulted.

But this was not the case, Nora and Jim had anticipated nothing. And the pregnancy that her mother feared might disgrace the whole family did not result, even after many years of marriage.

Month after month Nora Kelly reported to her husband that there was no reason to hope for a conception this time either. They shrugged and said it would happen sooner or later. That was for the first three years. Then they consoled each other in a brittle way. Why should two schoolteachers who had the entire child population of Shancarrig to cope with want to bring any more children into the world?

Then they decided to ask for help.

It was not easy for Nora Kelly to approach Dr Jims. He was a courteous man and kind to everyone. She knew that he would not be coy, or too inquisitive. He would reach for his pad and write, as he nodded thoughtfully.

Nora Kelly was pale at the best of times and this was not the best of times. She was a slight young woman with flyaway fair hair. She did it in a braid, which she rolled loosely at the back of her neck.

Nobody in Shancarrig had seen her with hair loose and flowing. They thought her expression a little stern, but that was appropriate for the schoolmistress. Her big husband looked more like a local farmer than the master – it was good to have some authority written on the face of the family.

Someone who had known Nora before she married said she was one of three young girls always dashing about and riding precarious bicycles, in a town some sixty miles away. They were three young harum-scarums, it was said. But it didn't sound likely.

She had no relations there now, she had no identity or past. She was just the schoolmistress – a sensible woman, not given to fancy dressing or notions. Not too fancy a cook either, to judge by what she bought in the butcher's, but a perfectly qualified woman to be teaching their children. It was of course a terrible cross to bear that the Lord hadn't given her children, but who ever knew the full story in these cases?

As she had expected, Dr Jims was kindness itself. The examination was swift and impersonal, the advice gentle and practical – some very simple, maybe even folk, remedies. Dr Jims said that he never despised wisdom handed down through the generations. He had got a cure from the tinkers once, he told her. They knew a lot of things that modern medicine hadn't discovered yet. But they were a people who kept their ways to themselves.

The old wives' advice hadn't worked. There were tests in the hospital in the big town. Jim had to give samples of his sperm. It was wearying, embarrassing, and ultimately depressing. The Kellys were told that, as far as medical science could determine in 1946, there was no reason why they should not conceive. They must live in hope.

Nora Kelly knew that Dr Jims found it hard to deliver this news to her, in an autumn where his own wife was pregnant again. Their little girls were already up at the school, this was another family starting. She saw his sympathy and appreciated it all the more because he didn't speak it aloud. It wasn't easy to be a childless woman in a small town; she had been aware of the sideways glances for a long time. Nora knew that the ways of God were strange and past understanding by ordinary people, but it did seem hard to understand why he kept giving more and more children to the Brennans and the Dunnes in the cottages, families who couldn't feed or care for the children they already had, and passing her by.

Sometimes when she saw the little round faces coming in to start a new life at school the pain she felt in her heart was as real as if it had been a physical one. She watched their little wobbly legs and the way the poorest of them came in shoes that were too big and clothes that were too long. If she and Jim had a child of their own they would look after it so well. It seemed every other woman in the village only had to think about conception to become pregnant – women who claimed to have enough already, women who sighed and said, 'Here we go again.'

When the doctor's baby son was born, in the coldest winter that Shancarrig ever knew, the year that the River Grane had frozen solid for three long months, his wife died at the birth.

Nora Kelly held the infant child in her arms and wished that she could take the little boy home. She and Jim would rear him so well. They would take out the baby clothes, bought and made many years ago, now smelling of mothballs. He would grow up in their school. He would not be over-favoured in front of the others just because he was the teachers' son.

For a wild moment that day in the doctor's nursery, when she had come to sympathise at the funeral, she thought that the doctor was going to give her the baby. But of course it was fantasy.

Nora had heard that couples who didn't have children often grew very close to each other. It was as if the disappointment had united them and the shared lifestyle, without the distractions of a family, made it easier for them to establish an intimacy.

She wished it had happened in her case, but in honesty she couldn't say that it had.

Jim grew more aloof. His walks of an evening became longer and longer. She found herself sitting alone by the fire, or even returning to the schoolroom to draw maps for the next day.

By the time she was twenty-eight years old her husband reached towards her to make love very rarely.

'Sure what's the point?' he said to her one night as she snuggled up to him. And after that she kept very much to her own side of the bed.

They had agreed not to say it was anyone's fault, but Nora looked to her side of the family. Her own two sisters had given birth to small families; one had only two, the other had an only child, while the sisters and sisters-in-law of Jim Kelly seemed to breed like rabbits.

Her sister Kay, who lived in Dublin, had two little boys. Sometimes they came to stay. Nora would feel her heart lurch when she saw how eagerly Jim reached for them and how happily he took them on walks. It was different entirely to the way he taught the children in the school. In the classroom he was patient and fair, but he was formal; there was no happy wildness like with her nephews. He used to take the small boys by the hand, and let them wade through the shallows of the River Grane and bring them to pick mushrooms up near the Old Rock, or to prowl through Barna Woods looking for bears and tigers.

Nora's sister never failed to say: 'He's a born father, isn't he?' Nora's teeth never failed to be set on edge.

She had more contact with her twin sister Helen, even though Helen lived on the other side of the world in Chicago.

She had sent grainy photographs of the baby, little Maria. Helen had gone to Chicago when Nora went to the training college. She didn't have the brains, she said, and she wanted no more studying. She wanted to see the world and make sure she didn't end up in some one-horse town like the one they'd come from.

In fact, Shancarrig was a much smaller one-horse town than their native place. Nora was sure that Helen must pity her. What had she got with all her brains? Marriage, to the increasingly silent Jim, schoolmistress in a tiny backwater, and no children.

Helen's life had been much more exciting. She had worked as a waitress in Stouffers. It was a coffee house – one of the many coffee houses of that name – and they had restaurants as well. She met Lexi when he was delivering the meat from the yards.

Big, blond, handsome Lexi, Polish Catholic, silent, whose dark blue eyes followed her everywhere she went. Helen had written about how he asked her out, how she had been taken to meet his family. They spoke Polish in the home, but in broken English told Helen she was welcome.

When they married in one of the big Polish churches in Chicago no one of Helen's family was there to give her courage. Who could afford a journey halfway across the world in 1942, when that world was at war?

And then Maria was born in 1944, baptised by a Polish priest. There were potato cakes served at the christening party, except they called them latkes, and there was a terrible soup called polewka, which they all drank at the drop of a hat.

Maria was beautiful. Helen wrote this over and over. Nora knew from experience that there wasn't much point in believing old wives' tales – they certainly hadn't been much use in her predicament – but she did believe that twins sort of knew about each other, even when they were almost five thousand miles apart.

She read and reread Helen's letters for some hint of what was troubling her, because Nora Kelly knew that life on Chicago's Southside was not as it was described in the very frequent letters.

On an impulse she wrote to her one spring day in 1948.

'I know it sounds like a tall order, but why don't you bring Maria over to see us in the summer? When the school closes Jim and I have all the time in the world and there's nothing that would please us more.'

Nora wrote warmly inviting Lexi too, but the implication was that he would not be able to take the time. Helen, working only part time in the restaurant now, could arrange leave.

Nora described the flowers and the hedges around Shancarrig. She made the river sound full of sparkle and the woods as if they were on the lid of a box of chocolates.

Helen replied by return of post. Lexi wouldn't be able to make the trip, but she and Maria would come to Shancarrig.

Nora could hardly wait. Their elder sister Kay said that Helen must have money to burn if she could just leap on a plane and fly off to Dublin on the spur of the moment. But Nora felt that it might well have taken a lot of explanations and excuses, as well as unimaginable scrimping and saving. She kept quiet about this. She would hear everything when Helen came home.

It was a relief to the twins when, after the big reunion in Dublin, they were able to leave Kay and travel together on the train to Shancarrig. They held hands and talked to each other, words tumbling and falling, finishing each other's sentences and beginning new ones . . . and mainly they said that the camera had not done the little girl justice.

Maria was beautiful.

She was four and a half, with a smile that went all the way around her face. She sang and hummed to herself, and was happy with the piece of cardboard and colouring pencils which Nora had brought to greet her.

'Aren't you great!' Helen exclaimed. 'Everyone else gives her these ridiculous ornaments or lacy things that she breaks or tears up.'

'Everyone else?'

'The Poles,' confessed Helen, and they giggled like the children they had been when they said goodbye so many years ago.

The sun shone as the train pulled into Shancarrig. There on the platform stood the master, Jim Kelly, waiting to meet his sister-in-law and little niece.

Maria took to him straight away. She reached up with her small chubby hand and he held it firmly while carrying the heavy suitcase in the other.

'Oh Nora.' Helen's eyes were full of tears. 'Oh Nora, you're so lucky.'

As they left the station and walked down to the row of shops where of late she had felt that she had been an object of pity, the childless schoolteacher Nora *did* feel lucky.

Nellie Dunne looked out of her door.

'Aren't you looking well today, Mrs Kelly!' she said.

'This is my sister, Miss Dunne.'

'And you have a little girl, do you?' Nellie Dunne asked. She wanted to have all the news for whoever came in next.

'That's my Maria,' said Helen proudly.

When Nellie was out of hearing Nora said, 'It'll be a nine days wonder in the place that someone belonging to me produced a child.'

Helen laid her hand on her twin sister's arm.

'Shush now. We'll have weeks on end to talk about all that.'

They walked companionably through Shancarrig, and home to make the tea.

But Nora Kelly did not have weeks on end to talk to her twin sister about life in Chicago and life in Shancarrig. Five days after she arrived Helen was killed when a runaway horse and cart went across the path of the bus which, swerving to avoid them, hit Helen, killing her outright.

Nora Kelly was in Nellie Dunne's with Maria when it happened. The child was trying to decide between a red and a green lollipop, holding them up against her yellow Viyella dress with the smocking on it, as if somehow one would look better with the outfit than the other.

The sounds were never to leave Nora's mind. She could hear them over and over, each one separate, the wheels of the cart, the whinnying of the horse, the irregular sound of the bus scraping the wrong way, and the long scream. Then silence, before the cries and shouts and everyone running to see what could be done.

Afterwards people said there was no scream, that Helen made no sound.

But Nora heard it.

They took her into Ryan's Hotel. She was given brandy, people's arms were around her, everywhere there were running footsteps. Someone had been sent up to the schoolhouse for Jim. There was Major Murphy from The Glen, a military man trying to organise things on some kind of military lines.

There was Father Gunn with his stole around his neck. He had run from the church to say the Act of Contrition into the lifeless ear of the dead woman.

'She's in heaven now,' Father Gunn told Nora. 'She's there, praying for us all.'

A great sense of the unfairness of it all rose in Nora. Helen didn't want to be in heaven praying for them all, she wanted to be here in Shancarrig telling the long complicated tale of a strange marriage to a silent man who drank, not like the Irish people drink, but differently. She wanted to arrange that her daughter came to Ireland regularly rather than grow up speaking Polish, hardly noticed amid the great crowds of other children in the family. Lexi's brothers and sisters had produced great numbers of new Chicagoans, apparently. Helen had begun to fear that Maria might get lost and never know a life of her own, be a personality and character in her own right like all the children in Shancarrig were. Nora had told her about the children who filled the classrooms during term time, each one with a history and a future.

Nora could not take it in. It couldn't have happened. Every minute seemed like half an hour as she sat in the lounge and a procession advanced and retired.

The voice of Sergeant Keane seemed a hundred miles away when he spoke of the telegram to Chicago, or the possibility of a phone call.

'We can't wire that man and say Helen is dead.' She heard her own voice as if it was someone else's. The words sounded unreal. The Sergeant explained that they could send a telegram asking him to phone Ryan's Hotel and someone would be here to give the message.

'I'll stay,' said Nora Kelly.

No one could dissuade her. It was not three o'clock in the afternoon in Chicago, it was early morning. Lexi was on his meat delivery rounds. It might be many hours before he got the telegram. She would be in the hotel, whatever time he phoned. Mrs Ryan organised a bed to be brought to the commercial lounge; the commercial travellers would understand that this was an emergency, that Mrs Kelly had to be near the phone, day or night.

She drank tea and they brought jelly for Maria. Red jelly, with the top of the milk. Every spoonful seemed to be in slow motion.

Then, at ten o'clock at night, she heard them coming to tell her that the call had been put through. She spoke to the man with the broken English. She had lain on the bed with the curtains pulled to keep out the evening sunlight of Shancarrig. And now it was almost dark. She spoke as she had drilled herself to speak, without tears, trying to give him all the information as calmly as possible.

'Why do you not weep for your sister?' He had a broken English accent, like a foreigner in a film.

'Because my sister would want me to be strong for you,' she said simply.

She asked did he want to speak to Maria, but he said no. She told him that Helen's body would be brought to Shancarrig church the next night, and the funeral would be on the following day, and that Mr Hayes had found out about flights. He had been on the phone to Shannon Airport all day . . .

She was cut short. Lexi would not come to the funeral.

Nora was literally unable to speak.

The slow voice spoke on. It would not be possible, they were not people who had unlimited money. Who would he know to walk with him behind his wife's coffin? There would be prayers said for her in his own parish, in his church. He returned again to the accident and how it had happened. Who was at fault? What part of Helen had been hurt to kill her?

The nightmare continued for what Nora Kelly thought was an endless time. It was only when the operator said six minutes that she realised how little time had actually passed.

'Will you ring again tomorrow?' she said.

'To say what?'

'To talk.'

'There is nothing to talk about,' he said.

'And Maria . . . ?'

'Will you look after her until we can come for her?'

'Of course . . . but if you are going to come for her, could you not come for Helen's funeral?'

'It will be later.'

The days of the funeral passed without Nora being really aware of what was going on. Always she saw Jim, his big hand stretched out to little Maria, whose crying for her mama grew less and less. They told her Mama was with the angels in heaven, and showed her the holy pictures on the wall and in the church to identify where her mother had gone.

And as the days passed Nora went through her sister's possessions, while Jim took little Maria up to Barna Woods to pick flowers.

Nora sat on her bed and looked at her sister's passport and official-looking cards for work and insurance. She could find no return air ticket. Was it possible that Helen had intended to stay here and not to return? There were letters from a solicitor 'regarding the matter we spoke of'. Could this solicitor have been arranging an American divorce? Did the strange tone of voice mean that Lexi was too upset to talk? Or that all love and feeling had gone from his marriage with Helen? Her head was whirling. Why had they not talked at once, she and Helen? It had been part of the slow getting back to knowing each other, the delighted realisation that each had only to begin a thought and the other could finish it.

What a cruel God to have taken this away from them five days after they had found it.

Kay the eldest sister was as usual practical.

'Don't grow too fond of the child,' she warned Nora. 'That unfeeling lout will be back for her the day it suits him.'

What did people mean . . . don't grow too fond of? How could anyone put a limit to the love she felt for this little girl with the big dark blue eyes, the head of curls and the endearing habit of stroking her cheek?

After a week Nora found herself saying to Jim, 'Is the child asleep yet?' and realised she was certainly coming to regard Maria as her child.

His reply was tender. 'I read her a story but she wants another from No, she says No has better stories.'

He was smiling at her affectionately, like before. He didn't turn away from her in bed any more, he reached for her like before. It was as if Maria had made their life complete.

'I suppose Kay's right about not getting too fond of her,' Nora said one summer evening, as they sat watching Maria play with the three baby chickens that Mrs Barton, the dressmaker, had brought along in a box as something to entertain the little girl.

'I keep hoping he won't want her back,' Jim said. It was the first time in four weeks it had been mentioned.

'We shouldn't get up our hopes . . . any man would want his only child.'

'Any man would have come to his wife's funeral,' Jim said.

Nora wrote letters regularly. She described the funeral, the flowers, the sermon. She told about the grave under a tree in the churchyard, and how on Sundays she went there with Maria to lay flowers on it. In a year a stone would be put up, Lexi must let her know what he would like written on the tombstone.

She told him about the bus driver who would never be the same again after the accident; the man who walked alone up to Shancarrig Rock. Everyone had told him that it had not been his fault. No one could have faulted him, it was an Act of God that the horse had shied at that very time. But he said that he would never drive again, and had come with flowers to the grave when he thought no one was looking.

She wrote that Maria said God Bless Daddy and a lot of other names every night, so she assumed that these were grandparents or relations. She didn't want him to think that that side of the family had been forgotten. She said that when the term started in September Maria would join the Mixed Infants. She was almost five – five was the age the children began coming to school.

She wrote and told him about the place, the huge big copper beech tree in the playground, and the maps on the schoolroom walls. She stopped saying 'until you come for her' and 'for the present time'. Instead she just wrote as if it was all agreed that Maria would stay here for an unspecified amount of time.

The children accepted her totally. They never thought it odd that she called Mrs Kelly 'No'. They thought it was just because she was babyish and younger than they were. Geraldine Brennan from the cottages decided to be her protector. Nora Kelly had to watch carefully in case part of the protecting might also mean eating Maria's little sandwich lunch.

The communications from Lexi were minimal. He wrote to say that he was grateful for her letters. His hand was not educated, and his grasp of grammar poor. He told her little or nothing about his intentions. He asked many times about the accident, what court case had resulted and whether the compensation had arrived. Once he enquired whether Helen had any valuables with her that needed to be looked after.

In Shancarrig too, people began to think of Maria as belonging to Jim and Nora. She was even called by their name.

'Hey, Maria Kelly, come over here and see the tadpoles!' Nora heard one day during dinner hour, when they played in the yard. Her heart soared with pleasure.

By accident she did have a child, a child of her own.

A child who had a fifth birthday party with a cake and candles. A child who had her first Christmas in Shancarrig and sang carols by the crib in the church.

'Do you remember the church back in Chicago at Christmas?' Nora asked, as she wrapped the child up in a warm scarf before taking her back up the road home from the church.

Maria shook her curly head. 'I can't think,' she said, and Nora smiled in the dark. The less Maria thought, the greater seemed the likelihood of her remaining with them.

Mr Hayes, father of Niall, an easy-going boy often put upon by the others, came to see her.

'My wife says he's being bullied by the other boys. Your husband will probably say it'll make a man of him. I wonder would you and I be better able to reach some kind of consensus?' he asked.

Nora Kelly smiled at him. It was typical of the way he did things, seeing was there a gentle way around things before you went in guns blazing.

'I think he needs to make a friend of Foxy Dunne,' she said after some thought.

'Foxy? That little divil from the cottages?'

'He's as smart as paint, that Foxy. He'll get himself out of that place, and away from the mess he's growing up in.'

'How should he make a friend of this fellow, so? Ethel would be afraid he'd lift the silver.' Bill Hayes looked rueful.

'He won't. He'd be a good ally for Niall. Niall's gentle. He doesn't need another gentle friend like Eddie, he needs a fighter in his court.'

'You can solve it all, Mrs Kelly.'

'I wish I could. I wish I knew how to keep my sister's child. I wish I believed that possession is nine tenths of the law.'

'You're too honourable for that.'

'I think my sister was going to leave her husband. I have letters from a solicitor . . . They don't say much, though.'

'They never do,' Bill Hayes admitted ruefully.

She sighed. He was telling her what Father Gunn and Dr Jims were telling her. Do nothing. Live in hope. If the man hadn't come over in six months it was a good sign.

When a year had passed it was even better.

When the time came for the Holy Year ceremonies at the school and the big dedication ceremony, Maria Kelly was part of their family and part of Shancarrig. She called Jim Daddy and she called Nora Mama No.

'It sounds like something from Japan, or from *Madam Butterfly*!' Jim said to Nora. He was always good-natured these days.

'She can't call me Mother, she remembers her mother,' Nora said.

'She seems to have forgotten her father though.' Jim spoke in a whisper.

At night Maria's prayers included a litany of friends at school, and the chickens – now hens – that Mrs Barton had given her. She prayed for all kinds of unlikely people, like little Declan Blake, who was pushed in his pram by that strange, abstracted maid, Carrie. Maria loved Carrie and Declan, and often asked Mama No if they could have a baby like Declan to play with. She prayed for Leo Murphy's dog, Jessica, which had broken its paw, and she prayed that Foxy Dunne would give her one of his worms in a jam jar. But the Polish names and her father's name had gone from the list.

It didn't take her long to realise she was in a privileged position being the daughter of the school.

'What would happen if you didn't know your tables?' Geraldine Brennan asked with great interest. 'Would you get your hand slapped like the rest of us?'

'No, she wouldn't.' Catherine Ryan from the hotel knew everything. 'She can grow up knowing nothing if she likes.'

'That's very unfair,' Geraldine Brennan complained. 'Just because my mam and dad aren't teachers I can get belted to bits, but you can do what you like.'

Maria Kelly didn't like Dad and Mama No being criticised. She worked harder than ever.

'Go to bed, child. You'll hurt your eyes,' Jim Kelly said, as Maria was learning her poem by the light of the oil lamp.

'I have to know it, I *have* to. It's much worse on me than any of the others. If I'm not word perfect I *must* be beaten, or else they'll be giving out about you and Mama No.'

Jim and Nora Kelly spoke in whispers that night. No child of their own could have brought them greater pleasure and happiness. It was as if she had been given to them as a gift from God in 1948, five long years ago.

Mattie, the postman, had delivered good and bad news to every house in Shancarrig. He knew when the emigrants' remittances arrived, he knew when a letter was unwelcome. He always hesitated slightly before handing Mrs Kelly any letter with a Chicago postmark.

When he was delivering an envelope with American stamps that was bigger and bulkier than usual, and looked more serious than the short scrappy-looking ones which had come before, Mattie asked if he could come in for a drop of water. Mrs Kelly poured him a cup of tea.

'I don't want to be in the way or anything . . . it's just in case it was bad news. I know that you're on your own today. Hasn't the master taken the children up to the Old Rock?'

It was true. Early in each summer term Jim organised an outing. The whole school would go – all fifty-six children. Father Gunn used to go too, and bring the elderly Monsignor O'Toole when he felt able. The old Monsignor liked to know that the children didn't think of the Old Rock as some kind of pagan place. That was the trouble with ancient monuments that dated back to before St Patrick ... people didn't relate them to God.

Nora Kelly had decided not to go today, and here, as ill luck would have it, was the news from Chicago. Could they be legal papers? Her hand trembled. She opened it. There were newspaper cuttings, a description of how Maria's father Lexi, had opened his own shop, his own butcher's place, a beautiful meat shop. He wanted his daughter to know this, to be proud of him.

Would Nora please show them to Maria? And perhaps she might write. 'She is a big girl now, it is strange that she does not write.' Nora Kelly put her head in her hands and wept at her kitchen table.

Mattie, who bitterly regretted not dropping the letter on the table as he would have done ordinarily, reached out and patted her heaving shoulders.

'It'll be all right, Mrs Kelly. You were meant to have her,' he kept saying, over and over.

Nora Kelly pulled herself together, washed her face and combed her hair. She put on her summer hat, a black straw one, and set off down the road to The Terrace, the row of houses in Shancarrig where Dr Jims Blake and Mr Bill Hayes, the solicitor, lived.

Nellie Dunne, looking out her open door over her counter, saw the schoolmistress walking briskly, cheeks flushed, face determined. Maybe she was heading for the doctor's? She might have news for him. They often said when you stopped worrying about having a child of your own that was the very time you conceived.

But Nora Kelly went up the steps to the Hayes household. Her business was legal, not medical.

Mr Hayes seemed to notice a change in her, a determination to have the compensation settled and done with.

'Has anything happened, Mrs Kelly?' he asked gently. 'It's just that up to now you were the one to put it on the long finger, saying that money couldn't bring your sister back and that the child lacked for nothing.' He was polite but questioning.

'I know,' Nora Kelly agreed. 'That's what I did think. But now I think my only hope is to get the compensation, whatever it is, and give it to him.'

'Him?'

'Her father. He's not interested in anything else, believe me.'

'But the compensation is for Maria as well as for him.'

'We'll give it all to him if he'll let us keep the child.'

'Ah Nora, Nora ...' Normally Niall Hayes' father didn't call her by her first name. He seemed upset.

'What are you trying to say to me, Mr Hayes?'

'I suppose I'm saying that you can't buy the child.'

'And I'm saying that that's exactly what I'm going to do,' she said, face flushed and eyes bright, much too bright.

Wearily Bill Hayes took out the file and together they went through the letters from CIE – the transport company – the solicitors for the insurance, and copies of his own to them. There was a sum. It would be agreed eventually. At most it would be £2,000, at the least £1,200. If they agreed to take something nearer the lower figure it would be sooner rather than later. But perhaps, after all this time, they should hold out for more.

'Take whatever you can get, Mr Hayes.'

'Forgive me, but should your husband perhaps . . . ?'

'Jim is as desperate to keep her as I am. More so, if that's possible.'

'There is absolutely no guarantee . . .'

'I know, but I have to have *something* to offer him. He's written to say he owns a shop. He's as proud as punch of it. Now he's started wanting her to write to him . . .' Her lip was trembling.

'Perhaps this is the first time he feels able to. You know Americans, they set a lot of store on having their own business . . .'

'Please don't stand up for him. I could have borne it if he had come over and taken her away at once. Not now. Not all those years of ignoring and neglect and now . . .'

'She might come for holidays . . .'

Nora Kelly's mouth was a thin line. 'You mean very well, Mr Hayes, but it's not a help.'

'Fine, Mrs Kelly. I'll get it moving, inasmuch as anything ever moves in the law.' Bill Hayes waved his hand around shelves filled with envelopes and documents tied up in pale pink tape.

'Will you write a little note to your father?' Nora asked Maria that night.

'What for? To thank him for the day up at the Old Rock?' She looked surprised.

Nora swallowed, and could hardly speak. Maria thought of Jim as her father. The man who was so proud of the new shop selling best meats in Chicago didn't even exist for her.

A few days later she brought it up again.

'We've had a letter from your Papa Lexi in Chicago. He wanted you to see the pictures of his new meat shop.'

Maria took the newspaper cutting.

'Ugh! Look at the dead animals hanging there,' she said, handing it back.

'That's his job. Like Jimmy Morrissey's father.' Nora wished she could leave it, but she knew that she dare not. 'Anyway Maria, it would be good to write him a letter and say the shop looks very nice.'

'It doesn't!' Maria said, giggling her infectious laugh.

Her hair, long now but still curly, was tied with a coloured ribbon. She always had her head in a book – the early years of long bedtime story sessions had paid off. She was tall and suntanned and strong. She was nearly ten years old, a girl that anyone would love to claim as a daughter.

'But he'd like to hear,' Nora insisted.

'It would only be pretending.' She pulled the newspaper cutting towards her again and looked, as Nora knew she must, at the picture of the tall, handsome man standing beside his shop.

'Is this him?' she asked.

'Yes.'

She looked uneasy, her dark blue eyes seeming troubled.

'What will I say?'

'Oh. Whatever you think. Whatever comes into your mind to say. I can't be dictating it for you.'

'But, nothing comes into my mind to say. I don't know. I don't feel safe when I think about . . . all this.'

Nora Kelly put her arms around Maria. 'We'll make you safe, pet. Believe me, we will.'

Maria wriggled away. It was too emotional.

'Yes. Fine. Okay, I'll say something. Will I say "you look fine and rich"?'

'*No*, Maria. Whatever else you say, I beg you not to say that.'

'Ah Mama No, I don't know what to say. I think you are going to have to dictate it to me.'

'I think I am,' agreed Nora.

They kept the letters respectful and distant, telling little about life in Shancarrig, mentioning nothing of the Kellys who were her real parents, but giving vague sentiments of goodwill to a stranger in Chicago.

Nora noticed with delight how briefly and casually Maria read the stilted letters which came back, each one beginning 'My dear daughter Maria'.

The man had little to say, and said it badly.

'He's not much at spelling, is Papa Lexi,' Maria said.

'Now, now!' Jim corrected her.

'Is he a secret? Do people know about him?'

'Of course he's not a secret, love. Why do you think that?'

'Because we don't talk about him. And nobody else has another papa miles away.'

'We do talk about him, and you write to him. Of course he's not a secret.' Nora was very anxious to take any glamour or mystery away.

'Do you write to him, Mama No?'

'I do, love. But about business.'

'The meat business?' She was genuinely puzzled.

'No. Legal things, you know, after your mother's accident . . .'

'Why do you have to write about that?'

'Oh, you know. Red Tape. Formalities. All that.' Nora was vague.

Maria lost interest. Instead she wanted to tell Mama No about Miss Ross.

'I saw her climbing the tree this morning,' she said, giggling at the thought of the elegant Miss Ross actually getting her leg up on the lower branch and hauling herself up into the higher parts of the tree.

'Nonsense! You imagined it.'

'No, I didn't. I was looking out my window at six o'clock this morning, and she came into the school yard. I swear she did.'

'What on earth could she have been doing at that hour?'

'Well, I saw her. She'd been up all night. She was coming back from Barna Woods.'

'I think you've been reading too many stories – you can't tell what's true from what's made up.'

Nora shook her head. The very idea of Miss Ross climbing the beech tree. Really.

'Miss Ross?'

'Yes, Maria.'

'Miss Ross, did you climb the beech tree yesterday morning?'

Miss Ross's face was red. 'Did I what, child?'

'It's just ... it's just, I told Mama No, and she said "nonsense".'

'That's what it is too, Maria. Nonsense.'

Miss Ross turned and walked away.

Nora heard the conversation. There was something about the way the young teacher spoke that didn't ring true.

'I was wrong about Miss Ross,' Maria said.

'Maybe it was the light. It's full of odd shadows at that time of morning.' Nora spoke kindly.

They exchanged a glance and somehow Maria seemed to know that Nora knew it wasn't something that had been made up. That it was something which might indeed have happened.

'I never thanked you properly for putting us right about that young divil, Foxy Dunne,' Mr Hayes said to Nora Kelly when she called to see him next time. 'It was absolutely the right thing for young Niall. Foxy taught him to catch rabbits – we have six of them out in the back. All male. Foxy taught him how to work that out too.'

Nora laughed. 'There's not much that fellow doesn't know.'

Bill Hayes looked out his window at the back garden. 'Look at that. He showed Niall how to build a proper little house for them, and put up a wire run from the hutch. It's very professional, and he's only a child.'

'He'll go far,' Nora said. She knew too that visiting The Terrace had a civilising effect on Foxy Dunne. He combed his hair and washed his hands without being asked to. He ate slowly, like his hosts. He was a fast learner.

Nora liked talking to Bill Hayes. He was a quiet man and people who didn't know him well might think he was a little too precise and fussy. But nobody's life was easy. Nora Kelly knew it was not a bed of roses living with the gloomy Ethel Hayes, who hadn't smiled for a long time. She knew that everyone's business was safe and secret in Number Five The Terrace. And that she would get the best advice that she could be given.

'Well now, you didn't come to talk to me about rabbits and hutches. I'm being very remiss.' He moved back to his desk and picked up some papers. 'We do have an offer now ... they're delighted to be able to close the file after five and a half years.'

'How much?'

'Thirteen hundred. Now we could get ...'

'That's fine, and here's a note from Jim saying he agrees too, in case you think I'm doing all this on my own.'

'No, no . . .' But he took the note.

'I'll write tonight. When would we have the money?'

'Oh, in a week or two.'

'And would there be a certain percentage legally for him and for Maria?'

'I'd advise that half be for her, to be invested . . .'

'You do know what we are going to do with her portion, don't you?'

'Yes, and I must say again how very unwise it is from every point of view. Suppose the child does stay with you, will she thank you for handing away what is her legal inheritance?'

Nora Kelly wasn't listening . . . she would write tonight.

She went to the post office to get a stamp, and Katty Morrissey looked up from behind the grille.

'Well, isn't that the coincidence! There was a telegram for you half an hour ago. I was going to get Mattie to go out with it.'

Nora felt cold. Her hand trembled as she opened the envelope, and in full view of Katty Morrissey and Nellie Dunne, who had materialised as usual when any drama was about to unfold, she read that Lexi was arriving in Shannon Airport on Friday morning and would be with them on Friday afternoon.

'Would you like a glass of water, Mrs Kelly?'

'No, Miss Dunne, thank you very much. I would like nothing of the sort.' Nora Kelly gathered every ounce of strength and walked out of the post office, leaving Nellie and Katty to say to each other, before they said it to the rest of Shancarrig, that the schoolteachers' time was up. The real father was on his way from the United States to take his child home.

'You don't look well, Mrs Kelly.' Maddy Ross had come up behind her as she crossed the bridge on the way back up home.

'Neither do you, Miss Ross,' Nora countered. There would be no sympathy from this young teacher who had her life before her – a life with marriage and children in it.

'I'm fine. A little tired. I don't sleep at night. I walk a lot in the woods – it clears my head.' She had a strange, almost wild, look about her.

Jim had said, over and over, that it was essential for Shancarrig school to keep Miss Ross. Her salary was small, as the Department would only pay the minimum. And only Maddy Ross, who had a house, and a mother with private means of a sort, would be able to live on what went into her envelope every month.

But sometimes Nora thought that Miss Ross had a giddiness and light-headedness that none of their silliest fourteen-year-old girls had ever managed to reach. And more than once she thought, God forgive her, that Miss Ross was almost flirting with young Father Barry. Nora kept her own counsel about this, not even confiding to Jim.

'Do you sometimes feel the world is bursting with happiness?' Maddy Ross asked her as they walked together up the road.

Nora Kelly, who could well have done without this feverish conversation, replied tersely that she didn't think that at all, and particularly not today. So if Miss Ross would excuse her she would like to be left to her own thoughts.

She saw Maddy Ross shrink away like an animal that has received a blow.

Still, there was no time to think about that now, the young teacher's nonsense could be dealt with later. Right now she had to cope with the event that she had dreaded since the week after her sister died – the arrival of her brother-in-law in Shancarrig to take his daughter home.

She walked like a woman in a dream. Not since the time of Helen's death had Nora felt this sensation of being outside her body, as if she was watching another being going through the motions – of filling a kettle, of setting a table.

When Jim came in she was sitting motionless at the table. He saw the telegram and needed to ask very little.

'When is he coming?' he said.

'Friday.'

'Nora. Oh Nora, my love. What are we going to do?'

He put his hands over his face and wept like a baby.

She sat there stroking his arm, listing the possibilities. Could they leave Shancarrig and hide somewhere? No, that was ridiculous, he would get the guards. Could they pretend that Maria was too sick to travel? Could they get Mr Hayes to brief a barrister in Dublin who would fight a case against her being taken away from them? Each solution was more unlikely than the one which had gone before.

They could ask Maria to beg him. No. They must never do that.

Perhaps for the child it *was* the best. A comfortable living in the New World. A whole lot of cousins, a ready-made family, a welcome home as if the five years since she left Chicago airport in 1948 were just a pause in her real life.

Nora and Jim Kelly realised that this was one occasion when they could do absolutely nothing. They would have to wait for Friday and all it would bring.

By the time they showed Maria the telegram they had calmed each other sufficiently to speak without letting their emotions show.

'Is he going to take me away from here?' Maria asked.

'Well, we don't know what he plans, do we? After all, he just says "arriving to visit you". He doesn't say anything about ... anything after that.'

'I don't want to go.'

'Now, that's not the way to start,' Jim Kelly said.

'Well, what *is* the way to start ... ?' Maria was flushed. They hadn't realised how independent she had become, how strong in her own views. 'This is my home. You are my parents. I don't want to go away with someone I don't remember, someone who didn't come for me when my real mother died.'

'He couldn't. And you mustn't begin by making him an enemy.'

'He *is* an enemy. I don't want to meet him, I'll run away.'

'No, Maria, please. Please, that would be the worst thing.'

'What would be the best thing?'

'I suppose it would be to reason with him, tell him how much you think of Shancarrig as your home, and of us as your ... well, your people.'

'My parents,' Maria said stubbornly.

'He won't want to hear that,' Nora said.

'I don't care what he wants to hear. Why should I have to beg him to let me stay in my own home?'

'Because life isn't fair, and you're only ten years of age.'

Maria ran out the door through the yard, and across the fields towards Barna Woods.

When she came home later that night, she was very silent. And pale. Nora, who knew every heartbeat of this child, knew that it was something else, something not to do with what was going to happen on Friday.

'Did something happen to frighten you?'

'You know everything, Mama No.'

'Was it something you saw?'

'Yes.' She hung her head.

Nora's cheeks burned. How could life be so cruel, that someone must have exposed himself to the little girl on this of all days?

'You can tell me,' she said.

'Not really. It's really very bad. You won't believe me.'

'I will. I always do.'

'I saw Miss Ross and Father Barry kissing each other.' She blurted it out.

Immediately Nora knew she was telling the truth. Without a shadow of a doubt she realised that this was indeed what had been going on under her eyes.

A priest of God and their Junior Assistant Mistress.

But even the scandal, and the need to tell Father Gunn tactfully, and the whole attendant list of complications, faded away compared to the shock that it had all given to Maria.

'Do you remember when you told me Miss Ross had climbed the tree? I didn't really believe you, but I did later. And I most certainly believe you now. But Maria, we have so much to worry about, you and I. Let us put this to the very back of our minds, right back behind everything, and later we'll talk about it. Just you and I. It's best to tell nobody, nobody at all. These things have explanations.'

'Don't send me to Papa Lexi.'

'You'll be strong and good when he comes. I'll help you every step of the way. We'll ask him can you share your time between us. Hey, wouldn't that be great? Two countries. Two continents. And we all want you. Not everyone has that.'

'Will it work?'

'Yes,' said Nora Kelly, knowing that she had never spoken such an untruth in her whole life.

They survived the four days to Friday.

People were very kind, which they expected, but also very tactful which they hadn't expected. They did practical things.

Mrs Ryan in the hotel looked up the time of the flight, and since it would be arriving in the early hours of the morning, worked out what time he could be expected in Shancarrig. Maybe lunchtime. If it would be easier they could have lunch at Ryan's Commercial Hotel, she suggested, a private room.

Mr Hayes, the solicitor, offered to take him through the steps of the settlement one by one, pointing out how it had been the best thing to do.

Dr Jims dropped by with sleeping tablets in case they were finding the nights long.

Leo Murphy, daughter of the Major up at The Glen, said that Maria could come up and hit a ball around on the tennis court if she liked. Even though she was four years younger it would be all right, because of things being difficult.

Young Father Barry said, with eyes of glazing sincerity, that God was a God of Love above all, and that he would open this man's heart to see the love the Kellys had for Maria.

Nora Kelly preferred not to think too deeply about the God of Love that Father Barry interpreted, but she thanked him all the same.

Father Gunn said that Polish Catholics were very devoted to Our Lady, and that Mrs Kelly should show him the plaque on the wall, where the school had been dedicated to the Blessed Virgin.

Foxy Dunne said he had heard there was a bit of a problem, and he knew some very tough people, or his brothers did, if reinforcements were called for. Jim Kelly put on his sternest face when refusing this offer, but gripped Foxy by the arm and told him he was a great fellow for all that.

Eddie Barton told his mother that the gypsies were coming again – wouldn't it be great if they were to kidnap Maria and then for her to be found and brought back after the man had gone back to Chicago.

Mrs Barton was altering Nora Kelly's best dress for her, with a trim of lace down the front, and on the collar and cuffs. She wanted to look the equal of anyone in Chicago for the visit. 'I only tell you what Eddie said, just in case. It might work,' she said, mouth full of pins.

'God bless you both,' Nora Kelly said, looking at her pale reflection in the mirror.

In many ways it was like a Western where they are all waiting for the gunmen to come to town. Down by the station Mattie the postman happened to be waiting with his bicycle, just waiting, looking into the middle distance as it were. Sergeant Keane was sitting on a windowsill by the bus stop, throwing the odd word to Nellie Dunne who had come out from behind her counter to stand at her doorway.

The Morrisseys in the butcher's shop were making frequent sorties out on to the street, and Mrs Breda Ryan from the hotel seemed to find a lot of activity that took her to the entrance porch of their premises.

Although none of them would have admitted it, and no one pretended to see the curtains of the presbytery move as Mrs Kennedy watched from one window and Father Gunn from another ... they were all waiting.

Someone would let the Kellys know the moment the man came into the town. They never thought he would arrive by car, and because it was an ordinary car, not a big American Cadillac, nobody knew it was Lexi when he drove into Shancarrig and looked around him to see where the schoolhouse was.

Not seeing it in the centre or near the church he took the road over the Grane and arrived at a huge copper beech tree, where the one-storey building had the notice Shancarrig National School.

Behind was the small stone house of Jim and Nora Kelly. They were sitting waiting for the message that would tell them by which route he had arrived. They certainly had not expected the man himself.

He was big and handsome, fair curly hair around his ears, eyes dark blue. He must be thirty-six or thirty-seven. He looked years younger – he looked like a film star.

Nora and Jim stood in their doorway, their sides touching for strength. She longed to hold her husband's hand, but it would look too girlish. It wasn't in their manner to do a thing like that; hip to hip was enough.

'I am Alexis,' he said. 'You are Nora and Jim?'

'You're very welcome to Shancarrig,' Nora said, the untruthfulness of the words hidden, she hoped, by the smile she had nailed on her face.

'My daughter Maria?' he said.

'We thought it best that she go to a friend's house. We will take you to her whenever you like.' Jim spoke loudly to try and hide the shake in his voice.

'This house of her friend?' he asked.

'It's ten minutes' walk, maybe two or three minutes in your car. Don't worry. She's there, she knows you're coming,' Jim said. He thought he could sense suspicion in Lexi's voice.

'We felt it would be more fair on you not to have to tell her in her own home ... what she thinks of as her own home.' Nora looked around the kitchen of the small house where she had spent all her married life.

'Tell her?'

'Well, talk to her. Meet her, get to know her. Whatever it is you want to do.' Jim knew his voice was trailing lamely. These monosyllables from Lexi were hard to cope with. Somehow he had expected something totally different.

'It is good that she is not here for the moment. May I sit down?'

They rushed to get him a chair, and offer him tea, or whiskey.

'Do you have poitín?' he asked.

Nora's warning bells sounded. She remembered her sister Helen telling of this morose drinking, this silent swallowing of neat alcohol.

'No. The local teacher has to set a good example, I'm afraid. But I *do* have a bottle of Irish whiskey that I bought in a bar, if that would do.'

He smiled. Lexi, the man who had come to take their daughter, smiled as if he was a friend. 'I need a drink for what I am to tell you.'

Their hearts were like lead as they poured the three little glasses, lest he think them aloof. They proposed no toast.

'I am going to marry again,' Lexi told them. 'I am to marry a girl, Karina, who is also Polish. Her father owns a butcher's shop too, and we are going to combine the two. She is much more young than I am, Karina. She is twenty-two years of age.'

'Yes, yes.' Nora was holding her breath to know what would come next.

'I tell you the truth. It would be much more easy for our marriage if Karina and I were to start our own family . . . to begin like any other couple. To get to know each other, to make our own children . . .'

Nora felt the breath hissing between her teeth. She gripped her small glass so hard she feared it might shatter in her hands. 'And you were wondering . . . ?' she said.

'And I thought that perhaps, if my daughter Maria is happy here . . . then perhaps this is where she might like to be . . . But, you see, it is not fair that I leave her with you . . . you have your life. You have been so good to her for so long . . .'

The tears were running down Nora's face. She didn't even try to wipe them away.

Lexi continued, 'I have made many enquiries about the finances because I want you to have the money to do so. But always when I talk of the money you do not reply. I fear there may be no money. I fear to give you money in case you think I am trying to give you a bribe . . .'

Jim Kelly was on his feet. 'Oh Lexi, sir, we'd *love* to keep her here. She'll always be your daughter. Whenever you want her she'll go on a holiday to you . . . but it's our hearts' desire that she stay with us.'

Nora spoke very calmly. 'And maybe she would see you as Uncle Lexi more than Papa Lexi, don't you think?' She didn't know where she found the strength to say the words that Lexi wanted to hear. She didn't dare to believe that she had got them right until she saw his face light up.

'Yes, yes. This would be much better for Karina, that she think of her as a niece, not a daughter. Because, in many ways now, that is what she is.'

Nora saw, out of the corner of her eyes, a shadow move on the beech tree in the school yard. It was Foxy Dunne, hovering. He had seen the car and guessed the driver.

'Foxy!' she called. He came swaggering in. This man was an enemy, he wouldn't be civil to him. 'Foxy, could you do us a favour? Maria is over at The Glen with Leo Murphy. Would you go over and tell her to come home, and tell her everything's fine.'

'It's a long journey over to The Glen,' Foxy said unexpectedly.

'It's ten minutes, you little pup,' said Jim Kelly.

'It'd be easier if you let me drive over for her.' He looked at the car keys on the table.

'Hey, how old are you?' Lexi asked.

'I've driven everything. That's dead easy.'

'He's thirteen and a half,' said Nora.

'That's a grown man,' said Lexi. 'But don't you put a scratch on it. I have to take it back to Shannon airport tonight.' He threw him the keys.

Tonight. The man was going back to his new life tonight. Without Maria.

The sunlight streamed into the kitchen as they talked, as they sat as friends and spoke of the past and the future, until Maria arrived, white-faced from the journey. Foxy had driven her three times round Shancarrig to get value from the drive, and then spotted Sergeant Keane so had put his foot down to get her back to the schoolhouse.

Nora put her arms around the girl.

'We've had a great chat, my love,' she said. 'This is Lexi, maybe even Uncle Lexi. He'll be going back to America tonight, and he wants to meet you and get to know you a little bit before he goes.'

Maria's eyes were wide trying to take it in.

'Before he goes off and leaves you here with us. Which is what we all agreed is where you want to be,' said Nora Kelly, who had told her daughter Maria that everything would be all right, and had now delivered on her promise.

Nessa

It was Mrs Ryan who wore the trousers in Ryan's Commercial Hotel. Everyone knew that. And just as well, because if Conor Ryan had married a mouse the place would have gone to the wall years ago.

Conor Ryan certainly hadn't married a mouse when he wed Breda O'Connor. A small, thin girl with restless eyes and straight black shiny hair, she was a distant cousin of the Ryans. They met at a family wedding. Conor Ryan told her that he was thinking of going off to England and joining the British army. Anything to get out from under his parents' feet – they ran this hole-in-the-wall hotel in a real backward town.

'What do you want going into the army? There might be a war and you'd get killed,' she said.

Conor Ryan implied that it mightn't be a huge choice between that and staying put with his parents.

'They can't be *that* bad,' Breda said.

'They are. The place is like the ark. No, the ark was safe and dry and people wanted to get into it. This is like a morgue.'

'Why don't you improve it?'

'I'm only twenty-three, they'd never let me,' he said.

Breda O'Connor decided there and then that she would marry him. By the time Britain declared war on Germany they were already engaged.

'*Now*, aren't you glad I didn't let you join the army?' Breda said.

'You haven't lived with my father and mother yet,' he said, with a look of defeat and resignation that she was determined to take out of him.

'Nor will I,' she said with spirit. 'We'll build a place of our own.'

Conor Ryan's father said that he had picked a wastrel, a girl who thought they were made of money, when the outhouse was converted into a small dwelling for the newly-weds.

Conor Ryan's mother said there would be no interfering from a fancy young one who thought she was the divil and all because she had a domestic science diploma. Conor reported none of these views to the bride-to-be. Breda would find out soon enough what they were like. She had assured him that she had been given fair warning.

As it happened she never really found out how much they had resented her coming to their house, and marrying their only son while he was still a child.

Breda never heard how his parents prophesied that when she had a few children out in that cement hut she was getting built for herself in the yard it would soften her cough.

The Ryan parents fell victim to a bad flu that swept the countryside in the winter of 1939.

Two weeks after the winter wedding of Conor and Breda the same congregation stood in the church for the double funeral of the groom's parents.

There was a lot of head-shaking. How hard it was for a young girl to step in like that. It would be too much for her. She was only a little bit of a thing. And you'd need to light a bonfire under Conor Ryan to get any kind of action out of him. It was the end of Ryan's Commercial Hotel for Shancarrig.

Never were people so wrong.

Breda Ryan took control at once. Even on the very day of the funeral. She assured the mourners that they would be very welcome to come back to the hotel bar for drinks rather than going up to Johnny Finn's pub, as they thought they should do out of some kind of respect.

'The best respect that you could give my parents-in-law is to come to their hotel,' Breda Ryan said.

Within a week she made it known that she didn't like to be referred to as the *young* Mrs Ryan.

'My husband's mother has gone to her reward, and the Lord have mercy on her she is no longer here to need her name. I am Mrs Ryan now,' she said.

And so she was. Mrs Ryan of Shancarrig's only hotel, a part of the triangle that people called the heart of the town – one side The Terrace where the rich people like the doctor and Mr Hayes the solicitor lived, one side the row of shops – Nellie Dunne's the grocery, Mr Connors the chemist, the other Dunnes who ran the hardware business, the butcher, the draper – the few small places that got a meagre living from Shancarrig and its outlying farms. The third side of the triangle was Ryan's Hotel.

Not very prepossessing, dark brown throughout, floors covered in linoleum. The rooms all had heavy oak fireplaces, the pictures on the walls were in dark heavy frames. Most of them were of unlikely romantic scenes with men in frock coats, never seen in Shancarrig or even in the county, offering their arms to ladies in outfits similarly unknown.

There were some religious pictures in the hall ... the one of the Sacred Heart had a small red lamp burning in front of it. The sideboards in the hall and dining room were stuffed with glass never used on the table, and Belleek china.

Mrs Ryan had plans to change and improve it all but first she must see that people came to it as it was.

She made sure that the smell of cooking didn't meet guests at the hall door by putting heavy curtains outside the kitchen doors. She installed a glass-fronted noticeboard near the reception desk and put up details of concerts, hunt balls or other high-class events in neighbouring towns.

She intended to make the hotel the very centre of Shancarrig, the place where people would come to look for information. The bus and train times were there too for all to see, in the hopes that it would encourage travellers to come and have a drink or a coffee as they waited.

Her plans had only just begun when she realised she was pregnant.

Her first child was born in 1940, a little girl, delivered by young Dr Jims because the baby arrived in the middle of the night and Dr Nolan was getting too old to come out at all hours.

'A lovely daughter,' he said. 'Is that what you wanted?'

'Indeed it's not. I wanted a strong son to run the hotel for me.' She was laughing as she held the baby.

'Well, maybe she'll run it till she gets a brother.' Dr Jims had a warm way with him.

'It's no life for a woman. We'll find a better job for Vanessa.' She held the child close.

'Vanessa! Now there's a name.'

'Oh, think big, Doctor. That's what I always believed.'

Conor Ryan poured a brandy for the doctor, and the two men sat companionably in the bar at 4.30 a.m. to drink to the new life in Shancarrig.

'May Vanessa live to see the year two thousand,' said Dr Jims.

'Won't Nessa only be a young one of sixty then! Why are you wishing her a short life?' said the new father.

She was Nessa from the start. Even her strong-willed mother was not able to impose her will on the people of Shancarrig on this point. And when her sister was born the baby was Catherine, and the third girl Nuala. There were no strong sons to run the hotel. But by the time they realised there never would be, the women were so well established in Ryan's that the absence of a boy wasn't even noticed.

Nessa always thought she had got the worst possible combination of looks from her parents.

She had her mother's dead-straight hair. No amount of pipe cleaners would put even the hint of a wave or a kink in it. And she inherited her father's broad shoulders and big feet. Why could she not have got his curly hair and her mother's tiny proportions? Life was very unfair. Everyone admired people with curly hair.

Like Leo's hair.

Since Nessa could remember she had been best friends with Leo Murphy. Leo was the girl who lived up at The Glen. She was almost an only child. Lucky thing. Not a real only child like Eddie Barton, the son of the dressmaker, but Leo's two brothers were very old and didn't live at home.

Nessa had even known Leo before the day they both started at Shancarrig school. Leo had been invited to come and play with her. Mrs Ryan had said she wanted Vanessa to have a proper friend before she started in there and had to consort with the Dunnes and the Brennans.

'What's consorting?' Nessa asked her mother.

'Never mind, but you won't be doing it anyway.'

'That's why you're off to school, to learn things like that,' said Conor

Ryan, folding back the paper at the race card to see could he pick a likely winner in the afternoon races.

The first day at school Nessa Ryan sat beside Maura Brennan. Together they learned to do pot hooks.

'Why are they called pot hooks?' Nessa asked, as the two girls slowly traced the S shapes in their headline copy books.

'They look a bit like the hooks that hang over the fire. You know . . . to hold the pots,' Maura explained.

Nessa told this information proudly to her mother.

'What! Have they got you sitting next to one of the Brennans from the cottages?' she said crossly.

'Don't be putting notions into her head. Isn't the poor Brennan child entitled to sit beside someone? Isn't she a human being?' Nessa's father was defending Maura Brennan for something. Her mother was still in a bad temper about it, whatever it was.

'That's not what you say when her father comes in here breaking all before him, and swearing like a soldier.'

'He takes his trade to Johnny Finn's after what you said to him that time . . .'

'You sound as if you're sorry, as if you miss that good-for-nothing drunk. It was a fine day for this house when I shifted him out. You agreed yourself.'

'I did, I did.'

'So what are you going on about?'

'I don't know, Breda . . .' He shook his head. Nessa realised whatever it was . . . her Daddy really didn't know. He didn't know about things like her mother did. About running a hotel, and being in charge.

'Will I not sit beside her?' Nessa asked.

Her mother's face softened. 'Don't mind me, your father is right. The child's not to be blamed.'

'We don't have pot hooks, do we?'

'No. We have a range, like any normal person would. The Brennans cook over an open fire, I expect. Did you not see Leo Murphy at school today?'

'She was sitting beside Eddie. They got told off for talking.'

'What else happened? Tell me all about it.'

'We played a game around the tree, you know, like a big ring o' roses.'

'I did that myself,' said her father.

She saw her mother going over and putting her arm around his shoulder. They were smiling. She felt safe. Maybe her mother *did* love her father even if he didn't know how to run a hotel. When anyone came to the hotel they asked for Mrs Ryan, not for Mr, that's if they knew the place. Otherwise it was a delay while Mr Ryan sent for his wife.

Nessa grew up knowing that she should get her mother, not her father, in any crisis. At the start she thought this was the same in all families.

But she learned it wasn't always the case. She discovered that Leo Murphy's mother didn't know where anything was, that Major Murphy and Biddy the maid ran The Glen between them. Leo never had to consult her mother about anything. It was a huge freedom.

She learned that Maura Brennan's mother had to go out begging because Mr Brennan drank whatever money he got. When Nessa wondered why Mrs Brennan didn't stop him with a word or a glance as her mother would have, Maura shrugged. Women weren't like that, she said.

Niall Hayes said that his mother didn't have any say in the house. His father paid all the bills, and dealt with things that happened. Foxy Dunne said that his mother hadn't been known to open her mouth on any subject, but of course his father had never been known to close his, so that made up a pair of them.

Only Eddie, whose father was dead or had gone away or something, said that his mother was in charge. But she didn't like being in charge, he said. She kept thinking there should be a man around the place.

Sometimes they even made jokes about Nessa's mother, about how different she was from the other women in Shancarrig. Nessa didn't like that very much but in her heart she had to admit it was true. Her mother was rather too interested in her for her liking. She wanted to know everything that happened.

'Why do you want to know so much?' Nessa asked her once.

'I want to make sure you don't make the same mistakes that I made. I want to try and help your childhood.' Her mother had seemed very simple and direct in that answer, as if she was talking to someone her own age, not talking down.

'Leave the child alone,' her father said, as he said so often. 'Aren't they only children for a very short time? Let them enjoy it.'

'I don't know about the very short time,' Nessa's mother said. 'There are quite a few people around here who never grew up.'

When people stopped to admire young Nessa Ryan on the street they often asked, 'And whose pet are you?' It was only a greeting, not a question, but Nessa took it seriously.

'Nobody's,' she would say firmly. 'There's so much work in a hotel there's no time to have pets.' People laughed at the solemn way the child spoke, in the parrot fashion she must have heard at home.

Her mother didn't approve. 'You're the most petted child in the country. Stop telling people that there's no one spoiling you,' she said.

But Nessa didn't think this was so. She wondered was she a foundling. Had the dark gypsies, the families who came through every year, left her on the hotel doorstep? Had she been found up at the Old Rock, left there by a wonderful kind noblewoman with long hair – someone who was in great secret trouble and left her baby while she escaped?

Nessa didn't know exactly what she wanted but she knew very definitely that it was something different from what she had got. She would never be able to please her mother, no matter what she did, and her father was too soft and easy-going for his views to count.

Sometimes when she was feeling particularly religious and near to God she used to ask him to make her popular and loved.

'I'm not asking to be pretty, God, I know we're not meant to pray for good looks. But I am asking to be liked more. People that are popular are very very happy. They can go around doing good all the time. Honestly God, even children. I'd be a great child and a great grown-up. Just try it and see.'

The years of Nessa Ryan's childhood saw a great change in Ryan's Commercial Hotel.

After endless rationing and petrol shortages brought about by the war in Europe, suddenly cars appeared on the road again. Instead of the hotel's visitors arriving at Shancarrig railway station and walking across to where Ryan's stood taking up one side of the three-cornered green that formed the centre and heart of the place, they now drew up outside the door. Most people were loath to leave their cars in the street, even though this was the best part of Shancarrig. Visitors didn't know that The Terrace where Dr Nolan and then Dr Jims lived in Number Three and where the Hayes family lived in Number Five was about the best address in the county. They wanted safe parking for their cars.

The hotel was no longer dark brown. The dark colours had been replaced by cream and what Breda called a lovely restful *eau de nil*. She had toured other smarter hotels and discovered that this pale greenish shade was high fashion.

The more sober of the heavy-framed pictures had been relegated to the master bedroom, out of view of any visitors.

More bathrooms had been installed, chamber pots were hidden discreetly in bedside cupboards rather than being placed expectantly under beds.

The women who served in the dining room of Ryan's Commercial Hotel wore smart green dresses now, with their white aprons and little white half caps. The days of black outfits were over. There were comfortable chairs in the entrance hall encouraging guests to think of it as it used to be.

When Nessa and her sisters, Catherine and Nuala, were young they were kept well out of sight of the hotel visitors, but were trained to say good morning or good evening to anyone they encountered, even scarlet-faced drunks who might not be able to reply.

Nessa's mother had cleared up the hotel yard. Old and broken machinery was removed, outhouses were painted. No longer was the place used as a dumping ground. Guests were told that ample parking facilities existed.

And the visitors changed too.

A trickle of American servicemen who had got to know Europe during the days of war, returned again in peacetime bringing their wives, particularly if there was any Irish heritage in the family tree. They would stay in hotels around the country and try to find it out. They became a familiar sight, sometimes still in uniform, and looking very dashing as they would book into Ryan's Commercial Hotel.

Father Gunn said he was worn out tracing roots from old church records.

There were the commercial travellers too. The same people coming regularly, once a month – once a fortnight sometimes. Usually two or three rooms would be booked by the various representatives coming to take orders in Shancarrig and outlying areas.

Nessa's mother treated them with great respect. They would be the backbone of their business, she told her husband. Conor Ryan shrugged. He often thought them a dull crowd, abstemious too, no bar profit from them. Pale, tired men, anxious about their sales, restless, uneasy.

It was Nessa's mother who insisted on the commercial room, and lighting a fire there. There were a few tables strewn around, they could fill their order books and smoke there. They could bring in a cup of tea or coffee.

Conor Ryan thought it a waste. Why couldn't they sit in the bar like any other person? He had noted that few of them followed either horses or dogs, there was little conversation with them at the best of times.

At school everyone was always interested in the hotel and its goings on. They always asked about what the farmers ate for breakfast on the fair days once a month, and whether any of the beasts had ever backed into the windows and broken them, as happened once down in Nellie Dunne's grocery when she forgot to put up the barriers.

Nessa told of the huge breakfasts served all morning, and of how fathers and sons would take turns, one to mind the animals while the other would eat bacon and eggs heaped high on plates.

'Who was your best friend when you were young?' Nessa asked her mother when Breda Ryan was brushing the dark shiny hair which she persisted in admiring so much despite all Nessa's complaints.

'We didn't have time for best friends then. Stay still, Vanessa.'

'Why do you call me Vanessa? Nobody else does.'

'It's your name. There, that looks great.'

'I look like the witch in the school play.'

'Why are you always saying such awful things about yourself, child? If you think these stupid things, other people will too.'

'That's funny. That's what Leo said too.'

'She's got her head screwed on her shoulders, that one,' Mrs Ryan said approvingly.

'We'll be going into the convent together next year, every day on the bus. Maybe she'll be more my friend then.'

In a rare moment of affection Nessa's mother held her eldest daughter close.

'You'll have plenty of friends. Wait and see!' she said.

'It had better start soon. I'm nearly fourteen,' Nessa said glumly.

In magazine stories Nessa had read of girls whose mothers were like friends. She wished she had a mother like that, not one so brisk and so sure of everything. Nessa had never known an occasion when her mother had been wrong, or at a loss for a word. Her father now, that was different, he was always scratching his head and saying he hadn't a clue about things. But Nessa felt her mother was born knowing all the answers.

On their last day at Shancarrig school Nessa Ryan stood between Niall Hayes and Foxy Dunne during the school photograph. Mrs Kelly always liked to have a picture taken on that day, and they were urged to dress themselves up well so that future generations could see how respectable had been the classes that had gone through these schoolrooms.

It had become a tradition now. The formal photograph taken under the tree outside the schoolhouse door. The very last moment of the year, organised to calm them down after the other tradition of name carving and the boisterous racing around the classroom collecting the books and pencils while singing:

> *No more Irish, no more French*
> *No more sitting on a hard school bench*
> *Kick up tables, kick up chairs*
> *Kick the master and the mistress down the stairs.*

That there had been no French ever learned in Shancarrig and that there were no stairs in the schoolhouse were details that didn't concern them. All over the world children sang that song on the last day.

Those who were only thirteen, and would have to return to school after the summer, looked on enviously. This was the day when they wrote their names on the tree. The boys had brought penknives. Everyone was busy digging at the wood of the old beech tree.

Nessa wished she could enjoy this like the others did. They all seemed very intense. Maura Brennan had been planning for weeks where she would put her name. Eddie Barton said he was going to carve his in a drawing of a flower so that it would look special in years to come. Foxy was saying nothing, but looked knowing all the same.

Nessa took the extra knife from Master Kelly and wrote Vanessa Ryan, June 1954. She felt there was more to say, but she didn't know what it was.

The sun was in their eyes as they squinted at Mrs Kelly's camera.

'Stand up straight! Stop fidgeting there!' She spoke knowing these were the last commands she would ever give them.

Foxy Dunne stroked Nessa's hair, which hung loose on her shoulders. 'Very nice,' he said.

'Take your hands off me, Foxy Dunne,' she snapped.

'Just admiring, Miss Bossy Boots. Admiring, that's all.' He didn't look the slightest bit put out.

Imagine Foxy, from that desperate house of Dunnes, daring to touch her hair.

'It is very nice, your hair,' Niall Hayes said. Square, dependable, dull Niall, who had never had an original thought. He said it as if he were trying to curry favour with Foxy and excuse him for his views.

'Well,' she said, at a loss for words. To her surprise she felt her face and neck redden at the praise. Nessa Ryan hadn't known a compliment from a boy before. She put her hand up to her face so that they wouldn't see her flush.

'Smile, everyone. Nessa, take your hand away from your face at once. Leo, if I see you put your tongue out once more there's going to be trouble. Great trouble.'

Everyone laughed, and it was a happy picture for the schoolhouse wall.

As they walked together for the last time from Shancarrig school, Nessa and Leo were arm in arm and Maura Brennan walked with them. Maura would get a job as a maid or in a factory, she had said she didn't want to go to England like her sisters. Nessa felt a flash of sympathy for the girl who hadn't the same chances as she had. Nessa's father had said about the Brennans and the Dunnes from the cottages that they had a poor hand dealt to them, very few aces there.

'Don't describe everything in terms of cards,' Mrs Ryan corrected him.

'Right. Then I'd say that the bookie's odds against the Brennans and Dunnes were fixed,' he said, grinning.

But Maura Brennan never complained.

She was always very agreeable and quiet, as if she had accepted long ago that her father was a disgrace and her mother was always asking for handouts. Foxy Dunne was different, he behaved as if his family were dukes and earls instead of drunks and layabouts. You'd never know from looking at Foxy Dunne that his father and brothers were barred from almost every establishment in the town. They weren't even allowed into their Uncle Jimmy's the hardware shop.

Foxy neither apologised for them nor defended them. It was as if he regarded them as separate people.

Nessa wished she could be like that sometimes. It hurt her when her mother was sharp to her easy-going father. It annoyed her when her father just shrugged and took none of the responsibility.

'There's a gypsy telling fortunes. They say she's terrific,' Maura said.

'Will we get our fortunes told?' Leo's eyes were sparkling.

Nessa knew that her mother would be very cross indeed if they went anywhere near the tinkers' camp. So would Leo's mother, but Leo didn't care. It would be wonderful to be as free as that.

'She'd only tell you back what you'd tell her,' Foxy said. 'That's what they do. They ask you what you want to be and then they tell you two minutes later that this is what's going to happen to you.'

'But that's dishonest,' Niall Hayes objected.

'That's life, Niall.' Foxy spoke as if he knew much more of the world from his broken-down cottage than did Niall Hayes, the lawyer's son who lived in The Terrace.

'So? Will we go?' Leo was on for any excitement.

'We could read palms to know what's going to happen to us,' Eddie said suddenly.

That seemed much safer to Nessa. Her mother need never know of this. 'How could we do it?' she asked.

'It's easy. There's a life line and a love line, and a whole lot of ridges for children.' Eddie sounded very confident.

'Where did you learn all this?' Foxy asked.

'I got interested in it through a friend,' he said.

'Is that your pen-friend?' Leo asked. He nodded.

A wave of jealousy flooded over Nessa. How did Leo know everything about everyone else and hardly anything about Nessa, who was meant to be her best friend?

'If we're going to do it, let's do it.' Nessa spoke sharply.

They walked up through Barna Woods, up towards the Old Rock.

No one needed to lead the way or decide where they were going. Once anything of importance had to be done, it was always at the Old Rock.

Eddie showed them their life lines. Everyone seemed to have a long one.

'How many years to the inch, do you think?' Foxy asked.

'I don't know,' Eddie admitted.

'Lots, I'd say.' Maura wanted to believe the best.

'Now. This is the heart line.' These varied. Nessa's seemed to have a break in hers.

'That means you'll have two loves,' Eddie explained.

'Or maybe love the same person twice. You know. Get your heart broken in the middle and then he'd come back to you,' Maura suggested.

'I might break *his* heart, whoever he is.' Nessa tossed her head.

'Yeah, sure. It doesn't say. Back to the lines.' Eddie moved away from troubled waters.

Foxy's heart line was faint.

So was Leo's. 'Is that good or bad?' Leo asked.

'It's good.' Foxy was firm. 'It means that neither of us will have much romance until it's time for us to marry each other.'

They all laughed.

Eddie moved to children. You'd know how many you were going to have by the number of tiny lines that went sideways at the base of your little finger. Maura was going to have six. She giggled. She'd be like her mother, she said, not knowing when to stop. Leo was going to have two. So was Foxy. He nodded approvingly. Eddie and Niall didn't look as if they were going to have any. They kept searching their hands and uttering great mock wails of despair.

Nessa had three little lines.

'That's three fine little Ryans to bring into the hotel with you,' Foxy said approvingly. He had already pointed out to Leo that they each had a matching score of two on their hands.

'Not Ryans,' Nessa corrected him sharply. 'They'll be my husband's name.'

'Yeah, but if you're anything like your ma they'll be thought of as Ryans,' Foxy said.

Nessa wouldn't let him see how annoyed she was. She fought back the tears of rage at his mockery.

'Don't let him upset you,' Leo said. 'Let it roll off.'

'It's all right for you. You don't care about your family,' Nessa snapped.

The others were still counting their future children. Leo and Nessa sat apart.

Although Nessa's eyes were bright, she would not allow herself to cry. She felt she had to keep talking, it might stop her starting to weep. 'If anyone says anything about your mother or father, Leo Murphy, you just laugh.'

'It wouldn't matter *what* they say, Nessa you eejit. It's only important if it upsets you, otherwise it's just words floating around in the air.'

Leo had lost interest as usual.

She went off to join the others, who had discovered the line in your hand that meant money. It looked as if the only one who would have any wealth to speak of was Maura Brennan from the cottages, the least likely one of them all.

Nessa didn't wait around to hear how her own future was mapped out in terms of wealth. Maybe Foxy would make some joke about her father's love of horses and greyhounds. It was so unfair, she raged. You couldn't answer back. You couldn't say that Foxy Dunne's father was even barred from Johnny Finn's, which meant he must have done something spectacular in terms of drunkenness.

Nor could you say that Foxy had one brother in gaol, and one who had got on the boat to England an hour ahead of the posse before *he* was in gaol too. It seemed that by being so really desperate Foxy's family had put themselves above being spoken badly of.

And yet she got annoyed at home when her mother would say those very things about the Dunnes. She found herself defending her friends in her home and defending her family when she was with her friends.

She couldn't bear it when Maura Brennan wiped her nose on her sleeve, because she knew her mother would sigh and shake her head.

But it was just as bad and even worse if Eddie and Niall were around when her mother would speak sharply to Dad, and tell him to clear the papers away, put on his jacket and make some pretence of running a hotel. She had seen them exchange glances once or twice at her mother's sharpness of tongue.

She longed to explain that it was needed, that Dad would sit there for ever telling long pedigrees of dogs and horses in faraway race tracks, while people waited to be served. She wished they knew that her father didn't take offence like other men might.

Nessa wanted her friends to be interested in tales she told about what her parents discussed over supper at home, but no one could care less. She wanted her mother and father to listen to stories about Foxy being mad enough to fancy Leo, without sniffing and saying something dismissive about both of them.

Up to now, she had felt safe in her family. It was one of the many bad things about growing up that you began to feel it wasn't as safe as it used to be.

A few days after the end of term the convent where Nessa would go to school sent a message saying that they would like to see the new pupils in advance.

'We'll dress you up smartly. It's important to make a good impression,' her mother said.

'But they're not going to refuse me, are they?'

'Will you ever learn? You want them to treat you as someone important, then *look* like someone important.'

'They're nuns, Mam. They don't look at things in that snobby way.'

'They don't, my foot.' Her mother was adamant.

They had a good outing. Leo went in her ordinary clothes, she hadn't dressed up at all.

'She doesn't need to,' Nessa's mother had said when they saw Leo arriving in her ordinary pink cotton frock, with its faded flower pattern and frayed collar.

'Why?'

'Because she is who she is.'

It was a mystery.

Leo was in great form that day, she and Nessa laughed and giggled at everything. They laughed all the more because they had to keep such solemn faces in the convent.

The corridors were long and smelled of floor polish. Little red lights burned in front of statues and pictures of the Sacred Heart, little blue lights in front of Our Lady.

Mother Dorothy, the Principal, spoke to them very earnestly about the need to behave well in school uniform. She told them that it would all be very very different from Shancarrig. She made Shancarrig sound as if it were on the back of the moon.

'Are you two great friends?' Mother Dorothy asked.

'Everyone's friends in our school,' Leo shrugged.

The nun's bright eyes seemed to take it all in.

Leo was all for exploring the town.

'We'd better go back,' Nessa said. 'They'll be wondering where we are.'

Leo looked at her in surprise. 'We're nearly fifteen, we've gone to see the convent where we are going to be imprisoned for the next three years. What can they be worried about?' she asked.

'They'll find something,' Nessa said.

'You're a scream.' Leo was affectionate.

And then, about three weeks later, Leo became almost a different person as far as Nessa was concerned. She was never around, and seemed unwilling to stir from The Glen at all. She'd gone off mysteriously for a holiday with her mother and father and the two great stupid dogs without even telling anyone where she was going.

The summer was endless. There was nobody to play with. Maura Brennan had gone around asking everyone could she be a maid in their house, and eventually Nessa's mother had given her a job, as a chambermaid in the hotel. Maura slept in, which was stupid because it was only ten minutes' walk to the cottages. But then again, Mother had said would Maura want to sleep in that place, and would you want to have her sleeping there?

Eddie Barton was lost in his old pressed flowers, and writing letters. Niall Hayes was complaining all the time about the school he was going to start in next September. He seemed to want reassurance that it was going to be all right.

Nessa wished that Leo was more like Niall, dependent on her, asking for advice. She thought Niall should be more like that tough little girl up in The Glen, able to survive on her own, fight her own battles.

Her mother noticed, like she always did.

'I've told you a dozen times, lead and they'll follow.'

'I could lead a thousand miles and Leo would never follow.' Nessa wished she hadn't admitted it, but it was out before she knew it. Breda Ryan sighed, she looked disappointed. 'I'm sorry, Mam, but it's different for you. You were always a born leader. Some people just have it in them.'

Her mother looked at her thoughtfully.

'I've been thinking about your hair,' she said unexpectedly.

'Well, don't think about it,' Nessa cried. 'Don't always think about how everyone else could do things better if only they did them like you.'

'Nessa!' Her mother was shocked at the outburst.

'I mean it. I'm fifteen. In some countries I could be married and have my own family. *You* always know best. *You* know Dad can't talk about greyhounds. *You* know that we can't call anyone a fella because you think it's vulgar, we have to say boy or man or something that no one else says.'

'I try to give you some manners. Style, that's all.'

'No. That's not all. You don't let us be normal. Maura is below us for some reason. Leo Murphy's family is above us because they live in a big house. You're *so* sure of everything, you just *know* you're right.' Nessa's face was red and angry.

'What brought this on, may I ask?'

'My hair. I was having an ordinary conversation with you and suddenly you said you wanted to talk to me about my hair. I don't care *what* you want, I won't do it. I won't do it. I'll go and tell Dad you want me to cut it or dye it or put it in an awful bun like yours. Whatever you want I won't do it.'

'Fine, fine . . . if that's the way you feel.' Her mother stood up to leave the sitting room.

Nessa was still in a temper. 'That's right. You'll go down now to Daddy and frighten him. You'll tell him I'm being so difficult you don't know how to handle me, and then poor Dad will come and plead with me, and ask me to apologise.'

'Is that what you think I'm going to do?' Her mother looked distant and surprised.

'It's what you've done for years.' She was in so far now it didn't matter what she said.

'As it happens I was *going* to tell you about your hair. That it never looked better, that you should get a good cut. I was going to suggest that we went to Dublin together and I took you to a good place that I asked about.'

'I don't believe you!'

'Well, believe what you like. The address is here on a piece of paper. I was going to say we could go on the cheap excursion on Wednesday. But go on your own.'

'How can I go on my own? I've no money.'

'I was going to ask your father to give you the money.'

'But you're not now. I see. You mean I lost it all by being badly behaved.' Nessa gave a mirthless laugh to show she knew the ways of adults.

'Ask him yourself, Nessa. You're too tiresome to talk to any more.'

Nessa didn't ask her father, so he mentioned it on Tuesday night. Why didn't she take the day trip up to Dublin and have a nice haircut. She said she didn't want to go, she said her mother hated her, she said her mother was only making her feel guilty, she said her hair was horrible, that it was like a horse's tail.

She said she wouldn't go to Dublin on her own.

'Take Leo. I'll stand you both,' he said.

'You can't, Dad.'

'Yes, I can. I make some of the decisions around here.'

'No, you don't.'

'I do, Nessa. I make the ones I want to.' There was something about his voice. She believed him utterly.

Leo went to Dublin with her.

The hairdresser spent ages cutting and styling. 'You should come back every three months.'

'What about in five years?' Nessa said.

'Don't mind her,' Leo interrupted. 'She looks so great now they'll have her up every week.'

'Do I really?' Nessa asked.

'Do you really what?'

'Look great? Were you just saying it to be polite to her?'

'But you're terrific-looking. You *must* know that. You're like Jean Simmons or someone.' Leo said this as if it was as obvious as that it was day rather than night.

'How would I know? No one ever told me.'

'I'm telling you.'

'You're just my friend. You could be telling me just to keep me quiet,' Nessa complained.

'Ah God, Nessa. You can be very tiresome sometimes,' Leo said.

It was the same word as her mother had used. She had better watch it.

It was an up and down relationship with her mother all the years that Nessa Ryan went to school every day in the big town.

It was no use talking to Leo because Leo didn't seem to consider her own mother as any part of her life. If Nessa couldn't go to the pictures it was because her mother wanted her to clean the silver. If Leo couldn't go to the pictures it was only because Lance and Jessica – the dogs – needed to go for a run, or because her father wanted help with something.

Mrs Murphy was never mentioned.

Nessa heard that Mrs Murphy of The Glen was not a strong woman and possibly suffered from her nerves, but this wasn't talked about much in front of children. Leo seemed very distracted, as if there was something wrong at home, but even in the cosiest of chats she couldn't be persuaded to talk about it.

And there were so few other people to talk to.

She wasn't encouraged to talk to Maura Brennan who worked as a chambermaid in the hotel. Every time she stopped in a corridor to speak to Maura, Maura looked around nervously.

'No, Nessa. Your mother wouldn't like us to be chatting.'

'That's bull, Maura. Anyway, I don't care what she wants.'

'I do. It's my bread and butter.'

And there was no answer to that.

Sometimes Mrs Ryan was terrific, like when she got them all dancing lessons – Leo, Nessa and her young sisters Catherine and Nuala, the two Blake girls. It had been the greatest of fun.

Sometimes Mother was horrible – when she had asked Father to leave the bar the night he won eighty-five pounds on a greyhound. 'I just didn't want to lose *two hundred* and eighty-five pounds, Nessa,' she had explained afterwards. 'He was going out in to the streets looking for greyhounds, or anything that approached them in shape, to buy them drinks.'

Nessa had fumed over it. Her father should have been allowed his dignity. He should have had his night of celebration.

Her mother had been wonderful about the record player, and Nessa built up her own collection – 'Three Coins in the Fountain', 'Rock Around the Clock', 'Whatever Will Be Will Be'. But by the time she bought Tab Hunter's 'Young Love' her mother had become horrible again, saying that Nessa was now leaving school with a very poor Leaving Certificate.

There was no question of university, no plan for a career, nothing except the usual refuge of those who couldn't think what to do – the secretarial course in the town.

Nessa became very mulish that summer. Several times her father asked her for the sake of peace to try and ensure they had a happy house.

'You're so weak, Daddy,' she snapped at him one day. She was sorry instantly. It was so like something she felt her mother would have said.

'No, I'm not weak actually. I just like a quiet life without the people I love fighting like tinkers, that's all.' He spoke mildly.

'Why do you nag me so much?' she asked her mother. 'I mean, it's not going to make either of us happier, and it's upsetting Daddy.'

'I don't think of it as nagging. I think of it as giving you courage and strength to live your own life. To be full of courage. Honestly.' She believed her mother too when she said that.

'Did you always have courage?'

'No I did not. I learned it when I came to this house. When I had to cope with the pair on the wall.'

'The what?'

'Your sainted grandparents,' her mother said crisply.

Nessa looked up in shock at the elderly Ryans who had always been spoken of with such admiration and respect in this house.

'Why did it need courage to cope with them?' she asked.

'They would have liked your father to have lived in a glass case and they could have thrown sugar at him,' Mrs Ryan said.

When she said things like this she seemed very normal, like someone you could talk to, but she didn't say them often enough.

So, the summer she was eighteen Nessa began her course in shorthand and typewriting with a very bad grace.

Leo Murphy wouldn't come with her, a series of vague and unsatisfactory excuses about being needed up at The Glen. It was a confused time in Shancarrig.

Eddie Barton was so depressed working in Dunne's that he could hardly raise his eyes when you went in to talk to him. Niall Hayes was in Dublin setting up his plans to study law. Foxy was in England on the building sites. The Blake girls were studying in Dublin. She wasn't meant to talk to Maura. Her mother asked so many questions about who she went to the pictures with in the big town it sometimes seemed hardly worth the whole business of going.

She was ready for something exciting to happen the weekend Richard Hayes came to town.

He was very handsome, not square like Niall. He was tall and slim and very grown up, seven or eight years older than Nessa – twenty-five or twenty-six. He had been sent away from Dublin because of some disgrace with a girl.

Everyone knew that.

He had been banished to Shancarrig. Where apparently there would be no girls. Or no girls worth looking at.

Nessa dressed herself very very carefully until she caught his eye.

'Things *are* looking up,' he said. 'I'm Richard Hayes.'

'Hello, Richard,' Nessa said in a voice she had been practising for weeks.

His smile was warm but it made her nervous. She longed to run away and ask someone for advice, and as it happened at that very moment her mother called for her.

'Now I know your name,' he said.

'Only my mother calls me Vanessa,' she said.

But she was glad to escape.

Her mother had seen it all. 'What a handsome young man,' she said.

'Yes.' Nessa bit her lip.

'You have absolutely no competition,' her mother assured her. 'That's a man who likes pretty girls, and you are the prettiest girl in Shancarrig.'

The next time he met her he suggested that she take him for a walk.

'I'd love to do that but I'm practising my awful grammalogues,' said Nessa.

'Shorthand is going out of fashion, it'll all be machines soon,' he said.

'You may very well be right, but not before I do my Certificate exams. So maybe I'll see you later in the evening,' she said. She could see by his eyes that she had done the right thing. He was more interested than ever before.

'Absolutely, Vanessa,' he said with a mock bow.

She took him for long walks around her country.

She brought him up to the Old Rock and told him all its legends. She brought him to the school and showed him the tree where they had carved their names. She took him to the graveyard and pointed out the oldest tombstones to him. She showed him the children fishing in the river, and explained how you caught little fish with your hands if you could trap them in the stones.

She told him about Mattie the postman, who didn't go to mass but could deliver any letter to anyone if it just had their name and Shancarrig on it. She brought him to meet Father Gunn and Father Barry, saying that she was being a guide. Mrs Kennedy, the priests' housekeeper, looked very disapproving so Nessa just laughed and sat up on her table, saying that she had brought Richard Hayes here especially to taste one of Mrs Kennedy's scones. They were legendary.

Privately she told Richard they were legendary because they were as heavy as stones.

Nessa took Richard Hayes to visit Miss Ross in her house, she brought him to Nellie Dunne's shop, she took him to every nook and cranny in about three days.

'It's your introduction,' she said to him cheerfully. 'So that you'll never say you weren't shown the place properly.' She could sense that he was delighted with her, that he thought her a confident, bright young woman.

And indeed, that is what she was.

She was proud of her dark thick hair, her clear skin, her bright yellow and red blouses, and most proud of all that she wasn't silly and giggling like so many others were with him. Her mother had given her this gift, this belief that she was the equal of any Adonis who came to Shancarrig.

But Nessa would not settle for a weaker man like her mother had done. She wouldn't take second best, which was obviously how her mother must regard her father. There would be no dull, plodding, average fellow for Nessa. Not now. Not now that she had seen the admiring glance of a man like Richard.

He was the kind of man who came through a town like this once every fifty years. She was lucky to have caught his eye, she must be absolutely certain not to lose it again. This was the kind of man you could dream about night and day, someone who would occupy all your thoughts. But for some reason she didn't really allow herself to think about what she felt for him, this charming attentive Richard Hayes, who seemed to want to spend every free minute he had in her company. Yes of course she wanted to think that he really liked her, but some warning voice made her think that she could only keep his attention if she didn't seem to care.

It was an act.

Life shouldn't be an act. Yet she felt that they were unequal somehow. She must play this one very carefully.

Of course she heard a lot of stories about why he had come to help his Uncle Bill in the office. Some people said that Mr Hayes was getting too busy to manage on his own and that he had little hopes of his son Niall ever learning enough about the business. Niall was off to University in Dublin where he would serve his time in a solicitor's office as well. It would be four or five years before he'd qualify – old Bill Hayes was quite right to take this bright young man into his firm.

There were others who said that Richard had been sent to Shancarrig to cool his heels – there had been talk of an incident in Dublin, an incident involving a judge's daughter. There was another story about a broken engagement and a breach of promise action settled at the last moment.

In the stories Richard Hayes, cousin of the solid Niall, was always shown as a playboy.

The feeling was that Shancarrig would be very small potatoes indeed for someone who had seen and done as much as this handsome young man of twenty-five or so who had taken the place by storm.

'Isn't he fantastic?' Leo had said when she saw him for the first time.

'He's very easy to talk to.' Nessa was quick to let her best friend know just how far she was ahead in the race which every woman in Shancarrig seemed to have joined.

'I wish he'd come into the bar more,' Nessa's mother said. 'He's such an attractive kind of fellow he'd be a great draw.'

'I'd say that boyo has been asked to leave more bars than a few,' Conor Ryan said with the voice of a man who has seen it all and knew it all.

Unexpectedly Gerry O'Sullivan, their personable young barman, agreed.

'Real lady killer,' he said. 'The kind they'd go for each other's throats over.'

'That's what we don't need,' Mrs Ryan said firmly. 'Maybe it's just as well he's not in here every night.'

'Who is there in Shancarrig that would cut anyone's throat over a fellow? There's not that kind of passion and spark around the place at all.' Conor Ryan was back reading the forecasts for race meetings in towns he would never visit, on courses he would never walk.

Breda Ryan looked thoughtfully out at the front desk where Nessa was painstakingly practising her typing. They were meant to do an hour a day homework, and she had covered up the keys of the hotel machine with Elastoplast so that she couldn't see the letters.

Nessa's hair was shiny, her eyes were bright, her neckline low. They didn't have to look far for any passion and spark as far as Richard Hayes was concerned.

Nessa fought off three attempts by her mother to talk about sex.

'I *know* all that, didn't you tell me that years ago when I got my periods first.'

'It's different kind of telling now, there are other things to be taken into consideration . . . please, Nessa.'

'There are no other things, I don't want to talk about it.' She wriggled away.

She didn't want to hear her mother say anything coarse or frightening. She was terrified enough already. These were problems that no mother could solve.

Richard Hayes told Nessa that she was beautiful. He called into the hotel and sat up on the reception desk to talk to her. It was the middle of the afternoon, a time when hotel business was slack and when Richard very probably should have been in his uncle's office.

He told Nessa that she had wonderful dark looks and she reminded him of Diana the huntress.

'Was she good or bad?'

'She was beautiful. Don't you know about her?'

'No, the nuns sort of dwelt more on the New Testament. She was the one that was extremely chaste, wasn't she?'

'That's her story and she's sticking to it,' he laughed, and she reddened. It seemed to her that he was eyeing her as if he was thinking along those lines himself.

He stroked her cheek thoughtfully.

'What happens if a girl is less than extremely chaste here?' he asked.

'They go to their grannies or to England.' She hoped that her cheeks didn't still look so red. It was just that he was looking at her breasts and appreciating her in a way that a man might if he wanted to make love.

Or maybe she was just fancying it. Nessa didn't know these days if anything was real or whether she was imagining a whole series of looks and gestures and feelings that didn't exist at all.

'I'd be very careful if we were . . . to do anything that might cause a trip to your Granny's,' he said. 'You know, really careful. There would be no danger at all.'

From somewhere she found a confident answer.

'Ah but there wouldn't be any question of that, Richard,' she said.

He was more interested than ever.

'Are you afraid?'

'No. There could be other reasons why people might say no to you.'

'But you do like me, that I know.' He was playful.

'But do I *love* you, and do you love *me*? That's what you'd have to ask yourself before going wherever people go.'

'Like up to the Old Rock?'

He had only been in Shancarrig ten days and already he knew where the lovers went. To the little hollow in Barna Woods where the road to the Old Rock began.

'If only we knew what love is, Vanessa Mary Ryan, then we could rule the world.' He sighed a heavy mock sigh.

'And would we rule it well, Richard Aloysius Hayes?' she laughed.

'How did you know that?'

'I asked Niall what the RAH stood for on your tennis bag.'

'And he told you? The swine!'

They were fencing now, and laughing. He caught her by the wrist.

'I'm not joking, you're the loveliest girl for miles around.'

'You haven't seen any others.'

'Excuse me but I have. I went on a tour of inspection, brought my tennis bag up to The Glen, got no game, and no great joy out of your so-called best friend, little bag of nerves with a frizzy head, she is.'

'Don't speak like that about Leo.'

'And I studied Madeleine Ross.'

'She's ancient.'

'She's three years older than I am. And let me see who else. Pretty little Maura Brennan who works in Ryan's Ritz, but I think she's been to the Old Rock with a young Mr O'Sullivan. We'll have wedding bells there if I'm not greatly mistaken.'

'Maura? Pregnant! I don't believe it.'

He held up his hands defensively.

'I could be wrong,' he said.

'She's a fool. Gerry O'Sullivan will never marry her . . .' Nessa had let it slip out.

'Aha . . . so it's not just a question of loving each other. It's a question of the chap marrying the girl, is it?'

Nessa had lost that one. 'I must be off,' she said.

She barely made it upstairs on shaking legs and went into her room. There she found her sisters Catherine and Nuala starting up guiltily from the dressing table where they had been reading her diary.

'I thought you were meant to be at the reception desk,' Catherine said, flying immediately to the attack.

'We hadn't read anything private really,' begged Nuala, who was younger and more frightened.

Frightened she had reason to be.

Nessa Ryan, eighteen and desired by the most handsome man in Ireland, drew herself up to her full height.

'You can explain all that later,' she said, taking the key out of the inside of the door. 'I'm locking you in until I find Mother.'

'Don't tell Mam,' roared Nuala.

'Mam won't like what you've been up to,' Catherine threatened.

But Nessa had the upper hand. She had written nothing in her diary, it was all in the back of her shorthand notebook which never left her side.

She had been coming up to write more, to tell herself of the passion in his voice, the tingles she had felt when he held her wrist, how he had said that he could love her.

She ignored the pleas and lamentations from her room and set off to find her mother.

In the corridor she met Maura Brennan carrying sheets.

'Is everything all right, Maura?' she asked.

'Why do you ask?'

'Well, I don't know. You look different.'

'I *am* different. I'm getting married next week to Gerry. I haven't told everyone else. It was only just arranged.'

'Married?'

'I know. Isn't it great!'

Nessa was dumbfounded. Perhaps there was a different set of rules, perhaps fellows *did* marry you if you went to the Old Rock with them. Maybe her mother and the nuns and Catholic Truth Society pamphlets had it all wrong. She pulled herself together.

'That's great, Maura,' she said. 'Congratulations.'

Nessa found her mother, and told her of the two criminals locked in the bedroom.

'Give them a very bad punishment,' she ordered.

'Did they find anything to read, anything they shouldn't have?' Her mother's eyes were anxious.

'If I have to say to you once more that there is nothing to find, nothing to discuss, I will go *mad*.' The words were almost shouted.

To her surprise her mother looked at her admiringly.

'You know, I think Richard may be good for you after all. You're getting to be confident at last. You'll be a leader yet.'

It was true. She did feel more in control. She was delighted to find that her mother took such a strong stand with Catherine and Nuala. And so, unexpectedly, did her father.

'A person must be allowed to have their private life and their dreams,' he told the two sulking girls, who were allowed no outings for a week. 'It's a monstrous thing to invade someone's life of dreams.'

'There was nothing there,' Catherine said.

'To say that is making it worse still.'

The two girls were startled.

There was Nessa, usually the one in trouble, Nessa who had been making calf's eyes at Niall Hayes's cousin, and all she was getting was praise for doing something as dangerous as locking them in a bedroom.

'Suppose there had been a fire?' Catherine even suggested as a possibility. She got little support.

'Then you would have burned to death,' said their mother.

Eddie Barton came in sometimes for a chat.

'Are you doing a line with Richard Hayes?' he asked Nessa.

'What's a line?'

'I don't know, I often wondered. But are you?'

'No I'm not. He comes in and out. He's very handsome, probably too handsome for me.'

'I know what you mean,' Eddie said unflatteringly.

'Thanks a lot, friend.'

'No, I didn't mean that. You're fine-looking and you've got much better-looking than when we were all young, honestly . . .' Eddie was flustered now and he saw he was making gestures to show how much better-looking Nessa had got. Gestures that indicated a bosom and a small waist. But she didn't seem offended. 'Looks are important, aren't they?' He seemed anxious.

'I suppose so, though people keep saying they're not.'

Eddie was running his hand through his spiky hair. 'I wish fellows improved, all fellows, like all girls seem to.'

'Aren't you a grand-looking fellow, Eddie?' Her voice was encouraging and light, she thought.

'Don't make fun of me.' His face was red.

'I'm not.'

'Yes you are. I've hair like God knows what, I'm pushing a brush around bloody Dunne's all day. Who'd look at me?'

He banged out of the hotel, leaving Nessa mystified. As far as she knew Eddie had never asked any girl in Shancarrig out, and had shown no interest at all in any of the females around the place. He did come in from time to time to make mysterious phone calls to Scotland. It was too hard to understand, and anyway she had far more important things on her mind.

Richard took Nessa to the pictures in the town in his uncle's car.

'He lets you drive this?'

'He doesn't go out at night.'

'Niall never drove it.'

'Niall never asked.'

Niall Hayes was staying with a schoolfriend of his. Together they were going to a three-week course in book-keeping. They hated it. Niall had sent several letters and postcards to Nessa saying how dreary it was. He hoped university would be better.

'I think Niall fancies you desperately,' Richard said as he kissed Nessa in his uncle's car.

She drew away.

'I don't think so,' she said, cool, ungiggly. Her mother was right. She had grown up a lot since Richard had come to Shancarrig.

'Oh I think he does. Doesn't he take you to the pictures? Doesn't Niall plan journeys to the Old Rock with you like I do?' He repeated his own words about his younger cousin.

'Niall never asked,' said Nessa.

'Niall will be back tomorrow, Ethel was telling me,' Mrs Ryan said to Nessa.

'That should shake the town to its foundations,' Nessa said.

'You and he were always good friends.' Her mother's voice was mild so Nessa became contrite.

'That's true, we were. He's got very mopey though, Mam. Not easy to talk to.'

'Everyone doesn't have the charm of his cousin Richard.'

'Richard's normal. He's nice to people, he's pleasant. He's not always grousing and groaning about things the way Niall is.'

'Maybe Niall has something to grouse and groan about.'

'What? What any more than the rest of us?'

'Well, his best girl is starry-eyed about his cousin, his place in the firm isn't nearly as secure as it used to be ... *and* he doesn't have a wonderful understanding mother like you do. He has dreary old Ethel.'

They laughed as they sometimes could nowadays like sisters, like friends.

'What would *you* do for Niall if you were his friend?' Nessa asked. She thought she saw her mother watching her very carefully, but she couldn't be sure.

'I'd encourage him to fight for his place over there. He's Bill's son. It's *his* business. I'd tell him that there are only a few chances and you should take them. Oh, I suppose I'd go on a bit about letting grass grow under your feet.'

'He mightn't listen to me.'

'No. People often don't listen when others are out for their good.'

'Did Dad listen to you?'

'Ah, yes. But that was different, I loved your father. Still do.'

'I don't *love* Niall, but I am very fond of him.'

'Then don't let him get walked on,' said Breda Ryan.

Nessa invited Niall to come over to the hotel and have a drink with her. It felt very grown up.

'You look great,' he said.

'Thanks, Niall. You look fine too.'

'I meant *pretty* like . . .' he said.

'What work are you doing in the office?' She changed the subject.

'Filing! Taking things out of torn envelopes and putting them into non-torn envelopes. God, Dinny Dunne could do that on one of his good days.'

Niall was full of misery and Nessa was full of impatience. Why hadn't he the fire to get up and go, the sheer charm of his cousin? They were the sons of brothers, after all. Richard's father must have been the one with the spirit.

Richard had told his uncle that a younger man should go around on home visits, which meant that he had the use of the car and could be out all day. Who knew how long it took to make a will or to get the details in a right-of-way claim? Who could measure how many hours it might involve talking to a publican about the extinguishing of a licence or to a woman about a marriage settlement involving a farm?

Richard was sunny and cheerful to everyone.

If he had been asked to do the files he would have made it into the most prestigious job in the office. Why could Niall not see this? Why did he hunch his shoulders and look defeated? Why didn't he throw back his head and laugh?

'Did you see much of Richard while I was away?' Niall asked, cutting across her thoughts.

'He's been around, he's been very lively.'

'He's not reliable, of course,' Niall said.

'Don't be such a tell-tale, Niall.' Her lightness of voice hid her annoyance. She wanted to hear nothing that would puncture her idea of Richard Hayes, no silly family story of shame or disgrace.

'It's just that you should know.'

'Oh, I know all about him,' she said airily.

'You do?' Niall seemed relieved.

'A girl in every town. We even had that Elaine down from Dublin last week. No, there are no secrets.'

'Elaine was here? After all that happened!'

'Right in front of your house. Dropped him off from a real posh car.'

'There'll be hell to pay if anyone knows that. She was the one.'

'The one?'

'The one that had the ... the one who got into ... the one.'

'Oh yes, I supposed she was.' Nessa's heart was leaden. Niall didn't have to finish any of his sentences. The stories had gone before, the judge's daughter who was reported to have been pregnant.

Imagine her coming down to Shancarrig, pursuing Richard after all that. She must be pretty desperate.

'So that's all right.' Niall looked at Nessa protectively, as if he was relieved that he didn't have to rescue her from a quagmire of misunderstanding.

'We're all fine here, it was a lovely summer. *You* sound as if you had a terrible time.' She led him into a further catalogue of his woes so that she could follow her own line of thought. Surely Richard couldn't still be involved with this girl. Then of course it was known that this girl, unlike Nessa, would go to bed with him. And had.

Is this all he wanted? Surely he wanted other things – fun and chat, and kissing, and a girl who was seven years younger than him who looked like Diana the huntress?

If only there was someone to ask. But there was no one.

On Maura Brennan's wedding day Leo suggested they go to the church.

'Maura won't like it. She doesn't want to mix because of working in the hotel.'

'That's pure rubbish,' Leo said. 'It's just your mother who doesn't want her to mix. Let's go.'

As they sat waiting for the sad little ceremony to begin Nessa was pleased to see Niall Hayes and Eddie Barton come in as well.

'I got an hour off from the desperate Dunnes,' Eddie whispered – he worked for the more respectable branch of the family in Foxy's uncle's hardware shop. He seemed very miserable about it.

'I'm allowed out from sticking labels on envelopes,' Niall said.

'I'm meant to be at the typing course but I told my mother we had a day off. I'm watched like a hawk,' Nessa complained.

'We weren't the most successful class ever to come out of Shancarrig school, were we?' asked Leo with a little laugh.

'Well, at least the rest of us ...' Nessa stopped. She had remembered before that Leo had looked very upset when she had been referred to as a lady of leisure.

Leo flashed her a smile of gratitude. They sat in supportive silence, the four of them, as they watched their schoolfriend Maura, pregnant and happy, marry Gerry O'Sullivan, small, handsome, with one best man but no other friend or family in the church.

'He doesn't look very reliable,' whispered Niall.

'Jesus, Mary and Holy Saint Joseph, who do you think *is* reliable these days?' Nessa hissed.

'*I* am, for what it's worth.' He looked at her and suddenly she saw that he did like her, much more than in the sort of hang-dog dependent way she had thought. Niall Hayes was keen on her. It didn't give her the kind of boost that she had thought it might. In the days when nobody fancied her she would love to have had a few notches on her gun, affections to play with, hearts to break.

But Niall was too much of a friend for that.

'Thank you,' she said very simply in a whisper.

Maura was delighted with the present they bought her, a little glass-fronted cabinet. Leo had remembered Maura saying that she would love to collect treasures and display them in a cabinet. There were tears of joy in her eyes when they delivered it to the cottage where she would be living – only a stone's throw from where her father still fell home drunk every night.

'You're great friends,' she said, her voice choked.

Nessa felt a blanket of guilt almost suffocate her. For years Maura had been working in Ryan's Hotel and hardly a sentence exchanged between them. If only she had the courage of a Leo Murphy she would have taken no heed of offending her mother, of crossing boundaries of familiarity between staff and owners.

But she *did* have courage these days and she would show it, use it. When she got back to the hotel her mother asked where the festivities were going to be held.

'You know that it will be a few drinks in Johnny Finn's and whatever bit of cold chicken poor Maura managed to put out on plates for those that will drag themselves back to her cottage for it.'

'Well, she should have thought of all that . . .' her mother began.

'No she shouldn't, she should be having a reception here by right. She was my schoolfriend, she and Gerry both work here. Anyone with a bit of decency would have given them that at least.'

Breda Ryan was taken aback.

'You don't understand . . .'

'I don't like what I do understand. It's so snobby, so ludicrous. Does it make us better people to be seen to be superior to Maura Brennan from the cottages? Is this what you always wanted, a place on some kind of ladder?'

'No. That's not what I always wanted.' Her mother was calm and didn't show the expected anger at being shouted at in the front hall of the hotel.

'Well, what did you want then?'

'I'll tell you if you take that puss off your face . . . and stop shouting like a fishwife. Come on.' Her mother was talking to her like an equal. They walked into the bar.

'Conor, why don't you take a fiver from the till and go up to Johnny Finn's to buy a few drinks for Gerry and Maura?'

Nessa's father looked up, pleased.

'Didn't I only suggest . . . ?'

'And you were right. Go on now while they're still sober enough to know you're treating them. Nessa and I'll look after the bar.'

They watched as Conor Ryan moved eagerly across to the festivities, hardly daring to believe his good luck. Nessa sat still and waited to be told. Mrs Ryan poured two small glasses of cream sherry, something that had never happened before. Nessa decided to make no comment; she raised the glass to her lips as if she and her mother had been knocking back drinks for years.

'People want things at different times. I wanted a man called Teddy Burke. I wanted him from the moment I saw him when I was sixteen until I was twenty-one. Five long years.' Nessa looked at this stranger sipping the sherry; she was afraid to speak. 'Teddy Burke had a word for everyone, but that's all it was . . . a word . . . I thought it was more. I thought I was special. I built a life of dreams on it. I couldn't eat. I lost my health and my looks, such as they were. They sent me away to do a domestic economy course.

'Do you know, I can't really remember those years. I suppose I must have followed the course – I got my exams and certificates – but I only thought of Teddy Burke.' She paused for such a long time that Nessa felt able to speak.

She spoke as a friend, as an equal. 'And did he know, did he have any idea . . . ?'

'I don't think so, truly. He was so used to everyone admiring, I was just one more.' Her mother's eyes were far away as she sat there in the empty hotel bar, her dark hair back in a loose coil with a mother-of-pearl clasp on it. Her pale pink blouse had its neat collar out over her dark pink cardigan – she looked every inch the successful businesswoman. This story of a thin frightened girl loving a man for five years – a man who didn't know she existed – was hard to believe.

'So anyway, one day I was told that Teddy Burke was going to marry Annie Lynch, the plainest girl for three parishes, with a bad temper and a cast in her eye. Everything changed. He was marrying her for her land, for her great acres running down to the lakes and over green valleys, for the fishing rights, for the stock. A man as handsome and loving as Teddy Burke could trade everything for land.

'It made me wonder what I really wanted.

'And I went to a cousin's wedding and met your father and I decided that I wanted to go far from where I lived, where I would remember Teddy Burke's laugh and his way with people. I decided that I wanted to make your father strong and confident like Teddy was when he got the land, like Annie Lynch always was because she had the land . . . I put my mind to it.'

There was a long silence. Nessa was taking it in.

'Were you ever sorry?'

'Not a day, not once I decided. And hasn't it turned out well? The hotel has survived, the pair out in the pictures in the hall would have let it run into the ground, and they'd have let your father go off to the British army.'

'Why are you telling me this now?'

'Because you thought that all I wanted was to put ourselves above other people. I may have done that by accident but it wasn't what I set out to do.'

'Does Dad know about Teddy Burke?'

'There was nothing for him to know but a young girl's silliness and dreams.'

Mattie came in, his sack of letters delivered.

'This town is going to hell, Mrs Ryan,' he said. 'A wedding party bawling "Bless this House" above in Johnny Finn's and the women of the house sipping sherry in Ryan's.'

'And no one to pour a pint for the postman,' laughed Nessa's mother.

The moment was over, it might never come again.

Nessa began to look at other people in a new light after this. Perhaps everyone had a huge love in their life, or something they thought was a huge love. Maybe Mr Kelly up at the school had fancied a night-club singer before he settled for Mrs Kelly. Maybe Nellie Dunne had once been head over heels in love with some travelling salesman who had come many years ago to Ryan's Commercial Hotel, but who had married someone else. Maybe one of those old men in the commercial room had been Nellie's heart's desire.

It wasn't so impossible.

Look at Eddie Barton, falling in love with someone in Scotland. It had never been exactly clear how he had got in touch with her in the first place, but apparently he had been writing to Christine Taylor for ages, and phoning her from the hotel.

And then she had arrived over and was living with his mother. Nessa was amazed at the change in Eddie. He was speaking to the Dunnes, cousins of Foxy, as if he was their equal. He was in the hotel with Christine discussing improvements and ways to decorate the bedrooms.

Love did extraordinary things to people.

Eileen Blake from The Terrace said that she was stopping for a coffee in Portlaoise on her way back from Dublin and who was there but Richard Hayes and a girl, and they were booking in. As man and wife.

Young Maria Kelly from Shancarrig schoolhouse was reported to have been at a dance with him in the big town, but her parents didn't know because she had climbed in and out her window through the branches of the old copper beech tree that grew in the yard.

Nessa Ryan heard both these facts in the space of three days. She came across them accidentally, they were not brought in as deliberate bad news to her door.

She felt, not as she had feared she might – no sense of cold betrayal, no rage that a man should tell her she was special and he wanted her to be his girl, and yet behave the same way with half the country. Very clearly and deliberately she felt her infatuation with him end. Perhaps she *was* her mother's daughter much more than she had ever believed. She was not ready to give him up but she would have him in her life under different terms.

Richard came into the commercial room of the hotel. There were no travellers staying and so Nessa was using the room to do her shorthand homework.

'I have to go into town tomorrow. I could pick you up outside your college,' he offered.

She could imagine the eyes of her classmates when Richard Hayes leant across to open the door of the car for her.

'And where would we go then?' she asked.

'I'm sure we'd find somewhere,' he said.

Nessa looked back into the bar where her mother and father were standing, well out of earshot.

'They're not listening.' Richard was impatient. But that wasn't what concerned Nessa. She looked at them and saw her mother stroke Dad's face gently, lovingly.

She saw that it really never mattered who talked to the men from the brewery, the biscuit salesmen, who hired or fired the barmen. It wasn't important that Sergeant Keane dealt with her mother over the licensing laws, not her father. Mother had forgotten Teddy whatever he was, he'd have been no good to her. She had found what she really wanted, someone she could share her own strength with. Nessa saw for the first time that her mother had got what she wanted. It wasn't a case of settling for second best.

And with a shock of recognition she felt that she was going to follow exactly the same path. It wouldn't be a question of aiming high and searching for fireworks. There might be an entirely different way to live your life. Unbidden, Niall's worried face came to mind. She longed to calm him and tell him it would all be all right.

She looked straight at Richard, right into his eyes.

'No thanks,' she said. 'No to everything. Thank you all the same.'

It wasn't at all easy to do.

But she would not live in fear of him and how he would react. Nothing was worth that.

'Well, well, well.' He looked around the room scornfully. 'So *this* is all you are ever going to amount to. A second-rate shabby hotel . . . a grown woman still a prisoner to her mother.' He looked very angry and put out. People didn't usually speak to Richard Hayes like this. Girls certainly didn't.

Nessa was furious.

'It is *not* a shabby hotel. It's my home. *My* home. I live here and I choose to live here. You can't even live where you want to because they run you out of town. Don't come down here and start criticising us. It doesn't sit well on you. And answer me one thing: how would I amount to any more if I were to go off to the glen with you and roll around for five minutes on the ground?'

'It would be longer than five minutes,' he said mischievously. She hadn't lost him. He fancied her all the more because she was refusing him.

What a wonderful power.

It was the making of Nessa Ryan.

She didn't flirt with him like every other woman within a hundred-mile radius seemed to. She did not want to be known as his girl.

It was as if she had turned around the relationship, made it businesslike, affectionate but in no way exclusive. She teased him about his latest conquests, real and supposed, she knew that her very lack of jealousy was driving him wild. She was happy in the knowledge that he desired her. When she met him it was always with other people.

She finished her course at the college and went to work full time for her mother and father.

It was she who decided to lift the hotel on to a higher level. She contacted the tourist board about grants, and organised that they got money advanced to improve their facilities. She asked visiting Americans to write letters to their local papers praising Ryan's so as to get them further custom.

She told her mother to drop the word Commercial from the title.

'Ryan's makes it sound like a pub,' her mother complained.

'Call it Ryan's Shancarrig Hotel,' said Nessa.

A few eyebrows were raised. Nellie Dunne presided over several conversations about the Ryans having notions.

'That young one is the cut of her mother,' said Nellie. 'I remember when Breda O'Connor came in and took the whole establishment from Conor's mother and father. That Nessa will do the same.'

But Nessa Ryan showed no signs of friction with her mother and father. She would laugh with her mother about the Sainted Grandparents who glared from the picture on the wall. She told her father that he looked handsome in a jacket and begged him to have nice framed pictures of racehorses on the wall, so that they might attract a few of the horsey set and give some legitimacy to her father's constant topic of conversation.

Catherine and Nuala were mystified by her. The most handsome man around seemed to be waiting on their sister Nessa and she barely gave him the time of day. They watched uncomprehending as Nessa became more and more attractive-looking, her dark shiny hair always loose and cut with a fringe. A style that owed nothing to the hairdresser but a lot to a picture in a children's book she had seen, a picture of Diana the huntress.

Nessa got on well with her mother. The two of them often drove to Dublin to look for fittings and fabrics. At an early age she seemed to have their trust, and to be allowed a lot of freedom that was later denied to the more spirited Catherine and Nuala.

'Why can't we go to Galway on our own? Nessa did,' Catherine complained.

'Because you're both so unreliable and untrustworthy you'd probably go under a hedge with the first pair of tinker boys you met,' Nessa said cheerfully to them. They felt it a great betrayal, there should be *some* solidarity between sisters. Imagine mentioning going under hedges in front of their mother, putting ideas in her mind.

'I have no solidarity with you,' Nessa said. 'You steal my make-up, you wear my nylons, you spray yourself with *my* perfume. You don't wash the bath, you do nothing to help in the hotel, you can't wait to get away from here. *Why* should I help you?'

Put like that it was hard to know why.

'Flesh and blood,' Catherine suggested.

'Overrated,' Nessa told her.

'Would you try for hotel management, do you think?' her mother suggested. 'It would teach you so much. There's a great course in Dublin.'

'I'm happy here,' Nessa said.

'I don't ask you about Richard . . .' her mother began.

'I know, Mother. It's one of the things I love about you.' Nessa headed her off before she could start.

She wondered how long would be his exile in Shancarrig, and on Niall's behalf she worried lest he had made too permanent and important a niche for himself with his Uncle Bill.

Mr Hayes came in to drink in Ryan's Shancarrig Bar with Major Murphy, Leo's father, sometimes. Nessa served behind the bar from time to time. She said it helped her to know what the customers wanted. Mr Hayes dropped no hint of how long his nephew would stay, but to Nessa's distress he showed little enthusiasm about his son's return.

'Hard to know what he learned up there, you couldn't get a word out of him,' she heard him say to Dr Jims Blake one evening. She didn't want to join in the conversation but later she brought up the subject.

'Niall seems to be enjoying university and studying hard,' she said.

'Divil a bit of a sign he gives of either.'

'Oh now. All fathers are the same. Still, business is good. There'll be plenty for Niall to take on when he comes back.'

'Oh, I don't know. What with Richard . . .' He let his voice trail away.

'But Richard won't be here for ever?' Her voice was clear and without guile.

Bill Hayes looked at her directly. 'There's something keeping him here. I had a notion it might be yourself?' he said.

'No, Mr Hayes, I'm not the girl for Richard.' There was no play-acting, nothing wistful – she seemed to be stating a fact.

'Well, something's keeping him here, Nessa. It's not the pay, and it's not the social life.'

'I expect he'll move on one day, like he moved in.' Her voice was bland, expressionless.

'I expect so.' He sounded troubled.

Niall was home the following week.

'I hear they're giving you a car for your twenty-first birthday,' he said to Nessa.

'It's meant to be a surprise, shut up about it,' she hissed.

'I didn't know it was a secret. Isn't it great though? A car of your own.'

'You could have one too.'

'How, might I ask? I'm not the doted-on daughter of the house.'

'No, but you're the eldest son of the house, and you never show the slightest interest in your father's business.'

'I'm only qualifying as a bloody solicitor, that's all.' Niall was offended.

'But what kind of a solicitor? You don't even ask him what's going on. You don't know about the competition.'

'Richard, I suppose.'

'No, you fool. He's the family, he's on your team. The competition. You know Gerry O'Neill the auctioneer in the town? Well, he has a brother who's taking a lot of the conveyancing, even out this way. You have to fight back.'

'I didn't know that.'

'You don't ask.'

'When I do ask can I help I'm told to tear up files and put labels on envelopes.'

'That was three years ago, silly.' She put her arm around his shoulder. 'Bring your father in here for a pint, treat him as an equal.'

'He wouldn't like that.'

'I used to be like that, I spent my whole childhood thinking my mother wouldn't like this or that. I was wrong. They want us to have minds of our own.'

'No. They want us to be reliable,' Niall insisted.

'Yes, well. You and I *are* reliable, so they've got that much. Now they want us to have views, opinions, be out for the common good.'

He looked at her with great admiration.

'Have you . . . ?' he began.

She knew he wanted to say something about Richard.

'Yes?' Her voice stopped him asking.

'Nothing,' Niall said.

'See you and your father tonight.'

When Nessa Ryan got her car for her twenty-first birthday she first took her mother and father for a drive around Shancarrig, waving to everyone they passed. She caught her mother's eye in the driving mirror more than once and they smiled. Friends. People who understood each other. She was doing the right thing. Thanking them publicly, showing Shancarrig that Breda O'Connor had come here twenty-two years ago and made a triumph of her life.

It was six o'clock and the angelus was ringing as she headed back home. People would be coming in to Ryan's Shancarrig now for a drink. There would be autumn tourists to check in – the coach buses arrived in the evening.

As they passed Eddie Barton's house Eddie and his Scottish Christine were in the garden. Nessa screeched to a halt.

'I'll come back for you later. I'll pick up Leo, Niall and Maura and take you all for a spin,' she called.

'Just Eddie,' Christine said. 'So it will be like old times.'

'You too.'

'No. Thanks, but no.'

'She knows what she's doing,' Nessa's mother said approvingly.

'Like all women, it seems to me,' Conor Ryan said. His sigh was happy, not resigned. Nessa knew this now. Once she thought he was yearning to be free, now she believed that her father had the life he wanted.

Maura wouldn't come, Nessa knew that, but she would love to be asked. She would be so pleased for the car to pull up at her cottage and for a group of the nobs, as Mrs Brennan would call them, to get out and beg her to join them.

But she would stay and mind Michael – her little boy, two-and-a-half-years old, a loving child, a child who never knew his father. Gerry O'Sullivan the handsome barman had been reliable enough to marry Nessa, but not reliable enough to stay when the child had been born handicapped.

Nessa ran up the steps of Number Five The Terrace. The door was never locked.

'Hello, Mr Hayes. I've come to take your right-hand man out for a drive in my new car,' she said.

'Congratulations, Nessa. I heard of the birthday and the car. Richard should be with you in a minute,' he said.

'I meant Niall,' she answered.

'Oh yes,' he said.

'I don't know *why* you're not out playing golf yourself, Mr Hayes, with all the help you have in here.' She was playful, confident, she knew he liked her. Three years ago she wouldn't have raised her glance to him, let alone her voice.

'Oh, my wife wouldn't like that,' he said.

Nessa thought of Niall's mother, a solid glum-looking woman, dressed always in browns or olive green. No spark, no life. Mr Hayes would have been better with a woman like Nessa's mother, or Nessa herself.

Niall had heard her voice. 'Did the car arrive?'

'It did. And I've come to drive you off in it.' She linked her arm in his and appeared not to notice as Richard arrived out of the other door, straightening his tie and assuming that all the fuss in the hall meant someone had called for him.

Richard Hayes was standing at the top of the steps as Nessa ushered Niall into the front seat.

'Didn't you want . . . ?' Niall began.

'Yeah. I wanted you but I waited till after six not to annoy your father. Let's pick up Eddie.'

If Niall had been going to say anything about Richard he didn't now. He settled back happily in the front seat. Eddie came, on his own. Chris had things to discuss with his mother. They drove up the long drive of The Glen. Leo was at the door waiting to meet them.

'Will I show the car to your parents?' Nessa asked.

'No. No, I'd rather not,' Leo said.

Possibly Leo's mother and father might not have been able to afford a car for her. Or maybe her mother wasn't well. Nobody had seen Mrs Murphy in ages, and Leo's brothers, Harry and James, never came home from wherever they were. Biddy their maid was as silent as the grave, as if she were defending the family. Perhaps they had their secrets. Nessa didn't mind. Not nowadays.

And she was right about Maura. Maura wouldn't come out with them, but she had a cake and they ate it together companionably in her cottage. The glass-fronted cabinet had a few items in it – a spoon in a purple velvet box, a piece of Connemara marble, and one of Eddie's pressed flowers that he had done under glass as a christening present for the baby Michael.

There was a picture of Gerry O'Sullivan in a small frame on the mantelpiece.

'Isn't it great how we all stuck together,' said Maura. And they nodded, unable to speak. 'All we need is Foxy to come home and we'd be complete.'

'He's doing very well,' Leo said unexpectedly. 'He'll be able to buy the town the way things are going.'

'Does he want to buy the town?' Niall asked.

'Well, he'd like to be a person of importance here, that's for certain,' Leo said.

'Wouldn't we all?' Niall said.

'You *are*, Niall. You're a solicitor. If ever I have any business I'll bring it to you,' Maura said.

They laughed good-naturedly, Maura most of all.

'But remember when we did our fortunes *you* were going to be the one who was going to be wealthy, not Foxy. Maybe you *will* have business,' Eddie Barton said. They all remembered the day they left Shancarrig school. It was seven years ago – it seemed a lifetime.

Nessa drove them up to the base of the Old Rock. They left the car and scampered up as they had done so often before.

It was hard to read their faces, but Nessa thought that Eddie's future seemed certain, bound up with the Scottish Chris who had come in some unexplained way into his life.

She knew that Maura would never consider herself unlucky. She would like a better house, maybe she was saving for one – there was no sign of her hard-earned wages in the cottage they had visited.

Leo would always be unfathomable but it was Niall, good dependable Niall, that Nessa was thinking about today. Leo and Eddie wandered off to stand on the stone where you were meant to be able to view four counties. Sometimes it was easier in this evening light. You could see a steeple that was in one county, a mountain that was in another.

Niall sat beside her, his jacket too small for him, his shirt crumpled. His hair was the same soft brown-black as his cousin Richard's, but jagged and not lying right. His eyes were troubled as he looked at her.

'We'll be very happy, Niall,' she said to him, patting his hand.

'I hope you will.' His voice was gruff with generosity and wishing her well, and loneliness. She could hear it, as her mother must have heard the eagerness in Conor Ryan's voice all those years ago, and coped with it.

'You and I,' Nessa said. 'We will get married, won't we? You will ask me eventually?'

'Don't make fun of me, Nessa.'

'I was never more serious in my life.'

'But Richard?'

'What about him?'

'Don't you . . . ?'

'No.'

'Well, didn't you . . . ?'

'No.'

'I thought that you didn't even *see* me,' he said.

'I've always seen you. Since the day you told me my hair was nice, the day we left Shancarrig school.'

'I wrote your name on the tree,' he said.

'You what?'

'I wrote JNH loves VR, very low down near a root. I did then, and I do now.'

'John Niall Hayes, Vanessa Ryan. You never did!'

'Will we go and see it?' he said. 'As proof.'

They had their first kiss in the sunset on her twenty-first birthday, on the hill that looked down over the town. Nessa knew that there would be a lot of work ahead. She would have to fight the apathy of his glum mother, the refusal to relinquish power by his father. She would have to decide where they would live and how they would live. Richard would move on sooner or later. Possibly sooner, now that this had all been planned.

Over the years she would reassure Niall Hayes that there had never been anything to fear from Richard, he was not a lover, nor even a love. He was someone who came in when she needed it and gave her the surge of confidence that her mother had never been given.

And yet, the reason that she felt so sure had a lot to do with being her mother's daughter.

Richard

Richard hated the sight of the Old Rock. It meant that they were back in Shancarrig for their miserable summer holiday. Back in Uncle Bill and Aunt Ethel's dark gloomy house, with the solicitor's office on the ground floor and the living quarters upstairs. Bedrooms with heavy furniture, nothing to see, nothing to do. A one-horse town and a pretty poor horse at that.

For as long as he could remember they had come here for a week in July. All through the war years, or the Emergency as it was called, they had travelled down from Dublin on a train fuelled by turf. If the weather was anyway bad the turf was bad and the journey was endless.

Richard's father would walk every night for miles with Uncle Bill. They both carried blackthorn sticks and pointed happily to places they had played when they were children – the gravelly shallows of the River Grane where they had caught their fish, the great Barna Woods which had got so small since they were young, the huge ugly heap of stones they called the Old Rock.

They would stand outside Shancarrig school and marvel at the old copper beech where they had carved their initials in 1914, twin boys aged fourteen, KH and WH – Kevin and William. It made Richard sick to see them so full of happy memories over nothing.

He was a handsome boy and a restless one. He thought this week of enforced idleness in his father's old village a waste of time. Even when he was very young he had asked if they really needed to go.

'Yes of course, we need to go. It's only one week out of fifty-two,' his mother had said.

It gave him hope that she didn't like it either. But she wasn't the soft touch on this as she was on other things. She was adamant.

'Your father doesn't ask much from us. Just this one week. We will do it and do it with a good grace.'

'But it's so boring, and Aunt Ethel is so awful.'

'She's not awful, she's just quiet. Bring something to entertain yourself – books, games.'

He noted his mother brought knitting. She usually managed to get two jumpers finished in their week in Shancarrig.

'You're a powerful knitter,' Aunt Ethel had said once.

'I love it. It's so restful,' his mother had murmured. Richard noticed that she didn't say that she hardly produced the needles and wool at all when she

459

was in Dublin. She regarded Shancarrig as her knitting time – her purgatory on earth.

Uncle Bill's children were all very young; the eldest boy Niall was a whole seven years younger than Richard, a child of five when Richard was twelve and looking for company.

By the year 1950 Richard was seventeen. It would be his last holiday in this terrible place.

As he stood at an endless school dedication with bishop and priest and self-important people from around he vowed he would never come back. It made him feel claustrophobic, as if he was being choked.

Richard Hayes was leaving his Jesuit boarding school that year. He would get his Leaving Certificate and Matriculation and go to university to study, not medicine like his father, but law. Next summer he could legitimately be away on some study course or be abroad.

They would never drag him to this village again. Let his sisters come, they seemed perfectly happy to play with the village children and run free. Richard Hayes had done his stint.

There was only one good-looking girl at the ceremony, in a blue and white dress, and a straw hat with the same material around the brim. She was shading her eyes from the sun and listening intently to the speeches. She was slim with a tiny waist and a pretty if pale face.

'Who's that, Uncle Bill?' he asked.

'Madeleine Ross. Nice girl, a bit under her mother's thumb though, and will probably go on that way.'

'She's going to stay here all her life?' Richard was horrified.

'Some of us do that willingly.' His uncle sounded huffy.

'Oh I know, Uncle Bill, I meant she seems so young.'

'I was young when I decided to come back here to live, all those years ago. If old Dr Nolan had wanted someone in the practice at that time then your father would have come back too. It's home, you see.'

Richard shuddered at the very thought.

The Dublin Hayeses lived in Waterloo Road, which was ideal for anyone with children at university. Richard was within walking distance of his lectures and, even more useful, within walking distance of all the night-time activities that went with being a student. The pubs in Leeson Street were literally on his way home, the student dances nearby, the parties in Baggot Street where fellows had flats only a stone's throw away.

Richard Hayes offered to do up the disused basement of his parents' house so that he could live there. To study, he said. To be out of the way.

His father and mother never heard or saw any sign of anything untoward. They were pleased with their son who was unfailingly charming as he came to sit at their table for supper at six and for weekend lunches. He was always smiling politely as he passed his bag of laundry to Lizzie to wash, and managed to make his own part of the house off limits.

'You've enough to do up here, honestly. I'll keep my own place tidy below,' he had said with his boyish smile. So without anyone realising it he had got his own little self-contained flat down in the basement. At eighteen years of age he had a freedom undreamed of by other undergraduates.

His parents had no idea that their son brought a series of girlfriends home and that not all of them left before morning. He had posters on his walls, chianti bottles that had been turned into lamps, coloured Indian bedspreads over chairs and sofas and his own bed.

There were very noisy studenty parties with loud songs and crashers. The kind of parties that Richard Hayes gave were usually for two people, and sometimes for four. There were two rooms in his little basement flat, and all you had to do was to leave confidently and authoritatively, as if you had every right to be there.

'Don't slink in and out,' Richard warned one girl. 'Walk out of the gate as if you had been delivering a note in my door. They wouldn't in their wildest dreams believe anything else.'

And he was totally correct in his belief that his parents knew nothing of his private life. They told their friends, and Richard's Uncle Bill down in Shancarrig, that the law studies seemed to be going very well, and that unlike a lot of young tearaways their son seemed to be a homebird, which was all they could have wanted for him and more.

So it came as a complete shock when shortly before Richard's finals there was the unpleasant business of Olive Kennedy and her parents.

It appeared that Olive was pregnant and that Richard Hayes was to blame.

Richard felt that the scene was like a play, a film of a court case. Nobody seemed to be speaking the truth.

Not Olive, who was crying and saying that she had thought it would be all right because Richard loved her and they were getting married. Not the Kennedy parents who said their daughter had been ruined. Not his own parents who kept protesting that their son could never have done anything like this. He lived at home for heaven's sake, he was under their watchful eye.

Olive made no mention of the many nights she had spent in the basement in Waterloo Road – perhaps she didn't want her family to know that. The location of the conception was not discussed, only the responsibility for it. And what was to be done now. Richard spoke clearly. He was very very sorry. He denied nothing, but he said that he and Olive were far too young to consider marriage. They had never committed themselves to it. He seemed to think that this was all that was needed.

His manner, respectful and firm, won the day. It now became a matter of negotiation: Olive was to go to England and have the child; she would return having given the baby for adoption and resume her studies. Some financial contribution should be expected for this. It was agreed between the fathers.

'Olive, I wouldn't have had this happen for the world,' Richard said as they left.

'Thank you, Richard.' She lowered her eyes, pleased that he still respected her and loved her even if they were too young to marry.

That was when Richard Hayes, as he let his breath out slowly in relief, began to realise that he must be by some kind of accident a bit of a lady-killer.

Richard kept his head down and studied hard for months after this event. He invited his parents down to his flat on several occasions so that they could see every sign of a blameless life and a hard-working son.

Bit by bit, without his having to tell any story, they began to see this Olive as a scheming wanton girl who had set out to get their Richard. They began to think he had behaved decently in the face of such temptation.

They watched proudly as he received his parchment, was admitted to practise as a solicitor and got a job in a first-rate office in Dublin. Even before his first month's salary they gave him money for clothes – he went to a tailor and his real good looks were obvious to everyone he met.

Particularly Elaine, one of the apprentices in the office. She was a niece of the senior partner, and the daughter of a judge. She wore the most expensive of twin-sets, her pearls were real ones, her handbags and silk scarves came from Paris. They looked a very elegant couple when they were seen together.

But they were rarely seen together because Richard said he wasn't a suitable escort for her. A penniless young solicitor starting off . . .

'You're not penniless, my uncle pays you a fortune . . .' She used to cling to his arm as if she never wanted him out of her sight.

'But we're too young, you and I . . .' he begged, knowing that she found him all the more irresistible the more he protested.

'We could grow up,' she said, looking at him directly.

So Richard Hayes saw a lot of Elaine the judge's daughter, but always in his flat where nobody else saw them.

For three years they lived a hidden life, behaving perfectly correctly to each other in the office, wrapped around each other passionately all night. It amazed him how easily she was able to tell her parents that she was staying with girlfriends.

As she stood in the sunlight barebottomed, wearing only the top of his pyjamas and frying eggs for their breakfast, he marvelled at his luck, that such a beautiful and clever girl should make him her choice in this way.

'Do you love me at all, Richard?' she asked as she turned the eggs on the pan.

He lay back on his bed, luxuriating and waiting for the breakfast that would be brought to him on a tray before they got up and dressed and made their separate ways to the office. He loved the very clandestine nature of it all, the fact that nobody in the office knew.

'What an extraordinary question! Why do you ask?' he said.

'It's always dangerous when people answer questions with another question.' She laughed, pretty Elaine with the golden hair and the expensive clothes thrown on the floor of his flat.

'No seriously, we loved each other twice last night and once this morning . . . and you ask me an odd thing like that?' He seemed puzzled.

'No, I meant real love.'

'That's real love. It seemed pretty real to me.'

'I'm pregnant,' she said.

'Oh shit,' he said.

'I see where we stand.' Elaine threw the plate of fried eggs into the sink and picked up her clothes.

'Elaine wait . . . I didn't mean . . .'

From the bathroom he heard over the running water her voice call back.

'You're so bloody right, you didn't mean it. You didn't mean any bloody word you said.'

She was out of the bathroom, dressed and furious. He came towards her.

'Don't touch me. You've said what you wanted to say.'

'I've said nothing. We have to talk.'

'You've talked. You said "shit". That's what you said.'

It was awkward in the office. She wouldn't catch his eye or agree to meet. Then she went missing for four days.

At home alone Richard didn't dare to let his thoughts follow the train they were heading down. Was it possible that she could have gone to have an abortion?

In the Dublin of 1958 such things were not unknown. There had been stories, none of them pleasant, of a nurse . . . He headed away from that thought. Elaine wouldn't have done that on her own.

But then, had he not shown how he didn't want to be involved? He telephoned her house; when he gave his name to the maid he was told that Elaine didn't want to speak to him.

This time there was no carpeting, no council of war as there had been in the case of Olive Kennedy. This time he was told by the senior partner that his position with the firm was now being terminated.

'But why?' Richard cried.

'I think you know.' The older man, Elaine's uncle, stood up and turned away.

It was the coldest gesture that Richard had ever seen. Now to explain to his parents.

He wanted to try to get another job first: to tell his parents that he had decided to change offices. This way it might not appear so bald. He had reckoned without the power of the senior partner, brother of the judge, and the smallness of Dublin legal circles. The word was out about him. He didn't know which word it was but it must have had something to do with being unreliable, a seducer of young women, someone unwilling to pay for his pleasure.

There were no jobs for Richard Hayes, whose record in the law was not so staggering that it would override the other considerations.

He told his parents.

It was not an easy conversation. There were very few solutions, and to his horror he realised that the only one which seemed possible was Shancarrig.

In July of 1958 he installed himself in Number Five The Terrace. He wandered disconsolately around the village, looking without interest at the church with its notices of upcoming events, like whist drives in aid of some villagers in South America who apparently needed a church . . . just like this one.

He walked hands in pockets across the River Grane and up towards the school where he remembered going to some tedious ceremony years ago. The place hadn't changed at all. Nor had the ill-kept river bank with its row of shabby dwellings, nor the clumps of trees they so proudly called Barna Woods. He couldn't bear to make the climb he had done so often as a child to the Old Rock. He came home shoulders hunched wearily and crossed the bridge back into the town.

A group of youngsters were playing on the bridge and turned to look at him as he passed. He realised that whatever he did in this village would be under the scrutiny of hundreds of eyes. It was an appalling thought.

Everything about Shancarrig depressed him.

The small fat beady-eyed priest welcoming him, and saying it would be a pleasure to have him in the congregation – what could he mean? And the wraith-like priests' housekeeper with a face like the Queen of Spades – a sour woman called Mrs Kennedy who looked straight through him and seemed to read his inner soul. She nodded dryly on being introduced, as if to say she knew his type and didn't like it.

His uncle's home offered little joy to him. Although Uncle Bill was a pleasant enough man and an efficient solicitor he had managed to encumber himself with such a mournful wife. Aunt Ethel saw little to celebrate in the world. And the children were not going to rate high on any ladder of companionship.

Niall was now about eighteen and at an age when he should have been full of the joys of spring, but he appeared disconsolate and without any fire. It didn't occur to Richard that his cousin Niall might merely be lacking in self-confidence; Richard had never known that state. He wondered why the boy didn't ask to borrow his father's Ford which was parked outside The Terrace. That way he could have toured the countryside and found wider horizons. There must be *some* social life for a boy in this place, but Niall had seemingly never found it; he stayed around the house, moving between The Terrace and Ryan's Hotel.

Richard looked at the bedroom he had been given – a huge heavy dark mahogany wardrobe which despite its great size found it difficult to hold the suits and coats of the young solicitor down from the city. His Aunt Ethel had proudly shown him the hot and cold running water; he had the only room with a hand basin. The bed would never welcome a companion. To manoeuvre a girl up those stairs past offices, kitchens, sitting rooms and bedrooms would be a feat that few would undertake. It would be celibacy, or else find someone else with a place of their own, which didn't look at all likely in Shancarrig.

There were, of course, pretty children.

Like Nessa from the hotel. He saw the huge interest in her eyes, the eagerness and shyness, the trying to please, the fear she was boring him.

He was not arrogant, he was realistic about this kind of response. If you were nice to girls, if you smiled at them and listened to them, just *liked* them, they opened up like flowers.

He supposed it helped being reasonably good-looking, but he truly thought it was a matter of liking them. Many a man in Dublin who had envied Richard's success had been so anxious for the conquest that he forgot to enjoy the chase. That must be where the secret, if there were a secret, lay.

He spent a lot of time wooing Vanessa Ryan. She was the best in town. He had been on an exploratory mission.

There was Madeleine Ross the schoolteacher, very intense and spiritual, deeply caught up in this attempt to convert some Spanish-named place that apparently meant Shancarrig in Peruvian or whatever. He suspected that she might harbour longings for the rather fey-looking priest, but he was very sure that neither of them had done anything about this hothouse passion if it existed.

There was a tough little girl who came from a falling-down Georgian mansion called The Glen, frizzy hair, good legs, strong face. There was some secret there too. Money, maybe, or a mad relative. He had called and been discouraged from calling again.

There were a few others, unsatisfactory.

Nessa with her clear eyes and dark good looks was the only one. To his surprise he didn't wear her down. He must be losing his touch, he thought. His winning Dublin ways didn't work here.

He threatened her that they wouldn't see each other any more . . . gentle loving threats of course, but she got the message . . . She said no.

And continued to say no.

It was a constant irritant to see her across the road in her parents' hotel, growing more attractive and confident by the week. Her dark hair shining as it hung framing her face, she wore clear yellows and reds that set off her colouring. She laughed and joked with the customers; he had even seen American men look at her approvingly.

The years passed slowly.

They were not as bad as he feared his years of exile would be, but still he yearned to be back in Dublin.

Elaine came to visit him.

'I'm getting married,' she told him.

'Do you love him?' he asked.

'You'd never have asked that question a few years ago. You didn't think love existed.'

'I know it exists. I haven't come across it, that's all.'

'You will.' She was gentle.

'About the baby . . . ?'

'There never was a baby,' she said.

'*What?*'

'There never was. I made it up.'

The colour drained from his face.

'You sent me here, you got me drummed out of Dublin on a lie.'

'There *could* have been a child, and your response would have been exactly the same. "Oh shit." That's all you would have said if we created a child between us.'

'But *you* . . . why did you let yourself be seen in that light by everyone . . . tell your father and your uncle . . . and let people think . . . ?'

'It seemed worth it at the time. It's a long time ago.'

'And why are you telling me *now*? Is the interdict lifted? Is the barring order called off? Can I crawl back to Dublin and they'll give me a job?'

'No, it's much more selfish. I wanted to tell you so that you'd know there never had been a child, no child born, no child aborted. I wanted you to know that in case . . .'

'In case what?'

'In case . . .' She seemed lost for words. He thought she was going to tell him that she worried lest he was thinking about this child, in case he felt ashamed. He had never thought of it as a child, real or imaginary as it now proved to be.

'In case Gerald ever heard. In case you might ever say . . .'

He realised she was more frightened of Gerald knowing about her past than anything to do with him.

'Tell Gerald you're white as the driven snow,' he said. He had been so right not to marry this devious lady.

It was around this time that his young cousin Niall asked him for advice.

'You sort of know everything, Richard.'

'Oh yeah?'

'Well, I know you're good-looking and everything but you know how to be nice to people and make them like you. Is there a trick?'

Richard looked at him, his hair unkempt, the jacket expensive but out of fashion, the trousers baggy. Mainly the boy's stance was what held him back: his shoulders were rounded, he looked down and not at the people he was talking to; it came from a natural diffidence but it made him look feeble and untrustworthy.

At another time and in another place Richard might have given the boy some brotherly advice; after all Niall *had* asked, which could not have been easy.

But this was the wrong time.

The business with Elaine had ruffled him. He began to doubt his own success with women, and there was also the fact that that little madam, Nessa Ryan across the road in the hotel, had become altogether too pert and self-confident. Richard Hayes didn't feel in the mood to give out advice.

'There's no trick,' he said gruffly. 'People either like you or they don't. That's the way it goes through life.' He looked away from the naked disappointment on the boy's face.

'You mean people can't get better, more popular, or successful?'

Richard shrugged. 'I never saw anyone change, did you?'

Niall had said nothing.

He looked increasingly mopey at meals in The Terrace. Richard wondered what work they would find for the lad to do when he came back to Shancarrig full time, as he undoubtedly would. It might make more sense for him to cut his teeth in a solicitor's office somewhere else. But this was his father's firm. He should come back and claim his inheritance lest Richard take it over from him. Not that Richard was going to stay here for ever. After Elaine's revelations he thought that it might well be time for him to go back to Dublin.

But that was when he got to know Gloria Darcy.

The Darcys were newcomers. This meant they hadn't been born and raised here for three generations like everyone else. They had been considered fly-by-nights when they came first, but that was before their small grocery shop became a larger grocery shop, and before they started selling light bulbs, saucepans and cutlery and began to bite into the profits of Dunne's Hardware. Mike and Gloria Darcy always smiled cheerfully in the face of any muttering.

'Isn't there plenty for everyone?' Mike would say with his big broad smile.

'This place is only starting out, it'll be a boom town in the middle sixties,' Gloria would say with a toss of her long dark curly hair and her gypsy smile.

She often wore a handkerchief tied around her neck so that she looked like a picture of a gypsy girl – not like the tall silent tinker girls who came into Shancarrig when they camped each year at Barna Woods, more like an illustration from a child's story book.

Bit by bit they were accepted.

Gloria was flashy, the women all agreed this. Richard heard his Aunt Ethel tut-tutting about her to Nellie Dunne and to Mrs Ryan, but there was nothing they could put their finger on. Her neckline wasn't so low as to raise a comment nor were her skirts too short. It was just that she walked with a swish and a certainty. Her eyes roamed around and lit up when they caught other eyes. There was nothing demure about Mrs Gloria Darcy.

Richard met her first when he bought a packet of razor blades. He didn't like the fussy Mr Connors the chemist – a small man with bad breath who was inclined to keep you half the day. When he saw packets of razor blades in the window of Darcy's he regarded it as a merciful escape.

'Anything else?' Gloria asked him, her smile wide and generous, her tongue moving slightly over her lower lip.

If it weren't for the fact that her husband stood not a foot away Richard would have thought she was flirting, being suggestive.

'Not for the moment,' he said in exactly the same tone, and their eyes met.

He warned himself not to be stupid as he walked back to The Terrace. This would be the silliest thing that a human could do.

What he must do now was sort out a new job in Dublin, and leave this town without having committed any major misdemeanour. He had been saving his salary quite methodically over the three years of his exile in the sticks. There was no point in buying finery to be paraded here, there were no places for meals, no going to the races. He had learned a lot about the rural practice, for all the use it would be to him in the future. But human nature was the same everywhere: perhaps his stay here might have been a better apprenticeship than he had ever thought possible.

It was early closing, the day his Uncle Bill usually walked up to The Glen and went for a stroll with the old Major Murphy. What the two of them talked about it would be hard to know. But today Bill Hayes was still in his office.

'I'm in a quandary,' he said to Richard.

'Tell me about it.' Richard sat down, legs stretched, face enthusiastic and receptive. He knew his uncle was pleased to be able to talk.

There was no one else in the house, not dour Aunt Ethel nor sulky Niall.

'It's up at The Glen. Miriam Murphy keeps telephoning me, saying she wants to set her affairs in order.'

'Well?'

'Well, Frank says not to take any notice of her – she's rambling.'

'She is a bit daft, isn't she?' Richard encouraged his uncle to speak.

'I suppose so, I mean it's not the kind of thing you'd ask a man. Not something that you'd talk about to a friend.' Bill Hayes looked troubled.

Richard thought that it should be the most important thing you might talk to a friend about, whether your wife was going off her head or not, but the more he heard of marriage the less likely anyone seemed to do anything normal within its bonds.

'So what do you think you should do?' he asked, expert as always in finding out what the other man wanted before giving his own view.

'You see, I think she has something pressing on her mind, some crime, even ... imaginary, of course.'

'Well, if it's imaginary ...'

'But suppose it's not, suppose it's something she wants to make restitution for?'

'You're not Father Gunn, Uncle Bill. You're not Sergeant Keane. All you have to do is make her will, or not be free to make it if that's what you'd prefer for Major Frank's sake.'

'It's worrying me.'

'Why don't I go and see her? Then you won't have failed either of them.'

'Would you, Richard?'

'I'll go today while you and Major Murphy take your constitutional.' His smile was bright.

'I don't know what I'd do without you, Richard.'

'You'll have a son of your own to help you in no time. You won't need me, I'll head off to Dublin soon.'

'Not too soon.'

'All right, not too soon, but soonish.' He stood up and clapped his uncle on the shoulder.

What was one more mad old bat of a woman confessing to the Lord knew what!

He had his lunch in the dark dining room of The Terrace; they talked of other things and he waited until his uncle and the Major would be well clear before he went to The Glen.

He didn't even have to go into the house to find her. Mrs Miriam Murphy half lay, half sat across the rockery. She was wearing a long white dress, possibly a nightgown; her hair streaked with grey was loose on her shoulders.

She was crying.

There was some garden furniture strewn about. Richard Hayes pulled up a chair for himself.

'I'm from Bill Hayes's office, I'm his nephew. He says you're anxious for us to sort something out for you.'

'You're too young,' she said.

'Ah no, Mrs Murphy, I'm older than I look. I'm twenty-eight, well on my way to thirty.' His smile would have broken down the reserve of any woman in Ireland, but Miriam Murphy's mind was miles away.

'That's what he was, twenty-eight, if you could believe him,' she said.

Richard was nonplussed. 'Well, what do you think we should do?' he said.

He knew his uncle wanted the woman to say that she had changed her mind, that she wanted no will made, no affairs sorted out. He must try to lead her in that direction.

'It's too late to do anything. It was done,' she said. He nodded uncomprehendingly.

There was a long silence between them. She seemed quite at ease lounging, half lying over the rock plants and the jagged edges of the stones that made up the rockery. He didn't suggest that she sit somewhere more comfortable – he knew that this was irrelevant.

'So perhaps we should leave things as they are?' He looked at her, pouring out reassurance.

'Is that enough?' she asked.

'I think it is.'

'You don't think we should leave them the place, The Glen, for themselves whenever they come this way?'

'Leave it to who exactly?'

'The gypsies.'

'No, no. Definitely not. People are always trying to leave them places. They want to be free,' he said.

'Free?'

'Yes, that's what they like best.' He stood up, anxious to be away from the mad staring eyes. It wasn't healthy for that girl Leo to stay here all the time. Why didn't she get a training, a job?

'If you think so.' Mrs Miriam Murphy didn't look relieved, she looked only resigned.

He walked down the long drive and was about to head down the hill to Shancarrig. God, the sooner he was out of a place like this the better. Walking along the road towards him was Gloria Darcy.

'Well, well, well. You have had a shave, I see.' She looked directly at his face.

'What do you mean?'

'I sold you razor blades this morning, don't tell me you've forgotten me already?' She was most definitely leading him on. Her laugh was unaffected, she could see the impression that she was making on him.

'No, Mrs Darcy, I imagine that very few people forget you,' he said. He was being equally gallant and flattering, giving as good as he got.

'And were you going to walk straight home down the hill or go the better way through the woods?'

He knew he stood at a crossroads. He could have said that he was needed back at the office, that he had work to catch up with, that he had to make a phone call to Dublin. He might have said anything.

But he said, 'I was hoping to find some attractive company to walk me through Barna Woods, and now I have.'

They laughed as they walked. She teased him about his city suit, he said she was dressing deliberately like a pantomime gypsy. She asked what he had been doing at The Glen, he said that there was a secrecy like the seal of Confession about matters between lawyer and client. He asked if the Darcys had a proper title to their shop, they hadn't bought it through his uncle's firm . . . She said the same seal of Confession applied to business deals.

By the time they came out into the sunshine again, and walked by the cottages to the bridge, they were well aware of each other. Much more than attractive faces and winning ways. They were people who could talk and play. They were a match for each other.

So when he went to buy things there he went knowing that it was a move, a degree of courtship. He bought more razor blades.

'My, what a strong beard we must have,' she said. Again within her husband's hearing.

When he bought a pound of tomatoes she asked him was he going on a picnic in the woods. Mike Darcy was serving another customer.

'No, my aunt wants some more, that's all.'

'No, she was in this morning and bought plenty,' said Gloria, eyes dancing and full of mischief.

The teasing visits and banter went on for some days.

'It's lovely of you to come and see me so often,' she said, pressing her body towards the counter. She wore a chain around her neck, the pendant was between her breasts, the eye followed it down as it was intended to.

'Yes, it's lovely of me, you never come to call on me,' Richard said.

'Ah, but I can't make excuses about civil bills and statements of claim,' she said. 'You can invent all the tomatoes and razor blades in the world.'

'So we'll have to meet on neutral ground,' he suggested.

They met two days later at the church when they both attended the funeral of Mrs Miriam Murphy.

It was pneumonia, Dr Jims Blake had said. Brought on by exposure, someone else had said, Mrs Murphy had taken to sleeping out on the rockery of their garden. It was a sure fact that money and position didn't bring you happiness.

Richard Hayes looked at the small wiry Leo as she walked down the church supporting her father. Two strange men, the brothers from abroad, had come for the funeral. They looked military, they knew hardly anyone.

There was a gathering in Ryan's Hotel. Young Nessa had done up one of the downstairs rooms as a special function room. It was exactly what was needed for this occasion. Coffee and sandwiches and some drinks. Those who wished to adjourn to the bar could do so. It had never been done before in Shancarrig; you either went back to someone's house or you went to the pub. This was a new respectability.

'Very clever of you to have thought this up, Nessa,' he said admiringly. Genuinely so.

'Leo is my friend. It's not easy for her to have people at the house.' Nessa hadn't time to talk to him – these days she was great with young Niall, and already the boy was beginning to look the better for it. His hair was smarter, he had got a new jacket. Somehow he even seemed to walk taller.

Gloria and Mike Darcy were in the gathering though somehow Richard wondered had they been invited in the strict sense of the word.

As people moved around offering sympathy and trying to place Harry and James who had long left Shancarrig, Gloria found herself next to Richard.

'So now we're on neutral ground,' she said.

'Yes, but very crowded neutral ground,' he said, shaking his head in exaggerated sorrow.

'Have you any suggestions for somewhere that's not crowded?' She couldn't have been more direct. Had she asked him to make love to her she could not have said it more clearly.

'Well, since your place, my place and this hotel are out of the question, let's think of somewhere that might be deserted at this moment.' He wasn't serious. There was nowhere they could go in Shancarrig, literally nowhere.

'There's The Glen,' she said. She saw the look of revulsion on his face. They were sympathising over the death of the woman who had lived all her life in The Glen; Gloria could not possibly be considering going there to use the empty house. 'Not the house, the gate lodge,' she said.

'How would we get in?' Already he had bypassed any moral objections to a place in the grounds. That was different.

'The back window is open, I checked.'

'Twenty minutes?' he asked. It would take him ten to say his goodbyes, two to go back to his room for condoms.

'Fifteen,' she said, and again she ran her tongue along her lower lip. His goodbyes were courteous and very swift.

There was a crotchety old farmer who lived out that direction. If he was asked he could say he got a message to visit him but then he had turned out not to be there. But why was he taking these kind of precautions? No one would ask him. Nobody would dream he was about to do what he was about to do.

She was there before him, lying on a divan covered with a rug. The place smelled musty but not of damp.

'Did you bring anything?'

'Yes, that's what delayed me. I had to go back to my room for them. I don't carry them always just in case,' he laughed, patting his pocket.

'Now don't be so unromantic. I meant champagne, something like that.'

'No, I'm afraid not.' He looked crestfallen.

'Never mind, I did.' Her white teeth flashed as she bit the foil from the top of the bottle, there were cups on the dresser. They laughed as they drank it too quickly so that the fizzy liquid went up their noses. And they kissed.

'Did you go back to the shop for this?' He marvelled at her speed.

'No. I had it with me in my big shoulder bag.' She laughed at her own wickedness and the confidence that it would have needed.

'Let me take off these dark respectable clothes. They don't suit you,' he said.

'Well, it was a funeral. I couldn't wear my red skirt but . . .' She was wearing a red petticoat, trimmed with white lace, she wore no brassiere, just a gold chain around her throat. She looked so abandoned and wild as she lay there laughing up at him he could scarcely bear the moments of waiting.

'I've longed for you, Richard Hayes,' she said. And he sank into her as if he had known her all his life.

After that it was always urgent and never easy. If only the Murphys lived a more regular life, Richard groaned to himself. If he could know they would stay in the big house, or stay out of it, then the gate lodge would have been the ideal place for his meetings with Gloria. But they could never be sure; they would have no excuse if they were seen going in and out of the window.

It took them weeks to work out some kind of a pattern to the curious ways of Leo and her father.

Leo eventually started a secretarial course which involved going to the town on the bus. This gave her day a shape. The Major, who walked the long avenue with his old dogs, that he kept calling Lance and Jessie, was less predictable. Richard tried to find out more of his movements by asking his uncle, but it seemed that a friendship of twenty-five years was based on Bill Hayes knowing nothing whatsoever about Frank Murphy. It was hard to believe, but that was the way it was.

And there was the time that Hayes and Son, Solicitors, were asked to see to a property. Richard and Gloria had many happy meetings there in the guise of showing it to clients.

Gloria could get away so easily it was almost frightening.

'Does Mike never ask where you're going?'

'Lord no. Why should he?'

'Well, if I had a beautiful wife like you I wouldn't let her wander off . . . to do the devil knows what . . .' He squeezed her and held her to him again.

'Then you wouldn't be a husband, you'd be a gaoler,' she laughed. He thought about it.

There was some truth in what she said. If you married someone just to guard her like a possession it was like an imprisonment. But look at it the other way, if Mike was more careful and caring about his wife then surely Gloria wouldn't wander free as she was.

Sometimes he spoke about her children, her little boys, Kevin and Sean.
'What is there to say?'

'Aren't you afraid they'll find out, that they'd hate you for this?'

'Darling Richard, you are riddled with guilt. I think we should make a regular thing of visiting Father Gunn together after we meet.'

'Don't tease me. I only say these things because I love you.'

'No, you don't.'

'I do. I never said it to anyone before.'

'We say it at the moment we make love, because at that moment everyone loves. But you don't love me in an everyday sort of way.'

'I could.'

'No, Richard.' She put her fingers on his lips and then into his mouth, and then she kissed him and soon the words were forgotten.

She was the ideal lover. He could never have dreamed of anyone so passionate and responsive, a beautiful woman who found him desirable and wasn't afraid to say so. A witty, flowing, secret love whose dark eyes flashed at him when they met in Ryan's Hotel, in the shops or at the church.

After years of girls wanting more from Richard here was someone who wanted no more at all. Not public recognition, not a commitment, and obviously because of the heavy band she already wore on her finger, not an engagement ring. For quite a time it was the perfect romance.

And then he began to notice small changes in his own attitude. He couldn't say that Gloria had changed, she had always been light-hearted in their daring and the fear of discovery . . . and enthusiastic about the pleasure they gave each other.

No. It was Richard who changed.

He couldn't bear to see her holding her little boys by the hand. He thought back to his own mother and father, the respectable Dublin doctor and his busy bridge-playing wife. Theirs had been a house of stability as he grew up in Waterloo Road. His mother had always been there for them. Suppose she had been someone who sneaked out to the arms of a lover while his father worked? He dismissed the thought as some kind of guilty fantasy.

There had been no way in which he had compared his life with that of his parents before, why was he holding up their staid and plodding existence as some kind of example now? Gloria was a wonderful mother to Kevin and Sean. What she had with Richard was something totally different, something separate entirely.

Then Richard found himself uneasy about Mike, big handsome Mike Darcy with his teeth as white and even as his wife's, who stood long hours in the grocery shop they were so busy building up together. Mike, who would go to endless trouble to find something Richard ordered, furrowing his brow to think where they might get that particular chamois leather Richard wanted. He didn't like the man being so generous with his time and help for him. Mike's innocent face was a reproach to Richard Hayes.

Gloria only laughed when he mentioned it. 'What Mike and I have is different to what you and I have . . . Let's keep them separate,' she said.

'But I know about him, he doesn't know about me.'

'Why do men have to think everything's a game, with rules?' she laughed.

And then there were times when he wondered if he *did* know about Mike and Gloria and what they had together. He would see the way they leant towards each other in the shop when they thought no one was looking. He saw the way Mike Darcy sometimes stroked his wife's body.

A very unfamiliar feeling of raging jealousy came over him when he saw them touch.

'You don't do this with Mike, do you?' he begged her one afternoon in their gate lodge.

'Nobody could do what you and I do. This is ours.'

'But does he want to . . . ? I mean do you and he . . . ?'

'You're so handsome when you look worried, Richard,' she said.

'I must know.'

Suddenly she sat up, eyes flashing. 'No, you must not know. There is no must about it. We are not master and slave . . . you have no right to know anything that I do not wish to tell you. Do I ask you any such questions . . . ?'

'But there's nothing to know about me.' He was wretched.

'That's because this is the way I choose to see things. I am not curious, suspicious, asking where I should ask nothing.' Her voice held an ultimatum.

Accept things as they were or there would be no more to accept. He longed to know if she had known other men since her marriage to Mike, if they failed at this test and had been sent away.

He would have killed any man, any traveller who walked into Ryan's Hotel, if he had said he shared a bed with Gloria Darcy. Yes, he would have taken this man by the throat and shaken him to squeeze out his life, uncaring about what onlookers or the law would say or do. Why then was Mike able to stand and fill bags with sugar and other bags with potatoes and not wonder where his beautiful wife went to in the afternoons?

It was becoming more difficult too for Richard to be free in the afternoons since young Niall had joined the firm. The boy had definitely gained a new confidence, which Richard suspected was due to the blossoming of a friendship and even courtship with the glossy young Nessa Ryan from the hotel.

Gone were the days when Niall Hayes was happy with the menial jobs, the work of a glorified clerk. Now he wanted to learn, to share, to study Richard's ways with clients. 'Can I come with you to the place that there's all the fuss about the title?' he would ask.

This was one of Richard's mythical excuses for being out of the office. He had described a difficult old farmer set in his ways who had to be cajoled and flattered into revealing his documents.

'No, Niall. It wouldn't work out . . . this fellow is as mad as a wasps' nest. You wouldn't know what he'd do if I brought anyone else. I've only got as far as I have because I go on my own and put in endless bloody hours with him.'

'Well, can I see the file on him?' Niall asked.

'Why? What do you want to bother yourself with that old fart for, there's plenty of other work to do . . .'

'But won't we need to know when . . . ?'

The words remained unfinished, the sentence hung in the air – when . . . Richard went back to Dublin – something they all knew would happen. There wasn't room for two partnerships in the firm. The business simply wasn't there; even two salaries was beginning to strain Bill Hayes. Niall was the son of the family.

Surely Richard would be going back any day now.

Only Richard knew that he could never leave Shancarrig and the woman he loved.

'I *do* love you,' he said defensively to Gloria, as they sat smoking a cigarette by their little oil stove one cold evening in the gate lodge.

'I know.' She sat hugging her knees.

'No, you don't know. You said we shouldn't talk of love, that I only felt it at the moment of taking you. That's what you said.'

'Stop sounding like a schoolboy, Richard.' She looked beautiful as she sat there in the flickering light.

'What are you thinking about?' he asked.

'About you and how good you make me feel.'

'What are we going to do, Gloria?'

'Well, get dressed and go home, I imagine.'

'About everything?'

'We can't solve everything, we can only solve things like not letting the light be seen through the windows and not getting our death of cold in all the rain.'

'What will you say . . . about where you've been?'

'That's not your concern.'

'But it is, you are my concern.'

'Then let me handle it.' Again he saw the warning in her eyes, and he felt frightened.

They had met in late summer and continued through autumn and a cold wet winter; soon it would be spring. Surely some solution would have to be found.

But for Gloria spring meant that she could wear fresh yellow and white flowery dresses, and white sandals and take her lover to hidden parts of Barna Woods, to dells with bluebells and soft springy grass. Again an ache came over him. How did she know where to find such places? She hadn't grown up in this place – had other men taken her here? Not only could he never ask, he must never think about it. He hated that the shop was doing so well, he wanted to be her provider and give her things but she would never take them.

'What would I say, Richard? I mean I could hardly say that the handsome young solicitor who drops in to buy an inordinate amount of razor blades bought me a silver bracelet, now could I?'

But with increased prosperity Mike Darcy bought his wife jewellery. There was an emerald pendant, there were diamonds. Nobody in Shancarrig had ever known such extravagance. Quite unsuitable, Richard's Aunt Ethel had said, shaking her head about it.

Richard agreed from the bottom of his heart but was careful not to express this.

To his surprise young Niall had the opposite view.

'What do people work for if it isn't to get themselves what they want?' he asked.

'I hope you wouldn't throw your money away on emeralds for Gloria Darcy and her like,' his father said in ritual dismissive vein to his son.

These days Niall Hayes answered back. 'I'm not sure what you mean "her like", but if I loved someone and I earned my money lawfully I would feel very justified in spending it on presents for her,' he said.

Suddenly the room was silent and drab. Aunt Ethel looked at her son in some surprise. On her cardigan there was no jewellery; there never had been any except the engagement ring, wedding ring and good watch. Perhaps life might have been better if Bill Hayes had visited a shop and looked at jewels.

'Let's celebrate our anniversary,' Richard said to Gloria.

'Like what? Dinner for two in Ryan's Shancarrig Hotel, a bottle of wine?'

'No, but let's do something festive.'

'I find what we do is fairly festive already.' She laughed at him.

'You must want more, you must want more than creeping around.'

She sighed. It was the weary sigh of a mother who can't explain to a toddler how to tie his shoe laces. 'No, I don't want any more,' she said resignedly. 'But you do, so we'll do whatever you like for the anniversary.'

It was hard to think what they could do. The mystery was that they had spent a year as lovers without being discovered. In a place of this size and curiosity it was a miracle.

Perhaps they could go to Dublin. He would find an excuse and she would surely be able to think of some reason to go away as well.

Before he suggested it he would plan what they would do, otherwise she would shrug and say that they might as well stay here. He wanted to take her into Dublin bars, restaurants, he wanted people to admire her and be attracted by her beautiful face and sparkling laugh. He wanted to see her against some other background, not just the grey shapeless forms of Shancarrig. In all his years there Richard had never been able to like the place, it was lit up only by Gloria and he wanted to take her away from it.

He planned the visit to Dublin, how he would meet her off the train in Kingsbridge in his car – he would have gone up the day before so that there would be even less suspicion – how he would show her the sights – she didn't know Dublin well, she had told him. He would be her guide.

They would check into one of the better hotels. He would check out the room first, make sure it was perfect . . . they would walk arm in arm down Grafton Street. If they met anyone from Shancarrig they would all laugh excitedly and say wasn't it great coming to Dublin how you ran into everyone from home.

The more he thought about it the more Richard realised that he did not want Gloria in Dublin just for one night, he wanted her there always. He didn't want them in a furtive hotel room, he wanted them in a home of their own. Together always.

There were the most enormous difficulties in the way. The biggest, most handsome and innocent was Mike Darcy, smiling and welcoming with no idea that his wife loved another.

There were the children. Richard loved the look of them, dark boys with enormous eyes like Gloria. They had their father's slow, lopsided grin too, but it was silly to work out characteristics and assign them to one parent or the other.

He wished he could get to know the children, but it had been impossible. If he could get to know them then they would find it easier to come as a little family to Dublin to live with him. Richard realised suddenly that he was no longer planning an illicit trip to celebrate an anniversary, he was planning a new life. He must take it more slowly.

He must not rush things and risk losing her.

The anniversary was all that he could have wanted and more.

The hotel welcomed them as Mr and Mrs Hayes with no difficulty. Gloria's large rings did not look as if they had been put on for the occasion, they had a right to sit on her hand.

They had champagne in their room, they walked the city. He showed her places that he had loved when he was a boy, the canal bank from Baggot Street to Leeson Street. It thrilled him to be so near Waterloo Road. It was quite possible that his father could walk by on his way to the bookshop on Baggot Street Bridge, or his mother going to the butcher's shop to say that last Sunday's joint had not been as tender as they would have expected and the Doctor had been very disappointed.

He didn't see his parents but he did see Elaine pregnant and contented-looking, getting out of her mother's car. She hadn't seen him, and under normal circumstances he would have let her go on without stopping her. But these were not normal times. He wanted to show her Gloria, he wanted her to see the magnificent woman on his arm.

He called and she waddled over.

'Oh, Mummy will be sorry to have missed you,' she said. He had waited carefully until her mother had driven off. He didn't think his name was held in any favour in that family.

'I'd like you to meet Gloria Darcy.' The pride in his voice was overpowering.

They talked easily. Gloria asked her was it the first baby. Looking Richard straight in the eye Elaine said yes it was, she was very excited.

Gloria said she had two little boys of her own, and that you wished they'd never grow up and yet you were so proud of every little thing they did. She was saying all the things that Elaine wanted to hear. She also told her that the old wives' tales about labour were greatly exaggerated – it was probably to put people off having children before they were married.

'Oh, very few of us would be foolish enough to do that,' Elaine said, looking again at Richard.

He realised with a shock that he had been a monster of selfishness. Suddenly he was glad that Elaine had lied to him, that she had never carried his baby. But Olive Kennedy had. She had gone to England and given birth to their child. Where was this child now? A boy or girl in an orphanage, in a foster family, adopted.

How could he have not cared before? He felt his eyes water.

They had drinks in the Shelbourne Bar, and lunch in a small restaurant near Grafton Street that he had heard was very good.

He managed to meet three people he knew slightly. That wasn't bad for a man four years in exile from the capital city. He had chosen the place well.

'Did you love that girl Elaine a lot?' Gloria asked.

'No, I have never loved anyone except you,' he said simply.

'I thought you looked sad when you left, your eyes were full of tears . . . but it's not my business. I'd be very cross with you for asking prying questions,' she said, squeezing his hand warmly.

He could barely speak.

'I'll die if I can't be with you always, Gloria,' he said.

'Shush now.' She put her finger in the little glass of Irish Mist that she was drinking and offered it to him to suck. Soon the familiar desire returned, banishing for the moment the sense of loss and anxiety about returning her to real life in Shancarrig. They went back to their hotel and celebrated their anniversary well and truly.

He never asked what excuse she had made to Mike, whether it was shopping, or a visit to a hospital, or seeing an old friend. He knew she didn't want him to be a party to her lies. It could not have been hard to lie to Mike, his enthusiasm and simplicity wouldn't take into account the deviousness of the world around him, a wife who would betray him, a casual friend Richard Hayes walking in and out of his shop not for the errands he pretended but to feast his eyes on Gloria, to remind himself of the last time and look forward to the next time.

Kevin Darcy was at Shancarrig school. Sometimes Richard stopped him on the road just for the excuse to talk to him.

'How's your mammy and daddy?' he'd say.

'They're all right.' Kevin hadn't much interest.

'What did you learn at school?' he might ask.

'Not much,' Kevin would say.

One day Richard saw him with a cut head. He fell off the tree, Christy Dunne explained. Richard went to the shop to sympathise. Mike was out in the yard supervising the building of the new extension. Darcy's was now almost three times the size it was when they had bought it first.

'Oh, for God's sake, Richard, it's only a scrape. Don't be such a clucking hen,' Gloria said.

'He was bleeding a lot, I was worried.'

'Well, don't worry, he's fine. I put a big plaster on him, and gave him two

Crunchies, one for him and one for Christy. There wasn't a bother out of him.' He looked at her with admiration. How was she so calm, so good and wise a mother as well as everything else?

He was still more admiring when the burglars came the following week and stole all the jewellery that Mike Darcy had bought for his wife.

Sergeant Keane was in and out of the place, enquiries were made everywhere, tinkers had been in Johnny Finn's pub, you couldn't watch the place all the time.

Gloria was philosophical. It was terrible, particularly the little emerald, she loved the way it glowed. But then what was the alternative? You watched them day and night, you made the place into something like Fort Knox. It would be like living in a prison; she shivered. Richard remembered how she had once said that to be married to a suspicious husband who checked up on her would be like living with a gaoler. She needed to be free.

Maura O'Sullivan, who minded the Darcy children and cleaned the house for them, also worked in his aunt's house. He tried to find out more about the household, but Maura, unlike the rest of Shancarrig, was not inclined to gossip.

'What was it exactly you wanted to know?' she would say in a way that ended all enquiries.

'I was just wondering how the family were getting over the loss,' he said lamely.

Maura nodded, satisfied. She always brought her son with her, an affectionate boy called Michael who had Down's syndrome. Richard liked him and the way he would run towards whoever came into the room.

'Daddy?' he said hopefully to Richard.

The first time he had said this Maura explained that the child's father had had to go to England, and that consequently he thought everyone he met was his father.

'Daddy, my daddy?' he asked Richard again and again.

'Sort of, we're all daddys and mammys to other people,' Richard said to him.

Niall had heard him.

'You're very kind, Richard. It comes naturally to you. I mean it, you're terribly nice to people, that's why you're so successful.' Richard was surprised, the boy had never made a speech like this.

'No I'm not. I'm quite selfish really. I'm surprised it doesn't show.'

'I never saw it. I was jealous of you of course with women, but I didn't think you were selfish.'

'Not jealous of me any more?'

'Well, I only like one person and she assures me that she's not under your spell ... so ...' Niall Hayes looked happy.

'She never was. I thought she was lovely like anyone would, but it was admiration from afar, I assure you.'

'That's what she says.' Niall sounded smug and content.

'I'm not cramping your style in work here, am I?' Richard wanted to have it out. This seemed a good time.

'No. No of course not, it's just that I suppose we expected . . . everyone thought that sooner or later . . .'

'Yes, and one day I will but . . . not just yet.'

'You're saving, I know.' Niall was understanding.

'How do you know?'

'Well, you never go anywhere, you only have a shabby car. You don't buy jazzy suits.'

'That's right,' Richard admitted. 'I'm saving.' This was his cover, he realised. He was putting together a stake to buy a practice in Dublin.

The months went on. Gloria bought him a silk tie.

'You said no presents.' He fingered the cream and gold tie lovingly.

'I said you weren't to buy *me* any, that's all.'

'I want to buy you a piece of jewellery. Not an emerald, a ruby – a very small ruby. Let me,' he begged.

'No, Richard. Seriously, when could I wear it? Be sensible.'

He bought it anyway. He gave it to her in the gate lodge.

Their Wednesday afternoons there were totally secure. Major Murphy walked with his uncle rain or shine, and Leo had got a job working in the office of one of the building contractors' firms in the town. It seemed an unlikely job, but Gloria told him that she heard Leo was still in touch with that mad Foxy Dunne, who was going from strength to strength on the building sites in England. The word was that he would come back and set up his own firm. The word was that he and Leo had an understanding.

'Foxy Dunne, son of Dinny Dunne?'

'Oh, Foxy Dunne is like the papal nuncio in terms of respectability compared to his father. You know him falling out of Johnny Finn's most nights.'

'Well, well, well.' He realised he was getting a small-town mentality; he was finding serious difficulty in believing that Major Murphy of The Glen would let his daughter contemplate one of the Dunnes from the cottages. He was glad however that it meant Leo worked far away. It left the coast much more clear.

Gloria looked at the ruby for a long time.

'You're not angry?'

'How could I be angry that you spent so much on me? I'm touched, but I'll never wear it.'

'Couldn't you say . . . ?'

'We both know there's nothing I could say.'

'You could wear it here with me.'

'Yes, I will.'

She took the ruby away and had it made into a tie pin, then she gave it back to him. 'I'll put on a chain to wear it when I am with you, but for the rest of the time you keep it. Wear it on the tie that I gave you, then you'll think of me.'

'I think of you always,' he said.

Too much perhaps.

It was the beginning of the withdrawal. He saw it and blinded himself to it. He feared that someone else had come to town, but he knew there could be no one. She didn't dream up schemes to meet him for five minutes any more, and although she lay and took his loving she didn't implore him to love her as she once had, begging, encouraging and exciting him to performances that he had thought impossible.

He felt it was the place, it was getting too much for them. There had been endless complications about builders' suppliers, and the building of the extension, and the hostility of the Dunnes who said that they weren't anxious to build the place that was going to be direct competition with them. There had been delays over the insurance money for the jewellery. There was a problem about the newspaper delivery they planned, Nellie Dunne had created difficulties.

In his uncle's office Niall was restless and urging that he be involved in more cases, have consultations with clients and barristers, and in general learn his trade. Richard felt he was putting him off at every turn.

It was time to take Gloria away.

He began to explain it and for once he wouldn't listen when she tried to stop him. 'No, I've shushed enough. We have to think. It's been nearly two years. We must have our own home, our own life together. I don't wish Mike any harm but he has to know, he has to be told. He's a decent man, he'll agree to whatever we suggest. Whatever's for the best . . . he can come to Dublin to see the boys, we'll never hide from them who their real father is . . . he'd prefer to be taken into our confidence from the start . . . well, not exactly from the start but from now . . .' His voice trailed away as he looked at her face.

They sat in the gate lodge. They hadn't undressed. Their cigarettes and the little tin they used as an ashtray and cleaned after each visit sat between them on the table. It was an odd place to be talking about their future. It was an odd expression on her face as she listened. It showed utter bewilderment and shock.

He thought first it was the enormity of what they were about to do . . . coupled with the disruption for the children. He must reassure her. 'I've been looking at houses in Dublin, a little out of the city so that we could have privacy and so that Kevin and Sean would have a local-type school, not somewhere huge like the big Christian Brothers in the city . . .' He stopped. He had not read her look right.

She didn't want reassurance, she wanted him to stop talking straight away. 'None of this is going to happen, you must know this. Richard, you *must* know.'

'But you love me . . .'

'Not like this, not to run away with you . . .'

'Why have we been doing all this . . . ?' He waved his hand wildly around the room where they had made love so often.

'It had nothing whatsoever to do with my leaving here. That was never promised, never on the cards.'

He was the one bewildered now, and confused. 'What was it all about?' he asked, begging to be told.

She stood up and walked around the room as she spoke. She had never looked more beautiful. She spoke of a happy time with Richard, how he had made her feel wonderful and needed, how she had given him no undertaking, no looking ahead.

She said that her future was here in Shancarrig or very possibly another small town. They might sell up to the Dunnes and move. She and Mike liked starting a place from scratch. They had done that in other places. It was a challenge, it kept everything exciting, new.

Richard Hayes listened amazed as she spoke of Mike with this respect and love.

She was totally enmeshed with Mike in a way Richard had never understood. Her concern had nothing to do with a fear that Mike might be hurt or made to suffer. It was much more an involvement, a caring what he would do and decide and where he would want to go.

'But you don't love him!' he gasped.

'Of course I love him, I've never loved anyone else.'

'But why . . . ?' He couldn't even finish the sentence.

'He couldn't give me everything I wanted. No one can do that for anybody. I love him because he lets me be free.'

Richard realised she spoke the truth. 'And does he know . . . ?'

'Know what?'

'About me, about us. Do you tell him?' His voice grew angry and loud. 'Is this what gets him excited, your coming home and telling him what you and I did together?'

'Don't be disgusting,' she said.

'You're the one who is disgusting, out like an alley cat and then pretending that you're the model wife and mother.'

She looked at him reproachfully. He knew it was over.

In the years when he had wriggled out of relationships and escaped from affairs he had not been as honest as she was being, he had been devious and avoided face-to-face contact except when it was utterly necessary. His heart was heavy when he thought of Olive Kennedy, and the way he had disowned her in front of her parents.

If only he could have his time all over again. He hung his head.

'Richard?' she said.

'I didn't mean it about the alley cat.'

'I know you didn't.'

'I don't know what to do, darling Gloria. I don't know what to do.'

'Go away and leave this place, have a good life in Dublin. One day I'll meet you there, we will talk in a civilised way like you and the girl in Baggot Street, the one who was having the baby.'

'No.'

'That's what you'll do.' She spoke soothingly.

'And if you go to another town will you find someone new?'

'I won't go out looking for anyone, that I assure you.'

'And will he ... will he put up with it, turn the other way...?' He couldn't even bear to speak Mike Darcy's name.

'He'll know I love him and will never leave him.'

There was nothing more to say.

There was a lot to be done.

He would go back to the office and telephone some solicitors' offices in Dublin. He would ask his mother if he could go back to the basement flat in Waterloo Road. He would work day and night to clear his files, and leave everything ship-shape for Niall. He could shake off his years here and start again.

They tidied up the little house that they were visiting for the last time. As usual they emptied the cigarette butts and ash into an envelope. They straightened the furniture to the way it had been when they first found the place. They left by the window as they had always done. They rearranged the branches that hung to hide it.

She wouldn't bring anyone else here after he had gone, he felt sure of that. With a little lurch he wondered had she ever brought anyone before.

But that was useless speculation.

'Now that we're legitimate we can walk home together,' he said.

'Why not?' She was easy and affectionate, as she was with everyone.

'The long way or the short way?' He offered her the choice.

'The scenic route,' she decided.

They went up past the open ground that led to the Old Rock, and back through the woods, past Maddy Ross's house where she sat at her little desk, maybe writing letters to that priest who had gone to the missions, the one that she might have fancied. Richard felt a huge wave of sympathy for her. What a wasted love that must have been. Compared to his own great passion.

They came to the bridge, children still playing there as they had been the day Richard Hayes had come to town five long years ago.

Different children, same game.

Imagine, only an hour ago he had been planning for Gloria's children to go to school in Dublin. He thought he had taken over a family.

And now everything was over.

Now they were free to talk to each other there was nothing to say. His thoughts went up the road to the old schoolhouse, to the big beech tree which was covered with people's initials and their names.

In the first weeks of loving Gloria he had gone there secretly and carved 'Gloria in Excelsis'.

It didn't seem blasphemous, it seemed a celebration. If anyone saw it in years to come they would think it was a hymn of praise to God. They might think a priest had put it there. He would not go and score it out. That would be childish. He could finish the story, of course. He could say that the glory of the world passed by; Sic Transit Gloria Mundi. Only a few would understand it and when they did they would never connect it with Gloria Darcy, loving wife of Mike Darcy, shopkeeper.

But that would be childish too.

Maura O'Sullivan and her son Michael passed them by as they stood on the bridge, Gloria and Richard who would never speak again.

'Good day Mrs Darcy, Mr Hayes,' she said.

'My daddy?' Michael ran up to him and hugged his leg.

Richard knelt down to return the hug properly.

'Go home, Gloria,' he said.

She went without a word. He could hear the sound of her high red heels tapping down the road towards the centre of Shancarrig.

'How are you, Michael? You're getting to be a very big fellow altogether,' he said and buried his head in the boy's shoulder so that no one would see his tears.

Leo

When Leonora Murphy was a toddler, her father used to sit her on his knee and tell her about the little girl who had a little curl *right* in the middle of her forehead. He would poke Leo's forehead on the word *right* to show her where the curl was. Then he would go on, *And when she was good she was very very good, but when she was bad she was HORRID.* At the last word he would make a terrible face and roar at her, *HORRID, HORRID.* It was always frightening, even though Leo knew it would end well with a big hug, and sometimes his throwing her up in the air.

She wasn't frightened of Daddy, just the rhyme. It seemed menacing, as if someone else was saying it.

Anyway it wasn't even suitable for her because she was a girl with much more than one little curl. She had a head full of them, red-gold curls. They got tangled when anyone tried to brush her hair. Her mother gave up in despair several times. 'Like a furze bush, like something you'd see on a tinker child.' Leo knew this was an insult. People were half afraid of the tinkers, who camped behind Barna Woods sometimes when they were on the way to the Galway races.

If Leo ever was bad and wouldn't eat her rice or fasten her shoes properly, Biddy would say that she'd be given to the tinkers next time one of them passed the door. It seemed a terrible fate.

But later when she was older, when she could go exploring, Leo Murphy thought that it might be exciting to go and live with the tinkers. They had open fires. The children ran around half dressed. They went through the woods finding rabbits.

She used to creep around with her friends from school, Nessa Ryan and Niall Hayes and Eddie Barton. Not daring to move they'd peep through the trees and the bushes and watch the marvellous free lifestyle of people who had no rules or no laws to tie them down.

Leo couldn't remember why she had been so afraid.

But then, that was when she was a child. Once she was eleven and grown up things could be viewed differently. She realised that there were a lot of things she hadn't understood properly while she was young.

She hadn't realised that she lived in the biggest house in Shancarrig, for one thing. The Glen was a Georgian house, with a wide hall leading back to the kitchen and pantry. On either side of the hall door were big beautifully proportioned rooms – the dining room where the table was covered with papers and books, since they rarely had anyone to dine – the drawing room where the old piano had not been tuned for many a year, and where the dogs slept on cushions behind the big baskets of logs for the fire.

There was a breakfast room behind where they ate their meals, and a sports room which had wellingtons and guns, and fishing tackle. This is where Leo kept her bicycle when she remembered, but often she left it outside the kitchen door. Sometimes the wild cats that Biddy loved to feed at the kitchen window came and perched on the bicycle. There was a time when a cat brought all her little kittens one by one and left them in the bicycle basket, thinking it might be a safe haven for them.

That was the day that Leo had watched stony-faced as her father drowned them in the rain barrel.

'It's for the best,' her father said. 'Life is about doing things for the best, things you don't like.'

Leo's father was Major Murphy. He had been in the British army. In fact, he had been away at the War when Leo was born. She knew that because every birthday he told her how he had been at Dunkirk and hadn't known if the new baby was a boy or a girl. Since there had been two boys already the news, when it did arrive, was great news.

Leo's brothers were away at school. They didn't go to Shancarrig school like other boys did, they were sent to a boarding school from the time they were very young. The school was in England, where Grandfather lived. Grandfather wanted some of his family near him and he paid the school fees, which were enormous. It was a famous school, where prime ministers had gone.

Leo knew that it wasn't a Catholic school, but that Harry and James did go to mass on Sundays. She also knew that, for some reason, she wasn't to talk about this to her friend Nessa Ryan, or to Miss Ross, or Mrs Kelly, or especially not to Father Gunn. It was all perfectly right and good, but not something you went on about.

She knew there were other ways in which she was different. Major Murphy didn't go out to work like other people's fathers did. He didn't have a business or a farm, just The Glen. He didn't go down to Ryan's Hotel in the evening like other men, or pop into Johnny Finn Noted for Best Drinks. He sometimes went for a walk with Niall Hayes's father, and he went to Dublin on the train for the day. But he didn't have a job.

Her mother didn't go shopping every morning. She didn't call to Dunne's or to the butcher's. She didn't get a blouse and skirt made with Eddie Barton's mother. She didn't get involved with arranging flowers on the altar for Father Gunn, or helping with the sale of work at the school. Leo's mother was very beautiful and gave the air of having a lot to do as she floated from room to room. She really was a very beautiful woman, everyone always said so. Mrs Murphy had red-gold hair like her daughter, but not those unruly curls. It was smooth and shiny and turned in naturally, as if it had always been like that. Once a month Mother went to Dublin and she had it trimmed then, in a place in St Stephen's Green.

Somehow Leo knew that Harry and James weren't going to come back to Shancarrig when they left school. They had been talking about Sandhurst for as long as she could remember. They were both accepted. Her father was delighted.

'We must tell everyone,' he said when the letter arrived.

'Who can we tell?' His wife looked at him almost dreamily across the breakfast table.

Father looked disappointed. 'Hayes will be pleased.'

'Your friend Bill Hayes is the only one who's heard of Sandhurst.' Miriam Murphy spoke sharply.

'Ah come on. They're not as bad as that.'

'They are, Frank. I've been the one who's always lived here, you're only the newcomer.'

'Eighteen years, and still a newcomer . . .' He smiled at her affectionately.

Leo's mother had been born in The Glen, and had played as a child in Barna Woods herself. She had gone fishing down to the River Grane, and taken picnics up to the Old Rock, from which Shancarrig got its name. She had been here all through the troubles after the Easter Rising, and through the Civil War. In fact, because there were so many upheavals at that time, her parents had sent her off to a convent school in England.

Shortly after she had left it she had met Frank Murphy and, as two Irish amid the croquet and tennis parties of the south of England in the early 1930s, they had been drawn together. Frank's knowledge of Ireland was sketchy, but romantic. He always hoped to settle there one day. Miriam Moore had been more practical. She had a falling down home, she said. It needed much more money than they would ever have to turn it into a dream.

Miriam's parents were old. They welcomed the bright son-in-law with open arms. They hoped he would be able to manage their beautiful but neglected house and estate. They hoped he would be able to keep their beautiful but restless daughter contented.

They died before they could judge whether he had been able to do either.

'Is Sandhurst on the sea?' Leo asked interestedly. If Harry and James were going to a beach next year, instead of back to school, she was very jealous indeed.

Her parents smiled indulgently at her. They told her it was in Surrey, nothing to do with sand as in Sandycove or Sandymount or any other seaside place she had been to. It was a great honour to get in there. They would be officers of the highest kind.

'Will they be a higher rank than Daddy if there's another war?' Leo asked.

'There won't be another war, not after the last one.'

He looked sad when he said that. Leo wished she hadn't brought the subject up. Her father walked with a stick and he had a lot of pain. She knew this because she could hear him groaning sometimes if he thought he was alone. Perhaps he didn't like being reminded of the War, which had damaged his spine.

'You should write to them, Leo,' her mother said. 'They'd like to get a letter from their little sister.'

It was like writing to strangers, but she wrote. She told them that she was sitting in the drawing room, and that Lance and Jessie were stretched in front of the fire. She told them about the school concert where they all wanted to sing 'I've Got a Lovely Bunch of Coconuts' and Mrs Kelly had said it was a filthy song. She told them how Eddie Barton had taught her how to draw different kinds of leaves, fishes and birds, and said she might do them a special drawing for Christmas if they ordered it.

She said she was glad they were going to be high-class officers in the army, even if there was never going to be another war. She said they would be glad to know that Daddy was walking a bit better and Mother looking a lot less sad.

To her surprise they both wrote almost by return and said that they loved her news. It was strange not being one thing or the other, they wrote.

Leo had a big bedroom that looked out over the garden. It was one of four large rooms around the big square landing. Nessa Ryan was always admiring the upstairs.

'It's like a room in itself, this landing,' she said in admiration. 'It's so poky in the hotel, all the rooms have numbers on them.'

Leo said that when her mother was young in The Glen there was breakfast on the landing. Imagine, people bringing all the food upstairs to save the family going down. Sometimes they used to eat in their dressing gowns, Mother had told her.

Nessa was very interested that Major and Mrs Murphy had different bedrooms; her parents slept in the same bed.

'Do they really?' Leo was fascinated. She broached the subject with Biddy. Somehow, it didn't seem right to ask directly.

'Don't go enquiring about where and how people sleep. Nothing but trouble comes out of that.'

'But *why*, Biddy?'

'Ah, people sleep where they want to sleep. Your parents sleep at each end of the house, that's what they want. Leave it at that.'

'But where did your parents sleep?'

'With all of us, in one room.' So it wasn't much help.

When Harry and James came home for a very quick visit she decided to ask them. They looked at each other.

'Well, you see. With Papa being wounded and everything . . .'

'All that sort of thing changed,' James finished.

'What sort of thing?' Leo asked.

They looked at each other in despair.

'All sorts of things. No sorts of things,' Harry said. And she knew the subject was over.

Mother never told Leo anything about the facts of life. If it hadn't been for Biddy and Nessa she would have been astonished by her first period. Although she knew how kittens, puppies and rabbits, and therefore babies, were born, she had no idea how they were conceived. She very much hoped that it was nothing to do with the behaviour of the dogs and cats at certain times. She didn't see how such a thing would be possible for humans anyway, even if any of them would agree to do it. She hated Nessa Ryan being so knowing so she didn't ask her, and she knew that Biddy in the kitchen flushed a dark red when the matter was mentioned...

When Leo Murphy was fourteen such matters had been sorted out, if not exactly satisfactorily, at least she felt that she had mastered whatever technical information there was about it from reading pamphlets and magazines.

She had agreed with Nessa and Maura Brennan that it was quite impossible to believe that your own parents could ever have done it, but then the living proof that they must have was all around.

Maura Brennan was able to add the information that a lot of it happened when the man was drunk, and Leo said it was very unfair that the woman shouldn't be allowed to get drunk as well, because it was bound to be so awful.

Maura was very nice. She never pushed herself on anyone. In ways Leo liked her better than she liked Nessa Ryan, who could be moody if she didn't get her own way. But Maura lived in the poorest of the cottages. Her father Paudie was often to be seen sitting on someone's steps with a bottle in his hand, having been out drinking all night.

Maura wouldn't go on to the convent with them next year when she and Nessa went into town on the bus to secondary school. And yet at fourteen Maura seemed to know a lot more about life than the rest of them did.

It seemed very unfair to Leo that families like Maura Brennan's and Foxy Dunne's had to live in the falling down cottages by the river and had such shabby clothes. Foxy Dunne was much brighter than Niall Hayes, much quicker when it came to giving answers in school, but Foxy had no bicycle, no proper clothes, and had never been known to wear shoes that fitted him. Maura Brennan was much kinder and more gentle than Nessa Ryan but she never got a dress like Nessa got for her birthday and she hadn't a winter coat.

Leo knew she wasn't meant to go into the cottages and so she didn't. No one ever said not to, but it was something that was unspoken.

Only Foxy ever challenged it.

'Aren't you coming in to see the Dunne family at leisure ...?' he asked.

They had learned the word leisure at school today. Mrs Kelly had written it on the board and talked about what it meant.

'No thanks. I've got to go home today,' Leo would say.

'But *I'm* allowed to come and see the Murphy family at leisure,' he would say.

Leo was well able for him. 'Yes you are, and very welcome too, when you want to . . .'

It was a stand-off.

They admired each other . . . it had always been like that, since they were in Mixed Infants together . . .

After the end of the summer term Leo and Nessa travelled on the bus to the convent school. They would meet the Reverend Mother, get a list of books and other items they would need, details of the school uniform and probably a string of rules as well. They thought that they would also be shown around the convent, but this did not materialise. They were tempted to spend the time idling round and sampling the pleasures of freedom of a place ten times the size of Shancarrig, but they felt that somehow they would be found out. It would be told back in Ryan's Hotel that they had been skitting and laughing on a corner with an idling lad, or licking ice creams in the street.

Better by far to get the early bus home and be shown to be reliable.

Nessa went into the hotel where she felt they weren't nearly grateful enough to see her.

'Are you back already?' Mrs Ryan said without enthusiasm.

'I hope you did everything you were meant to do,' her father said.

Leo grinned at her. 'It'll be the same in my place,' she said companionably. 'They'll have fed the dogs and won't have kept anything for me.'

She strolled up the hill, pausing to talk to Eddie Barton and tell him about the convent. He would be going to the Brothers. He said he wasn't looking forward to it. It was only games they cared about.

'In this place it's only prayers they care about,' Leo grumbled. 'There's statues leaping at you out of every wall.'

She trailed her shoulder bag behind her as she passed the old gate lodge that had been let once to people, who had left it like a pigsty. Now it was all boarded up in case any intruders got in.

It was a Thursday, and as soon as she was home Leo remembered that it was, of course, Biddy's half day. There would be food left under the meat safe. They usually had something cold for supper on a night when Biddy wasn't there. Leo knew that she should help herself because there was no one to greet her. Major Murphy had gone to Dublin that morning. He had caught the early train. Her mother must have gone walking in Barna Woods. Leo planned to take her food up to her bedroom and listen to her gramophone. She had written to James and Harry about the song 'I Love Paris in zee Springtime'. She could play it over and over. Some day she would go to Paris in 'zee Springtime or zee Fall' with someone who would sing that to her. She thought it would never go out of fashion. She closed herself into her room and before she even started on her milk and chicken sandwich she put on the record.

She threw herself on her windowseat and was singing along with it when, to her surprise, she heard a door bang and footsteps running up or down the stairs, she couldn't tell which.

Thinking she might be playing it too loudly, she went to take off the handle of the machine and as she did so her eye caught sight of a young man fleeing across the grass and into the shrubbery. As he ran he was pulling on a shirt.

Leo was very frightened. It must have been a robber. Could there be more of them downstairs? She didn't know whether to shout for help or pretend that she wasn't there.

Her mind raced. They must know she was there if they had heard the music playing. Perhaps one was waiting for her outside her bedroom door. She could feel her heart thumping. In the silence of the house she heard a door creak open. She had been right. There *was* someone else lying in wait for her. She prayed as she had never prayed before.

As if in direct answer to her, God had managed to make her mother's voice call out, 'Leo? Leo? Is that you?'

Mother was standing outside her bedroom door, flushed-looking and confused.

Leo ran to her. 'Mother. There were robbers . . . are you all right?'

'Shush, shush. Of course I am . . . what are you talking about?'

'I heard them running down the stairs . . . they went through the garden.'

'Nonsense, Leo. There were no robbers.'

'There *were*, Mother. I heard them, I saw them . . . I saw one of them.'

'What did you see?'

'I saw him pulling off or putting on a shirt. Mother, he ran over there behind the lilacs, over the back fence.'

'What on earth are you doing home anyway . . . weren't you meant to be on a tour of that school?'

'Yes, but they didn't show us. I saw him, Mother. There might be others in the house.'

Leo had never seen her mother so full of purpose. 'Come downstairs with me this moment and we'll put an end to this foolishness.' She flung open the doors of all the rooms. 'What burglar was here if he didn't take the silver, the glass? Or here, in the sports room, all your father's guns. Each one intact. Look, they didn't even take our supper, so let's have no chats about burglars and robbers.'

'But the feet on the stairs?' She was less sure of the figure now.

'I went downstairs myself and came back up to my room. I didn't know you were back . . .'

'But I was playing the record player . . .'

'Yes. That's what made me come out and look for you. To know what you were doing blasting it out and then turning it off.'

Mother looked excited. Different from the way she was normally.

Leo didn't know what made her think it was dangerous, but that is exactly what she felt it was. She had to walk just as delicately here as if there really were a robber hiding in the house.

*

She spoke nothing of the incident to her father, nor to Biddy. When Nessa Ryan asked whether Leo's welcome home had been any more cordial than the one that Nessa had got herself in the hotel, Leo said that she had made a sandwich and listened to 'I Love Paris'.

Nessa Ryan said that life was very unfair. She had been roped in to help polish silver, since she was back.

Imagine having all the freedom in the world in a big house like that.

Imagine. She didn't notice Leo shiver as she realised that she had denied the fright, and that somehow made the fright much bigger than it had been before.

Foxy Dunne came up the drive next day. His swagger showed a confidence that many of those twice his age might not have felt approaching The Glen.

But Foxy didn't push his luck; he went to the back door.

Biddy was most disapproving.

'Yes?' she said coldly.

'Ah, thank you, Biddy. It's good to get a real traditional Irish welcome everywhere, that's what I always say.'

'You and your breed never say anything except to make a jeer of other people who put their minds to work.'

Foxy looked without flinching.

'*I'm* different from my breed, as you call it, Biddy. I have every intention of putting my mind to work.'

'You'll be the first of the Dunnes who did, then.' She was still annoyed to see him sitting so confidently in her kitchen.

'There always has to be the first of some family who does. Where's Leo?'

'What's that to you?'

At that moment Leo came into the kitchen. She was pleased to see Foxy Dunne. She offered him one of Biddy's scones that were cooling on a wire tray.

'Will you like the place inside?' He was speaking about the secondary school.

'I think so. A bit Holy Mary, but you know.'

'A lot of people around here could do with being Holy Mary,' Biddy said.

Leo laughed. Everything seemed to be back to normal again.

'You'll work hard, won't you?' Foxy was concerned.

'Imagine one of Dinny Dunne's lads laying down the law on working hard,' Biddy snorted.

Foxy ignored her. 'It's important that you work as hard as I do,' he said to Leo. 'I have to, because I come from nothing. You have to because you come from everything.'

'I don't know what you mean,' Leo said.

'It would be dead easy for you to do nothing, for you to just drift about without doing anything, and end up just marrying someone.'

'Not for ages.' Leo was indignant.

'Not any time. You should get a job.'

'I might *want* to marry someone.'

'Yes, yes. But you'd be better off with a job, whether you married anyone or not.'

'I never heard such nonsensical talk.' Biddy was banging the saucepans around to show her disapproval.

'Come on, Foxy. We'll go out to the orchard,' Leo said.

They picked small gooseberries and put them in a basket that Leo's mother had left under a tree.

'It won't always be like this here, you know,' Foxy said.

'No. It'll be term time, and a list of books as long as your arm.'

'I meant this house, this way of going on.'

She looked at him, alarmed. The anxiety of the other night came back; things changing, not being safe any more.

'What do you mean?'

She looked very startled suddenly, and he didn't like the way her face got so alarmed, so he reassured her. He told her that if he could pretend to be sixteen or over he could get taken on by a man who was raising a crew for a builder in England – all fellows from round here, fellow countrymen . . . he'd start just doing odd jobs, but he'd work his way up.

'I wish you weren't going away,' Leo said. 'I know it's crazy, but I have this stupid feeling that something awful is going to happen.'

It was three weeks later that it happened. On a warm summer evening. The house was quiet. Biddy had gone on her annual summer holidays back to her family's farm. Leo had finished her letter to Harry and James, she had written how Daddy's back seemed much better and that Dr Jims had said that walking couldn't do him any harm – it couldn't hurt him any more than he had been hurt in the War – and that if he sat in a chair like an old man with a rug over his knees then he'd turn into one.

So he went off for long walks with Mr Hayes, even up as far as the Old Rock. That's where they had gone today. Leo decided to walk down to the town to post the letter. Once it was written she liked it to be on its way. It could sit on the hall table for days, with Biddy dusting around it. She found a stamp and headed off. Mrs Barton was ironing, Leo could see her through the window. She never went out to sit in her little garden. Surely she could have brought some of her sewing out of doors on a beautiful evening like this. Leo looked up to see if she could see Eddie's face at his window. He wrote almost as many letters as she did. She met him sometimes at the post office and Katty Morrissey said that between them they kept the whole of P&T going.

But there was no sign of Eddie. Maybe he was off finding odd shapes of wood and clumps of flowers to draw. She did meet Niall Hayes, however, walking disconsolately up and down The Terrace.

'God, that school I'm going to is like a prison,' Niall said. 'It's like *The Count of Monte Cristo*.'

'The convent's all right. It's choked with statues, though, all of them with cross faces.'

'Oh, I wouldn't mind if it was only the statues. You should see the faces on these fellows. All of them in long black dresses, and looking desperate.'

'Sure doesn't Father Gunn wear a long dress, and Father Barry. You're used to them.' Leo thought Niall Hayes was making heavy weather out of it all.

'They don't have faces like lighting devils.'

'Did your father go to school there?'

'Of course he did, and all my uncles. And they've forgotten how awful it is. They keep telling me of all the fun they had there.'

'Your father's gone for a walk with my father.' Leo was tired of all the gloom.

'Well, it must have been a short one then. My father's back in the house there, making some farmer's will. Leo, I don't think I could *bear* to be a solicitor here in Shancarrig.'

'You could always go somewhere else,' Leo said. There seemed to be no cheering Niall today.

She was sorry her father's walk had been cancelled, but maybe he was sitting with Mother in the orchard. She had seen sometimes they had a big jug of homemade lemonade, and they looked as if they were a bit happy.

She met Father Gunn, who said wasn't it amazing the way the time raced by. There was another whole class ready to leave Shancarrig and go out into the wide world. It was extraordinary how grown-ups thought time raced by. Leo found it went very slowly indeed.

As she came in the gate of The Glen she heard cries coming from the gate lodge, and at the same moment she saw her father hastening as fast as he was able down the drive. Leo shrank away from the sound of crashing furniture and screams.

But she knew without a shadow of a doubt that it was her mother's voice she heard screaming, 'No, no! You can't! No,' and a great long wail.

'Oh, my God, my God. Miriam. *Miriam.*'

Her father was stumbling. He had dropped his stick, and had to bend down for it.

Leo watched as if it was slow motion.

Then they heard the shots. Three of them. And at that moment Leo's mother came staggering to the door. Her blouse was covered with blood. Her hair and eyes were wild.

'My God . . . he tried to . . . he was trying to . . . he would have killed me,' she cried. She kept looking behind her where they could see a shape on the ground.

'Frank!' screamed Leo's mother. 'Oh, do something, Frank. For God's sake! He would have killed me.'

Leo shrank still further away from the scene which she could see unfolding, but yet could not take in.

Her father walked in exaggeratedly slow motion towards the door and took her mother in his arms.

He soothed her like a baby.

'It's over, Miriam, it's over,' he said.

'Is he dead?' Leo's mother didn't want to look.

Horrified, Leo saw her father bend to the shape on the floor and turn it over. Leo could see a man with dark hair, lying on the floor of the gate lodge. There was a big red stain all over the front of his shirt.

It was the man she had seen running towards the lilacs in the shrubbery three weeks ago, the day that she thought there had been robbers.

And now both her father and mother were crying.

'It's all right, Miriam darling. It's over. He's dead.' Her father was saying this over and over again.

Later they gave Leo a brandy too. With a little water in it. But that was well after they had come back to the house.

The door of the gate lodge had been closed. They all walked up the drive arm in arm and Mother had gone up to wash herself.

'You might need to, you know, not change anything,' Leo heard Daddy say, but Mother looked at him wildly.

'You mean . . . wear this? Wear *this* on my body? All this blood? What for? Frank, use your head. What for?' She was near hysteria.

'I'll wash you,' he offered.

'No. Please let me be on my own for a few moments.'

Mother had a wash basin in her room, with a mirror and a light over it, and little pink floral curtains.

Leo didn't want to be alone, so she followed her mother into the room. Their eyes met in the mirror.

'Are you all right, Mummy?' She rarely used that word.

Mother's face softened. 'It's all right, Leo. It's over.' She said Father's words like a parrot.

'What are we going to do? What's going to happen?'

'Shush. Let me get rid of all this. We'll put it out of our minds. It'll be like a bad dream.'

'But . . .'

'That's for the best, Leo, believe me.' Mother looked very young as she stood there just in her slip and skirt. She rubbed her neck and arms with a soapy flannel and warm water, even though there was no trace of blood. That was all streaked and hardening on the yellow blouse she had thrown into the wastepaper basket.

Mother was brushing her teeth, and she shook her tin of Tweed talcum powder into her hand and rubbed it into her skin.

'Go on, darling. Go down to your father. I want to finish dressing.'

Leo thought Mother only had to put on a blouse. And of course a brassiere. She had only just realised that for some reason Mother hadn't been wearing one as she stood beside the hand basin. Just the slip. Her silky peach-coloured one.

Everything was so strange and unreal. The fact that Mother had asked her to leave the room now was only one tiny fragment more in the whole thing.

Leo went into the drawing room. She felt something like this should not be discussed in the breakfast room where they lived on ordinary days. Her father must have felt the same thing. He had put a match to the fire and the two dogs, Lance and Jessie, seemed pleased. They stretched their big cream limbs in front of the grate.

Leo thought suddenly that Lance and Jessie didn't know what had happened. Then she remembered that nobody knew – not Niall Hayes, whom she had been talking to half an hour ago – nor Mrs Barton, who had waved from her ironing – nor Father Gunn, who had said that time passed so quickly.

Father Gunn? Why wasn't he here?

The moment someone died you sent for the priest. And Dr Jims, Eileen and Sheila's father, he should be here. That's what happened when people got sick or died, Father Gunn and Dr Jims arrived in their cars.

Mother was at the door. She shivered and hugged herself.

'That's lovely of you to light the fire,' she said.

They both looked up, Leo and her father. Mother sounded so ordinary – so normal. As if it all hadn't happened out there. Down in the gate lodge.

That was when Father poured the brandy for the two of them.

'Give Leo a little, too.' Mother sounded as if she was offering more soup at lunchtime.

'Come up here to the fire. Warm your hands. I'll phone Sergeant Keane. He'll be up in five minutes.'

'No.' It was like a whiplash.

'We have to call him, we should have phoned immediately.'

Leo was sipping the horrible and unfamiliar brandy. She didn't know how people like Maura Brennan's father wanted to drink alcohol all the time. It was disgusting.

'My nerves won't stand it, Frank. I've been through enough already.'

'Sergeant Keane's very gentle. He'll make it as quick as possible. It's just the formalities.'

'I won't *have* the formalities. There's no point in asking me to.'

'A man tried to kill you, he had one of my guns. He *could* have killed you.' Father's voice broke with emotion at the thought of it.

Mother became even more icily calm.

'But he didn't. What happened was that I killed him.'

'You defended yourself against him ... the gun went off. He killed himself.'

'No. I picked up the gun and shot him.'

'You don't know *what* happened. You're in shock.'

Major Murphy made a move as if to go out to the hall to the telephone.

Mother didn't even need to raise her voice to make her seriousness felt.

'If you ring him, Frank, I'm walking out of that door and you'll never see me again. Either of you.'

He put out his arms as if to hold her again, support her as he had up the drive, console her as he had done when he was holding her, telling her it was over.

Mother really seemed to believe that it *was* over.

Leo kept moving the glass around between her hands as she listened to her parents talking about the man who lay dead in their gate lodge.

Her mother's voice was strange and unnatural. It didn't sound like a voice, it sounded like a noise, a thin even noise, with no highs and lows.

She spoke as one who is being perfectly reasonable.

Frank had told her it was over, finished. So let it be forgotten. Why drag heavy-footed policemen in, and go over it and over it, and ask questions and give answers? The man had threatened her. He had got killed himself. It was an eye for an eye. Justice had been done. Let it be left as it was.

At every interruption she gave her strange disembodied threat: 'Or else I will disappear from this house and you will never see me again.'

It was as if they had forgotten she was here. Leo watched mesmerised as her mother, by sheer force of repetition, began to beat down the rational arguments. She saw her father change from the strong man comforting his wife caught in a terrible accident and become someone hunted and unsure. She saw him bite his lip and watched his eyes widen with fear at every repeated threat that Miriam Murphy would walk out the door and never be seen again.

She wanted to interrupt, to ask Mother where she would go. Why she would leave them, her home and her family?

But she didn't dare to move.

It was when her father had said, 'I couldn't *live* without you, Miriam, you couldn't leave knowing that . . .'

'Please . . .' She looked across at her fourteen-year-old daughter, as if a lapse of taste had been committed. A man shouldn't speak of his need, of his weakness, not in front of a child.

Major Murphy came over to the windowseat where Leo was sitting.

'Leo, dearest child.'

'What's going to happen, Daddy?'

'It's going to be all right. As your mother says, it's over, it's over. We mustn't . . .'

'Will we get Dr Jims? Father Gunn . . . ?'

'Leo, come with me. I'll bring you up to bed.'

'I want to stay here, Daddy, please . . .'

'You want to help us, you want to be big and brave and do the right thing . . .'

'No. I want to stay here. I'm afraid.'

Outside in the big garden darkness had fallen. The bushes were big shapes, not colours as they had been when the three of them walked back up, huddled together from the horrors they had left in the gate lodge.

He propelled her out of the door and to the kitchen where he warmed some milk in a saucepan. He took the big silver pepperpot and sprinkled some over the top of the milk when it was poured into a mug.

He walked up the stairs with her and led her to the room.

'Put on your nightie, like a good girl,' he said.

He turned his back as Leo slipped out of her green cotton dress and her summer vest and knickers, and pulled on the pink winceyette nightdress from the nightdress case shaped like a rabbit. Leo remembered with a shock that when she stuffed her nightie in there this morning nothing had happened. None of this nightmare had begun.

She got into bed and sipped the milk.

Her father sat on the bed and stroked her forehead. 'It will be all right, Leo,' he said.

'How can it be all right, Daddy?'

'I don't know. I used to wonder that in the War, but it was.'

'It wasn't really. You got wounded and you can't walk properly.'

'Yes, I can.' He stood up.

His face was so sad Leo wanted to cry aloud. She wanted to open the window in her room, kneel up on the windowseat and cry out for someone in Shancarrig to help them all.

But she bit her lip.

'I have to go down now, Leo,' he said.

It was as if they were allies. Allies to protect a strange silent mother downstairs who wasn't speaking in her ordinary voice.

She used to play that game of 'if'.

If I get up the stairs before the grandfather clock in the hall stops striking then Mrs Kelly won't be in a bad mood tomorrow. If the crocuses come up in front of the house by Tuesday I'll get a letter from Harry and James.

Now she sat in the dark bedroom with her arms around her knees. If I don't get out of bed it will be all right. Dr Jims will come and say he wasn't dead at all. If he is really dead then Father Gunn will say it wasn't Mother's fault.

If I don't get out of bed at all and if I sit like this all night without moving then it'll turn out not to have happened at all.

She woke in the morning stiff and awkward. She hadn't managed to stay awake. Now the charm wouldn't work. It *had* happened, all of it.

There was no point in holding her knees any more. None of it was going to work.

How could it be an ordinary day? A sunny day with Lance and Jessie rushing around outside, with Mattie the postman cycling up the drive, with smells of breakfast coming from downstairs.

Leo got out of bed and looked at her face in the wardrobe mirror. It was grey white and there were shadows under her frightened grey-green eyes. Her curly hair stood upright over her head.

She pulled on the clothes she had thrown on the floor last night, last night when Daddy had been standing with his frightened face.

At that moment the door opened and Mother came in. A different Mother from last night. Mother was dressed in a blue linen suit, her hair was combed, she wore her pink lipstick and she looked bright and enthusiastic.

'I have the most wonderful news,' she said.

Leo felt the colour rushing to her cheeks. The man wasn't dead. Dr Jims had cured him.

Before she could speak Mother had opened the wardrobe door and started to take out some of Leo's frocks.

'We're going on a holiday, all three of us,' she said. 'Your father and I suddenly decided that this was what we all needed. Now, isn't that a lovely surprise?'

'But . . .' Leo's voice dried in her throat.

'But we have to get going just after breakfast, it's a long drive.'

'Are we running away?' Leo's voice was a whisper.

'For a whole week we are . . . now, where are your bathing togs? We're going to a lovely hotel on a cliff, and we'll be able to run down and have a swim before breakfast every day. Imagine.'

Her father didn't catch her eye at breakfast, and Leo knew that she must not mention the events of last night. Her father had somehow bought the right for both of them to run away with Mother. That's what was happening.

They heard a knock at the back door. All three of them looked at each other in alarm, but it was Ned, who did the garden. Leo heard her father explaining about the sudden holiday . . . and giving instructions.

The glasshouses were in a terrible state – if Ned could concentrate entirely on clearing them, and sorting out what was to be done . . . .

'And what about the rockery, Major, sir?'

'It's very important that you leave that. There's a man coming down from the Botanic Gardens in Dublin to have a look at it. He said nothing was to be touched until he came.'

'I'm glad of that.' Ned sounded relieved. 'Will I fill in the hole we dug?'

'Oh, we've done that already . . .'

If Ned was surprised that a man with war injuries, and his frail wife, had covered in a pit that it had taken him two days to dig, he showed no sign of it.

'I'll leave it as it is then, Major, sir?'

'Just as it is, Ned. No disturbing it at all.'

Leo felt a cold horror spread all over her.

The memory of last night, hugging her knees in the dark. The sound of footsteps, of low urgent voices, of dragging and pulling. But her mother was calm as she listened to the conversation at the back door, and even laughed when Daddy came back into the room.

'Well, I expect that was welcome news for our Ned. Anything that he hasn't to do must come as a pleasant surprise.'

Leo beat back the wild fears.

Often her dreams seemed real to her . . . more real than ordinary life. This is what must be happening now. There was another knock at the door. Again the look of alarm was exchanged.

This time it was Foxy Dunne.

'Yes, Foxy?' Leo's father was unenthusiastic.

'How are you?' Foxy never addressed people by title. He wouldn't greet the priest as Father and he certainly wouldn't call Leo's father Major.

'I'm fine thank you, Foxy. How are you?'

'Great altogether. I came to say goodbye to Leo.'

Suddenly her father's voice sounded wary. 'And how, might I ask, did you know that she was going away?'

'I didn't.' Foxy was cheerful. 'I'm going away myself, that's why I came to say goodbye.'

'Well, I suppose you'd better come in.'

Foxy walked easily through the scullery and the kitchen and into the breakfast room.

'How're ya?' he said, nodding easily at Leo's mother.

She smiled at the small boy with the freckles and the red hair, the one Dunne boy that poverty and neglect had never managed to defeat.

'And where are you off to?' she asked politely.

Foxy ignored her and addressed Leo. 'I'm off to London, Leo. I didn't think I'd ever be able to do it. I thought I'd be hanging around here like an eejit, dragging a brush around someone's shop.'

'You're too young to go to England.'

'They won't ask. All they want is someone to make tea on a site.'

'Will you be frightened?'

'After my old fellow and Maura Brennan's old fellow? Both of them coming home drunk and both of them trying to beat me up . . . how could I be frightened?'

He talked as if Leo's parents weren't there. It wasn't deliberately rude, it was just that he didn't see them.

'Will you ever come back to Shancarrig again?'

'I'll come home every Christmas with fistfuls of pound notes, like everyone else on the buildings.'

Major Murphy asked whether Foxy would learn a trade.

'I'll learn everything,' Foxy told him.

'No, I mean a skilled trade, you know, an honourable trade, like a bricklayer . . . It would be very good to serve your time, to do an apprenticeship.'

'It'll be that all right.' Foxy didn't even look at the man, let alone heed him.

'Will you write and tell what it's like?' Leo knew her voice sounded shaky and not full of interest as Foxy would have liked.

'I was never one for the writing, but as I say, I'll see you every Christmas. I'll tell you then.'

'Good luck to you over there.' Leo's mother was standing up from the breakfast table. She was bringing the conversation to a close.

Foxy gave her a long look.

'Yeah. I suppose I'll need a bit of luck all right. But it's more a matter of working and letting them know you can work.'

'You're only a child. Don't let them ruin your health, tell them you're not able for heavy work.' The Major was kind.

But Foxy was having none of it. 'I'll tell them I'm seventeen. That's how I'll get on. Seventeen, and a bit stunted.' He was going in his own time, not in Mrs Murphy's. 'I'll see you at Christmas, Leo,' he said, and went.

Leo saw him fondling the ears of Lance, and throwing a stick for Jessie.

Other people were in awe of the two loudly barking labradors. Not Foxy Dunne.

She thought of him a few times during their holiday, that strange time in a faraway hotel, where there was nothing whatsoever for her to do except read the books that were in the library. Sometimes she walked with her father and mother along the sandy beaches, collecting cowrie shells. But usually she left Mother and Father to walk alone, with the dogs. They seemed very close together, sometimes even holding hands as Father limped along, and Mother sometimes bent to pick up some driftwood and throw it out into the sea so that Lance and Jessie could struggle to bring it back.

She didn't sleep too well at night in the small room with the diamond-shaped panes of glass in the window. The roar of the Atlantic Ocean down below the cliffs was very insistent. The stars looked different here from the way they looked in Shancarrig when she'd sit on her windowseat and watch at night – the familiar garden of The Glen, the lilacs, the shrubbery down to the big iron gates and the gate lodge.

She shivered when she thought of the gate lodge. She had not been able to look at it as they had driven past on the morning they had left home. She dreaded seeing it again when she went back, but she wanted to be away from this strange dreamlike place too, this holiday that never should have been.

Biddy would be at home now in The Glen. What might have happened? What might she have found? Yet neither Father nor Mother telephoned her or seemed remotely worried.

Leo felt a constriction in her throat. She couldn't eat the food that was put in front of her.

'My daughter hasn't been well. It has nothing to do with your lovely food.'

Leo looked at her mother in disbelief. How could she lie so easily and in such a matter-of-fact voice? If she could do that she could lie about anything. Nothing was as it used to be any more.

Leo was very afraid. She wanted a friend. Not Nessa whose eyes would widen in horror. Not Eddie Barton who would retreat into his woods, and his flowers, and his drawings. Not Niall Hayes who would say it was typical of grown-ups – they never did anything you could rely on.

She couldn't tell Father Gunn, not even in confession. Maura Brennan would be more frightened than she was herself.

For a moment she thought of Foxy Dunne, but even if he were at home he wasn't the kind of person you could tell. She wondered how he was standing up to life on a big building site in London. Did he seriously think that people would believe he was seventeen? But he was always so cocky, so confident, maybe they would.

She looked away to the other side of the car as they drove back in through the gates of The Glen. It was as if she was afraid that the door of the gate lodge would be swinging wide open and that Sergeant Keane and a lot of guards would be there waiting for them.

But everything was as it always had been. The dogs raced around, happy to be home and no longer cooped up in the station wagon. Biddy was bustling around full of interest in their sudden holiday. Old Ned, who was sitting smoking in the glasshouse, busied himself suddenly.

There had been no news, Biddy said. Everything had gone fine. There was a letter from Master Harry and Master James, and some other parcel that didn't have enough stamps on it and Mattie wanted money paid.

There had been cross words with the butcher because they had delivered the Sunday joint of beef as usual and been annoyed when told that the family were on holidays. Sergeant Keane had been up to know if there was any word of one of the tinkers who had gone missing.

Biddy had given them all short shrift.

She had told Mattie that enough money had been spent on stamps to and from this house for him to feel embarrassed even mentioning the question of underpayment. He had slunk away, as well he might. The butcher had felt the lash of Biddy's tongue as she told them that the new frontage on the shop had been paid for with money that Major Murphy and his family had spent on the best of meat, they should be ashamed to grumble.

She asked Sergeant Keane what he could have been thinking of to imagine that a tinker boy could even have crossed the lawns of The Glen.

At first Leo didn't want to meet anyone. She wanted to stay half sitting, half kneeling on her windowseat, looking out to where the dogs played, and old Ned made feeble attempts at hoeing, to where her father walked with his halting movements out to meet Mr Hayes, and where Mother drifted, her straw hat in her hand, through the shrubbery and past the lilacs.

No man came from the Botanic Gardens in Glasnevin to deal with the rockery that they had planned on top of the great pit that had been filled in.

When Mr O'Neill, the auctioneer from the big town, came to enquire whether they would be interested in letting the gate lodge, Leo's father and mother said not just now, some time certainly, but at the moment everything was quite undecided – perhaps one of the boys might come home and live in it.

There had never been any question of Harry or James coming back. Leo realised it was one more of these easy lies her mother told, like when she had told the people at the hotel that Leo had been unwell and that was why she hadn't been able to eat her meals.

One day Maura Brennan from school came and asked for a job as a maid in the house. She said she had to work somewhere and why not for someone like Leo, whom she liked. Leo had been awkward and frightened that day. It seemed another example of the world going mad: Maura, who had sat beside her at school, wanting to come and scrub floors in their house because that was the way things were.

But as the days turned into weeks Leo got the courage to leave The Glen. She called on Eddie Barton and his mother. They spoke to her as if things were normal. She began to believe they were. There was an ill-written postcard from London saying 'Wish you were here'. She knew it was from

Foxy, though it didn't say. And one Saturday at Confession Father Gunn had asked her was there anything troubling her.

Leo's heart leapt into her throat.

'Why do you ask that, Father?' she said in a whisper.

'You seem nervous, my child. If there's anything you want to say to me, remember you're saying it to God through me.'

'I know, Father.'

'So, if there is any worry . . .'

'I am worried about something, but it's not my worry, it's someone else's worry.'

'Is it your sin, my child?'

'No, Father. No. Not at all. It's just that I can't understand it. You see, it has to do with grown-ups.'

There was a silence.

Father Gunn was digesting this. He assumed that it was to do with a child's perception of adult sexuality and all the loathing and embarrassment that this could bring.

'Perhaps all these things will become clear later,' he said soothingly.

'So, I shouldn't worry, do you think, Father?'

'Not if it's something you have no control over, my child, something where it would not be appropriate for you to be involved,' said the priest.

Leo felt much better. She said her three Hail Marys, penance for her other small sins, and put the biggest thing as far to the back of her mind as possible. After all, the priest said that God would make it clear later; now was not the appropriate time to worry about it.

As she prepared for her years in the convent school in the town she tried to make life in The Glen seem normal. She had joined their game. She was pretending that nothing had ever happened on that summer evening when the world stopped.

Leo started to go down the hill to meet the people she had been at school with once more – her friend Nessa Ryan in the hotel, whose mother always found work for idle hands – Sheila and Eileen Blake, who were home from a posh boarding school and kept asking could they come and play tennis at The Glen. Leo told them the court needed a lot of work. She realised she was lying as smoothly as her mother these days. She met Niall Hayes, who told her that he thought he was in love.

'Everyone's doing everything too young,' Leo said reprovingly. 'Foxy's too young to be going to England to work, you're too young to be in love. Who is it anyway?'

He didn't say. Leo thought it might be Nessa. But no, surely not? He lived across the road from Nessa, he had known her all his life. That couldn't be what falling in love was like. It was too confusing.

She met Nancy Finn from the pub. Nancy was what they called a bold strap in Shancarrig. She was fifteen and had been accused of being forward and giving people the eye. Sometimes she helped serve behind the counter. It was a rough sort of place.

Nancy said she'd really love to go to America and work as a cocktail waitress. That was her goal but her father said it was lunacy. Nancy said her father, Johnny Finn Noted for Best Drinks, was fed up. The guards had been in every night for three weeks asking was there any brawl between tinkers and anyone, and her father said he wouldn't let a bloody tinker in the door. Sergeant Keane said that was a very unchristian attitude, and Nancy's father had said the guards would have another tune to play if he *did* let the tinkers in and took their money, so there had been hard words and the upshot was that the guards were watching Johnny Finn's pub night after night, ready to pounce if anyone was left with a drink in front of them for thirty seconds beyond the licensing hours.

The summer ended and a new life began, a life of getting the bus every day into school in the big town. The bus bounced along the roads through villages and woods, and stopped at junctions and crossroads where people came down long narrow tracks to the main road. Leo and Nessa Ryan learned their homework to the rhythm of the bus crossing the countryside. They heard each other's poems, they puzzled out theorems and algebra. Often they didn't even look out the window at the countryside passing by.

Sometimes Leo seemed as if she was looking out at the scenery. Anyone watching her would think that there was a dreamy schoolgirl looking out at the fields with the cattle grazing, the colours changing from season to season in the hedges and clusters of bushes that they passed.

But Leo Murphy's eyes might not have been focusing on these things at all. Her thoughts were often on her mother. Her pale delicate mother, who wandered more often through the gardens of The Glen no matter what the weather, with empty eyes, talking softly to herself.

Leo had seen her mother sit under the lilac tree picking the great purple flowers apart absently in her lap and crooning to herself, 'You had lilac eyes, Danny. Your eyes were like deep lilac. Your eyes are closed now.'

She spoke of Danny too when she half sat and half lay over the rockery. Every day, rain or shine, she tended it, and a weed could hardly put its head out before Mrs Murphy had snapped it away.

'At least I kept your grave for you, Danny boy,' she would cry. 'You can never say I didn't put flowers on your grave. No man in Ireland got more flowers.'

The first time Leo heard her mother speak like this she was frozen with horror. It was a known fact that the missing tinker was Danny. His family had told people that he must have a girl in Shancarrig. He used to be gone from the camp for long periods, and when he'd come back he was always smiling and saying nothing. There was the question he might have run off with someone from the locality. Sergeant Keane had assured the travellers that there were no unexplained disappearances of any of the girls of the village; he had made enquiries and there was no one missing from the area.

'No one except Danny,' said Mrs McDonagh, the sad-looking woman with the dark, lined face who was Danny's mother.

Leo heard all this from other people. Nessa Ryan heard it discussed a lot in the hotel, and reported it word for word. It was the only exciting thing that had happened in their lives. She couldn't understand why her friend Leo wasn't interested in it, and wouldn't speculate like everyone else about what might have happened.

The months went by and Leo's mother became less in touch with reality.

Leo had stopped trying to talk to her about school, and everyday things. Instead she spoke as if her mother was an invalid.

'How do you feel today, Mother?'

'Well . . . I don't know, I really don't know.' She spoke in a dull voice. The woman who used to be so elegant and graceful, the mother who would plan a picnic, correct bad grammar or a mispronounced word with cries of horror . . . that had all gone.

She barely touched her food, just smiled vaguely at Father, and Leo, and at Biddy as if they were people she used to know. She spoke to the dogs, Lance and Jessie, no longer the big gambolling pups, but more stately with years. She reminded them of how they had known Danny, and they would stand guard over his grave.

Biddy *must* have heard it. She would have had to be deaf not to have known what she was talking about.

But the conspiracy continued.

Mrs Murphy had been feeling under the weather, surely now the longer days, or the bright weather, or the good crisp winter without any damp . . . whichever season . . . she would show an improvement.

Old Ned had been pensioned off. Eddie Barton came and cut the grass sometimes, but there was nobody coming to do the gardens as they should have been done. Sometimes Leo and her father would struggle, but it was beyond them. Only the rockery bloomed. Mrs Murphy wandered outside The Glen with her secateurs in her pocket and took cuttings for it, or even dug up little plants that she thought might flourish.

In the increasingly jungle-like gardens of The Glen the rockery bloomed as a monument, as a memorial.

In her efforts to keep her mother out of anyone else's sight and hearing, Leo pieced together the story of horror, of what had happened in those weeks when she was fourteen and had understood nothing of the world. Those weeks before her world changed.

Mother remembered not only Danny's lilac eyes but his strong arms, and his young body. She remembered his laughter and his impatience and greed to have her, over and over. With a sick stomach Leo listened to her mother remembering and crying for a lost love. She hated the childlike coquettish enthusiasm in her mother's face when she spoke of the man she had welcomed on the mossy earth, in her bedroom on the rug, under the lilac trees, and in the gate lodge.

But it was when she mentioned the gate lodge that her face would harden and her questioning take a different turn. Why did he have to be so greedy?

What did he need with silver? Why had he demanded to take their treasures? What did he mean that he needed something to trade, some goods to deal in as they went towards Galway? Had he not taken her, was that not the greatest treasure of all? Miriam Murphy's eyes were like stone when she went through that part of the story of the last time they had met . . . of the silver he had wrapped in a tablecloth as he had roamed through the house, touching things, taking this, leaving that. She had begged him and pleaded.

'Say there was a robbery . . . say you came back and found it all gone.' His lilac eyes had laughed at her.

'I told him he must not go, he had been sent to me, and he could not leave.'

Leo knew the chant off by heart, she could say it with her mother as the woman stroked the earth of the rockery.

'You wouldn't listen, Danny. You called me old. You said you had given me my fun and my loving and that I should be grateful.

'You said you'd take some guns, that we had no need of them, but in your life you'd need to hunt in the forest . . . I asked you to take me with you . . . and you laughed, and you called me old. I couldn't let you leave, I had to keep you here, and that was why . . .' Her mother would smile then, and stroke the earth again. 'And you are here, Danny Boy. You'll never leave me now.'

Leo had known for years why her father had struggled that night, dragging and pulling with his wounds aching and his useless leg trailing behind. He knew why this woman had to be protected from telling this sing-song tale to the law. And Leo knew too.

At school they thought her a tense child. They spoke to her father about her since Mrs Murphy, the mother, never made any appearance.

Mother Dorothy, who was wise in the ways of the world, decided that the mother might have a drink problem. It had to be. Otherwise she'd have come in some time. Very tough on the child, a nice girl, but with a shell on her as hard as rock.

Leo told Father Gunn that Mother wasn't all that well, and that if they didn't see her at mass he wasn't to take any wrong meaning out of it.

Father Gunn asked would she like the sacraments brought up to The Glen.

'I'm not too sure, Father.' Leo bit her lip.

Father Gunn also knew the ways of the world.

'Why don't we leave it for the moment?' he suggested. 'And if there's any change in that department then all you have to do is ask me.'

Leo thought to herself that in Shancarrig it was really quite easy to hide anything from anybody.

Or maybe it was only if you happened to live in The Glen, a big house surrounded by high walls, with its own gardens and shrubberies and gate lodge.

It might be different trying to keep your secrets if you lived in the cottages down by the river, or in The Terrace with everyone seeing your front entrance, or in the hotel with half of Shancarrig in and out of your doors every day.

She felt watchful about her mother, but not always on edge. No long-term anxiety like that can be felt at the pain level all the time. There were many hours when Leo didn't even think about her mother's telling and re-telling the story. There were the school outings, there were the parties, the times when Niall Hayes kissed her and their noses kept bumping, and later when quite suddenly Richard Hayes, who was Niall's older cousin, kissed her and there was no nose-bumping at all.

Richard Hayes was very handsome, he had stirred the place up since he arrived. Leo felt sorry for Niall because deep in her heart she thought Niall still had a very soft spot for Nessa, and Nessa was of course crazy about the new arrival in town.

And it had to be said that Richard was paying a lot of attention to Nessa. There were walks, drives and trips to the pictures in the town. Leo thought he was rather dangerous, but then she shrugged. Who was she to know? Her views on love and attraction were extremely suspect.

Some of the girls at school were going to be nurses; they had applied to hospitals in Dublin and in Britain for places.

'Should I be a nurse, Daddy?' she asked.

They were walking, as they often did in the evening. Mother was safely talking to the rockery, and if you counted Biddy as the silent rock she had been for three long years, then there was no one around to hear the chant that had begun again.

'Would you *like* to be a nurse?'

'Only if it would help.'

Her father looked old and grey. Much of his time was spent persuading his sons not to come back to Shancarrig, and telling them that their mother was in poor mental health.

Naturally they had written and asked why was nothing being done about this. They had written to Dr Jims, which Major Murphy thought an outrageous interference. But fortunately Jims Blake had agreed with him that arrogant young men thought they knew everything. If Frank Murphy said there was nothing wrong with Miriam, then that was that. The doctor had seen the thin pale face and the over-brilliant eyes of Miriam Murphy, always a fairly obsessional person he would have thought, checking light switches, refusing to throw out old papers. This is what he had noticed on his visits to The Glen, and assumed that like many a nervy woman there was nothing asked and therefore nothing that could be answered. This was not a household where he would be asked to refer her to a psychiatrist in order to work out the cause of the unease. At least he wasn't being asked for ever-increasing prescriptions of tranquillisers or sleeping pills. This in itself was something to be thankful for.

Foxy Dunne came home every Christmas as he had promised. When he arrived on his first visit home, wearing a new zippered jacket with a tartan lining, at the back door of The Glen, he was surprised at the frostiness of his reception. Not that he had ever been warmly welcomed there, but this was out of that league ... 'Well, tell my friend Leo. She knows where I live,' he said haughtily to Biddy.

'And I'm sure, like everyone, she knows only too well where the Dunnes live and would want to avoid it,' Biddy said.

Leo had heard. She called to the Dunnes' cottage that afternoon.

'I came to ask if you'd like to go for a walk in Barna Woods,' she said.

Foxy looked very pleased. He was at a loss for words. The quick shrugging reaction or the smart joke deserted him.

'Well, I won't ask you into my house either,' he said. 'Let's go and be babes in the wood.'

He told her of living in a house with eleven men from their own country. He told her of the drinking and how so many of them spent everything they had nearly killed themselves earning.

'Why do you stay there?' she asked.

'To learn ... to save. But mainly to learn.'

'What can you learn from old men like that drinking their lives away?'

'I can learn what not to do, I suppose, or how it could have been done right.'

Foxy sat on a fallen tree and told her about the chances, the men who had made it, the small contractors who did things right and did them quickly. He told her how you had to watch out for the fellow who was a great electrician, a good plumber, a couple of bright brickies, a class carpenter. Then all you needed was someone to get them together and you had your own team – someone who had a head for figures, someone who could cost a job and make the contacts.

'And who would you get to do that?' She was genuinely interested.

'God, Leo, that's what *I'm* going to do. That's what it's all about,' he said.

She felt ashamed that she hadn't the confidence in him.

'Did you know my father was in gaol?' he asked defensively.

'I heard. I think Biddy told me.'

'She would have.'

She was torn between being sympathetic and telling him it didn't matter.

'Did he hate it?' she asked.

'I don't know, he doesn't talk to me. He should have been there longer. He hit a fellow with a plank that had nails in it. He's dangerous.'

'You're not like that,' she said suddenly.

'I know, but I didn't want you to forget where I come from.'

'You are what you are, so am I.'

'And do you have any tales to tell me?' he asked.

'No. Why?' Her voice was clipped.

He shrugged. It was as if he had been offering her the chance to trade confessions.

But he didn't know they were not equal confessions. What his father had done was known the length and breadth of the county. What her mother had done was known by only three people.

He looked at her for a while, as if waiting.

Then he said, 'No reason, no reason at all.'

She saw him looking at her, with her belted raincoat, hands stuck deep in her pockets. The wind made her cheeks red. Her red-gold curls stood out around her head like a furze. She felt he was looking straight through her, that he could see everything, knew everything.

'I hate my hair,' she said suddenly.

'It's like a halo,' he said.

And she grinned.

Every Christmas he came home. He called to The Glen and she would take him walking. For the week that he was home they would meet every day.

Nessa Ryan was very disapproving. 'You *do* know his father was in gaol,' she told Leo.

'I do,' Leo sighed. She had heard it all from Biddy, over and over.

'I'd be surprised you'd go walking with him, then.'

'I know you would.' Leo had heard the same thing from her father. But that particular time she had answered back. 'Well, if everyone knew about us, Daddy, maybe people wouldn't want to go walking with us either.' Her father looked as if she had struck him. Immediately she had repented. 'I'm so sorry, I didn't mean it . . . I just think that Foxy is lonely when he comes home. I don't ask him in here. I'm seventeen, nearly eighteen, Daddy. Why can't we let people alone? We, of all people?'

Her father had tears in his eyes. 'Go and walk with whoever you like in the woods,' he had said, his voice choked.

That was the Christmas when Foxy told her that he was on the way to the big time. He was working with two others. They were setting up their own contracts, they would hire men, get a team together. No more working for cheats and fellows who took all the profit.

'I'll soon have enough saved to come back a rich man,' he said. 'Then I'll drive up your avenue in a big car, hand my coat and gloves to Biddy, and ask your father for your hand in marriage. Your mother will take out the sherry and plan your wedding dress.'

'I'll never marry,' Leo told him.

'You sure as anything didn't take my advice about getting trained for a career or a job,' he said.

'I can't leave The Glen.'

'Will you tell me why?' His eyes still had that power to look as if they could see right through her, and know everything.

'I will, one day,' she promised, and she knew she would.

This year at least she had an address for Foxy. She wrote to him, he sent a very short note back.

'Why don't you learn to type, Leo? Your writing is worse than my own. We can't have that when we're in the big time, neither of us able to write a letter.'

She laughed.

She didn't tell Nessa Ryan that she had just got a sort of proposal from Foxy Dunne.

She didn't tell her parents.

Her mother died on an autumn night. They said it was of exposure. Her lungs filled up with the damp night air and, added to a chest infection ... There was no hope for a woman whose health had always been so frail.

She had been found in her nightdress, lying over the rockery in the garden.

The church was crowded. Major Murphy asked people to come back to Ryan's Hotel for a drink and some sandwiches afterwards. This was very unusual and had never been known in Shancarrig. But he said that The Glen was too sad for him and for Leo just now. He was sure people would understand.

Then Leo went to the town every day on the bus and learned to type in the big secretarial college where Nessa had done a course.

'Why couldn't you have done it with me?' Nessa grumbled.

'It wasn't the right time.'

There had been no note from Foxy Dunne about her mother's death.

She didn't write to tell him. Surely some member of his awful family was in touch, surely there would have been a mention that Mrs Murphy of The Glen had been found dead in her nightdress, and that her wits must have been astray. Everyone else knew about it.

When he came back at Christmas it was clear that he hadn't known. He was sympathetic and sad.

She asked him in, not to the breakfast room but the drawing room. Together they lit the fire.

The old dogs lay down, pleased that the room was being opened up.

Biddy was beyond complaining now. Too much had happened in this house. That Foxy Dunne be invited into the Major's drawing room seemed minor these days.

He told Leo of his plans. He had seen so much in England of how places could be developed. Take The Glen. They could sell off most of the land, build maybe eight houses, and still keep their own home.

'I expect your father would like that,' he said.

Outside they could see the sad lonely figure of Major Murphy walking up and down to the gate and back in the darkening evening.

'We can never sell the land,' Leo said.

'Is this part of what you told me you'd tell me one day?'

'Yes.'

'Are you ready to tell me now?'

'No. Not yet, Foxy.'

'Does your mother's death not make it different?' Again that feeling that he knew everything.

'No. You see, Daddy still lives here. Nothing could be ... interfered with.'

She thought of the big diggers, the excavators, the rockery going, as it would one day, when The Glen would disappear like so much of Ireland, and make way for houses for the Irish who were coming back to live in their own land, having worked hard in other countries.

People like Foxy coming back to their inheritances.

The body of Danny McDonagh which had lain so long under its mausoleum of flowers would be disturbed. The questions would be asked.

'We're over twenty-one. We can do what we like,' he said.

'I could always do what I liked, for all the good it did me.'

'So could I,' he answered her with spirit. 'And it did me a lot of good. I never wanted anyone else but you, not since we were children. What did you want?'

'I wanted to be safe,' she said.

He promised her that was exactly what he would do for her. They talked a little that night, and more the next day in Barna Woods. He left her at the gate of The Glen, and saw her look away from the gate lodge.

'Something happened here,' he said.

'I always knew you had second sight.'

'Tell me, Leo. We're not people to have secrets from each other.'

Through the window of The Glen they could see her father sitting at the drawing-room fire. He must have got the idea of sitting in that room after seeing them there yesterday. She told Foxy the story.

'Let's get the key,' he said.

She went through the kitchen and took it from the rack in the hall. Together, with candles, they walked through the gate lodge, a blameless place that didn't know what had happened there.

He raised her face towards him and looked into her eyes.

'Your hair is like a halo again. You're doing it to drive me mad,' he said.

'Don't you see all the problems, all the terrible problems?'

'I see nothing that won't be solved by a load of concrete on where that rockery stands now,' Foxy Dunne said.

A Stone House
and a Big Tree

The decision to close the school was known in 1969; National Schools all over Ireland were giving way to Community Schools in the towns. But still it was a shock to see the building advertised for sale in the summer of 1970.

FOR SALE
Traditional stone schoolhouse. Built 1899. School accommodation comprises three large classrooms, toilet facilities and outer hall. Accompanying cottage: two bedrooms, one living room/kitchen with
stanley range.
For sale by Public Auction June 24th if not disposed of by Private Treaty.
Auctioneers: O'Neill and Blake.

Nessa and Niall Hayes read it over breakfast.

From their dining room they could look over at Ryan's Shancarrig Hotel and see the early tour buses leaving on their excursions. Nessa worked flexible hours across the road in her family business. Neither of her sisters had shown any interest in hotel work.

'They will when they see there's money in it,' her mother had said darkly.

'Imagine the school for sale. We'd never have thought that possible.' Niall was thirty now. Nobody ever referred to him as young Mr Hayes any more, in fact his father took the back seat in almost every aspect of the business nowadays.

'What's not possible?' Danny Hayes was four, and very inquisitive. He loved long words and would pronounce them carefully.

'That you're not going to go to the same school we went to.' Nessa wiped his chin expertly of the runny bits of egg. 'You'll go on a big yellow bus to school. You won't walk over the bridge like we did.'

'Can I go today?' Danny asked.

'After Christmas,' Nessa promised.

'Won't he be a bit young?' Niall looked worried.

'If *your* mother had had her way you wouldn't have been allowed up the road to Shancarrig school until you were twenty.' There was a laugh in Nessa's voice, but also a tinge of bitterness.

It had not been quite as simple moving into The Terrace as she had thought it would be. Although her father-in-law had handed over the reins quite willingly to his son, Ethel Hayes had been less anxious to let go the gloomy rein over the family.

There were dire warnings of pneumonia, rheumatic fever, spoiled children, temper tantrums, all directed at Nessa. Danny and Brenda would suffer for it all later, was Mrs Hayes's prediction – the children were allowed too much freedom, too little discipline, and a severe absence of cod liver oil.

'Would we buy it?' Nessa asked suddenly.

'What on earth for?' Niall was genuinely surprised.

'To live in. It would be a great place for the children to play . . . the tree and everything. It would be lovely.'

'I don't know.' Niall bit his lip. It was his usual reaction to a new idea, to something totally unexpected.

Nessa knew him well enough.

'Well, let's not think about it now. It's a month to the auction,' she said.

Deftly she forced Danny to finish his egg and toast by cutting it into tiny cubes and eating one alternately with him. She settled Brenda into her carrycot. Niall was still sitting at his place pondering the bombshell.

'It's only an idea,' Nessa said airily. 'But if you're talking to Declan Blake at all, ask him how much he thinks they'll get for it.'

Niall looked out of the window, and saw Nessa moving into her parents' hotel. The carrycot was taken from her at the door by the porter. Danny had run to the hotel back yard where Nessa and her mother had built a sandpit, and swings and a see-saw to entertain the children who came to stay.

It had been yet one more excellent marketing notion for Ryan's Shancarrig Hotel.

Jim and Nora Kelly read it in Galway. They were staying with Maria and Hugh. They had wanted to be away when it was announced and by wonderful chance it coincided with the very time they were badly needed. Maria's first baby was due. She wanted her parents to be with her.

'It's the end of an era,' Maria said. 'There must be people all over Ireland saying that.'

'Not only Ireland – didn't our people go all over the world?' Jim Kelly said.

He was fifty years of age, and had been re-employed in the school in the town. It wasn't the same of course, nothing would ever be the same. But he knew a great number of the children, and he came trailing clouds of respect. A man who had run his own show, even in a small village, was a man to be reckoned with.

Nora had taken early retirement. And taken many a train to visit Maria over on the Atlantic coast. They walked along the beach together, the pregnant girl and the woman who was as good as her mother, with so much to say. Jim was pleased that his wife had taken the closing of the school so well. It might have been too much of a change for her to have gone to teach in the town.

Maria patted her stomach. 'It'll be so strange that she won't know the place as a school,' she said wonderingly.

'Or he. Remember, you could have a boy.' Jim Kelly knew that none of them minded whether it was a boy or girl.

They were so happy that Maria had found the steady Hugh after a series of wilder boyfriends had broken their hearts. Hugh seemed to know how much Maria needed her background in Shancarrig; he was always finding excuses to bring her there.

'Still, when the baby's born I'll wheel her . . . or him, up to the school and say that this is where Grandpa or Grandma used to live, where every child lived for a while.' Maria looked sad. 'Oh, come on. I'm being stupidly sentimental,' she said with a little shake. 'And anyway, aren't you better off by far living in that fine house near everything, instead of having to toil up and down the hill?'

The Kellys had settled in one of the cottages that had been vastly changed and upgraded. The row of houses by the Grane that had once held the most unruly Brennans and Dunnes were now what young Declan Blake called Highly Des Res material.

'I wish there were going to be children there,' Nora Kelly said. 'I suppose it's unlikely that anyone who has children could afford to buy it, but somehow the place cries out for them. Or am I the one being sentimental now?'

'There'd be nobody local who could think of it.' Jim was ticking off people in his mind.

'Maybe when Hugh makes a fortune we'll buy it ourselves . . . and let little Nora play under the copper beech like I did.'

There was a lump in their throats. It hadn't been said that Maria was going to call her child after Nora Kelly.

'I thought maybe Helen after your mother.' Nora felt she should say it anyway.

'The second one will be Helen!' said Maria.

And the matter was left there.

Chris Barton read the notice out to her mother-in-law. She always called Eddie's mother Una. It was yet another bond between them, the fact that she thought of the older woman as her sister.

'Well, Una. Is this our big chance?' Chris asked. 'Is this the famous opportunity that is meant to present itself to people? A ready-made craft centre . . . get Foxy to build a few more outhouses that we could rent out as studios . . . is this it or is it madness?'

'You're the one with the courage. I'd still be turning up hems for people and letting out their winter skirts if you hadn't come along.' Mrs Barton declared that she said an extra decade of the rosary every single night of her life to thank the Lord and His Mother for sending Chris to Shancarrig.

'I don't know, I really don't know. I'll ask Eddie. He has a great instinct for these things. We might be running before we can walk, or we might regret it all our lives. I trust his nose for this sort of thing.'

It was true. Mrs Barton realised that her daughter-in-law really did defer to Eddie's instincts and tastes. It wasn't a case of pretending to take his advice like Mrs Ryan in the hotel did, and indeed her daughter young Nessa who was busy pushing Niall Hayes into some kind of confidence. Chris genuinely thought Eddie the brains of the outfit. It made Una Barton's heart soar.

She thought less and less about the husband who had left her all those years ago – a quarter of a century – but sometimes she wished that Ted Barton could know how well his son had done and how splendidly they had managed without him.

Eddie came in holding the twins by the hand. He laughed as he saw his wife and mother automatically reach to protect everything on the table that was in danger of being pulled to the floor.

'Can we leave them with you, Una? I want to talk to Eddie in Barna Woods.'

'The last time you did that you proposed to me. I hope this doesn't mean you're going to leave.' He laughed confidently. He didn't think it was likely.

The children were strapped into their high chairs, and fussed over by their grandmother. Chris and Eddie walked as they so often walked together, shoulders touching, talking so that they finished each other's sentences, at ease with each other and the world. There was nobody in Shancarrig who noticed that Chris had a Scottish accent now, any more than they saw that she had a lame leg and a built-up shoe. She had been there since she was eighteen or nineteen. Part of the scenery.

They sat in the wood and she asked him about the centre. Was it exactly the right time? Or was this folly? Her eyes looked at him for an answer and she saw his face light up. He would never have thought of it, he said . . . to him it would always have been the school, the place that he had gone, rain or shine, where he had played and studied. Of course it was the answer.

'Would we live there, or just work there?' Chris wondered.

'It would be great for the children.'

'We could sell the pink house.' Chris had always called it that, since the moment she had arrived.

'But my mother?'

'She said she'd leave it to us.'

'Where would she go? She's so used to being beside us . . .' Mrs Barton lived in her own little wing of the pink house, beside them but not on top of them.

'She'd come with us, you big nellie. We'd be building a whole lot of places and she could choose the kind of place she'd like. It's no bigger a hill for her to climb than the one that she's been on all her life.'

Eddie's eyes were dancing. 'We could invite people in . . . like the pottery couple, or the weavers . . .'

'We could have a small shop there, selling everyone's work. Not only ours, but everyone's.'

'Nessa would get them up here from the hotel for a start, and Leo's got all sorts of contacts all over the place.'

'Will we do it?'

They embraced, as they had embraced in these woods years ago at the thought of being married and living happily ever after.

Richard saw the advertisement.

He wondered would whoever bought it cut down the tree in the yard. What would they make of the things that were written on it? He was prepared to bet that his wasn't the only carving that told a story.

He thought about the school all day in the office.

It was a tiring journey home, a lot of traffic. He was hot and tired. He hoped that Vera hadn't arranged anything for tonight. What he really would like to do was . . . he paused. He didn't know what he would really like to do. It had been so long since he had allowed himself a thought like that.

He knew what he would really *not* like to do, and that would be to go to the club. Vera might have set up a little evening, a few drinks at the bar, dinner. He would know when he got in. If she had been to the hairdresser this is what she had planned.

He nosed the car into the garage beside Vera's.

Jimmy the gardener was edging the lawn. 'Good evening, Mr Hayes,' he said, touching his forehead.

'That looks great, Jimmy. Great work.' Richard knew his voice was automatic; he didn't see what the man had done or what needed to be done. He thought that a full-time gardener was a bit excessive in a Dublin garden.

Still, it was Vera's decision. It was after all she who had bought the house, and filled it with valuable things. It was Vera who made the day-to-day decisions about how they spent the money which was mainly her money.

She was sitting in the conservatory. He noticed sadly that she had been to the hairdresser.

'You look lovely,' he said.

'Thank you, darling. I thought we might meet some of the others at the club . . . you know, rather than just sitting looking at each other all night?' She smiled.

She was very attractive in her lemon-coloured dress, her blonde upswept hair and her even suntan.

She did not look in her late thirties any more than he did. But unlike him she never seemed to find their life empty. She filled it with acquaintances, parties given, parties attended, a group of what she called like-minded people at the golf club.

Vera had taken their childlessness with what Richard considered a disturbing lack of concern. If the question was ever raised between themselves or when other people were present she always said the same thing. She said that if it happened it did, and if it didn't it didn't. No point in having all those exhaustive tests to discover whose *fault* it was, as if someone was to blame.

Since Richard knew from the past, only too well from his drama with Olive, that there could be nothing lacking on his side, he wished that Vera would go for an examination. But she refused.

She had the newspaper open in front of her.

'Look! There's a simply lovely place for sale, in that Shancarrig where you spent all those years.'

'I know. I saw it.'

'Should we buy it, do you think? It has tons of potential. It would make a nice weekend place, we could have people to stay. You know, it might be fun.'

'No.'

'What do you mean, *no*?'

'I mean NO, Vera,' he said.

Her face flushed. 'Well, I don't know what you're turning on *me* for, I only thought *you'd* like it. I do everything that I think you'd like. It's becoming impossible to please you.'

He moved over to reach for her but she stood up and pulled away.

'Seriously, Richard. Nobody could please you. There isn't a woman on earth that could hold you. Maybe you should never have married, just been a desirable bachelor all your life.' She was very hurt, he could see.

'Please. Please forgive me, I've had a horrible day. I'm tired, that's all. Please, I'm a pig.'

She was softening. 'Have a bath and a drink and we'll go out. You'll feel much better then.'

'Yes. Yes, of course. I'm sorry for snapping.' His voice was dead, he could hear it in his own ears.

'And you really don't think we should pick up this little house as a weekend place?'

'No, Vera. No, I wasn't happy there. It wouldn't make me happy to go back.'

'Right. It will never be mentioned again,' she said.

And he knew that she would look for somewhere else, a place where they could invite people for the weekend – fill their life with even more half strangers. Maybe she might even pick on whatever town Gloria had settled in. He knew the Darcys had left Shancarrig not long after he had.

Leo sat in the kitchen of The Glen making a very unsuccessful effort to comb Moore's hair. He had inherited the frizz from his mother and the colour from his father. He was six years old and in the last pageant that Shancarrig school had put on he had been asked to play The Burning Bush. This was apparently his own choice.

Foxy was delighted. Leo was less sure.

Moore Dunne was turning out to be a bigger handful than anyone could have believed. Foxy had insisted on the name. While he worked in England he said that he had discovered it was very classy to use one family name added to another. Leo's mother had been Miriam Moore, this had been the Moore household.

Moore's younger sister, Frances, was altogether more tractable. 'We'll liven her up yet,' Foxy had said ominously.

Unlike many of the builders who had returned from England in the prosperous sixties with their savings and their ideas of a quick killing, Foxy

Dunne had decided to go the route of befriending rather than alienating architects.

The eight small houses he had built within the grounds of The Glen had a style and a character that was noticeably missing in such similar small developments in other towns. A huge row of semi-mature trees had been planted to give the new houses privacy, but also to maintain the long sweep of The Glen's avenue.

Major Murphy had lived to see his grandchildren but was buried now in the graveyard beside his wife.

From the big drawing room of The Glen Leo ran the ever-increasing building empire that Foxy had set up. All his cousins in the town now worked for him, the cousins who had once barred his father from crossing the doors of their shops. His cousins Brian and Liam waited on his every word and his uncle treated him with huge respect.

Foxy's father was not around to see the fruits of having totally ignored his son. Old Dinny had died in the county home some years previously. Foxy's own brothers, never men to have held down jobs for any notable length of time, most of them with some kind of prison record, were now regarded as remittance men. Small allowances were paid as long as they stayed far away from Shancarrig.

The main alterations that had put Ryan's Shancarrig Hotel on the map for tourism had been done by Foxy Dunne. It was he who had transformed the cottages by the River Grane, his only concession to any sentimentality or revenge having been his own personal presence as they levelled to the ground the house he grew up in.

The church hall, which was the pride of Father Gunn's life, was built by Foxy at such a reduced rate that it might even have been called his gift to the parish.

Foxy kept proper accounts. The books that Leo kept were regularly audited. The leases to the property he bought and sold were handled by his friend Niall Hayes. Maura came up from the gate lodge every day to do some of the housework and to mind the children. As always, her son Michael came with her. Michael was growing up big and strong but with the mind and loving heart of a small child.

Moore Dunne was particularly fond of him. 'He's much more interesting than other big people,' Moore pronounced.

Leo made sure she told that to Maura.

'I've always thought that myself,' Maura agreed.

Leo and Maura had a cup of tea together every morning before both went to their work – Leo to cope with Foxy's deals and Maura to polish and shine The Glen. Together they looked at the advertisement offering their old school for sale.

'Who would buy it, unless to set up another school?' Maura wondered.

'I'm very much afraid Foxy wants to,' said Leo. He hadn't said it yet, but she knew it was on his mind. It was as if he could never burn out the memory of the way things used to be. Not until he owned the whole town.

They heard the sound of his car outside the door. 'How's Squire Dunne?' he said to his son.

'I'm all *right*,' said Moore doubtfully.

'Only all *right*. You should be tip top,' Foxy said.

'Well yes, but I think there's another cat growing inside Flossie.' Moore was delighted.

'That's great,' said Foxy. 'It'll be a kitten, or maybe five kittens even.'

'But how are they going to get out?' Moore was puzzled. Maura giggled.

'That's your mother's department,' said Foxy, heading for the office. 'I have to think of other things like planning permissions, son.'

'For the school?' Leo asked.

'Aha, you're there before me,' he said.

She looked at him, small and quick, eager as ever, nowadays dressed in clothes that were made to measure, but still the endearing Foxy of their childhood. She followed him into the room that was once their drawing room, where her father had paced, and her mother had sat distracted, and Lance and Jessie had slept uncaring by the fire.

'Do we need it, Foxy?' she asked.

'What's need?' He put his arms around her shoulders and looked into her eyes.

'Haven't we enough?' she said.

'Love, it's a gold mine. It's *made* for us. The right kind of cottages, classy stuff, the kind rich Dubliners might even have as a summer place, or for visiting at the weekends. Do them up really well, let Chris and Eddie loose on them. Slate floors . . . you know the kind of thing.' He looked so eager. He would love the challenge.

Perhaps he was right, it *was* made for them. Why did she keep thinking he was doing everything just to show? To show some anonymous invisible people who didn't care.

Maddy Ross thought it was wonderful that God moved so mysteriously. Look at how he had closed the school just at exactly the right time for Maddy.

Now she could be quite free to spend all her time with the Family. The wonderful Family of Hope. Madeleine Ross had been a member of the Family of Hope for three years. And it had not been easy.

For one thing there had been all that adverse publicity in the papers about the castle they had been given, and the misunderstanding over the deeds.

There had been no intention at all to defraud or deceive, but the way the papers wrote it all up you'd think that the Family of Hope was some kind of international confidence tricksters' organisation.

And there had been the whole attitude of Father Gunn. Maddy had never really liked Father Gunn, not since that time long ago when he had been so patronising and so judgemental about her friendship with Father Barry. If Father Gunn had been more understanding or open and liberal about the place of Love in God's scheme of things then a lot of events would have worked out differently.

Still, that was water under the bridge. The big problem was Father Gunn's attitude today.

He had said that the Family of Hope was not a wonderful way of doing God's work on earth, that it was a dangerous cult, that it was brainwashing people like Maddy, that God wanted love and honour to be shown to him through the conventional channels of the church.

It was just exactly what you would have expected him to say. It was what people had said to Our Lord when he went to the temple to drive out the scribes and the Pharisees. They had said to him that this wasn't the way. They had been wrong, just as Father Gunn was wrong. But it didn't matter. Father Gunn couldn't rule her life for her. It was 1970 now, it wasn't the bad old days when poor Father Barry could be sent away before he knew his mind to a missionary place where they weren't ready for him.

And Father Gunn didn't know about the insurance policy that Mother had left her. The money she had been going to give to the people of Vieja Piedra before they had been abandoned and the work stopped in midstream.

Maddy Ross still walked by herself in Barna Woods and hugged herself thinking of the money she could give to the Family of Hope.

They wanted to buy a place to be their centre.

She had wondered for a long time if there might be anywhere near here. She wanted to live on in Mother's house and near the woods and river that were so dear to her, and held so many memories. And now at last she had found the very place.

The schoolhouse was for sale.

Maura showed the picture of the school to Michael that evening in their little home – the gate lodge of The Glen.

'Do you know where it is, Michael?' she asked.

He held it in both his hands. 'Is my school,' he said.

'That's right, Michael. It's your school,' she said and she stroked his head.

Michael had never attended a lesson inside the school, but he had gone sometimes to play with the children in the yard. Maura had often stood, lump in throat, watching him pick up the beech leaves as she had done before him, and all his uncles and aunts – the Brennans who had gone away.

'We might walk up there tonight, Michael, and have a look at it again. Would you like that?'

'Will we have tea early so?' He looked at her anxiously.

'We'll have tea early so,' she agreed.

He got his own plate and mug, made of Bakelite that wouldn't crack. Michael dropped things sometimes. His mother's china he never touched. Some of it was in a little cabinet that hung on the wall, other pieces were wrapped in tissue paper.

Maura O'Sullivan went to local auctions, always buying bargains in bone china. She never had a full set, or even a half set, but it didn't matter since she didn't ever invite anyone to dine. It was all for her.

They walked past the pink house and waved to the Bartons.

'Can I go in and play with the twins?' Michael said.

'Aren't we going to look at your old school?' They crossed the bridge where the children called out a greeting to Michael, as they had done for many years. And would always do. As long as Maura was there to look after him. Suppose Maura weren't there?

She gave a little shudder.

At the school she saw Dr Jims and his son Declan. The *For Sale* sign was there in the sunset. It would look big in other places; under the copper beech it looked tiny.

'Good evening, Doctor.' She was formal.

'Hello, Declan . . .' Michael embraced the doctor's son, whom he had known since he was a boy in his pram.

'Changing times,' Dr Jims said. 'Lord, I never thought I'd see this day.'

'Don't be denying me my bit of business, Dad . . .' Declan laughed.

They got on so well these days, Maura realised. It must have been that nice girl Ruth that Declan had married. Some people had great luck altogether out of their marriages. But hadn't she got as much love and happiness as anyone had ever got in the whole world?

Michael was looking at the names on the tree. 'Is my name there, Mammy?' he asked.

'If it's not it should be,' Dr Jims said. 'Weren't you here as much as any child in Shancarrig?'

'I'll write it if you like,' Declan offered.

'What will you put?'

'Let's see. I'll put it near my initials. There, see DB 1961? That's me.'

'You've no heart drawn,' Michael complained.

'I didn't love anyone then,' Declan said. His voice seemed full of emotion. The two of them had made a great production of getting out Declan's penknife and choosing a spot.

Dr Jims said to Maura, 'Are you feeling all right? You're a bit pale.'

'You know me, I worry about things. Nothing maybe . . .'

'It's a while since you've been to see me.'

'No, Doctor. Not my health, the future.'

'Ah. There's divil a thing you can do about the future.' Jims Blake smiled at her.

'It's like . . . I wonder sometimes in case something happened to me, what would happen . . . you know,' Maura looked over at Michael.

'Child, you're not thirty years of age!'

'I am that. Last week.'

'Maura, all I can say is that every mother in Ireland worries about her child. It's both a wonder and a waste. Life goes on.'

'For ordinary people, yes.'

Michael gave a cry of pleasure, and came to tug at her.

'Look at what he's written. Look, Mammy.'

Declan Blake had drawn a heart, and on one side he had *MO'S*. On the other he said he was going to put *All his friends in Shancarrig*.

'See what I mean?' said Dr Jims.

*

Maddy Ross invited Sister Judith of the Family of Hope to come and see the schoolhouse. Sister Judith said it was perfect. She asked how much would it cost. Maddy said she had heard in the area of five thousand pounds. With her mother's insurance policy, Maddy explained, there would be that and plenty more. She would get the deeds drawn up with a solicitor. Not with Niall Hayes. After all, she had taught Niall Hayes at school; it wouldn't be appropriate.

Maria's child was born in Galway. It was a girl. She was to be called Nora. Nora Kelly telephoned Una Barton with the good news. The old habits die hard and they still addressed each other formally.

'Mrs Kelly, I'm so *very* pleased. I'll make the baby a little dress with smocking on it,' she said.

'Maria'll bring her back to Shancarrig on a triumphal tour, and you'll be the first port of call, Mrs Barton,' she cried. The Kellys enquired about the school and was there any word about buyers.

Mrs Barton paused. She didn't know whether the children wanted it known or not. Still, she couldn't lie to a woman like Mrs Kelly.

'Between ourselves, Eddie and Chris are trying to get the money together, with grants and everything. They hope to turn it into an arts centre.' There was a silence. 'Aren't you pleased to hear that?'

'Yes, yes. It's just I suppose we were hoping there would be children there.'

'But there will. They're going to live there with the twins, and me as well. That's the hope, Mrs Kelly, but it may come to nothing.'

'That would be great, Mrs Barton. I'll say a prayer to St Anne for you. I'd love to think of your grandchildren and mine playing under that tree.'

The Dixons were just driving through when they saw the schoolhouse. They were enchanted by it, and called in to Niall Hayes to enquire more about it.

They found him singularly unhelpful.

'There's an auctioneer's name and telephone number on the sign,' he said brusquely.

'But seeing that you are the local solicitor we thought you'd know, might shortcut it a bit.' The Dixons were wealthy Dublin people looking for a weekend home; they were used to shortcutting things a bit.

'There could be a conflict of interests,' Niall Hayes said.

'If you want to buy it then why is the board still up?' asked Mr Dixon.

'Good afternoon,' Niall Hayes said.

'Terrifying, these country bumpkins,' said Mrs Dixon, well within his hearing.

'We've never fought about anything, Foxy, have we?' Leo said to him in bed.

'What do you mean? Our life is one long fight!' he said.

'I don't want us to buy the school.'

'Give me one good reason.'

'We don't need it, Foxy. Truly we don't. It'd be a hassle.'

He stroked her face, but she got up and sat on the edge of the bed.

'Things are always a hassle, love. That's the fun. That's what it was always about. *You* know that.'

'No. This time it's different. Lots of others want it too.'

'So? We *get* it.'

'No, not just rivals, real people. Chris and Eddie, Nessa and Niall, Miss Ross, and I think Maura has hopes of it.'

'Miss Ross!' He laughed and rolled around the bed. 'Miss Ross is away with the fairies. It would be a *kindness* not to let her have it.'

'But the others! I'm serious.'

'Look. Niall and Nessa are business people, they know about deals. That's what Niall does all day. Same with Chris and Eddie, they'd understand. Some things you go for, some you get.'

Leo began to pace around the room. She reminded herself of her parents. They had paced in this house too.

She shivered at the thought. He was out of bed, concerned. He put a dressing gown around her shoulders.

'I told you. Give me one good reason, one *real* reason, and I'll stop.'

'Maura.'

'Aw, come on, Leo, give me a break! Maura hasn't a penny. We practically *gave* her the gate lodge. Where would she get the money? What would she want it for?'

'I don't know, but she has Michael up there every evening, the two of them staring at it. She wants it for something.'

'Nessa, come in to me a moment, will you?'

'Why do I always feel like a child, instead of the best help you ever had in this hotel, when you use that tone of voice?' Nessa laughed at her mother.

Breda Ryan poured them a glass of sherry each, always a sign of something significant.

'Has Daddy gone on the tear?'

'No, cynical child.' They sat companionably. Nessa waited. She knew her mother had something to say.

She was right. Her mother said she was going to give her one piece of advice and then withdraw and let Nessa think about it. She had heard that Nessa and Niall were thinking of buying the schoolhouse as a place to live. Now, there was no way she was going to say how she had heard, nor any need for Nessa to bridle and say it was her own business. But all Breda Ryan wanted to put on the table, for what it was worth, was the following:

It would be an act of singular folly to leave The Terrace, to abandon that beautiful house just because old Ethel was a lighting devil and Nessa didn't feel mistress of her own home. The solution was a simple matter of relocation, banishing both parents to the basement.

But not, of course, describing it as that. Describing it in fact as Foxy Dunne and his architect having come up with this amazing idea about making a self-contained flat for the older folk.

Nessa fidgeted as she listened.

'It's only a matter of time,' her mother told her. 'Suppose you went up to the schoolhouse and his parents were dead next year, think how cross you'd be. Losing the high ground like that. Keep the place, don't let them divide it up with his sisters. It's the best house in the town.'

'I wonder are you right.' Nessa spoke thoughtfully, as to an equal.

'I'm right,' said her mother.

Eddie came back from his travels. He had found enough people to make the whole centre work. Exactly the kind of people they had always wanted to work with, some of whom had known their work too. It was flattering how well Chris and Eddie Barton were becoming known in Ireland.

The next thing was to visit the bank manager.

And the projections.

Eddie had asked the potential tenants to write their stories so that he and Chris could work out the costings. He also asked them to tell what had been successful or unsatisfactory in the previous places they had been.

He and Chris together read their reports.

They read of places where no visitors came because it wasn't near enough to the town, places that the tour buses passed by because there was no time on the itinerary. They learned that it was best to be part of a community, not outside it. They sat together and realised that in many ways the schoolhouse was not the dream location they had thought.

'That's if we take notice of them,' Chris said.

'We *have* to take notice of them. That's our research.' Eddie's face was sad.

'Aren't we better to know now than after?' Chris said. 'Though it's awful to see a dream go up like that.'

'What do you mean a dream go up like that? Haven't we our eye on Nellie Dunne's place after her time? That place is like a warren at the back.'

She saw Eddie smile again and that pleased her. 'Come on, let's tell Una.' She leapt up and went to Eddie's mother's quarters.

'I don't mind *where* I am as long as I'm with the pair of you,' said Mrs Barton. She also told them that she heard that both Foxy Dunne *and* Niall Hayes were said to have their eye on the school.

'Then we're better off not alienating good friends who happen to be good customers as well,' said Chris. The two women laughed happily, like conspirators.

Father Gunn twisted and turned in his narrow bed. In his mind he was trying to write the letter to the Bishop, the letter that would get him a ruling about the Family of Hope. It now seemed definite that Madeleine Ross had given these sinister people the money to set up a centre in Shancarrig schoolhouse. They would be here in the midst of his parish, taking away his flock, preaching to them, in long robes, by the river.

Please let the Bishop know what to do.

Why had he made all those moves years ago to prevent a scandal? Wouldn't God and the parish have been far better served if that half-cracked Father Brian Barry and that entirely cracked Maddy Ross had been encouraged to run away with each other? None of this desperate mess about the Family of Bloody Hope would ever have happened.

Terry and Nancy Dixon called in on Vera and Richard Hayes's house on their way back home after their ramble.

'We saw the most perfect schoolhouse. I think we should buy it together,' Terry said. 'It's in that place you worked for a while, Shancarrig.'

'We saw it advertised,' Vera said, glancing at Richard.

'And?' The Dixons looked from one to the other. Richard's eyes were far away.

'Richard said he wasn't happy in Shancarrig.' Vera spoke for him.

'I'm not surprised,' said Nancy Dixon. 'But you wouldn't have to mix all that much. It would be just the perfect place to get away from it all. There's a really marvellous tree.'

'A copper beech,' Richard said.

'Yes, that's right. It should go for a song. We talked to the solicitor but he wasn't very forthcoming.'

'That's my uncle,' Richard said.

The Dixons looked embarrassed. They said it was a younger man, must have been his son. Not someone who was going to set the world on fire? they ventured.

Richard wasn't responding. 'They all wrote their names on that tree,' he said.

'Aha! Perhaps you wrote *your* name on the tree, that's why we can't go back there.' Vera was coquettish.

'No. I never wrote my name there,' Richard said. His eyes were still very far away.

'Is there much interest from Dublin?' Dr Jims asked his son.

'No, I thought there'd be more. Maybe if we advertised it again.'

The two men walked regularly together in Shancarrig. Declan and Ruth were having a house built there now. They didn't want the place in The Terrace. They wanted somewhere with more space, space for rabbits and a donkey, for the children they would have. Ruth was pregnant. They also felt that it was time to have a sub-office of O'Neill and Blake Estate Agents in Shancarrig. Many of the visitors who came to Ryan's Shancarrig Hotel now wanted to buy sites. Foxy Dunne was only too ready to build on them.

'What will it go for?' Dr Jims had the school on his mind a lot.

'We've had an offer of five. You know that.' Declan Blake jerked his head across at Maddy Ross's cottage.

'We don't want them, Declan.'

'I can't play God, Dad. I have to get the best price for my client.'

'Your client is only the old Department of Education, son. They're being done left, right and centre, or making killings all over the place. They don't count.'

'You're honourable in your trade. I have to be in mine.'

'I'm also human in mine.' There was a silence.

If either of them was remembering how Dr Jims had bent the rules to help his son all those years ago neither of them said it.

'Perhaps they'll get outbidden.' Declan didn't seem very hopeful.

'Has Niall Hayes dropped out?'

'Yes. And Foxy Dunne – that's a relief in a way. And so has Eddie. I wouldn't want them raising the price on each other.'

'There. You do have a heart.' Dr Jims seemed pleased.

'And nobody else?'

'Nobody serious.'

'Who knows what's serious?'

'All right, Dad. Maura. Michael's mother. She says that she wants the place to be a home, a home for children like Michael, with someone to run it. And she'd help in it too. People like Michael who have no mothers . . . that's what she wants.'

'Well, isn't that what we'd all want?' said Dr Jims. 'And if we want it, it can be done.'

Nobody ever knew what negotiation went on behind the scenes, how the Family of Hope were persuaded that it would be very damaging publicity to cross swords with a community which wanted to provide a home for Down's syndrome children – and had raised the money for it. Maddy Ross was heard to say that she was just as glad that Sister Judith hadn't been forced to meet the collective ignorance, superstition and bigotry of Shancarrig.

Foxy and Leo had provided a sister for Moore and Frances – Chris and Eddie a brother for the twins – Nessa and Niall a brother for Danny and Breda – Mr and Mrs Hayes had decided of their own volition to move downstairs to the basement of The Terrace and had their own front door by which they came and went – Declan and Ruth Blake had built their house and called their son James – the Kellys' granddaughter Nora was walking – when the Shancarrig Home was opened.

There were photographs of it in all the papers and nice little pieces describing it.

But it was hard to do it justice, because all anyone could see was a stone house and a big tree.

Tara Road

To my dearest Gordon, with all my love

1

Ria's mother had always been very fond of film stars. It was a matter of sadness to her that Clark Gable had died on the day Ria was born. Tyrone Power had died on the day Hilary had been born just two years earlier. But somehow that wasn't as bad. Hilary hadn't seen off the great king of cinema as Ria had. Ria could never see *Gone with the Wind* without feeling somehow guilty.

She told this to Ken Murray, the first boy who kissed her. She told him in the cinema. Just as he was kissing her, in fact.

'You're very boring,' he said, trying to open her blouse.

'I'm not boring,' Ria cried with some spirit. 'Clark Gable is there on the screen and I've told you something interesting. A coincidence. It's not boring.'

Ken Murray was embarrassed as so much attention had been called to them. People were shushing them and others were laughing. Ken moved away and huddled down in his seat as if he didn't want to be seen with her.

Ria could have kicked herself. She was almost sixteen. Everyone at school liked kissing, or said they did. Now she was starting to do it and she had made such a mess of it. She reached out her hand for him.

'I thought you wanted to look at the film,' he muttered.

'I thought *you* wanted to put your arm around me,' Ria said hopefully.

He took out a bag of toffees and ate one. Without even passing her the bag. The romantic bit was over.

Sometimes you could talk to Hilary, Ria had noticed. This wasn't one of those nights.

'Should you not talk when people kiss you?' she asked her sister.

'Jesus, Mary and Holy St Joseph,' said Hilary, who was getting dressed to go out.

'I just asked,' Ria said. 'You'd know, with all your experience with fellows.'

Hilary looked around nervously in case anyone had heard. 'Will you *shut up* about my experience with fellows,' she hissed. 'Mam will hear you and that will put paid to either of us going anywhere ever again.'

Their mother had warned them many times that she was not going to stand for any cheap behaviour in the family. A widow woman left with two daughters had enough to worry her without thinking that her girls were tramps and would never get a husband. She would die happy if Hilary and

Ria had nice respectable men and homes of their own. Nice homes, in a classier part of Dublin, places with a garden even. Nora Johnson had great hopes that they would all be able to move a little upwards. Somewhere nicer than the big sprawling housing estate where they lived now. And the way to find a good man was not by flaunting yourself at every man that came along.

'Sorry, Hilary,' Ria looked contrite. 'But anyway she didn't hear, she's looking at telly.'

Their mother did little else of an evening. She was tired, she said, when she got back from the dry cleaners where she worked at the counter. All day on your feet, it was nice to sit down and get transported to another world. Mam wouldn't have heard anything untoward about experience with fellows from upstairs.

Hilary forgave her – after all, she needed Ria to help her tonight. Mam had a system that as soon as Hilary got in she was to leave her handbag on the landing floor. That way when Mam got up to go to the bathroom in the night she'd know Hilary was home and would go to sleep happily. Sometimes it was Ria's job to leave the handbag out there at midnight, allowing Hilary to creep in at any hour, having taken only her keys and lipstick in her pocket.

'Who'll do it for me when the time comes?' Ria wondered.

'You won't need it if you're going to be blabbing and yattering on to fellows when they try to kiss you,' Hilary said. 'You'll not want to stay out late because you'll have nowhere to go.'

'I bet I will,' Ria said, but she didn't feel as confident as she sounded. There was a stinging behind her eyes.

She was sure she didn't look *too* bad. Her friends at school said she was very lucky to have all that dark curly hair and blue eyes. She wasn't fat or anything and her spots weren't out of control. But people didn't pick her out; she didn't have any kind of sparkle like other girls in the class did.

Hilary saw her despondent face. 'Listen, you're fine, you've got naturally curly hair, that's a plus for a start. And you're small, fellows like that. It will get better. Sixteen is the worst age, no matter what they tell you.' Sometimes Hilary could be very nice indeed. Usually on the nights she wanted her handbag left on the landing.

And of course Hilary was right. It *did* get better. Ria left school and like her elder sister did a secretarial course. There were plenty of fellows, it turned out. Nobody particularly special, but she wasn't in any rush. She would travel the world possibly before she settled down to marry.

'Not too much travelling,' her mother warned.

Nora Johnson thought that men might regard travel as fast. Men preferred to marry safer, calmer women. Women who didn't go gallivanting too much. It was only sensible to have advance information about men, Nora Johnson told her daughters. This way you could go armed into the struggle. There was a hint that she may not have been adequately informed herself. The late Mr Johnson, though he had a bright smile and wore his hat at a rakish angle, was not a good provider. He had not been a believer in nor a subscriber to life insurance policies. Nora Johnson did not want the same thing for her daughters when the time came.

'When do you think the time will come?' Ria asked Hilary.

'For what?' Hilary was frowning a lot at her reflection in the mirror. The thing about applying blusher was that you had to get it just right. Too much and you looked consumptive, too little and you looked dirty and as if you hadn't washed your face.

'I mean, when do you think either of us will get married? You know the way Mam's always talking about when the time comes.'

'Well, I hope it comes to me first, I'm the eldest. You're not even to consider doing it ahead of me.'

'No, I have nobody in mind. It's just I'd love to be able to look into the future and see where we'll be in two years' time. Wouldn't it be great if we could have a peep?'

'Well, go to a fortune-teller then if you're that anxious.'

'They don't know anything.' Ria was scornful.

'It depends. If you get the right one they do. A lot of the girls at work found this great one. It would make you shiver the way she knows things.'

'You've never been to her?' Ria was astounded.

'Yes I have actually, just for fun. The others were all going, I didn't want to be the only one disapproving.'

'And?'

'And what?'

'What did she tell you? Don't be mean, go on.' Ria's eyes were dancing.

'She said I would marry within two years . . .'

'Great, can I be the bridesmaid?'

'And that I'd live in a place surrounded by trees and that his name began with an M, and that we'd both have good health all our lives.'

'Michael, Matthew, Maurice, Marcello?' Ria rolled them all around to try them out. 'How many children?'

'She said no children,' Hilary said.

'You don't believe her, do you?'

'Of course I do, what's the point giving up a week's wages if I don't believe her?'

'You *never* paid that!'

'She's good. You know, she has the gift.'

'Come *on.*'

'No, she does have a gift. All kinds of high-up people consult her. They wouldn't if she didn't have the power.'

'And where did she see all this good health and the fellow called M and no children? In tea-leaves?'

'No, on my hand. Look at the little lines under your little finger around the side of your hand. You've got two, I've got none.'

'Hilary, don't be ridiculous. Mam has three lines . . .'

'And remember there was another baby who died, so that makes three, right.'

'You are serious! You do believe it.'

'You asked so I'm telling you.'

'And everyone who is going to have children has those little lines and those who aren't haven't?'

'You have to know how to look.' Hilary was defensive.

'You have to know how to charge, it seems.' Ria was distressed to see the normally level-headed Hilary so easily taken in.

'It's not that dear when you consider . . .' Hilary began.

'Ah, Hilary, please. A week's wages to hear that kind of rubbish! Where does she live, in a penthouse?'

'No, a caravan as it happens, on a halting site.'

'You're joking me?'

'True, she doesn't care about money. It's not a racket or a job, it's a gift.'

'Yeah.'

'So it looks like I can do what I like without getting pregnant.' Hilary sounded very confident.

'It might be dangerous to throw out the pill,' said Ria. 'I wouldn't rely totally on Madame Fifi or whatever she's called.'

'Mrs Connor.'

'Mrs Connor,' Ria repeated. 'Isn't that amazing. Mam used to consult Saint Ann or someone when she was young. We thought that was mad enough, now it's Mrs Connor in the halting site.'

'Wait until you need to know something, you'll be along to her like a flash.'

It was very hard to know what a job was going to be like until you were in it and then it was too late.

Hilary had office jobs in a bakery, a laundry and then settled in a school. There wasn't much chance of meeting a husband there, she said, but the pay was a bit better and she got her lunch free, which meant she could save a bit more. She was determined to have something to put towards a house when the time came.

Ria was saving too, but to travel the world. She worked first in the office of a hardware shop, then in a company which made hairdressing supplies. And then settled in a big, busy estate agency. Ria was on the reception desk and answered the phone. It was a world she knew nothing of when she went in, but it was obviously a business with a huge buzz. Prosperity had come to Ireland in the early eighties and the property market was the first to reflect this. There was huge competition between the various estate agents and Ria found they worked closely as a team.

On the first day she met Rosemary. Slim, blonde, and gorgeous, but as friendly as any of the girls she had ever met at school or secretarial college. Rosemary also lived at home with her mother and sister, so there was an immediate bond. Rosemary was so confident and well up in everything that was happening. Ria assumed that she must be a graduate or someone with huge knowledge of the property market. But no, Rosemary had only worked there for six months; it was her second job.

'There's no point in working anywhere unless we know what it's all about,'

Rosemary said. 'It makes it twice as interesting if you know all that's going on.'

It also made Rosemary twice as interesting to all the fellows who worked there. They found it very difficult to get to first base with her: in fact, Ria had heard that there was a sweepstake being run secretly on who would be the first to score. Rosemary had heard this too. She and Ria laughed over it.

'It's only a game,' Rosemary said. 'They don't really want me at all.' Ria was not sure that she was right; almost any man in the office would have been proud to escort Rosemary Ryan. But she was adamant, a career first, fellows later. Ria listened with interest. It was such a different message from the one she got at home, where her mother and Hilary seemed to put a much greater emphasis on the marriage side of things.

Ria's mother said that 1982 was a terrible year for film stars dying. Ingrid Bergman died, and Romy Schneider and Henry Fonda, then there was the terrible accident when Princess Grace was killed. All the people you really wanted to see, they were dying off like flies.

It was also the year that Hilary Johnson got engaged to Martin Moran, a teacher at the school where she worked in the office.

Martin was pale and anxious and originally from the west of Ireland. He always said his father was a small farmer, not just a farmer but a *small* one. Since Martin was six foot one it was hard to imagine this. He was courteous and obviously very fond of Hilary, yet there was something about him that lacked enthusiasm and fire. He looked slightly worried about things and spoke pessimistically when he came to the house for Sunday lunch.

There was a problem connected with everything. The Pope would get assassinated when he visited England, Martin was sure of it. And when he didn't, it was just lucky and his visit hadn't done all the good that people had hoped it would. The war in the Falklands would have repercussions for Ireland, mark his word. And the trouble in the Middle East was going to get worse, and the IRA bombs in London were only the tip of the iceberg. Teachers' salaries were too low; house prices were too high.

Ria looked at the man her sister was going to marry with wonder.

Hilary, who had once been able to throw away a week's salary on a fortune-teller, was now talking about the cost of having shoes repaired and the folly of making a telephone call outside the cheap times.

Eventually a selection was made and a deposit was paid on a very small house. It was impossible to imagine what the area might look like in the future. At present it was full of mud, cement mixers, diggers, unfinished roads and unmade footpaths. And yet it seemed exactly what her elder sister wanted out of life. Never had Ria seen her so happy.

Hilary was always smiling and holding Martin's hand as they talked, even on very worrying subjects like stamp duty and auctioneers' fees. She kept turning and examining the very small diamond which had been very carefully chosen and bought from a jeweller where Martin's cousin worked so that a good price had been arranged.

Hilary was excited about the wedding, which would be two days before her twenty-fourth birthday. For Hilary the time had come. She celebrated it by manic frugality. She and Martin vied with each other to save money on the whole project.

A winter wedding was much more sensible. Hilary could wear a cream-coloured suit and hat, something that could be worn again and again, and eventually dyed a dark colour and worn still further. As a wedding feast they would have a small lunch in a Dublin hotel, just family. Martin's father and brothers, being small farmers, could not afford to be away from the land for any longer than a day. It would be impossible to be anything but pleased for her. It was so obviously what Hilary wanted. But Ria knew that it was nothing at all like what she wanted herself.

Ria wore a bright scarlet coat to the wedding, and a red velvet hairband and bow in her black curly hair. She must have been one of the most colourful bridesmaids at the drabbest wedding in Europe, she thought.

When Monday came she decided to wear her scarlet bridesmaid's coat to the office. Rosemary was amazed. 'Hey, you look *terrific*. I've never seen you dressed up before, Ria. Seriously, you should get interested in clothes, you know. What a pity we have nowhere to go to lunch and show you off, we mustn't waste this.'

'Come on, Rosemary, it's only clothes.' Ria was embarrassed. She felt now that she must have been dressed like a tramp before.

'No, I'm not joking. You must always wear those knock-them-dead colours, I bet you were the hit of the wedding!'

'I'd like to think so, but maybe I was a bit too loud, made them colour-blind. You've no idea what Martin's people were like.'

'Like Martin?' Rosemary guessed.

'Compared to them Martin's a ball of fire,' Ria said.

'Look, I can't believe you're the same person as yesterday.' Rosemary stood in her immaculate lilac-coloured knitted suit, her make-up perfect and amazed admiration written all over her.

'Well, you've really put it up to me. Now I'll have to get a whole new wardrobe.' Ria twirled around once more before taking off her scarlet coat and caught the eye of the new man in the office.

She had heard there was a Mr Lynch coming from the Cork branch. He had obviously arrived. He wasn't tall, about her own height. He was handsome, and he had blue eyes and straight fair hair that fell into his eyes. He had a smile that lit up the room. 'Hallo, I'm Danny Lynch,' he said. Ria looked at him, embarrassed to have been caught pirouetting around in her new coat. 'Aren't you just *gorgeous*?' he said. She felt a very odd sensation in her throat, as if she had been running up a hill and couldn't catch her breath.

Rosemary spoke, which was just as well because Ria would not have been able to answer at all.

'Well *hallo* there, Danny Lynch,' she said with a bit of a smile. 'And you are very welcome to our office. You know, we *were* told that there was a Mr Lynch arriving, but why did we think it was going to be some old guy?'

Ria felt a pang of jealousy as she had never before felt about her friend.

Why did Rosemary always know exactly what to say, how to be funny and flattering and warm at the same time?

'I'm Rosemary, this is Ria, and we are the workforce that keeps this place going, so you have to be very nice to us.'

'Oh I will,' Danny promised.

And Ria knew he would probably join the sweepstake as to who would score first with Rosemary. Probably would win, as well. Oddly he seemed to be talking to Ria when he spoke, but maybe she was just imagining it. Rosemary went on, 'We were just looking for somewhere to go out and celebrate Ria's new coat.'

'Great! Well, we have the excuse, all we need is the place and to know how long a lunch break so that I don't make a bad impression on my first day.' His extraordinary smile went from one to the other; they were the only three people in the world.

Ria couldn't say anything; her mouth was too dry.

'If we're out and back in under an hour then I think we'll do well,' said Rosemary.

'So now it's only where?' Danny Lynch said, looking straight at Ria. This time there were only two of them in the world. She still couldn't speak.

'There's an Italian place across the road,' Rosemary said. 'It would cut down on time getting there and back.'

'Let's go there,' said Danny Lynch, without taking his eyes away from Ria Johnson.

Danny was twenty-three. His uncle had been an auctioneer. Well, he had been a bit of everything in a small town, a publican, an undertaker, but he also had an auctioneer's licence and that's where Danny had gone to work when he left school. They had sold grain and fertiliser and hay as well as cattle and small farms, but as Ireland changed, property became important. And then he had gone to Cork City and he loved it all, and now he had just got this job in Dublin.

He was as excited as a child on Christmas Day, and Rosemary and Ria were carried along with him all the way. He said he hated being in the office and loved being out with clients, but then didn't everyone? He knew it would take time before he'd get that kind of freedom in Dublin. He had been to Dublin often but never lived there.

And where was he staying? Rosemary had never seemed so interested in anyone before. Ria watched glumly. Every man in the office would have killed to see the light in the eyes, the interest in every word. She never enquired where any of her other colleagues lived, she didn't seem to know if they had any accommodation at all. But with Danny it was different. 'Tell us now that you don't live miles and miles away, do you?' Rosemary had her head on one side. No man on earth could resist giving Rosemary his address and finding out where *she* lived too. But Danny didn't seem to regard it as a personal exchange; it was part of the general conversation. He spoke looking from one to the other as he told them how he had fallen on his feet. He had really had the most amazing bit of luck. There was this man he had met, a sort of madman really called Sean O'Brien, old and confused. A real recluse. And he had inherited a great big house in Tara Road, and he wasn't capable of doing it up, and he didn't want all the bother and the discussing of it and all, so what he really wanted was a few fellows to go in and live there. Fellows were easier than girls, they didn't want things neat and clean and organised. He smiled apologetically at them as if to say he knew that fellows were hopeless.

So that's where Danny and two other lads lived. They had a bedsitter each, and kept an eye on the place until poor old Sean decided what he was going to do. Suited everybody.

What kind of a house was it, the girls wanted to know?

Tara Road was very higgledy-piggledy. Big houses with gardens full of trees, small houses facing right on to the street. Number 16 was a great old house, Danny said. Falling down, damp, shabby now. Poor Sean O'Brien's old uncle must have been a bit of a no-hoper like Sean himself, it must have been a great house once. You got a feel for houses, didn't you? Otherwise why be in this business at all?

Ria sat with her chin in her hands listening to Danny and looking at him and looking at him. He was so enthusiastic. The place had a big overrun garden at the back. It was one of those houses that just put out its arms and hugged you.

Rosemary must have kept the conversation going and called for the bill. They walked across the road back to work and Ria sat down at her desk. Things don't happen like this in real life. It's only a crush or an infatuation. He's a perfectly ordinary small guy with a line of chatter. He is exactly like this to everyone else. So why on earth did she feel that he was so special, and that if he got to share all his plans and dreams with anyone else she would kill the other person? This wasn't the kind of way people went on. Then she remembered her sister's wedding two days ago. *That* wasn't the way people went on either.

Before the office closed Ria went over to Danny Lynch's desk. 'I'm going to be twenty-two tomorrow,' she said. 'I wondered . . .' Then she got stuck.

He helped her out. 'Are you having a party?'

'Not really, no.'

'Then can we celebrate it together? Today the coat, tomorrow being twenty-two. Who knows what we'll have to celebrate by Wednesday?'

And then Ria knew that it wasn't a crush or an infatuation, it was love. The kind of thing she had only read about, heard about, sung about or seen at the cinema. And it had come to find her in her own office.

At first Ria tried to keep Danny to herself, not wanting to tell anyone about him or to share him with other people. She clung to him when they said goodbye as if she never wanted him to leave her arms.

'You're sending me very funny signals, my Maria,' he said to her. 'You want to be with me and yet you don't. Or am I just a thick man who can't understand?' His head was on one side, looking at her quizzically.

'That's exactly the way I feel,' she said simply. 'Very confused.'

'Well we can simplify it all, can't we?'

'Not really. You see for me it would be a very big step. I don't want to make a production out of it all, but you see I haven't with anyone else. Yet I mean . . .' She bit her lip. She didn't dare tell him that she wouldn't sleep with him until she knew that he loved her. It would be putting words in his mouth.

Danny Lynch held her face in his hands. 'I love you, Ria, you are utterly adorable.'

'*Do* you love me?'

'You know I do.'

The next time he asked her to go back to the big rambling house she would go. But, oddly, he didn't ask her at all in the days and nights that followed. He told her about himself, his time at school where he was picked on because he was small and how his elder brothers taught him to fight. His brothers were in London, both of them. One married, one living with a girl. They didn't come home much. Usually went to Spain or Greece on their holidays now.

His parents lived in the same house as they had always done. They were very self-contained, went for long walks with their red setter. She felt that he didn't get on well with his father, but even though Ria ached to ask she didn't probe. Men hated that kind of intimate chat. She and Rosemary knew this from reading magazine articles and even from their own experience. Fellows didn't like being questioned about feelings. So she did not ask him about his childhood and why he spoke so little of his parents and rarely went to see them.

Danny didn't ask questions about her family, so she forced herself not to prattle about how her father had died when she was eight, how her mother was still bitter and disappointed by the memory of him. And how dull Hilary and Martin's wedding had been.

There was no shortage of things to talk about in those heady days. Danny did ask about what music she liked, and what she read and where she had been on holidays, and what films she went to see, and what kind of houses she liked. He showed her books about houses, and pointed out things that she would never have noticed. He would love to own the old house, Number 16 Tara Road, he told her. He would do it up and take such care of it. He would put so much love into the house that the house would return his love.

It was wonderful having Rosemary to talk to. At first Ria held back. She was so afraid that if Rosemary smiled just once more, Danny would leave Ria's side and join her, but as the days went by she began to have a little more confidence. And then she told Rosemary everything, where they went, what he was interested in, about his strange lonely family in the country.

Rosemary listened with interest. 'You've got it very bad,' she said eventually.

'Do you think it's foolish, just a crush or something? You know a lot about these things.' Ria wished for an oval face and high cheekbones so desperately it almost hurt.

'He seems to have it just as bad,' Rosemary pronounced.

'He *says* he loves me, certainly,' Ria said. She was answering Rosemary's question but she didn't want to sound too confident.

'Of course he loves you, that was obvious the very first day,' Rosemary said, twirling her long blonde hair around her finger. 'It's the most romantic thing I've ever seen. I can't tell you how envious we all are. Total love at first sight and the whole office knows. What nobody knows is are you sleeping with him?'

'No,' said Ria firmly. And then, in a much smaller voice, 'Not yet.'

Ria's mother wondered was she ever going to meet him.

'Soon, Mam. Don't rush things, please.'

'I'm not rushing anything, Ria. I'm just pointing out that you have been going out with this fellow every single night, week after week, and common courtesy would suggest that you might invite him home with you once in a while.'

'I will, Mam. Honestly.'

'I mean, Hilary brought Martin back to meet us, didn't she?'

'Oh she did, Mam.'

'So?'

'So, I will.'

'Are you going home for Christmas?' Ria asked Danny.

'Here is home.' He embraced all of Dublin in a gesture.

'Yes, I know. I meant to your parents' home.'

'I don't know yet.'

'Won't they expect you to go back?'

'They'll leave it to me.'

She wanted to ask about his brothers over in England and what kind of a family *was* it if they didn't all gather around a table for a turkey on Christmas Day. But she knew she must not sound too inquisitive. 'Sure,' she said unconvincingly.

Danny took both her hands in his. 'Listen to me, Ria. It will be different when you and I have a home. It will be a real home, one that people will want to come running back to. That's what I see ahead for us. Don't you?'

'Oh yes, Danny,' she said, with her face glowing. She did understand. The real Danny was a loving person like herself. She was the luckiest woman in the world.

'Ask him for Christmas Day so that we can get a look at him,' her mother begged.

'No, Mam. Thank you, but no.'

'Is he going back down the country to his own people?'

'I'm not sure, he's not sure.'

'He sounds a real fly-by-night to me,' her mother sniffed.

'No, Mam, he's not that.'

'Well, a mystery man . . . he won't even put in an appearance to give the time of day to his girlfriend's family.'

'He will, Mam, when the time comes,' Ria said.

Someone always behaved badly at the office party.

This year it was Orla King, a girl who had drunk half a bottle of vodka before the festivities had even started. She tried to sing, 'In the jungle the mighty jungle the lion sleeps tonight'.

'Get her out before the top guys see her,' Danny hissed.

It was easier said than done. Ria tried to urge Orla to come with her to the ladies' room.

'Piss off!' was the response.

Danny was there. 'Hey sweetheart, you and I have never danced,' he said.

She looked at him with interest. 'That's true,' she agreed.

'Why don't we go out and dance a bit where there's more room?'

'Yesh,' said the girl, surprised and pleased.

In seconds Danny had her out on the street. Ria brought her coat. The cold fresh air made her feel sick. They directed her to a quiet corner.

'I want to go home,' she cried afterwards.

'Come on, we'll walk you,' Danny said.

Between them they supported her. From time to time Orla tried a chorus of 'The lion sleeps tonight' without much success.

When they let her in the door of her flat she looked at them in surprise. 'How did I get home?' she asked with interest.

'You're fine, sweetheart,' Danny said soothingly.

'Will you come in with me?' Orla ignored Ria entirely.

'No, honey, see you tomorrow,' he said, and they were gone.

'You saved her job, getting her out of there,' Ria said as they walked back to the office party. 'She's such a clown . . . I hope she knows how much she owes you.'

'She's not a clown, she's just young and lonely,' he said.

Ria got a stab of jealousy as sharp as a real pain. Orla was eighteen and pretty; even drunk and with a tear-stained face she looked well. Suppose Danny was attracted to her? No, don't suppose that.

Back at the party they hadn't been missed. 'That was very smart of you, Danny,' Rosemary said with approval. 'And even smarter, you missed the speeches.'

'Anything we should know?'

'Oh, that we had a profitable year and there would be a bonus. Onwards and upwards sort of thing.'

Rosemary looked magnificent, with her blonde hair swept up in a jewelled comb, a white satin blouse, tight black skirt and those long slim legs. For the second time that evening Ria felt a pang of envy. She was dumpy and fuzzy-looking. How could she keep a man as gorgeous as Danny Lynch? She was foolish even to try.

He whispered in her ear, 'Let's circulate, talk to the suits for a bit and then get away.'

She watched him joke easily with the senior figures in the agency, nod respectfully to the managing director, listen courteously to their wives. Danny had only been there a matter of weeks. Already they liked him and thought he would do well.

'I'm getting the Christmas Eve bus tomorrow.'

'I'm sure it'll be nice, lots of returned emigrants and everything,' she said.

'I'll miss you,' he said.

'Me too.'

'I'll hitch-hike back the day after Christmas . . . there's no buses.'

'That's great.'

'I wonder could I come and see you at home and, you know, meet your mother maybe?'

He was asking, she hadn't dragged him or forced him.

'That would be great. Come and have lunch with us on the Tuesday.' All she had to do now was force herself not to be ashamed of her mother and her sister and her dreary brother-in-law.

It wasn't a military inspection on Tuesday. It was only lunch. They were going to have soup and sandwiches.

Ria tried to see their home through Danny's eyes. It was not the kind of place where he would have liked to live, a corner house in a long road of the big estate. He's coming to see me not the house, she told herself. Her mother said she hoped he wouldn't stay after three because there was a great movie starting on the television then. Ria gritted her teeth and said no, indeed, she was sure that he wouldn't.

Hilary said she was sure he was used to fancier meals but he'd have to put up with this like anyone else. With a huge effort Ria said that he would be delighted to put up with it. Martin read the paper and didn't look up at all.

She wondered would Danny bring a bottle of wine or a box of chocolates or a plant. Or maybe nothing at all. Three times she changed her dress. That was too smart, this was too dowdy. She was struggling into the third outfit when she heard the doorbell ring.

He had arrived.

'Hallo Nora, I'm Danny,' she heard him say. Oh God, he was calling her mother by her first name. Martin always called her Mrs J. Mam would just hate this.

But she heard in her mother's voice the kind of pleased response that Danny always got. 'You're very, very welcome,' she said, in a tone that hadn't been used in that house for as long as Ria could remember.

And the magic worked with Hilary and Martin too. Eager to hear about their wedding, interested in the school where they worked, relaxed and easygoing. Ria watched the whole thing with amazement.

And he had brought no wine, chocolates or flowers. Instead he gave them a game of Trivial Pursuit. Ria's heart sank when she saw it. This was not a family where games were played. But she had reckoned without Danny. Their heads were bent over the questions. Nora knew all the ones about film stars and Martin shone in general knowledge.

'What hope have I against a teacher?' Danny groaned in despair.

He said he was leaving long before they wanted him to go. 'Ria promised to come and see the place I live,' he said apologetically. 'I want us to go while there's still light.'

'He's gorgeous,' Hilary whispered.

'Very nice manners,' her mother hissed.

And then they were free.

'That was a lovely lunch,' Danny said as they waited for the bus to Tara Road. And that was all he would say. There would be no analysis, no defining. Men like Danny were straightforward and not complicated.

And then they were there. And they stood together in the overgrown front garden and looked up at the house in Tara Road.

'Look at the shape of the house,' Danny begged her. 'See how perfect the proportions are. It was built in 1870, a gentleman's residence.' The steps up to the hall door were huge blocks of granite. 'Look how even they were, they were perfectly matched.' The bow windows had all the original woodwork. 'Those shutters are over a hundred years old. The leaded glass over the door has no cracks in it. This house was a jewel,' Danny Lynch said.

There he was living in it, well, more or less camping in a room in it.

'Let's remember today, the first day that we walked together into this house,' he said. His eyes were bright. He was just as sentimental and romantic as she was in so many ways. He was about to open the peeling front door with his key and paused to kiss her. 'This will be our home, Ria, won't it? Tell me you love it too.' He meant it. He wanted to marry her. Danny Lynch, a man who could have any woman. And he meant he was going to own a huge house like this. A boy of twenty-three with no assets. Only rich people could buy houses like this, even one in such poor repair.

Ria didn't want to pour cold water on his dreams, and particularly she didn't want to sound too like her sister Hilary with her new obsession with the cost of everything. But this was fantasy. 'It's not possible to own a place like this surely?' she said.

'When you come in and see it you'll know this is where we are going to live. And we'll find a way to buy it.' He talked her through the hallway with its high ceiling. He pointed out the original mouldings on the ceiling to take her eyes off the bicycles clogging the hallway. He showed her the gentle curve of the stairs, and made no mention of the rotting floorboards. They passed the big room with its folding doors. They couldn't go into it. Sean O'Brien, the eccentric landlord, was using it as some kind of storeroom for giant-size containers.

They went down the steps to the huge kitchen with its old black range. There was a side door here out to the garden, and numerous storage rooms, pantries and sculleries. The magnitude of it all was too great for Ria to take in. This boy with the laughing eyes really thought that he and she could find the money and skills to do up a house of this size.

If it were on their books back at the office it would have the customary warnings printed all over it. In need of extensive renovation, suitable for structural remodelling, ready for inventive redesign. Only a builder or developer or someone with real money would buy a property like this.

The kitchen had an uneven tiled floor. A small cheap tabletop cooker had been laid on the old black range.

'I'll make us some coffee,' Danny said. 'And in years to come we'll remember the first time we had coffee here together in Tara Road . . .' At that moment, as if on some kind of cue, the kitchen was suddenly lit up with one of those rays of watery winter sunshine. It came slanting in at the window through all the briars and brambles. It was like a sign.

'Yes, yes I will remember my first coffee with you in Tara Road,' Ria said.

'We'll be able to tell people it was a lovely sunny day, December the twenty-eighth 1982,' said Danny.

As it happened it also turned out to be the date of the first time Ria Johnson ever made love to anybody. And as she lay beside Danny in the small narrow bed she wished she could see into the future. Just for a moment. A quick look to see would they live here together for years and have children and make it the home of their dreams.

She wondered if Hilary's friend Mrs Connor, the fortune-teller on the halting site, would know. She smiled at the thought of going to consult her. Danny stirred from his sleep on her shoulder, and saw her smiling.

'Are you happy?' he asked.

'Never more so.'

'I love you, Ria. I'll never let you down,' he promised.

She was the luckiest woman in the country. No, she told herself, think generously, who was luckier anywhere? Make that the world.

2

The next weeks went by in a blur.

They knew that Sean O'Brien would be glad to get rid of the place.

They knew that he would prefer to deal with them, young people who wouldn't make a fuss about the damp and the roof, and would not tut-tut over the decay. But they still had to give him what the house was worth. So how could they get it together?

There were sheets of paper building up into piles as they did their sums. Four bedsitters upstairs would bring in enough to pay the mortgage. It would have to be done very quietly of course. No need to burden the planning authorities with any details, or indeed the tax people either. Then they would approach the bank with their proposition. Ria had a thousand pounds saved; Danny had two-and-a-half thousand. They had both seen couples with less than they had get their hands on property. It all depended on timing and presentation. They would do it.

They invested the price of a bottle of whiskey when inviting the landlord to discuss the future. Sean O'Brien proved to be no trouble. He told them again and again the story they knew already. He had inherited the house when his uncle died some years back. He didn't want to live in it, he had a small cottage by a lake in Wicklow where he fished and drank with congenial people. That's where he wanted to be. He'd only held on to Tara Road in case there was going to be a property boom. And indeed there had been. It was worth much more now than it had been ten years ago, so he had been clever, hadn't he? A lot of people said he was an eejit but that wasn't so. Danny and Ria nodded and praised him and filled his glass.

Sean O'Brien said he had never been able to keep the house up to any standard. It was too much effort and he didn't have the skills to restore it and let it properly to people who would look after it. That was why he had been happy to hand it to young fellows like Danny and his pals. But he took their point that it wasn't going to be such a great investment if it kept falling down and deteriorating the way it was.

He thought that the going rate would be in the neighbourhood of seventy thousand pounds. He had asked around and this is what he had heard. However he would take sixty thousand for a quick sale, and he'd get rid of all the old furniture and containers and boxes that he was storing for friends. Danny could have it when he produced sixty thousand.

It would have been a bargain for anyone with the money to restore it. For

Danny and Ria it was impossible. For a start they would need fifteen per cent of the price as a deposit. And nine thousand pounds was like nine million to them.

Ria was prepared to change the dream, not Danny. He didn't fret or complain. He just wouldn't let go of the idea. It was too good a house, too beautiful a place to let slip from their hands into the possession of some builder. Now that Sean O'Brien had faced the notion of selling, he would want to sell.

It was hard to keep their minds on the sales they had to handle in the office. Doubly hard because every day they were dealing with people who could buy Tara Road without any trouble at all.

People like Barney McCarthy, for example. The big bluff businessman who had made his money in England as a builder and who bought and sold houses almost on a whim. He was in the process of selling a large mansion that had been a mistake. One of his rare mistakes.

Barney was unexpectedly honest as to why it was a mistake. He had seen himself momentarily as a country squire, living in a huge Georgian house with a tree-lined avenue. The house was indeed elegant but it turned out to be too remote, too far from Dublin. It had been an ill-considered decision and he was prepared to lose a little on the whole deal, but not a lot. He needed to sell this white elephant.

He had already bought the comfortable big square family residence that he should have bought in the first place. His wife was settled there. He was involved in buying pubs and investing in golf courses but the issue that was uppermost was to sell the mansion which now seemed just like a monument to his folly. He was a man who cared about the public image of himself.

He also loved to drop the names of famous people he had met, and in the estate agency they were greatly in awe of him. But they had a huge problem in selling this property at anything like the price he expected. Quite simply Barney had spent too much on it and there were just not the buyers. He was not going to see a profit, and he was a man who hated to take a humiliating loss on this deal. Senior partners in the estate agency, smooth-talking men, pointed out to Barney that the upkeep of such a house was enormous and that they could count on the fingers of one hand the likely buyers in Ireland. They had looked outside the country too, but with no success.

There was a conference in the agency about it. Danny and Ria sat with the others listening to the worrying news that Barney might be taking his business elsewhere. Ria's mind was far from Barney's problems and more on their own. But Danny was thinking. He opened his mouth to say something and then changed his mind.

'What is it, Danny?' He was popular and successful. They wanted to hear what he would say.

'No, it's nothing. You've thought of all the angles,' Danny said.

And the conversation went around aimlessly in the same circle for another half an hour.

Ria knew that Danny had thought of something. She knew from the way his eyes danced. After the meeting he whispered that he had to get out of the office. She was to cover for him.

'If you pray to anyone, pray now,' he said.

'Tell me, Danny. Tell me.'

'I can't, there isn't time. Say I got a phone call . . . from the nuns down the road. Anything.'

'I can't sit here and not know.'

'I've got an idea how Barney can sell his house.'

'Why didn't you tell them?'

'I'm telling *him*. That's how we'll get our money. If I tell them we'll only get a pat on the back.'

'Oh God, Danny. Be careful, they could sack you.'

'If I'm right it won't matter,' he said. And he was gone.

Rosemary called Ria. 'Come into the ladies' room. I want to tell you something.'

'I can't. I'm waiting for a call.' Ria couldn't leave her post in case he rang, or needed her co-operation.

'Orla can cover for you, come on, it's important,' Rosemary said.

'No, tell me here, there's no one around.'

'Well, it's very hush-hush.'

'Speak in a whisper, then.'

'I'm leaving, I've got a new job.' Rosemary pulled back, waiting to see the amazement and shock on Ria's face. She saw very little reaction at all. Perhaps she hadn't explained it properly.

She explained it all again. It had just been agreed. It was very exciting. She would tell them here in the agency this evening. She had been offered a better job in a printing company. It wasn't far away; they could still have lunch. Ria barely listened, she was so sick with worry.

Rosemary was not unnaturally offended. 'Well, if you can't be bothered to listen,' she said.

'I'm sorry, Rosemary, really I am. It's just that I have something on my mind.'

'God, you're so bloody dull, Ria. You've nothing on your mind but Danny this, Danny that. It's like as if you were his mother. Do you know that you haven't the remotest interest in anyone else these days!'

Ria was stricken. 'Look, I can't tell you how sorry I am. Please forgive me. Tell me again.'

'No, I won't tell you again. You don't care if I go or stay. You're *still* not listening to me. You've your eyes on the door in case he's coming back in. Where is he, by the way?'

'With the nuns, they rang.'

'No, they didn't. I was talking to them an hour ago. There's no movement there, they have to wait for some Mother General to say yes from Rome.'

'I'll tell you all about it later. Please tell me about your new job, please.'

'Ria, will you *shut up*,' Rosemary hissed. 'I haven't told them yet and there you go bleating about my new job. I think you're unhinged.'

She saw Danny come in the door, walking quickly, lightly, as he always did. She knew by his face that it was all right. He slid into his desk and gave her a thumbs-up sign. Immediately she dialled his phone extension.

'Don't say you were with the nuns. Apparently there's nothing happening on that sale,' she whispered.

'Thanks, you're brilliant.'

'What happens now, Danny?'

'We sit tight for a week. Then all systems go.'

Ria hung up. She thought the day would never end, the hands of the clock were crawling past. Rosemary went in and came out having given her notice. Everything seemed to be in slow motion. Across the room Danny seemed to be perfectly normal in his conversations, chatting to people, laughing, working on the phone. Only Ria, who knew his every heartbeat, could see the suppressed excitement.

They went to the pub across the road and without asking her what she wanted he bought them both a large brandy.

'I told Barney McCarthy he should put in a sound-proofed recording studio, with all that stuff on the walls. Cost him another twenty thousand.'

'Why on earth . . . ?'

'He could sell it to pop stars. It's the kind of a place they'd want, carve out a helicopter pad as well.'

'And he thought it was a good idea?' Ria was weak.

'He asked why did those swanky auctioneers I worked for not come up with this idea.'

'What did you say?'

'I said they would probably think it was a bit of a young man's idea, that they were more conservative. And Ria, wait for this, I looked him in the eye and I said, "And another thing, Mr McCarthy, I thought if I came to you directly with this idea that maybe I could sell it for you myself."' Danny sipped his brandy. 'He asked me was I trying to take his business away from my employers. I said yes, I was, and he said he'd give me a week.'

'Oh God, Danny.'

'I know. Isn't it wonderful? Well, we can't do it from their place so I'll develop flu tomorrow, after I've taken all the addresses and contacts I need home. I've begun to make a list already and then I'll get on the phone. I may need you to send some faxes from the office for me.'

'We'll be killed.'

'Don't be ridiculous, of course we won't. This is what business is about.'

'How much will . . . ?'

'If I sell Barney's bloody house by next week we'll have the deposit on Tara Road and more. *Then* we can go to the bank, honeybun. *Then* we can go to the bank.'

'But they'll sack you, you won't have a job.'

'If I have Barney McCarthy's business any auctioneers in Ireland will take me. Just a week of iron-hard nerve, Ria, and we're there.'

'Iron nerve,' she agreed.

'And remember this day, sweetheart. March the twenty-fifth 1983, the day our luck changed.'

'Will Danny be back for my going-away drinks?' Rosemary asked Ria.

'Yes, I think his flu will be better by then,' Ria said loudly.

'Sorry, it slipped out. How is he, by the way?'

'Fine, he rings at night.' Ria didn't say how often he telephoned during the day too, asking for information.

'And did he find what he's looking for?' Rosemary asked.

Ria thought for a moment. 'He sounds cheerful enough. I think he is just in the process of finding it,' she said.

An hour previously Danny had rung to say that Barney's forces had sound-proofed a wine cellar already and the equipment was being installed today. Tomorrow the manager of a legendary pop group was flying over to inspect it; Danny would be travelling with him. It was looking very good.

And it was very good. Barney McCarthy got his price. And Danny Lynch got his commission. And Sean O'Brien got his sixty thousand pounds. And Danny told his employers what he had done, and that he would leave as soon as they wanted him to. They invited him to stay and keep Barney's business with them, but Danny said it would be awkward. They would always be watching him, he would feel uneasy.

They parted on good terms, as Danny Lynch did with everyone and everything in life.

They were like excited children as they wandered about the house planning this and that.

'This front room could be something *really* special,' Danny said. Now that the boxes and containers that held the secrets of poor old Sean O'Brien and his friends had been moved out, anyone could see what perfect proportions it had: the high ceiling, the tall windows, the big fireplace.

It didn't matter at all that a naked light bulb hung on an old knotted flex from the middle of the ceiling, or that some window-panes had been broken in the past and replaced with cheap and irregular bits of glass.

The stained and chipped mantelpiece could be renewed and made to look as it must once have looked when it was a gentleman's residence.

'We'll get a gorgeous soft wool Indian carpet,' Danny said. 'And look here, beside the fireplace do you know what we'll have – one of those big Japanese Imari vases. Perfect for a room like this.'

Ria looked at him with stunned admiration.

'How on earth do you know all this, Danny? You sound as if you'd done a course in fine arts or something.'

'I look at places, sweetheart. I'm in and out of houses like this all day. I see what people with taste and style have done, I just look, that's all.'

'A lot of people look but they don't see properly.'

'We'll have such a good time doing it up.' His eyes were shining.

Ria nodded, not trusting herself to speak.

The excitement of it all was nearly too much for her. Sometimes she felt dizzy, physically dizzy with the magnitude of what they were taking on.

The pregnancy test was positive. The timing could not be worse. As she lay awake at night, either in her mother's home or in the shambles that was now Tara Road, she rehearsed how she would tell him that she was pregnant.

The fear that he might not want the child was so great it stopped her opening her mouth. The days went by and Ria felt she was acting everywhere and to everyone, and that she had long ceased to be a real person with normal responses.

When she did tell him it was completely by accident. Danny said that the hall was much bigger than they had thought now that they had got the bicycles out of it and into the shed. Maybe they should have a painting party at the weekend, get everyone to do a bit of wall each. It wouldn't be permanent or anything but it might give them a bit of pride in the place.

'What do you think, sweetheart? I know the smell of paint will make us all sick for a day or two but it will be worth it.'

'I'm going to have a baby,' she said suddenly.

'What?'

'Yes, I mean it. Oh Jesus, Danny, I'm so sorry. I'm so sorry now in the middle of all this.' And she burst into tears.

He laid down his coffee cup and came over to hold her tight. 'Ria, Ria. Stop, stop. Don't cry.'

But she went on sobbing and shaking in his arms. He stroked her hair and soothed her as you would a child. 'Shush, shush, Ria. I'm here, it's all right.'

'No, it's not all right, it couldn't be worse. What a time for this to happen. I don't know how it happened.'

'I do, and it was all lovely,' he said.

'Oh Danny, please don't make a joke about it, it's a nightmare. I've never been so upset. I couldn't tell you, not with all this going on.'

'Why is it a nightmare?' he asked.

Oh please, please, may he not say that an abortion was no trouble. That he had the money now. They could go to London at the weekend. Please may he not say that. Because Ria knew that she didn't trust herself. She might do it just to keep him. Then she would hate him as well as loving him, which would be absurd but she could see it happening.

He was smiling his big wide smile. 'Where's the nightmare, Ria my sweet, sweet heart? We wanted children. We were going to get married. So it happened sooner rather than later. That's all.'

She looked at him in wonder. In as much as she could understand anything, he really did seem overjoyed.

'Danny . . .'

'What were all the tears about?'

'I thought, I thought . . .'

'Shush.'

'Rosemary? Can we have lunch? I've some marvellous news.'

'What makes me think it has to do with lover boy?' Rosemary laughed.
'Lunch or not?'

'Of course.'

They went to the Italian restaurant where they had gone that day with
Danny last November – only a few months ago but imagine all that had
happened since.

Rosemary looked better than ever. How it was that no drop of oil or spill
of sauce would ever land on her light grey cashmere sweater Ria would never
know.

'Well, tell me,' Rosemary said. 'Stop pretending to look at the menu.'

'Danny and I are getting married, and we want you to be the bridesmaid.'
Rosemary was speechless. 'Yes, isn't it wonderful! We own the house and we
thought it silly to wait any longer.'

'Married?' Rosemary said. 'Well, aren't you the dark horse. All I can say is
well done, Ria. Well done!'

Ria felt slightly that she would have preferred Rosemary to say that this
was great; 'well done' sort of implied that she had won by trickery. 'Yes.
Aren't you happy for us?'

'Of course I am.' Rosemary hugged her. 'Stunned but very happy for you.
You got the man of your dreams *and* a beautiful house as well.'

Ria decided to play it down a little. 'There's years of work to get it right.
No one else but us would be as mad as to take it on.'

'Nonsense, it's worth a fortune; you and Danny know that. You certainly
moved fast on that one, you got the bargain of the century.' She spoke with
true praise.

Ria felt a stab of guilt as if they had somehow conned poor Sean O'Brien
and given him less than he deserved.

'Nobody's seen the house yet but you. I'm almost afraid of what the
families will say when they do.' Ria could see the jealousy in Hilary's face
already.

'Nonsense, they'll be dead impressed. What are they like, Danny's
parents?'

'I haven't met them yet, but I gather not at all like Danny,' Ria said.

Rosemary made a face. 'Still, maybe the brothers are okay. Are they
coming home from England? I might make off with one of them.
Bridesmaid's privilege, you know!'

'No mention of them coming back.'

'Never mind. I'll find something to entertain me. Now, down to serious
things. What will we wear?'

'Rosemary?'

'What?'

'You know I'm pregnant?'

'I thought you might be. But that's good, isn't it? It's what you want?'

'Yes, it is.'

'So?'

'So, we shouldn't really be thinking of big white weddings and veils and all
that stuff. And anyway, his family is very quiet, low key. It wouldn't work.'

'What would Danny like? Isn't that all that matters? Would he like the whole works or a few sandwiches in the pub?'

Ria didn't even pause to think. 'He'd like the full works,' she said.

'Then that is exactly what we'll have,' said Rosemary, getting out pen and paper and starting to make a list.

She met Barney McCarthy before she met Danny's parents. She was invited to lunch. In fact it was a little like a royal command.

Danny was excited. 'You'll like him, Ria, he's marvellous. And he'll love you, I know he will.'

'I'm nervous of going to that restaurant, it will all be in French and we won't know what all the things are.'

'Nonsense, just be yourself. And never apologise or write yourself down. We are as good as anyone else. Barney knows that, that's how he got on, by knowing it about himself.' She noticed with a little stab of worry that Danny seemed more anxious about her meeting with Barney than with his parents. 'Oh we'll go down to them any time,' he said.

Nora Johnson was amazed at the news. 'You do surprise me,' she said twice.

Ria was irritated by this response. 'Why do I surprise you, Mam? You know I love him, you know he loves me. What else would we do but get married?'

'Oh certainly, certainly.'

'What have you against him, Mam? You said you liked him, you admired the fact that he bought a big house and is planning to do it up. He's got good prospects, we won't be penniless. What objection do you have to him?'

'He's too good-looking,' her mother said.

Hilary was no more enthusiastic. 'You'd want to be careful of him, Ria.'

'Thank you very much, Hilary. When you were marrying Martin I didn't say that to you. I said I was delighted for you and I was sure you were going to be very happy.'

'But that was true.' Hilary was smug in her excellent choice of a mate.

'It's true for me, too,' Ria cried.

'Yes, Ria. But you'd have to watch him; he's a high-flyer. He's not going to be content with earning a living like normal people do; he'll want the moon. It's written all over him.'

Danny, who never fussed about anything, went to great trouble discussing what Ria should wear when meeting Barney McCarthy.

Eventually it made her impatient. 'Listen, you were the one who said I should be myself. I'll wear something nice and smart and I'll be myself. It's not a fashion parade or a beauty contest, it's a lunch.' Her eyes flashed with the kind of spirit she hadn't shown for a while.

He looked at her admiringly. 'That's my girl, that's the way to go,' he said. She wore the scarlet coat she had bought for Hilary's wedding, and a new silk scarf that Rosemary had helped her to choose.

Barney was a large square man of about forty-five in a very well-cut suit.

He wore an expensive watch and he carried himself well and confidently. Slightly balding now, he had the face of a working man, someone who had been out in all weathers. He had an easy manner; he was neither impressed by the restaurant nor trying to put it down. They talked effortlessly all three of them.

Still, despite the pleasant, inconsequential conversation, Ria couldn't avoid the feeling that she was being given an interview. And with a sense of satisfaction after the coffee she realised that she had done very well.

Orla King was the one who told Ria that people in the office didn't really like her working there any more. Not now that she was engaged to marry Danny Lynch. People said that she would be telling him everything, giving him leads.

'I had no idea.' Ria was shocked.

'Well, I'm only telling you because you two were very nice to me when I was being an eejit last Christmas.' Orla was all right. She couldn't help looking so good. Ria wondered why she had felt so stupidly jealous of her.

Danny told Barney McCarthy that Ria had decided to leave the company, to go before they asked her to.

Barney was unexpectedly sympathetic. 'That's very hard on her. She was in that firm long before you went in and rocked the boat.'

'That's true,' Danny said, surprised. He hadn't thought of it that way.

'So is she upset?'

'A little, but you know Ria, she's out looking for another job already.' He was proud of her.

'Maybe I'd have a job for her,' said Barney McCarthy.

One of his business interests was a new dress-hire firm. A very classy outfit called 'Polly's'. They took Ria immediately.

'Should I not have a week's trial or something?' Ria asked Gertie, the tall pale manageress with her long dark hair tied in a simple ribbon behind her neck.

'No need,' said Gertie with a grin. 'Instructions from Mr McCarthy to hire you, so you're hired.'

'I'm sorry. That's an awful way to come in anywhere,' Ria apologised.

'Listen, it's fine, and you're fine and we'll get along great,' said Gertie. 'I'm only telling it to you the way it is.'

They went to see Danny's parents. It was a three-hour journey by bus. Ria felt very sick but forced herself to be in good spirits. Danny's father waited in the square where the bus came in. He drove an old shabby van with a trailer attached to it.

'This is my Ria, Dad.' Danny was proud and pleased to show her off.

'You're very welcome.' The man looked old, stooped and shabby. He had worked all his life for his elder and brighter brother, the man who had given Danny a start in the business. Danny's father was involved in delivering canisters of bottled gas around the countryside. He was about the same age as Barney McCarthy but he looked a different generation.

They drove the two miles through narrow roads with high hedges to where Danny had been born. Ria looked around her, pleased to know his past and the place that had made him. But Danny hardly looked out at all.

'Did you have friends living in these places we pass by?'

'I knew them, yes,' Danny said. 'I went to school with them.'

'And will we meet them?' she wanted to know.

'They've all gone away, nearly everyone emigrated,' he said.

His mother seemed old too, much older than Ria had expected. They had ham and tomatoes, shop bread and a packet of chocolate biscuits. They were not really sure if they could come to Dublin for the wedding, it was a long way and there might be work here that would be hard to get away from.

It was obvious that this was not so. Ria protested, 'It would be wonderful to have you there for such a big day. We're going to have the reception in Tara Road and you'll see the new house.'

'We're not great people for parties,' Danny's mother said.

'But this is family,' Ria begged.

'You know, it's a bit rattly in the bus and my back isn't what it was.'

Ria looked at Danny. To her surprise he wasn't pushing and coaxing as much as she was. Surely he wanted them there? Didn't he? She waited for him to speak.

'Ah, go on. Come on, can't you. It's only once in a lifetime.' They looked at each other doubtfully. 'Now, I know you didn't go to Rich's wedding because that was in London,' Danny continued.

'But London's much further away than here, and that would have meant planes and boats,' Ria cried.

But the Lynches had been thrown the lifebelt they needed, the excuse not to go to the wedding.

'You see, child . . .' Danny's mother said, clutching Ria's arm. 'You see, if we didn't go to the one wedding it would look like favouring Danny more if we went to the other.'

'And we'll come up and see the house another time,' Danny's father said.

They looked at her hopefully and there was no more to be said.

'Of course you will,' she said soothingly. And they all smiled, Danny as much as anyone.

'Did you not want them to come?' she asked on the long bus journey home.

'Sweetheart, you could see yourself they didn't want to come,' he said.

She felt disappointed in him. He should have persuaded them. But then men were different, everyone knew this.

After only a week at Polly's Gertie told her something most unexpected. She told her that as one of the perks of the job Ria could rent a wedding dress for herself free.

'Are you serious?' Ria's face lit up with joy. She would never have been able to afford anything like this.

'I tell you it straight up . . . Mr McCarthy's instructions,' said Gertie. 'The whole wedding party is to be kitted out, so choose what you like. Go on, Ria, it's what he wants. Take it.'

Danny took a morning suit for himself and his best man. Rosemary chose a slinky silver dress with little pearl buttons. Ria had a few problems convincing her mother and sister that they should pick something for the day.

'Come on, Mam, Hilary. It's free, for heaven's sake. We'll never get an opportunity like this again,' she pleaded. She was nearly there. 'And why doesn't Martin wear a morning suit?' Ria suggested. 'He'd look terrific in it. Go on, Hilary, you know he would.'

That's what did it. Her mother wore a smart grey dress and jacket, with a black feathered hat, Hilary a wine-coloured suit with pale pink lapels and a huge pink hat.

Since there was no outlay on wedding clothes, they paid for a tenor to sing 'Panis Angelicus' *and* a soprano to sing 'Ave Maria'.

It was a very mixed gathering. They invited Orla from the old office and Gertie from Polly's. One of Danny's brothers, Larry, came over from London and was best man. He looked like Danny, same fair hair and lopsided smile, only taller, and spoke now with a London accent.

'Will you be going home to see your parents?' Ria asked.

'Not this time,' Larry said. He hadn't been back to the place where he grew up to see his father and mother for four years.

Ria knew this, but she knew not to comment even by a glance. 'There'll be plenty of other times,' she said.

Larry looked at her with approval. 'That's it, Ria,' he said.

To Ria's huge relief her sister and brother-in-law made no mention at all of anything being a waste of money. The smell of paint had well left Tara Road and the big trestle tables covered with long white tablecloths held chicken salads and ice cream as well as the big wedding cake.

Barney McCarthy was there. He apologised that his wife Mona had not been able to come. She had gone to Lourdes with three friends, it had been long arranged. Gertie had giggled a bit at this information, but Ria had hushed her quickly. Barney had sent two cases of champagne in advance and he stood chatting easily among the forty people who toasted the bride and groom, handsome Danny Lynch and his beautiful bride.

Ria had never thought she could look as well as this with her dark curls swept up into a head-dress and a long veil trailing behind her. The dress had never been worn before, thick embroidery and lace from head to toe, the richest fabric she had ever seen.

Rosemary had been there to advise and suggest throughout. 'Stand very straight, Ria. Hold your shoulders right back. Don't scuttle up the church; when you get in there walk much more slowly.'

'Look, it's not Westminster Abbey,' Ria protested.

'It's your day, every eye in the place is on you, walk like you want to give them something to look at.'

'That's easy if you look like *you*. With me it's different. They'd die if they thought I was taking myself seriously.' Ria felt nervous, as if she was going to look affected, as if she were playing a part. She was so afraid of having them all laugh at her.

'Why shouldn't you take yourself seriously? You look gorgeous. You've got proper make-up on for once. You're a dream, go for it, Ria.' The bridesmaid's enthusiasm was infectious. Ria walked almost regally into the church on the arm of her brother-in-law who was giving her away.

Danny had actually gasped when she came up the aisle.

'I love you so much,' he said as they posed by the wedding cake for pictures. And Ria suddenly felt sorry for whoever else was going to wear this dress when it was cleaned and back out in the agency.

No other bride could ever look as well or be so happy.

They had no honeymoon. Danny went back to looking for work and Ria went back to her job at Polly's. She enjoyed working there and the extraordinarily varied streams of customers they met. There were many more rich people in Dublin than she had known about, and also people who were not rich but who were prepared to spend huge amounts on a wedding day.

Gertie was kind to the brides and didn't fuss them. She helped them choose but didn't steer them towards the most expensive outfits. She encouraged them to be more daring. A wedding was for dressing-up, she said, like a rainbow or fireworks.

'Why is it called Polly's? It's a silly name,' a bride asked Ria one day.

'I think it's to do with Pretty Polly . . . something like that,' Ria explained.

'That was very diplomatic,' Gertie said admiringly afterwards.

'What do you mean? I hadn't a clue why he called it Polly's. Do you know?'

'After his fancy woman. It's hers; he bought it for her. You know that.'

'I didn't, actually. I hardly know him at all. I thought he was a pillar of the Church and all that.'

'Oh yes, he is when he's with the wife. But with Polly Callaghan . . . that's something else.'

'Oh, that's why the cheques are all to P. Callaghan. I see.'

'What did you think it was?'

'I thought it might be a tax thing.'

'But wasn't he at your wedding and all? I thought you were great pals with him.'

'No, Danny sold his house for him, that's all.'

'Well, he told me to give you the job and to organise all the gear for your wedding, so he must think very highly of your Danny.'

'He's not the only one. Danny's out at lunch today with two fellows who are thinking of setting up their own firm. They want him to join them.'

'And will he?'

'I hope not, Gertie, it would be too risky. He has no capital; he'd have to put the house up with a second mortgage as a security or something. It would be very dangerous. I'd love him to go somewhere where he'd be paid.'

'Do you tell him this?' Gertie asked.

'Not really. He's such a dreamer, and he thinks big, and he's been right so often. I stay out of it a lot of the time. I don't want to be the one who is holding him back.'

'You have it all worked out,' Gertie said with admiration. Gertie had a boyfriend, Jack, who drank too much. She had tried to finish with him many times, but she always went back.

'No, I don't really have it worked out,' Ria said. 'I *look* placid, you see, that's why people think I'm fine. Inside I worry a lot.'

'Did you say yes to them?' Ria hoped that Danny couldn't hear the anxiety in her voice.

'No, I didn't. Actually, I didn't say anything. I listened to them instead.'

Danny was good at that. It looked as if he was talking but in fact he was nodding his head and listening.

'And what did you hear?'

'How much they wanted Barney's business and how seriously they thought I could deliver it. They know all about him, like what he eats for breakfast sort of thing. They told me about companies and businesses he has that I never knew about.'

'And what are you going to do?'

'I've done it,' Danny said.

'What on earth did you do?'

'I went to Barney. I told him that anything I had was due to him and that I had this offer from fellows who knew a bit too much about him for his comfort.'

'And what did he say?'

'He thanked me and said he'd come back to me.'

'Danny, aren't you amazing! And when will he come back to you?'

'I don't know. I had to pretend not to mind. Maybe next week, maybe tomorrow. You see, he might advise me to take it or not to. I'll listen to him. He could ring tomorrow. I might be wrong but I feel he'll ring tomorrow.'

Danny was wrong. Barney McCarthy called that night. He had been thinking of setting up a small estate agency business himself. All he really needed was to be prompted to do it. Now he had. Would Danny Lynch manage it for him? On a salary, of course, but part of the profits as well.

Not long after this they were invited to a party at the McCarthys' home. Ria recognised a lot of faces there. Politicians, a man who read the news on television, a well-known golfer.

Barney's wife was a large comfortable-looking woman. Mona moved with ease and confidence amongst the guests. She wore a navy wool dress and had what must have been real pearls around her plump neck. She was probably in her mid-forties, like her husband. Could Barney *really* have a fancy woman called Polly Callaghan? Ria wondered. A settled married man with this comfortable home and grown-up children? It seemed unlikely. Yet Gertie had been very definite about it. Ria tried to imagine what Polly Callaghan looked like, what age she was.

Just at that moment Mona McCarthy came up to her. 'I understand you work at Polly's,' she said pleasantly.

Ria suddenly felt an insane urge to deny it and say she had never heard of Polly. She told Barney McCarthy's wife that it was a most interesting job and that she and Gertie loved getting involved in all the dramas of the people who came in and out.

'Will you continue working after you've had the baby?' Mona asked.

'Oh yes, we need the money and we thought we'd give a foreign student one of the bedsitters and she could look after the baby.'

Mona frowned. 'You don't need the money surely?'

'Well, Mrs McCarthy, your husband has been most generous to Danny but we have a huge house to keep up.'

'When Barney was starting out I went out to work. It was to make money to keep Barney's builder's van on the road. I always regret it. The children grew up without me. You can't have that time back again.'

'I'm sure you're right, we'll certainly talk about it. Maybe the moment I see the baby I won't want to go out to work ever again.'

'I didn't certainly, but I went out after six weeks.'

'Was he very grateful, Mr McCarthy? Did he know how hard it was for you?'

'Grateful? No, I don't think so. Things were different then. We were so anxious to make a go of it, you know, we just did what had to be done.'

She was nice, this woman. No airs and graces, and they must have been a little like herself and Danny years ago. How sad that now when they were old he fancied someone else.

She looked across the room. Danny was at the centre of a little circle telling them some funny story.

Danny's parents could never have been guests in a house like this. Barney McCarthy when he was growing up would not have been in places of this grandeur. Perhaps he saw in Danny some of the same push and drive that he had in his youth, and that was why he was encouraging him. In years to come they might be entertaining at Tara Road and everyone would know that Danny had another lady somewhere.

She gave a little shiver. Nobody knew what the future had in store.

'What does she look like, this Polly?' Ria asked Gertie.

'Mid-thirties, I imagine. Red hair, very smart, keeps herself well. She comes in about once a month. You'll like her, she's really nice.'

'I don't think I will like her. I liked the wife.'

'But she's old the wife, isn't she, I mean really old?'

'I suppose she's about the same age as her husband. She went out to work, you know, so that he could afford a van.'

Gertie shrugged. 'That's life,' she said. 'It's hard on old Polly too at Christmas-time and Sunday lunches, he doing the family man bit. I suppose I should be congratulating myself that at least my Jack is single. He may not be much else but single he is.'

Gertie was back with Jack again. He was meant to be seriously off the drink this time but nobody was holding their breath.

Barney McCarthy was looking at some land in Galway and he needed Danny to go with him. Barney drove fast and they crossed the country quickly.

A table had been booked in advance and waiting for them was an attractive woman in a cream-coloured suit.

'This is Polly Callaghan.' Barney gave her a kiss on the cheek and introduced her to Danny.

Danny swallowed. He had heard about her from Ria. He hadn't expected her to be so glamorous.

'How do you do,' he said.

'The boy wonder, I'm told,' she smiled at him.

'No, just born lucky.'

'Was it Napoleon who said he wanted generals that were lucky?' she asked.

'He was bloody right if that's what he said. Now, what drinks?'

'Diet Coke, please,' Danny said.

'No vices at all?' she asked.

'I want to keep a clear head if I'm to work out how much apartments would go for in the area.'

'You weren't born lucky,' Polly Callaghan said. 'You were born sharp, that's much better.'

'And did they have the same room?' Ria asked.

'I don't know, I didn't check.'

'But, you know, were they lovey-dovey?' she was eager to know.

'Not so you'd notice. They were more like a married couple really. They acted as if they knew each other very well.'

'Poor Mona, I wonder does she know,' Ria said.

'Poor Mona, as you call her, probably doesn't give a damn. Hasn't she a palace of a house and everything she wants?'

'She may want not to share him with a mistress.'

'I liked Polly Callaghan, actually. She was nice.'

'I'm sure,' said Ria, a little sourly.

Polly came into the shop next day. 'I met your husband in Galway, did he tell you?'

'No, Mrs Callaghan, he didn't.' For some reason Ria lied.

Polly seemed pleased, she nodded approvingly. 'Discreet as well as everything else, or maybe you are. Anyway he's a bright lad.'

'He is indeed.' Ria smiled proudly.

Polly looked at Gertie carefully. 'What happened to your face, Gertie? That's a terrible bruise.'

'I know, Mrs Callaghan. Didn't I have a fall off my bicycle. I hoped it wasn't too noticeable.'

'Did you have to have a stitch?'

'Two, but it's nothing. Will I get you a cup of coffee?'

'Please.' Polly looked after Gertie as she went upstairs for the coffee tray. 'Are you two friends, Ria?'

'Yes, yes indeed.'

'Then talk her out of that lout she's involved with. He did that to her, you know.'

'Oh, he couldn't have . . .' Ria was shocked.

'Well he did it before, that's why she wears her hair long to hide it. He'll kill her in the end. But she won't be told, not by me anyway. She thinks I'm an interfering old bat. She might listen to you.'

'Where's *Mister* Callaghan?' Ria asked Gertie when Polly had left the shop.

'There never was one, it's only a courtesy title. Did she tell you that Jack did this to me?'

'Yes. How do you know?'

'Because I see it in your face. And she's always on at me to get rid of him.'

'But you can't go back to him if he hit you.'

'He doesn't mean it. He's so sorry, you have no idea.'

'Did he just come in and punch you in the face?'

'No, it wasn't like that. It was an argument, he lost his temper. He didn't mean it.'

'You can't take him back.'

'Look, everyone in the world's given up on Jack, I'm not going to.'

'But you can see why everyone in the world's given up.'

'I tell you, he cried like a baby he was so ashamed. He said he didn't remember picking up the chair.'

'He hit you with a chair? Jesus, Mary and Joseph.'

'Don't start, Ria. Please don't start. I've had my mother and my friends and Polly Callaghan. Not you as well.'

Just then Rosemary came in to look at wedding hats and the matter had to be dropped. Rosemary had been invited to a society wedding, she said. It was now seriously time to get a man. She wanted a hat that would take every eye in the place away from the bride.

'Poor bride,' said Ria.

'It's a jungle out there,' said Rosemary.

The baby was due in the first week of October.

'That will be Libra, that's a good star sign. It's got to do with being balanced,' Gertie said.

'You don't believe all of that, do you?'

'Of course I do.'

Ria laughed. 'You're as bad as my sister, Hilary. She and her friends spent a fortune on some woman in a caravan, they believed every word out of her.'

'Oh, where is she? Let's go to her.'

'I will in my foot go to her.'

'She might tell you if it's going to be a girl or a boy.'

'Stop it. I don't want to know that badly.'

'Ah, come on. And we'll get Rosemary to come too. What'll she say?'

'She'll tell me that I'm pregnant, she'll see that from my stomach. That you're involved with a fellow who can't keep his fists to himself; she'll see that from your face. And that Rosemary's going to marry a rich man, it's written all over her. And we'll have given her good money for that.'

'*Please*,' Gertie said. 'It'll be a laugh.'

Mrs Connor had a thin, haunted face. She did not look like someone who was being handed fistfuls of fivers and tenners by foolish women in exchange for a bit of news about the future. She looked like someone who had seen too much. Maybe that was all part of the mystique, Ria thought, as she sat down and stretched out her hand.

The baby would be a girl, a healthy girl, followed some years later by a boy.

'Aren't there going to be three? I have three little lines here,' Ria asked.

'No, one of them isn't a real child-line. It could be a miscarriage, I don't know.'

'And my husband's business, is it going to do well?'

'I'd have to see his hand for that. Your own business will do well, I can see there's a lot of travel, across the sea. Yes, a lot of travel.'

Ria giggled to herself. It was twenty pounds wasted, and the baby would probably be a boy. She wondered how the others had got on.

'Well, Gertie, what did she tell you?'

'Not much, you were right. She was no good really.'

Rosemary and Ria looked at each other. Rosemary was aware of Jack and his lifestyle by now.

'I expect she told you to walk out on your current dark stranger,' Rosemary said.

'Don't be so cruel, Rosemary, she did *not* say that.' Gertie's voice sounded shaky.

'Listen, I didn't mean it,' Rosemary said.

There was a silence.

'And what about you, Rosemary?' Ria wanted to break the tension.

'A load of old nonsense, nothing I wanted to know at all.'

'No husband?'

'No, but a whole rake of other problems. You don't want to be bothered with it.' She fell silent again and concentrated on driving the car. As an outing it had not been a success.

'I told you we were mad to go,' Ria said.

The others said nothing at all.

Barney McCarthy was a frequent visitor to Tara Road. Ria learned that he had two married daughters who lived in big modern houses out near the sea. Barney said that neither house had a tenth of the character that this one had. But the girls had insisted. They wanted places that had never heard of damp. They got no pleasure from going to auctions and sales and finding treasures. They just liked to accept delivery of brand-new suites of furniture, fitted kitchens, built-in bedroom cupboards. He spoke with an air of resignation, it was simply the way people were.

'It sounds as if he pays for it all,' Ria suggested to Danny.

'You can be sure he does, those two guys aren't lighting any fires anywhere – getting married to rich women, that's the only energy they used up.'

'Are they nice?'

'Not really, anyway not to me. And why should they be? They're not in business with him like I am. They resent me like hell.'

'Don't you mind?'

Danny shrugged.

'Why should I mind? Listen, Barney's got us a perfect Victorian brass fender from an old house his people are demolishing, and proper fire-irons. He says they're just right, the genuine article; the fender would cost two hundred pounds at a sale.'

'And why do we get them for nothing?' Ria asked.

'Because to everyone else they're just junk from a house. They'd go on a scrap pile. We really are getting that front room into shape.'

Danny was right. It was unrecognisable now. Ria often wondered what would happen if old Sean came back and saw what they had done to his shabby old storeroom. They hadn't got the carpet of Danny's dreams yet, though they kept looking, but they *had* found what they thought was the perfect table. It was called a 'mahogany tripodular breakfast table' in the catalogue. That meant it had three feet, they realised; it was exactly right for this room. They discussed it for ages. Was it too small, should they go for a real, *proper* dining table? But four could sit around it easily and even six at a pinch. They would be entertaining more as time went on.

Ria said that she had lost all contact with what was real and what was fantasy. 'I never saw ourselves as owning anything like this, Danny.' Her arms swept in the whole house. 'I never thought we'd have a front room like this in a million years. How do I know whether we might not end up with a dining table for twelve and a butler.'

They laughed and hugged each other.

Danny Lynch from the broken-down cottage in the back of beyond, and Ria Johnson from the corner house in the big shabby estate were not only living like gentry in a big Tara Road mansion, they were actually debating what style of dining table to buy.

The day the round table was delivered they brought up two kitchen chairs and a bowl of flowers and sat across from each other holding hands. It was a warm evening, their hall door was open and when Barney McCarthy called he stood for a few moments looking in at them, happy and excited.

'You do my heart good, the pair of you,' he said.

And Ria realised how his two sons-in-law must indeed hate Danny, the favoured one, in many ways the heir apparent.

Barney said that Danny and Ria needed a car. They began to look at the ads for second-hand motors. 'I meant a company car,' he said. And they got a new one.

'I'm really afraid to let Hilary see this,' Ria said, patting the new upholstery.

'Let me think . . . she'll say that the depreciation starts the moment you put it on the road,' Danny guessed.

'And my mother would say there was a car like this in *Coronation Street* or something.' Ria laughed. 'I wonder what *your* parents would say if they saw it?'

Danny thought for moment. 'It would worry them. It would be too much. They'd have to put coats on and take the dog for a walk.' He sounded sad but accepting that this was the way things would always be.

'They'll become more joyful in time. We won't give up on them,' Ria said. She thought she sounded a bit like Gertie, who despite everything was not going to give up on Jack. She was actually wearing his ring now and they would marry soon. That would give him confidence, she said.

They were invited to Sunday lunch at the McCarthys. Not a big party this time, just the four of them. Barney and Danny talked buildings and property all the time. Mona and Ria talked about the baby.

'I thought about your advice, and I think I am going to stay at home and look after the baby,' Ria said.

'Will you be able to rely on grandmothers for a bit of help?'

'Not really. My mother goes out to work and Danny's parents are miles down the country.'

'But they'll come up to see the child?'

'I hope so. They're very quiet you know, not like Danny.'

Mona nodded as if she understood very well. 'They'll mellow when the baby arrives.'

'Did that happen with you too?' You could ask Mona McCarthy anything, and she never minded talking about their humble origins.

'Yes, you see Barney was very different to the rest of his family. I think his parents didn't understand why he pushed himself so hard. They didn't do much; his father just made tea in the builder's yard all his life. But they loved it when we brought the children round at a weekend. I used to be tired and could have done without it. They never knew why Barney worked so hard and they couldn't understand his head for business. But it's different when it comes to grandchildren. Maybe it will be the same in their case.'

Ria wished this kind woman didn't have the well-groomed Polly Callaghan as a rival. For the hundredth time she wondered whether Mona McCarthy knew about the situation. Almost everyone else in Dublin did.

Danny had to go to London with Barney. Ria drove him to the airport. Just as she kissed him goodbye she saw the smart figure of Polly Callaghan get out of a taxi. Ria deliberately looked the other way.

But Polly had no such niceties; she came straight over. 'So this is the new car. Very nice too.'

'Oh hallo, Mrs Callaghan. Danny, I'm not meant to park here, I should move off. Anyway I should be at work.'

'I'll keep an eye on him for you in London. I won't let him get distracted by any little glamour-puss over there.'

'Thanks,' Ria gulped.

'Come on, Danny. The great man has the tickets, he'll start to fuss in a moment.' They were gone.

Ria thought of Mona McCarthy and how she had taken Barney's children every weekend to see their grandparents even though she was tired from working all week.

Life was hard on people.

Ria gave up work a week before the baby was due. They were all very supportive, these people she had not even known a year ago. Barney McCarthy said that Danny must be around Dublin, not touring the country so that he would be nearby for the birth. Barney's wife Mona said that they shouldn't waste money buying cots and prams. She had kept plenty for grandchildren; it was just that her own daughters hadn't provided her with any yet.

Barney's mistress Polly Callaghan said that Ria must know there would always be a part-time job for her when and if she wanted to come back, and gave her an outlandish pink-and-black bed-jacket to wear in hospital.

Rosemary, who had been promoted to run a bigger branch of the printing company, came to see her from time to time.

'I'm just no good at all this deep breathing and waters breaking and everything,' Rosemary apologised. 'I've no experience of it.'

'Nor I,' Ria said ruefully. 'I've never had anything to do with it either, and I'm the one who's going to have to go through with it.'

'Ah well,' Rosemary wagged her finger as if to say that we all knew why. 'Does Danny go to these prenatal classes with you? I can't imagine him . . .'

'Yes, he's as good as gold, it's idiotic really, but very exciting all the same; he loves it in a way.'

'Of course he does, and he'll love you too again when you get your figure back.' Rosemary was wearing her very slim-fitting trouser suit and looked like a tall elegant reed. She meant it to be reassuring, Ria thought, but because she felt like a tank herself it was unsettling.

As were the visits from pretty little Orla from the big estate agency, that would have been greatly frowned on had her bosses known of them. And Ria's mother came too, full of advice and warnings.

The only one who didn't come was Hilary. She was so envious of Tara Road that it pained her to come inside the door and see the renovations. Ria had tried to involve her in the whole business of looking for bargains at auctions, but that didn't work either. Hilary became so discontented at the size and scope of her own house compared to Ria's that the outings would end in disaster. The wonderful day when they bought the huge sideboard was almost ruined because of Hilary's tantrum.

'It's so unfair,' she said. 'Just because you have a great big empty room, you can buy great furniture dirt cheap. It's only because nobody else has these mansions that nobody wants it.'

'Well, isn't that our good luck?' Ria was stung.

'No, it's the system – you're going to get that sideboard for nothing . . .'

'Shush, Hilary, it's coming up in a minute. I have to concentrate. Danny says we can go to three hundred pounds – it's worth eight hundred, he thinks.'

'You're going to pay three *hundred* pounds for one piece of furniture for a parlour you don't even use? You're completely mad.'

'Hilary, *please*, people are looking at us.'

'And so well they might be looking at us, that thing could be crawling with woodworm.'

'It's not, I checked.'

'It's daft this, believe me.'

The bidding had started. Nobody was interested. One dealer that Ria knew by sight was raising it slowly against a man who ran a second-hand furniture shop. But they would both have the same problem unloading it. Whose house would have room for it?

'A hundred and fifty.' Ria's voice was clear and strong.

The others stayed in for a minute or two and then dropped out. She had the Victorian serving table, as it was described, for one hundred and eighty pounds.

'Now! Wasn't that marvellous?' Ria said, but the dead, disappointed face of her sister gave no answering flicker.

'Look, Hilary, I just saved a hundred and twenty pounds, why don't we celebrate? Isn't there something you'd like – you and Martin? Go on, we'll bid for that if there is.'

'No thank you.' The voice was stiff.

Ria thought of the huge celebration there would be in Tara Road when she told Danny the good news about the sideboard. She couldn't bear to think of her sister going back to that pokey little house, to that sad, joyless Martin. But she knew there was nothing she could do. She would have liked to stay, and with the money she had saved maybe spend fifty pounds on some nice glass. There were a couple of decanters that might go cheaply. But the mockery would be too great. Hilary would remind her that they were people who had had tomato ketchup and a bottle of Chef mayonnaise on their sideboard when they were young. Not a ship's decanter. It would take the joy out of it.

'Let's go then, Hilary,' she had said.

And since then Hilary had not been around to the house at all. It was childish and hurtful, but Ria felt that she had been given so much she could afford to be forgiving and tolerant. She wanted to see her sister and talk to her the way they used to before all this money and style got in the way.

Danny was working late in the office, there were still five days to go before the baby. Ria decided she would drive to see Hilary. She didn't care what snide remarks would be made by her sister about the smart car. She wanted to talk to her.

Martin was out; he was at a residents' meeting where they were organising a protest. Hilary looked tired and discontented.

'Oh it's you,' she said when she saw Ria. Her eye was drawn to the car at the gate. 'Hope that will still have tyres on it when you leave,' she added.

'Hilary, can I come in?'

'Sure.'

'You and I didn't have a fight about anything, did we?'

'What are you going on about?'

'Well, it's just that you never come and see me. I ask you so often it's embarrassing. You're not there when I go to Mam. Not one word of good wishes over all this. We used to be pals. What happened?'

Hilary's face was mutinous like a child. 'You don't need pals any more.'

Ria was not going to let this go. 'Like hell I don't need a pal. I'm scared stiff of having the baby in the first place. People say it's terrifying and that no one admits it. I'm worried that I mightn't be able to look after it properly and I'm afraid that Danny's taken on too much and that we'll lose everything. At times I'm afraid he'll stop loving me if I start whingeing about things, and you *dare* to tell me I don't need a pal.'

Things changed then. Hilary's frown had gone. 'I'll put on the kettle,' she said.

Orla called round to Tara Road. One of the bedsitter tenants explained that both the Lynches were out. Danny was probably at his office. Ria had taken the car somewhere. Orla thought she would call on Danny at his office. She had been drinking since she left work; she didn't feel like going home yet. And Danny might like to go for a pint. And he was extraordinarily attractive.

Nora Johnson read the letter for the third time. They were selling the shop where she worked. There were some expressions of regret. And explanations of the changing needs of consumers. But the bottom line was that, come the beginning of November, Nora Johnson was going to have no job.

Rosemary smiled at the man across the table. He was a big customer at the print shop. He had asked her out many times. Tonight was the first time she had said yes and they were having dinner in a very expensive restaurant. They were doing a colour brochure for him. It was for a charity heavily supported by businessmen. It would be a good point of contact. Others might see and admire their work. Rosemary had spent a lot of time and trouble making sure that the finished product would be right.

'And do you have the full list of your sponsors so that we can set them out for you with some suitable artwork?'

'I have them back at my hotel,' he said.

'But you don't have a hotel room,' Rosemary said. 'You *live* in Dublin.'

'That's right.' He had an easy, confident smile. 'But tonight I have a hotel room.' He raised his glass at her.

Rosemary raised her glass back. 'What an extravagant gesture,' she said.

'You're worth only the very best,' he said.

'I meant extravagant not to have checked first whether the room would be called on.'

He laughed at what he thought was her grudging admiration. 'You know, I had this premonition that you would come to dinner with me and end the evening with a drink back at the hotel.'

'And your premonition was exactly half right. Thank you for a delightful dinner.' She stood up ready to leave.

He was genuinely amazed. 'What makes you come on like this all promises and teasing and then a bucket of cold water?'

Rosemary spoke clearly. She could be heard at the nearby tables. 'There were no promises and no teasings. There was an invitation to dinner to discuss business, which was accepted. There was no question of going to your hotel room. We don't need business that badly.'

She walked head high from the restaurant, with all the confidence that being twenty-three, blonde and beautiful brings with it.

'I didn't mean to be stand-offish,' Hilary was saying. 'It's just that you have everything, Ria, really everything . . . a fellow like a film star . . . Mam says he's too good-looking . . .'

'What does Mam know about men?'

'*And* you've got that house and the flash car outside the door here and you go to places and meet celebrities. How was I to know that you might want someone like me around . . . ?'

As she was about to answer that, Ria got the dart of pain that she knew was waiting for her some time next week. The baby was on the way.

Gertie had been out to get fish and chips. She laid the package on the kitchen table while she went to get the plates that were warming in the bottom of the oven. She had a tray with tomato ketchup, knives, forks and napkins ready.

She had not understood Jack's humour. With his arm he swept the paper-wrapped parcel off the table. 'You're only a slut,' he shouted at her. 'You're not fit for any decent man's house. A woman who can't put dinner on the table but has to go out to the chipper to buy it.'

'Oh no. Jack, please, *please*,' Gertie cried.

He had picked up what was nearest to hand. As ill luck would have it, it was a heavy, long-handled scrubbing brush.

When Martin Moran came back from the residents' association a young boy from next door was waiting with the news. 'There's a baby being born,' he said excitedly. 'Your missus didn't know how to drive the car so my da drove them to the hospital. You missed all the fun.'

They couldn't find Danny. He wasn't at Tara Road. He wasn't at the office. Ria gave Hilary Barney McCarthy's telephone number in case he might be there but his wife Mona said that he wasn't at home, and she hadn't seen Danny at all. He had wanted to be at the hospital. They had been through it all so many times.

Ria wanted him beside her now. '*Danny!*' she screamed with her eyes closed. He had said so often that this was *their* baby, he would be there for the birth. Where in God's name was he?

Danny had been about to leave his office when Orla King arrived. Pretty as a picture but definitely slurring her words. He didn't need a conversation with her just now. But Danny Lynch was never rude.

'Would you like to go to the pub for the one?' Orla asked.

'No, sweetheart. I'm bushed,' he said.

'A pub livens you up. Come on, please.'

'You'll have to forgive me tonight, Orla.'

'What night then?' she asked. She ran her tongue over her lips as she smiled at him.

He could either go at once, risking a scene and possibly leaving unfinished business, or he could offer her a drink from the bottle of brandy he kept for Barney. 'A small brandy then, Orla. But just three minutes to drink it then we both have to go.'

She had won, she thought. She sat on his desk with her legs crossed as Danny went to the cupboard and found the bottle. Just then the phone rang.

'Oh leave it, Danny. It's only work,' Orla pleaded.

'Not this time of night,' he said, picking it up.

'Danny, are you alone? This is Polly Callaghan. It's urgent.'

'Not really, no.'

'Can you be alone?'

'It will take a few minutes.'

'I haven't time ... Can you just listen?'

'Of course.'

'Have you your car?'

'No.'

'Right, Barney's here. He has chest pains. I can't call the cardiac ambulance to come here, I want to call it to your house.'

'Yes, of course.'

'But it's a question of my getting him there.'

'I'll get a taxi to you. I'll make the other call first.'

At this stage the petulant voice of Orla could be heard. '*Dan–ny*, come off the phone, come over here.'

'And you'll get rid of whatever companion you have with you?'

'Yes.' He was clipped.

And even more clipped dealing with Orla. 'I'm sorry, Orla sweetheart. Brandy's over ... I have an emergency.'

'You don't call me sweetheart and then ask me to leave,' she began.

She found herself propelled towards the door, while Danny grabbed his jacket and phoned an ambulance all at the same time.

She heard him give the Tara Road address. 'Who's sick? Is it the baby arriving?' she asked, frightened by his intensity.

'Goodbye, Orla,' he said, and she saw him running down the street to hail a taxi.

Barney was a very grey shade of white. He lay in a chair beside the bed. Polly had made unsuccessful attempts to dress him.

'Don't worry about the tie,' Danny barked. 'Go down and tell the taxi man to come up . . . to help me get him down the stairs.'

Polly hesitated for a second. 'You know the way Barney hates anyone knowing his business.'

'This is a taxi man, for Christ's sake, Polly. Not MI5. Barney'd want to get there quicker.'

Barney spoke with his hand firmly holding his chest. 'Don't talk about me as if I'm not here, for Christ's sake. Yes, get the taxi man, Polly, quick as you can.' To Danny he spoke gently. 'Thank you for getting here, thank you for sorting it out.'

'You're going to be fine.' Danny supported the older man easily and warmly in a way he would never have been able to hold his own father.

'You'll look after everything for me, the way it should be?'

'You'll be doing it yourself in forty-eight hours,' Danny said.

'But just in case . . .'

'Just in case, then. Yes, I will.' Danny spoke briskly, knowing that was what was wanted.

At that moment the taxi man arrived. If he recognised the face of Barney McCarthy he gave no sign. Instead he got down to the job of easing a heavy man with heart pains down the narrow stairs of an expensive apartment block to take him to another address from which the ambulance would collect him. If he had worked out the situation he had seen too much and been too long in the taxi game to let on anything at all.

Hilary waited in the big shabby room outside the labour ward. From time to time she made further unsuccessful stabs at finding Danny. There was no reply from her mother's house when Hilary rang. She didn't know her mother was sitting there with the letter telling her that her working life was over.

Nora Johnson was too despondent to answer the telephone until she had pulled herself together and decided what she would do next.

'*Danny!*' That was the scream before the baby's head appeared. The sister was speaking and she could hardly hear. 'All right, Ria. It's over, you have a beautiful little baby girl. She's perfect.'

Ria felt more tired than she had ever been. Danny had not been here to see his daughter born. The fortune-teller had been right, it *was* a little girl.

Orla King felt that she was now losing her mind because of drink. Not only did the guilt of trying to seduce a man on the night that his wife was having their first baby hang heavily on her, but the subsequent confusion in her brain worried her. She knew that Ria must have been at home because she heard Danny call the ambulance to Tara Road. But then she heard from everyone else that Ria was at her sister's house and they had to get a neighbour to drive Ria's car to the hospital as Hilary couldn't drive. Orla knew now that she was hallucinating and having memory failure. She went to her first Alcoholics Anonymous meeting.

And on the first night she met a man called Colm Barry. He was single, handsome and worked in the bank. Colm had dark curly hair and dark sad eyes.

'You don't look like a banker,' Orla said to him.

'I don't feel like a bank clerk, I'd rather be a chef.'

'I don't feel like being a typist in an estate agency, I'd like to be a model or a singer,' Orla said.

'There's no reason why we shouldn't be these things, is there?' Colm asked with a smile.

Orla didn't know whether he was making fun of her or being nice, but she didn't mind. He was going to make these meetings bearable.

On that night when Gertie saw Jack raising the great scrubbing brush that might have split her head, she picked up a knife and stuck it straight into his arm. They both watched helplessly and amazed as the blood poured on to the packet of fish and chips he had flung to the floor. Then she took off her engagement ring, laid it on the table, got her coat and walked out of the house. From a phone box at the corner of the road, she rang the police and told them what she had done. In the emergency ward Jack assured everyone that it had been purely domestic and that nobody was making any accusation against anyone whatsoever.

For a very long time Gertie refused to see Jack, and then, to everyone's disappointment, she agreed to meet him just once. Jack had been put off the road for drunken driving and consequently sacked from his job. Gertie found a chastened and sober man. They talked and she remembered why she loved him. They asked two strangers to be their witnesses and they were married in a cold church at eight o'clock one morning.

Gertie left Polly's just before Polly Callaghan sacked her. She was absent too often; it was no longer reasonable to expect them to keep her on the payroll. Jack had bouts of sobriety, never lasting very long. Gertie grew white-faced and anxious. She got a job in a launderette just round the corner from Tara Road where there was a flat upstairs. It was a living but only a bare living.

Gertie's own mother washed her hands of the whole situation. She said that she just hoped Gertie had good friends who would tide her over when times got really bad. Gertie had one friend who tided her over a great deal: Ria Lynch.

Hilary Moran never fully forgave Danny Lynch for not being with his wife that night. Oh, she had heard that there were explanations and confidences that had to be kept, and Ria certainly bore no grudge. But nobody else had heard the great wailing as Ria had waited for him to come to her during the long hours of labour. It made her feel even more strongly that she had got a good man in Martin. He might never reach the dizzy heights of Danny Lynch; he was certainly not as easy on the eye. But you could rely on him. He would always be there. And when Hilary had a child Martin would not be missing. She hoped that they would have children. The fortune-teller had been wrong about living amid trees. She might be wrong about them having no children as well.

Barney McCarthy recovered from his heart attack. Everyone said that he had been so fortunate to have it come upon him when he was with quick-witted, resourceful Danny Lynch who wasted no time in getting him to hospital. He had to take things a little more easily these days.

He had wanted to involve Danny more in his business, but met with unexpected resistance from his family. Perfectly natural resentment, Barney thought to himself. They obviously feared that Danny was getting too close to him. He would have to be more diplomatic. Show them that he was not going outside the family.

Sometimes he felt that his daughters seemed sharper with him, less loving. Less uncritically supportive. But Barney did not allow himself the luxury of brooding about people's moods. These girls owed him everything. He had slaved long hours and years to get them their superior education and degrees. Even if they had heard something about Polly Callaghan they were unlikely to rock the boat. They knew that he would not leave Mona, that the household would continue undisturbed. He enjoyed his dealings with Danny Lynch, but for everyone's sake he just had to make sure they were less public as time went on.

For Nora Johnson the day that her granddaughter was born was also the date that she had been told her job was over. She made a decision not to tell any of the family about it, not until she had tried to find another position at any rate. But it wasn't easy, and in the first weeks of Annie Lynch's life her grandmother was facing rejection after rejection. There were few openings for a woman of fifty-one with no qualifications.

Wearily and without much hope she went for an interview as a carer-companion to an elderly lady who lived in a big house in Tara Road which had a purpose-built little granny cottage in the grounds. It turned out extremely well. They took to each other on sight. When it became known that Nora had a daughter living in Tara Road the old lady's family suggested that maybe the post should be a residential one. Nora could sell her own house, have a nest egg and live close to her daughter Ria.

Ah, but what about her security and her future? Nora had wondered. Where would she live when, in the fullness of time, the old lady she was looking after had left this earth? It was arranged that she should have first refusal on buying the little house when that day came.

Polly Callaghan remembered the night that Annie was born because it was the night she thought she was going to lose Barney for ever. She had loved him without pausing to count the cost for twelve years, since she was twenty-five years old. Not once did she stop and say that it was folly to love a man who would never be free.

She did not weigh up the very likely possibility of finding herself a single man who would be delighted to provide her with a home and family. Polly Callaghan, glamorous, articulate and successful, would have been the object of interest to many a man.

But the thought had not crossed her mind. She knew she had had a lucky escape that night. Barney had only just been got to Intensive Care in time, but he had agreed to change his lifestyle, give up the cigarettes and brandy. Walk more, behave like he might actually be mortal instead of invincible. Polly had been urging this for years, while his wife had provided comfort food and no such structure.

Now at last he had got the warning that he needed to jolt him into action. Barney McCarthy was only in his forties; he had years of living ahead of him.

Polly had been grateful to Danny Lynch for his speedy response. Grateful yet disappointed in him. He obviously had a girl with him in his office when she had called that night. Polly had heard her giggling. Polly was not one to sit in judgement on a man having an affair outside marriage. But she thought that Danny was fairly young to have started. *And* it was, after all, a night when you might have expected him to be with his wife who was having their first baby. Still, Polly was philosophical. That's men.

Rosemary remembered very well the time that Annie Lynch was born. It had been something of a turning-point in her life. First there was that loutish man who had booked a hotel bedroom and had assumed that she was going to share it. And this was the time she felt unexpectedly attracted to a man called Colm Barry who worked in the bank near where she worked. He had always been helpful and encouraging about how she should handle her business. Unlike some people in that branch he had never urged caution and restraint, which was the immediate response of others in the bank. He seemed even a little disenchanted with the whole idea of the bank. He was just genuinely helpful, and seemed admiring of Rosemary's skills in expanding the business. He must be about thirty, a tall man with black curly hair which he wore a little long on his collar. The bank didn't approve, he said with some satisfaction.

'Does it bother you what the bank thinks?' Rosemary asked.

'Not a bit. Does it bother *you* what other people think?' he asked in return.

'It has to a bit at work because if they see a youngish woman they're inclined to ask to speak to a man. Still! In this day and age I have to try and give off some kind of vibes of confidence I suppose. So in *that* way it bothers me. Not about other things though.'

He was easy to talk to. Some men had that way of listening to you and looking at you, men who really liked women. Men like Danny Lynch. Colm had sorrowful eyes, Rosemary thought. But she really liked him. Why should women always wait to be asked out? She invited Colm Barry to have dinner with her.

'I'd love to,' he said. 'But sadly I'm going to a meeting tonight.'

'Come on, Colm. The bank will survive without your being at one meeting,' she said.

'No, it's AA,' he said.

'Really, what kind of car do you have?' she asked.

'No, the other lot, Alcoholics,' he said simply.

'Oops.'

'No, don't worry. Think me lucky that I do go, that I get the support that's there. That's why I'm able to refuse a beautiful blonde like you.'

'For tonight,' she said with a big smile. 'There'll be another night, won't there?'

'Yes, of course there could be another night. But now that you know the score you might be a little less interested in having dinner with me.' He was wry but not apologetic, just preparing himself for a change in attitude. Rosemary paused long enough for Colm to feel that he could speak again and end things before they had begun. 'We both know that you must find someone who is ... let's say substantial. Don't waste time on a loser like a drinky bank clerk.'

'You're very cynical,' Rosemary said.

'And very realistic. I'll watch you with interest.'

'I'll watch you with interest too,' she said.

Mona McCarthy always remembered where she was when she heard that Barney had been taken into Intensive Care. She was in the attic rooting out a children's cot for young Ria Lynch. She had just got an anxious phone call from Ria's sister saying that the girl had gone into labour and they were looking for Danny. Then half an hour later Danny had rung to say that Barney was absolutely fine but they had thought it wise to err on the side of caution and have an ECG. And she could come into the hospital whenever she liked; he was sending a car for her straight away.

'Where did it happen? Is it bad?' Mona asked.

Danny was calm and soothing. 'He was at home with me, in Tara Road, we were working all evening. It's fine, Mona. Believe me, he's in great shape, telling you not to worry. You'll see for yourself when you come in.'

She felt better already. He was an amazing boy, Danny, so well able to calm her down while he should be in high panic himself over his wife's labour.

'And Danny, I'm delighted to hear the baby's on the way, how is she?'

'What?'

'Ria's sister brought her in, she ...'

'Oh shit, I don't believe it.' He had hung up.

'Danny?' Mona McCarthy was confused. Hilary had said she couldn't find Danny at Tara Road. Now Danny had said he had been there all evening. It was a mystery.

Whenever Mona McCarthy had been faced with a mystery she reminded herself that she was not a detective and there was probably some explanation. And then she put it out of her mind. She had found this to be a satisfactory way of coping with a few mysteries over the years. And after Barney recovered, she never asked him any details about that night.

Any more than she ever asked him to tell her about where he had dinner when he came home late or how he spent his time in hotels when he travelled. On several occasions she had to side-step conversations with her husband, conversations which looked as if they were heading towards a definition of mysteries and even confrontations. Mona McCarthy was much less simple-minded than most people believed.

Danny Lynch never forgot the frantic rush from one hospital to the other. And the look of reproach in his sister-in-law's face and the sight of his little daughter in the arms of an exhausted and tearful Ria.

He cried into Ria's dark hair and took the baby gingerly into his arms. 'I'll never be able to make it up to you but there *is* a reason.' And of course she understood. He had to do what he did, he hadn't known her time had come.

He had not known it was possible to love a little human being as he loved Annie. He was going to make his little princess a home that was like a palace. Princesses deserve palaces, he said.

'You'd never think we lived in a Republic with all this chat about princesses,' Ria would tease him.

'You know what I mean, it's all like a fairy tale,' Danny would say.

And in so many ways it was.

There was enough business coming in. It meant plenty of hard work but Danny was able for that. Barney was being a little more discreet about his involvement with him.

Ria was wonderful with little Annie. She even put her into the car regularly and drove her down to see her grandparents in the country. Danny's parents seemed very touched by that. His mother knitted the baby silly hats and his father carved her little toys. There had been no knitted hats and carved toys when Danny and his brothers were growing up.

He had a truly beautiful daughter, a house that someone of his education and chances could only have dreamed about. He had a wife who was loving and good to him.

Life had been very good to Danny Lynch.

Ria had never forgotten that Danny was not at her side when the baby was born, but she had heard the story of how Barney McCarthy's life and reputation had been saved. There was no way Danny could have known that the baby would come so early. Ria had very mixed feelings about the way Barney was being protected in his double life. She hated being a party to deceiving the kindly Mona McCarthy.

But all this took very much the back seat compared to her love for the new baby. Ann Hilary Lynch weighed seven pounds one ounce at birth and was adorable. She looked up trustingly at Ria with her huge eyes. She smiled at everyone and they passed her around from one to another, a sea of delighted faces, all of them thinking that they were special to the baby.

And all Ria's fears and worries that she had blurted out to her sister Hilary seemed to have been groundless. She was able to manage her baby, and Danny loved her more and more as time went on. He was a doting father and her heart was full as she saw him take his little daughter by the hand through the big wild garden which they had never tamed. There were too many other things to do and so little time.

She grew up a sunny child in a happy home, her blonde straight hair like her father's falling into her eyes.

There had never been proper pictures of Ria as she grew up. Often she had wished she had snapshots of herself as a toddler, as a ten-year-old, as a teenager. But apart from the occasional picture of a first communion, confirmation and a visit to the zoo her mother had not kept any real record. It would be different for Annie. Everything would be there, from the hospital to her triumphant arrival in Tara Road, her first Christmas at home . . . all the way along the line.

And Ria took pictures of the house too. So that they would all remember the changes, so that Annie would not grow up thinking things had always been luxurious. Ria wanted her to see how she and the house had in a way grown together.

The day before the carpet arrived, and then the day it was in place; the day they finally got the Japanese vase Danny had always known would be right; the huge velvet curtains which Danny had spotted at the windows of a house which was being sold at an executor's sale. They measured them and found they fitted exactly. Danny knew they'd go for nothing, it was always the same when distant relatives were selling up. They just wanted the place cleared quickly; there were massive bargains to be had.

Ria sometimes felt a little guilty about it, but Danny said that was nonsense. Things were only valuable to those who wanted them.

Most of their life was lived in the big warm kitchen downstairs, but Danny and Ria spent some time every day in the drawing room, the room they had created from their dreams. They delighted in finding further little treasures for it. When Danny got a raise in salary they went out and bought something else. The old candlesticks that were transformed into lamps, more glass, a French clock.

There was no sense that this room was kept to impress people. It was not a parlour as Hilary had so scornfully dismissed it. The heavy framed portraits that they bought for the walls were other people's ancestors not their own. But there was no pretence, they were just big pictures of people who had been forgotten by their own. Now they came to rest on Danny and Ria's walls.

Ria did not go back to work. There were so many reasons why it made more sense to be at home. There was always a need to drive someone somewhere, or pick them up. She did one day a week in a charity shop and another morning in the hospital helping to entertain the children who had come with their mothers because there was nobody else to mind them.

Danny's office wasn't far away. Sometimes he liked to come home to lunch, or even to have a cup of coffee and relax. Barney McCarthy came to see him there too. For some reason the two of them didn't meet in hotels as much as they used to. She knew the kind of food he liked to eat nowadays and always gave him a healthy salad and some poached chicken breast.

Ria would leave the men to talk.

Barney McCarthy often said admiringly in her presence, 'You were very lucky in the wife you got, Danny. I hope you appreciate her.'

Danny always said he did, and as the years went by Ria Lynch knew this was true. Not only did her handsome Danny love her; as the years went by he loved her more than ever.

3

Rosemary's mother said that Ria Lynch was as sharp a little madam as you'd meet in a day's walk.

'I don't know why you say that,' Rosemary said. But she knew very well what caused her mother's irritation. Ria was married, well married too. This is what Mrs Ryan wanted for her daughter and she transferred her disappointment to attacking Ria Lynch.

'Well, she came from nothing, from nowhere, a corporation estate. And look at her now, mixing with Barney McCarthy and the wife and living in a big house on Tara Road.' Mrs Ryan sniffed with disapproval.

'Honestly, you'd find fault with anyone, Mother.' Since she was a toddler Rosemary had been told to say Mother not Mam like other girls did. They were people with class, she had been led to believe.

But as she grew up Rosemary realised that there really wasn't much sign of classiness in their lives. It was much more in her mother's mind and dreams, memories of a grander lifestyle when she was young and resentment that her husband had never lived up to her hopes.

Rosemary's father was a salesman who spent more and more time away from a home where he never felt welcome. His two daughters grew up hardly knowing him except through the severe thin-lipped disappointment of their mother who managed to make sure they realised that he had let them all down.

Mrs Ryan had great hopes for her two elegant daughters, and believed that they would marry well and restore her to some kind of position in Dublin society. She was bitterly disappointed when Rosemary's sister, Eileen, announced that she was going to live with a woman from work called Stephanie, and that they were lovers. They were lesbians and there would be no secrecy or glossing anything over. This was the 1980s and not the Dark Ages. Mrs Ryan cried for weeks over it and agonised as to where she had gone wrong. Her eldest daughter was having unnatural sex with a woman. And Rosemary was showing no sign at all of landing the kind of husband who might change everyone's fortunes.

No wonder she resented the good luck of Ria, a successful husband, a house in a part of Dublin that was becoming increasingly elegant, and an entry to the best homes in the city because of the patronage of the McCarthys.

Rosemary had moved into a small flat as soon as she could afford to. Life at home was no fun at all but Rosemary visited her mother every week for a lecture and a harangue about her failure to deliver the goods.

'I'm sure you're sleeping with men,' Mrs Ryan would say. 'A mother knows these things. It's such a foolish way to go on, letting yourself be cheap and easily available. Why should anyone want to marry you if they can get it for free?'

'Mother, don't be ridiculous,' Rosemary said, neither confirming nor denying anything that had been said. There was not a great deal to confirm or deny. Rosemary had slept with very few men, only three in fact. This was more because of her own personality, which was aloof and distant, than from any sense of virtue or innate cunning.

She had enjoyed sex with a young French student and had not enjoyed it with an office colleague. She had been drunk on the two occasions when she had made love with a well-known journalist after Christmas parties, but then so had he been drunk so she didn't imagine it had been very successful.

But she didn't burden her mother with any of these details.

'I saw that Ria coming out of the Shelbourne Hotel as if she owned it the other day,' Mrs Ryan said.

'Why don't you like her, Mother?'

'I didn't say I didn't like her, I just said she played her cards right. That's all.'

'I think she played them accidentally,' Rosemary said thoughtfully. 'Ria had no idea it was all going to turn out for her as well as it did.'

'That kind always know they don't take a step without seeing where it leads. I suppose she was pregnant when she married him.'

'I don't really know, Mother,' Rosemary said wearily.

'Of course you know. Still, she was lucky, he could easily have left her there.'

'They're very happy, Mother.'

'So you say.'

'Would you like to come out and have lunch in Quentin's one day next week, Mother?'

'What for?'

'To cheer you up. We could get dressed up, look at all the famous people there.'

'There's no point, Rosemary. You mean well but who would know us? Who would know what we came from or anything about us? We'd just be two women sitting there. It's all jumped-up people these days, we'd only be on the outside looking in.'

'I have lunch there about once a week. I like it. It's expensive, of course, but then I don't eat lunch any other day so it works out fine.'

'You have lunch there every week and you haven't found a husband yet?'

Rosemary laughed. 'I'm not going there looking for a husband, it's not that kind of a place. But you do see a different world there. Come on. Say yes, you'd enjoy it.'

Her mother agreed. They would go on Wednesday. It would be something to look forward to in a world that held few other pleasures.

In Quentin's Rosemary pointed out to her mother the tucked-away booth where people went when they were being discreet. A government minister and his lady friend often dined there. It was a place where businessmen took someone from a rival organisation if they were going to offer him a job.

'I wonder who's in there today,' her mother said, drawn into the excitement of it all.

'I'll have a peep when I go to the loo,' Rosemary promised.

At a window table she saw Barney McCarthy and Polly Callaghan. They never bothered with a private booth. Their relationship was known to everyone in the business world. She saw the journalist that she had met so spectacularly at two Christmas parties; he was interviewing an author and taking some scrawled notes which he would probably never decipher later. She saw a television personality and pointed him out to her mother who was pleased to note that he was much smaller and more insignificant than he looked on the box.

Eventually she went to the ladies' room, deliberately taking the wrong route so that she could pass the secluded table. You would have to look in carefully to see who was there. With a shock that was like a physical blow Rosemary saw Danny Lynch and Orla King from the office.

'Who was there?' her mother asked when Rosemary returned to the table.

'Nobody at all, two old bankers or something.'

'Jumped-up people,' her mother said.

'Exactly,' said Rosemary.

Ria was anxious to show off the new cappuccino machine to Rosemary.

'It's magic, but I'll still have mine black,' Rosemary said, patting her slim hips.

'You have a will of iron,' Ria said, looking at her friend with admiration. Rosemary, so tall and blonde and groomed, even at the end of a day when everyone else would be flaking. 'Barney McCarthy brought it round, he's so generous you wouldn't believe it.'

'He must think very highly of you.' Rosemary managed to lay a tea towel across her lap just in time to avoid Annie's little sticky fingers getting on to her pale skirt.

'Well, of course Danny nearly kills himself working all the hours God sends.'

'Of course.' Rosemary was grim.

'He's so tired when he gets home he often falls asleep in the chair before I can put his supper on the table for him.'

'Imagine,' Rosemary said.

'Still, it's well worth it, and he loves the work, and you're just the same; you don't mind how many hours you put in to be successful in the end.'

'Ah yes, but I take time off too. I reward myself, go out to smart places as a treat.'

Ria smiled fondly at the armchair where Danny often slept after all the tiring things he had been doing. 'I think after a busy day Danny regards getting back to Number Sixteen Tara Road as a treat. He has everything he wants here.'

'Yes, of course he has,' said Rosemary Ryan.

Hilary told Ria that one of the girls in fourth year was pregnant. A bold strap of fourteen, and she was the heroine of the hour. All the children envied her, and the staff said wasn't it great that she didn't go to England and have an abortion. The girl's mother would bring up the baby as her own so that the fourteen-year-old could return to her studies. Wasn't it very unfair, Hilary said, that some people could have a child quick as look at you, while others in stable marriages who could give a child everything didn't seem to be so lucky.

'I'm not complaining,' Hilary said, even though she rarely did anything but complain. 'But it does seem an odd way for God to have sorted out the whole business of continuing the human race. Wouldn't you think He would have arranged something much more sensible, like people going to an agency and giving proof that they could bring up a child properly, instead of teenagers getting pregnant from gropings in the bicycle sheds.'

'Yes, in a way,' Ria said.

'I don't expect *you* to agree with me. Look at what getting pregnant did for you, a marriage to a fellow like a film star, a house like something out of *Homes and Gardens*...'

'Now hardly that, Hilary,' Ria laughed.

Nora Johnson pushed her granddaughter up and down Tara Road in a pram, getting to know the neighbours and everyone's business. She had settled very well into the compact mews at Number 48A Tara Road. Small, dark, energetic, almost bird-like, she was an authority on nearly everything. Ria was amazed at how much her mother discovered about people.

'You just need to be interested, that's all,' Nora said.

In fact, as Ria knew very well, you just needed to be outrageously inquisitive and direct in your approach. Her mother told her about the Sullivan family in Number 26; he was a dentist, she ran a thrift shop. They had a daughter called Kitty just a year older than Annie, who might be a nice playmate in time. She told Ria about the old people's home at Number 68, St Rita's, where she called from time to time. It did old people a lot of good to see a baby; it made them think there was some continuity in life. Too many of them saw little of their own grandchildren and great-grandchildren.

Nora brought her clothes to Gertie's launderette for the sociability of it, she said. She knew she could use Ria's washing machine but there was a great buzz in a place like that. She said that Jack Brennan should be strung up from a lamppost and Gertie was that extraordinary mixture of half-eejit half-saint for putting up with him. Gertie's little boy John spent most of his time with his grandmother.

She reported that the big house, Number 2 on the corner, was for sale, and people said it might be a restaurant. Imagine having their own restaurant in

Tara Road! Nora hoped it would be one they could all afford, not something fancy, but she doubted it. The place was becoming trendy, she said darkly.

Nora Johnson was soon much in demand as a babysitter, a dog walker and an ironer. She had always loved the smell of clean shirts, she said, and why not turn an interest into a little pocket money?

She seemed to know well in advance who was going to sell, who was going to build. Danny said she was invaluable. His eyes and ears on the road. He had managed to get two sales through his mother-in-law. He called her his secret weapon.

He also pretended a far greater interest in film stars than he really felt. Ria loved to watch him struggling for a name or to remember who had played opposite Grace Kelly in this film or who Lana Turner's leading man was in that one.

'You remind me very much of Audrey Hepburn, Mother-in-law,' he said once to her.

'Nonsense, Danny.' She was brisk.

'No, I mean it. You have the same shaped face, honestly, and long neck, doesn't she, Ria?'

'Well, Mam has a grand swan's neck all right. Hilary and I were always jealous of that,' Ria said.

'That's what I mean, like Audrey Hepburn in *Breakfast at Tiffany's*.' Nora was pleased but she wouldn't show it. Danny Lynch was a professional charmer; he wouldn't get round her. No way would she fall for his patter. But he insisted. He showed her a picture of Audrey Hepburn with her hand under her chin. 'Go on, pose like that and I'll take a snap of you and then you'll see what I mean .. Put your hand under your chin, come on, Holly . . .'

'What are you calling me?'

'Holly Golightly, the part Audrey plays in the film, you look just like her.' He called her Holly from that day on.

Nora Johnson who wouldn't fall for that kind of patter was totally under his spell.

Rosemary went to the bank on Friday mornings. The girls there admired her a lot. Always dressed immaculately, and it seemed as if she were wearing a different outfit each time until you looked carefully. She had three very well-cut jackets and a lot of different-coloured blouses and scarves. That's why it looked different. And she was so much on top of her business. The man who ran the print shop left everything to her. It was Rosemary Ryan who arranged the rates for deposit and the loans for new machinery. It was Rosemary who got the statement for the tax returns, and who tendered successfully for the bank calendar.

Young bank officials looked at her enviously. She was only the same age as they were and look at all the power and responsibility she had managed to get for herself. They thought she sort of mildly fancied Colm Barry, but then that couldn't be possible. Colm was the last man someone like Rosemary Ryan would go for. He had no ambition or sense of survival, even in the bank. He never kept from his boss the fact that he didn't really admire the ethics of the bank and that he went to Alcoholics Anonymous meetings. And these kinds of revelations were not the road to promotion. Rosemary would want a much higher achiever than Colm Barry, even if she did always wait until his window was empty and asked for him if he wasn't there.

Rosemary had all her documentation done before she came to the bank each weekend. As she stood in line that Friday she saw to her amazement Orla King in animated conversation with Colm Barry over the desk. Orla had what Rosemary considered cheap and obvious good looks. Too tight a top, too short a skirt, the heels on her shoes too high. Still, men didn't see anything too flashy in it; they appeared to like it. As Orla was leaving she saw Rosemary and her face lit up. 'Well now, it's a small world. I was only talking about you yesterday,' she said.

Rosemary's face was cold and disapproving but she forced her public smile. Orla must know she had been spotted in the private booth of Quentin's. 'All full of praise I hope?' she said lightly.

'Well yes, praise and puzzlement. Why such a beautiful woman like you isn't married. That was one of the strands.'

'What an extraordinary thing to talk about.' Rosemary was very cold.

Orla didn't seem to notice the tone. 'No, you're quite well known now, even people who don't know you know of you. They were all interested.'

'What very empty lives they must all live,' Rosemary said.

'You know the way people go on, they didn't mean any harm.'

'Oh, I'm certain that's true, why should they?' Her voice was so disdainful that anyone but Orla would have been put off.

'Well, why is it, Rosemary?'

'Probably like you I haven't found the right person yet.' Rosemary hoped her voice wasn't as glacial as it felt from inside.

'Ah yeah but I'm just a fun girl, you're a serious woman.'

'We're both in our twenties, Orla. Hardly over the hill yet.'

'No, but this man said, and honestly he was out for your good, he wasn't putting you down or anything, he said that you'd want to be looking round soon, the millionaires will be looking for younger models, next year's models, if you don't get in there quick.' Orla laughed happily. She meant no insult. In fact, talking to someone as beautiful as Rosemary you could only assume that saying such a thing was a joke and not to be taken seriously.

But Rosemary's face remained cold. That was exactly what Danny Lynch had said to her jokingly only a few days ago at Sunday lunch in Tara Road. Rosemary hadn't minded then but she minded now. She minded very much that he was saying such things about her to Orla King over lunch the previous day.

Orla was heading off for work without a care in the world. 'Cheers, Colm, see you Tuesday night,' she called.

'I gather that you and the lovely Ms King are going out socially,' Rosemary said to Colm.

'Yes, well that's right, sort of . . .' He was vague.

Rosemary realised that it must be at an AA meeting. People would tell you of their own involvement but they never told you who else went to the meetings. She was glad in a way that he had not fallen immediately for the tight sweaters and the skirt stretched across the small round bottom. 'Anyway, it's a very small forest, Dublin, isn't it? We all find out about everyone else sooner or later.' She was only making conversation but she saw a wary look come across his face.

'What do you mean?' he asked.

'I only meant if we were in London or New York we'd never know half the queue in the bank, that's all.'

'Sure. By the way, I'm leaving here at the end of the month.'

'Are you, Colm? Where are they sending you?'

'I'm brave as a lion. I'm leaving the bank altogether,' he said.

'Now that *is* brave. Are there farewell drinks or anything?' She could have bitten off her tongue.

'No, but I'll tell you what there will be. I'm going to open a restaurant in Tara Road. And as soon as I get started I'll send you an invitation to the launch.'

'I'll tell you what I'll do, I'll print the invites for you as a present,' she said.

'It's a done deal,' he said, and they shook hands warmly. He had a lovely smile. What a pity he was such a loser, Rosemary thought. He would have been a very restful man to have teamed up with. But a restaurant in Tara Road? He must be out of his mind. There was no catchment area there, no passing trade. As an enterprise it was doomed before it began.

Danny and Barney McCarthy were going to look at property very near Danny's old home.

'Will we all go together and take Annie to see her grandparents?' Ria suggested.

'No, love. It's not a good idea this time. I'm going to be flat out looking at places, and making notes, meeting local fellows who are all mad to make a quick killing. There's going to be nothing but meetings and more meetings in the hotel.'

'Well, you will go and see them?'

'I might, I might not. You know the way it's more hurtful to go in somewhere for five minutes than not to go at all.'

Ria didn't know. 'You could drive down a couple of hours earlier.'

'I have to go when Barney goes, sweetheart.'

Ria knew not to push it. 'Fine. When the weather gets better I'll drive her down to see them, we might both go.'

'What? Yes, great.' She knew he wouldn't. He had separated himself from them a long time ago, they were no longer part of his life. Sometimes Danny and his single-mindedness were a mystery and a slight worry to Ria.

'Would you like to drive down to the country with me to see Danny's parents?' Ria asked her mother.

'Well, maybe. Would Annie be carsick?'

'Not at all, doesn't she love going in the car? Will you make them an apple tart?'

'Why?'

'Oh Mam, out of niceness, that's why. They'll be apologising about everything. You know the way they go on. And if I bring too much they get sort of overwhelmed. You bringing an apple tart is different somehow.'

'You're very complicated, Ria. You always were,' said Nora, but she was pleased to make one, and did a lot of fancy lattice-work with the pastry.

Ria had written well in advance and the Lynches were expecting them. They were pleased to see little Annie, and Ria took a picture of them with her to add to the ones she had already framed and given to them. They *would* be part of Annie's life and future in spite of their distance and reserve. She had resolved this. They never saw their other grandchild in England. Rich didn't come back. It was hard, they said. Ria wondered why it was hard for a man who was meant to be doing well in London to come home even just once and show his son to his own parents.

Rosemary had said she should leave them to it and be glad that she didn't have nagging in-laws. But Ria was determined that they stay involved.

They had cold ham, tomatoes and shop bread, which was all they ever served. 'Will I warm up the apple tart, do you think?' Mrs Lynch asked fearfully, as if faced with an insuperable problem.

How had these timid people begotten Danny Lynch who travelled the country with Barney McCarthy, confident and authoritative, talking to businessmen and county families that would have had his parents doffing their caps and bending their knees?

'And you were down here a few weeks ago and never told us,' Danny's father said.

'No indeed I was not. I think Danny may have been nearby, but of course he would have to stay with Barney McCarthy all the time.' Ria was annoyed. She had known that somehow it would get back to them. He had only been a few short miles away, why couldn't he have come over for an hour?

'Well, now, when I was in the creamery there, Marty was saying that his daughter works in the hotel and that the pair of you were there.'

'No, it was Barney who was with him,' Ria said patiently. 'She got it wrong.'

'Oh well, fair enough,' said Danny's father. The incident had lost any interest for him.

Ria knew what had confused the girl; Barney McCarthy had brought Polly with him on the trip. So that's where the mistake lay.

In September 1987, shortly before Annie's fourth birthday party, they were planning a party for the grown-ups in Tara Road.

Danny and Ria were making the list, and Rosemary was there as she so often was.

'Remember a few millionaires for me, I'm getting to my sell-by date,' Rosemary said.

'Oh that will be the day,' Ria laughed.

'Seriously though, has Barney any friends?'

'No, they're all sharks. You'd hate them, Rosemary,' Danny laughed.

'Okay, who else is on the list?'

'Gertie,' said Ria.

'No,' said Danny.

'Of course, Gertie,' said Ria.

'You can't have a party and not have Gertie,' Rosemary supported her.

'But that mad eejit Jack Brennan will turn up looking for a fight or a bottle of brandy or both,' Danny protested.

'Let him, we've coped before,' Ria said. There were the bedsitter tenants, they'd be in the house anyway, and they were nice lads. They would ask Martin and Hilary who would not come but would need the invitation. Ria's mother would come just for half an hour and stay all night. 'Barney and Mona obviously,' Ria said.

'Barney and Polly actually,' Danny said.

There was a two-second pause and then Ria wrote down Barney and Polly.

'Jimmy Sullivan, the dentist, and his wife,' Ria suggested. 'And let's ask Orla King.'

Both Danny and Rosemary frowned. 'Too drinky,' Rosemary said. 'Unreliable.'

'No, she's in AA now. But still too unpredictable,' Danny agreed.

'No, I like her. She's fun.' Ria wrote her down.

'We could ask Colm Barry, the fellow who's going to open a restaurant in the house on the corner.'

'In his dreams he is,' Danny said.

'He *is*, you know, I'm doing the invitations to the first night.'

'Which may easily be his last night,' Danny said.

Rosemary was annoyed at the way he dismissed Colm, even if it was exactly her own feeling about it all. She decided to say something to irritate Danny. 'Let's ask him anyway, Ria. He has the hots for Orla King, like all those fellows who see no further than the sticky-out bosom and bum.'

Ria giggled. 'We're all turning into matchmakers, aren't we?' she said happily.

Rosemary felt a great wish to smack Ria. Very hard. There she stood, cosy and smug in her married state. She was totally confident and sure of her husband and it never occurred to her that a man like Danny would have many people attracted to him. Orla King might not be the only player on the stage. But did Ria do anything about it? Make any attempt at all to keep his interest and attention?

Of course not. She filled this big kitchen with people and casseroles and trays of fattening cakes. She polished the furniture they bought at auctions for their front room upstairs, but the beautiful round table was covered with catalogues and papers. Ria wouldn't think in a million years of lighting two candles and putting on a good dress to cook dinner for Danny and serve it there.

No, it was this big noisy kitchen with half the road passing through and Danny's armchair for him to fall asleep in when he came home from whatever the day had brought. She looked at Danny and admired his handsome smiling face. He stood there in the kitchen of his big house holding his beautiful daughter in his arms while his wife planned a party for him. A man so confident that he could take a girlfriend to within a few short miles of where his own mother and father lived. And in front of Barney McCarthy too. Rosemary had heard the laughing tale of how Ria's father-in-law had got the wrong end of the stick as usual. Why was it that some men led such lucky lives that nobody would blow a whistle on them? Things were very, very unfair.

Ria baked night and day to have a great spread for the party. Twice she had to refuse invitations from Mona McCarthy and remember not to tell her why she was so busy. She hated doing this to the kind woman who had shown her such generosity. But Danny had been adamant. This was a do that Polly would enjoy. The party would not be mentioned to Mona.

Ria's mother knew the score and would not say anything untoward. Living now so close to Ria meant that she was a constant visitor and aware of everything that went on in the household. Nora Johnson never came to Number 16 Tara Road for an actual meal, she was not a lunch guest or a dinner guest. That way you made yourself unpopular, she always said. Instead she was a presence just before or after every meal, hovering, rattling her keys, planning her departure and next visit. It would have been vastly easier had she come in properly and sat down with everyone else. Ria sighed over it but she put up with her mother. It was comforting, too, to have someone around who knew the whole background to things. Like the Barney McCarthy saga.

'Close your eyes to it, Ria,' she advised on several occasions. 'Men like that have their needs, you know.' It seemed unusually tolerant and forgiving on her mother's part. Usually people's needs were dismissed with a sniff. But Nora Johnson was a very practical person. She said once to Ria and Hilary that she would have forgiven her late husband much more if he had had his needs and dealt with them rather than doing what he did, which was failing to provide her with an adequate life insurance or pension.

'We must have plenty of soft drinks,' Ria said to Danny on the morning of the party.

'Sure, with people like Orla and Colm off the sauce,' he agreed.

'How did you know she was in AA?' Ria asked.

'I don't know, didn't you or Rosemary say? Someone did.'

'I didn't know; I won't say anything,' Ria said.

'Neither will I,' Danny promised her.

As it happened it was a night when Orla lapsed from her rule. She had arrived early, the first guest in fact, to find Danny Lynch and the wife that he had said meant nothing to him in a deep embrace in their kitchen. The home where Danny Lynch claimed he felt stifled was decorated, warm and welcoming, and about to fill up with their friends. The little girl in a new dress toddled around. She would be four shortly, she told everyone, and she thought that this was her party. She was constantly trying to hold her daddy's hand. This was not the scene that Orla had expected. She thought she might have one whiskey.

When Colm arrived she was already very drunk. 'Let me take you home,' he begged.

'No, I don't want anyone to preach at me,' Orla said, tears running down her face.

'I won't preach, I'll just stay with you. You'd do that for me,' he said.

'No I wouldn't, I'd support you if your fellow was behaving like a shit. If your fellow was here and behaving like a hypocritical rat I'd have a whiskey with you, that's what I'd do, not a rake of sanctimonious claptrap about Higher Powers.'

'I don't have a fellow.' He made a weak joke.

'You don't have anything, Colm, that's your problem.'

'Could be,' he said.

'Where's your sister?'

'Why do you ask?'

'Because she's the only one you give a tuppenny damn about. I expect you're sleeping with her.'

'Orla, this isn't helping you and it isn't hurting me.'

'You've never loved anybody.'

'Yes I have.' Colm was aware that Rosemary was beside them. He looked at her for help. 'Should we try and find whoever this fellow is that she thinks she loves?'

'No, that would be singularly inappropriate,' Rosemary said.

'Why?'

'It's the host,' she said succinctly.

'I see.' He gave a grin. 'What do you suggest?'

Rosemary wasted no time. 'A further couple of drinks until she passes out.'

'I couldn't go along with that, I really couldn't.'

'Okay, look the other way. I'll do it.'

'No.'

'Go, Colm. You're not helping.'

'You think I'm very weak,' he said.

'No, I don't for Christ's sake. If you're in AA you're not meant to get a fellow member to pass out. I'll do it.' He stood aside and watched Rosemary pour a large whiskey. 'Go on, drink it, it's only tonight, Orla. One day at a time, isn't that what they say? Tomorrow you need have none. But tonight you need one.'

'I love him,' wept Orla.

'I know you do, but he's a liar, Orla. He takes you to Quentin's; he takes you down the country to hotels with Barney McCarthy and then he plays housey-housey with his wife in front of you. It's not fair.'

'How do you know all this?' Orla was round-mouthed.

'You *told* me, remember?'

'I never told you. You're Ria's friend.'

'Of course you told me, Orla. How else would I know?'

'When did I tell ...?'

'A while back. Listen, come up here and sit in this alcove, it's very quiet and you and I'll have a drink.'

'I hate talking to women at parties.'

'I know, Orla, so do I. But not for long. I'll send one of those nice boys who lives in this house up to talk to you. They were all asking who you were.'

'Were they?'

'Yes, everyone is. You don't want to waste your time on Danny Lynch, professional liar.'

'You're right, Rosemary.'

'I am, believe me.'

'I always thought you were stuck-up, I'm sorry.'

'No you didn't. You always liked me deep down.' Rosemary went to find the boys who rented the rooms in Danny and Ria's house. 'There's a real goer up in the alcove on the stairs, she keeps asking where are the good-looking men she met when she came in.'

Colm moved out of the background. 'You should be in the United Nations,' he said to Rosemary.

'But you don't fancy me?' she said archly.

'I admire you too much, I'd be afraid of you.'

'Then you'd be no use to me.' She laughed, and kissed him gently on the cheek.

'I don't sleep with my sister, you know,' he said.

'I didn't think you did for a minute. Don't I know you're having a thing with that publican's wife?'

'How do you know that?' He was amazed.

'I told you it's a small forest and I know everything,' she said with a laugh.

Nora Johnson said afterwards it was amazing how much drink they put away, young fresh-faced people. And wasn't it extraordinary that young, very drunk, girl shouting at everyone. And she had gone into one of the boys' bedsitters. And what a funny chance that someone had opened the door and they had been seen in bed. Danny had said he hadn't thought that any of it was funny. Orla was obviously unused to drink and had reacted badly. She hadn't meant to go to bed with one of those kids. It was out of character for her.

'Oh come on, Danny. She's anybody's, we all knew that back when we worked in the agency,' Rosemary said in her cool voice.

'I didn't know.' He was clipped.

'Oh she was.' Rosemary listed half a dozen names.

'I thought you said that nice man Colm Barry fancied her,' Ria said.

'Oh I think he did a bit back a while, but not after last night's performance.' Rosemary seemed to know everything.

Danny glowered about it all.

'Didn't you enjoy last night?' Ria looked anxiously at him.

'Yes, yes of course I did.' But he was absent, distracted. He had been startled, frightened even, by Orla's behaviour. Barney had been unexpectedly cold and asked him to get her out as quickly and quietly as possible. Polly had looked at him as if he had somehow broken the rules.

That wet Colm Barry had been no help at all. The kids who rented the rooms had been useful at the time but why, oh why, had someone left the door of a bedroom open? Only Rosemary Ryan had been of any practical use, shepherding people on and off stage as if she knew everything that was going on. Which of course she couldn't have.

A couple of weeks later, Hilary arrived with a birthday present for Annie; the first thing she wanted to know was if Barney McCarthy had been wiped out in the stock-market crash.

'I don't think so; Danny never said a word.' Ria was surprised at such a thought.

'Martin said that fellows like Barney who make all their money in England always keep it there, that he'd have lost his shirt,' Hilary said grimly.

'Well he can't have done because we'd have known,' Ria said. 'He seems to be doing just as much if not more.'

'Oh well, that's all right then,' said Hilary.

Sometimes Ria felt that Hilary would have been pleased if there was bad news – she and Martin, who had no money at all, watched the ebb and flow of the stock market with so much interest.

Gertie had been quiet and watchful during the party at Tara Road. Jack was with her, dressed in his one good suit. They had a babysitter and they couldn't stay late. Jack drank orange juice. Gertie's sister Sheila was going to come home from the United States this Christmas. It had never been made clear to Sheila and her American husband Max the extent of the problems with Jack Brennan.

Sheila was inclined to be boastful of her life in New England. Their wealth and status was always treated to an impressive show in her letters home. The fact that Gertie had married such an unstable man had never been mentioned in her own letters or phone calls. Gertie was hoping that the three-week visit could hold without one of Jack's moods.

It depressed her to see that pretty girl Orla behaving so badly. If someone like that could lose control, what hope was there for her Jack? But against all the odds he remained sober. Restless and anxious, but sober. There was a God after all, Gertie confided to Ria as she helped her serve the hot spicy soup and pitta bread.

'I know, Gertie, I know. Every time I look at Danny and little Annie I know this.'

Gertie winced slightly because she had heard one of the girls who worked for her at the launderette say that the good-looking Danny Lynch who lived at the posh end of Tara Road had a fancy woman just like his boss Barney McCarthy had a fancy woman. Gertie had so much wanted it not to be true, she had refused to listen or enquire anything at all about it.

*

Barney McCarthy never mentioned again the behaviour of Orla King at the party in Tara Road. He had assumed that the relationship would now be at an end. And he had assumed correctly. Danny called to Orla's flat to tell her so. He spoke very directly and left no area for doubt.

'You don't think you're going to get rid of me like that,' Orla cried. She had indeed managed to stay sober after the upsetting events of the night in Tara Road, but this news was not helping her resolution.

'I don't know what you mean,' Danny said. 'We both went into this knowing the limitations, I was never going to leave Ria for you, we agreed that it would be fun and would hurt nobody.'

'I never agreed to that,' Orla wept.

'Yes, you did, Orla.'

'Well I don't feel that way now,' she said. 'I love you. You're treating me like shit.'

'No, that's not true, and if anyone is treating anyone like shit, it's you. You come to my house, you get as pissed as a fart, you insult my boss, you go to bed with at least one and possibly two of my tenants in full view of everyone. Who's treating whom badly, may I ask?'

'You've not done with me, Danny Lynch. I can still make trouble for you,' Orla said.

'Who'd believe you, Orla? After your behaviour in our house, who'd believe I touched you? Even with a forty-foot pole?'

'Hallo, Rosemary? Orla King here.'

'Hi Orla. Feeling okay again?'

'Yes, I didn't go back on the drink.'

'There. I knew you wouldn't. I told you, didn't I?'

'Yes, you did. I'm not a good judge of people as it turns out. I didn't know you were so nice.'

'Come on, of course you did.'

'No I didn't. Danny Lynch is a cheat and a liar and I'm going round to his house to tell his wife what he's been up to.'

'Don't do that, Orla.'

'Why not, he *is* a liar. She should know.'

'Listen. You've just agreed I'm your friend, so listen to the advice of a friend.'

'Okay. What is it?'

'Danny's very dangerous. Suppose you did that, he'd hit back. He'd get you sacked.'

'He couldn't do that.'

'He could, Orla, he really could. He could tell your bosses that you photocopied stuff for him, gave them details of deals that were coming up.'

'He wouldn't.'

'What has he to lose? He's secure with Barney. Barney doesn't owe you any favours for what you said to him about that trip to the country.'

'Oh God, did I?'

'Yes I'm afraid you did.'

'I don't remember.'

'That's the problem, isn't it. Listen, believe me, I haven't steered you wrong. You're going to give yourself nothing but grief if you go round to Tara Road with the story. Danny will go for you bald-headed. You know how determined he is. You know how ambitious, how much he wants to get ahead, he won't let you stand in his way.'

'So what do you think . . . ?'

'I think you should let him know you'd like to cool it a bit, men love that sort of thing. Agree to keep it on the back burner, some phrase like that, and once he knows you won't be any problem he'll start coming round to see you again and it will all restore itself to where it was.'

Rosemary could hear the tears of gratitude in Orla's voice. 'You're really so helpful, Rosemary. I don't know why I thought you were stuck-up and difficult. That's exactly what I'll do. And of course he'll come round when he knows there's going to be no drama.'

'That's it, it may take a bit of time of course,' Rosemary warned.

'How much time do you think?'

'Who knows with men? Maybe a few weeks.'

'*Weeks?*' Orla sounded horrified.

'I know, but it's for the best in the end, isn't it?'

'You're right.' Orla hung up.

Nora Johnson had been to bridge lessons. She was greatly taken by the game and somewhat inclined to tell lengthy tales about some hand that was dealt, called and played. She seemed to have the same kind of recall for bridge as she had about every film star she had ever seen on the screen.

Ria had refused absolutely to learn. 'I've seen too many people get obsessed by it, Mam. I'm bad enough already, I don't want myself spending five hours every afternoon wondering are all the diamonds out or who has the seven of spades.'

'It's not like that at all,' Nora scoffed. 'But it's your loss. I'm going to suggest that I get some games going for them up in St Rita's.'

And it was a huge success. There were demon bridge sessions in one of the residents' lounges at the retirement home, often with as many as three tables playing. Nora Johnson played there almost every afternoon wherever they needed to make up a four. There were not enough hours in the day for her.

And as well as organising their games she organised the lives of the residents, advising them, cajoling and contradicting them. She was never happier than laying down rules and making decisions for other people. Including her daughter Ria.

'I wish you'd pray to Saint Ann,' Nora Johnson told her daughter.

'Oh Mam, there's no Saint Ann,' Ria said exasperated.

'Of course there's a Saint Ann,' said her mother scornfully. 'Who else do you think was the mother of Our Lady. And her husband was Saint Joachim. Saint Ann's feast is at the end of July and I always pray to her for you then, and say that basically you're a good girl and you'll remember your name-day.'

'But it's *not* my name-day. We're not in Russia or Greece, Mam, we're in Ireland and my name is Ria anyway, or Maria. Not Ann.'

'You were baptised Ann Maria, your own daughter is called Ann after the mother of Our Lady.'

'No, it's because we like the name.'

'There!' her mother was triumphant.

'But what should I be praying for, even supposing she was there listening? Haven't we got everything?'

'You need another child.' Her mother spoke with pursed lips. 'Saint Ann could do it. You may think it's superstitious but believe me it's true.'

Ria knew that if she stopped taking the contraceptive pill that would do it too. Something she had been thinking about a lot, and must discuss with Danny. He had seemed preoccupied about business recently, but maybe this was the time to bring the subject up.

'I might pray to Saint Ann,' she said gently to her mother.

'That's the girl,' said Nora Johnson.

Gertie's sister Sheila came home for Christmas.

'I must have her to a lunch here,' said Ria.

'Oh God no,' Danny said. 'Not over Christmas. Not that fellow with his fists here over Christmas, please.'

'Don't give a dog a bad name, Danny. Wasn't he great now at the party?'

'Well, if standing like a block of wood was great then he was.'

'Don't be an old grouch, it's not like you.'

Danny sighed. 'Sweetheart, you're always filling the house with people. We get no peace.'

'I am not.' She was hurt.

'But you are, this is one of the few times there's just us and Annie here. There are people coming and going all the time.'

'That's the meanest thing I ever heard. Who's here more often than Barney? He's here about four times a week, and with Polly one day or Mona another. Now I don't ask them, do I?'

'No.'

'So?'

'So it's not very restful, that's all.'

'Forget Gertie's sister then,' Ria said. 'It was just an idea.'

'Look ... I don't mean ...'

'No, I said forget it, we'll be restful.'

'Ria, come here ...' He dragged her towards him. 'You are the world's worst sulker,' he said and kissed her on the nose. 'All right, what day will we have them?'

'I knew you'd be reasonable. What about the Sunday after Christmas Day?'

'No, that's the McCarthys. We can't miss that.'

'Right, the Monday then, no one will have gone back to work. It will be stay-at-home Ireland. Will we ask your mother and father?'

'What for?' Danny asked.

'They can see Annie, see all that we've done to the place, meet these Americans, you know.'

'They'd be no good, and honestly I don't think they'd enjoy it,' Danny said.

Ria paused. 'Sure,' she said. And, after all, she had won over Gertie's sister.

Sheila Maine and her husband Max had not been in Ireland for six years. Not since their wedding day. They now had a son Sean, the same age as Annie. Sheila seemed astounded at how well Ireland was doing, how prosperous the people were, and how successful were the small businesses she saw everywhere. When she had left to go to America to seek her fortune at the age of eighteen, Ireland had been a much poorer country. 'Look what has happened in less than ten years!'

Ria felt that, not unlike her own sister Hilary who seemed to rejoice in bad news rather than good, Sheila Maine was not entirely pleased to see the upturn in the economy. What Sheila really seemed to resent was the great social life that people had in Dublin. 'It's not at all like this in the States,' she confided on the evening before Christmas Eve when there was a girls' dinner out in Colm's new restaurant. 'I can't imagine all these people laughing and talking to each other at different tables. It's all changed a great deal from my time.'

Colm had been having a series of rehearsals, inexpensive meals where friends would try out the recipes and the ambience at a very reduced cost. This way they could iron out some of the wrinkles before the restaurant opened officially in March. Only those who were within his group were allowed in. Colm's beautiful and silent sister Caroline worked with him, serving and acting as hostess. 'Smile a little more, Caroline,' they heard him urging her from time to time. She was a nervous girl, she might never be seen as fronting a successful restaurant for her brother.

Sheila was thrilled with it all. And on Christmas Eve they were going in to Grafton Street where a live radio broadcast was done on *The Gay Byrne Show*. Perhaps she might even be called upon to speak as a returned emigrant. Anything was possible in the Ireland of today. Look at all Gertie's smart friends, with their good jobs or their beautiful houses. Gertie herself was not particularly well off; her launderette was at the less smart end of Tara Road. And her husband Jack, though charming and handsome, seemed vague about his prospects. But they had a business, and a two-year-old baby boy. And everyone was so confident. Sheila Maine's sigh was so like Hilary Moran's sigh that Ria could hardly wait for the two women to meet at lunch in her house.

And indeed they did get on very well. Gertie and Ria stood back and watched them bonding together. The quiet husband, Max Maine, who came from a Ukrainian background and knew little or nothing about Ireland, seemed ill at ease. Only Danny of course was able to draw him out with his warm smile and his interest in everything new. 'Tell me about the kind of houses you have out there, Max. Are they all that whiteboard we see pictures of?'

Max was frank and explained that in the part of Connecticut where he and Sheila lived, there weren't many dream houses standing in their own grounds. Danny was equally frank and expanded on how they had managed to get a big house like this one in Tara Road by being in the right place at the right time, and by having three of their rooms occupied by youngsters who helped to pay the mortgage. Visibly Max relaxed with half a bottle of Russian vodka which they sipped from small glasses. Ria watched as Danny captivated her friend's brother-in-law. He hadn't wanted them to come and yet he was now giving his all. Jack, having been frightened into some kind of truce, sat drinkless and wordless in a corner.

Afterwards, as they washed up, Ria gave Danny a hug. 'You are marvellous, and weren't you rewarded in the end? He is a nice man, Max, isn't he?'

'Sweetheart, he hasn't a word to throw to a dog. But you're so good to people when they come here for me, I thought I'd be nice to him for you, and for poor Gertie, who isn't a bad old stick. That's all.'

Somehow Ria felt cheated. She had really believed that Danny was enjoying his conversation with Max Maine. It was upsetting to realise that it had all been an act.

Sheila wanted to know was there a good fortune-teller around before she went back home. A lot of her neighbours in America went to psychics, some of them very powerful, but they wouldn't know you like an Irishwoman would. 'I'll take all you three girls ... my treat,' she said. You couldn't not like Sheila. Bigger and much more untidy than Gertie, she had the same anxious eyes and the edges of her mouth turned down in sadness to leave this place where everyone was having such a good time.

Ria longed to tell her that they were all putting on a show for her, but that would have been to let Gertie down.

'Come on, let's all go to Mrs Connor,' Gertie suggested.

'She didn't get things right for me years back, but I hear she's red-hot at the moment. Why not, it's an adventure, isn't it?' Rosemary agreed. The last time they had been there, Rosemary had said nothing about what had been predicted, just that it was not relevant to her life plans. Maybe it would be different now.

'Well, she did tell me my baby would be a girl. I know it was a fifty-fifty chance but she was right. Let's go to her,' Ria said. She had stopped taking the pill back in September. But as yet the time had not been ripe to tell Danny. She was waiting for the proper moment.

Mrs Connor must have had five or ten people a night coming to her since they were there last. Hundreds of eager faces watching her, thousands of hopeful hands held out, and many more thousands of paper banknotes crossing the table. There was no evidence whatsoever of any increased affluence in her caravan. Her face showed no sign of any contentment in having seen the futures of so many people.

She told Sheila, having heard her accent, that she lived across the sea possibly in the United States, that she was married reasonably happily, but that she would like to live back in Ireland.

'And will I live back in Ireland?' Sheila asked beseechingly.

'Your future is in your own hands,' Mrs Connor said gravely, and somehow this cheered Sheila a lot. She considered the money well spent.

To Gertie, with her anxious eyes, Mrs Connor said that there was an element of sadness and danger in her life and she should be watchful for those she loved. Since Gertie was never anything but watchful for Jack this seemed a good summing-up of affairs.

Rosemary sat and held out her hand, marvelling as she looked around her at the squalor of the surroundings. This woman must take in, tax-free, something like a hundred thousand pounds a year. How could she bear to live like this? 'You were here before,' the woman said to her.

'That's right, some years back.'

'And did what I saw happen for you?'

'No, you saw me in deep trouble; unsuccessful and a bad friend. It couldn't have been more wrong. I'm in no trouble, I have lots of friends and my business is thriving. But you can't win them all and you got the others right.' Rosemary smiled at her, one professional woman to another.

Mrs Connor raised her eyes from the palm. 'I didn't see that, I saw you had no real friends, and that there was something you wanted which you couldn't get. That's what I still see.' Her voice was certain and sad.

Rosemary was a little shaken. 'Well, do you see me getting married?' she asked, forcing a lightness into her voice.

'No,' Mrs Connor said.

Ria was the last to go in. She looked at the fortune-teller with sympathy. 'Aren't you very damp here? That old heater isn't great for you.'

'I'm fine,' Mrs Connor said.

'Couldn't you live somewhere better, Mrs Connor? Can't you see that in your hand?' Ria was concerned.

'We don't read our own hands. It's a tradition.'

'Well, somebody else might . . .'

'Can you show me your palm, please, lady. We're here for you to know are you pregnant again?'

Ria's jaw fell open in amazement. 'And am I?' she said in a whisper.

'Yes, you are, lady. A little boy this time.' Ria felt a stinging behind her eyes. No more than her mother's famous Saint Ann, dead and gone for two thousand years, Mrs Connor barely alive in her caravan couldn't know the future, but she was mightily convincing. She had been right about Annie, remember, and right about Hilary having no children at all. Possibly there were ways outside the normal channels of knowing these things. She stood up as if to go. 'Don't you want to hear about your business and the travel overseas?'

'No, that's not on. That's somebody else's life creeping in on my palm,' Ria said kindly.

Mrs Connor shrugged. 'I see it, you know. A successful business, where you are very good at it and happy too.'

Ria laughed. 'Well, my husband will be pleased, I'll tell him. He's working very hard these days, he'll be glad I'm going to be a tycoon.'

'And tell him about the baby that's coming, lady. He doesn't know that yet,' said Mrs Connor, coughing and drawing her cardigan around her for warmth.

Danny was not really pleased when he heard the news. 'This was something we said we would discuss together, sweetheart.'

'I know, but there never is time to discuss anything, Danny, you work so hard.'

'Well, isn't that all the more reason we *should* discuss things? Barney's so stretched these days, money is tight, and some of the projects have huge risk attached to them. We might not be able to *afford* another baby.'

'Be reasonable. How much is a baby going to cost? We have all the baby things for him. We don't have to get a cot, a pram or any of the things that cost money.' She was stung with disappointment.

'Ria, it's not that I don't want another child – you know that – it's just that we did agree to discuss it, and this isn't the best time. In three or four years we could afford it better.'

'We won't have to pay anything for him, I tell you, until he is three or four.'

'Stop calling it him, Ria. We can't know at this stage.'

'I know already.'

'Because of some fortune-teller! Sweetheart, will you give me a break?'

'She was right about my being pregnant. I went to the doctor next day.'

'So much for joint decisions.'

'Danny, that's not fair. That's the most unfair thing I ever heard. Do I ask to be part of all the decisions you make for this house? I do bloody not. I don't know when you're going to be in or out, when Barney McCarthy will come and closet himself with you for hours. I don't know if we are to see his wife or his mistress with him each time he turns up. I don't ask to discuss if I can go out to work again, and let Mam look after Annie for us, because you like the house comfortable for you whatever time you come home. I'd like a cat but you're not crazy about them, so that's that. I'd like us to have more time on our own, the two of us, but you need to have Barney around, so that's *that*. And I forgot to take the pill for a bit and suddenly it's a matter of joint decisions. Where are the other joint decisions, I ask you? Where are they?' The tears were running down her face. The delight in the new life that was starting inside her seemed almost wiped out.

Danny looked at her in amazement. His own face crumpled as he realised the extent of her loneliness and how much she had felt excluded. 'I can't tell you how sorry I am. I truly can't tell you how cheap and selfish I feel listening to you. Everything you say is true. I have been ludicrous about work. I worry so much in case we'll lose what we've got. I'm so sorry, Ria.' He buried his face in her and she stroked his head with sounds of reassurance. 'And I'm delighted we're having a little boy. And suppose the little boy's a little girl like Annie, I'll be delighted with that too.'

Ria thought about telling him what the fortune-teller had said about her having a business of her own one day, and overseas travel. But she decided it would break the mood. And it was nonsense anyway.

'I know you're pregnant again, Ria. Mam told me,' Hilary said when she came to call.

'I was about to tell you. I forgot what a bush telegraph Mam is. It's probably being broadcast on the midday news by now,' Ria said apologetically.

'Are you pleased?' Hilary asked.

'Very. And it will be good for Annie to have someone to play with, though she'll probably hate him at first.'

'Him?'

'Yes, I'm pretty sure. Listen, Hilary, it's hard for me to talk about this with you. You never want to talk about, well, about your own situation, and there was a time when we could talk about anything, you and I.'

'I don't mind talking about it.' Hilary was offhand.

'Well, have you thought of adopting a baby?'

'I have,' Hilary said. 'But Martin hasn't.'

'Why ever not?'

'It might be too expensive. He thinks that the cost of educating and clothing a child is prohibitive these days. And suppose it went to third-level education, well, you're talking thousands and thousands over a lifetime.'

'But if you'd had your own you'd have paid that.'

'With difficulty you know, and the other way there'd be the feeling we're doing it for someone else's child.'

'Oh there wouldn't. Of course there wouldn't. Once you get the baby it's yours.'

'So they say, but I don't know.' Hilary nodded doubtfully over her mug of tea.

'And is it easy to adopt?' Ria persisted.

'Not nowadays, they're all keeping their kids, you see, and getting an allowance from the State. I'd put an end to that, I tell you.'

'And have them terrified out of their lives, like when we were young.'

'It didn't terrify *you*,' Hilary said as she so often did.

'Well, I mean the generation before us then. Remember all the stories, girls committing suicide or running off to England and everything, never knowing what happened. Surely it's much better the way it is?'

'Easy for you to say, Ria. If you saw that little rossie up at the school, with her stomach stuck out in front of her, and now it appears that her mother doesn't want to bring it up, so there's more drama.'

'Maybe you and Martin . . .'

'Live in the real world, Ria. Could you imagine us working in that school, bringing up that little tinker's baby, paying through the nose for everything for it? Right pair of laughing-stocks we'd be.'

Ria thought that Hilary found the world too harsh and unloving a place but then she was in a poor position to try and console her sister. Ria had so much and in many ways Hilary really did have so little.

Orla King was back at her AA meetings again. Colm was as friendly to her as ever. But she felt awkward, particularly with imperfect recollection of the party in Tara Road. Finally she brought the subject up.

'I meant to thank you for trying to help me that night, Colm.' It wasn't easy to find the words.

'It's okay, Orla. We all go through it, that's why we're here. That was then, this is now.'

'Now is a bit bleak though.'

'Only if you allow it to be. Try something different. I've felt so tired since I left the bank, trying to set up this restaurant business, that I haven't had time to miss the drink and feel sorry for myself.'

'What can I do except type?'

'You said once you'd like to be a model.'

'I'm too old and too fat, you have to be sixteen and look half-starved.'

'You don't sing badly. Can you play the piano?'

'Yes, but I only sing when I'm drunk.'

'Have you tried it sober? It might be more tuneful and you'd remember the words.'

'Sorry to be so helpless, Colm. I'm like a tiresome child, I know. But suppose I *could* get a few songs together, then where would I try for a job?'

'I could give you the odd spot when my place opens . . . not real money, but you might get discovered. And of course Rosemary knows half of Dublin. She might know people in restaurants, hotels, clubs.'

'I don't think Rosemary's too keen on me these days. I did fool around with her best friend's husband.'

Colm grinned. 'Well, at least that's all you're describing it as now, fooling around, not the great love affair of the century.'

'He's a shit,' Orla said.

'He's all right really, he just couldn't resist you. Very few of us could.' He grinned at her and she thought again what an attractive man he was. Since he had left the bank he wore much more casual clothes, open-necked shirts in bright colours; his black curly hair and big dark eyes made him look slightly foreign, Spanish or Italian. And he was a rock of sense too. Handsome, single, sensible.

Orla sighed. 'You make me feel much better, Colm. Why couldn't I fall in love with someone normal like you?'

'Oh I'm not normal at all, we all know that,' Colm joked.

A look of unease crossed Orla's pretty round face. She hoped that when she had been drunk she had said nothing about the overprotectiveness Colm always had about his silent beautiful sister. No, surely bad and all as she had been that night she'd never have hinted at anything as dark as that.

Brian was born on the 15th of June and this time Danny was beside Ria and holding her hand.

Annie said to everyone that she was quite pleased with her new brother, but not *very* pleased. This made people laugh so she said it over and over. Brian was all right, she said, but he wasn't able to go to the bathroom on his own, and he couldn't talk and he took up a lot of Mum and Dad's time. Still, Dad had assured her again and again that she was his little princess, the only princess he would ever have or want. And Mam had said that Annie was the very best girl not only in Ireland, or Europe, but on Earth and quite possibly the planets as well. So Annie Lynch didn't have anything to worry about. And Brian was going to take ages before he could do anything like catch up on her. So she was very relaxed about the whole thing.

Gertie's baby Katy was born just after Brian, and Sheila Maine's daughter Kelly around the same time.

'Maybe they'll all be friends when they grow older.' The future was always happy and filled with people for Ria.

'They might all hate each other, you can just see Brian saying she wants me to be friends with these awful people . . . They'll make their own friends no matter what you say.'

'I know, it's just that it would be nice.'

Rosemary showed her irritation. 'Ria, you're amazing, you're so into never changing things, never moving on. It's ridiculous. You're not friendly with the children of your mother's friends, are you?'

'Mam didn't have any friends,' Ria said.

'Nonsense, I never met anyone with more friends, she knows the whole neighbourhood.'

'They're only acquaintances,' Ria said. 'Anyway, there's nothing wrong with my hoping that friendships will continue into the next generation.'

'No, but not very adventurous.'

'When *you* have children won't you want them to be friends with Annie and Brian?'

'They'll be far too young if they ever materialise, which is unlikely,' Rosemary said.

Annie had been listening carefully; these days she understood a lot of what was going on. 'Why don't you have children?' she asked.

'Because I'm too busy,' Rosemary said truthfully. 'I work very hard and it takes up a lot of time. You see, all the time your mummy spends on you and Brian? I don't think I could be unselfish enough to do that.'

'I bet you'd love it if you tried it,' Ria said.

'Stop it, Ria. You sound like my mother.'

'I mean it.'

'So does she. So does Gertie, for God's sake, she was trying to get me broody the other day. Imagine the Brennan family being held up to anyone as an example of domestic bliss!'

Gertie didn't bring her two children to Tara Road. They lived over the launderette not far away, and she always felt that they would be discontented if they saw how others lived. Also the atmosphere in Ria's house was so different from their own. A big kitchen where everyone gathered, something always cooking in the big stove, the smell of newly baked cinnamon cakes, or fresh herb bread.

Not like Gertie's house where nothing was ever left out on the gas cooker. Just in case, just in case it might coincide with one of the times that Jack was upset. Because if Jack was upset it could be thrown at anyone. But Gertie came on her own to Number 16 from time to time and did a little housework for Ria. Anything that would give her the few pounds that Jack didn't know about. Just something that might tide them over when there was trouble.

Rosemary's business was now very high profile. She was often photographed at the races, gallery openings or at theatre first nights. She dressed very well and she kept her clothes immaculately. Whenever she visited, Ria had taken to offering her a nylon housecoat to wear in case the children smeared her with whatever they had their hands in.

'Come on, that's going a bit far,' Rosemary laughed the first time.

'No it isn't. I'm the one who'd have to spend six years apologising if they got ice cream or puréed carrots all over that gorgeous cream wool. Put it on, Rosemary, and give me some peace.'

Rosemary thought they could have more peace if they went upstairs to that magnificent front room and drank their wine there rather than being in what was like a giant playpen with children's toys and things all over the floor and Ria leaping up to stir things and lift more and more trays of baking out of the oven. But it was useless to try and change her ways. Ria Lynch believed that the world revolved around her family and her kitchen.

Danny saw her in the pink nylon coat and was annoyed. 'Rosemary, you don't need to dress up to play with the children.'

'Your wife's idea,' Rosemary shrugged.

'I didn't want them messing up her lovely clothes.'

'Wait till she has kids of her own,' Danny said darkly. 'Then we'll see some messed-up clothes.'

'I wouldn't bet on it, Danny,' Rosemary said. Her smile was bright, but she felt that she was being put under a lot of pressure from all sides. It wasn't enough apparently to look well, dress well, and run a successful business. No, not nearly enough. Apparently there was no such thing as a private life in this city. Rosemary resented the excessive interest people had in marrying others off. Why was she not allowed to have a lover that no one knew of, or indeed a series of them? She was successful and glamorous but so what? You had to find a mate and breed children as well, otherwise it counted for nothing in people's eyes. She was getting it everywhere, but particularly on her weekly visits to her mother's house.

Mrs Ryan was becoming intolerable. Rosemary was now in her late twenties and with no marriage prospects. Her sister Eileen was no consolation to her. Just be yourself, be free. Don't listen to the old voices, Eileen would say if ever Rosemary grumbled about their mother. Which was fine for Eileen living as she did with the powerful Stephanie, a lawyer, and working for her as her clerk. They had an apartment where they had a regular Sunday afternoon drinks party. It was almost like a salon where everyone was welcome, men and women, but Rosemary felt they despised her for dressing so well. The term 'frocky' was used a lot as a derogatory description for women that Eileen and Stephanie thought were dressing just to please male egos.

Yet in ways Rosemary envied them. They were sure and happy in their lives and they wished her well. 'I'm demented with Eileen and Stephanie producing soulful ladies for me, my mother despairing that I'm a lost cause, and every customer that I'm nice to thinking I'm about to perform every known kind of sexual favour to keep his business.'

'Why don't you sign up with a marriage agency?' Ria said unexpectedly.

'You have to be joking me! Now you've joined them all.'

'No, I mean it. At least you'd meet the right kind of person, someone who wants to settle down.'

'You're daft as a brush, Ria,' Rosemary said.

'I know, but you did ask me what I thought.' Ria shrugged. It seemed perfectly sensible to her.

Rosemary met Polly Callaghan at several gatherings. Their paths would cross at press receptions and the openings of art galleries or even at the theatre. 'Did you ever think of a marriage agency? No, I'm not joking, someone suggested it to me as a reasonable option and I wonder is it barking mad?'

'Depends on what you want, I suppose.' Polly took the suggestion seriously. 'You don't look like the kind of woman who wants to be dependent on a man.'

'No, I don't think I am,' Rosemary said thoughtfully.

But it *would* be nice to have someone to come home to in the evening. Someone who was interested and in your corner, someone who would fight your battles. Somehow Rosemary had always thought he would turn up. But this was ridiculous, why should he? Business opportunities didn't fall into your lap, you had to make them.

Good dress sense wasn't just guesswork, you had to consult experts. Rosemary was on first-name terms with all the buyers in the smart Dublin shops. She told them exactly how much she could spend and discussed what she needed. They enjoyed doing the research for her, an elegant woman like that who paid them the courtesy of recognising that they were indeed experts in their field.

So why shouldn't she go to a marriage agency?

She approached it in her usual businesslike way and went to meet her first introduction. He was handsome in a slightly dishevelled way, came from a wealthy family but it took her forty minutes to realise that he was a compulsive gambler. With her practised charm she managed to manoeuvre the conversation far away from the actual reason why they were meeting – possible marriage. Instead she discussed stock markets, national hunt racing, the greyhound track. Then at the coffee stage she looked at her watch and said she had to have an early night; it had been delightful and she hoped they would meet again. She left without having given him her address or phone number but also without his having asked for it. She was pleased that she had handled it so well, but annoyed that she had wasted a night.

Her second introduction was to Richard Roche, the head of an advertising agency. She met him in Quentin's and they talked about a wide range of subjects. He was pleasant, easy company and she felt that he found her attractive. Nothing prepared her for the way it ended.

'I can't tell you when I've enjoyed a meal as much,' he began.

'I feel the same,' she smiled warmly.

'So I do hope we remain friends.'

'Well, yes.'

'You're not at all interested in getting married, Rosemary, but we can regard this dinner as a happy accident. All friends have to meet somewhere.' His smile was equally warm and sincere.

'What do you mean, I'm not interested in getting married?'

'Of course you're not, you don't want children, a home, anything like that.'

'Is that what you think?'

'It's what I can see. But as I say it was my good fortune to meet you and as I continue my search I'm sure I'll be unlikely to have such an elegant and charming dinner companion again.'

He was saying he didn't want her. Men didn't do that to Rosemary Ryan. 'You're playing hard to get, Richard,' she said, looking at him from under her eyelashes.

'No, you're the mystery woman. You must have a thousand friends and yet you chose to have dinner with a stranger. I'm what I say I am, a man who wants a wife and children, you are the puzzle.'

He was serious. He didn't want to continue. Well, she would get out with dignity if it killed her. 'It makes life a little adventurous, don't you think, to dine with a stranger?' She would *not* let him see how humiliated she felt, she would end the evening with style.

She nodded at Brenda Brennan to get her a taxi, and somehow got herself home.

She sat shaking in her small apartment. How dare he treat her like that! Damn him to hell. She had been prepared to go a bit of the distance with this Richard Roche. What made him think he could tell her she didn't want marriage and children?

She resolved to watch the paper for news of his eventual wedding plans and she would manage to circulate the story that he had found his bride through a marriage agency. She would let his colleagues know; she would wipe this night of embarrassment and failure from her mind. She would get a new apartment, somewhere elegant where she could relax. Nobody was going to treat Rosemary Ryan like this.

A year later she did see a gossip column item about him. He was going to marry a glamorous widow with two small children. They had met in Galway apparently with mutual friends. Rosemary didn't write to his colleagues or the wedding guests. The rage and hurt had long died down. She had taken up no further introductions after that night but instead concentrated on looking for somewhere new to live.

Colm's restaurant started very slowly. He devised the menus and did most of the cooking himself; and he had a *sous-chef*, a waiter, a washer-up and his sister Caroline to help him. But it didn't take off as he had hoped it would. This was 1989, a lot of new restaurants were opening in Dublin. Rosemary invited as many influential people as she could rustle up to come to the opening.

Ria was disappointed that Danny would not try to do the same. 'You know an awful lot of people through Barney,' she said pleadingly.

'Sweetheart, let's wait until it's a success, then we'll invite lots of people there.'

'But it's now he needs them otherwise how else will it *be* a success?'

'I don't suppose for a moment that Colm is expecting the charity of his friends. In fact he'd probably find that just a little patronising.'

Ria didn't agree, she thought it was small-minded and over-cautious of him. Don't risk getting your name associated with something that might fail. It was a shabby attitude, out of character with Danny's cheerful optimistic approach to life, and she said as much to Rosemary.

'Now don't be so quick to attack him. He may be right in a way. Much more useful to take business people there for meals when it's up and running.' Rosemary spoke soothingly but in reality she knew very well why Danny Lynch didn't want to go to the opening and why he forced Ria to go to a business dinner that night.

Danny knew that Orla King was going to sit at a piano in the background and sing well-established favourites. She would not have a spotlight but if the place was successful she would have a platform.

Orla had worn a demure black dress and sipped a Diet Coke through the many rehearsals. But she had proved herself once to be a very loose cannon on the deck, and unpredictability was the last thing Danny Lynch wanted around him. Especially since Barney McCarthy's finances had taken such a battering recently and there were heavy rumours of much speculative building to try and recoup the losses.

Rosemary went to Colm's opening night and reported that it had been very successful. A lot of the customers had been neighbours; it boded well for the future.

'This really is a great area, you two were very lucky to come in here when you did,' Rosemary said approvingly.

Ria wished that she didn't sound so surprised, as if she hadn't expected it of them.

'Not lucky, just far-seeing,' said Danny, who must have felt the same.

'Not a bit of it. The secret of the universe is timing, you know that,' Rosemary laughed. She wasn't letting them get away with anything except random good fortune. 'Isn't it a pity that there aren't any proper apartments or little mews flats around here? I could become your neighbour!'

'You could afford a whole house on the road the way you're going,' Danny said.

'I don't *need* a whole house. I don't want to be worrying about tenants. What I need is a house just like the one your mother has, Ria, a little mews like that.'

'Oh that's a one-off,' Danny explained. 'Holly was certainly in the right place at the right time. You see she looked after the old trout who lived in the big house and then, when she went to her reward, the family sold Holly the little mews. It's so valuable now you wouldn't believe it.'

'Would she like to sell and move in with you?' Rosemary wondered.

'No way,' Ria said. 'She loves her independence.'

'And we want ours too,' Danny added. 'Much as I love Holly, and I do love her, I wouldn't want her here all the time.'

'Well, if there are no more of those around perhaps something like a penthouse for want of a better word, something with a nice view.'

'Not too many of those in a Victorian road.'

'But there are a lot of conversions happening.' Rosemary knew the property scene as well as anyone.

'Indeed there are, expensive but you'd always see your money back. Two bedroom?' Danny was into sales mode now.

'Yes, and a big room for entertaining, I could have a lot of functions there. A roof garden I'd like if possible.'

'There's nothing like that around here at the moment, but a lot of the upcoming sales are going to want to do huge renovations,' Danny said.

'Keep an eye out for me, Danny; it doesn't have to be Tara Road, somewhere nearby.'

'I'll get it for you,' Danny promised.

In three weeks Danny came back with news of two properties. Neither owner was willing to build. It would be a question of Barney McCarthy buying the building, his men doing the renovation and, subject to planning permission, getting a penthouse-style apartment custom built for Rosemary. They could start drawing up plans as soon as she liked.

Danny expected Rosemary to be very pleased but she was cool. 'We are talking about an outright buy not just renting? And I could see the titles for all the other flats in the house?'

'Well yes,' Danny said.

'And my architect and surveyor could look at the plans?'

'Yes, of course.'

'And inspect the building specifications and work throughout?'

'I don't see why not.'

'What's the word on a roof garden?'

'If there's not too much heavy earth brought up there the structural engineers say that both houses could take the load.'

Rosemary smiled one of her all-embracing smiles that lit up the whole room. 'Well, Danny, that's great, lead me to the properties,' she said.

*

Ria was shocked that Rosemary had been so ungracious about it all. 'Imagine her interrogating you like that!' she said, outraged, to Danny.

'I didn't mind,' he said.

'But you're a friend, you went out on a limb for her, persuaded Barney to buy a place.' Ria was still stunned by the ingratitude.

'Nonsense, Ria, Barney doesn't do things just for friendship; it's a business thing for him too, you know.'

'But the way she said it, saying she'd have to inspect Barney's building methods and everything . . . I didn't know where to look when she said it.'

Danny laughed. 'Sweetheart, Barney has been known to cut corners with the best of them. Rosemary would know that. She's just thorough, covering everything. That's what has her where she is.'

Hilary sniffed when she heard that Rosemary was coming to live in Tara Road. 'That's the final seal of approval, if *she's* coming to live in the area,' she said.

'Why don't you like her? She never says a word against you,' Ria complained.

'Did I say a word against her?' Hilary asked innocently.

'No, but it's the tone of voice. I think Rosemary is quite lonely, you know. It's all very well for you, you have Martin, and I have the children . . . and Danny too when I see him, but she doesn't have anybody.'

'Well, I'm sure she's had offers,' Hilary said.

'Yes, I'm sure she has, and so had you and I in a way when we were young, but they were no use if they were from eejits like Ken Murray.'

'Rosemary could get better than Ken Murray interested in her.'

'Yes but she hasn't found the right one, so isn't it grand that she's coming to live here halfway between Mam and ourselves? All we need is for you to come and live here too then we'd have taken over.'

'Where would Martin and I get the repayment on a house in Tara Road?' Hilary began.

Ria moved off the subject. 'Gertie's mother's being difficult.'

'All mothers are difficult,' Hilary said.

'Ours isn't too bad.'

'That's because she babysits for you all the time,' Hilary said.

'No, very rarely, she's got far too busy a life. But Gertie's mother won't take the children any more, she says if she'd wanted a late family she'd have had one.'

'What will Gertie do?'

'Struggle like she always has. I told her they could come here for a while but . . .' Ria paused and bit her lip.

'But Danny wouldn't like it.'

'He's afraid Jack Brennan will come round looking for them and for a fight and that it would frighten Annie and Brian.'

'So what happens now?'

'I go up and take them out for the day for her, but you see it's the nights are the really bad times. That's the time she wants them out of the house.'

'What a desperate mess,' Hilary said, her face soft in sympathy and quite unlike the envious Hilary who normally talked about how much everybody earned.

'You'd never take them for this weekend, you and Martin, just till their grandmother comes round again, or that lunatic breaks his skull with drink and has to go to hospital again? I know Gertie would die with gratitude.'

'All right,' said Hilary surprisingly. 'What kind of things do they eat?'

'Beans and fish fingers, chips and ice cream,' Ria said.

'We can manage that.'

'I'd love to have them myself,' Ria apologised. She did in fact sound wistful.

Hilary forgave her. 'I know you would but it just happens that I'm married to a much more generous man than you are, that's the way things turn out.'

Ria paused to think of the spontaneous, loving Danny Lynch being considered less generous than the amazingly mean, penny-pinching Martin Moran. Wasn't it wonderful the way people saw their own situations?

'So Lady Ryan is going to grace us with her presence on the road,' Nora Johnson said. She had come to introduce the new element in her life, a puppy of indeterminate breed. Even the children, who loved animals, were puzzled by it. It seemed to have too many legs yet there were only four, its head looked as if it were bigger than its body but that could not possibly be so. It flopped unsteadily around the kitchen and then ran upstairs to relieve itself against the legs of the chairs in the front room. Annie reported this gleefully and Brian thought it was the funniest thing he had ever known.

Ria hid her irritation. 'Does it have a name, Mam?' she asked.

'Oh it's just thirty-two, no fancy name.'

'You're going to call the dog Thirty-Two?' Ria was astounded.

'No, I mean where Lady Ryan's penthouse is being built. The dog is called Pliers, I told you that.' She hadn't but it didn't matter. 'They all know she's coming to Tara Road, everyone's heard of her.'

'That's good, anyway they'd know her from visiting.'

'No, they read about her in the papers. There's as much about her as there is about your friend Barney McCarthy.' Nora didn't approve of him either so there was another sniff.

'It's extraordinary, Rosemary being so famous,' Ria said. 'You know, her mother thinks of her still as a thirteen-year-old and says she should be more like me. Rosemary of all people.'

Rosemary Ryan was featuring now in the financial pages as well as the women's pages. The company was going from strength to strength, and had taken on several foreign contracts in recent months. They printed picture postcards for some of the major tourist resorts in the Mediterranean, they had successfully tendered for sporting events as far afield as the West Coast of America. She had bought shares in the firm and it was only a matter of time before she would take it over entirely. The man who had employed her as a young girl to help in a very small print shop looked in amazement at the confident poised woman who had transformed his business. He was more interested in lowering his golf handicap nowadays than taking the early-morning train to Belfast, having two meetings and a lunch, and coming back on the afternoon train with a signed contract for work worth more than he ever dreamed possible.

Rosemary saw no reason at all why people in Northern Ireland should not have their printing done in the South, if the service was professional, the price was right and the quality high. She had long ago persuaded the company to change its name from Shamrock Printing to the more generally acceptable if equally meaningless Partners Printing.

And still no man. Well, there were plenty of men but no one man. Or at least no one available man. She puzzled people, so attractive, flirtatious even. It was not that she was frigid, she quite enjoyed dalliances and encounters on the few occasions that she allowed them to develop. People thought she had a much more adventurous and colourful sex life than she had. And Rosemary allowed this view to be widely held.

For one thing it discouraged people from thinking that she was lesbian like her sister. 'Would that be so terrible if they thought you were?' Eileen had asked.

'No. And don't get all sensitive and prickly on me, of course it wouldn't. It's just that if I'm not, then there's no point in having to carry all the defensive stuff that goes with it. You and Stephanie can do that because it's part of your life, it's not my cause.'

'Fair enough,' Eileen said. 'But I don't see what you're so hot under the collar about. It's not the 1950s for heaven's sake, you're free to do your own thing.'

'Sure. It's people's expectations that annoy me.'

'Maybe you've met him already and didn't know.'

'What do you mean?'

'Maybe Mr Perfect is out there under your nose, and you just didn't recognise him. One night you'll fall into each other's arms.'

Rosemary considered it. 'It's possible,' she said.

'So who do you think it might be? It can't be anyone who rejected you because nobody could, Ro. Maybe someone you never started with ... can you think of anyone?'

Rosemary had told nobody about Richard Roche, her date from the introductions agency whom she had since met briefly at various gatherings. It had been so hurtful when he claimed to read in her face that she had no interest in finding a life mate. 'I did fancy that Colm Barry a bit, you know, the one who has the restaurant. But I don't think he's the marrying kind.'

'Gay?' Eileen said.

'No, just messy, complicated.'

'I'd leave it, Ro, honestly. Stick to doing up this palace and building the business.'

'I think I will,' Rosemary agreed.

When Gertie had another accident her mother gave in and took the children back to live with her. 'You think I'm doing this for you, but I'm not, I'm doing it for those two defenceless children that you and that drunken sot managed to produce.'

'You're not helping me, Mam.'

'I am helping. I'm taking two children out of a possible death-house. If you were a normal woman instead of half crazed yourself you'd be able to realise that what I'm doing is helping you.'

'I have other friends, Mam, who would take them when Jack's upset.'

'Jack is upset every day and every night of the week these days. And decent though that Moran pair are, the odd weekend is all they'll manage.'

'You're very good, Mam, it's just that you don't understand.'

'You can say that again! Indeed I don't understand, two terrified little children who jump at the slightest sound, and you won't get a barring order and throw that lout out of their lives.'

'You're the religious one, you believe in a vow, for better for worse. We'd all stay when it's for better, it's when it's for worse it's harder, you see.'

'It's harder on a lot of people all right.' Her mother's mouth was a thin hard line as she packed John and Katy's things for yet another trip to their granny's in their disturbed young lives.

Rosemary came round to Danny and Ria several evenings a week. There were always plans to be discussed, reports to be given. She never stayed long, just long enough for everyone to know she was on the case and that no shoddy workmanship would escape her sharp eye. Ria tried to give her supper but she always said she had eaten a gigantic lunch and couldn't possibly swallow another thing. Ria knew this was not true. Once a week Rosemary went to Quentin's, the rest of the time she had low-fat yoghurt and an apple at her desk. Business meetings that had a social side to them would involve a wine and soda spritzer in the Shelbourne Hotel. Rosemary Ryan didn't remain greyhound slim without an effort of will. Sometimes Ria wondered why on earth she did it, why she pushed herself so hard. The gym and a swim before work, the jogging at the weekends, the permanent diet, the early nights, the regular hair appointments. What was it all *for*?

Rosemary would say it was for personal satisfaction, if she asked her. But it seemed such an odd and even a lonely answer that Ria didn't ask any more. It was like the way they didn't talk about sex these days. Once they had talked of nothing else. That was way back, before Ria had slept with Danny, but now they never mentioned the subject at all. Ria never said how Danny still had the power to thrill her just like in the early days. And Rosemary didn't tell of her numerous conquests. Ria knew that she was on the pill and she had a lot of lovers. She had seen the plans for the large bedroom in Rosemary's apartment with its luxurious bathroom, jacuzzi and twin hand-basins. This wasn't the bathroom of a woman who went to bed too often on her own. Ria longed to ask but didn't. If Rosemary wanted to tell her she would.

'It's all taking longer than we thought,' Rosemary said.

'Look at the contract, you'll see there are contingency clauses,' Danny laughed.

'*You* covered your back, didn't you?' She was admiring.

'No more than you did.'

'I just insured against shoddy workmanship.'

'And I just insured against wet weather, which indeed we had,' he said.

Ria was cutting out pastry shapes at the kitchen table with the children. Brian just wanted them round, Annie liked to shape hers.

'What are they talking about?' Brian asked.

'Business,' Annie explained. 'Daddy and Rosemary are talking business.'

'Why are they talking it in the kitchen? The kitchen's for playing in,' Brian said loudly.

'He's right,' said Rosemary. 'Let's take all these papers up to the beautiful room upstairs. If I had a room like that I wouldn't let it grow cold and musty like an old-fashioned parlour, I tell you that for nothing.'

Good-naturedly Danny carried the papers upstairs.

Ria stood with her hands floury and her eyes stinging. How *dare* Rosemary make her feel like that? In front of everybody! A woman who had let an upstairs parlour get musty. Tomorrow she would make sure that that room was never again allowed to lie idle.

'Are you okay, Mam?' Annie asked.

'Sure I am, of course.'

'Would you like to be in business too?'

For no reason Ria remembered the fortune-teller, Mrs Connor, prophesying that she would run a successful company or something. 'Not really, darling,' Ria said. 'But thanks all the same for asking.'

The next day Gertie came. She looked very tired and had huge black circles under her eyes.

'Don't start on at me. *Please*, Ria.'

'I hadn't a notion of it, we all lead our own lives.'

'Well, that's a change in the way the wind blows, I'm very glad to say.'

'Gertie, I want us both to tidy the front room, air it and polish it up properly.'

'Is anyone coming?' Gertie asked innocently.

'No,' Ria answered crisply. Gertie paused and looked at her. 'Sorry,' said Ria.

'Okay, you're kind enough not to ask me my business, I won't ask you yours.'

They worked in silence, Gertie doing the brass on the fender, Ria rubbing beeswax into the chairs. Ria put down her cloth. 'It's just I feel so useless, so wet and stupid.'

'*You* do?' Gertie was amazed.

'I do. We have this gorgeous room and we never sit in it.' Gertie looked at her thoughtfully. Someone had upset Ria. It wasn't her mother; Nora Johnson's stream of consciousness just washed over her all the time. It was hardly Frances Sullivan, the mother of Annie's friend Kitty; she wouldn't upset anyone. Hilary talked about nothing except the cost of this and the price of that; Ria wasn't going to get put down by her own sister. It had to be Rosemary. Gertie opened her mouth and closed it again. Ria would never hear a word against her friend; there was nothing Gertie could say that would be helpful.

'Well, don't you agree it's idiotic?' Ria asked.

Gertie spoke slowly. 'You know, compared to what I have this whole house is a palace, and everyone respects it. That would be enough for me. But on top of all that you and Danny went out and found all this beautiful furniture. And maybe you're right . . . you *should* use this room more. Why not start tonight?'

'I'd be afraid the children would pull it to bits.'

'No they won't. Make it into a sort of a treat for them to come up here. Like a halfway house to bed or something. If they're beautifully behaved here they can stay up a bit longer. Do you think that might work?' Gertie's eyes were enormous in her dark haunted face.

Ria wanted to cry. 'That's a great idea,' she said briskly. 'Right, let's finish this lot in twenty minutes then we'll go downstairs and have hot currant bread.'

'Barney's coming round for a drink before dinner this evening, we'll go to my study,' Danny said.

'Why don't you go to the front room instead, I'll leave coffee for you there. Gertie and I cleaned it up today and it looks terrific. I tidied away a lot of the rubbish. The table's free for you to put your papers.'

Together they went up to examine the room. The six o'clock sunshine was slanting in through the window. There were flowers on the mantelpiece.

'It's almost as if you were psychic. This isn't an easy discussion so it's good to have it in a nice place.'

'Nothing wrong?' She was anxious.

'Not really, just the perpetual Barney McCarthy cash-flow problem. Never lasts long but it would give you ulcers while it's there.'

'Is it best if I just keep the kids downstairs out of the way?'

'That would be terrific, sweetheart.' He looked tired and strained.

Barney came at seven and left at eight.

Ria had the children tidy and ready for bed. When they heard the hall door close they came up the stairs together, all three of them, the children slightly tentative. This room wasn't part of their territory. They sat and played a game of snakes and ladders. And possibly because they were overawed by the room Annie and Brian didn't shout at each other. They played it carefully as if it were a very important game. When the children were going to bed, for once without protest, Danny hugged them both very tight.

'You make everything worthwhile, all of you,' he said in a slightly choked voice.

Ria said she would be up to see that they had brushed their teeth. 'Was it bad?'

'No, not bad at all. Typical Barney, must have it now. Must have everything this minute. Overextended himself yet again. He's desperate to make Number thirty-two a real show house, you know. It's going to be his flagship, people will take him seriously with this one. It's just that it's costing a packet.'

'So?'

'So he needed a personal guarantee, you know, putting this house up as collateral.'

'*This* house?'

'Yes, his own are all in the frame already.'

'And what did you say?' Ria was frightened. Barney was a gambler; they could lose everything if he went down.

'I told him we owned it jointly, that I'd ask you.'

'Well, you'd better ring him straight away and say that I said it's fine,' she said.

'Do you mean that?'

'Listen, we wouldn't have ever had this place without him; we wouldn't have had anything without him. You should have told me earlier. Ring him on his mobile. So that he'll know we're not debating it.'

That night after they had made love Ria couldn't sleep. Suppose the cash-flow problem was serious this time. Suppose they lost their beautiful home. Danny lay beside her in an untroubled sleep. Several times she looked at his face and by the time dawn came she knew that even if they did lose the house it wouldn't matter just as long as she didn't lose Danny.

'Come on, Mam, we'll have our tea in the front room,' Ria said to her mother.

'It's far from a place like this you were reared.' Nora Johnson looked around the room which Ria had now resolved to use properly. She still smarted slightly from Rosemary's remark, yet in a way her friend had done her a favour. Danny didn't fall asleep when he sat here, he looked around him with pleasure at the treasures they had managed to gather. The children were quieter and kept their games neatly in one of the sideboard drawers rather than leaving them strewn around the place. Gertie enjoyed cleaning the place, she said it was like stepping into the cover of a magazine. Hilary went through the cost of every item of furniture and pronounced that they had made a killing.

Even Ria's mother seemed happy to sit there, although she would never admit it. She compared it to rooms in other houses where she ironed and said it was much more elegant. She wouldn't allow the dog to come into this territory and so Pliers slept glumly in a basket in the kitchen. When Rosemary called she always admired the room. She had probably forgotten her cruel words saying it had been kept like a musty front parlour that no one used. Instead she saw virtue in its high ceiling, its two tall windows, its lovely warm colours. It was a real gem, she said several times over.

Ria realised that there was great satisfaction in having lovely possessions. If you couldn't have a streamlined figure, flawless make-up and exquisite clothes, then having a perfect room was a substitute. For the first time she knew why people bought books on style and decoration and period furniture.

It was interesting however to see that Rosemary's own design plans were as different from the room she admired so much in Number 16 Tara Road as could possibly be. Number 32 had been gutted entirely and the long top-floor apartment had a wraparound roof garden with a view stretching out towards the Dublin mountains. At night it would look magnificent with all the city lights in between. The interiors were cool and spare, a lot of empty wall space, pale wooden floors, kitchen fittings that were uncluttered and minimalist.

It was about as unlike Ria's house as anyone could imagine. Ria fought to like the clean lines seen in the artist's impressions, and as the project proceeded she visited the site often and forced out words of praise for a place that seemed to her like a modern art gallery.

Danny spent a lot of time on Number 32. Sometimes, Ria felt, too much time. There were other properties out there, this was only one of them.

'I told you, if we get the right kind of tenants in here Barney's home and dry. He's into the prestige end of things not the Mickey Mouse conversion. We need a good write-up in the property pages, and Rosemary can organise that. We need a politician, a showbiz person, a sports star or something to buy up the other flats.'

'Can you pick and choose?'

'Not really, but we want the word to get about. I asked Colm to tell the nobs who come into his restaurant.'

'And has he?'

'Yes, but sadly his ignoramus brother-in-law Monto Mackey is the only one who came enquiring.'

'Monto and Caroline want to live in a flat in Tara Road?'

'I didn't think he'd have the cash but he does. And cash is what he offered, you know, suitcases of it.'

'No!' Ria was astounded. Colm's beautiful but withdrawn sister was married to an unattractive car dealer, a large florid man interested more in going to race meetings than in his wife or his business. He seemed the last kind of person to buy a property like this.

'Barney was delighted, of course, always a man for the suitcase of money, but I convinced him to watch it, that it was quality we wanted here, not dross like Monto Mackey.'

'And did he listen? Are things all right with him these days?' Ria never actually said aloud that she was anxious about the guarantee they had given to Barney, but it was always there.

'Don't worry, sweetheart, the bailiffs aren't at the door. Barney's fine, just has to be steered away from quick money without the small annoyance of tax.' Danny seemed amused and quite unimpressed by his boss. They had a very relaxed relationship.

When Rosemary spoke in front of Barney about getting some garden furniture he offered an introduction to a friend. 'No need to trouble the VAT man at all, pay cash and everyone's happy,' Barney had said.

'Not everyone.' Rosemary had been cool. 'Not the government, not the people who have to pay VAT, not my accountant.'

'Oh pardon *me*,' Barney had said. But nobody had been embarrassed. You met all sorts in this world. That's what business was about.

'Is Lady Ryan having a housewarming party? She might like me to take the coats for her.' Nora wanted to know every last detail of it all.

'Don't stir up trouble, Holly.' Danny was affectionate to his mother-in-law. 'You only call her Lady Ryan to get a rise out of Ria. No, I didn't hear of any party. She didn't say anything to you, did she, sweetheart?'

'She's going to wait until she has a proper roof garden apparently,' Ria explained. 'She says the place will look nothing until she has lighting and tubs of this and trellises of that. She's such a perfectionist.'

'How long will that take her? It took me three years to get anything to grow in my place,' Nora Johnson said.

'Oh Holly, we're just not in Rosemary Ryan's world. The garden will be ready in three weeks, that's part of the schedule.'

'It can't be,' Nora gasped.

'Yes it can if you hire good nurseries and have everything in containers.'

'I wonder could I clean for Rosemary do you think?' Gertie asked Ria.

'Gertie, you run a business, you haven't time to go out cleaning for people. You don't *have* to either.'

'I do.' Gertie was short.

'But who's looking after the launderette?'

'I told you it looks after itself; your mother's dog Pliers could run it. I have kids in there doing it for me, I make much more per hour cleaning than I pay them.'

'That's ludicrous.'

'Has she got anyone already to clean?'

'Ask her, Gertie.'

'No, Ria, you ask her for me, will you? As a friend?' said Gertie.

'Of course I won't have Gertie cleaning for me. She should be managing that run-down washeteria of hers for a start, and minding her own children for another thing.'

'She'd like the hours.'

'You give her the hours then.'

'I can't. Danny wonders what on earth I do all day that I then have to go and pay Gertie.'

'Yes. Quite.'

'Rosemary, go on, you need someone you can trust.'

'I'll have a firm, contract cleaners twice a week.'

'But they're total strangers, they might steal everything, root around amongst your things.'

'Oh Ria, please. How do you think these places survive? They have to employ honest people, you're absolutely guaranteed that. Otherwise they go out of business.'

And that was it as far as Rosemary was concerned. She was now much more interested in creating her garden. The trellis arrived and was erected immediately. Days later the instant climbers in containers were carried upstairs.

'Lots of roses, of course,' Rosemary explained to Ria. 'Bush Rambler, that's a nice pink here on this side and Muscosa and Madame Pierre Oger, all on this side. What else do you think?' she consulted Ria as if she wanted her view.

'Well, I see you have Golden Showers, that's nice.' Ria picked the only name she recognised.

'Yes, but that's yellow. I thought I'd go for blocks of colour, more dramatic to look out at.'

Rosemary never once said that it would look well or tasteful or dramatic for other people, it was always for herself. But surely she'd want other people to admire it too, Ria thought. She wasn't sure. She wasn't sure of anything about Rosemary sometimes. Ria knew for a fact that Rosemary hadn't known one flower from another three months ago and here she was helping the men from the nurseries to trail the honeysuckle, the jasmine, the wisteria as if she had been doing nothing else all her life. It was amazing the grasp she had of anything she touched.

She did indeed have a housewarming. Ria knew hardly anybody there; Danny and Barney knew a few. Polly was in attendance that night, so Ria had to be sure not to mention the party to Mona. Colm had hoped that he might tender to do the catering but Rosemary had chosen some other firm. 'Clients, you know,' she said lightly as if that covered everything.

Gertie had asked her directly did she want any help at all during the function and Rosemary had answered equally directly that she didn't. 'I can't risk having Jack turn up looking for his conjugal rights or his dinner or both,' she said.

Rosemary's mother and Eileen and Stephanie were there. 'Do you know any of this crowd?' Mrs Ryan asked her daughter querulously.

'No, Mother. I only know lawyers these days and protesters, and Rosemary *is* in business.'

'I don't think they come from anything, you know.' Mrs Ryan sighed. Rosemary was passing behind her mother. She mouthed the phrase at her sister that she knew was hovering on her mother's lips. 'Jumped-up people, you know.' Eileen and Stephanie burst out laughing. Mrs Ryan was startled. 'Look, you two are eccentric enough already, don't be drawing attention to yourselves.'

'At least we didn't wear our boiler suits, Mrs R,' said Stephanie who was willowy with long chestnut hair and quite gorgeous.

'Or our bowler hats,' giggled Eileen.

Mrs Ryan sighed again. Nobody had her problems, nobody at all. For all this wealth and style there wasn't a whisper of a husband for Rosemary anywhere in sight. There were photographers there, however, and Rosemary was photographed with a politician. Barney and Danny were taken with an actress, out on the roof garden with a bank of flowers and a panoramic view in the background. Rosemary was on the financial pages, the others on the property pages. Enquiries about Number 32 Tara Road came flooding in. Everyone was happy.

Because she was now such a near neighbour Danny and Ria saw a lot more of Rosemary. She often called in around seven in the evening for an hour or so and they would all have a glass of wine mixed with soda in the front room. Ria made hot cheese savouries, or bacon slices wrapped around almonds and prunes. It didn't matter that Rosemary waved them away; Danny would have a few, she and the children would eat the rest, and anyway it gave her a chance to bring out the Victorian china that she had bought at auctions.

The children stayed down in the kitchen, with strict warnings not to fight and not to touch anything on the stove. Ria found herself fixing her hair regularly and putting on some make-up. She really couldn't face the elegant Rosemary night after night without making some effort.

'Dressing up for Lady Ryan!' her mother scoffed.

'You always dress nicely, Mother, I note,' Ria said.

Her mother had taken to wearing little pillbox hats like Audrey Hepburn's headgear. She bought these in thrift shops. Danny had commented on them with huge admiration. 'Now you dare tell me, Holly, that you don't look like Audrey Hepburn, you could be her younger sister.'

Gertie was also disapproving of Rosemary's visits. 'You wait on her as if you were her maid, Ria,' she said.

'I do nothing of the sort, I don't go out to work like they do, that's all. Anyway, it's nice for me to have a room to show off and everything.'

'Sure.' Gertie had gone off Rosemary. It would have been a handy few quid just down the road, and she would like to have seen the inside of a place that had featured in the newspapers. Even as a cleaner. 'Is it lovely above there in Number thirty-two?' Gertie asked Ria. It would be nice to tell the customers in the launderette about it, even second hand.

Ria didn't often take Brian up to Rosemary's apartment. He was three now; he upset the calm of this place with his endless noise and perpetual toddling and constant sticky hugs and demands for attention. Annie wouldn't have wanted to come. There was nothing to entertain her at Rosemary's and too many areas that seemed off limits.

'You *must* bring the children with you,' Rosemary would insist. But Ria knew that it was easier not to. She loved them so much that it would kill her to apologise for what she considered their totally natural behaviour. So instead she left the children with her mother on one of the many Saturday afternoons that Danny was working and walked up to see Rosemary on her own. It was so peaceful and elegant, as if she hadn't unmade a bed, cooked a meal, or done any washing since the day it had been shown off at the housewarming. Even the roof garden looked as if every flower had been painted into place.

Despite the smart surroundings, Rosemary was in so many ways exactly the same as she had been years ago when they had started work at the estate agency. She could still laugh in the same infectious way about the things that had made them laugh back then, Hilary's obsession with money, Mrs Ryan's fear of jumped-up people, Nora Johnson's living her life through the world of movies.

Rosemary had told Ria about some of the problems at work, the girl who was excellent at everything and would have been a superb personal assistant but had such bad body odour she had to let her go; the man who had changed his mind at the last moment and cancelled a huge print job and Rosemary had to take him to court; charity leaflets she had printed for nothing for a function which turned out to be a rave where everyone was on Ecstasy and the police were called.

They would sit on the terrace with their feet up, and the heavy scent of the flowers all around them.

'What's that lovely green one with the gorgeous smell?' Ria asked.

'Tobacco plant,' Rosemary said.

'And the big purple one a bit like lilac?'

'*Solanum crispum.*'

'How on earth do you know them all, and remember them, Rosemary? You have so many other things in your mind as well.'

'It's all in a book, Ria. There's no point in having these things if you don't know what they are.' Rosemary's voice was slightly impatient.

Ria knew how to head impatience off at the pass. 'You're absolutely right. I've got plenty of books, next time I'll talk just as authoritatively as you do.'

'That's my girl.' Rosemary was approving. The moment of irritation was over.

Maybe if their place was less untamed and wild, she and Danny could sit like this on a Saturday afternoon and watch the children play. Maybe they could just talk to each other, read the papers together sometimes. It had been so long since they sat in their garden.

'Is there a lot of work keeping all this the way it is?'

'No, I have a man once a week for four hours, that's all.'

'And how do you know what to tell him to do?'

'I don't. I hired him from a garden centre, *he* knows what to do. But you see the whole trick was in making it labour-saving. It was the builders who did it all. Once you don't have sprawling herbaceous borders that would break your back weeding them you're fine. Just nice easy-care bushes and shrubs which sort of bring themselves up.' It always seemed so effortless when Rosemary described things.

As she walked down Tara Road Ria thought about it. Brian was old enough now, she could get a job, but Danny didn't seem to want her to. 'Sweetheart, isn't it wonderful for me to know you are here and in charge of everything . . .' he would say if she brought the subject up. Or else he would frown with worry and concern. 'Aren't you happy, love? That's terrible. I suppose I'm very selfish, I thought your life seemed very full, lots of friends and everything . . . but of course we'll talk about it.'

That wasn't what she wanted either.

It was a particularly lovely road just as the summer was starting. The cherry trees were in bloom everywhere, their petals starting to make a pink carpet. She never stopped marvelling at the variety of life you could find in Tara Road – houses where students lived in great numbers in small flats and bedsitters, their bicycles up against the railings just as they had been outside their own house until this year when Danny and Ria had been able to reclaim all the rented rooms for themselves. If she turned right outside Rosemary's house the road would go past equally mixed housing, high houses like their own, lower ones half hidden by trees, then on past the small lock-up workshop where the road changed again into big houses in their own grounds until it came to the corner with a busy street. And round the corner to where Gertie lived and worked, where the handy launderette had plenty of clientele among the bedsitterland around, and Gertie and Jack lived their mysterious life where you were considered a much better friend if you asked no questions at all.

Her mind full of gardens, Ria noticed that almost every house had made more effort than they had. But it was so hard to know where to start. Some of that undergrowth really needed someone with a saw to cut it down, and then what? She didn't want to be one of those women who, leaving a friend's house, immediately wanted new kitchen work surfaces or a change of curtains, but it seemed ludicrous that she and Danny had managed to close their eyes somehow to a huge aspect of the life they could have together.

Ria didn't want to admit it to herself but she knew that she had got out of the habit of initiating things. When they were first married she would go down to the main road, buy two pots of polish and the scullery would be immaculate when Danny got back from work. Now perhaps he had higher standards. He bought and sold and therefore got to know the houses of the rich and those with taste and style. She would never go ahead on her own with any plan. Yet if Danny didn't see that their garden was dragging the place down perhaps it was up to her to make the move.

Barney McCarthy was just parking his car in their cluttered driveway. It wasn't an easy manoeuvre, he had to negotiate it in beside their car, Annie's bicycle, Brian's tricycle, a wheelbarrow that had been there for weeks, several crates that had been ignored by the dustmen but had never been taken to the dump.

'You look lovely, Ria,' he said as he got out. He was a man who admired women but he never paid an idle compliment. If he said you looked well he meant it.

Ria patted her hair, pleased. 'Thank you, Barney. I don't feel lovely, actually I feel a bit annoyed with myself. I think I'm getting rather slovenly.'

'You?' He was amazed.

'When you think that we have lived here for nearly nine years and it's still a bit like a building site.'

'Oh no, no,' Barney murmured soothingly.

'But it *is*, Barney. And I'm the one who's around here all the time. I should be doing something about it, and I'm going to, I've decided that. Poor Danny shouldn't have to take that on as well as everything else. Already he works all the hours God sends . . .' She thought Barney looked at her sympathetically.

'Ria, you can't go talking like that, there's years of undergrowth there.'

'Don't I know it? No, I meant maybe you could tell me how much it would cost to get your men to come in and clear the place out, then we could arrange what to plant . . . Just tell me what it will be, don't bother Danny at all, and I'll build it into the household expenses. At least that's something I'd be able to do.'

'I think we should bring Danny in on this, ask him what he wants.'

'But he'll say: "In time, in time", and we'll never get it done. Let's just clear it, Barney, and then we can decide what we should plant and how to decorate it.'

Barney stood stroking his chin. 'I don't know, Ria, there's a lot to be thought of before you bring in the diggers. Suppose you wanted to build here, for example. It would be silly to have put in a lot of fancy flower beds and suchlike, which would only have to be taken out again.'

'*Build?*' Ria was astonished. 'But what would we want to build? Haven't we a huge three-and-a-half-storey house already! We haven't any furniture in some of the tenants' rooms yet. We're going to make a bigger study for Danny and maybe a sort of playroom for the children, but we don't need any more space.'

'You never know how people's plans change as the years go on,' Barney said.

She felt a chill. She didn't want things to change, only get better. She took a sudden decision. She was not going to discuss it any more with this man. Much as he liked and admired her he thought of her only as Danny's little wife. Pretty, possibly a good mother and homemaker, tactful and always ready with the right kind of food when they needed it, equally pleasant to his wife and his mistress. He did not consider her a person who would be able to make a decision about the home she lived in.

'You're absolutely right, Barney, I don't know what got into me,' she said. 'Will I make a little snack for you and Danny? Iced tea maybe and a tomato sandwich on wholemeal bread?'

'You're a genius,' he said.

Ria's mother was in the kitchen with the children. 'Oh there you are, back from Lady Ryan's place.' Nora Johnson had never liked Rosemary.

Ria had now forgotten where the resentment began and why. She had long ceased to try and convince her mother of Rosemary's worth. 'Yes indeed, and she was asking for you too, Mam.'

'Huh,' snorted Nora Johnson. 'Was that Barney I heard you talking to?'

Ria was bending over to see the picture that Annie had been painting, there was water all over the kitchen. 'I painted a picture of you, Mam,' she said proudly. A creature like a golliwog stood surrounded by saucepans and frying pans.

'Lovely,' said Ria. 'That's really beautiful, Annie, you're so clever.'

'I'm a clever boy,' Brian insisted.

'No, you're a very stupid boy,' Annie said.

'Annie, really! Brian's very clever too.'

'I don't think he has a brain in his head,' Annie said seriously. 'If you don't give him any paints he screams and if you do he just makes big splashes.'

'Rubbish, Annie. He's just not as old as you are, that's all. Wait until he's your age and he'll be able to do all the same things.'

'When you get older will you be as clever as Gran?' Annie asked.

'I hope so,' Ria smiled.

'Never in a million years,' her mother said. 'I expect you'll be whipping up some little delicacy for that adulterer upstairs.'

'It's a word I don't use really in general conversation myself,' Ria said, flashing her a look.

Annie was learning new phrases all the time. 'What's a dutterer?' she asked.

'Oh, a dutterer is like a sort of drain, you know, another word for a gutter,' Ria said quickly.

Annie accepted this and went back to her painting.

'Sorry,' her mother said a little later.

Ria patted her on the arm. 'It doesn't matter, I agree with you as it happens. Then I would, wouldn't I? Wives always do. Can you get me those big iced-tea glasses please, Mam?'

'Mad idea this, you should either have a nice cold gin and tonic or a nice hot cup of tea, I say, not mixing the two up. It's not natural.'

Later that evening Ria said to Danny that they should really try to do something with the wilderness of the garden.

'Not now, sweetheart,' Danny said, as she knew he was going to.

'I'm not going to nag, let *me* do it, I'll ask Barney for a price.'

'You already did,' Danny said.

'That's because I was trying to take things off your shoulders.'

'Sweetheart, don't do that, please. He'd only do it for nothing, and it's not necessary.'

'But Danny, you're the one who says we must keep up the value of the property.'

'We don't know what we're going to *do* with it yet, Ria.'

'Do with it? We want a place for people to park their cars when they come to see us, for us to park our car without it being like an obstacle race . . . we want it to look like a home where people are settling down for their life. Not some kind of a transit camp.'

'But we haven't thought it through . . . what the future may bring.'

'Now don't start talking like Barney about building here.' Ria was very cross.

'Barney said that?'

'Yes, and I don't know what the hell he was talking about.'

Danny saw her red angry face and her confusion. 'Listen, if there is any building to be done, it's way way down the road yet. You're right. We must do something . . . a sort of patch-up job on it.'

'But what do we need to build?'

'Nothing yet, you're quite right.'

'Yet? Haven't we got a huge house?'

'Who knows what the future will bring?'

'That's not fair, Danny. I must know what you think the future will bring.'

'Okay then, I'll tell you what I mean. Suppose, just suppose we fell on hard times, we wouldn't want to lose this house. If we had a chance to build in the garden, maybe a small unit, two self-contained flats, little maisonettes they used to be called, or town houses, there would be room . . .'

'Two flats in our garden? Outside our front door?' Ria looked at him as if he were mad.

'If we left the possibility of doing so then it would be like an insurance policy.'

'But it would be terrible.'

'Better than losing the house if that were the choice. It's not, but suppose it were.'

'Why should I suppose any such thing? You're always looking on the bright side, so why are we looking at doom and gloom and building horrible flats in our garden in case we're poor? If there's something you're not telling me then you'd better tell me now. It's not fair to leave me not bothering my pretty little head. It's not fair and I won't stand for it.'

Danny took her in his arms. 'I swear I'm not hiding things from you. It's just in this business you see so many people who believed that the future was going to be fine and that everything would go on slightly upwards each year . . . and then something happens, some swing in the market, and they lose everything.'

'But we don't have any stocks and shares, Danny.'

'I know, sweetheart, *we* don't.'

'What does that mean?'

'Barney does, did, and our fortunes are very much tied up with his.'

'But you said that the whole business of the guarantee was over, that once he had made his money on Number thirty-two he'd got out of that worry.'

'And he has.' Danny was soothing. 'So he's more cautious now.'

'Barney was never cautious in his life. He had a heart attack and he still smokes and drinks brandy, and anyway why does it mean that *we* should be cautious and edgy?'

'Because our fortunes are tied in with his. Barney knows that and he wants the best for us, so *that's* why he likes to think there's a chance of our building . . . suppose things go badly for him . . . of us getting more bricks and mortar, the only thing that's definitely going to keep its value. Do you see?'

'Not really, to be honest,' Ria said. 'If Barney's business collapsed couldn't you work in any estate agent in town?'

'Yes, I suppose I could,' Danny said with that quick bright smile that Ria had learned to dread. It was the kind of smile he had when he was showing somebody a doubtful property. When he was anxious to close on something, when he had a completion date but not an exchange date, when he was afraid that the chain wouldn't hold and somebody somewhere along the line wouldn't get their loan and so it would all collapse like a house of cards.

But there was no more to be discovered or discussed or gained. A patch-up job and a legacy of worry for the future. That was what had come out of the conversation.

Sheila Maine wrote from America to say that the papers were full of the great opportunities in Ireland, and the numbers of people who were relocating there. She wondered if any of the girls she knew in Dublin would advise her. She had so much enjoyed meeting them all when she had been there. And hadn't that been a fun day when they had gone to the psychic in her caravan? Mrs Connor had told Sheila that her future was in her own hands and really and truly this was very sound. Everywhere she looked now she read the same advice, the same counsel. Why hadn't they known it years ago when they were just swept along with what everyone else thought, and did what other people did?

Sheila wrote that her son Sean who was Annie's age was learning Irish dancing at a nearby class, and her daughter Kelly who was a very demanding three-year-old would join the babies' class in it next year. She was determined that the children would not grow up ignorant of their Irish heritage. She copied the letter to her sister Gertie, to Rosemary, to Ria and to Hilary. Sheila had particularly liked Hilary during her visit to Ireland and she urged her to come out to visit her in the school holidays.

'How could I do that? She must be mad, they've no idea of money over there.' Hilary showed the invitation.

'I don't know, Hilary.' Ria sometimes felt that she spent her life assuring her sister that some things actually *were* within her reach. 'Suppose you were to book three months in advance, you'd get a great reduction and Sheila says it would cost you nothing out there.'

'But what about Martin?' Hilary always had an argument against everything that was suggested.

'Well, he could go with you if he'd like two weeks out in Connecticut which he very well might, or else go home and see his parents in the country. You know he says he wants to go back there more than you do.'

Hilary frowned. It made sense only if you were as rich as Ria and Danny with no financial worries at all. Life was very strange the way the cards were dealt, she said again.

Ria's patience was limited that day. Mona McCarthy had been around wondering would Ria help at a coffee morning, which was fine except that it meant she would have to ask someone to look after Brian for her. She couldn't ask her mother. Nora Johnson had such a network of social and professional activities that you had to book her days in advance. Today she would be ironing in one place, delivering leaflets about the Bring and Buy sale in aid of the animal refuge, visiting some of the old ladies in St Rita's. She couldn't break into all that.

Gertie said it wasn't a good morning to leave Brian at the launderette for a couple of hours, because ... well let's say ... it wasn't a good morning. Gertie's own children were with her mother. That said it all. And never in a million years would Ria ask a neighbour like Frances Sullivan to look after him. It would be admitting that even as a non-working wife she couldn't organise her life. If only that pale wan Caroline, the strange sister of Colm in the restaurant, was more together then she could be drafted in for a couple of hours, but it always took her about three seconds too long to understand what you were saying, and Ria hadn't the time for it today.

Hilary sat there turning the letter this way and that. Ria decided to take the chance. 'I'm going to ask you a favour, say no if you want to. I am very anxious to go up to Mona McCarthy's house for a variety of reasons.'

'I'm sure you are,' Hilary sniffed.

'None of them like you think, but it would suit me greatly if you minded Brian for me for three hours, then I'll come back and make you a huge gorgeous lunch. Yes or no?'

'Why do you want to go there?'

'That's a "no", I suppose,' Ria said.

'Not necessarily. If you tell me why you want to go, then I'll stay.'

'All right I will. I'm worried that the McCarthys might be in some kind of financial trouble. I want to see what I can find out, because if they are then it will affect Danny. Now that's the truth – take it or leave it. Yes or no?'

'Yes,' said Hilary with a smile.

Ria phoned a taxi, put on her good suit, her best silk scarf, took a freshly baked walnut cake from the wire tray where it was cooling and headed off to the McCarthys' large house six miles from Dublin. The drive was filled with smart cars and the sound of women's chatter was loud as she approached the door. It was touching to see Mona's face light up when she came in. Ria slipped out of her jacket and began to help with the practised smile of one who had been to many coffee mornings. It was all about making sure these comfortably off and often fairly lonely women had a good time and were warmly welcomed into a group. Their ten-pound entrance fee was not in itself so important as making them feel they belonged. This way they could later be persuaded to part with much larger sums of money at fashion shows, at glittering dinner dances, at film premières.

An elegant woman was introduced to Ria as Margaret Murray. 'You may know my husband, Ken. He's in the property business,' she said.

Ria longed to tell her that Ken Murray was the first boy she had ever kissed many years ago, when she was fifteen and a half. That it had been horrible and he had told her she was boring. But she thought that Margaret Murray might not find this as funny in retrospect as she did, so she said nothing but had a little giggle to herself.

'You're in good form,' Mona McCarthy said approvingly.

'Remind me to tell you why later. This is all going very well, isn't it?'

'Yes, I think they like coming here as a curiosity,' Mona said.

'Why so?'

'Well they speculate a lot, you know, about whether we are still solvent or not. Rumours around the place have us in the workhouse.' Mona looked remarkably calm as she refilled the coffee pot from the two percolators.

'And aren't you worried about this?' Ria asked.

'No, Ria, if I worried every time that I hear something about Barney I'd be a very worried woman indeed. We've been poor before, and if it happens I imagine we could cope with it again. But I don't think it will happen. Barney is always a contingency-plan person, I feel sure there are a lot of safety nets along the way.' She was serene, almost like a ship as she sailed back into the room full of women whom she knew to be rather overinterested in what kept this extravagant lifestyle afloat.

Colm Barry called when Ria and Hilary were having the promised enormous lunch. 'Well you two don't stint yourselves, I'm glad to see.' He seemed happy to accept their invitation to join them.

'Oh, Ria can afford to buy the best cuts of meat,' Hilary said, reverting to type.

'It's what she does with them that's so delicious.' Colm appreciated the cooking. 'And the way they're served.'

'It's hard to get good fresh vegetables round here,' Ria said. 'They're very tired up at the corner and nowhere else is in a pram's walk really.'

'Why don't you grow your own?' Colm suggested.

'Oh Lord no. It would be such hard work digging it all out back there. Even to get the front tidied up was a major undertaking. Neither Danny nor I have the souls of gardeners, I'm afraid.'

'I'd do it for you at the back if you like,' Colm offered.

'Oh you can't do that,' Ria protested.

'I have an ulterior motive. Suppose I was to make a proper kitchen garden out there and grow all the things I want for the restaurant in it, then you could have some too.'

'Would it work?'

'Yes, of course it would, that is if you don't have plans to have velvet lawns, water features, fountains or pergolas out there.'

'No. I think we can safely say those aren't on the agenda,' Ria laughed easily.

'Great, then we'll do it.'

Ria noted with pleasure that Colm hadn't said they should wait to consult Danny. Unlike Barney McCarthy he seemed to regard her as a responsible adult capable of making a decision on her own. 'Will it be very heavy work, preparing the soil?'

'I don't know yet.'

'It's such a wilderness out there we have no real idea how much awful stuff there might be buried with old roots and rubble.'

'But I need the exercise anyway so it's going to be something that benefits everyone. We all win, no one loses.'

'Very few of those deals about, let me tell you,' Hilary said.

And from that time on Colm became part of the background in their house in Tara Road. He let himself in silently through the wooden door that opened on to the back lane; he kept his gardening tools in a small makeshift hut at the back. He dug an area half the width of the house and the whole length of the garden. This left plenty of space for the children to play in. And as the months went on he erected a fence and covered it with a plant he called Mile a Minute or Russian vine.

'It really looks rather nice you know,' Danny said thoughtfully one day. 'And the whole notion of mature kitchen garden at rear is a good selling-point.'

'If we were to sell, which we're not going to do. I wish you wouldn't frighten me saying things like that, Danny,' Ria complained.

'Listen, sweetheart, if you worked in a world where hardly anything else is discussed then you'd talk in auctioneer-speak too.' He was right, and what's more he was good-tempered and happy. He was very loving to Ria sometimes, dashing home from work saying he thought of her so much and deeply that he couldn't concentrate on anything else. They would go upstairs and draw the curtains. Once or twice Ria wondered what Colm working in the garden might think.

They didn't talk much about it but she knew that in Gertie's case it was a nightmare, usually only attempted by Jack when drunk. For Hilary it had almost ceased to exist. Martin had once said the only real reason for a man and woman to mate was the hope of producing a child, and that the urge and impetus just weren't there otherwise. He had only said it once, and afterwards confessed that he had been a bit depressed at the time and didn't really mean it, Hilary confided. But somehow it was there always in the air.

Ria didn't know any details of Rosemary's sex life. But she was sure it must be very active in those perfect surroundings that she had created for herself. Everywhere she went men were attracted by her. Ria had sometimes seen Rosemary leave parties with men. Did she take them home, upstairs to that apartment which had featured in so many magazines? Probably. Rosemary wouldn't live like a nun. Still, it must be very unsettling to have to get to know different people in that way. To learn the intricacies and familiarities of another body instead of knowing exactly what worked for you. And for Danny. Ria knew that she was very, very lucky.

The anxiety over the McCarthy finances seemed to have subsided. Danny didn't work so late at night. He took his little princess, Annie, out on walks and visits to the sea. He held the hand of his chubby son Brian as the child changed from stumbling to waddling and eventually to running away ahead of them.

The back garden changed slowly and laboriously. Ria knew that it was much easier to learn the names of twenty plants for containers on a roof terrace than to understand Colm's discussion about double cropping and pest-proof barriers. She tried to sympathise when his sprouts all failed, when his great bamboo bean supports blew down in the wind and when the peas that he had tried to grow in hanging baskets produced hardly anything at all.

'Why didn't you grow them in the ground?' Ria had asked innocently.

'I was trying to make it nice for you to look out on. You know, a lot of hanging baskets on the back wall. They looked good, I thought.' He was very disappointed.

She wished she could share his enthusiasm but to her it was back-breaking and unyielding and there were mountains of healthy sprouts and peas in the shops. Still, he battled on and he even gave the children little tubs where they could grow tomatoes and peppers. He was good with Annie and Brian, and seemed to understand the age difference between them well. Brian got a simple tomato plant which just had to be watered, Annie was encouraged to grow lettuce and basil. But mainly he didn't take part in their lives, he kept to himself on his side of the huge Russian vine fence.

On the other side there was a swing, a garden seat and even a home-made barbecue pit. At the front of the house the area had been tarmacadamed by Barney's men, and what had been described as a patch-up job had blossomed well. People admired the coloured heathers that grew in the makeshift flower bed.

'I don't know where the heathers came from, honestly,' Ria said once.

'You *must* have planted them, sweetheart. Little and all as I know about gardening I know that flowers don't appear by magic! And anyway don't you have to have special soil for heathers?'

Colm was there as they spoke. 'That's me, I'm afraid. I bought a bag of the wrong kind of soil, you know ericaceous, lime hating.' They didn't know but they nodded sagely. 'So I had to put it somewhere and I dumped it there. Hope it's all right.'

'It's great.' Danny approved. 'And did you plant the heathers too?'

'Someone gave me a present of them. You see, because I put in the menu that all vegetables are home grown, the customers think I have a great deal of land behind my place. They often give me plants instead of a tip.'

'But we should pay you for those . . .' Ria began.

'Nonsense, Ria. As I told you both I have a very good deal being able to use your garden and honestly the vegetables are a huge success. I have rows of courgettes planted this week, the trick is to come up with some clever recipes for them now.'

'You're doing better these days?' Danny was interested.

'Much better and we got a great review. That helped a lot.' Colm never complained even when times were slack. 'I was wondering if you'd consider a small greenhouse an eyesore? I'd disguise it well, you know, build it up against the back wall . . .'

'Go ahead, Colm. Do you want a contribution?'

'Only the right to use a bit of electricity for it, it won't take much.'

'Oh, would that all business deals could be like this!' Danny said, shaking Colm's hand.

Brian was seven in the summer of 1995. Danny and Ria had a barbecue for his friends. They only wanted sausages, Brian said. People didn't eat other things.

'Not lovely lamb chops?' Danny said. He liked the idea of standing with an apron and chef's hat turning something a little more ambitious than sausages.

'Ugh,' Brian said.

'Or those lovely green peppers Colm grew, we could thread them all on a skewer and make kebabs.'

'My friends don't like kebabs,' Brian said.

'Your friends have never had kebabs,' Annie said. She was close to being twelve, only three months away from it. It was really hard having to deal with someone as infantile as Brian. Very strangely it seemed that her mother and father appeared as delighted with his babyish ramblings as they were with anything she said.

The arrangements for his party were very tedious. Annie had suggested giving Brian two pounds of cooked sausages and letting all his friends heat them up. They'd never know the difference and all they cared about was lots of tomato ketchup.

'No, it must be right. We had a great party for your seventh birthday, don't you remember?' her mother said.

Annie didn't remember, all the birthdays had merged into one. But she knew that they must have made a fuss over it like over all celebrations. 'That's right, it was terrific,' she said grudgingly.

'You are beautiful, Annie Lynch, you're an adorable girl.' Her mother hugged her until it hurt.

'I'm awful, look at my desperate straight hair.'

'And I spend my life saying look at my frizzy hair,' Ria said. 'It's a very annoying part of being a woman, we're never really satisfied with the way we look.'

'Some people are.'

'Oh all the film stars your gran goes on about, all these beauties, I expect they're happy with themselves, but nobody *we* know.'

'I'd say that Rosemary is okay with the way she looks.'

Rosemary Ryan had refused to be called Aunty by her friends' children, she said she was quite old enough already without any of that sort of thing, thank you. 'She's super-looking I know, but she's always on this diet or that diet so maybe in her heart she isn't totally satisfied either.'

'No, she's very pleased with the way she looks, you can see it the way she looks at herself in mirrors.'

'What?'

'She sort of smiles at herself, Mam. You must see it, not only in mirrors, but in pictures, anywhere there's glass.'

Ria laughed. 'Aren't you a funny little article, Annie, the things you see.'

Annie didn't like being patted on the head. 'It's true, isn't it, Dad?'

'Totally true, Princess,' said Danny.

'You didn't hear what was said,' they both accused him.

'Yes I did, Annie said Rosemary smiles at her reflection in mirrors and indeed she does, always has. Years ago in the old agency she was at it.'

Annie looked pleased, Ria felt put out. It was such a criticism of her friend and she had never been aware of it. 'Well, she's so good-looking she's entitled to admire herself,' she said eventually.

'Good-looking? I think she's like a bird of prey,' Annie said.

'A handsome bird of prey, though,' Danny corrected her.

'Mam looks much better,' Annie said.

'That goes without saying,' Danny said, kissing each of them on the tops of their heads.

It was a very sunny day on Brian's birthday. The preparations went on all morning. Nora Johnson was there fussing, Gertie had come to ask could she help. She looked as if she hadn't slept for a month.

'Only if you stay for the party properly, if you go home and get the children,' Ria said.

'No, not today.' She was so strained it almost hurt to look at her.

'What's wrong, Gertie?'

'Nothing.' The word was like a scream.

'Where are the children?'

'With my mother.'

'Who's running the launderette?'

'A sixteen-year-old schoolgirl who wants a holiday job. Have you finished the interrogation, Ria? Can I get on with helping you?'

'Ah hey that's not fair, it's not an interrogation.' Ria looked upset.

'No, sorry.'

'It's just you don't look too well. Why do you want to help here?'

'Why do you think?'

'Gertie, I don't know. Truly I don't.'

'Then you're as thick as two short planks, Ria. I need the money.'

Ria's face paled. 'You're my friend, for God's sake. If you want some money ask me, don't come round expecting me to be inspired. How much do you want?' She reached for her handbag.

'I won't take money from you, Ria.'

'Am I going mad, didn't you just ask for it?'

'Yes, but I won't take it as charity.'

'Well, all right. Pay it back to me some time.'

'I won't be able to do that.'

'So, it doesn't matter then.'

'It does. I want to earn it, I want to scrub and clean. I'll start with the oven, then I'll do all the kitchen surfaces and the bathrooms. I need the tenner.'

Ria sat down with the shock of it all. 'You must have ten pounds. You *must* have that much, Gertie. You run a business, for God's sake.'

'I have to keep the float in the shop, he knows that. I told him I'd be back with ten pounds before lunch, he won't go near the shop.'

'Jesus Christ, Gertie, take the ten pounds. Do you think I'm going to watch you for two hours earning this.'

'I won't take it.'

'Well, get out then.'

'What?'

'You heard me. You're my friend, I'm not going to pay you five pounds an hour for sloshing about in my kitchen, and putting a brush down my lavatories today. I'm sorry but that's it.' Ria's eyes were blazing.

Gertie had tears in her eyes. 'Oh Ria, don't be full of principle, have a little understanding instead.'

'I have plenty of understanding ... why don't you have a little dignity?'

'I'm trying to, you're taking it away from me.' Gertie looked as if a puff of wind would blow her over. 'You're very upset.'

'Of course I am upset. Now will you please take the ten-pound note and if you try to give it back to me or lift one hand towards any cleaning whatsoever I'll ram the bloody money down your throat.'

'You have no reason to be upset with me or with anyone, Ria. You have a charmed life. I don't envy you it, you deserve it and you work hard for it, and you're nice to everybody but everything's going right for you. You might just *think* about how hard it might be when everything's going wrong.'

Ria swallowed. 'It's my son's seventh birthday, the sun is shining, of course I'm happy. I'm not happy every day, nobody is. Listen, you are my friend. You and I know everything about each other.'

'We don't know everything about each other,' Gertie said quietly. 'We're not schoolgirls any more, we are women in our mid-thirties, grown-ups. I thought that if I did the work somehow we'd be quits. I'm sorry. And I'm also sorry for upsetting you on Brian's birthday.' She turned to leave.

'If you don't take the ten pounds you'll have really upset me.'

'Sure. Thank you, Ria.'

'No, not coldly. With a bit of a hug anyway.' There was a stiff little hug. Gertie's thin body was like a board. 'You know what would be the best? If you were to come back later with the kids. Would you do that?'

'No thank you. But not because of sulking or anything. Just no.'

'Sure. Right.'

'Thanks again, Ria.'

'You're full of dignity, you always have been.'

'You deserve all you have, and even more. Enjoy the day.' She was gone.

Nora Johnson came into the kitchen from the garden. 'I've been tying the balloons to the front gate so that they'll know where the party is and I see Lady Ryan coming down the road wearing a designer outfit. Coming to help no doubt. Where's Gertie got to? She said she was going to clean some of those old baking tins for the sausages.'

'She had to go home, Mam.'

'Well honestly, talk about helpful friends when you need them! If you hadn't Hilary and myself you'd be lost.'

'Haven't I always said it, Mam?'

'And will Annie help to entertain them when they get here?'

'No, I don't think a dozen seven-year-old boys is Annie's idea of a good summer afternoon, she'll keep her distance. Danny has a whole lot of games planned for them.'

'He's not off about His Master's Business then, is he?' Nora sniffed.

'No, Mam, he's not.'

'You look a bit pale, are you all right?'

'Never better.'

Ria escaped in relief to greet Rosemary who had come to count the numbers. She had bought a great amount of individually wrapped chocolate ice creams which were at home in her freezer. 'I'll come back in an hour so you don't have to bother putting them into the freezer. Was there a problem with Gertie?'

'Why do you ask?' Ria wanted to know.

'She ran past me on the road crying and she didn't see me, she genuinely didn't.'

'Oh nothing more than the usual problem she has.' Ria looked grim.

'Roll on the divorce referendum,' Rosemary said.

'You don't think that's going to make the slightest difference in Gertie's way of thinking, do you?' Ria asked. 'I mean, if there was divorce introduced into this country tomorrow morning you don't think she'd leave Jack. Abandon him? Give up on him, like everyone else has? Of course she wouldn't.'

'Well, what's the point of having it on the statute-books at all if people are going to react like that?' Rosemary wondered.

'Search me.' Ria was at a loss. 'The two families we know who should avail themselves of it won't go near it. You don't think Barney McCarthy is going to disturb his nice comfortable little situation if divorce is introduced, do you?'

'No I don't indeed, but I didn't know that *you* would see things so clearly.' Rosemary laughed almost admiringly – sometimes Ria could be very surprising – and went back to Number 32 to change into something more suitable for a children's party.

The party guests had begun to arrive. Very soon they were punching each other good-naturedly. All of them. There didn't seem to be any reason for this, no real aggression or gangs or hostility, that was the way boys behaved. Annie's friends were much gentler, she said to her mother as they separated one pair of warring boys before they crashed into Colm's vegetable garden, locked into their fight.

'Where *is* Annie by the way?'

'In her room, I think. There's no point in dragging her down to join them. She's too old for them and not old enough to find them funny. She'll come when she hears there's birthday cake.'

'Or sausages. Two to one she gets the smell of sausages and she's down like a greyhound out of a trap,' said Nora sagely.

Annie was not in her room as it happened, she had gone out the back gate and was walking up the lane that ran parallel to Tara Road. She had seen a small thin ginger kitten there the other day. It might not belong to anyone. It had looked frightened, not as if it were used to being petted. Perhaps it was abandoned and she might keep it. They would say no of course, as people said no to everything. If she could get it into her room for a few days without anyone noticing, give it a litter tray and some food, then they wouldn't have the heart to turn it out. Today would be a good day to smuggle it in, nobody would notice. There was so much fuss about Brian and all his brain-dead friends, shouting and pushing and shoving around the garden. You could bring a giraffe upstairs today and no one would notice. Annie tried to remember which was the back gate where she had seen the little kitten. It wasn't as far up the road as Rosemary's. It was hard to identify them from the back.

Annie Lynch stood in the lane in her blue check summer dress squinting into the afternoon sun, pushing her straight blonde hair out of her eyes. Perhaps she could peep through the keyholes of these wooden doors. Some of them were quite rickety and it was easy to see through the cracks anyway. One of the back gates was a smart painted wooden door you couldn't see through at all. Annie stood back a little. This must be Number 32 where Rosemary Ryan lived.

She had a very posh garden upstairs on the roof but there was a garden with an ornamental pool and a summerhouse at the back. This might well be where the poor kitten had wandered in to have a look at the fish in the pond.

Annie knelt down and looked in the keyhole. No sign of a cat. But there were people there in the summerhouse. They seemed to be fighting over something. She looked more carefully. It was Rosemary Ryan struggling with a man. Annie's heart leapt into her throat. Was she being attacked? Should Annie rattle at the gate and shout, or would the attacker come out and hurt her as well? Rosemary Ryan had her skirt right up around her waist, and the man was pushing at her. With an even greater shock than the first one Annie realised what they were doing. But this wasn't the way it was done. Not what she and Kitty Sullivan had giggled about in school. Not what people almost did at the cinema and on television. That was different. They kissed each other and lay down, it was all gentle. It wasn't like this, all this shoving and grunting. Rosemary Ryan couldn't be making love with someone. This isn't the way it was meant to be. The whole thing wasn't possible!

Annie pulled back from the keyhole, her heart racing. She tried to make sense of the situation. To be honest, nobody *could* see them unless they were actually looking through the keyhole of the back gate. The summerhouse faced away from the main house and towards the back wall.

Annie couldn't see who the man was; he had his back to her. All she had seen was Rosemary's face. All screwed up and angry, upset. Not dreamy like it was in the movies. Maybe she had got it totally wrong, this mightn't be what they were doing at all. Annie looked once more.

Rosemary's arms were around the man's neck, her eyes were closed, she wasn't pushing him away, she was pulling him towards her. 'That's it, yes, yes, that's it!' she was crying out.

Annie straightened up in horror. She couldn't believe what she had seen. She started to run down the lane. When passing Number 16 she could hear the noise coming from Brian's party. But she didn't stop. She didn't want to go in knowing what she knew now. She couldn't bear them all expecting her to be normal. Things would never be the same again and she could never tell anybody. On she ran, tears blinding her eyes until, just as she was getting to the main road and back to normality, she fell, one of those unexpected falls where the earth just jumped up to meet you with a thud.

It winded her totally and she had trouble in getting her breath. When she struggled to stand she saw she had grazed both knees which were bleeding as well as her arm. She leaned against the wall of the end house and sobbed as if her heart would break.

Colm heard the noise and came out. 'Annie, what happened?' No reply, just heaving shoulders. 'Annie, I'll run and get your mother.'

'*No.* Please don't. *Please*, Colm.'

Colm wasn't like other grown-ups, he didn't always automatically know what was best for you. 'Okay, but look at you . . . you've had a horrible fall, let me see.' He held her arm gently. 'No, it's only the skin, what about your knees? Don't you look at them, I'll examine them without touching, and I'll report to you.'

Annie stood there while he knelt down and studied them. Eventually he said, 'Lots of blood but I don't think you need a stitch. Let me walk you home, Annie.'

She shook her head. 'No. Brian's having a party, I don't want to go home.'

Colm took this on board. 'If you like you could come into my house, into the bathroom and wash your poor knees. I'll be in the restaurant out of your way but there if you need me, and you could come in and out and I'll give you a nice lemonade or whatever you like.' He smiled at her.

It worked. 'Yes, I'd like that, Colm.'

Together they went in, and he showed her the bathroom. 'There's a whole lot of face-cloths there, and if you put a little Dettol in the water . . .' She seemed helpless, unsure of how to start. 'If you like I could dab them for you, take any grit out?'

'I don't know . . .'

'Yes, sometimes it's easier if you do it yourself. Would I stay here on this chair while you do it, and tell you if I see more bits that need to be done?'

He got the first smile. 'That would be great.' He watched while the child touched her knee tentatively with the diluted disinfectant, and wiped away all the grit and earth. It was only a surface scratch, the bleeding was slight. 'I can't reach my elbow, will you do that, Colm?'

Gently he cleaned her arm and handed her a big fluffy towel. 'Now, pat it dry.'

'There might be spots of blood on the towel.' She looked anxious.

'All the more work for Gertie's launderette then,' he smiled.

They went into the cool dark bar of his restaurant. At the bar there were four high stools. He gestured her to one of them. 'Now, Miss Lynch, what's your pleasure?' he said.

'What do you think is nice, Colm?'

'Well, they say that in times of shock something with a lot of sugar is good. In fact they always recommend hot, sweet tea.'

'Ugh,' said Annie.

'I know, that's my view too. I'll tell you . . . what I always have is a St Clement's. It's a mixture of orange and lemon. How does that sound?'

'Great. I'd like that,' said Annie. 'Do you not drink real drinks then?'

'No, you see they don't agree with me. Something to do with my personality or metabolism or whatever . . . it's not clear exactly what causes it but they don't suit me.'

'How did you find out they didn't suit you?'

'I got a few little hints like once I started I couldn't stop.' He smiled wryly.

'Like drugs?' Annie asked.

'Just like drugs. So I had to stop altogether.'

'Do you miss not being able to drink real drinks, at parties and things?' Annie was interested.

'Do I miss it? No. I don't miss the way I was, which was out of control, I'm very glad not to be like that. But I suppose I wish I was the way other people are – you know, having a nice glass of wine or two of an evening, a couple of beers on a summer day. But I'm not able to stop after that so I can't start.' Annie looked sympathetic. 'However, there are lots of things I can do that others can't,' Colm said cheerfully. 'I can make wonderful sauces and great desserts that would take the sight out of your eyes.'

'Brian's awful friends want ice creams in silver-paper wrappers! Imagine!' Annie said disparagingly.

'I know. Isn't it disgusting!' Colm said, and they both began to laugh. Annie's laugh had a slightly hysterical tinge in it.

'Nothing happened out in the lane to make you fall, did it?' Colm asked.

The child's expression was guarded. 'No. Why?'

'No reason. Listen, will I walk home with you now?'

'I'm all right really, Colm.'

'Of course you are, don't we know that? But I have to go for a walk every day, all chefs must, it's a kind of rule, stops them getting big stomachs that keep falling into their saucepans.'

Annie laughed. It wasn't possible to think of Colm Barry having a tummy like that. He was nearly as slim as Dad. They set off together. Just as they came to the gate they saw Rosemary Ryan unloading the ice creams in a cool-bag from the back of her car. Annie stiffened. Colm noticed but said nothing.

'Heavens, Annie, what a terrible cut! Did you fall?'

'Yes.'

'She's okay now,' Colm said.

'It looks dreadful, where did it happen?'

'On the road in front of Colm's restaurant,' Annie said quickly.

Colm was surprised.

'And Colm came to your rescue.' Rosemary always smiled at Colm flirtatiously though it never did her any good.

'Exactly. I can't have people falling down in front of my premises. Bad for business,' he joked.

'You were lucky you didn't fall in front of the traffic.' Rosemary had lost interest in it, now she was hauling out the boxes of ice creams. They could hear the shouting and screaming of Brian's friends from the back garden.

'My public is waiting for me and the ice cream,' Rosemary laughed. 'I think we know which they are waiting for more.' She moved ahead of them through the basement and out to the back.

'Thanks, Colm.'

'Don't mention it.'

'It's just that it's . . . well, it's nobody's business really where I fell, is it?'

'Absolutely not.'

She felt he was owed some kind of explanation. 'I was looking for a cat, you see. I thought if I got a kitten and sort of kept it secretly for a bit . . . you know?'

'I know.' Colm was grave.

'So thanks for all the St Clement's and everything.'

'I'll see you round, Annie.'

Gran was terrific, she had kept sausages for Annie. 'I couldn't find you so I put them in the oven to keep warm.'

'You're great. Where are they all?'

'They're about to have the cake, Lady Ryan arranged sparklers.'

'Mam hates it when you call her that.' Annie giggled and then she winced at the pain in her elbow.

Her grandmother was full of concern. 'Let me wash that for you.'

'It's okay, Gran, it's done, Dettol and all. Look at Aunty Hilary with all those awful boys.'

'She loves them, she's brought a big dartboard where you throw rings on. There's fierce competition.'

'What's the prize?'

'Oh some game, Hilary knows what electronic games children of that age want from being up at the school, you know.'

'Why didn't Aunty Hilary have any children, Gran?'

'The Lord didn't send her any, that's all.'

'The Lord doesn't send children, Gran, you know that.'

'No not directly, but indirectly He does, and in your Aunty Hilary's case He just didn't.'

'Maybe she didn't like mating,' Annie said thoughtfully.

'What?' Nora Johnson was at a loss for words, which was very unlike her.

'Maybe she decided not to go through the whole business of getting them, like cats and rabbits you know. There must be some people who just don't like the thought of it.'

'Not many,' her grandmother said dryly.

'I bet that's it, you could ask her.'

'It's not the thing you ask people, Annie, believe me.'

'I do, Gran, I know you couldn't ask her. There are some things you don't talk about at all, you just put away at the back of your mind. Isn't that right?'

'Absolutely right,' her grandmother said with enormous relief.

Later on the parents of Brian's friends came to collect their sons, and they stood in the warm summer evening in the back garden of Tara Road while the boys played and pummelled on, tiring themselves and each other out for bedtime. Annie watched her mother and father stand there in the centre of the group, passing around a tray of wine and little smoked salmon sandwiches. Dad's arm was around Mam's shoulder a lot of the time. Ria knew from the girls at school that parents still want to be with each other and make love and all that, even when they didn't want children. It seemed such an unlikely thing to want to do. Horrible even.

There was much sympathy about the grazed knee, and when she went to bed, Mam came into her room. She sat in Annie's big armchair, moving the furry toy animals out of the way.

'You've been very quiet all afternoon and evening, Annie. Are those knees all right?'

'Fine, Mam, don't fuss.'

'I'm not fussing, I'm just sorry for your poor old knees and your elbow too. Like you would be if I fell.'

'I know, Mam. Sorry. You weren't fussing, but I'm fine.'

'And how did it happen?'

'I was running, I told you.'

'It's not like you to fall, you're such a graceful girl. When Hilary and I were your age we were falling all the time, but you never do. I think it's because your dad calls you a princess you decided to behave like one.'

Her mother's look was so fond and warm that Annie reached out for her hand. 'Thanks, Mam,' she said, eyes full.

'I was so exhausted out there today, Annie, with those tomboys. Honestly they're like young bullocks head-butting each other, not like children at all. When I think what an ease it's always been to have your friends, but that's the difference between the sexes for you. Would you like a hot drink? You've had a bad shock today.'

'What do you mean?' Annie's eyes were wary.

'The fall, it jars the system even at your age.'

'Oh that. No, no I'm fine.'

Ria kissed her daughter's flushed face and closed the door. She had spoken only the truth, it *had* been a killing day. But then wasn't she so well off compared to everyone else? Her mother going home alone with that absurd little dog. Hilary crossing the city with her dartboard in a big carrier bag to a man who wouldn't hold her in his arms any more because they couldn't make children. Gertie facing who knew what horrors in the flat above the launderette. Rosemary alone in that marble palace of a penthouse.

While she, Ria, had everything she could ever have wanted.

4

Sometimes they saw mothers and daughters together in the shops. Talking normally, holding up a skirt or a dress. Nodding or frowning but concerned. Like friends. One going into a cubicle to try something on, the other holding four more outfits outside. Perhaps they weren't real people, Ria told herself. Maybe they were actresses or from advertising. Judging from the eleven confrontations she had had with her own daughter in an hour and a half it was very hard to believe that any teenager and her mother would go shopping together from choice. These other people were only playing at being Happy Families. Surely?

Annie had this gift token from her grandmother. It was for more money than she had ever spent before on clothes. Up to now Annie had only bought shoes, jeans and T-shirts on her own. But this was different, it was for something to wear for all the parties this summer. It had seemed normal for Ria to go with her and help her choose. It had even seemed like fun. That was some hours ago. Now it seemed like the most foolish thing either of them had ever done in their lives.

When Annie had looked at something with leather and chains, Ria had gasped aloud. 'I knew you were going to be like that, I knew it in my bones,' Annie cried.

'No, I mean, it's just ... I thought. . .' Ria was wordless.

'*What* did you think? Go on, Mam, say what you thought, don't just stand there gulping.' Annie's face was red and angry.

Ria was not going to say that she thought the outfit was like an illustration in a magazine article called 'Sado-Masochistic Wardrobe Unearthed'. 'Why don't you try it on?' she said weakly.

'If you think I'm going to put it on now that I've seen your face, and let you make fun of me . . .'

'Annie, I'm *not* making fun of you. We don't know what it looks like until you put it on, maybe it's . . .'

'Oh Mam, for God's sake.'

'But I mean it, and it's your token.'

'I know it is. Gran gave it to me to buy something I liked, not some awful revolting thing with a butch tartan waistcoat like you want me to wear.'

'No, no. Be reasonable, Annie, I haven't steered you towards anything at all, have I?'

'Well, what are you here for then, Mam? Answer me that. If you have nothing to suggest, what are you doing? What are *we* doing here?'

'Well, I thought we were looking . . .'

'But you never look. You never look at anything or anyone, otherwise you wouldn't wear the kind of clothes you do.'

'Look, I know you don't want the same clothes as I do.'

'*Nobody* wants the same clothes as you do, Mam, honestly. I mean, have you thought about it for one minute?'

Ria looked in one of the many mirrors around. She saw reflected a flushed angry teenager, slim with straight blonde hair, holding what appeared to be a bondage garment. Beside her was a tired-looking woman with a great head of frizzy hair tumbling on to her shoulders, and a black V-neck sweater worn over a flowing black-and-white skirt. She had put on comfortable flat shoes for shopping. This was not a day when Ria had rushed thoughtlessly out of the house, she had remembered the mirrors that came on you suddenly in dress shops. She had combed her hair, put on make-up and even rubbed shoe cream into her shoes and handbag. It had all looked fine in the hall mirror before they had left Tara Road. It didn't look great here.

'I mean, it's not even as if you were really old,' Ria's daughter Annie said. 'Lots of people your age haven't given up.'

With great difficulty Ria forced herself not to take her daughter by the hair and drag her from the shop. Instead she looked thoughtfully back into the mirror. She was thirty-seven. How old did she look? Thirty-five? That's all. Her curly hair made her young, she didn't look forty or anything. But then what did she know?

'Oh Mam, stop sucking in your cheeks and making silly faces, you look ridiculous.' When had it happened, whatever it was that made Annie hate her, scorn her? They used to get on so well.

Ria made one more superhuman effort. 'Listen we mustn't talk about me, it's *your* treat, your gran wants you to get something nice and suitable.'

'No she doesn't, Mam. Do you never listen? She said I was to get whatever I wanted, she never said one word about it being suitable.'

'I meant . . .'

'You mean anything that would look well on a poodle at a dog show.' Annie turned away with tears in her eyes.

Near by a woman and her daughter were looking through a rail of shirts. 'They must have a pink one,' the girl was saying excitedly. 'Come on, we'll ask the assistant. You look terrific in pink. Then we'll go and have a coffee.'

They seemed an ordinary mother and daughter, not just a couple sent over by central casting to depress real people. Ria turned away so that nobody could see the tears of envy in her eyes.

Danny had organised the people to deliver the sander at eleven o'clock. Ria wanted to be home to greet them. It was such a peculiar idea, to take up their carpets and bring out the beauty of the wooden floors. They didn't look a bit beautiful to her, full of nails and discoloration. But Danny knew about these things, she accepted this. His work and his skill was selling houses to people who knew everything, and these people knew that exposed wooden floors and carefully chosen rugs were good, while wall-to-wall carpeting was bad, and obviously concealed unmerciful horrors beneath. You could rent a sander for a weekend and walk around behind it while it juddered and peeled off the worst bit of your floor. That was what lay ahead today and tomorrow.

Would Annie think she was sulking if she left her now? Would she be relieved? 'Annie, you know your father arranged that this sanding machine come today?' she began tentatively.

'Mam, I'm *not* spending the weekend doing that, it's not fair.'

'No, no, of course not, I wasn't going to suggest it. I was going to say I should go home and be there when they arrive, but I don't want to abandon you.' Annie stared at her wordlessly. 'Not that I'm much help, really. I'm inclined to get confused when I see a lot of clothes together,' Ria said.

Annie's face changed. Suddenly she reached out and gave her mother an unexpected hug. 'You're not the worst, Mam,' she said grudgingly. From Annie this was high, high praise these days.

Ria went home with a lighter heart.

Ria had just got in the door of her house in Tara Road when she heard the gate rattle and the familiar cry: 'Ree-ya, Ree-ya'. A call known all over the area, as regular as the Angelus or the sound of the ice-cream van. It was her mother and the dog, the misshapen and unsettled animal Pliers, a dog never at ease in Ria and Danny's home in Tara Road, but because of circumstances forced to spend a lot of his disturbed life there. Ria's mother was always going somewhere where dogs weren't allowed, and Pliers pined if left at home alone. Pliers yowled in Ria's house, but for some reason this was not regarded as pining and was considered preferable.

Ria's mother never came in unannounced or uninvited. She had made a great production out of this from the time she had moved to the little house near them. Never assume that you are automatically welcome in your children's homes. That was her motto, she always said. It seemed a loveless kind of motto and also totally inappropriate since she called unannounced and uninvited almost every day at Ria and Danny's house. She thought that this shout at the gate was somehow enough warning and preparation. Today reminded Ria of being back at school when her mother would come to the playground or to the park where her pals had gathered, always calling 'Ree-ya'. Her school friends used to take up the cry. And now here she was, a middle-aged woman and nothing had changed, her mother still calling her name as if it were some kind of a war cry.

'Come in, Mam.' She tried to put a welcome in her voice. The dog would worry at the sanding machine when it arrived and bark at it, then he would set up one of his yowls so plaintively that they would assume his paw had been trapped in it. Of all days to have to babysit Pliers this must be one of the worst.

Nora Johnson bustled in, sure as always of her welcome. Hadn't she called out from the gate to say she was on her way? 'There was a young pup on the bus, asked me for my bus pass. I said to him to keep a civil tongue in his head.' Ria wondered why her mother, such a known dog lover, always used the word pup as a term of abuse. There were pups everywhere these days, in shops, driving vans, hanging about.

'What was so bad about him asking you that?'

'How dare he assume that I am at the age to have a bus pass? There's no way that he should think with only half a look out of his slits of eyes that I am a pensioner.' Of course Ria's mother despite her lemon-coloured linen suit and black polka-dot scarf looked exactly the age she was, the young pup on the bus had just been thoughtless. At his age he assumed everyone over forty was geriatric. But there was no point in trying to explain any of this to her mother. Ria busied herself getting out the tray of shortbread she had made the night before. The coffee mugs were ready. Soon the kitchen would be full of people, the men with the sanding machine, Danny wanting to learn how it worked, Brian and some of his school friends; there was always something on offer to eat in the Lynches' kitchen, unlike their own. Annie might be back with some amazing outfit and Kitty Sullivan whom she had met in the shopping mall.

Rosemary always came in on a Saturday, and sometimes Gertie escaped from the flat over the launderette. Gertie came twice a week to do the cleaning, it was a professional arrangement. But she could drop in socially on a Saturday. There would always be an excuse, she had left something behind or she wanted to check the times for next week.

Colm Barry might come in with vegetables. Every Saturday he brought them in armfuls of whatever he had collected. Sometimes he even scrubbed big earth-covered parsnips and carrots, or trimmed spinach for them. Ria made soups and casseroles with the freshest produce possible, all grown with no effort a few feet away from her own kitchen.

Other people came and went. Ria Lynch's kitchen was a place with a welcome. So unlike the way things had been when Ria was young herself and nobody was allowed out to their kitchen, a dark murky place with its torn linoleum on the floor. Visitors weren't really encouraged to come to her mother's house at all. Her mother and, from what she could remember, her father also were restless people, unable to relax themselves and incapable of seeing that others might want to.

Even when her mother visited her here in Tara Road she hardly ever settled, she was constantly rattling keys or struggling out of or into coats, just arriving or about to leave, unable to give in to the magic of this warm, inviting place.

It had been the same in Danny's family. His mother and father had sat in their very functional farmhouse kitchen drinking mug after mug of tea and welcoming no disturbance. Their sons grew up out of doors or in their own rooms, and lived their own lives. To this day Danny's parents lived that kind of life; they didn't mix with neighbours or friends, they held no family gatherings. Ria looked around with pride at her big cheerful kitchen where there was always life and company, and where she presided over everything at its heart.

Danny never noticed Nora Johnson's keys rattling, nor was he irritated by the way she called from the gate. He seemed delighted to see his mother-in-law when he came into the kitchen and gave her a big hug. He wore a blue sports shirt that he had bought for himself when he was in London. It was the kind of thing that Ria would never have chosen for him in a million years, yet she had to admit it made him look impossibly young like a handsome schoolboy. Perhaps she *was* the worst in the world at choosing clothes. She tugged uneasily at the floppy black top that Annie had mocked.

'Holly, I know why you're here, you came to help with the sanding,' Danny said. 'Not only do you give our daughter a small fortune for clothes but now you're coming to help us do the floors.'

'I did not, Daniel. I came to leave poor Pliers with you for an hour. They're so intolerant down at St Rita's, they won't allow a dog inside the door, and isn't it just what those old people there need, four-legged company! But those young pups of doctors say it's unhygienic, or that they'd fall over animals. Typical.'

'But it's our gain to have Pliers here. Hallo, fellow.' Could Danny really like the terrible hound, about to open his mouth and drown everything with his wail? Pliers' teeth were stained and yellow, there were flecks of foam around his mouth. Danny looked at him with what definitely seemed like affection. But then so much of Danny's life depended on being polite to those who wanted to buy or sell property, it was hard to know when he was being genuinely enthusiastic or faking it. His was not a world where you said what you thought too positively.

Ria's mother had downed her coffee and was on her way. She had become very involved in the whole life of St Rita's, the retirement home at Number 68. Hilary was convinced that their mother was actually ready to book herself in as a resident. Nora had taught Annie to play bridge and sometimes took her granddaughter along to St Rita's to join in the game. Annie said it was marvellous fun, the old people were as noisy as anyone at school and had just the same kind of feuds and squabbles. Annie reported that everyone in the home held Granny in high regard. Of course, compared to them Granny was very young.

Nora said it was only sensible to examine the options about ageing. She dropped many hints that Ria should do the same; one day she too would be old and on her own, she would be sorry then that she hadn't given more time to the elderly. It wasn't as if she had any real work to go out to like other people, she had plenty of time on her hands.

'You must drive the old fellows mad down in St Rita's, a young spring chicken like yourself in lemon coming in to dazzle them,' Danny said.

'Go on with your flattery, Danny.' But Nora Johnson loved it.

'I mean it, Holly, you'd take the sight out of their eyes,' Danny teased her. Pleased, his mother-in-law patted her hair and bustled out again, smart and trim in her suit. 'Your mother's wearing well,' Danny said. 'We'd be lucky to look as spry at her age.'

'I'm sure we will. And aren't you like a boy rather than a man free-wheeling down to forty,' Ria laughed. But Danny didn't laugh back. That had been the wrong thing to say. He was thirty-seven going on thirty-eight.

Foolish Ria, to have made a joke that annoyed him. She pretended not to have noticed her mistake. 'And look at me, you said that when you met me first you took a good look at my mother before you let yourself fancy me – women always turn into their mothers, you said.' Ria was babbling a lot but she wanted to take that strained look off his face.

'Did I say that?' He sounded surprised.

'Yes, you did. You must remember?'

'No.'

Ria wished she hadn't begun this, he seemed confused and not at all flattered by her total recall. 'I must ring Rosemary,' she said suddenly.

'Why?'

The real reason was so that she didn't have to stand alone with him in the kitchen with a feeling of dread that she was boring him, irritating him. 'To see is she coming round,' Ria said brightly.

'She's always coming round,' said Danny. 'Like half the world.' He seemed to say that in mock impatience but Ria knew he loved it all, the busy, warm, laughing life of their kitchen in Tara Road, so different to the loveless house where he had grown up in the country, with the crows cawing to each other in the trees outside.

Danny was as happy here as she was: it was the life of their dreams. It was a pity they were so tired and rushed that they had not been making love as often as they used to, but this was just because there was so much happening at the moment. Things would be back to normal soon enough.

Rosemary wanted to know all about the shopping expedition when she arrived. 'It's wonderful seeing them coming into their own,' she said. 'Knowing what they want, and defining their style.' She didn't sit down, she prowled around the kitchen picking up bits of pottery and looking at the name underneath, fingering the strings of onions on the wall, reading the recipe taped to the fridge, examining everything and vaguely admiring it all.

She clutched her mug of black coffee with such gratitude you would think that nobody had ever handed her one before in her life. Naturally she waved away the shortbread, she had just stood up from a disgustingly huge breakfast she said, even though her slim hips and girlish figure showed anyone that this was unlikely to have been the truth. Rosemary wore smart well-cut jeans and a white silk shirt, what she called weekend clothes. Her hair was freshly done, the salon's first client every Saturday morning week in week out. Rosemary always sighed enviously over those people who could go any day of the week, lucky people like Ria who didn't go out to work.

Rosemary now owned the printing company. She had won a Small Business Award. If she were not her longest-standing best friend Ria could have choked her. She seemed to be the actual proof that a woman could do everything and look terrific as well. But then, she and Rosemary went back a long way. She had been there the very day Ria had met Danny, for heaven's sake. She had listened to all the dramas over the years, as Ria had listened to hers. They had very few secrets.

In fact Gertie was the only subject where they really differed.

'You're only encouraging her to think her lifestyle is normal by giving her tenners for that drunk.'

'She's not going to leave him. You could put all kinds of work her way, I wish you would,' Ria pleaded.

'No, Ria, can't you see you're making the situation worse? If Gertie thinks you go along with this business of her head being like a punchbag and her terrified children living up in her mother's house, then you're just making sure the whole scene goes on and on. Suppose you said one day "Enough is enough", it would bring her to her senses, give her courage.'

'No it wouldn't, it would only make her feel she hadn't one friend left on earth.'

Rosemary would sigh. They agreed on so much, the sheer impossibility of mothers, the problems with sisters, the wisdom of living in the lovely tree-lined Tara Road. And Rosemary had always been incredibly supportive to Ria, about everything. Too many other women told Ria straight out that they would go mad if they didn't have a job to go to and money that they earned themselves. Rosemary never did that, any more than she would ask Ria, like other working wives often did, 'What do you *do* all day?' especially in front of Danny.

For the last five years of course Annie and Brian didn't need as much minding, but somehow the thought of a job outside the home had not really been a serious one. And anyway, realistically, what job could Ria have done? There was no real training or qualification to fall back on. Better by far to keep the show on the road here. Ria rarely felt defensive about being a stay-at-home wife, and she genuinely felt that it must be a good life if Rosemary, who had everything that it was possible to have in life, said she envied her.

'Well go on, Ria, tell me, what did she buy?' Rosemary really thought it had been fun and that Annie and she had agreed and bought something.

'I'm no good at knowing what to look for, where to point her,' Ria said, biting her lip.

She thought she saw a small flash of impatience in Rosemary's face. 'Of course you are. Haven't you all the time in the world to look around shops?'

Then the van containing the sander arrived and the men who delivered it were offered coffee, and ten-year-old Brian, looking as if he had been sent out as child labourer digging in a builder's site instead of having just got out of bed, came in with his two even scruffier friends, scooping up cans of Coke and shortbread to take upstairs. And Gertie, with her big anxious eyes and some rambling explanation about how she hadn't cleaned the copper saucepan yesterday, began to scrub at its base which meant that she needed a loan of at least five pounds.

Pliers whined and there on cue was Ria's mother back unexpectedly from St Rita's. They hadn't told her that there was a funeral there that morning so she wasn't needed after all. And Colm Barry knocked on the window to show Ria that he was leaving her a large basket of vegetables. She waved him in to join the group and felt the customary surge of pride at being the centre of such a happy home. She saw Danny standing at the kitchen door watching everything. He was so boyish and handsome, why had she made that silly remark about him approaching forty?

Still he had got over it, it had passed. His face didn't look troubled now, he just stood there watching almost as if he were an objective observer, as if he were an outsider, someone viewing it all for the first time.

They all took turns at doing the floors, and it wasn't as easy as it looked. Not just a matter of standing behind a machine that knew its own mind, you had to steer it and point it and negotiate corners and heavy objects. Danny supervised it, full of enthusiasm. This was going to change the house, he said. Ria felt an unexpected shiver in her back. The house was wonderful, why did he want to change it?

Ria's mother wouldn't stay for lunch. 'I don't care how many tons of vegetables you say that Colm left out for you, I know what troubles result from people moving in on top of other people. Sit down with your own family, Ria, and look after that husband of yours. It's a miracle that you've held on to him so long. I've always said that you were born lucky to catch a man like Danny Lynch when all was said and done.'

'Now, Holly, stop giving me a swollen head, I'm a very mixed blessing let me tell you. Here, if you really won't stay let me get you some of Colm's tomatoes to take with you. I can just see you serving delicate thin tomato sandwiches and vodka martinis to gentlemen callers all afternoon.'

Nora Johnson pealed with laughter. 'Oh, chance would be a fine thing, but I will take some of those tomatoes to get them out of your way.' Ria's mother could never take anything that was offered to her graciously, she would only accept something if there was an air of doing you a favour about it.

Rosemary was disappointed that there were no clothes to examine. She wondered had they caught sight of the gorgeous scarlet outfit in the corner window just where the two streets joined? No? Absolutely heavenly, no good for people of our age, Rosemary said, patting her own flat stomach, but great for someone like Annie who had a figure like an angel and wasn't getting droppy and droopy like the rest of us. Rosemary must have known that she wasn't getting droppy and droopy. She must have.

Brian and his friends Dekko and Myles had a problem. They had been going to watch a match on cable television up in Dekko's house but there was a new baby and so the television couldn't be put on.

'Can't you watch it here?' Ria had asked.

Brian looked at her, embarrassed. 'No. Do you not understand anything? We can't watch it here.'

'But of course you can. It's your home as much as Dad's and mine, you can take a tray into the sitting room.'

Brian's face was purple trying to explain. '*We don't have it here, Ma*, we don't have cable like Dekko's family.'

Ria remembered. There had been a long argument some months ago, she and Danny had said the children already watched too much television.

'Not that it's any good having it now,' Dekko said glumly. 'Not if we can't turn it on because of the awful baby.'

'Come on, Dekko, a little brother can't be awful,' Ria said.

'It is, Mrs Lynch, it's disgusting and embarrassing. What on earth did they have to have one for after all these years? I'm ten, for heaven's sake.' The boys shook their heads and began to debate the possibilities of getting an extension lead to add to the flex. If they moved it twelve feet outside the house and kept the sound down lowish, would that do? Dekko was doubtful. His mother had gone ballistic about this desperate baby.

This was not good news for Ria. She had been thinking long and hard about their having another child. The estate agency was now going from strength to strength. Danny had been made Auctioneer of the Year. They were still young, they had a big house; another baby was just what she had been hoping they might consider.

The copper saucepan was gleaming. Gertie showed it proudly to Ria. 'You could look at your face in it, Ria, and it would be better than a mirror.'

Ria wondered why anyone would want to lift a huge saucepan to look at a reflection but didn't say so. Neither did she say anything about the bruise down the side of Gertie's face, a dark mark that she was trying to hide with her hair. 'My goodness, it's shining like gold. You are so good to come in on a Saturday, Gertie.' The routine was that Ria would now offer the money and Gertie would refuse, but then take it. It was a matter of dignity, and that was the way they played it now.

But not today. 'You know why I did.'

'Well, I mean it's still very good of you.' Ria reached for her handbag, surprised by the directness.

'Ria, we both know I'm desperate. Can I have ten pounds, please? I'll work it all off next week.'

'Don't give it to him, Gertie.'

Gertie held back her hair until Ria could see the long red scab of a cut. 'Please, Ria.'

'He'll only do it again. Leave him, it's the only thing.'

'And go where, tell me that? Where could I go with two kids?'

'Change the locks, get a barring order.'

'Ria, I'm on my knees to you, he's waiting on the road.'

Ria gave her the ten pounds.

From the hall Ria could hear Annie speaking to her friend Kitty. 'No, of course we didn't get anything, what do you think? Just standing there gasping, eyes rolling up to heaven, you're *not* going to wear this, you're *not* going to wear that . . . no, not actually saying it but written all over her face . . . It was gross I tell you. No, I'm not going to get anything at all. I swear it's the easiest. It's not worth the hassle. I don't know what I'll tell Gran though, she's so generous and *she* doesn't mind what I wear.'

Ria looked for Danny. Just to be with him for a moment would make her feel better, it might mean a return of some of the strength and confidence that seemed to be seeping out of her. He was bent slightly over the sanding machine, his body juddering with it as it ground through to the good wood he wanted to expose. He was totally involved in it and yet there was something about him that seemed as if he were doing it for somebody else. As if he had been asked by one of his clients to improve a property.

Ria found her hand going to her throat and wondered was she getting flu. This was a marvellous Saturday morning in Tara Road. Why was everything upsetting her? Ria wondered what would happen if she were to write to a problem page? Or talk to a counsellor? Would the advice be that she should go out and get a job? Yes, that would on the face of it be a very reasonable response. Outside people would think that a job took your mind off things, less time to brood, might make you feel a bit more independent, important. It would seem like nit-picking to explain that it wasn't the answer. Ria *had* a job. There was no sense in going out somewhere every morning just for the sake of it, to make some point. And Danny had often said that a working wife would play hell with his tax situation. And there were ways that the children needed a home presence more than ever at this stage.

And her mother needed her to be there when she came in every day. And Gertie did, not just for the few pounds she earned from cleaning but for the solidarity. And who would do the charity work if Ria were to have a full-time job? It had nothing to do with smart fund-raising lunches like some middle-class women spent their time organising. This was real work, serving in a shop selling things to make money, turning up at the hospital to mind the toddlers whose mothers were being told they had breast cancer. It was collecting old clothes, storing them in the garage then getting them dry-cleaned at a cheap bulk rate, it was finding containers and making chutneys and sauces, it was standing outside the supermarket for four hours with a flag tin.

And the house itself needed her. Danny had said so often that she was a one-person line of defence, rooting out woodworm, fighting damp, dry rot. And suppose, just suppose that getting a job *was* the answer, what job would she do? The very mention of the Internet sent a chill through Ria. She would have to learn basic keyboard skills and how to work office machinery before she could even ask for a job as some kind of receptionist.

Perhaps the empty anxious feeling would go. Maybe the solution had nothing to do with looking for a job. The answer could be as old as time. It was simply that she was broody.

She wanted another baby, a little head cradled at her breast, two trusting eyes looking up at her, Danny at her side. It wasn't a ridiculous notion, it was exactly what they needed. Despite the scorn and ridicule from Brian and his friends, it was time to have another baby.

They were having dinner with Rosemary. Tonight it was not a party, there were just the three of them. Ria knew what would be served: a chilled soup, grilled fish and salad. Fruit and cheese afterwards, served by the big picture window that looked out on to the large well-lit roof garden.

Rosemary's apartment, Number 32 Tara Road, was worth a small fortune now, Danny always said, and of course immaculately kept. With the success of Rosemary's company there was no shortage of money and even though she was not a serious cook like Ria, Rosemary could always put an elegant meal on the table without any apparent effort.

Ria would know of course how much had come directly from the delicatessen, but nobody else would. When people praised the delicious brown bread Rosemary would just smile. And it was always arranged so well. Grapes and figs tumbling around on some cool modernistic tray, a huge tall blue glass jug of iced water, white tulips in a black vase. Stylish beyond anyone's dreams. Modern jazz at a low volume on the player, and Rosemary dressed as if she were going out to a première. Ria was constantly amazed at her energy and her high standards.

She walked with Danny along Tara Road. Sometimes she wished he didn't speculate so much about what the retail value of each house was. But then that was his business. It was only natural. As they had said to each other so often, this road stood out alone in Dublin. Any other street was either up-market or down-market, this was the exception. There were houses in Tara Road which changed hands for fortunes. There were dilapidated terraces, each house having several bedsitters where the dustbins and the bicycles spelled out shabby rented property. There were red-brick middle-class houses where civil servants and bank officials had lived for generations; there were more and more houses like their own, places that had been splendid once and were gradually coming back to the elegance that they had previously known.

There was a row of shops down by the launderette on the corner where Gertie lived, the shops getting gradually smarter as the years went by. There was Colm Barry's smart restaurant in its own grounds. There were little places like her mother's which defied description and definition.

Every time Ria came in the gate of Number 32 she marvelled at how elegant the whole front looked. Her thought processes went in exactly the same well-travelled channels. She would love their house to have a big expansive welcoming area like this, a place where more than one car could park, where everything seemed to sweep up towards the door, flowers getting taller and turning into bushes as they approached the granite steps. As if the house was some kind of temple. In their own house there was no air of permanency. It was as if the whole place could be dismantled in minutes. True, a few years back Danny had agreed to some small rockeries and a basic tarmacadam on the surface. But compared to Number 32 theirs was absolutely nothing.

Nobody would imagine that anyone in Number 32 would ever build flats or anything in their drive, but that could easily happen in the Lynch establishment the way it looked now. Danny had said several times that this just added to the charm, mystery and value of their property. Ria had said the money value of your property was only important when you came to sell it, otherwise the value was surely only what made you feel good while you lived there. They talked about this from time to time but it was one of the rare subjects where Ria had never been able to communicate how strongly she felt about it all. This business of wanting to make a more definite permanent entrance to the house always sounded superficial. It came out as nagging or envying what someone else had just for the sake of it.

Ria liked to think that she was able to know what was really important and what wasn't. She would use all her powers of persuasion in suggesting that Danny should be a father again. A garden was much lower on the list of priorities and she didn't want to hassle him about everything. He had been looking tired and pale lately. He worked too hard.

Ria looked around her as Rosemary went out to get them their drinks. This was a truly perfect setting for her friend. No sign whatsoever that the owner was a shrewd businesswoman. Rosemary kept all her files and work at the office. Tara Road was for relaxing in. And it looked as pristine as the day she had moved in. The paintwork was not scuffed, the furniture had not known the wear and tear of the young. Ria noticed that there were art books and magazines arranged on a low table. They wouldn't remain there long in her house, they would be covered with someone's homework or jacket or tennis shoes or the evening newspaper. Always Ria felt that Rosemary's house didn't really feel like a home. More like something you would photograph for a magazine.

She was about to say that to Danny as they walked home along Tara Road, peering in at the other houses as they passed by and, as always, congratulating themselves on having been so clever as to buy in this area when they were young and desperate. But Danny spoke first. 'I love going to that house,' he said unexpectedly. 'It's so calm and peaceful, there are no demands on you.'

Ria looked at him walking with his jacket half over his shoulder in the warm spring evening, his hair falling into his eyes as always, no barber had ever been able to deal with it. Why did he like the feel of Rosemary's apartment? It wasn't Danny's taste at all. Much too spare. It was probably just because it was valuable. You couldn't spend all your working day dealing with property prices and not get affected by those kinds of values and standards. Deep down Danny wanted a house with warm colours and full of people.

If they had been having Rosemary to dinner tonight it would have been seven or eight people around the kitchen table. The children would have come in and out with their friends. Gertie might have come to help serve and eventually joined them at the table. There would be music in the background, the telephone ringing, possibly Clement the inquisitive cat would come in and examine the guest-list, people would shout and interrupt each other. There would be large bottles of wine already open at each end of the table, a big fish chowder filled with mussels to start, and large prawns, and thick chunky bread. A roast as main course and at least two desserts. Ria always made a wonderful treacle tart that no one could resist. That was the kind of evening they all enjoyed. Not something that could have been part of a tasteful French movie.

But it was a silly thing to argue about and it might seem as if she were trying to praise herself so Ria, as she did so often, took the point of view she thought would please him. She tucked her arm into Danny's and said he was right. It had been nice to be able to sit and talk in such a relaxed way. Nothing about thinking that Rosemary had dressed and made up as if she were going to a television interview rather than to welcome Danny and Ria, probably the people closest to her.

'We're lucky we have such good friends and neighbours,' she said with a sigh of pleasure. That much she meant. As they turned in to their own garden they saw that the light was on in the sitting room.

'They're still up.' Danny sounded pleased.

'I hope they are nothing of the sort, it's nearly one o'clock.'

'Well, if it's not the children then we have burglars.' Danny sounded not at all worried. Burglars would hardly be watching television and waiting for the occupants to return.

Ria was annoyed. She had hoped that tonight she and Danny could have a drink together in the kitchen and they might talk about the possibility of another baby. She had her arguments ready in case there was resistance. They had been close tonight, physically anyway, even if she would never understand his pleasure in that cool remote home of Rosemary's. Why did the children have to be up tonight of all nights?

It was Annie, of course, and her friend, Kitty. There had been no mention of Kitty coming around, no request that they could take Ria's bottles of nail varnish to paint each other's toenails or borrow her fitness video which was blaring from the machine. They looked up as if mildly annoyed to see the adults returning to their own home.

'Hi, Mr Lynch,' said Kitty, who rarely acknowledged other women but smiled broadly at any man she saw. Kitty looked like something in a documentary television programme about the dangers of life in a big city. She was waif-thin and had dark circles under her eyes. These were a result of late nights at the disco. Ria knew just how many because Annie had railed at the unfairness of not being able to get similar freedom.

Danny thought she was a funny little thing, a real character. 'Hi Kitty, hi Annie, why look you've painted each toenail a different colour. How marvellous!'

The girls smiled at him, pleased. 'Of course there isn't a great range,' Annie said apologetically. 'No blues and black or anything. Just pink and reds.' Kitty's frown of disapproval was terrible to see.

'Oh I *am* sorry,' Ria said sarcastically, but somehow it came out all sharp and bitter. She had meant it to be exasperated funny but it sounded wrong. The unfairness of this annoyed her. It was *her* make-up drawer they had ransacked without permission, and she was meant to be flattered but also to feel inadequate at not having a technicolour choice for them. The girls shrugged and looked at Danny for some kind of back-up. 'Brian in bed?' she asked crisply before Danny said anything that would make it all worse.

'No, he's taken the car, and he and Myles and Dekko have gone out to a few clubs,' Annie said.

'Annie, really.'

'Oh Mam, what do you expect? You don't think Kitty or I know where Brian is, or care, do you?'

Kitty decided to rescue it. 'Now, please don't worry about a thing, Mrs Lynch, he went to bed at nine o'clock. He's all tucked up and asleep. Really he is.' She managed to cast Ria in the role of a fussing geriatric mother who wasn't all there in the head.

'Of course that's where he is, Ria.' Danny had joined in patting her down.

'Was it a nice night?' Annie asked her father. Not because she wanted to know but because she wanted to punish her mother.

'Lovely. No fussing, no rushing around.'

'Um.' Even in her present mood of doing anything to annoy her mother Annie couldn't appear to see much to enthuse about there.

Ria decided not to notice the angry resentment that Annie felt about everything these days. Like so many things she let it pass. 'Well, I suppose you'll both want to go to bed now. Is Kitty staying the night?'

'It's Saturday, Mam. You *do* realise there's no school tomorrow.'

'We still have some sit-ups to do.' Kitty's voice was whining, wheedling as if she feared that Mrs Lynch might strike her a blow.

'You girls don't need sit-ups.' Danny's smile was flattering but yet couldn't be accepted. He was after all a doting and elderly father.

'Oh Dad, but we do.'

'Come here, let's see what does she tell us to do.'

Ria stood with a small hard smile and watched her husband doing a ridiculous exercise to flatten his already flat stomach with two teenagers. They all laughed at each other's attempts as they fell over. She would not join them, nor would she leave them. It was probably only ten minutes yet it felt like two hours. And then there was no warm chat in the kitchen, and no chance of loving when they went upstairs. Danny said he needed a shower. He was so unfit, so out of training these days, a few minutes' mild exercise nearly knocked him out. 'I'm turning into a real middle-aged tub of lard,' he said.

'No you're not, you're beautiful,' she said to him truthfully, as he took off his clothes and she yearned for him to come straight to bed. But instead he went to shower and came back in pyjamas; there would be no loving tonight. Just before she went to sleep Ria remembered how long it had been since there had been any loving. But she wasn't going to start worrying about that now on top of everything else. It was just that they were busy. Everyone said that's what happened to people for a while, and then it sorted itself out.

On Sunday Danny was gone all day. There were clients looking at the new apartments. They were aiming for a young professional kind of market, Danny had said. The developers had asked why bother having a health club and coffee bar attached unless the young singles could meet similarly-minded people there. He had to go and supervise the whole sales approach. No, he wouldn't be back for lunch.

Brian was going to Dekko's house; there was a christening. Dekko wasn't going to go at all but there would be his grandmother and people from his mum and dad's work there, and apparently it was essential that he be there.

For some reason. Anyway it had been agreed that if Myles and Brian and he wore clean shirts and passed round the sandwiches, they would get five pounds each.

'It's a lot of money,' Dekko said solemnly. 'They must be mad investing fifteen pounds in us all being there.'

'I would have thought normal people would have paid us fifteen pounds for us all *not* to be there,' Brian said.

'Nobody's normal in a house where there's a baby,' Dekko had said sagely and they all sighed.

Annie said that she and Kitty were going to the Career Forum at school and that of course they had told everyone this ages ago, over and over. It was just that nobody ever listened.

'You didn't go to any of the other Career Forums,' her mother protested.

'But those were only about the bank, and insurance and law and awful things.' Annie was amazed that it wasn't clear.

'And what is it this week that you have to go?'

'Well it's real careers, like the music industry and modelling and things.'

'What about your lunch, Annie? I defrosted a whole leg of lamb and now it seems there'll be no one here.'

'Only you, Mam, would think that an old leg of lamb was important compared to someone's whole future.' She banged out of the room in a temper.

Ria rang her mother.

'No, don't be ridiculous, Ria, why would I drop everything and come to eat huge quantities of red meat with you? Why did you defrost it anyway until you knew whether your family was going to be there to eat it? That's you all over, you never think about anything.'

Ria rang Gertie. Jack answered. 'What?'

'Oh ... um ... Jack, it's Ria Lynch.'

'What do you want? As if I didn't know.'

'Well I wanted to talk to Gertie.'

'Yeah, with a load of feminist advice, I suppose.'

'No, I was going to invite her to lunch, as it happens.'

'Well we can't go.'

'*She* might be able to go.'

'She's not able to go, Mrs Burn-your-bra.'

'Perhaps she and I could talk about that, Jack.'

'Perhaps you'd like to go and take a ...' There was the sound of a scuffle.

'Ria, it's Gertie ... sorry I can't go.'

'You can't go to what?'

'To whatever it is you're asking me to ... thanks but I can't.'

'It was only lunch, Gertie, just a bloody leg of lamb.'

There was a sob at the other end. Then, 'If that's all it bloody was, Ria, why on earth did you ring me and cause all this trouble?'

'This is Martin and Hilary's answering machine, please leave a message after the bleep.'

'It's nothing, Hilary, it's only Ria. If you're not there on a Sunday at ten o'clock in the morning then it's not likely you'll be there at lunchtime . . . heigh ho, no message.'

Ria rang Colm Barry at the restaurant. He was often there on a Sunday, he had told her that he took advantage of the peace and quiet to do his accounts and paperwork.

'Hallo.' Colm's sister Caroline always spoke so softly you had to strain to hear what she said. She said that Colm wasn't there, he had gone out to do something, well he wasn't there. Caroline sounded so unsure that Ria began to wonder whether Colm was actually standing beside her mouthing that he wouldn't take the call.

'It doesn't matter, I was just going to ask him if he'd like to come to lunch, that's all.'

'Lunch? Today?' Caroline managed to make both words contain an amazing amount of incredulity.

'Well yes.'

'With your family?'

'Here, yes.'

'And had you asked him? Did he forget?'

'No, it was a spur of the moment thing, you too of course if you were free.'

Caroline seemed totally incapable of taking in such a concept. 'Lunch? Today?'

She said the words again and Ria wanted to smack her very hard. 'Forget it, Caroline, it was just a passing idea.'

'I'm sure Colm will be very sorry to have missed the invitation. He loves going to your house, it's just that he's . . . well he is . . . well he's out.'

'Yes I know, doing something, you said.' Ria felt her voice had sounded unduly impatient. 'And you're not free, Caroline, yourself? You and Monto?' She hoped fervently that they were not free. And she was in luck.

'No I'm very sorry, truly I am, Ria, I can't tell you how sorry I am but it's just not possible today. Any other day would have been.'

'That's fine, Caroline. It was short notice, as I said.' Ria hung up.

The phone rang and Ria answered it hopefully.

'Ria? Barney McCarthy.'

'Oh, he's already gone to meet you there, Barney.'

'He has?'

'Yes, up at the new development, the posh flats.'

'Oh, of course, yes.'

'Are you not there?'

'No, I was delayed. If he calls back tell him that. I'll catch him up along the way.'

'Sure.'

'And you're fine, Ria?'

'Fine,' she lied.

Would she cook the lamb anyway, and have it cold with salad when they all came home? Gertie said you could refreeze things if they hadn't thawed completely. But what did Gertie know? Colm would know but he was out somewhere doing something, according to that dithering sister of his. Rosemary would know but Ria hated having to ask her. Was she in fact becoming very boring, as Annie had said? Was she as thoughtless as her mother had suggested? Ria knew now why people who lived on their own found Sunday a long lonely day. It would be different when they had a new baby . . . then there wouldn't be enough hours in the day.

Brian had been sick at the christening. He said it was bad enough to let him off school. He was pretty sure that Myles and Dekko would have kinder, more understanding families who wouldn't force invalids to go out when they were feeling rotten. Annie said that it was just a punishment since they had all been drinking champagne and obviously they were sick. Brian, red-faced with annoyance, said that she had no proof of this at all. That she was only trying to make trouble to take attention away from the fact that she and Kitty had been out so late and caused such alarm.

'I was talking about my career, about the future, jobs and things, something a drunk like you will never have,' Annie said coldly to Brian.

Ria tried to keep the peace, looking in vain for any support from Danny who had his head stuck in brochures and press releases about the new apartment blocks. He had been tired when he came back last night. Too tired to respond when she had reached out for him. It had been a long day, he said. For Ria too it had been a long day, pushing a heavy sanding machine around the floor, but she hadn't complained. Now they were back in familiar territory, a big noisy breakfast, a real family starting the week together in the big bright kitchen.

And everything had simmered down by the time they were ready to leave. Brian said he thought he *could* face school, possibly the fresh air would do him good and there was no proof that a court of law would accept that any alcohol had been taken. Annie said that possibly, yes, she *should* have telephoned to say that it was all going on longer, but she hadn't thought that anyone would be waiting. Honestly.

Danny dragged himself out of the world of executive apartments. 'You couldn't *give* away anything with carpet wall to wall nowadays,' he said. 'Everything has to have sprung oak floors or they won't consider it. Where did all the money come from in this society? Tell me that and I'll die happy.'

'Not for decades yet, I have great plans for you first,' Ria laughed.

'Yes, well none for tonight, I hope,' he said. 'There's a dinner, investors, I have to be there.'

'Oh, not again!'

'Oh yes, again. And many times again before we're through with this. If the estate agents don't go to the promotions then what confidence will they think we have in it all?'

She made a face. 'I know, I know. And after all it won't be for long.'

'What do you mean?'

'Well, eventually they'll all be sold, won't they? Isn't that what it's about?'

'This phase . . . but this is only phase one, remember we were talking about it on Saturday with Barney?'

'Did Barney get you yesterday?'

'No, why?'

'He got delayed, I told him he'd find you at the development.'

'I was with people all day. I expect someone took a message. I'll get it when I get into the office and ring him then.'

'You work too hard, Danny.'

'So do you.' His smile was sympathetic. 'Look, I brought home that sander and you had to do most of it as it turned out.'

'Still, if you think it looks nice?' Ria was doubtful.

'Sweetheart, no question. It adds thousands to the resale value already and that's only in one weekend. Wait till we get those children of ours working properly, nice bit of slave labour, and do the upstairs as well. This place will be worth a fortune.'

'But we don't want to sell it,' Ria said, alarmed.

'I know, I know. But one day when we're old and grey and we want a nice apartment by the sea or on the planet Mars, or something . . .' He ruffled her hair and left.

Ria smiled to herself. Things were normal again.

'Ree-ya?'

'Hallo, Mam. Where's Pliers?'

'I see. You have no interest in seeing your own mother any more, only the dog.'

'No, I just thought he'd be with you, that's all.'

'Well he's not. Your friend Gertie's taken him for a walk, that's where he is. Gone for a nice morning run down by the canal.'

'Gertie?'

'Yes, she said that she heard dogs like Pliers needed a run now and then to shake them up. And of course though I have been able to keep myself reasonably trim, I'm not really able to do anything like that for Pliers any more, so Gertie offered.' Ria was astounded. Gertie didn't run, she barely walked these days, living in such dread of her drunken husband. Ria's mother had lost interest in the conversation. 'Anyway I only came in because I was passing to tell Annie that it's seven o'clock tonight.'

'What is?'

'They're coming down to St Rita's with me this evening, Annie and her friend Kitty. We're teaching Kitty bridge.'

Ria's mind was churning. 'But that will be during supper.'

'I suppose they manage to think that some things are more important because they're nice and normal and they actually like people,' said Ria's mother. She sat at her daughter's table waiting for coffee to be served to her, her face thunderous with the heavy implication that Ria was neither nice nor normal and positively hated meeting people.

The washing machine had just begun to swirl and hum when Rosemary rang. 'Oh Lord, Ria, how I envy you, relaxed in your own home while I'm stuck at work.'

'That's the way things are.' Ria knew there was an edge to her voice. She was becoming sharp with people for no reason. She rushed on to take the harm out of her words. 'We all think the grass is greener in the other place. Often when I'm picking up things from the floor here I envy you being at work and out of the house all day.'

'No, of course you don't.'

'Why do you say that?'

'Because, as I keep telling you, if you *did* feel like that, cabin fever and everything, then you'd *get* a job. Listen, what I rang to say is that I saw Jack being taken off in a Garda car this morning, some disturbance outside a pub. I thought you'd want to know. If you have nothing to do you might check whether Gertie's in bits or anything.'

'Gertie's not in bits, she's out walking my mother's dog.'

'You're not serious, aren't people amazing?' Rosemary sounded pleased at this surprise news. 'She didn't ask for a dog-walking fee, did she?'

'No, I don't think so, my mother would have said.'

'Oh well, that's all right then. It's not as if she's doing it to get a couple of quid to buy him more drink when the fuzz lets him go.'

'Mrs Lynch?'

'Yes, that's right.' All day odd things had been happening.

'Mrs Danny Lynch?'

'Yes?'

'Oh, oh I'm sorry. No, I think I may have the wrong number.'

'No, that's who I am, Ria Lynch.' The phone went dead.

Her sister Hilary rang just then. 'You sounded like the Mother of Sorrows on the answering machine,' she said.

'No I didn't. I just spoke and said it didn't matter. We both say that people who don't leave messages should be hanged.'

'I keep saying that the answering machine was a sheer waste of money. Who ever calls? What messages are there that you'd want to hear?'

'Thanks, Hilary.'

Hilary was unaware of any sarcasm. 'What was it you wanted to talk about anyway? Mam, I suppose?'

'No, not at all.'

'She's really going loopy you know, Ria. You don't see that because you don't want to. You always want to believe that everything's fine in the world, there's no famine, no war, politicians are all honest and mean well, and the climate's great.'

'Hilary, did you ring up just to attack me in general or is there anything specific?'

'Very funny. But going back to Mam, I worry about her.'

'But why? We've been over this a dozen times, she's fit and healthy, she's busy and happy.'

'Well, she should feel needed by her own family.'

'Hilary, she is needed by her family. Isn't she in here every single day of her life, sometimes twice a day? I ask her to stay to meals, I ask her to stay the night. She is out with Annie and Brian more than I am . . .'

'I suppose you're saying now that I don't do enough.'

'I'm not saying anything of the sort, and she's never done talking about you and Martin and how good you are to her.'

'Well, that's as may be.'

'So what is it really that's worrying you?'

'She's trying to sell her house.'

There was a silence. 'Of course she's not, Hilary, she'd have talked to Danny about it.'

'Only if she was selling it through him.'

'Well, who else would she go to? No, Hilary, you've got this all wrong.'

'We'll see,' said Hilary and hung up.

'Sweetheart?'

'Yes, Danny?'

'Was anyone looking for me at home, any peculiar sort of person?'

'No. Nobody at all, why?'

'Oh, there's some crazy ringing up about the apartments, she says she's being refused as a client . . . total paranoia. She's ringing everyone at home as well.'

'A woman did ring, but she didn't leave any message. That might have been her . . .'

'What did she say?'

'Nothing, just kept checking who I was.'

'And who did you say you were?'

Suddenly Ria snapped. It had been a stressful weekend, filled with silly unrelated things that just didn't make sense. 'I told her that I was an axe murderer passing through. God, Danny, who do you think I told her I was? She asked was I Mrs Lynch and I said I was. Then she said she had the wrong number and hung up.'

'I'm telling the Guards about it, it's nuisance calls.'

'And did you say that in the office . . . you know who she is?'

'Listen, honey, I'll be late tonight, you know I told you.'

'A dinner, yes I know.'

'I have to run, sweetheart.'

He called everyone sweetheart. There was nothing particularly special about it. It was ludicrous but she would have to make an appointment with her husband to discuss having a baby, and a further appointment to do something about it if he agreed that it *was* a good idea.

Ria had a mug of soup and a slice of toast for her supper at seven o'clock. She sat alone in her enormous kitchen. The blustery April wind blew the washing on the line, but she left it there. Brian had gone to Dekko's house to do his homework. Annie was going to have a pizza with her gran after bridge at St Rita's, hugely preferable to spending any time at all with her mother obviously. Even sharing space with an unwelcome baby seemed like a better bet for Brian than his own house. Colm Barry had waved to her from the vegetable garden before he left for his restaurant. Her friend Rosemary was at home no doubt cooking something minimalist. Her other friend, Gertie, had been avoiding a drunken husband by walking that ridiculous dog all day, or so Ria's mother said. How had it happened . . . the empty nest? Why was there nobody at home any more?

They all came back together when she least expected it. Annie and her grandmother, laughing as if they were the same age. There was over half a century between them and yet they were relaxed and easy together. The ladies had been great fun, Annie said. They were going to lend her some genuine fifties clothes, even one of those fun fake furs. Some of them had come with them to the Pizza House.

'They're allowed out?' Ria said in surprise.

'It's not a prison, Ria, it's a retirement home. And people are very lucky who can get in there.'

'But you're too young to go to a place like that, much too young,' Ria said.

'I was speaking generally.' Her mother looked lofty.

'So you're not planning to go in there yourself?'

Her mother looked astounded. 'Are you interrogating me?' she asked.

'Oh Mam, for heaven's sake don't always cause a row about everything,' Annie groaned.

Brian came in. He seemed pleased but not surprised to see his grandmother. 'I saw Pliers tied to the gate, I knew you were here.'

'Pliers? Tied to the gate?' Ria's mother was out of the house like a shot. 'Poor dog, darling Pliers. Did she abandon you?'

They heard the sound of a car. Danny was home. Early, unexpected.

'Dad, Dad, do you know where we'd find the colours of the flags of Italy and Hungary and India? Dekko's father doesn't know. It would be great if you knew, Dad.'

'That friend of yours is even more scattered than you are, Ria.' Nora Johnson was still smarting over the dog. 'Imagine, Gertie left poor Pliers tied to the gate. He could have been there for hours.'

'He wasn't there when we came in a few minutes ago, Gran,' Annie reassured her.

'No, I saw Gertie running up Tara Road. It could only be a couple of minutes at the most.' Danny was reassuring too. 'Hey, where's supper anyway?'

'No one came home.' Ria's voice sounded small and tired. 'You said you had a business dinner.'

'I cancelled it.' He was eager, like a child.

Ria had an idea. 'Why don't we go to Colm's restaurant, the two of us?'

'Oh well I don't know, anything will do . . .'

'No, I'd love to, I'd simply love to. It would be a treat for me.'

'It would be a treat for *anyone* to go to Colm's,' Annie sniffed. 'Better than a pizza.'

'Better than sausages in Dekko's,' Brian grumbled.

'Wish I'd been able to go out to four-star restaurants when I didn't feel like cooking,' said her mother.

'I'll phone him and book a table.' Ria was on her feet.

'Honestly, sweetheart, anything ... a steak, an omelette ...'

'It wouldn't do you at all. No, *you* deserve a treat too.'

'I eat out too much, being at home's a treat for me,' he begged.

But she had the phone to her ear and made the booking. Then she ran lightly upstairs and changed into her black dress and put on her gold chain. Ria would have loved the time to have a bath and dress properly but she knew she must seize the moment. This was the very best chance she would have to talk to her husband about future plans. Ria moved swiftly before she could be sabotaged by either her mother or daughter putting sausages and tinned beans in front of Danny.

They walked companionably down Tara Road to the corner. The lights of Colm's restaurant were welcoming. Ria admired the way that it was done. You couldn't really see who was inside but you got the impression of people sitting down together. She was glad that Colm seemed to have tables full on a Monday night. It would be so dispiriting to cook for people and have shining glassware and silver out there and then for nobody to turn up. That was one of the reasons she would never like to run a restaurant, you would feel so hurt if people didn't come to it.

'Very few cars outside,' said Danny, cutting across her thoughts. 'I wonder how he makes any kind of living.'

'He loves cooking,' Ria said.

'Well, just as well that he does because there can't be much profit in tonight's takings from the look of the place.' She hated it when Danny reduced everything to money. It seemed to be his only way of measuring things nowadays.

Caroline took their coats. She was dressed in a smart black dress with long sleeves and she wore a black turban covering her hair. Only someone with beautiful bone structure could get away with something as severe, Ria thought to herself. 'You look so elegant tonight, the turban's a new touch.' Was she imagining it or did Caroline's hand fly to her face defensively?

'Yes, well I thought that perhaps ...' She didn't finish her sentence.

She had been so odd on the telephone yesterday Ria had wondered if there was anything seriously wrong. And even tonight, despite the serene way she smiled and seemed to glide across to show them to their table, there was something tense and pent-up there. They were a strange pair, the brother and sister: Caroline with her overweight husband Monto Mackey, always in a smart suit and an even smarter car; Colm with his discreet relationship. He was nowadays involved with the wife of a well-known businessman, but it was something that was never spoken of. Colm and Caroline seemed to look out for each other, as if the world was somehow preparing to do one of them down.

Ria would have liked that kind of loyalty. Hilary was a complicated sister; she blew hot and cold, sometimes envious and carping, sometimes surprisingly understanding. But there was never this united front that Colm and Caroline wore.

'You're miles away,' Danny said to her.

She glanced at him, handsome, tired-looking, boyish still, puzzling over the menu. Wondering if he would go for the crispy duck or be sensible about his health and have the grilled sole. She could read the decisions all over his face. 'I was just thinking about Hilary,' she said.

'What has she done now?'

'Nothing, except get the wrong end of the stick about everything as usual. Burbling on about you and about Mam wanting to sell the house.'

'She told you that?'

'You know Hilary, she never listens to anyone.'

'She said I wanted to sell the house?'

'She said Mam wasn't even asking you, that she wanted to sell it herself.'

'I don't understand.'

'Would anyone? The whole thing is nonsense.'

'Your *mother*'s house! I see.'

'Well you see more than I do, it's totally cracked.'

Colm came to the table to greet them. He made a point of spending only forty seconds and putting a huge amount of warmth and information into that time. 'There's some very nice Wicklow lamb, and I got fish straight off the boat down in the harbour this morning. The vegetables as you know come from the finest garden in the land, and if you're not sick of eating them yourselves, I suggest courgettes. Can I give you a glass of champagne to welcome you? And then I'll get out of your way and let you enjoy your evening.'

Colm had once told Ria that too many restaurant owners made the great mistake of believing that the guests enjoyed the Mine Host figure spending a lot of time at the table. He always felt that if people had come out to dine then that's what they should be allowed to do. Tonight she valued it especially.

She chose the lamb and Danny said that because he really was as fat as a fool these days he must have plain grilled fish with lemon juice and no creamy sauce. 'You're not fat, Danny, you're beautiful. You know you are, I told you the other night.'

He looked embarrassed. 'A man can't be beautiful, sweetheart,' he said awkwardly.

'Yes indeed he can, and you are.' She reached out and touched his hand. Danny looked around. 'It's all right, we're allowed to hold hands, we're married. Now that couple over there, they're the ones who shouldn't be caught.' She laughed over at a couple where the older man was being very playful with his much younger companion.

'Ria?' Danny said.

'Listen, let me speak first. I'm delighted your dinner was cancelled tonight, delighted. I wanted you on your own without half the country being in our kitchen and all joining in.'

'But that's what you like,' he said.

'Yes, it's what I like a lot of the time but not tonight. I wanted to talk to you. We don't have time to talk these days, no time to do anything, not even make love.'

'Ria!'

'I know. I'm not blaming either of us, it just happens, but what I wanted to tell you was this . . . and I needed time and space to tell you . . . what I wanted to say was . . .' She stopped suddenly, unsure how to go on. Danny was looking at her, confused. 'You know how I said you look young, I mean it. You *are* young, you *are* like a boy, you could pass for someone in his twenties. You're just like you looked when Annie was a baby, with your hair falling into your eyes, unable to believe that you could be a father. You have that look in your eyes.'

'What are you saying? What in God's name are you saying?'

'I'm saying that honestly, Danny, I can see these things. It's time for another baby. Another start of a life. You're more sure and comfortable now, you want to see another son or daughter grow up.' A waiter approached them with plates of figs and Parma ham, but something about the way they sat facing each other made him veer away. These were cold starters, they could wait a little. 'It's *time* for you to have another child, to be a father again. I'm not thinking of myself only but of you, that's all I'm saying,' Ria said, smiling at the strange shocked look on Danny's face.

'Why are you saying it like this?' His voice was barely above a whisper. His face was snow-white. Surely he couldn't find it such a staggering idea. On and off she had been saying this over the years. Only this time she had phrased it in terms of fatherhood rather than her own need or their joint life with a new baby.

'Danny, let me explain . . .'

'I don't believe you're saying this. Why? Why this way?'

'But I'm just saying that it's the right time. That's all. I'm thinking of you and your future, your life.'

'But you're so calm . . . this isn't happening.' He shook his head as if to clear it.

'Well of course, I want it too, you know that, but I swear I'm thinking of you. A baby is what you need just now. It will put things into perspective, you won't be rushing and fussing about developments and market share and everything, not with a new baby.'

'How long have you known?' he asked.

It was an odd question. 'Well, I suppose I've always known that with the other two grown-up almost the day would come.'

'They'll always be special, nothing would change that.' His voice was choked.

'Well don't I *know* that, for heaven's sake, this would be different, not better.' Ria sat back from her position hunched up and leaning over the table. The waiter seized the opportunity and slid in their plates without any comment. Ria picked up her fork but Danny didn't move.

'I can't understand why you're so calm, so bloody calm,' he said. His voice trembled, he could hardly speak.

Ria looked at her husband in astonishment. 'I'm not very calm, Danny my darling, I'm telling you I think it's time we had another baby and you seem to agree ... so I'm very excited.'

'You're telling me *what*?'

'Danny, keep your voice down. We don't want the whole restaurant to know.' She was a little alarmed by his face.

'Oh my God,' he said. 'Oh God, I don't believe it.'

'What is it?' Now her alarm was very real. He had his head in his hands. 'Danny, what is it? Please? Stop making that sound, please.'

'You said you understood. You said you'd been thinking about my future and my life. And now you say that *you* want another baby! That *you* do, that's what you were talking about.' He looked anguished.

Ria was going to say that the way it normally happened was that the woman had the baby but something stopped her. In a voice that came from very far away she heard herself ask the question that she knew was going to change her life. 'What exactly were *you* talking about, Danny?'

'I thought you had found out and for a mad moment I thought you were going along with it.'

'What?' Her voice, impossibly, was steady.

'You know, Ria, you must know that I'm seeing someone, and well, we've just discovered she's pregnant. I am going to be a father again. She's going to have a baby and we are very happy about it. I was going to tell you next weekend. I thought suddenly that you must have known.'

The noise in the restaurant changed. People's cutlery started to clatter more and bang loudly off people's plates. Glasses tinkled and seemed about to smash. Voices came and went in a type of roar. The sound of laughter from the tables was very raucous. She could hear his voice from a long way off. 'Ria. Listen to me, Ree-ah.' She can't have said anything. 'I wouldn't have had this happen for the world, it wasn't part of any plan. I wanted us to be ... I didn't go looking for something like this...'

He looked boyish all right, helplessly boyish. This was too much to cope with. It wasn't fair that she should have to cope with something like this. 'Tell me it's not true,' she said.

'You know it's true, Ria sweetheart. You know we haven't been getting on, you know there's nothing there any more.'

'I don't believe it. I *won't* believe it.'

'I didn't think it would happen either, I thought we'd grow old together, like people did.'

'And indeed like people do,' she said.

'Yes, some do. But we're different people, we're not the same people who married all those years ago. We have different needs.'

'How old is she?'

'Ria, this has nothing to do with ...'

'How old?'

'Twenty-two, not that it matters ... or has anything to do with anything.'

'Of course not,' she said dully.

'I was going to tell you, maybe it's better that it's out now.' There was a silence. 'We have to talk about it, Ria.' Still she said nothing. 'Aren't you going to say anything, anything at all?' he begged.

'Seven years older than your daughter.'

'Sweetheart, can I tell you this has nothing to do with age.'

'No?'

'I don't want to hurt you.' Silence. 'Any more than I already have hurt you and honestly I was wondering could we be the only two people in the whole world who'd do it right? Could we manage to be the couple who actually *don't* tear each other to pieces . . . ?'

'What?'

'We love Annie and we love Brian. This is going to be hell for them. We won't make it a worse hell, tell me we won't.'

'Pardon?'

'What?'

'I said, I beg your pardon. What am I to tell you? I didn't understand.'

'Sweetheart.'

Ria stood up. She was trembling and had to hold the table to keep upright. She spoke in a very low carrying voice. 'If you ever . . . if *ever* in your life you call me sweetheart again I will take a fork in my hand, just like this one, and I will stick it into your eye.' She walked unsteadily towards the door of the restaurant while Danny stood helplessly at the table watching her go. But her legs felt weak, and she began to sway. She wasn't going to make the door after all. Colm Barry put down two plates hastily and moved towards her. He caught her just as she fell and moving swiftly he pulled her into the kitchen.

Danny had followed them in and watched, standing uncertainly as Ria's face and wrists were sponged with cold water by Caroline.

'Are you part of the problem, Danny? Is this about you?' Colm asked.

'Yes, in a way.'

'Then perhaps you should leave.' Colm was perfectly courteous but firm.

'What do you mean . . . ?'

'I'll take her home. When she's ready and if she wants to go, that is.'

'Where else would she go?'

'Please, Danny.' Colm's voice was firm. This was his kitchen, his territory.

Danny left. He let himself into the house with his front-door key. In the kitchen Danny's mother-in-law, her dog and the two children were watching television. He paused in the hall for a minute considering what explanation to make. But this was Ria's choice, not his, how to tell and what to tell. Quietly he moved up the stairs. He stood in the bedroom, uncertain again. After all, she might not want him here when she returned. But suppose he went elsewhere? Might not this be another blow? He wrote a note and left it on her pillow.

Ria, I am ready to talk whenever you are. I didn't think you'd want me here so I've taken a duvet to the study. Wake me any time. Believe me I'm more sorry about all this than you'll ever know. You will always be very, very dear to me and I want the best for you.

Danny

He reached for the phone and made the first of two calls.

'Hallo Caroline, it's Danny Lynch. Can I speak to Colm?'

'I'll see.'

'Well, can you ask him to tell her that I've said nothing to the children and I'm in the study at home. Not the bedroom, the study, if she wants to talk to me. Thank you, Caroline.'

Then he dialled another number. 'Hallo, sweetheart, it's me . . . Yes I told her . . . Not great . . . Yes, of course about the baby . . . I don't know . . . No, she's not here . . . No, I can't come over, I have to wait for her to get back . . . Sweetheart, if you think I'm going to change my mind now . . . I love you too, honey.'

In the kitchen of Colm's restaurant the business of preparing and serving food went on around them. Colm Barry gave Ria a small brandy. She sipped it slowly, her face blank. He asked her nothing about what had happened.

'I should go,' she said from time to time.

'No hurry,' Colm said.

Eventually she said it with more determination. 'The children will worry,' she said.

'I'll get your coat.'

They walked from the restaurant in silence. At the gate of the house she stopped and looked at him. 'It's like as if it's happening to other people,' Ria said. 'Not to me at all.'

'I know.'

'Do you, Colm?'

'Yes, it's to cushion the shock or something. We think first that it's all happening to someone else.'

'And then?'

'I suppose then we realise it's not,' he said.

'That's what I thought,' Ria said.

They could have been talking about the vegetables or when to spray the fruit trees. There was no hug of solidarity or even a word of goodbye. Colm went back to his restaurant, and Ria went into her home.

She sat down in the kitchen. The table had crumbs and some apple cores in a dish. A carton of milk had been left out of the fridge. There were newspapers and magazines on the chairs. Ria saw everything very clearly, but not from where she was sitting. It was as if she were way up in the sky and looking down. She saw herself, a tiny figure sitting down there in this untidy kitchen in the dark house while everyone else slept. She watched as the old clock chimed hour after hour. She didn't think about what to do now. It was as if it hadn't sunk in that it was happening to her.

'Mam, it's the drill display today,' Annie said.

'Is it?'

'Where's breakfast, Mam?'

'I don't know.'

'Oh Mam, not today. I need a white shirt, there isn't one ironed.'

'No?'

'Where were you, were you at the shops?'

'Why?'

'You're in your coat. I could iron it myself, I suppose.'

'Yes.'

'Has Dad gone yet?'

'I don't know, is his car there?'

'Hey Mam, why isn't there any breakfast?' Brian wanted to know.

Annie turned on him. 'Don't be such a pig, Brian. Are you too drunk to get your own breakfast for once?'

'I'm not drunk.'

'You were yesterday, you stank of drink.' They looked at Ria, waiting for her to stop the fight. She said nothing. 'Put on the kettle, Brian, you big useless lump,' Annie said.

'You're just sucking up to Mam because you want her to do something, make you sandwiches, drive you somewhere, iron something. You're never nice to Mam.'

'I am nice to her. Aren't I nice to you, Mam?'

'What?' Ria asked.

'Aw here, where's the iron?' Annie said in desperation.

'Why have you your coat on, Mam?' Brian asked.

'Get the cornflakes and shut up, Brian,' Annie said. Ria didn't have any tea or coffee. 'She had some before she went out,' Annie explained.

'Where did she go?' Brian, struggling with cutting the bread, seemed puzzled.

'She doesn't have to account to you for her movements,' Annie said. Her voice sounded very far away.

''Bye Mam.'

'What?'

'I said, goodbye Mam.' Brian looked at Annie for reassurance.

'Oh goodbye love, 'bye Annie.'

They went round to get their bicycles. Usually they did everything to avoid leaving the house together but today was different.

'What is it, do you think?' Brian asked.

Annie was nonchalant. 'They could be drunk, they went out to Colm's restaurant, maybe the pair of them got pissed. Dad's not up yet, you'll note.'

'That's probably it all right,' said Brian sagely.

Danny came into the kitchen. 'I waited until the children left,' he said.

'What?'

'I didn't know what you'd want to say to them. You know? I thought it was better to talk to you first.' He looked anxious and uneasy. Danny's hair was tousled and his face pale and unshaven. He had slept in his clothes. She still felt the strange sense of not being here, of watching it all happen. That feeling hadn't gone during the long wakeful hours of night. She said nothing but looked at him expectantly.

'Ria, are you all right? Why have you your coat on?'

'I don't think I took it off,' she said.

'What? Not even to go to bed?'

'I didn't go to bed. Did you?'

'Sit down, sweetheart . . .'

'What?'

'I know, I'm sorry, it doesn't mean anything. It's just something I call you. I meant sit down, Ria.'

Suddenly her head began to clear. They were no longer little matchstick figures way down below, people she was watching from far away. She was here in this messy kitchen wearing her coat over her good black party dress. Danny her husband, the only man she had ever loved, had got some twenty-two-year-old pregnant and was going to leave home and set up a new family. He was actually trying to tell her to sit down in her own house. A very great coldness came over her. 'Go now, Danny, please. Leave the house and go to work.'

'You can't order me out, Ria, and take this attitude . . . we have to talk. We have to plan what to do, what to say.'

'I will take whatever attitude I like to take, and I would like you not to be here any more until I am ready to talk to you.' Her voice sounded very normal from inside. Possibly to him too.

He nodded, relieved. 'When will that be? When will you be . . . ready to talk?'

'I don't know, I'll let you know.'

'Do you mean today? Tonight, or . . . um . . . later?'

'I'm not sure yet.'

'But Ria, listen sweet . . . listen Ria, there are things you have to know. I have to tell you what happened.'

'I think you did.'

'No, no. No, I have to tell you what it was about and discuss what we do.'

'I imagine I know what happened.'

'I want to explain . . .'

'Go now.' He was undecided. 'Now,' she said again.

He went upstairs and she stood listening to the sound of a quick splash wash, and his opening drawers to get clean clothes. He didn't shave, he looked hangdog and at a loss. 'Will you be all right?' he asked. She looked at him witheringly. 'No, I know it sounds a stupid thing . . . but I do care and you won't let me talk. You don't want to know what happened, or anything.'

She spoke slowly. 'Just her name.'

'Bernadette,' he said.

'Bernadette,' she repeated slowly. There was a long silence then Ria looked at the door and Danny walked out, got into his car and drove away.

When he had gone Ria realised that she was very hungry. She had eaten almost nothing since lunchtime yesterday. The figs and Parma ham had not been touched last night. She cleared the table swiftly and got herself a tray ready. She would need all her strength for what lay ahead, this was no time to think about diets and calories. She cut two slices of wholemeal bread and a banana. She made some strong coffee. Whatever happened now she would need some fuel to give her energy.

She had just begun to eat when she heard a tap at the back door. Rosemary came in carrying a yellow dress. It was something they had discussed the other night. Was that only Saturday night? Less than three days ago? Rosemary always dressed for work as if she were going to be on prime-time television, groomed and made up. Her short straight hair with its immaculate cut looked as if she had come from a salon. The dress that she had brought to lend to Ria was one she had bought but hardly ever worn. She didn't have the right colouring, she had said, it needed someone dark.

Rosemary held the dress out as if she were in a dress shop convincing a doubtful buyer. 'It looks nothing in the hand but try it on, it's absolutely right for the opening of the flats.' Ria looked at her wordlessly. 'No, don't give me that look, you think it's too wishy-washy but honestly with your dark hair and say a black scarf . . .' Rosemary stopped suddenly and looked at Ria properly. She was sitting white-faced, wearing a black velvet dress and gold chain, and eating a huge banana sandwich at eight thirty in the morning. 'What is it?' Rosemary's voice was a whisper.

'Nothing, why?'

'Ria, what's happened? What are you doing?'

'I'm having my breakfast, what do you think I'm doing?'

'What is it? Your dress . . . ?'

'You're not the only one who can get dressed in the mornings,' Ria said, her lip trembling. Her voice sounded to her a bit like a mutinous five-year-old. She saw Rosemary look at her face, aghast. Then it was all too much. 'Oh God, Rosemary, he has a girlfriend, a girlfriend who's pregnant. She's twenty-two, she's going to have his baby.'

'No!' Rosemary had dropped the dress on the floor and come over to embrace her.

'Yes. It's true. She's called Bernadette.' Ria's voice was high now and hysterical. 'Bernadette! Can you imagine it! I didn't know they still called people of twenty-two that. He's left me, he's going to live with her. It's all over. Danny's gone. Oh Jesus, Rosemary, what am I going to do? I love him so much, Rosemary. What am I going to do?'

Rosemary held her friend in her arms and muttered into the dark curly hair, 'Shush, shush, it can't be over, it's all right, it's all right.'

Ria pulled away. 'It's not going to be all right. He's leaving me. For her. For Bernadette.'

'And would you have him back?' Rosemary was always very practical.

'Of course I would. You know that.' Ria wept.

'Then we must get him back,' said Rosemary, picking up a table napkin and wiping Ria's tear-stained face just as you would a baby's.

'Gertie, can I come in?'

'Oh Rosemary, it's not such a good time. I wonder if I could leave it to another time . . . it's just . . .' Rosemary walked past her. Gertie's home was a mess. That was nothing new but this time there actually seemed to be broken furniture. A lamp was at a rakish angle and a small table now in three pieces stood in the corner. Broken china and glass seemed to have been swept to one side. There was a stain of spilled coffee or something on the carpet.

'I'm sorry, you see . . .' Gertie began.

'Gertie, I haven't come here at nine o'clock in the morning to give your home marks out of ten. I've come for your help.'

'What is it?' Gertie was justifiably alarmed. What kind of help could she possibly give to Rosemary Ryan who ran her life like clockwork, who looked like a fashion model, had a home like something from a magazine and a successful job? Something terrible must have happened if she had come to Gertie for help.

'You're needed up in Ria's house now. You have to come, I'll drive you. Come on, get your coat.'

'I can't, I can't today.'

'You have to, Gertie. It's as simple as this, Ria needs you. Look at all she does for you when you need her.'

'No, not now. You see, there was a bit of trouble here last night.'

'You do surprise me.' Rosemary looked around the room scornfully.

'And we made it all up and I said to Jack I wouldn't go running to the two of you any more.' Gertie lowered her voice. 'He said that it was the women friends I had who were coming between us . . . making the problems.'

'Bullshit,' Rosemary said.

'Shush, he's asleep. Don't wake him.'

'I don't care if he wakes or not. Your friend who has never once asked you a favour in her whole life wants you to come round to her house and you're bloody coming.'

'Not today, tell her I'm sorry. She'll understand. Ria knows what the problems are in this house, she'll forgive me for not coming this once.'

'She might, I won't. Ever.'

'But friends forgive and understand. Ria's my friend, you're my friend.'

'And that big ignorant bruiser in a drunken sleep is not a friend, we have to assume? Is that what you're telling me? Get sense, Gertie, what's the worst he can do to you? Another couple of teeth? Maybe you should have them *all* out next time you go to Jimmy Sullivan. Make it easier. Just whip out your dentures as soon as lover boy starts looking crooked.'

'You're a very hard, cruel woman, Rosemary,' Gertie said.

'Am I? A moment ago I was a sympathetic understanding friend. Well, I'll tell you what *you* are, Gertie. You are a weak, selfish, whingeing victim and you deserve to get beaten up as much as you do, and possibly more because you haven't a shred of kindness or decency in you. If someone told anyone else on God's earth that Ria Lynch needed them they'd be there like a shot. But not you of course, not Gertie.'

Rosemary had never been so angry. She walked to the door without even looking back to see how Gertie was taking it. Before she got to her car she heard steps behind her. Out in the daylight she saw the marks on Gertie's face, bruises that had not been visible indoors because of the dim light in the house. The women looked at each other for a moment.

'He's left her. The bastard.'

'Danny? Never! He wouldn't.'

'He has,' said Rosemary, starting up the car.

Ria was still sitting in her party dress. That, more than anything, underlined the seriousness of it all. 'I haven't told Gertie anything except that Danny *says* he's moving out. I don't know any more anyway, and we don't want to, or have to. All we want is to help you get through today.' Rosemary was completely in charge.

'You're very good to come, Gertie.' Ria's voice was small.

'Why wouldn't I? Look at all you do for me.' Gertie looked at the floor as she spoke, hating to catch Rosemary's eye. 'So where do we start?'

'I don't know.' The normally confident Ria was at a loss. 'It's just that I couldn't bear to talk to anyone else except you two.'

'Well, who might come in on top of you? Colm?'

'No, he stays in the garden. He knows anyway, I fainted in the restaurant last night.'

Rosemary and Gertie exchanged quick glances. 'So who else is likely to come?' Rosemary asked and then with one voice she and Gertie said, 'Your mother!'

'Oh sweet Jesus, I couldn't face my mother today,' Ria said.

'Right,' Gertie said. 'Do we head her off at the pass? I could do that. I could go and thank her for lending me the dog, tell her I'm sorry I tied him up at the gate.'

'Why did you want him?' Ria asked.

It was no time for disguises. 'For protection. Jack's a bit afraid of dogs. He was very upset yesterday what with being taken in by the Guards.'

'But not *kept* in, unfortunately,' said Rosemary.

'Yes, but what kind of gaols would they need if you took in every drunk?' Gertie was philosophical. 'I could tell your mother you had flu or something.'

Rosemary shook her head. 'No, that would be worse than ever. She'd come over like Florence Nightingale with potions and try to book you into that geriatric home of hers. We could say you'd gone out shopping, that there'd be no one at home. Or would that be an odd sort of thing to say?'

Ria didn't seem to know. 'She might come round to see what I bought,' she said.

'Could you say you have to go out and meet someone?'

'Who?' Ria asked. There was a silence.

Rosemary spoke. 'We'll say that there's a free voucher in Quentin's, that you and I were meant to be going there today but now we can't. And since it's only valid today your mother and Hilary are to go instead. How about that?' She was crisp and decisive, as she must be at work, looking around to see how the suggestion was received.

'You don't know how slow they are,' Ria said. 'They'd never do anything unexpected like that.'

'Hilary would hate to miss the bargain, she'd go just to get value. Your mother would love to see the style. They'll go. I'll book it.'

Gertie was reassuring. 'Anyone would get dressed up and go to Quentin's. I'd even stir myself for that, and that's saying something.' She managed a watery smile from her poor bruised face.

Ria felt a lump in her throat. 'Sure, sure they'll go,' she said.

'I'll pick up Annie and Brian from school and take them back to my place, to have supper and watch a video.' Rosemary saw the look of doubt on Ria's face about this and said quickly, 'I'll make it such a good video that they won't be able to refuse, oh and I'll invite the awful Kitty as well.' Ria grinned. That would do it. 'And lastly, Ria, I'll also book you a hair appointment in my place, they really are very good.'

'It's too late for hairdos and makeovers, Rosemary. We're way beyond all that. I couldn't do it, it would be meaningless to me.'

'How else are you going to fill in the hours until he comes home?' she asked. There was no answer. Rosemary made two brisk phone calls to busy professionals like herself. No time was wasted in long, detailed explanations. To Brenda at Quentin's who heard that a Mrs Johnson and a Mrs Moran would be going as her guests, and were to be treated royally as winners of a voucher, given everything they asked for. Then to the hairdressing salon, where she booked Mrs Lynch in for a style cut and shampoo and also a manicure.

'I'm not usually so feeble, but I don't think I have the energy to explain all this about Quentin's to my mother and Hilary,' Ria began.

'You don't have to, I will,' Rosemary said.

'The house is a mess.'

'It won't be when you get back,' promised Gertie.

'I don't believe any of this is happening,' Ria said slowly.

'That's what happens, it's nature's way of coping. It's so you can get on with other things,' said Gertie who knew what she was talking about.

'It's like an anaesthetic, you have to go on autopilot for a while,' said Rosemary, who had an explanation for everything but would have had no idea what it felt like to see a huge pit of despair open in front of you.

Ria didn't really remember the visit to the hairdressing salon. She told them she was very tired and hadn't slept all night, they would have to excuse her if she was a little distracted. She tried to show an interest in the hot oil treatment for her thick curly hair, and tried to make a decision about the shape and colour of her nails. But mainly she let them get on with it, and when it came to paying they said that it was on Rosemary Ryan's account.

Ria looked at her watch. It was lunchtime. If everything had gone according to plan her mother and sister would be sitting in one of Dublin's grandest restaurants having a meal they believed to be free. It was yet one more extraordinary aspect to this totally unreal day.

In Quentin's Hilary and her mother were offered an Irish coffee after their lunch. 'Do you think it's included on the voucher?' Mrs Johnson hissed. Emboldened by the excellent Italian wine Hilary decided to be assertive. 'I rather think it is. A place like this wouldn't stint on little extras.' It turned out to be very much included, the elegant lady who ran the place told them, and a second was brought to the table without their having to decide.

While they waited for the taxi, they were asked as a favour to taste a new liqueur that the restaurant was thinking of putting on the menu; they needed some valued customers' views before they made a final decision. The taxi journey back to Nora Johnson's house was something of a blur. She was relieved to have been told by that bossy Rosemary that Ria wouldn't be at home. Otherwise she might have felt she should call around and give a report on how the lunch had gone. She would telephone instead, when she had had a little rest.

There were two more hours before Danny came home. Ria had never known time pass so slowly. She walked aimlessly around the house touching things, the table in the hall where Danny left his keys. She ran her hand over the back of the chair where he sat at night and often fell asleep with papers from work on his lap. She picked up the glass jug he had given her for her birthday. It had the word Ria engraved on it. He had loved her enough last November to have her name put on a jug and yet in April another woman was pregnant with his child. It was too much to take in.

Ria looked at the cushion she had embroidered for him. The two words 'Danny Boy'. It had taken her weeks of unpicking the stitches to finish it. She could remember his face when she gave it to him. 'You must love me nearly as much as I love you to do something like that for me,' he had said. Nearly as much!

She looked at their new music centre. Only last Christmas, less than six months ago, he had spent hour after hour testing where the speakers would be best. He had bought her so many compact discs, all the Ella Fitzgeralds she had loved, and she had got him the big band sound he liked, the Dorsey brothers, Glenn Miller. The children had groaned at their taste. Perhaps the youthful Bernadette played the strange music that Annie and Kitty liked. Perhaps Danny Lynch pretended he liked it too. Soon he would be home to tell her things like this.

Ria saw Colm Barry in the garden. He was turning the soil but in a desultory way, as if he weren't really there to dig vegetables but to look after her in case she needed it.

Gertie phoned Rosemary at seven o'clock. 'I just rang to say . . . well, I don't know why I rang,' she said.

'You know why you rang, you rang because it's seven o'clock and we're both mad with worry.'

'Are the children there?'

'Yes, that bit worked anyway. I nearly had to give my body to get that video but I got it.'

'That'll keep them entertained. Do you think they'll patch it up?'

'They'll have to,' said Rosemary. 'They've too much to lose, both of them.'

'But what about the baby? The girl who's pregnant?'

'That's probably what they're talking about this minute.'

'Do you say prayers at all, Rosemary?'

'No, not these days. Do you?'

'No, I do deals, I suppose. I promise God to do things if Jack stops, whatever.'

Rosemary bit her lip. It must have cost Gertie a lot to admit this. 'Do they work, these deals?'

'What do *you* think?'

'No, I suppose not all the time.' Rosemary was being diplomatic.

'I've done a deal today. I've told God that if he gets Danny back for Ria, I'll well ... I'll do something I've been promising to do for a long time.'

'I hope it's not to turn the other cheek again or anything,' Rosemary said before she could stop herself.

'No, quite the contrary as it happens,' Gertie said and hung up.

At seven o'clock Ria turned down the volume control on the answering machine. She didn't want to be disturbed by any more drunken messages from her mother and sister who appeared to have become legless at the restaurant where they had lunch. There were also messages from other people. A query from her brother-in-law Martin to know where Hilary was. Dekko's mother to say that there would be a babysitting opportunity for Brian at the weekend. The hire shop confirming the rental of the sanding machine for next weekend. A woman organising a class reunion lunch who wanted addresses of others who had been at school with them.

Ria would not have been able to talk to any one of them today. What *did* people do without answering machines? She remembered the day they had installed it and how they had laughed at Danny's attempts to record a convincing message. 'We have to face it, I'm just not an actor,' he had said. But he had been an actor, a very successful one for months. Years maybe.

She sat down and waited for Danny Lynch to come back to Tara Road.

He didn't call out as he usually did. There was no, 'Yoo hoo, sweetheart, I'm back.' He didn't leave his keys on the hall table. He looked pale and anxious. If things were normal she would have worried, wondered if he was getting flu, begged him to take more time off from the office, to relax more. But things were not normal so she just looked at him and waited for him to speak.

'It's very quiet here,' he said eventually.

'Yes, isn't it?'

They could have been strangers who had just met. He sat down and put his head in his hands. Ria said nothing. 'How do you want to do this?' he said.

'You said we must talk, Danny, so talk.'

'You're making it very hard for me.'

'I'm sorry, did you say that *I* am making it hard? Is that what you said?'

'Please, I'm going to try to be as honest as I can, there will be no more lies or hiding things. I'm not proud of any of this but don't try and trip me up with words and phrases. It's only going to make it worse.' She looked at him and said nothing. 'Ria, I beg you. We know each other too well, we know what every word means, every silence even.'

She spoke slowly and carefully. 'No, I don't know you at all. You say there'll be no more lies, no more hiding things. You see, I didn't know there had been any lies or any hiding things, I thought we were fine.'

'No, you didn't. You can't have. Be honest.'

'I am, Danny. I'm being as honest as I ever have been. If you know me as you claim you do, then you must see that.'

'You thought that this was all there was?'

'Yes.'

'And you didn't think it had all changed. You thought we were just the same as when we got married?' He seemed astounded.

'Yes, the same. Older, busier. More tired, but mainly the same.'

'But . . .' He couldn't go on.

'But what?'

'But we have nothing to say to each other any more, Ria. We make household arrangements, we rent a sander, we get things out of the freezer, we make lists. That's not living. That's not a real life.'

'You rented the sander,' she said. 'I never wanted it.'

'That's about the level of our conversation nowadays, sweetheart. You know this, you're just not admitting it.'

'You're going to leave, leave this house and me and Annie and Brian . . . is that what's happening?'

'You know it's not the same any more, like it was.'

'I don't, I don't know that.'

'You can't tell me that for you everything's perfect?'

'It's not totally perfect, you work too hard. Well, you're out too much, maybe it's not work after all. I thought it was.'

'A lot of it is,' he said ruefully.

'But apart from that I thought everything was fine, and I had no idea that you weren't happy here with us all.'

'It's not that.'

She leaned over and looked him right in the eyes. 'But *what* is it, Danny? Please? Look, you wanted to talk, we're talking. You wanted me to be calm, I'm being calm. I'm being as honest as you are. What is it? If you say you weren't unhappy then why are you going? Tell me so that I'll understand. Tell me.'

'There's nothing left, Ria. It's nobody's fault, it happens all the time to people.'

'It hasn't happened to me,' she said simply.

'Yes it has but you won't face it. You just want to go on acting.'

'I was never acting, not for one minute.'

'I don't mean in a bad sense, I mean playing Happy Families.'

'But we *are* a happy family, Danny.'

'No, sweetheart, there's more, for both of us. We're not old people, we don't have to ruin ourselves and put up with the way it all turned out.'

'It turned out fine. Don't we have the most marvellous children and a lovely home? Tell me, what more do you want?'

'Oh Ria, Ria. I want to be somebody, to have a future and a dream and to start over and get things right.'

'And a new baby?'

'That's part of it, yes, a new beginning.'

'Will you tell me about her, about Bernadette? About what you and she have that we don't have, I don't mean glorious sex of course. Calm I may be but not quite calm enough to hear about that.'

'I beg you, don't bring bitter accusing words into it.'

'I beg *you* to think about what you say. Is there anything bitter and accusing about asking you in a totally non-hysterical way why you are suddenly ending a life that I thought was perfectly satisfactory? I just asked you to tell me what you are going to that's so much better. I'm sorry I mentioned sex but you did tell me that you and Bernadette are going to have a child and so forgive me but there must have been some sex involved.'

'I hate you to be sarcastic like this. I know you so well and you know me, we shouldn't be talking like this. We shouldn't truly.'

'Danny, is this just something that's happened to us, something that we might sort of get through like people do? I know it's serious and there's a child involved, but people have survived such things.'

'No, it's not like that.'

'You can't feel that it's all over. You got involved with somebody much younger, you were flattered. Of course I'm furious and upset but I can get over it, we all get over things. It doesn't have to be the end.'

'All day I said to myself . . . please may Ria be calm. I don't expect her to forgive me but may she be calm enough for us to discuss this and see what's best for the children. You are calm, I don't deserve this but it's the wrong kind of calm. You think it's just a fling.'

'A fling?' she said.

'Yes, remember we used to go through all the degrees of relationships, a whirl, a fling, a romance, a relationship, and then the real thing.' He smiled as he said this. He was looking at his wife very affectionately.

Ria was bewildered. 'So?'

'So this is not a fling, it's the real thing. I love Bernadette, I want to spend the rest of my life with her, and she with me.'

Ria nodded as if this was a reasonable thing for the man she loved to be saying about somebody else. She spoke carefully. 'During the day when you were thinking please let her be calm, what else did you think? What did you think would be the best end to this discussion?'

'Oh, Ria, please. Don't play games.'

'I have never felt less like playing games in my life. I mean this utterly seriously, how do you want it to end?'

'With dignity I suppose. With respect for each other.'

'What?'

'No, you asked me, you asked what did I hope for. I suppose I hoped you'd agree that what we had was very good at the time but it was over and that ... we could talk about what to do that would hurt Annie and Brian least.'

'I've done nothing at all to hurt them.'

'I know.'

'And you didn't think there was anything that you and I could talk about which would get us back together the way it used to be – well, used to be for you.'

'No, love, that's over, that's gone.'

'So when you said talk, it wasn't talk about us, it was talk about what I am to do when you go, is that it?'

'About what we both do. It's not their fault, Annie and Brian don't deserve any hardship.'

'No they don't. Do I, though?'

'That's different, Ria. You and I fell out of love.'

'I didn't.'

'You did, you just won't admit it.'

'That's not true. And I won't say I did to make you feel better.'

'Please.'

'No, I love you. I love the way you look and the way you smile, I love your face and I want to have your arms around me and hear you telling me that this is all a nightmare.'

'This isn't the way it is, Ria, it's the way it was.'

'You don't love me any more?'

'I'll always admire you.'

'I don't want your admiration, I want you to love me.'

'You only think you do ... deep down you don't.'

'Don't give me this, Danny, trying to make me say that I'm tired of it all too.'

'We can't have everything we want,' he began.

'You're having a pretty good stab at it though.'

'I want us to be civilised, decide what we'll do about where we all live ...'

'What do you mean?'

'Before we tell the children we should be able to give them an idea what the future is going to be like.'

'I'm not telling the children anything, I have nothing to tell them. You tell them what you want to.'

'But the whole point is not to upset them ...'

'Then stay at home and live with them and give up this other thing ... that's the way not to upset them.'

'I can't do that, Ria,' Danny said. 'My mind's made up.'

That was the moment she believed that all this was actually happening. Up to then it had all been words, and nightmares. Now she knew and she felt very, very weary. 'Right,' she said. 'Your mind's made up.'

He seemed relieved at the change in her. He was right, they did know each other very well, he could see that somehow she had accepted it was going to happen. Their conversation would now be on a different level, the level he had wanted, discussion of details, who would live where. 'There wouldn't be any hurry to move and change everything immediately, disrupting their school term, but maybe by the end of the summer?'

'Maybe what by the end of the summer?' Ria asked.

'We should have thought of what will happen, where we'll all live.'

'I'll be living here, won't I?' Ria said, surprised.

'Well, sweetheart, we'll have to sell the place. I mean it would be much too big for . . .'

'Sell Tara Road?' She was astounded.

'Eventually, of course, because . . .'

'But Danny, this is our home. This is where we live, we can't sell it.'

'We're going to have to. How else can . . . well . . . everybody be provided for?'

'I'm not moving from here so that you can provide for a twenty-two-year-old.'

'Please Ria, we must think what we tell Annie and Brian.'

'No, *you* must think. I've told you I'm telling them nothing, and I am not moving out of my home.'

There was a silence.

'Is this how you're going to play it?' he said eventually. 'Daddy, wicked monster Daddy, is going away and abandoning you, and good saintly poor Mummy is staying . . .'

'Well that's more or less the way it *is*, Danny.'

He was angry now. 'No, it's not. We're meant to be trying to be constructive and make things more bearable for them.'

'Okay, let's wait here until they come home and let's watch you making it bearable for them.'

'Where are they?'

'At Rosemary's, watching a video.'

'Does Rosemary know?'

'Yes.'

'And what time will they be back?'

Ria shrugged. 'Nine or ten, I imagine.'

'Can you ring and get them back sooner?'

'You mean you can't even wait a couple of hours in your own home for them.'

'I don't mean that, it's just if you're going to be so hostile . . . I suppose I'm afraid it will make things worse.'

'I won't be hostile. I'll sit and read or something.'

He looked around wonderingly. 'You know I've never known this house so peaceful, I've never known you sit and read. The place is always like a shopping centre in the city with doors opening and closing, people coming in and out and food and cups of coffee. It's always like a beer garden here, with your mother and the dog and Gertie and Rosemary and all the children's friends. This of all times must be the very first time in this house that you can hear yourself think.'

'I thought you liked the place being full of people.'

'There was never any calm here, Ria, too much rushing round playing house.'

'I don't believe this, you're just rewriting history.' She got up from the table and went over to the big armchair. She still felt this huge tiredness. She closed her eyes and knew that she could sleep there and then in the middle of this conversation that was about to end her marriage and the life she had lived up to now. Her eyelids were very heavy.

'I'm so sorry, Ria,' he said. She said nothing. 'Will I go and pack some things, do you think?'

'I don't know, Danny. Do whatever you think.'

'I'm happy to sit and talk to you.'

Her eyes were still closed. 'Well do then.'

'But there's nothing more to say,' he said sadly. 'I can't keep on saying that I'm sorry things turned out like this, I can't keep saying that over and over.'

'No, no you can't,' she agreed.

'So maybe it *would* be better if I were to go up and pack a few things.'

'Maybe it would.'

'Ria?'

'Yes?'

'Nothing.'

For a while she could hear him upstairs moving from his study to the bedroom. And then she fell asleep in the chair.

She woke to the sound of voices in the kitchen.

'Usually it's Dad fast asleep,' said Brian.

'Did you have a nice time?' Ria asked.

'It's not even in the cinemas for another three weeks.' Brian's eyes were shining.

'And you, Annie?'

'It was okay. Can Kitty stay the night?' Annie asked.

'No, not tonight.'

'But Mam, *why*? Why do you always make life hell for everyone? We told Kitty's mother that she'd be staying.'

'Not tonight. Your father and I want to talk to you and Brian about something.'

'Kitty can talk too.'

'You heard me, Annie.' There was something about her voice. Something different. Grudgingly Annie escorted her friend to the door. Ria could hear muttered remarks about people who spoiled everything.

Danny had come downstairs. He looked pale and anxious. 'We want to talk to you, your mother and I,' he began. 'But I'll do most of the talking because this is about . . . well, it's up to me to explain it all really.' He looked from one to the other as they stood alarmed by the table. Ria still sat in her armchair. 'It's very hard to know where to start, so if you don't think it's very sentimental and slushy I'll start by saying that we love you very, very much, you're a smashing daughter and son . . .'

'You're not sick or anything, Daddy?' Annie interrupted.

'No, no, nothing like that.'

'Or going to gaol? You have that kind of voice.'

'No, sweetheart. But there are going to be some changes, and I wanted to tell . . .'

'I *know* what it is.' Brian's face was contorted with horror. 'I know. It was just the same in Dekko's house when they told him, they told *him* they loved him. Are we going to have a baby? Is that it?'

Annie looked revolted. 'Don't be disgusting, Brian.'

But they both looked at Ria for confirmation that this wasn't the problem. She gave a funny little laugh. '*We're* not, but Daddy is,' she said.

'Ria!' He looked as if she had hit him. His face was ashen. 'Ria, how could you?'

'I answered a question. You said we should answer their questions.'

'What is it, Daddy? What are you saying?' Annie looked from one to the other.

'I'm saying that for some of the time I won't be living here any more, well, for most of the time really. And that in the future, well, we'll all probably move house, but you will have a place with me and also with Mummy for as long as you like, always, for ever and ever. So nothing about us will change as far as you're concerned.'

'Are you getting divorced?' Brian asked.

'Eventually yes. But that's a long way down the line. The main thing to establish is that everyone knows everything and there are no secrets, nobody getting hurt.'

'That's what your father wants to establish,' Ria said.

'Ria, please . . .' He looked hurt and annoyed.

'And is Mam making it up about you having a baby? That's not true, is it, Dad?'

Danny looked at Ria in exasperation. 'That's not the point at the moment. The point is that you are my children and nothing can change that, nothing at all. You are my daughter and my son.'

'So it *is* true!' Annie said in horror.

'Not a baby!' Brian said.

'Shut up, Brian, the baby's not coming here. Dad's going away to it. Isn't that what's happening?' Danny said nothing, just looked miserably at the two stricken young faces. 'Well, is it, Dad? Are you going to leave us for someone else?'

'I can never leave you, Annie. You're my daughter, we'll never leave each other.'

'But you're leaving home and going to live with someone who's pregnant?'

'Your mother and I have agreed that we are not the same people we once were . . . we have different needs . . .'

Ria gave a little strangled laugh from the armchair.

'Who is she, Daddy? Do we know her?'

'No, Annie, not yet.'

'Don't you care, Mam? Won't you stop him? Won't you tell him you don't want him to go?' Annie was blazing with rage.

Ria wanted to leap up and hold her hurt angry daughter to her and tell her just how bad it all was, how unreal. 'No, Annie. Your father knows that already, but he has made up his mind.'

'Ah, Ria, we agreed, you promised that this shouldn't be a slanging match between us.'

'We agreed nothing, I promised nothing. I am not telling my children that I have different "needs". It's just not true. I need you and want you at home.'

'Oh Mam, everything's ending, Mam.' Brian's face was white. He had never heard his capable mother admitting that she was adrift.

'Brian, it's all right, that's what I'm trying to say to you. Nothing's changing. I'm still Dad, still the same Dad I was all the time.'

'You can't leave Mam, Dad. You can't go off with some other one, and leave Mam and us here.' Brian was very near tears.

Annie spoke. 'She doesn't care, Mam doesn't give a damn. She's just letting him go, she's letting him walk out. She's not even trying to stop him.'

'Thank you very much, Ria, that was terrific.' Danny was near to tears.

She found her voice. 'I will not tell the children that I don't mind and that it's all fine. It is *not* all fine, Danny.'

'You promised . . .' he began.

'I promised nothing.'

'We said we didn't want to hurt the children.'

'I'm not walking out on them, I'm not talking about selling this house over their heads. Where am I hurting them? I only heard about your plans last night and suddenly I'm meant to be all sweetness and light. Saying this is all for the best; we're different people with different needs. I'm the *same* person, I have the same needs. I need you to stay here with us.'

'Ria, have some dignity *please*,' he shouted at her.

They seemed to realise that the children hadn't spoken. They looked at the faces of their son and daughter, white and disbelieving and both of them with tears falling unchecked. They were beginning to realise that their life in Tara Road was over. Nothing would ever be the same. An eerie stillness settled on the kitchen. They watched each other fearfully. It was always Ria who broke a silence, who made the first move, who jollied people along. But not tonight. It was as if she were more shocked than any of them.

Danny spoke eventually. 'I don't know what to do for the best,' he said helplessly. 'I wanted it told differently but maybe there's no good way of telling it.' They said nothing. 'What would you like me to do? Will I stay here in the study tonight so things will be sort of normal, or will I leave and come back tomorrow? You tell me and I'll do what you say.'

It was obvious that Ria was going to say nothing.

He looked at the children. 'Go,' said Brian. 'Stay,' said Annie. 'Not if you're going to leave anyway, go now,' Brian said. They all looked at Annie. She shrugged. 'Why not?' she said in a small hurt voice. 'If you're going to leave tomorrow, what's the point of hanging about?'

'It's not goodbye, sweetheart . . .' Danny began. 'Can you understand that?'

'No, I can't, Daddy, to be honest,' she said, and she picked up her school bag and without a backward glance went out the kitchen door and up the stairs.

Brian watched her go. 'What's going to happen to us all?' he asked.

'We'll all survive,' Danny said. 'People do.'

'Mam?' Her son looked at her.

'As your dad says ... people do, we will too.' The look that Danny gave her was grateful. She didn't want his gratitude. 'The children have said they'd like you to go, Danny. Will you, please?'

He went quietly and the three of them heard him starting his car and driving down Tara Road.

Ria had a little speech ready for them at breakfast.

'I wasn't much help last night,' she said.

'Is it all really going to happen, Mam? Isn't there anything we can do to stop it?' Brian's face was hopeful.

'Apparently it *is* going to happen, but I wanted to tell you it's not quite as sad and awful as it seemed last night.'

'What *do* you mean?' Annie was scornful.

'I mean that what your father said was quite true. We both do love you very much and we'll be here, or around if not here, whenever you need us until you get bored with us and want lives of your own. But until then I'm not going to shout at your father like I did and he's not going to sneer at me. And if you want to be with him, at a weekend say, then that's where you'll be and if you want to be with me, then I'll be here or wherever and delighted for you to be with me. That's a promise.' They didn't rate it much. 'And what I suggest is that you ring your dad at the office today and ask him where he'd like to meet you tonight and talk to you and tell you about everything.'

'Can't you tell us, Mam?' Brian begged.

'I can't really, Brian. I don't know it all and I'd tell it wrong. Let him tell you, then you won't feel worried and there won't be any grey areas.'

'But if he tells us one thing and you tell us another?' Annie wanted to know.

'We'll try not to do that any more.'

'And does everyone know about it?'

'No, I don't think many people do.'

'Well, do they or don't they?' Annie was abrupt and rude. 'I mean does Gran know, Aunty Hilary, Mr McCarthy – people like that?'

'Gran and Hilary don't know, but I expect Mr McCarthy does. I didn't think of it before but I imagine he knows all about it.' Her face was like stone.

'And are we to tell anyone? Do I tell Kitty what's happened or is it all a terrible secret?'

'Kitty's your friend. You must tell her whatever you want to, Annie.'

'I don't want to tell Dekko and Myles, they'd tell the whole class,' Brian said.

'Well don't tell them then, for goodness' sake.' Annie was impatient.

'Do you get custody of us, Mam, or does Dad?'

'I've told you we won't fight over you, you'll be welcome with both of us always. But I would think you would probably live with me during the week in term-time.'

'Because she wouldn't want us, is that it?' Annie was instantly suspicious.

'No, no. She knows your father has two children, she must want to welcome them.'

'But she's having her own,' Brian grumbled.

'What's her name?' Annie wanted to know.

'I don't know,' Ria lied.

'You *must* know, of course you know,' Annie persisted.

'I don't. Ask your father.'

'Why won't you tell us?' Annie wouldn't let go.

'Leave Mam alone. Why do you think she knows?'

'Because it's the first thing I'd have asked, that anyone would ask,' said Annie.

Danny used to laugh at the way Ria made a list of things to do. She always headed it *List*. Old habits die hard. She headed it *List* and sat at the table when the children had gone. Their hugs had been awkward but some pretence at normality had been restored. The tears and silences of last night were over. The list covered many phone calls.

She must ring her mother first and prevent her coming anywhere near the house, then ring Hilary, then at ten o'clock when the charity shop where she was meant to be working opened she would ring and cancel her shift. She would ring Rosemary at the printing company and Gertie at the launderette, and Colm to thank him for minding her.

And lastly she would ring Danny. Beside Danny's name she wrote firmly: *Do not apologise.*

Nora Johnson started to explain about the lunch. 'There may be a question on the bill at the restaurant. They *said* we could have three Irish coffees. In fact, Ria, they more or less insisted. But if there's any dispute . . .'

'Mam, could you stop talking *please*?'

'That's an extraordinary tone to take with your own mother.'

'Listen to me please, Mam. This is not a good day for me. Danny and I are going to have a trial separation. We told the children last night. It didn't go well.'

'And has he moved out?' Her mother sounded very calm.

'Yes. We haven't decided what to do about the house yet but he has moved out for the moment.'

'Keep the house,' her mother said, in a voice like a trap closing.

'Well, all that has to be discussed. If you don't mind I don't feel much like talking about it now.'

'No, but talk to a lawyer and keep that property.'

'Ah, Mam, that's not the point. The point is that Danny's leaving. Aren't you sorry? Aren't you upset for me?'

'I suppose I saw it coming.'

'No, you couldn't have seen it coming.'

'He has very small eyes,' said Ria's mother.

'Can I speak to Mrs Hilary Moran?'

'Jesus, Ria, think yourself lucky you didn't use that voucher, I have such a hangover.'

'Listen, can you talk?'

'Of course I can't talk. I can't think and I certainly can't be in a school with all these screeching voices but this is where I am, and where I have to stay until four thirty. God, you don't know how lucky you are having nothing to do all day but sit in a big house . . .'

'Hilary, shut up and listen to me . . .'

'What?'

'Danny has another woman, a girl he got pregnant.'

'I don't believe it.'

'It's true. I wanted to tell you before Mam did, she's possibly trying to ring you at this minute.' Ria felt her voice tremble a little.

'I'm very sorry, Ria, more sorry than I can say.'

'I know you are.'

'And what happens now?'

'We sell the house, I suppose. He goes his way, I go mine. I don't *know* what happens now.'

'And the children?'

'Like weasels of course. In total shock, as am I.'

'You didn't know or suspect anything?'

'No, and if you tell me he has small eyes like Mam did I'll go round and kill you.'

They giggled. In the middle of it all they were able to laugh at their mother.

'I could tell them I'm sick and come round to you?' Hilary was doubtful.

'No, honestly, I have a million things to do.'

'I hope one of them's getting your hands on the deeds of that house,' Hilary said before they hung up.

Frances Sullivan, who was married to their dentist Jimmy, ran the charity shop. 'Ria . . . of course . . . we'll find someone else for this morning, don't give it a thought. Going anywhere nice?'

'No, bit of a family crisis, something I want to work out.'

'You do that. Is it Annie and my Kitty?'

'No, why do you say that?' Alarm bells sounded in Ria's head.

'Nothing.' Frances was backing off.

'Go on, Frances. I'd tell you it if *I* knew.'

'It's probably nothing, it's just that Kitty let out that she and Annie were going off on a motorbike rally on Saturday next. I wondered had you found out.'

'Not next Saturday surely? They have another Career Forum.'

'I think not,' said Frances Sullivan. 'But you didn't hear it from me.'

Rosemary's secretary put her through at once. 'Is it a good time, Rosemary?'

'Is he giving her up?' Rosemary said.

'No, not a chance.'

'And the children?'

'Took it very badly, of course. Danny and I made a real mess of it.'

'Are you all right, Ria?'

'I am at the moment, I'm on autopilot. And thank you so much for all the things, I forgot to thank you for anything.'

'Like what?'

'The hairdo, the lunch for Mam and Hilary – they got pissed there by the way, the bill might be a bit more than we thought.'

'Oh, for heaven's sake, Ria.'

'And for coming around, and all the encouragement. That's the best bit, I'm sorry for not making a better go of it.'

'You and he'll be back together.'

'No, it's not likely.'

'You're still in Tara Road, aren't you?'

'Yes, for the moment.'

'Stay there, Ria. He's not going to leave that house.'

'Gertie, I truly appreciated your coming round, I knew it wasn't such a good day for you.'

'And you sorted it all out, didn't you?'

'No, I'm afraid not.'

'Listen, there's nothing I don't know about family rows, he'll be as sorry as anything, he'll put it right. He'll let your one, whoever she is, have her baby or an abortion or whatever. You and he are . . . well, I know you don't like the example but, you're like Jack and myself. Some people are meant for each other.'

'I know you think this is helping, Gertie, but . . .'

'Listen, can you ever imagine either of you living anywhere on earth but Tara Road? You're made for that house, that's a sure guarantee it will work out all right.'

'Colm? It's Ria Lynch.'

'Ah yes, Ria.'

'You were very kind to me. I realised I never thanked you.'

'There's no need for thanks between friends, it's assumed.'

'Yes, but we don't want to take friends for granted either.'

'You wouldn't do that.'

'I don't know. I seem to have been a bit spaced out.'

'There's days we're all like that,' he said.

'Thank you for not enquiring if it sorted itself out.'

'These things take time.' He was so soothing, making no demands that she tell him. After all the others that she had talked to this was very restful.

'Danny?'

'It was awful,' he said. 'I'm so sorry.'

Ria looked at her little piece of paper. *Do not apologise*, it ordered her. She had wanted to cry and say she was sorry, that they were not the kind of people who snarled at each other like that. She wanted him to come home and wrap her in his arms. *Do not apologise*, she read, and she knew she had been right to write it down. Danny was not coming home to her. Ever.

'There was hardly any way it couldn't have been awful,' she said in matter-of-fact tones. 'Now let's see what we can salvage. I've told the children to call you today and that maybe you could meet them one evening on some neutral ground. Tell them about things, tell them what it's going to be like. The summer and everything.'

'But it's all still so up in the air, you and I have to . . .'

'No, you must tell them what they can expect. Whether you'll be able to cook dinner for them, have them to stay for weekends. You see they know they'll be welcome here, they don't know what you can offer them.'

'But you won't want to let them . . . ?'

'Danny, they're ten and fifteen. Do you think I'm going to try to tell people of that age where they can go to see their father and where they can't? Nor would I want to. They must hear as much good news from you as possible.'

'You sound very calm.' He was impressed.

'Of course I'm not calm. But you will let them know they're welcome with you wherever you go, not just phrases, actual plans?'

'Plans?'

'Well, you do have a place to live, I imagine?'

'Yes, yes.'

'And would it have enough room for them to stay?'

'Stay?'

'When they go to see you.'

'It's just a small flat at the moment.'

'And is it nearby?' She kept her voice interested and without any emotion.

'It's in Bantry Court, you know, the block . . . that we . . . that Barney developed a few years back?'

'I do,' Ria said. 'That was handy, your being able to get a flat in Bantry Court.' She hoped the bitterness wasn't too obvious in her voice.

'No, it's not mine, it's Bernadette's. She got it from her father when she was eighteen. You see, it was an investment.'

'It certainly was,' Ria said grimly.

'He's dead now,' Danny said.

'Oh, I see.'

'And her mother's sort of worried about the whole situation.'

'I imagine so.'

'She rang you that time, you know, the woman that didn't give her name? She was sort of checking up on me, I suppose.'

'But she knew you were married, I presume?'

'Yes.' He sounded wretched.

Ria continued to speak brightly. 'And you're getting a house soon, is that right?'

'Yes, you know, a house. For everybody.'

'For everybody. Quite.'

There was a silence. He spoke again. 'You know it will take time to get everything sorted out.'

'I think they'd love to know some immediate sort of plans so that they'll know they haven't lost you.'

'But won't you . . . ?'

'I'll have them lots. And the same about summer. Tell them the weeks you can take them away. Remember you once talked of renting a boat on the Shannon?'

'Do you think they'd like that? I mean, you know, without you?'

'Without me? But they're going to have to learn that it will be without me from now on when it's with you. We *all* have to learn that. Let them learn it soon before they panic and think that you have gone away.'

At no stage did Ria mention Bernadette's name or the child that she was carrying. It was clear that she expected that Annie and Brian would be part of the new household. She wanted only that he would close no doors on his daughter and son.

'Another thing. Do your parents know about . . . about all this?'

'Lord no,' he said, startled at the very idea.

'Don't worry. I'll tell them in time,' she said.

'I don't know what to say . . .' he began.

'Oh, and Barney and Mona and Polly and people . . . do they know?'

'Not Mona,' Danny Lynch said quickly.

'But Barney is up to date?'

'Yes, well he helped us to get a house, you see.'

'Like he helped to get us this one,' Ria said. A wave of irritation about Barney McCarthy swept over her. She realised she had never liked him. She had liked both of his women but not him. How odd that she hadn't known this before. She decided to change the subject. 'Children are easily distracted, be sure to emphasise holidays to them.'

'But what would you do? If we all went away?'

'I'd go on a holiday myself maybe.'

'But sweetheart . . . where would you . . . ?'

'Danny, can I ask you not to call me that?'

'I'm so sorry. Yes, you did ask me, but you know it means nothing.'

'I know *now* it means nothing. I didn't always.'

'Please, Ria.'

'Okay, Danny. We'll say goodbye now.'

'Where will I take them, McDonald's, Planet Hollywood?'

'I don't know. It might be a bit difficult to talk in those places, but decide all of you.'

They hung up.

It had been less upsetting than she had thought. Funny how annoyed she was about Barney's complicity. It wasn't unreasonable to be annoyed. After all she and Danny had kept Barney's secret for years. They had never told Mona McCarthy where her husband really was on the night that little Annie Lynch was born.

5

Ria lost all sense of time. Sometimes when she went to bed she awoke thinking it was morning and realising that she had only been asleep for half an hour. The empty side of the bed seemed an enormous vast space. Ria would get up and walk to the window, hugging herself as if to try and ease the pain. Just after midnight and he was asleep in some apartment block wrapped around this child. It was too much to bear. Perhaps her mind would give up under the strain. That's what happened to people. As she sat long hours staring out the window while stars disappeared and dawn came, Ria thought that perhaps her mind had actually broken down already without her noticing it. Yet she appeared to function during daylight hours. The house was cleaned, the meals were cooked, people came and went. She spoke normally, she believed, to those who spoke to her.

But it was all totally unreal. And she couldn't remember anything at all from a day just over. Was it today that Myles and Dekko had brought three frogs to play in the bath – or was that yesterday or last week? Which was the day that she had the huge row with Annie about Kitty? And how had it started? Had Hilary come with six parsnips and a request that Ria make a parsnip soup to take home with her, or had Ria just imagined this?

He was going to come back of course, that was obvious. But when? How long did this humiliating, hurtful, waiting period have to go on before he threw his keys on to the hall table and said, *Sweetheart, I'm home. Everyone has a silly fling and mine is over, now will you forgive me or will I have to walk on my knees?*

And she would forgive him immediately. A great hug, a holiday maybe. The name of Bernadette would not be mentioned for a while and then it would come into the conversation as a kind of risqué joke.

But when was all this healing process going to start? Sometimes during the day Ria would stop whatever she was doing with a physical sense of shock as she remembered something else that had been a lie. That coloured shirt that he had bought in London. The girl had chosen it for him, hadn't she? Bernadette had been in London with him. Ria had to sit down when she realised that. Then the bill for the mobile phone. Almost every call was to her number, the number that was his now in case of emergencies. The duty-free perfume, a guilt present from a trip with Bernadette. The day when they were all at the zoo, just going into the lion house, and he got a call to go back to the office. That wasn't the office, that had been Bernadette. There were so many times and Ria had never suspected. What a fool, what a simple trusting fool she had been. Then she would argue that view. Who wanted to be a gaoler watching every move? If you loved someone you trusted him. Surely it was as simple as that.

And everyone knew, of course they did. When she telephoned him at work they must have raised their eyes to heaven, in sympathy as well as irritation. The staid stay-at-home wife who didn't know her husband had another woman. Even Trudy, the girl who answered the phone, must have put Bernadette through as often as Ria. Possibly Bernadette knew her name too, and asked about her diet which was a way of getting into her good books.

And then of course there was Barney McCarthy coming to this house praising Ria's delicious food. He had been out many, many times with Danny and Bernadette. In Quentin's where Ria went once a year on their wedding anniversary, that nice Brenda Brennan who ran the place would have known too. She must really have pitied Ria, the once-a-year mousy wife who suspected nothing.

And Polly knew, and of course she must have scorned, not pitied, Ria, because she was in exactly the same position as Mona. Mona? Did she know? Ria had spent so long deceiving Mona and hiding Polly's existence and all the time Mona might have been doing just the same about Bernadette.

It would be funny if it were not so terrible. And when you thought about it, if all these people knew, didn't Rosemary know? She knew everything that happened in Dublin. But no, Ria had to believe that her performance could not have been an act. And a true friend would have told her. If Rosemary and Gertie had known they would have had to give Ria some warning and not allow her world to be blown apart. From time to time Ria wondered if Rosemary *had* been giving her warnings. Was all this advice about clothes and getting a job some kind of hint that all was not well?

The Sullivans obviously knew. Frances had been brisk and supportive. 'It's probably a passing thing, Ria. Men approaching forty behave very oddly. If you can sit it out then I'm sure it will all be for the best.'

'Did you know?' Ria had asked her directly.

The answer had not been equally straightforward. 'This is a city full of rumours and stories. You would be addled in the head if you listened to them all. I have enough problems of my own trying to keep Kitty on the rails.'

Colm Barry probably hadn't known. Danny wouldn't have been so foolish as to take that child to a restaurant a few doors from his own house. But so many others did know. It was humiliating to think just how many. Taxi-drivers would have known, the man in the petrol station, Larry the bank manager, he probably knew. Maybe Bernadette had moved her account to Larry's branch for togetherness.

The window-cleaner asked about Danny. 'Where's himself?' he enquired. It was a day when she felt in a mood to talk.

'He's gone, he left me for a young one as it happens.'

'He always had a bit of a roving eye, your man had, you're well rid of him,' the window-cleaner had said. Now why had he said that? *Why?*

Why did people in the charity thrift shop press her hand and say that she was a great woman? Who had told them? Had they always known? Oh how she wished she could get away from all these people who knew. People who pitied her, patted her on the head and talked about her. She *knew* it would end when he gave up Bernadette and came home, but how long would she have to wait while all these people smiled indulgently as if Danny had a dose of the flu?

And of course she had to cope with the children. Annie's mood-swings went the whole way from blaming her mother to blaming herself. 'If you'd only been a bit more normal, Mam, you know, if you'd stopped yacking and cooking he wouldn't have gone away.' The next day it might be, 'It's all my fault . . . he called me his princess but I didn't spend any time with him, I was always in Kitty's house. He knew I didn't love him enough, that's why he went and found someone else not much older than me.'

Once or twice she asked Ria if they might write a letter to Dad saying how lonely they were without him. 'I don't think he knows,' Annie wept.

'He knows.' Ria was stony.

'If he knows why doesn't he come back?' Annie asked.

'He will, but only when he's ready. Honestly Annie, I don't think we can hurry him up.' And for once she noticed Annie nodding as if on this rare occasion she agreed with her mother.

Brian had his views as well. 'It was probably all my fault, Mam. I didn't really wash enough, I know.'

'I don't think that was it, Brian.'

'No, it could have been, you know the way Dad was always washing himself and wearing a clean shirt every day and everything?'

'People do that, you know.'

'Well, could we tell him that I wash more now. And I will, I promise.'

'If Dad left just because you were filthy he'd have left ages ago, you've been filthy for years,' Annie said gloomily.

Then Brian decided that his father had left on account of sex. 'That's what Myles and Dekko say. They say that he went off to her because she's interested in having sex night and day.'

'I don't think that's right,' Ria said.

'No, but it might be part of it. Could you telephone him and say you'd be interested in having it night and day too?' He looked a bit embarrassed and awkward to be talking to his mother about such things, but he obviously felt that they had to be said.

'Not really, Brian.' Ria was glad that Annie wasn't in the room.

Annie was in the room however when Brian came up with his trump card. 'Mam, *I* know how to get Dad back,' he said.

'This should be interesting,' Annie said.

'You and he should have a baby.' The silence was deafening. 'You could,' Brian went on. 'And I wouldn't mind, I've talked about it with Myles and Dekko, it's not as bad as you'd think. And we could babysit, Myles, Dekko and myself. It would be a great way of getting pocket money.' He looked at his mother's stricken face. 'Or listen, Mam, if Dad came back, I'd do it for nothing. No charge at all,' he said.

Wouldn't it be wonderful, Ria thought, if she could be miles away from here, not to have to reassure people that she was fine, and that everything was fine, when in fact the whole world was as far from fine as it would ever be. She put off going out because of the people she would meet, yet she knew it was dangerous to hole up in Tara Road and be the reclusive, betrayed wife.

She heard a sound at the hall door and her heart lifted for a moment. Sometimes Danny used to run back during the day. 'Missed you, sweetheart, have you a cuddle for a working man?' And she always had. When had it stopped? Why had she not noticed? How could the sound of a leaflet being pushed through a hall door still make her think that he had come back? She must make a big effort today to live in the real world. Like knowing what she was doing and what time it was. She looked at the clock automatically when she heard the Angelus bell ringing. Everyone did that, it was almost as if you were checking whether the church had got it right. At the same time the telephone rang.

It was a woman with an American accent. 'I do hope you'll forgive me calling a private home, but this was the only listing I could get for a Mr Danny Lynch, realtor and estate agent. Enquiries didn't have a commercial listing.'

'Yes?' Ria was lacklustre.

'Briefly, my name is Marilyn Vine and we were in Ireland fifteen years ago. We met Mr Danny Lynch and he tried to interest us in some property . . .'

'Yes, well do you mind if I give you his office number, he's not here at the moment . . . ?'

'Of course, but if I could take one more minute of your time to ask you is this something he might do. There isn't really any money in it.'

'Oh, then I doubt it very much,' Ria said.

'I'm sorry?'

'I mean he only cares about the value of this and the price of that nowadays – but then I'm just a little jaundiced today.'

'I beg your pardon, did I get you at a bad time?'

'There aren't going to be any good times from now on, but that's neither here nor there. What exactly was it that you wanted Danny to do for charity?'

'It wasn't that precisely. He was such a pleasant, personable young man I wondered did he know anyone who might like to do a house exchange this summer. I can offer a comfortable and I think pleasant home with a swimming pool in Westville – it's a college town in Connecticut – and I was looking for somewhere within walking distance of the city but with a garden . . .'

'This summer?' Ria asked.

'Yes. July and August. I know it's not much notice . . . but I really felt that I wanted to be there last night. I couldn't sleep and I thought I'd make this call, just in case.'

'And why did you think of Danny?' Ria asked in a slow, measured voice.

'He was so knowledgeable and he was my only contact. I felt sure he might put me on to someone else if it wasn't his particular scene.'

'And would it be a big house or a small house you'd want?' Ria asked.

'I don't really mind, I wouldn't be lonely in a large place and anyone coming here to Westville would have a house with plenty of room for four or five people. They could have the car too, of course, and there are very attractive places to go.'

'And aren't there agencies and things?'

'Yes of course, and I can go through the Internet . . . it's just that when you actually met a person all those years ago, and remembered a friendly face, it seemed a little easier. He wouldn't remember me, us, at all. But just at the moment I don't feel like talking to strangers much, negotiating with them. I guess it does sound a little odd.'

'No, oddly enough I know exactly how you feel.'

'Am I talking to Mrs Lynch?'

'I don't know.'

'I beg your pardon?'

'We are going to get separated, divorced. There's divorce now in Ireland, did you know that?'

'This really was not a good time to ring. I can't tell you how sorry I am.'

'No, it was a great time. We'll do it.'

'Do what?'

'I'll go to your house, you come to mine, July and August. It's a deal.'

'Well, I suppose we should . . .'

'Of course we should, I'll send you a photo of it and all the details. It's lovely; you'll love it. It's in Tara Road, it's got all kinds of trees in the garden and lovely polished wooden floors and it's got some old stained-glass windows, and . . . and . . . and . . . the original mouldings on the ceilings and . . . and . . .' She was crying now. There was a silence at the other end of the line. Ria pulled herself together. 'Please forgive me, Marion is it?'

'Marilyn. Marilyn Vine.'

'I'm Ria Lynch and I can't think of anything I'd like to do more than get away from here and go to a quiet place with a swimming pool and nice drives. I could take my children for one month and the other month I could spend on my own, thinking out my future. That's why I got a bit carried away.'

'Your house sounds just what I want, Ria. Let's do it.'

You mightn't have known from her voice that she was standing in her kitchen looking out of her white wooden house and tears were running down her face also. When Marilyn Vine at last put down the telephone on her kitchen counter, she went out into her garden with her cup of coffee. She sat by the pool where she had swum earlier. Fifteen lengths morning and afternoon; it was as routine now as brushing her teeth. It was ten minutes past seven in the morning. She had just agreed to exchange houses with an extremely agitated woman going through some kind of life crisis. A woman whom she had never met who lived three thousand miles away. A woman who might well not have the right to exchange houses, whose property could well be under some kind of legal review pending divorce.

All Marilyn knew was that it was very foolish to make early-morning, spontaneous, spur-of-the-moment decisions. It was so unlike her to make a telephone call like that at this hour of the morning. And even less like her to go along with the plans of the hysterical woman at the other end of the line. She would never do anything remotely like this again. The only question now was whether she should call back and unpick the entirely impractical arrangement before it had begun to take root in this woman's mind, or just write a letter?

She could call immediately, it might be a cleaner break, and say the home exchange was no longer possible from her end, that she had family duties which she could not ignore. Marilyn smiled wryly at the thought of her being someone with family responsibilities. But Ria in Ireland wouldn't know this. It would be easier to write or send an e-mail – anything not to have to hear the disappointment in that voice. But there was no technology in Tara Road and Ria Lynch would not have had access to her husband's office where presumably such things existed.

She had sounded gutsy and lively as well as slightly unhinged. Marilyn tried to work out how old she was. That good-looking young estate agent must be about forty now, this woman was probably the same age. She mentioned having a daughter of fourteen and a son who was almost ten. Marilyn's face hardened. So her marriage was ending, but she hated her husband: that much was obvious – she spoke about him so disparagingly to a total stranger. She was going to be much better off without him.

Marilyn would not allow herself to brood. Very soon now she would need to go to work. She would drive up to the college campus and take her place in the car park. Then, greeting this person and that, she would walk to the Alumni Office where she worked, cool and self-sufficient in her crisp lemon-and-white suit.

They would look at her with interest. How strange she hadn't gone to Hawaii with her husband. Greg Vine's visiting lectureship had seemed exactly what the couple needed. But Marilyn had been adamant she would not go, and had been equally resolute in giving no explanation to her colleagues and friends. By now they had stopped enquiring and trying to persuade her. She knew she was an object of interest and speculation. Their interest was genuine but so was their mystification that she would not go to a sunny island with the urging of a loving husband and the support of a caring department in the college that would hold the job open for her until her return.

What would they say if they knew what an extraordinary alternative she had been contemplating? To exchange homes for two months with a woman who owned, or claimed she owned, a four-storey Victorian house in Dublin. They would say it was a foolish decision, and must under no circumstances be allowed to go ahead.

Marilyn finished her coffee, straightened her shoulders and squared up to what she had done. She was an adult woman, very adult indeed. She would have her fortieth birthday this summer, on the first of August. She would make whatever decisions she felt like making. Who else was going to tell her what was best for her?

She nodded towards the telephone as if affirming the conversation she had made on it earlier. She looked at her reflection in the hall mirror. Short auburn hair, cut so that she could swim and leave it to dry naturally, green anxious eyes, tense shoulders but otherwise perfectly normal. Not at all the kind of person who would have decided something so unbalanced.

Marilyn picked up her keys and drove to work.

Ria sat down and held on to the table very tightly. Not since she was a teenager had she been abroad alone. And with Danny very few times. Well, at least she had a passport and a few weeks to get everything organised at this end.

Marilyn had said she was perfectly happy to feed Annie's cat. The children would love a trip to America, a house with a swimming pool. Marilyn said it was easy to learn to drive on the wrong side of the road because the place was so quiet. Ria had warned Marilyn against any such foolhardy courage in Dublin, which was filled with traffic hazards and mad drivers.

Marilyn had said she would prefer to walk anyway.

From force of habit, Ria got a piece of paper, wrote the word *List* and underlined it. As she began to write down what she had to do, her chest tightened. Was she completely mad? She knew nothing about this woman. Nothing at all except they had both cried on the telephone. When you paused to think about it, wasn't it very odd that she should approach the business of exchanging her house this way? There were agencies, firms specialising in such things. There was the whole Internet waiting for the opportunity to match people together, find them the ideal house-swap.

What kind of a person would remember Danny's handsome face from years ago and try to track him down? Perhaps she had fancied him all that time ago; he was a striking-looking man after all. Maybe she had in fact been closer to him than she was saying; it might have been a fling, a whirl or whatever. This whole idea of taking his house could be a ploy, a ruse to get involved in his life.

Ria had seen so many movies where mad people sounded totally plausible, where innocent trusting folk admitted them willingly into their lives. These could be the first hours of a nightmare that could wreck them. She must try and be rational about all this and work out what she wanted. Why did it seem such a good idea? Was it only so that she wouldn't have to look at Hilary, her mother, Rosemary, Frances and Gertie and see the sympathy in their eyes? Was there any other reason that was taking her across the Atlantic Ocean?

I might half forget him out there, Ria told herself. I might actually not see his face everywhere I look. Suppose she was sleeping in a strange bed in America she might not wake up at four o'clock frightened, thinking he was very late, could he have been in a car crash, and then with the even more sickening realisation that he was not coming back at all. America might cure that.

And the awful belief that there may have been other Bernadettes. People always said that the man doesn't leave on the first affair. There could have been other people entertained in this house, even that had slept with her husband. How great to go to a place where nobody had met Danny, heard of him, and certainly not slept with him.

But still it was a very sudden decision to have made. Promising a total stranger that she could live here in Tara Road. In normal times she would not have done anything so wildly lacking in caution. But these were not normal times, they were times when two months in America might actually be what was needed. And it was idiotic really to think that this woman Marilyn might be a serial killer.

Ria remembered that Marilyn had not wanted this house in particular, and it was Ria who had pushed Tara Road. Marilyn had sounded apologetic and had tried several times to end the conversation, it was Ria who had made all the running. She had said she would send photographs and banker's references, and Ria would do the same. Of course she was above-board and normal. She wanted to escape and have time to get her head together; that was American-speak for exactly what Ria wanted to do. It wasn't *so* outrageous a coincidence that two people with identical needs should meet accidentally at the right time.

Why do I want it so much? Ria asked herself. When I got up this morning I hadn't a notion of going to a house in Connecticut for the summer. Is it for the children so that I'll be able to offer them something the equivalent of their father's trip on the Shannon? Is it that I want to be somewhere where Danny Lynch isn't the centre of the world and we are all waiting for what he will do next so that we can react?

She felt the answer was a mixture of all these things, but she still wasn't sure that she had the strength to go ahead with it. Should she talk to Rosemary about it? Rosemary was so clear-headed she cut straight to the chase on everything.

But Ria firmed up her shoulders. She *was* a strong person despite a lot of evidence to the contrary. She would not allow circumstances to turn her into one of those dithering women she despised so much when she served them at the charity shop. The ones who couldn't make up their mind between a blue tablecloth and a yellow one; they'd have to talk to a husband, a daughter, a neighbour about it all before they came back and paid three whole pounds.

She liked the sound of Marilyn; this woman was not a psychotic, deranged killer coming over to waste the neighbourhood of Tara Road. She was someone who had appeared just when she was needed. With bleak determination Ria applied herself to the list.

The meal with Annie and Brian was not going well.

Danny had taken them to Quentin's which he thought would be a treat for them, but was turning out to be a great mistake. For one thing they weren't dressed properly. Any other young people having an early dinner there with parents and grandparents were elegantly turned out. Brian wore scruffy jeans and a very grubby T-shirt. His zipped jacket had a lot of writing on it, the names of footballers and dead pop stars; he looked very like a young tearaway who might have been harassing tourists in Grafton Street. Annie was also in jeans, far too tight in Danny's opinion. Her blonde hair was not washed and shiny, it was greasy and pushed behind her ears. She wore an old sequinned jacket to which she was inordinately attached. It belonged to some old lady in St Rita's and was described as a genuine fifties garment if you commented on it at all.

'Would you look at the prices!' Brian said, astounded. '*Look* what they charge for steak and kidney pie. Mam makes that for free at home.'

'Not for free, you eejit,' Annie said. 'She has to buy the steak and the kidney and the flour and the butter for the pastry.'

'But that's all there already,' Brian protested.

'No, it's not. It doesn't grow in the kitchen, you fool. That's so typical of a man. She has to go out and pay for it in the shops and then there's the cost of her labour; that *has* to be taken into consideration.'

Danny saw that in a way Annie was trying to justify the cost of the expensive meal that he was treating them to, but as a conversation it was going nowhere. 'Right, now do we see anything we like?' He looked from one of them to the other hopefully.

'What are porcini, is it roast pork?' Brian asked.

'No, it's mushrooms,' his father explained.

'Eejit,' Annie said again, even though she hadn't known either.

'I might have a hamburger but I don't see it on the menu,' Brian said.

Danny hid his annoyance. 'Look here, they say ground beef served with a tomato and basil salsa, that's more or less it,' he pointed it out.

'Why don't they *call* it a burger, like normal places?' Brian grumbled.

'They expect people to be able to read and understand things,' Annie said dismissively. 'Do they have vegetarian things, Dad?'

Eventually the choice was made and Brenda Brennan, the suave manageress, came and took their order personally.

'Pleasure to see you with your family, Mr Lynch,' she said, showing not an iota of displeasure at the fact that the children were dressed like tramps.

Danny smiled his gratitude.

'Is that her?' Brian whispered when Brenda Brennan had gone.

'Who?' Danny was genuinely bewildered.

'The one, the one who's going to have the baby, the one that you're going to live with?'

'Don't be *ridiculous*, Brian.' Annie's patience was now exhausted. 'She's as old as Mam, for God's sake. Of course she's not the one.'

Danny felt the time had come to reclaim the purpose of the evening. 'Your mother and I have had a very good conversation today, very good. We had none of those silly fights that have been so upsetting for us and indeed specially for you.'

'Well, that makes a change,' Annie grumbled.

'Yes it *does* make a change, these have been a bad couple of days for us all, but now we're all able to talk again.'

'Are you coming back?' Brian asked hopefully.

'Brian, this is what your mother and I were talking about. It's a question of what words we use. I've not gone away, I haven't left you two, of course I haven't. I'm going to be living in a different place, that's all.'

'What kind of place?' Annie asked.

'Well it's only a flat at the moment, but it will be a house very soon and you'll come to stay there as often as you like. It's got a lovely garden, and it will be your home too.'

'We've got a lovely garden in Tara Road,' Annie said.

'Yes, well now you'll have two.' He beamed with pleasure at the thought of it.

They looked at him doubtfully.

'Will we each have our own room?' Annie asked.

'Yes, of course. Not quite immediately, not the day we move in, but there'll be alterations done. Mr McCarthy's people will divide a room for you. In the meantime when you come to stay one of you can sleep on the sofa in the sitting room.'

'Doesn't sound much like a second home to me, sleeping on the sofa,' Annie said.

'No, well it's only temporary and then it will be sorted out.' He kept his smile bright.

'And how many days will we stay there, in the house with the divided room?' Brian asked.

'As many as you like. Your mother and I talked about that very thing today. You'll be delighted when you go home and discuss it with her, we both agree that you are the important people in all this . . .'

Annie cut across his speech. 'And could one of us stay in one place, and one in the other? I mean I don't have to be joined at the hip to Brian or anything?'

'No, of course not.'

Annie looked pleased by this.

'And when the baby comes if it's crying and annoying us, can we go back to Tara Road?' Brian asked.

'Yes, of course.'

'Well that's all right then.' Brian seemed satisfied.

'And will she be like Mam and say keep your room tidy and you can't come in at this hour?'

'Bernadette will make you very welcome. She's so looking forward to meeting you. When will we arrange that, do you think?'

'You didn't say if she'd be making rules and regulations,' Annie persisted.

'You'll be as courteous and helpful in this new house as you are in Tara Road. That's all that's expected of you.'

'But we're *not* helpful in Tara Road,' Brian said, as if this was something his father had misunderstood.

Danny sighed. 'Suppose we decide a time and place to meet Bernadette?'

'Does she have a big bump? Does she look very pregnant?' Annie wanted to know.

'Not particularly. Why do you ask?'

Annie shrugged. 'Does it make any difference where we meet?' Danny felt a tic of impatience; this was much harder than he had expected it would be. 'Do we have to meet her?' Annie asked. 'Wouldn't it be better to wait until the baby's born and everything, get all that out of the way?'

'Of course you'll meet her,' Danny cried. 'We're all going away on a boat on the Shannon for a holiday, all of us. We want to meet together long before that.'

They looked at him dumbfounded.

'The Shannon?' Annie said.

'All of us?' Brian asked.

'Can Kitty come too?' Annie put in quickly. 'And don't even think of asking about Myles and Dekko, Brian, don't think of it.'

'I don't honestly think Mam would like a holiday with . . . you know, *her* coming too,' Brian said slowly.

Annie and her father exchanged glances. It was the one moment of solidarity in a nightmare meal. At least his daughter understood some of the problems ahead. Annie said nothing about Brian being brain-dead. Instead they both began to explain to the boy who was, after all, only ten years of age, that his mother would not be coming with them on this long-planned, much discussed holiday.

In Marilyn's office there was much talk of the annual alumni picnic in August. They had to get a list of accommodation addresses ready. Hotels, guest houses, dormitories, private homes where the past students could stay. Many of them looked forward to this weekend as the high spot of the year. It was a highly successful fund-raiser for the college and maintained close contacts between present and past.

It had always been a tradition that those who worked in the Alumni Office would offer hospitality in their own homes. Marilyn and Greg had hosted many a family in 1024 Tudor Drive. Pleasant people all of them. They had always been delighted with the pool in the hot August weather and many had kept in touch over the years. The Vines had invitations in return to stay in Boston, New York City and Washington DC any time they liked.

The plans for the picnic were under way, the wording of the appeal in the first notifications, the details of tax deductions in any gift made to an alumni library and arts centre. They would have to debate the nature of the entertainment, the number of people allowed to address the gathering, the need to keep the speeches even shorter than they were. Soon work would be apportioned. Marilyn knew she must speak before then. She would not accept any tasks and projects which she would be unable to carry through.

She cleared her throat and addressed the Professor of Education who was taking the meeting. 'Chair, I must explain that I will not be here during the months of July and August. I have accepted the leave of absence so kindly offered to me by the college. I leave at the end of June and will be back after

Labor Day, so can I ask you to give me maximum input to the early preparation work in the knowledge that I will not be here for the event itself?'

A group of faces looked up, smiling. This was good news. The taut, tense Marilyn Vine was finally giving in. At last she was going to join Greg, her bewildered husband, in Hawaii.

Almost two months before she left. That would give Ria plenty of time. And she wouldn't tell anybody anything until she was ready. The list had been invaluable. She couldn't understand why Danny had laughed at her, ruffled her hair and said she was a funny little thing. It was what people *did*, for heaven's sake. All right, if they were at work or in an office they used computers, personal organisers, filofaxes. But basically the process was the same. You wrote down what had to be done, and you clutched it to you. That way you didn't forget anything.

It would take a week at least before she got the documents from Marilyn. She didn't want to spring this on everyone without being able to show them something to back up that this was a good idea. She had prepared a little dossier of her own, which she would send off today or tomorrow. She had photographs of the house both inside and out and cuttings from the *Irish Times* newspaper's property section showing the kind of place that Tara Road was. She put in a map of Dublin, an up-to-date tourist guide to the city, a restaurant guide, a list of books Marilyn might like to read before she came. She gave the address of her bank, the name, telephone number and fax of their bank manager. Also a terse and unemotional note to say that the house was owned jointly between her and Danny; its ownership was not in dispute. He would look after the children for the month of July and later she would send a list of friends and contacts that would be of help to Marilyn when she arrived.

Perhaps a week was too optimistic; she might have to keep her secret for a little longer than she had hoped. She imagined that the whole business could even take as long as ten days. But Ria had reckoned without the speed of the United States and the existence of courier firms. A Fedex van turned up the very next day at her house with all of Marilyn's details. Hardly daring to breathe she looked at the pictures of the swimming pool, the low white house with the flowers in the porch, the map of the area, the local newspaper, and the details of the car, shopping facilities and membership of a leisure centre and club which could be transferred to Ria while she was in residence. There were golf, tennis and bowling near by, and Marilyn also said she would give her a list of contacts with telephone numbers for any emergency that might occur.

In a note as terse and unemotional as Ria's own letter Marilyn explained that she needed some space to think out her future. She had not joined her husband on a short sabbatical in Hawaii, because there were still matters she had to think through. With her bank details she also added that she had not yet told her husband about the exchange but that there would be no problem and she would confirm this within twenty-four hours. She didn't like to call him and tell him it had been organised just like that. Some things need a little diplomacy, as she was sure Ria would understand.

Ria understood. She still had to tell Danny. Did they all know in his office, she wondered again, as she rang and asked to be put through to him? It was very, very hard to dial the office now. As Danny's wife she had had some kind of automatic status in their eyes, now what had she? It was easy to read sympathy, scorn or embarrassment into the voice of the receptionist. Perhaps it was none of these things.

'Can you come around and collect your things soon, Danny? I want to try and organise the place a bit.'

'There's no huge hurry, is there?'

'No, not from my point of view, but for the children . . . they really should get used to knowing that your things are where you stay.'

'Well, as I said, the flat's a bit small at the moment.'

'But didn't you say Barney was organising you a new house?'

'Finding us one I said, not buying one, Ria.'

'Sure I know that, but doesn't it exist?'

'It's not in great shape yet.'

'But it's probably in good enough shape to hold your golf clubs, your books, the rest of your clothes . . . you know, the music centre, that's yours.'

'No, sweet . . . No, it's not *mine*, it's ours. We're not down to dividing things up item by item.'

'We have to some time.'

'But not . . . no, not this minute.'

'Come today if you can, with the car. And there are a few other things I want to talk to you about anyway. Come before the children get back, won't you?'

'But I'd like to see them.'

'Sure, and you can any time, but it's not a good idea to see them here.'

'Ria, don't start laying down rules.'

'But we agreed not to confuse them; they're to be equally welcome in each home. I'm not going to be over in your place when they visit you, and it makes sense for you not to be in my place.'

There was a silence.

'It's a bit different.'

'No it's not, there'll be no sign of me or all my make-up and clothes and sewing machine dotted around in Bernadette's house, so why should all your things be here?'

'I'll come over,' Danny said.

Heidi Franks could hardly wait for the alumni picnic meeting to be over so that she could talk to Marilyn. She was overjoyed to know that the woman had finally seen sense. She would offer to go and keep an eye on her garden for her. She knew it was Marilyn's pride and joy and that the neighbours were not green-fingered. But this decision had been long in the making. Heidi would not rush in with cries of delight; she would take it as casually as Marilyn herself. That announcement at the meeting had been deliberately cool and unfussy, even in an environment where she knew they were all very interested and concerned about her plans.

'I'll be so happy to drop in and adjust the sprinklers for you,' she said as soon as they had a moment to talk.

'You're too good, Heidi, but truly they are totally automatic; they work themselves.'

'Well, just to make sure that there are no little bugs or aphids attacking all your lovely beds.'

'No, actually there'll be someone there, that's why I couldn't offer any accommodation for the picnic.'

'Really, someone to house-sit? That's a good idea, who's going to do it?'

'Oh you wouldn't know her, she's from Ireland – Ria Lynch.'

'*Ireland?*' Heidi said.

'I know. I expect she'll find it very different here. I must rush, Heidi, I have to hand this lot in. I'll talk to you later and tell you all about it.' She had left the office.

Heidi smiled fondly after her. Greg would be so pleased. He had been distraught when Marilyn wouldn't accompany him to Hawaii. He had moved heaven and earth to get the position and the professorial exchange; once it had been achieved he couldn't go back on it. Now Marilyn was going to join him at last.

Ria had never used a courier service before. It was surprisingly easy; they just came around and took the package. How foolish she had been, thinking that people used ordinary mail any more when things were important. She had a lot to learn. But maybe this summer would teach her quite a few of them.

She saw Colm in the garden being watched through sleepy eyes by Clement the cat that he had given to Annie when it was a little kitten. He worked so hard and was always so even-tempered and pleasant. She yearned to invite him in for coffee and tell him her plans.

But she couldn't, not until she had spoken to Danny. Danny, who was going to go through the roof when he heard how she intended to spend the summer. Danny, who had obviously had a disastrous evening with the children in Quentin's . . . what a stupid place to have taken them in the first place. They hadn't told her it was bad but they didn't have to, it was written all over their faces.

Heidi picked up the telephone on Marilyn's desk.

'Good afternoon, Marilyn Vine's phone, Heidi Franks speaking . . . Oh, Greg, nice to talk with you, no you've just missed her. She'll be back in ten minutes. Can I take a message? Sure, sure. I'll tell her. Oh and Greg, we're all thrilled she's going out to you. It's a great decision. Today. At the meeting. Yes, for July and August. No? You don't? Could it be a surprise or anything? Oh I'm really so sorry I spoke. No I don't *think* I got it wrong, Greg. She says there's an Irishwoman coming to house-sit up in Tudor Drive while she's out with you. Listen, better let her talk to you about it. I know, Greg. Things *do* get confused.' Heidi replaced the receiver slowly and turned around.

At the door stood Marilyn listening with a white face. *Why* had she told the faculty before she had told Greg? She was such a fool. It was partly because of the time-difference between here and Hawaii, partly because she had been considering what to say. Now things would be worse than ever.

Danny didn't even lift the envelope of pictures, brochure and maps. He just looked at Ria, astounded.

'This is *not* going to happen. Believe me, this is so mad that I can't even take it in.'

Ria was calm. On her list she had written: *Don't plead, don't beg.* It was working, she was doing neither.

'It's only going to cost our fares, and I've been on to the travel agency. They're not crippling.'

'And what exactly would you call crippling, might I ask?' he said with a sneer in his voice.

'The price of a meal in Quentin's for two children who only wanted a burger and a pizza,' she said.

'Aha, I *knew* something like this would come up, I *knew* it,' he said triumphantly.

'Good, it's nice to be proved right,' Ria said.

'I beg of you don't get all silly and smug on me. We're trying God damn it, we're trying for the kids' sake not to make them into footballs. You sounded fine on the phone. Why have you changed?'

'I'm still fine. I haven't changed. I *am* thinking of the children. You're going to be able to hire a lovely cruiser on the Shannon for them; I don't have the money for that. In fact I don't know *what* money I'll have so I've arranged a grand holiday for them in a place with a lovely pool. *Look* at it, Danny, at no cost except the fare. We'll just go out to the grocery and I'll cook there instead of here. I thought you'd be pleased.'

'*Pleased?* You thought I'd be pleased to let a madwoman that none of us know into my house . . .'

'Our house . . .'

'It's not on, Ria, believe me.'

'We've arranged it.'

'Then unarrange it.'

'Will you explain to the children that there'll be no holiday for them with me, no chance to see the United States? Will you look after them for two months instead of one? Well, *will* you Danny? That's what this is about.'

'No, it's not about this, it's about you putting a gun to my head, that's what it's about.'

'I am *not* doing that, I am trying my very best to pick up all the pieces that *you* broke. I was perfectly happy to go on here for ever and ever. You weren't. *That's* what it's all about.' She was as flushed as he was.

His voice was calmer now, and she noticed that he wasn't calling her 'sweetheart' any more. That much had sunk in anyway. 'We don't know anything about this person, Ria, even suppose for a moment that I thought it was a good idea. Running away is never a good idea.' She looked at him quizzically, her head on one side. 'I didn't run away, I made a decision about life and I told you openly and honestly,' he blustered slightly.

'Yes, I forgot. Of course you did.' She was totally calm now.

'So now will you agree that maybe *some* year we could talk about your doing this, you know, organising a house exchange to the States. It's a big market actually, and safer than timeshare. Barney was only talking...'

'I'm going on July the first, she's coming that day. The children can come out to me on August the first. I've checked the flights, there are seats available, but we need to book soon.' Her voice was very steady and she seemed very sure of what she was saying.

Danny reached out and unwillingly dragged Marilyn Vine's envelope to him to look at the contents. That was the moment when Ria knew she had won and that the trip was on.

Marilyn sent a very short e-mail to Greg at the University in Hawaii:

> *Very much regret not getting in touch about my summer plans. Please call me at home tonight at any time that suits you and I will explain everything.*
>
> *Again many sincere regrets,*
>
> *Marilyn*

He called at 8.00 p.m. She was waiting and answered immediately.

'It must be about three o'clock in the afternoon there,' Marilyn said.

'Marilyn, I didn't call to discuss the different time zones, what's happening?'

'I'm truly very sorry and Heidi is distraught over it all, as you can imagine. Another hour and I would have e-mailed you asking you to call.'

'Well I'm calling now.'

'I want to get away from here. I find it very stifling.'

'I know, so did I. That's why I arranged for us to come here.' His voice was uncomprehending. He had been so sure she would go to Hawaii with him, so devastated when she had said she wasn't able to face it.

'We've been through all that before, Greg.'

'We have most certainly *not* been through it as you say. I am sitting out here six thousand miles away without any understanding of why you are not here with me.'

'Please, Greg?'

'No, you can't just say "Please Greg" and expect me to understand, be somehow inspired. And what *are* your summer plans as you call them? Am I going to be told about them or must I wait for more conflicting messages from half the faculty to tell me that you're joining me here or not?'

'I can't apologise enough for that.'

'Where are you going, Marilyn?' His voice was cold now.

'I'm going to Ireland on July the first.'

'*Ireland?*' he said.

She could see his face, lined and sun-tanned, and his glasses pushed up on his forehead, his hair beginning to thin a little in the front. He would be wearing a pair of faded chinos and maybe one of those very bright primary-colour shirts which looked just fine in the glare and heat of the islands but looked overdone and touristy anywhere else.

'We were there years ago together. Do you remember?'

'Of course I remember, we were on a conference for three days and then three days touring the west, where it rained all the time.'

'I'm not going for the weather, I'm going for some peace.'

'Marilyn, it's very dangerous in your state of mind to go and bury yourself in some cabin on the side of a mountain there.'

'No I'm not doing that. It's a big suburban house actually, in a classy part of Dublin, old Victorian building. It looks lovely, four storeys altogether and there's a big garden. I'll be very happy there.'

'You can't be serious.'

'But I am. I've arranged an exchange with the woman that owns it, she's coming here to Tudor Drive.'

'You're giving our house to a total stranger?'

'I've told her that you may possibly come back, that it's not likely but that work may bring you back, she quite realises that.'

'Oh, very generous of her, and will her husband be coming back from time to time to visit you possibly?'

'No, they're separated.'

'Like us I suppose,' he said. 'For all the phrases we wrap it up in, we are separated, aren't we, Marilyn?' He sounded very bleak.

'Not in my mind, we're not. We are just having time apart this year; we've been through that a hundred times. Do you want to hear about Ria?'

'Who?'

'Ria Lynch, the woman who's coming.'

'No, I don't.' Greg hung up.

Heidi Franks was so upset at having opened her mouth to Greg Vine in Hawaii that she had to go to the restroom and have a weep at her own stupidity. She had obviously created a very awkward situation. And yet how was she meant to have guessed that the husband knew nothing of the wife's plans?

They were an immensely compatible couple, and nobody thought for a moment that this temporary separation while Greg was in Hawaii meant any rift in the marriage. For one thing he called and sent e-mails regularly, and also sent postcards to various faculty members always reporting some little bit of news he had learned from Marilyn. So how could *anyone* be blamed for assuming that Greg knew his wife's plans?

Still it was very upsetting, and that grey drained look on Marilyn's face as she realised that Heidi had been blabbing away on the telephone would be hard to forget. Heidi dabbed her eyes; her face looked blotchy and dry. Her hair was a mess. Oh, how she wished that Marilyn were the kind of person that she could apologise to properly. And maybe they might even both be a bit tearful together. Then Marilyn would tell her what it was all about, swear her to secrecy over whatever it was that was happening, and Heidi would be totally diplomatic. Because the maddening thing was that normally she actually *was* discreet. But this would not happen. Marilyn was stoic and unbending. Nonsense, she had said. Please don't mention it, it was a matter of timing. Then the subject had been closed.

Heidi felt wretched. Tonight there was a cocktail party to say farewell to a lecturer in the Mathematics Department. Henry had said he would like her to go. These were occasions when the older wives always dressed up to kill. Heidi looked once more with displeasure at her flaking skin and bird's-nest hair. It would take more than cold eye-pads to restore those sad red eyes to anything approaching elegance. She made a sudden and rare decision to take the afternoon off and go to Carlotta's Beauty Salon out in Westville. Carlotta, who specialised in 'treatments for the maturer skin', would look after her.

It was wonderful to lie back and let Carlotta get on with the repair job. Heidi felt herself relaxing and feeling better by the moment. Carlotta, with her big dark eyes, was both attractive and motherly-looking at the same time. She was immaculately groomed, a perfect advertisement for her own salon. She had come to live in Westville from California over ten years ago and opened a very smart and successful salon, employing six local women.

She had been married, it was rumoured at least three times, in her youth. Children were not spoken of. There was no husband around at the present time. But everyone knew that if Carlotta wanted one, one would appear. One might even detach himself from where he was already meant to be secured. She was a very exotic, charming, not to mention financially secure, woman. Whichever side of forty she was, and this was often debated in Westville, Carlotta would have few problems in finding husband number four when she set out to look for him.

She suggested a herbal facial for Heidi, and a scalp massage. Nothing too rushed, nothing too expensive. Heidi vowed that she would come to this restful place regularly. She owed it to herself. Henry had his golf; it was only fair that she should have something relaxing also. As the firm capable hands massaged her throat and neck Heidi began to forget the sad, strained face of Marilyn Vine who had planned to take two months off travelling somewhere without informing her husband.

'How is Marilyn getting along these days?' Carlotta asked unexpectedly.

Carlotta lived next door to the Vines. Heidi had totally forgotten. But she was not going to be caught twice in one day. This time she would say absolutely nothing about Marilyn's plan and intentions. 'I do see her from time to time in the office, but I don't really know how she's getting along. She keeps herself very much to herself. You know her much better than I do, Carlotta, living so near and everything. Do you see much of her?'

Carlotta spoke easily about everyone but she never actually gave out any detailed information. She spoke in warm generalities. They were wonderful neighbours, she said. You couldn't live beside better people than the Vines. And they kept their property so well. Everyone else on Tudor Drive had begun to smarten themselves up since Marilyn got going. She just loved those trees and flowers.

'Does she come to the salon?' Heidi asked.

'No, she's not really into skin care.'

'Still, this would be such a treat for her,' Heidi said.

'I'm glad you feel it relaxing.' Carlotta was pleased. 'But anyway, even if I were thinking about it, this isn't the time with her trip and everything.'

'Her trip?'

'Didn't she tell you? She's going to Ireland for two months, exchanging homes with a friend of hers there or something.'

'*When* did she tell you this?'

'This morning when we were putting out the trash. She had just fixed it up, she seemed very pleased. Longest conversation I've had with her for a long time.'

'Ireland . . .' Heidi said thoughtfully. 'What on earth is taking her all the way to Ireland?'

'America!' said Rosemary. 'I don't believe it.'

'I hardly believe it myself,' Ria admitted.

'And what does everyone say?' Rosemary wanted to know.

'You mean what does Danny say?'

'Yes I suppose I do, to be honest.'

'Well, he's horrified of course. But mainly I think because of having the children for a month, that doesn't suit the little love-nest at all.'

'So what's he going to do?'

'Well, *he* is going to have to work that out. I'll be at Kennedy to meet them on August the first. July is *his* business.' She sounded much stronger, more resourceful somehow.

Rosemary looked at her with admiration. 'You really have thought this through, haven't you? You'll have the whole place sussed out by the time the children get there, you'll know where to take them, how to entertain them and everything. You'll really *need* a month to get it together.'

'I need the month to get myself together. This month is for me, they'll find plenty to do when they get there. Here, let me show you pictures of the house.'

Rosemary was as fascinated with the change in her friend as she was with the pictures of a beautiful garden and a swimming pool in a small town in Connecticut. It might be just false energy but Ria certainly looked as if she had some life in her. Up to now she had been like somebody sleep-walking.

'I'm not going,' Annie said.

'Fine,' her mother replied.

This startled Annie. She had expected that she would be persuaded and coaxed. Things were certainly changing round here.

Brian was looking at the photographs. 'Look, they have a basket beside their garage, I wonder do they have a ball or should we bring one?'

'Of course they have a ball,' Annie said loftily.

'Look at the pool, it's like something in a hotel.'

Annie reached for the picture again. But her face was still mutinous. 'It's ridiculous us going out there,' she said.

Ria said nothing in reply, she just continued to set the table for breakfast. She had moved the big chair with the carved arms where Danny used to sit. Not a big public statement, she had just put it in a corner with a pile of magazines and newspapers on it. She always sat at different parts of the table herself trying to vary things, trying not to leave the yawning gap where the children's father used to sit.

It was surprising how she still expected him to come in the door saying: 'Sweetheart, did I have one awful day, it's good to be home.' Had he said that on the days when he had been making love to Bernadette? The thought made her shiver sometimes. How little she had known him and what he wanted in life. Ria found it almost impossible to concentrate on the trip to America at times, there was so much buzzing around in her head. Those times he had been working late, she had been so understanding and planned food that wouldn't be dried up when he came back. All those nights when he fell asleep exhausted in the big chair, perhaps it was exhaustion from making love to a young girl.

Weeks of waking with a shock at 4.00 a.m. in her empty bed and trying to remember the last time they had made love there, and wondering what he thought as he was planning to leave her and live in another home.

If she lived on her own Ria knew that she would almost certainly be quite mad by now. It was having to put on a face for the children that kept some hold of her sanity. She looked at them as they sat at the table, Brian looking at the pictures of a big basketball net fixed to a wall and the swimming pool with its tiled surrounds, Annie pushing the cuttings and pictures around sulkily. A wave of pity for them came over her. These were children who were having to face an entirely different summer than the one they had a right to expect. Ria would be very gentle with them.

She answered Annie thoughtfully. 'Yes, I know it sounds ridiculous to go there, but it has a lot going for it as well. It would be a new experience for us all to see America and no hotel bills to pay. And then of course there would be someone who would come here and mind this house for us all, that's important.'

'But who is she?' Annie groused.

'It's all there in the letter, love. I left it for you to read.'

'It doesn't *tell* us anything,' Annie said.

And in a way she was right. It didn't tell all that much. It didn't say why Marilyn wanted to leave this paradise and come to Dublin, and whether her husband would come too. It didn't speak of any friends or relations in Westville, nothing about a circle of people she knew, just an emergency list of locksmiths, plumbers, electricians and gardeners.

Ria's list had been much more people-orientated. But nothing would please Annie anyway so this wasn't relevant. She was still shuffling the papers around on the kitchen table, her face discontented.

'Has Dad fixed up the date of the Shannon trip?' Ria asked them.

They looked at each other guiltily as if there was something to hide.

'He says the boats are all booked,' Brian said.

'Ah, surely not?'

'That's what he *says*,' Annie said.

'Well, there must have been great demand for them then,' Ria said, pretending not to notice the disbelief.

'But he may be making it up,' Brian said.

'No, Brian, of course he wouldn't make it up, he's dying for a trip on the Shannon.'

'Yeah, but *she* wasn't,' Annie said.

'We don't know that now.' Ria struggled to be fair.

'We do actually, Mam.'

'Did she tell you to your faces?'

'No, we haven't met her yet,' Brian said.

'Well then . . .'

'We're meeting her today,' Annie said. 'After school.'

'That's good,' Ria said emptily.

'Why is it good?' Annie would fight with her shadow today.

'It's good because if you're going to be spending July with her, then the sooner you meet Bernadette the better. So that you'll get to know her.'

'I don't want to know her,' Annie said.

'Neither do I.' Brian was in rare agreement with his sister.

'Where are you all meeting?'

'Her flat, well, their flat,' Annie said. 'For tea, apparently.' She made it sound like the most unusual and bizarre thing to offer in the afternoon.

Part of Ria was pleased to see the resentment against the woman who had taken their father away. Yet another part of her knew that the only hope of peace ahead was if the children were co-operative. 'You know it would be nice if . . .' she began. She had been about to say that they should take a little potted plant or a small gift. It would break the ice and please Danny as well. But then she stopped herself. This was ridiculous. She would *not* make smooth the path of the meeting between her children and their father's pregnant mistress. Let Danny do it whatever way he wanted to.

'What would be nice?' Annie sensed a change of heart.

'If all this hadn't happened I suppose, but it has so we have to cope as best we can.' She was brisk.

She scooped up the contents of Marilyn's envelope.

'Are you putting those away?' Annie asked.

'Yes, Brian's seen them, you're not coming with us so I'll just keep them with my things. Okay?'

'What will I do while you're there?'

'I don't know, Annie. Stay with Dad and Bernadette, I suppose. You'll work it out.' She knew it was unfair, but she just wasn't going to go down the road of pleading and begging.

Annie would go to Westville when the time came, they all knew that.

Bantry Court, the apartment block that Bernadette lived in, had been developed by Barney about five years ago. Danny had sold many of the flats.

Perhaps this was how he had met Bernadette. Ria had never asked. There were so many questions she had not asked. Like what she looked like. What they talked about. What she cooked for him. If she held him and stroked his forehead when he woke with a nightmare and his heart racing.

She had coped by pushing these things out of her mind. But today her daughter and son were going to this woman's apartment for tea. Somehow it was important that she had to see Bernadette first. Before Annie and Brian did.

As soon as they left for school Ria got into her car and drove there. She noticed that it took fifteen minutes. On the many nights when he came home so late, Danny must have driven this route. Had he hated coming back to Tara Road all that time or was he happy to keep both lives going? If this girl had not become pregnant would it have just gone along like that for ever? Bantry Court, Tara Road, two different compartments of his life?

She parked in the forecourt and looked up at the windows. Behind one of those sat Bernadette who was going to entertain Danny's children to tea this afternoon and get to know them, tell them about the new half-sister or brother that would be born. Would she call Danny darling or even sweetheart? Would she upset them by putting her hand on his arm?

They weren't going to like her no matter what she did. There was no way she could get it right. Annie and Brian wanted what they could never have because Bernadette existed. They wanted things to be the way they were.

Her name was Bernadette Dunne. That much Ria did know. The children had told her. The name was stuck there at the back of her mind. Like a weight, a very heavy object.

Ria went to the list of bells. There it was. Dunne, Number 12, top floor. Would she press it? What would she say? Suppose Bernadette let her in, which she very probably would not, what on earth would Ria say? She realised that she hadn't thought it out at all, she had come here purely on instinct.

So she paused and moved back a little and while she did a woman came along and went up to the row of bells. She pressed Number 12.

A voice answered. 'Halloo!' A thin young voice.

'Ber, it's Mummy,' the woman said.

'Oh good.' She must have pressed a buzzer because the door snapped open.

Ria shrank back.

'Are you coming in?' The woman was pleasant and a little puzzled at Ria dithering and hovering there.

'What? Oh no, no. I've changed my mind. Thank you.' Ria turned to go back to her car but first she looked hard at Danny's new mother-in-law. Small and quite smart, wearing a beige suit and a white blouse, and carrying a large brown leather handbag. She had short well-cut brown hair, and copper-coloured high-heeled shoes. She looked somewhere between forty and forty-five. Not much older than Ria and Danny. And she was Bernadette's mother.

Ria sat in the car. It had been very foolish to come here and upset herself.

Now she was too shaky to drive. She would have to sit in this car park until she felt calm enough to move. What had possessed her to come and realise that Mrs Dunne visiting her pregnant daughter was of their generation, not an older woman like her own mother or Danny's mother?

How did Danny rationalise this to himself? Or was he so besotted that he didn't even notice? She had not got very far along this road of thought when she saw the woman coming out of the big glass doors of Bantry Court. This time she was with her daughter. Ria strained forward to see. The girl had long straight hair, shiny and soft like an advertisement for shampoo. Ria felt her own hand go automatically to her frizzy curls.

She had a pale, heart-shaped face, and dark eyes. It was the kind of face you might see on the front of a CD of some folk singer. It was a soulful face. She wore a long black velvet sweater and a short pink skirt and childish black shoes with pink laces in them. Ria knew that Bernadette Dunne was twenty-two going on twenty-three and that she was a music teacher. She looked about seventeen and being marched to school by her mother who had found her playing truant. They got into a smart new Toyota Starlet and Bernadette's mother backed expertly out.

Ria found her strength and her car key, and followed them as they drove out of Bantry Court. She simply had to know where they were going, nothing else mattered. The two cars went slowly in the morning traffic through the crowded streets, and then the one in front indicated and stopped. Bernadette leapt out and waved as her mother went to find a parking place. She didn't look remotely pregnant yet, but possibly the big floppy sweater hid that. Ria noticed where she was going. A big, well-known delicatessen. She was buying the supper for her future stepchildren. She was going to make a spread for Annie and Brian Lynch tonight.

Ria ached to park her car on the footpath, leaving its hazard lights on, and run into the shop. Then she would point out the vegetarian pâté that Annie would like, the little chorizo sausage that was Brian's current favourite, and nice runny Brie with bran biscuits for Danny. Or else she could just stand there and get drawn into conversation with this girl, as people do in shops.

But it was dangerous. Possibly Bernadette had seen a picture of Ria and knew what she looked like. And anyway her mother would be back shortly to help and advise about the purchases. She would recognise Ria as the dithering woman outside Bantry Court. What kind of a mother was she anyway, encouraging her daughter in breaking up another man's family, having a baby with a married man? Some help and example she must have been to Bernadette if this was the way things turned out.

But then Ria realised that it could not have been what that woman wanted for her daughter either. Possibly she had been horrified by it all, as Ria would be horrified if her own Annie were to get involved with a middle-aged married man. Possibly the mother hadn't been told that Danny was married at the start. And had then become suspicious.

Suddenly Ria remembered the woman who had telephoned her, the voice demanding to know if she were Mrs Danny Lynch. This was the woman. Danny had concocted some cock-and-bull story at the time, but had later admitted it. Ria would have done the same if Annie were to be involved with a married man. She would have called the house to check if his wife really existed. To speak to the enemy. This woman probably loved her daughter too. She would have wished for a boyfriend who was young and single. But who could know what a daughter was going to do?

Was seeing Bernadette better than not seeing her? She sat in the car biting her lip and wondering. Possibly better. It meant that now there was no more imagining. It had cleared that area of speculation from her mind. It didn't make it any more bearable that she was so young. Or forgivable.

There was a knock on the car window and Ria jumped. For a mad moment she thought Bernadette and her mother were about to confront her. But it was the anxious face of a traffic warden. 'You were not even thinking about parking here, were you?' she asked.

'No, I was thinking about men and women and how they want different things.'

'Well, you chose an extraordinary place to sit and think about that.' The warden looked as if she were itching to take out her notebook and issue a ticket.

'You're right,' Ria agreed. 'But these thoughts come on you suddenly. However I'm out of here now.'

'Very wise.' The traffic warden put her notebook away regretfully.

At noon Ria telephoned Marilyn.

'Nothing wrong, is there?' Marilyn's voice sounded anxious.

'No, I just wanted to check that it's all still on track at your end, that's all. I'm sorry, is it too early? I thought you might be up.'

'No, no. That's fine, I've just had a swim, this is a good time for me. So you're making all your plans?'

'Yes, yes I am indeed.' Ria's voice sounded very down.

'Nothing's changed, has it?'

'No, it's just something not connected. I saw the woman my husband is leaving me for today; she's just a child. It was a bit of a shock, you see.'

'I'm so sorry.'

'Thank you. I wanted to tell someone.'

'I can understand that.'

Ria's eyes filled with tears: it was as if this woman genuinely understood. She must reassure her that she wasn't going to be an emotional drain on her. 'I'm not cracking up or anything,' Ria began. 'I don't want you to get that impression, I just wanted to reassure myself that it's all going to happen, this business of going to Westville. You know, I wanted something to hang on to.'

'Sure it's going to happen,' Marilyn said. 'Because if it doesn't then I'm going to crack up also. I've had the most awful telephone conversation with my husband, such coldness, and bitter things we said . . . and I don't want to tell anyone about it here because they'd pat me down and say it didn't matter. But it did.'

'Of course it did. How did it end?'

'He hung up.'

'And you couldn't call him back because it would only be more of the same.'

'Precisely,' Marilyn said.

There was a silence between them. Neither of them offered a consolation.

'What kind of a day are you going to have?' Ria asked.

'A busy one, I'm filling up every moment of time. It may not be healthy but it's all I can do. And you?'

'Almost exactly the same, no point in sitting down to have a rest, taking it easy as they all say. The pictures keep coming back to your mind if you start taking things easy, I find.'

'Yes, I find that's exactly what they do,' Marilyn agreed.

There was no more to say. They said goodbye easily, like old friends who have shorthand between them.

Ria made good her promise to have a busy day. She would clean out cupboards first; it was an ideal opportunity for some hard physical work. Now that a stranger was coming to live in her house all those long-promised clearances would be made. Most of Danny's things were gone already, but she would get the last lot out now. There would be no sentimental pausing to remember when times were better. It would be as if she were part of a removals business.

She began with the big airing cupboard in the bathroom. There were still some of his pyjamas, socks and old T-shirts. *She* was not going to look after them; let Bernadette find the space for them now. All were neatly folded and placed in one of the specially bought carrier bags with handles. Danny could not say that she had flung them into a garbage bag, they were as carefully arranged as if he were taking them on a vacation. She included old sports towels of his, a winter dressing gown, a shabby track suit and some very out-of-date swimming trunks. He would not thank her for these things but still he could not fault her.

Then she telephoned her mother and asked her to come for lunch.

'Have you got over this nonsensical idea of emigrating to the USA?' Nora Johnson asked.

'Two months' holidays, Mam, a rest, a change, it's exactly what I need. Do me all the good in the world.'

'Well, it's certainly cheered you up a bit,' her mother admitted unwillingly.

'Come up to me, Mam, I need your help. I'm sorting out the kitchen cupboards, it needs two.'

'You're mad, Ria, you know that, clinically mad. Imagine tidying the kitchen cupboards at a time like this.'

'What would you prefer, that I get Danny arrested for not loving me any more? That I lie on a long sofa and weep?'

'No.'

'All right, I'll make us a great energy-giving soup and we'll have it as a reward after an hour-and-a-half's work.' Ria was killing two birds with one stone. Her mother would need explanations and reassurance that this was not a mad endeavour. What better time to do it than while they were sorting out her kitchen?

She was utterly exhausted when it was over. But at least her mother was placated, reassured of the sanity of the enterprise, cordially invited to come out and visit Westville and also had helped in the clearing out of kitchen cupboards.

But still Ria would not stop, she wanted to wear herself out. She didn't want to lie wakeful in that big lonely bed tonight and think of Danny and that child asleep in Bantry Court. She wanted to fall straight into a weary sleep the moment she got there. So after her mother had left Ria called Gertie. She was another who needed a one-to-one explanation of what Ria was doing. Better by far to do it while they were working. 'Gertie, I know I sound like the Diary of a Mad Housewife but I don't suppose that if you could get away you could give me two hours this afternoon? It would be such a help. I need to polish all the silver, wrap it up and put it into the bank. Marilyn doesn't want the responsibility of having it around when she comes. And anyway I suppose I'll have to divide it with Danny later so it's no harm that it's all put away.'

'I'd love to, because I want to talk to you about something else, and it's fairly quiet here just now. I could come up now, straight away?'

'Great, and listen, Gertie, I can give you twenty quid. It's worth that to me, honestly.'

'You don't have to . . .'

'No, this is a professional agreement; you're doing me a service.'

Gertie came, pale as ever, eyes darting anxiously round her. 'There's nobody here, is there?'

'No one but me.'

'You know what I wanted to tell you. This place you're going to, I looked it up on the map. It's only about thirty miles away from where Sheila lives.'

'Sheila? Your sister? Isn't that marvellous.' Ria was delighted. 'I'll be able to see her.'

Gertie wasn't so pleased. 'You'd never tell her, would you, Ria? You'd never let anything slip?'

'About what?'

'About me and Jack. You know, about the situation?' Gertie's eyes were haunted-looking.

Ria felt such a wave of pity for her friend that she could hardly speak. 'Of course I wouldn't, Gertie, you know that.'

'It's just that you being out on your own there and a bit low and everything after all you've been through, you know the way people confide . . . ?'

'No, Gertie, I *wouldn't* confide, believe me.'

'It's hard to say this, Ria, but you see it sort of keeps me going that Sheila envies me; nobody else does. It's nice to hold on to the fact that my smart sister who went out to the United States thinks that I have a great life back here, handsome husband, terrific family, great friends and all.'

'But in many ways you *do* have all that, Gertie,' Ria said. And was rewarded by the old smile, the smile Gertie used to have when she worked in Polly's.

'I do,' she said. 'You're quite right. I do have all that, depending on how you look at it.'

Together they polished the silver, and kept off topics that would hurt either of them. When it was done Ria handed over an envelope.

'I hate taking this because I've enjoyed it so much. This is a lovely happy house, that man is so stupid. What can he get from her that he can't have here?'

'Another crack at being young, I think,' Ria said. 'That's all I can make of it.'

'You're tired, Ria. Aren't you going to have a lie-down before the children come home?'

'No, I'm not tired and anyway they're with their father this evening.'

'Is he taking them to Quentin's again, I wonder?'

'No. He's taking them to meet their new stepmother as it happens,' Ria said in a dangerously calm voice.

'She'll *never* be that, mark my words. That will all be blown over long before there's any question of marriage, divorce referendum or no divorce referendum.'

'That doesn't help any, Gertie. Really it doesn't,' Ria pleaded.

'It wasn't meant to help, it's just a fact, it's what's going to happen. Polly met her apparently, she says she gives it three months.'

Ria hated the thought of Polly talking about her, but not nearly as much as she hated the thought of Barney and Polly having met Bernadette socially. Probably many times, as a foursome. It made Ria want to do some very hard work indeed, until her brain stopped functioning. She wondered would she scrub the kitchen floor when Gertie went, or was that going over the top entirely?

As a compromise she went into the front room and sat at the circular table looking around. What would the American woman make of this old-fashioned room? Her place seemed to be so modern and open-plan. She would possibly consider this a fusty, silly room with its heavy framed pictures and the over-formal sideboard. But these pieces had been bought with love and care at auction rooms over the years. She remembered the day that each of them had been eased through the doors. They were polished regularly by Gertie, when she came to earn Jack's extra drinking money. Surely Marilyn would like them. And feel happy in this room.

Ria opened the drawers of the sideboard. It would be interesting to know what they *should* contain. Possibly this was the place for table napkins, corkscrews, salad servers. But then, since they had their meals in the kitchen, what was the point of stacking things you needed where you didn't eat? Ria wondered what the drawers actually did contain.

The answer was in fact everything that had no place there. There were children's drawings, a broken watch, pencils, an old calendar, a knitted beret that her mother had made, sticky tape, a torch without a battery, a restaurant guide, a tape of Bob Marley songs, some cheap plastic toys from Christmas crackers, an old diary of Annie's, a couple of receipts, and a picture of Ria and Hilary when they were in their teens. Ria put everything on a tray and cleaned out the drawers with a damp cloth. She would put nothing back in again; none of these things belonged there.

Idly she picked up Annie's diary; the funny slanted writing was small and crowded so that she could fit more in. Ria smiled over the lists of hit singles, the Top Ten, the names and birth dates of various singers. Then there were bits about school and the fact that Annie wasn't allowed to sit beside Kitty because they talked too much. Some of the teachers were hateful, some weren't too bad but a bit pathetic. It was exactly the kind of thing that Ria used to write herself. She wondered where her old diaries were and whether her mother had ever read them.

Then she came to Brian's birthday party that time they had a barbecue for him. The writing was very small and crabbed here, as if every word was important and it must all be included. It was very hard to understand as well as to read.

Ria felt no compunction at all about reading the private diary. She had to know what had occurred that day. Annie wrote about it in veiled terms. Whatever it was it had happened in the lane and nobody knew and it was truly the most horrifying thing in the world. She wrote that it most definitely was not her fault. All she had been doing was looking for the kitten. There was no crime in that.

I don't care how marvellous Kitty says it is, I don't care what these feelings are. I don't believe them. Her face was all screwed up as if she was cross about something. I wouldn't tell Kitty because she'd laugh, and of course I couldn't tell Mam because she wouldn't believe me or she'd make some awful remark. I nearly told Colm. He's so nice, he knew something was wrong. But I couldn't tell him. He has too many things to worry about anyway and it's not a thing you could tell anybody. There aren't words to tell it. It was something I wish I'd never seen. But I did and I can't unsee it now. I didn't know that's the way it was done, I thought you did it lying down. And her of all people. I never liked her, and I like her less now. In fact I think she's disgusting. There's ways I'd like her to know I saw, have some power over her, but that's not right either. She'd just laugh and be superior about it as she is about everything.

Ria caught her breath. What could Annie have seen? Who was it? And where? It couldn't have been Kitty since she was mentioned in other contexts. The memory of the day of Brian's birthday came back to Ria. Annie had come home after a fall outside Colm's restaurant. Could she have seen Colm Barry and that publican's wife? No, she mentioned Colm as a nice person, and it was the woman she resented, someone superior, someone scornful. Possibly it was Caroline. Could she have stumbled across that strange withdrawn sister of Colm and her big ignorant husband? Or even Caroline and someone else? Would there be any clue?

Ria read on.

I don't care how marvellous they say Love is, I'm not going to have any part of it. I wish Daddy would stop saying that one day some man will come and carry away his little Princess. It's not going to happen. Sometimes I wish I had never been born.

Ria sat down suddenly at the table that was strewn with all the clutter from the sideboard. She would have to return it all to where it came from. Annie must have stuffed the diary away hastily one time and meant to collect it later. Annie must never know that her mother had seen this diary.

Marilyn looked around her house with an objective eye. How would it appear to someone who lived in a house that was over a hundred years old? The items of furniture pictured in Ria's home looked as if they were all antiques. That Danny Lynch must have done very well at his business. This house had been built in the early 1970s. Tudor Drive was part of an area developed for the increasing number of academics and business people who wanted to enjoy a quiet and deliberately simple lifestyle. The homes all stood in their own grounds; the lawns and frontage were communally looked after. It was an affluent neighbourhood. Here and there small white wooden churches dotted around made it look like a picture postcard saying *Welcome to Connecticut.* But it would all look very new and recent to someone who came from a civilisation as old as the one that Ria was leaving.

In one of the books about Dublin that she was reading Marilyn saw that they recommended an outing to see where Saint Kevin had lived the life of a hermit on a beautiful lake south of Dublin. That was in the year six something, not sixteen something but the actual seventh century, and it was on their doorstep. Marilyn hoped that Ria and her children wouldn't think that they had seen everything that Westville could offer in the first half-hour and would then wonder how to spend the rest of the time.

Marilyn was tired from her constant clearing out of closets and leaving things ready for the new family. There would be plenty of room for them all. Ria would sleep in the main bedroom, and there were three other bedrooms. The people who designed this house must have had a more sociable and hospitable family than the Vines in mind.

The guest rooms had hardly ever been used. They had been so content on their own that they rarely invited visitors. Family came at Thanksgiving, and they put up people for the alumni picnic but that was all. Now two Irish children would sleep in these rooms and play in the garden. The boy was ten. Marilyn hoped he wouldn't throw a football or anything on to her flower beds, but it wasn't something you could actually make rules about. It would be suggesting to Ria that she thought the boy would be out of control. Better to assume perfect behaviour rather than try and legislate for it.

Marilyn paused with her hand on the door of one room. Should she lock it? Yes, of course she should. She didn't want strangers in here amongst these things. They wouldn't want to see it either. They would respect her for keeping her private memories behind a locked door. They would not feel excluded. But then wasn't it *odd* somehow to lock a room in the house which was meant to be these people's home?

Marilyn wished there were someone she could ask, someone whose advice she could seek out and take. But who could she ask? Not Greg, he was still very cold and hurt. Mystified by her decision to go to Ireland, irritated by Ria coming to Tudor Drive, and unable to talk about any of it.

Not Carlotta next door who had been forever anxious to come in and be part of their lives. Marilyn had spent a long time carefully and courteously building up a relationship based on distance and respect rather than neighbourly visits. She could not ruin it now by asking advice on a matter so intimate and personal that it would change everything between them.

Not Heidi at the office. Whatever she did she must not encourage Heidi who was always asking Marilyn to join this or that, Beginners' Bridge, Feng Shui groups, embroidery circles. Heidi and Henry were so kind they would have come around to Tudor Drive every single evening and picked her up to take her somewhere if she had allowed them to. But they had never really known what it was like to feel so restless. They had both been married before and now found contentment in a mature second marriage. They were always entertaining in their home and attending the college functions. They couldn't understand someone who wanted to be alone. Marilyn thought she might lock the room but leave the key somewhere for Ria so that it didn't look so like an action of exclusion. She wouldn't decide now, she'd see how she felt the morning she left.

And the time raced by. Summer came to Tara Road and Tudor Drive. Ria marshalled her troops well in advance and encouraged them to welcome Marilyn and invite her into their homes. That's what Americans liked, visiting someone's home.

'Even mine?' Hilary was unsure.

'Particularly yours. I want her to meet my sister and get to know her.'

'Isn't she getting enough? Do you know what someone would pay for the use of that fine house for two months? Martin and I were saying that if you let it in Horse Show week alone you'd get a small fortune.'

'Sure, Hilary. I wish you'd come out to see me there, we could meet Sheila Maine and have great times.'

'Millionaires can have great times certainly,' Hilary said.

Ria ignored her. 'You will keep an eye out for Marilyn, won't you?'

'Ah, don't you know I will.'

And all the others had promised too. Her mother was going to take Marilyn to visit St Rita's; she might enjoy meeting elderly Irish people with lots of memories. Frances Sullivan would ask her to tea and possibly to come to the theatre one night. Rosemary was having a summer party, she would include Marilyn.

Polly Callaghan called unexpectedly. 'I hear there's an American woman coming to stay here; if she wants any chauffeuring around at weekends tell her to get in touch.'

'How did you know she was coming?' Ria asked.

'Danny told me.'

'Danny doesn't approve.'

Polly shrugged. 'He can't have it every way.'

'He mainly has, I think.'

'Bernadette's not going to stay the distance, Ria,' Polly said.

Ria's heart leapt. This was what she so desperately wanted to hear. Someone who knew them all and could make a judgement on who would win in the end. Someone like Polly who would be in her corner and tell her what was going on in the enemy camp. Ria was about to ask her what they were like together. Was it true that Bernadette didn't talk at all but sat with her hair falling over her face? She yearned to know that Danny looked sad and lost and like a man who had made a wrong turning.

But she pulled herself together sharply. Polly was Barney McCarthy's woman, she was in their camp when all was said and done. Ria must not give in to the need she felt to confide. 'Who knows whether it will last or not? Anyway, it's not important. He wants her, we're not enough for him, so be it.'

'All men want more than they can have. Who knows that better than I do?'

'Well you went the distance, Polly. You and Barney lasted, didn't you?' It was the first time Ria had ever mentioned the relationship and she felt a little nervous at having done so.

'Yes, true, but only unofficially. I mean, I'm still the woman in the background; that's all I'll ever be. Mona is the wife, the person of status.'

'I don't think so actually, I think Mona is a fool,' Ria said. 'If he loved you then she should have let him go to you.'

Polly pealed with laughter. 'Come on, you know better than that, he didn't *want* to leave her, he wanted us both. Just like Danny possibly wanted you both, you and the girl as well.'

Ria played that conversation over in her mind many times. She didn't think that Polly was correct. Danny had been anxious to leave, to start again. And of course times were so different now to what they were when Barney McCarthy and Polly Callaghan had fallen in love.

She was surprised to get a telephone call from Mona wishing her luck in the States and offering her a loan of suitcases. 'You have great courage, Ria. I admire you more than I can say.'

'No, you don't, Mona, you think I'm running away, making a feeble gesture – that's what most of Danny's friends think.'

'I hope I'm your friend too. I didn't know one thing about this other woman, you know, I wasn't part of any cover-up.'

'No, I'm sure that's true, Mona.' Ria felt guilty then. For years she herself had been part of a cover-up.

'And Ria, I think you are quite right to take a strong stand, I wish I had done that years ago, I really do.'

Ria could hardly believe this conversation was taking place. All the taboos with Polly and Mona suddenly broken after all the years. 'You did what was right then,' she said.

'I only did what made less waves, it wasn't necessarily what was right,'

Mona said. 'But great good luck to you out there and if I can take your American friend anywhere just ask her to call me.'

Yes, they were all going to rally round when Marilyn arrived. Gertie was going to come and clean for her. Colm had said he would invite her to the restaurant, introduce her to a few people.

'Colm, can I ask you a strange question?'

'Anything.'

'It's ages ago now, but Annie had a fall outside your restaurant, it was on the day of Brian's birthday and you cleaned up her knee for her.'

'Yes, I remember.'

'And you made her a nice drink called a St Clement's, and that's why she called the cat Clement.'

'Yes?' He looked wary.

'It's just that . . . well, do you think Annie was upset by anything else that day? Not just the fall. Like some incident or something?'

'Why do you ask all this, Ria?'

'It's hard to say. Something came to my notice as they say, and I was just wondering if you could throw any light on it.'

'Well, couldn't you ask her yourself?'

'No.' There was a silence. 'It came to my notice reading her diary,' Ria admitted.

'Ah.'

'You're shocked,' she said.

'Not really, a little maybe.'

'Every mother does, believe me.'

'I'm sure you're right. But what did you learn?'

'That she saw something that upset her, that's all.'

'She didn't tell me. And I hope you don't think that I upset her?' He looked stern now.

'God no. I've made a desperate mess of this. No, no of course I don't think that. She said in her diary that you were so kind and helpful and she was going to tell you about it but couldn't. I just wondered did she see anything here?'

'Here?'

'She fell outside your restaurant, didn't she?'

Colm remembered that Annie had fallen in the back lane. But that was her secret which he had kept. One she obviously had not shared with anyone except what she thought was her private diary.

'No,' Colm said thoughtfully. 'There was nothing upsetting she could have seen here. Nothing at all.'

Ria pulled herself together. 'I feel very cheap admitting all this but you'll have to forgive me. I'm saying goodbye to the children for a month tonight. It's a bit emotional.'

'They seem to be coping very well, you are too.' He admired her.

'Oh, who knows how people cope?' Ria said. 'When my father died years and years ago I used to keep searching the house in case he had left us some treasure and then my mother would stop going on about him and how badly he had provided for us. But to the outside world people thought I had got over it fine.'

'I know.' Colm was sympathetic. 'Caroline and I had a very drunken father, and I used to wish that there was some kind of magic potion that we could give him and that he would stop drinking and be a real dad. But there wasn't.' His face was empty as he spoke.

Ria had never known this about his background. 'We *do* let our children down, we read their diaries, we lose their fathers . . . we're hopeless! I think I'll be able to make their world all right just by having a barbecue in the garden for them tonight.' She gave a little laugh.

'No, it will be fine. I'll leave over some vegetables for Annie, she's still into that, isn't she?'

'She is, Colm. Thank you, you've been a great friend through all this.'

'I'll miss you.'

'Maybe Marilyn will be a dish and you and she will be a number when I get back.'

'I'll let you know,' he promised.

And Ria went home to face the evening when she would say goodbye to her children.

They had told her little or nothing about their meeting with Bernadette. Ria had been longing to know every detail but wouldn't ask. She must not make them feel that they had to report back from one camp to another. She learned only practical things like that the holiday on the Shannon cruiser was back on course, that the new house had been hurried on – Barney McCarthy's men were there night and day finishing the renovations and it was now finally ready. Smelling of paint but ready; they would sleep there tomorrow night.

Ria learned that there would be two beds in Annie's room and there was a bunk bed being installed for Brian in a sort of outhouse that was once going to have appliances, whatever they were. Washing machines, dryers, Ria had explained. Brian was disappointed; he thought they might be scientific things.

And they had met Bernadette's mother who was all right really and would drive them to a swimming pool for a course of six lessons. It was so that they could get themselves ready for the one in America. Ria felt she knew everything and yet nothing about the life that her children would live without her. It was an uncanny feeling, as if she had died and was hovering overhead like a ghost, again anxious to intervene but unable to speak because she didn't have a body.

They had supper in the garden, kebabs, with sausages for Brian and lots of little vegetables that Colm had left in a basket for Annie. Clement seemed to know they were going; he came and looked at them all reproachfully.

'I hope she'll play with him you know, entertain him a bit,' Annie said. 'Clement is not a cat who should be left to brood too much; it doesn't suit him.'

'Well, you can come and visit Marilyn and tell her about his personality, can't you?' Ria suggested.

'This isn't our house any more, not after tomorrow morning when you go,' Annie said.

'No, that's true, but on the other hand it will be lived in by someone whose own house *you* are going to visit and it would be nice to introduce yourselves to her.'

'Do we have to?' Brian saw tedious conversations with adults ahead.

'No of course not, it might be nice, that's all.'

'Anyway, Colm will keep an eye on Clement, Colm loves him as much as I do,' Annie said, cheering up.

There was no point whatsoever in hoping for any confidences from Annie. And she must never in a million years confide what she had read. Any possible trust that might grow between them would have been destroyed if that were ever known.

They talked on easily in the warm night about plans.

Rosemary had offered to drive the children to Danny's new house tomorrow morning so that Ria would have time to leave the house unfussed. Most of their things were there already. Ria had taped to the inside of their suitcases lists of clothes that they were to pack for the boat-trip. They were to check these carefully before they left.

'She said you were very organised,' Brian said.

'Bernadette said that?' Ria tried not to sound too interested.

'When she saw the suitcases, and Dad said you were the Queen of the Lists.' Brian looked at her eagerly hoping she would be pleased. But Annie, who was sharper, knew that her mother would not like to hear of this discussion.

'And so I am, your dad's right,' Ria said with a brightness she certainly didn't feel. She hated the thought of Danny mocking her list-making activities with this child Bernadette.

'Dad's coming round here later to say goodbye, isn't he?' Brian's face was still hoping for some reassurance that things were normal.

'That's right, when you've gone to bed, there are a few last-minute things we have to discuss.'

'You won't have awful fights or anything?' Annie checked.

'No, we don't do that any more, you know that.'

'Not in front of us you don't, but you obviously drive each other mad,' Annie pronounced.

'I don't think that's so at all, but then we all look at people's lives differently. I often think that your gran is crazy to spend so much time with those old people in St Rita's instead of with people of her own age but she's as happy as a songbird there.'

'Well, that's because they depend on her there, they need her. And she's only a young thing up in St Rita's, not an old bag as she is with other people,' said Annie as if it were dead simple to understand.

Ria told them she would telephone every Saturday and they could ring any time because there was an answering machine. But not to waste Dad and Bernadette's money on long calls.

'I don't think she has much money,' Brian said. 'I think it's mainly Dad's.'

'Brian, you have the brain of a flea,' Annie said.

Danny arrived at ten o'clock. With a shock Ria realised how physically attractive he still was to her and would always be. Nothing had changed very much since those first days when she had met him at the estate agency and the heady discovery that he had eyes for her rather than for Rosemary. The line of his face had something about it that made you want to stroke him. She had to control herself before she stretched out a hand to touch him. She must behave calmly, he must not know how much power he had to move her.

'We'll go out to the garden in a minute, it's so peaceful. But first what would you like? Tea? A drink?'

'Any lager?'

'Sorry, no. Is that a new taste?'

'I'll have tea,' he said.

'Do we drive each other mad?' Ria asked companionably as she put on the kettle.

'No, I don't think so. Why do you ask?'

'The kids think we do.'

'What do they know?' he grinned.

'They say the new house is very nice,' she said.

'Good, good.'

'Can I ask you to keep a sharp eye on that Kitty? All right, so we know I never liked her, but she is a little madam and she really could lead Annie astray.'

'Sure, anything else?'

'Brian is by nature filthy, I mean truly filthy. You wouldn't believe it, it could be very unpleasant in close quarters like a boat. You might just *insist* on clean clothes every day, otherwise he'll wear the same things for a month.'

Danny smiled. 'I'll note that.'

'And is there anything for me to look out for when they come to Westville? Is there anything you don't want them to do?'

He looked surprised to be asked. And pleased. 'I don't know. The traffic I imagine, to warn them that it will be coming from a different side when they cross the road.'

'That's very sensible, I will warn them all the time.'

'And maybe they could do some educational things there, you know, museums or art galleries. Things that would help them at school.'

'Sure, Danny.'

They brought their mugs of tea out to the garden and sat on the stone bench. There was a silence.

'About money,' he said.

'Well *I* bought *my* air ticket, you've bought theirs. The rest is just as if we were here, isn't it? I mean the same household expenses except I'll be paying them there.'

'Yes.' His voice seemed a bit flat.

'That's all right, isn't it?'

'Yes, of course.'

'And the electricity, gas and phone are all paid by banker's order here . . .'

'Yes,' he said again.

'So that's money sorted out, is it?' Ria asked.

'I suppose so.'

'And I hope you all have a lovely time on the Shannon. Are you going south or north when you get on the boat?'

'South to Lough Derg. Lots of lovely little places to moor, it would be fabulous if we got the weather.'

They were talking like two strangers.

'I'm sure you will, the long-range forecast is good,' Ria said cheerfully. Another silence.

'And I hope this place works out very well for you too,' he said.

'I'm sure it will, Danny, thank you for accepting it all. I appreciate that.'

'No, no it's only fair,' he said.

'I've left your telephone number for Marilyn.'

'Good, good.'

'And perhaps you might bring the children round here to meet her one day?'

'What? Oh yes, certainly.'

'Probably best to ring in advance.'

'Indeed.'

There was nothing left to say. They walked up the stairs and stood awkwardly in the hall which had been full of crates and boxes and bicycles on the day they had vowed to make it a great home for ever and ever.

Now the polished floor with its two good rugs glowed warmly in the evening light. The door to the front room was open. There on their table was a bowl of roses that Colm had picked to welcome the American guest. They reflected in the wood, the clock on the mantelpiece chimed and the wind moved the heavy velvet curtains.

Danny went in and looked around him. Surely he was full of regret not just for these pieces but for the time and energy and love that had gone into gathering them. He seemed to be swallowing as he looked around. He was very still. None of his usual quick movement and almost quivering approach to the world. He was like a photograph of himself.

Ria knew she would never forget him standing here like this, his hand on the back of one of the chairs. He looked as if he had just thought of the one final thing that this room needed. Maybe a grandfather clock? Possibly another mirror to reflect the window. His face had that kind of look. He did *not* look like a man about to go away from all that he had built up here to stay with a pregnant girl called Bernadette. He looked like someone about to put down his car keys and say he was home and that it had all been a ridiculous mistake. It would be too late now of course to stop Marilyn but they would find her another place to stay and everything would be as it was. And they wouldn't wake the children now to tell them, let them find out tomorrow. That was the kind of look he had and the aura that surrounded him.

Ria said nothing; she stood holding her breath as if waiting for him to begin to rebuild the dream. It was very important not to say the wrong thing now. She had been brilliant so far this evening, calm and undramatic. She knew he had valued it. His smile was warm, not strained. He had laughed aloud when she told him how smelly and dirty his son was, his arm had brushed against hers on the stairs and he had not flinched away as he had done during all their prickly conversations.

He stood almost transfixed in this room, Ria didn't know for how long; it felt like a long time. The room was working a magic of its own. He would speak, he would say it was madness, all of this total madness, he was so sorry that he had hurt so many people. And she would forgive him, gently and soothingly, and he would know that he had come back home where he belonged.

Why was he taking so long to find the words? Should she help him, give him a pointer in the right direction? And then he looked at her directly and she saw he was biting his lip, he really was struggling to say what was almost too huge to be said. How could she let him know how great would be her forgiveness and understanding, how much she would do to have him home with her again?

Words had been her undoing in the past apparently; he had thought she was babbling and prattling. Horrible, horrible phrases when she thought she had been talking, confiding. She knew that whatever the temptation she must say nothing. Their whole future depended on this.

She moved very slightly towards him, just one step, and it seemed to have been enough. He came and put his arms around her, his head on her shoulder. He wasn't actually crying but he was trembling and shaking so heavily that she could feel it all through his body.

'Ria, Ria, what a mess, what a waste and a mess,' he said.

'It doesn't have to be.' She was very gentle into his ear.

'Oh God I wish it had all been different. I wish that so much.' He wasn't looking at her, still talking to her hair.

'It can be. It can all be what we make it,' she said.

Slowly, Ria, slowly, she warned herself. Don't gabble; don't come out with a long list of promises and resolutions and entreaties. Let him do the asking and say yes. Stroke his forehead and say that it will all be all right in the end; that's what he wants to hear. He moved his face from her neck and he was about to kiss her.

She must respond as the old passionate Ria would have. She raised her arms from his shaking shoulders and almost clenched him around the neck. Her lips sought his, searching and demanding. It was so good to hold him again. She felt herself carried away in what could only be called a flood of passion, and didn't realise for an instant that he was tugging at her hands behind his neck.

'Ria, what are you doing? Ria, stop!' He seemed shocked and appalled.

She pulled away, mystified. He had reached for her; he had laid his head on her shoulder and said it was a waste, a mess. He had said he wanted to undo it, hadn't he? Why was he looking at her like this?

'It will be all right,' she said, flustered now but sure that her role must still be one of making smooth his homecoming. 'I promise you, Danny, it will be all right, it will all sort itself out. This is where you belong.'

'*Ria!*' He was horrified now.

'This is your room, you created this. It's yours, like we are your family, you know that.'

'I beg you, Ria . . .'

'And I beg *you* . . . come back. We won't talk about it now, just stay, it will all be as it was. I'll understand you have responsibilities to Bernadette and even affection . . .'

'Stop this . . .'

'She'll get over it, Danny. She's a child, she has her whole life ahead of her, with someone of her own age. She'll look back on it as something foolish, wonderful but foolish . . . and we'll just accept it into our lives the way people do.'

'This is not possible . . . that you should . . . I don't know, suddenly change like this.' He did look bewildered.

But this was madness. *He* was the one who had reached out for her. 'You held me. You told me it was all a mess and a mistake and a waste and you were sorry you did it.'

'I didn't, Ria. I said I was sorry, but I didn't say the other things.'

'You said you wished it hadn't turned out like this, I'm saying come back. I won't ask you where you are if you stay out late, I swear I won't. Please, Danny. Please.' The tears were pouring down her face now and he was standing there horrified. 'Danny, I love you so much I'd forgive anything you did, you *know* that. I'd do anything on earth that it takes to have you back.' She was gulping now and she stretched her arms out to him.

He took her hands in both of his. 'Look, love, I'm going now. This minute. You don't mean any of this, not a word of it. You meant all the things we talked about for half an hour in the garden. You meant about wishing us all a good holiday on the Shannon and I meant about hoping it goes well for you in America.' He looked at her hopefully, as if praying that his nice practical soothing words would stop her tears and prevent the danger of her clutching him again.

'I'll always be here waiting for you to come back, just remember that.'

'No you won't, you'll be in America having a great time.' He tried to jolly her along. 'A strange woman will be here trying to make head or tail of our funny ways.'

'I'll be here, this room will always be here for you.'

'No, Ria, that's not the way things are, and I'm going now but I want you to know how . . .'

'How what?' she asked.

'How generous it would have been of you to make that offer, if there had been any question of it. It would have been a very unselfish thing to do.'

She looked at him in amazement. He didn't see that there was no unselfishness or generosity involved. It was what she ached for. He would never realise that, and now she had made a total fool of herself on top of everything else.

The weeks of planning and driving herself and discipline had been thrown away. Why had they come into this room anyway? If she had not seen that look on his face she might not have seen a possible lifeline. But she had seen it; she had not imagined it. That's what she would hug to herself always.

'Yes, it's late, of course you must go,' she said. The tears had stopped. She was not the calm Ria who had walked up the stairs from the kitchen with him, her face was too tear-stained for that. But she was in control again, and she could sense his relief.

'Safe journey,' he said to her on the steps.

'Oh yes, thank you, I'm sure it will be fine.'

'And we did make a lovely house, Ria, we really did.' He looked past her back into the hall.

'Yes, yes indeed, and two marvellous children,' she said.

On the steps of the house they had spent so long creating, Danny and Ria kissed each other cautiously on the cheek. Then Danny got into his car and drove away and Ria went into her home in Tara Road and sat for a long time at her round table, staring sightless in front of her.

6

'They didn't fight,' Annie said to Brian as she helped him close his suitcase.

'How do you know?'

'I listened for a bit at the bathroom window, they talked about holidays.'

'Oh good,' Brian said.

'She said to Dad that you were filthy, though.'

Brian looked surprised but unconvinced. 'No she didn't, she wouldn't say that about me. What would make her say that?' His face looked round with worry.

Annie took pity on him. 'No, I made it up,' she lied.

'I knew.' Brian's faith in his mother was restored.

'I wish she weren't going,' Annie said.

'So do I.'

It was such a rare thing for the brother and sister to be joined in any emotion that it startled them. They looked at each other uncertainly. These were very troubled times.

Rosemary arrived earlier than expected. Ria handed her a cup of coffee.

'You look fine,' Rosemary said approvingly.

'Sure.'

'I came early to leave you less time for tearful farewells. Where are they anyway?'

'Finishing their packing.' Ria sounded very muted.

'They'll be okay.'

'I know.'

Rosemary looked at her friend sharply. 'Was it all right last night with Danny and everything?'

'What? Oh yes, very civilised.' Never in a million years would anyone know how it had been last night with Danny. Ria would not allow it to be spoken of even in her own heart.

'Well, then that's good.' There was a silence. 'Ria?'

'Yes?'

'You know they'll never see Bernadette as anything ... as anything except what she is.'

'I know, of course.'

'They won't bond with her or anything like that. Can you *imagine* what she feels like having to replace you for a month? What a task that would be

721

for anyone let alone a dumb kid like that.' There was no reply so Rosemary just carried on. 'You know, I did think this whole jaunt to America was mad, but now I think it's the cleverest thing you could have done. You're really much sharper than anyone gives you credit for. Hey, here come the kids. What do you want, lingering or brisk?'

'Brisk, and you're wonderful,' Ria said gratefully.

In minutes Ria was waving goodbye as Rosemary drove the children to stay in a strange house for the month of July. Who would ever have believed that any of this could happen? And what was even more incredible was that Rosemary actually thought that Ria had been somehow clever to engineer this situation.

Bernadette's mother was sitting at the kitchen table in the new house. 'Well, she's a fine hard-hearted-Hannah, isn't she, sweeping off to the United States and leaving you to look after her children.'

'I know, Mum, but in a way it's for the best.'

'How is it for the best?' Finola Dunne couldn't see any silver lining.

'Well, I suppose she won't be there in Tara Road any more as a kind of centre for him, you know.'

'She wasn't much of a centre for him when she was there, judging from the amount of time he spent with you.' Bernadette's mother always managed to sound disapproving of her daughter's affair with a married man while equally proud that the matter had been so satisfactorily sorted out.

'It was his home for sixteen years, it still has a great draw for him, the place.'

'This place will too in time, child. Wait till it gets a bit more settled.' Finola Dunne looked around the luxury fitted kitchen which Barney McCarthy's men had installed at double speed. This was an expensive house in one of the more fashionable southern suburbs of Dublin. It must have cost a packet. It was a sheltered avenue, a good place to bring up a new baby, and a lot of other young couples around.

Finola Dunne knew that Danny Lynch was a hotshot estate agent. But she felt that the sooner he sold the Tara Road house, realised his money and got some small, more suitable place for his first wife, the better. The boy worked hard, she gave him that, and he obviously adored Bernadette, but he would wear himself out unless he sorted out his finances. He had left this morning for a meeting at 6.00 a.m. to avoid the traffic.

'Any mention of his selling Tara Road?' she asked.

'No, and it's not something I ask about. I think he was more attached to that house than to any woman. It gives me the shivers,' Bernadette said.

'No time for that, they'll be here any minute and a long summer of entertaining them begins.'

'Only thirty days, and they're not too bad,' said Bernadette with a grin.

Ria's children were very quiet in Rosemary's car.

'What kind of things will you do all day, do you imagine?' Rosemary asked brightly.

'No idea,' Annie shrugged.

'They don't have cable television,' Brian said.

'Maybe they'll take you out to places?' Rosemary was optimistic.

'She's very quiet, she doesn't go to places,' Brian said.

'Is she nice, I mean interesting to talk to?'

'Not very,' Brian said.

'She's okay, just you know nothing much to say,' Annie said.

'I prefer her mother actually,' Brian said. 'You'd like her, Rosemary, she's full of chat and more your age.'

'I'm sure I would,' said Rosemary Ryan who could cope with any boardroom committee meeting or television discussion, but was finding this conversation very hard going indeed.

At Dublin airport Ria looked around. So many people heading off in so many directions. She wondered whether any of them could be travelling in such a confused state of mind as she was. In the line next to her she saw a good-looking man with the collar of his raincoat turned up. He had fair hair that fell into his eyes. She looked at him wildly. For an instant she thought it was Danny, racing out to stop her leaving, a last-minute plea that she change her mind. She remembered with the feeling of a shower of cold water that this was the last thing on earth he would do. She could still feel him tugging at her hands which she had clasped around his neck. Her face burned at the shame of it.

She walked through the duty-free shop wondering what she should buy. It seemed such a pity to waste the value that was there on all those shelves. But she didn't smoke, she drank little, she didn't need anything electronic, Marilyn's house would be full of more equipment than she would ever learn to use. She stopped by the perfumes.

'I want something very new, something I've never smelled before, which will have no memories,' she said.

The assistant seemed used to such requests. Together they examined the new scents, and settled on one that was light and flowery. It cost £40.

'It seems rather a lot,' Ria said doubtfully.

'Well it is, but then it depends. Do you *have* that kind of money to spend on a good perfume?' The girl clearly wanted to move on.

'I don't know whether I do or not,' Ria spoke with wonder. 'Isn't that odd? I actually don't know what my financial situation will be. I never thought about it until this minute. I might be the kind of person who could afford this and more, or I might never be able to buy anything remotely like it in my whole life.'

'I should take it then,' said the sales assistant, quickly trying to head off too much philosophy.

'You're right, I will,' said Ria.

She fell asleep on the plane and dreamed that Marilyn had not left Tudor Drive after all but was sitting waiting for her in the garden. Marilyn had brown hair and copper shoes and was wearing a beige suit just like Bernadette's mother had worn. She spoke with a cackle when Ria arrived.

'I'm not Marilyn, you stupid woman, I'm Danny's new mother-in-law. I've got you out here so that they can all move into Tara Road. It was all a trick, a trick, a trick.' Ria woke sweating. Her heart was racing. It was an extraordinary sensation to be on a plane thousands of feet up in the air, people around her eating lunch.

The air hostess was concerned. 'Are you all right? You're as white as anything.'

'Yes ... I had a bad dream, that's all.' Ria smiled her gratitude for the concern.

'Have you anyone meeting you at Kennedy?'

'No, but I know the bus to take. I'll be fine.'

'A holiday, is it?'

'Yes, I think it is, I'm sure that's what you'd call it, what I call it. It will be certainly a holiday.' Ria saw the nervous smile of the courteous girl in her stewardess uniform. Really, she must stop this habit of analysing what she was doing. It was just that simple questions caught her unawares.

She lay back and closed her eyes. How ridiculous of her subconscious to have made Marilyn look like Bernadette's mother when of course she looked totally different. Ria opened her eyes suddenly in shock. She had no idea whatsoever what Marilyn looked like. She knew the measurements of her swimming pool, the voltage of her electricity, the weight of laundry that the dryer could handle, the times of church services in Westville and the days of the week the garbage was collected. She had the names and phone numbers of two women called Carlotta and Heidi. She had photographs of the rock garden, the main bedroom, the swimming pool and carport.

She knew that Marilyn would have her fortieth birthday while she was in Ireland but she did not know whether she was fair or dark, tall or small, thin or fat. Extraordinary to think that an entirely unknown woman had set out for Tara Road last night and nobody knew what she looked like.

The flights to Dublin were at night and there was a coach service to Kennedy Airport from a nearby town. Marilyn accepted Heidi's offer to drive her there. She closed the door and left the keys and an envelope of instructions with Carlotta. Ria would call to collect them when she arrived in the early evening. She had left her house in perfect order. Clean, freshly laundered linen and towels everywhere, food in the icebox, flowers on the table and the breakfast bar.

She decided about locking the room only when she heard Heidi's car pull up outside the house. She left the door closed but not locked. Ria would understand; she would treat it appropriately. She would probably dust it and open the windows during the two months. There were some things you didn't need to say or to write down.

Heidi chattered and asked questions all the way to the coach terminal. Did Ria play bridge by any chance? Would Marilyn take any courses in Trinity College while she was in Dublin? What was the weather going to be like? And casually, very casually, Would Greg be joining her there at all? Or might he be coming back to Westville during the vacation? To none of these questions did Marilyn give any satisfactory reply. But she did hug her friend Heidi just before she got on the coach.

'You're very generous, and I do hope to be generous myself one day, when I come out of this forest, this awful forest.'

Heidi looked after the bus as it pulled out of the station. Marilyn sat there, bolt upright and reading a letter. Her eyes were very bright. It was the nearest that Marilyn had come to being human for a long time.

Marilyn read the letter she had written to Greg again and again.

She had put as much of her soul into it as she could and she realised that she was still holding back a lot. It was as if there was some kind of brake refusing her permission to explain too much. Or maybe there was no more to explain. It was quite possible that she had lost the capacity to love and care any more and that this is how she was going to be for the rest of her life.

She took out the little wallet of pictures that Ria had sent. Every one of them had people in them. And little notes on the back. Annie doing her homework in our front room. Brian serving a pizza in the kitchen. My mother and sister Hilary. Me with my friend Gertie who also helps with the cleaning, hanging out the washing. Our friend Rosemary who lives up the road. Colm Barry who runs a kitchen garden at the back of our house and a restaurant at the corner of Tara Road. The best picture of the house itself also showed a family of four squinting into the sun. On the back Ria had written 'In Happier Times'.

Marilyn studied Danny Lynch carefully. He was handsome certainly. And very unchanged from the boyish enthusiastic salesman she had met all those years ago. Then she looked at Ria, small, dark and always smiling. Her whole face was lit up with goodwill in every single snapshot. Very different in a lot of ways to the voice she talked to on the phone. There Ria sounded tense and anxious. Anxious to please, that her house should be good enough, anxious to reassure that her children were going to be no trouble when they came to Westville.

And most of all anxious that Marilyn would be swept immediately into this huge group of family friends and acquaintances. Never had anything been a more unlikely starter. Marilyn Vine who kept herself so withdrawn from colleagues, family, friends and neighbours that they all called her a recluse. Marilyn Vine, unable to talk to her own husband and tell him why she was making this strange journey. She would be polite to these people, of course, but she didn't want anything at all to do with their lives.

'Can I ask Kitty to supper please, Bernadette?' Annie asked.

Bernadette raised her eyes from the book she was reading. 'No, sorry, your father said no.'

'She always comes at home. When Dad was at home he liked her.'

'Well he must have gone off her.' Bernadette was not very concerned.

'Will Mam be in America yet?' asked Brian.

'Don't go on about Mam,' Annie corrected him with a hiss.

'It's okay,' Bernadette shrugged. She was back in her book. She really didn't seem to mind.

'Well, will she?' Brian wanted his question answered.

Bernadette looked up again perfectly pleasantly but they felt she would have preferred there to be silence in the house. 'Let me see, it takes about five or six hours. Yes, I'd say she'd be there now, on a bus to wherever the place she's going is.'

'Westville,' Annie said.

'Yes, that's right.' Bernadette was reading again.

There didn't seem to be any more to say. Dad wouldn't be home until eight o'clock. It was a long sort of an evening. Out of sheer desperation Annie took out *Animal Farm*, one of the books that her mother had given her to pack. I don't think I'd like it, Annie had said at the time, but surprisingly she did, very much. And Brian read his book of soccer heroes.

So when Danny came home tired and apprehensive he found them all sitting in armchairs reading peacefully. Annie looked up and saw the pleasure in her father's face. This was so different to Tara Road. But he must miss it all there, surely he did, even if he didn't love Mam any more, and preferred Bernadette and all that. There was no bustle of dinner being prepared here, Bernadette would take out two frozen dishes shortly and put them in the microwave. There was no endless stream of people passing through. No Gertie coming and going. No Rosemary popping in and out, no Kitty, no awful Myles and Dekko, no Gran with Pliers or Colm with his basket of vegetables. Surely Dad must miss all that very much.

But as Annie looked at her father she knew with a great certainty that he preferred things like this. He laid his keys in a long oval dish. 'I'm home,' he said and everyone sprang into action to welcome him. When he said he was home in Tara Road there was so much going on that nobody seemed to notice.

All the instructions had worked like a dream. The bus was where Marilyn had said it would be, the fare was exactly as she had described. The weather was warm and sunny, much hotter than back in Dublin. The noise, and the variety of people everywhere was extraordinary. Yet despite it all Ria felt well able to cope, she had expert guidelines and the whole system seemed to be working perfectly.

The first coach driver told her when they got to the big town where to find the next and smaller bus to Westville. Ria took a deep breath when she saw the sign for Westville coming up. This was going to be her home now. She almost wanted to look at it unobserved for a while, so she took her two suitcases into an ice-cream parlour and sat down to get her bearings. The menu was exotic – Marilyn would find the range of ice-cream sodas, floats and specials so much less extensive in Dublin. Still, she wasn't going there for ice cream. Ria watched the people come and go. A lot of them knew each other. The woman behind the counter seemed a real personality, wisecracking with the customers just like they did in the television comedies.

She was in America now, she would not start comparing and contrasting everything with the way it was at home. She would even try to think in dollars rather than converting it back to pounds all the time. From her window seat in the Happy Soda House, Ria could see Carlotta's Beauty Salon. It looked elegant, and a discreet sort of place where a woman might go in and, behind those heavy cream-coloured curtains and all that gold lettering, get good advice about keeping old age at bay and keeping your man at home. She wondered what Carlotta herself looked like; there had been no pictures, no pictures of any person at all.

Steeling herself Ria crossed the road, her dark green travelling outfit of jumper and skirt and her two suitcases looking out of place here. Everyone else seemed to wear Bermuda shorts or crisp cotton dresses. They all looked as if they had been to other beauty salons already. Ria felt travel-stained and tired. She pushed the door and went in. Carlotta was the tall, full-bosomed, almost Mexican-looking woman at the desk. She excused herself from the client she was talking to and came over at once.

'Ria, welcome to the United States, I hope you're going to love Westville. We are just delighted that you're here.' It was so warm, so genuine and so utterly unexpected that Ria felt a prickle of tears in her eyes. Carlotta was looking at her with an expert eye. 'I was keeping an eye out for those buses, they come in every twenty minutes but I guess one must have come now without my noticing it.'

'I went into the Happy Soda House,' Ria confessed. She realised it was a dull and indeed ungracious thing to say in response to all this welcome and kindness. And Ria did want to respond. This woman was so outgoing compared to Marilyn who had sometimes been a little terse on the telephone. Carlotta was making such overtures of friendship that Ria was appalled at her own inability to find the proper words. 'You'll have to forgive me, I seem to be sort of shell-shocked. I'm not used to long flights . . . and things . . .' Her voice trailed away.

'Do you know what I was going to suggest to you, Ria? Suppose you relax here, have a nice shower, a relaxing aromatherapy massage, Katie doesn't have a client at the moment, then you go and have a lie-down in a dark room and I come and wake you up in a couple of hours and we go back home? Or would you prefer if I drove you straight out to Marilyn's home? Either is fine with me.'

Ria thought that she would love to stay in the salon.

Katie was one of those women who made no small talk and asked no questions. Ria felt no need to apologise for her tired neglected skin, for the lines appearing around her eyes, for the chin that was definitely more slack than it used to be. The healing soothing oils were gently and insistently massaged into the various pressure points, temples, shoulders, scalp. It felt wonderful. Once before Ria had gone for this aromatherapy with Rosemary as a treat, and Ria had promised it to herself every month. Twelve times a year. But she never had. It was too expensive and there were always things she wanted to buy for the children or the house. Her mind started to go down that channel again about what she could afford from now on but she forced it back. Anyway, here in this cool dark place with that wonderful rhythmic massage of her shoulders and back, with that intense satisfying smell of the oils, it was easy to banish worries and to fall into a deep sleep.

'I hardly liked to wake you up.' Carlotta was handing her a glass of fruit juice. 'But otherwise your sleeping pattern will go astray.'

Ria was now her old self again. She got up from her relaxation bed in the pink cotton robe that had been provided and came out to shake Carlotta's hand. 'I can't thank you enough for this terrific welcome. It was exactly what I needed and I didn't know. You couldn't have arranged anything that I would have liked more.'

Carlotta knew genuine appreciation when she saw it. 'Get your clothes on, Ria, and I'll take you home. You're going to have a great summer here, believe me.'

Ria was about to leave when Katie handed her a piece of paper. She wondered if it was some advice about future skin care that she would study later, but she looked at it anyway. It was a bill for an amount of money that Ria would never in her whole life have spent in a beauty salon. She had thought it was a complimentary treatment. How humiliating. She must show no hint that she was surprised.

'Of course,' she said.

'Carlotta wanted you to have a fifteen per cent discount so that's all built into the check and service is included,' Katie said.

Ria handed over the money with a sickening feeling that she was a great fool. Why should she have thought that this woman was giving her a free treatment? She was living amongst people who took beauty salons as a matter of course. Possibly if she had done so years ago she might not be in the position she was in now.

Gertie had arranged to be in Tara Road when Marilyn arrived. Ria had said that there just had to be someone here to open the door. It was a high priority.

'Suppose, just suppose, Gertie, that there's any crisis or anything, you will make sure that my mother's installed here instead of you, won't you?'

'Crisis?' Gertie had asked as if such a thing had never occurred in her life.

'Well you know, anything could happen.'

'Listen, there's going to be someone to meet her.' Gertie spoke very definitely. And just as Gertie was leaving her house to head to Ria's she got the message that Jack was in hospital. There had been a fight somewhere last night and Jack had only recovered consciousness now. Gertie ran down the road to the little house where Nora Johnson lived but she wasn't at home. Possibly gone to St Rita's, her neighbour didn't know. Gertie damned Danny Lynch to the pit of hell. All her anger was directed at him. If he hadn't abandoned his wife for some pale-faced child none of this would be happening. Gertie would not be running from house to house looking for someone to open Ria's door and greet some American woman. Jimmy Sullivan said that Frances was at the thrift shop and wouldn't be able to get away.

Gertie ran to the restaurant. Please, please let Colm not have gone to a market or anything. Please, God, if you are there, and really I know you are there, let Colm Barry be at home. He's fond of the Lynches, he'd do it. And he'd be nice to the woman. Please.

Gertie never prayed to God to ask him to make Jack behave like a normal man. Some things were too big even for the Almighty to undertake. But something like Colm being in could happen. And did happen. 'Let me drive you somewhere first, Gertie. She won't be in for another half-hour.'

'No, no, I couldn't let Ria down.'

'We know she's going to come in to the city, look around for a few hours and then come here at twelve, that's the arrangement.'

'She might come early. Anyway I can go on the bus.'

'I'll drive you. Which hospital?'

As they sat in the car Gertie twisted a handkerchief in her hands, but there was no conversation. 'You're very restful, Colm, really you are. Anyone else would be asking questions.'

'What's there to ask?'

'Like why does he do it?'

'Why ask that question? I did it for so long myself, people were possibly asking that question fairly uselessly about me all over the shop.' He was very reassuring, just what she needed. She stopped tearing at the piece of cotton in her hands.

'Maybe people would ask why I stay with him?'

'Oh well, that's easy. He's very lucky, that's all.'

'How do you mean?'

'I had nobody to stay with me, no one to cushion things, so eventually I had to face it, what a lousy life I had.'

'Well, doesn't that mean being on your own might have made you strong?' Gertie's face was anguished. 'That's what my mother's always telling me. She says give him up and he'll come to his senses.'

Colm shrugged. 'It could work, who knows. But I'll tell you one thing, coming to *my* senses was no bloody fun at all because all I came to was a hollow, empty life.' He left her at the gate of the hospital and drove back to welcome Ria's American.

Marilyn told herself that Ria's instructions about what to do on arriving in Dublin had been excellent. They had agreed not to meet, since it would be a rushed, hopeless meeting, with one arriving and the other leaving. Marilyn's overnight plane would be in by seven o'clock, Ria advised that she should get a bus to the city, leave her bags and walk up to have breakfast in a Grafton Street coffee shop. This way she would pass O'Connell Bridge on the River Liffey, the entrance to Trinity College, and she would see the various bookshops and gift stores which she might like to explore later. After breakfast she should go up and walk around St Stephen's Green. A few statues and points of interest were listed and a gentle itinerary, ending up at a taxi rank where she should take a cab, pick up her luggage and head for Tara Road. One of the people already mentioned would be there to welcome her in and show her around.

It had all gone extremely well. The city began to fall back into place for Marilyn; she had not properly remembered the whole layout from the brief visit before. It had certainly changed and become much more prosperous in the intervening years. The traffic was much denser, the cars bigger, the people better dressed. Around her were foreign accents, different languages. It was not only the American tourists who came to the craft shops nowadays, the places seemed full of other Europeans.

Around eleven thirty her feet were beginning to feel tired. Ria would be boarding her plane just about now. It was time to find her new home. The taxi-driver told her a long complicated tale of woe about there being too many taxis allowed on the streets of the city and not enough work for them. He said that most people were on the take all the world over, that he was sorry that he hadn't emigrated to America like his brother who now had a toupee and a German wife. He said that Tara Road was the fastest-moving bit of property in Dublin. A regular gold mine.

'If your friends own that house, ma'am, they're sitting on half a million,' he said confidently as he drove in the gateway and drew up at the foot of the steps.

The door was opened by a dark, good-looking man in his early forties. He came down the steps, hand stretched out. 'On Ria's behalf you're very welcome to Tara Road,' he said, while Marilyn frantically searched for his name from the cast of thousands she had been presented with. Somehow she had thought it would be the sister Hilary, or one of the two women friends. 'I'm Colm Barry, neighbour and friend. I also dig the back garden but I use a back gate so I'll be no intrusion in your time here.'

Marilyn looked at him gratefully. He seemed to tell her what she needed to know and not too much. He was courteous but also he was cool in a way that she very much liked. 'Indeed, the man who runs the restaurant,' she said, placing him at last.

'The very one,' he agreed. He carried her cases up the granite steps.

Ria's photographs had not lied. The hall was glorious with its deep glowing wooden floor, and elegant hall table. The door to a front room was open, Colm pushed it slightly. 'If it were my house I would never leave this room,' he said simply. 'It runs the whole depth of the house, windows at each end. It's just lovely.' On the table was a huge bowl of roses. 'Ria asked me to leave those for you.'

Marilyn felt a gulp in her voice as she thanked him. The place was so beautiful and these rich pink and red roses on such a beautiful table were the final touch.

He carried her bag upstairs and showed her the main bedroom. 'I expect this is where you'll be, I'm sure all the details were written out for you. Ria's been getting ready for weeks. I know she's gone to huge trouble.'

Marilyn knew it too. Her eyes took in the immaculate white bedcover, brand new, must have been put on this morning, the folded towels, the shiny paintwork and the empty closet. This woman had worked at getting her house ready. Marilyn hoped guiltily that hers would match up. They went down to the kitchen and at that moment the cat flap opened and a large ginger cat came in.

'This is Clement.' Colm introduced the cat formally. 'An excellent cat, he has a little weakness sometimes of killing a perfectly innocent bird for no reason, and then he'll bring it back to you as a trophy.'

'I know, I have to say well done Clement how lovely,' Marilyn said with a smile.

'Good, just so long as you know the drill. Anyway Clement isn't very competitive, usually he just opens one eye and looks at the birds, then goes back to sleep.' Colm continued his tour of the kitchen, opening the fridge. 'Ah, she's left you some basics I see, including a soup made from vegetables grown in that very garden. Shall I take some out for you to heat up? You've had a long journey, you'll want to settle in.' And he was gone.

What a restful pleasant neighbour, Marilyn thought, exactly the person she would like to live near. There would be no problem in keeping someone like Colm Barry out of your life. He would never be like Carlotta, aching to come over the fence and get involved. And he was right, she did want to settle in. She was pleased that it had been this man rather than one of the women she had expected. He was a fellow spirit, a soul mate. He somehow understood that she wanted to be alone. She was glad he had been there to welcome her.

She wandered slowly about the house that would be hers until September. The children's rooms had been tidied, pictures of soccer players on Brian's wall, pop stars on Annie's. Plastic models of wrestlers on Brian's window-sills, soft furry toys on Annie's. Two well-kept bathrooms, one with what looked like genuine Victorian bathroom fittings. And one empty, lifeless room, a lot of shelving on the wall but nothing on display. This must have been a study or office that belonged to Danny in what Ria would have called happier times.

A warm, almost crowded kitchen, shelves of cookbooks, cupboards full of pans and baking dishes, a kitchen where people baked, ate and lived. A house full of beautiful objects but first and foremost a home. There was very little wall space that did not have pictures of the family, mainly of the children but some which included the handsome Danny Lynch as well. He had not been cut out of their lives because he had gone away. Marilyn looked at his face for some clues about this man. One thing she knew from being in his home: he must love this new woman very much or have been very unhappy in his marriage to Ria to enable him to leave all this without a backward glance.

'I wonder should I go and call on her?' Nora Johnson said to Hilary.

'Ah, isn't she perfectly all right where she is. Hasn't she a valuable house worth a fortune to sit in all summer for nothing?' Hilary sniffed.

'Yes, well, she still might be a bit lonely, and Ria said . . .'

'Oh Ria said, Ria said . . . there's many people she could have given that house to, to mind, if she had wanted to.'

Nora looked at her elder daughter with a flash of impatience. 'Listen to me, Hilary, if you're suggesting that you could have looked after the house and fed that very dim cat for Ria . . .'

'Yes, or you could have, Mam. She didn't have to go and get a perfectly strange American.'

'But Hilary, you great silly girl, the whole point of it was that Ria wanted to go to America. She didn't want to exchange houses with me down the road, and you across the city.'

Hilary listened, feeling very foolish. Somehow in her flurry of resentment she had forgotten this fact. 'We should give her tonight and tomorrow to rest anyway and maybe we might get in touch then,' she said.

'I'd hate her to think she wasn't welcome,' Ria's mother said. While Ria's sister hid the sniff she had been about to indulge in.

Carlotta pointed out all the amenities as she drove Ria to Tudor Drive.

Ria marvelled as they passed all the houses with their communal lawns in front. 'No fences,' she noticed.

'Well, it's neighbourly I guess,' Carlotta said.

'Is it like that in Tudor Drive?'

'Not our part, no, it's more closed in.'

Carlotta told her the names of streets and drives that would become familiar in the next days and weeks. She pointed out the two hotels, the club and the library, the good gas station, the one where the guy was a pain in the butt, the two antique shops, the florist, the okay deli, the truly great deli. And of course the garden centre, Carlotta gestured triumphantly.

'Oh well, that's not going to be of much interest to me, I barely know flower from weed.'

Carlotta was puzzled. 'But I thought you were crazy about gardening, that that's how you got to know each other.'

'Not at all, the reverse in fact.'

'Well, well, well. Just goes to show how you can get things wrong. It's just that Marilyn doesn't have any other interests, so I just assumed . . .'

They were nearly there.

'Look, I'd love you to come in and have something to eat and drink with me in my place, but you're here for the summer, you'll want to get into your own place, and see what it's like.' Carlotta took out the envelope with the keys in it and prepared to hand them over.

'But aren't you going to come in with me?' Ria was surprised.

'Well, no, honey, not really. I mean this is your house, Marilyn and Greg's house.'

'No, come in please, I'd love you to come in and show me around, won't you?'

Carlotta bit her lip in indecision. 'I don't really know where their things are . . .' she began.

'Oh please do, Carlotta. I'd feel much more at home if you showed me everything. And Marilyn said she was going to leave me a bottle of wine in her fridge. I left her one in mine. So it would be a lovely start for me.'

'I wouldn't want her to think . . .'

But further protest was useless. Ria was already out of the car and looking up at her new home. 'Do we go in this little gate or round by the carport do you think?'

'I'm not sure.' The previously suave and confident Carlotta looked flustered.

'But which way is the front door?'

'Ria, I've never been in this house in my life,' said Carlotta.

The pause was minimal. Then Ria spoke. 'So, it will be a new experience for both of us,' she said.

And taking a suitcase each they went in to explore Number 1024 Tudor Drive, home of the Vines.

'Heidi? It's Greg Vine.'

'Oh hallo, Greg. And how are you?' Heidi was so relieved that he was still speaking to her after her indiscretion to him on the telephone some weeks back she didn't even pause to wonder why he had called.

'Well, I'm basically okay, Heidi, but a little confused. You did see Marilyn off to the airport, didn't you? I mean, she *did* go?'

'Yes, yes of course. And you do have her number there? She said you did?' Heidi's voice was rising a little anxiously.

'Sure, I have all that. I was just wondering if this person . . . has arrived in Westville? You know, the one who's going to be living in our home.'

'I'm not sure of all the details, but I think she should have got there an hour or two ago, Greg.' Heidi wasn't saying so but it had been like drawing teeth out of Marilyn getting any information whatsoever about the arrival of Ria.

'I see.'

'Was there anything?'

'No, not really.' He sounded very bleak. Despairing almost.

Heidi's heart went out to him. She tried hard to guess what he might want to know. 'You'd like to know if she arrived safely and got in, is that it?'

'In a way, I suppose,' he said.

'So would you like *me* to call and see is she there?'

'It's going to be on the answering machine apparently for the first week with our message on it, and then if this person wants to change it she may.' He sounded very bitter and hurt.

'You want to know if she has arrived and what she's like, what kind of a person she is, Greg? Is *that* it?'

'Well, I think it's more it than anything I've come up with so far,' he said. And there was a wry near-laugh in his voice.

'I'm not sure if I should drive by, she may be asleep. But if I call and then it's only the machine . . . ?'

'Look, whenever you can, Heidi, that's all. I feel so helpless out here, it's so strange, things sort of multiply in your mind.'

'I know.' She was sympathetic.

'I don't think you do. You and Henry can talk about anything and I think we used to once also. But now we can talk about nothing without upsetting each other . . .' He broke off.

'It'll get better, Greg.'

'I'm sorry, I sound like someone on the Oprah show.'

'Is that so bad?'

'No, it's just not the way I am. Listen, I don't want to upset any kind of confidence between you and Marilyn, believe me I don't.'

'There is nothing to upset, just give me the numbers to call and I'll get in touch as soon as I have something to report.'

'Call collect, Heidi.'

'No, I will not do that, but you buy me a nice bright-coloured muu-muu to wear at the alumni picnic.'

'Oh God, I'd forgotten that.'

'You'll be back for it, Greg. You've never missed one yet. We rely on the History Department.'

'But where would I live even supposing I did come back for it?' He sounded totally bewildered.

'Listen, Greg, that's not for weeks yet. Let me report on the situation in Tudor Drive before you make any decisions.'

'You're a real friend, Heidi.'

'We all were and all will be, the four of us, mark my words,' she said with no conviction whatsoever.

Carlotta and Ria toured the house.

'Everything is so beautiful and she had no help coming in, she must have had contract cleaners,' Carlotta said admiringly.

They moved from the big open-plan living room with its coloured rugs on the floor, also three white leather sofas circling an open fireplace, into the huge kitchen with its breakfast bar and dining table, into Greg's study room lined with books from ceiling to floor on three walls and with a red leather desk and big black swivel chair under one window. There was no room for pictures on the walls but three tables stood around, all of them with little sculptures, ornaments, treasures of some sort.

'What a beautiful room,' Ria said. 'If you could see *my* husband's study now ... it's like, well it's like a shell.'

'Why is that?' Carlotta asked reasonably.

Ria paused and looked at her. 'Sorry, he's my ex-husband, and he's just moved out so his study's empty. But it was never like this, not even in our heyday. Should we tour the garden, do you think?'

'The garden will be there tomorrow,' Carlotta said.

'Then let's hit Marilyn's bottle of Chardonnay,' Ria suggested.

'If aromatherapy can cope with jet lag the way it's working with you, we're only in the foothills of discovery,' Carlotta said and they went into the kitchen.

Just at that moment there was a knock on the door. Carlotta and Ria looked at each other, and went together to answer it. A woman in her forties stood there carrying a gift-wrapped bottle.

'I'm Heidi Franks, I work with Marilyn and I wanted to welcome you ... well, hallo Carlotta, I didn't know you'd be here ...'

'Ria insisted that I came by.' Carlotta seemed to be apologising, as if she had been discovered intruding.

'Come on in, Heidi,' Ria said. 'You arrived at a great time, we were just about to have a drink.'

'Well I don't really like to . . .'

Ria wondered what made them both apologise for coming into this home. Americans were meant to be legendary for their friendliness and their ease yet both Carlotta and Heidi seemed to be looking over their shoulders in case the shadow of Marilyn Vine might fall on the place and they would have to run away.

She put away the fanciful thoughts and ushered them back into the kitchen.

Marilyn unpacked everything and had her soup. And a glass of the expensive French wine that Ria had left her. Then she lay for a long time upstairs in the claw-foot bath and soaked away the hours of travel followed by hours of walking around Dublin.

She thought she might sleep, but no, all during the long afternoon her eyes were open and her mind was racing. Why had she come to this house, full of the past and the future? This was a Victorian house, for heaven's sake. Marilyn didn't know exactly what date it was, but people could well have lived here when the Civil War was taking place, when Gettysburg was being fought!

There was hope in this house, which there was never going to be in 1024 Tudor Drive. Two sunny children smiled out of photographs in every room in Tara Road. A boy with a grin as wide as a water melon, and a girl who would be almost the same age as Dale. Marilyn lay under the white bedspread in the master bedroom of this house which had everything, and thought of her life which had nothing.

There was a small sound and the anxious face of the great marmalade cat came around the door. With a leap he landed and laid himself on the bed beside her. He had a purr like the engine of a small boat on the lakes in Upper New York State. Marilyn neither loved nor hated cats, she approved of all animals in a vague way. But Clement was a knowing sort of cat. He seemed to understand that she was not happy. He nestled in beside her, purring louder and louder. Like some kind of lullaby or a mantra it sent Marilyn Vine to sleep and when she woke it was twelve midnight.

In Westville it must be seven o'clock in the evening. She would call Ria and thank her for this restful home. The arrangement was that Ria would pick up if she wanted to answer the call. Marilyn dialled the number. After three rings she heard her own voice respond. 'It's Marilyn,' she said. 'It's midnight here and everything's wonderful. I just wanted to thank you.'

Then Ria's voice came on the line. 'It's only twilight here, but it's even more wonderful. Thank you very, very much.'

'You found the Chardonnay?' Marilyn asked.

'Yes indeed I finished it, and you found the Chablis?'

'Sure I did. I haven't finished it yet but I will.'

'And Gertie let you in?'

'I got in fine and I love the place. You have one beautiful home. And Carlotta gave you the keys and everything?'

'She did, it's a dream house, you undersold it.'

There was a little pause. Then they both said goodnight. Marilyn did not know why she had pretended Gertie had been there. Ria had no idea why she did not say to Marilyn that her friends Carlotta and Heidi were about to open a third bottle of wine. If anyone had asked them they would have been hard put to explain.

'I'm going to see my granny today, Bernadette.'

'Oh good.'

'So I don't know *exactly* what time I'll be back.'

'Sure.' Annie gathered up her tote bag of things which included a very short lycra skirt and a halter-neck top. 'Before you go, call your dad in the office, will you?'

'Why should I do that?'

'Because you forgot to tell him at breakfast that you were going to your grandmother's.'

'Oh, he doesn't want to be bothered with every detail.'

'He does actually.'

'I'll tell him tonight.'

'Would you prefer *me* to tell him for you?' Bernadette's voice was without any threat. It sounded like a simple question, which it most definitely was not.

'There's no need to behave like a gaoler, Bernadette.'

'And there's no need to lie to me either, Annie. You're not going to your grandmother's with all that gear. You and Kitty are off somewhere entirely different.'

'What's it to you if we are?'

'It's nothing to me, I couldn't care less where you go or what you do, but your father's going to be upset and *that* I don't want.'

It was the longest sentence that Annie had ever heard from Bernadette. She considered it for a while then she said enquiringly, 'He won't be upset if he doesn't know.'

'Nice try. No way,' Bernadette said.

'I have to ring Kitty,' Annie said, defeated.

Bernadette nodded to the phone. 'Go ahead,' she said and went back to her book.

Annie looked around once or twice during the conversation but there was no evidence that Bernadette was listening. 'No, I can't explain,' Annie said mutinously. 'Of course I tried. Don't you think I did? Who do you think? Yeah. Yeah. Even worse than Mam if you ask me.'

She hung up disconsolately and looked over at Bernadette curled up in her armchair. She thought she had seen a flicker of a smile but she might have only imagined it.

*

'What's she like?' Myles and Dekko wanted to know.

'She's all right, I suppose,' Brian said grudgingly.

'Do they have lots of sex all the time?'

'Oh no, of course they don't.'

'Well, why else did he go and live with her and get her pregnant?' Dekko asked.

'That was all in the past. I don't think they do that sort of thing now.' Brian was puzzled at the notion.

'They never stop doing it.' Myles was still gloomy about the new baby that had blighted his own life. 'They go on and on until they drop dead from it.'

'Do they?' Dekko was interested.

'I know they do.' Myles was an authority on this. 'But in your house, Brian, they must be at it all the time. What with the situation and everything.'

'Yeah, I see what you mean.' Brian considered it carefully.

'Don't you hear them gasping and being out of breath from it?'

'No,' he shook his head. 'Not in front of us anyway.'

'Of course it's not in front of you, you eejit. It's when they go to bed . . . that's when you'd hear it.'

'No, they just talk in low voices about money.'

'How do you know?'

'Annie and I listened. We wanted to know if they were talking about Mam, but they never mentioned her, not once.'

'What kind of talk about money?'

'Oh, desperate boring things about second mortgages. For hours and hours,' said Brian.

'Are they total monsters?' Finola Dunne asked her daughter on the phone.

Bernadette laughed. 'They're not too bad, very loud of course, and restless.'

'That's all ahead of you,' her mother said sagely.

'I know.'

'Anyway, it's swimming today. I'll be able to report myself. I like the boy, he's got a sense of humour.'

'It's much harder on Annie.' Bernadette sounded sympathetic.

'Yes, she needs watching.'

'That's always been your motto, Mum.'

'Fine lot of good it did me with you!' Bernadette's mother rang off.

At the swimming pool Annie was astounded to see her friend Kitty.

'What a coincidence!' she said four times.

Kitty was equally amazed. 'Who would have thought it?' she asked the air around her.

'This is my friend Mary, Mrs Dunne.' Annie introduced her. 'She's been feeding my cat Clement. Can I go around to Tara Road with her to see Clement after the swimming lesson?'

'I don't see why not,' Finola Dunne said. There was an easy bus service back to Danny and Ria's house. Mary seemed a nice little thing, kind of the child to feed the cat.

'Why are you calling her Mary?' Brian asked.

'Because it's her name, you fool,' Annie hissed.

'It never was before,' Brian protested.

'It is now, so will you shut up?'

The swimming coach was blowing a whistle to get their attention.

'See you later, Kitty,' Annie called.

'I'm sorry, I got her name wrong, I called her Mary,' Finola Dunne said.

'Oh, um, she's both . . . really.' Annie's face was red.

Brian grinned in triumph.

While the swimming lesson was in progress Finola Dunne made a phone call. Her eyes were steely when it was time to go. 'Tell Mary that the American lady is feeding the cat in Tara Road and that you won't need to go and visit it at all.'

Annie hung her head. 'Did you ring Bernadette?' she said eventually.

'Yes, and she had a message for you.'

'What did she say?' Annie was apprehensive.

'She said I was to say to you nice second try, third try your dad deals with it.'

Heidi and Carlotta told Ria that they had never in their whole lives drunk a bottle of wine each. They were astounded with themselves and each other. They blamed it entirely, they said, on the bad influence of their new Irish friend. Ria assured them that she had never done anything so outrageous herself and that at home she was very much a one-drink-a-night person.

'But this is the United States,' wailed Carlotta. 'We count units, we count calories, we all know people like about half my clients in the salon at a rough guess . . . who are in recovery and de-tox and now we're heading that way ourselves.'

'And I'm a middle-aged faculty wife. We all hear tales of how *they* go on the bottle at exactly this time of life. And rot away. Our husbands don't have the salary cheques to get us into the Betty Ford Clinic.'

'Ah, but I'm a sadder case than either of you,' Ria laughed. 'I'm a deserted wife from Ireland over here to sort out my head and on my first day in America I fall in with two lushes and get pissed out of my brains.'

They had learned a great deal about each other. Carlotta's alimony from her three husbands, all paid at the time in large, agreed lump sums, was revealed and even details of how well it had been invested. Heidi's first marriage was described. It had been to a man so totally unsatisfactory in every way that he was only equalled in horror by Henry's first wife. It would have been a wonderful poetic justice had they met and married each other but they had gone on to marry and upset other people. And of course Danny Lynch was introduced to Westville. The story was told of how Ria met him the day before her twenty-second birthday, the afternoon she first slept with him in Tara Road and the night he told her that he was indeed planning to be a father but not of her baby.

'Let's see what Marilyn left in the icebox,' Heidi said.

They could have talked for ever. But when they had eaten a spinach quiche which they found in the icebox, and had two sobering cups of coffee, Ria felt they were both slightly guilty and even embarrassed at the confidences shared. It was not that they regretted having talked so openly, more that this was an inappropriate place to have done so. She was disappointed to see the warmth of the evening beginning to trickle away. She had thought she had found two wonderful new friends the moment she arrived. Perhaps it wasn't going to be like that. She must learn to move more slowly, not to assume huge warmth where it might not exist. She let the evening wind down without begging to meet them again. This seemed to suit them. And Ria also felt that they were very pleased she had not mentioned to Marilyn that they were all sitting together having a little party in 1024 Tudor Drive. In all their revelations and discussions and debates, they had mentioned not once the woman who lived in this house.

When they left at about ten o'clock, which was three o'clock in the morning at home, Ria walked slowly around Marilyn's house. In Ireland her husband Danny was in bed with a child who was expecting his child. Her son Brian was lying on his back with the bedclothes in a twist at the end of the bed, and the light on. Her daughter Annie would have filled her diary with impossible plans of how to escape to somewhere dangerous with Kitty. Her mother would be asleep surrounded by pictures of the saints and vague unformed plans to sell her little house and move herself into St Rita's.

Hilary and Martin would be asleep in their pokey little house in the bed they had bought at a fire sale, the bed where they no longer made love because Martin said that unless you thought you were conceiving a child there was no point in it. Their big round red alarm clock would be set for six thirty. During the vacation Hilary still had to go up to the school to do secretarial work and Martin had a job marking exam papers to make ends meet. Rosemary would have been asleep now for four hours and as Gertie's life had obviously been tranquil enough to allow her to be at Tara Road to welcome Marilyn, so perhaps she too was asleep beside the big drunken boor that she thought of as some kind of precious and fragile treasure which it was her mission to protect.

Clement would be asleep somewhere in the kitchen on a chair. He chose a different one every night with great care, and a sense of hurt. He was never allowed upstairs to the bedrooms no matter how much he had tried or no matter how often Annie had pleaded.

Was Marilyn asleep? Maybe she was awake thinking about her. Ria went into the room that she had just glimpsed before she had somehow instinctively shut the door against Carlotta. She turned on the light. The walls were covered with pictures of motorbikes, Electra Glides, Hondas.

A bed had boy's clothes strewn on it, jackets, jeans, big shoes . . . as if a fifteen-year-old had come in, rummaged for something to wear and then gone out. The closet had clothes hanging neatly on a rail and on the shelves were piles of shirts and shorts and socks. The desk at the window had school papers on it, magazines, books. There were photographs too, of a boy, a good-looking teenage boy with hair that stuck up in spikes and a smile not at all impaired by the braces on his teeth, always with a group of friends. They were playing basketball in one, they were swimming in another, they were out in the snow, they were in costume for a school play. The pictures were laid out casually.

She looked at the photographs. It must have been intentional. She longed to know more about the woman who was asleep in her bed back in Tara Road. There must be something in this house which would give her an image of what Marilyn Vine looked like. And then she found it. It was attached with sticky tape to the inside of his sports bag. A summer picture of a threesome; the boy in tennis clothes, all smiles, with his arm around the shoulders of a man with thinning hair and a check open-necked shirt. The woman was tall and thin and she wore a yellow track suit. She had high cheekbones, short, darkish hair and she wore her sunglasses on her head. They were like an advertisement for healthy living, all three of them.

Rosemary left a note in the letterbox.

Dear Marilyn,

Welcome to Dublin. When you wake up I'm sure you may want to go straight back to sleep and not to get involved with nosy neighbours but this is just a word to say that whenever you would like to come round for a drink or even to have a lunch with me in Quentin's which you might enjoy, all you have to do is telephone.

I don't want to overpower you with invitations and demands but I do want you to know that as Ria's oldest and I hope dearest friend I wanted to welcome you and hope you have a good time here. I know she is very excited about going to your home.

Most sincerely,
Rosemary Ryan.

Marilyn had the note in her hand before Rosemary had run back to her car which was parked outside the gate. She had felt wide awake after her conversation with Ria in the night, and knew that sleep would not come again, despite the hugely affectionate purring of Clement who had reluctantly come downstairs again to be with her and sat on one of the chairs in this beautiful old room. Through the window Marilyn saw the tall blonde elegant woman in a very well-cut suit that was most definitely power-dressing. With a flash of very elegant smoky tights and high heels she was getting into a black BMW and driving away. This was the woman that Ria had described in her letters as her great friend, who was a business tycoon and Ms Perfect but absolutely delightful at the same time.

Marilyn read the letter with approval. No pressure but generous. This was a woman who went to work at six thirty in the morning, owned her own business and looked like a film star. Rosemary Ryan drove the streets in her BMW. Marilyn read the note again. She didn't want to meet this woman, make conversation with her. It didn't matter how important these people were in Ria's life, they weren't part of hers. She would leave the letter unanswered and eventually if Rosemary called again they would have a brief meeting.

Marilyn hadn't come to Ireland to make a whole set of superficial acquaintances.

'I dreamed about you, Colm,' Orla King said as he came into the restaurant.

'No you didn't. You decided you wanted to ask me could you sing here on Friday and you needed an excuse to come and see me.' He smiled at her to take the harm out of his words.

Orla laughed good-naturedly. 'Of course I want to sing here on Friday and Saturday, and every night in August during Horse Show week when you'll be full. But I actually did dream about you.'

'Was I a successful restaurant owner, tell me that?'

'No, you were in gaol for life for murdering your brother-in-law Monto,' Orla said.

'Always very melodramatic, Orla,' Colm said, but his smile didn't quite go to his eyes.

'Yeah, but we don't choose what we dream, it just happens,' Orla said with a shrug. 'It must mean something.'

'I don't *think* I murdered my brother-in-law,' Colm said as if trying to remember. 'No, I'm sure I didn't. He was here last night with a big crowd from the races.'

'He's a real shit, isn't he?' Orla said.

'I'm not crazy about him certainly, but I definitely didn't murder him.' Colm seemed to find it hard to hold on to the light banter of this conversation.

'No, I know you didn't, he was on the phone to me today trying to get me to go to a stag night. Singing, he said. We all know what he means by singing at a stag night.'

'What *does* he mean, Orla?'

'It means show us your tits, Orla.'

'How unpleasant,' Colm said.

'Not everyone thinks so, Colm.'

'No, I mean how deeply unpleasant of the man who is married to my sister asking a professional singer to do anything like that at a stag night. You misunderstood me totally. I'm obviously sure that the sight of your breasts would be a great delight to anyone but not under such circumstances.'

'You speak like a barrister sometimes.'

'Well I might need one if your dreams come true.' Colm spoke in a slightly tinny voice.

'Monto told me that ... well, he sort of said that ...' Orla stopped.

'Yes?'

'He sort of hinted that he had a few problems with your sister Caroline.'

'Yes, I think he has a problem remembering he is married to her.'

'He says more than that. He sort of says there's a dark secret.'

'There is, you know, it's called Bad Judgement. She married a man whom you so rightly describe as a shit. Not much of a dark secret, but there you go. Anyway, Orla, you'd like to sing on Friday? A couple of pointers. You sing as background not as foreground. They want to talk to each other as well as listen to you. Is that understood?'

'Right, boss.'

'You'll sing much more Ella and lots less Lloyd Webber. Okay?'

'You're wrong, but yes, boss.'

'You keep your hands and eyes off Danny Lynch. He'll be here with his new wife and his two kids and his mother-in-law.'

'It's not a new wife, it's his pregnant girlfriend so don't be pompous, Colm.'

'Hands and eyes. A promise or no slot and you never work again here or anywhere else.'

'A promise, boss.'

Colm wondered why he had warned Orla off, after all it might be some small pleasure for Ria out in America to hear that the love-nest was less secure than everyone imagined. But business was business and who wanted a scene in a restaurant on a Friday night?

'We're going to take Mrs Dunne out to dinner on Friday night,' Danny told his children.

'Mam's going to ring on Friday night,' Brian objected.

'She told us to call her Finola, not Mrs Dunne,' Annie objected.

'She told *me* to call her Finola, she didn't tell you.'

'Yes, she did.'

'No, Annie, she didn't. She's a different generation.'

'We call Rosemary Rosemary, don't we?'

'Yes, but that's because she's a feminist.'

'But Finola's a feminist too, she said she was,' Annie insisted.

'Okay, so she's Finola. Fine, fine. Now I thought we might go to Quentin's, but it turns out that she . . . Finola . . . wants to go to Colm's so that's where we're going.'

'Dead right too,' Annie said. 'Colm has proper vegetarian food not some awful poncy thing that costs what would keep a poor family for a month like the token vegetarian dish in Quentin's costs.'

'But what if Mam rings?' Brian asked.

'There's an answering machine and if we miss her we'll call her back.' Danny was bright about it all.

'She might have been looking forward to talking to us though,' Brian said.

'We could change the message and say we were all at Colm's maybe?' Annie suggested.

'No, I think we'll leave the message as it is.' Danny was firm.

'But it's so easy, Dad.'

'People ring Bernadette too, and they wouldn't want to hear all about our fumblings and foosterings.'

'It's not fumbling just to let Mam know that we hadn't forgotten she was going to call,' Annie said.

'Well, call her! Say we're going out.'

'We can't afford to phone her,' Brian said.

'I just told you you can. A quick call, okay?'

'But what about the second mortgage and all the debts and everything?' Brian asked.

'What do you mean?' His father was anxious.

Annie spoke quickly. 'You know you often said that everything costs so much we might have to get a second mortgage, but Brian doesn't realise how cheap it is to call for thirty seconds.'

'I didn't say anything about . . .'

'Dad, we're just going to love a night out in Colm's, and Finola will love it and so will you. Stop worrying about Brian, who as I have so often told you, is totally brain-dead. And let's get on with it.'

'You're a great girl, Princess,' he said. 'I look around Dublin and I see all the bright young men who are going to take you away from me one day.'

'Come on, Dad, who are you fooling? You don't meet kids of my age anywhere.'

'No, but you're not going to run off with a kid, are you, Princess?' her father asked.

'You did, Dad.'

There was a silence.

'Who will I marry?' Brian asked.

'A person who has been deprived of all their senses, but very particularly the sense of smell,' Annie said.

'That's not right, is it Dad?'

'Of course not, Brian. Your sister is only making a joke. You'll marry a great person when the time comes.'

'A lady wrestler, maybe,' Annie suggested.

Brian ignored her again. 'Is there any way of knowing it's the right person, Dad?'

'You'll know.' His father was soothing.

'You didn't, Dad. You thought Mam was the right person and she turned out not to be.'

'She *was* the right person at the time, Brian.'

'And how long's the right time, Dad?' Brian asked.

'About fifteen years, apparently,' Annie said.

'Supper everyone, I have bought lovely fish and chips,' Bernadette called from the kitchen.

Marilyn had taken a chair and a cup of coffee out to the front steps; she sat in the sun examining the garden.

There was so much that could be done with it. Such a pity they hadn't given it any real love and care, unlike the house itself. She saw there *had* been interesting trees planted. Somebody at some stage had known what would flourish and had wanted to make an impression, but the arbutus had not been pruned or shaped, it had been allowed to become rough and woody, it was almost beyond saving. The palm tree was scraggy and untidy and almost unseen because other bushes had grown up around it and taken it over.

Outside the gate she noticed a woman in her sixties with a very misshapen and unattractive dog. The woman was staring in with interest.

'Good morning,' Marilyn said politely.

'And good morning to you too, I expect you're the American visitor.'

'Yes, I'm Marilyn Vine. Are you a neighbour?'

'I'm Ria's mother Nora, and this is Pliers.'

'How do you do?' Marilyn said.

'Ria said most definitely that we should not call in on top of you unannounced.' Nora had come up the step to continue the conversation but she looked doubtful. Pliers gave a wide and very unpleasant yawn as if he could sense a tedious exchange of courtesies ahead. Marilyn remembered her from the photograph, she knew the woman lived near by. 'I can tell you one thing for a start, Ria didn't grow up in a home like this with all those antiques around her.'

Marilyn could hear the resentment in the woman's voice. 'Really, Mrs Johnson?'

Nora looked at her watch with a scream and said she'd be late for St Rita's. 'You must come with me one day . . . it's an old people's home, a visit would be a great thing,' she said.

'It's very kind of you but *why* exactly?' Marilyn was bewildered.

'Well, they like unusual things to happen in their day. I take my grandchildren there sometimes, and I once brought a juggler I met in Grafton Street. They like Pliers as a new face, I'm sure they'd enjoy meeting an American, it would be different anyway.'

'Well, thank you. Some time, perhaps.'

'Has Lady Ryan been around yet?'

'I beg your pardon?'

'Ria's friend, Rosemary?'

'No, she left a note though. People have been so kind.'

'Well, they're interested in you, Marilyn, it's only natural.' Nora Johnson was gone, having said she wanted to know every little detail about Marilyn Vine and having asked or discovered absolutely nothing at all.

After Ria's mother left Marilyn took out again the wallet of photographs that she had been given. She had to know who these people were when they all turned up as they would, so when Gertie arrived, slightly hesitantly, Marilyn recognised her at once.

'Let's not be awkward about this,' Gertie began. 'I know Ria told you I need a few extra pounds a week, but it seems unfair on you to have to dig into your holiday money . . .'

'No, that's perfectly fine and I'd love to know that this beautiful house is being kept the way it always is.'

Gertie looked around her. 'But you've got the place looking great, there's not a thing out of place. It's just putting out my hand and asking for charity.'

'No, that's not the way I see it.'

'I'm not sure if Ria explained . . .' Gertie began.

'Oh, sure she did. You are kind enough to come and help to keep her house in its fine condition twice a week.'

'Yes, but if that's all right with you?' Gertie had big black circles under her eyes. There was some background of dependency here. Marilyn knew Gertie was both friend and employee, still, it was none of her business. 'And would you like me to make you a cup of coffee?' Gertie began.

'No thank you.'

'Well, shall I start doing the cleaning then?'

'I'm sure you know this house very well, whatever you think . . .'

'Well, she always liked the front room polished.'

'Sure, that would be fine.'

'And would you like me to do anything for you like ironing maybe?'

'That's very kind. I hate ironing. I'm going out now, so shall I see you next time?'

'That's fine, and you're very welcome here, Marilyn.'

'Thank you,' Marilyn said. She took her keys and walked up Tara Road. Lord but this house was going to be full of people. Not exactly the rest she had been looking for.

Gertie thought that for a woman who absolutely hated ironing all Marilyn's clothes were very crisp and well pressed, and that she had already found time to take out Ria's iron since her arrival. But she decided not to argue it any further. There was something about Marilyn that appealed to her. She didn't seem to want to know why Gertie, who already ran a launderette, needed extra money in cash, nor did she seem anxious to talk about her own situation. In a life where too many people wanted to move in and alter the situation, Gertie found this lack of involvement very pleasing indeed.

'What does it say?' Brian asked.

'It's an American woman's voice saying she's not there and to leave a message for the people who are there,' Annie replied.

'There aren't any people . . . there's only Mam.'

'Shut up, Brian. Hallo Mam, it's Annie and Brian, and everything's fine and it's just that we'll be going out to a big dinner with Dad and . . . well, what I mean is that we'll be going out to dinner in Colm's restaurant on Friday so we won't be back until maybe eleven o'clock our time. We didn't want you to ring and find nobody at home. That's it, Mam. Brian's okay too.'

'Let me say I'm okay,' Brian cried.

'You're not to waste the call, Mam *knows* you're okay.'

Brian snatched the phone. 'I'm okay, Mam, and getting on at the swimming. Finola says the coach told her that I'm making fine progress. Oh, Finola's Bernadette's mother by the way. She's coming to the dinner too.'

Annie snatched the phone back and hung up. 'Aren't you the greatest eejit in the whole wide world to mention Finola? Aren't you a fool of the first order?' she said to him, her eyes blazing.

'I'm sorry.' Brian was crestfallen. 'I'm so sorry, I just didn't think. I was excited leaving the message for Mam.'

He looked so upset that even Annie Lynch's hard heart relented. 'It's not the end of the world, I suppose,' she said gruffly. 'Mam won't mind.'

Ria came in from the pool wearing one of Marilyn's towelling jackets. For the first few times she had just flopped around luxuriating in the cold water and the beautiful flowers and the lovingly kept garden all around her. But she had taken to reading Dale's sports books all laid out so neatly in his room. There had been a swimming notebook recording how many lengths he and his friends had done on different days. One entry said: 'Mom has decided to stop behaving like a dolphin and be a proper swimmer. So she's doing four lengths each time, it's nothing but she's going to build it up.'

By the time Dale stopped writing his records Marilyn Vine was doing thirty lengths. Ria felt there was a message for her here. By the time her children came out she wouldn't be like a dolphin any more, she would be purposeful, competitive even. She had done six lengths today and was utterly exhausted. What she needed was a cup of tea and a rest.

She saw the little red light flickering on the phone and rushed to play back the message. She sat at the breakfast bar listening to her children speaking to her from thousands of miles away. The tears poured down her face. What was she *doing* out in this place wearing herself out playing silly games in a swimming pool? Why was she not at home with them instead of leaving them to become bosom pals with Bernadette's bloody mother? And why was Danny being so cruel and insensitive as to go back to the very restaurant where they had had such a scene on the night she first learned of Bernadette? And would Colm make a fuss over them and offer them a complimentary drink as he always did?

The Lynch family on an outing the same as usual, only a few small things changed. The wives, for example. The one put out to grass and a newer model installed. The mothers-in-law. Nora Johnson wouldn't be there but Mrs Dunne with her shiny copper shoes and her smart suit would. Like probing a sore tooth she insisted on playing the message over and over. She couldn't even smile at the argument between the children. She knew that once they had hung up Annie had laid into Brian for his tactlessness. At this very minute some huge argument was taking place. How would Bernadette react? Would she stop them fighting or would she pretend not to notice?

Ria didn't care which she did. It would be the wrong thing to do anyway. And maybe this woman who was somehow Finola to Ria's children and yet was Mummy to Bernadette was now a huge influence in their lives. She was going out to dinner with them, for heaven's sake. That hurt more than anything.

It was too much to bear. Ria put her head down on the breakfast bar in the sunny kitchen and cried and cried. She didn't see a man come to the glass doors and pause before knocking. He, however, saw a woman doubled over in grief. He couldn't hear her sobs or the choked words. He picked up his canvas bag and moved silently away. This was not the time to call and say that he was Greg Vine's brother passing through and that he had come to see Marilyn. He walked down to his rented car and drove to a motel.

It had been such a house of tragedy since the accident he had hardly been able to bear visiting it. And now he had come across a strange woman in a pool wrap, crying with a kind of intensity he had never known. Still, he had promised his brother that if work took him east he would look up Marilyn. He had thought, wrongly, that it would be better to come without warning, otherwise she would have certainly found some excuse not to meet him.

He had a shower, a cool beer at the motel and then he telephoned his brother's house. The words said Marilyn and Greg were both away but to leave a message for the people staying in the house. On a whim he spoke.

'My name is Andy Vine. I'm Greg's brother, passing through Westville staying at the . . . sorry . . .' he hunted for the name and number of the motel. 'I know Greg's in Hawaii obviously, but perhaps you might kindly call me and tell me where Marilyn is? I would much appreciate this. Many thanks in advance.'

Ria sat listening to the message. She did not pick up the receiver. Marilyn had mentioned no brother-in-law. Perhaps there was a coldness. If he was a brother of Greg Vine then surely he'd know that Greg's wife was in Dublin. If he was a brother-in-law of Marilyn and had thought she was at home, why had he not called around? But then was she being ridiculously suspicious over nothing? And would it be childish and nit-picking to call Marilyn in Ireland and check? It would also be somehow involving herself in Marilyn's doings, which she realised now was the last thing Marilyn seemed to want. She couldn't ask Carlotta and Heidi since they seemed to know nothing whatsoever about their friend Marilyn's lifestyle. She decided she would call Greg Vine in Hawaii.

She was put through to him with great ease. He sounded younger and more relaxed than his photograph had suggested.

'Yes, of course,' he said when she gave her name.

'First, I must assure you that there's no problem here. Everything in your beautiful house is in fine shape,' she said.

'That's a relief, I thought you were going to tell me the plumbing wasn't working.'

'No, nothing like that, and I suppose in a way because I'm living in your home . . . I wanted to introduce myself to you . . . but not at length on your phone bill.'

'That's most courteous of you, I hope you have everything you need.' His voice was polite but cold.

Ria told him about the call from the motel. Greg assured her that he did have a highly respectable brother called Andy who worked in Los Angeles but came to Boston and New York City on business from time to time.

'That's fine then, I'll call him, I thought it wiser to check it out because he didn't seem to know anything about Marilyn's movements.'

'I appreciate your caution very much. But Marilyn was, let us say, a trifle reserved in telling people anything about her movements.' He sounded bitter.

Ria decided to ignore the tone. 'Well, you'll be glad to know she's arrived there safely and is as well installed as I am in Tudor Drive. It would be good if you had the chance to go over there yourself.'

'Oh, I don't think that's in the master plan.' Again his voice sounded icy.

'I asked would you be going, she said she didn't know.'

'Really? And will your husband be joining you in Westville?' he asked.

Ria took a deep breath. Marilyn had certainly been fairly short on her explanations of anything to anyone. 'No, Danny is now my ex-husband. He is living with a much younger woman called Bernadette. It's the reason why I am actually here in your house. My son and daughter will however be joining me here next month. Did Marilyn not even tell you that much?'

There was a pause, then he spoke. 'Yes, she did, and I apologise for my manner. It was uncalled for. I was confused by Marilyn not wanting to come here, I still am.'

'That's perfectly all right. I think it was a search for somewhere completely different.'

'Obviously.'

There was another pause.

'And your son?'

'Yes?'

'He likes Hawaii?'

'I beg your pardon?'

'I suppose it's a place that all young people would like.' Ria felt flustered, although she did not know why.

'Oh yes. Certainly.'

'I expect he's missing his mother.'

'I'm sorry?'

'They never pretend, but they do in a way that they can't even define.' She knew she was gushing. 'Boys . . .' said Ria nervously.

'Well, yes.' He seemed anxious to end the conversation.

'I won't keep you any longer,' she said. 'I'm not clear about what's going on in anyone's lives these days, but just be sure that your house is in fine shape. I had hoped to reassure you of that anyway.'

'Of course, of course. And is it working for you being over here?'

'It was,' Ria said truthfully. 'It was working quite well but I just got a message from my children on your answering machine.'

'Are they missing you? Is that the problem?'

'No, Greg. They're not missing me, *that's* the problem.'

'Marilyn? This is Rosemary Ryan.'

'Oh yes, thank you for your note.'

Rosemary was to the point. 'I wondered can I take you and Gertie to Colm's restaurant on Friday for dinner? He has a special seafood evening, and you might enjoy it.'

'I don't want to intrude.'

'This would be a casual easy girls' night out. Gertie doesn't go out socially. Do say yes.'

'Thank you so much, Rosemary, I'd love to join you,' said Marilyn Vine.

Ria called Andy Vine at the motel, told him who she was and where Marilyn had gone.

'We both needed a little space in our lives and thought it would be a good idea,' she said.

He seemed happy enough with the explanation.

'And in the normal turn of events would you be staying here in Tudor Drive, I mean if Marilyn had been at home and everything?'

'Well, I might,' he said.

'So you shouldn't be paying for a motel really, should you? If you expected to stay here in your brother's house?' She was eager to do the right thing.

'No, please, Maria. Please don't think like that. It's your house now just as the house in Ireland belongs to Marilyn.'

'I feel bad about it. How long are you going to be in Westville anyway?'

'I had thought that maybe I'd spend tonight and Saturday night here, you know, if Marilyn were about ... then drive up to Boston on Sunday. The conference starts on Monday morning.'

'I'm sorry she didn't think of telling you. It was all arranged in a bit of a hurry,' Ria apologised.

This couldn't be the woman he had seen crying like no one had ever cried before. 'I had been going to ask Marilyn out to dinner in a new Thai restaurant.'

'Maybe next time,' she said.

'Would *you* like a Thai dinner, Maria?' he asked.

She paused. It was the last thing on earth she thought would happen to her in America, a man who hadn't even seen her inviting her out to dinner within a week of her arrival. But it was a Friday night. Back in Ireland her children were being taken to Colm's restaurant with a lot of strangers. 'Thank you so much, Andy, I'd be delighted to accept,' Ria Lynch said.

'Monto wants to bring in a crowd tonight,' Colm said.

'What did you tell him?' Caroline was immediately anxious.

'I told him we were full.'

'Oh.'

'He said I was to have a word with Caroline and that he'd call back later and see if we had an unexpected cancellation for six people.'

'Give it to him, Colm.'

'Why? It upsets you when they're here. We don't need the business those guys bring in, six overdone steaks and round after round of double gins.'

'Please, Colm . . . ?'

'It's utterly terrifying for me to see you so afraid of him.' He looked at her big sad eyes with such compassion that he could see the tears form in the corners. 'Still I'll do what you say. Which table will they be least noticeable at, do you think?'

She gave him a watery smile. 'Look, do you think I'd be like this about him if there was any other solution?'

'There *is* a solution.'

'We've had this conversation a thousand times.'

'I'm so sorry, Caroline.' He put his arms around his sister and she laid her head on his shoulder.

'What have you to be sorry for? You've done everything for me, you've saved my life.'

He patted her on the back as he held her and behind him he heard the cheery voice of Orla King.

'Well, hallo everybody. I thought I'd be on time to show you my sheet music but, boy, did I come a little early.'

Bernadette's mother had decided to teach Brian Lynch to play chess.

'Isn't it hard?' Brian asked suspiciously.

'No, it's not hard at all to learn to play, it's hard to be good at it. You'd pick it up in half an hour then you'd know it for life.'

'Right then,' said Brian agreeably.

'Would you like to learn too, Annie?'

'No thanks, Finola, if you don't mind.'

'Not at all.' She had known Annie would refuse to do anything in tandem with her younger brother, and also she might have felt it somehow disloyal to her mother. Bernadette was right. Annie was a complicated child, and of course fourteen-and-a-half was the very worst age in the whole world.

Danny and Bernadette were out with Barney McCarthy meeting some possible investors in a new development. It had not gone well, they had asked rather too searching questions about previous financial returns and too many details about building specifications. Bernadette had been quiet and respectful, looking from one to another with interest but no understanding. Ria would have had some kind of sparky input into the conversation which might have taken the dead edge of an unsuccessful pitch for unlikely business off the whole thing.

Danny was tired when they got up to leave. 'Will we go to Quentin's tonight?' Barney suggested.

'No. A family dinner. Long arranged.'

'Never mind, I just thought it would be relaxing to drop into Tara Road, have a drink, a shower, and then just the two of us head off and sort out the financial problems of the world.'

'It would have been,' Danny said.

Then they both looked at each other in alarm. They had both actually forgotten that Danny didn't live in Tara Road any more.

Possibly that was what made Danny drive home that way. It was only slightly out of his way to cut through that neighbourhood. As he looked out at the house that had been his home Danny Lynch saw a tall slim woman in dark jeans and a white shirt, quite striking in a sporty kind of way, digging urgently at the undergrowth in his front garden. On the tarmacadam drive was a huge sheet of plastic that held what she had already hacked out.

'What the hell does she think she's doing?' he said, slowing down immediately.

'Drive on, Danny.' Bernadette's voice was calm but insistent.

'No I won't. She's tearing my garden to bits.'

'Drive on a little bit further anyway so that she won't see you.'

'She'll see me, by God she'll see me. I'm not letting her get away with that.'

But he did go on further, and parked near Rosemary's house.

'Don't go in, you're upset.'

'But she'll have the whole place cut down,' he protested.

'Don't upset her. She might storm back to America.'

'Good.'

'Then there'd be nowhere for the children to go on holiday,' said Bernadette.

'They're having a bloody holiday with us next week on the Shannon, isn't that enough for them?' But he took her advice and drove home.

'I brought you Martinis in honour of the visiting American,' Colm said. It proved to be a great success.

Marilyn told them about her happy day in the garden, she was never happier than when up to her elbows in earth. If the other two thought that she might have checked with Ria before embarking on it they said nothing. And of course it was quite possible that she had. Gertie told them about a man in the launderette who came there every Saturday and washed an entire bag of women's black lacy underwear. Quite unconcerned as people saw him taking them out and folding them neatly into a big carrier bag. Gertie said that she'd love to be able to tell these little things to Jack but that sadly you never knew how he would take them, he might come rushing in and calling the man a pervert. And if the other two thought it was a poor life if you couldn't even tell your husband a pleasant story about work they gave no hint of it.

And when a good-looking blonde began to sing 'Someone to Watch Over Me', they told Marilyn that this was about the most troublesome woman in Dublin and that she had been known to cause spectacular scenes in her time.

'She's a good singer, though,' Marilyn said, struggling to be fair and looking at the girl who played and sang as if every word had a huge meaning for her.

'Bit of a high-risk factor. I always tell Colm but when does anyone listen to me?' Rosemary said in a tone that suggested almost everyone else listened to her and was wise to do so.

'Maybe he just likes giving her a chance, Colm's great at helping the underdog,' Gertie said.

'She doesn't look like much of an underdog to me,' Marilyn volunteered. At that moment Danny Lynch and his party came into the restaurant and they were settled at a table across the room. Marilyn recognised them immediately from the photographs on the walls and in the wallet Ria had sent her. 'Is that Ria's husband?' she asked very directly. And the other two nodded glumly.

Until this stage in the meal Ria had not been spoken of at all. Now her whole personal story was here in the restaurant and they couldn't skirt around it any more. A glamorous, well-made-up woman in a black sequinned jacket was being very much the centre of things, pointing at where people were to sit.

'She doesn't look like a twenty-two-year-old to me, she's my age if she's a day,' Marilyn whispered.

'You're not going to believe this, Marilyn, but that's the twenty-two-year-old's mother,' whispered Rosemary.

'Mother!' said Marilyn in disbelief.

Then she saw, beside the two animated children familiar from their pictures, the waif in the shapeless blue jumper and skirt. A pale child with long straight hair who could definitely be taken for Annie's not very much older sister. Marilyn felt a pain that was almost physical to think that Ria Lynch had to endure this. Danny Lynch was still the excitable boy that he had been all those years ago. And Ria loved him deeply still. How could anyone bear the pain of losing a man to this, this strange unformed young girl? No wonder poor Ria had run three thousand miles away to get over the grief of it all.

Orla began to sing 'The Man I Love'. Colm frowned. He frowned even more deeply when she went straight into 'They're Singing Songs of Love but Not for Me'. 'Cool it, Orla,' he said as he passed with the steaks for Monto's table.

'Pure Gershwin, boss, as you suggested. Coming up with "Nice Work if You Can Get It". That should set a few hearts fluttering, don't you think?'

'You have a reasonably nice voice but you don't have all that much of a career. And while you're at it, if you go on like you're going on tonight, forget the Horse Show next month.'

'Be fair, Colm. You said Cole Porter and Gershwin. George I've done, they liked it. I'm coming up to Cole now. "I Get a Kick outa You". "I've Got You under My Skin". "The Lady Is a Tramp". Can I help it, boss, if the titles have a bit of innuendo? I don't write them, I'm only singing them at your request.'

'Don't be a fool, Orla, please.'

'Hey, who are you to ask me not to be a fool? A man who's in love with his sister. Great bloody role model, Colm Barry.'

'I warn you, you'll be so very, very sorry tomorrow. I'll still have a restaurant, you won't have a job or a chance of ever getting one in Dublin.'

'Do you remember something we used to hear every week called "One Day at a Time"? Okay, this is my day, this is my time.' Her eyes were too bright.

'Don't do it, Orla.'

'He left me, he could have had me and he went for an old trout in a sequinned jacket.'

'That's not who's with Danny.'

'He's holding her bloody arm, who else is he with? The others are children.'

'The one in the blue sweater; the black sequins is his mother-in-law.'

She looked over again, astounded. 'You're making it up.'

'I'm not, but you're not going to have a chance to check it.'

'She's under the age of consent, it's not legal. Any more than you and

Caroline are.' She was standing up now, prepared to go over to Danny Lynch's table.

'Orla, sit down, this minute. Play. Don't sing. Play "Smoke Gets in Your Eyes".'

'It's the kind of shitty philosophy you believe in.'

'Play it, Orla, or leave. Now.'

'You and whose army will make me?'

'Monto's army.' He looked over at their table. Six rough vulgar men whom he disliked intensely.

'They like me, why would they throw me out?'

'I'd ask them nicely.'

'And I'd tell Monto that you're screwing his wife.'

'And who would believe you, Orla? Out-of-control weakling that you are.'

'Hey, where's the solidarity tonight?'

'Where did you put it? The drink? I was on to you the moment you came in, I checked your grapefruit juice.'

She threw her head back at him and laughed. 'It's in the flower vase, you fool. First line of defence. Half-bottle of vodka in with the carnations.'

He picked up the vase and emptied the contents into an empty wine bucket and indicated to a waiter to take it away.

'What will I do with it, Mr Barry?'

'Down the drain outside. Save the flowers, wipe the stems.'

'You believed me.' She looked both anxious and triumphant at the very same time.

'Not until I saw your eyes when I threw it out. Then I knew it was there all right.'

'Self-righteous prick,' she said.

'Hey Colm, are you going to stand there looking down the singer's tits all night, or serve us our steaks?' Monto called from his table.

A few people laughed nervously. Others looked away.

Orla got up, and taking her microphone with her began to wander around the room. 'I'd like to do requests for people,' she said. 'I think this is what makes a night out special. But so often people don't always quite know exactly what they want to hear. So I thought that possibly tonight I could *choose* songs for people, something that could be appropriate. And sing a few bars at each table.'

People were laughing and encouraging her. To the customers who didn't know her, Orla King was an attractive, professional singer. Now she was doing something a little more personal, that was all there was to it. But many people in the room froze and they watched her edgily.

First she came to Rosemary's table. 'We have three lovely ladies here,' she said. 'Feminists, oh definitely. Lesbians? Very possibly. Anyway, no men. My grandmother used to sing a song called "There Were Three Lovely Lassies from Bannion". But it's a little too old even for this group. Suppose I were to sing "Sisters" for them . . . ?'

'Did I do anything except help you all your life?' Rosemary asked, with the mask of a frozen smile on her face.

'You had your reasons,' Orla said. She judged that a few bars were enough and moved to Monto's table. 'Six men, powerful men, rich men. Nothing poofy about these men, believe me, I know.' She smiled radiantly around the room. 'Now what song should we choose for them? Oh I know, there was one they all sang at this stag night, they asked me to perform and they loved it. No, it was not "Eskimo Nell", everyone knows that. No, it was "The Ball of Kirriemuir". "Four and twenty virgins came down from Inverness and when the ball was over there were four and twenty less."' She smiled and moved to the Lynches' table.

At the same time Colm Barry was at Monto's table, whispering feverishly. 'Well well, what a wonderful family group. Let me see.' She smiled at them all, playing them like little fishes on a line. 'What would you like?'

Only Brian thought it was a real question. He chose a Spice Girls song. 'Do you know "Whaddya Want, Whaddya Really Want"?' he asked eagerly.

His innocent face halted her in her tracks. Just for one moment, but for long enough to throw her. 'What about "Love and Marriage"? No, that's not permanent enough. What about that nice song "She Was Only Sixteen"? No, she must be older than that. This *is* your new wife, isn't it, Danny?' She was just turning to point to Finola, but as she turned Monto and one of his henchmen had lifted her bodily and were carrying her to the door. 'Don't think people don't know, Danny. They know what you and I had, just as they know what Monto's wife had ... and still has ...'

Her voice was no longer heard. She was outside the restaurant. If Colm had hoped that he could get by with the help of some of his friends he was disappointed. The embarrassed silence that fell on the restaurant seemed to last for ever. Rosemary, usually so quick to know what to do in a crisis, sat white-faced and furious at her table, with the new American woman from Ria's house confused and bewildered beside her. And with them was Gertie, terrified to see yet again at first hand the damage drink could do.

Monto's party were more triumphant and hilarious than could be imagined, imitating some of Orla's more drunken lurches.

Jimmy and Frances Sullivan, entertaining some guests up from Cork, embarrassed at the turn the evening had taken. Two fellow restaurateurs that Colm knew who had come in specially to see how his business was getting on. A party of two families getting to know each other before a wedding at the weekend. His sister Caroline standing stricken by the accusations that had been made. And Danny Lynch's party he didn't even dare to look at. All of them upset by that destructive little Orla King. *Why* had she done it? Because she was unhappy.

But we're all unhappy, he told himself. Why should she have the luxury of throwing a scene and upsetting everyone else? He saw his waiters looking at him as if waiting for a lead. It could only have been seconds, he realised, since Orla's struggling body had been carried out of his restaurant. It felt like a lifetime. Colm straightened his shoulders, indicated by a gesture that one table should be cleared, that the wine bucket should be placed nearer to another. He touched Caroline's shoulder and looked at the kitchen, and zombie-like she walked towards it.

Then he approached Rosemary Ryan's table. 'Well well,' he said, looking directly at Marilyn Vine. 'You can't say we don't show you life in the fast lane in Dublin.'

'No, indeed.' Her face was impassive. He wished she didn't have to be so po-faced. She was the guest, she should have said something warm-hearted and funny to show that she was a good sport, to show that it didn't matter. But she didn't.

'I'm embarrassed that this should have happened the first time you come to my place,' he said. Marilyn nodded her head as if accepting his apology. He felt a dark flush of annoyance at being dismissed so regally.

'She'll never work again, Colm,' Rosemary said, but not with the solidarity he might have liked. There was a hint that he might have known this would happen, that the fault was partially his.

'It was all a bit like a cabaret really,' said poor Gertie, trying to put some favourable gloss on it.

At the Lynch table they hadn't quite recovered either. 'Sorry about the cabaret.' Colm had decided to play it low key, he wasn't going to crawl to these people.

'Was it something she ate, do you think?' Brian Lynch asked with interest.

'I very much hope not, speaking as a restaurant owner.' Colm forced a smile.

'More like something you gave her to drink.' Danny Lynch's voice was cold.

'No, Danny, you know I wouldn't do that. Like myself, Orla can't drink like all you people can, but she was upset by something and she had hidden vodka in the flower vase.'

Bernadette clapped her hand over her mouth to stop the giggle. 'The flower vase? It must have tasted *awful*,' she said.

'I hope it did.' Colm smiled at the strange girl that he had thought he would never speak to. She really *was* only a child, more a friend for Annie than for Annie's father. What a nightmare for Ria to take on board. 'Anyway, you'll have to rely on conversation rather than music,' he said.

'That's better in a way,' Annie said. 'You can hear music anywhere, we'd rather chat as it happens.'

'Yes, we were asking Bernadette whether the baby inside her had webbed feet,' Brian said. 'And we were wondering was that the American? You know, Mam's friend Mrs Vine, over there with Rosemary and Gertie?'

'Yes, that's Marilyn Vine,' Colm said.

'Some welcome to Tara Road for her,' Danny said.

'That's what I told her, she thought it was very funny,' Colm lied and moved on to placate the next table.

Somehow the night ended for everyone. Monto and his friend came back.

'Where exactly?' Colm hated having to talk to this man.

'We thought of a lot of places, but settled on an Out-Patients' in a hospital eventually,' Monto said with a smirk.

'She'll leave, she'll come back. Close the door of the restaurant.'

'No, we gave a folding note or two to someone there who will make sure she doesn't.'

'Thank you, Monto, I owe you for tonight.'

'You owe me for a lot more than just tonight and you know that. So you'll never tell me again that your restaurant is full.'

'No, of course not, a mistake.'

'Exactly.'

At Danny's table they had paid the bill and were leaving. 'I took the price of the wine off to compensate for the unpleasantness involved,' Colm said.

'Thank you.' Danny was cold.

'It wasn't Colm's fault,' Annie said.

'Of course not.' Danny was still chilly.

'Nor was it your father's fault that Orla picked on him specifically,' Colm said in an even icier voice.

'No indeed, and thank you very much for your generous gesture about the wine,' said Danny Lynch, changing his tack so swiftly it knocked them all off course.

'Was it a great dinner?' Ria asked her daughter.

'It was extraordinary, Mam. This singer got pissed or stoned or something and started going around with her bosom falling out upsetting everyone. Then she was sort of carried out. Mrs Vine was there and the drunk singer headed straight for her table and said they were all lesbians! Honestly, Mrs Vine, Gertie and Rosemary.'

Ria held her head in her hand. 'Come again, Annie? Gertie, Rosemary . . . I don't believe any of this, Annie.'

'Well, Mam, the only one who's going to confirm it to you is that brilliant observer Brian Lynch, who was there for it all and who's waiting to get on the phone.'

'I'm sorry, Annie, of course I believe you, love. It just seems so unlikely. And did Bernadette and . . . um . . . Finola enjoy it all too?'

'Well I think they were a bit stunned.'

'I love you, Annie,' said Ria.

'Oh Mam, for heaven's sake. I'll put Brian on now.'

'Mam?'

'Brian, was it a great night?'

'It was mad, Mam. You just wouldn't believe it. Mam, what's a lebsian? Nobody will tell me.'

'A lesbian, is it?'

'Yes, whatever.'

'It's a lady who likes other ladies more than she likes men.'

'So, is that a big deal?'

'Not a bit. Tell me about the night in the restaurant.'

'Do you know any lebsians?'

'Yes, I know a few, sure.'

'Are they awful?'

'No, of course not.'

'So why do people whisper about them?'

'They don't, believe me.'

'They did, Mam, tonight. Believe me.'

'I'm sure you misunderstood.'

'I don't think so. Do you want to say goodnight to Finola? She's just off.' Ria could hear Annie scream.

'Brian, you are so stupid,' she could hear Annie crying.

'Yes, sure, I'd love to say goodnight to Finola,' Ria heard herself say.

There was a fluster and then a woman came on the line. 'Well, I just want to say that your children are great company,' she said desperately.

'Thank you for saying that. They seem to have taken to you greatly also,' Ria gulped. 'And I gather there was some kind of night to remember?'

Finola considered. 'Unless there had been someone there with a video camera you would never believe it.'

Neither used the other's name. Perhaps it was always going to be like that between them. 'Good luck to you,' Ria said.

'And great good luck to you too,' said Bernadette's mother.

Ria hung up the telephone. She had two hours to get ready for her date with a man who was in technical publishing in Los Angeles and was en route to a conference in Boston. She had just finished a pleasant conversation with the mother of her husband's mistress. The apparently manic-depressive woman with whom she had exchanged homes had been out partying in Colm's restaurant. The world had tilted.

Andy Vine didn't look at all like his brother when he came in and had a lemon drink by the pool, so she was glad she had telephoned Hawaii about him. About her own age or younger, slight and red-haired. Somewhat academic and assuming that she knew much more about college life than she did. 'Forgive me, I keep making the wrong assumptions,' he said when she knew nothing of any faculty or alumni association in either Ireland or Connecticut. 'I thought that's how you and Marilyn met.'

'No, not at all. Other people thought we met over an obsession about gardens, in which I have no interest at all.' She was all smiles and wearing her best summer outfit, a blue-and-white dress that she had got for a wedding last summer and had never worn since. It had looked great with a hat from Polly Callaghan, but there was never anywhere smart enough to wear it since. She should have dressed better. Would everything have been all right had she been an elegant wife?

'Do you know Thai food at all?' he was asking.

'Well, there *are* Thai restaurants in Ireland now, we are very international. But I've only been twice so I don't remember it all and I'd love you to choose for me when we get there.'

This seemed to go down well. Maybe it was easier making fellows interested in you when you were old and way past it and it didn't matter any more.

They talked easily in the Thai restaurant. He told her about the kind of publishing his company was involved in. Books that you would never hear of unless you happened to be in that field, and then you not only heard about them, you bought them because you had to. He explained how it had all changed so radically because of technology and CD-roms. His grandfather had been a door-to-door salesman for encyclopaedias. The man would spin in his grave if he saw the size of an encyclopaedia now and knew how they were sold. Andy lived in LA in an apartment. He had been married, and was now divorced. There were no children.

'Did you leave her or did she leave you?' Ria asked.

'It's never as simple as that,' he smiled.

'Oh it is,' she insisted.

'Okay, I had an affair, she found out and she threw me out.'

Ria nodded. 'So you left really, by ending the marriage.'

'So you say, so she said. I didn't want it to end but who listened to me?'

'Would you have forgiven her, if she were the one who had the affair?'

'Sure I would.'

'You'd have gone on as if nothing had happened?'

'Look, Maria, people let each other down all the time, don't they? It's not a perfect life with everyone delivering on every promise. Marriages survive affairs if there's something there in the marriage itself that's bigger than the affair. I thought there was in our case, I was wrong.'

'If you had your time all over again . . . ?' She was keen to know.

'You can't rewrite history, I have no idea what I'd do. Tell me, are you divorced also?'

'I think so,' Ria said. He looked at her, startled. 'That's not as mad as it sounds. You see, divorce was only recently introduced in Ireland. We're still not entirely used to it. But the answer is yes, I am about to be.'

'Did you leave him or . . . ?'

'Oh, he left me.'

'And you won't forgive him?'

'I'm not being given the chance.' There was a pause. 'Andy, can I ask you about Dale?'

'What do you want to know exactly?'

'It's just that when I talked to Greg, well, I think I may have somehow said the wrong thing. He seemed a bit startled, upset almost.'

'What on earth did you say?'

'I don't know, ordinary things, you know, good wishes, and so on.'

Andy shook his head. 'Well, of course people are not all the same the way they respond. Everyone takes things differently. Marilyn's never really accepted it, that's the way she copes.'

'Can't she and Greg talk about it?'

'Greg wants to but she won't apparently.'

Ria felt stung by the way men shrugged things off. Dale was in Hawaii, his mother clearly missed him and yet things were stuck in this impasse. She and Danny hadn't made a brilliant job of sorting their children out, but they had tried. Both of them, she gave Danny that much. This matter of Dale was very baffling. 'Surely all Greg has to do is to work it out with her, dates and times of visits.'

'He was trying to and then she disappeared to Ireland.'

'But when does she think he will come back?'

'In the fall.'

'That's a long time and she still leaves that room like that?' Ria was puzzled.

'What did she tell you about it all?' Andy asked.

'Nothing at all. She never mentioned she had a son at all.'

Andy looked upset and a little silence fell between them. And then they didn't speak about the matter again. There were plenty of other things to talk about. He told her about his childhood in Pennsylvania, she told him about her mother's obsession with the movies, he explained the passion for baseball and she told him about hurling and the big final every year in Croke Park. He told her how to make a great Caesar salad and she explained about potato cakes. She enjoyed the evening and knew he had too.

He drove her back to Tudor Drive and they sat awkwardly for a few moments in the car. She did not like to invite him in in case it would be misunderstood. Then they both spoke at once.

'If ever business takes you to Ireland . . .' Ria began.

'The conference ends on Wednesday at lunchtime . . .' Andy said.

'Please go on . . .' she said.

So he finished what he was going to say. 'And I was wondering if I drove back this way and made you a Caesar salad would you cook those potato cakes?'

'It's a deal,' Ria said with a big smile and got out of the car.

Years ago when they went out with fellows the big question always asked was 'Are you seeing him again?' And now she was back in that situation, a fellow had asked to see her again. With all that implied.

Ria stood in her bedroom and looked out on the beautiful garden that this strange woman had created. From what she had heard, Marilyn Vine spent every waking moment with her hands in the earth pulling and changing and turning the soil and coaxing the flowers and climbers to come up out of the ground.

She felt very out of place here. The friendship that she had thought she might have with Carlotta and Heidi had not bloomed. Both women seemed embarrassed at the effusion of the first night, and had made no attempt to arrange another jolly threesome. Despite the admiration in Andy Vine's eyes she felt no real sense of being pleased and flattered. He was just a strange man from a different world to hers. True, Westville was peaceful and beautiful, a place of trees and a river and a gracious easygoing lifestyle with superficial courtesy and warmth everywhere. But it wasn't home. And at home her children had gone out to Colm's restaurant for a hilarious evening with their new family. And Marilyn Vine had been across the room at a table with Rosemary. And I was here alone. Tears came down her face. She must have been mad to think this was a good idea. Totally mad.

It was dawn in Tara Road. Marilyn had not slept well. What an ugly scene that had been at the restaurant. Everything had suddenly slipped out of control. All these people were like characters playing their parts in a drama. And not a very pleasant drama. Rosemary and Gertie had filled her in on some of the background. Stories of Ria's broken marriage, the new relationship, the puzzlement of the children, the known unreliability of that offensive drunken singer, the possible criminal connection of the heavy men who had eventually taken her away. These people knew everything about everyone and were not slow in discussing it. There was no dignity, reserve, self-preservation.

Rosemary had talked about it being natural that people might assume she was gay since she was single and had a sister who was already 'out' with a partner who was a lawyer. Gertie had told her about her husband's problems coping with drink and violence. She spoke as if Jack had been prone to getting chest colds in the winter. Colm had approached their table with a casual apology over the incident as if it had not been the most excruciatingly embarrassing moment of her life. The two women had told her how they had initially thought Ria was mad to go to America and leave her children but they hoped it would all work out for the best.

Marilyn could not take in the degree of involvement and indeed interference that these people felt confident to have in everyone else's life. They thought nothing of discussing the motives and private sorrows of their friend with Marilyn who was after all a complete stranger, here purely because of an accidental home exchange. While she felt sympathy for Ria and all that had happened to her, she also felt a sense of annoyance.

Why had she not kept her dignity, and refused to allow all these people into her life? The only way to cope with tragedy and grief was to refuse to permit it to be articulated and acknowledged. Deny its existence and you had some hope of survival. Marilyn got out of bed and looked down on the messy garden and the other large red-brick houses of the neighbourhood. She felt very lost and alone in this place where garrulous people wanted to know everything about you and expected you to need the details of their lives too.

She ached for the cool house and beautiful garden in Westville. If she were there now she could go and swim lengths of her pool safe in the knowledge that no one would call and burden her with post-mortems about last night. Clement the cat who slept on her bed every night woke up and stretched and came over to her hopefully. He was purring loudly. The day was about to begin, he was expecting a game and a bowl of something.

Marilyn looked at him sadly. 'I don't usually talk to animals, Clement, but I'm making an exception in your case. I made the wrong decision coming here. It was the worst decision I ever made in my life.'

7

'Do you think when we're talking to Granny we should call her Nora?' Brian asked.

'What?' Annie looked up from her book.

'You know . . . if we call Bernadette's mother by her first name maybe we should do the same with Granny.' Brian wanted to be fair.

'No, Brian, and shut up,' said Annie.

'You always say shut up, you never say anything nice, not ever at all.'

'Who could say anything nice to you, Brian, honestly?'

'Well, some people do.'

'Who apart from Mam and Dad? And they *have* to because you're what they got.'

'Finola often says nice things.'

'Tell me one nice thing she said to you today, go on tell me.'

'She said it was good that I had remembered to let my knights command the centre of the board.'

'And had you?' Annie still refused chess lessons and she couldn't accept that Brian had mastered it.

'Well, only by accident in a way. I just sort of put them out there and they were commanding and she was very pleased with me.' Brian smiled at the triumph of it all.

Sometimes he was more pathetic than awful, Annie thought, you'd feel sorry for him. And he didn't really understand that their lives were going to change. He thought that after the summer everyone would go back to their own homes. He had even asked Bernadette's mother if they could go on playing chess in the autumn when they came back from America. Their games wouldn't have to end then, would they? Finola had said that they could surely continue to play whenever he came to visit his dad and she happened to be around. Stupid Brian had just looked bewildered. In his heart he thought that Dad might be coming home. He hadn't taken on board that this was the way things were always going to be.

Kitty had said that Bernadette must be very, very clever to have got her claws into Annie's father. Despite the ban Annie still managed to see Kitty by dint of visiting the library. Since Annie read a lot now, from sheer lack of anything else to do as she kept telling them, it was considered legitimate that she visit the library. Kitty would come along too and report on the real world of motorbike rallies, of discos and of great crowds who hung out in bars. Annie listened wistfully to the freedom of it all.

But Kitty was more interested in the sexual side of it all, and was fascinated by Bernadette. 'She looks so dumb and half asleep you'd never have thought it. She must be like one of these sirens, one of these famous courtesans who had captured people by wiles. There *were* women who could make men their sexual slaves. It would be interesting to know exactly how.'

'She's hardly likely to tell me,' Annie said dryly.

'But you all get on so well,' Kitty said, amazed. 'I thought you'd hate her taking your mother's place and everything.'

'No, she hasn't taken Mam's place, she's just made a new place. It's hard to explain.'

'And she lets you do what you want, that's good anyway.'

'No, I said she doesn't bother us, that's a different thing. She doesn't make any rules except about you. She's obviously got a heavy message from Dad that you're a no-go area,' Annie grinned.

Kitty was puzzled. 'I always thought he liked me, I even thought he fancied me a bit, that I was in there with a chance. Your mother was on to me – that's why *she* didn't want me round the place.'

Annie was shocked. 'Kitty, you wouldn't have.'

'I wouldn't have wanted to be your stepmother. I thought a bit of clubbing, going to fancy places . . .' Kitty wiggled her hips. 'A bit of you know . . . he's a good-looking man, your dad.'

Annie looked at her with a sick feeling. Kitty had had sex with fellows, and she said it was usually great. Sometimes it was boring but mainly it was great. Annie shouldn't knock it until she'd tried it. But Annie knew she was never going to try it, it was frightening and urgent and out of control and horrible. Like what she had seen in the lane that day. And like Orla King, the woman who sang and made all the trouble in Colm's, she had been singing and talking about sex. It was a horrible, upsetting, confusing business. She remembered her mother explaining it all to her years back and saying that it was very good because it made you feel specially close and warm when you loved someone.

Some good it had done poor Mam feeling close and warm. And it wasn't as if at her age she was ever going to feel close and warm to anyone again, like Dad had done. So easily.

Ria decided to have her hair done for her date with Andy on Wednesday night. But she would not go to Carlotta's. She would not let these women think that she was clingy and dependent even if it were true.

There were other beauty salons in Westville or nearby. In fact she remembered seeing one in a shopping mall that she had driven to not long ago. She would go and investigate. Expertly she backed Marilyn Vine's car out of the carport and by chance met Carlotta who was collecting her mail.

The greeting was warm. 'Hi! Now isn't this a bit of luck, I was hoping to see you.'

'Here I am,' Ria said with a smile fixed to her face.

What did the woman *mean*, she was hoping to see her? She lived next door for heaven's sake. 'Yes, well, I didn't want to keep coming on top of you. I know Marilyn values her privacy...'

'Marilyn is Marilyn,' Ria said tartly. 'I'm Ria.' She felt it was a childish, petulant outburst, something Brian would have said a few years ago. She must be getting unhinged.

If Carlotta was startled she managed to hide it. 'Sure, well what I was going to say was that Tuesday evening we have a hair product company coming to the salon, you know? They want us to buy their line so, as an encouragement, they offer four or five of our regular customers a Special, shampoo, treatment, conditioner, the works ... then if we all like what we see we buy into their range. It happens with various companies a couple of times a year. I wondered would you like to take part? It's not being a guinea-pig or anything, they won't turn your hair purple!'

Ria was astounded. 'But you must have more regular clients.'

'Do come,' Carlotta pleaded.

'Well of course, what time?' It was all arranged. Ria wished she could feel more pleased.

Carlotta was obviously not being cold and distant as she had thought, and it would be good to meet some neighbours. But her heart wasn't in it. Her feelings from Friday night were still with her. This was a strange place, not her home. It was foolish to build up hopes that she would fit in and get to know everyone.

She had been meaning to ring Marilyn in Ireland but couldn't think of anything to say. Still, she shrugged to herself, it was something. And as Hilary would say, it was a free hairdo.

Marilyn braced herself for endless discussions about the scenes in the restaurant when Gertie next arrived. But the woman looked frail and anxious, and wasn't at all eager to speak. Possibly Jack had not appreciated the girls' night out and had showed it in the way he knew best. Gertie for once seemed relieved to be left alone to iron and kneel down and polish the legs of the beautiful table in the front room.

Marilyn worked on in the front garden. She always left Gertie's money in an envelope on the hall table with a card saying thank you. Colm worked in the back garden; there was no communication there either. Rosemary had driven by but hadn't felt it necessary to call. Ria's mother and the insane dog hadn't been in for two days.

Marilyn felt her shoulders getting tense. Perhaps she had managed to persuade them that she didn't want to be part of some big holiday camp with them all.

As Gertie was leaving, she paused and congratulated Marilyn on the work she had done. 'You have a fierce amount of energy, Marilyn,' she said.

'Thank you.'

'I hope it gets better for you, whatever it is that's wrong,' Gertie said, and then she was gone.

Marilyn flushed a dark red. How *dare* these people assume there was something wrong? She had confided nothing to them, answered their very intrusive questions vaguely and distantly. They had no right to presume that there was anything wrong. She had been tempted to tell Ria during that very first conversation the extent of her grief, but now she was glad she hadn't. If she had told Ria Lynch, nerve centre of all the information and concern of the city it appeared, then it would probably have been published in the newspapers by now.

Marilyn had intended to call Ria in Westville but held off. There was nothing to say.

The phone rang in the sunny kitchen where Ria was busy making her scrapbook of Things to Do for when the children arrived.

'Hi Ria? It's Heidi! I've found a course for beginners on the Internet. Shall we sign on?'

'I'm sorry to be so wet, Heidi. I don't know if I'd understand it, I might be left behind.'

'But it's *for* people like us who aren't computer literate. It's not for bright kids. All we need is basic keyboard skills, you've got those.'

'If I can remember them.'

'Of course you can, and it's only five lessons.'

'Is it very expensive, Heidi? I hate sounding like my clinically mean sister and brother-in-law but I do have to hold on to my dollars for when the kids come out.'

'No it's not expensive at all, but anyway it's my treat. We get a reduction through the Faculty Office and anyway I want someone to go with.'

'I can't.'

'Wednesday and Friday this week and then three days the following week and hey we're on the World Wide Web.'

'Oh, I'm not sure about this Wednesday,' Ria began.

'Come on, Ria, you're not doing anything else are you?'

'No, no, it's not that ... it's just ...'

'I'd love you to come, it's only for an hour – they think rightly that we can't concentrate any longer ... it's twelve to one.'

'Oh it's in the *day*time,' Ria said with relief. 'Then of course I'll come, Heidi. You tell me where to go.'

Greg telephoned Marilyn from Hawaii.

'Thank you for your letter,' he said.

'It was still very stilted, I tried to say more,' she said.

'Still, we're talking, writing. That's good. Better anyway.'

She didn't want him to begin defining things too much. 'And are *you* all right, Greg?'

'I'm okay ... summer courses, kids who know nothing, then graduate. Then there are graduate students, far too many bright kids who'll never get appointments. What else is new in university?' He sounded relaxed. This was as near as they had been to a real conversation for a long time.

'I wish they had e-mail here,' Marilyn said.

'You could have taken your laptop, I suppose?' he said.

'I know. I didn't think of it at the time.'

'I spoke to Ria Lynch by the way. She called me here, she sounded very pleasant.'

'Nothing wrong?'

'No, just to check if Andy was who he said he was. He was passing through Westville and wanted to contact you.'

'That was good of Andy. And did Ria meet him?'

'No, no she just called him at the motel.'

'I hope she's getting on okay. I don't want to call her there too often; it sounds as if I'm checking up on her,' Marilyn said.

'I know what you mean,' Greg said. 'And what sort of feeling do you get about her, from being in her home?'

'What do you mean, feeling?'

'Does she sound a bit odd or anything?'

'Why do you ask that?' Marilyn's voice was cold now. 'I thought you said you had a conversation with her yourself?'

'Sure. I just got the impression that she might be very religious, spiritual or something.'

'I never got that,' Marilyn said, puzzled. 'In Ireland of course the place is coming down with churches and bells ringing and statues but I didn't think she was into all that.'

'No, maybe I got it wrong. It was just something she said.'

'What exactly?'

'Well, no, nothing important I guess. As I said, I got it wrong. What's the place you're staying in like?'

'It's a beautiful house, everything's so old here. People are different, they keep dropping by but they don't stay long. Oh, and there's a cat, Clement, an enormous ginger cat.'

'That sounds good, and have you things to do?'

'Yes, I garden a lot, and I walk and . . . it's all okay, Greg.'

'I'm glad you're happy,' he said.

'Yes. Well.'

'But you're all right anyway?' He sounded anxious.

'Sure, Greg, I'm all right,' she said.

Marilyn went back into the garden and dug with renewed vigour. She would not ask Greg why Ria had sounded odd. It didn't matter. Nothing mattered except that she put in her time here and got on to whatever happened next.

A shadow fell over her and there was Colm standing beside her. She put up a hand to keep the sun out of her eyes.

'Hallo,' he said.

'Hi,' Marilyn said.

'I'm not a great believer in words as apologies, so I brought you some flowers instead.'

'It wasn't your fault.'

'It was my place where it all happened. Anyway it's over. Please Almighty

God may it be over! In all my anxiety-dreams about running a restaurant, and they were pretty vivid let me tell you, I never thought up that particular scenario.'

In spite of herself Marilyn found that she was smiling. 'As you say, it's over. Thanks for the flowers. I also need your advice about where to get soil and fertiliser when I've cleared that undergrowth.'

'I'll take you.' Colm looked amazed at her achievement. She had done the work of three men uprooting and cutting back. Soon the earth would be ready to function.

'Danny Lynch must be very grateful to you.'

'What on earth for?' She was genuinely surprised.

'For improving the value of his property, that sort of thing is a big priority in his life.'

'You don't like him very much.'

'I don't like what he did to Ria and how he did it, that's true. But I don't know now whether I liked him before or not. I think I probably did.' Colm tried to remember.

'I'm not doing it for him, I'm doing it for Ria and the house,' Marilyn said.

'Well, same thing. They'll have to sell it eventually.'

'Never!' Marilyn was shocked.

'Well, how can he keep two families *and* keep this place going? But enough about Danny Lynch and all the trouble he causes everywhere he goes.'

'Was he the problem with the little blonde chantoosie as my dad used to call them.'

'Chantoosie! That's a marvellous word. Yes, he was one of her problems, another was a carnation vase filled with vodka.' She looked at him open-mouthed. 'Come to Ireland, Marilyn, and see it all, nature red in tooth and claw. Will you come out to dinner tonight? I want to check out some of the opposition. I'd love your company.'

'Thank you so much,' said Marilyn Vine.

She would not mention it, however, when Gertie next came in to clean the house and iron her clothes. Nor did she refer to it in the thank-you note she wrote and left at Rosemary's elegant house. No need to overburden people with information.

'I was wondering would you like me to call you Nora, Granny?'

'Have you gone off your head, Brian?' his grandmother answered.

'Told you but you wouldn't listen,' Annie said triumphantly.

'What's all this about?' Nora Johnson looked from one to the other suspiciously.

'It's one more sign that he should be in a straitjacket,' said Annie.

'Well I know you're pretty old, Granny, but you're not *that* old, are you? And I thought it would be more friendly, make us all the same somehow.'

Annie raised her eyes to heaven. 'And will you call Dad "Danny" when we go down to the boat tonight? And will you have a few more upsetting things to say to your friend "Ria" when she rings up from America next?'

Nora Johnson looked at her grandson. His face was troubled. 'You know what, Brian? I'd actually like to be called Nora, on reflection I would. That's what they call me in St Rita's.'

'But they're a hundred and ten in St Rita's,' cried Annie in rage. 'Of course they call you Nora.'

'And of course Pliers calls me Nora,' said her grandmother.

Annie looked at her in horror. 'The *dog* calls you Nora, Granny?'

'In his heart he does, he doesn't think of me as a Mrs Johnson figure. Yes, Brian, I'm Nora to you from now on.'

'Thanks, Granny, I knew it was for the best,' said Brian happily.

The entire family was going mad, Annie decided. And now they had to go to Tara Road and say hallo to Mrs Vine before they left for the boat on the Shannon. Mam wanted it. It would be friendly she said, and courteous. Mam lived in a different world when all was said and done.

Mrs Vine had a plate of horrible ginger-snap biscuits that would break your teeth and she had made some ham sandwiches.

'Nothing, thank you,' Annie said firmly.

'But please do, I got them ready for you.'

'I'm very sorry, Mrs Vine, I don't eat dead animals, and I find the biscuits a bit hard, so is it all right if I just drink the tea?'

'Of course, let me see . . . I have some frozen cheesecake, I could defrost that for you, it won't take long.'

'I eat ham sandwiches,' Brian said. 'I'll eat them all so that they won't go to waste. I mean apart from the ones you'll be eating yourself.' He reached out for the plate. 'We could divide them up.'

Annie didn't have to say 'Brian', her face said it fairly loudly.

'Or indeed leave them where they are and eat them as the urge comes on us,' he said apologetically.

Marilyn felt that she couldn't have made a worse start. 'I hope you'll both enjoy your visit to Westville,' she began.

'Do they have proper biscuits there?' Brian wondered.

'Yes, quite a range,' Marilyn assured him.

He nodded, pleased.

'I'm sure it will be great, Mam says she loves it. We were talking to her on Friday night.' Annie was trying hard to be polite and to make up for rejecting both kinds of hospitality. 'I think she's getting to know the place. She was going out to dinner in a Thai restaurant.'

This was puzzling. Who could have invited Ria to that new place that had opened a couple of months back? Or would she have gone on her own? 'Does your mother like different food tastes?'

'She's always cooking certainly.'

Brian looked around the kitchen of Tara Road, empty of its normal wire trays filled with scones, breads and cakes. 'You don't do much cooking yourself, Mrs Vine?' he said slightly censoriously. 'Daddy's friend Bernadette doesn't either. Her mother Finola does but only when she's in her own place. Though I think she's going to cook on the boat . . . do you think she is, Annie?'

'I hadn't given it much thought,' Annie said through gritted teeth. 'And I'm not sure Mrs Vine wants to hear all about it either.'

'I wonder if I could ask you both to call me Marilyn?' she asked them suddenly. The much-repeated address of Mrs Vine was beginning to grate on her nerves. The girl resented her somehow for being in their mother's house. Or maybe she resented her mother for having gone away.

Brian accepted that eagerly. 'Yes I think it's much better, if you ask me,' he said.

'Is that you digging up the garden or is it Colm? We saw an awful lot of stuff out there.'

'Well it's mainly me, I just love it. But Colm *is* going to help me get new soil and plant things where they can reach the light. Maybe you'd like to choose some plants?' she asked without much hope.

The telephone rang just then. They heard the sound of their mother's voice on the machine. 'Hi Marilyn, it's Ria. I was just calling to say...'

'It's Mam,' cried Brian, running for the phone.

'Brian, wait,' Annie called.

'No, please,' Marilyn insisted.

'Mam, Mam, it's Brian, we're here, how did you know?'

Marilyn and Annie's eyes met. Somehow in that moment Marilyn felt the hostility beginning to depart. It was as if they were both adults looking at the baby Brian who thought his mother had tracked him down.

'Yeah she's fine, she's chopped down most of the front garden.'

Annie sighed. 'You get to expect a lot of that sort of thing with Brian,' she explained to Marilyn. 'He always manages to say the one thing you don't want him to say. I'll sort it out.'

And to give her great credit she did sort it out.

'Hi Mam. It's Annie. Yes, we're here having tea. Yes, very nice indeed. I read a lot... it's all so boring in Dad's place I've had to become a compulsive reader. *Catch-22* and *The Thorn Birds*. Yes, she did ask us to call her Marilyn. No, that is not Brian being mad this time, but don't mind him about the garden, it's only a few weeds, and Colm's helping her so stop panicking. And we're off tonight but we'll ring you on Saturday.'

When Marilyn finally did get on the telephone Ria was very apologetic.

'I'm so sorry, I didn't mean to make it a family conference.'

'It was just good timing, and it's all going well?'

'Oh yes, brilliantly, and with you?'

'Couldn't be better.'

'You were at Colm's restaurant, I hear?'

'Yes, the resident pianist drank a vase of vodka. And they tell me *you* went to the new Thai restaurant in Westville. You liked it?'

'Yes, terrific, lovely green shrimp curry.' Ria didn't say that she had been there with Marilyn's brother-in-law. 'Look, it's silly us talking now, why don't you call me back later tonight using my phone?'

'I'm going out tonight.'

'Oh good, where are you off to?'

'I arranged to go out to the cinema, there's a movie I really want to see,' lied Marilyn who did not want to say she was going out to dinner with Colm Barry.

They agreed to talk later in the week.

'Is Bernadette up to high doh packing and everything for the holiday?' Barney asked.

'No, not at all.' Danny was constantly surprised at how gently she moved through life. There would be no lists, no plans, checking through things, emptying fridges, cancelling people, phone calls. Twenty minutes before they left she would put a few items in a bag. He would pack his own case. The children had lists of what they should take taped to their cases by Ria. 'No, she's amazing, Barney. I don't know where she gets her serenity. It's infectious too, seriously, it's catching. Sometimes when I get fussed, I only have to be with her for ten minutes and it's all all right again.'

'What do you get fussed about, Danny?'

'Lots of things. Money, work, a madwoman living in my house cutting down my front garden, Ria being so unaccepting of everything that's happened.'

'Hey, is it that bad?' Barney asked.

'I don't usually give a long list of moans, but you did ask and today's not a good day. There's a long drive ahead, then a cramped cruiser for seven days that I can ill afford to be out of the office, Bernadette's mother thinking I'm made of money, and the kids seem to be on top of us all the time.'

'And there was a bit of trouble with Orla King on Friday night?'

'God, you know everything, Barney! How did you hear that?'

'A friend of Polly's was with Monto's party. He said the owner came over to them with barked instructions that Orla be got out before she got to your table. It wasn't quite in time.'

'No, but nearly.'

'You'd want to watch it, Danny.'

'Tell me about it. I'm watching it so feverishly I'd need a dozen eyes.'

The river was full of families getting on to their Shannon cruisers.

Bernadette's mother had arranged a box of groceries from a local store. 'I telephoned ahead to order them,' she explained to Danny.

'Great, Finola.' He seemed relieved.

It had been a long car journey. In the beginning, as they left the Dublin late-afternoon traffic, he was tense. His shoulders were cramped, he had a dozen worries and his conversation with Barney had not helped. Twice he had made foolish mistakes pulling out of the traffic without checking. Tactfully Finola had offered to drive and eventually he accepted.

Bernadette sat in the front and played them tapes which she had assembled specially for the holiday. It was a restful choice, gentle Irish music, harpists or uileann pipes, non-strident Greek bouzouki, nocturnes by Chopin, deep soulful French songs that none of them understood, pan-pipes, violin music that no one recognised. Danny sat in the back of his own car between his daughter and son and slept fitfully as Finola Dunne drove them to the Midlands.

He dreamed that Ria was waiting for them on the boat. 'Aren't you going to go home?' she asked Bernadette in the dream. And Bernadette had just shrugged, and said 'If you like.' Danny had wanted to run after her but his feet were rooted to the ground. The dream was still very real to him as they got out of the car and began to settle into their boat.

'So will you then?' Finola said to him.

'Will I what?' Danny was genuinely puzzled.

'Will you pay this man for the groceries?'

'What? Yes, of course.' He took out his credit card; the man shook his head, so he took out a cheque-book. He saw the last cheque stub. It was a payment for their mortgage to the building society. The grocery bill was enormous. The cost of the cruiser was on his credit card. He didn't even want to think about it.

But he knew he would *have* to think about it one day soon.

Colm took Marilyn to Quentin's. He said he wanted to show off Dublin's finest. Also he knew the Brennans who ran the place.

'Very full for a Monday, that's the booming economy for you,' he said approvingly, looking around the many tables that were occupied.

'Nonsense, Colm. You should explain to Mrs Vine that they come because the food is so brilliant,' said Brenda Brennan.

'This I can believe,' Marilyn murmured politely.

'I see you've got Barney McCarthy in with a crowd,' Colm observed.

A shadow crossed Brenda's face. 'Yes, indeed we have,' she said. Colm raised his eyebrow as if to ask what was the problem. 'I'll let you study the menu,' Brenda Brennan said, and moved away.

'Does she not like those people?' Marilyn had picked up a vibe.

'No, it's not that. I think she may have had the same problem as I've had.'

'Which is?'

'A very big cheque returned from the bank.'

'Really!' Marilyn put on her glasses and studied the party by the window. 'They look very substantial people, not the kind that would bounce a cheque.'

'No, they never did before. And the problem is they're important. They know everyone; you wouldn't want to insult them, *and* also to be fair they have brought in big business in the past. So it's all a bit tricky.' He looked over at the large man who was being expansive as a host to nine other people. A smart, much younger woman was laughing.

'Is that his wife?'

'No, that's Polly. His wife's at home in a mansion.'

'Will you sue him?'

'No. I'll be full next time he books, I'll just kiss one big bill goodbye. No point in going to court over one dinner.'

Marilyn looked at him admiringly. 'You're so right. In the States we are much too litigation-conscious. You're sensible to think of it as one big dinner and not to worry too much about it.'

'But I do worry about it. Barney McCarthy more or less owns Danny Lynch. If he goes down so will Danny, and what will happen to Ria then?'

Rosemary was legendary for the speed of her weekly business meetings. They were held early in the morning, a large dish of fresh fruit, a lot of strong coffee and a rapid agenda. Accountant, office manager, marketing manager, and her own personal assistant, all trained to present speedily their reports and follow-ups. They went rapidly through Accounts, New Business, Overtime and What the Rivals Are Up To. Then it came to Problems.

'A really big cheque returned from the bank, I'm afraid,' the accountant said.

'How much? Who?'

'Eleven thousand, Barney McCarthy.'

'That's an error, that's a bank oversight,' Rosemary said, about to go on to the next item.

'I see Polly's Dress Hire is for sale in this morning's paper.' The accountant was laconic.

'Thanks. Then it's not an oversight. I'll call the bank.'

'They won't tell you anything.'

'They'll tell *me*,' said Rosemary.

When the meeting was over she dialled Danny Lynch's mobile phone. It was not picking up. 'You're not doing this to me, Danny, you little bastard. You've done enough to everyone, and I can tell you straight out you're not doing this to me, not after all we've been through.' But she was speaking to herself not to Danny, since he was on the Shannon without a care in the world.

Hilary said that she was going to invite Marilyn to come for a swim out in the Forty Foot. They could go out on the DART.

'That's an unusual idea,' her mother said.

'Martin suggested it. He said it would save the cost of buying her a meal.'

'True,' said Nora Johnson.

'And still be entertaining her.'

'It would.'

Nora Johnson sighed a deep sigh. How had she raised a daughter who thought only in terms of saving money? Hilary hadn't been like that as a child, surely she hadn't. They never had much when she worked in the dry cleaners and the mother and two daughters were all slightly wistful about what they would buy had they the money, but it had not been obsessive. Martin had changed her, dragged her down. Still, at least he hadn't abandoned her for a teenage waif. Nora sighed again. Sometimes she felt it was all very hard.

Hilary looked at her in concern. She didn't like all this sighing. 'Mam, don't you think it's about time you moved into Ria's house?'

'*What?*'

'Well, not when Marilyn's there, of course, but as soon as she goes.'

'What would I do that for?'

'To have company for you and to pay Ria some rent.'

'I don't need company.'

'Of course you do, Mam. But whether you do or not Ria will definitely need someone to pay her something when Danny's grand plans are all sorted out.'

'You can't be serious.'

'I am. Get in there, Mam, before she asks someone else.'

'Hilary, have you a brain in your head? Poor Ria will be out of that house by Christmas.'

'*What!*'

'Barney McCarthy's on his uppers. I saw in today's paper that Polly Callaghan's business is for sale. If he's selling the floozy's dress-hire outfit he must be down to looking in kiddies' money boxes. And when he goes for the high jump then so will Danny Boy. Your brother-in-law will have one of his boards up outside that house before Ria gets back.'

They all took turns at steering the boat. It was simple while you were still in the river, but when it broadened into a lake there were real rules. You had to keep the black buoys on one side and the red on the other. They waved to Germans and Dutch people they had met already, more expert at mooring and casting off than they were. They bought ice creams when they drew in and tied up at the small villages, or went to pubs where they played darts.

'Wouldn't Mam love this!' Brian said once as a flight of birds came out of the reeds and soared above them. The silence was worse than any number of people telling him to shut up.

'Sorry,' he said.

Bernadette spoke dreamily. 'Brian, of course you must mention your mother, she's not dead or anything. And maybe one day you'll take her on a trip like this.'

Annie and Brian saw Danny reach out and stroke Bernadette's face in gratitude. He sort of traced it with his fingers and pushed her hair back. There was such love and tenderness in the gesture it was almost embarrassing to watch.

The boy Hubie who taught the course 'Don't Fear the Internet' looked about sixteen. In fact he was not much older. This was his first venture into business, he said, and he wanted to make sure all the customers were satisfied so if there were any areas they didn't understand then he wasn't doing his job right.

Ria found to her surprise that she seemed to understand it. It wasn't a world that only people like Rosemary understood, it was quite ordinary. A way of getting in touch. She saw how easy it would be to get sucked in and to spend all day browsing, looking up amazing facts and talking to strangers on the screen.

She had lunch with Heidi afterwards and they went over what they had learned and what they should practise before meeting Hubie again on Friday. He had asked them to send him messages which he would answer. It was easy for Heidi, she had all the computers and word processors in the Alumni Office. But where would Ria go?

'Marilyn has a laptop that she didn't take away with her. You could use that.'

'Oh, I'd be afraid I might break it.'

'No, of course not. Tell her on the phone you want to use it and I'll set it up for you.'

'Do you think it wouldn't be intrusive?'

'No, it's only machinery. But Ria . . . I don't think you should mention that Hubie is our teacher.'

'Why ever not?'

'Well, he was a friend of Dale's, you see.'

'Well, what's so bad about that?'

'You know . . .'

'I don't know. All I know is that Dale's in Hawaii . . .'

'What?'

'Well, with his father. Isn't he?'

Heidi was silent.

'Heidi, where else is he? He's not here, he's not in Ireland. His room is there waiting for him.'

'Dale's dead,' Heidi said.

'No, he can't be dead. You should see his room, that's not the room of someone dead.'

'Dale's dead, that's what it's all about. Marilyn won't accept it.'

Ria was more shocked than she had been for a very long time. 'Why didn't she tell me?'

'She won't speak about it. Not to anyone. Not even to Greg. That's why he's in Hawaii.'

'He left her?'

'No, he thought she'd come with him but apparently not, they had been there once with Dale.'

'How old was Dale?'

'Not quite sixteen.'

Oh God, thought Ria, Annie's age. 'How did he die?'

'A motorcycle accident.'

'But surely he was too young to ride a . . . ?'

'Exactly.'

'Why on earth didn't she tell me?' Ria shook her head. 'I was coming to live in her home after all. She'd know I'd see his room. I even dust it, for heaven's sake.'

Heidi was gentle. 'She doesn't have the words to tell people.'

'When did it happen?'

'March of last year. They turned off the machine in August.'

'The machine?'

'Life-support machine.'

'Poor Marilyn. What a decision to have to make.'

'She thinks they made the wrong one, that's why she has no peace.'

'Well, if she has no peace, I sure as hell wonder whether she'll find it in Tara Road,' said Ria.

Marilyn lay in her bath and Clement sat on the bathroom chair as if he were somehow guarding her. Gertie had told her that Clement didn't normally go upstairs.

'Well, he does now,' Marilyn had said.

'It's just that when Ria comes back, he might you know, being only a cat, still think he's welcome up here.' Gertie had tried to be tactful, but wasn't making a good fist of it.

'I'm sure Ria's doing things in my house that I don't approve of either but we agreed that we would put up with that for the summer.' Marilyn sounded brisk and firm.

'But are there any living things in your house?' Gertie wanted to know.

'No living things,' Marilyn had said.

As Marilyn added more hot water to her bath Clement yawned a great yawn.

'I fought for you, Clement. Don't yawn at me like that,' she said.

Clement closed his mouth and went back to sleep. Marilyn wondered at all the living things that Ria had left behind her.

Andy arrived with a cold-bag full of food. He had also brought a bottle of wine. 'You look very nice,' he said appreciatively. 'Very nice indeed.'

'Thank you.' It had been so long since anyone had paid her a compliment. *You look fine, sweetheart* was the most Danny had said to her for ages. And in the last years Annie had said little except *You look absolutely terrible in that colour*. Rosemary had said she looked well when she dressed up but the implication was that it was not often enough. Hilary had remarked that fine feathers make fine birds. Her mother had said there was nothing to beat a good navy costume and a white blouse and that it was a pity when people with as much class and opportunity as Ria wore streelish-looking things that you wouldn't see on a halting site. True, Colm sometimes said she looked well. But it was more a compliment to the house or the garden, or Ria as part of the scene, than to herself.

So it was unusual to be admired openly by a man.

Then the cooking began by rubbing the garlic around the bowl for the Caesar salad. There was a lot of gesture, flourish and fuss but it tasted very good. And then they began on the potato cakes.

'Oh, they're latkes,' Andy said, a little disappointed. He had thought it was something totally unknown.

'Are they?' Ria was disappointed too.

'But I actually like them a lot. And these are Irish latkes so that makes them special,' he said.

So they laughed over that and over a lot of things. He told her about the conference and the madwoman organising it who was at such a level of stress she was almost ready to ignite. Arranging the seating plan for the conference dinner, a matter of no importance whatsoever, had her on heavy sedation.

'How did it go, the dinner, in the end?' Ria asked.

'No idea, it's tonight.'

'And you didn't wait for it?'

'I thought this would be more fun, and I was right,' he said.

Ria had made a strawberry shortcake which they had with coffee.

'You mean you didn't buy this at the gourmet shop?'

'No, my own two hands,' she laughed and stretched out her newly manicured hands.

'But you bought the pastry surely?'

'No way. I make pastry quick as looking at you.' Andy was very impressed. She was enjoying this in a childish way. She told him about the Internet lessons and asked did he think Marilyn would mind her using the laptop.

'Not a bit, I'll set it up for you.'

'I should ask first.'

'Look, it's like using someone's telephone, or the vacuum . . . it's not like a finely tuned piano or anything.'

'But suppose . . . ?'

'Come on, where does she keep it?'

'It's in the study.'

They went into the pleasant book-lined room and Andy opened the machine. 'I'll show you how to boot it up then you'll be able to do it for yourself.' As he spoke the telephone rang and because they were not in the room with the answering machine Ria answered it automatically.

'Hallo?' she said as if she were back in Dublin and this was her phone.

'Ria? It's Greg Vine.'

'Oh Greg. How are you?' Her eyes met Andy's across the desk. The natural thing, the normal thing would have been to say 'You won't believe it but your brother is here.' That's what people would say if it were an ordinary situation surely. But then it might need a lot more explanation than was necessary. And might imply things which didn't need to be implied. So she said nothing about Andy Vine being four feet away from her with a half-smile on his face as he watched her.

Ria listened to Greg's apologetic request that she find a file for him. It was in the study. 'I'm in the study as we speak,' Ria said.

'Oh good.' He sounded pleased. 'Very technical books I'm afraid and lots of student papers. That's what I want you to get for me, can I direct you?'

'Sure.'

From Hawaii Greg Vine directed her to the wall with Student Notes on it and gave her a year, then a name, then a subject. Each time she repeated them Andy moved and found the document.

'It's just the first page and title of the publications this kid has done, and we need it today.'

'Today?'

'I was going to ask Heidi and Henry as a huge favour to call round and pick it up and e-mail it to me.'

'Heidi and Henry to come round here to pick it up and e-mail it to you tonight?' She repeated every word as if she were a halfwit but she wanted Andy to get the other end of the conversation. He understood immediately. He pointed to the piece of paper, and to the laptop and to his own chest. 'I could send it to you by e-mail myself if you let me use Marilyn's laptop.'

'You know how to e-mail?' He was surprised and pleased.

'Well yes, by chance I do, I went to a lesson this morning with Heidi.'

'Well, well, what amazing luck. I don't need to get Heidi and Henry out at all.' He was overjoyed at the good timing.

Andy had written down 'Get the password and his e-mail address'. And in moments the information was put in, and the message sent.

'It's on my screen now, I can't thank you enough. Who is giving this course anyway? You learned pretty quick.'

Ria remembered that Hubie had been a friend of the dead Dale. 'Oh some man . . . I didn't get his name.'

'Never mind. He saved us all tonight whoever he was.'

When she hung up they looked at each other. One bridge had been crossed almost accidentally.

'Well now, since they think in Hawaii that you're an expert at this, let's make you one,' he said.

Was he sitting a little too close to her? she wondered. 'Let me get my notes.' She jumped up and went for the sheet of paper that Hubie had given them all at the class.

Andy looked at them. 'My God, Hubie Green, he was one of the kids with Dale on the night of the accident.'

Ria looked at him levelly. 'Why didn't you tell me Dale was dead?'

He was shocked. 'But you knew, surely?'

'No, I didn't. I had to wait until Heidi told me.'

'But you mentioned his room, the way it was all laid out.'

'I thought he was in Hawaii. I asked you when was he coming back, you said in the fall.'

'Oh my God, I thought you meant Greg.'

There was a silence while they each realised how the misunderstanding had happened.

'You see they're so very cut up they can't even bring themselves to talk about it. To mention that you knew Hubie Green would bring it all back.'

'I know,' said Ria. 'That's why I pretended I didn't know his name.'

'You did it very well.' Andy was admiring.

'You know a funny thing? At home I am always so honest and undevious, and since I came out here I haven't stopped pretending and covering up things for no reason at all.'

'Oh, there's always a reason,' he smiled.

'Pure misguided niceness, I think,' she said ruefully.

'Okay, so we have to pretend one more thing, which is that you understood this whole getting-on-the-Net thing by yourself and then we can stop pretending, okay?'

'Okay,' she said a little anxiously.

He was definitely sitting too close for friendship. 'Who do we know with e-mail?' he asked.

'Hubie! He said we could send messages any time.'

'Hubie. Yeah.'

'What's wrong? He's a nice kid.'

'Sure.'

'Tell me. I know nothing about what happened, nothing at all. Well, I get the feeling that Marilyn's so private. I felt she wouldn't want me to go round asking questions, that she'd tell me what she wanted me to know, and it's not very much.'

'Do you resent that?'

'I think she should have told me her son was dead. I don't want half of Dublin telling her about poor Ria, poor old Ria whose husband took off with a teenager. So since I get the feeling she's not going to be demanding information from my friends I shouldn't from hers ... it's just ... it's just ...'

'It's just what, Maria?' He had never got the shortened version of her name and somehow she quite liked him calling her something different. It made whatever there was or might be between them something that was out of time.

'It's just that there's a mystery here. There's no mystery in my case, it's as old as time. Man marries wife, man sees newer younger fresher model, man says goodbye to wife. The only mystery is that there's not more of it.'

'Maria, please, you sound so bitter.'

'What, should I be overjoyed about it? At least it's plain to see what happened. Here it's different, quite different. There's like a conspiracy of silence about it all. That room is like a shrine to him. The fact that nobody mentions the accident.'

'But you see ...' Andy began.

'No, to be honest I don't see. Do you know what I said to your brother Greg when I was talking to him in Hawaii? I'll tell you what I said, I asked him how Dale was enjoying it out there. My flesh is creeping when I try to think why he thinks I said what I did.'

'He'll know.' Andy soothed her. 'He'll realise that Marilyn couldn't have told you.'

'Look, I'm as sorry as hell that it all happened. I went into that room again and I cried over the child that I thought was out surfing in Honolulu. I cried to think he's dead and buried, but still we should be able to talk about it. Not all the time, as people say we do in Ireland, but just acknowledge it. She left his room like that and didn't tell me. That's not natural, Andy. Even you freeze up at the mention of that kid Hubie's name. Maybe if nobody else tells me what happened I'll talk to Hubie about it.'

'Don't do that.'

'No, of course I wouldn't but I am pointing out that it's odd.'

'Don't you think we all know that?'

'What do you mean?'

'Listen, in this world there was only one marriage that any of us could think was truly happy and that was Greg and Marilyn's. And yet from the night of the accident they were never able to relate to each other as human beings again.'

'Did they blame each other or something?'

'Well, there's no way they could have. Hubie and two other kids and Dale were all crazy about motorbikes, but they were too young and they all had parents who would have as soon let heroin into the house as let a motorbike into their backyards. So on Hubie's birthday the kids went out somewhere. It was meant to be a picnic, I know because I was here at the time.' He got up and started to walk around the study. 'And they drank some beer and they found two bikes and they decided that this was a gift from the gods.'

'They *found* them?'

'Yes, found as in stole them outside a restaurant. Hubie and the other kid who died, Johnny, were a little bit on the wild side. Not hugely wild but the signs were there. Older too, but not much. But at that age a few months counts.'

'I know.' Ria thought suddenly of Kitty, a year older than Annie but several years ahead of her always.

'And they went for what was described at the inquest as a kind of test drive and they went round a corner and one of the bikes was hit by a truck. Which wasn't surprising really because the bike where Dale was hanging on to Johnny was on the wrong side of the road. Johnny was killed instantly. Dale was on a life-support machine for six months and then they agreed to let him go.'

They sat in silence at the tragedy that had come to this house.

'And Marilyn said that she would never forgive any of them as long as she lived, and Greg said that they would have no peace until they learned to forgive.'

Ria had tears in her eyes. 'And is that what drove them apart?'

'I imagine so. Greg doesn't say much about it. You know how hopeless we men are for talking about feelings.'

'You're not too bad; you've told me that story very sympathetically and it wasn't just idle curiosity on my part, you know.'

'I know,' he said.

'Do you understand how I felt sort of protective about her, how I didn't want to ask Carlotta and Heidi and anyone else?'

'Sure I do, and you understand also why it wouldn't be good to ask Hubie. That kid has had a lot to live with: his birthday, he got them drunk, his friend Johnny driving a stolen bike, and he and another kid walk away alive. I'm kind of impressed with him that he's setting up something like this to make his college tuition.'

'I know, and of course you feel bitter about him,' Ria said.

'It wasn't his fault; he didn't set out to kill Dale or anything,' Andy soothed her.

'But it's awkward, isn't it? I'm sorry to have become involved.'

'Look, it's got nothing to do with you. Come on, Maria, homework time; let's get our assignments done.'

They sent Hubie a message and he sent back *Congratulations Mrs Lynch! You're a natural.* Then they sent one to Heidi.

'She's going to die when they tell her in the Alumni Office tomorrow that there's a message for her from me!' Ria pealed with laughter.

'I wish we knew someone else with an e-mail,' she said.

'Well, we could send one to my laptop back in the motel,' he said.

'And you could ring me tonight to say that it had arrived,' she said.

'Or tomorrow?' he suggested gently. It took a moment for it to dawn on her what he was saying. 'It's so nice here, so good to hear laughter in this house again,' Andy said. 'And you and I have no ties, nobody who will be betrayed or hurt. Wouldn't it be nice if we spent the rest of the evening together?' He had a hand under her chin, lifting her face up towards his.

She swallowed and tried to speak. He took the opportunity of her not speaking to kiss her. Gently but firmly. And he put his arm around her shoulder.

She pulled away, startled. Ria Lynch would be thirty-eight this year. In November, on the anniversary of Clark Gable's death. Nobody had kissed her since she was twenty-two except the man who had tired of her and told her that there was nothing left in what she thought was a fine happy marriage.

'I must explain,' she began.

'Must you?'

'Yes. I've had a lovely, lovely evening, but you see I don't . . .'

'I know, I know.' He was kissing her ear now, gently nuzzling in fact, and it was rather nice.

'Andy, you have to forgive me if I have been giving the wrong signals. I couldn't have had a happier evening. I mean that truly, truly I do, but I don't want it to go any further. I'm not playing games, I never did, not ever, even when I was a kid going out with fellows. But I was often misunderstood and the fault is all mine if you thought things were different. I'm a bit inexperienced, you see.'

'I had hopes when you didn't tell my brother that I was here, you see,' he explained.

'I know, I know.' She knew that was a fair perception.

'But I agree it was a delightful evening. It doesn't *have* to end in bed, it would be much much nicer if it did, but if it's not going to let's remember the good bits.'

'They were all good bits.' She smiled at him, grateful that he hadn't turned on her, outraged that he had been misled.

'Those Irish latkes. Eat-your-heart-out Jewish cookery,' he said.

'That Caesar salad, Emperor of Caesar salads,' she said.

'And that strawberry shortcake. Home-baked pastry already.'

'And the stylish wine in its cool-bag.'

'Hey, there's lots of good bits,' he said.

'Look in your machine tonight, there may well be a Message Pending,' he said, and left.

She cleared up everything and went into the study to see if there were any e-mails for her. There were two. One from Hubie. *Just a test Mrs Lynch to see can you retrieve as well as send! Hubie Green.* And then there was one from Andy. *Thank you so much for the most enjoyable dinner I have had in years. I will definitely be back at the alumni weekend as will Greg but if there's a chance we could meet again before that I would so much enjoy it. Your new friend, Andy Vine.*

Imagine! Boring old Ria Lynch, poor deserted Ria, dreary mumsy tiresome Ria had a new friend called Andy Vine. And had she not said a persuasive no, then she could have had a lover of the same name as well. She looked at herself in the hall mirror and wondered what it would have been like. She had never made love with any man except Danny. Danny, who knew her body so well and brought her such pleasure.

It would have been awkward getting undressed in front of this man. How did people do it? Be so instantly intimate with people they hardly knew? People like Rosemary. But then Rosemary looked like Rosemary. As near perfect as possible. Ria was afraid that her own bottom might be a bit saggy, that she would look floppy when naked. In a way it was a relief not to have to go through the motions of getting to know another body and fear the possible criticism of her own. Yet it would have been nice to have had arms around her and someone wanting her again.

She sighed and went into Dale's room. She turned over the pages of Dale Vine's scrapbook, the pictures of motorbikes, the advertisements, the cuttings about various motorcycle heroes. Marilyn had been strong enough to leave these here, reminders of the machines that had killed her only child, and yet she had not been able to tell the woman who was going to live in her house that her son was dead. This was a very complicated person indeed.

Marilyn had refused so many invitations that she feared she might now be causing offence. She had better go out with Hilary, Ria's discontented and unprepossessing sister. The woman had been very insistent, she had called several times to mention a picnic on the coast. It would be good to swim again, and Marilyn told herself she was a match for any of these inquisitive Irish. Just answer vaguely and ask them about themselves, then they were off, all you had to do was sit back and listen.

Hilary arrived bristling with energy and fuss. 'We'll miss the rush hour on the train which will be good,' she said.

'Good. I'm ready whenever you are.'

'Merciful God, Ria'll go mad when she sees all that work in the garden. Are they digging for treasure or what?'

'Just a bit of clearing-out the undergrowth, it will be perfect when she comes back. Your sister has a very beautiful house, hasn't she?' Marilyn said.

'I'll tell you straight out what I think. I think that Ria and Danny got their money too easy and these things have a habit of coming home to roost.'

'How do you mean exactly? Should we have a cup of coffee or would you like to get on the road, the train?'

'We could have a cup of coffee, I suppose. Were you not cooking, baking like?' Hilary seemed to look around the kitchen with the same disapproval as Brian had, searching for something which was not there.

'Well no. We're going out, aren't we?' Marilyn was startled.

'I thought we might have a picnic out there.'

'Yes, yes what a good idea, will we pass a delicacy shop on the way?'

'A what?'

'You know, somewhere we could buy the picnic.'

'But it would cost as much to buy a picnic in one of those places as to have a meal out. I really meant sandwiches.' Marilyn was beginning to regret this bitterly, but it was too late to turn back. 'We could hard-boil two of those eggs, and take a couple of tomatoes and two slices of ham, bread and butter, and aren't we fine then?'

Hilary seemed to be restored to good humour. The two of them prepared the very basic picnic and caught a bus to the station and then took the little electric train out to Dun Laoghaire. It travelled south along the coast and Marilyn commented with pleasure on all that she saw.

'Martin and I knew you'd enjoy this.' Hilary was pleased.

'Tell me how you met Martin,' Marilyn asked. She listened to the strange downbeat story, told with great pride, of a house saved for and bought, investments made, savings tucked away, economies arranged. They got out of the train and walked along the coast to the place where they were going to swim. And as they walked by the shining but very cold-looking sea Hilary talked about property prices, about Martin's brothers getting the small farm in the west, about the children of fourteen getting pregnant in the school where Martin taught and where she worked in the office.

When they got to the swimming place Marilyn cried out in delight. 'Look at the Martello tower, and the Joyce Museum! I know where we are. This is where *Ulysses* opened. It's the very spot.'

'Yeah, that's right.' Hilary was not very interested in James Joyce.

She pointed out the much photographed sign that said Forty Foot Gentlemen Only, and said she remembered her mother telling her about the feminists first swimming in there to claim it back for everyone.

'But that can't have been in your mother's time surely?'

'It was probably in *my* time! I'll be forty this year,' Hilary said gloomily.

'So will I,' Marilyn said.

A first mark of solidarity between two totally different women. They had a swim which froze Marilyn's blood to the marrow, and then ate their makeshift picnic. Hilary did most of the talking.

'Tell me about Ria's marriage,' Marilyn asked.

They talked about Ria. Hilary told the whole story as she knew it. The sudden announcement and he was gone overnight. The utter folly of it all, the comeuppance which was near at hand. Barney McCarthy wasn't a golden boy any more, and his political pals were not in power. It was curtains for Mr Danny Lynch.

'Did you ever like him?'

'I was nervous about him, he was too smart for Ria, too good-looking. I always said it and it turned out I was right in the end. It gave me no pleasure being right. I'm happily married myself, I'd prefer her to have been. Are you happily married?' Hilary asked suddenly.

'I don't know,' Marilyn said.

'You *must* know.'

'No I don't.'

'And what does your husband think?'

'He thinks we're happily married. We have nothing to say to each other. But he wants to go on as normal.'

'Sex, do you mean?' Hilary asked.

'Yes. It was good once. But no, it would be empty. I had a hysterectomy two years ago, so even if a forty-year-old woman could conceive, which they can, there's no chance for me.'

'I think you're lucky that he still wants to be with you in that way. I can't have children and so Martin thinks we shouldn't have sex. And so we don't.'

'I don't believe you,' Marilyn said.

'It's true.'

'But since when?'

'We're married sixteen years . . . about eight years I'd say, since he knew we couldn't have children.'

'And did you know before?'

'I always knew. I went to a fortune-teller, you see. She told me.'

'Did you believe her?'

'Totally. She's been right about everybody.' Hilary tidied up the remains of their food, and put it into a paper bag.

She was so sure and confident in everything, including the fact that this psychic had told her she wasn't fertile. This was a very strange country. 'Is she a psychic?'

'I don't know, she just knows what's going to happen.'

'Is she a medium? Does she get in touch with the dead?'

'I don't think so,' Hilary said. 'I didn't want to anyway, I only wanted to know about the living.'

'And what else did she tell you?'

'She said I'd be happily married, which is true, and that I'd live in a place with trees but that hasn't happened yet.'

Marilyn paused for a moment to think about a woman who considered herself happily married to a man who thought about nothing except interest rates and didn't believe in sex without the possibility of procreation.

'Is she still around, this woman?' Marilyn asked.

They were getting the best weather ever known for a week in July. Everyone said so. The children were sun-tanned and loving it all.

'Can we take the dinghy out, Dad?' Annie asked.

'No, Annie, it's too dangerous.'

'Why did they give it to us then?'

'They gave it to *us*, Princess, not to you, not to children.'

'Let them, Danny,' Bernadette said.

'No, sweetheart, they don't know about boats.'

'Well, how will they ever learn?' Bernadette asked. 'Suppose they go where we can see them, would that do?' It was a compromise that did fine. Danny looked on proudly as his son and daughter rowed the little boat along the shore.

'You're so good with them, but you're fearless. Ria would have wanted to swim along beside them like a mother duck.'

'You have to let children go free,' she said. 'They hate you otherwise.'

'I know but when we have our baby will you feel the same?' He laid his hand on her stomach and thought about the son or daughter that would be in their home, a real person, by Christmas.

'Of course!' She looked at him in surprise. 'You don't want children, free spirits, all herded into some kind of corral, do you?'

Danny realised that this was exactly what he and Ria had built and why he so badly needed to escape. He lay with his head in her lap and closed his eyes. 'Sleep on, I'll look out at the dinghy,' she said.

'Isn't that amazing?' Finola Dunne was reading them extracts from the newspaper.

'What's amazing?' Danny asked. He was still lying in the grass and Bernadette was making a series of daisy chains which she was spreading over him like threads tying him to the earth.

'Polly's is for sale! That's been the main dress-hire place in Dublin for years.'

'It's never for sale.' Danny sat up suddenly.

'Well, so it says here.'

He took the paper and read the paragraph. 'I have to make a phone call,' he said. 'Where are those goddamn children on their bloody boat, and what the hell did you let them go off for?'

'Danny, they've tied up the dinghy. You were asleep. They've gone to get ice creams. Please, please be calm. You have no idea what's going on.'

'I have a fair idea.'

'Well, what do you think it is? Do you think that if Polly's is being sold Barney's running out of money?' Bernadette asked.

'And you can sit there making daisy chains if you think that?'

'I'd prefer to make daisy chains than to have a heart attack,' Bernadette said.

'Darling darling Bernadette, the world might be about to end for us. You don't understand, you're just a child.'

'I wish you wouldn't say that, you've always known what age I am,' she said.

'I have to talk to Barney, find out what's happening.' Danny's face was white.

'I should wait until you are calmer. You won't understand anything the way you are now.'

'I won't *be* any calmer, not until I know. And maybe not even then. I can't believe he wouldn't tell me, we're friends. I'm like a son to him, he's said so often.'

'Then if he *is* in trouble maybe it was harder to tell you than anyone else.' She saw it quite simply.

'And aren't you worried, frightened?'

'Of what?'

'Of what might be ahead?'

'You mean being poor? Of course not. You've been poor before, Danny. You'll live, you did before.'

'That was then, this is now.'

'You've a lot more to live for now.'

He held both her hands in his. 'I want to give you everything. I want the sun, the moon and the stars for you and our baby.'

She smiled at him, that slow smile that always made him feel weak. She said nothing more. This was what made him feel ten feet tall.

Bernadette didn't busy herself wondering was this strategy better than that. Having urged him to be calm she was now staying out of it. She was leaving it all to him.

'Where's Dad? Annie asked. 'We got him a choc-ice.'

'He went to make a phone call,' Bernadette said.

'Will he be long do you think or should we eat it?' Brian wanted a ruling.

'I think we should eat it,' said Bernadette.

'It's Danny.'

'Didn't *you* get the weather! I bet it's beautiful down there.' Barney sounded pleased for him.

'Barney, what's happening?'

'You're worse than I am about not being able to cut off and take a holiday.'

'Were you looking for me? My mobile's not charged up, I'm ringing from a bar.'

'No, I wasn't looking for you, I was letting you have your holiday in peace.' He sounded very unruffled.

'I saw the paper,' Danny said.

'The paper?'

'I saw Polly's is on the market.'

'That's right. Yes.'

'What does it mean, Barney?'

'It means that Polly wants a break from it, she got a good offer and we're just testing the market in case there's an even better one out there.'

'That's bullshit. Polly doesn't want a break, she's hardly ever in there anyway.'

'Well, that's what she says. You know women . . . unpredictable.'

Danny had heard Barney so often talking to clients like this. Or when speaking to accountants, lawyers, politicians, bank managers. Anyone who had to be kept at bay. Simple, homespun, cheerful, even a little bewildered. It had always worked in the past. But then he had never talked like that to Danny before. Suddenly he thought of something. 'Is there anyone with you as we speak?'

'No, no one at all, why?'

'Are we okay, Barney? Tell me straight out.'

'How do you mean?'

'You know what I mean. Have we our heads above water? Are we in the black?'

Barney laughed. 'Come *on*, Danny, has the sun softened your head? When were we ever in the black? The red is where we live.'

'I mean will we be able to climb out this time?'

'We always did before.'

'You've never had to sell Polly's before.'

'I don't *have* to sell it now.' There was a slightly steely sound to Barney's voice. Danny said nothing. 'So if that's all, will you get on with having a holiday, and be in good shape when you're back here on Monday.'

'I could come back now if you needed me. I'd just drive straight up, leave the others here.'

'See you Monday,' said Barney McCarthy, and hung up.

Danny bought himself a small brandy to stop the slight tremor in his hand. The barman looked at him sympathetically. 'Family life all cooped up in a small boat can get a bit ropey,' he said.

'Yes.' Danny spoke absently. His mind was far away in Barney McCarthy's office. He had been dismissed on the phone, that was not an exaggeration. He had seen Barney do it so often to other people. Now he was at the receiving end.

'How many kids?' the barman asked.

'Two, and one on the way.'

'God, it must be pure hell for you,' said the man who had seen a lot of human nature in running a lakeside pub, but had never seen a face as white and strained as this fellow's.

'I'm going to go to a psychic with your sister,' Marilyn said to Ria on the phone. 'May I use your car?'

'I'm going to lessons on the Internet with your friend Heidi. Can I use your laptop to practise on?'

Sheila Maine was delighted to hear from Ria. Gertie hadn't told her that she was coming, what a marvellous surprise.

'Does Gertie write a lot then?'

'Usually an air letter every week. She fills me in on all that's going on.'

Ria's heart lurched to think of the fantasy life poor Gertie needed that she had to write a catalogue of imaginary goings-on. 'Gertie's great, I see a lot of her,' Ria said.

'I know, she tells me. She's in and out of your house all the time, she tells me.'

'That's right,' Ria said. Gertie didn't write and say *why* she was in and out of the house in Tara Road, that she was usually down on her hands and knees scrubbing floors in it to make Jack's drinking money. Still, people had to have some area of dignity. This was Gertie's.

'Will you come and visit me in Westville? I've a lovely house for the summer. The children will be coming out too in a couple of weeks' time.'

Sheila said she'd love to visit and that she'd drive over on Saturday with her children; Max was working shifts so he wouldn't be able to come. It was only an hour away. 'And you tell that handsome husband of yours that I'm really looking forward to seeing him again. He was so welcoming to us when we were in Tara Road that time.'

With a shock Ria realised that Gertie's letters about the never-never land that was Dublin must have failed to include mention of *any* kind of marital disharmony. Not only her own. She decided to wait until Sheila Maine arrived before telling her the story. It was too long and wearying for the telephone. It was a story told too often and becoming more incomprehensible with each telling. People thought she was over it all by now, they didn't realise that Ria still felt the phone would ring and it would be Danny. 'Sweetheart, forgive me' is what he would say, or 'Can we start again?'

Ria had answers for both questions. She would say yes and mean it. He was the man she loved and this had all been a terrible mistake. A series of incidents that had escalated and got out of control. Ria told herself that if she didn't think about, pray for it, and hope for it too much, it would happen.

Rosemary said that Mrs Connor was amazing, Marilyn would be astounded by her. Rosemary looked particularly well today, Marilyn thought, in a very dressy rose silk dress. It was the kind of thing you might wear to a wedding rather than to entertain a neighbour. She poured tea in the beautiful roof garden where they had been admiring the planting that had been done by a nursery. Rosemary said that Mrs Connor should be investigated by the Fraud Squad. She saw nothing, revealed nothing about the future, charged a fortune and looked more and more poverty-stricken and tubercular.

'You've been to her?' Marilyn was surprised.

'Yes, a couple of times when we were kids. I went with Ria and Gertie.'

'And what did she tell you?'

'Nothing at all, but she told it with great pain and anguish in her face. She puts on a good show, I give her that.' Rosemary was being fair.

'But she must have told you something specific?'

'Interestingly she told me that I was a bad friend.' Rosemary laughed.

'And were you?' Marilyn had a slightly disconcerting way of asking questions directly.

'No, I don't think so particularly. Look, I'm in business, you have to be a bad friend to someone every hour doing deals.'

'I guess.'

'But I was a very good friend to Polly Callaghan last week. She came in and wanted a brochure printed. You know, full colour, big pic and everything. And I knew somehow that the bill might *just* not be paid. Now I like Polly. I didn't want to lose her friendship over this so I said let's do a straight swap. I take something from your stock and you have the printing free. And I got this dress. How about that for enterprise and the barter system?'

'And did she know why you did it?'

'She may have.' Rosemary was thoughtful. 'Barney McCarthy would know certainly when she tells him. Anyway enough about all that. Why are *you* going to Mrs Connor anyway?' she asked Marilyn.

'To talk to the dead,' Marilyn said.

And for once in her life the cool confident Rosemary Ryan was at a loss for anything to say.

Marilyn realised that if she were to drive Hilary to this remote place where cars parked in a field she had better put in a little practice in driving. Even though she drove an automatic car at home she had been used to driving a stick shift too, so the gears were not beyond her. She had been warned by everyone about Dublin traffic, the way people fought for parking places and were leisurely about indicating when they moved from one lane to another. Nothing prepared her for the number of near incidents she encountered on her first outing. Shaking, she came back to Number 16 Tara Road. Colm saw her getting rather unsteadily out of the car and asked was she all right.

'I swear they pull out right in front of you,' she said. 'I nearly wasted a dozen pedestrians. They just roll across the road no matter what colour the lights are.'

He laughed easily. 'The first day is always the worst, anyway you're home now and are going to have visitors by the look of things.' He nodded towards the gate where Nora Johnson and Pliers were making their entrance.

'Yoo-hoo, Marilyn,' called Nora.

'Oh hell,' Marilyn said.

'Tut-tut, Marilyn,' said Colm in mock disapproval, but he slipped away out to the back garden and let her cope with the visit on her own.

'Hilary and I were going to have lunch together, we wondered would you like to join us?'

'Thanks, Mrs Johnson, but I don't really feel like going out just now . . .' Marilyn began.

'Well, never mind, we can eat here.'

'Here?' Marilyn looked wildly around the garden.

Nora Johnson was almost inside the house already. 'Wouldn't it be much nicer, easier for us all?' she said. She was not a person who would sense when she might not be welcome. Not anyone to be rebuffed by a little coldness. There was no hint heavy enough to move her.

Aw, what the hell, Marilyn said to herself. I coped with Dublin traffic, I can make a lunch, can't I? Forcing a smile on her face she beckoned Ria's mother to come in.

Hilary came along not long after. 'Mam said we'd meet here, where are we going?'

'Marilyn's going to cook for us,' Nora said, pleased.

'It'll be like old times in this kitchen then,' said Hilary, settling down happily. 'What are we going to eat?' There were chicken pieces in Ria's fridge and some potatoes from the garden in a wire basket. 'I'll peel those,' Hilary offered.

'Thank you,' Marilyn said, struggling to take in a recipe pinned to the inside of the store cupboard. It didn't look too daunting, it involved honey, soya sauce and ginger, all of which seemed to be on hand.

Pliers had settled down in his own corner, Clement on his own chair. It was, as Hilary said, like old times in this kitchen, only with a different woman standing at the cooker.

Annie and Brian had remembered something very important. If they were to enter Clement for the cat show the form had to be handed in today.

'You'll be back in Dublin in two days,' Finola protested.

'But that's too late,' Annie wailed. 'We thought Clement could get a Highly Commended. The form's probably on the hall table with all the mail in Tara Road.'

Bernadette shrugged. It was one of the many things in life good and bad that just happened. She was sympathetic but offered no solution. Danny was out phoning, he wasn't there to help.

Finola Dunne recognised a crisis when she saw one. 'Go and ring Mrs Vine,' she suggested.

Gertie rang on the door of Number 16 Tara Road. 'This has to be the most embarrassing moment of my life, Marilyn.'

'Yes?' Marilyn was flushed and anxious. The mixture of honey, soya sauce and ginger looked very glutinous and was sticking to the bottom of the saucepan while the chicken still seemed raw.

'But you know the way I come tomorrow . . . could I come today instead?'

'It's not really suitable Gertie, I'm cooking a lunch.'

'It's just . . . it's just it would help matters greatly at home if I were to . . .'

'I'm so sorry. But if you want to be away from home would you care to join Ria's mother and sister for lunch?' Marilyn felt her head buzzing. She was dizzy from her first attempt to cope with Dublin traffic. She was cooking a complicated dish for people she had not wanted to entertain, under the eyes of a menagerie of watchful animals. Now she was asking a third and very stressed woman to join them.

'Ah, no thank you, Marilyn, that's not what it was at all.' Gertie was fidgeting with her hands, her eyes looked frightened.

'Then what is it, Gertie? I'm sorry, I'm not sure . . .'

'Marilyn, could you give me the money for tomorrow and I'll do the work of course later . . . ?' It was so hard for her to ask.

So hard to hear. Marilyn flushed. 'Yes, yes,' she muttered, embarrassed, and went to find her wallet. 'Do you have any change?' she asked without thinking.

'Marilyn, if I had any change would I be here like this asking you for tomorrow's money?'

'No, how stupid of me. Please take this.'

'This will cover tomorrow and all of next week,' Gertie said.

'Sure, fine, whatever you say.'

'You could ring Ria in America and she'll tell you I always honour it.'

'I know you will, and well . . . goodbye now.'

Marilyn came downstairs flustered and unsettled by the conversation. 'That was Gertie,' she said brightly. 'She couldn't stay.'

'No, she had to get Jack's drinking money to him,' said Nora Johnson succinctly.

At that moment they all realised that one of the saucepans seemed to be on fire with what looked like a toffee coating on the bottom.

'That will never come off,' said Hilary. 'And those are very expensive saucepans.'

They left the saucepan to soak and Marilyn began again. As Hilary had said, it was a mercy she hadn't wasted the chicken fillets, the other bit was only old sauces.

The telephone rang. It was Annie and Brian from the River Shannon. Could Marilyn please find this form? She went upstairs again to the front room where she kept all the mail neatly on the sideboard. She found the form and called them back at the pub where they were waiting for news.

'Great,' Brian said. 'All you have to do now is drive it around to the address with the one-pound entrance fee.'

'Yes, well . . .'

'Thanks very much, we'd hate for him not to enter.' Annie had taken the phone by now.

'I don't have to take Clement to the show myself?' Marilyn asked anxiously. 'Walk him around a ring or anything?'

'No, they sit in cages actually, and to be honest I'd quite like to do that myself, but if you'd like to come along or anything . . . ?'

'Yes well, we'll see.' Marilyn ended the conversation.

'Are they having a good holiday?' Nora sniffed at the unlikely prospect of this.

'I didn't ask them,' Marilyn cried with a great wail because she saw that the second saucepan was burning and neither of these two women who were used to Ria Lynch being in total charge had lifted a finger to rescue it.

Was this what she had come all the way to Ireland for? This ludicrous, exhausting kind of day? Getting more and more enmeshed and involved in the lives of total strangers?

There was a letter from Mam in the mailbox on Tudor Drive.

Dear Ria,

I should have been better about writing letters but somehow God does not put enough hours in the day. And talking of God as we were, I hope you've found a Catholic church out in that place for my grandchildren to go to on Sundays. Marilyn said that she gave you all the details, phone numbers and Mass times and everything, but you don't have to pretend to me that you are a regular Mass-goer, I know better. Marilyn doesn't go to the Protestant church here, and of course she might be of the Jewish faith, but I didn't like to suggest the synagogue to her. She's a grown woman and can make her own choices. I'd be the last one to interfere in anyone else's life.

She was a bit stiff in the beginning but I think she's getting used to our ways all right. A mother should not criticise her daughter's friends, and I don't intend to but you know I don't like Lady Ryan and never will, and I regard Gertie as a weak slob who deserves what she gets by putting up with it. Marilyn is different, she's very interesting to talk to about everything, and very knowledgeable about the cinema. She drives your car like a maniac and has burned two saucepans which she has replaced. She's going to be forty on August 1st. I'm twenty-seven years older than her but I get on with her just fine. I think she's sleeping with Colm Barry but I'm not certain. The Adulterer Barney McCarthy is still prancing around the place. The children get back from the ludicrous boat holiday tomorrow. I'm going to take Annie out for a pizza and hear all the gory details. Annie's anxious to bring her friend Kitty as well, so we may include her in the party and then let them go home together.

Lots of love from your Mam

Ria looked at the postmark wildly. Five days since her mother had written all this. Five whole days. And she hadn't known anything that had been going on. What kind of friends' support system was there that nobody had told her all of this vital information? It was eight o'clock in the morning. She reached for the phone and realised that since it was lunchtime in Ireland her mother would be out on one of her insane perambulations. Why did people write letters like this that took five days and five nights to get there instead of using e-mail? She realised that it was a little unfair of her to blame her mother for not being on the Net since she herself had hardly heard of it a couple of weeks ago. But honestly.

She rang Marilyn. The answering machine was on but she had changed the message. 'This is Ria Lynch's house but she is not here at present. Messages will be taken and relayed to her. Marilyn Vine speaking. I will return your call.' How *dare* she do that? Ria felt a huge surge of rage. She could hardly contain her hatred of Marilyn.

This woman had gone into her house, driven her car into the ground, chopped down the garden, burned Ria's saucepans, slept with Colm Barry. What else was there to discover about her?

Ria rang Rosemary. She was at a meeting, her secretary said. She rang Gertie in the launderette.

'You're so good to entertain Sheila and the children, she loved her visit to you. She phoned and told me all about it. Loved it she did.' Gertie's voice was happy. What she was really thanking Ria for was keeping up the fiction that Gertie and Jack lived a normal life.

More lies, fantasy, pretence. Ria was so impatient she could hardly keep it out of her tone. 'What's Marilyn up to, Gertie?'

'She's great, isn't she?'

'I don't know, I never met her.'

'Is she sleeping with Colm?'

'Is she *what*?' Gertie's laugh from the busy lunchtime launderette was like an explosion.

'My mother says she is.'

'Ria, your mother! You never listened to a word your mother said before.'

'I know, did she burn my saucepans?'

'Yes, and replaced them with much better ones. You'll be delighted. She got herself a couple of cheap ones in case she burned them again.'

'What is she . . . accident prone?'

'No, just not any good as a cook. But you should see what she's done with the garden!'

'Is there any of it left?'

'Ria, it's fantastic.'

'Like are there any trees or bushes? Anything I'd recognise? Brian told me she'd cut it all down.'

'You listened to Brian?' Gertie asked.

'She's not working in my thrift shop with Frances Sullivan as well, is she? I mean, in between doing tunnel excavations in my garden.'

'What *is* all this, Ria? She's a lovely person, she's *your* friend.'

'No, she's not. I never laid eyes on her.'

'Are you upset about something?'

'She's taken over my house.'

'Ria, you gave her your house, you took hers.'

'She changed the message on the phone.'

'You told her to when she was ready.'

'She's ready all right.'

'Annie helped her decide what to say.'

'Annie?'

'Yes, she comes round to the house a lot.'

'To Tara Road?' Ria asked through gritted teeth.

'Well I think she misses you, Ria, that's why she comes round.' Gertie sounded desperate to reassure her.

'Yeah, I'm sure she does,' Ria said.

'She does, Ria, she said that the holiday on the Shannon was bizarre, that was the word she used. She said that Brian said every day "Mam would like this" and she agreed.'

'Did she?' Ria brightened a little.

'Honestly she did. I was talking to her this morning when I went up to the house. She's actually gone out with Marilyn today. The two of them have gone shopping.'

'What?'

'Yes. Apparently Annie has some voucher or something for clothes which your mother gave her. She wanted to use it so they went off to Grafton Street.'

'I suppose she's there now, ploughing up and down the pedestrian precinct in my car.'

'No, she went on the bus. I honestly don't know why you've turned against her, Ria, I really don't.'

'Neither do I,' said Ria.

And she hung up and burst into tears.

There had been three false attempts to meet Mrs Connor. Each time the line of cars had been too long. The anxious-looking boys who protected the vehicles said that it wouldn't be worth their while to wait. Fourth time lucky.

Marilyn looked into the haunted face of the thin woman.

'You're welcome to our country,' she said.

'Thank you.'

'You came to find something here.'

'Yes, I suppose we all do.'

'It's not here, it's where you came from.'

'Can you talk to my son for me?'

'Is he dead?'

'Yes.'

'It wasn't your fault, madam.'

'It *was* my fault, I should never have let him go.'

'I can't talk to the dead, madam.' The woman's eyes were very bright in her thin face. 'They're at peace. They are sleeping and that's how we must leave them.'

'I want to tell him I'm sorry.'

'No, madam, it's not possible. And it's not what the people who are sleeping would want.'

'It *is* possible.'

'Not for me. Would you like me to look at your hand?'

'Why can't you talk to my son, tell him I'm so very sorry? That I let him go that day, that I agreed they should pull out the plug? I took him off the life-support machine. After only a few months. They might have found a way to get him back. I sat there and watched him take his last breath.' Mrs Connor looked at her with great sympathy. 'I held his hand in mine at the end and in case he could hear, I said, "Dale, your father and I are turning this off to release your spirit. That's what it will do." But it *didn't* release his spirit, I know that. It's trapped somewhere and I'll have no peace unless I can talk to him just once to tell him. Can't you find him for me?'

'No.'

'I beg you.'

'You have to find your own peace.'

'Well, why am I here?'

'Like everyone else who comes in here. People come because they are unhappy.'

'And they're hoping for a little magic, I suppose?'

'I suppose so, madam.'

'Well, thank you for your time and your honesty, Mrs Connor.' Marilyn stood up to go.

'Take your money, madam, I gave you nothing.'

'No, I insist.'

'No, madam, I insist too. One day you will find your peace. That day, go out and give this money to someone who needs it.'

In the car going home Hilary asked almost nervously, 'Was she any help to you, Marilyn?'

'She's very wise.'

'But she didn't get to talk to the dead for you?' Marilyn felt a rush of affection for Ria's lonely, ungracious sister.

'No, she said he was asleep. Well, we agreed why wake him if he's peacefully asleep.'

'And was that worth it? I mean you didn't think you paid her too much?'

'No, not at all, it was good to know he was asleep.'

'And do you feel better now?' Hilary was hopeful.

'Much better,' lied Marilyn Vine. 'And now tell me, what did she tell you?'

'She told me that it was up to me to find the trees, that we had enough put by to choose where we lived.'

'And would you *like* to live somewhere with trees?' Marilyn asked.

'Not particularly, I've nothing against them, mind, but I never yearned for them either. Still if it's what's meant to be out there for me I think I should look for them.'

The line of cars waiting for Mrs Connor had been still long as they left. People all looking for a little magic to help them through. That woman had said that everyone who came to her caravan was unhappy. What a sad procession. But somehow there was a curious strength about it. Everyone sitting in those cars had a sorrow. Marilyn Vine wasn't the only woman in the world racked with guilt and loss. Others had survived it too. Like people needing medicine, they had to go to a caravan or something similar occasionally just in case there was any magic floating by that would help.

She smiled to herself. Hilary saw the smile and was pleased.

Ria changed the message. 'This is the home of Greg Vine who is in Hawaii, and Marilyn Vine who is in Ireland. Ria Lynch is living here at the moment and will be happy to forward your messages to the Vines or return your calls.'

She played it back several times and nodded. Two could play at that game. That would sort Ms Marilyn out.

She called Heidi. 'I'm having a little supper party here, won't you and Henry come? Carlotta's coming and that nice couple we met at the Internet class, and those two men who run the gourmet shop you told me about. I've got friendly with them but I have to show off to them seriously with my home-cooked food. I'm hoping they may give me a job.'

'Mam?'

'Hi, Annie.'

'Mam, aren't you funny, you say Hi instead of Hallo.'

'I know, I'm a scream.'

'You didn't call us so we called you.'

'I did call you. And I also left a message for your father. To which he hasn't replied yet, you might tell him.'

'He's out, Mam, he's out all the time.'

'Well, when next he comes in tell him that I'm waiting.'

'But it's only a message about business, Mam.'

'I know, but I'd still like to hear his answer.'

'Will it be a fight?'

'Not if he returns my call, no.'

'And how are you, Mam?'

'I'm fine. How was your outing to the pizza place with Granny?' Ria had a bit of steel in her voice that Annie recognised.

'It was fine. Gran gave me a marvellous waistcoat. You'll see it, I'll take it over with me.'

'And did Kitty join you there?'

'No, she didn't as it happens.'

'How did that happen?'

'Because Bernadette rang Granny and said Dad had a rooted objection to Kitty.'

'How disappointing.'

'Well I was disappointed, Mam, but there you go. You and Dad don't like Kitty so what can I do?'

'I'm glad your father's looking after that side of things anyway.'

'He didn't do it, he wouldn't know what day it was these times. I tell you, it was Bernadette.'

'And tell me about your shopping expedition with Marilyn.'

'Have you a fleet of detectives on me or something, Mam?'

'No, just friends and family who tell me about things I'm interested in, that's all.'

'You're not interested in clothes, Mam, you hate clothes.'

'What did you buy?' Ria hissed at her daughter.

'Pink jeans and a navy-and-pink shirt.'

'Sounds great,' Ria said.

'Mam, are you in a bad mood at me over something?'

'Should I be?'

'I don't think so, I'm having a shitty summer to be honest, everyone's upset the whole time. I'm not allowed to see my friend Kitty. Granny's going to live in an old people's home. Mr McCarthy's gone off somewhere without letting Dad know where. Rosemary Ryan is like something wired to the moon looking for Dad to give him urgent messages. Brian has Dekko and Myles back in tow again roaring and bawling and driving everyone mad. Dad had some kind of row with Finola and she's not around any more. Bernadette's asleep most of the time. Aunt Hilary's lost her marbles and keeps looking up into trees. Clement was coughing up fur balls and he had to go to the vet. Colm took him. It's not serious . . . but it was very frightening at the time. And then I ring you and you're in a snot with me about something that I don't know about. And honestly if it weren't for Marilyn I'd go mad.'

'She's helpful, is she?'

'Well, at least she's normal. And she recommends me books to read. She gave me *To Kill a Mockingbird*. Did you ever read it, Mam?'

'I love you, Annie.'

'Are you drunk, Mam?'

'Of course I'm not drunk. Why do you ask?'

'I asked you did you read a book and you said you loved me. That's not a conversation.'

'No, but it's a fact.'

'Well I suppose, thank you, Mam. Thanks anyway.'

'And you? Do you perhaps love me?'

'You've been too long in America, Mam,' said Annie.

Danny Lynch was standing on the steps ringing the doorbell of what used to be his own house.

Marilyn, kneeling under the huge tree inside the gate, was invisible to him as he stood fidgeting and looking at his watch. He *was* a handsome man with all that nervous energy that she remembered from years back but now there was something else, something she had seen in the restaurant that night. Something anxious, almost hunted. Then he took out some door keys and let himself in. Marilyn had been about to get up and approach him but now she moved very sharply from her planting and ran lightly up to the house and followed him inside.

He was standing in the front room looking around. He called out: 'It's only me, Danny Lynch.'

'You startled me,' she said with her hand on her chest, pretending a great sense of alarm and shock. After all if she *had* come in without knowing he was inside she would have been very shocked.

'I'm sorry, I did ring the bell but there was no answer. And you're Marilyn. You're very welcome to Ireland.' Despite his restlessness he had great charm. He looked at her as he welcomed her. He was a man who would look at every woman he talked to and make them feel special. That's why she had remembered him, after all, when she had forgotten so many other people.

'Thank you,' she said.

'And you're happy here?' He looked around the room, taking it all in as if he were going to do an examination on its contents.

'Very. Who wouldn't be?' She wished she hadn't said that. Danny Lynch had obviously not been happy enough to stay here. Why, out of courtesy, had she made that stupid remark?

He didn't seem to have noticed it. 'My daughter says you've been very kind to her.'

'She's a delightful girl. I hope she and Brian will enjoy visiting my home as much as I like being in theirs.'

'It's a great opportunity for them. When I was Brian's age I had only been ten miles down the road.' He was very engaging.

And yet she didn't like the fact that he had let himself in. 'I didn't actually know that there was another key to the house out. I thought Gertie and I had the only two.'

'Well, it's not exactly having a key *out*,' he said. 'Not *my* having one surely?'

'No, it's just I misunderstood, that's all. I didn't realise that you come and go here, Danny. There were very precise notes about Colm having a key to the back gate and everything. I'll tell Ria that she forgot to tell me about you and how I thought you were an intruder.' She laughed at the silly mistake but she watched him carefully at the same time.

He understood what she was saying. Carefully he took the key to Tara Road off his key-ring and laid it on the table beside the bowl of roses. 'I don't come and go actually. It was just today I needed something and since you weren't in I thought . . . well you know, old habits die hard. It was my front door for a long time.' His smile and apology were practised but none the less genuine.

'Of course.' She was gracious, she could afford to be. She had won in this little battle, she had got Ria's door key back too. 'And what was it you wanted?'

'The car keys actually. Mine has packed up so I need to take the second car.'

'Ria's car?'

'The second car, yes.'

'For how long? I'd need it back in an hour.'

'No, I mean take it, for the duration.'

'Oh that's impossible,' she said pleasantly.

'What do you mean?'

'I mean I paid the insurance company an extra premium to cover my driving that car for eight weeks. Ria will be driving your children around Connecticut in my car. My husband can't suddenly appear and claim the car from *her* . . .' She paused. The rest of the sentence hung there unspoken.

'I'm sorry, Marilyn, very sorry if you'll be inconvenienced but I have to have it. You don't need it, you're here all day digging in the garden. I have to go out and make calls on people, earn a living.'

'I'm sure your company will provide you with another car.'

'It suits me to have this one, and since you don't need . . .'

'Excuse me, you don't know what I need a car for. Today as it happens I'm meeting Colm to arrange that some organic fertiliser for your garden be delivered, and the nursery where we are meeting is not on a bus route. I am driving your *first* mother-in-law and three old ladies from St Rita's to a bridge tournament in Dalkey. Then I'm picking up your daughter and son and driving them to meet your *second* mother-in-law, with whom you have apparently had some quarrel, for swimming lessons. Then I meet Rosemary Ryan, who has been trying to get in touch with you urgently by the way, and she and I are going to a charity fashion show. I agreed to drive.' He looked at her open-mouthed. 'So can we *now* agree that regretfully there isn't a question of my giving you Ria's car?' Marilyn asked.

'Danny?'

'Jesus, Barney, where are you?'

Barney laughed. 'I told you, a business trip.'

'No, that's what we tell the bank, the suppliers, other people, it's not what you tell me.'

'That's exactly what I'm doing, on the business of raising money.'

'And tell me you've managed to raise some, Barney, because otherwise we're going to lose two contracts this afternoon.'

'Easy, easy. It's raised.'

'Where are you?'

'It doesn't matter, ring Larry at the bank and check. The money's there.'

'It wasn't there an hour ago.'

'It's there now.'

'Where are you, Barney?'

'I'm in Málaga,' Barney McCarthy said and hung up.

Danny was shaking. He hadn't the courage to ring the bank. Suppose Larry said he knew nothing of any money. Suppose Barney was in the south of Spain with Polly and wasn't coming back. It was preposterous of course but then people did that sort of thing. They left their wives and children without a backward glance. Hadn't he done it himself?

'Ms Ryan on the line for you, *again*,' the secretary said to him, rolling her eyes to heaven, pleading with him to take the call this time.

'Put her through. Sweetheart, how are you?' he said.

'Five calls, Danny, what's this?' Her voice was clipped.

'It's been hell in here.'

'So I read in the papers and hear everywhere,' she said.

'It's okay now, we're out of the fire.'

'Says who?'

'Says Barney. He's saying it from Spain, rather alarmingly.'

Rosemary laughed and Danny relaxed.

'We have to meet. There are a few things we must talk about.'

'Very difficult, sweetheart.'

'Tonight I'm going to one of Mona's dreary charity things with the woman who's living in your house.'

'Marilyn?'

'Yes. Have you met her?'

'I don't like her, she's a real ball-breaker.'

'Come round after ten,' Rosemary said and hung up.

Somewhere Danny found the courage to ring the bank. He must sound cheerful and confident.

'Hi Larry, Danny Lynch here. Is the red alert over? Can we come out of the bunkers?'

'Yes, some last-ditch Mafia money turned up.'

Danny went weak with relief but he pretended to be shocked. 'Larry, is that any way to talk to respectable property people?'

'There are some respectable property people, you and Barney aren't amongst them.'

'Why are you being so heavy?' Danny was startled.

'He left a lot of small people who could ill afford it without their cash, and then when it started to get ropey he went down to the Costa del Crime and got some laundered drug money from his pals.'

'We don't know that, Larry.'

'We do.'

Danny remembered hearing that Larry's son was in a de-tox centre. He would have very strong feelings about money that might have been made through the sale of heroin.

Greg called Marilyn. 'No reason. Just to chat. I miss the e-mails.'

'So do I, but I gather Ria's making great progress on my little laptop. She sent an e-mail to Rosemary Ryan, a woman here – I'm going out to a fashion show with her shortly – and one to her ex-husband's office. They nearly collapsed.'

'Oh I know, she sends them to me too.'

'She does? What about?'

'Oh this and that . . . arrangements for the alumni weekend . . . Andy will be coming up too, and her children will be there, so it will be a full house.'

'Yes.' Marilyn couldn't quite explain why this slightly irritated her, but it did.

'Anyway, she seems to be getting on very well, she's cooking in John and Gerry's a couple of hours a day.'

'She's *not!*'

'Yes. Isn't she amazing? And Henry told me that he and Heidi were at a dinner party round there . . .'

'Round where?'

'In the house. In Tudor Drive. There were eight of them apparently and . . .'

'In our house? She had eight people in our house? To dinner?'

'Well, she knows them all pretty well now. Carlotta comes in for a swim every morning, Heidi's round there for coffee after work. It didn't take her long . . .'

'It did *not*,' said Marilyn grimly.

Mona McCarthy was on the committee. She sat smiling at the desk and had their tickets ready for them when they went in. People often wondered how much she knew about her husband's activities both in business and in his private life. But they would never learn from Mona's large face. There were no hints there. A big serene woman, dull even, constantly raising money for good causes. It might have been trying to put something back in order to compensate for the many sharp deals where Barney might have taken too much out.

'And a glass of champagne?' she offered.

'I'd love one,' Rosemary said. '*And* I have a chauffeur.' She introduced Marilyn.

Marilyn was being unusually silent tonight as if she were thinking about something miles away.

Mona's face lit up. 'And little Ria's out in your house at the moment, isn't she?'

Marilyn nodded with a bright smile. She was wondering what percentage of the population of Westville was now installed in Tudor Drive tonight. Oh no, it was just after lunch back home, maybe a buffet party for thirty at the swimming pool. But she had to say something pleasant. 'Yes, I gather she's having a good time, settling in well.'

Mona was pleased. 'She really needs that, how wonderful you were able to provide it for her.'

'She's even got a job, I hear, in our local gourmet shop.' Marilyn wondered whether there was a tinny note in her voice, and she wondered further why there should be.

'Ria should have got a job years ago,' Rosemary said. 'That's why she lost everything she had.'

'She didn't lose everything,' Mona said quietly. 'She still has the children.'

Rosemary realised it had not been the right remark to make in front of the stay-at-home wife of Barney McCarthy who was in the south of Spain with his mistress. 'Yes, of course. That's right, she has the children, and of course the house.'

'Do you think that Danny Lynch's liaison, for want of a better word, is . . . permanent?' Marilyn wondered.

'No way,' Rosemary said.

'Not at all,' Mona said at the same time.

'And would Ria have him back when it does end, do you think?' Marilyn couldn't believe that she was asking these personal questions. Marilyn who was legendary about her reserve had changed entirely in this country, she had become a blabbermouth and busybody in a matter of weeks.

'Oh, I think so,' Mona said.

'No question of it,' said Rosemary.

If everyone seemed so sure . . . if it were all going to end with everyone back in their own boxes as they had been . . . then what a terrible amount of pain and hurt for the whole summer! And what would happen to the baby that was waiting to be born?

As they drove back through the warm Dublin night Marilyn talked easily to Rosemary. She spoke about Greg out in Hawaii. At no stage did she give any explanation why he was on one side of the earth and she was on the other.

When Marilyn stopped the car outside Number 32 Rosemary thanked her for the lift. 'It was wonderful, it meant I could have four glasses of champagne. And I loved them. I would ask you in for coffee but I have such an early start . . . I thought I'd give the plants in the garden a drink of water and then go to bed.'

'Heavens no, and I want to get an early night too.'

Marilyn drove back and parked the car outside Number 16.

Just then she remembered that she had left the signed programmes she had got for Annie in Rosemary's purse. Annie and her friend Kitty were mad about two of the models. Marilyn had gone to the trouble to get the right ones, now she had stupidly left them in Rosemary's elegant black leather bag. She looked at her watch. Rosemary wouldn't be in bed yet. She had only left her two minutes ago, she would be watering the garden. Marilyn would just run up the lane, it would be quicker. They didn't lock their back gate in Number 32.

It was such a pleasant neighbourhood, this, in ways; she had been very lucky to find it. She looked up at the sky, slightly rosy from the lights of the city, a big moon hidden from time to time by racing black clouds that looked like chariots hastening across.

She wished that she didn't feel so mean-spirited about Ria's antics in Westville, but it was really most unfair of her. She was setting up precedents, establishing patterns which could now not be broken. Marilyn didn't *want* Carlotta's voluptuous figure diving into her swimming pool, she didn't *need* Heidi coming for coffee every day. And she felt absurdly jealous of what Ria would do for everyone at the alumni picnic.

She was at the back gate of Number 32 now and she pushed it open. She expected to see Rosemary in her bare feet, having taken off her expensive shoes, directing the hose towards the beautifully planted herbaceous border.

But there was nobody there. She walked quietly across the grass and then she heard two people talking in the summerhouse. Not so much talking, she realised as she got nearer, more kissing. Rosemary had indeed taken off her expensive shoes and also her expensive rose silk dress, the one she had got from Polly Callaghan in exchange for a printing job. She lay in a coffee-coloured silk slip across Danny Lynch and she had his face in her hands.

She was speaking to him urgently. 'Never, never again as long as you live, leave me with five phone calls unreturned.'

'Sweetheart, I told you . . .' he was stroking her thigh and raising the lacy edge of the slip.

Marilyn stood there frozen. This was the second time she had watched Danny Lynch without him seeing her. She seemed to be condemned to spy on this man. She was utterly unsure of which way to move.

Rosemary was angry. 'Don't, Danny. Don't play with me. There's too much history here. I've put up with too much, saved you, warned you too often.'

'You and I are special, we've always agreed that what we have is something that's outside everything else,' he said.

'Yes, I put up with your housey-housey marriage, with your affairs, I even put up with you getting that child pregnant and moving away from this road. God knows why.'

'You know why, Rosemary,' Danny said.

And Marilyn fled. Back to the safety of her garden where she watered Colm's vegetables and everything else in sight with a ferocity that they had never known and might not indeed have needed.

Clement came and watched her gravely, sitting at a safe distance. She was using that hose like a weapon. She was astounded at how shocked and revolted she felt. This was the falsest friend she had ever known. Poor, poor Ria, so unlucky in her man, which could happen to anyone. But so doubly unlucky to be advised and betrayed by her best friend as well. It was beyond understanding.

In a fit of generosity Marilyn decided she didn't care if Ria was entertaining whole coachloads of people in 1024 Tudor Drive, serving them platefuls of home-made delicacies. She deserved it. She deserved whatever bit of pleasure she could get.

Ria was in fact on her own in Tudor Drive bent over Marilyn's laptop.

Hubie Green had given her a computer game. She was going to master it and be able to show it to them when they got here. Sheila Maine's children had lots of these and both Annie and Brian did of course work on computers at school, but Ria had known nothing about them and had never been interested. Still this game was defeating her.

She sent Hubie an e-mail. '*Hubie, it would only take you thirty minutes to explain this game to me. It's worth ten dollars of my time to learn it. Do you think you could come by at some stage? A seriously confused Ria Lynch.*'

The kid must live beside his screen: he answered immediately. '*It's a done deal. Can you call me on the telephone at this number and tell me where you live?*'

She called him and gave the address.

There was a silence. 'But that's Dale's house. Dale Vine.'

'That's right.' She was solemn now. She had somehow thought he would have known. But then why should he know?

'Oh I couldn't go there, Mrs Lynch.'

'But why not?'

'Mr and Mrs Vine wouldn't like it.'

'They're not here, Hubie, I'm living in the house. Marilyn's in my house in Ireland, Greg's in Hawaii.'

'Did they split up?' He sounded concerned.

'I don't know,' she said truthfully.

'You must know.'

'I don't as it happens, they don't tell me. I think after Dale's death they needed to get away.'

'Yeah, sure.'

'But of course I understand, Hubie, if you don't want to come round here, if it has bad memories for you. I'm sorry, I should really have thought.'

She heard him take a breath. 'Hey, it's only a house, they're not there to get upset. Your kids have to play this game and ten dollars is ten dollars. Sure I'll come, Mrs Lynch.'

It was so simple once he explained it, and also quite exciting. They played on and on.

'That was much more than half an hour, I'd better give you twenty.'

'No, we agreed ten. I stayed because I enjoyed it.'

'Would you like some supper?' She brought him into the kitchen and opened the fridge.

'Hey, you've got one of those lovely Irish flag quiches they sell at John and Gerry's.'

'I make them,' she said, pleased.

'You *make* them? Fantastic,' he said. 'My mother bought two of them for a party.'

'Good, well I'll give you some Irish soda bread with currants in it to take home to her when you leave, then I don't feel too bad keeping you out for so long.'

He walked around the kitchen, restless, uneasy maybe to be in this home again. Ria said nothing about the past. Instead she busied herself talking about the visit of Annie and Brian. Hubie picked up a picture of the children. Ria kept it out where she could see it.

'Is this her? Your daughter? She's real cute,' he said.

'Yes, she's lovely but then I would think so, and that's Brian.' She looked proudly at the son who would be here soon. Hubie showed no interest at all. They sat and talked companionably over the meal. Hubie used to come here a lot, he said. Great swimming pool and always a welcome. Not food like this, mind you, but cookies from the store and this was the house where the kids came. In fact his parents were quite friendly with Mr and Mrs Vine before everything.

'And now?' Ria was gentle.

'Well you see how she is, Mrs Lynch. You know what she's like now.'

'No, the funny thing is I don't know what she's like, I've never met her and I've only seen one photograph of her.'

'You don't know her? You're not a friend?'

'No, it was a home exchange, that's all, she's in my house you see, digging up my garden, buying my daughter pink jeans.'

'You don't want her to do that? Why don't you tell her?' To Hubie it was simple.

'Because we're old and complicated, that's why. Anyway to be fair I'm doing something now that she mightn't like, having you to supper.'

'She wouldn't like this, believe me, Mrs Lynch.'

'It wasn't your fault.'

'Not the way she sees it.'

'I don't know all about it, people don't talk and I don't like to ask. I just heard it was your birthday.'

'Yeah it was.'

'But why is she upset with you?'

'You really don't know her?' He wanted to be reassured. 'You're not a friend of theirs?'

'No, I promise you, we just got in touch by accident. I had problems of my own, you see.'

'Did someone die?'

'No, but my husband left me and I felt bad and upset over there.'

'Oh.'

'And Dale's mother obviously couldn't come to terms with what had happened around here so . . .'

'Yes, that's true. She went insane, I think.'

'People do for a while, but a lot of them get better.' Ria tried to be encouraging.

'She hates me.'

'Why should she hate you?'

'Because I'm alive, I guess.' He looked very young and sad as he sat there trying to make sense of what had happened. And the lights went on in the garden as the darkness came down, as it did so quickly here in America, unlike at home where everything seemed to move much more slowly.

'But surely if she were to hate anyone it would be the other boy, the one who died?'

'Johnny?'

'Yes, Johnny. I mean he was the one driving. *He* was the one who killed her son.'

He said nothing, just looked out at the garden lights and the sprinklers beginning to play on the lawn.

'She can't hate Johnny. Johnny is dead, there's no point in hating him. We're alive, David and I. She can hate us, it gives her life some purpose.'

'You sound very, very bitter about her.'

'I do, yes.'

'But it must have been so terrible for her, Hubie. So hard to forgive. If Johnny hadn't been drunk . . .'

'Johnny wasn't driving. Dale was driving.' She looked at him in horror. 'Dale stole the bikes, Dale set it up. It was Dale who killed Johnny.'

Ria felt her heart turn over. 'That can't be true.'

He nodded sadly. 'It's true.'

'But why? Why did nobody . . . how did they not know?'

'You don't want to think what that wreck looked like, you don't want to think about it. I saw it and David saw it so we have to think about it for the rest of our lives.'

'But why didn't you . . . ?'

'Everyone assumed it was Johnny driving and at that time we thought Dale was going to get better. They said he might survive; they had him on this machine. I went in once to see him before she had orders issued that I wasn't to be let near. I told him in case he could hear me that we'd let people go on thinking it was Johnny. He was under-age, you see, and also he had these parents that worshipped him. Johnny had nobody.'

'Oh God,' said Ria.

'Yes, I know, and now I don't think what we did was right but we did it for the best. We did it to help goddamn Mrs Vine and then she wouldn't even let me come to Dale's funeral.'

'Oh God Almighty,' Ria said.

'You won't tell her, will you?' he asked.

Ria thought of the room along the corridor, the shrine to the dead son. 'No, Hubie, whatever else I may do in my life I won't tell her,' Ria said.

8

'Marilyn, this is Ria. Sorry to miss you. Nothing really. Just to say that the Dublin Horse Show will be on next month, you might enjoy it. And Rosemary can get you tickets for the show-jumping which is very spectacular. She's terrific about things like that, she'd do anything to help. She sent me an e-mail on your laptop and she's dead impressed that I know how to do it. Then maybe you might hate the Horse Show. I don't know why I'm burbling on, I think it's just I want to make sure you're having a good time. I hear from Gertie that you've done wonders in the garden, thank you so much. Okay. 'Bye now.'

Marilyn listened to the message. She felt such a surge of rage against Rosemary Ryan that she was glad she wasn't holding her coffee mug in her hand. She would surely have crushed it into her palm. She would not return the call yet because she didn't trust herself to speak about Ria's friend who was so terrific about things that she would do anything to help.

'Ria, this is Marilyn, sorry I missed you. Our machines are playing tag as they say. No, I won't ask Rosemary for any tickets to the show-jumping but I may well go to the Horse Show when it's on. I see a lot of advertisements for it already. You must tell me more about your Internet lessons. They seem to have worked very well for you, it took me ages to get familiar with it all. Glad to hear that you are getting to know people in Westville. Annie and Brian are coming to supper here tomorrow. I was terrified of cooking for them but Colm said he'd leave something suitable. The children are really looking forward to seeing you again. 'Bye for now.'

Ria listened to the message. For the first time she didn't feel excluded and annoyed that the children were going to supper with Marilyn. That woman needed any bit of consolation she could get. And she couldn't return the call because she had to work out with Heidi what they would say about Hubie Green.

'What did you and Dad fall out about, Finola?' Brian asked.
    'Brian!'
    'No, Annie, it's a reasonable question. And the answer is money.'
    'Oh,' said Brian.
    'People often do fall out about that.' Finola was brisk and matter-of-fact. 'I

asked your father to tell me how his company was doing. I wanted to know whether he had enough funds to look after you both, your mother and Bernadette as well.'

'And has he?' Brian asked fearfully.

'I don't know, he asked me to mind my own business, which was fair enough in a way. It's actually *not* my business, but that's why we fell out.'

'Will you ever make it up?' Annie asked.

'Oh yes, I'm sure we will.' Finola was bright. 'And anyway I want to thank you both very much indeed for coming to say goodbye, I really appreciate that.'

'You were very good to us, with the swimming lessons and everything,' Annie said.

'And with talking to us when Dad and Bernadette were being all sentimental and soppy on the boat.' Brian remembered it all with some distaste.

'I was going to give you a little present for the trip but I thought I'd give you twenty dollars each instead,' Finola Dunne said.

Their faces lit up. 'We shouldn't really take it.' Annie sounded doubtful.

'Why not, we're friends aren't we?'

'Yes but if you and Dad . . .'

'That will be blown over by the time you come back, believe me.' They believed her at once and pocketed the money with big smiles. 'And . . . I do hope it's all nice for you out there, the holiday with your mother.' Finola meant it.

'It will be,' Brian said. 'I mean she's quite old, Finola, like you are, there won't be any soppiness going on out there.'

'*Brian!*' Annie said.

'I'll see you both in September.' Finola had never thought she would like Danny Lynch's children and be sorry to see them leave Ireland for a whole month.

Greg Vine telephoned to say that he would like to stay in Tudor Drive for the alumni weekend in August. 'Normally I would leave you the house to yourself and stay in a motel, but there won't be a bed for miles around. Even Heidi and Henry won't have any room.'

'Heavens, no, you must stay here. And Andy too.'

'We can't all descend on you surely?'

'Why not? Annie and I can sleep in one room. You have two guest rooms, you and Andy have one each. Brian would sleep standing up, he doesn't have to be taken into consideration. And anyway there's a canvas bed that we can put anywhere for him.'

'That's very good of you, it will only be for two nights.'

'No, please, it's your house, stay as long as you like.'

'And when do your children arrive?'

'Tomorrow, I can hardly wait.'

When he had replaced the receiver Greg realised that she hadn't suggested that Brian sleep in Dale's room. It would have been perfectly acceptable. To him anyway. But not to Marilyn. Ria Lynch must have worked that out. She had been so odd the first time, talking about Dale's spirit being in Hawaii and the dead boy missing his mother. But maybe he had misunderstood her. This time she seemed highly practical and down-to-earth.

Marilyn went to Colm's to collect the food.

'I'd have brought it down to you,' he said.

'Nonsense, I'm grateful enough to you already. What have I got here?'

'A light vegetable korma for Annie, with some brown rice. Just sausage, peas and chips for Brian, I'm afraid. I did nothing special for you, I presumed you'd eat from both not to show favouritism.'

Marilyn said that seemed an excellent scheme. 'Let me get my billfold.'

'Please, Marilyn.'

There was something in his face that stopped her. 'Well, thank you so much, Colm, truly.'

'Let me get you a basket to carry them.' He called out to Caroline, and his pale, dark-haired sister whom Marilyn had only seen in the distance before came in carrying the ideal container, with a couple of check dinner napkins. 'You have met Caroline, haven't you?'

'I don't think so, not properly anyway. How do you do, I'm Marilyn Vine.'

Caroline put out her hand hesitantly. Marilyn glanced at her face and realised that she was looking straight into the eyes of someone with a problem. She didn't consider herself an expert but as a young graduate she had worked for three years on a rehab project. She had not a shadow of doubt that she was being introduced to a heroin addict.

'Do you think Dad has lost all his money?' Brian asked on the bus from Finola's house.

'No, don't be an eejit,' Annie said.

'But why does Finola think he has?'

'She doesn't know. Anyway, all old people like Finola and Gran ever think about is money.'

'We could ask Rosemary, she'd know,' Brian suggested. 'We'll be passing her house anyway.'

'If you so much as open your mouth to Rosemary about it I'll take your tonsils out with an ice-cream scoop, and no anaesthetic,' Annie said.

'All right, all right.' Brian wasn't going to risk it.

'But if we *are* going to Tara Road we might as well call in on Gertie,' Annie suggested.

'Would she know about Dad's money?'

'Not about Dad's money, you moron, to say goodbye, like we did to Finola.'

'Oh, do you think she'd give us anything too?' Brian was interested.

'Of course she wouldn't, Brian, you *are* a clown. You get worse all the time.' Annie was exasperated with him.

'No, well, I don't suppose she'd be cleaning the house for Mam if she had any money herself.' Brian had worked it out.

'I think Mam would like it if we called on her,' Annie said.

Gertie was very pleased to see them. 'You tell your Mam that the house is fine, won't you?' Gertie said.

'I think she's forgotten all about the house,' Brian said philosophically.

'She remembered that you told her the whole garden was cut down,' Gertie said.

Brian felt there was some criticism implied here but was not sure why. 'I was going to tell her that Myles and Dekko got into an over-eighteen film because they said they were dwarves, but I thought she might prefer to hear about the garden,' he said by way of explanation.

'We're going to be meeting your relations out there, Gertie, Mam told us.' Annie was hoping to steer the conversation into safer channels.

But Gertie didn't seem all that pleased. 'Won't there be plenty of young American boys and girls for you in your own place without going all the way to Sheila's place or dragging them over to you?'

Annie shrugged. It was impossible to please people sometimes. 'Sure,' she said.

'And will you be sure to tell your mother that everything's fine with me too, just fine, for weeks on end. She'll know what I mean.'

Annie agreed that she'd tell that to her mother. She knew what Gertie meant: Jack hadn't lifted a fist to her recently. Gertie was right, Mam would be pleased. Annie felt her eyes fill with tears. Mam was so kind in many ways, it was just that she didn't understand anything at all that was going on in the world. She knew nothing about clothes, and people's friendships, and how to keep Dad or get him back once he had gone away. And Mam didn't understand why she should put Brian down more and how awful Rosemary was. And she'd probably be terrific for the first ten minutes and then go back to being hopeless and understanding nothing. Annie sighed a deep sigh.

'Won't you have a great trip the pair of you?' Gertie said.

'We will. Finola gave us twenty dollars each to spend on the way,' Brian said cheerfully. Annie tried to stand on his foot but he was too far away.

'That was grand. Tell me, who is Finola?' Gertie asked.

'You know, Bernadette's mother,' Brian said. Annie rolled her eyes.

'That was kind of her, she must have plenty of money to give you all that.'

'No, she's broke, that's why she fought with Dad.'

'I don't think Brian quite understands the whole scene,' Annie began.

'But she told us, Annie, she *told* us, you're always saying *I'm* a moron and I'm brain-dead, but you must be deaf. She said she fought with Dad over money.'

'Brian, we'd better go now. Marilyn's expecting us, and we have to call in on Granny as well,' Annie pleaded.

'Well I hope she'll have more than those ginger-snaps,' he grumbled, red-faced and annoyed.

'No, don't worry, Colm's making your dinner,' Gertie said.

'Oh good.' Brian brightened up. Maybe he could talk to Colm about football and videos and not have to listen to Marilyn Vine and Annie talking about clothes.

'Listen, maybe I shouldn't have said that. If she doesn't tell you that he made it, don't say I told you. She might be passing it off as her own.' Gertie was contrite now.

'Oh, I'm sure Brian Lynch would be able to cope with that, Gertie – tactful, diplomatic, he'll handle it beautifully.'

'She's always picking on me, even before I do anything,' Brian said. 'Don't worry, Gertie, I'll say, "It's terrific, Marilyn, haven't you become a good cook!" That's what I'll say.'

Gertie put her hand into the pocket of the pink overall she wore in the launderette. 'Here's a pound each, I'd love to be able to give you more, but it'll get you an ice cream at the airport.'

'Thanks, Gertie, that's terrific,' said Brian. 'Hey, I wonder if Marilyn will give us anything.'

'Why don't we just stand at the gate of our house at Tara Road and shout out how much we want? Wouldn't that be a good idea?' Annie said with her face set in a fury as she marched her brother out of the launderette.

'Sheila, won't you come up this weekend?' Ria asked Gertie's sister on the phone.

'But you'll want to be alone with the children.'

'Don't believe it, they'll be bored with me in twenty minutes. I'd love you to bring your two over again.'

'They won't wait to be asked twice, they've never stopped talking about the pool,' Sheila said. 'So if you're sure?'

'I'm sure. Imagine, in only a few hours they'll be getting on the plane. I can't believe it.'

'You know I've been going over and over the conversation we had when you first came. I'm so sorry about thinking Danny was with you and asking about him. You must have thought I was so crass.'

'No, no.' Ria remembered her own conversation with Greg Vine. 'How could you expect to be inspired? If people aren't told things how would they know?'

'Gertie certainly keeps things very secretly to herself,' Sheila Maine said.

It was all quite clear now to Marilyn why Colm was so protective of his sister. The woman was hooked on drugs. Her husband, a coarse and flashily dressed man who had been present on the night of the restaurant débâcle, did not look as if he would be any great help in such a situation. In fact he might well be part of it. Marilyn wished now that she had listened when Rosemary and Gertie had gone wittering on about Monto or whatever the man was called. She couldn't remember what he had done for a living or if it had been at all clear. Perhaps he might even have been involved in what his wife was addicted to.

What a truly extraordinary cast of people she had met since she had come to Ireland. Not for the first time she wished she were talking to Greg properly and could tell him about them. But at the moment she couldn't tell him anything.

'There's going to be a party in my house next weekend, Mrs Lynch, if your daughter would like to come along.'

Ria bit her lip. Hubie had been so helpful and straight with her. Yet she didn't want to let Annie go to a party with a whole lot of young people that she didn't know. All she *did* know was that some of them had been involved in drinking and stealing motorbikes.

Hubie saw her reluctance. 'Hey, it's not going to be anything wild,' he said.

'No, of course not.' Suppose Annie got to know that her mother had refused a party for her before she even arrived, the summer would be off to a very poor start. And that appalling Kitty wouldn't be here to lead her astray. Ria forced a cheerful smile to her face. 'Hubie, that would be great, but we will have friends staying here that weekend and the boy Sean is about Annie's age . . . can he be included too?'

'Why not?' Hubie was easy.

Annie's social life was hotting up already. At least she would enjoy it more than the boat trip, Ria thought with some satisfaction.

'When we go in to Granny, if you ask for money I'll kill you there and then and let Pliers drag your body up and down the street before he devours it,' Annie said.

'I never ask anyone for money, they keep giving it to me,' Brian said. 'Howarya, Nora,' he said cheerfully as his grandmother opened the door. Annie still insisted on addressing her grandmother in a more traditional way.

'I'm fine,' Nora Johnson said. 'You don't have Kitty hidden in the hedge or anything?'

'No,' Annie sighed. 'I suppose Bernadette was on red alert about that. God, she missed her vocation, she shouldn't be teaching music, she should be running a prison.'

Nora Johnson smothered a laugh. She had been amused by the phone calls from that strange waif-like girl that Danny Lynch was shacked up with. Bernadette Dunne was no better herself than Kitty. What was she but a fast little piece making off with someone else's husband, proud as punch to be an unmarried mother?

Still, to give her her due, she did follow Ria's instructions, which was more than Danny did. Danny seemed to be on another planet, and everywhere Nora Johnson went heads were wagging over his future. She had even broken the habit of a lifetime and asked Lady Ryan if there was any truth in the rumours. Rosemary Ryan had bitten the head off her. 'There's nothing wrong with Danny and Barney's business except gossiping old biddies trying to spread scandal about him because he left Ria.' Nora hoped that she was right.

'Imagine, this time tomorrow night you'll be in America.'

'I wish Marilyn had children,' Brian grumbled.

'If she had she'd have brought them with her, you wouldn't have them to play with out there,' Nora said.

'Mam didn't take us with *her*,' Brian said unanswerably.

'She does have a child but he's with his father in Hawaii, Mam told us ages ago, you just didn't listen,' Annie put in.

'Well, he's no use to us in Hawaii,' Brian said. 'Were you about to make tea, Nora?'

'I thought the pair of you were going down home for your supper.'

'Yes, well . . .'

Nora got out orange squash and biscuits.

'Why did you never go to America, Granny?' Annie asked.

'In my day working-class people only went to America to emigrate, they didn't go on holidays.'

'Are we working class?' Brian asked with interest.

Nora Johnson looked at her two confident, bright grandchildren and wondered what class they might consider themselves at the end of the summer when, according to informed opinion, their beautiful home would be sold. But she said nothing of that.

'You're to have a great holiday and you're to send me four postcards, one a week, do you hear?'

'I think postcards are dear out there,' Brian said.

'You're as bad as your Aunty Hilary . . . I was going to give you a fiver anyway for spending money.'

At that time by chance Pliers gave a great wail.

'I didn't ask for the money,' Brian cried out, remembering that Annie had threatened to feed his body to the dog.

'No, Brian, of course you didn't,' Annie said menacingly.

It was very odd to go into their own home as guests. And even more odd to find the place so quiet. When they had been here with Mam only a month ago there were always people coming in and out. It wasn't like that now.

'Where's Clement?' Annie asked. 'He's not in his chair.'

'He may be upstairs, I'm sure he'll come down when he smells the food.'

'Clement doesn't go upstairs,' Brian began, then catching Annie's eye he changed tack hastily. 'What I mean is . . . he used not to be much interested in going upstairs. But maybe he's changed now.'

Marilyn hid a smile. 'I've got a wonderful supper for us from Colm,' she said. 'I checked what you'd both like.'

They helped her set the table as the food was warming in the oven. It was so different to the time when they had come first and she had found them hard going.

'Have you packed everything?'

'I think so,' Annie said. 'Mam e-mailed a list of what we should take to Dad's office. Imagine her being able to use machines.'

'She uses all these machines here.' Marilyn waved around at the food processors and high-tech kitchen equipment. Recently she had felt a very strong protective sense about Ria. She wouldn't have anyone criticise her, enough bad luck had come into her life already.

'Oh that's just kitchen stuff,' Annie said loftily. 'Mam would learn anything if it had to do with the house.'

'Maybe she's broadening out.'

'Are you broadening out here?' Brian was interested.

'In a way yes, I'm doing things that I wouldn't normally do at home. It's probably the same for your mother.'

'What do you do that's so different?' Annie was interested. 'I mean you liked gardening and walking and reading at home, you said, and you're doing all that here.'

'That's true,' Marilyn said thoughtfully. 'But I feel different inside somehow. Maybe it's the same with your mother.'

'I hope she feels more cheerful about Dad and everything,' Brian said.

'Well, being away from the problem is a help certainly.'

'Did it help you feel better about your husband?' Brian wanted to know. He looked nervously at Annie, waiting for her to tell him to shut up and call him a thicko but she obviously wanted to know too, so for once she said nothing.

Marilyn shifted a little uncomfortably at the direct question. 'It's a bit complicated. You see I'm not separated from my husband. Well, I am of course, since he's in Hawaii and I'm here, but we didn't have an argument, a fight or anything.'

'Did you just go off him?' Brian was trying to be helpful.

'No, it wasn't that, and before you ask I don't think he went off me. It's just we needed some time to be alone and then perhaps it will be all right, maybe at the end of the summer.'

'Do you think Mam and Dad might be all right after the summer too?' Poor Brian's face was so eager that Marilyn felt a lump in her throat. She couldn't think of anything helpful to say.

'There's the little matter of Bernadette and the baby,' Annie said, but she spoke more gently than usual.

'And did your husband not have anyone young who was going to have a baby?' Brian was clutching at straws.

'No, that wasn't it at all.'

'Well then there's not much hope,' Brian said. He looked as if he was about to cry.

'Brian, can you do me a favour? I have a horrible feeling that Clement may have gone to sleep on my bed, on your mother's bed, and we don't want him to get into bad habits. Do you think you could go up and rescue him?'

'He's really Annie's cat.' Brian's lip was trembling but he knew too well Annie's territorial attitude to Clement and didn't want to risk being bawled out over it.

'It's okay, get him down,' Annie agreed. When he had gone upstairs Annie apologised for him. 'He's very dumb,' she said.

'And young,' Marilyn added.

'He still thinks it will end all right,' Annie sighed.

'And you, Annie, what do you think?'

'I think as long as Mam is able to keep this house, she'll survive somehow.'

Danny came home late. Bernadette sat curled in her armchair, the table was set for two. 'Where are the children?' he asked.

Bernadette raised her eyes slowly to him. 'I beg your pardon?' she said.

'Where are Annie and Brian?'

'Oh. *I* see. Not . . . hallo Bernadette, or I love you sweetheart, or it's good to be home. Well, since you ask where the children are, try to remember back as far as breakfast when they said they were going to make a series of calls saying goodbye to people like your mother-in-law, my mother, Marilyn, whoever, and you said they were to be home by ten at the latest.'

He was instantly contrite. 'Jesus, Bernadette, I'm so sorry, I'm so sorry and crass and stupid and selfish. I had a day – boy, did I have a day, but that's not your fault. Forgive me.'

'Nothing to forgive,' she shrugged.

'But there is,' he cried. 'You've given up everything for me and I come in and behave like a boor.'

'I gave up nothing for you, it was you who gave up a lot for me.' Her voice was calm and matter-of-fact as if she were explaining something to a child. 'Let me get you a drink, Danny.'

'It might make me worse.'

'Not a long, cool, very weak whiskey sour, it's mainly lemonade.'

'I'm no company for you, a grumpy old man harassed by work.'

'Shush.' She handed him the drink and raised the level on the player a little. 'Brahms, he works magic all the time.'

Danny was restless, he wanted to talk. But Brahms and the whiskey sour did their work. He felt his shoulders relaxing, the frown-lines going from between his eyes. In many ways there was nothing to talk about. What was the point of giving Bernadette a blow-by-blow account of the unpleasantness in the office today? How Larry their bank manager had been downright discourteous on the telephone. How a big businessman had pulled out of a consortium that was going to do a major development in Wicklow because he said Barney and Danny were unreliable, possibly tainted partners. How Polly had called to warn them that the word was out they were on the skids. How Barney had proved elusive and distant over all these matters as if it didn't really concern him.

And, worst of all, Danny's niggling fear that the personal guarantee he had given to Barney on Number 16 Tara Road would be called in and that he would lose the house. And not only would there be no home for Ria and the children but there would be nothing to sell. Some things were too huge to talk about, Bernadette was quite right not even to attempt it.

Clement sat in his chair but glanced wistfully at the door that would take him back to the big comfortable bed with its white counterpane where he had been sleeping happily for so long.

As she served Colm's food, Marilyn told them more about Westville. She explained the alumni weekend and how everyone would come back and tell each other how young they looked. 'My husband will be coming back from Hawaii so you'll meet him then.'

'Will he be staying in the house, your house?' Annie asked.

'Yes, apparently your mother very kindly said he could.'

'Will your son be coming back too?'

'I beg your pardon?'

'Your son? Isn't he in Hawaii with Mr Vine?'

'My son?'

Annie didn't like the look on Marilyn's face. 'Um yes.'

'Who told you that?'

'Mam did.'

'Your mother said that Dale was in Hawaii?'

'She didn't say his name but she said his room was all there ready for him to come back.'

Marilyn had gone very white.

Brian didn't notice. 'Will he be there when we're there? Maybe we could have competitions with the basketball?'

'Did your mother say anything more?' Marilyn's voice was scarcely above a whisper now.

Annie was very alarmed. 'I think she said she'd asked Mr Vine about him but she didn't get any details so she doesn't know if he's going to be coming back or not.'

'Oh my God,' Marilyn said.

'I'm very sorry . . . should I not have asked? Is anything . . . wrong?' Annie began.

'What is it?' Brian asked. 'Is he not in Hawaii? Did he run away?'

'I see *now* what he meant,' Marilyn said.

'What?'

'Greg said that your mother sounded very religious . . .'

'She's not a bit religious,' Brian said disapprovingly. 'Nora always says she's heading for the hob of hell.'

'Shut up, Brian,' Annie said automatically.

'What a stupid thing to do. I never stopped to think that of course that's what she would imagine.' Marilyn looked utterly anguished.

'So he's *not* in Hawaii?' Annie asked.

'No.'

'Where is he then?' Brian was getting tired of this.

'He's dead,' Marilyn Vine said. 'My son Dale is dead.'

Danny felt a lot calmer after an hour. Perhaps he was just exaggerating the situation. Bernadette drifted into the kitchen to prepare the smoked chicken salad. There was never any hiss of pots boiling, soufflés rising, pastry-making covering the whole place with flour. He had never known how gentle and undemanding life could be, how free from frenzied activity. And there was more than enough of that in the office.

'Have I three minutes to make a call?' he asked.

'Of course.'

He dialled Finola. 'This is Danny Lynch. I wanted to apologise very sincerely for my bad temper with you.'

'I expect the children asked you to do this.'

'No, not at all, they're not here.'

'Or Bernadette?'

'You know your daughter better than that, she has never mentioned it. Not once. No, this is from me. I was out of order.'

'Well, Danny, what can I say?' She sounded totally nonplussed.

'The answer to your question is that our company *is* in financial trouble, but I am utterly certain we will get out of it. We have plenty of assets. Bernadette will not be left destitute, believe me.'

'I believe you, Danny, and thank you. Perhaps I should not have asked. It's just that you have so many other responsibilities as well as Bernadette.'

'They'll be looked after, Finola. Are we friends now?'

'We always were,' she said.

He hung up and saw Bernadette watching him from the doorway. 'You are a hero,' she said. 'It's just as simple as that.'

In the kitchen of Number 16 Tara Road a silence had fallen.

Eventually it was broken by Brian. 'Did he have an awful disease or something?' he asked.

'No, he was killed. A motorcycle wreck.'

'What did he look like? Did he have red hair like you?' Annie asked.

'Yes. Even though we have no Irish blood at all, both Greg and I have reddish hair, so for poor Dale there was no escape. We're both tall, so he was tall too. And lean. And sporty. He had braces on his teeth, you know lots of the kids in the States do.'

'It's coming in here a bit too,' Brian said, not wanting Ireland to be left behind.

'Sure it is. He was one great kid. Every mother thinks her son is the best in the world, I was no different.'

'Have you a picture of him, a photograph?' Annie asked.

'No, none at all.'

'Why not?'

'I don't know. It would make me too sad, I suppose.'

'But you have pictures of him at home; Mam said he was very good-looking and he had a lovely smile. That's why I was sort of hoping he'd be there,' Annie said.

'Yes.'

'I'm sorry.'

'No, it's all right, he was good-looking.'

'Did he have any girlfriends?'

'No, Annie, I don't think so, but then what does a mother know?'

'Bet he did, you can see it in all the movies. They start very young over in America,' Brian said wisely.

And they sat and talked on about the dead Dale until Annie realised that

Commanding Officer Bernadette would be on the warpath and they'd better go.

'I'll drive you,' Marilyn offered.

They saw Rosemary on the street. Marilyn looked at Annie as if asking whether she wanted to stop and say goodbye to her mother's friend. Imperceptibly Annie shook her head. Marilyn accelerated so they wouldn't be noticed. She was very relieved. She found it increasingly hard to give the barely civil greetings that were required between neighbours. Interesting that Annie seemed to feel the same way.

Marilyn left the children at the end of their road. She had no wish to engage in any kind of conversation with Danny Lynch or his new love. She drove back to Tara Road, her mind churning.

When she parked at Number 16 she realised with a sense of shock that she didn't really remember the journey. Yet she must have taken the correct turns and given the appropriate signals. Marilyn felt very ashamed. This was how accidents were caused, just as much as by speeding, people driving with their minds somewhere else. She was shaking as she parked Ria's car and let herself into the house. She went and sat down at the table. Ria had left three cut-crystal decanters on the sideboard. In her note she had said that they were mainly for show, since she and Danny had always drunk bottles of inexpensive wine. She hoped that the contents were still drinkable and if so Marilyn was to help herself. There was a little brandy in one, something that looked like port in another and sherry in the third. With a shaking hand Marilyn poured herself a brandy.

What had happened today? What had changed so that she could talk about Dale, tell strangers that he had freckles on his nose and braces on his teeth? Admit that she couldn't carry a picture of him in case she would convulse with grief just by looking at it? Why had the direct questions of two children whom she hardly knew released these responses that her husband, friends, colleagues could not make her give?

It was almost dark now but the reds and gold of the sunset had not disappeared totally from the sky. She was living in a house and a city that Dale had never seen. Nobody here had known her when she was a mother, a loving fulfilled mother with a future ahead of her. They only knew her as frosty, buttoned-up Marilyn Vine, and yet some of them still liked her. She had met people who had problems as bad as hers. For the very first time since the tragedy she now knew this was true.

People had told her to count her blessings but had not been able to think of one blessing that was worth mentioning in the context of her own great loss. And nothing Greg or anyone had said had helped at all.

It was stupid to think that she had turned a corner in one night. Marilyn was not a person who believed in miracle cures. It was an emotional occasion, that was all. These two living children were going to go to 1024 Tudor Drive where Dale Vine had played and slept and studied in his short life. They would make friends as he had done, and swim in the swimming pool where he had dived. They might even find the stopwatch and time each other and their mother as he had timed her when he was alive. 'Come on, Mom, you can do better than that,' he would shout. And she had done better.

She sipped her brandy and noticed that there were tears on her hand. She hadn't even realised she was crying. She had never let herself cry before and had dismissed as pop psychologists those who told her she must let go and give in to sorrow. Now she sat weeping in this darkening room with the sounds of a foreign city around her, the different traffic noises, the cries of children with Irish accents, and the birds with unfamiliar calls.

The great ginger cat sat looking at her on another chair. She was drinking brandy and crying. She had said his name aloud, and the world had not ended. Annie and Brian had asked questions about him. What would he have done as a career? Did he eat meat, which were his favourite film stars, what books did he read? They had even asked what kind of a motorbike he was riding when he was killed. She had answered all these questions and volunteered more information, told them stories about funny things that had happened at Thanksgiving, or Dale's school play or the time of the great snowstorms.

Dale. She tried again, fearfully, but no, it hadn't disappeared. She could say his name now. It was extraordinary. It must have been there the whole time and she hadn't known. And now that she knew, there was nobody she could tell. It would be cruel and unfair to telephone her husband, poor baffled hurt Greg wondering what he had done wrong and how he had failed her. It would be so wrong to call him in Hawaii, and say that something had happened to unlock her prison. It might just be because she was here in a place he had never known. But Marilyn believed that it was more than that. She needn't fear going to a place where Dale had been, somewhere where she had seen him smile and rush up with yet another new enthusiasm.

She always knew that Dale had loved her own spirit of adventure, her willingness to learn. She had followed his lead in everything, to be a stronger swimmer, a demon at computer games, Sumo wrestling fan, and gin rummy player. Only at motorbikes had she turned away from him. For month after weary month she had agonised in case it had all been her fault. Suppose she had promised him a bike when he was the age to drive one, then he might not have gone along with those wild boys and their dangerous drunken plans. But tonight somehow she felt a little differently.

Annie had said in a matter-of-fact way that of course you couldn't let him mess around with motorbikes, it would have been like letting him play with a gun. And Brian had said, 'I expect he's up in heaven and he's very sorry he caused you all this trouble.'

And nothing anyone had said before, since the moment she had been told the news about the accident, had made any sense at all until this. She put her head down on the table and cried all the tears that she knew she should have cried in the past year and a half. But they weren't ready then, they were now.

Ria drove to the next town and got the bus to Kennedy Airport. A month ago Marilyn had made this journey, a whole month. And in another thirty days

Ria would be going home. She closed her eyes and wished hard that this would be a wonderful, unforgettable month for the children. It was no longer a matter of trying to outdo what Danny and Bernadette had given them. That seemed unimportant just now. They deserved a holiday, a good time, the feeling of hope, the prospect that the future might not be grim.

She would *not* lose her patience with Annie and boss her and tell her what to do. Annie was a young woman, she would let her find her own level in this quiet sheltered place. Much, much safer in many ways than a capital city like Dublin. And, mercifully, three thousand miles away from Kitty. She would *not* let Brian's gaffes irritate her. There was no way you could impress anyone with Brian, she must learn to stop trying. He would say the most insensitive things to everyone. He would ask John and Gerry why they weren't married, Heidi why she didn't have children, Carlotta why she spoke funny English. There were acres of minefields for Brian to plough through. At no stage would she be ashamed of him or urge him to be more thoughtful.

She ached to put her arms around him and for him not to pull away in embarrassment. She yearned for Annie to say, 'Mam, you look terrific you've got a suntan, I really missed you.' All the way to the airport Ria forced herself not to live in a world of dreams. It wasn't going to be perfect just because they hadn't seen her for thirty days.

Remember that, Ria, remember it. Grow up, grow up and live in the real world.

Danny rang the bell of Rosemary's flat. It was ten o'clock at night. Rosemary was working at her desk, she put away her papers. She looked at herself in the mirror, fluffed up her hair, sprayed on some expensive perfume and pressed the buzzer to let him come up.

'Why won't you take a key, Danny? I've asked you often enough.'

'You know why, it would be too much temptation, I'd be here all the time.' He gave her the lopsided smile that always turned her heart over.

'I wish.' Rosemary smiled at him.

'No, I suppose the truth is I'd be afraid I'd come in and find you *in flagrante* with someone else.'

'Unlikely.' She was crisp.

'Well, you have been known to indulge,' he accused.

'Unlike yourself,' Rosemary said. 'Drink?'

'Yes, and you'll need one too.'

Rosemary stood calm and elegant in her navy dress by the drinks trolley. She poured them two large Irish whiskeys then sat down on her white sofa, her back straight and ankles crossed like a model.

'You were born graceful,' he said.

'You should have married me,' she said.

'Our timing was wrong. You're a businesswoman – you know that the secret of the universe is timing.'

'All this philosophy didn't stop you leaving Ria for someone else, and not for me, but we've been through all that. What are we drinking to? A success or a disaster?'

'You never lose control, do you?' He seemed both admiring and annoyed at the same time.

'You know I do, Danny.'

'I'm finished . . .'

'You can't be. You've a lot of fire insurance.'

'We've called it all in.'

'What about the Lara development?' This was their flagship, the forty-unit apartment block with the leisure club. The publicity had been enormous, every unit had been sold and resold long before completion. It was what was going to make them turn the corner.

'We lost it today.'

'What in God's name is Barney at? He's meant to have these hotshot advisers.'

'Yes, but apparently they need collateral . . . that we're not so strong on.' He looked tired and a little rueful.

Rosemary could not accept the seriousness of what he was saying. Anyone else whose business had been wiped out would be hysterical, fuming with rage, or frightened. Danny looked like a small boy who had been caught in somebody's orchard. Regretful, that was how he appeared.

'What are you going to do? she asked.

'What *can* I do, Rosemary?'

'Well you can stop being so bloody defeatist, you can go out there and ask. Ask somebody for the support. Stop being so goddamn noble about it, it's only money when all's said and done.'

'Do you think so?' He looked unsure now, not the cocky Danny who could conquer the world.

'I *know* so. And you know it too. We are two of a kind, we didn't get where we are by bleating. We've all had to humble ourselves from time to time. By God I know I have, and you've had to too.'

'All right, I will,' he said suddenly. His voice was stronger than before.

'That's better,' she said.

'Lend me the money, Rosemary, lend it to me now. I'll double it as I did with everything.' She looked at him open-mouthed in shock. He went on. 'I won't let Barney near it, he's past it and I owe him nothing. This will be my investment, our investment. I'll tell you what we'll do. I have a complete business plan . . .' He took out two sheets of paper with columns of figures written on them.

She looked at him, aghast. 'You're serious?' Rosemary said. 'You really are.'

He appeared not to notice her shock. 'Nothing's typed up, I didn't want to use the machines in the office but it's all here . . .' He moved to sit beside her on the sofa to show her what he had written.

Rosemary leapt to her feet. 'Don't be ridiculous, Danny, you're embarrassing us both.'

'I don't understand . . .' He was bewildered.

'You're demeaning us, what we have, what we were to each other. I beg you don't ask again.'

'But you have money, Rosemary, property, a business . . .'

'Yes.' Her voice was cold.

'You have all that, I have nothing. You have no dependants, I have people hanging out of me at every turn.'

'That's your choice to have people hanging out of you.'

'If you were in trouble, Rosemary, I'd be in there helping you.'

'No you wouldn't. Don't give me that line, it's sentimental and it's not worthy of you.'

'But I would, you know I would,' he cried. 'You're my great friend, we all help friends.'

'Neither of us helped Colm Barry. He asked us both to invest and we wouldn't. You wouldn't even bring clients there until it was successful.'

'That's different.'

'It's not. It's exactly the same.'

'Colm was a loser, I'm not a loser.'

'He's not a loser now but by God you will be, Danny, if you go round asking your lovers for support to help you keep your wife and your pregnant mistress.'

'I don't *have* any lovers except you, I never did.'

'Of course. Perhaps Orla King has hit the big time now as an international singer and *she* might bankroll you. Grow up, Danny.'

'I love you, Rosemary. I always have loved you. Don't throw everything back in my face. I just made a mistake, that's all. Surely you've done that occasionally?'

'You made two mistakes, one called Ria and one called Bernadette.'

He smiled slowly. 'Yet you didn't leave me over either of them, now did you?'

'If that's your trump card, Danny, it's a poor one. I stayed with you for sex, from desire not love. We both know that.'

'Well even then, can't you see that this would work . . . ?' He indicated the papers again, thinking even at this late stage that she might read them and reconsider. She put her glass down firmly, showing that it was time to go.

'Rosemary, don't be like this. Listen, we're friends as well as . . . as well as the passion and desire bit. Won't that make you think that you might be able . . . ?' His voice trailed away as he looked at her cold face. He made one last try. 'If I had my own business, sweetheart, and you were involved in it, we'd be able to see each other much more often.'

'I've never had to pay for sex in my life and I don't intend to start now.' She opened the door of the apartment that they had so long planned for. They had spent hours on their own, planning what they jokily called a love-nest, while in front of Barney it was a stylish investment property, and for Ria they had called it an elegant new home for Ria's friend.

'You're throwing me out,' he said, looking at her, head on one side.

'I think it's time you left, Danny.'

'You know how to kick someone so that it hurts.'

'You did that twice to me. You didn't know you were doing it when you married Ria, but you sure as hell knew it when you couldn't even tell me about Bernadette and I had to hear it from your wife.'

'I'm sorry,' he said. 'There are some things which are so difficult . . .'

'I know.' Her voice was momentarily softer. 'I do know. It's not that easy for me to let you go to the wall. But Danny, I will not even contemplate financing two different homes for you, while I sit here alone. If you can't understand that then you understand nothing and you deserve to go under.'

When he was gone she went out on her roof garden terrace. She needed the air to clear her head. There was almost too much to take in. The only man she had ever fancied in her whole life had grovelled to her. He had not been his old slick, confident self. He had really begged her to help him. It gave her no pleasure to remember how she had refused him. There was no sense of power in withholding money from him. But there would have been terrible weakness in giving it to him, in paying him for his mistakes.

It gave her no satisfaction to let him go under. What she wanted was for things to be different. For Danny to desire her so strongly and permanently that he would give up everything else for that alone. This, she realised, is what she must have wanted him to do all the time. Rosemary had always thought that she was so strong, she was a woman like Polly who could live her life and keep love in its place.

In so many ways Barney and Danny were alike, urgent and ambitious, men for whom one woman would never be enough. What they needed were tough strong partners, women who could provide them with passion without making irritating demands. Danny and Barney were so alike in their belief that they could conquer the world.

And suddenly she realised that they were alike in other ways too. They loved two kinds of women, the ones they married and those they kept on the side. They married Madonnas – the quiet, worthy Mona and the earnest, optimistic Ria. But to her great annoyance, Rosemary realised that Bernadette had been cast in the Madonna-role too. She hadn't realised how angry that made her feel. How had Bernadette sneaked in there somehow?

Was it possible that after all Rosemary did love Danny Lynch? She had told herself a million times that the words she would use were desire, appreciate and fancy. Love was never meant to be any part of it. Surely it couldn't be developing at this entirely inappropriate stage?

At times like these Ria wished she were taller. It was infuriating to have to jump up and down but unless she did she couldn't see the passengers coming through. And then she saw them. They wheeled a luggage trolley with their two suitcases on it, their eyes raking the crowds. They each carried a small grip bag. Those were new. Ria wondered with a pang who had bought those particular gifts. It was a good idea to have something that would hold sweaters, books, comics, games. Why had *she* not thought of that?

She forced herself not to shout out their names, neither of them would want the attention called to them. Instead she ran to a corner where she could reach out when they passed by. Don't hold them too long or too tight, she told herself. She waved with all the Irish Americans who waved for their families and friends. And they saw her. With a lump in her throat Ria saw their faces light up and they both broke into a run.

'*Mam!*' Brian cried, and ran towards her. It was he who hugged longer.

Ria had to release him to reach for Annie. She seemed taller, slimmer, but this couldn't be. Not in four weeks. 'You're beautiful, Annie,' Ria said.

'We missed you, Mam,' Annie said into her mother's hair.

It was as good a reunion as Ria could have wished for as she had sat on the bus impatient for their arrival. Ria had decided she would take them into Manhattan, show them the big sights, take them on the Circle Line tour, and behave like a native New Yorker pointing out everything from the Hudson and East Rivers. She had already done this tour herself, she knew what it could offer. But then she thought, they'll be tired, and everything in America will be new for them anyway, even being on a bus over here will be exciting. Take them home to Tudor Drive, let them swim, let them see their new home.

Back in Tara Road Ria would have had many people to discuss this with over the past few days. There would have been phone calls and cups of coffee and the whole thing would have been argued to the bone. Here there was nobody. It would seem feeble somehow to lay such issues in front of Carlotta, and Heidi, young Hubie Green, John and Gerry from the gourmet shop. Nowadays Ria Lynch made up her own mind about things, matters were no longer arranged by long committee discussions with coffee and shortbread.

'We're going straight back to Westville,' she said, an arm lightly round each of their shoulders. 'I want to show you your summer home.'

They seemed pleased, and with her heart light and happy Ria marched her little family to the bus.

Heidi was looking at her e-mail with amazement. There was a message from Marilyn in Dublin.

Heidi, I found a Cyber café and decided to seize the opportunity. Thank you so much for your air letters, you are good to keep in touch. I miss you and Henry. There are lots of things I imagine myself telling you about Dublin and the way people live. I've been through Trinity College which is quite beautiful, and absolutely in the centre of the city, it's as if Dublin was built all around it. I'm glad to hear that you have been socialising with Ria, she sounds a great cook and a wonderful homemaker. Her children are going over to Tudor Drive today, a very bright girl called Annie just a year younger than Dale, and Brian who should be the hero of some cartoon series and one day will be. I'll miss them. I wonder if you could possibly arrange some kind of treat for them? If there's anything like a circus or a pop star or Wild West Show coming to the area. It's just that I'm afraid they'll find Tudor Drive a bit dull after Dublin and I really do want them to have a good time. I'd so much appreciate it, Heidi. You can't mail me back here sadly but I'll be in touch again. Love Marilyn.

Heidi read the screen three times then she printed it out to take home and show to her husband. Marilyn Vine wanted people to get involved in her life. She thought Tudor Drive might be dull for two strange children. But most startling of all she had mentioned Dale. She had actually used his name.

Polly Callaghan heard Barney's key in the lock. He looked a little tired but not as tired as he deserved to look with all that was happening to him.

'Come in, you poor divil,' she said with a big warm smile.

'It's not good news, Poll.'

'I know it's not,' she said. 'Look, I've got the evening paper, I've been looking through Accommodation to Let for places to stay.'

He put his hand on hers. 'I'm so ashamed. First your business, now your apartment.'

'They were never mine, Barney, they were yours.'

'They were ours,' he said.

'So what's the bottom line? What date do I leave?'

'By September the first.'

'And your own house?'

'Is in Mona's name.'

'As this flat is in mine.'

'I know.' He looked wretched.

'And is she being as good a sport as I am? Giving it up without a murmur?'

'I don't know, she's not in possession of all the facts, if you understand.'

'Well, she will be this week, you'll be declared a bankrupt.'

'Yes. Yes. We'll get back, Poll, we always did before.'

'I think this may be a bit heavy,' she said.

'They tell us to take risks, they advise us to be adventurous, entrepreneurs even, and then when we do they bloody leave us in the gutter.' He sounded very bitter.

'Who do? Banks?'

'Yes, banks, big business consortiums, civil servants, architects, politicians . . .'

'Will you go to gaol?'

'No, not a possibility.'

'And you do have some money outside the country?'

'No, Poll, hardly anything. I was vain you know, I believed my own publicity. I brought it all back for schemes like Number 32 Tara Road, like the Lara development. And look where it got me.'

'Talking about Tara Road . . .' Polly Callaghan began.

'Don't remind me, Poll, telling them is as bad as telling Mona.'

They chattered all the time on the bus.

There had been a well-known singer on the plane, up in the front in first class, but Brian and Annie had seen him as they went to view the flight deck. They asked him to sign his menu. Annie had seen him first but he could see Brian's disappointment so he had signed another for him. The pilots did nothing on the plane at all except sit there apparently. The whole thing was done by radar and computers on the ground. You didn't have to pay for Coke or Pepsi or orange on the plane, it was free.

Granny was fine, they hadn't seen Hilary but apparently she and Martin were looking for a new house. Gertie had sent a message. What was it? Brian couldn't remember.

'She said to tell you Jack wasn't belting her,' Annie said. Ria was startled.

Brian looked up with interest. 'She didn't say that, I'd have remembered,' he said.

Ria intervened. 'That was just a joke,' she said.

Annie caught the tone. 'Of course it was a joke, Brian, you've no sense of humour,' she said. 'What Gertie said was to tell you that everything was going fine in the launderette and everywhere, and that you'd be glad to know that.'

Ria smiled at her daughter. Annie was growing up. 'And how's your dad?' She kept the question light.

'Fussed,' Annie said.

'Broke,' Brian said.

'I'm sorry to hear both of those things.' Ria knew this was a slippery slope and she must leave it as soon as possible. 'Look, I brought a map to show you where we're going.' She pointed out the route and told them about thruways and highways and turnpikes, but all the time her mind kept going back to these two words. Fussed and broke. Danny had been neither of those things when he lived with her. What a fool he was! What a stupid fool to leave her and his children, and to end up not blissfully happy as he had thought but broke and fussed.

They couldn't believe that Mam could drive on the wrong side of the road. 'It's sort of automatic unless you're coming out of a gas station, then it's dangerously easy to set off on the left instead of the right.'

'Coming out of a what?' Annie asked.

'Petrol station. Sorry, I'm picking up the language,' Ria said, laughing.

They loved the house. 'My God, that's like a film star's swimming pool,' Annie said.

'Will we have a swim now?' Brian wanted to know.

'Why not? I'll show you your rooms and we'll all change.'

'You're going to swim too?' Annie was surprised.

'Oh, I swim twice a day,' Ria said. With her first earnings from the delicatessen she had bought a smart new swimsuit. She was anxious to show it off to the children. 'Annie, this is your room, I put flowers in it, there's lots of closet space ... lots of presses in it. And Brian you're over here.'

They flung their suitcases on their beds and began to throw the clothes out. Ria was touched to see the e-mail that she had sent to Danny's office telling them what to pack taped inside the lid of Annie's suitcase. 'Did Dad do that for you, help you pack?' she asked.

'No, Bernadette did. Mam, you wouldn't believe Dad these days ... he honestly hardly noticed we were leaving.'

'And *is* he broke, do you think?'

'I don't know, Mam, there's a lot of chat about it certainly but if he were he'd tell you, wouldn't he?' Ria was silent. 'He'd have to, Mam.'

'Yes, of course he would. Let's all get changed and go swim.'

Brian, already in his bathing trunks, was investigating the house. He opened the door to Dale's room that Ria had meant to lock until she could explain. 'Hey, look at all this!' he said in amazement, looking at the posters on the wall, the books, the music centre, the clothes and the brightly coloured cushions and rug on the bed. '*This* is a room.'

'Well I must explain . . .' Ria began.

Annie was in there too, she was running her hand across the photographs framed on the wall. 'He *is* good-looking, isn't he?'

'Look at all the pictures of wrestlers! Aren't they enormous!' Brian was examining pictures of giant Sumos.

'And this must have been his school play,' Annie said. 'Let me see, oh *there* he is.'

'I must tell you about this room,' Ria began.

'I know, it's Dale's room.' Annie was lofty, she knew everything.

'But what you don't understand is that he won't be coming back.'

'No, he's dead, he was killed on a motorbike,' Brian said.

'How do you know?'

'Marilyn told us all about it. Let's see, can you see the braces on his teeth? Look, they're only like little dots.' Annie was examining a close-up picture of Dale shovelling snow. 'That must have been when they had the snowstorm and Dale dug out a path for them in the middle of the night as a surprise.'

'She told you all this?' Ria was astounded.

'Yes, why did *you* tell us he was in Hawaii?' Annie wanted to know.

'Not to upset us maybe?' Brian suggested.

'I got it wrong,' Ria said humbly.

'Typical Mam,' said Annie as if this was no surprise to her but no big deal either. 'Come on, Mam, let's swim. Hey that's a nice swimming cozzy. And you're much browner than we are, but we'll catch up, won't we, Brian?'

'Sure we will.'

Gertie was walking past Number 32 Tara Road when Rosemary came out.

'You're the very person I wanted to meet,' Rosemary called.

Gertie was surprised. Rosemary rarely wanted to meet her and when she did she seemed very scornful of Gertie's lifestyle. Also, there was a telephone in the launderette if she needed her. But life was good these days. She had asked those children to tell Ria, it wasn't a thing you'd put in writing but Jack hadn't touched a drop for a week and he had even given the launderette a coat of paint. Her children were at home again, watchful and wary but at least they were home. 'So now you found me,' Gertie said brightly.

'Yes, I was wondering when Ria's children are off to the States. You see Ria sent me an e-mail no less, and she was talking about a big faculty picnic or some other college thing in the town she's living in. Anyway I thought I'd send her over a couple of dresses, you know, things I don't need any more.

She might find them useful for socialising. She doesn't have anything particularly stylish herself.'

Rosemary's eye always seemed to go up and down you as she talked. It began at your feet and went as far as the crown of your head, as if she were a teacher inspecting pupils to see if they were suitable for a public parade. Gertie had known it for many years, and the eye always seemed to linger on the stained part of the pink nylon overall or the hair when it was uncombed and greasy. 'But they've gone already,' Gertie said. 'They went the day before yesterday, they'll be settled in now.'

Rosemary was irritated. 'I didn't know that.'

'It was always August the first that they were going out there, remember?'

'No I don't. How can I hold everything in my head? They never called to say goodbye.'

'They came to say goodbye to me,' Gertie said. She had very few satisfactions, she would savour this one.

'Maybe I was out,' Rosemary said.

'Could be.' Gertie put a lot of doubt in her voice.

'And where are you off to?' Rosemary wanted to change the subject.

'I have a busy morning.' Gertie sounded on top of the world. 'I've hired a girl to do ironing and I want to ask Colm if he'd give me a trial to do his tablecloths and napkins. We do his towels already.'

'Oh I think for a restaurant like that he'd need a proper laundry, and particularly for Horse Show week.' Rosemary poured cold water on the scheme.

'Colm will know, and then I go in to Marilyn, do her floors and ironing. And she's going to drive me to this place where they do cheap electrical signs, and we're going to have one put up over the launderette.'

Gertie looked so pleased with the modest plans for the day that Rosemary was touched. Gertie, who used to be so handsome when she worked in Polly's all those years ago with Ria, Gertie who had lost everything for loving that madman. 'And Jack. How is he these days?'

'He's fine, Rosemary, thank you. He gave up drink entirely and it suits him,' said Gertie with a big broad smile.

Hubie telephoned to know if he could call by the house and welcome Annie to Westville. Brian too, of course, he added as an afterthought.

'Please do, Hubie. They both love it here and they've been playing that game you set up every evening.'

'Great.'

The admiration in his eyes for shapely blonde Annie was obvious. 'You're even cuter than your picture,' he said.

'Thank you,' Annie said. 'That's very nice of you.'

Where had Annie, who was not quite fifteen, learned such composure? Ria wondered over and over. Certainly not from her mother who was still unable to accept a compliment. Possibly from Danny who had managed to appear calm no matter what was happening. She was very worried to hear the children say that he was broke and fussed.

As Hubie, Brian and Annie went up to the pool she decided she would call Rosemary about it. It would be nine o'clock at night at home. Rosemary would be in the cool elegant penthouse. At her desk maybe with papers. Watering the plants in her roof garden. Entertaining three people to one of her brilliant and apparently effortless meals? In bed with a lover?

Ria had realised this summer for the first time how lonely parts of Rosemary's seemingly perfect lifestyle must be. When you live by yourself your life is not dictated by others, you have to choose. And if you don't plan something you sit staring at the walls. No wonder Rosemary spent so much time with them in Number 16.

There was nobody at home. Rosemary might be out at Quentin's, or in Colm's? Possibly she was with Marilyn, they had become friendly and gone to a fashion show organised by Mona.

'Rosemary, it's Ria. Nothing really. Only a chat. The children have arrived and everything's just wonderful. I wanted to talk to you about whether Danny and Barney's business is in any trouble. I can't call Danny obviously, and I thought you might know. Don't call me back about it because the kids will be here and if there is anything to tell I don't want them to hear. But you can see how I'm a bit out on a limb here and you're the only one I can ask.'

Barney had asked Danny to meet him in Quentin's.

'We can't go there, Barney, we owe them, remember?'

'I remember. That's been settled, and I told Brenda it would be cash tonight.'

'With Bernadette or without?'

'Without. Nine o'clock okay?' He was gone.

Perhaps at the very last moment he had pulled something out of the fire. Barney was an old-time wheeler and dealer. He had come from working on building sites all over England to being the most-talked-of builder and property developer in Ireland. It was inconceivable that he would declare himself and the company bankrupt next week, which was now on the cards.

Danny wore his best jacket and his brightest tie. Whoever he was being brought to meet would need to see a buoyant Danny Lynch, nothing hangdog. He had been putting on an act for years, that's how you bought and sold houses for heaven's sake. Tonight would be the biggest act because so much depended on it.

'I might be late, sweetheart,' he said to Bernadette. 'Big Chiefs' meeting called by Barney, sounds like light at the end of the tunnel.'

'I knew there would be,' she said.

Brenda Brennan directed him towards the booth. Danny knew that this is where they would be. Whoever he was going to meet might not want to be seen supping publicly with McCarthy and Lynch. Their names were not so good at the moment. He was surprised to see only Barney there, the other person or people hadn't turned up yet. He was even more surprised to see that the table was only set for two.

'Sit down, Danny,' Barney said to him. 'This is the day we hoped never to have to see.'

'Everything?' Danny said.

'Everything, including Number 16 Tara Road,' said Barney McCarthy.

Rosemary was also having dinner in Quentin's. With her accountant, her manager and two men from a multinational printing company who wanted to buy her out. They had approached her, she had not gone to them. They were suggesting very attractive terms but were finding it difficult to persuade her how lucky she was to be approached in this way.

One man was American, one was English, but they knew that their nationality had nothing to do with their incomprehension about this beautiful blonde Irishwoman with her flawless make-up, shining hair and designer outfit.

'I don't think you'll ever be able to realise capital in this way again,' the Englishman said.

'No, that's true, nobody wants to take me over as much as you do,' she smiled.

'And there's nobody apart from us with the money to do so, as well as the will, so it's not as if you can play us off against anyone else,' said the American.

'Quite true,' she agreed.

Rosemary had seen Danny go into the booth with Barney McCarthy. Nobody had joined them. That was a bad sign. She knew that if she agreed to this deal, if she sold her business, she could save them. It was almost dizzying to think that she had that much power. She lost track of what the two men were saying.

'I beg your pardon?' She went back to the conversation.

'We were just saying that time is moving on and as you approach forty you may want to get a life for yourself, rest after all this hard work. Put your feet up, take a cruise, live a little.'

It had been the wrong thing to suggest to Rosemary Ryan. She didn't see herself as a person putting her feet up. She didn't like strangers telling her that she was approaching forty. She looked pleasantly from one to the other. 'Come back to me in about six years. You will of course have worked out that by then I'll be half of ninety. Ask me again then, won't you? Because it really has been such a pleasure talking to you.'

Her mind wasn't fully on what she was saying, she had just seen Barney McCarthy, white-faced, storming out of the restaurant. Danny was not with him. He must be still sitting in that booth where people went when they wanted really private conversations. Rosemary Ryan would not rescue him from bankruptcy but neither would she leave him on his own after a body-blow.

'Gentlemen, I'll let you finish your coffees and brandies on your own. I'm so grateful for your interest and enthusiasm, but as you said for me time is moving on and I can't afford to waste any of it. So I'll say goodnight.'

The men were only struggling to get to their feet when she was gone.

'Rosemary?'

'Brandy?'

'Why are you here?'

'Have you eaten?'

'No, no there wasn't time to eat.' She ordered a large brandy for him and a bowl of soup and some olive bread. A mineral water for herself. 'Stop playing nursemaid, I don't want to eat, I asked you what are you doing here?'

'You need to eat. You're in shock. I was at another table and saw Barney leaving . . . that's why I'm here.'

'My house is gone.'

'I'm so sorry.'

'You're not sorry, Rosemary, you're glad.'

'Shut the hell up . . . pitying yourself and attacking me. What did I ever do bad to you except betray your wife, my friend, by sleeping with you?'

'It's a bit late to be getting all remorseful about that, you knew what you were doing at the time.'

'Yes I did, and you knew what you were doing playing with Barney McCarthy.'

'Why are you here?'

'To get you home.'

'To your home or my home?'

'To your home. My car is outside, I'll drive you.'

'I don't want your pity or this soup,' he shouted as the waiter laid down a bowl of parsnip and apple soup.

'Eat it, Danny. You're not functioning properly.'

'What do you care?'

'I care because you are a friend, more than a friend.'

'I told Barney McCarthy I never wanted to lay eyes on him again. You're right, that wasn't functioning properly.'

'That's business talk, panicky business talk, that's all. It will sort itself out.'

'No, some things can never be forgotten.'

'Come on, you and I were bawling at each other the other night and here we are sitting talking as friends. It will happen with Barney too.'

'No it won't, he's very shabby, he told me he'd settled up the bill here and it turns out he hasn't.'

'Why did he want to tell you here?'

'He said he needed neutral ground. All he was doing was humiliating me here in front of the Brennans, people I know and like.'

'How much is the bill?'

'Over six hundred.'

'I'll pay that now on my card.'

'I don't want your charity. What I want is your investment, I told you.'

'I can't do it, Danny, it's not there. Everything's tied up.' Out of the corner of her eye she saw the group of four leaving, her own office manager, her accountant and two bewildered people who had come to offer her a huge sum of money, more than enough to bail Danny Lynch out and leave her plenty to live on. She caught Brenda Brennan's eye. They had known each other a long time. 'Brenda, there was a misunderstanding. An old bill. It was never settled. Here, can we do it now on my card? No receipt to be sent to Barney McCarthy, this is Danny paying if you get my drift.'

Brenda got Rosemary's drift. 'The table was booked in your name, Mr Lynch, otherwise Mr McCarthy would not have been able to get a reservation,' she said crisply. 'He said that he was your guest when he arrived.'

'Which, as it turned out, he was,' said Rosemary.

'Drive along Tara Road,' Danny asked her.

'Stop punishing yourself.'

'No, please, it's not taking us out of the way.'

They approached Tara Road from the top end, the corner near Gertie's launderette.

'Look, she's got a new sign up: GERTIE'S. What a stupid name,' Rosemary said.

'Well, it's better than calling it Gertie and Jack's, I suppose.' He managed a weak smile.

They passed Number 68, the old people's home. 'They're all asleep in St Rita's, and it's not even ten o'clock,' Rosemary said.

'They're all asleep there at seven. Imagine, I won't even be able to afford to go there when I'm old and mad.' They passed Nora Johnson's little house at Number 48A. 'It must be about time for Pliers to go out and foul the footpath,' Danny said. 'Pliers always likes to go where it will cause maximum discomfort to everyone.'

The little laugh they managed over that got them past Number 32, the elegant renovation with its beautiful penthouse where Danny and Rosemary had spent so many hours together. Frances and Jimmy Sullivan were putting out their dustbins at Number 26. 'Kitty is pregnant, did you know that?' Rosemary asked.

'No! She's only a kid, Annie's age.' He was shocked.

'There you go,' Rosemary said.

They were at Number 16. 'It was a beautiful house,' Danny said. 'It always will be. But I won't be living there any more.'

'You'd moved out already,' Rosemary reminded him.

'I don't like that woman Marilyn at all, I can't bear to think she's living there in the last few weeks that I own it,' he said.

'She's gone off me,' Rosemary said. 'I don't know why, she used to be perfectly pleasant, but she's curt to the point of rudeness now.'

'Madwoman,' Danny said. They were passing Colm's restaurant. 'Plenty of cars,' he said. 'We were mad not to give him a start. Look where I'd be tonight if I had a piece of that restaurant.'

'We weren't mad, we were careful.'

'You may have been. I was never careful, I was just wrong, that's all,' Danny Lynch said.

'I know. How did I fancy you so much?' Rosemary said wonderingly.

'Can you turn the car?'

'Why? This is the way.'

'I want to come home with you. Please.'

'No, Danny, it would be pointless.'

'Nothing between us was ever pointless. Please, Rosemary, I need you tonight. Don't make me beg.'

She looked at him. It had always been impossible to resist him. Rosemary had already been congratulating herself that her infatuation had not let her sell her company for this man. And he wanted her. As he had always wanted her more than his prattling little wife and the strange wan girl he lived with. She turned her car in the entrance of Colm's restaurant and drove back to Number 32.

Nora Johnson taking Pliers for his nightly walk saw Lady Ryan driving up the road with a man in the passenger seat. Nora squinted but couldn't see who it was. For a moment she thought it was Danny Lynch. Lots of people looked like that. She had liked Danny and loved him calling her Holly. And she had thought he was handsome when she met him first. But when all was said and done what Danny had was cheap good looks.

Danny started to caress Rosemary before she had even put the key into the front door of Number 32.

'Don't be idiotic,' she hissed. 'We've been so careful for so long, don't blow it now.'

'You understand me, Rosemary, you're the only one who does.'

They went upstairs in the lift and as soon as they were in the door he reached for her.

'Danny, stop.'

'You don't usually say that.' He was kissing her throat.

'I don't usually refuse to save your business either.'

'But you told me you couldn't, that your funds were all tied up.' He was trying to hold her and stop her slipping away.

'No, Danny, we have to talk.'

'We never had to talk before.'

She saw her message light winking on the answering machine but she would not press the button. It might be one of the men she had had dinner with increasing the offer, raising the stakes. Danny must never know what had been turned down only feet away from him in the restaurant.

'What about Bernadette?'

'It's early, she won't expect me for a long time.'

'It's foolish.'

'It was always foolish,' he said. 'Foolish, dangerous *and* wonderful.'

Afterwards they had a shower together.

'Won't Bernadette think it odd that you smell of sandalwood?' Rosemary asked.

'Whatever soap you get I get the same for our bathroom.' He wasn't being smug or proud of his cunning, just practical.

'I remember Ria always had the same soap as I did,' she said. 'I used to think that she was copying me but it was you all the time. My, my.'

Rosemary wore a white towelling robe. She glanced at herself in the bathroom mirror. She did *not* look like someone for whom time was marching on, nor a woman approaching forty. Those men would never get their hands on her company.

'I'll call you a taxi,' she said.

'I needed you tonight,' he said.

'I suppose I need you too in ways otherwise you wouldn't have stayed. I don't do anything out of kindness.'

'So I notice,' he said dryly.

She called a cab company, giving her own account number. 'Remember to get out at the end of your road, not your house, the less these drivers know the better.'

'Yes, boss.'

'You'll survive, Danny.'

'I wish I could see how.'

'Talk to Barney tomorrow. You're both up the same creek, there's nothing to be gained by fighting each other in it.'

'You're right as usual. I'll go down and wait for the cab.' He held her very close to him. Over her shoulder he saw the light on her machine. 'You have a message,' he said.

'I'll listen to it later, probably my mother demanding that I find a suitable man and get married.'

He grinned at her, head on one side. 'I know I should hope you will, but I really hope you don't.'

'Don't worry, even if I did I expect we'd cheat on him as we have on everyone else.'

The honeymoon period was still on in Tudor Drive. Ria could hardly believe it though she walked on eggshells. Sean and Kelly Maine proved to be perfectly satisfactory friends for Annie and Brian.

'I wish Sean was younger,' Brian complained. 'It's the wrong way round. Kelly's okay but she *is* a girl.'

'I'm glad Sean's not your age. I think he's fine the age he is,' Annie said with a little laugh.

Ria opened her mouth to say that Annie wouldn't want to do anything silly with both Hubie and Sean fighting for her attention but she closed it again. These weeks of having to think before she spoke were paying dividends. It had been no harm learning to live in entirely new and different surroundings where people might judge you by what you actually did and said here and now and not in the context of years of friendship. Ria felt she had grown up a lot in a way she had never had to at home. After all she had never lived alone, she had gone straight from her mother's house to Danny's. No years in between like girls who lived in flats might have known. Girls like Rosemary.

She had got an e-mail from Rosemary saying that Dublin was Rumour

City and that it was impossible to separate the truth from the fiction but it had always been that way. Still if there was anything to tell, she *would* tell it, and of course Danny wouldn't keep her in the dark if there was anything serious. Rosemary wrote that the children had disappeared without saying goodbye which was a pity because she had intended to send out a couple of dresses for Ria to wear at the picnic.

'You didn't say goodbye to Rosemary?' Ria asked them before she headed out to the gourmet shop.

Annie shrugged.

Brian said, 'We forgot her, we called on everyone else.' He seemed to think that it was a source of income they had overlooked.

'Brian, she wouldn't have given you a penny,' Annie said.

'You don't like Rosemary, Annie, do you?' Ria was surprised.

'You don't like Kitty,' Annie countered.

'Ah, but that's different. Kitty's a bad influence.'

'So is Lady Ryan on you, Mam, giving you things, patting you on the head. You can earn money to buy your own dresses, not wear her cast-offs.'

'Thanks, Annie, that's true. Now will you two be all right, I'll only be gone three hours?'

'It's so funny to see you going out to work, Mam, you're like a normal person,' said Brian.

Ria drove Marilyn's car to John and Gerry's, her knuckles white with rage. This was the thanks she got for staying in Tara Road to make the place into a home for them all. Danny had left her saying she was as dull as ditchwater and they had nothing to talk about. Annie thought she was pathetic and Brian thought she was abnormal. Well, by God, she was going to make a success of business anyway.

She parked with a screech of brakes and marched into the kitchen.

'What thought have we given to making special alumni cakes?' she barked. The two men looked up, startled. 'None I see,' she said. 'Well I suggest we have two kinds, one with a mortar board and scroll of parchment, and one with hands of friendship entwined.'

'Special cakes for the weekend?' Gerry said slowly.

'Everyone will be entertaining, won't they need something festive? Something with a theme?'

'Yes but . . . ?'

'So we'd better get started on them at once, hadn't we? Then I can get the graphics up and running and get young people at home to do work on the advertisements, posters for the window and leaflets.' They looked at her open-mouthed.

'Don't you think?' Ria said, wondering had she gone too far.

'We think,' said John and Gerry.

'I'm finding it real hard to see you alone,' Hubie said to Annie. 'Last weekend there was the party with all the other guys around, and then Sean Maine was everywhere like a shadow, next weekend is the alumni weekend and then you're going off to stay with the Maines.'

'There's plenty of time left.' They were lying by the pool sailing a paper boat from one side to the other by flapping the water with their hands.

Brian was practising his basketball at the net.

'Perhaps I could take you to New York City?' Hubie asked.

'I'd better not. Mam wants to show it to us herself, it's a big deal for her.'

'Do you never say no to her, Annie, and do what you want to do?' Hubie wanted to know.

'Yes I do, quite a lot. But not at the moment. Things are hard for her. My dad went off, you see, with someone not much older than me, it must make her feel a hundred.'

'Sure I know. But somewhere else then?' He was very eager that they should have a date.

'Look, Hubie, I'd love to but not at the moment, we've just got here, okay?'

'Okay.'

'And another thing, I was writing to Marilyn and Mam said I wasn't to say you come here.'

'Marilyn?'

'Mrs Vine. This is her house, you *know* that.'

'You call her Marilyn?'

'That's what she wanted.'

'You like her?'

'Yes, she's terrific.'

'You're so wrong. You have no idea how wrong you are, she's horrible and she's mad.' Hubie got up and gathered his things. 'I have to go now,' he said.

'I'm sorry you're going. I like you being here but I have no idea what all this is about.'

'Think yourself lucky.'

'I know you were with Dale when the accident happened, my mother told me, but that's all. And I'm not going to say that Marilyn is horrible and mad just to please you, that would be weak and stupid.' Annie had stood up too, eyes flashing.

Hubie looked at her in admiration. 'You're really something,' he said. 'Do you know what I'd really like?'

Annie never discovered what Hubie would really have liked just then because at that moment Brian arrived on the scene. 'You were very quiet up here, I came to see were you necking,' he said.

'What?' Hubie looked at him, startled.

'Necking, snogging, you know, soul kissing. What do you call it here in America exactly?' He stood there, his shoulders and face red, his spiky hair sticking up and his round face as always interested in something entirely inappropriate.

'Hubie . . .' said Annie in a dangerously level voice '. . . is just leaving and the way things are he may never come back.'

'Oh, I most definitely will be back,' said Hubie Green. 'And as a matter of interest I would like you to know that the way things are is just fine with me.'

*

'Hubie fancies Annie,' Brian said at lunch.

'Of course he does. He fancied her before he met her, he was always looking at that photograph.'

'That's nonsense, Mam. Stop encouraging Brian.' Annie was pink with pleasure from it all.

'Well, we need Hubie here tonight, so you'll have to use all your powers of persuasion to get him to come over.'

'Sorry, Mam, impossible.'

'I need him, Annie. I want him to design a poster for my cakes on the computer.'

'No way, Mam, he'll think I put you up to it.'

'No, he won't. It will be a professional job, I'll pay him.'

'*Mam*, he'll think you're paying him to come and visit me. It would be terrible. It's not going to happen.'

'But it's my job, Annie, I need him here,' she stopped suddenly. 'I'll tell you . . . suppose you go out somewhere then he can't think that you're after him, can he?'

Annie thought about it. 'No, that's true.'

'In fact it might be playing hard to get, he'd wonder where you might be.'

'And where *would* I be, Mam?'

Ria paused to think up a solution to this problem and then suddenly it came to her. 'You could go to work in Carlotta's salon for two or three hours, you know, folding towels, sterilising hairbrushes, sweeping up, making coffee . . . you know the kind of thing?'

'Would she let me?'

'She might if I asked her nicely, as a favour for tonight, since I know you want to be out of the house.'

'Please, Mam, would you? Please?'

Ria went to the telephone. Carlotta had suggested it days back, but Ria knew better nowadays than to tell her daughter straight out. She came back from the phone. 'Carlotta says yes.'

'Mam, I *love* you,' Annie cried.

Barney McCarthy said he would meet Danny any place and any time. How could there be hard feelings about what was said last night? By either of them. They had both been in shock, they knew each other far too well for mere words to create a barrier. They met in Stephen's Green and walked around the park where children were playing and lovers were dawdling. Two men walking, hands clasped behind their backs, talking about their futures and their past.

On the surface they were friends. Danny said that he would never have had the start in business without Barney McCarthy. Barney said *he* owed Danny a great deal for his insights and hard work, not to mention his quick thinking the night of the heart attack in Polly's flat.

'How's Polly taking it?' Danny asked.

'On the chin, you know Poll.' They both thought for a few moments about the elegant dark-haired woman who had let any chance of marriage pass her by just waiting in the background for Barney. 'Of course she's still young, Poll,' Barney said.

'And with no dependants,' Danny agreed. There was another silence. 'Have you told Mona?' Danny asked.

Barney shook his head. 'Not yet.'

He looked at Danny. 'And Ria?'

'Not yet.'

And then they walked in silence because there was nothing left to say.

'I think Sean is greatly taken with your Annie,' Sheila said on the telephone.

'I know, isn't it amazing?' Ria said. 'It only seems such a short time since they were both in prams, now they're talking romance.'

'I guess we'll have to keep an eye on them.'

'Much good it did anyone keeping an eye on us,' Ria laughed.

'But we weren't as young as they are,' Sheila said. 'I don't expect Annie's on the pill?'

Ria was shocked. 'Lord no, Sheila. For heaven's sake, she's not sixteen yet. I was only talking about kissing at the cinema and all that.'

'Let's hope that's all they're talking about too. Anyway you're coming to stay with us the weekend after next.'

'Indeed we are.'

Ria was troubled by this conversation, but she hadn't much time to think too deeply about it. The orders for her alumni cakes were unprecedented, they had to take on extra help in the shop, *and* she had to organise the house for her guests *and* prepare a huge buffet lunch for the friends of Greg and Andy Vine while trying to keep a low profile so that Marilyn's nose would not be put out of joint by it all. Apparently Marilyn had served olives and pretzels any time people came at alumni weekend.

And she had to make sure that the children had activities. Oddly, Annie and Brian were the least of her worries. Brian had found a new friend called Zach four houses away, and had taken to wearing a baseball cap backwards and using phrases he didn't understand at all. Hubie was always calling for Annie and taking her out to see cultural things, and since it was always in broad daylight Ria could not object. Every afternoon at four o'clock Annie went to Carlotta's salon, and came home with amazing stories about the clientele. Ria had rented a chest freezer for a week and she cooked, labelled and stored way into the night.

As she was going to bed at 2.00 a.m. on the Thursday before the big weekend she remembered suddenly that she hadn't thought about Danny all day. She wondered could it be that she was getting over him, but then when his face did come back to her, the whole bitter loss was as hurtful, lonely and sad as ever. She missed him as much as she always had, it was just that she had been too busy to think about it until now. Maybe this was as good as it was ever going to get.

Marilyn brought a cup of coffee out to Colm in the garden. 'What are you on today?' she asked.

'Sweet fennel,' he said. 'It's only to please myself, prove I can grow it. Nobody asks for it much in the restaurant.' He grinned ruefully.

Marilyn thought again what an attractive man he was and wondered why he hadn't married. She knew about his love affair with alcohol, but that never stopped people marrying. 'How long does it take?'

'About four months, or thereabouts. The books say fifteen weeks from sowing.'

'The books? You learned your gardening from books?'

'Where else?'

'I thought you came from a long line of committed gardeners, that you grew up with your hands in the soil.'

'Nothing as nice and normal as that, I'm afraid.'

Marilyn sighed. 'Well, which of us ever had the childhood we deserved?'

'It's true, sorry for the self-pity.'

'Hey, you don't have any of that.'

'Have you heard how they're all getting on, Annie and Brian?'

'Well just great, they seem to know half the neighbourhood, dozens of kids in our pool.'

'That doesn't bother you?'

'Why should it, it's their house for the summer.'

'But you're a very private person.'

'I have been since my son died last year.'

'That's a terrible tragedy for you. I'm very sorry. You didn't speak of it before, I didn't know.'

'No, I didn't speak of it at all.'

'Some things can be almost too hard to talk about, let's leave the subject if you prefer.' He was very easygoing, Marilyn knew that he would have left it.

'No, strangely. I find recently when I *do* talk about it now it becomes a little easier to bear.'

'Some people say that, they say let some light in on it, like plants your problems need light and air.'

'But you don't agree?'

'I'm not sure.'

'Which is why you don't talk about Caroline?'

'Caroline?'

'This country has unhinged me, Colm. In a million years I would never have interfered or intruded in anyone's life like this. But I'll be away from here in less than three weeks; I'll never see you again. I think you should let a little light and air into what you're doing for your sister?'

'What am I doing for her?' His face was hard and cold.

'You're running a restaurant to feed her habit.'

There was a silence. 'No, Marilyn you've got it wrong, she works in my restaurant so that I can keep an eye on her. Her habit is paid for by somebody else entirely.' Marilyn stared at him. 'She is very well supplied by her husband Monto, a businessman – one of whose most thriving businesses is heroin.'

*

'Maria?'

'Hallo, Andy?'

'Just a quick question. When I come to stay next week are we meant to have met?'

'Oh I think so, don't you?'

'Certainly I do, but I was letting you call the shots.'

'It will be good to see you again, and have you meet my children.'

'Sure. Will we have any time alone together, do you think?'

'I feel that's going to be very unlikely, simply because I have so much to do.'

'I'll keep hoping. See you Friday.'

'Zach says they're going to be very old and very boring,' Brian pronounced.

'Isn't it amazing the way Brian crosses the Atlantic Ocean and in minutes he finds a friend like Myles and Dekko!' Annie sighed.

Brian saw no insult in this, in fact he saw huge possibilities for the future. 'Can Zach come to stay in Tara Road?' he asked.

'Certainly, we'll discuss it next year,' Ria said.

'Do you think we'll still be in Tara Road next year, Mam?' Annie was thoughtful.

'Why ever not? Did you have plans for moving anywhere?' Ria laughed.

'No, it's just . . . it's quite dear and everything . . . I was wondering would we all, Dad and everyone, be able to afford it?'

'Oh that will be fine, I'm going to work when we get back to Dublin,' Ria said airily.

'*Work*, Mam . . . ? What on earth would you do?' Annie looked at her mother surrounded by food.

'Something a bit like this probably,' Ria said.

Greg Vine was tall, slightly stooped and gentle. He was courteous and formal to the children. He seemed overcome at the hospitality that Ria was providing for his friends. 'You must have been slaving for weeks,' he said as she took him on a tour of the freezers, and the rented trestle tables and linen.

'I didn't want to use Marilyn's cloths in case something happened to them.'

'No, I don't think she'd mind,' he said, unsure, uncertain.

'She has been meticulous about my home they all tell me, I don't want to be any less with hers.' She showed him all the replies to the guest-list he had sent out. 'I'll leave you to settle in your own house,' she said. 'I didn't put anyone to sleep in Dale's room . . . and on that subject I must apologise.'

He cut straight across her. 'No, it is we who must apologise, it was unpardonable for you to come here without being told the whole story. I'm very, very sorry. All I can say in explanation is that she doesn't talk about it to anyone, anyone at all.' His face was full of grief as he spoke. 'I think she genuinely believes that if you don't talk about a thing it hasn't happened . . . if you don't mention Dale at all then his horrific death didn't occur.'

'Everyone's different,' Ria said.

'But this has gone beyond reason, to let you into this house, to see that room without knowing what happened. It probably doesn't matter now what she and I have left to say to each other, but for Marilyn's own health she will *have* to acknowledge what has happened and talk about it. To someone.'

'She's talking about it now,' Ria said. 'She told my children all about him, everything. From when he got braces on his teeth to the time you all went to the Grand Canyon and he cried at the sunset.'

Greg's voice was a whisper. 'She said all this?'

'Yes.'

His eyes were full of tears. 'Maybe, maybe I should go to Ireland.'

Ria felt a pang of jealousy like she had never known before. Marilyn was going to be all right. Her husband still loved her and he was going to go over to Tara Road. Lucky, lucky Marilyn Vine.

'I can't ask anything at all about his business,' Finola Dunne said to her daughter.

'No, that's true.'

'I accepted his apology for sharp words and he gave it generously so now you see my hands are tied. But you can, and you *must*, ask him, Ber. It's only fair, on you and the baby. You have to know is he bankrupt.'

'He'll tell me, Mum, when he thinks I need to know.'

The alumni picnic party in Tudor Drive was long talked of as one of *the* events of Westville. Ria had asked Greg if Hubie Green could come to the house as a waiter, and young Zach as an assistant.

'Hubie?'

'Yes, he taught us the Internet, and has been most helpful.'

'He's a wild and irresponsible young man,' Greg said.

'I know that he was with Dale that day. He says it was the worst day of his life.'

'I have no objection to his being here, I never had. Those were all Marilyn's . . . I suppose in a way I'm advising you to keep him away from your daughter.' Ria felt a shiver of anxiety but she couldn't allow it to develop, there was too much to do.

When Hubie arrived he went straight to Greg. 'Mr Vine, if my presence here is unwelcome I quite understand.'

'No, son, I'm glad to see you in our home again,' said Greg.

Ria let out a slow sigh of relief. That was one hurdle safely crossed. And then, surrounded by friendly faces and food, Ria felt very much at home. She made sure that Marilyn's name was constantly mentioned. She said that she had been speaking to her the previous evening and she had sent her love to everyone.

'I think Greg's brother sort of fancies you, Mam,' Annie said after the party.

Annie and Hubie had been a delightful double-act filling the wineglasses and serving huge slices of the mouth-watering cake that had been such a success.

'Nonsense, we're geriatric people. There's no fancying at our age.' Ria laughed, admiring the sharp young eyes of her daughter.

'Dad was able to find someone else – why wouldn't you?'

'What a matchmaker you are. Now don't go encouraging me or I might stay over here cooking and fancying old men. What would you do then?'

'I suppose I could stay here studying and fancying young men,' Annie said.

There was no time for Andy to meet Ria properly on her own. 'I could come back another weekend?' he said.

'It wouldn't be fair to ask you, Andy. I'll be up to my elbows in cooking and children and I couldn't concentrate on you.'

'You didn't, even when you could.' He was reproachful.

'I was very flattered to be invited to concentrate.'

'I'm not giving up, I'll think of something.'

'Thank you, Andy.' She looked around to make sure there was nobody in sight and kissed him playfully on the nose.

'I wish you weren't going off to that hicksville town to see the Maines,' Hubie said to Annie.

'No, it will be fun, they're nice people.'

'And Sean's a good-looking guy,' Hubie said gloomily.

'Is he?' Annie pretended to be surprised.

'Remember . . . I'm in Westville, he's in the boondocks,' Hubie said.

'I'll remember,' Annie promised. Kitty wouldn't believe all this. Two men fighting over her. But then Kitty would ask, 'Which of them did you sleep with?' And Annie wasn't going to sleep with either of them.

'What did Mona say?' Danny asked.

'Nothing at all.'

'Nothing?'

'Total silence,' Barney said. 'It was much worse than any words. And Ria?'

'I haven't told her yet.'

'But Danny, you'll have to tell her. She'll hear.'

'I must tell her face to face, I owe her that much.'

'You're going to get her home?'

'No, I'm going out there.'

'On whose money, might I ask?'

'On your money, Barney. You've got my house, for Christ's sake. You can give me a lousy air ticket.'

They were sitting by the pool planning what to pack to go to the Maines.

'Are you still into lists, Mam?'

'I think so,' Ria said. 'It makes life easier.' The telephone rang, Ria went to get it.

'Sweetheart, it's Danny.'

'I did ask you not to call me that.'

'Sorry. Force of habit.'

'I'll get the children.'

'No, it's you I want to talk to. I'm coming out there tomorrow.'

'You're what?'

'I'm coming out to see you all for the weekend.'

'Why?'

'Why not?'

'And is Bernadette coming too?'

'Of course not.' He sounded irritated.

'Forgive me, Danny, but you do live with each other . . .'

'No, I mean, I'm coming to talk to you and Annie and Brian. Is that all right or has America been put off-limits?'

He sounded very edgy. Something in her throat began to constrict. Was it over with Bernadette? Was he coming to ask her forgiveness? A new start. 'When do you arrive? Do you know how to get here?'

'I have all the details you gave the children about the buses and everything. I'll call from Kennedy.'

'Yes but Danny we were going away for the weekend . . . up to Gertie's sister.'

'Gertie's sister! That can be changed surely.' He was very impatient.

'Yes,' she said.

'See you tomorrow,' he said.

Ria went slowly back to the pool. This was too big to blurt out. The new Ria nowadays thought before she spoke. She wouldn't tell them until she had thought about it. She wouldn't cancel Sheila Maine either. Perhaps the children could go for one night. And leave her alone with Danny.

It was her that he was coming to see. That's what he had said on the phone. 'It's you I want to talk to.' He was coming back to her.

9

The doorbell rang in Number 16 Tara Road. It was Danny Lynch. The smile was very warm. 'I hope I'm not disturbing you, Marilyn?'

'Not at all, won't you come in?'

'Thank you.'

They went into the front room where Marilyn had been sitting reading. Her book and glasses were on the table.

'You like this room,' he said.

'Very much, it's so peaceful.'

'I liked it too. We didn't live here enough, it was always down in the kitchen. I'd like to have sat here of an evening reading too.'

'Yes, well of course it's easy for me, I'm on my own. When there's a family it's different.'

'True,' he said. She looked at him enquiringly. 'I'm flying to New York tomorrow, I'll be staying in Tudor Drive. I thought I'd pay you the courtesy of telling you.'

'That's very kind of you, but not at all necessary. Ria's free to have whoever she likes, but thank you anyway.'

'And I need some documents to take with me.'

'Documents?'

'Yes, they're upstairs. I wonder if I can go and collect them?'

'Ria didn't say anything about . . .'

'Look, I appreciate your caution, but pick up the phone now and call her. This is kosher, Marilyn, she knows I'm coming.'

'I don't doubt it for a moment.'

'You do. Call her.'

'Please, Danny, please don't speak like that. Why shouldn't I believe you? You've given me no reason to think you might be deceiving Ria in any way.' Her voice was cold and her eyes were hard.

He seemed to flinch a little. 'You can come with me, I know where they are.'

'Thank you.'

They walked up the stairs in silence to the bedroom. Clement lay asleep on the bed. 'Hey, how did you get up here, fellow?' Danny said, tickling the cat under the chin. Then he went to the chest of drawers, and opened the bottom one. There was a plastic envelope called House Documents. He picked out four sheets of paper and returned the rest.

Marilyn watched him wordlessly. 'And if I'm talking to Ria tonight what shall I say you took?'

'Some correspondence about the ownership of this house . . . she and I need to discuss it.'

'She'll be home in under three weeks.'

'We need to discuss it now,' he said. He looked around the big airy bedroom with its high ceiling and long window. Marilyn wondered what he was thinking about. Did he remember fifteen years spent here with Ria or was he in fact working out what price the house would go for?

Marilyn hoped that in this complicated network of friends Ria had a good lawyer. She was going to need one. It was only too clear why Danny was going out to Westville to ruin the rest of Ria's visit. He was going to tell her that they had to sell Tara Road.

Ria was singing as she made breakfast.

'You never sing, Mam,' Brian said.

'She is now.' Annie defended her mother's right to croon tunelessly.

'Bernadette sings a lot,' Brian said.

'That's so interesting, Brian, thank you for sharing that with us,' Annie said.

'What kind of things does she sing?'

'I don't know. Foreign things.' Brian was vague.

'She only hums, Mam,' Annie said. 'Not real singing.'

Ria poured another cup of coffee and sat down with them.

'You'll be late for work,' Brian said disapprovingly.

'Well, at least Mam and I *do* go out to work,' Annie said. 'Unlike some people who throw a ball with Zach all day.'

'I'd go out to work if there was a job,' Brian said earnestly. 'Honest I would.'

'I think you're safe enough for the next twenty years, Brian. I mean who'd want to close down their business by employing you?' Annie consoled him.

'I have something marvellous to tell you,' Ria said. 'Something you'll be very pleased to hear.'

'What is it?' Brian asked.

'You have a boyfriend?' Annie suggested.

Brian looked appalled. 'Don't be disgusting,' he said to Annie. 'Mam wouldn't do anything like that.' He felt that somehow he had said the wrong thing as he looked at their faces. Slowly to his mind came the notion that his father after all had a new girlfriend and everyone was going along with that. Perhaps he shouldn't have said it was disgusting. 'Without telling us, I mean,' he said lamely.

'Your dad is coming to stay for the weekend,' she said.

Their mouths were open with shock.

'*Here*, here in Westville?' Annie said.

'But he said goodbye to us and he didn't say,' Brian said. 'Isn't that fantastic? When does he get here? Where will they sleep?'

'They?' Annie said.

'Well, isn't Bernadette coming too?'

'No, of course she's not, eejit,' Annie said.

'Does that mean he's left her and he's coming back to us?' Brian wanted to be clear about what was happening.

'Oh Brian, we've been through this a thousand times. Your dad didn't leave *you*, he went to live in another place, he'll always be your dad.'

'But has he given her up?' Brian insisted on knowing.

'No, of course not. He wanted to come out and see you both and he got a chance . . . through work.'

'So they can't be broke after all,' Annie said with relief.

'He'll be here about five o'clock. He didn't want us to go and meet him, he said he'd take a taxi from the bus station.'

'But we're going to the Maines this weekend,' Annie remembered in horror.

'I've spoken to Sheila. You're going up on the bus tomorrow just for one night then come back on Sunday and we'll all have a big goodbye dinner for your dad.'

'I can't believe it. Dad coming here. He'll even meet Zach.'

'Well worth flying thousands of miles for,' Annie said.

'Dad could well put a stop to you and Hubie and your goings-on when he comes,' cried Brian, stung by the attack on his friend.

'Mam, there *are* no goings-on,' Annie appealed.

But Ria didn't seem interested in whether there were or there weren't. 'Let's think what we'll do tonight when your dad comes. Will we drive him around Westville and show him the sights? Would he like a barbecue here by the pool? What do you think?'

'Dad's got much quieter, you know,' Annie said thoughtfully. 'He sits and does nothing a lot nowadays.'

For some reason that made Ria feel uneasy. The picture of Danny sitting still wasn't an easy one to create. Danny who never sat down, who was always on the go. What was making him quiet these days? Annie was observant, she wouldn't have imagined that. And from what Ria had heard, Bernadette was no ball of fun at keeping the conversation going. It seemed to be a silent house just as it had been an eventless holiday on the boat. So different to what the energetic quick-moving Danny Lynch had wanted all his life.

But she gave no hint of her anxiety. 'Well, if your dad would like to be quiet . . . then hasn't he picked a great place for it? Now I'm out of here, as they say at the shop, while I still have a job to go to. See you lunchtime.'

When she had gone the children looked at each other across the table.

'You're a little thug, a combination of a rat and a thug and that's saying something.'

Brian looked at her mutinously. 'And you're nothing but a jeer, a horrible old scornful jeer. What has Zach done to annoy you? Nothing at all, and you're always making fun of him.' His face was red and upset.

'Okay, peace?'

'No, not peace. It's only peace until you see Zach again and start groaning.'

'Okay, not peace, but it's going to be great to have us fighting when Dad arrives.'

'Why do you think he's coming?' Brian asked.

'I have no idea. But I don't think it could be anything bad,' Annie said reflectively.

'No, like he's given all the bad news already. It might be something good though, mightn't it?'

'Like what?' Annie wondered.

'Like he's leaving Bernadette?' Brian sounded hopeful.

'Didn't look much like it, did it though?' Annie said. 'They're very lovey-dovey.'

'Do you think Dad will sleep with Mam when he's here?' Brian asked suddenly.

'I don't know, Brian, but can I beg you on bended knees not to ask them if they're going to? Either of them.'

'What do you think I am?' Brian asked indignantly.

Ria came home from the gourmet shop with two big brown paper bags. 'Now we've lots of work to do, will I make a list?' she asked them.

They exchanged glances. 'What needs to be done?' Annie asked.

'We want to clean the place up and show Dad what a great house this is, scoop the leaves off the pool, make a super meal, and make up the bed . . .'

'Will he not be sleeping with you, Mam, in the same bed?' Brian asked. There was a pause. 'Sorry,' he said. 'I didn't mean to say that.'

Danny was packing his things in the office when the phone rang.

'Rosemary Ryan?' The girl raised her eyebrows questioningly.

'Put her through,' Danny said.

'I hear that you're going out to America,' she said.

'You could hear the grass grow, sweetheart.'

'I didn't hear it from you,' she said crisply, 'when we were last talking. In bed.'

'I gather you're not in the office,' he said.

'You gather right, I'm on my mobile in my car very near your office. I'll drive you to the airport.'

'There's no need, honestly.'

'Every need,' she said. 'Ten minutes' time I'll be parked outside.'

He came out of the building where he would probably never work again. The offices would be repossessed on Monday. Danny carried the grip bag he was taking to Westville, and two large carrier-bags, the contents of his desk. 'Do you know what would be wonderful? If you could keep these for me until I come back, save me going out to Bernadette and dropping them at home. And I can't leave them in Tara Road; that Kamp Kommandant will hardly let me past the door.'

'It was actually she who told me you were going to America,' Rosemary said as she negotiated the traffic along the canal.

'Did she now?' He wasn't pleased.

'Yes, I met her this morning in Tara Road and she asked me whether I had heard anything of your plans. I told her she could call Ria to check. She said she didn't want to make waves. That was her expression.'

'Was it?' he grunted.

'You don't think she could *know* about us do you, Danny?'

'I certainly didn't tell her.'

'No, it's just that she looks at me coldly and says things like "your good friend Ria" . . . with what sounds like heavy sarcasm. Did she say anything to you?'

'She said something about . . . you've never done anything that would make me think you weren't trustworthy, have you? It seemed a bit odd at the time, I'm trying to remember the words. But . . . no, I think we're only imagining things.'

'Why are you going, Danny?'

'You know why I'm going. I have to tell Ria face to face.'

'It won't make it any better for either of you, it's a wasted journey.'

'Why do you say that?'

'Even if you do tell her she still won't believe that it's going to happen. Ria doesn't believe unpleasant things. She's going to say "Never mind, it will all turn out fine".' Rosemary put on a childish voice to imitate the way Ria might speak.

Danny looked at her. 'What did Ria ever do to you to make you despise her so much? She never says anything except good things about you.'

'I suppose she let me walk off with her husband under her nose and didn't notice. That's not a clever way to be.'

'Most people don't have to be so watchful of people that they think are their friends.' Rosemary said nothing. 'I'm sorry, that was smug and hypocritical.'

'I never loved you for your fine spirit, Danny.'

'It's not easy, what I'm going to do, but fine spirit or no fine spirit, I think she deserves to hear it from me straight out.'

'Did you tell her what you were coming out for?'

'No.'

'She probably thinks you're going back to her,' Rosemary said.

'Why on earth would she think that? She knows it's over.'

'Ria doesn't know it's over. In twenty years she still won't believe it's over,' said Rosemary.

At the airport Danny met Polly Callaghan.

'Fleeing the country?' she asked him.

'No, going out to discuss the whole sad tale with Ria. And you? Deserting the sinking ship?'

'No, Danny.' Her eyes were cold. 'You know better than that. I'm giving Barney a little space with Mona for the weekend, he needs it. You're not the only one with a long sad tale to discuss.'

'Polly, I have spent the morning apologising to people for things. I'm upset, I lash out. Forgive me.'

'People will always forgive you, Danny. You're young and charming and you have a whole life still ahead of you. You'll be forgiven and you'll start again. Barney may not be so lucky.'

And she was gone before he could say any more.

The taxi drew up outside the carport. Danny stared up at the house where his family was spending the summer. It was much more splendid than he had imagined. He wondered would he have liked Marilyn Vine under more normal circumstances. Possibly. After all, she had remembered him from a chance meeting half a lifetime ago. They might well have been friends, business associates. And now he was walking into her home.

He could hear Brian shouting: 'He's here!' and his son hurtled down the slope to meet him and hug him.

A boy with a ball and a baseball cap on backwards stood watching closely. Brian's new friend no doubt. Annie, slim and tanned in her pink jeans, was right behind him. The hug was as warm as when she was four years of age. At least he hadn't lost them.

Danny had tears in his eyes when he saw Ria. She had come out too to meet him but she didn't run to him as she would have done in times gone by. She stood there serene, pleased to see him, a big smile all over her face. This was the Ria who hadn't realised that the marriage was over, the Ria who had lost all dignity and control the night before she left for America and who had begged him to leave Bernadette. But she was a different woman now surely. Confident and aware of the real world for the first time.

'Ria,' he said and stretched out his arms to her. He knew the children were watching.

She hugged him as she would have hugged a woman friend, and her cheek was against his. 'Welcome to Westville,' she said.

Danny let his breath out slowly. Thank God Rosemary had been wrong. All during the flight he had been wondering had he given the wrong message to Ria on the phone. But no, he knew that she saw him coming just as a friend. What a tragedy that he would have to change this mood entirely when he told her about Tara Road.

There was no opportunity to tell her the first night. Too much, far too much happening. There was a swim in the pool, a couple of neighbours or friends dropping in. Trust Ria to have got to know everyone. Admittedly these people didn't stay long, they were introduced, Heidi, Carlotta, two cultured gay men who ran a business in the town, a student who obviously had great designs on Annie. They had all dropped by, they said, to say Hi to Annie and Brian's father. He wasn't being presented in some cosy way as a current husband, Danny noted with relief. A glass of wine and club sodas in the garden and a platter of smoked salmon, then they were gone and there was a family barbecue beside the pool.

Danny learned that the children were going to stay with the Maines the following night. Ria must have realised that they needed to talk alone and she was packing them off there on a bus. He looked at her with admiration. She was handling it all so much better than he could ever have hoped. All he had to do now was to give her some realistic options about the very bleak financial future that lay ahead of them, something that wouldn't make her believe that her whole world was ending.

'It's eleven o'clock for us but four a.m. for your dad, I think we should let him go to bed,' Ria said, and they all carried the dishes back down to the house.

'Thank you for making it so easy, Ria,' he said as she showed him into the guest room.

'It *is* easy,' she smiled. 'I've always been delighted to see you, so why not now and in this lovely place?'

'It's worked well for you then?'

'Oh very much so.' She kissed his cheek. 'See you in the morning,' she said and left. He was asleep in under a minute.

Ria spent much of the night in her chair staring out into the garden. She saw a little chipmunk run across the grass. Amazing that she had never seen an animal like this before she came to America. There were squirrels in the trees, and Carlotta had a racoon which she was trying not to feed because you shouldn't encourage them, yet he had a lovely face. Brian was going to smuggle one home, he said, and start a chipmunk shop in Dublin.

'You'd need two if you were going to breed them,' Annie had said. 'Even you should know that.'

'I'm going to bring a pregnant one,' Brian said.

Ria forced herself to think about things like this rather than about the man who was sleeping in the room next door. Several times during the evening she had had to shake herself to remember the events of the past few months. They had seemed such a normal happy family, the four of them. It was almost impossible to believe that he had left them.

Surely he realised that it had all been a terrible mistake. That was the only reason he could be here. Ria wondered why he hadn't said it straight out. Asked her to forgive him and take him home. He had already thanked her for making things easy for him. She must continue in the same manner, rather than throw herself into his arms and tell him that nothing mattered any more. It was like some kind of game, you had to play it by the rules. Danny was coming back to her and this time she was going to keep him.

Mona McCarthy listened to the story without interrupting. Her face was impassive as she heard the events unfolding.

'Say something, Mona,' he said eventually.

She shrugged her shoulders slightly. 'What is there to say, Barney? I'm sorry, that's all. You put so much into it I'm sorry that in the end you won't be able to sit back and enjoy it.'

'I was never one for sitting back,' he said. 'You haven't asked how bad it is.'

'You'll tell me.'

'This house is in your name, that's one thing anyway.'

'But we can't keep it surely?'

'It's all we have, Mona.'

'You're going to let all those people lose their jobs, all those suppliers go without payment and Ria Lynch lose her home and expect me to live in this mansion?'

'That's not the way it is.'

'What way is it then?' she asked.

He couldn't answer. 'I'm sorry, Mona,' he said.

'I don't mind being poor, we've been poor before, but I won't be dishonest.'

'It's business. You don't understand, you're not a businesswoman.'

'You'd be surprised,' said Mona. 'Very surprised.'

Early next morning Ria took Danny a cup of coffee to his room.

'We usually have a swim before breakfast, will you join us?'

'I didn't bring any swimming trunks.'

'Now that was bad, if you'd only made one of my lists . . .' she mocked herself. 'I'll get you something from Dale's room.'

'Dale?'

'Their son.'

'Will he mind?'

'No, he's dead.' Ria went off and found him a pair of swimming shorts.

'Dead?' Danny said.

'Killed. That's why Marilyn wanted to get away from here.'

'I thought her marriage broke up,' Danny said.

'No, I think her marriage is fine actually.'

'But isn't he in Hawaii? That doesn't look very fine to me.'

'I think he's on the way to Ireland this weekend,' Ria said.

'Can't you stay longer, Dad?' Brian asked.

'No, I have to go on Monday night, but I have three full days here,' Danny said as they came down from the pool to the omelettes that Ria had made for breakfast.

'What did you come for really?' Brian asked.

'To see you all. I told you that.'

'It's a long way,' Brian said thoughtfully.

'True. But you're worth it.'

'Mam said your visit had to do with your work.'

'In a way yes.'

'So when will you do it? The work part?'

'Oh it will get done, don't worry.' Danny ruffled his son's hair affectionately.

'Dad, what would you like me to be when I grow up?'

'I don't mind. What would *you* like?'

'I don't really know. Mam says I might be a journalist or a lawyer because I have an enquiring mind. Annie says I should be a bouncer in a casino. Would you like me to be an auctioneer and work in your office with you?'

'Not really, Brian. I think people should choose their own line of work, follow their own star.'

'What did your parents want *you* to do?'

'I think they hoped I'd marry a rich farmer's daughter and get my hands on some land.'

'I'm glad you didn't. But suppose I did want to be an auctioneer I could, couldn't I? Then I could see you every day in the office, even if you didn't come home to live again.'

'Sure, Brian, I'd love to see you every day, we'll work something out.'

'And even when Bernadette's baby comes you'll still have time for us?' Brian's face was anxious.

Danny couldn't find the words to speak. He gripped Brian's shoulder very hard. When he did speak his voice was choked. 'I'll always have time for you and Annie, Brian, believe me. Always.'

'I knew you would, I was just checking,' said Brian.

They took Danny on a tour, pointing out all the sights of Westville and ending up at the burger bar beside the bus station where Annie and Brian were catching the bus to the Maines.

Zach and Hubie turned up to say goodbye. 'It's going to be real dull with you gone,' Zach said.

'It's going to be fairly dull with Kelly, she's a girl, you know,' Brian said. Zach nodded sympathetically.

'If that guy Sean Maine puts a hand on you, I'll know and I'll be up there so quick . . .' Hubie said.

'Will you stop talking about people putting hands on me? My parents are listening to you,' hissed Annie.

Danny and Ria got into the car and drove back to Tudor Drive.

'You were right to bring them out here, it's a great holiday for them.'

'Well, you paid their fares.' She was giving credit where it was due. In her list she had written down: *Make it easy for him. Be cool and calm rather than eager. Don't let him think he is a villain. Don't gush. Don't say that you knew he'd come back. Make no plans for Bernadette's future, that's up to him.* Ria smiled to herself. They might laugh at her lists, but they had their uses.

'You're happy here?' Danny said.

'I'm fine,' she agreed.

'What's that place over there?' He pointed to a cluster of trees in the distance.

'That's Memorial Park, they keep it beautifully.'

'Could we go and walk there, sit there for a bit?'

'Sure, but would you not prefer to go home? The garden in Tudor Drive is as good as it gets.'

'I'd prefer somewhere . . . I don't know . . . somewhere a bit separate from things.'

'Right, Memorial Park it is. There's car parking around this way.'

They walked together and looked at the names of the men from Westville who had died in the World Wars, in Korea and Vietnam.

'What a waste war is. Look, that boy was only four years older than Annie,' Ria said.

'I know, he could have been one of those old men playing chess there instead of a name on a piece of stone,' Danny said.

She longed to touch him but she remembered her advice to herself. They sat down on a wooden seat and he reached out to hold her hand in his.

'You probably know what I have to say,' he said.

She worried slightly, just a little. Surely he should say what he *wanted* to say not what he *had* to say. Still it was only words. 'Say it, Danny.'

'I admire you so much, I really do . . . and I hate to have to tell you bad news. I can't tell you how much I hate it. The only one thing you'll have to give me some little credit for is that I came out to tell you myself.'

She felt a big heavy stone suddenly develop below her throat, under the jaunty scarf that she had tied so cheerfully that morning.

'So?' she said, not trusting herself to say anything more.

'It's very bad, Ria.'

'No, it can't be all that bad.' Ria realised that he was not coming back to her. This was not what this was all about. Her list hadn't been necessary at all. It didn't matter now whether she was calm or cool or gushy, he wasn't coming back.

She heard herself speaking. 'Danny, I've already *had* the worst news, nothing will ever be as bad as that. There can't be anything else you have to tell me.'

'There is,' he said.

And on a wooden seat in Memorial Park, Westville, he told Ria that her home was gone. Part of the assets in the estate of Barney McCarthy, which would be put into the hands of the receiver very shortly.

'There's a party tonight, we can go to it,' Sean Maine said the moment Annie arrived.

'Do we have to take Brian and Kelly?'

'No way. My mom got them a video to watch.'

'I don't have any party clothes,' Annie said sadly.

'You look just great.' The admiration in Sean's eyes was plain.

Kitty wouldn't believe it. What a pity she wasn't here to watch this triumph! But of course Kitty would have the jeans off him by this stage, Annie thought disapprovingly. There would be none of that sort of thing as far as Annie was concerned; she must make that very clear from the start. Hubie had said it was totally unfair to look as good as she did and then not play. It was like putting delicious food on the table and then taking it away before people could eat it, he said. Really it was all very complicated.

'All right, Hilary, what is it? What are you trying to tell me?'

'And how did you know that I wanted to tell you anything, Mam?' Hilary asked.

'You're like Pliers. He goes round in a circle when he's trying to let you know he wants to go for a walk, you're doing the same.'

'Nothing's written in stone, Mam.'

'Tell me.'

'I mean if Ria were only here I'd sound her out before telling you anything at all . . .'

'Do I have to beat it out of you, Hilary?'

'Martin and I were wondering would you mind if we went to live in the country?'

'The *country*?'

'I knew you'd mind. Martin said you wouldn't.'

'Whereabouts in the country?' Nora Johnson was astounded.

'Well, Martin's old home. You know, none of his brothers want to live there and the house is falling down and there's a teacher's job in the local school, and I'd be able to get a job there as well.'

'You'd live in the west?' Nora Johnson as a Dubliner regarded the country as a place you went for holidays.

'If you wouldn't be upset by it, Mam, yes we would.'

'I wouldn't be upset by anything. But Hilary, child, in the name of God what would possess you to go over there?' She should have known.

'It's going to be much cheaper, Mam. We've done our sums, the cost of living is much lower there, less petrol on commuting, and of course we'll get a little nest egg from selling our own house.'

'And what will you do with the little nest egg?'

'We'll just hold on to it, Mam, it would be a great comfort to us as we grow older.'

Nora nodded her head. For Martin and Hilary it might be the only comfort. 'And what made you make up your mind?'

'When we were there last I looked up and wasn't the place all surrounded by trees,' Hilary said. 'I knew then it was right for us.'

'I suppose you have sex with the customers?' Jack roared at Gertie.

'Ah, Jack, will you give over.' Gertie struggled to get herself free of his grip. 'What are you talking about?'

'You're my woman and you're not going out like any old cheap tart just to have a tenner in your handbag.'

'Let me go. You're hurting me, Jack, I beg you.'

'Where do you do it? Up against the wall, is it?'

'You know this is only madness.' She was terrified now; she hadn't seen him like this for a long time. She knew that Ria and the children were up visiting the Maines this weekend. What a different story Ria would tell. Suppose Sheila could see her now.

'You knew I'd discover, didn't you?'

'Jack, there's nothing to discover.'

'Why did you send the kids to your mother's last night then? Answer me that.'

'Because I could see you are a bit . . . under the weather. I didn't want anyone getting upset.'

'You didn't want them hearing that their mother did it for a tenner with anyone who came in.' He hit her.

'*Jack.*'

'I'm a normal man, this is what a normal man would feel about a wife who couldn't explain ten-pound notes in her handbag.'

'I scrub floors for them, Jack.'

'Where? Where do you do that?'

'In Marilyn Vine's house where Ria lives, for Polly Callaghan sometimes, for Frances Sullivan . . .'

He laughed. 'You don't expect me to believe that.'

Gertie wept with her head in her arms. 'Well if you don't believe me, Jack, then kill me now, because there's not much point in going on,' she said through her tears.

'I've never had a real girlfriend before,' said Sean Maine to Annie. They sat on a windowseat at the party. There was dancing in the room and they were building the barbecue in the garden. Sean had his arm around her shoulder proudly, protectively almost. Annie smiled at him, remembering that she must not encourage him to think she was going to go any great distance. 'It's just my luck that the girl I like is going back to Ireland in a short time.'

'We can write to each other,' she said.

'Or maybe I could come over to Ireland, stay with my Aunt Gertie and Uncle Jack, go to school and be near you.'

'Yes, I suppose.' Annie sounded doubtful.

'Would you not like that?'

'Oh I would, it's just . . . it's just . . .' She wasn't sure how to finish. Mam had told her not to go into details about Gertie's life, it wasn't necessarily known over here. She knew that somehow it was important. 'It's just that I think Gertie's pretty busy,' she said lamely.

'She'd find room for family.' He was confident.

'Sure.'

'It was a big surprise your dad coming back?' Sean knew the story.

'I'm not sure he is actually back.'

'But Brian said . . .'

'Oh Sean, what does Brian know? It's just that Dad looked a bit sad. And he *was* very taken with Bernadette. I can't see he's given her up already, with the baby and everything.'

'Still he's at home there in Westville with your mom, that can't be bad.'

'No,' Annie agreed. 'That can't be bad at all.'

The shadows of the trees in Memorial Park grew longer as Danny and Ria sat on the wooden bench. They held hands, not like they used to do when they were young. Not even like friends, but like people in a shipwreck, holding on for fear of letting go and being totally alone. Sometimes they sat and said nothing at all. Other times Ria asked questions in a flat voice and Danny answered. At no stage did he call her sweetheart, and he offered no false hopes and glib reassurances that they would be all right.

'Why did you come over to America to tell us?' she asked. 'Couldn't it have waited until we came home?'

'I didn't want you to hear from anyone else.'

They were still holding hands, and she squeezed his as thanks. There were no recriminations. They had both known that the personal guarantee was there. It was just something that neither of them ever thought would be called in.

'Was he very sorry about us and Tara Road?' Ria asked.

Danny struggled to be truthful. 'He's so shell-shocked about himself, to be honest, that it's only one part of it.'

'Still he sent you out here to tell me, he must care a bit?'

'No, I insisted on coming out.'

'And Mona?'

'Barney said Mona said nothing. Nothing at all.'

'She must have said *something*.'

'If she did, he didn't tell me.' This was a very different Danny. No longer certain of anyone, anything. Even the great Barney McCarthy was no longer a fixed point in his life.

They spoke idly of what Danny would do now. There were other estate agencies where he might get a job. But he would go in on a very low rung of the ladder.

'What about Polly?'

'She's giving up her flat, getting a job, Barney says she's a brick or a sport, I can't remember which.'

Ria nodded. 'Yes, it would be one or the other.'

'And the staff, that's another very hard bit,' he said.

'Who told them?'

'*I* did as it happens.'

'You've had a lot of the telling to do.'

'Yes, well, I rode high and had a lot of the good times when they were there too.'

'I know you did, we both did.'

The silences that fell were not anxious or uneasy. It was as if they were both trying to take it all in.

'And what does Bernadette say about it all?'

'She doesn't know.'

'Danny?'

'No, she doesn't, truly, I'll tell her when I get back. She'll be calm. Her mother won't, but she will.'

A wind blew, lifting some of the leaves and blossoms up from their feet.

'Let's go back to the house, Danny.'

'Thank you so much.'

'For what?'

'For not screaming at me. I've had to give you the worst news anyone could ever give anyone.'

'Oh no,' she said.

'What do you mean?'

'You gave me much worse news than that before.'

He said nothing. They walked together across Memorial Park back to Marilyn Vine's car.

Colm Barry called at Number 16 Tara Road.

'You really did work on a rehab programme?'

'Oh yes, certainly.'

'So can you help?'

'You know I can't. Caroline will have to want to do it herself, *then* I can help.'

'But we can't drag her there.' He sounded very lost.

'There is a place, a centre?'

Colm nodded. 'Yes, a fine place. But what use is it?'

'You could go there, check out the programme, meet some of the people. Tell her about it.'

'She'd only close her ears.'

'She doesn't love that guy Monto?'

'No, but she loves what he provides for her, and now he's doing deals in my restaurant.'

'You're not serious.'

'Last night, I know that's what they were doing, I know it.'

'You can't have this, Colm. He'll get the place closed down, what hope for you or Caroline then?'

'What can I do? I can shop him, but that would be to destroy her.'

'You and Caroline have shared enough and have had enough history for you to be able to talk to her. Tell her that you may lose your restaurant, beg her to give this centre a try. Tell her I'll go with her and sit through the assessment with her if she likes.'

When he left, Marilyn looked at herself in the mirror. She still had the same auburn hair, slightly longer now than when she arrived. Her eyes were still watchful, her jaw firm. Yet she was totally different inside. How could she possibly have changed so much in these few short weeks? Getting involved with strangers and trying to alter the course of their lives. Greg wouldn't believe it was possible.

Greg. She decided to telephone him, but to her surprise they told her that he was taking some reading days. That wasn't like Greg, but she called him at home. His machine said that he would be away for a week.

For the first time in their married lives he had not told her where he was going or what he was doing.

Suddenly she felt very lonely indeed.

When they got back to Tudor Drive, Ria suggested they have tea.

'No, Ria, sit down, talk to me ... try to talk, don't bustle about doing things like you used to do at home.'

'Is that what I did at home?' She felt very hurt, annoyed.

'Well, you know whenever I came in and wanted to talk there was this in the oven and that on the burner and something else coming out of the deep-freeze and people coming and going.'

'Only the family, our children if I remember.'

'And half the neighbourhood. You were never there to talk to me.'

'Is that what a lot of this was about?'

'I suppose it was to cover what wasn't there,' he said sadly.

'Do you really believe that?'

'Yes I do.'

'Well, of course, I won't get tea, I'll sit down and talk to you now.'

That didn't please him either. 'Now I do feel a shit,' he said. 'Come on, let's have tea.'

'You make it,' she said. 'I'll sit here.'

He put on the kettle and took out the tea bags. Maybe she should have let him do this kind of thing more.

'You have a message on the machine,' he said.

'Take it for us, Danny, will you?' The old Ria would have leapt up with a pencil and paper.

'It's Hubie Green, Mrs Lynch. I didn't catch Annie's telephone number and I thought it would be good to give her a call during her weekend away. I did leave you an e-mail about it but I guess you don't have time to look at your messages now with all the action going on. Say Hi to Mr Lynch for me.'

'Do you want to call him with her number?' Danny asked.

'No. If Annie had wanted him to have it then she'd have given it to him,' Ria said.

Danny looked at her admiringly. 'You're right. Shall we check your e-mail in case there are any more messages?'

'I thought you wanted to talk, now who is putting it off?'

'We have the evening, the night to ourselves.'

The old Ria would have started to fuss about what they would eat for supper and whether it should be earlier or later. But now she just shrugged. 'Right, come into Greg's study and see how good I am at it.'

Expertly she went for her Mailbox and saw three messages. One from Hubie, one from Danny's office, and one from Rosemary Ryan.

'Do you want the office?' she asked.

'No, who needs any more grief?'

'Well, will I see what Rosemary says?'

'More bad news surely,' he said.

'She knows? Rosemary knows?' Ria was startled.

'She had heard already from her own sources, then I met her yesterday just as I was leaving. She drove me to the airport.'

Ria brought Rosemary's message up on the screen. Ria read the message over several times, as if trying to read between the lines. She didn't want to raise their hopes unnecessarily.

Ria, Danny, you should access the Irish Times *this morning. There's an*

*item about Barney that would interest you. All may not be lost after all.
Enjoy New England.*

'She says we should look up the *Irish Times*, the business gossip column,'
she finally said.

'Can you do that?' he asked, impressed.

'Yes, hold on a minute.'

Very shortly they had the website and got the item. The paragraph said
that rumours around the city seemed to suggest that Barney McCarthy's
financial death might be like that of Mark Twain, somewhat premature. The
word was that there had been a rescue package from sources outside his
company. Things didn't look as dire as had been thought. Ria read it aloud,
her voice getting lighter all the time.

'Danny, isn't that magic?'

'Yes.'

'Why aren't you more pleased?'

'If there *was* anything, Barney would have phoned me here; he has the
number. This is just him doing the PR job.'

'Well, let's see what your office says on this. He might have sent you an
e-mail.'

'I doubt it, but let's call it up anyway.'

'Message for Danny Lynch could he please phone Mrs Finola Dunne at her
home number urgently.'

'I *told* you it would be grief,' Danny said.

'Do you want to call her?'

'No, I can get the earful about how irresponsible I am when I get back,' he
said.

'You'll probably get a similar earful from *my* mother too,' Ria said ruefully.

'No, to give poor old Holly her due, she'd put it all down to That
Adulterer, as she calls him. Though these days it's hard to know who she'd
describe as that.'

They had gone back into the kitchen and picked up their mugs of tea. The
garden lights went on automatically, lighting up the place. Ria sat down and
waited. She ached to speak, to reassure him about that paragraph in the
newspaper, to encourage him to ring Barney and Mona at home. But she
would do none of these things, she would wait. As, apparently, she should
have waited in the past.

Eventually he spoke. 'What are you saddest about?' he asked.

She would *not* say that she was most sad because she thought he had been
coming back to her. That would be the end of any meaningful conversation
between them again. She tried to think what was the next most awful thing
on the list.

'I suppose I'm sad that your dreams and hopes are ended. You wanted so
much for the children and indeed for us all. It will be different now.'

'Will we tell them together tomorrow, do you think?' he asked.

'Yes, I suppose so. I was wondering if we should let them have their
holiday in peace but that would be lying to them.'

'And I don't want you to have to do it on your own, make excuses for me as I know you would,' he said.

'There are no excuses to make. Everything you did, you did for us all,' she said. Danny looked quite wretched. She was determined to cheer him up. 'Right, they'll be home tomorrow, let's try and guess what horrific thing Brian will say.' He forced a smile and Ria went on determinedly. 'Whatever we guess it won't be *quite* as bad as what he'll come up with.'

'Poor Brian, he's such an innocent,' Danny said.

Ria looked at him, calmer than she had been for a long time. He really did love his family, and this was Danny without any disguises. Why did she not know what to do to help him or make things better? She just knew what *not* to do. Almost everything that her instinct told her would be right would only annoy him.

Tears fell down her face and splashed off the table. She didn't lift her hand to wipe them away, half hoping that in the fading light he would not see. But he came up to her and gently took her tea mug out of her hand and placed it on the table, then he pulled her up from the chair, held her close to him and stroked her hair.

'Poor Ria, dear, dear Ria,' he said. She could feel his heart beating as she lay against him. 'Ria, don't cry.' He kissed the tears from her cheeks. But more came in their place.

'I'm sorry,' she said into his chest. 'I don't mean to.'

'I know, I know. The shock, the terrible awful shock.' He still stroked her and held her away from him, smiling at her to cheer her up.

'I think I am a bit shocked, Danny, maybe I should lie down for a bit.'

They went to the bedroom where she had been hoping he might join her tonight. He sat down and gently he took off her lilac-and-cream-coloured blouse, which he hung carefully on the back of the chair. Then she stepped out of her silk skirt and he folded that too. She stood in a white slip like a child being put to bed with a fever, and he turned back the sheet and counterpane for her.

'I don't want to miss your visit. I want to get value out of your being here,' she said.

'Shush, shush, I'll stay here beside you until you get a little sleep,' he said.

He brought a face flannel from the bathroom wrung out with water and wiped her face. Then he stroked her hand as he sat beside her in the chair. 'Try to sleep, dear Ria, and to know how fond of you I am, how very fond of you.'

'I know that, Danny.'

'That never changed, you do know that?'

'Yes I do.' Her eyelids were heavy. He looked so tired as he sat there minding her, his face half in the light that came in from the garden. She sat up on her elbow and said, 'It will be sort of all right, won't it?'

He put his arms around her and held her again. 'Yes, Ria, it will be sort of all right.' His voice was weary.

'Danny, lie down on the bed and sleep too, just close your eyes. It's been worse for you.' She didn't mean any more than that, lie down in his clothes on top of the bedspread and sleep beside her for a couple of hours.

But he clung to her and she realised that he wasn't going to leave her go. Ria didn't allow herself to think about what might be happening. She lay back in Marilyn Vine's bed and closed her eyes while the only man she had ever loved gently removed the rest of her clothes and made love to her again.

Greg decided to tell Ria that he was going to Ireland but the answering machine was on. He debated whether to leave a message and decided against it. He stood in the phone booth at Kennedy Airport and considered calling Marilyn. But suppose she told him not to come? Then they would be worse than they had ever been. His only hope was to call her and say he was in Dublin. Which he would be very soon.

He heard his flight being called. It was now too late to call his wife even if it were a good idea.

There had been no reply from Danny. Rosemary was very annoyed. She had driven him to the airport, he was in a house with an e-mail facility, a telephone. He would have known what to make of that cryptic piece in the paper. He would be tired of playing Happy Families and trying to bolster up Ria. Why didn't he call her? Rosemary told herself, as she had told herself many times before, this was not going to continue.

What she felt for Danny Lynch was neither sensible nor in any game plan. It was in fact the most basic urge imaginable. No other man would do. She had put up with sharing him with Ria for years, and with others like that disgusting Orla King. She had even put up with the infatuation for the wraith-like Bernadette. But he had always been civil and courteous before. He wasn't even that these days.

She was glad that she had not rescued him; she was just quivering with curiosity to know who had. The woman who wrote this column in the *Irish Times* was very informed. It would not be a flyer, something deliberately planted. Rosemary believed that Danny Lynch and Barney McCarthy were genuinely going to be pulled out of the fire. All she needed to know was by whom.

'Frances, you know the way I told you never to tell Jack I did a bit of cleaning for you?' Gertie said.

'And I never have,' Frances Sullivan said.

'No, but things have changed now. Now I do need him to know I come here, you see he thinks I get the money somewhere else.'

'Yes, but surely he won't come and ask me?' Frances looked fearful.

'No, but suppose he does, it's all right now, I'd prefer him to think that this is where I get the money.'

'Yes, Gertie.' Like a lot of people Frances was becoming increasingly wearied by the menacing presence of Gertie's Jack Brennan in her life.

'Thanks, Frances, I'll just go and tell Marilyn and then Polly and it will all be out of the way.'

Marilyn was in the front garden in jeans and T-shirt. She looked very young and fit for her years, Gertie thought.

'I hate having to burden you with my problems.'

'Sure, what is it, Gertie?' Marilyn listened and with great difficulty controlled her impatience. In her newly directive mood, she could easily have urged Gertie not to be so foolish, such a hapless victim encouraging more senseless violence and even neglecting her own children in the process. But one look at that haunted face made Marilyn retreat from any such action. 'Right,' she sighed. 'It's okay this week to tell him, let me know if it changes next week.'

'You're lucky and strong, Marilyn, I'm neither, but thank you.' She left to go to the bus stop across the road. Polly Callaghan was the third person she must warn.

Rosemary drew up her car. 'Can I drive you anywhere, Gertie?'

'I was going over to Polly, I wanted to give her a message.'

'She's in London, back after the weekend.'

'Well I am glad I met you. Thanks, Rosemary, you saved me a trip, I'll just walk up home then.'

'They did invent a telephone system, you know, you could have called her,' Rosemary said. It sounded somehow very dismissive and cruel.

'Are you cross with me about something, Rosemary?'

'No, I'm in a bad mood. Sorry, I didn't mean to bark.'

'That's all right.' Gertie never held a grudge for long. 'Man trouble is it?'

'What kind of man trouble do you think I might have?' Rosemary asked with some interest.

'I don't know, choosing between them I imagine,' Gertie shrugged.

'No, it's not that. I'm sort of restless, I don't know why, and people are being difficult. Your woman in there hasn't spoken to me for ages. What did I do to get up her nose?'

'I don't know. I thought you were great friends, going to fashion shows and all together.'

'Yes we were, that was the last time she spoke to me,' Rosemary said in wonder.

'So was there any coldness?'

'None at all. She drove me home ... I didn't ask her in.'

'Well, she'd not be sulking about that.'

Rosemary remembered back to the night, and Danny coming to the summerhouse. But there was no way, no possible way that Marilyn could have ... She pulled herself together. 'You're absolutely right, Gertie, I'm imagining it. All well at home?'

'Oh fine, thank you, just fine,' said Gertie who was relieved that Rosemary wasn't really interested anyway.

They slept wrapped up together as they had done for years in Tara Road. When Ria woke she knew she must not stir. So she lay there going back over all the events of the day and evening. She could see the time; it was eleven o'clock at night. She would like to get up, have a shower, and make them both an omelette. Together they would sit and talk about what was to be done. They would make their plans as they had long ago. And it was all going to be all right. Money wasn't important. Even the house they had built up together could be replaced. They could get another one, a smaller one. But she would take no initiative, she would lie there until he moved.

She pretended to be asleep when he got out of bed, picked up his clothes and went to the bathroom. When she heard the shower being turned on she joined him there with a towel wrapped around her. She sat down on one of Marilyn's cork-and-wrought-iron bathroom chairs. She would let him speak first.

'You're very quiet, Ria,' he said.

'How are *you*?' she said. There would be no more taking the initiative. The wrong initiative.

'Where do we go now?' he asked.

'A shower, a little supper?'

He seemed relieved. 'Sandalwood?' he said of the soap.

'You like it, don't you?'

'Yes I do.' He seemed sad about something, she didn't know what. He went to his own room to get clothes. She followed him into the shower, then put on yellow trousers and a black sweater.

'Very smart,' he said as they met in the kitchen.

'Annie says I look like a wasp in this outfit.'

'Annie! What does she know?'

They were walking on eggshells. Not a mention of what had happened. Or of what might happen next. Nor did they talk of Barney McCarthy or Bernadette, or the future or the past. But somehow they filled the time quite easily. Together they made a herb omelette and a salad; they each drank a glass of wine from the fridge. They ignored the message light winking on the answering machine. Whoever it was could be dealt with tomorrow.

And when it was half past midnight, they went back to bed. In the big double bed that belonged to Greg and Marilyn Vine.

The phone kept ringing, as if someone was refusing to accept that there was nobody going to take the call.

'Technology,' yawned Danny.

'Hubie Green, desperate for our daughter's telephone number,' giggled Ria.

'I'll get coffee for us. Will I put whoever it is out of their misery?' Danny suggested.

'Do, of course.' Ria was chirpy and cheerful as she heard the message tape winding backwards. Anything at all he did was all right with her today. She was just pulling on her swimsuit, ready to go to the pool, when she heard the fevered voice on the answering machine. 'Danny, I don't care what time it is, or Ria or whoever is there, you've got to pick up, you have to. This is an emergency. Please pick up, Danny. It's Finola here. Bernadette's been taken to hospital, Danny, she's had a haemorrhage. She's calling out for you. You've got to talk to me, you've got to come home.'

Ria put a dress on over her swimsuit and went quietly out to the kitchen. She filled the percolator and switched it on. Then she took out a directory with the numbers of airlines in it and passed it to Danny without comment. He would go home today, and she must do absolutely nothing to stop him.

She caught sight of her reflection in the mirror. She had a half-smile on her face. She must lose this immediately. She must not let a hint of what she was feeling escape. If Bernadette was losing the baby then their problems might be over.

Danny looked at her with anguished eyes.

'Get dressed,' she said. 'We'll get you on a plane.'

He came over to her and held her very tight. 'There never was and never will be anyone like you, Ria,' he said in a broken voice.

'I'll always be here for you, you know that,' she said into his hair.

Marilyn had seen Rosemary stop and talk to Gertie at the bus stop. She was relieved that she hadn't used the opportunity to come and call. It was getting harder to disguise her resentment of such a betrayal. She dug on furiously, wondering whether in this Catholic country they would think she was breaking the Sabbath by working in the garden. But Colm Barry had reassured her, it would be regarded as purely recreational, and weren't all the shops open on Sundays now, football games played.

She heard another car draw up outside. Surely not a caller, she didn't want to talk to anyone now. She wanted to lose herself in this work. There were so many things she did not want to think about. Strange that. Once there had only been one topic that had to be forced away. But today, as well as banishing Dale from her mind, she did not want to think about Gertie's violent husband, Colm's addicted sister, or Rosemary the faithless friend.

She heard voices outside the gate of Number 16. And as she knelt, trowel in hand, Marilyn Vine saw the slightly stooped figure of her husband come into the drive and look up at the house. She dropped the trowel and ran to him, crying out, 'Greg ... Greg!'

He pulled back from her first. Months of rejection had taken their toll. 'I hope it's all right ...' he began apologetically.

'Greg?'

'I did plan to call you from the airport. I sat there until it was a civilised time,' he explained.

'It's all right.'

'I didn't want to disturb you, or invade your time, your space. It's just ... it's just ... well it's only for two or three days.'

She looked at him in wonder. He was apologising for being there, how terrible must have been the coldness she had shown to him. 'Greg, I'm delighted you're here,' she said.

'You are?'

'Of course I am. I don't suppose you'd think of giving me a hug?'

Hardly able to believe it, Greg Vine embraced his wife.

There were bus timetables there too, so Ria looked up an earlier bus back for the children, then she called Sheila. 'Could you be very tactful and get them on it for me? I'll explain everything tomorrow.'

Sheila knew an emergency when she heard one. 'No bad news?' she asked.

'Not really, very complicated. But Danny has to leave tonight and I want him to be able to say goodbye to the children himself.'

'How much will I tell them?'

'Just that plans have changed.'

'I'll do it, of course, but I want you to know the courage it will take to tell that to Sean Maine and Annie Lynch.'

'Dad, it's Annie. I can't believe what Mrs Maine has told me, she says you're going back tonight.'

'That's right, Princess, I'd love it if you could get back.'

'But why, Dad, *why*?'

'I'll explain everything when I see you, Princess.'

'We were going to go to have a picnic and then come back this evening *and* we were all going to go to Manhattan tomorrow for the day. Now it's all changed.'

'I'm afraid so, my love.'

'Did you have some awful row with Mam? Did *she* send you home, is that it?'

'Absolutely not, Annie. Your mother and I have had a wonderful time here together and we both want to talk to the two of you this evening, that's all.'

'Okay then.'

'Sorry to upset all the romance,' he said.

'What romance, Dad? Don't be old-fashioned.'

'Sorry,' he said and hung up.

On the bus Annie and Brian tried to work it out.

'He's coming back to live at home?' Brian was hopeful.

'They wouldn't bring us back to tell us that,' Annie grumbled. She had missed a marvellous picnic by a lake. Sean had been very sulky about her departure. Even suggested she wanted to go back to Westville to meet Hubie Green.

'Well, what then?' Brian asked.

'He's broke, I think that's it.'

'I always said that.' Brian was triumphant.

'No you didn't, you kept bleating that Finola was saying it.'

'We'll know soon.' Brian was philosophical. 'We're on the edge of Westville now.'

When they got off the bus Hubie Green was waiting. 'Your mom asked me to pick you up and drive you back to Tudor Drive,' he said.

'Are you sure, you're not just kidnapping us?' Annie asked.

'No. I *was* glad of the chance to see you again, but truly she did ask me.' They climbed into Hubie's car. 'Did you have a good time?'

'It was all right . . .' Annie began with a careless shrug.

Brian decided that more information should be given. 'She and Sean

Maine were disgusting, almost as bad as the two of you. I can't understand it myself, I think it would choke you and I honestly don't know how you'd breathe while you're doing it.'

Bernadette's face was very white. 'Tell me again, Mum, what did he say?'

'He said I was to listen carefully and repeat these words: "He was flying home tonight, he'd be here tomorrow and nothing had changed".'

'Did he say he loved me?' Her voice was very weak.

'He said "Nothing has changed". He said it three times.'

'Why do you think he said that instead of that he loved me?'

'Because his ex-wife may have been there, and because he wanted to tell you that if you *did* lose the baby, which you won't, Ber, it would still be the same.'

'Do you believe that, Mum?'

'Yes. I listened to him say it three times and I believe him,' said Finola Dunne.

'Sit down, Barney, we have to talk,' Mona McCarthy said.

'But you wouldn't talk at all when I was trying to,' he complained.

'I didn't want to then, but we have to talk now. A lot of things have changed.'

'Like what?'

'Like that paragraph in the newspaper.'

'Well, you *said* that you had something put by over the years and you were prepared to rescue things.'

'We haven't yet discussed in what way. And I certainly didn't expect you to start telling the newspapers.' She was calm and confident as always, but this time with a steely hint that he didn't like.

'Mona, you know just as well as I do the need to build up confidence at a time like this,' he began.

'You'd be most unwise to build up anyone's confidence until we have discussed the terms.'

'Look, love, stop talking in mysteries. What do you mean *terms*? You told me you'd put something away, something that would rescue us.'

'No, that's not what I said.' She was placid. She could have been talking about a knitting pattern or a charity fashion show.

'What *did* you say then, Mona?'

'I said I had something, a way which *could* rescue you, that's a very different thing.'

'Don't play word games, this isn't the time.' There was a tic in his forehead. She couldn't have been fooling him, leading him along. It wasn't her style.

'No games, I assure you.' She was very cold.

'I'm listening, Mona.'

'I hope you are,' she said. Then in very level tones she told him that she had enough money saved over the years in reputable pension funds and insurance policies which, when cashed in, would bale him out. But they were all in her name and they would only be cashed if Barney agreed to pay his debtors. *And* to sell this mansion they lived in and buy a much smaller and less pretentious house. *And* to return the personal guarantee on Number 16 Tara Road to the Lynches. *And* that Miss Callaghan be assured that any relationship with her, financial, sexual or social, was at an end.

Barney listened open-mouthed. 'You can't make these demands,' he said eventually.

'You don't *have* to accept them,' she countered.

He looked at her for a long time. 'You hold all the cards,' he said.

'People can always get up and leave the card table, they don't have to play.'

'Why are you doing this, you don't need me, Mona? You don't have to have me hanging around the place as some kind of an accessory.'

'You have no idea what I need and what I don't need, Barney.'

'Have some dignity, woman, for God's sake. At this stage everyone knows about me and Polly, we're not hushing anything up that isn't widely known already.'

'And they'll know when it's over too,' she said.

'This will give you pleasure?'

'These are my terms.'

'Do we have lawyers to fix it up?' He was scathing.

'No, but we do have the newspapers. You've used them already, I can do the same.'

If anyone had ever suggested to Barney McCarthy that his quiet compliant wife would have spoken like this to him Barney would have laughed aloud.

'What's brought this on, the thought of being poor?' His lip was twisted as he spoke.

'I pity you if you really think that. I never wanted to be rich. Never. It always sat uneasily on me. But anyway as it happens I *am* rich, and I'll be richer if I don't help you out of the hole that you are in.'

'So why then?'

'Partly from a sense of fairness. You did work hard for what you got, very hard, and I enjoyed a comfortable life as a result. But mainly because I would like us to move with some grace into this period of our lives.'

He looked at her with tears in his eyes. 'It will be done,' he said.

'As you choose, Barney.'

Hubie left them at the carport.

'Nothing is ever the way Brian says it is,' Annie said to him sadly.

'I know.'

'So will I see you again?'

'Of course. Anyway neither Sean bloody Maine nor I will ever see you again after this summer, so what the hell?'

'I'd hate to think that,' she said.

'About which of us?'

'About both of you,' she said.

And they ran inside. They saw Danny's grip bag packed.

'You really are going then?' Annie said.

'Did you think I was making it up?'

'I thought you might want to get us back from the Maines,' Annie said.

'You'd want to have seen Annie and Sean Maine . . .' Brian began.

'No we wouldn't,' Ria said. 'We wouldn't have wanted to at all, any more than we'd want to have seen the way you left your bedroom here, Brian. But let's not waste time, we only have an hour before I take your dad to the bus station. There are a lot of things to be said so we must all talk now.'

'Zach might have seen me coming home, he could call in,' Brian began.

'Well, he'll just be asked to call out again,' Annie said.

Danny took control. 'I came over here to tell you that there are going to be a lot of changes, not all for the better.'

'Are any of them for the better?' Brian asked.

'No, as a matter of fact,' his father said. 'They're not.'

They sat silent, waiting. Danny's voice seemed to have failed him. They looked at their mother, but Ria said nothing, she just smiled encouragingly at Danny. At least she wasn't fighting with him and it reassured them. A little.

He cleared his throat and found the words. He told them the story. The debts, the gambles that hadn't worked, the lack of confidence, the end result. Number 16 Tara Road would have to be sold.

'Will you and Bernadette sell the new house too?' Brian asked.

'Yes, yes of course.'

'But Barney doesn't own that one?' Annie asked.

'No.'

'Well, maybe we could *all* live there, couldn't we?' Brian enclosed the whole room in his expansive gesture. 'Or maybe not,' he said, remembering.

'And I would have told you all this tonight, with more time for us to discuss what was best and to tell you how sorry I am, but I have to go home.'

'Is Mr McCarthy in gaol?' Brian asked.

'No, no it's not that at all, it's something else.' There was a silence. They looked at Ria again; again she offered nothing but a look of encouragement for Danny to speak. 'Bernadette isn't well. We've had a message from Finola. She's had a lot of bleeding and she may be losing the baby, she's in hospital. So that's why I'm going home early.'

'Like it's not going to be born after all, is that it?' Brian wanted to make sure he had it straight.

'It's not totally formed yet so it would be very weak and might not live if it were born now,' Danny explained.

Annie looked at her mother as she listened to this explanation, and bit her lip. Never had things been so raw and honest before. And Dad had been telling the truth on the phone, they were not rowing and fighting.

Brian let out a great sigh. 'Well, wouldn't that solve everything if Bernadette's baby wasn't born at all?' he said. 'Then we could all go back to being like we were.'

Danny gave the taxi-driver the address of the maternity hospital. 'As quick as you can, and I have to pay you in US dollars, I don't have any real money.'

'Dollars are real enough for me,' said the taxi-driver, pulling out in the early-morning sunshine and putting his foot down on the empty road.

'Is this the first baby?' the driver asked.

'No.' Danny was curt.

'Still it's always the same excitement, isn't it? And every one of them different. We have five ourselves, but that's it. Tie a knot in it, they told me.' He laughed happily at the pleasantry and caught Danny's eye in the mirror. 'Maybe you're a bit tired and want to have a bit of a rest after the flight.'

'Something like that,' Danny said with relief, and closed his eyes.

'Well, make the most of it, you'll have plenty of broken sleep for the next bit, there's a promise,' said the driver, a man of experience.

Orla King was having a routine check-up at the hospital. Something had shown up on a smear test but it had proved to be benign. Her blood tests had also shown much improved liver function. Apart from the catastrophic lapse at Colm's restaurant she was keeping off alcohol.

'Good girl,' said the kindly woman specialist. 'It's not easy but you're in there winning.'

'It's a funny old world. I stay off the booze and God says: okay, Orla, you don't have cancer this time.' Orla was cynical.

'Some people find that kind of attitude helps.' The doctor had seen it all and heard it all.

'Fantasists.' Orla dismissed them.

'What would help you?'

'I don't know. A singing career, the one fellow I fancied to fancy me . . .'

'There are other fellows.'

'So they say.' Orla went out into the corridor and walked straight into Danny Lynch. 'We do meet in the strangest places,' she said.

'Not now, Orla.' His voice was hard.

'It can't be baby time *yet* surely?'

'Please, excuse me.' He was trying to step past her.

'Come and have a coffee in the canteen and tell me all about it,' she pleaded.

'No. I'm meeting someone, I'm waiting.'

'Go on, Danny. I'm sober, that's one bit of good news, and a better one I don't have cancer.'

'I'm very pleased for you,' he said, still trying to escape.

'Look, I behaved badly some time back. I didn't ring or write or anything, but you know I didn't mean it, it's not the real me when the drink takes over.'

Across the corridor was a men's toilet. 'I'm sorry, Orla,' he said and went in the door. When he was inside he just leaned over the hand basin and looked at his haggard face, sunken eyes from a sleepless night on the plane, crumpled shirt.

He had been told she was still in Intensive Care, and he could see her in an hour or two. Her mother would be back shortly, she had been there most of the night. Oh yes, she had lost the baby; there had been no possibility of anything else. Bernadette would tell him everything herself, it wasn't hospital policy to tell him whether it had been a boy or a girl, the woman would do all that. In time. Go and have a coffee, they had urged him, and then he had met Orla King of all people in the universe.

His shoulders began to heave and the tears wouldn't stop. Another man, a big burly young fellow, came in and saw him.

'Were you there for it?' he asked. Danny couldn't speak and the proud young father thought he had nodded agreement. 'I was too. Jesus, it blew my mind. I couldn't believe it. I had to come in here to get over it. My son, and I saw him coming into the world.' He put an awkward arm around Danny's shoulder and gave him a squeeze of solidarity. 'And they say it's the women who go through it all,' he said.

Polly Callaghan came back from London early on Monday morning. Barney was waiting in his car outside her flat.

Polly was thrilled to see him. 'I didn't call you or anything, I wanted to leave you a bit of space. Aren't you good to come and meet me?'

'No, no not at all.' He seemed very down.

Polly wasn't going to allow that. 'Hey, I bought the *Irish Times* at Victoria Station in London and I saw that piece about you, it's wonderful.'

'Yes,' he said.

'Well, isn't it?'

'In a way.'

'Well, get out of that car, come in and I'll make us coffee.'

'No, Poll, we must talk here.'

'In your car, don't be ridiculous.'

'Please. Humour me this once.'

'Haven't I spent a lifetime humouring you? Tell me before I burst. Is it true, are you being rescued?'

'Yes, Poll, I am.'

'So why haven't we the champagne out?'

'But at a price. A terrible price.'

'Polly, it's Gertie here. Is this a good time to talk? I have a bit of a favour to ask you.'

'No, Gertie, it's not a good time to talk.'

'Sorry. Is Barney there?'

'No, and he's never going to be here again.'

'I don't believe it! I knew he was in a bit of trouble but . . .'

'He's in no trouble now, it's all been smoothed out for him, but he's not ever going to be here again, that's part of the deal. Actually *I'm* not going to be here much longer, that's part of the deal too.'

'But how?'

'His wife. Wives always win in the end.'

'No they don't. Ria didn't win, did she?'

'Ah shit, Gertie. Who cares?'

'I do, I'm very sorry. Maybe he doesn't mean it.'

'He means it. It was either or. What was your problem by the way?'

'Just . . . it doesn't matter, it's not big compared to yours.'

'What was it, Gertie?'

'It's just that Jack got some silly notion in his head that I was earning the extra money, well you won't believe how he thought I was earning it, so I had to tell him I was working for you. He might come round to check so can you say yes?'

'Is that all? Is that the big problem?'

'It was quite big at the time, and might be again if he's still brooding about it.'

'Were there any stitches this time?'

'No, no.'

'Gertie you're *such* a fool, such a mad fool. I'd love to come over and shake every remaining tooth out of your head.'

'That wouldn't help me. Not a bit.'

'No, I know that.'

'It's only because he loves me you see, he gets notions.'

'I see.'

'And you know that Barney loves you, Polly, he'll be back.'

'Of course he will,' said Polly Callaghan and hung up.

Marilyn Vine said to Greg that they were going to drive out to Wicklow for the day on Monday. It was less than an hour's journey, and very beautiful. She was going to make what would pass for a picnic.

'Here, I'll show you a map, you love maps,' she said as she got out Ria's picnic basket. 'Now, you can see where we're going and navigate if I take the wrong turning.'

He looked at her in amazement. The transformation was extraordinary. The old enthusiasms were back. 'We can go to the country in one hour?' he said, surprised.

'This is an extraordinary city, it's got sea and mountains right on the doorstep,' she said. 'And I want to take you to this place I found. You can park the car and walk over the hills for miles and meet no one, see no one. You can't even see any dwelling places. It's like Arizona without the desert.'

'Why are we going there?' he asked gently.

'So that nobody can interrupt us. If we stay here in Number sixteen Tara Road we might as well be in Grand Central Station,' said Marilyn, with the easy laugh that Greg Vine had thought he would never hear again.

Bernadette looked very white. His stomach nearly turned over when he saw her. 'Go on, talk to her. She's been counting the moments till you got here,' the nurse said.

'She's asleep,' he said, almost afraid to approach the bed.

'Is that you, Danny?'

'I'm here beside you, darling, don't speak. You're tired and weak. You've lost a lot of blood, but you're going to be fine.'

'Kiss me,' she said. He kissed her thin white face. 'Properly.' He kissed her on the lips. 'Do you still love me, Danny?'

'Darling Bernadette, of course I do.'

'You know about the baby?'

'I'm sad we've lost our baby, very sad,' he said, eyes full of tears. 'And, God, I'm sad I wasn't here to be with you when it happened. But *you* are all right and *I'm* here for you and that's what's going to make us strong for ever and ever.'

'You're not glad or anything, you don't think it sort of solves things just now?'

'Jesus, Bernadette, how could you even *think* that?' His face was anguished.

'Well . . . you know . . .'

'No, I don't know. Our baby is dead, the baby we were building a home for, and you're so weak and hurt. How could I be glad about anything like that?'

'It's just that I was afraid, you being out in America . . .' her voice trailed away.

'You know I had to go out to America to tell them face to face about the business. And that's done and I'm home now, home with you.'

'And did it go all right?' Bernadette asked.

'Yes, it went all right,' said Danny Lynch.

Ria rang Rosemary. 'You haven't set out for work yet?'

'No. Hey, what time *is* it out there? It must be the middle of the night.'

'It is, I couldn't sleep.' Ria sounded flat.

'Is anything wrong?'

'Well, yes and no.'

And Ria confided to her good friend Rosemary that Danny had gone home early because of Bernadette's miscarriage. She had nobody in Dublin to keep her informed of what was going on, could Rosemary keep an ear to the ground? Nobody else would tell her what was happening, but Rosemary saw Danny from time to time and she would be in a position to know.

Ria also told her how she hoped to get into some kind of catering job when she got home. Everyone here had been pleased with her work, she would try to get commissions from Colm for desserts and from the big delicatessen to do specialist work. She said she thought that everything was going to be all right again.

'And how was Danny when he was out there?'

'He was fine, it was a bit like the old days,' Ria said. She didn't go into details but Rosemary got the distinct feeling that more had happened than was being said. But even Danny Lynch wouldn't be so foolish as to sleep with his ex-wife under such circumstances. Surely?

When Rosemary went out to get into her car, still concerned about it, she met Jack Brennan. He did not smell of drink – but he wasn't sober. 'Just a quick question, Rosemary. Do you pay my wife to clean your house?'

'Certainly not, Jack. Gertie is my friend not my cleaner. I have cleaners who come from an agency twice a week.'

'And do other people pay her? Ria and that one staying in Ria's house, Polly, Frances?'

'Don't be ridiculous, Jack, of course they don't,' said Rosemary as she slammed her car door and drove to work.

Finola Dunne drove Danny to his office.

'I have to talk to Barney about what this rescue business is all about. It may be nothing, only puff, but it just might be something we can cling on to. I'll be back to Bernadette before lunch.'

'You'll need some sleep, you look terrible,' Finola said.

'I can't sleep, not at a time like this.'

'Ber losing the baby . . . at this time . . . ?' Finola was tentative.

'Makes me love her still more and want to look after her even more desperately than I did before . . .' Danny finished the sentence for her.

'But there must be ways . . . ?'

'Surely you know, Finola, that I adore her, that I wouldn't have left my wife and children for her if I didn't love her more than anything else in the whole world. You *must* know that.'

In the office a full-scale meeting was taking place. The receptionist was surprised to see him. 'They didn't think you were coming back until tomorrow,' she said, startled at his dishevelled appearance.

'Yes, well I'm here now, who's in there?'

'The accountant, the lawyers, the bank manager, and Mrs McCarthy.'

'Mona?'

'Yes.'

'And was anyone going to tell me about this summit or was I to hear about it when it was all over?'

'Don't ask me, Mr Lynch. I'm on notice like everyone else here, I don't get told what's happening either.'

'Right, I'm going in there.'

'Mr Lynch?'

'Yes?'

'If I could suggest you sort of . . . well . . . cleaned yourself up a bit.'

'Thank you, sweetheart,' he said. The girl was right. Five minutes in the men's room would take the worst edges off.

The sun shone through the trees as Greg and Marilyn sat at a wooden table and unpacked their picnic. They had walked and talked easily in the hills, looking at the sheep that barely gave them a second glance.

'Why did you come here?' Marilyn asked.

'Because Ria said you had talked to her children about Dale. I thought you might be able to talk to me about him too.'

'Yes, of course I can. I'm sorry it took so long.'

'It takes what time it takes,' Greg said. He laid his hand on hers. Last night he had slept in the big white bed beside Marilyn. They really hadn't touched each other, not reached out towards the other, but they had held hands for a little. He knew he must be very gentle in asking questions. He wouldn't ask what had changed her. She would tell him.

And then she did. 'There's always some stupid unimportant thing, isn't there?' Marilyn said with the tears that he had never seen her shed in her eyes.

'I mean it's so idiotic that I can hardly bear to tell you. But it was all to do with those children. Annie said that of course we couldn't have let him play with motorbikes any more than you'd let someone play with guns. And Brian said that he imagined Dale was up in heaven looking down, sorry for all the trouble he had caused.' The tears fell down on to their joined hands. 'Then it all made sense somehow, Greg,' she said through her sobs. 'I mean, I don't think there's a real heaven or anything, but his spirit is somewhere, sorry for all the trouble. And I must listen to him and tell him it's all right.'

'The wanderer returns,' Danny said, coming in with a false smile and confident stance to the boardroom where the meeting was going on. The stolid figure of Mona McCarthy sat beside Larry from the bank and the two lawyers.

'I'm sorry, we didn't know you were going to be in the country, Danny, there was no attempt to exclude you,' Mona said. Mona was speaking at a meeting like this?

'Well, tell the prodigal if the story in the *Irish Times* about a fatted calf was true.' Barney seemed curiously mute, so Danny was playing to the gallery now, trying to take control, or raise it a little anyway.

'Less of the jokes, Danny.' Larry from the bank had never liked him, but today he was speaking as if Danny were a schoolboy.

Danny was silent. And in the space of fifteen minutes he learned that Mrs McCarthy had, entirely without any legal or moral need to do so, decided to rescue the firm from bankruptcy. Everything would be wound up, the assets sold, the debtors paid. There would be no more work for Danny Lynch since the company no longer existed. The bank manager also managed to let Danny know that it might be extremely difficult for him to find a position in any reputable estate agency. The word about the financial mishandling was well known.

The good news was that the personal guarantee on Number 16 Tara Road was now rescinded. The house would not be sold to pay Barney McCarthy's debts. Danny could feel his breath slowly beginning to return to normal. But Larry added that on the Tara Road front there was also, on a practical level, bad news. Danny had no assets, no job and a considerable personal overdraft. The house would have to be sold anyway.

Fergal, a man that Colm knew slightly from the AA, called to see him. He was a detective as far as Colm could remember. 'You know the way we're all meant to be like the Masons or the Knights looking out for each other?' Fergal said, slightly awkwardly.

'I know. And are you telling me something or asking?' Colm made it easy.

'Telling. The word is that your brother-in-law is dealing here in this restaurant. There could be a raid.'

'Thank you.'

'You knew?'

'I suspected.'

'Will you warn him, move him on somewhere else or what?'

'I'd like to see him moved on to gaol but I have to do something else first.'

'Will it take long, what you have to do? You haven't got long,' Fergal said.

'Then it will have to be done quickly,' said Colm and prepared for the worst conversation in his life. He had promised his sister that he would look after her. Looking after her had long involved turning a blind eye to her addiction. Colm hoped that Marilyn Vine would deliver on her promise to help.

Mona was still talking in the boardroom. Barney and Danny walked out together. They weren't necessary any more.

Danny was determined to be bright. 'In better times we'd have said this was the day to ring Polly and book Quentin's for lunch,' he said.

'There won't be any more days like that.' Barney was subdued.

'Part of the deal?'

'Absolutely. And how did it go with you out there?'

Danny shrugged. 'You know . . .'

'Well, at least Ria will get something now this way.'

'Yes.'

'So what brought you back early anyway?'

'Bernadette lost the baby.'

'Oh dear, oh dear. Still there are ways that it might all be for the best.'

'There are no ways that it's in any way for the best,' said Danny coldly and went out to get a taxi back to the hospital.

Greg had gone back to America. Marilyn had longed to get the plane with him. 'I can't leave her house, I can't abandon ship now, leave a house she's going to lose anyway, it would be too cruel.'

'Of course not,' he had said.

'I'll be back on September the first, back in Tudor Drive,' she promised.

'So will I, in that week anyway,' he said.

'Hawaii?'

'They'll understand.' Greg was confident. 'It was a compassionate posting anyway. They'll be glad we got better.'

'It's just a pity that Ria didn't get better,' Marilyn said.

'We don't know, maybe she did.' Greg was hopeful.

'No, she wants that guy back and she's not getting him. I hear from the network here that he's back and glued to the girlfriend again.'

'She'll survive,' said Greg.

'What's she like?' Marilyn asked suddenly. 'As a person?'

'I forgot you don't know her. She's very warm, innocent in ways. She isn't short of a word. There was a time I didn't think you'd like her but now I think you would. I think my brother Andy did too.'

'There!' Marilyn cried. 'We might end up being sisters-in-law.'

'Don't hold your breath,' said Greg.

After he had gone, she sat at the table talking to Clement. 'You know we're going to get a cat, just like you, you foolish animal.'

Colm came in from the garden. His face was pale. 'Glad to see you talking to the cat,' he said. Marilyn was startled. Normally he never came in unannounced. He didn't wait for her to speak. 'I've got to do it, I'm telling her today. Will you help?'

'You've been to the centre?'

'Yes.'

'And they'll take her if she's willing.'

'Yes.'

'Then of course I will,' said Marilyn Vine.

'Ria, it's Danny.'

'Oh thank God, I was hoping to hear from you.'

'Well, it was a bit fraught.'

'How are you . . . ?'

'Well, we lost the baby but that was to be expected.'

'I am sorry.'

'Yes, I know you are, Ria.'

'But in a way . . .'

'I know you're not going to be like these people who wrongly say it's all for the best,' he interrupted her.

'No, of course I wasn't going to say that,' Ria lied.

'I know you weren't, but people do and it's very upsetting for us both.'

'I'm sure.' She was confused but she must never show it. 'Anyway the children are fine, they're winding down to go home now, and then we'll all meet and make plans about the future.'

'Yes, it's not quite as bleak as it looked on that scene,' he said.

'What do you mean?'

'Mona had some savings, Barney doesn't get our house after all.'

'*Danny!*' She was overjoyed.

'We'll still have to sell it, but at least this way you and I get the money, we'll find somewhere for you to live.'

'Sure.'

'So that's what I rang to tell you.'

'Yes . . .'

'Are you okay?' He sounded concerned.

'Fine, why?'

'I thought you'd be so pleased. Out of all this misery something good has emerged in the form of Mona McCarthy.'

'Yes, of course I'm pleased,' she said. 'Sorry, Danny, I have to go, someone's ringing at the door.' She hung up. There was nobody at the door but she needed to go without him hearing the tears in her voice. And the total wretched realisation that it had all meant nothing to him and that there were no plans for them for the future.

'Monto will have a table for six tonight and he'd like the one near the door,' said one of the nameless friends who accompanied Colm's brother-in-law.

'We have no reservations,' Colm said carefully.

'I think you have.'

'Ask Monto to talk to me himself if he's in any doubt,' Colm said.

He had asked his friend Fergal to tell the Drugs Squad that Caroline was safely installed on a rehabilitation programme. She could not be reached by Monto, offering her more supplies.

'Monto doesn't like people playing games.'

'Of course he doesn't.' Colm was pleasant.

'He'll be round.'

'I'm sure he'll believe *you* that there's no room for him here tonight. Why shouldn't he take your word?'

'You'll be hearing from him.'

Colm knew he would. Fergal said he'd make sure there were a couple of guys in the vicinity, in an unmarked car.

'Very good of you, Fergal, there'll always be a dinner for you and whoever here.'

'Ah, my whoever didn't hang around after the drinking days,' Fergal said sadly.

'And I never found a whoever at all. Right pair of eejits we were. Still, this should be the year.' Colm pretended a much greater sense of ease than he felt.

Marilyn called to the restaurant. 'I thought I'd invite Gertie here for dinner tonight.'

'On the house and with pleasure,' he said.

'I wouldn't hear of it.'

'Look what you did for Caroline.'

'She *was* ready, truly she was, she thought you'd feel let down if she went in, that's all.'

'Aren't we all mad in our ways?' he said.

'Sure,' she agreed with a laugh. 'Still Gertie and I will have a nice quiet time here compared to the first visit. Remember the singer who drank the carnations?'

'I'm not likely to forget her, but I wouldn't put money on it being quiet tonight.'

'Can we have the Maines to stay? Our visit *was* cut a bit short when we were there.'

'I know, Annie, but there was a reason.'

'Still. Please?'

'I don't know . . .'

'But Mam, this is the last good holiday we might ever have, you know if

874

we're going to be broke, and Dad gone and everything. It would be nice to have something to remember.'

'It would,' Ria said.

'Are you all right, Mam?'

'Yes. I don't want you getting too fond of a boy that you're going to have to say goodbye to in ten days' time.'

'No, Mam, you'd much prefer that than one I might see every day and night for the rest of my life,' Annie said, her eyes dancing.

'Ask them,' Ria said. It didn't really matter now. Nothing did.

Rosemary called at Number 16. 'Just passing by, I heard from Gertie that your husband came over.'

'That's right.'

'Good visit?'

'Very nice, thank you.'

'And is there any news of Ria?' If Rosemary thought it odd that she was being left on the doorstep to ask these questions she showed nothing of it.

Suddenly Marilyn opened the door wider. 'Yes, there is as it happens. Come in and I'll tell you about her news.'

Bernadette was home from hospital. She lay on a sofa and Danny brought her a bowl of soup.

'That's nice,' she said. 'What is it?'

'It's just a tin of consommé and a little brandy in it. To make you strong.' He stroked her face.

'You're the kindest man on earth,' she said.

'I'm useless. I have to sell our new home before we've even begun to pay for it.'

'I don't care. You know that.'

'Yes, I do.'

'And what about Ria?' It was the first time she had asked. 'Is she all right about selling Tara Road?'

'I think she is,' Danny said. 'She seemed all right about it when I was out there but she sounded different on the phone, I don't know why.'

'Phones are bad,' Bernadette reassured him. 'Did she say anything about the baby?'

'She said she was very sorry.'

'I'm sure she is,' Bernadette said. 'And the children too. Remember when Brian asked did he have webbed feet?' She smiled at the memory and cried at the thought of the little boy they had lost.

Marilyn sat opposite Rosemary in the beautiful drawing room. 'Would you care for a glass of sherry?' she asked in a very formal and courteous tone. She picked up a decanter and filled two of the small cut-crystal glasses that stood on a tray. 'Ria is thinking of going into business when she comes back.'

'So she told me.'

'She won't need a premises or kitchens or anything but she's a very talented cook, as I suppose you know.'

'She's good, yes.'

'And Colm's pastry-cook has left so she can do that. I gather she'll have an introduction to Quentin's, too, to do something different that won't compete.' Marilyn looked quite fierce and determined. Rosemary wondered where all this was leading. 'She'll also approach that big delicacy shop, you know the one I mean on the junction of three roads?' Rosemary supplied its name. 'Exactly . . . and do cakes for St Rita's. Her mother and I have been there already discussing it.'

'You *have* been busy.' Rosemary was impressed.

'But what she really needs, Rosemary, is someone to help her professionally, someone like you.'

'I can't cook. Heavens, I can barely open a tin,' Rosemary said.

'To write and print a brochure for her, business cards, menu suggestions.'

'Well, of course . . . if there's anything I can do to help . . .'

'And to give her a series of introductions, small receptions in your office, in places you visit.'

'Come on, Marilyn, you're making it sound like a full-time job.'

'I think you should invest a fair amount of time in it, yes certainly.' Marilyn's voice was steely now. 'And even some money, Rosemary.'

'I'm sorry but I don't really know what business . . .'

Marilyn cut straight across her. 'I'll be talking to Ria again tomorrow on the phone. I'd like her to know how much is being set up in advance for her. She needs all the practical help she can get just now. She has loads of goodwill already, that's falling off the trees for her, what she needs is the hard practical help that you can give her.'

'I don't invest in friends' schemes, Marilyn,' Rosemary said. 'I never have. It's just been a policy I've always had. I worked hard enough for my money and I want to keep my friends. If you don't lose money in their businesses then you've a better chance of keeping them *as* friends, if you see what I mean.'

There was a silence.

'Of course I'll be happy to mention her name,' Rosemary said. Still silence. 'And if ever I hear of anything . . .'

'I think we should get a list ready now of exactly what you'll do. We could write down what a good kind friend like you has done for Ria while she was away.' It sounded like a threat. Rosemary looked at her wildly. It couldn't be a threat, could it? 'Because she needs to know that friends can do things as well as say them. What good would a friend be, who betrayed her?'

'I beg your pardon?'

'Well it would be a betrayal, wouldn't it, if a friend took the things she most wanted in the world, while still pretending to be a friend?'

Rosemary's voice was almost a whisper now. 'What do you mean?'

'What do *you* think she wants most in the world, Rosemary?'

'I don't know. This house? Her children? Danny?'

'Yes. And of course you can't restore the house to her, her children she has already. So?' Marilyn paused.

'So?' Rosemary said shakily. The woman knew, she bloody knew.

'So, what you can help with is her dignity and self-respect,' Marilyn said brightly.

Danny's name had been left out of the list.

They began to write down what Rosemary would do to help Ria's career.

Gertie had been ironing a dress for Marilyn. 'That's a beautiful shade. Fuchsia, is it?'

'I think so. It doesn't fit me properly, I rarely wear it.'

'That's a shame, it's a gorgeous colour. Years ago when I worked in Polly's dress-hire place we had an outfit that colour; people were always renting it for weddings.'

'Would you like it?' Marilyn asked suddenly. 'Seriously I don't wear it, I'd love you to have it.'

'Well, if you're sure.'

'Wear it tonight to Colm's, the colour would suit you.' Gertie's face seemed to have a shadow. 'It's still on, tonight, isn't it?' Marilyn thought she would kill Gertie if she chickened out now.

'But of course it's on, Jack's pleased for me. I don't think he'd like to see me wearing such a classy dress though. One he didn't buy for me himself.'

'Change here on our way to the restaurant then.'

'Why not? Won't it do me good to dress up?' said Gertie with that heart-breaking smile which made Marilyn glad she hadn't said anything terrible about Jack.

At seven o'clock Monto and two friends arrived at the restaurant. And headed for the table that they thought they had booked. The restaurant was still empty. No one would arrive for at least thirty minutes. This was better than Colm had believed possible.

'Sorry, Colm, there was some mistake. You didn't get the message that we are meeting some friends here. Two are coming over from England and one down from the North. We have an important meeting and this is where we are having it.'

'Not tonight, Monto.'

'Tell me a little more.' Monto smiled a slow smile. He had very short hair and a fat neck. His expensive suit did nothing to hide his shape, and the regular manicures little to help his pudgy hands and square nails. Colm looked at him levelly.

'You have a short memory, not long ago you told me you owed me.'

'And I paid you. You've done enough deals in this place.'

'Deals?' Monto looked at the other two associates and laughed. 'Isn't the word "meals", Colm? That's what you run, it's a restaurant isn't it? They serve meals, not deals.'

'Goodbye, Monto.'

'Don't think you can talk to me like that.'

'I just have and if you know what's good and wise you'll go.'

'Give me a reason or two.'

'The number of the car from Northern Ireland has already been taken down. Your guests from the UK will be interviewed. Everything you have will be searched.'

'Big talk, Colm . . . and who'll look after your sister? She hasn't enough to get her to the weekend.'

'She's being looked after, thank you.'

'Nobody in this city will supply your sister, they know she's my wife. They know she's with me.'

'Well, they know more than you do. She hasn't been with you for three days.' Colm sounded very calm.

'You'd start a drugs war in your own place just because you got her a new source?'

'No, I'm starting nothing, I'm asking you to leave.'

'And what makes you think I will?'

'The Guards in the car just outside.'

'You set me up.'

'No, I didn't as it happens. I told them that there would be no meeting, no deal here tonight or ever again.'

'And they believed you?'

'They felt pretty sure that I meant it all right. Goodnight, Monto.'

When Marilyn and Gertie arrived Colm was calm again.

'Gertie, don't you look lovely! That's a colour you should always wear.'

'I will, Colm, thank you,' she said, delighted with the compliment.

'And are we going to have fireworks tonight?' Marilyn asked.

'It's over, amazingly. All wilted at the first touch of winter frost,' he said.

'You two have lots of secrets,' Gertie giggled.

'Only the secrets of those who share a garden,' Colm said.

Across the restaurant they saw Polly Callaghan. She was with a very distinguished-looking man.

'Isn't Barney very understanding that he lets her go out to dinner with other men.' Gertie was full of admiration.

'I don't think Barney is in the picture these days,' Colm said.

'Of course you're right. Come to think of it she's leaving her flat tomorrow I hear.' Gertie had forgotten.

'Now how on *earth* do you know all these things, Colm?' asked Marilyn Vine who would not have been remotely interested a few weeks ago.

'In a restaurant you see and hear everything and say nothing,' he said, and left them the menus and moved on.

Rosemary Ryan waved at them from another table.

'Who is she with? Marilyn asked.

'Her sister Eileen and her sister's girlfriend Stephanie. And now they really *are* lesbians,' Gertie giggled.

'Let's hope the lady who drank the carnations doesn't come back and out them all,' Marilyn said.

'They're so out you wouldn't believe it, Rosemary hates it.'

'Does she now?' Marilyn smiled.

Jack was sitting up waiting when Gertie came home. 'Nice evening, was it?'

'Yes, Jack, it was a nice girls' night out.'

'And who gave you the whore's purple dress?'

'Marilyn did, it doesn't suit her.'

'It wouldn't suit anyone except a whore,' he said.

'Ah Jack, don't say that.'

'All my life I loved you and all you did was betray me and let me down.' He had never spoken like this before.

'That's not so, Jack. I never looked at another man, never.'

'Prove that to me.'

'Well, would I have stayed with you all these times you've been under the weather?' she asked.

'No, that's true,' he said. 'That's very true.'

They went to bed. She lay there hardly daring to move in case she might feel his fist. Out of the corner of her eye she saw him. Jack Brennan was awake and looking at the ceiling. He was dangerously calm.

'Hallo Marilyn, it's only Ria. Don't bother to ring back, I'll be here and there and everywhere. I've no news. Sorry I sound a bit down. It's stupid to ring up and then sound like something from a depressives' ward. It's just . . . it's just . . . Anyway the real reason I rang was to thank you *so* much for the e-mail you sent from the Cyber café. Isn't Rosemary wonderful to do all that? Wouldn't we all be lost without our friends? I'll say goodbye now, I've got to drive the Maine children back home, and Annie's heartbroken, she seems to be crazy over Gertie's nephew. Everyone just laughs at first love, but then Danny was my first love and look how long it lasted. For me anyway. All the best, Ria.'

The next morning Jack Brennan got very drunk very early. He went first to Nora Johnson's house at Number 48A. 'Does my wife clear up after your daughter and all her friends?' he shouted.

'I have nothing to say to you drunk or sober,' Ria's mother said with some spirit. 'I have never met your wife without telling her that she should leave you. I'll bid you good-day.'

He moved on to Rosemary's house. 'Swear to me on a stack of bibles that Gertie never cleaned for you or anyone.'

'Oh get the hell out of here before I call the Guards,' Rosemary said, and pushed past him.

Next he stopped at the dentist's house. Jimmy Sullivan saw him from the window and answered the door himself.

'Tell me.'

'I'll tell you nothing, Jack Brennan, except that I fix your wife's teeth every time you hit her and I'm not in a mood to do so again.'

Then he went and knocked loudly on Marilyn's door. 'Did you give Gertie a whore's dress?'

'Did she say I did?'

'Stop being Mrs Clever with me.'

'I think you should go, Jack.' She slammed the door and looked out the window to see where he went. She saw him run across the road to the bus stop.

Polly Callaghan had everything ready. Today she was moving to rented accommodation. An unfurnished flat so she could take her own things with her. Those at least had not been seized by that woman, Barney's mouse-like wife, who had been stacking away thousands upon thousands.

Last night Polly had gone to dinner with a pleasant man who had long been pestering her for a date. It had been a deadly dull evening. She dreaded to think of a lifetime without Barney. She wished she could hate him but she couldn't. She just hated herself for having taken the wrong decision so long ago.

The furniture vans had arrived. Polly sighed and began to give the directions that would dismantle a large part of her life. The phone was disconnected but her mobile was still in operation. It rang just at that moment.

'Poll, I love you.'

'No you don't, Barney, but it doesn't matter.'

'What do you mean it doesn't matter?'

'It doesn't,' she said, and clicked off.

She was going to drive ahead of the van to direct them to the new address. One final look and she was ready to close the door. Polly sighed. It was hard to say to Barney that it didn't matter, but she must be practical. She had always known Barney for what he was. He was like Danny Lynch, although as far as she knew Danny had never had any strong partner-figure like herself. Barney would always remain married to a safe-haven person like Mona. Danny had moved from his safe haven, the faithful, loving Ria, to safe, compliant Bernadette. There had been some little dramas in between like that wild Orla King and one or two others. But that's the way things were. Polly did not think she had been fooled or betrayed. She had always known the score. And there was plenty of life ahead.

She gave one last glance out the window at the removal van. Everything was packed now, she only had her hand luggage to take. There were sounds of shouting, some drunk was yelling abusively. Polly couldn't quite see what was happening. Then there was a thump, an impact followed by a screech of brakes. There were screams from everywhere. The boy who was driving was being helped from his seat.

'I couldn't help it, he threw himself, I swear,' he was stammering.

It was Jack Brennan. And he was dead.

10

The launderette was busy when they arrived. The shirt-ironing service had been a big success, and Gertie had got orders from several business concerns as well. Colm had been high in his praise of her and personal recommendation was always very important. She looked up when she saw Polly Callaghan coming in and her hand flew to her throat when she saw that Polly was followed by two Guards.

'Jack?' she cried in a strangled voice. 'Has Jack done something? He was grand last night, very quiet, not a word out of him. What did he do?'

'Sit down, Gertie,' Polly said. One of the Guards had organised a glass of water from amongst the inquisitive staff and clientele. 'There's been an accident. It was very quick, he didn't feel a thing,' Polly said. 'The ambulancemen said it would have been over in a second.'

'What are you saying?' Gertie was white-faced.

'We would all be lucky to go so quickly and painlessly, Gertie, honestly, when you think of the length it takes some people to die.'

The young Guard handed her the glass of water. She had only been in uniform for a week. This was the first occasion when she had been sent to break bad news to someone about an accident. She was very glad that this Miss Callaghan had come with them. The poor woman who ran the launderette looked as if she were going to keel over and die herself.

'But Jack can't be dead,' Gertie kept saying. 'Jack's not even forty, he has years of good living ahead of him, ahead of both of us.'

'Mrs Vine, Marilyn, we met briefly. I'm Polly Callaghan. I'm with Gertie Brennan now.'

'Yes?'

'There's been a most awful accident. Gertie's husband Jack was killed and of course she's devastated, I'm here with her now, and they're getting her mother and everything ... but I do have to go to let people into a new apartment and I was wondering...'

'Would you like me to come to the launderette?' Marilyn asked.

'If you can, please.'

Marilyn heard the urgency, almost desperation, in the voice. 'I'll come right away.' She called out to Colm in the garden, 'I'm going out to Gertie, Jack had an accident.'

'Nothing trivial, I hope?' Colm said.

'Fatal, I believe,' Marilyn said tersely.

To her surprise Colm threw down his fork and rushed into the house. 'Jesus, what a stupid remark to make, I'll come with you,' he said. 'But I'll run on ahead and tell Nora Johnson, she'd want to come too.'

Marilyn thought to herself, not for the first time, that these really were extraordinary people. The very time when you wanted to be left alone with your grief they started assembling half the country around you. She tried to take it in. Jack Brennan who had called at this door under two hours ago was *dead*? Her last words to him had been, 'I think you should go.' Suppose she had asked him in for coffee, suppose she had tried to reassure him, would he be alive now? But Marilyn had been down that road before: she wasn't going to travel it again. What had happened to Gertie's husband was not her fault. She would no longer take on the guilt and responsibility of the universe. She would go and see what could be done for the living.

Ria's mother was exactly the right person to have alerted. She knew precisely what to do. She encouraged the launderette staff to continue working. It's what Gertie would want if she were able to speak, Nora Johnson said. No, it wasn't at all heartless to keep the business going, in fact it was only fair to customers. But if the staff would all like to give her fifty pence each she would go out now and buy a big bunch of flowers and a card so that they could be seen to be the very first to sympathise. They rooted in their apron pockets and Nora came back with a bouquet, which had cost three times what she had collected.

'What exactly would you write in a case like this?' one of the girls asked.

'Suppose you say: "For Gertie with love and sympathy", would that cover it?' Nora Johnson knew that none of them, any more than herself, could bear to mention the name Jack on a card. Only a couple of hours ago she had shouted at him herself and said that she had always urged Gertie to leave him. Nora didn't regret it at all, it was what she had always felt. Not of course that there would be any need to say anything like that now to Gertie.

Marilyn watched in amazement as the little flat above the launderette filled with people. A buffet table was set up with cold ham and pâté which came from Colm's restaurant. Jimmy and Frances Sullivan had sent a crate of wine, and bottles of soda. Hilary had sent a message saying she'd come over after work and bring a bag of black clothes which Gertie could borrow. The children John and Katy had arrived, stunned, confused and taken from the summer course where their grandmother had paid for them to have some kind of normal holiday. Gertie's mother was there, her mouth a thin hard line, but her words kind as she went along with the general fiction that Gertie had tragically lost a great man, a loving husband and devoted father.

It was entirely surreal, but Marilyn told herself over and over that this is what Gertie ached to hear and it was being delivered to her.

Ria was having coffee with Sheila Maine when the call came from Sheila and Gertie's mother with the news of Jack's death. She said it was hard to speak because there were so many people there. Ria realised that it was also hard to speak since she too had been sworn to support the story of the fairy-tale marriage.

Sheila was appalled. 'What on earth will she do without him, she'll be devastated,' she cried. 'I mean, other people *think* they have happy marriages but this is one we all dreamed about and never knew.'

Polly left a message in Rosemary Ryan's office. They told her that Rosemary was on another line and couldn't be interrupted.

'Just tell her that Gertie Brennan's husband is dead.'

'Any more details, Ms Callaghan?' Rosemary Ryan's assistant was as cool as she was herself.

'No, she'll know what to do,' said Polly.

'Danny, I have to talk to you.' Rosemary had phoned Danny Lynch's mobile.

'It's not appropriate now, Rosemary.' He was sitting holding Bernadette's hand, as she drifted off to sleep.

'Go on, Danny, take the call if it's business,' Bernadette said.

He took his phone into the next room.

'What is it, Rosemary?'

'You haven't got in touch since you got back.'

'Well, quite a lot has been happening,' he said.

'I know, and didn't I alert you out there?'

'Not about work. We lost the baby.'

'Oh.'

'Is that all you can say?'

'I'm sorry.'

'Thank you.'

'But life goes on, Danny, and you and I have a lot of worries which you should know about. Can you meet me?'

'Absolutely not.'

'We have to talk.'

'No, we don't.'

'Is your business safe, your house?'

'The business has closed, the house will have to be sold, but at least not as part of Barney's estate. Now I have to go back to . . .'

'But you, Danny, what will you do? You must tell me. I have a right to know.'

'You have no right to know. You couldn't help me when I was in trouble. You made that clear, and I accepted it.'

'But there's more . . . wait . . . Marilyn knows.'

'Knows what?'

'She knows about us.'

'Really?'

'Don't go all distant on me, Danny Lynch.'

'Please, Rosemary, leave me alone, I have too much to worry about.'

'I don't believe this,' she said.

'Rosemary, stop the drama. It's over.'

She hung up, shaking.

Her assistant came in. 'Ms Ryan, I have a message here. Some bad news. It's to tell you that Gertie Brennan's husband is dead.'

'Good,' said Rosemary.

'We're going home two days early,' Ria said. 'I was able to get cancellations.'

'Oh *no* Mam, no. Not for awful Jack Brennan's funeral. You never liked him, it's so hypocritical.'

'Gertie's my friend though, I like her,' Ria said.

'You *promised* we could stay here until September.'

'Well, I'd have thought you would like to be going on the same plane as Sean Maine, but what do I know?' Ria said.

'What?'

'Sheila's taking the two children over to the funeral, we'll all travel together ... but of course if you're violently opposed to that then I suppose ...'

'Oh Mam, shut up, you'd never win a prize for acting,' Annie said, overjoyed.

Andy had a business meeting nearby. Or so he said. 'Can I take your mother out to the Thai restaurant on her own?' he asked Annie and Brian when he came to the house.

'On a date like?' Brian asked.

'No, just for boring grown-up conversation.'

'Oh, sure, I'll go to Zach's house. Will it be overnight?' Brian asked.

'No, Brian, it will *not* be overnight,' Ria said.

'I can go to the movies with Hubie,' Annie said. 'And before you ask, Brian, that's not a date and neither is it overnight.'

'You have a delightful family,' Andy said.

Ria sighed. 'I must remind myself not to cling to them too much, not to be the mother from hell.'

'You couldn't be that,' he laughed.

'Oh easily. I don't know what we're going back to; it's real uncharted territory. I must not use them as my pair of crutches through it.'

'You don't need any crutches, Maria,' he said. 'Will you keep in touch with me, do you think?'

'I'd love to.'

'But just as a friend ... that's all, isn't it?' He was disappointed but realistic.

'I need friends, Andy, I'd love to think you were one.'

'That's what it will be then. *And* I'll send you recipes, I'll actively seek them out for you to make you a legend in Irish cuisine.'

'You know, I really do think it might get off the ground. My friend Rosemary is putting herself right behind it and she's a real dynamo.'

'I don't doubt it for one minute,' said Andy Vine.

*

'I didn't have sex with Sean Maine and I'm not going to have sex with you either, Hubie. Are we clear on both these matters?' Annie said.

'You're making the point very forcibly, yes,' he said. 'But the thing that really bugs me is that one day soon you *are* going to have sex with somebody and it won't be me because you're going to be miles away.'

'I might *not,* you know.' Annie spoke very seriously. 'I don't mean become a nun or anything but I might just not do it, ever.'

'Unlikely.' Hubie dismissed the notion.

'I once saw two people doing it . . . years and years ago. I don't know how to describe it . . . it wasn't nice. It wasn't the way I thought it would be.'

'But you were very young then,' he said. She nodded. 'And you probably didn't understand it.'

'Do *you* understand it?' she asked him.

'A bit, I suppose, well better than when I was a kid. Then it seemed full of mystery and excitement and you had to have it and yet you were afraid of it.' He smiled at the recollection of how silly he had been when young.

'And now?'

'Well, now it seems more natural, do you know? Like the thing to do with someone you like.'

'Oh?' She wasn't convinced.

'I haven't done it all that often, Annie, believe me. I'm not bull-shitting you.'

'But it was nice?'

'It was, and that's the truth,' said Hubie Green who knew they were having a conversation about abstracts and not about how the evening was going to end.

'Will you be living in a trailer park when you get back?' Zach asked.

'No, I don't think so, why?' Brian was interested.

'Well, if your house is gone?'

'I don't know where we'll live, maybe with Dad but I think *his* house is gone too.'

'It's a real adventure, isn't it?' Zach said. 'Will there be somewhere for me to stay when I come over there next year?'

'Oh, there'll have to be,' Brian said airily.

'And will I meet Myles and Dekko?'

'Certainly.'

'That's great,' Zach said. 'I never thought I'd be a person who would travel.'

'That's funny,' Brian said. 'I always knew I'd travel, I'll probably go to planets and all. I was going to be an auctioneer like my dad and work with him but now that he's lost his business I think I'll be an astronaut instead.'

'I'll miss you,' Carlotta said. 'I wish I'd got to know you better. Earlier on I suppose I felt inhibited. Marilyn has kept us all at such arm's length, we thought that as her friend . . .'

'I think you'll find that she has changed a lot in a couple of months. She talks about Dale now, and Greg's coming back here to live. Things will be much more open now.'

'Does she know Hubie visits here?'

'Yes, I told her. She has no objection, though I don't think he'll be around so much when my Annie leaves!'

'And did you find what you came here for, Ria?' Carlotta asked.

'No, but I was looking for the moon,' she said.

'I kinda thought you had found the moon that weekend when your husband was here,' Carlotta said.

'Yes, so did I for a little while, but it wasn't the moon after all,' Ria said.

'Greg has told us how wonderful your home in Ireland is, I'm so sorry you won't be able to go on living there,' Heidi said.

'It's only a house, Heidi, only bricks and mortar,' Ria said.

'That's such a very wise thing to be able to say.' Heidi was admiring.

'I'm just practising, rehearsing my lines,' Ria admitted. 'I think that if I say it often enough then I might believe it when I walk around it and have to say goodbye to it.'

'And do you know where you'll go?'

'House property is very expensive in Dublin at the moment, so we'll get a good price for it but then we won't be able to buy anything in the area. I imagine that we'll have to move out a long way.'

'It does seem such a waste. He and you got along so well when he was here ... but then I'm only saying things you must have thought a thousand times in your head.'

'A million times, Heidi.'

John and Gerry said they really would miss her in their shop. Ria was to go home, set up a food export business, get written up in *Bon Appetit*, and they would be amongst her first clients.

'That's what I love about America. You really do believe dreams come true here,' Ria said to them.

She telephoned Gertie just before they left.

'I can't believe you're coming home early for Jack's funeral, you changed your tickets and all to be here.'

'Well of course I would, Gertie. You'd do it for me if things were different.'

'Thank you, Ria, and you do know that Jack was always very admiring of you. Remember the party in your house that he came to where he drank lemonade and helped serve the food?'

'I do indeed, Gertie.' Ria bit her lip.

'They're taking him to the church tonight,' Gertie said. 'You wouldn't believe all the lovely flowers. Jack was very popular and well-liked in his own way.'

'Of course he was, and we'll see you tomorrow morning,' said Ria, who would be hard put to it to find one person who could say one good word about the late Jack Brennan.

Sheila Maine slept in the plane. Kelly and Brian played cards and watched the movie. Annie and Sean whispered plans for the future to each other.

Ria could not sleep. Her mind was full of pictures. The funeral, and the sustained pretence that Jack Brennan had been very different. The meeting with Danny to discuss their future. Arranging to sell Number 16 Tara Road. Finding a new place to live. The whole business of starting to cook for a living. Meeting Marilyn face to face after all this time.

Ria hoped she would like her. She knew so much about her now, more than Marilyn even dreamed she knew. There was a time when Ria had thought she would hate her, when she heard of Marilyn taking over her garden, her house, her friends and her daughter. That was when she had thought Marilyn cold and unfeeling, wearing a prickly armour about her son's death and shutting out so much goodwill everywhere.

But the summer had changed that. Now she was touched by little secrets she knew about this woman. How she had a bottle of hair colourant labelled in her own writing 'Special Shampoo'. How she had inexpensive discount toilet tissue in her storeroom, and instant cake mixes in her larder. Ria knew that Marilyn's friends had been hurt and repelled by her, and that her love of the garden was not considered admirable but obsessive.

And Ria also knew a far bigger secret. Something that would never be told. She knew what had happened on the day of Dale Vine's accident. To know that would never make Marilyn stronger, it would ruin everything. She had reassured Hubie that it would never be mentioned and he believed her.

Ria hadn't told everyone else that she was coming home. She would meet them all at the funeral anyway.

Marilyn had promised to have breakfast ready for them when they arrived at Tara Road. They would have time for that, to get changed, and then they would all go to the church together. Ria smiled as she remembered their conversation. 'The one good thing about this dreadful accident is that you and I get a chance to meet. Otherwise we would have passed in mid-air again,' she had said to Marilyn.

'I think there's a lot more than one good thing about this dreadful accident,' Marilyn had said. 'Not of course that any of us will ever admit it.' Marilyn had been in Ireland for two months. She was learning.

Just then the captain announced that due to weather conditions they were being diverted to Shannon Airport. He apologised for the delay which would not be more than a couple of hours. They would certainly be in Dublin by 11.00 a.m.

'My God,' said Ria. 'We'll miss the funeral.'

'I'm going to that eejit Jack Brennan's funeral,' Danny Lynch said.

Bernadette looked up. 'Who was he?'

'A drunken bully. His wife Gertie was always in and out of Tara Road. If Ria and the children were here they'd have gone; I suppose in a way I'm going to represent them.'

'That's very good of you,' said Bernadette. 'You're always thinking of other people.'

'I met Lady Ryan on the road,' Nora Johnson told Hilary. 'She said she was going to Jack's funeral.'

'Well, I suppose like the rest of us she's only going as a bit of solidarity for poor Gertie.'

'She never had the civility to throw the time of day to poor Gertie,' Nora sniffed.

'Ah, be fair, Mam, didn't we all say that Gertie should have thrown him out years ago?'

'We did and we were right, but we didn't say it with the scorn that Lady Ryan did. She treated Gertie like dirt, like something she found stuck to her shoe.'

'You never liked her, Mam.'

'Do you?'

'She's all right, she's funny I suppose and she jazzes us all up,' Hilary admitted grudgingly.

'No she doesn't, she pats you all on the head, and you're all worth ten of her.' Some of Nora's opinions would never change.

The delay at Shannon Airport seemed interminable. Sheila Maine telephoned her sister. 'If we're not in time for the church, we'll go straight to the graveyard,' she said.

Gertie wept her gratitude on the phone. 'Oh Sheila, if you knew how kind everyone's being. And if only poor Jack knew how much it turned out that people loved him.'

'Well, of course he did. Didn't everyone know you had a great marriage?' Sheila said.

Ria rang Marilyn. 'It seems we won't have that breakfast after all,' she said.

'Then you'll never know what a bad cook I am,' Marilyn said.

'I wish you didn't have to leave tomorrow, that you could spend a couple more days.'

'I might easily do that. We'll talk later ... Oh and another thing ... Welcome home!'

'Jimmy, would you sing "Panis Angelicus" at the funeral?' Gertie had asked on the phone.

'Now you wouldn't want me croaking away...' he began.

'Oh Jimmy, please. Jack just loved that hymn, he really did. It would make it lovely for me if you sang it.'

'I think it's more a wedding hymn really, Gertie, rather than a funeral one.'

'No, it's about Holy Communion so it would be equally suitable at both.'

'Well, if you'd like me to then certainly I will,' said Jimmy Sullivan. He put the phone down and raised his eyes to heaven. 'If there *is* a God, which I gravely doubt, then he should smite us all to the pit of hell for our hypocrisy.'

'What else can we do?' Frances shrugged.

'We could have the balls to say that Jack was a mad bollocks and that the world is better off without him,' Jimmy suggested.

'That would be *great* consolation to the widow and children,' Frances said.

There was a black-edged notice on the door of the launderette saying that Jack Brennan, proprietor, had died and giving the time of the funeral Mass, so quite a few of the customers came out of respect to Gertie.

The church was crowded when Gertie, her mother and her children arrived. Some of Jack's family, long-estranged, had turned up, with dark suits and white shirts and awkward handshakes. Gertie, pale and wearing the black dress she had borrowed from Hilary, walked up the aisle looking proudly from side to side at all the people who had come to say goodbye to Jack. At least now he might know that he had worth in people's eyes. Surely he was somewhere where he could see all this.

The Mass had only just begun when Sheila Maine and her two children came up and joined the family. A little ripple of approval went through the church. The relatives had flown in from America, a further sign that Gertie was being honoured and made much of.

Ria, Annie and Brian slipped into a bench a little further back. 'My God,' Nora Johnson said to Hilary. 'Ria came back. Isn't she a great girl.' Danny Lynch saw his wife and children. He bit his lip. It must have been hard to organise, Ria was certainly a loyal friend. Colm Barry saw them too. Ria looked magnificent, he thought, tanned, slimmer, holding herself taller somehow. He had known she would try to be here even though she wasn't meant to be back today. She and Gertie went back a long way.

Polly Callaghan sat by herself. She averted her eyes from the pew where Barney McCarthy sat with his wife. If Mona saw Polly in the church she gave no sign or acknowledgement, any more than she ever had.

Rosemary had dressed carefully for the occasion as always. A grey silk dress and jacket, very high heels and dark stockings. She was most surprised to see Ria and the children, nobody had told her they were coming back. But then she realised with a start there were few people to tell her anything. Apart from Ria herself, she didn't seem to have any friends any more.

Frances Sullivan stared ahead of her as her husband's deep rich voice sang 'Panis Angelicus'. She knew how much it cost him to do this. He had despised Jack Brennan and felt that singing this hymn was in some way letting him win.

Ria looked around the church to see could she identify Marilyn. She wasn't beside Rosemary, or Colm, or near Ria's mother. But surely one of them would have taken her under a wing. Ria couldn't concentrate on the prayers, she looked at the bouquets and wreaths all sent by people who had nothing but scorn for the deceased.

Where was Marilyn Vine?

It was when the congregation was singing 'The Lord's My Shepherd' that Ria saw her. Taller than she would have thought, auburn-haired from the Special Shampoo bottle, and wearing a simple navy dress. She was holding up the hymn sheet and singing along with the rest. Just at that moment she looked up and saw Ria looking at her. They gave each other a great smile across the crowded church. Two old friends meeting each other at last.

The sun was shining, the unexpected gales and rainstorms of the night before had blown away. The people stood and talked outside the church, a Dublin funeral where there weren't enough minutes in the hour for people to say what they wanted to say.

Ria was being embraced and welcomed home by everyone. She broke free to hug Gertie.

'You're such a true friend to come back early,' Gertie said.

'We travelled with Sheila and the children, we didn't notice the journey. And they'll be staying with you?'

'Yes, yes, we have the rooms ready. It's such a pity that they had to come for this reason, isn't it? I mean Jack would love to have welcomed them here again.'

Ria looked at Gertie with shock. She realised that history was being rewritten here. There was no longer any need to pretend to Sheila that everything had been wonderful with Jack. Gertie had bought the story herself, she really thought it had been a great marriage.

Danny looked curiously like someone on the outside. Not the man who used to dart from group to group, shaking this hand, slapping that shoulder. Ria told herself that she must not think about him and care what became of him. He was not part of her life, the notion that they could go back to the old life was only in her head. She stood looking at him across the crowds. Soon the children would spot him and run over. But she would make no move. This is the way it was always going to be.

Annie had gone to talk to Marilyn, to introduce her new friend Sean Maine, to talk about Westville. Brian had gone to his grandmother to tell her about Zach's visit next summer. Ria could hear him. 'We might be living on a halting site then but he's coming anyway,' Brian's clear, carrying tones were explaining.

Hilary was trying to tell Ria all about the move. They would leave in the autumn and settle in. Martin's post would begin in January. Ria couldn't quite understand where they were going.

'You'll come and stay, Ria . . . lots . . . won't you? It's full of trees. Like the fortune-teller said.'

'Yes, yes of course.' She was bewildered. There were too many people around, too much was going on.

'I'll give you twenty-four hours to get over your jet lag and then you start working for me,' Colm said. 'You look absolutely beautiful by the way.'

'Thank you, Colm.' She thought she saw something of the admiring look that had been in Andy Vine's eye, but she shook off the notion. She must not lose her marbles now and think everyone was fancying her.

Rosemary didn't come over, which was odd. She stood, a little like Danny stood, on the outside of a crowd where she knew many people. Ria went up to her, arms open wide. She saw Rosemary looking a little uneasily over her shoulder. Ria turned to follow her glance. Marilyn Vine had paused in her conversation with Annie and was watching them. Very carefully.

'Are you going to the graveyard?' Ria asked Rosemary.

'God no, here's bad enough.'

'Gertie's so pleased to see everyone,' Ria said.

'I know, and she's been on the phone to the Vatican to organise his canonisation too. Believe me, Ria, that is not beyond the bounds of possibility.'

Ria laughed. 'God, it's good to be back,' she said, putting her arm into Rosemary's. 'Tell me, was it a good summer?'

'No, it was a bloody awful summer one way and another.'

'You're so good to put so much effort into getting *me* started up,' Ria said. 'I really do appreciate it.'

'Least I could do,' Rosemary said gruffly, looking over at Marilyn Vine again.

'It's a really beautiful house, Marilyn,' Annie said. 'You never told us how great it was.'

'I'm so pleased you had a good time.'

'You have no idea, it was like a house in the movies, honestly. And we swam before breakfast and even at night.'

'Great.'

'And we went on roller-blades in Memorial Park and we ate huge pizzas, and we went to New York City twice and up to Sean's house on the bus all on our own. There was never a holiday like it.'

'I'm so very happy it went well,' Marilyn said.

She knew that she and Ria were almost putting off the moment when they would speak to each other. And yet every time they took a step in each other's direction someone came to claim one of them.

This time it was Colm. 'I didn't know Ria was coming back today. I'll leave you something over in the house, something from the restaurant. To save you cooking,' he said.

'To save them being poisoned, you mean.' Marilyn laughed at herself.

'You said it, not I.'

Barney McCarthy had sympathised briefly with the widow.

'You're very good to come, Mr McCarthy, Jack would have been very impressed at the quality of all the people who are here,' Gertie said.

'Yes, well. Very sad,' Barney mumbled.

'Polly Callaghan is devastated that it happened on her premises,' Mona McCarthy said unexpectedly.

Gertie nearly fell down on the ground. Mona didn't talk about Polly, she pretended that she didn't exist.

Barney looked startled too. 'Well, it wasn't exactly her premises...' he began.

'No, that's right, she was moving house and poor Jack, poor, poor Jack had called on her ... He wanted reassurance about something, you see.' Gertie's lower lip began to tremble.

Mona rescued her. 'I know, I heard the story. He wanted to be sure that you loved him. Aren't men like children in so many ways? They always like everything to be there in black and white.' Gertie looked from Barney to Mona, bewildered. But Mona sailed on. 'And Polly told him that of course you loved him, those were the last words he heard.'

'Polly told me, but I wasn't sure if she was just being kind you know, telling me what I wanted to hear.'

'No, no, whatever else you could call Polly, she isn't kind,' Mona said. And moved away.

'That wasn't necessary, Mona,' Barney hissed at her.

'Yes it was. Poor Gertie had no life while that savage was alive, she's going to have one after he's dead, believe me.'

'But how did you hear what Polly said or didn't say ... ?'

'I heard,' Mona said. 'And don't think I have anything against Polly, I think she did this city a huge service by allowing her furniture van to kill Jack Brennan. She should be decorated by the Lord Mayor.'

Then they finally met. They put their arms around each other. And said each other's names.

'I'll drive us to the graveyard,' Marilyn said.

'No, no.'

'I have your car, all shiny and clean from a car wash. I want to show it off to you.'

'We cleaned your car too, Marilyn,' Brian said. 'And we got all the pizza off the seat at the back.'

There was a pause and then Annie, Ria and Marilyn broke into near hysterical laughter.

Brian was startled. 'What on earth did I say now?' he asked, looking from one to the other and getting no answer.

When they did get back to Tara Road there wasn't nearly enough time for all they had to say to each other. The children eventually went to bed. Marilyn and Ria sat on at the table. It was unexpectedly easy to talk. They apologised for nothing. Not for encouraging Clement to sleep upstairs or for cutting back the garden, nor for inviting neighbours to become part of Tudor Drive and taking up again with Hubie Green. They asked each other about the visits of their husbands. And each spoke thoughtfully and honestly.

'I thought Greg looked tired and old, and that I had taken away a year of his life because I couldn't help him over the bits that were just as bad for him as for me.'

'And will it be all right from now on?' Ria asked.

'I guess he'll be cautious, even a little mistrustful of me from time to time. If I closed myself off so terribly before I could do it again. It will all take time to get back to where we were.'

'But at least you will.' Ria sounded wistful.

'And nothing happened when Danny was over there to make you think that *you* might get back together again?' Marilyn asked.

'Something happened that made me certain that we *were* back together already. But I wasn't right. He told me all about the financial disaster, and losing the house and everything, in Memorial Park under a big tree. Then we went back to Tudor Drive and . . . I suppose if I were being realistic I would say he consoled me in the way he knows best. But I took more from it than there was.'

'That's only reasonable, and he probably meant it all at the time,' Marilyn said.

'Timing is everything, isn't it?' Ria was rueful. 'Just after that came the news that Bernadette was losing the baby and he was off like a flash. Even if we had had another twenty-four hours . . .'

'Do you think that would have made a difference?'

'No, to be honest,' Ria admitted. 'It might only have made me feel worse. Maybe it was for the best. The stupid bit was I kept thinking that it was all tied up with the baby. Once that no longer existed, perhaps the whole infatuation would go. But again I was wrong.'

'Did you talk to him today at the funeral?' Marilyn asked.

'No. He looked as if he were going to speak but I didn't trust myself so I turned away. I couldn't think what he was doing there anyway, but he told Annie that he was there representing the family.'

'That was a good gesture anyway.' Marilyn's voice was soft and conciliatory.

'Danny's full of good gestures,' Ria said with a smile.

Marilyn had been able to change her ticket. Now she was going to stay for an extra three days. This way she could arrive back at Tudor Drive at the same time as Greg. It was to be symbolic of their starting a new life together. And Marilyn said that by staying on a few days she could help Ria settle in and start to face the whole business of selling the house.

They talked about Hilary's plans to move to the country, the pregnancy of young Kitty Sullivan. They spoke of Carlotta wanting a fourth husband and how John and Gerry's gourmet shop had really taken off this summer. They didn't shy away from personal questions. When they spoke of Colm Barry Ria asked whether Marilyn had been having a thing with him. 'That was what I heard from a probably ill-informed source,' Ria apologised.

'Totally wrong. I think he was much more interested in waiting until *you* came home,' Marilyn said. 'And on the subject, can I ask whether you had anything going with my brother-in-law?'

'No, your husband is quite wrong about that too,' Ria giggled.

'But he might have liked to, we think?' Marilyn wondered.

'We don't know at all because we didn't allow such a situation to develop,' Ria said.

And into the night they spoke of Gertie and how she was going to build a legend based on the dead Jack. They were both much more tolerant than they would have been a few weeks back. It wasn't just because Jack was dead.

They sat in the beautiful front room of Number 16 Tara Road as the moonlight came in at the window, and they each thought about the need to have some kind of legend in your life. Ria knew that for good or evil Marilyn must go on for ever without knowing it was her drunken son who had killed Johnny and himself that day. And Marilyn thought that for better or worse Ria should not learn how the husband she still loved and the friend she still trusted had conspired to betray her for so long.

'Aunt Gertie's not as well off as I thought she was,' Sean Maine said to Annie.

'Does it matter?' Annie shrugged.

'No, of course it doesn't, except I was just thinking it might work to our advantage.'

'How's that?'

'Well ... suppose I were to stay with her ... you know, pay board and lodging and go to school here?'

'It won't work, Sean.' Annie was practical.

'Not next week when school starts, okay I know it won't, but after Christmas I can find out what courses I'd get credits for ... organise a transfer ...'

Annie looked troubled. 'Yes, well ...'

'What is it? Would you not want me here? I thought you liked me.'

'I do like you, Sean, I like you a lot. It's just ... it's just I don't want to sort of lure you on with promises of things we might do, I might do, once you got here. It wouldn't be fair to let you think that ...'

He patted her hand. 'In time,' he said.

'But probably not in a short enough time for you,' she said.

'I've never done it either,' Sean said. 'I'm just as confused.'

'Really?'

'It mightn't be as good as they say. But we could see what we thought,' he said, and then, looking at her face, 'Not now, of course, but when the time seems right.'

'I bet Gertie'd just love having you to stay,' Annie said.

'I'm taking on more private pupils this year, Mum, can I do it in your house?' Bernadette asked.

'Of course, Ber. If you're well enough.'

'I'm fine. It's just that I don't want to start them off in one place and then have to transfer them when we move from here.'

'Does he know when he's going to sell?'

'No, Mum, and I don't ask him, he has enough pressures.'

'Does he have great pressures about Tara Road? Is she on at him all the time?' Finola Dunne was always protective of her daughter against the ex-wife.

Bernadette thought about it. 'I don't think so, I don't think she's even been in touch since she came back.'

'I wouldn't mind seeing those children again,' Finola said.

'Yes, I'd like to see them too, but Danny says they're all tied up with this

Marilyn until she leaves. They're mad about her apparently,' Bernadette reported gloomily.

'It's just because they stayed in her house which had a swimming pool, that's the only reason,' Finola tried to reassure her daughter.

'I know, Mum.'

'Do you mind if we have Gertie and Sheila around for lunch?' Ria asked Marilyn. 'Sheila's not staying long in Dublin and it would be nice for her to meet you ... she's been in your house, remember?'

'Of course,' Marilyn said. She would have preferred to talk to Ria on her own. There were still so many things to discuss, about Westville and about Tara Road. About the future and the past. But this was Ria's life and lunch with these ladies came first. Marilyn had learned this. And Ria had learned something too.

'I'm not going to spend the whole morning getting something ready. They want to talk not do a gourmet tasting, let's you and I walk down to the deli and get something simple.'

They walked up the road past Number 26 and waved at the swinging seat where Kitty Sullivan sat in the garden with her mother. Sixteen, anxious and pregnant, she had suddenly found a way of communicating with Frances which they never had before.

'Let's hope Annie doesn't find a similar one,' Ria said wryly.

'Do you think she might be sexually active, as they say at home?'

'And as they increasingly say here,' Ria confirmed. 'No I don't, but mothers know nothing, you'd know more about Annie than I would.'

'I know a bit about her hopes and dreams, but I truly don't know anything about that side of things,' Marilyn hastened to say.

'And if you did it would be sacred, you wouldn't have to tell me,' Ria said, anxious not to appear curious and trying to beat down the slight jealousy that was always there. Why could Annie Lynch tell Marilyn her hopes and dreams? It was beyond understanding.

They looked into the grounds of Number 32.

'Does Barney own any of that still?'

'No, they sold it all at huge prices, it was the talk of the place at the time. Rosemary really knew what she was doing going in there.' Ria was pleased for her friend.

Then they were at Number 48A. No sign of Nora Johnson and Pliers; they must have gone on one of their many adventures. 'Your mother will miss you if you move from here. Hilary going to the west, now you going too.'

'It's not *if* we move away from here, it's *when*. This is Millionaires' Row nowadays. Weren't we so clever to move in here when we did?'

'You weren't being clever, you went after a dream, didn't you?'

'I suppose Danny did. He wanted a grand house with high ceilings and deep colours. Often nowadays when I think about it I don't quite know why, but that's what he seemed to want when he was young.'

They walked on, an easy companionable silence between them. They passed the gates of St Rita's.

'Future home of nice soft cakes,' Ria said, laughing.

'Nothing too difficult to chew,' Marilyn giggled. 'Not like those ginger biscuits I bought Brian and Annie first time, they were horrific.'

They turned the corner and saw that Gertie's launderette was busy.

'I dare not mention the deceased but would he have left any insurance?' Marilyn asked.

'Gertie's mother paid some kind of a policy,' Ria said. 'I think it was just a burial one.'

'And will she be all right?'

'She'll be fine. She has the little flat upstairs there and of course she can have her children at home now that they won't be assaulted or have their poor nerves shot to pieces by that lunatic.'

Gertie was so used to cleaning in Number 16 Tara Road that it was hard to get her to sit down.

'Will I do a bit of ironing for you to have your clothes nice for packing, Marilyn?' she said.

'Lord, Sheila, don't you have the kindest sister. I simply hate ironing and Gertie often helped me out.'

'Yes . . . she was born caring about clothes, I never was,' said Sheila and the moment passed. Once or twice Gertie rose as if to clear the table but Ria's hand gently pressed her back. 'Sean is so anxious to come back and study in Ireland after Christmas and find his roots,' Sheila said. The other three women hid their smiles. 'He has been around to all the various schools and colleges and of course I'd just *love* him to come back here,' Sheila said.

'And Max?' Ria wondered.

'There's not much looking for roots in the Ukraine, they all came to the States from that village. Max will be okay about it.'

Gertie was excited about the proposition. 'There will be a small room in our flat, it's not very elegant but it's convenient for schools and libraries and everything.'

'Stop saying it's not elegant,' Sheila cried. 'Your property is in such a good area. It's a wonderful place for him to stay, it's a happy home. I'm only sorry his Uncle Jack won't be there to see him grow up.'

'Jack would have made him very welcome, that's one sure thing,' Gertie said, without any tinge of irony. 'But we'll paint up his room for him to have it ready when he comes back. He can tell us what colour he'd like. And maybe he'd get a bicycle. You know,' Gertie confided, 'a lot of people have asked me would I be financially able to manage without Jack?'

Ria wondered who had asked that and why. Surely they must have known that poor Gertie's finances would take an upturn now that she didn't have to find him an extra thirty or forty pounds' drinking money a week by cleaning houses. And now that she could concentrate on her business. But then perhaps other people didn't know the circumstances.

'And of course I am fine,' Gertie continued. 'My mother's looked through all the papers and there was a grand insurance policy there, and the business is going from strength to strength. There will be fine times ahead, that's what I have to think.'

Suddenly Ria remembered something. 'Talking of what lies ahead, I wonder what happened to Mrs Connor!'

'She told me she couldn't talk to the dead when I wanted to, and that one day I wouldn't want to any more,' Marilyn said. 'I'd like to tell her that day has come.'

'She told me I'd have a big business, I'd like to know how big,' Ria said, 'and travel the world. I've already done that.'

Sheila said that Mrs Connor had said the future was in her own hands, and look at the way it had all worked out. With her boy wanting to come back to Ireland to his own people!

Gertie tried to remember what Mrs Connor had told her. She had told her that there would be some sorrow but a happy life, she thought. 'Well, that was true enough,' Sheila said, patting her sister on the hand.

'Will I make myself scarce while you meet Danny?' Marilyn asked as they cleared the dishes after lunch.

'No need, there'll be plenty of time after you've gone home. Let's not waste what we have.'

'You should talk to him as soon as possible, listen to what he has to say and add what *you* have to say. The more you put it off the harder it is to do.'

'You're right,' sighed Ria. 'Yes, but it's a question of don't do as I *do*, just do as I *say*!'

'I'm only telling you what I didn't do myself.'

'I suppose I should ask him to come over.'

'I have to go and buy some gifts for people back home. I'll go down to that place I saw in Wicklow and leave you the morning.'

'That's an idea.'

'And you know what we'll do as a treat tomorrow afternoon?'

'I can't guess.'

'We'll go see Mrs Connor,' said Marilyn Vine, who wanted to pay her debt to the woman who had told her the truth. That the dead like to be left asleep. They want to be left in peace.

'I have to meet Ria this morning,' Danny said.

'Well, it's better that you get it over with,' Bernadette said. 'Are you very sad?'

'Not so much sad as anxious. I used to laugh at middle-aged men who had ulcers and said their stomachs were in a knot. I don't know why I laughed, that's the way I am all the time now.'

She was full of concern. 'But you *can't* be, Danny. None of this is *your* fault, and you are going to be able to give her half the proceeds of that house which is very big nowadays.'

'Yes, true.'

'And she knows all this; she doesn't have any expectations of anything else.'

'No,' said Danny Lynch. 'No, I don't suppose that she can have any expectations of anything else.'

'Brian, will you go and play with Dekko and Myles this morning? Your dad is coming here and we need to talk on our own.'

'Is it just *me* that you don't want to be here?' Brian wanted it clarified.

'No, Brian, it's not just you. Marilyn's going down to that craft shop, Annie's showing Sean the rest of Dublin. It's everyone.'

'You won't fight, will you?'

'We *don't* now, remember? So will you go to Dekko and Myles for a bit?'

'Would you think it was okay if I went to see Finola Dunne? I bought her a present when I was in America.'

'Yes, of course, that's a great idea.' She laughed at his anxiety.

'That's not just me being awful and doing the wrong thing, is it?'

'You're wonderful, Brian,' his mother said.

'But a bit different?' This was too much praise, he wanted it tempered.

'Very different, that's for sure,' said Ria.

He came at ten o'clock, and rang on the front door.

'Haven't you got your keys?' she asked.

'I turned them in to Mrs Jackboot,' he said.

'Don't call her that, Danny. What would she have done with them, do you think?'

'Search me, Ria. Cemented them to a stone maybe?'

'No, here they are, on the key-holder at the back of the hall. Shall I give them back to you?'

'What for?'

'For you to show people around, Danny. Please let's not make it more difficult than it is.'

He saw the sense in that. 'Sure,' he said and held his hands up as a sign of peace.

'Right, I have some coffee in a percolator up here in the front room, will we sit in there and if you'll forgive the expression . . . make a list?'

She had two lined pads ready on the round table and two pens. She brought the coffee over to them and waited expectantly.

'Look, I don't think that this is going to work,' he began.

'But it *has* to work. I mean, you said we'd have to be well out of here by Christmas. I made sure that the children and Marilyn were out so that we could get started.'

'She hasn't gone home yet?'

'Tomorrow.'

'Oh.'

'So who will we sell it through?'

'What?'

'The house, Danny? We can't use McCarthy and Lynch because they don't exist any more. Which agency will we ask?'

'There will be a line of them waiting to dance on my grave,' Danny said glumly.

'No, that's not the situation. Stop being so dramatic, there will be a line of people waiting to sell it so that they can get two per cent of the price. That's all. Which one will we choose?'

'You've been out of the business for a long time. It's not two per cent any more, it's cutthroat nowadays, all of them trying to shave off a bit here and there.'

'How do you mean?'

'It will be what they call the Beauty Parade, they all come in one by one, each one hoping to be chosen. This one says he'll take one point seven per cent, this one will do it for one point two five. Then there's going to be some so desperate for the commission they'll say a flat fee.'

'That's the way it is?'

'That's the way it is. Believe me I've been in it, may even be in it again one day, who knows?'

'So who, then?'

'Ria, I'm going to suggest something to you. These guys hate me, a lot of them. I've cut right across their deals, stolen their clients. You must sell it on your own, and give me half.'

'I can't do that.'

'I've thought about it, it's the only way, and we must pretend to be fighting as if I'm giving you nothing, and your only hope is to screw as much out of this as possible.'

'No, Danny.'

'It's for us, for the children. Do it, Ria.'

'I can't possibly hold a Beauty Parade, as you call it, of auctioneers here on my own.'

'Get someone to help you.'

'Well, I suppose Rosemary could come in and sit with me, she's a businesswoman.' Ria thought about it.

'Not Rosemary.' He was firm.

'Why not, Danny? You like her, she really does have a head for figures; look at her own company.'

'No, they'd walk over two women.'

'Come on. What do you think it is? People don't walk over women in business any more.'

'Get a man to help you, Ria, it's good advice.'

'Who, what man? I don't know any man.'

'You've got friends.'

'Colm?' she suggested.

He thought about it. 'Yes, why not? He's got valuable property himself, more or less by accident but he's sitting on it. They'd respect him.'

'All right.'

'So when should I start?'

'I suppose as soon as possible. And tell these guys that you'll be in the market to *buy* a house too. They'll be even more helpful if they think there are going to be two bites of the cherry.'

'The furniture and everything?' He shrugged. 'Well, what will we do with it?'

'If you buy somewhere that suits it then of course you must take it,' he said.

'But suppose *you* find somewhere that suits it?' she asked.

'I don't think we will, it will be small, and anyway . . . you know?'

'I know,' Ria said. 'Bernadette would prefer to start life with you having her own furniture.'

'I don't think she'd even notice what furniture was in the room,' he said. He sounded very sad.

She touched one of the balloon-backed chairs that they had found in the old presbytery, covered then with a rough and torn horsehair. Everything here had been searched for and found with such love. And now, less than two decades later, two people were shrugging about what would happen to it.

She didn't really trust herself to speak.

'So, it's not easy but we'll do it.'

'I'll do it apparently.' She hoped it didn't sound too bitter.

'You understand why?'

'Yes I do. And will you say I could have got more, or I shouldn't have chosen this or that one?'

'No, believe me I won't say anything like that.'

She believed him. 'Well, I'll ask Colm today. I'm anxious to get it done and start trying to work for a living.'

'You always worked hard,' he said appreciatively and annoyingly.

Ria found that this made her eyes water a little. 'And will you be able to get work?' she asked.

'Not as easily as I thought. In fact I was sort of advised to look into some other sector. Not too many estate agencies opening their doors, arms or books to me, I'm afraid. Still there's always something.'

'Like what?'

'Like PR for the building industry or property companies. Like buying furniture from dealers – there are still houses throwing out beautiful stuff and filling themselves up with pine and chrome.'

He was talking more cheerfully than he felt. Only someone who knew Danny Lynch would realise that. Ria gave no sign that she saw anything at all.

It was late in the afternoon when they went out to the halting site. Horses were tethered to fences, children played on the steps of caravans. Young boys hung around hopefully as cars drew up.

'Mrs Connor?' Ria asked.

'She went away,' said a red-haired boy with paper-white skin.

'Do you know where she went?' Marilyn asked.

'No, she just went overnight.'

'But you might have some idea where she went.' Ria made a move as if to open her handbag and look for a wallet.

'No, really, Missus, if we knew we'd tell you. There's people coming here all the time looking for her, but we can't say what we don't know.'

'And does she have any relations here?' Ria looked around the caravans that housed this particular travelling community.

'No, not to speak of.'

'But surely a lot of you are family cousins, we really do want to find her.'

'To thank her too,' Marilyn said.

'I know you do, aren't there droves of them coming at night. And even now there's two cars coming in asking after her, my brother's telling them we haven't a God clue where she is.'

'Was she sick, do you think?' Ria asked.

'She never said a word, Missus.'

'And no one else took over her ... um ... work or anything?' Marilyn wondered.

'No. Wouldn't they have had to have the gift?' said the boy with the nearly transparent face.

They went to a last dinner in Colm's. Sean and Annie held hands and ate an aubergine and red bean casserole. 'Sean doesn't eat dead animals now,' Annie said proudly.

'Sound man, Sean,' Colm said admiringly.

'Finola Dunne said she saw your sister in a hospital. Her friend is there,' Brian said.

Ria closed her eyes. Marilyn had told her the story. Brian was the last person in Ireland who should have learned it.

'Yes, that's right, she's been quite sick but getting a lot better now. Is Mrs Dunne's friend getting better too?' Colm was ice-calm.

Ria flashed him a glance of huge gratitude.

'I think her friend's a drug addict, to be absolutely honest. But I *suppose* she could get better. They do, don't they?'

'Oh they do, Brian,' Colm said. 'They do all the time.'

Barney and Mona McCarthy came up to the table. 'I just wanted to welcome you home, Ria, and to wish you *bon voyage*, Marilyn.' Mona spoke with confidence these days.

'Mam's going to be cooking things for money now if you still know any rich people who'd buy them,' Brian said helpfully.

'We know a few,' Mona said. 'And we'll certainly be able to put the word around.'

Barney McCarthy was anxious to end the conversation. Colm ushered them to their table. You would never think from his manner that Barney had ever been at this restaurant with another woman. Or that his bills had remained unpaid until a solicitor had asked for any outstanding invoices to be presented.

The solicitor had been engaged by Mrs and not Mr McCarthy.

'Do you want us to call so that you can say goodbye to Rosemary tonight?' Ria asked Marilyn.

Annie looked up.

'I think I'll just leave her a note,' Marilyn said.

'Sure, why not?' Ria was easy.

At that moment Colm asked Ria would she come into the kitchen. He wanted her to see the desserts that he had prepared for tonight so that they could discuss what she might dream up.

'Can I come into the kitchen?' Brian's eyes were excited.

'Only if you don't talk, Brian,' his mother said.

'Sean, would you ever go with them and clap your hand over his mouth if he says anything at all?' Annie begged.

Sean Maine was pleased to be seen as a hero and went willingly.

Annie and Marilyn looked at each other across the table. 'You don't like Rosemary,' Annie said.

'No I don't.'

'Why don't you like her?' Annie asked.

'I'm not sure. But it's not something I need to say to your mother, they're friends over many years. And you, Annie? Obviously you don't like her either. Why is that?'

'I couldn't explain.'

'I know. These things happen.'

The taxi was coming at ten thirty but Ria said Marilyn would not think she was getting away with leaving quietly. Colm was there with a gardening book for her, a very old one they had talked about; he had tracked it down in an antiquarian bookseller's. Nora had come to say goodbye too. Hilary came to show a photograph of Martin's old homestead. A bleak-looking place with great tall trees. 'There's a lovely sound in the evening when the rooks all come home,' Hilary said.

'We went to see Mrs Connor. I was going to tell her about you and the trees but it turns out that she's gone away,' Ria told her sister.

'Well, her work is done,' said Hilary as if it was obvious.

Gertie came to say goodbye. 'You were a great pal while you were here, and honestly, Marilyn, I wouldn't expect you to understand our ways, being a foreigner and everything, but you understood as well as anyone that Jack loved me and did the best for me. His problem was that he thought nobody really appreciated him.'

'But they did,' Marilyn said. 'You only had to look at the crowds at his funeral to know that.' Then it was time to go. 'I could get a taxi, Ria,' she began to protest.

'I'm driving you to the airport. Don't argue.' The telephone rang. 'Who now?' Ria groaned.

But it wasn't for her. It was Greg Vine from California. He was changing planes and about to check in for New York. He would wait for Marilyn in Kennedy Airport. They would go back to Tudor Drive together.

'Yes, you too.' Marilyn ended the conversation.

'Did he say I love you?' Ria asked.

'Yes, as it happens,' Marilyn said.

'Lucky Marilyn.'

'You have the children,' Marilyn said.

And they held each other tight in a way they wouldn't be able to do at the airport.

Annie was coming to say goodbye, accompanied by Sean Maine and Brian. As they got into the car Clement came out to say goodbye. It took the form of a huge yawn and stretch but they all knew what it was.

'I'm sorry about letting him into your bedroom,' Marilyn said.

'No you're not, but it doesn't matter, we'll be somewhere new soon and he'll have to relearn all his good habits.'

Colm was in the back garden, he came out to wave them off.

'You are still working in that garden even though other people will get the benefit?'

'No, they won't get the benefit, I'm moving it all up to Jimmy and Frances Sullivan's garden, that's what I'm at.'

'Why don't you dig up that awful concrete behind your restaurant? You could plant there.'

'I'm hoping to build there,' he said.

'Build?'

'Yes, proper accommodation at last, not just a bachelor flat.'

'Great idea.'

'Well, you never know.'

'I hate to go,' Marilyn said.

'When you come back we'll welcome you somewhere new.'

'I don't suppose you could take anything *live* on the plane, could you, Marilyn?' Brian asked.

'Not really, except myself,' she said.

'Then it's no use giving you a guinea pig for Zach, is it?'

'We can't go beyond here,' Ria said at the passenger check-in.

'Aren't we magnificent?' Marilyn said.

'Yes, we really took a chance, didn't we,' Ria said.

'And how very well it worked out,' said Marilyn.

They were still unable to say the goodbye.

Annie flung herself into Marilyn's arms. 'I hate you going, I just hate it, you're quite different to anyone else, you *know* that. Will you come back so that I'll have someone to talk to?'

'You live in a place where there are plenty of people to talk to.'

Ria Lynch wondered were people speaking about her over her head, but she must be imagining it.

'And you'll keep an eye on things from over there,' Annie said.

'Yes, and you from here?' Marilyn begged.

'Sure.'

Sean Maine shook her hand gravely and Brian gave her an embarrassed hug. Marilyn Vine looked at Annie Lynch. The blonde, beautiful, nearly fifteen-year-old Annie walked up to her mother and put an arm around Ria's waist. 'We'll keep the world ticking over until you get back,' she said. 'Won't we, Mam?'

'Of course we will,' said Ria, realising that it might be possible after all.

Preface

The social institutions are the major operative agencies of every community or society. They are the focal and strategic societal instruments by means of which the different common and recurrent relationships of the people of the society are subjected to systems of rules of behavior, with the result that their actions are patterned, stabilized, and made predictable. Institutions are also the means whereby all of the essential functions are organized, directed, and executed. These established and formalized requirements of individual and joint behavior produce the ways of life which are effective in maintaining societal order, harmony, and efficiency and certainty of operation.

Institutions, combining in themselves most of the essential structural-functional agencies and the instrumental processes of the society, epitomize social organization.

Every major functional department of social life is institutionalized; and whenever a body of activities becomes crucial, as society changes, it must be institutionalized. Our society has met and is meeting this need for institutionalization. Never before has there been such a multiplication of institutions in general, such an extension of institutions into areas of life heretofore non-institutionalized, such a specialization of institutions and at the same time an interinstitutional transfer of functions, and such a structural-functional reorganization of institutions.

This study has two main objectives: (1) to provide a general theoretical orientation consisting of the more important general facts and principles regarding the place, nature, formation, constitution, and operation of social institutions; and, (2) especially to analyze the major blocks of institutions found in every modern society, with special reference to those systems of institutions as they function in our over-all American social system.

In order to understand the setting and place of institutions, we will briefly examine the nature of man's societal life in an effort to see it as a systemic totality. Without some conception of society's architecture, we have a limited comprehension of the significance in the whole of any particular arch or angle, of any particular agency or activity. The basic contention—one universally accepted in science—is that the *principle of organization* prevails in the universe, and that every going concern in it, including human society, is a *system* which demonstrates this principle. These two related concepts are the basis of the present study.

The point of departure thus involves a skeletal treatment of systems in general and social systems in particular, of social organization, of the systems related to the societal system, and of the structural-functional systems instrumental in the organization of societal behavior and the operation of human society. The general institutional system, which combines and implements all of the general functionally differentiated ingredient subsystems, is then examined in fulfillment of the first objective of the study. The main body of the study (Part 3) consists of the somewhat extended treatment of the major blocks or sectors of institutions classified under the six functional categories: communication; acquisition, organization, and utilization of knowledge; maintenance; socialization and cultural transmission; over-all regulation and ordering; and expression. This part seeks to present a rather wide scope of both utilitarian and humanistic insights into, and understanding of, the major departments of societal life.

It is in the theory of institutions and in the examination of the inter-functioning of the major institutional sectors of society that sociology comes very near to fulfilling its strategic function as the general inter-relating social science. In the study of the institutional organization of society we get into clear focus the major parts and the major operations *of the whole*. It should also be pointed out that almost every institutional sector, or some important aspect of such a sector, examined in Part 3, is the subject matter of one or more of the present widely discussed "special" sociologies. Part 3 can, in fact, serve as a systematic treatment of most of the special sociologies. Specifically represented are the sociology of language, the sociology of science and technology, family sociology, occupational sociology or the sociology of work, the sociology of health and the closely related medical sociology, educational sociology, political sociology, the sociology of law, military sociology, the sociology of religion, and the sociology of art, literature, and music. The sociology of values and of knowledge are also peripherally involved. This situation occurs partly because these areas of sociological concern are functional areas of such importance that the activities in them must be institutionalized. Furthermore, certain special sociologies contribute to the understanding of certain institutional sectors or of certain institutions in the sectors.

I am grateful to the University of Nebraska Press, which holds the copyright of my *Social Institutions,* published in 1946, and now out of print, for permission to use in the present study a considerable body of materials from that work that still have theoretical pertinence.

There is no name index. Only authors quoted or paraphrased in the text are mentioned in the index. The important contributors of knowledge about institutions and their pertinent works are indicated in the rather extensive classified bibliographies appended to each chapter.

J. O. H.